GRAHAM MASTERTON OMNIBUS

Corroboree

Empress

Also by Graham Masterton

GRAHAM MASTERTON OMNIBUS

Corroboree
Empress

GRAHAM MASTERTON

timewarner
paperbacks

A *Time Warner* Paperback

This omnibus edition first published in Great Britain by
Time Warner Paperbacks in 2004
Graham Masterton Omnibus Copyright © Graham Masterton 2004

Previously published separately:
Corroboree first published in Great Britain by W. H. Allen & Co
First published in paperback by Sphere Books Ltd 1991
Reprinted by Sphere Books 1996
Copyright © 1984 by Graham Masterton

Empress first published in Great Britain by Hamish Hamilton Ltd 1990
Published by Sphere Books Ltd 1991
Copyright © by Graham Masterton 1988

The moral right of the author has been asserted.

A CIP catalogue record for this book
is available from the British Library.

ISBN 0 7515 3602 4

Printed and bound in Great Britain by
Clays Ltd, St Ives plc

Time Warner Paperbacks
An imprint of
Time Warner Books UK
Brettenham House
Lancaster Place
London WC2E 7EN

www.TimeWarnerBooks.co.uk

Corroboree

For Wiescka,
and for Roland, Daniel
and Luke,
with love

Prologue

More than anything else, said Netty, her mother would like a musical box for Christmas: one of those musical boxes with six or seven different and interchangeable cylinders, so that she could play 'Silent Night' and 'The Wonderful Polka' and 'Sweet Heart's Delight'; and think of all the days gone by, happy and sad, and how God had blessed her so, and punished her, too.

Eyre listened with amusement, smoking his cigar, his eyes bright; and at last he said. 'Very well, if that's what you want to give her, I'll ask Mr Granger,' and he reached out to lay his hand on the parting of his daughter's shining hair, as gently as a blessing. His only daughter, and although he didn't yet know it, his only child.

Outside, in the garden, the sun shone in brilliant skeins, like the straw in Rumpelstiltskin which had been spun into gold; and the birds whooped and laughed, and one of the grooms called 'Wayandah! Wayandah!' as he tried to lead Eyre's favourite stallion back into the stables. And across the lawns, watered and fed so that they looked unnaturally green in this dusty December landscape, Charlotte moved this way and that in her clotted-cream-coloured dress, bobbing now and again to pick a flower, stopping occasionally to scold the gardening-boy; Charlotte with her perfect bonnet and her perfect ribbons and her perfect parasol; a picture of perfection wherever she went, and whatever she did.

Only Eyre understood what pain and loss her perfection so perfectly concealed Only Eyre heard her sobbing at night, a thin, inconsolable whining; or knew what she was thinking about on those evenings when the sun was gradually burning itself out behind the branches of the stringy-bark trees, and she stared out across the river valley; silent, her face severe.

He said to Netty, 'She'd like some perfume, too, if I can get Mr McLaren to send some up.'

'Oh, *do*,' enthused Netty. 'And some lace, too, if there's any to be had. I could make a collar for that green velvet dress—the one she wore at Governor McConnell's birthday party.'

'Netty,' smiled Eyre, 'I sometimes think you were sent by the angels.' Netty took his hand, and pressed it against her cheek. 'Dear father,' she said. 'I hope I can be everything to you: friend, and son, and daughter, all three.'

Eyre drew her towards him, and kissed her twice, once on each cheek. 'You always look so much like your mother,' he smiled. 'There was one night, long ago . . . well, you look just like her, the way she did on that night.'

Netty said nothing. She knew that he was flattering her, for her mother was still a remarkably beautiful woman. But she also understood that he was thinking back to the time before her mother was sad, those few brief months before the loss of her son, Netty's brother, whom Netty had never known. His absence from their family, even after twenty years, was like an empty bedroom, or a photograph-frame with no picture in it. Every year, on his birthday, her mother would light candles for him. Every year, she would buy him a small Christmas gift, and lay it beside the others, in case he came back. A necktie, or a diary. Once, she had bought him a harmonica.

Eyre smoked for a while, and then said, 'There always used to be snow at Christmas, when I was a boy.'

8

Netty smiled, and shook her head. 'I can't imagine it. I've tried. I've looked at pictures. But I just can't imagine it.'

'Well,' he said, 'it isn't easy to describe. It isn't so much the whiteness, or the coldness, it's the *sound* of it. The whole world suddenly becomes muffled. Everything somehow seems to be more private. They say Eskimos are great natural philosophers, you know. Perhaps that's because the snow makes you turn in on yourself. Think more.'

'The desert must do that, too,' said Netty.

Eyre looked at her and his eyes were peculiarly remote. 'The desert?' he asked her. He was still smiling, but his smile had nothing at all to do with his eyes.

'Yes,' she said, uncertainly. 'It must be very silent out there.'

'No,' he told her. Then, after another long pause: 'No. The desert isn't silent at all. The desert is . . . Babel, a whole Babel of voices. All speaking at the same time. Never quiet. Thousands of them: the voices of the past and the voices of the future.'

'I don't understand what you mean. What voices?'

Eyre was about to say something more, but suddenly he stopped himself, and smiled instead, and stroked Netty's hair. 'A figure of speech,' he explained; but Netty wouldn't be put off.

'What do they say?' she asked him, intently.

'What does who say?'

'The voices. The ones in the desert.'

'They don't say anthing,' Eyre told her. 'Now, come on, let's forget all about it, and call your mother in for tea.'

'But they must say *something*,' Netty insisted. 'Otherwise you wouldn't have called them voices.'

Eyre twisted his side-whiskers thoughtfully. They were greying now, and made him look less saturnine than when he was young; although his eyebrows were still dark and swept-up; and his cheeks were still hollow. Charlotte had once teased him that he looked like the night-devil; but

9

that was before they had lost their son. She would never tease him like that now.

Eyre said, 'The voices tell stories. Everything that happened in the past, how the mountains were made, why the lakes are all dry, how the blue heron brought in the tide, how the no-drink bear lost his tail. And they tell what will happen in the future, too. Which years are going to be dry, which years are going to be happy. Who will die, who will lose his way. Who will honour his promises, and who will not.'

He was silent for a moment, and then he added, in a dead-sounding voice, 'Who will regret what he has done.'

Netty sat on the floor looking up at him. 'Do they really say things like that? Can you really hear them?'

'You hear whatever is inside your own head,' said Eyre. 'That is why the desert is never quiet.'

A whole hour seemed to pass between them in what could only have been a few seconds. Charlotte came in from the garden, and kissed them both, Eyre and Netty, and Eyre said, 'How's Yalagonga? Do you think he's going to make a good gardener?'

Charlotte put down her basket of flowers, and unlaced the ribbons of her bonnet. 'He's confident, I'll give him that! He wanted to clear all the wattle from the back fence and cut down my favourite apple tree. But, I think he's going to do. I'd rather have a boy who's going to be strict with the garden, than one who lets it grow wild. Do you remember Jackie? He wouldn't cut a single weed, in case it offended the spirits.'

'Shall we have some tea?' asked Eyre, in the manner of someone who has been asking the same question day after day for nearly twenty years.

'I think I deserve it,' replied Charlotte. 'In fact, I think I may have some of the coconut biscuits, too.'

Eyre nodded to Netty, who got up from the floor and went over to the large carved limestone fireplace, and rang the bell-cord.

'I suppose you two have been discussing politics again,' said Charlotte.

Eyre smiled. 'Actually, we've been trying to decide what to buy you for Christmas.'

'Well, that's easy enough. It doesn't need a discussion. I want a new hut for treating the children, more linseed oil, and as much tincture of catechu as you can get.'

'Don't be so practical,' said Eyre. 'I'm talking about perfume, and lace.'

'What on earth is the use of perfume and lace, out here at Moorundie? I'd rather have medicines.'

'Charlotte . . .' Eyre began, but then he sat back, and tried to keep on smiling as if he had only been teasing her about the perfume, and the lace. He knew that the children were her main preoccupation, with their sores and their runny noses and their shivering-fits. He knew why, too. And he knew that whatever he gave her for Christmas, it would never do anything to make up for the loss of their boy-child.

He could see it now, as clearly as if it had happened last night, instead of twenty years ago. The open window, the curtain blowing in the warm night wind. The empty crib, still warm and indented from the baby's sleeping body; still smelling of mother's milk and freshly-washed hair. And he could remember the pain, too: the pain that was so much greater than he had expected. More than a sense of loss; more than a sense of sacrifice, and duty. It had been like having his arm twisted and torn out of its socket by the roots. An actual physical tearing-away.

The black trackers had spent hours scouring the garden. 'Three,' they had said. 'Two men, one woman, all barefoot, blackfellow.' They had tried to follow the footprints into the bush, but the kidnappers had been too wily. They had backtracked, run through streams and brushed their trail with wattle-branches. The black trackers had come back four hours later glistening with sweat, and admitted that whoever had taken the boy had been an exceptionally skilful hunter; or a ghost.

11

Fly-posters offering rewards had been displayed all around Moorundie for weeks. But the boy seemed to have disappeared without a trace; melted into the setting sun. Eyre had offered £500 and a free pardon for his return. But there had been nothing, not a word; although the ironic part about it had been that Eyre had actually known where his son was; or at least who it was that had taken him. Yet he had been unable to speak, for fear of condemning himself, and for fear of destroying both his marriage and his career.

For somebody that night had left the main gates of the house unlocked. And somebody had carelessly (or thoughtfully) propped up a ladder by the child's bedroom window. And somebody had left the window unlatched, so that all an intruder had to do was ease up the sash, and climb straight into the room.

The blackfellows must have been ten miles to Woocalla before anybody had noticed that the boy was gone. And Eyre had known, as he had stood at the end of the crib, breathing in the very last vestiges of baby-smell, that any attempt to take the boy away from them would be suicidal, perhaps worse. An Aborigine uprising had always been on the cards. Any attempt to arrest blackfellows *en masse*, or take reprisals against them, would be madness.

Times had changed since he had first arrived in Australia. Your blackfellow nowadays was either a great deal more skilled and co-operative, or else a great deal more vicious.

When the last of the scouts and the trackers had reported no sign of the baby, Eyre had been obliged to say, 'That's it. Don't search any more. Whoever took him means to keep him.'

But of course life had never been the same since then; and Eyre had always felt that Charlotte was accusing him of carelessness, or cold-heartedness, or both. They wanted the baby because it was yours, she had insisted, over and over again. They wanted the baby because you're famous, and because you always show them that you understand

12

them. Perhaps they kidnapped him as a compliment. What a compliment, to lose your own flesh and blood. They probably worship him, as if he were the son of God.

'*Charlotte*!' Eyre had snapped at her, but the hurt had already been inflicted; and even through years of friendliness and sweetness and shared kisses, it was never undone. When they had lost their son, they had lost their first fresh love, and whatever came afterwards was a compromise, an attempt at living together with as little pain as possible.

Charlotte said, 'Can you call Molly, and ask her to arrange these flowers for me? I think I'm going to take a bath.'

'You're not tired, are you?' Eyre asked her. 'I mean, not too tired?'

'For tonight's dinner? Hmh! I think I'll be able to manage it.'

'Wear the white,' Eyre told her.

'The white?'

'I just want you to.'

'I don't know,' said Charlotte. Her eyes were so wide, her hair was so blonde; but somehow behind all that beauty there was nothing at all. Looking into Charlotte was like looking behind a magic-lantern screen; all you could see was the same picture you had seen on the front of the screen, in reverse.

Eyre touched Netty's shoulder. 'I think I'll take a bath, too. It's been so damned hot today.'

Charlotte stood up, with a rustle of skirts. But at that moment, there was shouting from outside, in the garden. Whoops, and cries, and someone saying, 'Biranga! They brought Biranga!'

Eyre was out of his chair immediately. He pulled aside the lace curtains and hurried out into the hot sunshine, followed by Netty. Charlotte called, 'Netty! Your bonnet!' but Netty took no notice.

Eyre strode across the lawns. His shadow followed him like the scissor-man in *Struwwelpeter*. A party of seven or

13

eight blackfellows had come to the front gate of his house, and were standing there, calling and clapping. He saw one of his principal helpers, Wawayran, and shouted out, 'Wawayran! What's going on?'

'They brought him in, sir! They brought in Biranga!'

Eyre pushed the Aborigines aside, and looked down at the ground. Lying in the dust, on a crumpled blanket that had obviously been used to carry him for several miles, was the blood-caked body of a young man. He was naked, except for a twisted string around his waist, and his chest and shoulders were patterned with decorative scars. His face was white with pipe-clay, although part of it had flaked off, and some of it was crusted with blood. It looked as if the man had been savagely beaten around the head and shoulders, and then speared in the stomach.

'Who killed this man?' asked Eyre.

'I did, sir,' said one of the Aborigines, quietly. He was a tall, stooped fellow, dressed in European clothes, a well-patched white shirt and drooping khaki trousers. 'I was looking after the sheep for Mr Mullett, sir, and I saw him by the fence. I knew he was Biranga, sir, because he was so white, sir, just like you said, just like a ghost.'

Eyre knelt down beside the body and lifted its limp, disjointed wrist.

'What was he doing by the fence?'

The Aborigine shook his head. 'Just standing, sir; just staring.'

'Was he alone?'

'There were five, six more, sir; but they ran off. I think towards Nunjikompita.'

Eyre was silent for a long time. Then he said to Wawayran, 'Fetch me a rag, soaked in water.'

'Yes, sir.'

Eyre stood up, and turned, and frowned against the sunlight. Charlotte was waiting on the verandah, one hand slightly raised as if she were about to call out to him. Netty was a step or two behind her. They could have been posing

14

for a daguerreotype of *Two Ladies At Moorundie, 1861*. One more faded colonial record.

Charlotte called, in a high-pitched voice, 'Is it Biranga?'

'I think so,' Eyre replied.

There was a short pause, and then Charlotte said, 'Is he quite dead?' 'Yes,' Eyre told her.

'Ten pounds bounty, sir,' said the Aborigine who had killed him.

'You speared him,' Eyre remarked. It was almost an accusation.

'Only to make sure, sir. First of all I hit him with my club.'

'Well, so I see.'

'He said nothing, sir. But I couldn't trust him. He didn't even put up his hand to save himself.'

Eyre thoughtfully put his hand over his mouth, and looked down at Biranga's battered body. Biranga had been a fugitive from the South Australian police for nearly six years now, ever since the trouble over at Broughton, when two Aborigines had been shot by white farmers as a vigilante punishment for rape and murder. Four days later the farmers had been speared to death themselves by Biranga and several other tribesmen, including Jacky Monday and a boy called Dencil.

Eyre had himself put up the offer of £10 for Biranga's capture, dead or alive. Eyre was fair and considerate when it came to dealing with the tribesmen of the Murray River district; but also firm. Some of the blackfellows called him 'Take-No-Nonsense' after one of his own favourite phrases.

Biranga, however, had successfully eluded Eyre and his constables, until today. He had been seen scores of times, although the majority of sightings had been very questionable, since a shilling was paid for each report, and most of the Aborigines around Moorundie would have sworn blind that they had seen a real live Bunyip for a penny, and a herd of Bunyips for twopence. Biranga had also been blamed for almost every unexplained theft or act of

15

vandalism for over four years. Eyre's black trackers would make a desultory search in the bush whenever something went missing, and then come back to say, 'Biranga took it. That's what we heard.' If Biranga had really been as industrious a larcenist as the Moorundie blackfellows tried to suggest, then he would have been walking around the bush with beehives, rifles, sheets of corrugated iron, and scores of blankets.

Some of the blackfellows had said that Biranga was a ghost, because of his unusually pale skin. Captain Billington had suggested that he might be an albino. Wawayran had declared that he was a real phantom. But everybody agreed that he had to be caught. It was unsettling for all of the civilised Aborigines who lived on the missions, or as servants in European homes, if a wild black tribesman was running free, doing whatever he pleased, and cocking a snook at the white authorities.

Governor McConnell had written to Eyre and added dryly, 'I expect you to be able to report within a few weeks that you have been able to apprehend the native they call the Ghost of Emu Downs, the fellow Biranga.'

The Ghost of Emu Downs, thought Eyre, as he looked down at Biranga's broken body. Some ghost. Wawayran came up with a wet rag, and Eyre took it, and knelt down again, and began carefully to wipe away the pipe-clay that encrusted the dead Biranga's forehead and cheeks.

The face that appeared through the smeary clay was startlingly calm, as if the man had died peacefully and without fear, in spite of his terrible injuries.

It was also an unusually cultured-looking face, almost European, although the forehead and the cheeks were decorated with welts and scars, marks which Eyre recognised as those of a warrior of the Wirangu. Eyre hesitated for a moment, and then peeled back one of the man's eyelids with his thumb. The irises were brown; although not that reddish-brown which distinguished the eyes of so many Aborigines. Carefully, Eyre pushed the eyelid back.

He was not squeamish about touching dead men: he had touched so many, and some he had embraced.

He suddenly became aware that Charlotte was standing close behind him, looking down at the body.

'Charlotte,' he said, 'this is not a place for you.' But there was very little hint of admonition in his voice. He knew that she had to look; that she would not be satisfied until she did.

Charlotte said quietly, 'He could almost be a white man.'

'Just pale, my dear. Some of them are. Sometimes it's caused by disease. Poor food, that kind of thing. I've seen some Aborigines who looked like snowmen.'

'Snowmen,' Charlotte whispered.

Eyre stood up. 'Come away now,' he said. 'There's nothing to be done. I'll have to make a report to the governor; and perhaps a note to Captain Billington, too.'

Charlotte stayed where she was, the warm wind blowing the hem of her cream-coloured dress into curls. 'Do you think—?' she began. But then she stopped herself, because she had asked the same question already in her mind, and so many times before, and the answer had always been the same: that she would never know. The desert does something to a child. It makes a child its own; as do the strange people who walk the desert asking neither for food nor for water; except what they themselves can discover from the ground.

Eyre had explained that to Charlotte time and time again, in different ways, perhaps to prepare her for this very moment.

She turned and looked at him, and there were so many anguished questions in her eyes that he had to look away—at the lawns, the kangaroos in the distance—at anything that would relieve him from the pain which she was using like a goad—forcing him to face up again and again to the most terrible secret of his whole life.

'It's not possible,' he said. Then he reached out his hand, and said, 'Come on. Come away. There's no profit to be had from staying here.'

'I always thought—' she blurted; and then she took a breath, and controlled herself, saying in a wavery voice, 'I always thought that he might have survived somehow, and been taken care of. I mean—why else would they have taken him? Except for money perhaps, and they never asked for that. I always imagined that he might have grown up amongst them; and lived a happy life, for all that had happened. Even Aborigines can be happy, can't they, Eyre? You know them better than I do. The men, I mean. They *can* be happy, can't they?'

'Yes,' said Eyre.

He took her sleeve, but she twisted away from him, and looked down again at the body lying in the lawn.

'He looks so contented,' she said. 'They killed him, and yet he looks so peaceful. As if he were at home, at last.'

Eyre frowned towards the Aborigine who had brought Biranga in; and thought of what he had said. *'He didn't even put up his hand to save himself. He was just standing, sir; just staring.'*

He said to Wawayran, 'Make sure this fellow gets buried; soon as you like.'

'Yes, sir.' Then, 'Please, sir?'

'What is it?'

'Well, sir, the burial, sir. Christian or Wirangu, sir?'

'This man's a Wirangu, isn't he?'

Wawayran didn't answer at first, but stared at Eyre in a peculiar way.

'He's a Wirangu?' Eyre repeated, sharply.

'Yes, sir.'

'Well, then, give him a Wirangu burial.'

'Yes, sir.'

Charlotte had already returned to the house. Eyre stood on the lawn for a moment, undecided about what he should do next. Before he could turn away, though, one of the black boys came towards him with his hand held out, and said, 'Mr Walker, sir, this was found in Biranga's bag.'

18

Eyre peered at it, and then picked it up. It was a fragment of stone, carved and painted with patterns.

'This is nothing unusual,' he said. 'It is only a spirit-stone.'

'But what it says, sir.'

'What do you mean?'

The boy pointed to the patterns and the pictures. 'The stone says, this is the mana stone which will be carried by the one spirit who comes back from the world beyond the setting sun; and by this stone you will know that it is truly him.'

Eyre turned the stone over and over in his hand.

'Yes,' he said, at last. 'I saw something like this before, once upon a time.'

'Well, sir, if Biranga was carrying the stone, do you think that was the spirit who come back from the world beyond the setting sun?'

Eyre looked at the boy, and then laid a hand on his shoulder.

'Do you believe in spirits coming back from the land beyond the setting sun?'

The boy hesitated, and then said, 'No sir.'

'No, sir,' Eyre repeated. Then, 'Neither do I.'

And the time will come when a dead spirit visits the earth from the place beyond the setting sun, so that he may see again how beautiful it was.

Many will be frightened by the spirit's white face; but he will be befriended by a simple boy, who will guide him through the world.

In return for this kindness, the spirit will try to teach the boy the magical ways of those who have passed into the sunset.

However, he will forget that the boy is only mortal, and in trying to teach the boy how to fly like a spirit, he will cause the boy to drop from the mountain called Wongyarra, and die.

And the spirit in his grief and remorse will seek out the cleverest of all clever-men, and will give him the magical knowledge of the dead; so that the clever-man may pass the knowledge on to every tribe; and to every tribesman.

And in this way the grief of the spirit will be assuaged; and the tribes of Australia will be invincible in their magical knowledge against men and devils and anyone who wishes them harm.

And this will be the beginning of an age that is greater and more heroic than the Dreaming.

> — Nyungar myth, first recorded by J. Morgan in Perth, 1833, from an account by the Aboriginal Galliput

One

There was an extraordinary commotion at the Lindsay
house when he arrived there on his bicycle. Mrs McMurtry
the cook was standing on the front lawn screaming shrilly;
while upstairs the sash-windows were banged open and
then banged shut again; and angry voices came first from
the west bedroom and then from the east; and footsteps
cantered up and down stairs; and doors slammed in
deafening salvoes. Yanluga the Aborigine groom scampered out of the front porch with his hair in a fright crying,
'Not me, sir! No, sir! Not me, sir!' and rushed through the
wattle bushes which bordered the garden, like a panicky
kangaroo with greyhounds snapping at his tail.

Eyre propped his bicycle against a hawthorn tree and
approached the house cautiously. Mrs McMurtry had
stopped screaming now and had flung up her apron over
her face, letting out an occasional anguished '*moooo*', as if
she were a shorthorn which urgently needed milking. The
front door of the house remained ajar, and inside Eyre
could just see the bright reflection from the waxed cedar
flooring, and the elegant curve of the white-painted banisters. Somewhere upstairs, a gale of a voice bellowed,
'You'll do what I tell you, my lady! You'll do whatever I
demand!'

Then a door banged; and another.

Eyre walked a little way up the garden path; then took off his Manila straw hat and held it over his chest, partly out of respect and partly as an unconscious gesture of self-protection. He was dressed in his Saturday afternoon best: a white cotton suit, with a sky-blue waistcoat with shiny brass buttons, from the tailoring shop next to Waterloo House. His high starched collar was embellished with a blue silk necktie which had taken him nearly twenty minutes to arrange.

'Is anything up?' he asked Mrs McMurtry.

Mrs McMurtry let out a throat-wrenching sob. Then she flapped down her apron, and her face was as hot and wretched as a bursting pudding.

'The mutton-and-turnip pie!' she exclaimed.

Eyre glanced, perplexed, towards the house. 'The mutton-and-turnip pie?' he repeated.

'*Moooo!*' sobbed Mrs McMurtry. Eyre came over and laid his arm around her shoulders, trying to be comforting. Her candy-striped kitchen-dress was drenched in perspiration, and her scrawny fair ringlets were stuck to the sides of her neck. In midsummer, cooking a family luncheon over a wood-burning stove was just as gruelling as stoking the boilers of a Port Lincoln coaster.

'That's not Mr Lindsay I hear?' asked Eyre.

Mrs McMurtry snuffled, and sobbed, and nodded frantically.

'But surely Mr Lindsay wasn't due home until Friday week!'

'Well, *mooo*, he's back now, aint he; came back this morning in the blackest of humours; too hot, says he, and nothing to show for a month's dealings in Sydney but expenses; and he kicks the boy for not grooming the horses as good as he wanted; and he kicks the dog for sleeping in the pantry while he was gone; and then he shouts at Mrs Lindsay for letting Miss Charlotte dress herself up like a fancy-woman, *mooo*, and for walking out without his say-so, with only the boy for chaperone; and then he sees that

22

it's mutton-and-turnip pie, and what he says is, *mooo*, what he says is, "I hates the very *sight* of mutton-and-turnip pie, so help me,' that's what he says, and he tosses it clean out of the kitchen window and upside-down it lands plonk in the veronica.'

Eyre took his hand away from Mrs McMurtry's sweaty shoulders and wiped it unobtrusively on his jacket. He looked towards the house again and bit his lip. This was extremely bad news. He had wanted to tell Lathrop Lindsay about his freshly flowered affection for Charlotte in his own particular way. Mr Lindsay was unpredictable, irascible, and no lover of 'sterlings', those who had newly arrived from England, or what he called 'the burrowing class', by which he meant clerks and salesmen and junior managers. Mr Lindsay had a special dislike of Eyre, and not just because Eyre was a 'sterling', or because he worked as a clerk for the South Australian Company down at the port. He disliked Eyre's manner, he disliked Eyre's smartly cut clothes, and he very much disliked Eyre's bicycle. It was probably fair to say that he disliked Eyre even more than he disliked mutton-and-turnip pie, and for that reason Eyre had wanted to prepare the ground for his announcement with ingenuity and care. He had already run two or three useful errands for Mrs Lindsay; and advised her where to find a reliable gardener, one who could conjure up English primroses as well as acacia. And back at his rooms on Hindley Street he had stored up five bottles of Lathrop Lindsay's favourite 1824 port-wine, which he had obtained in barter from the bo'sun of the *Illyria* in exchange for two nights' use of his bed, and an introduction to a benign and enormously fat Dutch girl called Mercuria.

Now all this expense and inconvenience had gallingly gone to waste; and Eyre cursed his rotten luck.

'I never saw Mr Lindsay in such a bate,' protested Mrs McMurtry.

One of the upstairs windows was lifted again. Mrs

Lindsay leaned out, white and fraught, with her primrose hair-ribbon halfway down the side of her head.

'Mr Walker!' she called, breathily. 'You'll have to make yourself scarce! My husband has come back, and I'm afraid that he's terribly angry at Charlotte for having stepped out with you. Please—you must go at once!'

At that moment, another window opened up, on the other side of the house. It was Lathrop Lindsay himself, crimson with indignation.

'What's all this calling-out?' he demanded. 'Phyllis!' Then he caught sight of Eyre standing in the garden with his hat over his heart and he roared incontinently, 'You! Mr Walker! You stay there! I want to have a word with you!'

His window banged down again. Mrs Lindsay waved to Eyre in mute despair, and then she closed her window, too. Eyre took two or three steps in retreat, towards the garden gate, but then stopped, and decided to stand his ground. If he were to flee, and pedal off on his bicycle, he would never have the chance to walk out with Charlotte again. He had to face up to Mr Lindsay; one way or another. Not only face up to him, but win him over.

My God, he thought. How am I going to convince a snorting bull like Lathrop Lindsay that I could make him a suitable son-in-law? He cleared his throat, and wiped sweat away from his upper lip with the back of his sleeve. Mrs McMurtry had stopped *mooo*-ing now, and was staring at him with her hands on her hips with a mixture of suspicion and pity.

'He'll eat you up alive,' Mrs McMurtry told him. 'The last fellow Charlotte walked out with, Billy Bonham, he was a new chum like you; and Mr Lindsay cracked three of his ribs with a walking-cane, so help me. And he was a lot better connected than what *you* are.'

Eyre gave her a quick, dismissive scowl. She hesitated, huffed, and then flounced off back to the house, swinging a cuff at Yanluga as he re-appeared through the shrubbery.

'Sterlings and Abbos,' she grumbled. 'Bad luck to the lot of 'em!'

Yanluga came cautiously up towards Eyre, biting his lips in apprehension. He was only fifteen but he had a natural way with horses, a way of calming them and whispering to them. Charlotte said that she had once seen him whistle to a kangaroo on the south lawn; and freeze the animal where it was, head raised, and then walk right up to it, and speak to it gently, although she hadn't been able to hear what he had said. He was very black, Yanluga, a wonderful inky black, with bushy hair and a face that defied you not to smile at him. Eyre's mother would have called him 'sonsy'.

Only Lathrop Lindsay found Yanluga irritating; but then Lathrop found the whole world irritating; and not only because of his inflamed piles. Lathrop had been dispatched to Australia by the Southwark Trading Company as a polite but very firm way of telling him that his books were not in order; and ever since then he had fought a ceaseless and irascible crusade to re-establish his self-esteem, both social and moral. Lathrop spoke a great deal of God, and Mary Magdalene, and also of Surrey, which he missed desperately; but more usually of the natural superiority of those who were neither clerks, nor black.

Yanluga said, gently, 'I'm sorry, Mr Walker, sir.'

'Sorry?' asked Eyre. 'What for?'

'Mr Lindsay asked me, did I take you and Miss Charlotte out for rides, sir, and I said yes. And then he asked me, did we have a chaperone, sir, and I said no.'

Eyre ruffled Yanluga's wiry hair. 'Don't you worry yourself,' he said, trying to be reassuring. 'It's better that you told the truth, in any case.'

'Sir, one of my cousins knows Steel Bullet the Mabarn Man.'

'Is that so? I didn't think that anybody knew Steel Bullet—not to speak to; I thought he hunted on his own; and never let anybody find out where he was.'

'I tell you the truth, sir. One of my cousins knows Steel

Bullet, sir, and maybe if you paid enough money, Steel Bullet would come in the night and kill Mr Lindsay for you, sir.'

Steel Bullet the Mabarn Man was a legend in South-Western Australia; and whalers had already brought tales of his horrifying behaviour as far east as Adelaide. He was an Aboriginal called Alex Birbarn, and he was said to possess the magical powers of a Mabarn Man—including the ability to fly hundreds of miles at night, and to change himself into anything he wished, such as a rock, or an anthill. So far he was credited with the murders of seventy people, and he was notorious for following kangaroo hunts, and making off with the kangaroo skin or sometimes the whole kangaroo before the exhausted hunters realised they had a thief in their midst.

Eyre said, 'I don't want to kill Mr Lindsay, Yanluga. I just want to persuade him to be reasonable.'

'Mr Lindsay never reasonable, sir. Never.' He shook his head violently.

'Well, yes, I know that, but what can I do?'

'Call the Mabarn Man, sir. Steel Bullet will chop him up into very small pieces for you, sir. Please, sir. Everybody would be very happy to see you marry Miss Charlotte, sir. Especially Miss Charlotte, sir.'

Eyre looked at Yanluga carefully. 'Miss Charlotte told you that?'

'Yes, sir.'

'You're not making it up?'

'Honour of Joseph, honour of Jesus, honour of God who always sees us.'

'Hm,' said Eyre. He pushed a finger and thumb into his tight waistcoat pocket, and took out sixpence, which he held up for a moment, so that Yanluga could see the sunlight wink on it; and which he then tossed up into the air, and smartly caught.

'You can do something for me, young Yanluga. You can go tell Miss Charlotte that I absolutely adore her; you know what adore means? Well, never mind, just say it. And you can tell her to meet me at ten o'clock tonight by the back fence, and not to worry about Old Face-Fungus.'

'Face-Fun-Gus?' Yanluga frowned. He was one of the better-educated Nyungars, but he found it difficult to follow what Eyre was saying when he spoke in his broadest Derbyshire accent.

Eyre slapped him on the back. 'Never mind about that,' he said, impatiently. 'Just make sure that Charlotte's outside the back gate at ten. Tell her to dress warmly: it can get devilish cold at that time of night. But I'll bring a blanket and a bottle of wine. Come on now, cut along, here's Mr Lindsay.'

Lathrop Lindsay was bustling down the front steps of the house, clutching a black-lacquered cane in both hands, his knuckles spotted with white. 'Now look here,' he called, and then he waved his stick at Yanluga, and cried, 'Be off with you! You idle black bastard!'

He steamed up to Eyre with all the boisterous energy of a small tug boat, his pale eyes bulging, his mouth tight. He wore tight white cotton trousers and a scarlet embroidered waistcoat, and a red necktie. His bald head was beaded with sweat.

'Now then, Mr Lindsay,' said Eyre, backing away a little, and lifting his hands to show that he surrendered.

'Now then yourself, you blackguard,' puffed Lathrop. 'You and your beguiling ways. You and your yessir nossir. And what happens the moment I'm away? Take advantage, don't you? Yessir. That's what you're interested in, isn't it, courting my daughter; nothing to do with shipping or business, nossir. And to think I believed you honest. To think I said to Mrs Lindsay, not a day before I went away, there's a trustworthy chap, albeit a new chum, and still white as milk. Yessir.'

'Mr Lindsay, please, I think there's been a frightful misunderstanding,' Eyre protested. Then, more persuasively, he said, 'Please.'

'Well, then?' Lathrop demanded. 'Did you go walking out with Charlotte or didn't you?'

27

'Yes, sir.'

'And did you take a chaperone with you?'

'No sir.'

'And what, pray, do you think that does for my daughter's reputation? Bad enough, by Heaven, that she walks out with one of the burrowing class. Bad enough, by God. But to walk out unattended, when anything might happen. *Anything*; and you know what *anything* means. Anything means shady goings-on, at least in the common mind, at least in the vulgar imagination, that's what anything means.'

'Mr Lindsay—' Eyre began.

'Mr Lindsay nothing,' Lathrop interrupted him. 'You'll be off at once, or I'll have the dogs on you. And you'll not be back, nossir. If I catch you once around this property; just once; if I catch you sniffing around my daughter; well you whelp I'll have you arrested by God and locked up, yessir, and beaten, too; whipped.'

'Eyre stood his ground. 'Mr Lindsay,' he said, 'I love your daughter. I love her with all my heart. And, what's more, I believe that she loves me in return.'

Lathrop stared at Eyre like a madman. His hairy nostrils widened, and his whole body seemed to quake uncontrollably.

'Mr Lindsay—' Eyre cautioned him. But Lathrop grew redder and redder, and his eyes popped, and with peculiarly stiff movements he raised his cane in his right hand, and began to advance on Eyre with dragging, paralytic steps; as if his entire nervous system had been congested by sheer rage.

'You dare to speak to me of love,' he boiled. 'You dare to come to my house on a bicycle and speak to me of love. By God, you young cur, I'll take the skin off your back.'

'Mr Lindsay, please, you're not yourself,' Eyre told him, retreating towards the garden gate. 'This is not you, Mr Lindsay. Not the calm and ordered Mr Lindsay, of Waikerie Lodge.'

He backed quickly out of the garden gate, and closed it.

The two of them faced each other over the low white-painted palings; Eyre trying every possible expression of appeasement in his facial repertoire; Lathrop Lindsay gradually coming to the point of spontaneous combustion.

'Mr Lindsay, I don't know what to say,' said Eyre. 'I imagined that I was a friend of the family. You gave me to *believe* that I was. I apologise if I mistook your charm and your courtesy for friendship. Perhaps you were just being nice to me for the sake of politeness. Please; it's all my fault and I apologise. Can't we start afresh?'

Lathrop threw open the garden gate and began to stalk after Eyre along the dusty sidewalk.

'You, sir, are trying my temper to the very utmost,' he trembled. 'And if you are not astride that contraption of yours, that ridiculous pedalling-machine, and gone; if you are not gone by the time I reach you with this cane, then, God help you, I will have that skin of yours; and I will stretch out that skin of yours on my fence.'

Eyre reached the hawthorn-tree and retrieved his bicycle. 'You can consider me gone already,' he said, tilting his nose up haughtily. 'If I'm not welcome, then I'll leave you. But a sadder man, let me tell you. And a disillusioned one, too. I used to respect you, Mr Lindsay, as a man of great social grace. I used to believe that you could charm the birds out of the trees.'

'By God,' Lathrop threatened him; but at that moment there was a dull dusty flopping sound on the sidewalk next to him; and then another. He looked around in surprise, and saw that two currawong birds had fallen unconscious out of the hawthorn-tree, one after the other, and were lying in the dirt with their legs in the air.

It was a common enough sight at this time of year, when the birds gorged themselves on dozens of fermented hawthorn berries and fell out of the trees in a drunken stupor. But the apt timing of their appearance led Lathrop and Eyre to stare at each other in utter surprise. Eyre couldn't help himself: he burst out laughing.

'I told you, Mr Lindsay! And it looks as if you can still do it!'

Lathrop let out an unearthly growling noise, and rushed towards Eyre with his cane lifted. Eyre pushed his bicycle four or five quick paces, then mounted the saddle and pedalled off along the street as rapidly as he could.

'I'll thrash you, you blackguard!' Lathrop screamed after him. 'You stay away from Charlotte, do you hear me! You burrower!'

Eyre raised his hat in mocking salute, and pedalled off between the rows of houses and hawthorn trees. Three Aborigine children in mission-school dresses stopped and stared at him as he balanced his way past them. He was whistling defiantly, a new popular song that had just found its way to Adelaide from London, 'Country Ribbons', and he sang the first verse of it as he turned right at the end of the road and bumped his way downhill on the dry ridgy track that led towards the centre of town.

'In her hair were country ribbons,
Tied in bows of pink and white;
In her hair were country ribbons
In her eyes a gentle light.'

But he stopped singing long before he reached the corner of Hindley Street; and as he approached his lodging-house he dismounted from his bicycle and walked the rest of the way. The truth was that he had grown far fonder of Charlotte than he had actually meant to. There was something so unusual and provocative about her; something that stirred him in the night, when he was curled up under his blanket and trying to sleep. Charlotte Lindsay was special, and Eyre was afraid that what he had said to Lathrop was painfully true: he loved her. In fact, he loved her so much that he almost wished that he didn't.

His landlady's husband, Dogger McConnell, was sitting in his red-painted rocking-chair on the porch, smoking his pipe. Dogger had once been a dingo-hunter, out beyond Broken Hill, and he reckoned that in his life he had killed thousands of them. 'Bloody thousands.' His face was as creased as a creek-bed, and his conversation was unremittingly laconic. He could tell tales of the outback that, in his own words, would 'shrivel your nuts', but he rarely did. He preferred instead to smoke his pipe in satisfied silence on the porch and watch the comings and goings along Hindley Street, and take a prurient interest in the activities of his wife's eleven lodgers, who were all male, and all clerks, and all desperate for female company, always.

'Back early, Mr Walker,' he remarked

'Yes. The young lady's father was home. Rather unexpectedly, I'm afraid; and not in the best of sorts.'

'Hm, I've heard tell of that Lathrop Lindsay. Old Douglas Moffitt used to do odd-jobs for him, painting and suchlike. Not an easy man, from what Douglas used to say.'

'No, certainly not,' said Eyre. He wheeled his bicycle into the cool dusty shadows under the verandah. He only left it there so that the leather saddle wouldn't get too hot in the afternoon sun, not because he was frightened that anyone might steal it. Apart from the severe punishments which met any kind of pilfering, hardly anybody in Adelaide apart from Eyre knew how to ride a bicycle, and even when they had seen him do it, many of the blackfellows still believed that it was impossible, or at the very least, magic. The children called him Not-Fall-Over.

Eyre came back out and sat on the steps.

'You're glum, chum,' said Dogger. He puffed his pipe and frayed fragments of smoke blew across the sunny street.

'Well,' said Eyre, 'you'd be glum if you were in love.'

'With her?' Dogger cackled, gesturing behind him with his thumb. 'You've got to be bloody joking.'

'I don't know why you're so hard on her,' said Eyre. 'She's a fine woman. She's always good to me, anyway.'

Dogger took his well-gnawed pipestem out of his mouth and leaned toward Eyre with a wink. 'She's good to me too, chum. Always has been and always will be. But as

31

for love. Well, no, love's in your head. You can't love any more, when you grow older, you don't have the brain for it. And the things I've seen, out at Broken Hill. Different values, you see, out beyond the black stump. And, to tell you the truth, you don't have the steam for it. Do you know what I mean? And she's had eleven children, Mrs McConnell. Eleven; nine still living, seven normal, two potty. Left her as capacious as the Gulf of St Vincent, without being indelicate.'

'Indelicate?' said Eyre, mildly amazed.

They sat together on the verandah for a while in silence. The sun began to nibble at the branches of the gum trees on the other side of the street and the dusty lanes and gardens began to glow with the amber light which Eyre could never quite get used to, even after a year in Australia; as though everything around them, houses, trees, and sun-dusted hills, had become theatrically holy.

Dogger said, 'There's a jug of beer in the kitchen, bring some out. Maybe I'll tell you about the time that poor old Gordon Smith had to cut his horse's throat, just for something to drink. And listen chum, I'd forget that girl of yours, I would, if I were you.'

Eyre turned to him, and looked for a moment into that brown, crumpled-handkerchief face, and then turned away again. 'Yes,' he said, 'I suppose I ought to.'

Two

But he couldn't, of course. He had the same obstinacy in him as his father; the same determination to have what he wanted in the face of every discouragement possible. And he very much wanted Charlotte.

That was why, at a quarter to ten that evening, he was crouched among the wattle bushes at the rear of Waikerie Lodge, whistling tonelessly from time to time so that if Charlotte had managed to venture out into the garden, she would be able to hear him over the sweatshop clamour of insects and night parrots.

He had brought a plaid blanket with him, as well as a bottle of sweet Madeira wine, which was Charlotte's favourite; and a handkerchief with a few of Mrs McConnell's apple turnovers tied up in it, in case they felt peckish.

He was probably being wildly over-optimistic. Lathrop would more than likely have kept Charlotte confined to her room, in disgrace. Lathrop was the kind of father who would allow his daughter every indulgence, except the freedom to choose her own lovers. Not that he was particularly unusual. Eyre had already discovered that most of the upper-quality families in Adelaide were stiff and virtuous, and kept a very short rein on their daughters, regardless of how plain they were.

Eyre felt tense and lustful at the same time; and his starched collar cut into his neck. He wished very much that he hadn't drunk quite so many glasses of Dogger's home-made beer; for if Charlotte didn't appear soon, he was going to be obliged to hide behind the stringy-bark gums which screened the end of the Lindsay's garden, and relieve himself.

He whistled again, low and flat. Still there was no reply.

The moon was not yet up, although the sky was a pale luminous purple, the colour of parakeelya flowers. Lathrop Lindsay's grand white-painted mansion had taken on the appearance of a house made of sugar, with gingerbread shingles and frosted verandahs. Like most of the statelier homes in Adelaide, it had been shipped from England piece by piece, pillars and newels and architraves all numbered and ready for reconstruction among the gums and wattles of the Lindsays' private estates.

The Lindsays lived to the north-west of Adelaide, in common with almost all of the richer and better-connected settlers; eschewing the streets and squares and parks that had been laid out for them by Adelaide's Surveyor-General, Colonel William Light, only five years ago. Last year, soon after Eyre had arrived, Adelaide had been declared Australia's first municipality, and land prices in the centre of town had soared, up to £10,000 a section, but the heart of Light's city was still neglected. Those brave souls who ventured for a walk into Victoria Square, the small park halfway along King William Street, were still quite liable to become frighteningly lost, and have to spend the night under the shelter of fallen gum-trees.

Lathrop had several times thrust his thumbs aggressively into his waistcoat, and told Eyre, 'Planners don't make cities; people do. And the manner of man who has chosen to make South Australia his home, free and self-determined, is going to build his house where he wishes. We're not convicts, by God; nor refugees political or religious; nor anybody's minion, neither.'

Eyre took out his silver pocket-watch and sprung open the case so that he could check the time. Ten o'clock and half-a-minute; and still no sign of Charlotte. He shivered, partly with cold and partly because he was bursting to empty his bladder. But supposing he went for a piss and missed Charlotte altogether? Or supposing she came out, all perfume and beauty, and caught him at it? He swore to God that he would never drink beer again.

He whistled again, and listened. A parrot creaked and chattered, and fluttered in the branches off to his left. One of the windows in the Lindsay house dimmed, and then the window next to it brightened, as if someone were carrying an oil-lamp from room to room. A window was closed, and then four or five shutters. It sounded as if the family were preparing to go to bed.

Eyre thought of the afternoon when he and Charlotte had walked in the abandoned Botanic Gardens, among the wild and scraggly bushes, down by the Company's bridge. A flock of sulphur-crested cockatoos had suddenly risen from the river-banks like a shower of snow, and circled around them, fluttering and crying, and then gradually settled again. And while Yanluga had sat placidly at the reins of the carriage, smoking his small clay pipe, Eyre had drawn Charlotte close to him, and kissed first her cheek, and then her forehead, and then her lips, until she had lifted her fingers gently and touched his mouth, to make him stop, because he was disturbing her so.

A dog barked three or four times, over by the mill. Then there was silence again, for endless minutes; except for the insects, and the night-birds, and the whispering of the trees.

Eyre decided that Charlotte wasn't coming; and that it was time to give up this amorous vigil as nothing but self-inflicted torture, both physical and mental. He collected up his blanket and his bottle of wine and his parcel of cakes, and retreated from his hide-out by the Lindsay's back gate at a slow backstepping crouch, until he was well beyond the stringy-bark gums. He paused for a clattering pee; and he was just buttoning himself up again when Yanluga appeared out of nowhere, the whites of his eyes as bright as a beast's, and his teeth shining in a disembodied grin.

Eyre let out a whoop of fright.

'Mr Walker, sir,' said Yanluga, clutching his sleeve.

'Yanluga! You scared me out of my skin.'

Yanluga couldn't help giggling. 'You were making *kumpa* on the dry tree-bark. Anybody could hear, for miles and miles.'

'Only if they had ears like a blackfellow; or a dingo. Where's Miss Charlotte?'

'Miss Charlotte had to go to her room, sir. Mr Face Fun-Gus say so.'

'Damn it,' said Eyre. 'I thought as much. Damn. Can you give me another message for me?'

'You shouldn't worry, sir,' said Yanluga. 'Miss Charlotte said, wait for just a little while, and she can escape from her room. Then she will come to the garden to see you. *Ngaiyeri* Face Fun-Gus is very tired from travelling; and from *ngraldi*, from anger.'

'*Ngraldi*,' Eyre repeated. 'I think that describes it perfectly. Will she be long?'

'One minute, two minutes. But wait here.'

Eyre laid down his blanket and his wine, and then reached out and took Yanluga's hand, and squeezed it. 'Teach me another word,' he said. 'The blackfellow for "friend." '

Yanluga kept on smiling, but he was silent for a very long time.

'What's the matter?' asked Eyre.

'No white sir ask me that before,' said Yanluga.

'Well, there's always a first time.'

Yanluga squeezed Eyre's hand in return. 'Friend is *ngaitye*, in my tongue, sir,' he said.

'*Ngaitye*,' Eyre pronounced; and then he said, 'That's you.'

Yanluga hesitated, and then he bowed his head, and said, 'I go find Miss Charlotte, Mr Walker, sir.'

'Good,' Eyre told him. 'And next time, don't come jumping out at me like a ghostly golliwog.'

Yanluga laughed, and raised both hands like a demon's claws. 'You be careful of Koobooboodgery, sir, the night spirit.'

'You be careful of yowcheroochee, the box on the ears,' Eyre retorted; and smiled to himself as Yanluga rustled quickly off into the golden wattles again and disappeared towards the house.

Eyre felt much more cheerful now, and spread out the blanket on top of the crisp, curled-up bark from the

surrounding gum-trees. He hummed to himself the chorus
from 'Country Ribbons'.

'*In her hair were country ribbons, tied in bows of pink
and white . . .*' and uncorked the bottle of Madeira and
took a mouthful straight from the neck to warm himself
up.

Over his right shoulder, the moon had risen over the
distant undulating peaks of the Mount Lofty Range, and
Mount Lofty itself, the mountain the Aborigines called
Yureidla. The dogs over at the new flour mill began to yip
and howl again; but probably because there were dingoes
around, hunting for Mr Cairns's poultry.

He thought of the morning he had first seen Charlotte,
seven months ago, when her father had brought her down
to the wharf to watch the unloading of pumping machinery
from England. It had been a bright, busy day, with a fresh
wind blowing across the mouth of the harbour; and Eyre
had been supervising the loading of a ripe-smelling cargo
of raw wool, bound for Yorkshire, with the stub of a pencil
stuck behind one ear, and his scruffiest britches on.

His fellow clerk Christopher Willis had nudged him, and
said, 'What do you think of that, then, Eyre, for a prize
ornament?'

Eyre had raised one hand to shield his eyes from the
sun; and had stared at Charlotte in complete fascination.
She was small, white-skinned, and angelically pretty, with
blonde curls straying out from the brim of her high straw
bonnet. At first she had appeared almost too doll-like to
be true, especially the way in which she was standing so
demurely beside her father in her pink fringed shawl; but
when she turned and looked towards Eyre he saw that
she had a mouth that was pouty and self-willed and a little
petulant; the mouth of a spoiled little rich girl who needed
taming as well as courting. The sort of girl who could
benefit from being put over a chap's knee, and spanked.

'Well, well,' Eyre had remarked, and grinned across the
wharf at her and winked.

'That's not for you, Master Walker,' Christopher had

chided him. 'That's Lathrop Lindsay's only and unsullied daughter; and he's keeping her in virginal isolation until royalty comes to Adelaide, or at the very least a duke; or an eligible governor, not like poor old George Gawler.'

'She scarcely looks real, does she?' Eyre had murmured. 'And by all the stars, look, she's smiling at me.'

'Scowling, more like, if she takes after papa,' Christopher had told him. 'Lathrop Lindsay's temper is one of the hazards that they warn settlers about, before they embark from Portsmouth; that, and the heat, and the death-adders, and the tubercular fever.'

'No, no, she's definitely smiling at me,' Eyre had insisted, and had ostentatiously doffed his hat, and bowed.

'Who's that impudent ruffian?' he had heard Lathrop demanding, in a voice like a blaring trumpet. 'You! Yes, *you*, you scoundrel! Be off with you before I have you thrashed!'

Eyre hadn't seen Charlotte for several weeks after that; although he had bicycled out several times to Waikerie Lodge, where the Lindsays lived, and sat on the wrought-iron seat across the road in the hope of catching a glimpse of her, occasionally smoking one of his brandy-flavoured cheroots, or eating an apple.

That was why it had been such a stroke of good fortune when Lathrop's senior manager, a morose man called Snipps, had visited the offices of the South Australian Company where Eyre was working, and had asked if Mr Lindsay could be expeditiously assisted with a cargo of wheat, which was lying at the dockside without a merchantman to take it. Eyre had immediately arranged for a Bristol ship which was already half-loaded with wool to be unloaded again, and for Mr Lindsay's cargo to be taken in preference; and at a preferential rate. The irate sheep-owner whose wool it was hadn't discovered that his cargo was still in the warehouse at Port Adelaide until the ship was already halfway across the Great Australian Bight; but

Eyre had been able to mollify him with the promise of the very next ship, and a case of good whisky.

Most important for Eyre, however, had been an invitation two weeks later to a garden-party at Waikerie Lodge, in gratitude for his assistance. There, on the green sunlit lawns, where peacocks clustered, he had been introduced formally to Lathrop; and to Mrs Lindsay, and at last to Charlotte. He and Charlotte had said nothing very much as Lathrop had brought them together; but there had been an exchange of looks between them, his challenging, hers provocative; and Eyre had known at once that they could be lovers.

Later, munching one of Mrs McMurtry's teacakes, Eyre had spoken for a while to Lathrop of shipping costs; and how those who knew friendly clerks in the South Australian Company could save themselves considerable amounts of money, especially if the bills of lading showed that cargoes weren't quite as weighty as one might have imagined them to be. And Lathrop (who hadn't once recognised Eyre as the 'impudent ruffian' from the wharf) gave him a sober and watery-eyed look that meant business.

From then on, Eyre had been a regular visitor at Waikerie Lodge, either on business or on social calls; and he and Charlotte had been drawn together like two dark solar bodies, feeling the tug of each other's sexual gravity and being unable and unwilling to resist it.

Eyre looked at his watch again. On the inside of the lid was engraved a crucifix, and the words '*Time flies, death urges, knells call, heaven invites, hell threatens,*' and then 'Henry L. Walker, 1811'. The watch was the only gift that his father had given him when he had decided to emigrate to Australia; and he both treasured it and resented it; but it told the time with perfect accuracy, and now it was eleven minutes past ten.

He heard a low call. Yanluga, skirting around the garden. Then he heard the back gate creak open, and the swishing of skirts on the grass. Before he knew it, Charlotte was there, in her shawl and her blue ruffled dress, pale-faced and smelling of lily-of-the-valley. Her blonde curls shone in the moonlight, and her eyes glistened with emotion. Eyre held out his arms to her, and she came to him, in a last quick rustle of silk; and then they were holding each other close, closer than ever before.

'Oh, Eyre,' she said. 'I'm so sorry about what happened. If only I had known that father was coming back so soon.'

He kissed her forehead, and then her eyes, and then her lips. 'Shush now; it wasn't your fault. If anybody's to blame, it's me, for upsetting your family so.'

'Hold me tight,' she begged him. 'I'm so frightened that father won't allow us to see each other again.'

'He can't do that.'

Charlotte shook her head. 'He can; and if he's really angry, he will.'

'Yanluga says he suffers from *ngraldi*.'

'*Ngraldi*?' asked Charlotte. She rested her face against his lapels, and held him tight around the waist, as if she were afraid that he might suddenly become lighter than air, and bob up into the night sky like a gas balloon. Eyre stroked the parting of her hair, and grunted with amusement.

'What's *ngraldi*?' she asked.

'Rage. I just like the sound of it. There's your father, getting into a *ngraldi* again.'

'But you've upset him terribly. He couldn't talk about anything else at dinner, except how you'd besmirched my reputation.'

Eyre kissed her again; right on her pouting mouth. 'Don't you worry about your father. He'll calm down, I'm sure of it; especially when he remembers how much money I'm saving him every month on shipping costs.'

'I don't know. He had a partner once, Thomas Weir, and even though he lost thousands of pounds, he refused to take Thomas Weir back, once they'd argued. He's so set in his ways; and he always believes he's so *right*.'

Eyre said, 'Sit down. I've brought a blanket. And some

Madeira wine, too, if you can manage to drink it out of the bottle. I couldn't work out a way of carrying glasses on my bicycle.'

Charlotte spread her skirt and sat down on the rug under the stringy-bark gums. She looked like a fantasy, in the unreal light of that cold and uncompromising moon; and the gums around her shone an unearthly blue-white, as if they were frightened spirits of the night, the slaves of Koobooboodgery.

Eyre flipped up his coat-tails and sat down close to her, taking her hands between his.

'It's so good to see you,' he said. 'This afternoon, I began to be worried that I might never set eyes on you again.'

Charlotte said, 'Dear Eyre. But it isn't going to be easy. Father doesn't go away again until just before Christmas, when he usually travels to Melbourne.'

'Surely he won't stay angry for as long as that.'

'Eyre, he wants me to marry into the aristocracy.'

'Of course he does. Every father in Adelaide wants to see his daughter married to a man who's wealthy, or famous, or well-bred; or all three. But the truth is that there aren't very many of those to be had. Some of those fathers will have to accept the fact that if their daughters are going to be married at all, they will have to put up with clerks for husbands, or farmers, or dingo-hunters, if they're not too quick off the mark.'

'Father said he would gladly see you hung,' Charlotte told him. She kissed him again, and he felt the softness of her cheek, and the disturbing lasciviousness of her lips. She was a girl of such contrasts: of such pretty mannerisms but such provoking sensuality; of bright and brittle intelligence but stunning directness; polite but candid; teasing but thoughtful; flirtatious but brimming with deeply felt emotions. Sometimes she was a woman who had not yet outgrown the coquettishness of girlhood; at other times she was an innocent girl whose life was slowly nudging out into the heady stream of sexual maturity, like a boat on the Torrens River. She was trembling on the cusp of

41

nineteen; and tonight she was probably more desirable than she would ever be again; sugar-candy and butterflies and claws. She knew how captivating she was; and yet she had not yet learned to use her attraction cruelly, or cynically, simply for the pleasure of seeing some poor beau dance on a string.

Eyre kissed her in return; much more forcefully, much more urgently. Their tongues wriggled together, until Eyre's tongue-tip penetrated Charlotte's slightly opened teeth, and probed inside her mouth, tasting the sweetness of it.

They parted for a few moments. Charlotte lay back on the blanket and stared up at him, without saying anything. Her mouth was still moist with their shared saliva, and she made no attempt to wipe it away.

Eyre said, 'Yanluga told me something today. I don't know how true it was; whether he was just trying to be nice to me.'

'Yanluga thinks the world of you. You're the only white man who has ever treated him with any respect. Men like my father don't think anything of the blackfellows; they don't even believe that they're human. Father's always striking Yanluga with his riding-crop. Once he made him pick up a coin that he had dropped, and then stepped on his fingers, just to hear him howl. He says they're like babies, the blackfellows, it's good for them to howl.'

Eyre was silent for a moment. Then he said, 'Yanluga told me you'd quite care to marry me, if you could.'

Charlotte slowly smiled.

'Is it true?' Eyre asked her.

She nodded. 'But he wasn't supposed to tell you. I shall whip him myself when I get back to the house.'

Eyre said, 'I want to marry you, too. And if that sounds like a proposal, well, I suppose it is. I very much like the sound of "Mrs Charlotte Walker." '

Charlotte said, 'Father won't allow it, you know. He won't even let you come near the house.'

'Can't your mother intervene?'

42

'She's tried. Poor dear mother. She was trying all evening to persuade father what a wonderful upright person you were; but he wasn't listening. He doesn't *want* to listen. He never thinks of my happiness, that's why. All he can think about is being the father-in-law to some English baron; or some famous explorer; or something that will give him glory.'

Eyre looked down at her, and stroked her cheek, and then her neck. 'What can we do, then?' he whispered.

'We could wait until I'm twenty-one; although he can make it difficult for me even then, because of my inheritance. Or you could go off and do some magnificent deed, and be knighted for it.'

'What magnificent deed could a clerk do?' asked Eyre. 'Fill in three thousand bills of lading in a week? Write up a record number of ledgers? And even if I *could* think of something magnificent to do, how are we to manage in the meantime, with a love that can't even be admitted in daylight?'

Charlotte reached up and held the hand that was stroking her cheek. She kissed his fingers, and then she said, 'We can manage. We must manage. But you mustn't be shocked.'

'Shocked?' he asked her.

She put her fingertip up to her pursed lips. 'Sssh,' she said; and then she reached down and unlaced the ribbon that held the bodice of her pale blue dress.

Eyre said, 'Charlotte?' but she shushed him again, and slowly drew out the criss-cross ribbon until her bodice was open to the waist. Then, eyes dreamily half-closed, she took his hand and slid it underneath the white silk lining until it was cupping her warm bare breast.

She whispered, 'You mustn't be shocked, or then I will shock myself. I love you, Eyre; I want you to touch me. I want you to love me just as much in return. Sometimes I tease you but I want you. I have dreams about you, dreams about kissing you; dreams that make me wake up feeling hot, and confused.'

43

Slowly, fascinated, he caressed her nipple between finger and thumb until he could feel it crinkle tight. Charlotte let her head drop back on to the blanket, her eyes completely closed now, her breath coming quick and harsh from between her parted lips.

'We must *make-believe* that we are married, if my father won't allow us,' she told him, in the same urgent, sleepy voice. 'If he discovers us, he will probably kill you, and he will most certainly whip me. But we don't mind the danger, do we, my darling lover? The risk is what makes us both so excited!'

Eyre was so aroused now that his britches could hardly contain him. He knelt over Charlotte, and drew the bodice of her dress wide apart, so that both her breasts were exposed to the moonlight. They were high young breasts, very white, well-rounded, and the nipples were as wide and pink as rose-petals stuck to a rainy window.

A night-parrot shrieked startlingly above them; and Eyre lifted his head for a moment in alarm. But then he realised that everything was quiet, and that they were still alone, and he bowed over her breasts, kissing them in quick, complicated patterns, teasing at her nipples with his teeth, pressing the soft flesh against his face.

'Eyre, I must be asleep; I must be dreaming,' sighed Charlotte, twisting and rustling beneath him, one arm raised so that he could see the pattern of blue veins on her thin white wrist, a single string of pearls around her neck. And all the time there was that needful sibilant whisper of silk, as she rubbed one thigh against the other.

'You've been sent to me ... from heaven,' he murmured, as he kissed her. 'And I *will* make you my wife . . . I promise it . . . one day.'

He reached downwards, and raised the frilly hems of her dress. At that moment, she opened her eyes and stared at him, and said in a high voice, 'I'm not at all sure what one does.' But Eyre leaned forward again, and brushed his lips against hers, and said, 'I'll show you.'

'But do you really *want* to?' she asked.

He smiled. 'Of all the people in all the world, upside down or right way up, I want to show *you* more than anybody.'

He paused, and then added, 'In fact, you're the *only* person I want to show.'

His hand caressed her silk-hosed knee, and then her thigh. Bloomers had not yet reached Australia as a universal fashion, and beneath her silk dress and her silk hooped underskirt, Charlotte wore nothing at all. Eyre's hand on her bare hip made her shudder, and when at last he ran his fingers around the curves of her bottom, and touched lightly the slipperiness between her legs, she cried out; a strange suppressed little cry like a shriek.

'You're safe,' Eyre comforted her. 'You're quite safe, and you're very beautiful.'

Wide-eyed, she lay back, and allowed him to touch her further; but she was tense now, and less sure of herself. She thought she heard a door banging over by the house, and she half-lifted her head, but Eyre gently pushed her back again, and said, 'It's nothing. You're safe. Just close your eyes and enjoy yourself.'

She flutteringly closed her eyes for a few seconds. She felt Eyre's fingers stroking her, and the sensation was so intense that she bit her lip. Then she could feel him peeling her sticky lips apart. His fingers were so tender! And then he slid one slowly right inside her; and she felt as if she were a geyser that was beginning to come to the boil, as if heat and bubbles were rising inside her and that they would have to come bursting out. The danger and the excitement and the lewdness of having a man's finger, Eyre's finger, right up inside her, right under her skirts! And she held his wrist tight between her silk-sheathed thighs, gripping him there, wanting to keep him there for ever, wanting him deeper, wanting him so much that it almost gave her backache.

'Eyre,' she garbled, and she could hardly understand her own voice. 'Eyre, please, whatever it is, show me, please.'

He knelt astride her. She heard him unbuckling his belt, and his britches buttons being pulled apart with a soft sound like an opening seed-pod. Then he took her hand, her small white uncertain hand, and brought it downwards; urged it downwards; and laid in it a hot thick sceptre of flesh. So hard, so demanding, so impossibly big. And she stared up at him for reassurance, and comfort; but all she saw in his eyes then was an inexplicably glazed look, as if he were somehow suddenly possessed; as if instead of being Eyre he were *all* men, at the moment of taking a woman.

Eyre said, '*Now*.' His throat was constricted, and he was shaking. Charlotte clutched him tighter, and tighter still, as if by clutching him so tight she could make him burst, and bring to a finish this strange and suddenly frightening act of passion; and exorcise the devils that had arisen in both of them, tongues and forks and fire, to stoke up their lust.

Eyre shifted his weight forwards, kneeling on the back of her dress, trapping her, and forcing her thighs apart, indecently wide. She released her hold on him, and desperately clutched at the blanket, and at the fragments of loose bark on the ground; and she thrashed her head from side to side in perplexity and fear and mounting desire. What was happening to her? She felt as if she were actually alight. She was going mad! Was this what it was like to go mad? She was burning! But she was chilled, too, sharply: she could feel the chill between her wide-apart thighs, exciting and terrifying at the same time. And Eyre was pushing against her, pushing and pushing, and urging himself into her. Not that! It was far too big! It would kill her, it would split her apart! It was like a huge crimson truncheon!

And then Eyre had fiercely grasped both of her shoulders, and tugged her towards him; so that the enormous crimson truncheon was forced right up between her legs; and she shrieked and shrieked at the top of her voice,

scattering parrots and jacks and galahs all through the
trees in a furious explosion of wings and feathers.

Three

A window banged; and then a door. Then they heard
somebody shouting in dialect. '*Naodaup*? What's the
matter? *Unkee*. A woman. *Tyintin*. Stay there.' And then
something about searching in the trees—'*Tuyulawarrin!*'

Eyre was already on his feet, swiftly buttoning up his
britches. Charlotte banged at her upraised dress with her
fists, as if it were a disobedient puppy that refused to lie
down. She was panting, and whimpering, embarrassed at
her own panic, and furious at Eyre for allowing her to
humiliate herself. 'You shouldn't have done!' she kept
flustering. 'Eyre, you *shouldn't!*'

Eyre tightened his belt, and then knelt down beside her
again. He felt shaky and breathless, and so irritable at
having been interrupted right at the very instant of posses-
sing her that his teeth were on edge, as if he had been
biting lemons.

Charlotte held on to his sleeve. 'I told you I didn't know
what was supposed to happen,' she persisted. 'You
shouldn't have done it, Eyre! It hurt so much!'

'You were frightened, that's all,' said Eyre, taking her
wrists and trying to coax her on to her feet. 'It doesn't
usually hurt, not like that. Usually, it's the most marvellous thing you can imagine. But you're right. I shouldn't
have led you on. Not here; and not tonight.'

'I just didn't *know*,' Charlotte told him; and now she
started to weep.

Eyre heard dogs barking, over by the stable-block. 'Come on, now,' he said. 'Your father's let the hounds out. We don't want to be caught here. Is there any way you can get back to your bedroom without him seeing you?'

Charlotte sniffed, and blew her nose on her little lace handkerchief. 'I think so. Once I get back through the garden gate, I can go along the ha-ha until I reach the kitchen. Then I can go up the back stairs.'

'Well you'd better hurry in that case,' said Eyre. 'It sounds as if he's brought out the whole pack. And if they can catch a red kangaroo, they can certainly catch us.'

'Eyre,' said Charlotte, lifting her face, wet with tears, to kiss him. 'Eyre, I'm sorry. You must think me so ridiculous.'

He kissed her, and then held her head close to his cheek, his fingers buried in her curls. 'It's my fault. I love you now and I always will. Now, please, you'd better go.'

The hounds were being led around the side of the house now, yipping and snapping. Eyre took Charlotte's arm and guided her swiftly to the garden gate; where he kissed her one last time before letting her go. She hurried off along by the stringy-bark gums at the end of the lawns, her blue ruffled dress shining pale in the moonlight, a fleeing ghost in a garden of ghostly trees.

Just before she could reach the ha-ha at the far side of the garden, however, and disappear from view; flashing lanterns appeared at the side of the house, and Eyre saw Lathrop's two Aborigine dog-handlers, Utyana and Captain Henry, struggling across the south-east patio with six greyhounds each. The dogs were straining at their leads until their eyes bulged, their claws scratching and skittering at the stone pathways.

'*Koola*! *Koola*!' Captain Henry shouted to his dogs, and they snarled and gnashed and writhed against their leads in a froth of hunting-lust. '*Koola*' was Aborigine for kangaroo, and these dogs had been trained for two years to chase after kangaroos and bring them down as quickly and as bloodily as possible. The dogs had to be strong and vicious because the kangaroos were strong and vicious; even the youngest kangaroo could run for miles before the hunt caught up with them, and a fully grown buck could fling a greyhound into the air and break its back. Kangaroos were unnervingly intelligent, too. Last season a big red had caught Lathrop's favourite hound Rocket with its front paws and held it under water at the Nguru waterhole until it had drowned.

Eyre shouted, 'Charlotte! Hurry!' and Charlotte at last reached the shelter of the ha-ha and began to run towards the house with her skirts raised. But the dog-handlers had already seen her, and must have thought she was an intruder, or even (knowing how superstitious they were) a Koobooboodgery. And now Lathrop himself appeared, in his flapping nightshirt, carrying a lantern in one hand and a musket in the other.

Captain Henry must have asked for permission to let the dogs loose; for Lathrop nodded, and in the next instant six of the greyhounds were streaking across the moonlit grass in sudden silence; pale shadows so quick that Eyre found it difficult to follow them.

He wrenched open the garden gate, and shouted at Lathrop, 'It's Charlotte! Call them off, Mr Lindsay! It's Charlotte!'

Lathrop stared at him from twenty yards away in complete amazement. 'Walker?' he demanded, lifting up his lantern. 'What the blue devil are you doing here?'

'It's Charlotte!' Eyre screamed at him.

'What?' Lathrop turned, frowned towards the ha-ha, frowned back at Eyre; and then said, 'Charlotte? What's Charlotte?'

'There! For the love of God, call those dogs off!'

It was then that they heard Charlotte scream, and the growling and snapping of the dogs.

Lathrop suddenly understood what was happening, and roared at Captain Henry, 'Call them off, man! Call them off! They'll kill her!'

Captain Henry held his hands on top of his head in complete misery. 'Can't do it, sir. Won't come now, sir. Not until they bring the *pipi*, sir.'

Eyre felt cold. He knew what *pipi* meant—entrails. Without thinking of anything at all, he began to run across the lawn towards the ha-ha, his vision a jumble of grass, gum-trees, flashes of moonlight. He could hear himself panting as he ran as if somebody else were running close beside him.

He reached the brink of the ha-ha, his shoes skidding on the dry grass. Charlotte had stopped screaming now; and was desperately trying to scramble up the side of the slope, one hand pressed to her face to keep the greyhounds from tearing at her nose and eyes. All six dogs were leaping and snapping and hurling themselves at her like suicidal acrobats. Two of them clung on to her petticoats to drag her down, while the others bit at her arms and her ankles and her bare shoulders.

Eyre roared at the top of his voice, and bounded down the ha-ha and right into the tussle of dogs, shouting, 'Off! You damned creatures! Get off! Damn you!'

He kicked one dog hard in the ribs, and it screamed like a child. Another went for his trousers, but he seized its hind leg and threw it end-over-end, howling, into a patch of bottlebrushes. But two more dogs launched themselves at his calves, and one of them bit right through into the muscle with an audible crunch of flesh, and the other scrabbled with sharpened claws at his ankles, ripping off skin in ribbons. Eyre shouted out loud, and yet another dog threw itself at his elbow, gripping the bone with relentless jaws and refusing to let go, even when he twisted its ear right around.

He dropped to the grass; first to his knees, then as the dogs went for him again, on to his back. He was too frightened even to cry out; and angry, too, in an extraordinary way.

Captain Henry reached the ha-ha, and managed to beat off two of the hounds with a stick; at least for long enough for Charlotte to be pulled, crying and bloody, to the safety of the dog-handler's side. But now the rest of the dogs hurled themselves at Eyre with redoubled fury, and one of them bit him right in the cheek, only an inch below his right eye, while two more of them ripped at his arms and his legs.

He thought, Jesus Christ, I'm dead. I'm already dead. These dogs are going to kill me. And his whole world was crowded with snapping and biting and flying saliva and flailing claws.

Quite suddenly, however, he felt the dogs stiffen, and lift their heads. One of them stepped back from him, and then the others followed, and in a moment all six of them changed from snarling beasts into elegant canine statues, standing in the light of the moon quite motionless, noses slightly lifted, as if they had inhaled some rare and indefinable essence that was undetectable by humans but which could instantly turn greyhounds into figures of limestone.

Lathrop said abruptly, 'Utyana. Tie the rest of those dogs up and bring Mr Walker up here. Captain Henry, do you hold your ground.'

'Yes, sir, Mr Lindsay.'

Digging his heels into the grass, Eyre managed to push himself a little way up the side of the ha-ha on his back. He was shocked and trembling and he felt as if his skin had been curried all over with a wire brush. Utyana hurried over and lifted him the rest of the way out of the ditch; and then he lay back on the grass, sniffing and shaking, and up above him the sky was impossibly rich with stars.

Utyana knelt beside him, taking off his wide felt hat so that he was wearing only a red headscarf over his scalp. He was big-nosed and ugly, and his breath smelled of sour fruit, but he smiled at Eyre and touched his forehead very gently.

'How's . . . Miss Charlotte?' asked Eyre.

'Yes, sir,' nodded Utyana.

'Going to be all right, no thanks to you,' remarked the

51

vinegar voice of Lathrop Lindsay, from somewhere out of sight.

'And me?' Eyre whispered. 'I'm not going to die, am I?'

'Yes, sir,' nodded Utyana.

'Only English the blighter ever learned,' said Lathrop. 'Understands it, doesn't speak it'.

Eyre reached down and felt his chest. His waistcoat was badly torn, and his lapels were hanging in shreds. Then suddenly he felt his stomach, and to his utmost horror he could feel something wet and stringy. He lifted it up in his hand, and raised his head a little way, and there between his fingers was a bloody mess of tatters, with something pulpy right in the middle of it all.

He let his head drop back on the grass. 'Oh my God,' he said, out loud. A feeling of nausea surged up in him, and his mouth flooded with blood and bile.

Lathrop came into view, on the right-hand side, and peered down at him. 'What's the matter with you?' Lathrop asked him, shortly.

Eyre took three or four quick breaths. 'I'm going to die, aren't I? Those dogs have ripped my guts out.'

Lathrop stared at him, and then down at his stomach. 'That, you mean?' he asked, poking at the stringy mess with his finger.

Eyre said nothing, but nodded rapidly. He was sure that he could already feel the coldness of death seeping into his legs; soon it would overtake him altogether.

'That's the lining of your jacket,' Lathrop told him. 'Got torn, that's all; and that bit there's your pocket, with your pocket-handkerchey. Ripped your guts out my Aunt Fanny. Wish they damn well had, the damage you've done.'

Eyre took another, longer breath, and then looked at Lathrop and attempted a friendly chuckle. It came out like a ghastly, irrational honk; and he was glad that Lathrop didn't hear it, and turned away.

It was then that Eyre realised how hushed the garden was; even the night-parrots were silent; and the insects had hesitated as if rain were expected, or an unfelt earth tremor had shaken the deeper levels of the surrounding hills.

Eyre said to Utyana, 'What's going on? Help me sit up.'

'Yes, sir.' Utyana smiled, and continued to stroke his forehead.

'For God's sake!' Eyre demanded. 'I want to sit up!'

Utyana at last realised what he wanted, and gripped him under the armpits with his thin black muscly hands, and helped him to sit. Eyre looked around, and the tableau that he saw in front of him was so strange that at first he couldn't believe that it was real.

The greyhounds were still poised in the ha-ha; with Captain Henry standing a little way back; and Lathrop commanding the scene with one hand firmly planted on his hip, his musket angled over his shoulder, and the evening breeze billowing his nightshirt around his thick white ankles. But it was Yanluga who caught Eyre's attention. He was sitting cross-legged on the far edge of the ha-ha, his back very straight, and he was whispering, a peculiar hollow whisper that gave Eyre a prickly feeling all the way down his back, the way some particularly plaintive music can.

Yanluga was charming the greyhounds as if they were children. They stood hypnotised, their ears and their tails depressed, their white eyes wide, watching him as if they couldn't bear to let him out of their sight for a single instant. Eyre didn't recognise the words that Yanluga was using; they didn't even sound like Wirangu. But the effect they had on the greyhounds was undeniable; they stood pale and still like dogs from the Bayeux Tapestry; and the moon which had now moved out from behind the stringy-bark gums gave the garden a look of enchantment. Yanluga would have called it a *mirang*, a place where magic is practised.

Lathrop took two or three steps back, so that he was standing next to Eyre.

'Remarkable, isn't it?' he said, without taking his eyes

off Yanluga. 'You'd be quite amazed at what some of these blackfellows can do. Sensitive to nature, that's what it is; only a step away from being animals themselves, and there's the proof of it. What civilised man could speak to a pack of greyhounds, so that they'd listen?'

Eyre said thickly, 'It seems that he saved my life.'

'Well, you're probably right,' replied Lathrop. 'After all, those are rare hounds, more than £50 apiece they cost me, and I'd have been loathe to shoot them, especially for the sake of a chap who's already trespassed twice in one day both on my property and on my patience; and abused my hospitality to the point of theft. You realise that if I speak to Captain Tennant, I could have you locked up; hanged, even. It wouldn't do you any harm at all, hanging. It might improve your manners.'

Eyre said, 'I am conscious, sir, that I owe you an apology. But I hardly think that being in love with Charlotte can be construed as a capital crime.'

'Abduction is a capital crime, sir.'

'There was no question of abduction, sir. Charlotte came to meet me of her own free will.'

Lathrop slowly turned his head to look at Eyre with small and shiny eyes.

'If I was the kind of father who was unaware of his daughter's extreme wilfulness; and was not quite accustomed to tantrums and foot-stamping and deliberate disobedience, especially during discussions about which young men are suitable companions for a girl of her quality and which young men are not; then I would be quite minded to whip you. But as it is, I *am* aware, and I *am* accustomed, and consequently I shan't.'

Eyre climbed slowly and painfully to his feet, with Utyana staying close by in case he needed help. He wiped his bloody mouth with the back of his bloody hand.

'I think I should go now,' he said. 'I'd like to wash out these bites before they go septic, and bandage myself up.'

Lathrop stared at him with a tight, forced smile. 'Of course you would, of course you would. Bandage yourself up, that's right. But there's one small aspect of this evening's amusements which still concerns me.'

Captain Henry called over, 'Can I leash the dogs now, sir? Seems as if they're growing restless.'

'In a moment,' Lathrop told him; then turned back to Eyre. 'What I'd like to know is, how was tonight's tryst arranged? That's what I'd like to know. And why is young Yanluga here? He was the one who drove you around with my own daughter in my own carriage while I was off in Sydney, wasn't he? Could it have been *he* who helped you to meet my daughter in the woods, in the dark, under the most improper of circumstances?'

Eyre glanced across the ha-ha. Yanluga had raised his arms now, and was chanting to the dogs, a long, repetitive chant. But there was no doubt that the hounds were beginning to twitch now, and lick their lips, and paw at the grass.

Lathrop said, 'I haven't punished him, you know; and until I discovered him here tonight I wasn't intending to. I like to think that I'm a forgiving employer, on occasions, as well as a stern one. But what he did tonight was really unforgivable.'

'He saved my life,' Eyre repeated.

'Ah,' said Lathrop. 'But had you not been here; had Yanluga not arranged a sweetheart's meeting for you; then there would have been no need for him to save your life, now would there? So, who do we have to blame for all of tonight's distress? Why, Yanluga.'

Eyre said, 'Leave him be. Please, for Charlotte's sake. For pity's sake.'

Lathrop peered at Eyre maliciously, as if he were trying to make out where he was in a particularly obnoxious fog. 'Let me tell you something, sir. I am an exemplary husband, a benevolent father, and a trustworthy businessman. But, I am not a monkey. I have never been a monkey and I never will be a monkey, and you won't make me one, I promise you.'

With that, he lifted his musket from his shoulder; and,

still smiling at Eyre, cocked it. Then he swung around, and aimed it directly at Yanluga.

'Boy!' he called.

Yanluga didn't look up at first; couldn't, because he was trying to keep the hounds calm. But then he glanced up quickly once; and then again and squinted at Lathrop in uncertainty and fear.

'What the devil are you doing?' Eyre demanded. 'You're not going to shoot him, not in cold blood!'

'Of course not,' said Lathrop. 'I am simply giving the chap a chance to leave my property, and my employ, as smartly as he likes. Boy!' he called again. 'Stop that singing and chanting now, and be off with you! That's it! Make yourself scarce!'

'Sir!' called Yanluga. 'Please ask Captain Henry to tie up the dogs first.'

'You just be off,' said Lathrop. 'Captain Henry will take care of the hounds when he pleases.'

'Sir, if I run, sir, the dogs will chase me.'

'As well they might. Now, let's have a look at those sandy-white heels of yours. And make it quick! I've lost enough sleep tonight as it is!'

'You can't do this,' said Eyre. 'Mr Lindsay, listen to me. Those dogs will tear him to pieces before he can get halfway across the garden.'

Lathrop continued to squint along his musket-barrel. 'There are several things you don't understand, Mr Walker; and one of those things is the meaning of justice. What you are seeing now is justice. The wronged employer gives the ungrateful servant the opportunity to leave his property as expeditiously as possible. You won't find one magistrate who won't congratulate me for my fairness and my magnanimity.'

'You windy old fraud!' Eyre shouted at him. 'That's a boy's life you're talking about! Now, put down your gun, tie up those dogs, and let him be.'

Lathrop turned back to Eyre with his face already darkening with anger. He poked the muzzle of the musket at him, and said, in a shaking voice, 'You, Mr Walker—*you*, Mr Walker—you by God have crossed me just once too often. And let me remind you that I could blow your brains out where you stand, and still be well within the law; because you're a trespasser, sir; an illegal interloper; and a known eccentric.'

'Don't you dare to wave that gun at me,' Eyre told him; but at that very instant, on the other side of the ha-ha, Yanluga twisted around and jumped to his feet, and with his head down began to run towards the distant shelter of the gum-trees.

'Ha! Ha!' shouted Lathrop. 'You see! You see what I mean! Doesn't that show you! Isn't that it! The guilty ones always take to their heels! Captain Henry—the dogs, Captain Henry!'

'Yes, sir, Mr Lindsay,' acknowledged Captain Henry, and whistled through the gap in his front teeth, a weird, loud, rising whistle that gave Eyre the irrational sensation that something was flying through the air towards him, like a boomerang. The greyhounds barked, and pranced, and Captain Henry called, '*Koola*! *Koola*! *Taiyin*! *Koola*!'

'No!' shouted Eyre; but Lathrop lifted his musket and discharged it in the air. There was a flat, ear-slapping bang; and a flash; and a sharp smell of gunpowder. Lathrop reappeared through the swirl of smoke with a look in his eyes that was so piggish and menacing the Eyre couldn't find the words to curse him. Instead, he turned to look across the lawns to see if Yanluga had managed to outrun the dogs.

Yanluga had almost reached the gum-trees; but the dogs had gone rushing off after him as soon as Captain Henry had given the word, and now they were only two or three yards behind him, swift as Yanluga's own shadow. Eyre breathed to Lathrop, 'By God, Mr Lindsay,' and hobbled down the side of the ha-ha, and then up the other slope, making his way as quickly as he could manage to the end of the garden. Under the trees, where the bone-white moonlight couldn't penetrate, it was difficult to see what was happening; but for a moment Yanluga's running silhouette was outlined against the pale bark of a large gum, followed hotly by the bobbing heads of the dogs.

'Koola! Hi! Hi!' whistled Captain Henry, off to Eyre's left.

Yanluga reached the trees. Eyre could hear his bare feet sprinting across the dry, crackling bark. Then, instantly afterwards, the rush of the dogs. With a high-pitched shout of effort, Yanluga leaped up and grasped an over-hanging branch; first with one hand, dangling for a moment, and then with the other. Two of the greyhounds jumped up at his feet, but he kicked them away, and then tried to swing his legs up so that he could work his way even higher into the tree, suspended underneath the branch like an opossum.

'Yanluga!' Eyre shouted, through swollen lips. 'Yanluga, hold on!'

'Now then, Mr Walker, sir,' called Lathrop, from the far side of the ha-ha. 'Don't give me any trouble.'

Eyre turned around, staggering on his lacerated leg. 'Trouble?' he yelled, almost screeching.

Yanluga was grimly silent, struggling to edge his way further up the blistery bark of the tree, while the dogs sprang and hurtled just beneath him. He had almost reached an elbow in the branch, where he would be able to perch well out of the reach of the greyhounds' jaws. Eyre had limped within ten yards now, and bent down painfully to pick up a dry fallen bough, to beat the dogs away. 'Yanluga!' he called again. 'Hold tight, Yanluga!'

The dogs spun around and around in a yapping frenzy; jumping up at Yanluga like vicious grey fish in a turbulent sea. One of them tore at the back of his shirt, and Yanluga beat at its snout with his hand. But that was all the other dogs needed. One of them sprang up and seized Yanluga's wrist in its jaws; and even though Yanluga shouted and thrashed, the dog hung on to him, its body twirling and swinging in the air, its sharp teeth deeply embedded in his flesh. Another jumped up, and then another, ripping at Yanluga's arm and shoulders. Yanluga held on for one more agonising second, and then dropped heavily to the ground with a cry more of hopeless resignation than of fear.

Eyre came limping forward, swishing his stick fiercely from side to side; but he was already too late. The dog which had first caught Yanluga was worrying and tearing at his wrist, and at last tore the boy's hand right away from his arm, in a grisly web of tendons, and snarled and tossed it. Another dog ripped at Yanluga's thighs, so that the flesh came away from the bone with a terrible noise like tearing linen; and it was then that Yanluga started to scream—a high, warbling scream.

'Off! Jesus! Get off, you devils!' Eyre shouted at the greyhounds, and struck out at them with his stick. But they had caught the smell of fresh blood now, *koola* or Aborigine; and a few glancing blows on the back weren't going to be enough to drive them away.

'Off! Get off! Get off!' Eyre roared at them; and one of them turned for a moment, so that Eyre could catch it a smart blow at the side of the head, and knock it aside. Savagely, it went for Eyre's arm; but Eyre struck it on the shoulder, and then the spine, and yelping it staggered and collapsed in front of him. Shuddering with anger, inflamed with pain, and with Yanluga's agonised screams tearing inside his mind like a fast-growing thorn-bush, Eyre hoisted the bough vertically upright, hesitated, and then brought it down in a piledriving blow right on top of the dog's skull. With a crack, the dog's eyes were squirted out of their sockets, and its head was smashed into fur, bone, blood, and a grey cream of brains.

The ferocity of the remaining five dogs was unabated. Eyre saw Yanluga lift the bloody stump of his wrist in a last attempt to beat them away; but they had already torn open his shirt, and tugged the muscles away from his ribs, and now one of them was stepping backwards, snarling and shaking its head, trying to free itself from a garland of yellow-purplish intestines. Another had torn off most

59

of his scalp, and half of his ear; while a third was chewing and tugging at the rags of his penis.

'*Ngura!*' Captain Henry commanded, from a little way across the lawns. '*Hi, hi, hi! Ngura!*'

The hounds were satisfied now. Bloody-snouted, trailing liver and muscles and intestines behind them, they bounded across to Captain Henry and laid their prizes at his feet. He patted each of them; and then commanded again, '*Ngura!* Back to your shelter!'

Eyre stood still for a moment or two, and then let his stick fall to the grass. He knelt down beside Yanluga; and quite magically Yanluga was still conscious, still alive, and staring at him out of bright red haemorrhaged eyes. His stomach gaped open, and his insides had been draped out for yards across the garden, so that he looked as if he had exploded. But he was still gasping a few last breaths; and his lips still moved.

'*Koppi unga,*' he whispered.

Eyre said, 'What is it? Tell me, what do you want?'

'*Koppi unga,*' Yanluga repeated. His eyes were like those of a demon.

'I don't understand you,' Eyre told him, miserably.

'Ah . . .' said Yanluga. He was silent for nearly a minute, but Eyre could hear him breathing, and hear the sticky sound of his lungs expanding and contracting. 'Water . . .' he said.

Utyana was now standing close by, and when Eyre turned around, he silently handed him a leather bottle full of warm water. Eyre shook a few drops on to his fingers, and touched Yanluga's lips with them. Yanluga said, with great difficulty, 'You are my *ngaitye*, my friend. You must not let them bury me here. This is important to me, sir. Do not let them bury me here, or take me to the hospital and cut me up. Please, sir. I shall never join my ancestors from the dreamtime . . .'

He coughed, a huge spout of blood. Then he said, 'Please sir, find the clever-man they called Yonguldye, he will bury me . . . Please. If I can call you friend.'

60

Eyre said huskily. 'I will find the man they call Yonguldye. I promise you. Do you know where he is? In Adelaide?'

Yanluga stared at him glassily.

'I have to know where to find him,' Eyre repeated. 'Please, Yanluga. Is Yonguldye in Adelaide?'

Yanluga coughed again, and then again. Lathrop had walked up to them now, and was standing watching over them with his gun crooked under his arm. 'Chap's gone, I should say,' he remarked.

Eyre said, 'Yanluga, please. You have to tell me.'

Yanluga's face was grey now, like a grate of burned-out ashes. A large shining bubble of blood formed on his lips, and then burst. The smell of blood and bile and faeces was almost more than Eyre could stomach. It was the terrible odour of real death; and Eyre closed his eyes and prayed and prayed that God would take Yanluga out of his pain.

Yanluga whispered, 'Yonguldye is northwards, sometimes; sometimes west; Yonguldye is The Darkness; that is his name.'

Lathrop said, 'Chap's raving. Think I ought to put him out of his misery?'

Yanluga tried to lift his head. His last words were, '. . . *kalyan . . . ungune . . .*' and then the blood poured from the side of his mouth like upturned treacle, and he died.

Eyre stayed on his knees for a long time. Lathrop watched him, whistling 'D'ye Ken John Peel' over and over again, tunelessly. At last Eyre turned to him, and said, 'You've killed a man. You understand that I'm going to have to report you.'

Lathrop shook his head. 'I don't think so, Mr Walker. Chap was mine, you see. My servant. My responsibility. Welfare, board and lodging; discipline too. Chap disobeyed me. You know it for yourself, for you were a party to it. Hence, chap gets punished.'

'You call this punishment?' Eyre demanded, spreading his hands to indicate the gruesome remains which were twisted across the lawns.

'I call it justice,' Lathrop retorted. 'And if I were such a stickler for punishment as you believe me to be, I'd have you reported for killing my dog. Lucky for you it was a slow one, long in the tooth. But that dog was worth £30 of any man's money; and you've killed it; no reason; no provocation. Whereas this chap, why, only paid him £3.2s. 6d the year; worth a damned sight less than the dog.'

Eyre stood in the moonlight, shaking. He was too shocked and too painfully injured to argue with Lathrop now about the value of a man's life. He knew, too, that Lathrop would be given no trouble by the law. At a time when Englishmen were still liable to be hung for stealing a hat, blackfellows had no rights to life whatsoever. It was only two years ago that twenty-eight Aborigines had been murdered at Myall Creek; and the defence put up at the trial of the settlers who had killed them had been that 'we were not aware that in killing blacks we were violating the law, as it has been so frequently done before'. Seven settlers had been hung; but the Myall Creek trial had done nothing to change the general view of Adelaide's colonists that blackfellows were little more than indigenous vermin, filthy and primitive.

Eyre said, 'I'll pay you for the dog, if you can accept recompense by the instalment. They don't pay me very much down at the South Australian Company.'

'Don't let me see hide nor hair of you again; that'll be recompense enough,' said Lathrop.

'One thing more,' said Eyre. 'I'd like to take this boy's body with me. If your servants could find a box for him, I'll come by with a cart in the morning.'

Lathrop stared at him. 'What's your game?' he wanted to know. 'You can't take that body; that belongs to me. What do you think you're going to do with it? Sell it to the hospital? Or show it to the magistrate, more like.'

'He asked me—just before he died—for a proper Aborigine burial.'

'A what?'

'A ritual burial, according to his own beliefs.'

'That's barbaric nonsense,' Lathrop protested. 'He'll have a Christian burial and like it.'

'But he wasn't a Christian,' Eyre insisted. 'And if you don't bury him according to his own beliefs, then his soul won't ever be able to rest. Can't you understand that?'

Lathrop eyed Eyre for a moment, and then pugnaciously bulged out his jowls, like a sand goanna. 'Captain Henry,' he said, quite quietly.

'Yes, sir, Mr Lindsay.'

'Mr Lindsay, please listen to me,' Eyre urged him.

'I have listened enough,' Lathrop retorted. 'Now clear off my property before I have the dogs let out again. Captain Henry, do you take out the pony-trap and take this gentleman back to his diggings, wherever they may be. Utyana!'

'Yes, sir.'

'Clear this rubbish off the lawn before it attracts the dingoes. You understand me? Sweep up.'

'Yes, sir.'

Captain Henry helped Eyre to limp over to the stables. Eyre stood against the stable gate with his eyes closed, his legs and his arms throbbing and swollen, while Captain Henry harnessed up one of Mr Lindsay's small bays, and wheeled out the trap.

'Captain Henry,' said Eyre, without opening his eyes.

'Mr Walker?' asked Captain Henry, softly, anxious that Lathrop should not overhear him.

'Captain Henry, tell me what *kalyan ungune* means.'

'*Kalyan ungune lewin*, sir. It means "goodbye".'

Four

Mrs McConnell had already girded herself to retire to bed
when Captain Henry brought Eyre back to his apartments
on Hindley Street. She came out on to the front verandah
in curling-papers and a voluminous dressing-gown of
flowered cotton, her lantern raised high, like a lighted
thicket of moths and flying insects; and a long pastry-pin
swinging from a string around her wrist, in case it was
blackfellows, or burglars, or drunken diggers.

High above the roof of the house, the Southern Cross
hung suspended, its two brightest stars, Alpha and Beta
Crucis, winking like the heliographs of distant civilisations.

Mrs McConnell said, 'God in his clouds, what's
happened?' and came down the steps to the pony-trap
with her pastry-pin rattling against the banisters. Captain
Henry climbed down from the trap and held the horse,
while Mrs McConnell lifted her lantern over Eyre's bruised
and bloodied face.

'What's happened to you?' demanded Mrs McConnell.
'Who did this? You, blackface, who did this? And no
demurring.'

Eyre said awkwardly, 'It's all right, Mrs McConnell. I
was involved in an accident, of sorts. Fell off my bicycle.'

'Fell off your bicycle into a passing tribe of cannibals,
more like it,' said Mrs McConnell. 'Look at you, you're
bitten all over. Those are *bites*!'

Eyre attempted to stand up and greet Mrs McConnell
with bravado. He almost managed it; but his legs closed
up like cheap penknives and he sat down very hard again
on the pony-trap's horsehair seat; and couldn't manage
anything more than a puffy, lopsided smile.

'Tie up that pony, blackface, and help me to carry the
poor gentleman inside,' Mrs McConnell told Captain
Henry. Captain Henry did as he was told, and then
between the two of them they managed to drag Eyre up

64

the wooden steps, across the verandah, and into the hallway, where they laid him down on the brocade-covered sofa on which it was Mrs McConnell's pleasure (believing herself to be quality) to keep all her visitors waiting, even her friends from the Sewing Circle.

'You look regularly chewed,' said Mrs McConnell. 'It's a wonder you're still with us. Who did this, blackface? Who's the folk responsible?'

'Not my position to say, madam,' said Captain Henry, uncomfortably.

Mrs McConnell brandished her pastry-pin at him, and Captain Henry squinted at it in alarm.

'How about a crack on the skull?' Mrs McConnell asked him. 'And believe you me, when you're cracked with *this*, you know it. Not like your clubs or your bangarangs.'

'Please, madam, all I can say is that I work for Mr Lindsay, madam; and that this gentleman was hurt by Mr Lindsay's greyhounds.'

'Lathrop Lindsay? That bullfrog? Well, then, be off with you and tell Mr Lindsay from Mrs McConnell that he had better not take Hindley Street for a year or so; unless he fancies a crack on the skull with Chumley here.'

Captain Henry gratefully retreated from the hallway; and out into the street, and turned the pony-trap around, and whipped up the pony with a high cry of 'whup! whup!' Mrs McConnell closed the door and came across to Eyre with a sweep of her dressing-gown, her forehead solicitously ribbed like a sand-dune.

'We're going to have to clean up these bites at once,' said Mrs McConnell. 'I remember a friend of Dogger's, Mr Loomis, he was bitten by dogs and died of the lockjaw in less than a week. Can you manage to climb the stairs?'

Eyre nodded; and with Mrs McConnell helping him, he managed to climb one stair at a time up to his room. He knew better than to ask if Dogger might not lend a hand. Dogger was invariably unconscious at this time of the evening, after three jugs of home-made beer. His snores were already reverberating across the landing, like a man giving poor imitations of a prowling lion. Mrs McConnell said, 'Off with your trousers, Mr Walker; and I'll fetch a basin.'

Eyre hesitated, but Mrs McConnell said, 'I've seen a few men in my day, Mr Walker; and I'm beyond embarrassment. There used to be a telescope at Brighthelmstone beach, you know, which the young girls used in order to spy on their young beaux bathing in the sea; and many a girl was saved from a disappointing marriage by being afforded a view in advance; although my aunt used to say that they were nothing more than so many whelks.'

With that strange non sequitur, she bustled off, all curling-papers and flowery skirts, to fetch the jug and the basin, and the Keatings Salve, which she always swore was so effective that it 'could heal a severed leg'.

Eyre lay back on his narrow iron-framed bed, still trembling with shock. The bite in his leg hurt the most; a penetrating ache that felt as if the metal teeth of a kangaroo-snare had been embedded in his thigh. His right eye had almost closed up, and when he touched his cheek, he could feel a crust of dried blood on it. He supposed that he ought to undress himself, ready for Mrs McConnell's nursing, but somehow he felt too sensitive, as if he wasn't going to be able to bear the sensation of moving his sleeves over his skin.

'Oh, God,' he whispered. Then, even more softly, 'Oh, Charlotte.'

He looked around him; and his room, through half-focused eyes, had the blurriness of a room in a dream. It was plain enough, wallpapered with brown-and-white flowers, with a cheap varnished bureau; and a bedside table that had once belonged on the SS *Titania*, complete with brass handles and tobacco-pipe burns; and a carved mahogany wardrobe that looked as if it had been the only entry in a competition for upright coffins. Beside him, enhancing the blurriness with a halo of light, stood an oil-lamp with an engraved glass globe, and beneath it, his small brass carriage-clock, and the two oval-framed daguerreotypes of his mother and his father; the first long dead and the second far away.

Eyre looked at the picture of his mother and for the first time in two years his eyes filled with tears. He felt suddenly alone, and hurt, and further away from Derbyshire than he could ever remember. He couldn't even assuage his grief by laying flowers on his mother's grave. But he could think of the rain, and the green silent hills of Baslow and Bakewell; and he could still remember those days as a boy when he had sat watching a distant rainbow, and his mother had gently touched his shoulder, and said, 'God's paintbox, Eyre, that's what it is.'

And now he lay here shivering, thinking of Charlotte, erotic but innocent, tempting but afraid; and of his mother, calm but dead. He thought of time, and how quickly it had passed and taken his mother's life away and how his small brass carriage-clock was measuring his own life away, second by second, month by month, unceasingly.

His father had been the vicar of St Crispin's, in Baslow. Thin-faced, with drawn-in cheeks, and old-fashioned side-whiskers, and a row of black silk-faced buttons in front that must have taken him ten minutes each morning to fasten. The Reverend Leonard Walker, dry and determined, the one and only messenger of God. Conscientious, grave, a believer in angels and Holy Grails; and also in the life everlasting, at least for those who were saved. And he, of course, was the only agency through which the people of Baslow could achieve salvation.

He would take Eyre for walks: miles across the Dales, in rain or sleet or misty sunshine. But the walks were not for enjoyment or for exercise; they were visits to the poor; to dribbling grannies or Mongol children; or to vermin-ridden cottages where filthy women suckled filthier children, and where fathers mounted their daughters, night after night, with the energy born of desperation, regardless of what the Bible might say; or of how many idiot children they might conceive. And the Reverend Leonard Walker would rest his dry, thin-fingered hands on their lousy heads, and bless them; and accept their gifts of salt pork and lardy-cakes; but leave them in no doubt whatsoever when he said goodbye tht he would expect them in church that Sunday, to save their miserable souls.

Eyre had been brought up in the gloom of the vicarage and the light of God. He had sat at his desk on hot summer afternoons, dressed in thick woollen socks and buttoned-up jackets, watching the days pass him by through closed windows, his nail-bitten hands resting on his open copy of *Pilgrim's Progress*. 'Then I saw that there was a way to hell, even from the gates of heaven.' And the pendulum-clock on the wall had measured his childish weariness hour by hour; until it was time for supper; and prayers; and bed.

By the time he was ten, Eyre had felt that life was nothing but tedious duty, of silent meals with grace to begin them and grace to end them, and of books with no pictures.

He had been quiet, friendless, and withdrawn. His only toys had been a whipping-top and a wooden Noah's Ark. On the few occasions when his father allowed him out to 'disport himself', as he put it, Eyre had walked down the muddy lane to talk to the neighbouring farmer's collie-dog, which stood chained and miserable by the fence. Eyre used to have daydreams about setting the dog free, and running away with it to sea. He had never seen the sea; but old Mr Woolley had been apprenticed to an East Indiaman, and had told Eyre with great earnestness that the sea was 'like glass, and like moving mountains, and sometimes like hell and damnation all put together'.

Eyre's mother had been a gentle quiet-spoken Derbyshire girl of no particular beauty. But although she had been completely overwhelmed by his father's strictness, she had graced Eyre's childhood with a warmth that had at least made it tolerable. He remembered the softness of his mother's cheek, the soapy-scenty smell of her neck, the sharpness of her starched aprons. One day, when Eyre was twelve, she had walked all the way to Bakewell market in the rain, and a week later she had died of pneumonia. So white! and not like his mother at all. And after that, life at the vicarage, already strict, had become an endless penance of catechism and parochial duties, to say nothing of the undercooked tripe and slippery onions with which Eyre had regularly been served by his father's housemaid, the turkey-necked Mrs Negus.

When he was twenty, Eyre had been sent by his father to Chesterfield, to study divinity under Dr Croker. But there, two people had changed his life forever. The first had been his landlady's daughter, a flirtatious and friendly young girl called Elaine, who had teased him and winked at him, and at last (the day after his twenty-first birthday) had taken his virginity from him, in his own rumpled bed, all giggles and perspiration, on a stormy afternoon when the thunder had rolled around and around Chesterfield's twisted spire, and the rain had clattered in the gutters outside his bedroom window. Eyre had delighted in her plump white pink-nippled breasts, sugar-mice he had called them; and in her chubby thighs, and the moist blonde hair between her legs; and most of all in the conspiratorial way she had whispered in his ear, her breath like the wind from a church-organ bellows, 'I'm glad you're a bit of a devil, Eyrey, as well as an angel.' Eyre had thought of his catechism, and of *Pilgrim's Progress*, but then he had smiled less than shyly and kissed her, and decided that God really could be bountiful, after all. And that His gifts could embrace more than fishes, and loaves of wheatmeal bread, and more than divine inspiration, too.

Then there had been John Hardesty, a fellow student, curly and serious; who had given up his theology studies after two terms to go to Australia, to raise sheep. John had been the son of a wealthy Derbyshire sheep farmer, and had been enthused for years with the idea of making his own fortune in a strange land. His father had stood against him, and insisted that at least one member of his family should be given to God, but at last John had decided that he would have to go. He had begged Eyre to emigrate with him. In South Australia they were all free men, and from what he had heard, they were making thousands. Thousands! And not a word of religion; thank God.

Eyre had been tempted. But whenever he had returned to the vicarage at Baslow, he had been unable to summon up the courage to tell his father that he was leaving. Four years had passed; four years of unhappiness and silent suppers; until the time had come for Eyre to be ordained. It was then that he had simply told his father, 'I'm leaving for Australia. I'm sorry. I think I'll probably go tomorrow.'

His father had stared at him. 'You're due to be ordained in three weeks.'

'Yes,' Eyre had told him. Then, quite gently, 'Nonetheless, I'm going.'

There had been a moment of unexpressed emotion; a moment which Eyre would remember for the whole of his life. His father had stared at him with such anger that Eyre almost believed that supernatural forks of lightning would flicker from his eyes; and thunder blare out of his mouth. But then he had reached across the table and laid his hand on top of Eyre's hand, and said, 'I shall pray for you. And I shall ask of you only one thing: that you always remember that I love you.'

In that one moment, Eyre began to understand for the first time the spirit of Christian tolerance; and also to see how lovingly, as well as how severely, his father had brought him up.

He and his father had taken a last walk together on Big Moor, the evening before Eyre was due to leave. The clouds had been dark and soft and a stirring wind had blown through the grass from the south-west. There had been rain in the air, and the moistness of the atmosphere made distant noises sound clearer: the barking of dogs, the jingling of bridles.

Eyre's father had stood a little way off, his face to the wind. 'Don't go believing what people tell you,' he had said. 'But never say you can't to anybody. What you want

70

to be done, through the power of God, can be done. What needs to be done, will be done.'

The next morning, with all of his bags packed, Eyre had held his father very tight. His father had seemed so bony and smelled of Latakia snuff. Patting Eyre's back, his father had said, 'Don't cry; for we shall never see each other again.'

Five

Eyre had sailed seven weeks later from Portsmouth, bound for Port Adelaide on the merchant-vessel *Asthoroth*. On a drizzling day in early September he had left behind him an England over which Queen Victoria had reigned for only a year; in which Charles Dickens had just launched a periodical called *Master Humphrey's Clock*; in which Gordon of Khartoum was a five-year-old boy living at Woolwich; and from which transportation to Australia for life was still a common punishment for stealing cheese, or sheep, or linen.

As the *Asthoroth* had sailed past Whale Island on a slackish wind, Eyre had seen at close quarters the hulk of the *York*, moored to a dismal row of other hulks. It was on these rotting hulls of old sailing-ships that convicts were held before they could be embarked at Spithead for Australia, and they were a particular Purgatory of their own. Eyre had watched the *York* in awe as the *Asthoroth* had slid silently by: the hulk had no masts or sails now, and her superstructure had been replaced by a crazy collection of wooden cabins, complete with smoking chimneys, ladders, balconies, walkways, and washing-lines. The stench of ordure and grease as they passed downwind made Eyre's stomach tighten with nausea and dread.

He had heard about the hulks; about the vicious whippings and the diet of rotten food; and how many sick and elderly convicts died in their bunks, still within sight of England.

The *York*'s sinister bulk had impressed him deeply. No sound had come from its decks and cabins, no singing; only the steady muffled throb of a drum. He had stood by the *Asthoroth*'s after-rail as she bent at last to the breeze beyond Southsea, watching the convicts' tattered washing as it idly flapped on the lines, and the fishy-smelling smoke of their midday meal, as it tumbled away to the east like vanishing hopes. Eyre had thought of the words of Jeremy Bentham's imaginary judge, as he sentenced a thief to transportation, 'I sentence you, but to what I know not; perhaps to storm and shipwreck; perhaps to infectious disorders; perhaps to famine; perhaps to be massacred by savages; perhaps to be devoured by wild beasts. Away—take your chance; perish or prosper; suffer or enjoy. I rid myself of the sight of you.'

He had turned away at last to find one of the *Asthoroth*'s crew watching him, a red-headed Hampshire man with striped pants and earrings, and eyes as sharp as whalebone needles.

'You hear that drum?' he had remarked, in an oddly challenging voice. 'They're flogging a man, and that drum marks the time. Fifty lashes, by the count so far.'

'Well, God have mercy on him,' Eyre had replied.

The red-headed sailor had snorted mucus from his nose, and wiped it on his arm. 'Don't you go feeling sorry for them wretches,' he had said. 'You'll have trouble enough looking out for yourself, once we reach Australee.'

'I was thinking how they're treated as refuse; as men without souls,' Eyre had said.

'Yes,' the red-headed sailor had agreed. 'For once sentenced, that's what they be.'

It had taken the *Asthoroth* eight-and-a-half months to

reach Port Adelaide, in the last week of June 1839. During the voyage Eyre had become a stone thinner and his dark hair had become streaked by the sun. He had also become more confident, more sure of himself, although he had still been uncertain what he would do to make his fortune once he reached Australia.

He had rounded the Cape of Good Hope on a spanking bright day, and seen Table Mountain with her grey-and-white crown of clouds. He had crossed the Indian ocean under a sun that was as hot as a blacksmith's hammer. He had eaten fresh pineapples in Colombo, in Ceylon, on a night when the rain thundered down among the leaves; and had his fortune told in Singapore, in the hush of a Buddhist temple, with incense drifting across the court-yards like ghosts. The fortune-teller had warned him, 'Beware of your own fortitude. Beware of your own faith. Your own determination is your greatest weakness. Beware, too, of the sun; for the sun will be your most implacable enemy, and you will learn to curse it.'

He had seen parakeets and leaping dolphins and the sleek fins of cruising sharks. He had awoken one morning off Tandjung Puting, in Borneo, to find the ocean as still and steamy as a laundry, with no wind, and no sound but the cries of invisible fishermen in the fog. And he had sighted Australia at last, *Australia Felix*, as Major Thomas Mitchell had named it, 'Happy Australia'; a long low coast-line with a cream of surf, and clusters of dark green trees.

'Don't be tricked by what you see on the coast,' the red-headed sailor had told him sharply, as the *Asthoroth* had tacked across the green seas of the Great Australian Bight on her last leg to Port Adelaide. 'Beyond that there coast-line is nothing but desert; at least, as far as anybody's gone, and lived to tell about it. Some say the land has a great freshwater ocean, right in the middle of it, for many rivers run that way, inland. But I wouldn't trust my chances to find it. Not me, sir. Some's even gone off into the desert with boats. Boats, if you please! And they've

73

found the boats later on the sand-dunes, crewed by skellingtons.'

Eyre had listened, and eaten a pomegranate, and said nothing. The red-headed sailor had seemed to have a down on Australia, in any case; and had complained ever since they had left Portsmouth that Australia was the Lord's joke.

'Why, what can you make of a land where winter is summer, and summer is winter; a land in which there are birds with wings but don't fly; and animals with heads like rabbits which bounce instead of walking; and evergreen trees which are no use at all for building, but are always crowded with birds—birds that sit still all day and laugh. Laugh! They can drive you clean mad with their laughing.'

He had often spoken, too, of the blackfellows. 'A less Godly race of human animals there never was; bare-bum naked most of them, women too; but they paint their faces and smear themselves with ashes and grease, so you wouldn't take a fancy to any of them. They think that rocks and trees and pools of water all have souls of their own; that *places* have souls, and a sadder lot you could never meet. They sleep at night with wild dogs for blankets, when it's cold, but don't ever suppose that they're friendly. Most of them will spear you through, just like that, like a pork-chop if you give them the chance.'

The red-headed sailor had sniffed loudly, and said, 'If you ask me, Australia was the land which the Lord used for practice, before He created the rest of the Earth; and so learned by His mistakes. Not a land to love, Australia.'

They had sailed into Port Adelaide on a cool, still, overcast afternoon. The port itself was a collection of long wharves and tall warehouses, and a few untidy stores and office-buildings. The water had been lapping up to the silty edge of the shore, cluttered with nodding beer-bottles and discarded spars and empty broken baskets. In the far distance, off to the east, barely visible through the cloud, Eyre had been able to make out the greenish-blue peaks of the Mount Lofty range, dark with grass after the winter rains.

The red-headed sailor had watched Eyre from the quarter-deck as he disembarked; and grinned; and spat noisily into the water. Eyre had hesitated, and looked back at him; but then he had turned his face away, towards the land he would now have to call his own.

He had written to his college friend John Hardesty the Christmas before last, telling him that he was considering coming out to Australia, but of course he had left England well before any reply could have reached him, if John had replied at all. But he had an address at Angaston, and tomorrow he would hire a carter to take him out there.

He had been looking for a baggage-porter to carry his trunks for him, and to advise him where he might spend the night, when he had caught sight of his first Aborigines; two of them, standing by the unloaded luggage; and he had stopped where he was, jostled by disembarking passengers and messenger-boys and busy men in tall hats and bright waistcoats, and he had openly stared.

There had been a tall bearded man, quite upright and handsome, except that his face was smeared with grease and wilga, a thick red ochre. The man had been wearing a European jacket, but he had fastened it around himself like a cloak, and tucked up the superfluous sleeves. He had worn a loin-cloth, fastened with bone pins, and a band of stringy fur around his head. In one hand he had held a long spear. His other hand had rested on the shoulders of a young girl; small, broad-faced, and shaggy-haired, but surprisingly handsome. She had been wearing a rough cloth cloak tied up in the same way as the man's jacket, with an untrimmed hem; but to Eyre's disturbance, nothing else. One breast had been bared like a glossy black aubergine, and her curly pubic hair had been visible to all who crowded the wharf.

'Carry your trunks, sir?' a bald old man had demanded.

'Yes. Yes, please,' Eyre had replied, distracted.

The bald man had loaded Eyre's baggage on to a small

two-wheeled cart, drawn by a moth-eaten donkey, and had bidden Eyre to climb up on to the seat. But as they had trundled away from the *Asthoroth*, Eyre had been unable to take his eyes off the two Aborigines, standing in such a striking pose, attenuated black figures against the pearl-grey water of the harbour, half-wild, mysterious, magic, sexual; like no people that Eyre had ever seen before.

'First time?' the old man had asked. He had boasted scarcely any teeth at all and his bald head had been as brown and wrinkled as a pickled walnut.

Eyre had nodded. The cart had bounced and rattled out of the port; and south-eastwards towards the settlement of Adelaide itself. The rough muddy road was lined with scrubby bushes; and off to the right Eyre could see rows of sand-dunes, and hear the waters of the Gulf of St Vincent slurring against the beach.

'Got a place to kip, squire?' the old man had asked.

'No,' Eyre had told him. It had begun to drizzle; a thin, fine, rain from the mountains.

'Well then,' the old man had decided. 'It's Mrs Dedham's for you. Every boy's mother, Mrs Dedham. Solid cooking, clean sheets, and Bible-reading afore bedtime.'

They had driven through the low-lying outskirts of Adelaide, the donkey slipping from time to time on the boggy road, and the rain growing steadier and heavier; until the old man took a sugar-sack, which he had ingeniously rolled up into a kind of huge beret, and tugged it on to his head. Eyre had watched the rain drip from the brim of his hat, and shivered.

They had rolled slowly past sheds, mud-huts with calico roofs and calico-covered windows and even an upturned jolly-boat, with windows cut into its sides, and a tin chimney. But then at last they had reached the wide, muddy streets of the city centre, where there were rows of plain, flat-fronted houses, and shops, and courtyards; all interspersed with groves of gum-trees and acacias; and quite handsomely laid out. Although it was a wet afternoon, Eyre had been impressed by the number of people in the streets, and the scores of bullock-carts and carriages. He had expected the people to be roughly-dressed, but apart from a group of bearded men in tied-up trousers who were probably prospectors, most of the passers-by were smartly turned-out in tail-coats and top-hats. The women looked a little old-fashioned in their bonnets and shawls, but what they lacked in modishness they made up for in the self-assured way they promenaded along the wooden sidewalks, mistresses of a new and confident country.

Eyre had seen more Aborigines, most of them dressed in *bukas*, or native capes, but a few of them in European clothes, although one girl had been wearing an English skirt with her head and one arm through the waist, and the other arm protruding from the open placket.

Mrs Dedham had owned a fine large house at the east end of Rundle Street, built like its neighbours out of lime-stone, brick, and pisé. She had come bustling out to greet Eyre as if he were her prodigal son; even hugged him against her huge starched bosom; and offered him steak-and-kidney pudding at once. In the kitchen, as he had eaten with determined unhungriness, she had told him how she had come to Australia from Yorkshire with her dear husband Stanley, and how Stanley had started a sheep-farm at Teatree Gully, only to be taken at the peak of his success by 'shrinking of the mesenteric glands', an ailment that would later be diagnosed as peritonitis. Mrs Dedham had sold off the farm and bought herself what she like to call 'a gentleman's hotel'; three good meals a day, no visiting women, no whistling, and a communal Sunday lunch after church.

That night, in his unfamiliar bed, with an unfamiliar light shining across the ceiling, Eyre had lain awake and thought of his father. Outside in the street he had heard laughter, and a woman calling, 'Fancy yourself, then, do you?' Then more laughter.

The following day, he had paid Mrs Dedham's

handyman four shillings to drive him out to Hope Valley, to find John Hardesty. It had still been raining as they had followed the narrow rutted track between dripping gums and wet sparkling spinifex grass; until at last they had arrived at the sheep farm, and the rain had begun to ease off.

The farm's owner had been a stocky man in a wide leather hat, his face mottled by drink and weather. He had said very little, but taken Eyre to the back of the house, and shown him the wooden-paled enclosure where John Hardesty had been buried, over two years ago.

Eyre had stood by the grave for five or ten minutes, then returned to the farmhouse. 'Had he been ill?' he had asked.

The farmer had shrugged. 'You could say that.'

Eyre had replaced his hat. The farmer had stared at him for a while, and then said, 'Did away with himself. Hung himself with wire in his own barn. Nobody knows why.'

'I see,' Eyre had said; and then, 'Thank you for showing me.'

He had decided to stay on at Mrs Dedham's; and so that he could pay her rent of 2s 0½d the week, he had found himself a job in the tea department of M. & S. Marks' Grocery Stores, on Hindley Street, scooping out fragrant Formosas and Assams, and also brewing up tea in barrels, since some customers still preferred to buy their tea the old-fashioned way, ready infused, for warming up at home. Just after the New Year, however, he had met Christopher Willis at a party given by Marks' for all of their suppliers; and Christopher had arranged for him to take up a clerical post with the South Australian Company, for 1s 3d more per week. 'And far more future, old man, than tea.'

His first sweetheart in Adelaide had been a saucy young Wiltshire girl called Clara, daughter of one of the aides to the Governor and Commissioner, Colonel George Gawler. Clara was green-eyed and chubbily pretty and Eyre had courted her with the frustrated enthusiasm that only a

78

single man living at Mrs Dedham's could have mustered. He had bought his bicycle solely to impress her, even though it had cost him two weeks' wages; and he had taken her for a wobbling ride on the handlebars from one end of King William Street to the other, with Clara shrieking and kicking her ankles.

On his return to Mrs Dedham's that evening, he had found a note waiting for him, to the effect that Clara's father had complained that Eyre had made 'an unforgivable public exhibition of his daughter's virtue'. Mrs Dedham herself had told him the following morning, over veal pudding, that she considered it best if he sought alternative accommodation.

'I don't expect my gentlemen to be bishops,' she said, bulging out her neck, and lacing her fingers tightly together under her bosoms. 'But I don't expect them to be hooligans, or peculiars, either.'

That was how he had found himself staying with Mrs McConnell, on Hindley Street; and from the beginning Mrs McConnell had taken a special shine to him, and pampered him so much that in three weeks he had put on all the weight he had lost on the voyage from Portsmouth. She cooked marvellous pies, with glazed and decorated crusts, and washed his shirts and starched them until they creaked. All he had to do in return was call her 'Mother', and accompany her once or twice a month to the Methodist chapel by Adelaide barracks. She did so like to go to chapel in company; and Dogger wouldn't go for anything. Dogger said that he had carried on quite enough conversations with the Lord in the outback; and that if he went to chapel, the Lord would only say, 'Christ, Dogger, not you again.'

'You have to understand that a fellow needed God, in the outback,' Dogger had frequently explained. 'You didn't have anybody else, after all. The kowaris didn't talk to you; the dingoes didn't talk to you; and the damned skinks and shinglebacks, they'd either puff themselves up or yawn at you something terrible.'

Eyre had nodded sagely, although it was not until later

that he had learned that kowaris were desert rats, which preyed ferociously on insects and lizards and smaller rodents; and that skinks and shinglebacks were both prehistoric-looking species of lizard.

Mrs McConnell came back with the jug and the basin and the pale green jar of Keatings Salve.

'You've not undressed,' she said.

Eyre started to unbutton his shirt. 'I felt too sore,' he confessed. 'And a little too tired, too.'

'The salve will soon make you feel better.'

She tugged off his clothes in a businesslike way, until he lay naked on the bed. Then she carefully washed out his bites, and sponged the rest of his body, his chest, his back; and laid a cool wet cloth on his forehead. 'You sometimes remind me of my son Geoffrey,' she said.

'Yes,' Eyre acknowledged. She had told him that several times before.

'Geoffrey always used to say that life was like a sugar-basin.'

'Yes,' Eyre agreed.

Mrs McConnell washed the dark crucifix of hair on his chest, so that it was stuck to his skin in whorls. Quite matter-of-factly, she held his penis, and rolled back the foreskin, and washed that, too. He looked at her through puffy, half-closed eyes, and he was sure that for a second he saw something in her expression that was more than matronly; but then she smiled, and clapped her hands, and said, 'You must have a clean nightshirt. I'll bring you one of Geoffrey's.'

He lay on the bed waiting for her. He smelled of camomile and vanilla and tincture of zinc, which seemed to be the principal ingredients of Keating's Salve. He found himself thinking of Geoffrey. Poor Geoffrey who had said that life was like a sugar-basin, because every taste of it was so sweet. Geoffrey had gone riding, a keen and straightforward young boy of eighteen; so far as Eyre could gather; and been bitten in the ankle by a death-adder, the snake the Aborigines called *tityowe*. Mrs McConnell had stayed in her back parlour with the drapes drawn for nearly three months, until Dogger had at last come home from Broken Hill, and persuaded her to start living her own life again.

That night, Eyre dreamed of Yanluga, sobbing, crying for help. He dreamed of Charlotte, too, gliding across the lawns of Waikerie Lodge as if she were on oiled wheels, instead of feet. He dreamed that Mrs McConnell came into his room naked, but with the black body of an Aborigine woman, and that she knelt astride his face and buried him between her thighs.

He woke up at dawn; when the sky was a thin, cold colour; and he was shivering. He climbed stiff-legged out of bed in his ankle-length nightshirt and went shuffling to the window, and leaned against the frame. Hindley Street was deserted. The only signs of life were the lighted window of Keith's Fancy Bakery across the street, and a single Aborigine boy sitting close to the bakery steps wrapped up in his *buka*, a puppy crouching between his bare feet.

Eyre began to feel that something momentous was about to happen, and that his life had already changed beyond recall. He sat down on the side of the bed, frowning, still shivering, not understanding why he felt this way. And the morning breeze which lifted the dust in the street also rattled the casement like a secret message from one prisoner to another, 'it's time to be free.'

Six

Mrs McConnell brought him a breakfast of oat cakes, ham, and soft-boiled eggs, with honey from old Mr Jellop's apiary. She parked her big bottom on the bed and watched him eat; smiling and nodding in encouragement each time he forked a piece of ham into his mouth, or bit into an oat cake.

'You're going to have to rest for a few days, get your strength back,' she said.

'Mrs McConnell, I'm a little bruised, but that's all. I really want to go and get my bicycle back, before some blackfellow steals it, or Lathrop Lindsay finds it and smashes it to bits.'

'You're not thinking of going out there today?'

'As soon as I've finished my breakfast, as a matter of fact. And then I'm going to cycle over and see Christopher.'

'But you're still invalid! I can't allow it! Supposing you came over queer?'

'Mrs McConnell, I can't tell you how much I appreciate your nursing. You've been more than kind. But I'm really quite well.'

'*Well*? Do you call that *well*? Your eye looks like a—like a squashed cycad fruit.'

At that moment, Dogger appeared in the doorway, his hair sticking wildly up in the air, his face in a condition of chronic disassembly, his striped nightshirt as crumpled as if he had been tossed into a wool-baler.

'Constance,' he said. 'Don't mollycoddle the boy. He's not your boy. And besides, my brains won't stand arguing.'

'Just because you've drunk yourself silly, don't go picking at me.' Mrs McConnell retorted. 'I've had boys, I know what's best for them. And what's best for this boy is a day or two in bed.'

Eyre took hold of her hand. 'Mrs McConnell, I'll come to a compromise. If you let me go out this morning, I'll make a point of coming back to bed this evening early; and you can dress the bites for me, too, if you please.'

Dogger sniffed, and ran his hand through his hair, making it look even wilder. 'There you are, you see,' he remarked, to an invisible referee who was standing next to the wardrobe. 'The voice of sanity prevails. Thank God for that. Now, where's my breakfast?'

Mrs McConnell patted Eyre's mouth with his napkin, kissed him on the forehead, and stood up. 'I'll make it for you now,' she told Dogger, still smiling at Eyre. 'The fish, I'll be bound.'

Dogger gave a twisted, exaggerated grimace. After an evening of heavy drinking, the only breakfast which he could physically stomach was salted sea-perch, with red pepper; and a large glass of buttermilk. About an hour after that, he would be ready for another jug of home-made beer.

Eyre walked up to Waikerie Lodge. The morning was bright and dusty. The twin plagues of Adelaide were dust in the summer and mud in the winter; apart from the flies, and the fog, and the occasional outbreak of typhus, or 'mesenteric fever'. The dust rose up with the wind and whistled softly through the sugar-gums like hurrying ghosts, and everything it touched it turned to white; so that after it had died away the countryside looked as if it had been blanched, and aged, as if by some terrible experience.

His bicycle was exactly where he had left it, propped up against a bush, untouched except for a splash of parrot guano on the saddle. He walked cautiously up to the back gate of Lindsay's house, and looked across the lawns, but apart from a few scuff-marks on the grass, there was no trace of last night's horror. There was no trace of Charlotte, either, although he skirted through the bushes so that he could see up to her bedroom window. The family had probably gone to church. If so, Eyre hoped without cynicism that they would pray for Yanluga. They had certainly done nothing else to assure that their servant's spirit would rejoin his dreamtime ancestors.

Captain Henry came out on to the patio, wearing a red string headband and a shabby frock-coat, and leading half-a-dozen of Mr Lindsay's greyhounds. He was probably doing nothing more than taking them out for a walk, but Eyre decided that retreat was more sensible than suicide, and crept away from the perimeter of Waikerie Lodge, and retrieved his bicycle, and pedalled off to visit Christopher Willis.

A little way off, though, he stopped, and looked back towards Waikerie Lodge. All he could see through the surrounding trees was the edge of its brown shingled roof, and the white columns that flanked its grandiose porch. It was like an impregnable castle in a Grimm's fairy tale; ruled over by a king who had set impossible standards for his daughter, the Princess Charlotte. She would probably die an old maid, imprisoned by her father's ambition, particularly since South Australia's economy, buoyant at first, had gradually begun to collapse; so that week by week, the likelihood of a visit from an eligible English baronet was becoming increasingly remote.

Down at the South Australian Company, Eyre had already seen three major merchant banks withdraw their money from Adelaide; and more letters of withdrawal were expected by the end of the year. The returns had not been high enough, or quick enough, and the general feeling in the City of London, which in the early days had been adventurous and optimistic, was that Australia, on the whole, was 'a damned odd duck'.

These days, the only English quality that Adelaide saw were the exiled sons of shabby Sussex landowners; or botanical eccentrics whose trunks were crammed with magnifying-glasses, and tweeds. Nobody suitable for a girl like Charlotte.

Eyre cycled off towards the racecourse. It was warm now, and the wind had dropped, although high creamy clouds had mounted in the east, and there was a chance of thunder. The mid-morning light had become curiously metallic; as though the landscape had been cured in spirits of silver, and the spokes of Eyre's bicycle wheels flashed brightly along the pathway towards the racecourse. He usually sang as he cycled. This morning he was silent. A distant church-bell clanged from the centre of the city; and he allowed himself to whisper a verse from the 62nd Psalm, one of his father's favourites.

'How long will you assail a man, that you may murder him, all of you, like a leaning wall, like a tottering fence? Men of low degree are only vanity, and men of rank are a lie; in the balances they go up; and they are together lighter than breath.'

Eyre repeated, with relish, 'a tottering fence', and tried to swerve so that he ran over a Holy Cross frog that was squatting on the track, but missed it.

Christopher Willis was packing his horse-panniers to go out fishing when Eyre arrived on his bicycle, and he didn't look particularly pleased to see him. Nonetheless, he put down his nets, and said, 'Hullo, Eyre; you look as if you've been boxing with kangaroos.' Then, as Eyre parked his bicycle, he peered at him more attentively, and said, 'And the kangaroos won, by the look of it. Are you all right?'

Eyre said, 'I'm recovering, thank you. My dear Mrs McConnell is taking care of me better than I have any right to expect.'

'Ah,' said Christopher. 'Your dear Mrs McConnell. I always suspected that she wanted to adopt you. In fact, I rather believe that she thinks you're Geoffrey—Geoffrey, is it?—returned from the grave.'

He sniggered. That was the type of joke he always enjoyed. He had the appearance of a very disjointed public schoolboy, and the humour to match. He was big-nosed, with wide-apart eyes, and he always seemed to be growing out of his clothes, even though he was twenty-five. He parted his hair severely in the middle, and sometimes stuck it down with bay rum, or violet essence, especially when he was going to meet a young lady, which he did with unexpected regularity. They were never young ladies of the very best breeding, but they were invariably willing, and giggly, and of course they always wanted him to marry them, at once, which he wouldn't.

Eyre grudgingly admired Christopher's lack of sensitivity. He didn't very often feel like courting a girl himself, and when he did, it was invariably a painful and caustically romantic experience. How could you love a girl at all without wanting to love her for ever? He still thought of Clara with regret, the girl for whom he had first bought his bicycle.

He sat down on one of the frayed basketwork chairs on Christopher's untidy verandah. 'If you want to know the truth, I was attacked by Lathrop Lindsay's dogs. Worse than that, they set on Yanluga, too, his Aborigine groom, and killed him.'

Christopher took off his wide straw hat. 'Well, now,' he said. 'That *is* bad luck. Killed him, hey? My dear chap. Won't you have a glass of something? Old Thomas came past yesterday with four bottles of brandy.'

'Thank you,' said Eyre.

Christopher looked at him closely, as if he were testing his eyesight, and then said, 'You *are* all right? That's a frightful bite on your phizzog. If I were you, I'd sue the bugger.'

'I can't do that. I was trespassing. In law, he had every right.'

'Hm,' said Christopher. 'He's a bugger, nonetheless. Didn't I tell you that Charlotte wasn't for you? You can't beat a bugger; not when it comes to a bugger's one and only daughter; and he's a bugger all right, his lordship Lathrop Lindsay. Everybody says so.'

'Who's everybody?'

'Well, *I* say so. Who else do you need?'

Eyre couldn't help smiling. 'Go and get me that brandy,' he admonished Christopher.

They sat and drank for a while in silence, secure in their

companionship. A few hundred yards to their right, a dull chestnut yearling was being cantered and turned, in training for the winter season. The rider lifted his crop in salute to Christopher, and shouted, 'halloo', and then galloped off towards the billowing white tents which formed the major part of the racecourse.

'Sam Gorringe,' Christopher remarked. 'Terrible rider. Rotten horse, too. Just in case you were ever tempted to back him.'

Eyre sipped his brandy; and let it burn its way slowly over his tongue, and down his throat.

'My father disapproved of gambling,' he said. 'A short-cut to hell, that's what he called it.'

'Oh, well, yes.' said Christopher.

There was another silence, less relaxed this time. Then Eyre said, 'I've decided to bury him.'

'Bury him? Who? Lathrop Lindsay?'

'No, you lummox. Yanluga.'

'Yanluga? Isn't that Lindsay's responsibility?'

'Lindsay is going to give him a Christian burial.'

'Well?' asked Christopher, swilling his brandy around and around in his glass.

'Well, he wasn't a Christian, was he?' Eyre retorted.

'He was a heathen,' Christopher declared.

'Heathen? How can you say that? You've lived here longer than I have. You know how religious the blackfellows are. They have all kinds of religious rites; especially when it comes to burial. Don't they break the body's bones, and then burn it? And don't they sometimes have dances, and processions on the river? The poor chap should at least be given the ceremony that his beliefs demand, don't you think? Or perhaps you don't.'

Christopher balanced his glass on the warped verandah table. 'Well,' he said, 'I must say that you're really getting yourself in rather deep. Especially for the son of an Anglican vicar.'

'What my father believes is nothing to do with it. My

father hasn't met any Aborigines; he doesn't know how magical they are.'

'They're *superstitious*, I'll give you that. Do you know that boy from Moomindie mission? The one who came up here to mend my fences? He was supposed to have been converted to Christianity, *and* cricket, but he wouldn't stay here after dark because of the Yowie. The Yowie! Can you imagine it? A completely mythical monster, and the poor lad went beetling back to the mission as soon as the sun went down, as if all the devils in hell were after him.'

Eyre looked at Christopher sharply. 'But of course,' he said, 'there *are* devils.'

Christopher frowned, and then pouted. 'You can actually be rather tiresome at times, Eyre, did you know that?'

'Is it tiresome to want to give Yanluga the burial he begged me for?'

'Not entirely. Although it might be a bit too saintly.'

'I'm not a saint, Christopher,' Eyre smiled at him. 'I never will be, either. But the boy liked me, and respected me, and I liked and respected him. And I think that's reason enough.'

'If you say so. But how will you go about it?'

'I need to find an Aborigine chief called Yonguldye. Apparently he knows what to do.'

'Hm,' said Christopher. He stood up, and pushed his hands into the pockets of his baggy white trousers, and walked to the end of the verandah, where he stood looking out over the windy racecourse with his lank hair flapping across his forehead.

'I suppose it's no use telling you that you're really wasting your time?' he asked Eyre. 'In fact, more than that, you're doing yourself a positive disfavour. A chap like Lathrop Lindsay can make or break you. And it doesn't do one's reputation much good to be associated with blackfellows. They're a miserable lot, on the whole.'

Eyre said, 'I think I'd be miserable, too, if I was treated worse than vermin, and dispossessed of my hunting grounds, and shot for the sport of it. And I care very little for Lathrop Lindsay, thank you. What man can set dogs on to a boy, in the sure knowledge that they will tear him to pieces? My only regret is that it was my rash affection for Charlotte which led him to die; and for that reason I feel as responsible towards him as if he were my own brother.'

Christopher turned around, and folded his arms over his grubby yellow waistcoat. 'I was right, y'know,' he said. 'You're *far* too saintly; and it will be the death of you.'

'Perhaps,' Eyre replied, conscious that he was being melodramatic.

'Well, then,' said Christopher, 'what's to be done? Have you heard at all from Charlotte?'

'Nothing.'

'Do you think that you will?'

'I don't know,' said Eyre. 'It depends whether or not she still feels any passion for me; and whether or not her father has managed to prevent her from geting in touch.'

'Is she yours?' Christopher asked, bluntly.

Eyre glanced up. 'I suppose so, in a manner of speaking.'

'What? You've been fiddling, and that's all?'

'Christopher, don't be so damned indelicate.'

'Indelicate? I thought we always shared our confidences; and our conquests. Didn't I tell you absolutely everything about Anne-Marie? My God, apart from me, and a captain at Adelaide barracks, you're the only person on the entire continent who knows that Anne-Marie has a mole right next to her left nipple.'

Eyre lifted his empty glass. 'What about some more brandy?'

Christopher went to fetch the bottle. 'I hope you're not *really* in love with this Charlotte girl,' he said.

'And what if I am?'

'You'll have *pain*, my dear fellow, that's what, and nothing else. From what you tell me, Lathrop Lindsay would rather see you cremated alive than have you court his daughter. Perhaps the very best thing you can do is tell me everything about her, and then try to put her out

89

of your mind; and that goes for that Aborigine fellow, too. Exorcise your feelings of romantic lust; and your guilt, as well; and start tomorrow morning with a clean slate, determined to do nothing more complicated with pretty girls than take ungentlemanly advantage of them; and nothing more with blackfellows than kick them very hard in the arse, whenever the feeling takes you.'

Eyre swallowed more brandy; then wiped his mouth with the back of his hand. 'I can't,' he said, shaking his head, and Christopher saw then that he meant it.

'Well,' he said, 'damn it. I knew you couldn't. Damn it.'

'Why do you say "damn it"?'

'I say "damn it" because from the very moment I first met you I knew you were one of these chaps who has to do something *noble* in life. I knew you'd never be satisfied with fun, not for its own sake. No, you're the kind of chap who has to have a cause, and I do believe now that you may have found it. You're going to go off searching for this Aborigine chief and that's probably the last we'll ever hear of you.'

'I'm not afraid of the Aborigines,' said Eyre.

'You ought to be. Captain Sturt was.'

'That was ten years ago.'

'Well—let me tell you—Captain Sturt will be at Colonel Gawler's house on Thursday evening, for the Spring Celebratory Ball.'

'I didn't know that Captain Sturt was even in Adelaide.'

'He came in on Friday, on the *Albany*. He's staying with the Bromleys. A quiet, private visit, supposedly; but he's too much of a showman to let it stay quiet and private for very long. And I do think, since he's here, that you ought to meet him. *He'll* tell you what scoundrels the blackfellows can be.'

Eyre said, 'I'm not sure that I want to hear such a thing.'

'Nonetheless, don't tell me you're going to go looking for this chief of yours completely unprepared; and without asking South Australia's greatest living explorer what you might hope to find. It's an opportunity, let's be honest.'

'I haven't got a ticket.'

'Aha. There I can help you. Daisy Frockford has six, and two to spare.'

'I suppose you're going to ask Captain Sturt to dissuade me from seeking Yonguldye out altogether.'

Christopher finished his second glass of brandy. 'I'll try, believe me,' he said, frankly. 'But, even if he won't; or even if he *will* and you still decide that you want to go off on your wild Aborigine chase; then at least you'll have some idea of what dangers you may be up against.'

Eyre said, 'Christopher, I do believe you're a true friend.'

'I am, God help me.'

'In fact,' said Eyre, 'if I do make up my mind to go and look for Yonguldye, I'd very much like you to come with me.'

Christopher hesitated. Then he said, 'Oh, no. Not I. You won't ever catch *me* looking for Aborigine chiefs; not a hope of it.' And then, when Eyre kept on smiling, 'Listen, Eyre, I'm going to do my level best to make sure that *you* don't go; let alone me.'

Seven

Eyre had a busy week down at the port. Two vessels had docked from England, with ploughs and shovels and timber; and there were five separate consignments of wheat to be loaded. It rained heavily, too, the last heavy rains of the winter, and the offices he shared with Christopher and four other clerks were dark and humid and thick with tobacco-smoke. On Wednesday morning, he stood

91

on the wharf in his oily rain-cape, waiting for the fat wife of a newly appointed government official to be rowed ashore in a jolly-boat, rotund and placid under her umbrella, a red plaid shawl around her shoulders, and he wished very much that he was away from here, and out in the bush, where the problems of life were uncomplicated, and the only threats to life and sanity were the sun, and the snakes, and the lack of water.

Perhaps Christopher had been right about him all the time. Perhaps his life *was* committed to some noble and historic adventure. After all, there must have been some saintly determination inside his father, to make him such a dedicated priest. And saintly determination could well be hereditary.

Yet he felt that it was no more than a sense of ordinary justice that had outraged about what had happened to Yanluga; a plain conviction that no matter how wealthy or influential Lathrop Lindsay might be, he had no right to deny Yanluga the burial ceremony that all Aborigines considered essential, not only to protect the living from his spirit's anger, but to avenge his death, and to ensure that he returned by way of the sky to the spiritual centre of his tribal life.

Like most white men, Eyre knew practically nothing about the blackfellows; and until now, he had felt no particular need to. The only blackfellows he had ever spoken to were dressed-up servants like Yanluga and Captain Henry; or those dissolute families who had become dependent on the Europeans for food and whisky, and lived in sorry brushwood shelters on the outskirts of the municipality, miserably exiled from their own nomadic way of life, and even more miserably attached to the *amerjig*, the white man.

Even the tamest of Aborigines talked very little of their magic, and their rituals, since to divulge their songs and their secret places to the white men was to disenchant them, and lose them forever. Yanluga had often spoken to Eyre about a place he called *Yeppa mure*, the dust hole, where he had spoken with his ancestors from the dream-time; but he had never told Eyre where it was, nor invited him to see it, for all of their mutual respect.

The fat wife of the newly appointed government official arrived at the wharf. Eyre helped her disembark, and the jolly-boat swayed dangerously.

'Well,' she piped, as she clambered heavily on to the wharf. 'I was told that the climate of Adelaide was amenable. I might just as well be back in Manchester.'

Eyre drew back his rain-cape and offered her his arm. 'Indeed, ma'am, you might,' he told her, although she missed the meaningful sharpness in his voice. She was too busy shaking the rain from her heavy ruffles.

'Such a voyage,' she said. 'If I was unwell once, I was unwell a hundred thousand times.'

'I'm frightfully sorry to hear it,' said Eyre.

The woman abruptly stopped, and clutched at Eyre's arm. 'Are you one of those lonely Australian bachelors?' she asked him. 'You won't mind my asking.'

'I am a bachelor, ma'am.'

'Well, in that case, before I leave the dock you must write down your name for me. I have a sister back at Audenshaw who has been trying to find a husband for nigh on eighteen years, without success; and you would certainly suit her nicely, even if you are a little tender.'

'You're very complimentary, ma'am.'

'It has been said,' the woman bustled; pleased with herself.

A black carriage drew up, slick with rain, and the woman's husband alighted, thin and whiskery and looking tired. He accepted her kisses as if he were being rhythmically slapped in the face with a soaking-wet duster. Eyre raised his hat, and said, 'Good morning, sir. Good morning, ma'am. Welcome to Adelaide, ma'am.'

The government official gave Eyre a tight, twisted smile, and handed him a shilling.

'Come along, dear,' he told his wife. 'You don't want to catch your death.'

Eyre was just about to go back to his office when some-body else caught his sleeve. He turned quickly and to his complete surprise it was Charlotte, in a hooded cloak, her eyes wide, the front curls of her hair stuck against her forehead with rainwater.

'Eyre,' she appealed, clinging on to his cape.

'Charlotte! My God! I thought I'd never see you again.'

'Eyre, oh Eyre! Oh look! Your poor dear face.' She hesi-tantly touched the triangular scar under his eye. 'You don't know how desperate I've been to see you. And it was all my fault. Why did I scream so, when you were all that I wanted? Oh, your face. Does it hurt still?'

Eyre took hold of her wrist, and hurried her across the slippery planking of the wharf; until they were sheltering under a lean-to roof where kegs of nails and ship's caulking were usually stored. There was a pungent smell of tar, and hempen rope.

'Charlotte,' said Eyre, and held her close to him, and kissed her. He felt absurdly breathless, as if he had just been running; and confused, too, so that none of his words seemed to come out straight. 'Charlotte, my God. I thought that was the end of us.'

She took a breath, and patted the lapels of his cape with her fingertips, quickly, fussily, like something she had to do for luck.

'Father's furious. I won't be able to see you again; not for ages; if at all. He says you're a devil. Oh, please don't be angry. He says you're a devil and that he should have set the dogs on you, as well as poor Yanluga.'

'Yes,' said Eyre. 'Poor Yanluga.'

'Oh, please, Eyre. He was only an Aborigine.'

Eyre looked at her for a long time, while the rain dripped along the rim of the lean-to roof in sparkling droplets, one after the other, each droplet a tiny winking life of its own.

Out in the harbour, a sailing-ship silently glided through the rain, with wet sails, a ghost on a ghostly voyage.

Eyre said, 'Yanluga was a boy; a human being. Your father deliberately had him killed.'

Charlotte looked at him oddly, and then shuddered, as if she had wet herself a little.

'I love you,' said Eyre. 'Despite everything that's happened.'

Charlotte turned away; but he loved her profile just as much. Those long, curled lashes; and those high, well-rounded cheeks, like two young clouds. She said distractedly, 'I love you, too; although I have resisted it. I think I was probably very shallow until you showed me that I could be deeper, and more thoughtful, and you still make me ashamed of some of the things I say. I suppose the trouble is that girls are not brought up to be thoughtful, or even to be considerate, especially not in Australia. We have to think of the marriages that will advance us best; of lords and viscounts, and men with money. All my friends do. Some of them say that they don't even mind if their husband is ugly, as long as he is titled, and rich.'

She looked back at Eyre, and there were tears shining in her eyes, more droplets, more sparkles.

'I screamed because you frightened me. Well, I think I frightened myself even more. I thought you were going to—*damage* me. I know now that you couldn't have done. I talked to Mrs McMurtry, the cook. She said that the first time was always difficult. And I didn't really know what to expect. It was, you know, the very first time.'

She paused again, and now the tears slid freely down her cheeks. 'I don't know what to say, Eyre. I feel so unhappy. I was so wrong; so stupid. And I have to tell you why. So please forgive me. And please believe that I'm trying to love you, very hard. And poor Yanluga. I feel so sorry for poor Yanluga.'

Eyre held her close. He could feel the warmth of her tears against his shirt. 'Well,' he said, a little tightly. 'I expect that Yanluga will appreciate your sorrow, wherever he is.'

'Oh, Eyre, don't blame me. Please.'

'I blame myself.'

They stood for almost five minutes under the lean-to,

while the rain fell across Kangaroo Island in slow, persistent draperies.

Eyre said, 'Do you know what your father has done with Yanluga's body?'

'Buried it, of course. Out at the back, where the mulga grows. He buried his horse there, too, do you remember Kookaburra? Dear Kookaburra. It shows how sorry he felt.'

'It also shows that he thought of Yanluga as somewhat less than a human being.'

Charlotte reached up on tiptoe and kissed his lips. 'You mustn't be bitter, my love. I do believe that father means well. It's just that he sees life so differently from you and me.'

'Yes,' said Eyre. He held her very close. He could have held her all day, feeling the softness of her breasts against him, and breathing in her perfume. He twisted one of her damp curls of hair around his finger, and then kissed her forehead.

'Shall I see you again?' he asked her.

'Whenever I can get away; but we may have to go to Angaston for a week or so; and father's started to drop hints that he might be taking me to Melbourne.'

'I shall wait for you. You know that, don't you?'

'Oh, Eyre,' said Charlotte.

At that moment, Robert Pope, one of Eyre's assistants, appeared on the wharf with a large umbrella. 'Eyre? Sorry to interrupt you, old man, but Mr Duffy wants to know when you can arrange to ship that wool of his. He's in the office now.'

Eyre squeezed Charlotte's arm, and kissed her once more, on the lips. 'I shall have to go,' he told her. 'But remember that I love you.'

'Please say you forgive me,' Charlotte begged him.

'There's nothing to forgive.'

Eyre followed Robert back to the office. The rain blew in his face as he turned the corner on to the wharf. Charlotte remained under the lean-to for a while, until an unshaven matelot in an oilskin hat stopped and stared at her, and hitched up his trousers, and said, 'What ho, my darlin'.'

Eight

Mrs McConnell knocked excitedly on the door of Eyre's bedroom to tell him that their hired carriage had arrived outside. He knew, he had seen it, but he dutifully said, 'Oh! Excellent!' Mrs McConnell also announced that Christopher was downstairs in the front parlour, drinking small beer with Dogger, although he knew that, too. He had heard Christopher's giggling through his red-patterned carpet, and guessed that Dogger was relating his favourite story of the Nyungar Aborigines at New Norcia. These proud and independent tribesmen had been given trousers and sandals by the missionaries there, and told to cover their shamefulness; only to return the following week with their trousers on their heads, and their sandals ostentatiously buckled around their penises.

Eyre had just finished tying his black silk cravat, and he pivoted around on his heel for Mrs McConnell to admire him. He was dressed in a magnificently cut black tailcoat, and double-breasted waistcoat, with satin-trimmed britches and black-kid slippers. Severe, but correct, and very handsome. His collar was extravagantly high, which he understood to be the latest fashion in England; but it did require him to keep his head rather loftily raised, and Dogger had described it as a Patent Double-Chin Cutter-Offer.

'Lord have mercy,' said Mrs McConnell. 'You could be the King of South Australia.'

'Well, Mrs McConnell, if only I were. The things I wouldn't put right.'

'You're not still worrying yourself about the blackfellow? You'd be best off forgetting about that.'

Eyre picked up his cane and his gloves. 'I can't, Mrs McConnell. I would that I could.'

'But you're such a gay fellow, Mr Walker. Why should you let such a grave affair distress you?'

Eyre took her hand, and affectionately pressed it, and kissed her cheek. 'A man can only be gay when his conscience is at ease, my dear. I saw Yanluga die, and it was my fault that Mr Lindsay set his dogs on him. Therefore, the task with which Yanluga charged me is a most serious responsibility. He must be buried according to the dignity of his own beliefs, and not laid to rest in some pet's graveyard, with foreign words spoken over him by a man who had nothing but contempt for the sanctity of his life.'

Mrs McConnell looked a little flustered. 'Well,' she exclaimed, 'I can only say that your father must have been a rare preacher.'

Eyre said nothing. He tried to look happy, but it wasn't especially easy. The truth was that every night since Sunday, he had been having grotesque nightmares about Yanluga's death, and about frightening Aboriginal rituals in which he had been somehow compelled to take part. He had heard weird ululating voices, and seen black flickering silhouettes, and hooked devices that tumbled over and over in the air, whistling as they went. And every morning he had woken up with his nightshirt tangled and sweaty, and the vision of Yanluga's ripped-open entrails vivid in front of his eyes.

To dress up for this ball tonight was a marvellous relief; quite apart from the fact that he wanted to meet Captain Sturt. He led Mrs McConnell down the stairs, and into the front parlour. Christopher was waiting for him there in a bright peacock-blue coat and yellow britches, his hair frizzed up with curling-tongs; and Dogger was just pouring out two more small beers. Mrs McConnell said happily, 'Doesn't Mr Willis look the very picture?'

'Smartest I've ever seen you,' Eyre grinned, and shook Christopher's hand. 'Not sure about the hair, though. You look as if you've been struck by lightning.'

'I'm glad you've come down to rescue me.' Christopher replied. 'Any more of Mr McConnell's small beer and I do believe I wouldn't have been able to stand up tonight; let alone dance.'

Dogger stood up, sniffed dryly and lifted his glass. 'Since I myself have no dancing to do, I'll venture a toast. To the young Queen who promises to be good; and to Britannia herself who needs no bulwarks; and to the man who said that black's not so black, nor white so very white.'

Mrs McConnell, unusually indulgent, poured a glass of beer both for herself and for Eyre, and with all the self-conscious solemnity of the English during moments of extreme patriotism, they drank. Eyre thought that the small beer tasted exactly like the thinned-down varnish with which the verger at St Crispin's used to refurbish the pews, but he smiled at Dogger nonetheless, and said, 'Excellent.'

'Now,' put in Christopher, rubbing his hands, 'we must be on our way to collect Daisy Frockford. And you'll be delighted to hear, my dear Eyre, that May Cameron will be accompanying us, too.'

The muscles in Eyre's cheeks tightened a little. 'Why should I be delighted to hear that?'

'Why? My dear fellow, you must have heard that May's engagement to Peter Harris was broken off, after Peter lost all that money at the races. And apparently she's desperately anxious to be seen walking out with somebody else, just to spite him. And when I say *desperately* anxious, well, please excuse my implications, Mrs McConnell. May Cameron's a healthy girl.'

Mrs McConnell furrowed up her forehead, this time in disapproval. 'Remember this is a Methodist home, Mr Willis.'

'I apologise,' said Christopher, bowing his fluffed-up head. 'We do live in practical times, however. Not all appetites can be satisfied with hymn-books.'

Dogger cackled. 'That reminds me of another story they told me at Mallala; how they found some of the Aborigine women taking Bibles back to their camp in their dilly-bags, and stripping off the leather bindings for a tasty chew. They even boiled the glue off the spines, and drank it like soup.'

'Now then, you're right, Christopher, we really must go,' said Eyre; who was afraid that Dogger's beer had already made Christopher too pompous and Dogger himself too reminiscent. He took Mrs McConnell's hand, in its fine crochet mitten, and kissed her neat little cuticles. Then he took Christopher's arm and led him out on to the verandah. The carriage was waiting under the lamplight; a hired phaeton from Meredith's, rather dilapidated, and leaning askew on its worn-out suspension, but brought up to a high polish nonetheless, and harnessed up with two quite respectable-looking bays. The coachman was a stout, broad-shouldered fellow with a high hat and a face like a Mile End prizefighter, with scarred eyebrows and a twisted nose. He climbed down as Eyre and Christopher came out of the house, and put down the step for them, so that they mount up and take their places on the dusty green upholstery.

'You know where to go first, don't you?' Christopher asked him.

'Flinders Street, sir, no need to remind me,' the coachman told him, with undisguised aggression. He climbed back up on to his box, and snapped his whip, and the phaeton began to lurch off with an eccentric up-and-down motion which caused Eyre and Christopher to look at each other and laugh in amusement.

'You may walk if you wish, gents,' the coachman told them.

'I wouldn't dream of it,' Christopher replied. 'This

100

carriage has all the safety and comfort of a vehicle which travels on land; and yet all the general hilarity of a boat.'

'Well, sir, in that case, you've nothing to complain of,' replied the coachman, in a voice as hoarse as a parrot.

'Nothing but your manners,' Christopher told him.

'My manners, sir?' The coachman shifted himself around in his seat and stared at Christopher with eyes as black as waistcoat-buttons. 'Well, sir, you'll have to forgive me for being one of the blunter sort. But then bluntness was never on the catalogue of criminal offences, was it, sir?'

'Your employer may have different views,' said Eyre, who was beginning to find this fellow irritating. 'Now trot along, and let's have less of this chatter. We've come out this evening for amusement, and we don't want any sourness, especially from you.'

The coachman looked as if he might have a less than courteous reply to that remark; but he closed his mouth tight, like a doctor's portmanteau, and shifted around on his seat again, and stung the horses' ears with the tip of his whip. 'Hee up, you shamblers.'

'I hope you haven't made a mistake, hiring this coach,' Eyre said to Christopher, under his breath, as they wallowed towards the end of Hindley Street. He inclined his head towards the coachman. 'He may very well be perfectly respectable, but he looks like a legitimate to me.'

'Nonsense,' said Christopher, running his hand through his fuzzed-up hair. But then he leaned across and said, 'He does seem a trifle uncouth, though, for a coachman.'

'Legitimate' was the generally accepted euphemism for 'ex-convict'. There were comparatively few in Adelaide, which had been founded as a free settlement; but a few score of pardoned men had sailed here from Sydney to seek their fortune in farming and prospecting and keeping sheep, and most of all to try to escape the social stigma of having been 'sent out'.

Eyre said, 'I suppose it's all right. The firm where you hired the coach was respectable enough, wasn't it?'

'Of course it was; although this isn't one of their usual carriages. Everything else was taken for the ball.'

Eyre raised an eyebrow at Christopher, and sat back on the seat in a conscious attempt to appear relaxed; although he wasn't.

'Well, this is all nonsense,' Christopher repeated. 'You're just trying to put the wind up me.'

Eyre looked around. They were now in a particularly deserted part of Pulteney Street, by an area of waste ground; and the only inhabited houses that he could see were a group of small workers' cottages behind a high picket fence, and the lamps were lit in only one of them. There was a tippling-house called the Cockatoo a hundred yards further along the street; and three or four men were sitting out on the verandah with bottles of rum, singing and laughing. But apart from these, and apart from the ghostly pale gum-trees which rustled in the evening wind, they appeared to be all alone.

The coachman eased out his reins, and said, 'Ho, now,' to his horses, and gradually the lop-sided carriage began to slow down, almost to walking-pace.

'What's going on?' Christopher asked him. 'What have we slowed down for?'

The coachman didn't turn around; but said something in a hoarse mutter, like 'traces slipped', or 'braces tripped', or 'brakes is stripped'. Eyre said loudly, 'What?' but at that moment the coachman applied the phaeton's brake and the whole assembly jingled to an awkward halt.

Eyre heard running feet, and at once said to Christopher, 'Out, and make a dash for it!' But the coachman just as quickly swung himself down from his box, and hurried back to their door, wrestling the handle open and banging down the step. He jumped up into the carriage, and Eyre saw that there was a heavy hardwood truncheon in his hand, which he brandished under Christopher's nose. 'Legitimate indeed!' he snapped, roughly. 'I'll break your nose for you; see how *you* care for it!'

Three more men appeared, as promptly as Jack-in-the-boxes, a trio of hardened old ruffians in baggy sailcloth britches and woollen hats. One of them hoisted himself up on to the opposite side of the carriage, and grinned up at Eyre with a face like a withered red pepper. Eyre raised his arm defensively and said, 'Get away!' but the man simply grinned and swung up a shining machete, and said, 'I'll geld you first, mate.' Another man, limping, went around to hold the horses' bridles, sniffing as he went.

'It's your money and your timepieces, that's all, sirs,' said the coachman. 'And it's your promise of silence, too; for we have too many loyal friends for you to think of grassing on us. Go to the military, and say one single word, sirs, and our friends will have your gizzards slit within the hour. A friendly warning, sirs, that's all; for what you're losing tonight is nothing as painful as your life.'

Eyre looked at Christopher, and said, 'I think, under the circumstances, we'd be better off doing what he says, don't you?'

Red-pepper-face grinned even more broadly, and spat, and said, 'You're cool enough, aren't you, mate?'

Eyre unfastened his watch-chain, and held up the watch that his father had given him. 'That's only because the Lord is with me,' he said. 'And because you'll most certainly get your punishment in Heaven, even if they fail to catch you in Adelaide.'

The coachman snatched the swinging watch, and stuffed it into his pocket. 'Don't preach, sir,' he advised. 'I'm not partial to being preached at, especially when I'm hoisting.'

Christopher handed over his purse. 'I hope you're damn well satisfied,' he told the coachman. 'I worked a month of late hours for that.'

'Oh, *well* satisfied, sir,' said the coachman. Then he turned to his fellow thieves, and whistled, and said, 'Come on, now, we're set.'

Just then, however, Eyre heard another whistling; softer and lower. It sounded as if something were flying towards them through the air, like a fast and predatory hawk. And then the coachman was suddenly knocked in the side of the head by a whirling piece of wood, and shouted, '*Ah!*'—just that—and somersaulted right over the side of the phaeton and fell heavily on to the dust.

Red-pepper-face stepped back in surprise, but then there was another whistle, sharper this time, and a long stone-tipped spear flashed right throught his throat, in one side and out of the other. He looked up at Eyre in outrage, his eyes crimson with shock; and then he raised his hands and clung on to the shaft which protruded from either side of his neck, and opened his mouth in an enormous bloody yawn.

A second spear hit the bodywork of the coach, so violently that the phaeton rocked on its worn-out springs. The limping man who had been holding the horses began to shuffle-*kick*-shuffle-*kick* back across the street, in the direction of the Cockatoo tippling-house; but a third spear struck him squarely in the back, and he dropped flat on his face.

The last of the thieves ran off so fast that a kangaroo couldn't have caught him, his sailcloth trousers flapping in panic.

There was a moment of utmost tension. Eyre slowly raised his head, and peered into the darkness of the waste ground. The insects were still singing, and the moths still pattered around the carriage-lamp. Over at the Cockatoo, one of the men had fallen dead-drunk off his chair, and the others were bawling at him to *wake up, Jack, you idle sod*, and hooting with laughter.

Down on the roadway, the coachman stirred and moaned. 'Christ Almighty.'

'What happened?' Christopher asked, floury-faced.

'I'm not sure,' said Eyre. 'Wait.'

They stayed where they were, with Christopher gripping Eyre's wrist, listening and sweating. Then, unexpectedly close, a skeleton appeared out of the darkness; or what looked like a skeleton. When it came nearer, Eyre saw that it was a blackfellow, his ribs and his bones outlined on his grease-smeared body in chalky white. He was naked except for a headband of kangaroo fur and feathers, and he carried two spears and a spear-thrower.

One by one, silently, like remembered shadows from a prehistoric past, other Aborigines appeared, until there were seven in all, standing around the carriage naked and painted. Eyre could smell them on the wind; that distinctive fatty pungent odour, mingled with the fragrance of woodsmoke.

One of them, the tallest, leaned over and picked up the fighting boomerang which he had used to knock down the coachman.

Eyre stood up in the coach, holding on to the door for support. 'You came to our rescue,' he said, his voice off-key. 'We thank you for that.' He rubbed at his shoulder with his free hand and suddenly realised that he was cold.

The skeleton Aborigine came forward and stood close to the coach. He raised his fingers in a quick series of complicated signs, without saying a word. Then he solemnly reached into a small kangaroo-skin pouch which hung around his neck, and took out a piece of stone. He handed it to Eyre, bowed his head slightly, and then retreated into the darkness. The other Aborigines followed him; until within a few moments they were all gone.

'Well, now,' said Christopher, sounding shaken. 'What the devil was all *that* about? I'd like to know?'

Eyre sat down, and examined the fragment of stone. It was a piece of granite, sharpened and pointed, with curling decorations carved on it, and red ochre rubbed into the indentations.

'It looks like a token,' he said. 'Some sort of a sign.'

'But what's it all *about*, Eyre? For goodness' sake! And what are we going to do about these chaps? Dead as dodos, those chaps in the street, I should say. And the coachman looks rather more than out of sorts.'

Eyre dropped the stone into his pocket, and climbed down from the phaeton. The coachman was sitting up now, dusty and dazed; a huge red lump rising on the side of his forehead.

'Christ Almighty,' he cursed; and spat dust and saliva.

Eyre knelt down beside him, and retrieved his watch and Christopher's purse. 'You're fortunate you weren't killed,' he said. 'Your villainous friends were, though, two of them.'

The coachman squinted through unfocused eyes at the bodies of red-pepper face and the limping man lying in the road. His high hat had been knocked off by the boomerang, and Eyre could see now by the light of the coachlamp that his head was shaved, a lumpy skull covered with bone-white bristles. It gave him a brutish, half-human appearance; but at the same time there was something remarkably vulnerable about him; like a retarded child.

'Christ Almighty,' he spat again.

'You realise I'm going to have to call the police,' said Eyre.

Grunting, the coachman managed to heave himself up on to his feet, and lean unsteadily against the phaeton's rear wheel. He dragged a rag out of his pocket, and wiped his face. 'Well, then, sir,' he said, 'that, I suppose, is your privilege. But I should like to know what happened here. Was it *you* who knocked me down? And what are these spears?'

Red-pepper-face was lying legs-apart on his back, his dead hands still clutching the shaft of the spear which had skewered his neck. His eyes were wide open; and he looked as if he were just about to explain what had happened to him.

'It seems we have friends, this gentleman and I,' said Eyre.

'Blackfellows, sir?'

Eyre nodded. He was quite as confused and disoriented as the coachman must have been; but he thrust his hands into his pockets and did his best to walk confidently around the side of the coach as if he had expected this sudden rescue all along.

'I wish they had done for me too,' the coachman said, glumly. 'By God I do.'

Eyre looked at him questioningly.

'Well, sir,' the coachman said, 'they'll hang me this time, and no mistake; or worse.'

'What could be worse than hanging?' asked Eyre.

'You don't know the penal settlements, sir, if you don't know what's worse than hanging.'

Eyre said, curiously, 'What's your name, fellow?'

'Arthur Mortlock, sir.'

'Well, Arthur Mortlock, tell me why you tried to rob us tonight, if you're so much afraid of the penal settlements.'

Mortlock looked down at red-pepper-face, and his black dry blood in the dust. 'That man's Duncan Croucher, sir; and he and me was together for seven years at Macquarie Harbour. We're ticket-of-leave men, both of us; and we was supposed to stay within sight of Sydney; but there was no work for us there. So we absconded and came to Adelaide, I suppose to find ourselves a respectable living. They always told us that Adelaide was just the place for respectability, sir. The kind of town where a man isn't looked down on for being a Crown pensioner, sir; nor ostracised.'

'That doesn't explain why you tried to rob us.'

Mortlock dabbed gingerly at the lump on his forehead. 'No, sir. But I expect you understand. We tried to start up a carriage business between us, on account of Croucher was a cabbie, back in London; and I was a drayman for Bass. But the times aren't good, sir, and tonight was the first bit of legitimate business we'd had for a fortnight.'

Christopher, irritable and frightened, said, 'Come on, Eyre. We're frightfully late. Let's call the police and have this chap locked up where he belongs. Daisy and May will be quite frothing by now; and the Ball will have started.'

Eyre said, 'Just a moment, Christopher. I want to hear from Mr Mortlock what it is that is worse than hanging.'

Mortlock raised his eyes; and they were black and bright and a little mad. Not the madness of rage or felony; but the madness of fear. The madness that dogs' eyes show, when their owners whip them; and which drives their owners to whip them even harder.

'I was sent out for losing my temper at the brewery, sir, and beating my foreman; but one fine day I lost my temper again and beat my guard; and for that they sent me to Macquarie Harbour. There they flogged me four times in all; two hundred and seventy lashes altogether; but one day I lost my temper yet again and beat a fellow prisoner; and that was when they locked me into solitary confinement, for a year, Christmas to Christmas, with my face covered all the time in a helmet of rough grey felt, sir, with holes pierced for the eyes. And when they let me out of there, and eventually gave me my ticket-of-leave, I was still inclined to lose my temper, and act rash, as I have this evening. But the effect of that confinement, sir, was such that I would rather cut my own throat than go through it for one more hour. You have no idea, sir.'

Eyre put his hand across his mouth. Both Christopher and Mortlock watched him; Christopher with nervousness and badly disguised impatience, and Mortlock with dreadful fascination.

After a moment, Eyre asked, 'Do you think you can still manage to drive the carriage?'

'I don't understand, sir.'

'Come,' said Eyre. 'Let's drag these two bodies into the bushes, and leave them lie. We didn't murder them ourselves, after all; and they still have Aborigine spears in them. Let's leave Major O'Halloran's constables to think that they were slain by wandering tribesmen.'

Christopher burst out, 'This is preposterous! You're not going to let this fellow go free?'

'I was thinking of it,' said Eyre.

'But for goodness' sake, the fellow tried to rob us; he would have killed us himself if he'd half a mind to.'

'I don't suppose you've heard about the spirit of Christian forgiveness,' Eyre retorted.

'Well, of course I have. But I've also heard the commandment which says you shall not steal; and I should think that also includes *attempted* robbery, wouldn't you?'

Eyre said, 'For now, Christopher, I'm not going to argue with you. Mr Mortlock, help us pull these bodies into the bushes. Then let us get on our way exactly as if nothing had happened; and we can discuss the morals of it later. Let me tell you one thing, though, Mr Mortlock.'

Arthur Mortlock looked at Eyre disbelievingly, and nodded his head.

'From now,' said Eyre, 'from this very moment, in fact, you must live your life as if you were aspiring to be one of the angels. For if you do not, I will make quite sure that a letter is held in safekeeping which will condemn you at once. Do I make myself clear?'

Mortlock stood up straight. 'You're asking a lot of me, sir.'

'Of course. But I'm also *giving* you a lot. Your continued freedom; possibly your life.'

'I know that, sir.'

'Well, then, let's be quick. One of those boozy fellows at the Cockatoo is going to look across here soon and wonder what we're up to.'

Mortlock retrieved his high hat, and brushed it. 'Yes, sir, and God bless you, sir.'

It took them only a few minutes to drag the limping man and red-pepper-face into the thorn bushes. It was a grisly business; and they had to kick dust over the bloodstains on the road. But then they climbed up into the carriage again, and were driving lopsidedly off towards Daisy Frockford's house.

As they passed the Cockatoo, the men outside were swinging their bottles of rum in time to a filthy old song from the slums of London.

'If you ever want to charver wiv a leper,
Make sure you chooses one wiv biggish tits.

109

On account of when you charver wiv a leper,
Yer avridge leper usually falls to bits.'

From the carriage, Eyre could see in the men's faces a
desperate happy brightness; a terrible oblivious joy; and
he was disturbingly reminded of a young blind farm-
worker he had once seen on the road to Baslow, who was
laughing in desperation because his daughter could see a
rainbow.

Christopher was sulking. Even when they drew up
outside the smart imported-wood house on Flinders Street
where the Frockfords lived; with its sparkling lamps beside
the door, and its two dark spires of Araucaria pines in the
exact centre of each front lawn; he would do nothing more
than pull a face and say to Eyre, as Mortlock pulled down
the step for them, 'You're making a serious mistake, Eyre.
A *very* serious mistake. You mark my words.'

Nine

The driveway outside Colonel Gawler's residence on North
Terrace was impossibly cluttered with carriages when they
arrived; and as they jostled in through the gates, Eyre
could detect a certain lowering of Mortlock's head into his
shoulders, which suggested to Eyre a well-suppressed
urge in Mortlock to lay about him with his whip, and flick
off a few hats and ostrich feathers, and clear a way.

The lawns were lit with sparkling lanterns, which swung
prettily in the evening wind, and even the colonel's tame
kangaroos had been dressed up with white silk bows
around their necks. Two footmen in green frogged coats
stood by the door; one of them as tall as a Tasmanian pine,

110

the other almost a dwarf; and between them, awkwardly, they helped the ladies to alight from their barouches. Each lady as she stepped down glanced quickly around her like an alarmed emu, in case she should see a gown in the same design as hers, or (worse) a gown in the same particular shade of silk. Fine fabrics from London and Paris were in short supply in Adelaide this season, and there were only two dressmakers in King William Street capable of sewing a really fashionable gown; so for the past four or five weeks, fear and secrecy had been intense in the parlours and dressing-rooms of Rundle and Grenfell Streets.

Daisy Frockford, who now sat beside Christopher fanning herself furiously and uttering little yelps of impatience and disapproval, was dressed in a gown of vivid emerald-green, with white leaf patterns of pearls and diamante all around the hem. She wore a head-dress that looked to Eyre like an overgrown garden-gate, with creepers hanging from it; and it had the effect of making her fat little face seem even fatter, and even littler, like a vexatious baby.

May Cameron, Eyre's companion, was quieter, almost melancholy. She was wearing pale pink moiré silk, with seed-pearls sewn on to it in the pattern of butterflies. She was dark-haired, with a profile that reminded Eyre of engravings he had seen of the young Queen Victoria: just a little too plump to be beautiful. Her breasts were quite enormous, and lay side by side in her lace-trimmed décolletage with the gelatinous contentment of two vanilla puddings. Now and then she sighed, and attempted the smallest of small sad smiles, and Eyre supposed she was thinking of the wastrel Peter Harris.

Wedged in close to Daisy Frockford was an aunt of Daisy's who had been introduced to Eyre and Christopher as Mrs Palgrave; a talkative woman with a perfectly oval face and false teeth that clattered whenever she spoke, which was often.

At last, by jamming his dilapidated phaeton in between

111

two highly varnished landaus occupied by some of the wealthier local aristocracy; a manoeuvre which caused one of their coachmen to glare hotly at all of them, and scowl, 'Bustard,'; Arthur Mortlock brought them up to the entrance, and the two footmen opened their door for them and assisted them down. Mrs Palgrave caught her foot in her hem, and performed the most extraordinary little dance, but the dwarf footman managed to catch her around the waist, and hold her upright while she disentangled herself.

'I declare the silliest thing that ever happened,' Mrs Palgrave flapped. 'I shall have that seamstress in court see if I don't. Could have tumbled head-over-heels and broken my neck and then what.'

Eyre walked around to the front of the phaeton and spoke to Arthur Mortlock. Arthur Mortlock took off his high hat and looked down at him with unreadable eyes.

'I'd like you to be here when the Ball finishes, to take us home,' said Eyre. 'That's unless you want to make a run for it.'

'I'm done with running, sir,' said Mortlock.

'You realise that when the militia find your two companions, they may start making enquiries after you; and if they discover that you're a ticket-of-leave man, they'll take you directly back to Norfolk Island.'

'I repeat, sir, I'm done with running. All I ask is that you vouch for me, sir, if it comes to trouble. I suppose that's an impertinence to ask, after this evening's bit of business; but I've made you a promise, sir, that I'll stay on the straight and narrow, and that's all I can say.'

Mrs Palgrave said, 'Pushing and shoving, no wonder I tripped. Look at them all, like monkeys in the menagerie see if they aren't, supposed to be high-and-mighty and pushing away rude as you like.'

Eyre looked up at Arthur Mortlock and gave him a small nod of encouragement. 'Very well,' he said. 'Let's see if you really have been converted on the road to Damascus.'

Mortlock drove the phaeton away to the rear of the

stables, where the horses would be fed, and the coachmen would share a pipe or two of tobacco and play cards until it was time for carriages. Eyre and Christopher guided May and Daisy into the wide parquet-floored hallway, with its crystal chandelier and its idealistic paintings of Mount Lofty and the valley of the Torrens River; and there they were met by Colonel Gawler's head footman, all wig and catarrh, who took their invitations and hoarsely announced their arrival to the disinterested throng in the reception room.

There was music from a small orchestra which had been formed the previous year by Captain Wintergreen, a retired bandmaster from the New South Wales Corps: quadrilles played like cavalry charges, and waltzes so emphatic that it was obviously going to be easier to march to them than dance to them. At the far end of the room, with a distracted smile, Colonel Gawler himself was standing in his full regalia as Governor and Commissioner, his chest shining like a cutlery canteen with tiers of decorations, trying to make intelligent responses to a tall woman with an exceptionally meaty nose, whom Eyre recognised as Mrs Hillier, one of Adelaide's few schoolmarms. Captain Bromley was there, too, with his corn-coloured hair and his stutter; and the Farmer sisters, in a bright shade of blue; and the Reverend T.Q. Stow, with his hands clasped adamantly behind his back and his face squeezed up like a closed umbrella. Mrs Maria Gawler, the Governor's wife, was wearing an unbecoming brown dress, and fluttering her hands about like little birds.

The noise was tremendous. Not only the whomp-ti-bomping of the orchestra, but the screeching and laughing of the ladies, and the overblown boasting of the gentlemen: a strange relentless roar of competitive sound, as Adelaide's socialites did their absolute utmost to outcry, outpose, outshout, and out-amuse each other. Already the reception room was suffocatingly hot, and the ladies' fans were whirring everywhere, giving the impression that the

113

house was crowded with birds which couldn't quite manage to raise themselves into the air.

'What a din I declare, never heard the like,' complained Mrs Palgrave. 'Toss them nuts and apples I would, see if they scramble for them. Monkeys in the menagerie.'

'Is Sturt here yet?' Eyre asked Christopher, as they piloted their lady companions into the middle of the room. May nodded her head at one or two friends whom she hadn't seen since her engagement had been broken off. Daisy, who couldn't see anyone she knew, fanned herself even more violently.

Christopher lifted his head and looked around. 'Can't see him. But he'll be here, all right. Loves the admiration. We might have to wait until the end of the evening before we can talk to him, though.'

Daisy said, 'I'd adore a glass of punch.'

'Then you shall certainly have one,' said Christopher.

'And you, May, would you care for a glass?' Eyre asked her.

She nodded. 'But I'd prefer to drink it outside, if we may. The noise and the heat in here is making me feel dizzy already.'

They beckoned over a perspiring waiter, who handed them glasses of scarlet punch, rum and grenadine and pineapple-juice, and while Mrs Palgrave perched herself on a small gold-painted chair, and talked to Mrs Warburton about tattooing, and how there wasn't an ounce of civilized behaviour from Para Scarp to Port Adelaide, Christopher and Daisy went off to find somebody who might give Daisy a compliment, and Eyre took May out of the open French windows and on to the verandah.

May sat on a garden-chair, while Eyre leaned against the wooden balustrade. Beyond them, in the lantern-lit gardens, the kangaroos slowly hopped, like large animated £-signs; and the night parrots did their best to compete with the screeching ladies indoors.

The governor's new house was white-painted, and comparatively elegant, although only the east wing had

114

been fully completed. The original house had been built for Colonel Gawler's predecessor, Captain John Hindmarsh, out of mud and laths; but because he had employed sailors and ship's carpenters to put it up, they had forgotten to give him a fireplace, or a chimney. This house was more in keeping with the status of governor and commissioner of South Australia, and Eyre quite coveted it. Sitting on the balustrade with his drink, he felt successful and confident already; and he thought that May wasn't too bad a companion, either, even if she was a little solemn.

'You must learn to smile again,' he told her, lifting his glass.

'I do try,' she said.

'Were you so very upset about your engagement?'

She nodded. 'I loved Peter enough to want him for my husband. But after he lost all that money, father forbade it. Most of the money had been lent to him by my uncle; some by my mother. He said he was going to invest in a mining company, and that we should all be paid back a hundred times over.'

'And instead, he put it on horses?'

'I don't know why,' she said. There was a sparkle of tears in her eyes. 'I suppose he wanted to impress me, and win my father over.'

'Fathers can be a problem,' said Eyre. 'Especially fathers who worship their daughters, and want only the very best for them.'

May sipped her punch, and glanced up at Eyre, and tried to smile. Eyre didn't know if it was the effect of the heat, or the noise, or the music, but he suddenly began to think that he might have taken quite a fancy to May. There was something about her cupid's-bow lips, something tempting because they looked so sweet, and naive. And he found himself admiring her breasts, and imagining what they must look like when they were uncupped from her gown. And he thought of her body, too, white-skinned and chubby, with fleshy hips and thighs between which

115

a man could happily suffocate. A virgin, too. Well brought up and well protected; and sentimental to a fault.

'May,' he said, 'you and I must dance. We must endeavour to be happy together, even though we are both feeling sad. Just for tonight, we must forget what might have happened, and try to think of what *could* happen.'

May sipped a little more of her drink, and twiddled the stem of her glass around. 'Daisy said that you're a vicar's son.'

'Well, Daisy's quite right.'

'She said that you're very religious, when the mood takes you; or so Christopher told her.'

'Religious? Well, I believe in God, and the sacrament of Holy Communion, if that's what she meant.'

'Well, I don't know. She said that you could be rather *dogged*, at times. I hope you don't mind my saying that.'

Eyre stood up, and walked around the verandah. 'Dogged? I suppose I *can* be rather dogged when I feel seriously about something. But I don't count that altogether wrong, do you? Doggedness in the defence of what is right, and what is just, and in the upholding of Christian principles—well, you can hardly call that a vice.'

'Daisy said something about an Aborigine boy; how you wanted to give him an Aborigine funeral.'

Eyre nodded slowly. 'I do. That's one of the reasons I've come here tonight.'

'But Aborigines are *savages*.'

'You may think so. Most people do, and I suppose that they can be forgiven for it. The government does nothing to help us understand them. But it seems to me that the Aborigines are one of the most magical and religious of peoples on the face of the earth. Just because they live in innocence and nakedness, that doesn't mean that they're savages. Adam and Eve lived in innocence and nakedness; and far from being savages, *they* were the most divine of all human beings ever; nearer to God than anybody today could imagine. It could very well be that Aborigines are the results of God's attempt to start again: to create for a second time a perfectly innocent society. If that is so, and it *could* be so, then I believe that it is our duty to protect the Aborigines and to prevent them from losing their innocence. Perhaps the Garden of Eden now lies here, in the unexplored centre of Australia. Perhaps the significance of this strange country is divine, as well as geographical. Whatever it is, I believe that we should be cautious, and respectful, and that we should be very wary of imposing our own way of life on the blackfellows. We, after all, are the descendants of Adam and Eve: we are the sinful children of sinners. The Aborigines know no sin; and to that extent we should envy them. To that extent, they are our superiors.'

May stared at him. It was quite plain that she could hardly believe what he had said.

Eyre stopped pacing, and reached out his hand towards her. 'Don't let's talk of such serious matters tonight; why don't you dance with me? They're playing *Le Pantalon*.'

'I—ah—I think I'd rather not,' said May, considerably flustered. 'Really.'

'Because of what I said about Aborigines?'

'Well—how can you possibly suggest that an Aborigine could be your own superior? Or mine?' She was flushed, and she didn't know what to do with her glass of punch.

'May—what I said—it's only a theory. But Australia is such an extraordinary country that you can't close up your mind to *any* possibility. Why does it exist at all, this peculiar continent with foxes that fly but birds that won't? We know hardly anything of it, especially the interior; the very centre of it; how can we make any assumptions at all? It's a work of God; there's no doubt of that at all. But what a work!'

May said, 'Please, don't talk like that. It upsets me.'

'Why? Because it could be true?'

'It makes me feel . . . uncomfortable, that's all.'

Eyre knelt down beside her, on one knee. 'In that case, forgive me. I brought you here to enjoy yourself, not to feel uncomfortable. I know that I might sound rather odd, but the truth is that I adore Australia and all of its mysteries; and I truly believe that there's a meaning behind it being here; and a reason for its existence.'

May was just about to answer him, when they were interrupted by a spattering of applause from the garden. Eyre turned around in surprise, and saw a tall man in side-whiskers walking towards him across the lawn, clapping his hands as he came. The man had an intelligent, amused face; and eyes that were bright with self-confidence and pleasure. Nobody could have called him handsome. But his plainness was commanding in its own particular way; and as Eyre stood up to greet him, he knew at once that here was a man both to trust and to like.

'You must accept my apologies for eavesdropping on you,' the man said, warmly. 'But you are the first person I have heard for many a long month who has dared to question the very being of this continent; and to acknowledge what it has to offer us now as well as what it may surrender in the future.'

The man stepped up on to the verandah, bowed deeply to May and kissed her hand, and then shook hands with Eyre. His handshake was very firm and strong, and Eyre noticed that there was a white scar across the base of his thumb, and another scar across his forehead.

'Charles Sturt,' the man announced himself. 'I believe I was supposed to be guest of honour here tonight; but I'm afraid that my nerve rather failed me.'

'I'm honoured to know you, sir,' said Eyre. 'My name is Eyre Walker, and this young lady is Miss May Cameron.'

Sturt took May's hand again, and kissed it; allowing himself a closer inspection of her creamy-white cleavage. 'Charmed,' he said, richly.

Sturt dragged over a chair, and sat himself down on it, uninvited. 'I'm supposed to be the most social of creatures; but believe me that's only a façade. I enjoy applause, and general admiration. Don't we all? But the thought of spending the entire evening recounting my expeditions to endless numbers of open-mouthed ladies and their sceptical husbands . . . well, it's been almost enough to give me a headache.'

'You surprise me, sir,' said Eyre.

'Well, I often surprise myself,' Sturt replied. He reached into his pocket, and took out a silver cigar-case, and opened it. 'But I consider that to be one of the essentials of a worthwhile life; to keep on surprising everybody, including oneself.'

He said, 'You won't mind if I smoke?' and lit up a small cigar. 'I have a particular weakness for the indigenous tobacco. One of the tastes I acquired on the Murrumbidgee.'

Inside the reception room, another fierce quadrille had struck up; and the floor was drummed by dancing feet.

'I must say that I think your theory about Australia has some merit,' remarked Sturt, leaning back in his chair, and blowing out strong-smelling smoke. 'Whatever seems to hold good in the northern hemisphere seems to be quite reversed here; and I have wondered many times whether there is any divine logic behind such a reversal. The very essence of this land is its upside-downness, if I might call it that; and to discover its secrets one must first of all invert every interpretive facility that one possesses.'

'I read about your expedition of 1829,' Eyre told him. 'I was much impressed.'

Sturt's exploration of the Murrumbidgee and Murray Rivers was already legendary. He had set out from Sydney with a 27 foot whaleboat carried on horse-drawn drays; and in this and in another boat which they had hewn out a giant forest tree, he and his companions had rowed for six weeks along the Murrumbidgee and Murray Rivers, until they had reached the coast of the Indian Ocean, thirty minutes south of Adelaide at Lake Alexandrina. When they had arrived there, however, there had been no ship to meet them, and with their supplies dwindling, they had been obliged to row all the way back to where they had started from, over 800 miles, upstream.

Sturt had gone temporarily blind during the last days of

the expedition, and some of his companions had collapsed in delirium. But all had survived; and when Sturt returned to Sydney with his stories of the spectacular cliffs and idyllic lakes that they had seen, and the sweeping floods on the Murray, and the 'vast concourse' of Aborigines who had followed them, clamouring and shouting and shaking their spears he had immediately been fêted as a hero, and a great explorer.

His eyes were better now; although Eyre noticed that they still had a slightly stony look about them. His enthusiasm for exploration, though, was as fervent as ever.

'I long now to open up the interior,' he said, smoking in quick little puffs. 'If there is an inland sea there, I want to sail on it before I die. If there is a Garden of Eden there, as you suggest, then I wish to walk in it, close to God. It is one of the last great mysteries of the globe; a secret that only the Aborigines know; and perhaps even they have never succeeded in penetrating to the very core of the continent.'

Eyre said, 'It was about Aborigines that I wished to speak to you.'

'Well, I'm not sure that I'm your man,' said Sturt; still affable, but suddenly and noticeably less interested. 'Your Aborigine is a sad and particular creature, and there are many who know him better than I.'

'But you encountered so many of them when you were exploring the Murrumbidgee and the Murray. You said so in your reports.'

'I read them, too,' ventured May. 'They sounded an extraordinarily warlike people to say the least.'

Sturt coughed, and brushed ash from his trousers. 'They were threatening, and raucous, the first time we saw them. They lined up on the banks of the river, and up on the cliffs, and chanted war-songs at us; and for a time I must admit that we were very alarmed. They were shining with grease, and they had painted themselves like skeletons and ghosts. Their women appeared to have capsised a whole bucket of whitewash over their heads. But, in the end, they did little more than stamp at us, and shout, and then retreat. They didn't hurt us; not once; and when at last we did manage to make some kind of contact with them, and talk to them by signs and gestures, we found that they were a very unfortunate people indeed. Rich in superstition and myth, no doubt of that. But scratching a living from food that would horrify you, if I were to tell you of it, and wandering from place to place with a restlessness that totally precludes the development of any kind of civilisation. They were riddled with syphilitic diseases, even the very youngest of them; in fact some of the sufferers were so young that I can only pray that they were born in that diseased condition. I agree with you, Mr Walker, that the Garden of Eden may indeed be found in the centre of this continent; but I must say that I doubt very strongly whether the Aboriginals are the truly innocent people whom God intended to dwell there.'

May, who had been listening to this with some discomfort, took Eyre's arm and said, 'Shall we dance now? I really would rather dance.'

Eyre said, 'Of course. But please let me first ask Captain Sturt if he knows how a particular Aborigine might be found.'

'I beg your pardon?' asked Sturt. 'A *particular* Aborigine?'

'That is what I wanted to ask you. I have to find a chief, a Wirangu I think, whose name is Yonguldye, The Darkness.'

'Now then,' said Sturt, 'that may present some problems. The blackfellow will stay in each location for only a limited time, according to the season, and according to what magical and traditional obligations have brought him there. In September, for example, many of the Wirangu will be seen at Woocalla Rock; where they will hold a corroboree to mark the victory of Joolunga over the Lizard-Man, long ago in the time they call the dreaming.

121

Then, they will be gone. All you will find of them will be their ashes and the bones of the animals they have eaten.'

Eyre said, 'It may seem curious to you, Captain Sturt; even a little desperate, perhaps, but I recently made a promise to a dying Aborigine boy that I would ensure his burial according to Aborigine custom. He told me before he died that I should look for the one they called The Darkness.'

'Eyre,' said May, tugging at his arm again, 'can't you speak of this later? They're playing *'Dufftown Ladies'.*'

But Eyre held back for a moment, and waited for Sturt to answer him. After a while, Sturt looked up with a mixed expression on his face; as if only Eyre himself could resolve how Sturt was going to feel about him.

'Why should a young man like yourself feel obligated to a blackfellow?'

'I made a promise, sir, that's all. And I have to confess that, in a way, I was responsible for his dying.'

'Has he been buried already?'

'So I understand; but according to the Christian service.'

'But are you not a Christian yourself?'

'My father was a vicar, sir, in Derbyshire.'

Sturt sucked at his cigar, so that the tip of it brightened like a red-hot cinder. 'There is more to this, don't you think, than simply a promise of burial to one unfortunate black boy?'

Eyre stared at Sturt carefully. 'There may well be,' although he didn't fully understand what Sturt was implying.

Sturt nodded. 'I had with me two or three young men like you when I rowed down the Murray. You, Mr Walker, have the calling. You know that, don't you?'

'The calling, sir?'

Sturt raised an arm, and swept it around to suggest the far and unseen horizons of Australia. 'You have the calling of the great and terrible interior. You may be a new chum; you may be fresh to Australia; but you are not a coast-squatter, like so many; afraid even to contemplate the

122

Ghastly Blank that lies to the north of us. Ah, you have the vocation my boy! I can sense it! All you have to determine now is whether you have the strength.'

Eyre said nothing. Sturt had touched too many silent strings inside his mind; and for the first time played for him the inaudible but irresistible music of real ambition. He began to see that his promise to Yanluga may have been far more significant than a simple commitment to one dying boy; it may have been a promise to himself, and to his future life, and to the unknown continent of Australia.

His life of girls and bicycles seemed suddenly frivolous; and without any purpose or satisfaction. But even when he had been cycling, and flirting, and drinking home-made beer with Dogger McConnell, something must have been happening within him; some deep and vibrant change. Why had he felt so responsible to Yanluga? Why had he agreed to let Arthur Mortlock go free? Perhaps he had sensed in them, as Captain Sturt had sensed in him, that they were true children of the Australian continent, and that it was they and their descendants who would reveal at last the frightening and mystagogic significance of *Terra Australis Incognita*.

At that moment, Mr Brough stepped out on to the terrace, and cried, 'Why *there* you are, Captain Sturt! We've been a-hunting for you everywhere! Do come inside, the ladies are all agog to meet you.'

Sturt took a last suck at his cigar, and then tossed it glowing into the acacia bushes. 'Very well,' he agreed, trying not to sound too resigned about it. Then he took May's hand, and kissed it again, and shook hands with Eyre, and said, 'We must discuss this some more. Where do you think I might find you?'

'I work at the port, sir, for the South Australian Company.'

'Well, that's capital, for I shall be down at the wharf tomorrow morning. If you can persuade the company to allow you a few minutes' spare time; there are one or two

123

matters we could discuss. And I might be able to assist you in locating your mysterious Mr Darkness.'

Sturt went inside, to be greeted by spontaneous applause, and a quick burst from the orchestra of *For He's A Jolly Good Fellow*, immediately followed by *The Rose of Quebec*, which Eyre supposed to be an obscure acknowledgement of Sturt's military service in Canada, just before Waterloo.

'Now then,' he said to May, 'perhaps we can dance. I'm sorry to have spent so much time talking about exploration, and Aborigines.'

'Well, it was a pleasure to meet Captain Sturt,' said May. But then she squeezed Eyre's hand, and added, 'The only trouble is that men like you and he, well, you perplex me.'

Eyre ushered her in through the open French doors. The room was hot and crowded and even noisier than before, with a new and shriller chorus of voices now as the men drank too much punch and the women tried to attract the attention of Captain Sturt.

'You mustn't let such things worry you,' Eyre told May. 'Men like Captain Sturt and I, we perplex ourselves.'

Ten

Inexplicably, Christopher appeared to be bitterly put out that Eyre had already been speaking to Sturt, and that Sturt had done nothing to dissuade Eyre from going in search of Chief Yonguldye. To show his annoyance, he stamped his feet furiously as he danced a quadrille with Daisy, and glared at Eyre with such wrath that a dear old lady in a pearl head-dress rapped Eyre's elbow with her fan, and said, 'I do believe that gentleman is trying to attract your attention, young man. Do you think he might be in pain?'

After the quadrille, however, as Christopher came stalking over to argue with him some more, Eyre immediately swept May out on to the floor to dance a long, slow, clockwork waltz, around and around, with Christopher's indignant face appearing with bright-red regularity on the third beat of every tenth bar.

Eyre found May quite provocative; and his britches tightened as they danced. But provocative as she was, her conversation was nothing but a shopping-basket of confusions, worries, second-hand notions, and unrelated facts about nothing of any importance. With his imagination already widening to encompass the 'calling' which Captain Sturt had spoken about; with his mind's-eye repeating for him again and again the sweep of the arm with which Sturt had outlined the furthest reaches of the Ghastly Blank; Eyre found it difficult to follow what May was saying, and even more difficult to come up with any sensible replies.

'Everybody knows that Aborigines are little more than dirty children,' said May, as Christopher's face swung past her shoulder, followed by the glittering chandelier, and a footman carrying punch, and a white-faced young man with fiery red hair.

'I'm sorry?' said Eyre.

'They steal, and they lie, and they're no use at all to man or beast.'

'What? Who do?'

'Oh, *Eyre*,' protested May, 'you're being absolutely impossible.'

Eyre kissed her on the forehead, just at the moment that Mrs Palgrave was peering at them both like a custodial bandicoot. 'Forgive me: let's go and find something to eat.'

Christopher caught up with them in the dining-room, where the long walnut table had been laid out with terraces of food.

'Eyre, you're being quite impossible.'

'I know. May has just told me that.'

'But to talk to Captain Sturt like that; really. What on earth did he think?'

'He didn't think I was insane, or anything of that nature, if that's what you imagine.'

'But you're going through with this ridiculous idea?'

Eyre picked a chicken vol-au-vent from the very top of a mountain of vol-au-vents, and bit into it. 'Of course I am. Especially now that Captain Sturt seems to think that I could have all the makings of an explorer.'

'That's nonsense. He was only being polite.'

'I don't think so,' said Eyre, shaking his head.

'Well, even if he wasn't, what would you explore?'

Eyre stared at him. 'What do you *think* I would explore? Australia, of course! There are countless thousands of square miles of quite uncharted territory out there. For all we know, there may be a vast inland sea. Or a huge tropical forest. Or an undiscovered range of mountains.'

They walked along the whole length of the table. There were smoked hams, tureens of white cockatoo soup, wild ducks stuffed with beef and apricots, chickens, Goolwa cockles, roasted emu thighs, and lamb cutlets with crisp golden fat on beds of wild celery and spinach. There were boiled crabs, glistening oysters, and freshly-opened lampreys, as well as silvery smoked sea-perch, baked snapper, and steaming tureens of green-turtle broth. Eyre picked here and there; and forked up tidbits for May and Daisy; while Christopher hovered around him and sulked.

'I really can't understand why you're so upset,' said Eyre, with his mouth full.

'You're making a fool of yourself, that's why. Chasing off after Aborigines.'

'I've invited you to come with me. Then we can *both* make fools of ourselves.'

Christopher said nothing, but forked himself up a slice of emu meat, which was coarse and lean and rather like mutton; and chewed it with concentrated aggression.

Eyre said, 'I haven't really worked out what I'm going to do yet. Tomorrow, after I've spoken to Captain Sturt again, perhaps I shall know more clearly. But I shall go in search of Yonguldye; and, as I go, I shall chart whatever countryside I come across, and make maps.'

Christopher swallowed his meat, and looked away.

Eyre touched his back. 'You could come with me, you know. It would be quite an adventure; and, who knows, we might come back from it as heroes. Look at Captain Sturt.'

Christopher shrugged, and still didn't answer.

'I *have* to go,' said Eyre. 'I owe it not only to Yañluga, but to myself, too.'

'If you must,' retorted Christopher.

Eyre hesitated, and then took Christopher aside, where they could be overheard only by a large bronze bust of Matthew Flinders, the man who had discovered the site of Adelaide in 1801. 'Something is upsetting you,' said Eyre. 'I think you should explain to me just what it is.'

Christopher looked at him, watery-eyed. 'It is not an easy matter to explain without your misunderstanding it altogether.'

'Can you try?'

Christopher shrugged. 'The fact of the matter is that I have formed a considerable affection for you. Not a physical affection—please don't think that it is anything to do with matters of that nature. But, I suppose I must say that I love you.'

Eyre held his friend's hand. 'That's nothing to be ashamed of. I love you, too, with all my heart.'

'Not quite as I do, my dear chap. I love you—' and here he swallowed as if he were still trying to force down his mouthful of emu flesh, '—romantically.'

Eyre couldn't find any words to answer him; but he kept hold of his hand, and gripped it firmly, to show that he was neither disgusted nor repelled.

After a moment or two, Christopher said, 'This has only happened to me once before in my life, at college, and I

127

never imagined for a single instant that it would ever happen again. But during the year in which I have known you, I have become as attached to you as a young girl might have done. That is why the thought of your leaving on this incredible expedition to find Yonguldye fills me with such dread. There have been many explorers, Eyre; and very few of them have been as lucky and as successful as Captain Sturt. There may be an inland sea. There may be a wonderful forest. But those who have tried to penetrate the interior and survived have come back with stories of nothing but treeless desert, and of unimaginable heat, and death.'

Eyre licked his lips, to moisten them. The dining-room suddenly felt dry, and stuffy, like a brick oven. 'I have already said that you could come with me. Your feelings about me give me no cause whatsoever to change my mind.'

Christopher said, 'No. I am afraid that such ventures are not for me. If I were to go, I would die just as surely as you would survive. I am not a hero, Eyre, for all of my bombast, and for all of my womanising. You said to me once that you envied me and my ability to court girls without becoming over-attached to them. Well, now you know why.'

Eyre insisted, 'You *must* come with me; because you will never persuade me not to go.'

'No,' said Christopher.

'But we will be properly equipped. Captain Sturt will give us all the advice we need. We will take plenty of water with us, and at least two other companions; and an Aboriginal guide. How can we fail? And if we *do* fail, then all we have to do is to turn back.'

'Do you think that those poor souls whose bones lie out on the sand-dunes didn't believe the same thing? You know how hot it can be here in the summer: further north the heat becomes more and more intense. No, Eyre, it is a land of death, and when you speak about this expedition I can feel death itself on my shoulder.'

May came over, her white breasts bouncing, and said brightly, 'You two *do* look serious. For myself, I think this ball has quite recovered my spirits. And that dear Lance Baxter has asked me to dance with him, twice!'

'A cataclysm,' complained Mrs Palgrave, whose hair had begun to slip sideways. 'The way they fell upon the food like orang-utangs. All eating with their fingers, greasy lamb cutlets and all, even soup it wouldn't surprise me. Civilisation all gone to pot.'

Daisy pouted, 'Eyre, you haven't danced with me at *all* yet. I do believe that you're becoming miserable, and mean.'

'Very well, then, we shall dance,' Eyre agreed. He gave Christopher's hand one last reassuring press, and then he tugged on his white evening gloves so that he and Daisy could gavotte.

Daisy was a peculiarly cater-footed dancer, and Eyre kept finding himself in corners of the dance floor where he hadn't intended to be; but she chattered about all the latest scandal in Adelaide; Mimsy Giles had been sent by her parents to Perth for kissing one of the gardeners; and the Stewart family were in a terrible furore over Mr Stewart's affair with Doris King; and Eyre found the gavotte unusually instructive, even if it wasn't particularly accurate.

Christopher watched them morosely from the corner of the room, but Eyre determined to himself that nobody was going to be sad on his account, for any reason; and he made up his mind that he would persuade Christopher to come with him on his expedition to find Yonguldye, whatever happened.

It was odd, to find himself loved by a man, especially a man he knew so well. But he thought of his father's favourite proverb, from the Bible: 'Hatred stirs up strife, But love covers all transgressions.'

The gavotte was almost finished when Eyre noticed a familiar face on the far side of the room. Big, and boiled-looking, the face of Lathrop Lindsay. He twirled Daisy around, so extravagantly that she almost lost her balance; searching quickly from left to right for a sign of Charlotte. At first he couldn't see her there, and he began to think that Lathrop might have come to the Spring Ball with nobody but his wife, and left Charlotte at home at Waikerie Lodge.

When the music came to a scraping, irregular finish, however, and he escorted Daisy back to the custody of Mrs Palgrave, Christopher came over and said, tersely, 'Lathrop Lindsay's here.'

'Yes,' Eyre acknowledged. 'I've seen him.'

'Charlotte's here too.'

'I didn't see her.'

'She's taking some supper. But, Eyre—'

Eyre looked at Christopher sharply; but Christopher simply raised his hands in surrender. He wasn't going to interfere in Eyre's affections for Charlotte, no matter how tempted he might be. Nor was he going to allow this evening's admission of his unnatural love for Eyre destroy their friendship. Perhaps it would, in time. Perhaps it would strengthen it. It would certainly alter it irrevocably. But just for this evening, Christopher knew that it was better to leave well enough alone.

Eyre walked into the dining-room, looking around for Charlotte. He didn't recognise her at first, because she was wearing a white lace mantilla over her loose, fair curls. But then she turned, and he saw that remarkable profile, and those long eyelashes; and that half-dreamy innocent-sinful look of hers that had attracted him right from the very first moment he had caught sight of her on the wharf. She was helping herself to fillets of smoked fish, with whipped mayonnaise; and he said not loudly, but clearly 'Charlotte!'

She turned at once but so did the tall young man standing beside her, a square-faced fellow with the pale golden tan of a natural-born Australian. He was one of those vigorous, healthy, confident young colonists whom later arrivals skeptically called 'cornstalks', because of the upright way in which they walked about.

130

'Eyre!' said Charlotte, blushing. 'I didn't imagine that you would be here!'

Eyre defiantly looked across at Charlotte's escort, and kissed Charlotte on both cheeks. 'I came to see Captain Sturt,' he said. 'Christopher arranged it.'

Charlotte drew the young Australian boy forward, and in a flustered voice, announced, 'Eyre, this is Humphrey Clacy. Humphrey, this is Mr Eyre Walker. Humphrey is a friend of the family, Eyre; son of a Sydney family with whom father does business.'

'How do you do?' Eyre asked Clacy.

Humphrey Clacy said, uncertainly, 'Well, thanks.'

'Can we talk?' Eyre asked Charlotte. 'Your father's busy for the moment, trying to make himself known to Captain Sturt. Perhaps we could go out on the terrace.'

'Eyre, really, I don't think I can,' said Charlotte, hesitantly.

'Charlotte, we must talk; even if it's only for a moment or two.'

Charlotte took his hand. 'Eyre, please. It's all so difficult.'

'I'm only asking for two or three minutes, Charlotte. But I must tell you what I plan to do.'

'Eyre, you must understand. Father was so adamant that you and I should never see each other again. I've—I've grown resigned to it. Well, I've *tried* to grow resigned to it. You don't want me to go through any more pain, do you? You don't want me to suffer any more than I have already? Please, Eyre, I do love you; I'm terribly fond of you; but if we can never be together, what is the point of torturing ourselves so? Believe me, my dear, I'm thinking of you, too.'

Eyre breathed crossly, 'Charlotte, for goodness' sake. All I want to do is talk to you for five minutes.'

'Eyre, I'm sorry.'

Humphrey Clacy laid his arm around Charlotte's shoulders, and said in a strong 'flash' accent, 'I think you'd better leave the lydy alone, Mr Walker.'

131

Eyre stared at him in exaggerated surprise. 'He speaks!' he cried.

'Eyre, please, don't make one of your scenes,' begged Charlotte. 'We can talk later perhaps; or tomorrow. But, please, try to think of the pain that I've been feeling. It must be as sharp as your own. Please, let it be; and leave us.'

'Come on, Mr Walker,' Humphrey Clacy urged him; his cheeks suddenly firing up. The other guests were beginning to turn around now, and whisper to each other, and over in the far corner somebody dropped a plateful of potato salad on to the carpet.

'He speaks again!' Eyre shouted, angrily. 'Ladies and gentlemen, this indigenous animal has the power of communication!'

Charlotte hissed, 'Eyre, *please*! I must do what my father says. Eyre, please don't make me cry.'

'Ah, but that's the trouble,' said Eyre. 'I never make *anyone* cry. Not real tears, anyway. You can only cry for those you love, and those you respect; and neither you nor your father ever respected me, my love, for all of your sentimental words.'

'Eyre, of course I respect you.'

'You don't, Charlotte! You don't! Not for one moment! And I will never believe that you do until your father does; for you will never stand against him. A clerk, at the port? A newly-arrived burrower? You don't respect me in the least. All you cared for was my nonchalance, and my bicycle, and most of all the fact that I irritated your father.'

Humphrey Clacy took hold of Eyre's shoulder, and twisted his jacket. 'Mr Walker,' he said, in a tone which he obviously believed was very menacing, 'if you don't leave here immediately, and allow Miss Lindsay to finish her supper in peace, then I regret very much that I shall be obliged to hit you.'

Eyre looked this way and that, in furious mock-astonishment. 'I declare that it's miraculous! Why, I knew they could dig; and I knew that they could drink; and I knew that they could spit. But nobody told me that they could come along to parties, and make real conversation, even if it *is* offensive to listen to.'

There was sudden laughter. Eyre realised that he might be drunk. He was certainly very angry. The orchestra struck up with a polonaise, erratic and harsh. There was more laughter. And then Lathrop Lindsay appeared through the throng in the doorway of the dining-room, his face volcanic.

'Colonel Gawler, sir!' he called.

Somebody said, 'Fetch the Governor.'

Lathrop stepped forward like an elderly fighting-cock. He was dressed in full formal evening wear, with a wide pink cummerbund. He beckoned Charlotte to stand aside, and then he addressed himself directly to Eyre, his forehead shiny with perspiration, his lower lip protruding with stubborn rage.

'I tried to get him to leave, sir,' ventured Humphrey Clacy. 'He wouldn't hear of it.'

'That,' boiled Lathrop, 'is because he is chronically deaf. Deaf to advice, deaf to warnings and entreaties of all kinds, and above all deaf to the moral guidance of his betters, of whom there are very many.'

'I was simply asking to speak to Charlotte,' said Eyre.

'Well, you may not speak to Charlotte,' Lathrop retorted. 'You may neither speak to her nor see her. She has no desire to have any further to do with you. She finds you unspeakably offensive; as do I. I have called for Colonel Gawler, as I know that you will make trouble if any of us attempt to eject you forcibly; but you will probably understand that it would be far more satisfactory for you to leave quietly, and to leave at once, of your own volition.'

'I have a ticket and I shall stay,' Eyre declared. 'And let me say that if Charlotte does not wish to speak to me, then she can quite easily say so herself. She is an intelligent and spirited girl who has no need of a frothing father to speak for her; nor the company of a barely literate wheat-farmer with all the social graces of a duck-billed platypus.'

This was too much for Humphrey Clacy, who had already become over-excited by the appearance of Lathrop, and by the amusement of those who were standing around listening, and by the prospect of seeing Eyre ejected from the Ball by Colonel Gawler's footmen. He struck Eyre quite suddenly in the right ear, without warning, a sharp painful knock that sent Eyre staggering two or three steps sideways.

Eyre turned, stunned, not even sure what had happened. But then he saw Humphrey with his fists raised in the classic pose of a prizefighter, his blue eyes staring, his mouth pugnaciously pursed, and the frustration of everything that had happened to him in the past week burst out, with spectacular consequences.

He pushed Humphrey Clacy smartly in the chest; and Humphrey Clacy fell heavily backwards, the back of his legs striking the dining-table, so that he overbalanced. For one split-second everybody believed that he could save himself. But then he toppled with a tremendous crash of plates and silverware, right into a display of fresh fruit and shellfish and savoury jellies, bringing down rumbling pineapples and avalanches of ice and then a whole fragile castle of glass dishes filled with compôte of pears and charlotte russe. Some of the women screamed. Charlotte herself gave a cry like a wounded dove. Many of the drunker men gasped helplessly with laughter; and one of them, still laughing, offered Humphrey Clacy a hand up, only to let him slip back again, knocking over a tall arrangement of crab's-claws and plums and stuffed poussins.

'You are a walking disaster!' Lathrop roared at Eyre. 'You have brought down on me nothing but embarrassment and tragedy!'

'You're wrong!' Eyre shouted back at him. 'I have brought down on you *this*, as well!'

So saying, he lifted up from the table a huge cut-glass

dish of apple trifle, and promptly upturned it over Lathrop's head. Custard and apples splattered all over Lathrop's face and shoulders; and he stood for a moment like an unfinished clay statue, his eyes blinking out through the creamy sliding dessert in utter disbelief at what had happened.

Unsteadily, like a man on a tightrope, Eyre made his way across the food-strewn floor, and then crossed the reception-room at a pace that was almost a canter. He ran out through the french windows on to the verandah, and then down the stone steps into the garden. The first cries of 'Where is he? Where is the fellow?' were beginning to rise up from the house as he jogged around the corner of the stables, and found the carriages assembled there, and the coachmen drinking ginger-beer and playing cards.

Arthur Mortlock stood up immediately. 'Anything amiss, sir?' he asked, picking up his high hat.

'Nothing for you to worry yourself about,' Eyre panted. 'But I think it would be wiser if I were to leave directly. Take me back to my lodgings fast as you can; then come back and collect the rest of my party later.'

Arthur unhooked the feedbags from the horses' noses, and patted them.

'Trust it's nothing serious, sir,' he remarked, as he climbed up on to the box.

Men in evening dress were running this way and that across the lawns, some of them shouting, some of them laughing hysterically. There were cries from inside the house, and the off-key trumpeting of a French horn from the orchestra. One man had saddled up his grey mare, and was riding her backwards and forwards across the garden, trampling the acacia, frightening the kangaroos, and setting up a whooping and mewling among the peacocks.

As Arthur Mortlock's lopsided phaeton rolled noisily out of the gates, and turned back towards Hindley Street, Eyre heard the head footman shouting hoarsely. 'Stop him if you can! But be careful! He's violent!'

Eleven

Charles Sturt said, 'On an expedition, you know, you have to learn to control your emotions. You have to take the greatest triumphs and the greatest disasters with equal equanimity. There is no more terrible sight than to come across explorers whose fear has overtaken their judgement; to find their huddled bodies not five miles away from supplies, and food, because they eventually lost confidence in their ability to survive.'

He paused, and looked out towards the grey glittering waters of the Gulf of St Vincent. 'I will never forget when we arrived at last at Lake Alexandrina, the lake which I named for our young queen-to-be. It was separated from the Indian Ocean by nothing more than a few sand-bars; and the plan had been to carry our boats over the sand-bars to be loaded on to a ship. We could have sailed back to Sydney in complete comfort! But there was no ship there, and our food and water were almost exhausted. Now, the angry and emotional thing to do would have been to curse our luck, and wait for a ship to arrive. But, had we done that, we would most certainly have died. No: we had to resolve ourselves calmly to row back again, all the way up the Murray, and all the way up the Murrumbidgee.'

He watched Eyre closely; and his voice was so quiet that Eyre could scarcely hear it above the wind.

'We rowed,' Sturt said, 'from dawn until dusk, for six weeks, with a single mid-day break of one hour only. We had scarcely anything to eat, and we were too exhausted even to talk to each other. Our hands were blistered until they bled and then the raw flesh became blistered in its turn. Often we fell asleep while still rowing, and dreamed while we rowed. When we got back to Sydney, we were starving wrecks; and, as you know, I myself went blind for several months, through deficiency of diet. But we remained calm, and we never once railed at God, or at our terrible fortune, and all of us are still alive today.'

They walked a little further down the sand-dune, until they reached the shore. It was a grey, warm, overcast morning, a little after eleven o'clock, and they were strolling southwards on the beach at Port Adelaide. Eyre had arranged for Robert Pope to take care of his bills of lading while he talked with Captain Sturt; and fortunately the head wharfinger, Thomas Taylor, had been called up to Angaston for two days, to discuss the shipment of wool.

Eyre had half-expected that Sturt would not come, especially after the débâcle in the dining-room at last night's ball. What he hadn't known, however, at least until Sturt had told him, was that Sturt disliked Lathrop Lindsay more than almost any other man in South Australia; and that he and Lathrop had fallen out years ago, shortly after Sir Ralph Darling had appointed Sturt as Military Secretary of New South Wales. Sturt had counted the apple-trifle incident as one of the great amusements of the year, and had personally begged Colonel Gawler not to take the matter any further.

'Do you know what they're saying about you this morning?' Charles Sturt had said to Eyre, the very first moment he had walked into Eyre's office this morning. 'They're saying, "Beware of Eyre. He is definitely not a man to be trifled with. Especially apple-trifled with." '

Eyre said, as they walked on the beach, 'I'm disgusted with myself.'

'Well,' said Sturt, 'it *was* rather incontinent of you. But, it shows spirit.'

'I wish I'd never seen the girl. The trouble is, I still adore her.'

Sturt smiled at him. 'I'm sure that she still adores you. But she's very young, remember. She's bound to be influenced by what her father tells her. Give her a chance.'

Eyre went down on his haunches, his coat-tails trailing on the sand, and selectively picked up shells. 'I don't think it's up to *me* to give *her* a chance. I can't get near her. And after last night, I should think that Lathrop Lindsay would quite happily see me beheaded.'

'You need to become a hero,' said Sturt.

Eyre gathered up a handful of cockles, and stood up, and tossed them one by one into the breakers of the sea. 'Clerks,' he said, grunting with the effort of throwing, 'do not become heroes.'

'Come now! Last night you were full of heroism.'

'That was last night. Today, I have a serious headache.'

'Well, I hope you haven't lost your heroism permanently, because I have decided to put up a considerable sum of my own money to finance your expedition to find Yonguldye, and also to map the interior due north of Adelaide, and beyond; which is where you are most likely to find him.'

Eyre stared at him. 'You really believe that I *can* find him?'

Sturt nodded. 'There are several Aboriginals from the Murray River area who frequently help us with tracking, and letter-carrying, and even with escorting prisoners. The best of these is Joolonga; whom I met on my first expedition; and he will go along with you and help you to find the man you seek. He is an interpreter, too, and that should assist you in your search.'

'But will that be the sum of the expedition? Just Joolonga and I?'

'Of course not. You should take with you at least two reliable friends; and two more Aborigine bearers. You may take more, if you wish; but personally I believe it unnecessary, and of course it will add to the expense.'

Eyre tossed away the last of his shells, and then walked along the beach, close to the line where the surf sizzled, his shoes leaving water-filled tracks in the sand. Sturt followed, a few yards further off, climbing up and down the dunes as he went, holding his hat to prevent it from being blown away.

Eyre said, 'Supposing I find Yonguldye straight away,

within ten miles of Adelaide? What kind of an expedition will that be?'

'There has to be some give-and-take,' said Sturt. 'If I am to finance an exploration; then there must be some results.'

'What sort of results?'

'You spoke yourself of an inland sea, or a Garden of Eden. Perhaps Yonguldye knows how these may be reached, and will guide you there. Alternatively, he may be able to help you locate a good cattle-herding route to the north. To be able to drive cattle directly from Adelaide to the north coast of Australia would be of tremendous financial advantage. Then again, Yonguldye may know where there are opals to be found.'

'Opals?'

Sturt took off his hat, tired of keeping it clamped on his head with one hand. 'Several Aboriginals have spoken of secret opal diggings, rich beyond all imagination. Now think what you could be if you were to find one of those.'

Eyre turned around, and stopped where he was. Sturt stopped too. Eyre said, 'All I wanted to do to begin with was find Yonguldye, and bring him back here to Adelaide so that he could bury Yanluga. But now it seems as if I'm also supposed to go looking for seas, and gardens, and cattle-trails, and opals.'

Sturt came sliding awkwardly down the side of the sand-dune. Above him, a flight of black swans flew through the morning wind, crying that sad, silvery cry. He stood close to Eyre, and said, 'Australia is not a land for the selfish, Mr Walker. You have your own obligations to fulfil, I understand that. But when I spoke to you yesterday evening about the calling, I was talking about the greater good; the good of all Australians; and you have that calling, and all of the responsibilities that go with it.'

'Well,' said Eyre, feeling evasive and unsure of himself. 'I'm not sure that I do.'

He had dreamed those dreams again last night; in the first heavy sleep of drink; and he had heard those blurred, slow, extraordinary voices, speaking to him in tongues that he was unable to understand. Voices that spoke of *yonguldye*, the darkness, and *tityowe*, the death adder. And there were other noises: the hissing of sand in the wind, and the whirring of boomerangs, and that distinctive whip-like sound of a spear launched from a *woomera*. He had woken, at the very moment that Mrs McConnell's clock had struck three, and he had walked in his nightshirt to the window and seen that same Aborigine boy sitting across the street, with his scruffy wild dog lying at his feet, while the moon shone through the branches of the gum-trees like a prurient face. He had remembered then the stone that the Aborigine had given to him when their carriage had been ambushed, and he had gone to his wardrobe and searched in his jacket until he had found it.

He had heard of *tjuranga*, the sacred stones of the Aborigines, which were supposed to contain the spirits of ancient dreamtime people or animals. Perhaps this was one. Whatever it was, it must have some kind of mystical significance, something to do with Yanluga. Eyre had held it up to the moonlight, and traced the carved patterns on it with his fingertips. He had almost been able to convince himself that he felt a magnetic tug between the stone and the moon itself; as if the stone were an alien mineral, from somewhere unimaginably distant, carved and decorated according to protocols that were not of this earth.

It frightened him, although he didn't know why. But it also re-affirmed his determination to seek religious justice for Yanluga; and to discover as much as he could about the primaeval secrets of Australia.

Today, on the beach with Captain Sturt, he was no less determined to find Yonguldye and to embark on whatever exploration the search would demand. But he had become suspicious of Sturt himself: not only of Sturt's sudden and copious friendliness, and his immediate readiness to put up the money to send Eyre northwards, but of his repeated explanations that it was necessary for the expedition to be quickly profitable.

Sturt said, 'Whenever capital is invested, for whatever

140

purpose, there must always be some return. You appreciate that, don't you?'

'I'm not sure that the value of burying one black fellow according to his religious beliefs could be totted up in a balance-book,' replied Eyre, although he did his best not to sound sarcastic.

'Well, of course not,' said Sturt. 'But we're actually hoping for a little more than that; as I've been trying to tell you. I mean—I haven't misjudged you, have I? You *are* the exploring type? I thought I saw so much vision in you last night. So much imagination. It takes imagination, you know, to be a good explorer. What could lie beyond the next range of mountains? Where could that river run? That wasn't just liquor, was it, that sense of imagination? I mean—you won't think that I'm being offensive, or personal. But today you seem to be more—well, how can I put it?—*closed-up*, as it were. Inward, in your attitudes.'

Eyre said, 'I'm not lacking in gratitude, Captain Sturt. Please don't think that.'

'I don't, Mr Walker, not for a moment. But I do want you to understand that it wouldn't be possible for me to finance a venture like this solely for the purpose of finding one Aborigine chief, and bringing him back to Adelaide. There must be benefits for everyone, not just Yanluga; and let us not forget that Yanluga is already dead.'

Eyre thrust his hands into the pockets of his britches, and walked on a little further. He couldn't think why Sturt's proposition disturbed him so much. After all, he was a white man; and he worked for a commercial company which depended on South Australia flourishing, and on the exploitation of whatever riches and facilities the land had to offer. Yet he knew from what Yanluga had told him that the Aborigines had already been dispossessed of many of their magic places, and that scores of sacred caves and creeks had been lost to them for ever. And what the white man did not yet understand—if he ever would— was that the Aborigines depended on being able to visit these places in order to remind themselves of

141

their complicated and mystical past. None of their stories and songs were written down; none of their magic was recorded in books. The places themselves were the culture; the rocks and the creeks were invested with all the knowledge that the Aborigines needed in order to live and die according to what they believed. Once the places were gone, the culture was gone, irrevocably. To deny the Aborigines access to them was like burning down cathedrals.

Eyre watched a Dutch whaler sailing slowly around the point on its way to the waters of the South Indian Basin, its triangular sails shining in the morning sun. He said, 'Perhaps I'm just being eccentric. Mr Lindsay is always accusing me of eccentricity. It's just that I feel that whatever we find in Australia we ought to protect as well as exploit. Scores of Aborigines have died of the measles, because they were infected by British settlers. Some tribes have died out altogether. Who will ever know now what they believed, and why they lived the way they did? Each time we destroy something here, we destroy one more secret. I'm simply afraid that if I find opals, or gold, or even a passable cattle-trail—well, this Garden of Eden will very quickly go the way of all Gardens of Eden. Trampled underfoot.'

Sturt dragged a large red handkerchief out of his sleeve, and loudly blew his nose. When he had folded the handkerchief back up again, and tucked it out of sight, he said, 'You're quite right. Or at least Mr Lindsay's quite right. You *are* eccentric. In fact, you're eccentric enough to be a really great explorer.'

Eyre picked up more shells; and began to skip them over the surf.

Sturt said, 'Let me put it this way, Mr Walker. I have lived among your Aboriginal at very close quarters; and believe me there is no more wretched specimen of humanity. He survives on insects and frogs and all kinds of repulsive creatures; nourishment to which a civilised man could never turn, even in his direst need.'

142

'Alexander Pearce excepted,' commented Eyre, skipping another shell.

Sturt ignored that sharp remark. Alexander Pearce had been a Macquarie Harbour convict, a one-time pie-seller from Hobart, who had twice escaped from prison, and twice survived by eating his companions.

Sturt went on, 'Every Aboriginal I have come across who has encountered the white man has benefited from the experience. True, many of them have unfortunately caught diseases not endemic in Australia; but Doctor Clarke tells me that they will eventually form a satisfactory resistance to most of the commoner sicknesses. And a few hundred deaths, no matter how regrettable those deaths may be, is a small price to pay for the advantages of Christianity, and clothing, and a good wholesome diet. I must tell you, Mr Walker, that it has long been my dream to teach and train the Aboriginals, to make them into happy servants. Many of them are already useful as constables, and guides, and houseboys. And when they are properly housed, and taught the elements of agriculture and the keeping of sheep and cattle, they will at last be able to develop for themselves the rudiments of civilisation. Do you want to see them forever outcast from normal society? Do you want to see them live in hardship and poverty and shameful nakedness, ignorant and filthy, ridden with venereal diseases, for generation after generation? Do you call that protecting them? They are backward children, Mr Walker; and as such their condition begs every paternal care that we can offer them.'

Eyre said, 'Does that mean we have to overrun their land, and dig out of it everything and anything valuable? Does that mean we have to desecrate their sacred places?'

Sturt laid his hand on Eyre's shoulder, and smiled at him rather too closely, so that Eyre could see the hairs growing out of his nostrils.

'To use the natural gifts that the land of Australia holds within her bosom, to give succour and support to her natural inhabitants; that is scarcely destructive. Of what use to an Aborigine are opals? Or copper? Or gold, even? Far better that we should take the gold, and the opals, and whatever other minerals might be discovered, and sell them where they are most wanted, and in return give the Aborigines food, and education, and proper clothing, and Goulard's extract, and Holy Bibles. Come, Mr Walker; you are the son of a minister. What do you think *he* would have said? Your father?'

Eyre let his remaining shells fall to the beach, one by one. 'I suppose he would have agreed with you,' he said, quietly.

'Of course,' said Sturt. 'Of course he would. A Christian minister.'

'But I still don't believe that it's necessary to destroy the Aborigine beliefs, and their sacred grounds.'

Sturt smiled again, and shook his head. 'Omelettes can't be made without breaking eggs, Mr Walker. I know how strongly you respect the native superstitions. That, after all, is your motivation for seeking out this one chief Yonguldye. But sacredness is relative. And the sacred Christian nature of this one great mission, to explore and develop South Australia well, that simply *must* take precedence over the erratic beliefs of a few score of unschooled savages. I very much regret all those sacred places and magical artefacts which must have been lost; but I suppose one could express the same sort of regret about the Dissolution of the Monasteries. And in those historic days, we were dealing with the same God, weren't we, and not with peculiar creatures like the Bunyip and the Yowie, and the Kangaroo-Men. No, Mr Walker, much as we would prefer to preserve these places, we cannot; and if the Aborigines forget their gods because of it, well, they will have forgotten nothing more holy than the boogie-man.'

It was gradually becoming clear to Eyre why Captain Sturt had picked him so quickly, and with such certainty. If Sturt was going to mount an expedition to explore the territory north of Adelaide, and look for cattle-trails and natural riches (and he had obviously been considering such an expedition for quite a long time) then who better to lead it for him that a man with inspiration, unusual vision, and an uncommon sympathy for the Aborigines? Sturt must have decided that an expedition could be smaller, cheaper, and that it would have a far greater chance of survival, if only the Aborigines could be persuaded to give it every possible assistance along the way.

It occurred to Eyre that Captain Sturt didn't even like him very much. In fact the longer he spoke to him, the more sure of it he became. But like him or not, Sturt wanted him, and quite badly.

Eyre said, 'I'm interested to know why you don't want to lead this particular exploration yourself.'

Sturt laid a hand on his chest. 'My health, I'm afraid. I'm still not quite the man I was. Eyesight's poor; lungs still clog up a bit. My wife's not keen, either. And, besides, I feel confident that you would carry it out far more successfully than I.'

Eyre nodded, slowly. He really had no more questions. Not for Captain Sturt, anyway. There was one question, however, which he had to ask of himself; and that was whether he was prepared to search for Yonguldye on an expedition which was intended to bring about the eventual extinction of everything that the Aborigines held to be holy; of their gods, and their totems, and their hunting-grounds; in fact of their existence.

If he went, and if he were successful, Yanluga's spirit could at last be guided to its resting-place in the sky; but it was possible that his discoveries would hasten the white colonisation of South Australia by months, if not years, especially if he were to find opals, or gold. If he didn't go, then the Aborigine's lands might remain unexplored for decades, but Yanluga would have to remain where he was, buried like an animal next to Lathrop Lindsay's favourite horse, his soul unsettled for ever. And there was no guarantee that Sturt himself might not decide to undertake the expedition; or any one of half-a-dozen explorers, some of them far more inconsiderate towards Aborigines than Sturt.

To Eyre, the responsibility of making up his mind was like a physical pain, and he stood for almost five minutes on the shoreline, his fingertips pressed to his temples, staring out to sea. Sturt, however, seemed to be prepared to wait for him, and sat on a broken wooden bucket nearby, quite calm, and smoked a cigar.

Destiny, thought Eyre. The terrible *jug-a-nath* of destiny. One day he had been responsible for nothing and nobody more than himself, and for keeping the wheels of his bicycle well-greased with emu fat. Then he had fallen for Charlotte, and become acquainted with Yanluga. Now Yanluga was dead, and Eyre had become responsible not just for him, but for every Aboriginal in South Australia. He knew it: he sensed it. What had Christopher called him? 'One of these chaps who has to do something *noble*.' Why had he been unable to let Yanluga lie? Was it because he still loved Charlotte; and carrying out this expedition gave him one last tenuous connection with her? Or was it truly a Christian sense of duty? The need to do something noble?

He thought of his father, on the night when he had told him that he was going to emigrate; and that he was not going to take holy orders. 'I am extremely sad,' his father had admitted, 'but I have to say that I respect what you believe All I require of you is that you in your turn, always respect the beliefs of others.'

Had the words of an English country vicar, spoken over supper two years ago to his disobedient son, now become the *leitmotiv* for the gradual dismemberment of an entire primaeval civilisation? Perhaps they had. Perhaps that was the real devastating power of God's holy word, from halfway around the world.

Because what could Eyre believe? In Christ crucified, and the holy testaments? Or in Kinnie-Ger, the cat beast; and Yara Ma, who could swallow a human being whole, and suck up a creek so that a whole village would die of drought? And much of what Captain Sturt had said was true. The blackfellows in the bush were filthy, and undernourished, and appallingly ignorant. Could it be that Yanluga's death had set in motion an historic series of events that would at last bring them health, and contentment, and the spiritual satisfaction of knowing that they were the children both of Her Majesty the Queen, and of God?

Eyre turned his back on the sea, and walked across to Captain Sturt with his hands still pressed, a little melodramatically, to his temples. He was conscious of the melodrama, but Sturt was, too; and Sturt played his part by smoking his cigar with equanimity and saying nothing.

It was then that Eyre caught a glimpse of a movement among the distant sand-dunes. He slowly lowered his hands, and looked more carefully. At first there was nothing; but then he saw a thin stick, like a reed, or a wand, moving rhythmically behind the curves of the dunes. It began to rise higher and higher, and at last it revealed itself to be a long spear, being carried up the far side of the dune by an Aborigine warrior, fully decorated with ochre and feathers.

The Aborigine stood on the skyline for no more than a quarter of a minute, but it was plain to Eyre that he had meant to be seen; and that his presence there was not accidental. He made some kind of distant hand-signal, and then he disappeared from sight.

Captain Sturt turned around on his bucket just too late to see what Eyre had been looking at.

'Are you all right?' he asked. He glanced back once towards the dunes and then he tossed his cigar-butt into the surf. 'Perhaps we'd better be getting back.'

'Yes,' said Eyre. An extraordinary feeling passed over him, as if he were going to pass out. He blinked at Sturt and for a moment he couldn't think who he was; or what either of them were doing here.

They began to walk back towards the port. A sudden shower started to fall, but at the same time the sun came out, and the gulf was bridged by a three-quarter rainbow, intensely vivid against the graphite-coloured sky. Then a second rainbow appeared, but fainter.

'An omen, perhaps,' smiled Sturt.

Eyre turned his high coat-collar up against the spattering rain. He was wearing a new silk necktie, maroon, and he didn't want to get it wet.

'Perhaps,' he said. 'In any case, I accept your offer.'

Sturt looked at him, as if he were expecting him to say more. But when Eyre remained silent, he said, 'Very well. That's excellent.' Then, 'Good. I'm very pleased about that.'

They walked as far as the wharf, which was silvered with wet. They shook hands, and Sturt said, 'I want to have a talk to Colonel Gawler; then I'll be in touch with you again.'

Eyre said, 'You knew what I was going to decide, didn't you?'

'My dear fellow,' smiled Sturt. 'I never had any doubt of it.'

'You know what consequences this expedition may have? On Australia, I mean; and the Aborigines?'

Sturt kept on smiling, but the expression in his eyes was quite serious. 'The interior of this continent is quite uncharted,' he said. 'That means that the explorations of one man can have extraordinary effects on the lives of thousands. I myself discovered the second greatest river network in the entire world, after the Amazon. What you may discover on this expedition could be equally momentous. The great inland sea, perhaps; which could be wider than the Caspian. The greatest forest beyond the continent of Africa. You will be making history, Mr Walker; you will be finding rivers and mountains and deserts that no white man has ever found before.'

He paused, and then in quite a different voice, he said, 'You will be finding something else equally important—and I speak now from my own experience. You will be finding yourself.'

Twelve

After the offices of the South Australian Company had been locked up that evening, he bicycled home to Hindley Street. The day's showers had cleared the air; and it was one of those bright marmalade-coloured Adelaide evenings, with the fragrance of acacia in the air. His bicycle left criss-crossing tracks on the muddy streets.

He felt quiet, and rather depressed. He had explained to Christopher what Captain Sturt had said to him during their walk on the beach; and told him that he had decided to look for Yonguldye and whatever geographical or geological features Captain Sturt might be interested in. He hadn't told him about the appearance of the lone Aborigine warrior, but then he felt for the time being that he would prefer to keep it to himself. He didn't yet understand the visitation himself, and he didn't want to share it until he did.

He felt like Macbeth must have felt, after seeing Banquo's ghost.

As he turned into Hindley Street, three or four raga-muffin Aborigine children began to run after him, shouting 'No-Fall-Over! No-Fall-over!' and 'Come -To-Jesus!' which were the very first words that Aborigine children were taught at missionary school. The street was scattered with bright blue puddles, like mirrors, and the children skipped barefoot into the mirrors and smashed them into splashes.

Dogger McConnell was sitting on the verandah under a wet canvas tent, which he wore as if it were a particularly badly designed evening cloak. He raised a jug of beer, and called, 'Good evening, mate! Come and have a drink!'

Eyre dismounted and put away his bicycle. 'Why are you sitting out here?' he asked Dogger. 'You could have caught pneumonia, in all that rain.'

Dogger jerked his head towards the front door. 'We had a bit of a horse-and-cow, me and the estimable missus. I was told never again to darken the parlour. Well, it was my fault. She's a saint, really. A saint who's married an objectionable old devil. Want a drink? It's the first jug of the new batch; better than last time. Last one made you fart, didn't you find? All day on the dunny playing *Oh God Our Help In Ages Past* and never a shit to show for it.'

'I think I'll wait until the brew's matured a little, thank you,' said Eyre. 'Besides, I have some sensible thinking to do.'

'Ah,' said Dogger. 'Thinking. That's something I haven't done for a while. Well, never mind. There's plenty of beer here, once you've finished. Need your liquid, in this climate. Worse in the outback, of course, out beyond the black stump. Saw a fellow sitting under his mule once, waiting for it to piss, he was so thirsty. Saw another fellow squeezing shinglebacks in between his bare hands, just to get their juice.'

Eyre touched Dogger's shoulder. 'Perhaps I'll come out and talk to you later. Leave some for me.'

Mrs McConnell was in the kitchen, her sleeves rolled up, flouring a board so that she could roll out her pastry. There was a good strong aroma of mutton and carrots curling out of the big black pot on the front of the range; and a steamed pudding was clattering away at the back.

'A blackfellow called by,' said Mrs McConnell. She nodded towards the stained pine dresser. 'There's a letter for you there.'

Eyre took down the pale blue envelope and tore it open. He knew at once that it was from Charlotte. The writing was firm and clear, with loops like rows of croquet-hoops.

Eyre read it through quickly; then drew across one of Mrs McConnell's bentwood chairs, and sat down to read it again.

My darling Eyre, (Charlotte had written) after everything that occurred at the Spring Ball, I think that I owe you both an apology and an explanation. What I said to you on the wharf, my dear, that I would always love you, that was quite true, and remains true. Every moment that I am without you, you are dearer to my heart, and I miss you most dreadfully.

The day after poor Yanluga died, however, my father confided in me that he was seriously ill. He had suffered a seizure of the heart whilst in Sydney, and that was the reason why he came home before he was expected. His doctors have told him that he must take great care, otherwise his next seizure might prove fatal.

Of course, he is a volatile man, and it is difficult for him to keep his temper, but I know that he loves me in spite of everything and that he is trying in his own way to do his best for me. He is so sure that his time is short that he is anxious to put his family and his business affairs into order, and that I should be happily and appropriately settled.

To begin with, he had nothing against you personally, dear Eyre. It was just that he wanted to make sure that his only daughter should be secure and contented and well cared-for; and he did not believe that a mere clerk could do that for me. Of course, events since then have unhappily led to a personal argument between you, but father is not an unforgiving man, and the time may come when you will again be on speaking-terms with him.

In the meanwhile, please understand that I must do everything I can to keep my father rested and calm, and not to provoke him. It is my sacred duty as a daughter, I know you will realise that. That is why I spoke to you the way that I did at the Ball.

May I please beg of you not to disclose to anyone anything concerning my father's health, since his business interests would suffer badly if it were suspected that he were unwell. Please remember my darling that *whatever happens* I shall always love you and think of you, no matter how many years go by.

Your adoring Charlotte.

Eyre folded up the letter and tucked it into his pocket. Mrs McConnell said, 'Not bad news, is it?'

'Well,' said Eyre, 'good and bad.'

'Somebody's died and left you a fortune?

'Hm, I wish they had.' He stood up, and walked around to the range, lifting up the pot lids to see what was cooking. 'Is supper going to be very long?'

'You've time to change.'

Mrs McConnell wiped her hands on her apron, and reached across to touch Eyre's arm. 'It's that girl, isn't it, Miss Charlotte?'

Eyre nodded.

'I thought it was. I recognised the blackfellow who brought the letter. One of Mr Lindsay's boys. She hasn't written to say that she doesn't love you any more?'

'No,' said Eyre, and for some unaccountable reason he felt a lump in his throat as big as a crab-apple. 'She still loves me; but we may not be able to see each other for quite a long time.'

He paused, and then he said, 'We may not be able to see each other ever. Mr Lindsay is determined to marry her off to somebody wealthy.'

Mrs McConnell heard that downsloping, near-to-tears catch in his voice, and came around the kitchen table and held him, without any ceremony or affectation, and kissed him like a mother.

'You don't *always* have to be brave, you know,' she told him. Her eyes were pale blue, like a washed-out spring sky, with tiny pupils. 'It isn't necessary; not for women, nor for men, neither. I know how much you like her. She's a very pretty girl. Not much in her head, perhaps, except for fun and flattery, but what girl has. Well, I never had much more, when I was younger, and there were times when Dogger piped his eye over me, I can tell you, although you're on your honour not to tell him now. Why do you think I put up with him; what with his beer and his snoring; and he can't eat anything without making a crunching noise, not even porridge.'

Eyre looked down at Mrs McConnell and suddenly laughed. He kissed her on the nose, and then on both cheeks, and hugged her.

'You're a rare lady, Mrs McConnell. You've cheered me up.'

'Are you sure? Because you can cry if you feel the need.'

Eyre shook his head, and kissed her again. 'I don't think so. I'll go upstairs and get changed for supper.'

They sat around the dining-room table, under the slightly smoking oil-lamp, and ate mutton stew and suet dumplings and fresh greens cooked crunchy and bright. Dogger drank two pots of beer and told a long story about the Aborigines at Swan River; and how they had developed an insatiable enthusiasm for linen handkerchiefs, and broken into white men's huts and cottages searching for nothing else, not guns, not flour, but linen handkerchiefs.

'I suppose with hooters as big as theirs, linen handkerchiefs were quite a comfort,' Dogger ended up, obliquely.

While Mrs McConnell washed up the dishes, Dogger and Eyre played a game of draughts out on the verandah.

Dogger said, 'You're quiet tonight, mate. Something preying on your mind?'

Eyre crowned one of his draughts, and then shook his head. 'Nothing serious. But I may be going away for a while.'

'Away? Where?'

'Exploring. Well—partly exploring and partly looking for someone.'

'Not in the outback?'

'Yes.'

'But, Christ Almighty, you don't know the first thing about exploring! Do you have any idea at all what it's *like* out there? How hot it can be? How *dry*? You can walk for weeks and never see water. Who's going with you?'

'One or two friends. Christopher Willis, I hope.'

'You're not serious. Christopher Willis, that wilting plant? He wouldn't stay alive for three days in the outback.'

Eyre said, 'We're taking Aborigine guides along with us.' He felt quite hurt and embarrassed that Dogger should think so little of their chances. 'The main guide will be a blackfellow called Joolonga, if you've ever heard of him.'

'Joolonga? Joolonga Billy or Joolonga Jacky-Jack?'

Eyre shrugged. 'He's a constable, apparently.'

'That's Joolonga Billy, then. Lucky for you, I suppose. He's experienced enough. I met him a couple of times out at Eurinilla Creek. He used to teach some of the new chums how to track, how to tell one kind of footprint from another. He did it the same way they teach Aborigine children: making tracks for them to follow and then hiding behind a rock, to see if they could find him. He could make counterfeit tracks, could Joolonga Billy: snake-tracks with his kangaroo-hide whip, and dingo tracks with his knuckles. But he always said there was only one way to make counterfeit camel-tracks, and that was to use a bare baby's bottom.'

'Well,' said Eyre, 'it seems as if we'll be properly taken care of.'

Dogger looked down at the draughts board. Above his head, hanging from the rafters, the oil-lamp was thick with insects and moths, and their shadows flickered across the squares of the board like the shadows in Eyre's dreams.

'How far are you going?' asked Dogger, trying hard not to sound interested.

'I don't know. I have to find an Aborigine chief called Yonguldye. As far as I understand it, he could be absolutely anywhere north of Adelaide. Depending on whether I find him or not, and depending on what he tells me, if he tells me anything, I could go no further than fifty miles away. On the other hand, I may go hundreds of miles away—as far as the northern coast.'

Dogger moved one of his draughts. 'You'll die, you know,' he told Eyre, matter-of-factly.

He looked up at Eyre and there was such an expression of care and certainty on his face that Eyre didn't know what to say to him.

154

After a while, though, Eyre said, 'It was Captain Sturt who suggested we might get as far as the north. In fact, he's going to put up the money for the whole expedition.'

'Captain Sturt,' said Dogger.

'That's right, Captain Sturt. He came down to the port to talk to me this morning. He firmly believes that the centre of Australia is covered by an inland sea; as large as the Caspian, he said. All we have to do is reach its southernmost shore, and then we can sail for most of the way.'

'Sail,' said Dogger.

'You don't have to sound so sceptical,' Eyre retorted. 'There may not be an actual sea. There may be a forest, instead. But if there are trees there, we'll soon be able to find water, and fruit to eat; and only God can guess what manner of creatures might inhabit it.'

'Bunyips, I wouldn't be surprised,' said Dogger, pouring himself some more beer.

There was a long and difficult silence between them. Then Dogger wiped his mouth with the back of his hand, and said, 'There has to be a first time for everybody, I suppose. But you just make sure that your first time isn't your last. When you're out in that mallee scrub, with the wind blowing willy-willys all around you; and your horses scared to death; and you haven't had a drink of water for four days; you just remember what Dogger McConnell told you. There isn't any sea in the middle of Australia, and there isn't any forest. There's sand out there, that's what there is, because I've been there; or at least as far as anyone has; and all I've ever seen is sand, and scrub, and more sand; and sometimes I've seen skeletons, of dogs, and mutton-birds, and men.'

Eyre finished his beer. It was lukewarm, and flat. 'I'll remember what you said,' he told Dogger. Then, 'Seriously, I'll remember.'

Dogger grunted. 'Who's winning this damned game?' he wanted to know.

'I am,' said Eyre.

'Well, you damned well shouldn't be. You can't have everything.'

Eyre looked at Dogger with a smile. 'You're jealous,' he said.

'Jealous? What in hell do you mean?'

'You're jealous about my going on this expedition. That's what it is.'

'Why should I be jealous?' Dogger asked him, caustically. 'I've had enough of sand and rats and flies and murderous blackfellows to last me a lifetime.'

'I still think you're jealous.'

'Play the damned game,' Dogger growled.

Eyre crowned another of his draughts, and then said, 'You'd come, wouldn't you, if you were asked?'

Dogger was silent for a very long time. His head was bowed over the board but Eyre knew that he wasn't concentrating on the game. His face was completely concealed by the dark semi-circular shadow of his hat; but his hands were illuminated by the lamplight, hands with callouses and scars and broad, horny nails, and fine hairs that had been gilded by the sun.

Dogger sniffed, and then said, 'I can remember one morning I was camping up in the Flinders Range. I was lost, as a matter of fact, although I never admitted it to anybody. I woke up in the middle of the morning, round about nine or ten o'clock, and the sky was blue, deep blue; and up against it the mountains rose up like a fortress. Red they were, you've never seen such red. The Aborigines say that a giant emu used to live there, and that when it was slaughtered, its blood splashed all over the rocks. Actually, it's red ochre; the stuff they call *wilga*. They come from hundreds of miles to collect it, just to rub all over themselves; but that's the Aborigines for you.'

He picked up his beer-glass; realised it was empty; and set it down again.

'I woke up,' he said, 'and there was a blackfellow staring at me; with emu feathers in his headband, and *wilga* all over his face, silent he was, staring at me.'

Dogger lifted his head, so that the lamplight delineated the triangle of his nose.

'He could have killed me, you know, while I was sleeping. He could have killed me when I woke up. He was fully armed, with a spear and a boomerang and a kind of a club made out of animal bone, or a human bone, who knows. But instead he made a sign with his hand, three fingers down, one finger raised, and that means "who are you?" I knew that, so I said, "Dogger McConnell." '

'Well?' asked Eyre. 'What did he do?'

Dogger shrugged. 'He blinked at me, and then he made the sign again, "who are you?" as if he couldn't believe what I'd told him. So I said, "Dogger McConnell" and, damn me, do you know what he did?'

'Tell me,' Eyre insisted.

'He laughed, that's what he did. That damned impudent blackfellow, his face all covered in mud and ochre and God knows what else, stark naked, you certainly couldn't have taken him home to meet your mother. But he laughed and laughed; I thought he was going to be sick. And then he pointed at me, and said 'Dogger McConnell', clear as a bell, and laughed even more. And then, when he'd finished laughing, he rubbed his eyes, and walked off, and that was the last I ever saw of him.'

Eyre said, 'Dogger.'

Dogger gave a sharp sniff, and cleared his throat. 'Come on, now, Eyre. You know what I'm trying to tell you.'

There was another long silence between them. All around the house, the cicadas sang; and the moon that had haunted Eyre the previous night rose again behind the gums.

Dogger said, 'Once you've been there, once you've seen it, the colours, the trees, the smell of eucalyptus oil; once the Aborigines have laughed at you, and taken you for just a friend, well—'

He grasped Eyre's hand, tightly, quite unexpectedly. 'I'd do anything to come with you,' he said. 'Anything at all.'

Eyre said, 'I'll have to see. It depends on how much money Captain Sturt is able to raise.'

'But you'll consider it?'

Eyre looked down at the draughts board. Then he looked back up at Dogger. 'Play the damned game,' he told him.

Thirteen

Eyre was almost asleep that night when there was a rapping at his bedroom door. He opened his eyes, and lay still for a moment, unsure if the rapping had been real, or a dream. But then it came again: softly, almost furtively.

He threw back the quilt and walked across to the door. He leaned his head towards the door, and said, 'Who is it?'

Mrs McConnell whispered, 'It's me. Dogger's asleep.'

Eyre opened up the door. Mrs McConnell was standing on the landing in her capacious linen nightdress, with a frilly mob-cap covering her hair, a lamp in one hand, and a big white mug of steaming-hot meat stock held up in her other hand like the Holy Grail.

'I thought you might want a drink before you went to bed,' she told him.

'Oh. Well, thank you.'

He held out his hand for the mug but she kept it just out of his reach.'I wanted to have a little talk to you, too,' she said.

'Can't it wait until the morning? I must say I'm rather tired.'

'It won't take long, I promise.'

'Well, er—come in,' said Eyre, and opened his bedroom door wider.

Mrs McConnell bustled past him; after all the bedroom did belong to her; and set the mug of meat stock down on top of the bureau. Then she said, 'Close the door,' and when Eyre hesitated, 'It's quite all right. I can do what I like in my own house. I don't need anybody else in Hindley Street to tell me what morals are.'

Eyre stood there in his nightshirt, raking his fingers through his scratchy hair. He wished that he were wearing britches; or his new nightshirt at least; but this one was old and worn-out, with a hole on one side through which two weeks ago he had accidentally pushed his great toe. It didn't make any difference that Mrs McConnell always washed and ironed it for him: he felt shabby and ill-at-ease.

Mrs McConnell sat herself down on the end of the bed, and patted the quilt imperiously as an instruction to Eyre that he should sit beside her.

'Dogger was talking to me tonight,' she said. 'It seems that you're going off on some kind of an expedition.'

'Yes,' said Eyre. 'It looks as if I am.'

'Don't you think it was your duty to tell me first, before Dogger?'

'I don't really see why. It isn't definite yet; and when it is, you'll be the first to know. It was just one of those things that comes out in conversation.'

'Dogger says that you promised to take him along.'

Eyre shook his head. 'That's not true. I'm sorry, but it isn't. He asked me to consider taking him, but I don't even know yet how much money is going to be put up; or how many people I'll be able to take.'

'Dogger says that you're going to go north.'

'That's right. We'll be looking for minerals, and cattle-tracks, and whatever else we can find. Captain Sturt believes that we may be able to reach the inland sea.'

Mrs McConnell looked at him with motherly solicitude. The lamplight behind her head gave her mob-cap the appearance of a home-made halo; and lit up the stray wisps of hair that curled out from underneath it. The Madonna of the Boarding-House. She touched Eyre's hand and for some reason he shivered, not because she repelled him in any way, but because he suddenly remembered his mother; in fact, more than remembered her, felt her, smelled her, sensed her; all around him, like a warm and actual ghost.

Yet he knew it was only memory. His mother lay under her grey granite gravestone in St Crispin's churchyard; rained-on, snowed-on, lit by rainbows; gone forever. And thinking of that, he admitted to himself for the first time something that he had never been able to admit to himself before, that he would never return to England; ever.

Mrs McConnell said, 'Would you think me foolish if I asked you not to go?'

He frowned at her. 'Is there any particular reason?'

'If I were to give you one, would it make any difference?' Mrs McConnell asked him. Her hand still touching his.

Eyre shrugged. 'I don't know. I don't really think so.'

'Are you going because of her?'

'You mean Charlotte? Well, partly; but not really.'

'I lost my son, you know,' said Mrs McConnell. She lowered her head, so that Eyre found himself looking at the top of her mob-cap. There was a tiny silk bow in the middle, like a butterfly.

Eyre said, 'Do you still miss him so badly?'

'I haven't missed him so much since you've been here.'

There was a curious silence between them. No wind rattled at the window, no dogs barked, no moths tapped at the lampshade. It was so silent that they could hear each other breathing, and Eyre was suddenly embarrassed by a little gurgle in his stomach.

Mrs McConnell looked up again. Her face was glistening with tears. 'I'm a ridiculous woman,' she said, 'but I've grown to think of you as my second son, and that's why I don't want you to go. I beg you.'

'I'll come back,' Eyre told her. 'I promise you.'

'No,' she said. 'Either you'll die, which is what I'm really afraid of; or else you'll be acclaimed as a hero. And if you're acclaimed as a hero, you won't want to live here any more, not at Mrs McConnell's boarding-house. No, it'll be King William Street for you, or North Terrace. Eyre, think of what you're doing. You have a home here, and you always will.'

Eyre didn't know what to say. He tried to smile at her, and he laid his hand on her shoulder, but she wouldn't be comforted. The tears basted her cheeks, and her mouth was puckered miserably, and she trembled all over as if she were chilled.

He held her close to him. He felt slightly absurd and extremely uncomfortable, but she clung on to him tightly, quivering from time to time, and there was nothing he could do to break free. He found himself looking over her shoulder at the mug of meat stock on the bureau, with its wisp of steam like an advertisement for Twining's tea; and at his own face in the mirror where he kept his hairbrushes. A serious, thinnish young man, with well-trimmed side-whiskers, and anxious eyes. His nose was a little too narrow, he always thought; and his mouth too melancholy, especially for somebody who liked to laugh as much as he did. But he thought he looked eminently suitable for Charlotte. Handsome, particular, intelligent. Pity about the nightshirt with the toe-hole in it.

Mrs McConnell shivered. 'I'm cold,' she said. 'I don't know why. I feel as if the whole world is freezing.'

'Would you like to wrap my quilt around you?' asked Eyre.

She lifted her head and looked at him. Her face was full of questions. 'Could I lie with you in your bed for a little while? Could you hold me, and warm me up?'

Eyre smiled and then immediately stopped smiling. 'Well,' he said. 'Well.' Then, 'It's not quite—well.'

'Hold me,' Mrs McConnell pleaded.

With some difficulty, Eyre manoeuvered himself backwards, and lifted up the quilt, and pushed his legs beneath it. Mrs McConnell climbed in beside him, so that they were both sitting upright side by side in the rigid little brass bed. Eyre cleared his throat, and then awkwardly lifted his right arm, like a chicken-wing, and put it around Mrs McConnell's plump back. She kissed his cheek; and then smeared away her tears with her fingers, and said, 'You don't know how much you mean to me; I promise you that. You don't have the slightest idea.'

'Well,' said Eyre, 'nobody could have wished for a better landlady. Or, indeed, for better care.'

'Is that all?' asked Mrs McConnell.

'Oh, well, no—of course not. Affection as well as care. And sympathy, too. And consideration. And, well—'

'Yes?' asked Mrs McConnell, her eyes moist and bright, like newly opened cockles.

'Well, love,' he admitted.

There was a pause. She beamed at him beatifically. Then she patted the quilt, and said, 'Let's lie down. Hold me. Keep me warm.'

There was a prolonged bout of jostling and struggling, and at last they managed to position themselves face to face on the bed. Mrs McConnell, with sudden joviality, kissed Eyre on the nose.

Eyre said, 'What about the light?'

'Do you mind the light?' asked Mrs McConnell.

'Not particularly.'

'Well, then, let's leave it.'

'All right,' said Eyre.

They continued to lie side by side for several minutes. The meat stock on the bureau grew slowly cooler and steam no longer rose from the rim of the mug. Far away, out in the darkness, a night parrot cackled; and the wind began to rise again and lift the dust along the street, with a soft sifting noise that Eyre had sometimes mistaken for rain. Mrs McConnell said, 'I'm feeling warmer now, thank goodness.'

Eyre tried to reposition himself more comfortably, and found that his penis was suddenly resting against Mrs

McConnell's thigh. He gave her the thinnest of smiles, and tried his best to think of something else. He thought about Arthur Mortlock, and Lathrop Lindsay. He thought about his father, and *Pilgrim's Progress*, and even the words of John Selden. 'Pleasures are all alike simply considered in themselves. He that takes pleasure to hear sermons enjoys himself as much as he that hears plays.'

But all the time his penis wilfully unfolded itself, and rose, and then stiffened so hard that it was pressing against Mrs McConnell's bulging stomach through the material of her nightdress.

Eyre was sweating. He stared at Mrs McConnell at very close quarters and Mrs McConnell stared at him. Then suddenly he felt her fingers around him; and slowly she began to caress him, up and down.

He said nothing. To begin with, he didn't want to; and then later, he didn't need to. She rubbed him and rubbed him and he closed his eyes. There was a strong smell of meat stock in the room, and Mrs McConnell was panting lightly, under her breath.

Suddenly the room seemed to tighten, like the shrinking pupil of an owl's eye, and then Eyre anointed Mrs McConnell's hand, in three warm spurts.

'Ssh,' she said, kissing him again. She didn't seem to be at all embarrassed. Instead, what she had done for him was as kindly and as matter-of-fact as bathing a cut, or easing a headache with a cold compress.

After a while, though, Eyre said, 'We can't really stay like this all night, can we?'

Mrs McConnell smiled. 'In your own house, you can do whatever you wish.'

'But Dogger—'

'Don't you go worrying about Dogger. I've had no attention from Dogger these past five years. Dogger can sleep off that skinful of drink and mind his own business.'

At last, however, she climbed out of bed, and brushed down her nightdress, and went to collect her lamp.

'Your drink's gone cold,' she told him.

'Well,' he said. 'Never mind. I can always have some water if I'm thirsty in the night.'

'You'll think about staying?' she asked.

'I can't make you any promises.'

'I don't want to lose you, you know. Not like that.'

Eyre didn't say anything. There was nothing he could think of to say. How could you bluntly hurt the feelings of a woman who was prepared to treat you like her own son; nurse you and coddle you; and even relieve you sexually? He knew with a kind of detached amazement that if he had wanted to mount her, and fornicate with her, she probably would have let him. In fact she probably would have done anything at all. That was the measure of her emotional need.

She leaned over the bed and kissed his forehead. 'You sleep well now, and I'll see you at breakfast.'

'Goodnight, Mrs McConnell.'

She brushed back his hair with the tips of her fingers. 'When we're alone together, you can call me Constance.'

'Thank you.'

There was a lengthy pause, while she stood beside him with her upraised lamp. 'Goodnight, Constance,' he told her; and she kissed him again, and left, closing the door behind her as quietly as if it were a nursery, where her baby was sleeping; and hesitating just for a moment on the landing outside in case he should call for anything.

He lay awake for hours, thinking of what had happened; and when he did sleep, in the cold silent time before dawn, he dreamed of his mother laying out alphabet blocks for him, one after the other, and he dreaded what they might eventually spell out.

Fourteen

On Saturday morning, he received an unexpected visit from Captain Sturt and a man called Pickens, whose face was as yellow as custard, and who introduced himself as Captain Sturt's accountant. They sat in Mrs McConnell's front parlour, drinking Mrs McConnell's sherry-wine, and they told Eyre expansively that they had been able to raise from the Adelaide business community subscriptions amounting to £1,103 and some shillings, which would be more than adequate to finance a six-week expedition to the north, in search of precious minerals, passable stock-routes, and God favourable, the legendary inland sea. Or forest, Captain Sturt qualified himself. Or, indeed, swamp.

'Or desert,' remarked Dogger, who was sitting in the corner, refusing to mind his own business.

Captain Sturt turned around in his chair. 'My dear fellow, I know that you have an extensive knowledge of the country as far north as the Flinders Range, and Broken Hill; but when you go even further north, it becomes quite evident that all the rivers and natural drainage systems are flowing not towards the sea but in the opposite direction, towards the very heart of Australia. Where does all this water go? The very simplest mind can deduce that there must be an inland ocean.'

'Or forest,' said Dogger.

'Or swamp,' agreed Captain Sturt.

Dogger opened his small penknife-blade with his teeth, and began to cut at the hardened dottle in his pipe. 'All I can say, sir, is this: that there may well have been an ocean there once, just as there were lakes and creeks and rivers all over the outback. But these days it's fierce out there, sir; as hot as a furnace; and I never saw water survive for long in a furnace. That sun can make a man's blood boil dry; and I will lay you money that it can make an ocean boil dry, too, just as easy.'

Captain Sturt let out a peculiarly feminine laugh, and turned to Eyre and Pickens with amusement. 'He's quite a character, your Mr McConnell. Quite a character. Salt of the earth.'

Eyre glanced at Dogger in embarrassment, but Dogger was studiously cleaning out his pipe and ignoring Captain Sturt's patronising banter as if it were nothing more than the clacking of parrots.

Captain Sturt leaned forward and said to Eyre, 'You will take Joolonga and two more Aborigines, a carrier called Midgegooroo and a boy called Weeip. Then I suggest you take two companions of your own choosing; for although I know one or two fellows who are sturdy and helpful and ready to take part in whatever adventures might befall them, I believe from my own experience that your choice of travelling-companions must be your own. They must be men that you trust, and like, and with whom you feel easy. There will be exhausting days ahead of you; sometimes dangerous days; and to have with you men whom you dislike is to court disaster.'

Eyre said, 'I have one or two ideas for travelling-companions. It may depend on whether I can persuade them to come with me.'

'Well, don't take them if they require too much persuading, or you will find that, when times become difficult, which they assuredly will, they will blame you for every hardship and privation they have to endure. I truly believe that the qualities you have to look for are loyalty, and stamina, and a degree of personal courage. No man is experienced in exploring this territory, for no man has ever been there before. So what you need to look for are friends, rather than veterans.'

With that, he gave an odd jerk of his neck.

Eyre said, 'I beg your pardon?'

Captain Sturt smiled at him, and then jerked his neck again. Eyre suddenly realised that he was jerking his neck towards Dogger.

166

'You mean I shouldn't take Mr McConnell with me?' he asked Sturt, in a loud voice.

Captain Sturt frowned, and flushed. 'Nothing of the kind. I didn't mean that at all. I simply meant that you should consider your travelling companions with unusual care.'

'Is there any quality which Mr McConnell particularly lacks, which renders him unsuitable?' Eyre asked him.

Pickens said, in a nasal tone, 'I'm not sure that Captain Sturt was trying to suggest that Mr McConnell is in any way unsuitable. I believe that he was simply suggesting that one ought to consider how one's companions are going to behave in extreme circumstances.'

Eyre stood up, and walked around behind Pickens, so that the yellow-faced accountant was obliged to twist uncomfortably around in his chair in order to see him.

'I appreciate that Captain Sturt and several other businessmen in Adelaide have been generous enough to finance me, and to give me guidance,' he said, in almost schoolmasterly tones. 'However, the idea of looking for Yonguldye was mine, and remains my obligation; and it is *my* life that will be at risk. I have already told Captain Sturt that I will do my best to locate whatever minerals may be to hand; and that I will also attempt to find a reasonable track for driving stock. But that is as far as I will go in return for money. I expect to be able to choose whoever goes with me, for whatever reasons I wish, and which route I take, and when the expedition has gone far enough.'

Captain Sturt clapped his hands. 'Bravo!' he shouted.

Eyre looked across at him in surprise.

'I say "bravo!" because I know what kind of a fellow you really are,' Sturt enthused, standing up, and looking around him as if he were well pleased with himself. 'You are a young man of vision, and fortitude; and you will not give up until you have discovered everything which you set out to discover. I trust you, Mr Eyre Walker! By God, I trust you! You will be back here in Adelaide inside of eight weeks, with news that you have found opals, and copper, and even gold; and that you have sighted in the distance the glittering shores of the inland sea, even if you haven't actually sailed on it!'

He came over and clapped Eyre enthusiastically on the back, and then Pickens; but when he went towards Dogger, his hand lifted in gladsome welcome, Dogger glared at him with such a grotesque expression of contempt that he was obliged to skip and swivel and pretend that he had only stepped towards the corner of the room to adjust his necktie in the mirror.

'Well, now!' Sturt enthused. 'You must come to lunch on Monday, Mr Walker; and tell me what plans you have devised. We will go over the latest maps, and discuss the very best course of action. If you can, I would like you to tell me who you have chosen to go with you; so that I may talk to them too.'

'Very well,' said Eyre. He glanced towards Dogger, who was now carefully packing the bowl of his pipe with home-grown tobacco. 'Where are you staying?'

'On Grenfell Street, with the Wilsons. Come at half-past eleven, sharp. Mrs Wilson is a capital cook; you'll enjoy it.'

'Yes,' said Eyre. 'Mrs McConnell is a capital cook, too.'

'And more besides,' said Dogger, obliquely.

Captain Sturt and Pickens both left, raising their hats several times too often to Mrs McConnell. Eyre stood on the verandah watching them climb into their carriage, and then went back into the house.

'Well?' asked Dogger.

'Well, what?' Eyre replied.

'Well, are you going to take me with you? You said you had one or two ideas for travelling-companions.'

Eyre sat down opposite him, and laced his fingers together. Dogger watched him expectantly; but when Eyre didn't speak, and when the clock on the chimney-shelf at last struck half past ten, Dogger put down his pipe and his penknife and sat well back in his armchair, and looked at Eyre with an expression both of forgiveness and of desperate disappointment.

'I didn't think you would,' he told him. 'Too old, I suppose. Drink too much. Don't want a sodden old dingo-hunter on a smart expedition like this; not with Captain Charles Sturt putting up the money for it, no sir. Well, I can't say that I blame you; not completely. But I would be more of an asset than a liability, and I'd never drink a drop, not me. And it could be that I would save your life.'

Eyre said, 'Don't think that I haven't considered taking you, Dogger. I have; and very deeply. There's only one thing that prevents me.'

'The beer? Come on, now, Eyre, I can easily give up the beer.'

'It's not the beer, Dogger, it's Constance.'

Dogger was outraged for a moment, and bulged out his bristly cheeks, and planted his hands on his hips, and couldn't think of a single word to express how furious he felt.

'Constance?' he burst out, at last.

Eyre nodded. 'You and I both have a responsibility to Constance. You know that, because your responsibility is far greater than mine. But if both of us were to die on this adventure, then she would have nobody to take care of her at all, and that would be more than she could bear. You left her for years and years, while you went out hunting for wild dogs; but she's used to you now, used to having you around the house. Used to your grumbling, and your drinking, and your bad temper. And, believe me, Dogger, she loves you.'

'I don't need a raw carrot like you to tell me my wife loves me.'

Eyre shrugged. 'I don't know. Perhaps you do.'

Dogger said, 'You're a damned preacher, do you know that? Too damned religious by half.'

'Well,' said Eyre, amused, 'perhaps I am.' He raised his hand as if he were bestowing a blessing on Dogger, and intoned, ' "You husbands, live with your wives in an understanding way, as with a weaker vessel. You have pursued a course of sensuality, lust, drunkenness, carousals, drinking parties, and abominable idolatries." The first letter of Peter.'

'Oh, bollocks,' said Dogger.

He went to the window and lifted back the flower-patterned nets so that he could look out over the dusty street. Then he said, 'I'm sorry. I didn't mean to blaspheme. It's just that I feel so useless here; shut in, do you see, like a dog in a kennel.'

Eyre watched him sympathetically but said nothing.

Dogger said, 'I just wanted to see the outback one more time. All those twisted trees, like demons and devils. All those cracked rocks, and dry creeks. And smell that smell, when the sun gets really hot, and the eucalyptus oil comes up from the trees in a vapour. And most of all, the sky. You don't know what a really blue sky is, until you've been out beyond the black stump.'

'I'm sorry,' said Eyre.

'Well,' sighed Dogger, 'I suppose I can understand your reasons.'

Constance came in, and asked them, 'Do you want some luncheon? It's mutton cutlets, and soubise sauce.'

'Want a beer before you eat?' Dogger asked Eyre.

Eyre said, 'I'd love one.' Dogger went off to pour a jug out of his latest barrel; but Constance McConnell stayed where she was, wiping her hands on her apron, looking at Eyre with that expression of warning and concern.

'Did you and Captain Sturt come to any conclusions?' she asked.

'Conclusions?'

'Have you decided to go?'

Eyre nodded. 'Yes, I have.'

'I see,' she said. 'I suppose there's no further use in appealing to you.'

'No.'

She sat down, and stared at him for a very long time. Outside in the street they could hear dogs barking and the

170

cries of a man who would sharpen knives, and shears, and worm your cat.

'You're not taking Dogger with you, though?' asked Mrs McConnell.

'No. I'm afraid he's a little too old. We want to find water and cattle-trails and opals out there; not graves.'

'Well I suppose I can thank you for that.'

Eyre knelt down beside her chair, and held her arm. 'Constance,' he said, 'I'm going to make you one solemn promise. Whatever happens, I'll come back to you. Do you understand me? You've taken care of me. I promise in return that I'll take care of you.'

Constance McConnell lowered her head. Eyre stayed beside her for a little while, and then stood up. 'Shall we have some lunch?' he asked her.

At that moment, however, there was a sharp banging at the door-knocker. Dogger went to answer it with his jugful of beer in his hand, and it was Christopher Willis, in a baggy linen suit, and Arthur Mortlock, rather incongruously dressed as a waiter, with a red waistcoat and rows of shiny brass buttons.

'Sorry to barge in,' said Christopher, 'but do you think we could have a private word? Good morning, Mrs McConnell; fine day. Fine smell from the kitchen, too. Mutton stew?'

'Cutlets,' Mrs McConnell told him, snappily.

Arthur Mortlock took off his derby hat to reveal his prickly scalp, and grinned at Mrs McConnell with a clash of artificial teeth. 'Nothing to which I'm more partial than mutton cutlets,' he remarked. 'Especially when they've been cooked by a fair gentlewoman; near to raw; and then sprinkled with a little mustard-seed.'

Mrs McConnell blinked; unsure of what she ought to say. But Arthur bowed, and sniffed, and said, 'Please don't think that I was after inviting meself to lunch, mum. As it turns out, I don't have the time. I'm helping out a friend at the Adelaide Hotel just at the moment, waiting on table,

171

seeing as how he's short of fellows what knows the difference between a fish-fork and a kick in the nostril.'

Eyre reassuringly took Mrs McConnell's arm. 'Mr Mortlock is an acquaintance of mine, Mrs McConnell. He's quite respectable.'

'Well, then, a fine good morning to *him*', said Mrs McConnell, and bustled off back to her kitchen.

Dogger poured out beer for everybody, frowning at the jug when it was empty, and then ambled distractedly off to stoke up the kitchen range and lay the table. Christopher peered down the hallway to make sure that he was gone, and then closed the parlour door. He also went to the window, to see if there was anybody watching the house from the street outside.

'What's up?' asked Eyre.

'Arthur came to see me this morning and said that two men took rooms at the Adelaide Hotel late last night, presumably off the packet from Sydney. They told the porter they were on the lookout for ticket-of-leave men who had absconded from Botany Bay; and they gave the names Croucher, Philips, Bean, and Mortlock. Then this morning, over breakfast, they told another waiter that they had discovered already that Philips and Croucher were dead, killed and robbed by Aborigines; but that Bean and Mortlock were still at large, and that they were quite determined to run them to earth.'

Eyre said to Arthur, 'I presume Bean was the other man with you; the man who ran off.'

'Yes, sir,' said Arthur. 'I never knew his other name, sir, only Bean; and as far as I know that was the way his mother had him baptised, Bean and nothing more.'

'Have you heard from Bean since the night of the Ball?'

'No, sir. But he won't have gone far. He was never the adventurous kind. Nerves of seaweed, sir, had Bean.'

'If these men were to track Bean down, and question him, do you think you could rely on him not to tell them where you might be found?'

Arthur said, 'Hard to say, sir. But I doubt it. Bean was

never a hard case, sir, not in that sense of it. And if they threaten him with flogging, well, you can't blame a fellow for wanting to keep the flesh on his back, can you?'

'You must leave, then,' said Eyre.

Christopher fanned himself with his hat. 'It's a little more difficult than that, Eyre old chap. Apparently these fellows have got the roads watched, and they've been talking to all the Aborigine constables to make sure that nobody slips out of Adelaide through the bush. I was down at the port this morning, too—in fact, that's where Arthur came to find me—and all sea-captains and fishermen and boat owners have been told to keep a weather-eye open for men who want to leave Adelaide by sea in anything of a hurry. They've been offering rewards, too: bottles of rum for information; gold sovereigns for capture.'

'Well,' said Eyre, looking at Arthur warily. 'It seems as if they've made up their minds that they're going to run you down.'

'So it would seem, sir,' Arthur agreed.

'Of course, we have another little problem,' said Christopher. 'It's an offence to harbour a wanted criminal, and that means that both you and I are equally liable to be arrested and charged. And if this Bean decides to describe what happened on the night when Philips and Croucher were killed, why, we might very well find ourselves charged with aiding and abetting murder, too, and conspiracy, and obstructing justice.'

Eyre said, 'Come on, now, Christopher, we've done nothing criminal.'

'Oh, haven't we just? If you'd had the sense that night to call the police; or at least let Arthur run off, then we would have been quite all right. But here we are, almost as guilty of absconding from Botany Bay as he is.'

'Arthur will have to hide,' Eyre decided.

'Hide? But where?'

'There must be somewhere at the racecourse.'

'There's a hut there, which they use to keep the scythes

173

and the shovels in; but he won't be able to stay there for longer than two or three nights. There's a race meeting on Wednesday afternoon.'

'That may be as long as we need,' said Eyre.

Christopher frowned. 'I'm not sure that I follow you.'

'It's very simple,' said Eyre. 'In three days, we shall be able to assemble everything we need for my expedition. Food, water, horses; we shan't need to take anything particularly fancy. Joolonga is arriving in Adelaide tomorrow, and the other Aborigines are already here.'

'I hope you're not suggesting what I *think* you're suggesting,' said Christopher, in a pale voice.

'It seems to me the very best way of killing two birds with one stone,' said Eyre. 'I need two companions to come with me on this expedition. I was already thinking of you, Christopher, if I could persuade you; and of Robert Pope. But I am prepared to substitute Arthur here for Robert. After all, Arthur seems to have been something of an expert when it comes to surviving under harsh conditions. We could dress him up, and perhaps give him a large hat and a pair of spectacles to wear, and we could say that he was a cousin of mine from England. Then all three of us could ride out of Adelaide without any trouble or hindrance whatsoever. No bounty-hunters are going to question the departure of a geographical expedition financed by Captain Sturt, of all people.'

Christopher looked at Arthur closely, quite unconvinced. 'A cousin of yours from England?'

'Perhaps we can find him a wig,' Eyre suggested.

'Well, that's all very well,' Christopher protested, 'but what about me? I don't even want to go on this expedition. I was very much hoping that *you* wouldn't go.'

'Under the circumstances, I would think it wiser if you changed your mind,' said Eyre. 'Especially since *I* am intending to go, whatever happens; and no matter what anyone says to deter me.'

'You're inordinately stubborn, you know,' Christopher complained.

'Perhaps.'

'No *perhaps* about it. When it comes to stubbornness, I'd set you up against two mules and a kangaroo any day of the week.'

Arthur cleared his throat. 'Is it all right if I say something, sir?'

'Of course,' said Eyre.

'Well, sir, the thing is that there's no need for either of you gentlemen to feel in any way obligated to me, sir. I never did nothing for you but try to rob you of what was yours; and that's hardly a worthy recommendation for anyone. If I was to give myself up right away to these two gentlemen what seems to be searching for me, then there wouldn't be any need for either of you to get yourselves tangled up in it; and that would be the end of the matter.'

'Except that they could take you back to Norfolk Island and flog you so hard that they would probably kill you,' Eyre put in.

'I took my own risk, sir, when I jumped the boat for Adelaide. I always knew the consequences, should I be caught.'

Eyre was silent for a minute or two. Christopher sat crossing and uncrossing his legs; and staring at Eyre with such concentration that if it had been possible for him to persuade Eyre by thought-transference that Arthur should give himself up, then he certainly would have succeeded.

Eyre, at last, said, 'I'm not a judge, Arthur. I don't enforce the laws which sentence men to years of transportation for stealing hats, and sheep, and loaves of bread. Nor do I give the orders for men to be flogged, or kept in solitary confinement. It seems to me that you have served out your sentence, and yet the very fact that you have to remain here in Australia means that, in a way, you are serving your sentence still. You broke the conditions of your ticket-of-leave, I suppose, and you did attempt to rob us. But it is not for me to demand that you give yourself up; nor even to expect it; and if you wish to come along on this expedition, then you are welcome.'

175

Christopher covered his face with his hands. 'I *knew* it,' he said. 'I sensed it, the very moment you mentioned the idea of it. I hate camping; and I hate riding horses; and I hate discomfort of all kinds. And yet here I am, condemned to join an expedition into the very harshest country known to man. Eyre Walker, I wish I'd never set eyes on you.'

'No, you don't,' Eyre smiled at him.

'No,' said Christopher. 'The trouble is, I don't.'

Arthur said, 'If that's a genuine offer, sir, then I feel it in my water to take it, if that's agreeable.'

'You realise that I may be condemning you to a worse fate than any you might meet at Macquarie Harbour.'

Arthur sat up straight. 'I'd rather die ten times in the company of gentlemen, sir, than just once by myself, with a cloth bag over my head, in deep disgrace.'

'Well, wouldn't we all?' said Christopher. 'Or, I don't know. Perhaps we wouldn't.'

Just then, Mrs McConnell came in and announced that luncheon was almost ready.

'I don't suppose you'd find it in your heart to root around for a spare cutlet, would you mum?' Arthur spoke up.

Mrs McConnell glared at him; and then at Eyre. Eyre twinkled his eyes at her, and gave her the most winning smile he could manage. And a little nod of his head, as if to say, go on, just for me, give the man a cutlet.

Mrs McConnell hesitated. Then she turned and called down the hallway, 'Dogger! Lay the table for two more, please! Yes, soup spoons, too!'

Fifteen

On Monday, Eyre and Christopher ate lunch with Captain Sturt at the Wilson's house on Grenfell Street. Mrs Wilson was a plain, flustering woman who baked raised pies that could have been exhibited in a museum, and perhaps should have been: perfect to look at, but tasting of nothing very much at all, except shortening, possibly, and potatoes boiled without any salt. The dining-room was heavily curtained and painted in brown, and on the sideboard there was a huge sorry-looking salmon in a glass case.

Every time Captain Sturt said anything witty, Mrs Wilson would let out a sound like a stepped-on mouse; a quick, suppressed squeak; and then giggle. Captain Sturt obviously found her responses almost intolerable, for every time she squeaked he closed his eyes for a moment, and gripped his fork as if he could cheerfully jab her with it.

Christopher glanced across the table at Eyre with some unease. But Eyre was determined that the expedition should go ahead as he and Captain Sturt had agreed, and as quickly as possible.

Sturt, in fact, had been most industrious since he had last spoken to Eyre. He had already talked to Mr Townsend of the South Australian Company and arranged for Eyre to take whatever leave of absence might be required; and now he knew that Christopher was to accompany Eyre, he would make the same arrangement for him.

He had bought half-a-dozen horses; complete with saddles and saddle-packs; and leather bottles for the carrying of water. He had also arranged for the delivery of jerked meat, dried fruit, flour, salt, rice, and tea. These would be carried on a mule, although he hadn't yet been able to find a satisfactory mule.

The single item of provisions which he plainly considered to be the most valuable, however, was a leather-bound copy of his own *Expeditions*. This he laid reverently on the table in front of Eyre, and opened the cover to show him the inscription on the title-page. 'For Mr Eyre Walker, in Trust and Confidence, that he will follow in my footsteps to the very heart of the Australian continent.'

Eyre picked up the book, and leafed through it. He was actually very moved; because for all of Sturt's pomposity, he was still the greatest explorer the Australian continent had yet seen, and he was certainly the most celebrated man in Adelaide.

He said, 'Thank you, Captain Sturt. I shall treasure this above everything.

'Not above food and water, I hope,' Sturt grinned at him. 'Although you will notice that the binding is leather, and that it may always be good for nourishment. Before they started dining on themselves, you may remember, Alexander Pearce and his companions actually devoured their kangaroo-skin jackets. Did you know that? Men can be pushed to extraordinary extremes in the outback.'

Mrs Wilson squeaked and sniggered, and Captain Sturt pulled a twisted kind of a face.

'Do you think it will be possible for us to leave on Wednesday?' asked Eyre.

Sturt forked up the last of his pie, and washed it down with a liberal mouthful of red wine. 'I don't doubt it,' he said. 'Mrs Wilson, that was a capital pie. A pie by which all other pies should have to be judged.'

Squeak, and giggle, from Mrs Wilson's end of the table.

Eyre said, 'I'm sorry my cousin couldn't be here today. He likes his pie; and, of course, he was very anxious to make your acquaintance, Captain Sturt.'

'I've never met him, I suppose?' asked Sturt. 'Did you tell me his name?'

'His name? Well, yes, I believe I did. Mr Martin Ransome, that's it. One of the Clerkenwell Ransomes.'

Sturt buttered himself a large piece of soda-bread, and nodded, although it was plain that he wasn't really interested. That was just what Eyre had been counting on: a general lack of curiosity about his soon-to-be-bespectacled cousin that would allow them to set off from Adelaide unharassed by bounty-hunters or militia.

Today, Arthur was hiding in the hut out at Adelaide racecourse, with plenty of cold mutton sandwiches and a bottle of tea, and the day after tomorrow they would be riding northwards, well away from Aborigine constables and sea-captains who would tell anything for a bottle of rum; and all the other grasses with whom Adelaide was rife. Mrs Wilson rang the bell for the pie-plates to be removed, and her freckly Irish servant-girl brought in jaunemange and baked carrot pudding.

Christopher looked at Eyre with an expression which clearly illustrated the hope that the luncheon-table would be cleaved in half by a bolt of divine lightning, and that Mrs Wilson would be burned to a manageably small cinder.

'A very agreeable meal, Mrs Wilson,' said Captain Sturt, and Eyre began to understand that it took more than twelve weeks' rowing along wild and uncharted rivers to become, and remain, a hero.

That afternoon, excused from the office, Eyre and Christopher went for a long walk in the Botanic Gardens, neglected and abandoned now; and strolled among the tangled acacia bushes and discussed the expedition. Then they went to Coppius's Hotel and sat in the high-ceilinged lounge, and ordered rum punches. A new Axminster carpet was being carried into the hotel, freshly arrived from England, and the patrons in the lounge were continually being asked to move their chairs as the carpet-fitters manhandled it in.

Eyre and Christopher were standing next to the window, waiting for the carpet to be shouldered over their table, when they saw two men by the hotel's reception desk; two dark and unfamiliar men in frock coats and stovepipe hats and side-whiskers; and there was something about them which immediately led Eyre to suspect that they were the men who were looking for Arthur Mortlock.

One of them was smoking a small cigar and reading the messages which had been left for him at the desk; the other was leaning against the wall talking to the porter.

'You see those two fellows?' Eyre asked Christopher. 'Ten to one they're our bounty-hunters.'

Christopher glanced at Eyre, and nodded. 'That's what I was thinking. They don't look at all like salesmen, or government men. Too surly for salesmen; too smartly dressed for government men. And hard, too. Look at their faces. They'd just as soon hit you in the face as say good afternoon.'

Eyre finished his drink. 'Do you want another one?' he asked Christopher, 'or shall we call it a day?'

'Too late, I think,' said Christopher.

Eyre turned around. The two dark men had begun to walk towards them, stepping over the rolled-up carpet, and circling around the table. At last they came right up to Eyre and Christopher, and stood with their hands clasped in front of them, their faces bored and arrogant, their collars clean and sharp but unfashionably low, their black silk neckties sparkling with diamond stickpins.

'You'll excuse us, gentlemen,' said one of them, in a marked 'flash' accent. 'But do we have the privilege of addressing ourselves to Mr Eyre Walker and Mr Christopher Willis?'

Eyre looked at them. The one who had spoken was thin, with a high domed forehead and a drooping moustache. He was very pale and veiny; and he gave Eyre the impression that if he were to take off his shirt, you would be able to see his heart pulsing underneath his ribcage, and his blood coursing through every vein. His companion on the other hand was thick and ruddy, with a gingery moustache and a body like beef.

Eyre said, 'What can we do for you?'

The thin man inclined his head in a bow that was patently not meant to be subservient. 'My name is Mr Chatto; this is Mr Rose. We are here on the direction of the government of New South Wales, to look for two

180

ticket-of-leave men, one named Bean and the other named Mortlock.'

'Yes?' asked Christopher, with complete deadpan innocence.

Mr Chatto gave a thin smile, as transparent as a finger drawn through water. 'It came to our attention, Mr Walker, that you and Mr Willis were the last customers to hire Mr Mortlock's carriage; on the night of the Spring Ball at Government House; on Thursday last week.'

'Were we?' asked Eyre 'What of it?'

'We were hoping that you might have engaged Mr Mortlock in conversation,' said Mr Rose. 'Perhaps he might have told you where he lived, or where he was going.'

'Is he missing?' asked Eyre.

'He is not in immediate evidence, if we can put it that way,' said Mr Chatto. He cracked his knuckles one by one, ten distinct cracks, and looked around the hotel lounge as if he were expecting somebody; not Arthur, but somebody equally fateful. Then he turned back to Eyre and Christopher, and looked at them wanly, as if he didn't believe anything that either of them had told him, not for a moment.

'Would you recognise Mr Mortlock if you saw him again?' he asked, expressionlessly.

'Who?' Eyre frowned.

'Mr Mortlock,' Mr Chatto repeated, patiently. 'The coachman who took you to the Spring Ball.'

Eyre turned to Christopher in exaggerated bafflement.

'Mr Mortlock?' he said. 'Was that his name?'

'This gentleman seems to think so,' said Christopher.

'Come now, Mr Willis, you must recognise the name,' said Mr Chatto. 'It was you who went to Meredith's for the phaeton; and you who Meredith's sent around to Mr Mortlock, because all of their own fleet of carriages were out on hire.'

'Well, well, was that his name?' asked Christopher. 'Mortlock, hey? I could have sworn it was Keys, or Morton, or Locket, or something to do with padlocks. But Mortlock. Well, well.'

'He took you to the Ball, didn't he?' asked Mr Rose.

'Of course.'

'And then he took you home?'

'Well, naturally.'

'And in all that time, he didn't say anything at all that struck you as untoward?'

Eyre clamped his hand over his mouth as if he were thinking very deeply. Then suddenly he snapped his ·fingers, and said, 'There was one thing.'

Mr Chatto took out a notepad, and an indelible pencil, and licked the pencil with a tongue that was already a bright shade of laundry-purple.

'He said he was thinking of taking up the piano-accordion.'

Mr Chatto's pencil remained poised over the notepad; trembling very slightly, like the motion of a crane-fly on a late-summer porch.

He said, flatly, 'I don't think, Mr Walker, that you fully realise the gravity of our investigations; nor the weight of the authority we carry. We have been given special approval to hunt down these men by the Governor and Commissioner of South Australia himself.'

Eyre peered over the edge of his notepad. 'You haven't written down "piano-accordion",' he said, in a helpful tone.

Mr Rose put in, 'Our authority, sir, also extends to bringing to book those who may have given the fugitives succour and shelter.'

Eyre turned to Christopher, and said, 'The quality of the clientele here seems to have sunk rather low lately, wouldn't you say? I think a quiet drink at home is called for; among more civilised company.'

Mr Chatto put away his notepad and his pencil, and fastened up the buttons of his coat. 'I want you to know, Mr Walker,' he said, in a particularly drear voice, 'that your answers to my questions were not at all satisfactory, and that I regard you as under suspicion of knowing the whereabouts of Mortlock and Bean.'

'You may regard me however you like, that is your privilege,' said Eyre. 'But I had better remind you that I have influential friends; Captain Charles Sturt among them; and that if you attempt to harass me in any way at all, then he shall get to hear about it, and take whatever action he considers fit.'

Mr Chatto said, 'Even Captain Sturt is not above the law, Mr Walker. Look—this is my address—at the Torrens Hotel. Leave a message for me there if it should occur to you to change your mind about Mortlock.'

Eyre took the scrap of paper on which Mr Chatto had written the address, 75 King William Street. He crumpled it up between the palms of his hands, and tossed it on to the floor. Mr Chatto stared at him with eyes of a curiously neutral amber, in which his tiny black pupils were suspended like insects. He made no attempt to pick the paper up. Instead, he tugged at each of his cuffs; cracked at all of his knuckles; and then inclined his head to Eyre and Christopher, and said, 'Very well. I think you have made yourselves perfectly clear. Whatever it is that you know, I am to receive no help from you, whatsoever.'

Eyre smiled, and inclined his head in return, to indicate that no, he certainly *wouldn't* receive any help from them, whatsoever.

Mr Chatto and Mr Rose walked off, leaving Eyre and Christopher alone together.

'Well,' said Christopher, 'I think I could happily do with that second drink you offered me; particularly now that the air seems to have cleared itself a little. You know something, I never could abide the idea of hunting men for money. It's just not human.'

Eyre was silent. The truth was that he had found Mr Chatto and Mr Rose quite unsettling. If they were searching for Mortlock and Bean with the authority and the co-operation of Colonel Gawler, then it was entirely possible that they would find him: and then both Eyre and Christopher would be deeply implicated in aiding and abetting the escape of a wanted man. That could mean prison, or worse: particularly since these days Eyre was awkwardly short of good character-witnesses. Captain Sturt might speak up for him, but there was no guarantee of it. Eyre felt that Captain Sturt, despite his proven bravery and despite his urbanity, was something of an opportunist. The sort of friend, as Christopher had once put it, who could always be relied on to be absent in a crisis.

'I think we'd be better advised to warn Arthur Mortlock to lie exceedingly low,' Eyre replied. 'Why don't you go out to the racecourse and make sure that he's all right? Then come back to the McConnell's; and we'll see if we can't think of some way of hiding him more securely, at least until Wednesday.'

Christopher was not altogether enthusiastic about driving his waggonette all the way to the racecourse, but in the end he agreed that it would be safer. Eyre climbed on to his bicycle and pedalled his way slowly back to Hindley Street, pursued as usual by a happy little knot of dancing Aborigine children. It was a bright, sun-flecked afternoon; and kookaburras laughed madly at him as he rode over the company's bridge, and through the avenues of stringy-bark gums on the other side.

It was just as he was bouncing uncomfortably over a series of dry sunhardened ruts in the road that he caught sight of the Aborigine warrior again; standing black and tall and still as a heron by the side of a tumble-down squatter's shed. He should have been seen by everyone who passed him by, yet he was so completely motionless, and his colour was so close to the indigo colour of the afternoon shadows, that hardly anybody seemed to see him at all. The only reason that Eyre had seen him was because the Aborigine had obviously *wanted* him to.

Eyre stopped his bicycle by the side of the road, only a few yards away from the silent blackfellow and well within range of his spear. The blackfellow's hair was thickly greased and decorated with kangaroo bones, emu feathers, and dangling crab claws. His eyes were emphasised by wide circles of white painted around them, and there were *ngora*, or decorative scars, all over his chest. He wore a loincloth, in which were hung a bone axe, and a hardwood club, and a large steel knife. He watched Eyre carefully; neither inviting him nearer nor indicating that he should go away. There was something almost magical about him.

'You're following me,' Eyre called at him. 'Why?'

The blackfellow said nothing, but made some complicated hand-signs which Eyre found it impossible to follow. He shook his head, and said, more loudly, 'Is it because of Yanluga?'

A passing bush-farmer turned around in surprise to see who it was that Eyre was addressing himself to, and at first saw no one. It was only when he stopped and looked again that he made out the silhouette of the Aborigine, and then he turned back to look at Eyre, and shake his head.

'Thought you were talking to yourself, mate. No offence but.'

Eyre stayed where he was for two or three minutes, until the passing of a bullock-cart obliged him to move. By the time he had cycled around to the side of the road again, the Aborigine was gone; or at least he appeared to have gone. He was in that state of invisibility which the Aborigines usually entered when they were hunting. He may or may not have still been there. Either way, Eyre found it impossible to see him.

Eyre thoughtfully bicycled back to Hindley Street. There was no doubt in his mind now that the Aborigines expected something of him; that his seeking-out of Yonguldye was more than just an unpremeditated act of respect for a murdered boy. Eyre almost had the feeling that he was acting out a destiny which the Aborigines had already charted for him, centuries ago, as one of their dreamtime legends. *'A boy will die at the hands of a man with white skin . . . and the man with white skin will seek out Yonguldye the*

185

Darkness in order that he may be forgiven . . . and that the boy's soul may lie forever at rest . . .'

Eyre reached Mrs McConnell's house and wheeled his bicycle under the verandah. Humming to himself, he went up the steps and opened the front door. Mrs McConnell was waiting for him in the kitchen, and as soon as he closed the door behind him, she called, in a peremptory voice, 'Mr Walker!'

'Mrs McConnell?' asked Eyre.

Mrs McConnell came into the hallway, wiping flour from her hands on to her apron. She looked hot and disapproving.

'Mr Walker, there's a visitor for you in the parlour. He's been there for an hour or more.'

'Not Captain Sturt?' asked Eyre, in surprise.

Mrs McConnell opened the parlour door. 'See for yourself,' she said; and there he was. Arthur Mortlock, in his best britches and a bright red pair of suspenders. He stood up, and bowed his head.

'Mr Mortlock?' Eyre demanded. 'What on earth are you doing here?'

'My humble apologies, sir. Wouldn't have come for the world, excepting as I didn't have a choice. They came out to the racecourse looking for me, sir, with dogs. Well, I used a ripe-dead bandicoot to lay something of a false trail for them, sir; but they found the hut where I was hiding, and I think that they was fair certain that it was me who was billeted there, sir. So I didn't have no choice, sir, but to run for the only place where I knew I could find me some reasonable sanctuary, sir. Being this good lady's residence, as it were.'

Mrs McConnell flounced, 'Pff! I'll have you know that I'm not at all accustomed to giving shelter to runaway legitimates. Nor to any manner of legitimates for that matter.'

With an unexpected display of early-Victorian theatre, Arthur Mortlock threw himself heavily on to his knees on the Persian-patterned carpet, and grasped the hem of Mrs

McConnell's apron in his hands, and noisily kissed it. Mrs McConnell looked almost apoplectic, and cuffed him on both sides of his prickly head; but that didn't prevent him from bowing alarmingly low, his forehead touching the carpet, his broad bottom rising so high that it revealed a patch on the back of his black britches in green cotton, with red cobbled thread.

'Mum, I abases meself,' he pleaded. 'I hurls meself willy-nilly on your tenderest mercy, knowing as how you're sure to get what you deserve in the life hereafter.'

'Incinerated, I shouldn't wonder, you rogue, if I let you stay here,' protested Mrs McConnell. 'No, the only course that I can take with you, Mr Arthur Mortlock, is to call for the authorities, and have you locked up for life.'

Sixteen

Wednesday was hot and clear, and Eyre and Christopher arrived outside Government House early, nervously accompanied by Arthur Mortlock, whose distinctive Macquarie Harbour haircut was hidden under a wide-brimmed kangaroo-skin hat, and whose eyes were distorted by a small pair of wire-rimmed spectacles. If anything, Arthur looked even more disreputable than he had before, and Christopher said that he had all the appearance of a recently released lunatic; but he couldn't easily be recognised as Arthur Mortlock, and that was all that Eyre cared about.

After half an hour of argument, Mrs McConnell had reluctantly agreed to let Arthur stay until Wednesday morning, on the strict understanding that he kept himself locked up in his room, that he didn't show his face at any of the windows, and that once he had left he never breathed a word about staying with Mrs McConnell to anybody; nor admitted that he even knew the name McConnell.

Dogger hadn't appeared to say goodbye to Eyre; and Eyre had supposed that he was brooding about the outback. He had certainly been very uncommunicative over the past few days, and had taken to leaving the house for hours at a time, and not saying where he had been. The British Tavern, probably, for a few disgruntled drinks.

Mrs McConnell at the very last moment had melted. She had kissed Eyre again and again, and held him close to her, and at last said tearfully, 'Don't forget that you promised to come back to me.'

'I won't forget.'

'And if I've ever done you any kind of harm; or injustice; then I hope you find it within yourself to forgive me.'

He had kissed her tear-wet cheek. 'You've never been anything but good to me. There's nothing to forgive.'

She had stood on the verandah and waved her handker-chief until he had ridden out of sight. His bicycle stayed under the steps. Dogger had promised to grease it from time to time, although he had said that he would be 'utterly danged' if he would try to ride it. 'I only have to *look* at the bloody thing and I lose my balance.'

Eyre and Christopher were surprised to see twenty or thirty people already gathered in the roadway outside government house, including a party of finely dressed marines, and several notable Adelaide businessmen and merchants, in tall riding-hats and white britches. There were several carriages and waggonettes there, too, in which brightly dressed local ladies sat and twirled their parasols; and an untidy collection of children and Aborig-ines; shouting and kicking the dust.

Ship's bunting had been hung from the picket-fence, and from the tall flagpole the Union Jack smacked laconically in the warm morning wind.

There was a spattering of applause as Eyre and Christopher and Arthur Mortlock walked up to the front of the governor's house; and somebody even shouted, 'Huzza! huzza!'

The train of pack-horses was drawn up by the steps, and there, in a self-consciously magnificent tableau, stood Captain Sturt and Colonel Gawler and Captain Sturt's accountant Mr Pickens, as well as Mr David McLaren from the South Australian Company, Mr Ragless, and Mr Peter Percy from the Mineral Rights Board, and even the Reverend T.Q. Stow, looking flushed, and sneezing spasmodically, and wiping his nose. Colonel Gawler's five children ran around and around them all, shrieking and laughing.

'Mr Walker! Mr Willis!' called Captain Sturt. He came striding forward and shook both of them firmly by the hand. 'This is a great day! An historic occasion!'

'You seem to have drummed up plenty of enthusiasm for it,' Eyre remarked. He bowed his head to Colonel Gawler, and said, 'A very good morning to you, colonel.'

Colonel Gawler gave him a testy smile in response. It was clear that he hadn't yet forgiven Eyre for the fracas at the Spring Ball last week, however much economic hope he had invested in this expedition; however much he personally disliked Lathrop Lindsay; and however much Captain Sturt had impressed on him that he should at least be cordial to Eyre and his companions.

'In a moment I will introduce you to Joolonga, and your other black servants,' bustled Captain Sturt. Then he turned to Arthur Mortlock. 'Is this your cousin, Mr Walker? How do you do, sir, Mr Ransome, isn't it, as I remember? A fine adventure for you, Mr Ransome.'

Arthur muttered something unintelligible, and cleared his throat.

'I'm afraid my cousin has been suffering from a slight cold,' put in Eyre. 'However the dry air in the desert should do him some good.'

'I've been suffering from quite the same malady,'

complained the Reverend Stow. 'It always attacks me, at this time of year. Yesterday afternoon I was obliged to lie on the ottoman and sleep for an hour. All I could manage for breakfast this morning was a little clyster. It's quite exhausting.'

'You could try me old mum's fever draft,' suggested Arthur.

The Reverend Stow frowned at Arthur in surprise. Eyre nudged Arthur with his elbow to warn him to say no more; but it was too late. The Reverend Stow and one or two people around them had already heard Arthur's fruity East End accent.

'What, pray, is your "old mum's" fever draft?' asked the reverend.

Arthur shrugged, and shuffled his feet, and stared unhappily towards Eyre, his eyes unfocused and beady behind his borrowed spectacles.

'Please,' insisted the Reverend Stow. 'I'd love to know.'

'Well, your reverence,' said Arthur. 'It's powdered niter, and potash and two teaspoons of antimony wine, all mixed up with sweet spirits of nitre, and a pint of warm water. Very efficacious. Well, specially when you clap a bread poultice on to your bonce at the same time.'

He hesitated, and licked his lips, and then said quickly, 'I mean head. Not—' he hesitated again, and the last word came out as scarcely a whisper '—bonce.'

Captain Sturt looked across at Eyre and there was an emotionless, questioning expression on his face. He suspected Eyre of something, although he wasn't quite sure what it was. Eyre looked back at him and tried to convey by telepathy that 'Mr Ransome's' presence here was a private matter, and that it wouldn't jeopardise the expedition. But there was no flicker of an answer on Sturt's face; no indication that he had either received Eyre's silent message or understood it. But he made no attempt to question Eyre about Arthur; instead, he turned away and started talking to Mr Rutgers, of the *Adelaide Dispatch*, and telling him how Australia's great inland sea was going to be discovered at last; and that, no, if the people of South Australia insisted, he wouldn't object to them calling it Lake Sturt; or even Sturt Ocean.

Eyre, Christopher, and Arthur were called over to the train of pack-horses by the young artist George French Angas, who had come down from Angaston late the previous day in order to see them off, and to make sketches for Captain Sturt and for the press. He was a humorous, lively fellow, with a small dark moustache and irrepressible hair, and he drew them quickly and accurately.

The finished drawings that he would produce, long after the expedition had left Adelaide, would show in water-colour three serious-faced men, dressed in khaki twill shirts and wide hats and riding-britches, with high leather boots. Their faces would be shadowed by their hats, but one of them would appear to be dark, and angular, and handsome in a slightly untidy way; whereas the young man standing next to him would be fair, and lanky, and standing with one hand perched on his hip in an incongruously balletic pose, as if he were waiting impatiently to leap on to the stage during the second act of Mozart's *Les petits riens*; and the third man would appear oddly blurred, as if he were doing everything he could to avoid making a clear impression on the artist, so that all one would really be able to remember about him distinctly would be the sharp reflection on his spectacles, and the pugilistic flatness of his nose. Behind these three men would be a dappled frieze of pack-horses, heavily saddled and laden; and beyond the curves of the horses' backs would be stringy-bark gums, and the sky as clear-washed as only young George Angas could paint it.

There would be other drawings and paintings, too; some of which would be used as reference for woodcuts and steel engravings which would be sent all over the world for reproduction, to the *Illustrated London News* in England, to the *Spirit of the Times* in Philadelphia, and to *L'Histoire* in France. One of the most frequently reproduced would

191

be that of the expedition's three Aborigines. The tall, broad-faced Joolonga, dressed in a cockeyed midshipman's hat, a striped cotton shirt, and knee-britches, but with bare feet. The powerful, squat Midgegooroo, his head tied around with kangaroo-fur sweatbands, dressed in the customary *buka* and less-than-traditional loincloth. And beside them, in nothing but a small leather apron, a slender boy with wild long hair, and those hypnotically prehistoric features that had first aroused Eyre's sense of destiny and timelessness when he had arrived in Australia; and this was the boy Weeip.

Joolonga came up and saluted Eyre with a raised hand. He had small, glittery eyes, and a permanent grin. His cheeks were marked with V-shaped scars, and a white band of chalky paint was smeared across his forehead. He smelled strongly of lavender cologne.

'Mr Walker, sir, I am pleased to make your acquaintanceship.'

'And I yours,' said Eyre. 'It seems that we are going to be travelling companions for quite some time.'

'Yes , sir. Well, you will find that I speak all variety of English, sir, as well as many of the various languages, Wirangu, Nyungar, Ramindjeri. Captain Sturt tells me we are to seek the one they call Yonguldye.'

'That is part of the purpose of this expedition, yes. For me personally, it's the principal part. Finding Yonguldye is of the very greatest importance to me.'

Joolonga nodded, still grinning. 'I have heard word of this importance, sir. It is concerned with the burial of the boy Yanluga. Believe me, sir, you are not the only person who believes that it is necessary for the boy Yanluga to be buried in the accepted fashion.'

There was an inflection in the Aborigine's voice that somehow gave Eyre the impression that Joolonga was more than a little sceptical of the need for Yanluga to be given the traditional tribal burial rites. Eyre said nothing about it, not then, but it led him decide to treat Joolonga with more than the usual caution. Eyre had come across one or two of these 'civilised' Aborigines before, mostly when they had come down to the harbour on errands for their masters; and he had generally found them to be arrogant, especially to their own kind; and imbalanced; and very rarely trustworthy.

Once an Aborigine had been taken into a white man's home as a servant or a flunkey or even as nothing more than a fashionable curiosity; once he had eaten like a white man, dressed like a white man, and learned something of the scope of the world outside Australia; he was imprisoned for ever betwixt-and-between, like a wasp caught in a jar of jam. He would see his own tribespeople through white eyes: as filthy and ignorant and poverty-stricken—and yet he would find it impossible to be fully accepted into white society. Eventually, the effect on his character would be catastrophic. He would suffer from tempers, grinding bouts of bottomless depression, rum-drinking, and wild displays of infantile mischief. Quite often, he would try suicide.

Joolonga, however, appeared to be somewhat wilier than those tame Aborigines like the celebrated Bennelong, who had once been taken to England and presented to King George III by his patron, Governor Arthur Phillips of New South Wales, and who afterwards had always held a scented silk handkerchief over his nose whenever his tribal relatives came to call on him at government house; or like the boastful chieftain Bungaree, of the Broken Bay tribe, who had worn a naval coat resplendent with gold lace, but no shirt, and whose six wives had been given the whimsical and degrading names of Askabout, Boatman, Broomstick, Gooseberry, Onion and Pincher. Joolonga seemed just as culturally isolated, perhaps: but very much more hard-baked, and very much more knowledgeable. He grinned all day, and he wore a cock-eyed midshipman's hat, but there was nothing of Bennelong or Bungaree about him. He was not a strutting eccentric, nor a white man's mimic, and by the way he looked back at Eyre, it was plain that his life was his own, and that he danced on no man's string.

He spat tobacco-juice into the dusty flowerbed. 'You understand, sir, that Yonguldye is a Mabarn Man,' he told Eyre.

'You mean a medicine-man?'

'If that is how you wish to describe it, sir, yes.'

'Do you know him well?'

Joolonga shook his head. 'I have seen him only once, sir, when the troopers had to question him, on account of a killing.'

'Oh, yes?'

Joolonga raised his hand and pointed towards the north-west. 'He had tracked down Willy Williway, sir, over three hundred miles, after Willy Williway had stabbed and murdered one of the Mindemarra Brothers.'

'He tracked a man for three hundred miles?' asked Eyre, impressed, but a little disbelieving. He had been warned by Captain Sturt about the tall tales that Aborigines could tell; and he knew from the conversations that he had had with Yanluga that even quite 'civilised' Aborigines lived partly in the real world and partly in the dreamtime.

Joolonga said, 'Yonguldye is the strongest Mabarn Man, sir, as strong as the Steel Bullet, some believe. Many say that they have seen him fly.'

'Hm,' said Christopher. 'Many say that they have seen me fly, too, but only after a bottle-and-half of rum.'

'It is easy to disbelieve, sir,' replied Joolonga. 'But the magistrate's records show that Willy Williway murdered Jack Mindemarra in Nuriootpa, and that the medicine man Yonguldye followed him all the way to the head of the gulf; where Billy Mindemarra was able to kill him. There is a way of tracking wrongdoers, sir. The Mabarn Man will wear the *Kurdaitja* shoes, especially made of emu feathers, stuck together with human blood, and with these shoes he will be able to follow his quarry for miles and miles, sometimes with his eyes closed, over deserts and mountains and scrubs; and from the wearer of the *Kurdaitja* shoes there is no escape.'

Eyre laid his hand on Christopher's shoulder. 'It seems as if Yonguldye is a man worth finding. But tell me, Joolonga, do you think that he may be likely to help us? If I ask him to perform the necessary ritual for Yanluga to find peace, do you believe that he will do it?'

'You will have to ask him, sir,' said Joolonga, not altogether respectfully.

'Well, I can't ask him until I find him, can I? Where do you think he's likely to be?'

'The last word I had of Yonguldye's people was at the sacred place near Woocalla, sir. That is where we should go first.'

'How far is Woocalla? Many days?'

'Possibly five days, sir. Not more.'

'Very well, then,' said Eyre. 'Is everything ready for us to leave?'

'We have done our best, sir.'

Eyre said, 'You may stop calling me "sir" if you wish; since we have to live and travel together. I would prefer "Mr Walker", if you must be formal, or "boss" if you do not.'

Joolonga gave Eyre a glittery, sarcastic nod, and then went to tighten all the traces on the pack-horses, and chase away a young Aborigine boy who had discovered that one of the saddlebags contained sugar, and was dipping his hand into it. There were rifles in the packs, too: three Baker's models, which Captain Sturt had shown Eyre how to load, and fire.

Eyre beckoned to Midgegooroo, who came forward and raised his hand in salute.

'Do you speak any English?' Eyre asked him.

Midgegooroo stared at him respectfully, but said nothing.

'Joolonga!' called Eyre. 'Does Midgegooroo speak any English?'

'Midgegooroo speaks no language at all, Mr Walker-sir.

Midgegooroo has no tongue. But he understands simple orders, such as "stop", "go", "wait", "eat". And he is very strong, Mr Walker-sir. He can break limestones into chalk, just in his fist. And once he held up a carriage on his back while the wheel was changed.'

From the crowd around the picket-fence, which had now increased to nearly a hundred people, there came laughter and singing. A young boy in a green velvet suit had brought along a violin, and was playing 'All Around My Hat'. The sound of this tune had an obvious effect on Arthur Mortlock, who was becoming increasingly twitchy and impatient. The words of the tune spoke of 'my true love, who is far, far away', and 'far, far away' meant nothing more and nothing less than transportation as a convict.

Captain Sturt came forward and snapped open his gold half-hunter, peering at it officiously. 'Well, Mr Walker, nine of the clock. I believe it's time for you to leave us.'

'An admirable quest, if I might say so,' said the Reverend T. Q. Stow. 'Your father is a man of the cloth, I understand, Mr Walker? Quite admirable. The Lord has inspired so much, don't you agree?'

Eyre gave the Reverend Stow a tight little nod of agreement, and then called forward the boy Weeip. Weeip was in awe of all of them, and stood with his arms crossed over his bare chest like the wings of a fledgling galah bird, his eyes wide.

'Weeip, do you know any English?' Eyre asked him, kindly.

'Few words, boss. I went to mission last dry.'

'Well, that's something,' said Christopher. 'I was beginning to think that we would have nobody to listen to for two months but the miserable Mortlock and the jesting Joolonga.'

'Tell me what words you know,' Eyre encouraged Weeip.

Weeip closed his eyes, hesitated, and then rapidly recited in that high, clacking voice that Aborigines use whenever they become excited, 'One hour father, which are dinner then? hallo my name; give us this daily-daily breath; give us this dress purses; as we four give them their dress purses; and lead us knotting ten station; but the liver is from Beef Hill; fine in the king pond; how is the glory? ever-ever our men.'

The Reverend T. Q. Stow stared at the boy in utter astonishment. Christopher had to cover his mouth with his hand, and even Eyre, for all the tension he was feeling about Sturt and Arthur Mortlock, was unable to resist a smile.

'Well,' said Eyre, 'that was very well done. Now, why don't you go to that waggonette over there and fetch me my wooden case. The shiny wood box. Those are my medical supplies; and I want to make sure that we carry them with us.'

He ruffled Weeip's wild black curly hair. It was soft, but greasy, like a goat's. Weeip scampered off to do what he was told, and Eyre turned back to Captain Sturt and Colonel Gawler, who had now come forward to make a short official sending-off speech.

'We know that this expedition was first inspired by your personal sense of duty towards a single indigenous individual,' said Colonel Gawler, then lifted both his hands for silence, and raised his voice louder, so that the chattering crowd quietened down. 'But you have a wider duty, Mr Walker, a duty which I know you will do your utmost to discharge. And that is, towards the economic and geographical development of the free colony of South Australia; establishing its place in the world; and opening up for human investigation the unknown environment in which the municipality of Adelaide is set.

'You go with our blessing. You go with our heartfelt admiration. You go, of course, with a considerable amount of our money invested in you, and all your forthcoming endeavours. But we know that you will not disappoint us. In fact, so sure do we feel that you will accomplish everything which today you are setting out to achieve, that we are making you a presentation. Mrs Dunstable!'

'They're not going to present us with Mrs Dunstable, are they?' Christopher muttered in Eyre's ear. Eyre touched his finger with his lips to tell him to be quiet.

'Sorry,' said Christopher. 'Forgive me my dress purses.'

Mrs Dunstable was ushered forward by Mr Pickens. She was one of the prettiest young ladies in Adelaide, but a widow. Her husband had died during their second winter in Australia of pneumonia, and since that time she had devoted herself to charity work, and particularly to helping all the scores of women, young and old, handsome and plain, who regularly arrived from England in search of a husband and a new life. In the face of considerable local hilarity, she had converted her house on Grenfell Street into a hostel, and spent three days of each week driving eligible young Englishwomen around the neighbouring farms and sheep-stations in a bullock dray seeking to place them with a suitable husband. Her service was politely referred to as 'Cupid's Carriage', and less politely as 'Mrs Dunstable's Wholesale Harlots'.

She was dressed in black, as always, with a black bonnet and veil; but her heart-shaped face was bright and appealing, and she stepped up to Eyre with a smile that was both pretty and completely confident, as if she were minor royalty, about to bestow on Eyre an honour which he had earned in devoted service to her most gracious person.

'Mr Walker,' she said, in a bell-like voice, and handed him an empty glass bottle with a screw top.

Eyre looked at the bottle, and then at Mrs Dunstable, who blinked at him attractively, and then at Captain Sturt.

'This bottle is a measure of our confidence in you,' announced Colonel Gawler. He took the bottle out of Eyre's hands and held it up for everyone to see. 'In this bottle, you will bring home a sample of the water from the inland sea. In this bottle, you will bring back the proof that all of Captain Sturt's theories are true, and that there is a vast untapped reservoir of water, just waiting for brave

198

and adventurous men to push northwards and exploit its riches.'

He handed the bottle back to Eyre, and said, in a quieter voice, but with well-contrived sincerity. 'I have sent many expeditions northwards from Adelaide; all have been deterred by the conditions they have encountered soon after they have started their journey. But you, I know, will *not* be deterred. You have many compelling reasons for going, and many compelling reasons for finding those things that will make South Australia wealthy and great. Opals, perhaps. Diamonds. Lead, if you can locate it; and copper. But most of all I want you to bring back water, and that is why I have presented you with this bottle. For, once this bottle is full, it shall never again be emptied, not in my lifetime, nor yours, nor the lifetimes of anyone else who is present this morning.'

Now Mrs Dunstable was handed by one of her lady-friends a folded Union Jack, sewn of segments of silk. This she gave to Captain Sturt, who presented it to Eyre with a dramatic bow.

'This has been sewn for you by the ladies of Adelaide; so that you can carry it to the centre of the continent, there to leave it as a sign to the savage that the footsteps of civilised man have penetrated so far.'

There was a slight ripple of applause, which quickly died away. Then Captain Sturt turned, raised his arm, and cried, 'The time is arrived!' and from the side lawn of the house, a brass quintet struck up, for no discernible reason, with a ragged version of 'The March of the Davidsbündler against the Philistines'.

With the help of Colonel Gawler's Aborigine stable-boys, Eyre and Christopher and Arthur Mortlock mounted their horses; and were led by Joolonga to the front gates of Government House, and slowly through the applauding crowd. The brass quintet followed them at a slow march, alarming their mule so much that he kept braying and kicking out his heels, in spite of the weight of flour and bacon which he carried on his back.

The gentlemen in the crowd raised their hats; some tossed them into the air; and the ladies fluttered their fans and spun their parasols and giggled a great deal. Somebody let off a firecracker, which popped and danced and jumped all over the dusty road, and caused several of the horses to rear up and thrash their hooves.

They were right in the middle of the assembly, bowing and nodding and lifting their hats, when a small black gig drew up on the far side of the road. A flash of sun on its highly varnished door caught Eyre's attention, and when he saw who it was he reined his horse around and lifted a single warning finger towards Arthur Mortlock. Out of the gig stepped Mr Chatto and Mr Rose, both of them dressed in clashing check country suits, and they strode quickly and purposefully straight towards the procession as if they knew already what they had to do.

Mr Rose pushed his way through the crowd until he reached Eyre's horse, and without a word he reached up and held its bridle. He was followed closely by Mr Chatto, who came close up to Eyre and stood with his arms folded and his face peaky with satisfaction. 'Never heard of Arthur Mortlock, is that it, Mr Walker? Never knew what became of him? Well, sir, we beg to disagree, Mr Rose and I. We beg to venture that Mr Arthur Mortlock has been with you these past four days or more, and that he spent last evening with you at Mrs McConnell's lodging-house on Hindley Street. And what's more, we beg to suggest that the gentleman in the spectacles on the third horse there is none other than Arthur Mortlock himself, in person, disguised as a *bona-fide* member of this expedition.'

Captain Sturt elbowed his way up to the front of the procession. The crowd's cheers had now subsided to a discontented buzz; and a woman's voice shouted out tipsily, 'for shame!' Somebody made a ribald remark about the mule, and a shudder of amusement went through the company, but then there was silence.

'What's this?' Captain Sturt demanded, facing Mr Chatto with his fists on his hips. 'This is a government expedition!

How dare you attempt to delay it? These men must make a good distance before nightfall; and distance is money. *My* money, if you must know.'

Mr Chatto removed his hat; and Mr Rose touched his brim.

'My personal apologies, Captain,' said Mr Chatto. 'But we have reason to think that the gentleman in the spectacles is an absconded ticket-of-leave man by the name of Arthur Stanley Mortlock, wanted in New South Wales for breaking the conditions of his parole, and also for offences of violence and theft which were committed while making good his escape.'

Captain Sturt was silent. He glanced up at Eyre, and then back at Arthur Mortlock. Eyre's horse stepped nervously sideways, and its bridle clinked. Mr Rose patted its nose, and said, 'Steady, old thing, steady.'

At last, Sturt turned back to Mr Chatto, and said, 'You must be mistaken, I'm afraid.'

'I don't think so, sir,' Mr Chatto insisted. 'And the worst of it is that these two genetemen here, sir, Mr Willis and Mr Walker, are both guilty of having harboured the said Arthur Mortlock, giving him shelter and succour; and of assisting him to elude custody. You can see for yourself, captain. They're about to ride off with him right at this very moment. The felony is being committed in broad daylight, in front of a hundred witnesses.'

Eyre said, as boldly as he could, 'I'd like to see what evidence you have that this man is anything other than what he claims to be; and what *I* claim him to be. He is my cousin, not long ago arrived from England, Mr Martin Ransome.'

'This is nonsense,' replied Mr Chatto, coldly. 'I will have to detain you.'

'On whose authority?' snapped Captain Sturt.

'On the written personal authority of the Governor and Commissioner, Colonel George Gawler, if you'll forgive me, captain. Do you wish to examine it? We have been given a free hand to recapture all absconders, and to detain all those who have assisted them.'

Captain Sturt stared at Mr Chatto furiously, and then stamped his foot. 'Is this true?' he demanded. He spun around, and confronted Colonel Gawler. 'Is this true, George?'

Colonel Gawler blushed, like a young girl who has just confessed to a secret and intimate misdeed. 'Of course,' he said. 'These men came to me with letters of authority from Major Sir George Gipps himself, Charles I could hardly deny them. And, of course, one had no idea that—'

'If these men are detained, the entire expedition will have to be abandoned!' shouted Sturt. 'And that, George, is out of the question. That—is—quite—*out of the question*!'

'My dear Charles—' Colonel Gawler began.

' "My dear Charles!" What do you mean, "my dear Charles!" These whelpish hirelings are attempting to ruin the most important geographical expedition in the history of Australia! With the exception of *mine*, of course. But nonetheless!'

Mr Chatto remained where he was, unmoved by all of this blustering. 'I have the authority, captain,' he repeated, in a thin voice. 'And I must insist on exercising it.'

Eyre suddenly took off his hat, and held it against his chest. 'If I might make a remark, Captain Sturt, it seems that our detention depends entirely on this gentleman's assertion that my cousin Mr Martin Ransome is in fact an absconded ticket-of-leave man. Perhaps a few questions will satisfy him that he is mistaken.'

Colonel Gawler, anxiously tugging at the braid on his ceremonial jacket, said, 'Yes; well that might be a good idea. After all, if this isn't the man you seek—'

'I have no doubt that it is, sir,' said Mr Chatto.

'All the same,' put in Sturt, 'it seems to me fair that Mr Ransome here should not be branded as an offender until Mr Chatto has established his identity. It is hardly a cordial welcome for someone so recently arrived here.'

Mr Chatto paused for a moment, and systematically

clicked his knuckles. Then he said, 'Very well, if it's proof that you want,' and walked around Eyre's horse until he was standing close to Arthur. Arthur peered down at him through his tiny pebble glasses, and all he could see was a small curved figure with a looming head and a curled-up body, like a sinister sprouting bean. His horse shifted from one foot to the other, sensing Arthur's agitation.

Mr Chatto reached up and held the horse's throatlatch; and crooned a few words to it which settled it down. 'Shoosha, shoosha.' Then he looked up at Arthur, and said, 'You and I have no need of this pretence, do we, Mr Mortlock?'

Arthur said nothing, but noisily cleared his throat, as if it were full of dried peas.

'You *are* Mr Arthur Mortlock, late of Macquarie Harbour?' asked Mr Chatto.

'No, mate, I'm not,' Arthur managed to croak.

'Then forgive me, who are you? Surely you can't really be this gentleman's cousin. This gentleman, if you will pardon me for being so blunt, is a *gentleman*. He speaks like a gentleman, and bears himself like a gentleman; wheras you sir have the sound of the East End about you; a vulgar voice; and a ruffian's demeanour. If you'll forgive me, of course.'

Eyre said, 'Captain Sturt, I must protest about this.'

Sturt glanced up at him sharply, and said, 'I don't think you have any real justification for protesting, do you, Mr Walker? It was *your* idea that Mr Ransome should be questioned, after all; and I for one am interested to see how he answers.'

Eyre replaced his hat, and sat silent and uncomfortable on his fidgeting horse, sweating with the morning heat and with the fear that all of them were now at risk of arrest and imprisonment. Their prospects had not been helped at all by the way in which Captain Sturt had embarrassed Colonel Gawler in front of a large crowd of eminent Adelaide citizens.

Mr Chatto said to Arthur, 'Which ship did you come out on?'

'The *Beaumonde*, three weeks since.'

'The *Beaumonde* sailed from Portsmouth, did she not?'

'No, friend, she didn't. She sailed from Tilbury on the four o'clock tide on 2 March; which was a Monday.'

'Her master?'

'Captain Hoskins.'

Mr Chatto hesitated, and then he asked, 'Where did you live, in London?'

'Sixty-one Sumner's Rents.'

'And explain to us how you could be a relative of Mr Walker's.'

For the first time, Arthur looked across at Eyre, although his face was white and set, like an unpainted plaster death-mask, and his eyes were swollen from wearing Mrs McConnell's spare spectacles for too long. He said, without looking down at Mr Chatto, 'It's simple enough, friend. Mr Walker's father had an adopted brother, who ran away from home when he was ten, and made his way in London as a link-boy, and then as a brewer's man.'

'And *your* trade, Mr Ransome?'

'A little of several. Stevedore, porter, wherryman. Anything to do with the water, or the docks.'

Mr Chatto didn't seem to be able to think of any more questions; at least not questions that would catch Arthur out. He turned around, and cracked the knuckles of both hands; and then he walked back towards his colleague, Mr Rose. Eyre suddenly began to think that they had got away with it after all, and that last night's slow and painful coaching, hours of facts about the *Beaumonde*, and about childhood days in Derbyshire, and about Eyre's appeal to 'Martin' to come out and join him in Australia, might all have been worthwhile.

Captain Sturt said, in a brittle tone, 'That all seems to be satisfactory, Colonel. Do you think we might now get on?'

Colonel Gawler looked at Sturt dubiously, and then at

Mr Chatto. But Mr Chatto had been whispering in the ear of Mr Rose, and Mr Rose had been whispering in the ear of Mr Chatto; and after a minute or two Mr Chatto stood up straight and tugged at his cuffs and said to Arthur in a clear voice, 'Would you have any objections to showing us your bare back. Mr Ransome? Just to make sure that you're not wearing the red shirt?'

Eyre wheeled his horse around. 'This is quite outrageous!' he shouted. 'Mr Ransome is my cousin! Captain Sturt! I won't allow him to be subjected to these indignities! He may not speak as correctly as you and I, but he is a British subject, and a loyal servant of Her Majesty, and a Christian, and he has never committed any act of any kind that could possibly justify this manner of treatment!'

But Captain Sturt knew why Mr Chatto had asked to see Arthur's back. Arthur had been at Macquarie Harbour, and there was scarcely a single convict who had been imprisoned there who would have escaped the marks of the lash. Even the most docile of prisoners would have suffered floggings for talking, or shirking work, or singing, or sodomy.

'I'm afraid I have to say that Mr Chatto is within his rights, Mr Walker,' he said. 'To examine a man's back is quite an accepted and acceptable way of establishing what you might call his legal credentials. Mr Ransome, do you think you would be so kind?'

There was nothing that Eyre could say; because in approving the inspection of Arthur's back, Captain Sturt had actually declared his belief that Eyre was telling the truth, and that Arthur really *was* his rough-cut cousin from Clerkenwell. The trouble was, when Arthur's scars were revealed for everyone to see, Sturt would be fifty times more embarrassed and wrathful than Colonel Gawler had been and Eyre and his companions could expect very little in the way of leniency. To have broken the law was one thing; to have made a public mockery of Australia's greatest explorer was quite another. Eyre backed his horse towards Christopher, and said, out of the side of his mouth, 'Do you think we might make a run for it?'

Christopher was pallid, and there was a coronet of sweat on his forehead. 'With all these packs on our horses? And all those peppery young dragoons around? They'd catch us up and cut us down before you could say "penitentiary".' He paused, and wiped away the sweat from his face with his scarf. 'Damn it, Eyre,' he said, 'I told you this business with Mortlock would get us into trouble. I damn well told you.'

Arthur slowly climbed down from his horse, and removed his hat. An expectant, gossipy hush fell over the crowd of sightseers, and many of them shuffled nearer to get a better view. Captain Sturt folded his arms and looked handsome and stern; Colonel Gawler kept making impatient faces and planting his hands on his hips and blowing out his cheeks.

Arthur hung his kangaroo-skin hat on to his saddle-pommel. To Eyre's surprise, his scalp was no longer prickly but completely bald. But with an expression of complete resignation, Arthur took off his leather satchel, and his water flask, and unbuttoned his bush-jacket and took that off, too.

Mr Chatto approached him with the gliding self-satisfaction of a white-bellied shark that can smell blood in the water. 'That's an interesting style of haircut you have, Mr Ransome. Now, where would a man get himself a haircut like that?'

Arthur stared at him with pebbly little eyes. 'Ringworm Hall, mate, that's where.' He said it so quietly that few people in the crowd could hear him, but those that did let out a chuckle, and somebody said, 'Let the gentleman be!' and 'here's for the expedition, lads!'

Arthur now turned his back on Mr Chatto, and reached around behind him to tug the tail of his shirt out of his belt. Mr Chatto cracked his knuckles in anticipation, and smiled across at Mr Rose. For his part, Mr Rose had now released the bridle of Eyre's horse, and had walked around to cover Arthur's only way of escape, should he try to run.

Without any hesitation, however, Arthur hiked up the back of his shirt as far as he could, and revealed a brown, slightly blotchy back; but certainly not a back that bore any scars from flogging.

'Is that enough for you, friend?' he said roughly. 'Are you satisfied now? Or do you want to inspect me teeth, to see if there's any junk caught between them?'

That was a provocative, almost dangerous challenge. Few Englishmen who had never served time in a penal settlement would have known that the principal item of diet there was salted beef, either seething with maggots, or cured to the consistency of old saddle-leather, and that the common name for this delicacy was 'junk'.

But now Captain Sturt stepped forward, and took Mr Chatto almost rudely by the arm.

'I think this gentleman has made his point, sir, and clearly established his innocence. Now I require you to leave him be; and let this expedition be on its way.'

Mr Chatto stared at Sturt with undisguised horror. '*Captain!*' he protested, in a high voice.

'I have seen and heard enough, thank you,' insisted Sturt. 'George, will you be kind enough to tell these fellows to be on their way?'

Colonel Gawler humphed, and wuffled, and flapped his hand at Mr Chatto to clear off. There was a burst of applause in the crowd as Arthur tucked in his shirt, and buttoned up his bush-jacket; and at last gave everyone a sweeping bow.

'I know this man to be Arthur Mortlock!' Mr Chatto kept on. 'I can produce witnesses who will identify him quite positively!'

'Be off, for goodness' sake,' said the disgruntled Colonel Gawler.

'You cannot let him go!' shrilled Mr Chatto.

There was more laughter, and cheering, and the brass quintet began to play *King William's March* in double-time, and Mr Chatto and Mr Rose both had to retreat from the dust and the jostling spectators and the rearing pack horses. Arthur climbed back into his saddle, and lifted his hat as if he were King William himself. More firecrackers went off; more hats flew into the air; and then Captain Sturt cried out to Eyre, 'God speed, Mr Walker! God speed!' and there was a general cheer, and shouts of 'God be with you!'

With a sudden rush, the expedition was off, and trotting down the wide, rutted street. Everybody followed: dragoons, children, carriages, and dogs. Eyre and Joolonga rode side by side at the front, Christopher and Arthur a few steps behind, with Midgegooroo and Weeip keeping the horses and the mule in order. The noise and the dust were tremendous; and for a moment Eyre felt as if he were lost in a blinding golden fog, with the drumming of mysterious war-parties all around him. It was that strange sense of destiny again: that uniquely Australian feeling that he was living in two different ages simultaneously, both prehistoric and modern. A gig rattled up beside him, its young driver lifting his hat and calling 'The very best to you, sir!' and then there were more cheers, and more laughter, and the dogs yipped and barked and ran between the horses' trotting hooves.

They had crossed the river, and almost reached the northern outskirts of Adelaide, and most of their enthusiastic followers had already dropped back, when Eyre saw somebody waving with a handkerchief from a sugar-gum grove off to the left of the track. A girl, dressed in saffron-yellow chiffon, with a yellow-and-white bonnet.

'Joolonga!' he called. 'I'll catch you up!'

He veered his horse away from the main party, and trotted as quickly as he could towards the grove. Christopher shouted after him, 'Where are you going?' but he ignored him. Christopher could see very well where he was going; and while he was prepared to accept Christopher's affection, he wasn't prepared to accept his jealousy.

Under the bluey-green shadow of the gums, Charlotte

was waiting for him, accompanied by Captain Henry. He brushed the dust from his clothes with his hat, and dismounted, and Captain Henry came to hold the reins.

Neither of them said a word. They held each other tightly; and then kissed, deeply and warmly, with all the urgency of a kiss which would have to be remembered for months to come. Eyre breathed in the scent of her skin, the smell of her perfume, and felt her fine tickly hairs against his cheek.

'I couldn't let you leave without seeing you,' Charlotte told him.'I've tried so hard to be stern with you, and yet I can't be.'

'How's your father?' asked Eyre. 'Is he any better?'

'The doctor still insists that he must rest. He's taking syrup of squills every day, and mustard poultices, and he's not permitted fatty foods or fermented liquor, and of course that doesn't improve his temper. But I pray for him, Eyre. I pray for him most earnestly.'

Eyre kissed her forehead. 'In that case, so shall I, if my prayers will do any good at all. And I shall also pray that I shall soon discover everything which I am going out to find, and that I shall be back with you before the New Year.'

'Eyre,' she pleaded. 'Love me for ever. I shall always love you.'

He kissed her one last time, and then he returned to his horse and mounted up. They remained there motionless for a second or two; under the rustling trees; trying to imprint on their minds an impression which would last for all the months of separation which were to come. Then Eyre turned his horse, and trotted off through the crackly bark, and Charlotte turned back to her carriage.

Captain Henry removed his hat while Charlotte climbed up and seated herself; and when Eyre twisted around in his saddle to look back at them, he thought how much she looked like a girl who had recently been bereaved.

He caught up with Christopher and the others just as

the dragoons were wheeling their horses around and turning back.

'Bring us back a bunyip!' one of them laughed; and then they spurred their mounts and cantered back towards Adelaide with shouts and cries and more laughter.

The expedition rode on about a mile further, none of them saying very much, up through the low hilly countryside towards Pooraka. The weather had been dry for the past few days, and the mallee bushes and mulga trees were clinging with dust. Up above them, the sky was ribbed with thin stratospheric cloud, which screened a little of the sun, and gave the morning the appearance of a dull daguerreotype. Their pack-horses snorted and flicked their tails at the teeming grey flies which crawled into their nostrils and around their haunches; and their harnesses clanked and squeaked in an endless rhythm that reminded Eyre of a funeral procession.

Joolonga said, 'Advisable to stop here, Mr Walker-sir, to look over all the equipment, and tighten the girths. If we have omitted to take anything important with us, we can at least turn back now to fetch it; and if any girth is loose we can remedy that matter before there are sores.'

'Very well,' Eyre ageed, and called the expedition to a halt. They dismounted, and drank a mouthful of water each, and strolled around while Joolonga and Midgegooroo inspected their packs and their horses' bridles. A warm wind, so slight that they could scarcely feel it, flowed against their faces from the direction of the sea.

Arthur said, 'You'll excuse me, gents, if I just adjust my clothing.'

'Pardon?' asked Christopher; but without any further ado, Arthur took off his satchel again, and tugged off his bush-jacket, and then shook himself out of his shirt.

Eyre stared at him in fascination. On his back, Arthur was wearing a large square of pale pigskin, from his shoulders to his waist, and right around under his arms, tied across his chest and his stomach with bootlaces. He unfastened it, and peeled it carefully off, and rolled it up as if it were a treasure-map on a parchment.

'I made that for meself not long after I got to Adelaide,' he said, with a sniff. 'I wore it for most of the time, for all that it made me sweat like a pig. It stopped my shirts chafing my back, for one thing; and for another thing I knew that the scars from a flogging was what bounty-men always looked for first. I saw a man caught in Sydney that way, when his scars opened and he started to bleed through his shirt.'

Eyre said, 'That is quite astonishing. Show it to me.'

Arthur unrolled the pigskin again. On close inspection, it looked like nothing more than a thin sheet of bacon rind, very dried up, and not very much like human skin at all. But Mr Chatto had been looking for weals, and scars, and the notion that Arthur's back might have once belonged to a Large White had undoubtedly never occurred to him.

'A man sees what he expects to see,' Arthur remarked, sagely, and tucked the skin into his leather satchel.

He was about to pull on his shirt again, when Eyre touched his arm. 'You'll probably think me morbidly curious,' said Eyre, 'but would you show me your back as it really is?'

Arthur took of the spectacles he had been wearing and folded them up. 'Are you sure that you want to see it, Mr Walker? It's not a sight that does much for the appetite.'

'All the same. I want to know what they did to you; and I want to know what kind of a mark they made on you.'

Arthur shrugged, and said, 'If that's what you want.'

Silently, he turned around. Eyre and Christopher looked at his bare back and neither of them spoke. Eyre felt as if the air had become impossible to breathe, and the sweat ran down the sides of his face and chilled him. He had never known that human flesh could be reduced to such a livid ruin; not purposely, not deliberately, not at all. Arthur's shoulders were criss-crossed all over with shiny mauve scars, scar upon scar, until the flesh was knotted into ropes and ridges and twisted shapes like umbilical

211

cords. Further down, the flesh had been beaten away from his backbone until only a thin transparent covering of scar-tissue remained, through which his vertebrae could be seen as whitish lumps; and the fattier sides of his back had been cut up into diamond-shaped segments, red and angry and sore with sweat.

At last, Eyre whispered, 'Thank you, Arthur,' and Arthur put on his shirt again, and fastened up his jacket.

'I wasn't the worst, by no means,' said Arthur, matter-of-factly. 'Plenty of lads were killed by flogging, and some were flogged and had salt and vinegar rubbed into their backs. Some couldn't walk afterwards, and quite a few lost their manhood, if you understand me. They'd flog you for anything at all, at Macquarie Harbour, I can tell you.'

'I honestly don't know how you managed to bear it,' said Eyre. He felt deeply shocked. So shocked, in fact, that he didn't even know if he wanted to continue with this expedition. Why was he galloping off in search of a medic-ine-man to bury a dead blackfellow according to his tribal rites, when living white men were being so mercilessly punished in the name of Christianity?

'I'll tell you how I bore it,' said Arthur. 'I didn't bear it. I was just there while it was being done to me, and that was all. They tie you up to an X-frame, wrists and ankles, stripped to the waist, and then they flog you in front of the whole company, with the six-tailed cat. It's better if the cat is knotted; it bruises more but it doesn't cut. But some of the gentlemen preferred to cut you, and one or two of them were so expert they could cut you one way and then the other, so that the flesh flew off in perfect squares. I didn't bear it because no man can bear it. A flogging is beyond bearing. It is the nearest thing to hell on earth outside of the solitary. The second time they flogged me I looked down between the angle of the X-frame and saw the ants carrying off great pieces of my back. I came away that time and I had a hump like a hunchback, and it was eight weeks and a day before I could walk.'

Eyre took off his hat. He looked northwards, out towards the scrubby horizon. 'I think we'd better get on,' he said. 'If I hear any more of this, I'm going to start questioning the very basis of my life here, and the very motive behind our going.'

Both he and Christopher were silent as they remounted their horses, and set off. Arthur, however, was in good spirits, and started to sing.

'All around my hat, I will wear the green willow;
All around my hat, for a twelvemonth and a day.
And if anyone should ask me, the reason why I'm wearing
*   it,*
It's all for my true love who is far, far away.'

Seventeen

They were to follow the coastal plain between the Gulf of St Vincent and the foothills of the North Mount Lofty mountains until they reached the northernmost point of the gulf, where the Yorke Peninsula protruded into the Indian Ocean like the cocked leg of a saucy dancing-girl. They would carry on northwards across the 'thigh' of the peninsula until they reached the head of the next inlet, the Spencer Gulf; and it was here at Kurdnatta that the Indian Ocean thrust its deepest into the underbelly of the Australian continent. Beyond, to the north, lay nothing but 'The Ghastly Blank'. Unexplored, unmapped territory, into which only the bravest and foolhardiest of doggers and prospectors had ever penetrated. Those who had seen it and survived had brought back stories of mountains like the moon and deserts that never ended, of mysterious

213

glittering lakes that could never be reached, of dragons and monsters and extraordinary insects, and green fields that could appear and disappear overnight. It was at the same time the most alluring and the most frightening land on earth: and that night, as they camped amongst the mallee scrub, their lonely fire flickering in answer to the stars, Eyre felt the stirrings of its ancient and sun-wrinkled soul.

Joolonga sat and chewed tobacco, while Midgegooroo unloaded the horses and watered them, and Weeit squatted by the fire and cooked them up a potful of pork and brown beans. Although their fare was necessarily plain and filling, Weeip was a good enough cook. He had been taught baking at the mission, he said. Cakes, pies, and 'York Shark Pudding'. He could make a passable mug of tea, too, very hot, with molasses stirred into it.

Now that they were out of Adelaide, Weeip discarded his leather apron and went naked, except for a thin string of twined hair around his stomach. Midgegooroo kept his *buka*, but dispensed with his loincloth. Only Joolonga remained dressed in his white man's uniform and cocked hat; although on several occasions he would forget to put on his britches. Eyre had seen scores of naked Aborigine men before, but never at such close quarters, and he was fascinated to see that their penises were not only circumcised but slit open all the way from the urethral opening at the end, right back to the scrotum. He asked Joolonga about it, but Joolonga was evasive, and simply said that it was 'usual'. The sub-incision caused the Aborigines to urinate in a wide spray, but obviously it had not affected their sexual capacity, for later as young Weeip slept and dreamed, and Eyre kept watch, the boy's penis rose several times in a jutting erection.

On that first night out, they talked about Mr Chatto and Mr Rose, and Yonguldye, and what might lie ahead of them. They also talked about the penal colonies at Botany Bay and Macquarie Harbour, and Arthur gave them a long and unsettling account of his life as a 'guest of the Crown'.

'In particular, I think of Tom Killick—a young pale fellow fresh out from England; an accountant I think, transported for life for embezzling £2 from his employers. The first night at Macquarie Harbour, the guards amused themselves by treating him as if he was a master-criminal; and pretending they were afeared of him. They locked him up for the night with eleven of the worst knaves on the whole island; men who were little better than animals. They buggered him that night, all eleven of them, and most of them more than once; and the other unnatural acts they forced him into—well, I saw acts of that nature many a time, and I regret to say at times that I was party to them. But the effect on that delicate young fellow was to turn his mind, and by daybreak he was screaming and sobbing like a woman. You would have thought they were a-killing of him; the noises he made. And in the end, they did, in their usual way, because he killed himself. I saw him do it, in the exercise yard; stand on a box with a broom, and push the handle into his back-passage; then just let himself drop. Right through his guts, that handle went, right through his stomach and liver and lungs, and lodged inside his chest. Four of us tried to get it out, but we couldn't, so in the end we just sawed off the brush and left the rest inside of him.'

They listened to these stories seriously and unhappily. When he had finished, however, Arthur lifted his cup of rum, and said, 'There should be no long faces here, gentlemen, for you have rescued at least one wretch from that kind of life; and given him an opportunity for freedom. So here's your health, and may we find the success we're after.'

'Well, I'll drink to that,' said Christopher. 'I think I'll also drink to the hope that I never get to see the inside of one of Australia's prisons. The idea of being kept in chains!'

'Ah, it's not the chains you have to worry about, Mr Willis,' said Arthur. 'It's what they do to your mind.' He tapped his forehead, and said, 'It's up here that they do the damage. Inside your bonce. They make your brave man frightened, and your good man evil, and your weak man as wild as a snarling, snavelling beast. They corrupts the pure, and they spays the strong, and they makes your wisest man into a idiot. They knows their stuff, sir; but all I can say is, on reflection, that no man ever came out of those prison settlements a better man than what he went in.'

By ten o'clock that night, Arthur was asleep, wrapped up in his blankets, in his own words, 'as snug as a sossidge roll'. Eyre wondered how a man who had suffered so long and so acutely could ever sleep again, particularly since the danger of recapture was always close. He kept thinking about the 'young pale fellow' who had impaled himself, and wondered if he would have been driven to seek the same kind of terrible escape, if *he* had been imprisoned at Macquarie Harbour. He though of the scarred gristle of Arthur's back, and tried to imagine what pain Arthur must have felt.

Christopher came and sat beside him with a fresh mug of tea. 'Do you want some? Weeip's just brewed up some more.'

'Yes, I will.'

'You're not brooding,' said Christopher.

'No,' Eyre replied, shaking his head. 'I was just thinking about those penal settlements.'

'Well, yes,' said Christopher.

'Is that all you can say?' Eyre asked him.

'What do you want me to say? That they're cruel, and barbaric, and that no man should ever be allowed to inflict such pain and indignity on other men?'

'If you like.'

'It won't be any use. The law is the law; a sentence is a sentence; and if a sentence is carried out more harshly than it ought to be, well, my only reply to that is, abide by the law. Which we haven't, of course, bringing Arthur along with us, and I must say that Arthur's stories don't make me feel any happier about it.'

'There's nothing that Chatto can do now,' Eyre reassured him.

'I wouldn't lay any money on it.'

They sat in silence for a while, and the fire flickered and popped and lit their faces in kaleidoscopic orange. Up above them, the sky was rich as ink and prickled with stars. Cicadas sang, even though a cool wind was getting up; and there was a fragrant smell of woodsmoke in the air. Eyre was beginning to feel very tired now, exhausted not only by the day's travel and by this morning's send off, but by the enormity of what he was doing. He was seeking out a strange Aborigine medicine-man in an unknown land; quite apart from whatever riches he could discover; and more than that he was also beginning that longest of all journeys—the journey to discover his own soul. To understand at last what he actually *meant*—why he was here, what forces and reasons had brought him here, with these companions, on such a night—that would be the greatest discovery of all.

While they finished their tea, Joolonga came over, and said that everything was ready for their departure at sunrise. 'Today was a slow day, Mr Walker-sir. Tomorrow we must make much more distance.'

Eyre said, 'How far north have you travelled, Joolonga? What kind of country can we expect?'

Joolonga said, 'I have travelled as far as the place they call the diamond-sparrow-water, Edieowie. The country is difficult; flat land, salt water; mountains on the east side, salt marshes on the west.'

'And ahead?'

'They speak of a lake there, Mr Walker-sir. Sometimes they say that it is a magic lake, sometimes they say that there is no lake there at all, but just the memory of a lake. They call it Katitanda. But I have never been there, Mr Walker-sir.'

Eyre emptied out the dregs of his tea on to the ground. 'Well,' he said, 'if we are to find this lake, magical or not, we had better get some sleep.'

217

Christopher said, 'It would certainly solve some problems if there *were* a lake there. I'm not too keen on this bottled water, are you? It tastes as if it's been gently simmering in an unwashed stew-pot all afternoon.'

Joolonga took off his cocked hat. His hair was bound tightly with kangaroo-skin twine into a pigtail; and he looked to Eyre like a black-faced parody of a dandified lawyer he had once known in Baslow. What always struck him so forcibly about the Aborigines was that they did not resemble negroes in the least, in spite of their wide-spread noses and their thick lips. They were like an ugly variety of European; and Eyre always felt that they were far more intelligent and far more alert to what was going on around them than they ever allowed anyone to see.

Joolonga said, 'Midgegooroo told me that one of his brothers' families came from the west to Katitanda; but that they died there, and that Katitanda became their *wandalwallah*, their burial-place. He does not know why, exactly. It has become a story now, a legend, and his family have retold it so many times that nobody is sure what happened. All they know is that his brother, and his brother's two wives, and four of their children, all perished. Narahdarn swept his wing over them, and that is all they will say.'

'Narahdarn?' asked Eyre.

'Narahdarn is the Bringer of Death. Many tribes have stories about him. Captain Sturt says the story is like the beginning of the white man's Bible-book.'

'Tell me,' said Eyre.

Joolonga took out of his jacket pocket a small pipe made out of a crab's-claw, and filled it up with some of the sticky tobacco which he always carried with him. He picked a glowing twig out of the fire, and laboriously lit up. He was obviously considering at length whether he wanted to tell Eyre about Narahdarn or not.

Eventually, though, when the tarry fragrance of his tobacco was mingling with the smell of mallee scrub he said, 'All of this happened in the days of Ber-rook-boorn,

218

who was the very first man to live in Australia. He and his wife had been made by the great being Baiame; and had been permitted by Baiame to eat and drink everything that they could find, except honey from Baiame's own sacred yarran tree. But the wife of Ber-rook-boorn was tempted by the honey, and tasted it; and out of the tree with great black wings flew Narahdarn, the monster of death which Baiame had charged with guarding his honey.

'Ber-rook-boorn's wife hid in her *gunyah*, which in the northlands is what they call a *tantanoorla*, a brushwood shelter. But the harm was done. She had let out death into the world, and after that, men were no longer able to live for ever. The yarran tree was so sad that it wept, and some of my people still say today that the red gum on the trunk of the tree is the dried tears that it sometimes sheds for the dead.'

'Adam and Eve all over again,' remarked Christopher. 'That's remarkable, isn't it?'

'And the woman still gets the blame,' smiled Eyre, 'no matter what her name is; and no matter what language they tell the story in, English, Latin, or Aborigine!'

Joolonga smoked his pipe in silence, staring at the fire.

Eyre said to him, 'You don't seem particularly anxious to tell us much about the Aborigine.'

Joolonga frowned. He didn't seem to understand; or else he deliberately didn't want to.

'You don't appear to have any desire to tell us about your people,' Eyre repeated. 'Why is that?'

Joolonga took the crab's-claw pipe out of his mouth and spat into the fire.

'What white people know, they destroy. Their knowledge is more dangerous than their rifles. You see what they have done to me? What manner of a man am I? Blackfellow, or white? I can speak like white, dress like white, hold a knife and fork like white. I can think like a white man, too, which is my worst punishment of all. And everything I know, I destroy, just like white men do. They have destroyed me, and in my turn I destroy my people.'

He looked at Eyre and Christopher for a moment with a fierce, almost frightening pride. It was the wasp, making a last noisy effort to escape from the jar of jam.

'The dreamtime may be true and the dreamtime may not be true. It is not necessary for you to know about it. It is not necessary for you to hear about Narahdarn and Baiame and Priepiggie. You should close your ears to these things. And this expedition of yours to find Yonguldye . . . do you know how much you will destroy with this expedition? Thousands of years of sacred secrets. You may even destroy a people—a people who have no need of you, and who ask for nothing more than to be left to live their lives according to legend and tradition.'

Eyre stared at Joolonga for a long time over the leaping flames of the fire. Then he said, 'You're wrong. You're wrong about me in particular and about the white immigrants in general. I have set out on this expedition to do nothing more than find Yonguldye, and bring him back to Adelaide to bury the boy Yanluga. That's all. If I find the inland sea that Captain Sturt believes in; if I find opals; or copper; or gold; or a cattle-route to the north of Australia: well, I shall be lucky, and those who invested their money in this expedition shall be rewarded. But my principal aim is to see that justice is done to a single young Aborigine boy, and if by chance the expedition has other more profitable results, then I can only be doubly satisfied. This is a huge land, Joolonga. There is space in Australia for all of us, white and black. If we white people seem to be selfish, and destructive, it is only because we are struggling to survive here, just as your people have struggled to survive here for centuries. You must forgive us for that.'

Joolonga smiled. 'Of course. And shall I forgive you for my mother, who was cudgelled to death by British sailors because she refused to take off her *buka* for them? Or the friend with whom I grew up, whose name was Bundaleer, who was burned alive in his *tantanoorla*, he and his baby daughter, because a white bushman believed that he had taken his boots? Let me tell you something, Mr Walker-

220

sir, I despise the Aborigine because he is ignorant and filthy, and scratches the ground to survive in a country which could give him so much more; I despise him because he cannot and will not fight back against the white people, and for that reason I also despise myself. I have become their flunkey, yes Mr Walker-sir, no Mr Walker-sir. I am full of hate and yet I have to remain polite, and I will always remain faithful to you, as long as you need me. But never expect me to believe that this land is a better place because of the white man coming here. The white man has a power which is more dangerous than a bush-fire, and consumes everything it touches. After a bush-fire, the burned trees begin to grow again; but after the white man has passed, nothing grows. In a hundred years time, Mr Walker-sir, there will be no blackfellows here. The man I used to be has gone already. My father's son Joolonga has joined Ngurunderi in his place in the sky. This Joolonga who sits with you now is a white man's dog.'

Eyre took off his hat and ran his hand through his hair. 'Well,' he said, 'I don't know what to say to you.'

'It is not necessary to say anything. It is destiny.'

'Joolonga—' Eyre began.

But Joolonga raised his hand to ward off whatever Eyre was going to say. 'Say nothing, please, Mr Walker-sir. You will not hear me speak this way again. You will learn nothing from me; and come no closer to me. And whatever promises you make yourself, you cannot promise anything on behalf of any other white man. What has happened has happened; what is about to happen cannot be avoided. In this land it is better not to think of anything but your own survival. My mother's spirit rests in a certain rock; it will always be there. When the wind and the sun break the rock into dust, the dust will blow across the plain. My mother will always be there, long after the men who took her life are being punished by their own God.'

Eyre was silent. He turned to Christopher, but Christopher could do nothing but shrug. Joolonga finished his pipeful of tobacco, knocking the dottle into the fire. Then he said, 'We must sleep now. we have far to go tomorrow. I will watch first. Then Midgegooroo.'

Eyre brushed his teeth with dry liquorice-flavoured dentifrice, and then wrapped himself tiredly up in his blankets. The night seemed even darker and even windier when he was lying down; and the fire crackled like a fusillade of pistol-shots.

Christopher whispered, 'Eyre? What did you make of all that? He's quite a philosophical chap, isn't he, for a blackie? Never heard one speak like that before. Didn't know they could.'

'Well, he was well-educated,' Eyre remarked.

'Somewhat bitter, though, what?'

'Wouldn't you be, if your mother had been beaten to death; and everywhere you looked your lands were being taken over by strange people from a strange country?'

Christopher propped himself up on one elbow and stared at Eyre through the darkness. 'What do you mean "strange people from a strange country"? We're English.'

'Exactly,' said Eyre. 'Now, let me get some sleep, will you?'

Christopher was silent for a while, although he didn't lie down straight away. 'Eyre,' he said.

'Mmph?'

'Eyre, I beg of you, please don't get me wrong. I know that I've been complaining rather a lot today. You know—about bringing Arthur with us, and all that trouble we had with Chatto. But I wouldn't have missed coming along with you for anything.'

'That's all right, Christopher. Now, please get some sleep.'

'Very well. But just remember how much I admire you; how much loyalty I have for you. Just remember that in the final reckoning I dearly love you.'

Eyre was almost asleep. His mind was already beginning to swim in some deep dark silent *billa*. 'Yes, Christopher,' he said, and his voice sounded in his ears as if it were echoing across thirty centuries of lonely Australian nights.

Eighteen

It was a few minutes past five in the morning when Joolonga shook Eyre's shoulder and told him that they were being followed.

The day was chilly and grey, and there was a coastal mist over the landscape, so that Eyre felt as if he had been awakened into a world of phantoms. The fire had burned out, and Weeip was clearing away the ashes to build up a fresh one. Midgegooroo, stolid and silent, was feeding the horses. Arthur, already awake, was sitting on one of their packs, carefully scraping away at his scalp with a barber's razor.

Joolonga said, 'Two, perhaps three men are riding towards us from Tandarnya.' For some reason he used the Aborigine name for Adelaide. 'They are coming quickly, in the manner of riders who wish to catch up with us.'

Eyre pushed aside his blankets, and stood up, tugging at his tousled hair. He frowned through the mist in a south-easterly direction, but all he could see was the shifting silhouette of the horses, and the grey blotchy shadows of the mallee scrub.

'How do you know?' he asked Joolonga.

Joolonga touched his ear. 'The ground tells me.'

Eyre said, 'Show me.'

Flicking up the tails of his fancy coat, Joolonga knelt on the ground, and held his ear against it. He listened for a while, and then he said, 'Yes. I hear them still. They are closer now, maybe two miles, perhaps not so far. Two men.'

Eyre crouched down beside him, and pressed his ear to the earth, too. He closed his eyes and strained to pick up the slightest drumming, the slightest vibration. But all he could hear was the shuffling of their pack horses, and the crackle of the dry twigs as Weeip lit the fire, and the sharp scratching noise of Arthur's razor.

'Nothing,' he admitted, sitting up straight.

Joolonga stood up. 'You have to listen with your mind, Mr Walker-sir. The land will speak to you if you allow it to talk inside your head.'

Just then, Christopher came over, walking stiffly. 'What's up?' he asked. 'Do you know something, I don't think I'm ever going to get used to sleeping on the ground. I feel as if I've been pummelled all over by an entire company of dancing bears.'

Eyre said, 'Joolonga says there are two men following us, not more than two miles away.'

'Mr Chatto and Mr Rose?' Christopher suggested, at once.

'I don't know, but it's likely. I can't think of anyone else who would want to come chasing after us at five o'clock in the morning, can you?'

'Maybe we left something behind,' said Christopher. 'Maybe somebody's riding after us with extra food, or clean laundry.'

Eyre said, 'You checked our stores, Joolonga. Is there anything missing—anything that Captain Sturt would want to send out after us?'

Joolonga shook his head. 'Everything is in apple-pie order, Mr Walker-sir.'

'Well, they needn't necessarily be *chasing* us, need they?' said Christopher. 'They might just be travelling in this direction on business of their own.'

'I suppose that's possible,' said Eyre. But Joolonga shook his head again.

'They are coming after us, Mr Walker-sir. They are coming too quick for ordinary travellers. There is no settlement for twenty miles, and if they were ordinary travellers, they would be riding much more slowly. These two men are riding as if they do not think they will be going too far.'

'Then it must be Chatto and Rose,' said Eyre. He stood up, too, and brushed the knees of his britches. 'I should have realised they were too persistent to let us go. After

224

all, they won't be paid their bounty, will they, nor their travelling expenses, not until they take Arthur back to Botany Bay.'

Arthur came over, towelling his head. 'You lot look like a week of wet Wednesdays,' he said, cheerfully. 'Didn't you sleep?'

'Chatto and Rose are coming after us,' said Christopher. 'At least, that's what Joolonga seems to think.'

Arthur looked from Eyre to Christopher and then back again. 'How can he tell that?' he asked. 'It's as thick out there as a bowl of prison-house porridge.'

'He can hear the hoofbeats,' Eyre explained. 'There's a slight chance that it *isn't* them; but a far greater chance that it is.'

Arthur pulled a face. 'Well, then,' he said. 'It seems as if they won't let an old government pensioner go free after all.'

'We *can't* let the buggers have him; not now,' protested Christopher.

'I don't intend that they shall,' Eyre told him. 'Joolonga, how long would it take us to saddle up and get out of here? Could we do it before they reach us?'

'No, Mr Walker-sir. Five minutes, and they will be here.'

'In that case, break out two rifles; powder and ball.'

'Now then, Mr Walker, you can't go doing a thing like that,' Arthur spoke up. 'Those two fellows have letters of authority from the Governor of New South Wales, and from Colonel Gawler. If you were to harm them at all, sir, even a scratch, they'd have you locked up and flogged and sent out to Norfolk Island, before you could say cheese.'

Eyre turned to Christopher.

'Rather risky, I'd say,' Christopher told him. 'Not that I'm afraid, mind. Just judicious.'

'Break out the rifles,' Eyre instructed Joolonga. 'Make it quick, too, will you? They'll be on us in a minute or two.'

Joolonga called to Midgegooroo, and Midgegooroo unbuckled one of the horse-packs, and drew out two Baker rifles wrapped in waterproof oil-cloth. He brought them over, as well as a satchel filled with powder and shot. Eyre silently unwrapped one of the rifles, watched with solemnity by his companions, and then crouched down on the ground to load it, the way that Captain Sturt had shown him. He wrapped a lead ball in a patch of calico, rammed in into the barrel; then put a pinch of priming powder on the pan. Once the rifle was loaded, he handed it to Christopher, and loaded the second one.

'I'm not at all sure I'm going to be able to use this,' Christopher protested.

'Well, with good luck, you won't have to,' said Eyre.

Arthur said, 'Begging your pardon, Mr Walker, I'd much rather give meself up. *You* they may flog; *me* they'd hang.'

'I refuse to allow it,' Eyre insisted. 'You've come this far; and now you're an indispensable member of this expedition. Apart from that, you've served your time, and if they send you back to the penal colony then no justice will have been done, of any kind.'

Almost at that moment, they heard hoofbeats for the first time, muffled in the mist. Then two riders appeared, both wearing large bush hats and masked by scarves. They slowed down as they came past the line of pack-horses, and then drew their horses up only ten feet away. Their horses snuffled, and blew out vapour, and scraped at the ground. The riders themselves remained silent and upright, their eyes gleaming above their masks like the eyes of predatory animals, silvery and avaricious.

Eyre stepped forward, holding his rifle in one hand, upraised. The nearer of the two riders wheeled his horse around, so that he was well off to Eyre's left side; making it far more difficult for Eyre to shoot at both of them quickly. The rider seemed to have judged, probably rightly, that Christopher would not be inclined to fire, and that Eyre was the only man he had to worry himself about.

Eyre said, 'Show yourselves. Are you robbers, or what?'

The nearer rider pulled down his scarf. Eyre's suspicions had been correct. It was Mr Chatto, his face looking even more milky and translucent than ever, like a glass jug filled with cloudy water. There were sooty circles under his eyes, which was hardly surprising. He and Mr Rose must have ridden out of Adelaide a little after midnight to catch up with them here at dawn.

'You would be doing yourself a kindness, Mr Walker, if you laid down your rifle,' he called to Eyre.

Eyre said nothing, but lifted the muzzle of his rifle a little higher.

'We want Mortlock, that's all,' Mr Chatto declared. 'If you co-operate with us, and give us no trouble we will say nothing to the authorities about your own involvement in this affair. And I believe you already know that you could well be arrested for giving aid and succour to an absconded ticket-of-leave man.'

Eyre said, 'Turn your horses around, Mr Chatto, and go back to where you came from.'

'Not without Mortlock, I regret.'

'Your regret doesn't interest me in the slightest. Either you go back to Adelaide now, and tell your paymasters that you were unable to find any trace of Mr Mortlock at all; or else I will shoot first your horses and then you.'

'That, Mr Walker, would not be wise.'

'Perhaps not. But it would be wiser than letting you live.'

'That would be murder,' said Mr Rose.

Eyre shook his head. 'Whatever you believe, Mr Chatto, disinfestation is not a punishable offence. If you happen to kill a louse, or a leech, is anyone concerned about it? Killing you two would be no more criminal than ridding the mattress of Australia of two particularly unpleasant bedbugs.'

Mr Chatto's horse began to twitch, and shake its head. It could probably sense through the grip of his thighs that he was angry. But with Eyre, Chatto remained white-faced and utterly calm; although he never took his eyes away from Eyre's face, no matter which way his horse turned itself.

'Mortlock,' called Chatto, to Arthur.

'No Mortlock here, friend,' Arthur replied.

'Well, whatever you're calling yourself, step forward.'

Arthur came around the camp fire, and stood in front of Mr Chatto, quite close, with his arms folded.

'Will you give yourself up without protestation?' Mr Chatto asked, still keeping his eyes on Eyre.

'Mr Ransome is a member of this expedition,' Eyre answered firmly before Arthur could open his mouth. 'As such, he enjoys special protections and privileges, quite apart from the sponsorship of the Government of Southern Australia.'

'His name is Arthur Stanley Mortlock and he is under arrest; to be taken back to New South Wales in chains.'

Eyre cocked the hammer of his rifle; and in the misty atmosphere of the morning, it made a loud, flat click. He raised the gun and pointed it directly at Mr Chatto's head. Mr Chatto blinked slightly, and drew himself back, as if someone were waving their hand too closely in front of his face. 'You would be well advised to put that down, you know,' he told Eyre, his voice anxious and nasal.

'You, for your part, would be well advised to go back to Adelaide and forget about anyone called Mortlock,' Eyre cautioned him.

'That's impossible, I'm afraid. I have a job to do. Mr Rose has a job to do.'

'You have a count of five to turn around and start riding away,' said Eyre, in a constricted but level tone. 'Then, I will fire at you.'

Mr Chatto said, 'Killing me won't bring you anything but grief, Mr Walker.'

'You sound as if you don't mind the idea of being killed.'

'I have friends, Mr Walker. No matter what happens to me, my friends will always make sure that I am revenged. In a way, it is nearly as good as being immortal. They will tear you to pieces, Mr Walker, I assure you, and feed you raw to the dingoes. You will be dog meat, if you kill me; I warn you now.'

Eyre said, 'One.'

Mr Chatto stayed where he was, watching Eyre with that white-lantern face of his. Joolonga said, 'Mr Arthur should go, Mr Walker-sir. No good is going to come of shooting this man.'

'Two,' said Eyre.

'For goodness's sake, Eyre, think what you're doing,' put in Christopher. 'I mean, really. The poor fellow already offered to give himself up. There's going to be the very devil to pay if we open fire on these chaps.'

'Three,' said Eyre, and then, 'You, Christopher—*you* were the one who said we couldn't let the buggers have him now.'

'Yes, but I didn't think it would have to go as far as actually—'

'Four,' Eyre announced, quietly.

Mr Chatto loosened his horse's rein, and then unexpectedly swung himself out of the saddle, and in two steps was close beside Arthur, with one arm around Arthur's shoulder, as if they were the very best of friends, posing to have their picture taken.

'Now then, Mr Walker,' he called. 'Don't you think it would be foolhardy of you to shoot at me with your cousin here so close? A Baker's an accurate weapon, I'll give you that, but somewhat out-of-date. I'd hate to think what the consequences might be if you were to miss.'

'Step aside, Arthur,' Eyre instructed him, tautly.

'Ah! So you admit at last that he's Arthur!' grinned Mr Chatto. 'Well, now, that makes my task a little easier. Mr Rose, will you please take this gentleman's rifle away.'

Eyre took two or three steps back, and turned; but it was too late. Mr Rose had been shifting his horse right around behind him, and was now pointing a pistol at him from out of the folds of his riding-cape.

'The other rifle, too, Mr Willis, please,' said Mr Chatto.

Christopher hesitated, and then let the Baker fall to the ground with a clatter. Mr Rose dismounted, and came across to Eyre with his pistol now openly displayed, his hand held out for Eyre's rifle. 'There's no shame to it, sir,' he smiled, trying to be consoling. 'We're professionals, and you're an amateur. We don't expect you to be any sort of a match for us; not when it comes to tracking down beasts like our chum Mortlock here.'

'I object to you calling him a beast,' Eyre replied, coldly.

'Nonetheless, a beast he is,' said Mr Chatto. 'A beast that walks on two legs, and has the rudiments of speech. A beast that sometimes has wonderful charm; to beguile such unsuspecting people as may give him shelter and assistance. But a beast who is nothing much better than any other crawling, shambling creature of the Australian forest. A beast who thieves and kills in order to survive, and who has been condemned to Hell so thoroughly that he has no qualms about thieving and killing again. For what do you have to look forward to, Mr Mortlock, but the noose, and then the countenance of Satan?'

Arthur didn't answer. For all that he had offered to give himself up, he appeared to be stunned by his recapture. Mr Chatto said to him, 'Come here then, cully,' and led him across towards Mr Rose's horse, where there were chains and steel circlets hanging from the saddle; and as he walked across the campside, Arthur stumbled and almost lost his balance, like a Finniss Street drunk.

From the other side of the blazing fire, Joolonga and Midgegooroo and Weeip watched in respectful silence as Arthur was chained up. For South Australian Aborigines, the sight of a white man being treated as badly as a black-fellow was both frightening and fascinating. Arthur remained silent, his face set solid, his eyes already looking far beyond this misty morning to the cells in which they were going to lock him up; and the bloody wooden frames on which they would flog him; and further still to the tangled and rotting vegetation of Macquarie Harbour; and the suffocating madness of solitary confinement, and death.

Last night he had told Eyre and Christopher how the prisoners used to draw straws; one to be a 'murderer' and the other to play his 'victim'. Then, in full sight of the guards, the 'murderer' would cut his willing partner's throat, so that the guards would have no choice but to take him, and hang him. 'In that fashion, two men would get blessed relief for the effort of killing one,' Arthur had explained. 'And the rest of us would make book on who picked the straws, and at least have a little excitement to pass the day.'

He had described how a friend of his called Billy Pegler had laughed for joy as he had been slashed from one side of his neck to the other; and how he had still been laughing in bubbles of blood as he collapsed to the ground.

Eyre felt that he would almost be doing Arthur a service if he were to pick up his rifle and shoot the poor man dead before Chatto and Rose could take him back.

It took only four or five minutes for Arthur to be shackled, with circlets around his ankles, and handcuffs around his wrists, joined behind his back by a long running-chain. He stood beside Chatto's horse with his head bowed, averting his eyes from everyone around. He was an untouchable again, now that he was chained up; an old hand. He appeared to Eyre to have lost his humanity, and to have reverted to what Chatto believed him to be, a beast.

Christopher blurted out, in an agitated voice, 'Oh God, Eyre, is there nothing we can do?'

Without bitterness, Eyre said, 'You could have kept your eye on Rose, while I was warning off Chatto.'

'Eyre, I've *told* you, I'm not the kind of man who can point a rifle at anybody. and what would I have done anyway—even if I had seen him take out his pistol? Shot him, in cold blood? Killed him?'

Chatto came over and removed his hat. 'I have to take this man back to Adelaide now, Mr Walker, and thence to New South Wales, where the magistrates will decide what sentence to impose on him. Now, I would be quite within my authority if I were to require you to come back with me, too, and face charges of harbouring a convict. But as I understand it, this is Captain Sturt's expedition, and I have no desire to displease Captain Sturt. Therefore I will press the matter no further. But, if you and I should meet again, sir, under circumstances that are in any way similar; then, believe me, I will make sure that you pay the penalty for it. And that is as God is my saviour and judge.'

Eyre said, 'I should like to say a last word to Mr Mortlock, if I may.'

Chatto replaced his hat, and gave a white-lipped smile. 'Mortlock is not a "mister" now, sir; nor never will be, not again.'

'Nevertheless,' said Eyre.

Chatto stretched out a hand, to indicate to Eyre that he should do whatever he pleased.

Arthur was staring at the front fetlocks of Mr Rose's horse as if he had seen the animal dance, and did not want to miss it if it happened again, not for the world. When Eyre came up and laid a hand on his shoulder, he kept on staring; although a shudder went through his muscles like a man with a fatal chill. His shackles clanked dolefully, and Eyre could understand why men released from Botany Bay or Macquarie Harbour could never hear the sound of chain running upon chain without their teeth being set on edge.

Eyre said, softly, 'I fear that we've let you down.'

'Not your fault, Mr Walker,' Arthur replied. 'One of those things. Fate, in her winged whatsit. You did your level best, didn't you? Not your fault if Mr Willis doesn't have the necessary bottle. Not his, neither, some men are made that way. No—I was always at risk of being collared, right from the start. I should have known better than to try to make meself a respectable living. I should have known better than to get meself *born*, come to mention it.'

'As soon as we get back to Adelaide, I'll ask Captain Sturt to make representations through Government House to have you freed,' Eyre promised. 'If the expedition turns out to be a success, which I'm sure it will, then there isn't any doubt that they'll let you go. We'll be heroes.'

'Ah, heroes,' Arthur nodded. 'Well, I shouldn't bother

yourself too desperate, Mr Walker. By the time you get back, if there's anything left of you, there certainly won't be anything left of me. Not worth saving, anyhow. This time, I think that this is me lot. Called to lower service, as it were.'

He looked up at Eyre for the first time since he had been chained, and Eyre was shocked to see how drawn and grey his face had suddenly become, as if each link of each shackle had instantly aged him by another year. He could have been a man of seventy; or even older. There was the mark of pain on him already; the mark of a man who had been humbled to the ground, now facing the prospect of being humbled to the death. He knew what the prison authorities would do to him. How could he face it?

Eyre took Arthur's hand, and clasped it. In spite of the coolness of the morning, it was clammy with sweat.

'God go with you, Arthur. I shall pray for you.'

'Well, yes, sir, you might pray for me,' said Arthur. Then, through scarcely opened lips, 'But pray for yourself, besides. That Mr Chatto, he would have taken *you* today, too if he'd been able. He won't forget what you did to him yesterday morning. I know his type. He'll have you; even if he has to wait for the rest of his life.'

Eyre glanced over his shoulder at Chatto and Rose, who were standing a few yards away from the camp fire, talking to one another confidentially. Weeip had put the pot on the fire now, and the water was beginning to simmer for their morning tea. Presumably Chatto and Rose were waiting to have a cup themselves before they left for Adelaide. They had, after all, been riding since midnight at a fast trot, over the dry and dusty Adelaide Plain; and it would take them another four or five hours to get back, in the full heat of the day.

Eyre said to Arthur, 'Would you like some breakfast before you go? Some bacon, and a glass of rum?'

Arthur shrugged, and clanked his chains. 'I don't see that there's any point in it, Mr Walker, to be quite frank.

Whether I eat or not, what does that matter? I might just as well starve meself.'

'Arthur, you're going to need your strength.'

Arthur lowered his head, and then he said, 'You've been good to me, Mr Walker, that's all I can say. In twenty years you're the first man I ever met who had any time for me at all; the first man who wasn't a thief, or a convict, or a street beggar. The brewery sent for the peelers, as soon as I beat that foreman; and the peelers took me to the magistrate; and the magistrate sent me for transportation. I spoke up for meself; I told them that I was provoked. I told them that I wasn't the kind of man who broke the law heedless-like. But they sent me to Botany Bay, and from Botany Bay to Macquarie Harbour, and now they have me again, after all these years but. And out of the whole lot of them, you're the only man who helped me, and the only man who ever spoke up in my defence.'

Eyre was moved by what Arthur had said, and touched his arm. 'You're a man, Arthur, that's all; and every man is entitled to justice. That's what my father used to say.'

'Justice,' said Arthur. 'They'll kill me now. This is me lot, you wait and see.'

Weeip had made tea for Chatto and Rose, although he seemed disinclined to cook them any Scotch pancakes. Eyre went over to the fire, and said, 'Weeip—feed these gentlemen as they require. And make some pancakes for Mr Mortlock.'

'Yes, Mr Wahkasah,' said Weeip, and laid a flat iron sheet on top of the fire so that he could begin to cook their breakfast.

Chatto said to Eyre, as he drank his tea, and bit into his batter pancake, 'You surprise me, Mr Walker. You're not the man I thought you to be not when I first met you.'

'Oh?' Eyre asked him.

'You're more romantic; less practical. I don't know what you're doing on this expedition. I had imagined you to be harder; but you're not. You should sitffen up, you know,

Mr Walker, if you intend to survive what you have ahead of you.'

The sun was beginning to penetrate the mist, and the camp glowed with a supernatural light, yellow-silvery but still quite cold.

Eyre said, 'I have plenty of determination, if that's what you're talking about.'

'Hm,' said Chatto, wiping butter away from his mouth with a crumpled, blood-stained handkerchief. 'That's as may be. But determination and stamina, well, they're not the same thing. Never have been. To *think* you can do something; and to be *able* to do it—they're poles apart. I've found that out for myself.'

Eyre said to him, 'Where were you born, Mr Chatto?'

Chatto looked at him with suspicion. 'Is it anything to you, Mr Walker?'

Eyre shrugged. 'Not much.'

'Well,' said Chatto, 'I was born in Sydney, of exclusive stock.'

'Not an emancipist, then?'

Chatto said, with undisguised dislike, 'They should have kept them away. Not just by manners, but by law. Given them farms of their own, right out in the bush; anywhere to keep them separate from decent folk.'

'Are you trying to explain something to me?' asked Eyre.

'Explain something? What do you mean?'

'I don't know. You appear to be so angry.'

'Wouldn't *you* be angry, if your sister had been attacked and killed by convicts?'

For almost a minute, neither of them said anything. The fire popped and crackled, and Weeip turned over his Scotch pancakes, and the sun at last was bright enough to cast shadows across the ground; the pale, complicated shadows of pack-horses, and tents, and eight men, in various postures of fear and resignation. The shadow of Rose's rifle, too, as he kept Arthur casually covered.

Chatto said, 'My sister Audrey was caught one day in a side-alley off George Street. They assaulted her and strangled her and left her for dead. I was a clerk, Mr Walker, just like you; why do you think I decided to take up bounty-hunting? For Audrey's sake, God bless her, that's why I do it. To give her the satisfaction, as she sits there in Heaven Above, of knowing that every convict who escapes from New South Wales is always at risk. I became a bounty-hunter so that Audrey would smile, that's why. My dear and delicate Audrey. She has had her revenge, you know; but she will have more. She will have every convict who ever tried to escape his punishment. Every absconder; every ticket-of-leave man.'

He cracked his knuckles, one after the other; and then turned to Arthur, and said, 'Have you breakfasted? Mortlock?'

Eyre reached out and caught Chatto's sleeve. 'Mr Chatto, I appeal to you. Let this man go free. Tell them you found him dead. He can give you his rings to prove it.'

'Audrey begged for mercy,' said Chatto, sourly.

'What do you mean?' asked Eyre. 'How do you know?'

'I know because she was still begging for mercy when they found her; and she was still begging for mercy when I saw her in the hospital. She begged for mercy until she was dead, and that's the whole of it.'

Eyre said, 'Your own personal pain is no reason for taking this man back to Botany Bay. You know as well as I do that he will die there. At least give him this one chance to get away. He is doing nothing more heinous than helping us to track, and to put up tents, and to dig for water, when we need to.'

Chatto stared at Eyre with a face as grey as the front page of the *Southern Australian*.

'There is no question of it, Mr Walker.'

He raised his scarf over his face, and reached behind him to tighten the knot. And it was while he was standing in this position, with his elbows raised, that Eyre heard a sharp, vicious crack, off to his right; and saw Chatto's head blown noisily in half, right in front of his eyes,

236

leaving nothing but one wildly staring eye, and a skull like a bloody soup-bowl. Chatto made no sound at all, but pitched backwards on to the dust, his arms still raised. Blood was sprayed for ten yards across the camp-site, in blobs and squiggles and exclamation marks.

Rose, alarmed, raised his rifle. But almost immediately there was another crack, and he cried, '*Ooff!*' and dropped backwards as if somebody has struck him in the chest with a ten-pound hammer. His right hand fell into the fire, and for a few moments it twitched and jumped like a redback spider.

Arthur said, 'Heads down!' and cautiously, bewildered, one by one, they sank on to their knees, and looked around with anxious faces to see who had been shooting at them. But whoever it was, he didn't seem to be intending to shoot any more; because a silence fell over the scrub; and there was no movement from any direction.

Christopher said, 'Dead as mutton, both of them.'

Eyre looked back at Chatto's awkwardly tangled body. 'Whoever he is, he's a marksman. And he has a heavy rifle, too.'

'Bush-rangers, do you think?' asked Christopher. 'There's a lot of expensive tools and supplies on those horses; not to mention the food and the water.'

Eyre lifted his head a little, and strained his eyes in the direction from which he thought the two shots had come. 'I don't know. It seems odd that he should shoot only Chatto and Rose, and leave the rest of us unharmed.'

Just then, as if he had materialised out of a sudden whirl of wind-blown dust, a man appeared, walking towards them, only about two hundred yards away. He wore a dusty bush hat, and a worn blue shirt, and brown leather boots. He whistled as he came, and as he did so, a horse suddenly rose up from behind the bushes, where it must have been lying down on its side. Christopher looked at Eyre and made a face.

Even before he could see the man clearly, Eyre knew who it was. He stood up, and waited for him with his arms folded, the wind blowing through his hair. Hesitantly, Christopher stood up, too; and Joolonga and Midgegooroo and Weeip came out from behind the packs of supplies. Joolonga said something to Midgegooroo, and the Aborigine mute dragged Rose's body away from the fire. The smell of charring flesh was beginning to grow unpleasantly strong, and Rose's hand had already been reduced to a small blackened claw.

The man whistled to his horse again, and the horse trotted over so that he could take its reins. Then he walked up to Eyre, and slung his rifle on to his back, and held out his hand.

'Hallo, Dogger,' said Eyre.

'Hallo yourself.'

Dogger looked down at Chatto and Rose, and then lifted an eyebrow. 'Not bad shooting, what do you think? Must have been all of three hundred yards.'

'You realise you've murdered them,' said Eyre.

Dogger smiled. 'I've brought along some brandy. It's French, none of your home-made hotch. Mr Abbott gave it to me, at the Queen's Head. What you might call a going-away present.'

'Dogger, this is no joke,' Eyre protested. 'These two men had papers from the Governor of New South Wales, not to mention the full authority of Colonel Gawler. If they don't come back, then the troopers are going to come looking for them. And they'll find them, too, if they have trackers as good as Joolonga.'

Christopher stood with his hands on his hips, staring at Eyre and Dogger in despair. 'What on *earth* made you shoot them?' he asked, almost petulantly. 'You could have come up behind them and made them lay down their weapons. You could have—well, I don't know, you could have hit them on the head, couldn't you? Good God, man, now we'll be wanted for murder, as well as aiding and abetting an escaped convict.'

'Old hand, I'd prefer, if you don't mind, Mr Willis,' said Arthur.

'Well, whatever you like,' Christopher replied. 'But what you call yourself doesn't mean much, not when it comes to the law. You can call hanging a judicial termination of life by means of glottal suspension from entwined hemp; but that doesn't make it any less unpleasant. I saw Michael Magee hung. That was two years ago—the first man they ever hung in South Australia, and believe me I never want to see another. He was choking and gurgling and crying out, and the hangman was swinging from his legs to try and finish him off. I don't want to see that happen again, and I very particularly don't want it to happen to me.'

Joolonga came forward, chewing a large wodge of tobacco. 'Excuse me, Mr Walker-sir, I think we can hide this killing.'

'Hide it?' asked Eyre. 'What do you mean?'

'We can cut the bodies, Mr Walker-sir, so that it will look as if they have been killed by tribesmen. Some bad Murray River blackfellows passed this way not long ago, causing some damage. The troopers will believe it was them.'

Dogger lifted his rifle off his shoulder, and propped it carefully up against one of their supply packs. 'He's right, you know. That's the best way to do it. I was going to suggest it myself, as a matter of fact.'

'Nonetheless,' said Eyre caustically, 'the fact remains that you killed them.'

Dogger sniffed, and walked around his horse to find his bottle of brandy. '*You* would have shot them, too, if you'd had the chance. It's a question of staying alive, that's all. And if you have to kill the other bastard to protect your own life; well, that's what you do. There isn't any room for fellows with too much religion; not beyond the black stump.'

He found the bottle, and pulled the cork out with his teeth. 'You can call on the Lord Almighty as often as you wish when you're out here, all alone; and there are plenty of times when you get the feeling that the Lord Almighty is listening to you. Even answering back, bless Him. But when you're out of water and out of luck, then there's only you. You and you and you alone; and sometimes not even a shadow to talk to.'

Eyre rubbed his eyes. The grey sand-flies were already swarming over Chatto's broken skull, and crawling like a living grey waistcoat over Rose's chest.

'All right,' Eyre said to Joolonga. 'Do what you have to.'

Nineteen

They saw the last of the ocean at Kurdnatta, on the third day out from Adelaide. They stopped to rest there at midday, under an extraordinary dark sky the colour of dark-grey mussel shells. Weeip and Midgegooroo went down to the beach to collect Goolwa cockles from the rocks; which they baked in a charcoal pit in the sand. The wind from the Gulf of St Vincent whipped the charcoal smoke through the grassy dunes, and blew a stray cinder into Weeip's eye.

Eyre sat back on a blanket staring out to sea. The waves sparkled in the sunlight like a dazzling treasure-chest filled with shining coins; and against their dazzle the naked figures of Weeip and Midgegooroo darkly danced, gathering treasure of their own. Flocks of muttonbirds, which had just begun to migrate fom the north in large numbers, fluttered and wheeled in the sky. Weeip kept his eyes open for exhausted birds which had fallen into the sea, and might be washed ashore.

Joolonga was silently sitting a few yards away on a sand-dune, his midshipman's hat perched on his head. He seemed to have been in an oddly subdued and uncommunicative mood since Chatto and Rose had been shot. He had cut off the remains of Chatto's head with a sharpened stone knife, and slashed Rose's plump white chest into bloodless ribbons, so that it would be impossible for anyone to tell that he had been hit by a rifle ball. Then he had broken the bones of both bodies with a wooden club, and burned them. The fire had still been blazing fiercely when they rode out of camp; and as they had ridden northwards the oily black smoke that had risen from it had reminded them for miles and miles of what they had done.

It was only when Arthur had begun to sing,

'The miller, the dusty old miller
He carries his flour in a sack. . .'

one of his ribald songs from the East End markets, that the mood of the expedition had begun to lighten. Only Joolonga had remained silent.

'You shouldn't talk to a blackfellow if he's sulking,' Dogger had advised Eyre. 'He's probably thinking about one of his legends; some story from the dreamtime. What he had to do back there, burning those bodies, he probably thinks it was all told in a legend, hundreds and hundreds of years ago; and that he's going to have to pay for it, somehow. But don't worry. He'll get over it.'

Weeip, who had been listening, said, 'Joolonga believes that Wulgaru the devil-devil will chase him, because he cut off Mr Chatto's head.'

It had been accepted without any discussion between them that Dogger was to join them. After all, Dogger was an experienced bushman, and he had convincingly proved himself to be an excellent shot. He had also come supplied with all his own provisions. That was what he had been doing away from home on those last few evenings before Eyre and his companions had set off: preparing his packs and his food and choosing a horse.

'Right up until the last minute, I was still in two minds whether I ought to come with you or not,' he had explained over last night's camp-fire. 'But then I heard

241

Constance at the front door, talking to those bounty-hunter fellows. She was telling them that Arthur had been staying with us; and that he was about to leave on your expedition with you; and that if they wanted to catch him they should beetle around to Government House just about as fast as those spindly legs of theirs could carry them.'

'It was *Constance* who told Chatto and Rose where to find us?' Eyre had asked him, in astonishment.

'Why are you so surprised?' Dogger answered him, laconically. 'You know darn well that she didn't want you to go. She was always so afeared that you'd be killed by blackfellows, or bitten by a death adder, or that you'd run out of water and end up wearing nothing but your bones. She sent a boy to fetch Mr Chatto about ten minutes after you'd left the house. She told him she had some private information regarding Mr Mortlock here, but that she would only divulge it if the magistrate could be persuaded to keep you under a year's house arrest, for conspiracy, or whatnot. Anything to stop you going. She thought I wasn't around when she was a-talking to those fellows, but there I was up on the landing, and I'm like our friend Joolonga here. I was trained by practical experience. I can hear a bandicoot break wind from half-a-mile away; and I can certainly hear what Constance is a-whispering-of, even when she's out in the yard.'

'Well, I'm shocked,' Eyre had told him.

'Hm, no point in being shocked. A woman will do anything at all if she wants you serious enough.'

'You had every intention of coming along on this expedition right from the start, didn't you?' Eyre had asked. 'All that Constance gave you was a convenient excuse.'

'Constance is a convenient excuse in her own right, my friend,' Dogger had grinned. 'Is she a woman or is she a Yara-ma-yha-who?'

Weeip had giggled. Christopher had asked, with obvious impatience, 'What on earth is a Yara-ma-yha-who?'

Dogger's weatherbeaten face had crinkled up like a dry wash-leather. 'A Yara-ma-yha-who is a creature with such a big mouth that it can swallow a man up whole.' He had slapped his leg, and cackled out loud, and then he had said, 'That could call for a drink, couldn't it? What do you say?'

On the beach at Kurdnatta, among the drifting sands, they ate a meal of roasted muttonbird, baked cockles, which Weeip called '*pipi*', biscuits, and dried dates. Then they drank a little tea, and gathered up their supplies in preparation for their first strike inland.

Just before they mounted up again, Arthur came over to Eyre and said, 'Supposing they send the troopers after us?'

'Well,' said Eyre. 'Supposing they do?'

'You wouldn't want more killing, would you?'

'Not if I could possibly avoid it.'

'But you wouldn't let them take me?'

Eyre shaded his eyes so that he could see Arthur more clearly. The wind whistled through the spinifex grass, and blew the mane of Eyre's horse so that it stung his hand.

'I suppose I shouldn't have asked,' said Arthur, thrusting his hands into his pockets.

'No,' said Eyre. 'We have nature to contend with, just at this particular moment. Let's concern ourselves with troopers when we have to, but not before.'

Dogger was watching them, from a short distance away. With his long-barrelled rifle on his back, and his wide-brimmed hat tugged well down over his eyes, he looked like the archetypal Australian bushman. Eyre thought to himself that one day there would be a statue erected to men like him; and it would look exactly as Dogger did now, in bronze.

They rode slowly northwards under a high sun. There was no sound but the wind and the surf and the jingling of bridles. After a mile or so, Eyre turned in his saddle and listened and realised that he couldn't hear the surf any longer. Ahead of them lay miles and miles of yellow grassy plain, dotted with saltbush and scrub, and far off to their right the first pink peaks of the Flinders mountains, mysteriously rising in the endless sea of the plains like enchanted and inaccessible islands.

In the distance, scores of big red kangaroos flew through the grass; sending up sudden bursts of pipits. There could have been more than a hundred of them.

Dogger drew his horse close up to Eyre's, and pointed towards the Flinders. 'Those are the mountains I was telling you about. There, you can see them for yourself now. That's where the Aborigines go for their ochre. It's sacred, as far as they're concerned. Magic. They dig it up, and then they mix it with water; or sometimes with emu fat; and they use orchid juice to stop it from running.'

He rambled on, occasionally taking a swig from his bottle of French brandy, telling Eyre about the day that he had ridden into the Flinders and seen a thousand emus gathered together at once. 'I watched them for hours. I thought perhaps the end of the world had come. The strangest sight I ever saw.'

Eyre said, 'What will Constance say, when she finds that you've gone?'

Dogger sniffed. 'Ah, she won't mind. Well, she may. But what can she do about it? Besides, I was beginning to get suffocated, back there in Adelaide. It was like having a pillow pressed over my face. Too cosy and too polite for my liking.'

He was silent for a while. Then he said, 'Besides, she never loved me. She never believed that I was good enough.'

'That's not what she told me.'

'You? You're her darling. As far as Constance is concerned, you're the best thing that happened to her since her cousin Ada drowned in a vat of maroon dye and left her fifty pounds.' He sneezed, and added, 'I'm not blind, you know, Eyre; and I'm not deaf, either, although I'm sometimes drunk. A man knows what goes on inside his own house.'

Eyre looked at him cautiously, uncertain if he ought to say anything or not. He decided that it was probably wiser to keep quiet. Whatever Dogger's suspicions about him and Constance, his desire to come north on this expedition had plainly outweighed any husbandly outrage he might be feeling. He seemed more contented now than Eyre could ever remember him; sitting easily in his saddle, his eyes narrowed towards the horizon with an expression of deep and happy hunger, as if he could devour the distance just by staring at it.

Gradually, the sun began to sink on their left, and their shadows began to lean to their right. The Flinders Ranges, pink during the hottest part of the day, now began to glow a curious iridescent mauve. Eyre could see clumps of native pines on the foothills, and white, contorted gums. The ground itself wriggled with dry creekbeds and eroded gullies, most of which were bushy with bright lime-green acacia. More kangaroos fled across the plain like frightened waiters.

The grass began to give way to mallee scrub and clumps of sharp spinifex. Joolonga urged his horse a little way forward to catch up with Eyre and Christopher, and said, 'We should make camp soon, Mr Walker-sir. We have ridden far today. Tomorrow the land will become more difficult.'

'Another half-an-hour,' said Eyre. 'The horses seem still quite fresh.'

Christopher said, 'The *horses* may still be quite fresh, but *I'm* absolutely exhausted. I feel as if my backside has grown to twenty times its usual size.'

'In half-an-hour we can make four miles,' Eyre told him. 'That will be four miles fewer to ride tomorrow.'

Arthur put in, 'That's four miles further away from Jack Ketch, as far as I reckon it.'

They stopped at last. The plain was dark and warm; although the sky was still luminous and light, and prickled all over with stars. The horses shuffled and scraped their hoofs; and Weeip knelt on the ground, busying himself

245

with a firestick. Christopher had several times offered him lucifer-matches, but he had only stared at him mistrustfully, and shaken his curly head.

Eyre and Christopher walked around the campsite to stretch their legs. Eyre had sores on the insides of his thighs now, and his penis had become tender from grit which had lodged under the foreskin. There was a dryness in his mouth and throat quite unlike any dryness he had experienced before; he felt as if his tongue had turned to rough, brushed-up suede, and his sinuses had shrunk and shrivelled like cured tobacco-leaves. When he blew his nose now, his sinuses produced no phlegm. There didn't even seem to be any moisture between his eyeballs and his eyelids; and his eyes, like those of the rest of the party, were crimson from dust and glare.

'Somewhere out there is the man they call Yonguldye,' said Eyre reflectively, 'I wonder where he is tonight? I wonder if he's sensed that we're looking for him? They say that a Mabarn Man can feel you coming from twenty miles away.' Christopher slowly untied his scarf, with one hand, and then dragged it away from his dusty neck. 'I can't imagine how we're going to find him. One man, in country like this. It goes on for ever.'

Eyre was about to turn back to the fire when a slight movement in the darkness caught his eye. He gripped Christopher's wrist, and said, 'Ssh; there's something there.'

'As long as it's not a bunyip, or Wulgaru the devil-devil,' Christopher whispered; but all the same he stood still, and listened.

The fire crackled. Arthur was talking to Joolonga in an intensive murmur, something about 'I'll lay you odds. Well, I will. I'll lay you fifty-to-one.'

Christopher frowned. 'It's nothing. Come on, you're just tired. Probably nothing more frightening than a mallee fowl, raking a bit of extra soil on to its eggs. Got to keep the babies warm at night, after all.'

He strolled back to the fire, and asked Weeip, 'What's on the menu tonight, young man? I'm famished.'

'Me too,' said Arthur. 'I could eat a bloody horse.'

Dogger spat into the fire. 'Don't make jokes about it,' he said. 'One day you may have to.'

'Well, that's charm itself,' Arthur retorted. 'Gobbing in the fire like that. Good luck for you there wasn't no pot on it.'

'What are you, the Governor's chief advisor on campfire etiquette?' Dogger demanded.

'Oh, for God's sake stop arguing,' Christopher complained.

'Well, damn it, here's a man who's been flogged, and locked up in jail and here he is trying to teach me manners,' Dogger protested.

'My old mother taught me my manners, not the government of New South Wales,' Arthur shouted back at him. 'And you wouldn't catch my old mother gobbing in the fire. You wouldn't catch none of my family gobbing in the fire. My Uncle Joe fell in the fire once, and burned half of his ear off, but he never gobbed in it, not once.'

'What would you prefer?' Dogger snapped at him. 'Would you prefer me to throw *my* ear in the fire? Would that be polite enough for you? For Christ's pity, years in those prison made you soft in the head.'

Eyre said, 'Quiet,' and then, when the two of them continued to argue, he barked, '*Quiet!*'

They stopped bickering; and for one hallucinatory second, Eyre glimpsed four skeletons running through the scrub. He could hear nothing: no sound of feet running on hard-baked dust. No rustling of spinifex grass. Not even the soft clattering of spear-shafts. But he knew they were out there, daubed in their white pipe-clay bones; their faces reddened with the sacred ochre.

'Joolonga,' he called, quietly.

'Yes, Mr Walker-sir?'

Joolonga came up and stood beside him. He smelled strongly of fat and sweat and stale lavender-water.

247

'Joolonga, is anybody following us?'

Joolonga stared at him. The campfire was reflected in his eyes, two dancing orange sparks.

Eyre said, 'Are any blackfellows tracking us? Blackfellows painted like bone men?'

Joolonga looked out into the night. It was much darker now already, and the last luminosity was fading in the west, ushering in, for this day at least, the black wing of Narahdarn, the messenger of death. 'This is a *kybybolite*, nothing more,' he told Eyre, in a soft, hoarse voice. 'A place of ghosts, and unhappy spirits.'

'Twaddle,' snapped Eyre.

'No, Mr Walker-sir,' said Joolonga, calmly. 'There are men like ghosts; just as there are ghosts like men.'

'What are you talking about?'

'Yonguldye already knows that you are seeking him out, Mr Walker-sir. The bone-men you have seen are Yonguldye's messengers, the ghosts from Yonguldye's camp.'

'If they know where Yonguldye is, why don't they guide me to him?'

Joolonga shrugged, and took out his pipe. 'This journey means more than you understand, Mr Walker-sir. What you have decided to do has deep meaning both for your own people and also for the Aborigine. Both peoples see this journey with hope; both peoples see it with fear. Captain Sturt wants to find his inland sea, and his precious stones in the ground; but he is worried that the respect you will give to Aborigine magic may make it more difficult for him to take all of the land and the riches that he wants. Yonguldye is pleased that a white man is recognising the ancient beliefs from the dreamtime; but he also fears the other white men who will come after you. That is why his ghosts are following you. But, neither people can prevent this coming-together. It is something that *must* happen. It was prophesied in the dreamtime, and the story of it was written in the caves at Koonalda, in the desert called Bunda Bunda.'

Eyre felt as if the ground had shifted under his feet. Off-balance, perplexed, as if Joolonga's words had possessed the power to create a supernatural earth-tremor. The more he talked to Joolonga, the more unsure of himself he became; and the more he began to feel that as they journeyed forward into the interior, the further they were leaving behind them not just civilisation but time itself. Joolonga spoke like no Aborigine he had ever met before. It was not simply his wide European vocabulary that impressed Eyre: it was his ability to express Aboriginal ideas in white man's language, to make his own people understandable.

He had an inner perception, a clarity of thought, which even to Eyre was unexpected and disturbing. Eyre had never believed what most white settlers believed: that the Aborigines were idle, ignorant, savages; dirty and destructive; not even reliable enough to keep as servants. He had always seen magic in them, and understood something of their significance. But Joolonga was very different, and with each day they travelled deeper into tracklessness and timelessness, the difference became more apparent. It was like looking into the face of a wild animal, and suddenly realising that its eyes were knowing and human.

Joolonga said, 'Have you seen the bone-man before?'

Eyre nodded.

'Did they give you any signs? Any hand-signs? Or perhaps a bone?'

Eyre unbuttoned his shirt pocket and took out the stone talisman which the Aborigine warriors had given him on Hindley Street. He passed it to Joolonga, who made a protective sign with his hand before he touched it, rather like the sign of the cross. Then he examined it carefully, turning it over and over in his fingers.

'It is a magical stone,' he said at last. 'These marks on it show that it belongs to Yonguldye, the one they call the Darkness. The stone has the power to draw you towards its owner, It is quite like the *Kurdaitja* shoes, only it works the other way.'

Just then, Dogger came up, with his hands in his pockets. 'What's this, a Methodist prayer evening?'

'Not quite,' smiled Eyre.

'Well, tuck's ready when you are,' said Dogger. He caught sight of the stone which Joolonga was turning over in his hand. 'What's that, a *tjurunga*? Let's take a look.'

Without comment, Joolonga obediently handed the stone to Dogger, although he kept his attention fixed on Eyre. Dogger joggled the stone up and down in the palm of his hand, and then said, 'You know what this is, don't you? You know where it came from?'

Eyre shook his head.

'It's a shooting-star, or a piece of one. You can find them at the Yarrakina ochre mine, up at the place the blackfellows call Parakeelya. They think the stones were once the eyes of emus, back in the dreamtime, and that they give you power over all birds.'

Eyre looked at Joolonga. 'Didn't *you* know what it was?'

Joolonga's eyes were glittery but uncommunicative. 'I have never been to Yarrakina, Mr Walker-sir. I have never been further north than Edeowie.'

'But surely you've seen one of these stones before?'

Joolonga said nothing.

Eyre said, 'If this stone came from Yonguldye, then it seems likely that he must have been camped near Yarrakina. Perhaps he even sent it on purpose, to guide us.'

'Well, it's quite likely,' Dogger sniffed. 'The blackfellows travel from hundreds of miles away to dig out the ochre at Yarrakina. It's supposed to be first-class magic; the best ochre you can get.'

Eyre took the stone back, and dropped it into his pocket. 'How far is Yarrakina?'

'Couldn't tell you exactly,' Dogger admitted. 'I only went that far north because I was hunting emu.'

'You came all the way out here to hunt emu?'

'Well, I was a younger man then,' Dogger told them. He hesitated, and looked embarrassed, and then he said,

250

'Also, some sheep-farmer over at Quorn had told me that some emus have diamonds in their crops.'

'Diamonds?' asked Eyre, incredulously.

'That's what he said. He said he had met a bushman once who had shot an emu; and then, when he had cut it open, he had found a diamond inside it, a diamond as big as an egg. Well, a chicken's egg, not an emu's egg. And apparently the bushman had shot six more emu, and one of *those* had had a diamond in it, too. So he had ended up shooting two hundred of them, and making himself a fortune.'

'You really believed that story?' Eyre ribbed him.

Dogger scratched the criss-cross, weather-beaten skin on the back of his neck. 'Yes. I suppose I did. But who was to say it wasn't true? And when you've spent your whole life out beyond the black stump, well, you get to believe almost anything. But that's why I went up to Yarrakina. A blackfellow told me that there were thousands of emus there; he'd seen them whenever he went to mine for ochre. Only one thing, though: he warned me it was sacred ground there, especially around the ochre mine, and that if I didn't make sure I walked backwards, the monster Mondong would jump up and get me, and eat me up. They're very frightened of those ochre mines, the blackfellows. If you haven't been initiated, they won't let you anywhere near them.'

Joolonga said, 'That is simply because the ochre was left in the rock by our ancestral spirits.' His voice was flat and expressionless; neither mocking nor reverent.

Eyre looked towards the fire. 'You did say that Yonguldye had been heard of at Woocalla. Don't you think it would be better to go there first?'

'Of course, Mr Walker-sir. But my information was not new; and it is more likely that Yonguldye has moved on to Yarrakina; or perhaps beyond Yarrakina.'

'Nevertheless, it would be foolish of us to go past Woocalla; only to have to go back again.'

Dogger interrupted, 'Let's have something to eat. My belly feels like a *paringa*.'

Weeip giggled. *Paringa* meant whirlpool; and Dogger had already amused Weeip and Midgegooroo with his gurgling stomach. He seemed to Eyre to have an infinite capacity for food and drink which he shared with the Aborigines. Down at the beach, Weeip had eaten so many cockles that his stomach had protruded like a medicine ball; and Dogger had devoured almost as many—pushing twenty or thirty into his mouth at one go, and then swilling them down with tepid tea. Even Arthur had been revolted, and that was probably why he had complained to Dogger tonight about spitting in the fire.

They sat around and ate a meal of cockle broth, and four roasted mallee fowl. Weeip had kept the cockles fresh on their slow, hot ride north from the ocean by filling two sacks with damp sand, and then pushing handfuls of shellfish deep into the middle of them. The dampness had been sufficient to keep the cockles alive. Weeip said that his father used to bury hundreds of freshwater mussels in this way; and that he had been able to return to his larder months later to find them still fresh. Eyre found this fascinating; because he had heard that apart from smoking turtle meat for long canoe journeys, and sealing up wild figs in large balls of ochre, and leaving them in trees, Aborigines had almost no way of storing food at all.

After they had eaten, Joolonga went with Midgegooroo to prepare the horses and their packs for the next day's journey. Weeip, while he scoured their tin plates with handfuls of grass, and built up the fire to last them through the night, sang Aborigine songs in a clear, high-pitched voice.

Wyah, wyah, deereeree
Tree-runner made a rainbow for the woman he loved
Together they walked in the sky
On the road of many colours.
Wyah, wyah, deereeree.'

It occurred to Eyre as he listened that this was the first

252

Aborigine song that he had heard Weeip sing. He twisted himself around so that he could see the boy better. Against the firelight, naked and skinny, except for his protuberant stomach, his hair bound tight now with kangaroo skin thongs, he looked quite different from the boy who had recited the Lord's Prayer in Adelaide. Savage, wild, with that extraordinary prehistoric sexuality.

Arthur said, 'Gives me the creeps, hearing them blackfellows sing.'

Dogger sniffed. 'It's not their singing I object to. It's when they start screaming for blood. I saw an old mate of mine killed in front of my eyes once, because he struck a lucifer match on some sacred rock, without even knowing what it was. The chief came up and my old mate said, "how d'ye do," and the next thing I knew it was wallop right over the head with a war club. And the scream that went up, from all the rest of the blackfellows there. I ran a straight mile and I didn't stop. That was in Whyalla not more than five years ago. You wouldn't believe it, would you? Just for striking a match.'

They drank tea for a while and listened to Weeip singing more chants. Eventually, Arthur threw away his slops into the darkness, and wiped his mouth with the back of his hand.

'I suppose we *are* going to come out of this alive?' he said, in a noticeably off-key voice.

Eyre looked at him in surprise. Even Christopher lifted his head from the book he had been reading.

'What makes you think that we won't?' asked Christopher. 'I mean, why shouldn't we? It's all gone rather well up until now.'

'I dunno,' said Arthur. Then, 'I had a nightmare, last night that's all.'

'Describe it,' Eyre encouraged him.

'Well, there's not much to describe, really. I just dreamed I was drowning, but I wasn't drowning at all, because it was too dry. It was like being in that what-do-you-call-it, quicksand. And all the time I could feel that

253

something was pressing on me chest, so that I couldn't scarcely breathe.'

'I expect Midgegooroo came and sat on you in the night, thinking you were a sofa,' Christopher teased him.

'Well, you can laugh,' said Arthur. 'But I woke up in a muck sweat, and I was shaking like a horse with the blind staggers. Almost as bad as when I was in solitary.'

'You went through a terrible time in prison,' Eyre remarked. 'It isn't surprising that you have dreams about it. I'm surprised you stood up to it so well. Many men would have gone mad.'

'And did, Mr Walker. And did.'

A little after midnight, they rolled themselves up in their blankets around the fire, and tried to sleep. But although he was exhausted from the day's travelling, Eyre found it impossible to close his eyes. A dusty northerly wind had got up, uncomfortably warm; and it whistled in the spinifex grass. Fed by the wind, the fire glowed brighter, and its flames made breathy, feathery noises. Sparks flew across the scrubland, and were swallowed in the darkness. Eyre drew his blanket more tightly around him, and stared up at the stars.

He thought of Charlotte, and as if the ancient plains all around him were resonant with spiritual forces, he found that he could picture her with startling clarity, with those pretty blonde curls of hers blowing in another wind far away, and her eyes wide with affection. He could almost hear her speaking, and at times he was unsure if he could make out the words, 'Eyre . . . Eyre. . .' or if it was nothing more than the funnelling voice of the fire.

He wondered if he would ever see her again—if he would ever *live* to see her again. Would it really make any difference if he returned to Adelaide as a celebrated explorer? Would Lathrop Lindsay really take him by the hand and forgive him for everything—the secret courtship, the battered greyhound, and the apple trifle? Would she still love him, or would she have found herself another smart young suitor, a visiting baron from England or a wealthy stock-farmer from New South Wales?

Lying in the night, he felt painfully lonely for her; and he thought of the times they had walked out together, hand-in-hand, laughing, while Yanluga had sat on the carriage and whistled and waited for them. He thought of her body, too, of her full bare white breasts, and her slender waist, and of her vulva opening up for him like a sticky flower.

Supposing Lathrop forbade him to see her ever again, no matter what he had done? Supposing he died in the 'Ghastly Blank', like one of those boatloads of 'skellingtons' that the red-haired matelot had described to him. Supposing he were buried somewhere out in this wilderness in an unmarked grave, and Charlotte never even came to find out where he had died?

He slept for a few minutes, and then woke up again. He began to feel that the clock had deceived him; that an unseen corps of time- and scenery-shifters had been hustling around him while he slept; and that when he woke up the following morning he would find himself somewhere completely different.

From quite close by, Joolonga suddenly whispered, 'Are you all right, Mr Walker-sir?'

'Yes, thank you,' Eyre told him, quietly. 'I was just thinking, that's all.'

'This is not a place to think, Mr Walker-sir,' said Joolonga. 'There are too many ghosts and memories of ghosts, all waiting to rush inside your head. Remember what I told you; this place is a *kybybolite*.'

This time, Eyre didn't answer; but lay where he was; listening to the wind and the furtive noises of the night.

Twenty

In the morning, Arthur was hideously and spectacularly sick. He had only just climbed out of his bedroll, and stretched himself, when he jacknifed forward and clutched at his stomach.

Eyre said, 'Arthur? Are you all right? *Arthur!*'

Arthur did nothing but shake his head; and then suddenly brought up a splattering stream of dark brown bile and half-digested food. He retched again and again, and the fourth or fifth time he retched he brought up blood. He collapsed on to his knees, his face white and shiny with sweat.

Christopher exclaimed, 'For God's sake! What's the matter, Arthur? Arthur, are you all right?'

Midgegooroo hurried over to Arthur, and tried to lift him up, But Arthur was too bulky for him, and pitched sideways on to the dust and lay there shuddering and groaning.

Eyre knelt down beside Arthur and unbuttoned his shirt. 'Christopher!' he called. 'Fetch me a damp cloth, will you? Now then, Arthur, what's come over you? Do you think it's something you've been eating?'

'Perhaps it was the cockles,' suggested Christopher. 'There *are* people who come over all peculiar when they eat shellfish. My uncle Randolph only had to *look* at a whelk.'

'Arthur, do you think it was the cockles?' asked Eyre. But Arthur simply stared at him through pale misted eyes, and trembled, and said nothing.

'Well, whatever it is, he seems to have it rather badly,' said Christopher.

'Weeip, get me my medicine-chest,' said Eyre. 'Midgegooroo, bring me some water.'

Weeip ran over to the makeshift shelter in which they had stacked their packs, and began to search for the medicine-chest. Meanwhile Midgegooroo came over with a leather bottle of water.

Joolonga knelt down in the dust beside Eyre, and examined Arthur closely. He peeled back Arthur's eyelid with his black fingers, and looked at the jerking, twitching eyeball as dispassionately as if he were inspecting a freshly opened oyster.

'Do you think we ought to give him any water, Mr Walker-sir?' he asked blandly.

'What do you mean?' Eyre asked him. 'He's feverish; he's been vomiting. He's going to need water, especially in this heat. And especially if he's eaten something that's poisoned.'

'Hm,' said Joolonga.

'What do you mean, "hm"?' Eyre demanded. 'Do you know something about this that I don't?'

'I know simply that fresh water is scarce, and that the next water-hole is many miles from here, especially if we go to Woocalla.'

'So?'

'So, it is wiser not to waste it on a man who will soon be dead.'

Eyre said fiercely, 'He has an upset stomach. It can't be unusual, especially when you're living off any bird or fish or animal you happen to come across. Would *you* like to be deprived of water, just because you had an upset stomach?'

'This man will die,' said Joolonga, baldly.

'You're a doctor, I suppose, as well as a constable?'

'I know the bush, Mr Walker-sir. I have seen hundreds of men die here. This man has the mark of death on him, and that is all I can say to you.'

Eyre beckoned sharply to Midgegooroo, who had been standing watching them in perplexity. Midgegooroo gave him the water-bottle, and Eyre opened it and touched it to Arthur's greyish lips. A trickle of water slid across his mouth and dribbled into the white stubble of his beard.

'He has the mark of death, Mr Walker-sir,' Joolonga repeated.

'All right, then, he has the mark of death,' Eyre retorted. 'But what's wrong with him? Why is he sick? All the rest of us are quite healthy. And if it had been the cockles, why wasn't he sick yesterday?'

'Perhaps the ghost-men pointed the bone at him, Mr Walker-sir,' suggested Joolonga.

'Pointed the bone at him? What kind of nonsense is that?'

Joolonga stood up. He was wearing his gilt-buttoned overcoat this morning, but no britches, and he had strapped his penis and testicles up against his belly in an elaborate cat's-cradle of bast fibre. He looked down at Eyre with that wise-animal expression of his, and said, 'To point the bone brings death. Yonguldye's bone is more magical than that of any other Mabarn Man. If that is what has happened to your friend here, then he cannot avoid death. He will die before the sun sets again today.'

Eyre said cuttingly, 'I respect your religion, Joolonga, but I have no respect whatsoever for malicious mumbo-jumbo. I want you to load up the horses, but leave one horse completely free of baggage. That horse you will cover with blankets; and on those blankets we will tie Mr Mortlock, in the most comfortable position we can.'

Arthur shuddered again, and moaned. 'No, sir,' he whispered. 'I'm not a bolter. Not me, sir.'

'Arthur,' Eyre coaxed him. 'Arthur, can you hear me? It's Eyre Walker, Arthur.'

Joolonga said, 'He will die, sir. That is a certainty.'

'Joolonga!' Eyre barked. 'Do as you're bloody well told!'

There was a taut, elliptical moment. Weeip raised his head from the fire, where he was boiling up oats and left-over mallee fowl into a kind of thin meat gruel. Midge-gooroo glanced uneasily at Joolonga, and then lowered his eyes. Dogger and Christopher stayed well back; Dogger because he was a stowaway of sorts, Christopher because he had no stomach for angry confrontations. The sun had risen now, and in that moment they stood in oddly theatrical poses, seven dusty men in a vast and dusty landscape.

Joolonga said something in dialect to Midgegooroo, and then strode off towards the line of pack-horses; angry and obviously affronted. Midgegooroo knelt down beside Eyre and touched his shoulder. His broad face was wrinkled with worry and disapproval, and he made a three-fingered sign across his chest.

'Weeip,' said Eyre. 'What is Midgegooroo saying?'

Weeip shook his head. 'They did not teach me finger-talk at the mission Mr Wakasah.'

Midgegooroo touched Eyre's arm again, respectfully but urgently, and made a jabbing gesture. Then he sketched a triangular shape in the air, on top of his head.

'Joolonga?' asked Eyre, recognising the triangular shape of the cock-eyed midshipman's hat. Midgegooroo grinned, and nodded, and repeated the jabbing gesture.

'Joolonga points?' Eyre frowned at him.

Midgegooroo nodded again, more frantically this time; and then reached down into the dust and picked up the wing-bone of one of the mallee fowl they had eaten last night. Again, he jabbed, this time at Arthur.

'Joolonga pointed the bone at Mr Mortlock?' Eyre queried.

Midgegooroo raised his hand in the one sign that Eyre recognised; the sign for 'yes'. But then he looked around to make sure that Joolonga was still occupied with the pack-horses, and that he hadn't seen anything of the strange one-sided conversation that had taken place between them. Weeip said nothing; but went back to stirring his mallee fowl gruel.

Arthur trembled again, and snorted. 'Not a bolter, sir,' he repeated. 'Not past Doom Rock, sir. Not worth it, sir, what? And end up an uncooked banquet for Skillings here, sir. Ha ha. Not worth it, sir.'

He seemed to contract every muscle in his body for a moment, and then he abruptly squirted green and foul-smelling diarrhoea into his britches and then squeezed again, and squirted some more.

'Good Heavens above,' said Christopher, ostentatiously hiding his eyes behind his hands.

'Get some water down him, for pity's sake,' put in Dogger. 'Otherwise the poor sod's going to dry up like a quandong; and that'll be the end of him. And give him something to bind his bowels.'

Eyre opened his medicine-chest; the same medicine-chest that had been prepared for him by the chemist at Bakewell, including everything imaginable for the treatment of sickness while abroad. There had been a bottle of tincture of Kino, which was the most effective treatment for diarrhoea that Eyre knew; but he had taken all of it himself during his first few months in Adelaide. He still had a full bottle of Dalby's Carminative, however; and he quickly poured out a spoonful of it and held it over Arthur's half-open mouth.

'Pinch his nose,' he ordered Midgegooroo; and when Midgegooroo did so and Arthur opened his mouth to breathe, Eyre poured the syrup straight down his throat. Arthur choked, and retched, and for a moment Eyre thought he was going to vomit again; but then he shuddered, and lay back on the ground, and appeared to fall into a deep and fretful sleep.

Christopher came closer now. 'Well, then,' he said, 'what are we going to do now?'

'Do you have any suggestions?' asked Eyre.

'Well, we could turn back, and take poor old Arthur with us, and hand him over to the authorities.'

'What about the expedition?'

'Oh, come on, Eyre; you know what I think about the expedition. Doomed from the very beginning, and too dangerous by half. Just look up ahead of us. What do you think you're going to find there? More of the same, if you ask me. Grass and scrub and kangaroos, *ad infinitum*; emus without end, amen. At least if we go back now, we'll have the chance to redeem ourselves, by handing over poor old

260

Arthur. Come on, Eyre. I told you right at the very beginning that it was a mistake not to call the police, that night he tried to rob us. And wasn't I right? And look where his new-found emancipation has led him to; a smelly death on a scrubby plain.'

Eyre screwed the cap back on to the medicine bottle, and put it carefully away. 'In my view,' he said, in that precise voice he could use when he was being a little too pompous; 'in my view, we ought to continue. In fact, that's exactly what we're going to do, regardless.'

Dogger took off his hat and squinted up at the sun. 'You'll kill him, you know,' he said, pragmatically.

'I'll kill him just as certainly if I take him back to Adelaide. That's if he doesn't die on the way. They'll chain him up, and they'll flog him, and then they'll put him in solitary confinement, and that will turn his mind for ever.'

He looked down at Arthur lying in the dust, eyes closed, still convulsing, white and sweaty and somehow shrunken, and all he could think of to say was, 'Poor bastard.'

'Perhaps we should put it to a vote,' said Christopher. 'You know, draw straws.'

Eyre shook his head. 'We're going on. I'm the leader of this expedition and that's my decision. If you don't approve of it, Adelaide is back that way, and you can take enough food and water to get you there.'

Christopher stiffened, and looked at Eyre with an expression which Eyre had never seen on his face before; offended, in a nakedly womanly way; like a wife whose dignity has been shaken by her husband's coarseness and lack of understanding. Eyre began to see then that Christopher was not a sodomite or an ogler of young boys, although he had several times seen him admiring Weeip's naked body. He was instead a man who sought the companionship of other men in the way that a good and loyal woman seeks the companionship of a husband. His love of Eyre was far more emotional than sexual; and Eyre's sudden rejection of him in favour of the expedition

261

and everything that it meant (Charlotte, Yanluga, fame and possible riches) was to Christopher a hurtful surprise.

Eyre realised that he would have to treat Christopher with care if he was going to retain his loyalty; and out here on the wild and empty plains with a self-willed Aborigine guide and a sick ex-convict, Eyre was going to need all the loyalty that he could muster.

'I'm sorry,' he told Christopher. 'I didn't mean to be so abrupt. It's just that we can't turn back now, not after we've come so far.'

Christopher tried to look aloof and displeased for a moment longer; but he was too sensitive and too good-humoured not to be able to accept Eyre's apology, and he made a considerable show of disassembling his frown, and unpuckering his mouth, and at last managing to smile. 'All right,' he said. 'I can't say that I understand what has driven you out here; not completely. Not at all, really. But if you think we ought to continue—well, let's continue.' He added wryly, 'At least until we're *all* dead.'

He came forward and rested his hand on Eyre's shoulder, and shook his hand. 'Do you have any idea what's wrong with him?' he asked, nodding towards Arthur.

'Well, your first guess was probably correct,' said Eyre. 'He could have eaten a bad clam; or perhaps one of the mallee fowl was diseased. Then again the water might have been poisoned.'

'What was Joolonga saying about him?'

'Some ridiculous Aborigine mumbo-jumbo about someone having pointed a bone at him. That's why I shouted at him.'

'They do say that Aborigine medicine-men kill their enemies that way,' said Christopher.

'And do you believe it?'

Christopher shrugged. 'In this country, I think I could believe anything.'

Arthur mumbled, 'Not a bolter, sir, I'll swear to that. Swear on the Holy Bible.' Then he suddenly convulsed again, and lumpy strings of bloody white mucus slithered out of his mouth and on to his shoulder.

Christopher looked almost as sick as Arthur. 'My God, Eyre, the man's *dying*. What on earth is the matter with him?'

'I just pray that it's nothing contagious,' said Eyre. 'Otherwise, this is going to be the shortest expedition into the Australian interior that ever was.'

Midgegooroo and Weeip tugged off Arthur's clothes; and washed him with what little water they could spare. All the time he rambled on about 'bolting', which Eyre presumed to mean escaping from Macquarie Harbour, and vomiting great ropes of mucus, mingled with raw membrane. It was as if his entire insides were being gradually gagged out of his mouth. His face took on a grey ghastliness that Eyre could scarcely bear to look at; and his eyes seemed blind.

They decided not to leave the camp until noon, to see if Arthur showed any signs of recovery. Weeip made a shelter for him out of twigs and scrub; and the rest of them sat around the fire and listened with increasing despondency to his ramblings and chokings.

'I don't know what on earth to give him,' said Eyre. 'I tried a carminative, but he must have vomited that back up by now.'

Dogger said, 'What else have you got in that medicine-box of yours?'

Eyre opened the polished mahogany lid, displaying the neat bottles of antimonial wine, blister compound, extract of colocynth, Epsom salts, powdered jalap, myrrh-and-aloes pills, powdered opium, opodeldoc, and Turner's cerate. Dogger picked out one or two bottles, and then said, 'I don't know. Constance would know what to dose him with, if she were here, Heaven forbid it. Perhaps we ought to mix them all together, and see what happens. He wouldn't be any the worse off.'

At noon, the temperature rose to 92 degrees Fahrenheit, according to their thermometer. Heat rose up off the plain in extraordinary transparent French-curves, and high above their heads, they saw flocks of seagulls flying northwards.

'There,' said Eyre. 'That's evidence for you. If seagulls are flying to the north, that must mean that water lies there; Captain Sturt's inland sea.'

'Or swamp,' put in Dogger. His face was sparkling with sweat.

Joolonga came over, and took off his midshipman's hat.

'Yes?' Eyre asked him, trying to sound as testy as he could.

'Mr Walker-sir, it is no use staying here. We must go on. Mr Mortlock will not get better for days and days; maybe weeks; that is if he ever gets better at all. If we stay here, we are only suffering for no reason, and exploring no further.'

Eyre stood up, and shaded his eyes so that he could look northwards. The scrubby bushlands wavered and danced as if he were seeing them through water, a world drowned in heat. He felt that everything was being relentlessly baked, punished by the sun to see what it was made of. Every breath he took was hot and suffocating and dusty; every move he made produced chafing and sweat. Now, at midday, even the red-capped robins had stopped shrilling and chattering in the bush, and there was an overwhelming hot silence. In the distance, the Flinders Ranges rose like the ramparts of some strange red city.

'All right,' said Eyre. 'You and Midgegooroo tie Mr Mortlock on to his horse. Make sure he's tied fast. Then we'll go.'

Arthur was muttering and shaking as Midgegooroo hefted him over his shoulder, and then lifted him up on to his horse. Joolonga tied him to the saddle, and then ran a leather strap under the horse's chest which he fastened tightly to each of Arthur's dangling wrists, Even if Arthur did slip off the horse, he wouldn't fall to the ground. He would be dragged along, instead, like a sack of meal.

And the trouble is, thought Eyre, that is exactly what Arthur has become. A sack of meal. A dead weight, to be dragged through the bush whether he likes it or not; and whether *we* like it or not. And if I catch this sickness, then I'll be the same. This is land in which only those who can keep moving can ever survive; a land in which a nomadic existence is not just possible, but essential. A land in which, when anybody is stricken by sickness, they are sick unto death.

In the same way that God had been practising creation when he had devised Australia, perhaps he had also been practising His punishments. Death by isolation; death by hunger; death by evaporation of the body and spirit.

It took nearly a quarter of an hour, but at last they were ready to leave. Midgegooroo had rigged up over Arthur's horse a kind of makeshift parasol, an unsteady contraption of tent-poles and calico, which would at least protect him from the worst of the sun. Arthur was slumped over the horse's back as if he were already dead, a string of spittle swinging from his parted lips, his eyes closed.

Christopher said, 'You don't think it would be kinder to leave him here? I mean, simply to let him—'

Eyre stared at him; thin-faced; his dark hair already streaked with blond from the sun; the untanned crowsfeet around his eyes making him look even older and more anxious than he actually was. 'I can't,' he said.

'If I did, I don't think I would ever be able to forgive myself.'

'What do you think the poor fellow is going to suffer now, on the back of a horse?'

'Christopher, for God's sake, there's always hope. There's always prayer. Why do you think I'm here at all? I'm here because I'm trying to redeem what I did to Yanluga; I'm trying to find him peace. Now you're asking me to leave Arthur to die, without the benefit of help or prayer.'

'It seems your religious upbringing had quite an effect

on you,' said Christopher, taking care not to sound too sarcastic.

'Well, perhaps it did,' Eyre told him. 'But I'm not ashamed of it, and I'm not ashamed of having hope. "The prayer offered in faith will restore the one who is sick, and the Lord will raise him up, and if he has committed sins, they will be forgiven him." That's James.'

'The brother of Jesus,' said Christopher.

'Chapter five,' Eyre retorted. Then, when Christopher was silent, 'Verse fifteen.'

Dogger whistled sharply from across the campsite. 'Come on, Eyre. If we don't go now, there won't be any use in going at all.'

'All right,' said Eyre. 'Come on, Christopher; we have to do our utmost for Arthur, no matter how sick he is. Just for pity's sake, let's stay together. I need your help; and Dogger's help, too. If we start arguing between ourselves, we'll be finished.'

Christopher said nothing more, but followed Eyre back to the line of horses. Eyre mounted up, and they set off again, heading north-north-west, towards the place called Woocalla, the water-hole where the kangaroos come to drink. The sun had fallen to the west of its zenith now, so that it shone directly in their eyes. All they could see was dust and dazzle, and willy-willys twisting and hurrying through the scrub. There was no sign anywhere of the ghost-men whom Eyre had glimpsed the previous evening; but then the bush was not a difficult landscape in which to hide. As they rode, they frequently surprised mallee fowl and pipits, and once or twice they sprang euros out of their squats in the tussocks of spinifex grass.

Dogger had often talked to Eyre about euros, and so he knew what they were when he first saw them: solidly built little hill kangaroos, with black-tipped hair and pale snouts. They hurried off in front of the slow-moving train of pack-horses like busy little clerks.

The afternoon was enormous and cruelly hot. For a while they chatted to each other; about Adelaide; about

Captain Sturt; about all the nauseating medical treatments they had been given as children. But as the temperature rose over 100, their conversation died away; and for almost two hours there was nothing but the jangling of buckles, and the squeaking of saddles, and the occasional snort from one of the horses.

Arthur made no sound at all. He lay strapped flat to a thick grey blanket under the lurching shadow of his rectangular parasol, his eyes staring at nothing at all. Midgegooroo was solemnly leading Arthur's horse; and occasionally during the afternoon Eyre rode up alongside and asked Midgegooroo whether Arthur had shown any signs of life; but Midgegooroo shook his head, and raised his hand in the complicated finger-language which meant 'no hope'.

There was a time, just before four o'clock, when Eyre felt as if God Himself were pressing down on them with all the heat and brilliance He and His angels could summon up. There didn't even seem to be any point in breathing. The air outside his body was hotter than the air in his lungs. His shirt and his britches were clinging wet; and the salt from the sweat which dripped from his eyebrows made his eyes sting.

Behind them, there was nothing but miles of wavering scrub. In front of them, a dusty and invisible horizon. All that reminded Eyre that there *was* an end to the world, after all, was the distant red line of the Flinders mountains, off to the right.

The heat separated them; and caused them to draw in upon themselves. They began to ride further and further apart; their heads bowed; until the expedition was strung out over a quarter of a mile. Their shadows walked beside them with irritating persistence, on and on, mile after mile, seven spindly Don-Quixote figures which lengthened even more absurdly as the sun burned its way down the sky.

Eyre found himself daydreaming, in a welter of heat and sweat. He daydreamed about Charlotte; and about returning to Adelaide with flags flying and people cheering, and riding straight up to Waikerie Lodge and claiming Charlotte, with a sweep of his arm, as his bride-to-be.

Then, unaccountably, he found himself thinking about the new wharf and the new sheds that Mr McLaren of the South Australian Company had been building at Port Adelaide. They must almost be finished by now, he thought. He remembered that Mr McLaren had promised a grand opening, with a regatta, and a band, and refreshments; and Eyre was quite sorry that he wasn't going to be there. The quiet, scratchy afternoons of clerkdom; with ledgers and ink and bills of lading; now, in the scrub, seemed idyllic. He thought of the times when he and Christopher had sat in Dougal's Oyster Saloon on Hindley Street, opposite Elder's store, sometimes eating two dozen oysters at a time, with black stout to wash them down. They had talked then of being wealthy and famous, but Eyre had never imagined that fame would have to be earned as hard as this.

Christopher rode up beside him, his face sugar-pink and sweaty. 'I hope we're going to be able to stand up to this heat,' he said, in a hoarse, dry voice. 'I'm beginning to feel as if I haven't got any more perspiration left to perspire.'

'It's very good for you,' Eyre replied. 'It cleanses out the body's impurities. Just like a Turkish bath, without any steam.'

'I'm not sure I'd rather remain impure.'

Eyre gave a wry smile, and shrugged.

'Did Joolonga say how far it was to Woocalla?' Christopher asked him.

'Not too long now. We should be there by evening.'

Christopher nudged his horse a little closer. 'He's not—he's all right, isn't he, Joolonga? You can trust him?'

'What makes you say that?'

'I don't know. He hardly speaks to me at all. I mean, I've tried to treat the chap decently, for all that he's a native. But he seems to have thoughts of his own.'

'Well?' asked Eyre.

'Well, I don't know. I've never thought it was too healthy for natives to have thoughts of their own.'

'I don't see that there's any way in which you can stop them.'

Christopher turned around in his saddle, and looked back at Joolonga, who was riding with his midshipman's hat pulled far down over his eyes, his blue uniform so dusty that it was almost white. Joolonga gave no indication that he knew that Christopher was watching him; and his expression remained as abstracted and as arrogant as ever. Weeip, however, gave Christopher a wave of his fly-whisk; and Dogger raised his head in interest to see what Eyre and Christopher were doing.

'Captain Sturt said he trusted Joolonga, didn't he?' said Christopher.

'He didn't say anything about him: except that he'd met him on his first expedition.'

'Well,' said Christopher, 'the fellow seems strange to me. Not altogether friendly. I don't know. It's difficult to describe, exactly. But I rather get the feeling that he's *watching over us*, don't you see, instead of guiding us. He's not what you might call co-operative.'

'He's self-opinionated, I'll give you that,' Eyre agreed. 'But I must say that I find him quite interesting. He's the first Aborigine I've ever met who can describe ideas, as well as people, and events, and places. He seems to have a grasp of what this expedition means; not only to his own people, but to ours, too.'

'Is that likely to have made him any more friendly?' asked Christopher. He took off his hat, and dabbed the sweat away from his forehead with a scarf that was already soaked in sweat.

'I'm not sure,' said Eyre. 'But he's no fool; and he knows a lot more about this country than we do. He also seems to know where we might find Yonguldye.'

'I'd rather trust Dogger's opinion on that,' said Christopher.

Eyre narrowed his eyes, and looked up ahead of them,

towards the horizon. The north-west wind had stirred up so much dust there that it was impossible to distinguish where the plains ended and where the sky began. There could have been mountains ahead of them, for all they knew. And now that the sun was sinking, the horizon began to glower and boil, a dark scarlet colour, and the empty sky above them began to rage with red.

Dogger had once said to Eyre, out on the verandah in front of Mrs McConnell's house, 'Don't ever ask me to tell you what the sunset's like, out in the bush. You wouldn't believe me if I told you, and if you saw it for yourself you wouldn't believe it. And besides, it happens every evening; and after a few weeks you begin to grow tired of reds and oranges and ochres; and you begin to dream about green.'

Eyre was beginning to understand what Dogger had been talking about. Ever since they had struck inland from Kurdnatta they had been living in a world of brick-reds and purples and dusty yellows. And the further north they travelled, the harsher and redder the landscape became; and the fiercer the sun. If there was an ocean in the centre of Australia, there was no question in Eyre's mind now that it could only be reached by days of hot and uncomfortable travel. Perhaps that would enhance the relief it gave them, when they eventually reached it. Eyre had already begun to have dreams about shining blue water, and nodding palm trees; and dhows sailing from the inland shores of South Australia to the tropical inland beaches of the north.

Perhaps the inland sea was further away than Captain Sturt had imagined it to be. After all, Joolonga had been as far north as Edieowie, and Dogger had actually visited the northern ramparts of the Flinders Range, and neither of them had seen the glitter of an inland sea, even from a distance. But the geological fact remained that scores of rivers drained inland, rather than out towards the ocean, and that if they drained inland then they must drain somewhere. And then there were the seagulls, which Eyre had seen with his own eyes. Seagulls, flying north.

Eyre said to Christopher, 'Don't worry too much about Joolonga. As long as he leads us to Yonguldye, we'll be all right. It can't be more than three or four days' riding now, to the inland sea. Then, if Joolonga proves to be troublesome we can dispense with his services altogether. Personally, I don't think that he's going to be particularly difficult. He's a man caught between two civilisations, that's all; and sometimes he has trouble convincing himself that he belongs to either. Hence, the arrogance.'

The sun had now plunged itself so deeply into the dust that it was no brighter than a sore red eye. They had reached a gully, where mulga and ghost gums grew, and Eyre raised his arm and called to Joolonga, 'This is it. We'll camp here for tonight. Then we'll make an early start in the morning.'

Joolonga came riding up, and circled his horse around in front of Eyre. 'We have travelled only thirty miles today, Mr Walker-sir. If we travel so slowly, our water will run out before we can reach a water-hole.'

'We will make up for any lost time tomorrow,' said Eyre. 'But for tonight, we will pitch our camp here. I think that Mr Mortlock has probably suffered enough for one day, don't you?'

Joolonga stared at Eyre defiantly, and then he said, 'Mr Mortlock is dead, Mr Walker-sir.'

Eyre said nothing. Instead, he stared at Joolonga in shock. Then he climbed down from his horse; and walked back to the heavy-set chestnut on which Arthur had been strapped, under his parasol. One of Arthur's arms dangled lifelessly; and his head was slumped to one side of the chestnut's neck at such an awkward angle that he had to be dead, because no living man could have endured it. Beneath him, his grey blanket was caked with dried mucus, which buzzed with flies; and flies clustered all around Arthur's mouth and nose, giving him the appearance of a man with a dark grey beard. The crimson sunlight

271

illuminated the spectacle of Arthur's death with grisly theatricality; as if it had been staged as a carnival sideshow, the Horrible Demise of Arthur Mortlock.

Eyre stood for a long time looking at Arthur's body, and his restless horse, and the makeshift shelter which had protected him from the sun during the worst of his suffering. Then at last he turned back to Joolonga, and said, 'We'll bury him here, tonight. Then we'll pitch our camp. Weeip—you make up the fire. Midgegooroo, you start digging a grave for Mr Mortlock. Joolonga—'

A moment's tight pause. Then, 'Yes, Mr Walker-sir?'

'Joolonga, you check through the stores. I want an inventory of what we've consumed to date, including how much water we've been drinking; and I also want an idea of how long you think our supplies are going to last.' He glanced towards Arthur's body. 'Taking into account, of course, that Mr Mortlock is no longer with us.'

'Yes, Mr Walker-sir.'

Midgegooro was unstrapping Arthur's body, and lowering him down the side of his horse to the ground.

Eyre said, 'You don't know how this happened, do you, Joolonga?'

Joolonga's face remained impenetrable; and very black; and there was something in his eyes that was so haughty and self-possessed and yet so strangely prehistoric that Eyre, for the first time in days, felt a prickle of coldness. He felt that Joolonga knew far more about Arthur's death than he was prepared to volunteer, whether it had been magical or not. Perhaps Joolonga knew more about the entire expedition, and where it was going, and what it could expect to find. Or, on the other hand, perhaps he didn't. Perhaps Eyre was simply allowing himself to be frightened by his own lack of experience, and by the prospect of leading six men to their deaths in a fiery and unfamiliar landscape. When they had ridden out of Adelaide, it had seemed inconceivable that this expedition could be anything more than a stiff ride into the South Australian countryside, with a few picnics along the way.

But now that Eyre had seen for himself the devastating distances; and felt for himself the sun bearing down on him at 110 degrees; now that he had peered until his eyes watered at horizons that refused to materialise, and mountains that refused to come any closer; now at last he knew that they were confronting far more than tiredness, and saddle-sores, and disobedient Aborigines. They were confronting the entire meaning of Australia. These plains, these mountains, these endless miles of scrub, these were Australia's unforgiving heart, and her uncompromising character. She was like an old, old woman, who no longer considered that she was obliged to grant favours to anyone; an old, severe woman who castigated her children, and her children's children, and especially the new children who didn't understand her cruelty at all.

On that evening when they buried Arthur, Eyre felt closer to turning back than he ever had before; or ever would again. Midgegooroo dug a shallow pit in the dry ground, and then wrapped Arthur in his blanket, and laid him down like a grey mysterious totem. They gathered around him as the sun boiled through the clouds, and hundreds of emus rushed away to the east, so that it looked as if the whole earth was moving.

Eyre recited the Lord's Prayer, and then he quoted from Job. ' "Why did I not die at birth, come forth from the womb and expire? Why did the knee receive me, and why the breasts, that I should suck? For now I would have lain down and been quiet. There the wicked cease from raging, and the weary are at rest. The prisoners are at ease together; they do not hear the voice of the taskmaster. The small and the great are there, and the slave is free from his master." '

'Food poisoning,' said Christopher, as they slid down the sides of the gully, back to the camp fire. Weeip was cooking beans again, and what he called 'fat flaps', or flapjacks.

'Perhaps,' said Eyre. 'But none of the rest of us have

caught it; and we've all been eating the same food and drinking the same water.'

'It could have been some disease that he picked up in prison,' Christopher suggested. He held out his hand to Weeip for a hot mug of tea. 'You know how malaria comes and goes; perhaps this sickness was the same kind of thing.'

Eyre looked around the warm twilit gully. The stars were out; the cicadas were singing; and the ghost gums were playing statues. There was a dry smell of scrub on the wind; and the spinifex grass whistled softly and eerily to itself. He thought: we could turn back now, saddle up the horses in the morning and head straight back to Adelaide. After all, three men had died already, Chatto and Rose and the long-suffering Arthur. Do the rest of us have to risk our lives, simply to find an Aborigine medicine-man for a boy already dead, and wealth for Captain Sturt? We could always say that we ran out of water; that we rode for hundreds of miles and saw no sign of anywhere to fill our bottles, let alone an ocean, and how could anybody think of mining or farming or driving stock through territory as harsh as that?

But the seagulls had been flying north; and what was more, he had given Yanluga his word. There would be no chance of his claiming Charlotte, either, unless he came back triumphant. His moral and political destiny were all invested in this one expedition. It was his one opportunity to fulfil himself, his one chance of greatness. The seagulls had been flying north and he would have to follow them.

He looked up and saw Joolonga sitting by himself on the opposite rim of the gully, hungrily spooning up heaps of beans. He stood up, and climbed across to him under a white moon the size of a dinner-plate. Joolonga glanced towards him as Eyre came across; but said nothing, and continued to wolf down his beans.

'Touching, wasn't it?' Eyre asked him, standing over him, one elbow resting on his knee.

'Touching, Mr Walker-sir?'

'The funeral. The Christian interment of Mr Arthur Mortlock, lately departed.'

'It was sad, Mr Walker-sir.' Joolonga washed down the beans he was chewing with a mouthful of tea. 'It is always sad when a spirit leaves the real world.'

Eyre watched him for a moment, and then said, 'Midgegooroo told me that it was you who pointed the bone at him.'

'Midgegooroo cannot speak, Mr Walker-sir,' replied Joolonga, placidly.

'Midgegooroo *can* speak, and you know it. He uses hand-language.'

'Perhaps there was a misunderstanding, Mr Walker-sir.'

Eyre shook his head. 'I don't think so. Midgegooroo has a way of making himself quite explicit.'

There was a very long silence between them. Joolonga continued to eat his beans, occasionally taking a sip of tea or a bite of hard biscuit; his eyes darting around in the gathering darkness like two elusive white animals.

After a while, Eyre said, 'I want to know the truth, Joolonga.'

'There are many different truths, Mr Walker-sir. One truth for the white man, one truth for the Aborigine.'

'And for you? Mr Betwixt-and-Between? What is *your* truth?'

Joolonga swallowed quickly, and sniffed, and then said, 'Mr Mortlock *had* to die, Mr Walker-sir. The decision was not mine. It was Ngurunderi, the spirit of death, who lives in the sky. He accepted the souls of those two white men, Mr Chatto and Mr Rose; and when Ngurunderi accepts the soul of a murdered man, he demands revenge for those who killed him. Otherwise, he sends Wulgaru the devil to exact the punishment himself.'

Eyre stared at him. 'You mean to tell me that you killed Arthur because you thought that those two bounty-hunters had to be avenged?'

'Not I, Mr Walker-sir. Ngurunderi.'

'And how exactly did—*Ngurunderi* make this requirement known to you?'

'There have been signs, Mr Walker-sir, ever since those men were buried.'

'What signs, precisely?' Eyre snapped at him.

Joolonga said, 'In the sky, sir. That is where Ngurunderi made his home. Two clouds, shaped this way; then a single cloud.'

Eyre was both furious and frightened. If Joolonga had really killed Arthur; then the rest of them were equally at risk. Who knows what exotic excuses he could find to murder Dogger, or Christopher, or Eyre himself, when they were sleeping? The expedition would have to be called off; and they would have to take Joolonga back to Adelaide as their prisoner. Unless of course, they summarily executed him here.

'Why in God's name didn't you tell me about any of this?' Eyre demanded. 'What earthly right do you think you had to take this matter into your own hands? You're a danger to yourself and you're a danger to all the rest of us, as well. Damn it, Joolonga, if you believed you saw a sign from Ngurunderi, why didn't you say anything about it? That's what you've been brooding about, isn't it? And now you've killed Arthur, and brought the whole expedition to a useless halt. It's over. It's finished. And you're responsible.'

'Ngurunderi would have stopped us himself, sooner or later, Mr Walker-sir. Far better to sacrifice Mr Mortlock, and spare the rest of us.'

'Joolonga, I don't give a damn about Ngurunderi. I don't give a damn for your hocus-pocus and I don't give a damn for you. This is a Christian expedition and we shall abide by Christian morality.'

Joolonga put down his dish. 'An eye for an eye, Mr Walker-sir? Isn't that what it says in your good book?'

'Joolonga—you were supposed to be our guide. You were supposed to protect us in the bush. You were not supposed to set yourself up as our judge and executioner.'

Joolonga raised one hand, the light-coloured palm facing towards Eyre. 'This is my country, Mr Walker-sir, and in my country I know how to protect the people in my care. Believe me, Mr Walker-sir, there was no other way. Mr Mortlock's spirit was forfeit. When men die wrongly, the one who brought about their death has to die, too. It is the balance of life.'

Eyre said, with a dry throat, 'How did you kill him? Come on, Joolonga, I want to know.'

Joolonga reached into the pocket of his coat and produced a packet made of tanned kangaroo-hide. He unwrapped it, and then held out on the palm of his hand a pointed white bone, almost pistol-shaped, highly polished. It looked like the shin-bone of a euro, or a small red.

'I said from the first, sir, that he had the mark of death on him.'

'You didn't say that it was you who had pointed the bone.'

'Would you have believed me, Mr Walker-sir, if I had told you that this bone had brought about Mr Mortlock's sickness? Do you believe me now?'

'Give it to me,' said Eyre.

Joolonga carefully laid the pointing-bone on to Eyre's palm. Eyre felt the weight of it: it seemed to be unusually heavy for a bone so small. And even through the kangaroo-hide wrapping, he was sure that it felt cold. A dry, ancient artefact from a magical age. As cold as the night. As frigid as the Southern Cross.

'That was all you did to Arthur? Point this bone at him?'

'That was all that was necessary, Mr Walker-sir.'

Eyre slowly stood up straight. He didn't know what to say. Joolonga had suddenly confronted him with one of the greatest tests of his religious convictions since he had decided not to take holy orders. He had set out on this expedition with the unusual but firm belief that *all* faith, no matter how it was expressed, found equal favour in the eyes of God—that God's power and influence could be called upon in any language, by any ritual, and that God would answer any prayer, regardless of whether it was addressed to Yahweh or Allah or Baiame.

As long as those who called for help were ready to acknowledge the moral supremacy of a higher Being, then all of God's strength could be theirs.

Eyre had believed that Yanluga's spirit could be laid to rest by Yonguldye the medicine-man. But could he now bring himself to believe that Joolonga had killed Arthur Mortlock simply by pointing a bone at him? If he could, then Joolonga was a fearful threat to all of them, and to the whole expedition. Or perhaps he wasn't—because if he *had* killed Arthur, then everything he had said about Ngurunderi, and the necessity for avenging the killings of Chatto and Rose—well, it was conceivable that all that had some basis in reality, too.

If on the other hand Joolonga *hadn't* killed Arthur, he could still be very dangerous. After all, he had pointed the bone at him with the *intention* of killing him; and he seemed quite pleased that Arthur had died. Next time, he might try murdering his white companions with something less innocuous than a kangaroo's shin-bone—like a knife or a rifle.

Then there was the possibility that Joolonga was lying, and that he had deliberately poisoned Arthur's food. There were plenty of virulently poisonous fruits in the scrub, especially the brilliant red macrozamia nuts, and certain yams. Joolonga may even have stolen poison from Eyre's medical supplies. There were small bottles of salt of lemons and pearlash in his box, both of which could bring on bloody vomiting, and even madness.

At last, however, Eyre gave Joolonga back his bone. 'I'm going to put you on trust,' he said quietly. 'I cannot arrest you here, nor can I put you in irons. You would just become an encumbrance. Nor would there be any point in shooting you, since we need your guidance to continue. And we *are* going to continue. We are going to pursue this expedition of ours to wherever it may lead us. We are going to find Yonguldye and we are going to find the inland sea; and we are not going to return to Adelaide until we do. We have a great destiny to fulfil, and we shall fulfil it with glory.'

Joolonga watched him, warily. 'Yes, Mr Walker-sir,' he acknowledged.

'Yes, Mr Walker-sir,' Eyre repeated. 'Because you are going to behave yourself from this moment on. No more insolence, no more contemptuous behaviour, no more mumbo-jumbo or pointing of bones. If you try to harm any one of us in any way, then I warn you now that I will personally kill you, at once. You are a guide, and you will guide us, and that is all.'

'You accuse me of Mr Mortlock's murder, Mr Walker-sir?'

'Yes, Joolonga, I do.'

'Then what will you do when we return to Adelaide?'

'I will have you arrested and tried.'

Joolonga said, 'You are a brave man to tell me that, sir. Either brave or foolish.'

'Not as foolish as you think, Joolonga. If you see us through this expedition, and bring us back safely, then it may be possible for me to forget the way in which Mr Mortlock died; and simply to say that he was suffering from food-poisoning.'

Joolonga sat back, hugging his knees, and slowly grinned. 'You are an interesting man, Mr Walker-sir. You seem to be one who dreams, and yet your dreams move mountains. Perhaps we are all dreaming with you.'

Eyre said nothing; but slid cautiously back down the gully to the camp-fire, where Dogger and Christopher were finishing their supper.

'I was just telling Joolonga to buck his ideas up,' said Eyre.

'About time, too, coal-black bastard,' sniffed Dogger.

'I find him impossible,' said Christopher. 'He's the strongest case for keeping the blackfellows uneducated that I've ever come across. Obstinate, wilful, bad-tempered, and bloody ugly.'

'Don't imagine the blackfellows think very much of *your* looks,' grinned Dogger, nudging Christopher in the ribs. 'Whenever they see a bright-red fizzog like yours, they say, "Time to wake up, it's sunrise." They do have a sense of humour, you know.'

Christopher said, 'Are we going to go on, now that Arthur's dead?'

Eyre nodded. 'There's nothing to go back for; and every reason for going on.'

'And you're sure you can trust Joolonga? You seemed to be having rather a testy discussion with him up there.'

'I was simply reminding him that, out here, the first duty of each of us is to his companions, and to the whole expedition.'

Dogger spat into the fire. 'Eyre's right, you know. You don't have to worry about trust in the outback, Joolonga needs us just as much as we need him. The only time that you ever have to worry about trust is when you've run out of everything—food, horses, water, and leather boots That's when you start looking at each other and imagining each other as cutlets and chops.'

His spit sizzled in the fire, and he suddenly realised what he'd done. He looked up towards the night sky, and took off his hat, and said, in an apologetic voice, 'Sorry, Arthur. Forgot myself there, for a moment.'

Twenty-One

By noon the following day, the temperature had already risen to 100. They rode single file through a distorted landscape of brindled scrub and twisted bushes, under a sky that was as blue as a sudden shout.

Joolonga rode ahead, with Eyre a little way behind. Somehow, their talk yesterday evening had excited a fresh awareness between them; and although Eyre remained as suspicious of Joolonga as ever, he began to sense that the Aborigine guide was just as determined to see this expedition through as he was himself; and that for their different reasons they both needed to see this extraordinary act of social and geographical drama brought to whatever conclusion history might demand.

It might end in the bush, with exhaustion, and bones. It might end in frustration and giving-up. It might end in magnificent triumph. But both of them had made up their minds with equal strength that it would succeed.

Dogger said to Eyre, as they sat under the patient shade of their horse a little after midday, swatting at the flies which crawled all over their faces and arms, 'Do you know something, Eyre? About an hour ago, I asked myself a question.'

'What question was that?' Eyre wanted to know. He took a carefully measured mouthful of warm leathery water, swilled it around his mouth, and then swallowed it.

'I asked myself: Dogger, I asked, what in blazing hell are you doing here, sitting on this horse, sweating your way through the bush like a boiled bandicoot, when you could be back on Hindley Street in the comfortable arms of Mrs McC., well-drunk on ice-cold beer, and with a belly full of pot-pie? That's what I asked myself.'

Eyre looked at him, brushing away again and again a persistent fly that seemed determined to land on the same spot on the side of his nose, whatever happened. 'What was the answer?' he asked Dogger, with a smile.

'The answer was, I don't know. I suppose I'm like the sailor; who every time he went to sea, he was homesick; and every time he came home, he was seasick.'

From the shadow of his horse, where he was lying with his head back on his carefully rolled-up jacket, with the casual air of a reclining picnicker, Christopher said, 'I think I'd give a year of my life to be back at the racecourse now, eating an ice, and watching Mr Stewart's Why Not in the three o'clock. It would be a fine thing to see a decent elegant horse again, instead of these equine elephants.'

At that very moment, there was a loud clattering noise; and Christopher shrieked, and sprang up from under the horse, flapping his hands at his shirt and britches. 'Bloody thing pissed on me! Of all the bloody nerve!'

Eyre and Dogger laughed until they were weak, rolling and kicking around in the dust. Eyre at last stood up, coughing the dust out of his lungs, and put his arms around Christopher's shoulder. 'My dear chap. Don't you know that you should never malign a horse within earshot.'

'And especially not within pizzle-shot,' put in Dogger. 'By God, I've seen some fellows jump. But you!'

They rode on, into the afternoon. As they rode, the land subtly changed from mallee scrub to flat salt marshes, dried out in glittering swirls of pink and white, like ground glass, and dotted with tussocks of tough grass. The wind persisted hot north-westerly, keeping the temperature high, and a flock of bustards rose against it, and then circled lazily in the air.

By mid-afternoon, the land began to rise a little, and they were riding again through scrubby savannah, with an occasional scattering of stunted mulga trees on the low horizon. The spinifex grass was so sharp that sometimes it drew blood from the horses' legs; and the ground between each clump was uncompromisingly stony and hard. But shortly after four o'clock they reached a twisting gully; and at the far end of it was a small reflecting pool of water, its sides stained like a geological rainbow with the various minerals which had evaporated from it during the dry season. A frightened collection of red gums grew around the pool, and their branches were thick with zebra-finches.

Joolonga dismounted, and led his horse down to the edge of the water. Eyre followed him; then Christopher and Dogger. Weeip and Midgegooroo began to unpack some of the leather water-bottles, so that they could replenish their supplies.

The water in the pool was low, and tasted metallic; but it was cooler and fresher than the water they had been drinking from their bottles. Dogger knelt down by the edge of the pool and drank until water gushed out of the sides of his mouth; then washed his face in it.

Eyre said to Joolonga, 'No sign of Yonguldye.'

Joolonga replaced his midshipman's hat and looked around. Then he beckoned to Eyre, and the two of them climbed up the far side of the gully until they reached a second ravine, which must have been carved out centuries ago by the water which once flowed through these plains. There were signs of an Aborigine encampment here: a fire which had been left to burn after the nomads had left, and which had blackened the grass all up one side of the ravine. Bones, pieces of wood, and three shelters made out of mulga branches and woven grass.

Eyre looked back. The heads of the horses drinking at the pool were reflected like the heads of turned-over chess-pieces. Weeip was sitting by the far edge, filling up two or three water-bottles at once, while Christopher watched him contentedly, his hands in his pockets; and Dogger lit up his pipe.

'How long ago did Yonguldye leave here?' Eyre asked Joolonga. 'I mean—this was Yonguldye's camp, wasn't it?'

Joolonga nodded. 'Yonguldye was here. There, on the stone, are the marks of his totem.'

Eyre could made out nothing except a few criss-cross

streaks of ochre, but he was prepared to take Joolonga's word for it.

Joolonga said, 'He is not long gone. See the footprints are still clear. Here, and here. The north-westerly wind has been blowing hard enough to have swept these footprints away in a week or so. Perhaps he was here two days ago; perhaps only yesterday.'

'As recently as that? Are you sure? Then we've only just missed him.'

'The ashes of the fire are still fresh,' said Joolonga. 'If we are quick, we may catch up with him tomorrow. If not tomorrow, the day after that.'

Eyre cupped his hands around his mouth and called down to Christopher and Dogger, 'Halloo! Some luck, at last! Joolonga says that Yonguldye was camped here only two days ago. We could catch up with him by tomorrow!'

'Thank God for that,' said Christopher. 'Then we can all go home.'

Eyre turned back to Joolonga but he could see by the fiercely amused expression on Joolonga's face that he was not thinking of returning to Adelaide yet, any more than Eyre was. There were other mysteries to be solved, before they could head back south again. There were other discoveries to be made.

'Which way do you think he went?' Eyre asked.

Joolonga pointed north-east, across the salt marshes, towards the brick red line of the north Flinders mountains. 'The ochre mine,' he said. 'Mr McConnell was quite right. But we have only ridden half a day out of our way; and at least we know that we shall not have to retrace our steps. We have water, too; and we can find more water at Edieowie.'

Eyre said, 'All right. You can set up camp now. And before we leave in the morning, I want to make sure that every water-bottle is filled right up to the neck, and that the horses have all been watered. And one thing more. I want the rifles loaded, and holstered beside our saddles. One for Mr Willis and one for me.'

Joolonga looked back at Eyre with one hand raised against his eyes to shield them from the setting sun. 'Yong-uldye will not harm you, Mr Walker-sir. Not as long as you have Joolonga with you.'

'Nevertheless, I want the rifles loaded and holstered; and properly loaded too.'

'Yes, Mr Walker-sir.'

'*Yes*, Mr Walker-sir,' Eyre repeated, just to remind him that he was on probation.

They were reasonably lucky with food that night. Midge-gooroo speared a bandicoot that had come to the water-hole to drink; and they roasted it and ate it with salted beef and pressed apricots, and tea. Eyre thought that it tasted rather like lamb; although Christopher said that it was easily the most repulsive meat that he had ever tasted. It had probably been the sight of the small furry animal twisting and jerking on the end of Midgegooroo's spear that had upset him. He sucked a barley-sugar to take the taste away; while Weeip, to complete *his* meal, dug scores of fat white grubs from between the roots of the gums, and crammed them into his mouth as eagerly as if they were sweets.

Eyre stood beside Weeip as he dug deftly with the end of a pointed-stick. It was almost dark now, and the surface of the pool had turned to glutinous blood. 'They didn't teach you to eat those at the mission,' he said.

Weeip shook his curly head, and looked serious. 'The Lord is mice pepper,' he said. 'I shall knot one.'

Eyre squatted down beside him. The point of Weeip's stick flew into the loose-packed soil and quickly winnowed out the grubs with extraordinary speed; although Eyre was growing used to the boy's dexterity. He had seen him two days ago pick up a handful of ants and sand; let the sand slide slickly through his fingers, and then press the whole handful of ants straight into his open mouth, and crunch them between his teeth. The way in which he had done it had been so matter-of-fact, so practised, that for a moment Eyre hadn't thought that it was anything unusual.

Christopher looked determinedly in the opposite direction whenever any of their three Aborigines began to eat anything which he considered to be disgusting. He particularly complained about the way in which Midgegooroo would sit by the camp-fire, and suddenly scoop out of the flames any ghost-moths which had fluttered too close; plucking off their wings and devouring them ostentatiously.

Joolonga had told them that in the mountains of the far south-east, Aborigine tribes would soon be gathering for the aestivation—the summer equivalent of hibernation—of the Bogong moth. He called it 'the summer sleeping'. The moths would swarm together in rock crevices, thousand upon thousand of them, and the tribesmen would either scrape them down with a stick or, if they were nestling in very deep crevices, smoke them out. They would cook them quickly on a hot flat stone, brush away the burned wings, and eat them. The moths were tiny, no larger than peanuts, but full of fat; so that at the end of the season the tribesmen would come down from the mountains glossy and plump.

'It is a time for friendly tribes to meet together; to tell stories, and to trade, and to hold a great corroboree,' he had explained.

Eyre had looked up, interested. 'Captain Sturt mentioned corroborees. They're dances, aren't they? Religious meetings.'

'A corroboree can be held for any reason,' Joolonga had informed him. 'To celebrate a boy's initiation; or to tell sacred stories from the dreamtime or to give thanks for food. Sometimes a corroboree may be held because it has rained, and there is plenty of water. But many of the corroborees are secret, and may only be danced by initiated men. No white man or woman will ever see those dances; nor the magic that is performed there.'

'If the magic has anything at all to do with eating moths, I think I prefer to be exluded,' Christopher had remarked, wrinkling his nose.

Now Eyre watched Weeip dig out a whole handful of ten or twelve fat white grubs, which slowly twitched and wriggled in the palm of his hand.

'What do they taste like?' Eyre asked him.

Weeip poked at the grubs, and then looked up at Eyre with his wide reddish-brown eyes. 'Coomoorooguree,' he said, simply.

Over at the camp-fire, Joolonga laughed. 'He says they taste like grass-tree grubs. He is a connoisseur of grubs.'

'Let me taste one,' said Eyre.

'I cook it on the fire for you?' Weeip asked him.

Eyre said, 'Don't bother. I'll eat it the way you're eating them.'

'Oh God, as if I didn't feel sick enough already,' Christopher groaned. Dogger took his pipe out of his mouth and laughed like a dog barking. 'Trying to eat like a real bushman, are you?' he said. 'Wait until they give you that juice they squeeze out of green ants.'

Weeip dropped the grub on to Eyre's hand, and Eyre felt it squirm against his skin. It was semi-translucent, ringed with faint brownish markings, and there was a pattern of dots at one end of it which could almost have been an insect-like face. It seemed very much bigger and fatter now that he had offered to eat it.

Grinning, his own mouth full of grubs, Weeip watched and waited for Eyre to put it between his lips.

'Come on, Eyre,' Dogger coaxed him. 'Nothing ventured, nothing gained. You don't want some salt-and-pepper with it, do you? Or a dash of Worcestershire sauce?'

Eyre tilted his head back, closed his eyes, and opened his mouth. Then without any more hesitation, he clapped his hand over his mouth and let the grub tumble on to his tongue.

For one moment, as the grub twitched and wriggled against the insides of his cheeks, he felt a shudder of convulsive disgust. His stomach, already overfilled with half-digested bandicoot and dried apricots, let out an

287

audible groan. But then he sternly commanded his regurgitative muscles to behave themselves, and ordered his front teeth to bite through the slightly membranous exterior of the grub, into the grape-like insides.

The taste of the grub was bland, not dissimilar to undercooked pork fat, and Eyre supposed that it would be quite acceptable if you happened to be particularly short of food. The consistency of the flesh, however, was repulsively stringy and jellyish; and when he had finished chewing the grub and swallowing it, he had to sit down on a fallen gum-tree for four or five minutes, trying to discipline himself not to think about those ringed markings, or that insectlike face.

'Well?' asked Christopher. 'You haven't said much. Not even *delicieux*!'

'It's good Aborigine manners to belch out loud if you enjoyed something,' grinned Dogger.

'I think I'd bring it all up if I belched,' said Eyre.

'I have more here, Mr Wakasah,' enthused Weeip, who had been busy with his digging-stick. He opened up his cupped hands to reveal twelve or fifteen fresh, twitching grubs.

Dogger, without a word, opened up his satchel and took out a silver flask of home-distilled rum. Eyre took a long, sweet, fiery swallow; and then gargled with it.

'I don't think you're hungry enough for an Aborigine diet yet,' said Dogger dryly. 'Most of what they eat is what you might call an acquired taste.' He took a pull on the flask of rum himself, and sniffed. 'I remember we were down on the beach once, not far from Wallaroo, and a whale had been stranded there. Pilot whale, huge bastard. It must have been rotting for weeks, but about a hundred blackfellows found it, and hacked it to pieces, and roasted it there and then. Great rejoicing there was, that day. The stink would have blown you all the way to Tasmania and back.'

They bedded down early that evening: Eyre wanted to make an early start to track down Yonguldye. The moon and her reflection moved gracefully to rendezvous behind the black bank of the water-hole; and the insects began their repetitive timekeeping.

Twenty-Two

Eyre slept dreamlessly for two or three hours; and then suddenly woke up, his eyes wide, listening. The insects had stopped singing, and all he could hear was the wind, low and sibilant, like the breath of a hesitant flute-player. Everyone else was asleep, as far as he could make out; although the horses were shifting restlessly beside the gum trees. He sat up, and looked around. The water-hole was as dark as a memory, pricked with stars. The gums performed a motionless mime, white-faced dancers in the prehistoric night.

Then, he heard chanting. Very low, and quite far away; but vibrant enough to carry. He listened for a minute or two. Sometimes the chanting was blown away by the wind, but when the wind dropped he heard it quite clearly. It was accompanied from time to time by a sharp wooden clapping, and by a hollow pipe-like sound which inexplicably made the hair around Eyre's scalp prickle up like pins.

He shook Christopher's shoulder, and whispered, 'Christopher!' But Christopher was determined to carry on sleeping, and all he did was roll on to his back, open his mouth, and begin to snore. Eyre whispered, 'Christopher!' again, but when it was obvious that he was going to arouse no response, he quietly drew back his own blankets, and eased himself away from the camp-fire, which had now burned down to nothing more than hot grey ash.

Dressed in nothing but his shirt, he crossed to the other side of the gully, and climbed up it so that he could see out across the plain. Off to the north-east, over the peaks of the northern Flinders range, large clouds were banked, although there was no likelihood that they would bring any rain. Directly to the north, there was a tiny blue glitter; the light of a distant camp-fire. It was from there that the chanting was coming; and the clapping of sticks.

Eyre looked back at the gully. None of the others had stirred, and he decided not to wake them. Dogger and Christopher always made such a performance of unrolling themselves in the morning, scratching and yawning and stumbling around, and so Eyre preferred to investigate this chanting himself; quietly. He would have liked to have taken a rifle with him, but unpacking it and loading it would have made too much noise.

He crouched low, so that he would remain unseen behind the mulga bushes and spinifex grass, and headed diagonally away from the gully, towards the eastern side of the distant fire. The wind was a light north-westerly, and so from the eastern side he would be able to hear the chanting at its clearest. Apart from that, Aborigines could pick up scents as sharply as hounds, or so Captain Sturt had told him, and so he decided that it would probably be more prudent to stay downwind.

He ran stealthily and quickly through the grass. His feet were cut and his legs were stung, and he began to wonder whether it would have been more sensible simply to fire off a few rifle shots from far away, and scare the chanting tribesmen from a safe distance. But he thought; you never know with blackfellows. If he were to frighten them, or if he were to interrupt one of their sacred rituals, they might well take it into their heads to come after him, and pay him back with a swift death-spear in the heart; or some more arcane revenge, like that which had befallen Arthur Mortlock.

The thought of Arthur still alarmed him. He would probably have nightmares about Arthur gagging and vomiting for the rest of his life; however long *that* would last. And most disturbing of all was the thought that Arthur might actually have died from the magical effects of Joolonga's pointing-bone, no matter how unearthly or preposterous that seemed. Eyre had heard of Mabarn Men who could actually shout their enemies to death; by letting out a long and terrible roar that ruptured their hearts and stunned their minds.

As Eyre made his way closer to the fire, the chanting died away; and a ragged chorus of cries and responses was taken up, like a primitive version of a Church of England collect. The responses were accompanied by a loud sporadic clapping that sounded like boomerangs being slapped together. A voice shouted a hoarse incantation, and there was an answering cry that ended with an Aborigine word that Eyre recognised, '—*wynarka!*' It meant 'Stranger'—and judging from the ferocity with which it was cried out, these blackfellows plainly felt very little affection for the 'stranger' about whom they were singing.

Eyre crouched and half-crawled his way up behind a mulga bush, and pushed the branches apart with his hand so that he could see the corroboree more clearly. As far as he could make out, there were ten or twelve blackfellows there, gathered around the fire, all of them naked, all of them painted with horrific masks of white pipe-clay. Their hair was elaborately pulled up into high top-knots, and there were rows of wallaby's teeth hanging across their foreheads. Two of them were sitting cross-legged on the ground; one of them clapping two boomerangs together to produce the sharp wooden rhythm that had first woken Eyre up, the other playing a large wind instrument that looked like a decorated tree-trunk, but which obviously must have been hollow. The booming, flutey song that this instrument produced was the most scaring noise of all; it didn't even sound as if it could have been created by a human at all, but rather by the wind, blowing through some lonely curve of eroded limestone, or by a breathing

Bunyip, or by some other strange creature from Australian legend.

Eyre watched the ritual for nearly half-an-hour. The blackfellows sang and clapped, and then they took each other around the waist and danced in a circle, swaying and shuffling, and humming in an undertone which was even deeper and more vibrant than the voice of the wooden instrument. Eyre began to wish very much that he hadn't ventured out this far, because he was now faced with the difficult task of returning to the gully without being noticed. The sky was lighter now, and the singing and the humming and the clapping had died away; and he was much more likely to be seen or heard. And there was no doubt about it: the collection of weapons which lay stacked beside the fire included not only spears with pirri points, but 'death-spears' with rows of sharp quartz flakes stuck along the sides of them with gum—spears which could inflict terrible wounds and which could usually be removed from a victim's body only by being pushed right through.

'The Lord is mice pepper,' he breathed to himself, a self-mocking repetition of the prayer which Weeip had told him. Then he stealthily backed away from the mulga bush, and then began to hurry like a frightened hunchback towards the edge of the gully.

He was panting as he ran; and his footsteps sounded thunderous as he weaved through the scrub and the spin-ifex grass. He kept imagining that he would hear the noise that the north Australian Aborigines described as *bimblegumbie*—the sound made by a spear launched from a woomera—and that seven feet of quartz-tipped kalyra-wood would stick into his back and bring him down before he could even tell Christopher that he loved Charlotte irrationally but passionately, and that she could have his bicycle, if she wanted it.

He was almost there. He could see the gums that surrounded their makeshift encampment. But just as he was about to slide down the slope towards the *billa*, some-

292

thing attenuated and dark rose out of the bushes beside him and made him shout out, 'Jesus!' in uncontrollable fear and surprise.

'*Quiet*, Mr Walker-sir,' said Joolonga's urgent voice.

'Quiet? You scared me half to death.'

'I saw you had gone, Mr Walker-sir. Weeip was supposed to be keeping watch but Weeip was asleep. I was coming after you, in case you needed me.'

'You could have given me a heart-seizure, you black rogue. Have you heard all that singing and chanting? Have you heard those fellows? Out there, by the fire. They've been singing and dancing away there for hours.'

'Yes,' said Joolonga, enigmatically.

'Well, do you know what they're doing?' Eyre asked him, as they made their way down to the water.

Joolonga squatted down by the oil-black surface of the pool, scooped his hand into the water, and splashed his face; then the back of his neck. His eyes glittered in the night like coins glimpsed at the bottom of a sunless well. 'They are holding a corroboree, Mr Walker-sir. A sacred dance to celebrate the coming-alive of a dreamtime story. It is here, tonight, that the coming-alive of the story begins.'

'Out here? What are you talking about?'

'Out here is where it was always foretold that the story would begin.'

'I'm not at all sure that I understand you.'

Dogger rolled over testily in his blankets, and called out, 'If you two want to spend the night nattering, why don't you do it somewhere out of earshot? I'm uglier than both of you put together: I need my beauty-sleep.'

Joolonga stood up, and beckoned Eyre to follow him further down the gully, until they were out of sight of the camp behind an outcropping of rock, overgrown by mulga bushes. Then Joolonga lit up his crab's-claw pipe and filled the night air with the strange pungency of his tobacco. 'I can safely tell you now, Mr Walker-sir. Before tonight, you may not have understood why this expedition was so important to us; and you may have declined to embark on it, in spite of how you felt about young Yanluga.'

'Go on,' said Eyre, warily.

'Well, Mr Walker-sir, it was always said in the dreamtime that the spirits of the dead would one day return from the place of the setting sun. When the first white men came here, most of us believed that they were the ghosts of our forefathers, since they came from the west, and their skins were white. Dead people, you see, were thought to shed their earthly skin when they rose up to the skies. In the early days, white men were always called *djanga*, which is the same word we use for "spirits of the dead".'

'Well?' said Eyre, a little testily. 'What does that have to do with this expedition?'

'Simply that it was always foretold, Mr Walker-sir, that one of the *djanga* would visit Tandarnya, which is what we call Adelaide; and that he would accidentally take the life of a blackfellow whose name in the story is Utyana, which means a boy who has not yet been initiated. But the *djanga* would seek atonement for what he had done; and would seek out a clever-man in order to be forgiven for taking the boy's life. He would have to journey for many weeks across the plains in order to find the cleverman; just as you have been obliged to.'

'If this mythical spirit is supposed to be me, I think you're forgetting that it wasn't *I* who killed Yanluga; it was Lathrop Lindsay, and those hounds of his.'

Joolonga looked unperturbed. 'You have said yourself, Mr Walker-sir, that if you had not gone to meet with Mr Lindsay's daughter that night, Yanluga would still be alive. It was always foretold that you would cause his death, Mr Walker-sir, and no matter what you did, no matter how you tried to avoid it, the foretelling had to come to pass.'

'Rubbish,' Eyre snapped. He was silent for long, deafened seconds, while Joolonga attentively smoked. Then he said, 'How does the story end?'

Joolonga spat into the darkness. 'In the story, the *djanga* comes across the trail of the clever-man at a place where the kangaroos come to drink. That is why we have come here to Woocalla. I think that Mr Dogger is probably right, and that Yonguldye is already at Yarrakina, the place of the ochre-mine; but it was necessary for us to come here in order to fulfil the story. That is why my brothers are out there tonight, dancing. They know that the foretelling will soon come to pass. They are celebrating.'

'Does the story say what happens when the *djanga* meets the clever-man?'

Joolonga nodded. 'It is known all over South Australia as the Story of the Spirit's Gift; for when the *djanga* meets the clever-man, he gives him in atonement all the knowledge of the spirit-world, so that living men might at last know all the strange and marvellous secrets of the land beyond the setting sun. These days, however, the blackfellows realise that the story foretold the landing of the white man, rather than the return of ghosts from the world above, and they believe that the chosen white man will give to the clever-man all the magical knowledge that makes the white man so superior; and that the clever-man will pass this magical knowledge from tribe to tribe, so that at last the blackfellow will be able to stand as an equal to the *djanga*; and protect his lands and his secret places from the white man's thievery.

'You, Mr Walker-sir, are the *djanga* for whom the Aborigine people have been waiting for hundreds of years, ever since the dreamtime. On your shoulders, the future of the Aborigine people completely rests; and they look to you for their salvation. Do you now see why you have been followed and protected by Aborigine warriors ever since the day of Yanluga's death; ever since you first declared that you would give him the burial which you believed he deserved?'

Eyre smeared chilly sweat away from his forehead with the back of his hand. The sky was far lighter now; and the *billa* shone like a cold memory, its surface circled only by the beaks of early-rising zebra-finches which had come down to the water's edge to drink while it was cool.

Eyre said, 'Listen to me, Joolonga. I determined to come out on this expedition firstly to do my duty by Yanluga; and secondly to make my name; so that I can claim the bride I want, and the fortune I want. But those two goals are the beginning and the end of it; whatever interpretation you and your Aborigine chums wish to put on it. I am a Christian, and I am as a moral as the next man, although I have no pretensions to holiness. But, damn it, Joolonga, I am not a messiah. Nor ever shall be.'

'Captain Sturt doesn't seem to agree with you,' said Joolonga, with a sly smile.

'Captain Sturt? What does Captain Sturt know about it?'

'Everything, of course.'

'You mean he knows about the legend of the *djanga*?'

'Of course,' Joolonga nodded. 'That is why he chose you to lead this expedition. Do you think there could have been any other reason for choosing an inexperienced shipping clerk to plunge straight into the deserts of South Australia? Captain Sturt came directly to talk to you at the Spring Ball, do you remember? Why do you think he picked you out so readily?'

'*You*,' said Eyre, 'are the black devil.'

'No, Mr Walker-sir; I am Captain Sturt's man.'

'But how did Captain Sturt come to hear so quickly of what I wanted to do? How did he know that I wanted to find Yonguldye? And what possible good could it have done him, even if he *did* know?'

Joolonga waved a mud-wasp away from his ear. 'You remember Captain Henry, who took you home after Yanluga was killed? He heard what you promised Yanluga, and heard it clearly, and he believed right away that you were the *djanga* of whom the foretelling had always spoken. Captain Henry is a Wirangu, sir, and in his own time was a clever-man of a kind. He was very excited. He told Yagan, who is the head man of the Aborigines who camp by the Torrens River, in Adelaide, and Yagan in his turn told me. Yagan has believed all his life that the blackfellow must find a way to live with the white man, but that he must have strength, and knowledge, and understand the white man's power, in order to survive. Otherwise, he will be like nothing better than a possum attacked by dingoes. Torn apart, ripped to pieces, out of weakness and ignorance.'

Eyre said nothing. He felt both angry and humiliated. Angry most of all that Captain Sturt should have deceived him; but deeply humiliated that he hadn't been chosen for this expedition because of his determination to find Yonguldye or because of his confidence and clear-headedness, but because he had appeared to a few superstitious blackfellows to be the thunderous coming of some mythical messiah; a magnificent but stupendously ignorant delusion which Captain Sturt had obviously done his best to exploit to the very limit. Captain Sturt had known his Aborigines better than he had let on; and his white men, too.

Joolonga said, casually, 'I told Captain Sturt all about you; and Captain Sturt contrived for you to meet him at the Spring Ball.'

'How?' Eyre demanded.

'A friend of Captain Sturt's talked to *your* friend, Mr Willis. I think the friend persuaded Mr Willis that Captain Sturt would soon talk you out of any ideas of looking for Yonguldye. And, I think there was some money.'

Eyre felt as if the flesh were being boiled of his bones. '*Why*?' he hissed at Joolonga; too furious and too shocked even to shout.

Joolonga shrugged. 'Finance, Mr Walker-sir. That is the word for it, isn't it? South Australia is almost bankrupt: the whole colony. Lately, Captain Sturt has lost thousands of pounds of his own money in sheep and wheat farming; while Colonel Gawler has already drawn £200,000 on the London Commissioners to build new roads and houses in Adelaide, and they say they will order him back to England if he draws any more. South Australia has no money, sir, and things go from bad to worse, and worse to terrible.'

'And that is why Captain Sturt has decided to make the best of me, is it? That is why he sent me off to meet with the Aborigine clever-men, and find out anything I could about opals, or copper, or cattle-trails to the north; anything that would pull his financial chestnuts out of the fire? And in the guise of a dreamtime spirit!'

Eyre stood up, and he was shaking. 'My God,' he said. 'Captain Sturt knew how much I respected the Aborigine religion. He knew what guilt I felt for Yanluga's death. And yet he calmly deceived both me and blackfellows who take me for their *djanga*. They were out there all night, around their fire, dancing and singing and celebrating! You saw them yourself! They believe that I'm that legendary spirit of yours! They believe that I can help them against men like Gawler and Sturt and Lathrop Lindsay! And *you*, Joolonga, what the hell do *you* believe? Not in your own people; that's quite obvious. Not in your own religion and your own legends. Nor do you believe in me; or you wouldn't have tricked me for so long. Is it money you believe in? Is that it? Is that all? God, man, you have no morals at all!'

Joolonga tapped out his pipe. 'I have beliefs, Mr Walker-sir.'

'Oh, yes? What beliefs?'

'I believe that we must fulfil this expedition: that we must follow Yonguldye to Yarrakinna.'

'Even though you know damned well that whatever riches Yonguldye points us to; no matter how many stock-trails to the north he tells us about; in return I can give him nothing? What magical secrets do *I* know? You would deceive your own people so flagrantly?'

Tightly, Joolonga said, 'My own people, as you call them, Mr Walker-sir, are already doomed. They were doomed from the moment the first white man set foot on Australia. My own people are a sad, poor, filthy, people. They should have died out hundreds of years ago; before

298

the white man ever saw them. Perhaps they should never have been.'

'You don't believe that.' Eyre challenged him.

'What I believe is unimportant,' said Joolonga. 'The man who was Joolonga died many years ago. He cannot rise again. It is not foretold.'

Eyre looked up at the pale, sand-coloured sky. His anger at Captain Sturt's deception had died down a little; although he knew it would continue to grate inside him like a fractured rib, until he could face Captain Sturt again and have it out with him, shout for shout. His most critical dilemma now was not whether he ought to take revenge on Captain Sturt or not, but whether he should call off the expedition altogether. Whether he ought to return to Adelaide without wealth, without glory, and without any kind of discovery to honour his name; to face both a political and a financial scandal, not to mention disgrace in the eyes of everybody he knew, especially Charlotte; or whether he ought to press on, and find Yonguldye, and accomplish everything that both Sturt and the Aborigine people expected of him regardless of how he had been tricked; and regardless of how the Aborigines would eventually suffer. And, by God, how they would suffer, especially if Captain Charles Sturt had anything to do with it.

Joolonga had already taken sides. Joolonga had chosen inevitability. Why struggle to win a battle that has already been lost? Yet, in spite of himself, Joolonga still guarded some silent and secret faith in Ngurunderi, and Baiame, and the other dreamtime gods; and that faith gave Eyre an inkling of hope that if he continued the expedition, they would be able to bring to Yonguldye's *noora* not magical knowledge, perhaps; not even the promise that the black-fellows would be able to protect their hunting-grounds and their sacred places from the ravages of the whites but the possibility that they might at least be able to survive and eventually flourish in what was one day going to be predominantly a white man's country.

Dogger, from around the bushes, shouted, 'Eyre? What the *hell's* going on? Where are you? Not taking your morning shit already?'

'*Coming*!' Eyre called back, as lightly as he could. Then, to Joolonga, 'I'm not sure why you felt it necessary to tell me all of this. But, I appreciate your frankness. At least I know now why I'm here.'

Joolonga said flatly, 'It was necessary for you to know sooner or later. Captain Sturt said that I should tell you the night before we expected to reach Yonguldye's encampment. However, I saw that you were seeking an explanation for that corroboree which was held during the night; and that unless you were given an answer, you might decide to return to Adelaide.'

'What makes you think that I'm not going to return to Adelaide even now?'

'You are a young man, Mr Walker-sir. You have ideals that older men no longer have; and you are ready to believe things which older men no longer believe. But I have seen that you make your mistakes once only; and that you learn as quickly as a dingo. You know that you will go on, if only to prove to Captain Sturt that you can do everything he expected you to do, only better. Ahead, there is a chance of fame and wealth. Behind, only confusion and disgrace. This is not a country which rewards those who surrender, Mr Walker-sir, no matter what the perils may be.'

Eyre said, 'Very well, we're going on. But let me warn you, Joolonga, everything I said to you yesterday still applies. I've had enough of your secrets, and enough of your arrogant manners. We're going under *my* terms, not yours, and certainly not under Captain Sturt's. When we catch up with Yonguldye, it will be my decision how we approach him; and I will want nothing more from you than to act as my interpreter. Because, by God, if you cross me once more, Joolonga, I will have your head off for it.'

Joolonga bowed his head, and then trod heavily away to sort out the horses. Eyre stayed where he was for a while, breathing deeply, and wondering what in all Heaven he ought to do. The sharpest pain of all was that Christopher should have talked about him to Captain Sturt's friend before the Spring Ball; and that he should actually have taken money to persuade Eyre to come along with him that night. No wonder Christopher had seemed so angry when Captain Sturt had done nothing at all to dissuade Eyre from setting out to find Yonguldye. No wonder he had tried to say that night how much he loved Eyre; and how much he revered him.

It had been the love of Judas; the reverence of guilt.

Twenty-Three

They crossed the salt lake towards Parachilna like slowly-moving figures in a sparkling dream. The sun shone with such shattering brilliance on the swathes of dried-out, coloured minerals that made up the lakebed; almost blinding them; that Eyre devised himself a pair of spectacles made of smoked pieces of bottle glass and wire; and rode through the days of heat and dust like Mephistopheles.

He hardly spoke at all to any of his companions; and in return they kept well away from him, Dogger and Christopher and Midgegooroo and Weeip riding in a small, close bunch, with the pack-horses on either side of them, although Joolonga rode closer to Eyre, and a little off to the right, as if he were privy to his secrets, if not his thoughts.

During the whole length of those glaring days, Eyre could think about nothing but Captain Sturt, and how he had betrayed him; and Christopher, too, and how Christopher had hurt him more than Eyre could have imagined possible. He ate in silence at their evening fires; and slept apart in his bedroll. In the morning, with the sun rising over the crust of the lake like the unwelcome visitation of some incandescent Presence from heaven itself, he would mount up and ride ahead of them again, silently, blind-eyed, his face wrapped in scarves against the saline dust. Dogger began to talk of sunstroke, and bush-madness, and of turning back. But Christopher perversely began to talk about Eyre as if he were a doomed young knight from medieval days on a quest for the Holy Grail; and far from faltering, his enthusiasm for the expedition grew even more complicated, and more involved.

They reached Parachilna on a surprisingly mild evening, when a light dusty wind was blowing, and there were clouds moving along the horizon like sailing-ships in a nearby harbour. The rusty-coloured peaks of the north Flinders rose all around them now, the dry, wrinkled peaks of a once-forested mountain range. Eyre dismounted, and began to walk his horse up a twisting creek-bed; and there was no sound but the clinking of fragments of slate disturbed by its hoofs, and the *whirrr-whirrr-whirrr* of the cicadas.

Dogger gave his horse to Midgegooroo to lead, and hurried up the creekbed to overtake Eyre before they started climbing up the more gentle slope ahead of them.

'Eyre,' he said, taking hold of Eyre's bridle. 'Eyre, you can't continue like this. Come on, mate. You've got the rest of us to think about, apart from yourself.'

Eyre was silent for a while, standing very upright, his face floury with dust. His eyes were invisible behind the two darkened curves of smoked glass; like the eyes of an insect.

'I suppose you want me to sing and joke,' he said, at last.

'Well, why not?' Dogger told him. 'This is a miserable enough business as it is, without a little fun. And damn it, Eyre, you used to be fun. What about those evenings on Hindley Street? Two jugs of beer and you and me were laughing fit to bust our trousers. What happened to all that?'

'I don't know,' said Eyre. He truly didn't know. He felt as if all the fun had been evaporated out of him, by the sun; as if now he had been kippered into mirthlessness, sexlessness, and irascibility; a leathery ascetic in search of a dried-up ideal. He no longer knew why he was here; or what moral principle he was trying to uphold. He had lost his faith in Christopher; his trust in Joolonga; and his enjoyment of Dogger.

Dogger said bluntly, 'If you don't snap yourself out of this, old mate, I'm turning back. I know this territory, as far as here. I came out here once, looking for emu. But I'm not going any further; not unless I get some sign from you that things are jogging along as they ought to be. I'm game for adventure, Eyre. But I don't intend to die for no good reason; and especially not without a smile on my fizzog. Anyone who comes out beyond the black stump with a mien as miserable as what yours is; well, mate, they're certain dingo-fodder, that's all, and I didn't spend twenty years hunting down dogs to end up as dog's breakfast, nor dinner, nor *hoose-doovries* neither.'

Eyre lowered his head, and brushed white dust from his curls with the back of his hand. Then he carefully took off his dark glasses, and looked at Dogger, and grinned.

'You're right,' he said. 'I've been a sour and miserable bastard, and I'm sorry. But let's go on.'

'We can turn back if you want to. Nobody will think the less of you.'

Eyre shook his head. 'I've forgotten why I'm here. The whole desert is so overwhelming that I don't think I really care any more. But let's go on.'

'And you'll smile, now and then?' urged Dogger.

Eyre nodded.

'Not just at me and Weeip; but at Christopher, too. You've been giving *him* a pretty uncomfortable time, these past three days. Come on, Eyre, you know it.'

'I'll do my best.'

Christopher caught up with them, leading his horse with difficulty up the narrow, fragmented creek-bed. He frowned at Eyre from beneath the brim of his wide kangaroo-skin hat, and there was a look in his eyes which was a mixture of admiration and despair; a look to which Eyre was bound to respond. Bound not only by their friendship; but by plain human dignity; and by the circumstances in which they now found themselves, hundreds of miles from anything but scrub and salt and mountains as dry as a nine-hour sermon.

Eyre let go of his bridle, and came forward over the clattering slate, and put his arms around Christopher, and held him close; and then turned to Dogger, and held out an arm for him, and embraced him, too. And the three of them stood under the violet evening sky, on the side of a rust-red mountain, holding each other in the comradeship that would one day be known in the outback as 'mateship'; the love man-for-man that is blatantly forged on the battered anvil of self-preservation; the love that knows neither dignity nor suspicion; that asks no questions; and expresses no desires; but which fades in city streets as rapidly as an uprooted desert rose.

Joolonga watched this embrace dispassionately from the ridge above the creek-bed, among the vivid-green acacias. Weeip and Midgegooroo stood by their pack-horses, equally expressionless, both of them chewing on pitjuri leaves, which always made them placid and detached.,

At last, Eyre said, 'Let's get ahead. It's going to be dark before long and I want to find a decent place to camp.' He felt more encouraged now, especially since Christopher had made it quite clear that he would follow him and support him wherever he went. 'Joolonga,' he called, 'do you think there's any chance of catching up with Yonguldye before nightfall?'

'I smell an encampment close, Mr Walker-sir; big one. See, there is smoke over the ridge there.'

'Do you think it's a good idea just to go barging in to a

strange community of blackfellows?' asked Dogger. 'I've heard that some tribes are quite partial to explorer casserole.'

Eyre put on his dark glasses again. 'We'll carry the rifles with us; just in case. Midgegooroo, unpack three rifles for us, will you; three; and make sure that they're properly loaded, the way I showed you.'

He felt in his pocket and made sure he had one essential item: his magical *mana* stone. Weeip came up and brought them water. There were streams running through the Flinders, which the Aborigines called *aroona*; streams which bubbled up from underground springs and danced their way down between the limestone rocks, sometimes forming pools of stunning clarity. The water attracted seabirds, grey teal and white-faced tern, as well as wallabies and euros and emus, so there would be plenty of fresh food for them to eat while they were here.

Eyre led them up the creek-bed until they found themselves in a wide gorge, with overhanging rocks rising up on three sides; and extraordinarily, like a silently-shrieking governess throwing herself from an attic window, a single ghost-gum growing out from the rocks almost thirty feet above their heads.

Eyre said, 'We'll leave the horses here. Weeip, you keep watch on them. Joolonga, Midgegooroo, you come up with us. If we can find Yonguldye, we'll come back and fetch the horses; if we can't, we'll settle here for the night. Weeip?'

'Yes, Mr Wakasah?'

'Light yourself a fire. If we don't find Yonguldye, we'll be hungry by the time we get back.'

'Yes, Mr Wakasah. And—Mr Wakasah?'

'What is it, Weeip?'

Young Weeip covered his face with his hands, so that his dark eyes sparkled through the gaps between his fingers. 'Don't bring back the devil-devil, Mr Wakasah.'

Eyre knelt down beside him. Weeip kept his hands over his face, and his soft curly hair blew in the evening breeze.

305

'You're not scared of the devil-devil, are you?' Eyre asked him, kindly.

Dogger laughed; and snorted. But all the same, he looked around the gorge with sudden apprehension, as if Weeip's fear had attracted the first flickering coldness of Kooabooboodgery, the night spirit. Christopher coughed into his hand.

'I feel the devil-devil, Mr Wakasah. Something bad here. Yea though I walk through the alley of the valley of death.'

Eyre glanced up at Joolonga. 'Joolonga?' he asked. 'Do you sense anything?'

Joolonga took off his midshipman's hat and raised his flat nose to the wind. He remained like that for a few moments, his face concentrated and fierce, but then he said, 'Only fires, Mr Walker-sir. No evil spirits.'

'Well, then,' said Eyre, and stood up. 'Let's go and see if we can find our man. You know, I'm almost sorry I didn't bring my bicycle. Can you imagine what a rip it would be to cycle all the way down that creek-bed?'

Dogger picked up his rifle, and slung it on to his back. 'Surprising how a few hills can cheer a fellow up, isn't it? It's the flatness that makes you feel like giving up, and killing yourself. One old dogger I knew, Bill Hardcastle, he used to curse the desert for hours on end, because it was flat. You never heard such language in your whole life; and every insult for flat that you could think of. He used to say that it was all God's fault, the desert. God ran out of ideas, he said, and said to the Angel Gabriel, what shall I do with the rest of this world? And Gabriel said, "Oh, I shouldn't bother if I were you; leave it flat." So that's what He did. Mind you, he could catch dingoes, could Bill; even the ones that could sniff out a trap from a mile away. He'd set up scarecrows and windmills alongside his traps; just enough to catch the dog's attention, so that the dog wouldn't notice where it was walking. Then snap, and the dog was caught. God's featureless folly, that was one of the names he called the desert. Poor old Bill.'

'Why "poor old Bill"?' asked Christopher.

Dogger spat inaccurately at a lump of euro dung on the rocks. 'Gave up dogging, did Bill, went back to Melbourne, and tripped over a mounting-block by the side of the road and broke his neck.'

With Joolonga leading the way, and Eyre close behind him, they climbed the side of the gorge. The rock was flaky in places, and once or twice Eyre missed his footing and skidded backwards, sending showers of stones down on Christopher's head; but at last they crested the gorge and found themselves walking along a high spine of mauvish-coloured limestone, with the higher peaks around the Yarrakinna ochre-mine rising off to their left, blood-red against a blood-red sky.

They crossed a low, gentle valley of lemon-scented grasses. Here and there, they came across clumps of the startling red-and-black flowers which had been named for Captain Sturt—Sturt's desert pea. They had petals like the gaudy hoods of elfish cardinals, hung up in the vestry.

The air was aromatic with eucalyptus oil and the dryness of emu bushes but now Eyre, too, could pick out the distinctive smell of cooking-fires. Joolonga was twenty or thirty paces ahead of him now, his head down, following the tracks of Yonguldye's people through the grassy sand.

Christopher said, 'I hope we know what we're getting ourselves into.'

Eyre ran his hand through his tangled curls. 'Don't worry about it, old chum. I've talked to Joolonga, and Joolonga says that the Aborigines really want us here. To them, this expedition is vitally important. Apparently, it was foretold in the dreamtime; and it has some sort of magical significance for them.'

'I'm still not desperately happy about it,' remarked Dogger, laconically. 'They're a funny lot, these bush black-fellows. Different from the tame characters you see around town. Funny ideas; and very quick to take the huff.'

The ground had been steadily rising, and the grass becoming increasingly sparse, until they were walking on bare limestone again; over ridges that had been scoured by sand and worried by water. At last, they saw the bright blue haze of cooking-smoke rising up ahead of them; and Joolonga turned to Eyre and raised ten fingers twice, which meant twenty fires, at least.

'Quite a gathering,' said Eyre. 'It seems as if we're expected.'

Christopher held back. 'Eyre, listen—we ought to approach these people with the greatest of caution.'

Eyre walked back and took hold of the straps of Christopher's satchel, and drew him forward. 'They're not going to hurt us, I promise you. Tell him, Joolonga. They think that I'm a messenger from the spirit world, or something like that. Everything's going to be perfectly all right.'

Dogger said to Joolonga, 'What's your opinion, squash-face? You're supposed to be the guide. Do you know these people? What are they, Wirangu?'

'Some Wirangu, some Nyungar, maybe some from Murray River.'

'Are they friendly, or what? And what's all this about our friend here being a messenger from the spirit world?'

'It is what they believe, Mr Dogger. It is a long-ago story which they now seem to think has come true.'

'And has it?'

'We must see, Mr Dogger,' said Joolonga.

At that moment, so silently that even Joolonga was startled, three skeleton-figures rose up from the rocks nearby; three Aborigine warriors smeared with grease and pipe-clay and ochre, their hair wound with twine and decorated with scores of wind-twirled emu feathers. Each of them carried a long spear and a woomera; with clubs tied around their waists. One of them also had a dead tern hanging around his waist, a bird he must have caught while waiting and watching for Eyre's expedition to make its way up the mountains.

'Christopher, Dogger,' said Eyre, and beckoned them to stand closer to him. All three of them raised their rifles, and cocked them ready for firing. Midgegooroo remained where he was; but Joolonga raised one hand and stepped forward, until he was fewer than ten paces away from the nearest tribesman. He spoke quickly, first in Nyungar, which was the nearest that South Australia's tribes had to a common language; and then in Wirangu. The tribesman did not deign to reply at first, but looked haughtily from Joolonga to his three white companions, and then to Midgegooroo.

'What did you say to him?' asked Eyre.

'I said that you were the chosen *djanga*, and that you were seeking to talk to Yonguldye the Mabarn Man.'

'Tell him again,' said Eyre.

'Wait,' advised Joolonga.

They stood their ground. It was beginning to grow dark now; and against the gradually thickening sky, the three Aborigine warriors looked as wild and primaeval as Cro-Magnon men. One of them pointed with his spear at Midg-egooroo, and indicated that he should move closer to Eyre and Christopher and Dogger; and this Midgegooroo reluctantly did. Eyre lifted his rifle-stock up to his shoulder, and took aim at the tribesman who stood furthest off to the left. He was silhouetted sharply against the last of the daylight, and made by far the easiest target.

'Be careful, Mr Walker-sir,' said Joolonga. 'If you should shoot by mistake, there is no telling what they might do.'

'Tell them again that I am the *djanga* who has come to talk to Yonguldye, Eyre insisted. 'And also tell them that we are all *ngaitye*. We are all friends.'

Joolonga hesitated, but then rapidly spoke to the tribesmen again.

'If you want my opinion,' said Dogger, 'We should drop the lot of them here and now, before they know what's hit them; and then leg it back to the horses at top belt.'

'Ssh,' said Eyre. 'He's answering.'

Now, the leading tribesman was saying something to Joolonga. The language sounded to Eyre like Wirangu, although he couldn't be certain. There was a distinctive guttural clacking about Wirangu which Eyre recognised from the way in which Yanluga used to talk to his horses. The tribesman seemed to feel very vehemently about what he was saying, because he kept rapping his throwing-stick against the shaft of his spear, and ducking and nodding his head. Sometimes his voice was a breathy murmur; at other times he was shouting as if he were apoplectically furious that they had arrived here without asking his permission. All the time Joolonga remained impassive, his hat set very straight on his head, one arm tucked into his impressive coat like Napoleon, but trouserless, with his scrotum and his penis elaborately wound up with twine.

At last the tribesman's haranguing appeared to be over. He stepped back two or three paces, and stood quite still, the wind ruffling his feather head-dress. Joolonga made two or three quick gestures in sign-language, and then walked back to Eyre. To Eyre's surprise, Joolonga's forehead and cheekbones were shining with sweat, and he was shivering.

'What was all that about?' asked Eyre.

'He says that we must follow him, but that he expects us to observe certain proprieties.

'What proprieties?'

'We must leave all of our clothing here; and our weapons.'

'What?' demanded Dogger. 'You expect me to walk baby-bum-naked into a camp full of mad Aborigines, without even a rifle to guard my particulars. Come on, Eyre. This is ridiculous.'

Eyre looked towards the tribesman who had spoken to Joolonga. 'Ask him what his name is,' he said.

'Joolonga turned around and called out to the tribesman, who lifted his spear and said, 'Parilla.'

Joolonga translated, 'That is his familiar name, not his family name. It means "cold", or "the cold one".'

'Well, you can call *me* the cold one if I have to go down and meet those blackfellows without my clothes on,' put in Dogger.

But Eyre called out to Parilla, in a challenging voice,

'Parilla! You go without clothes! But what man would ever go without his weapons? Not you! Well, nor will we!'

Anxiously, gabbling sometimes, Joolonga translated. Parilla listened seriously, occasionally nodding his head; and then he turned and spoke to his two lieutenants. Joolonga murmured to Eyre, 'This could mean some trouble, Mr Walker-sir. Parilla is a fierce tribal warrior; he does not like to be ridiculed, especially by a white man. It seems to me that he does not believe that you are the *djanga*; or even if he does, he feels enmity towards you.'

Without any warning at all, Parilla stooped, picked up a stone, and hurled it straight at Eyre's face. Eyre didn't even have time to think about dodging away; but the stone was thrown so accurately that it did nothing more than graze his cheekbone, and flick an instant line of bright red blood across his skin.

There was a clockspring silence between them. Joolonga backed away a little. Christopher raised his rifle now, and aimed it directly at the second tribesman. Even Dogger kept quiet, except for a spasmodic sniff, and warily flicked his eyes from one warrior to another.

Below them, off to the right, where the cooking-smoke was coming from, they heard the first cry of a great chant. To Eyre, the sound was completely electrifying; because it must have come from the throats of a hundred Aborigines; and it made the entire evening vibrate, as if the limestone bedrock of the Flinders mountains themselves were humming like a tuning-fork. A flock of fairy martins, hunting insects in the dusk, swooped and turned as if the sound of human voices had deflected them in flight.

Eyre lifted his rifle again and pointed it at Parilla's head. the Aborigine remained motionless, his expression unreadable beneath the thick pipe-clay and ochre that striped his cheeks and his forehead. The rifle was heavy and Eyre knew that he would have to be quick before his aim started to waver. He was no marksman; and although the distance between them was only fifteen paces, it was so gloomy now that it would be easy to make a fatal mistake.

311

Dogger said, 'We'd be well advised to walk quietly away now, Eyre. I'm not funning with you.'

Eyre said, 'If we walk away now, they'll never let us go. And besides, we still have our duty.'

'I rather think our prime duty is to stay alive,' said Christopher, with deep unhappiness.

Eyre ignored him. He had been challenged by Parilla; only a glancing, childish blow with a stone; the kind of blow with which the tribesman would have teased an uninitiated youth. But he had done it to see whether Eyre really was the *djanga* he proclaimed himself to be, or just another scavenging white man. Eyre had no way of knowing it for certain, but he sensed that if they tried to retreat without accepting Parilla's challenge, they would be speared where they stood, like Weeip's writhing bandicoot.

Joolonga blurted, 'Mr Walker-sir—' But Eyre squeezed the rifle's trigger, and there was an abrupt loud report, as if two boomerangs had been slapped together right next to his ears, and a spurt of bright orange fire from the pan; and then a cloud of brown smoke.

Everybody turned to stare at Parilla in shock. But the Aborigine warrior was still standing, although he was swaying slightly in delayed reaction to being fired at. The most remarkable sight, however, was his head-dress of emu feathers. The shot had blown it completely to pieces, leaving his thickly-greased hair standing on end in a parody of utter fright, and the air around his head full of whirling, floating feathers.

The echo of the shot came back from the distant mountains, and far away there was a flurry of birds. But then came the laughter: first from Midgegooroo, then from Dogger and Christopher, and finally from Parilla's own tribesmen. The laughter subsided for a moment, but then Parilla himself reached up gingerly and patted his hair; and he began to laugh, too, an odd clacking high-pitched chuckle.

'By God I think you've rediscovered your sense of humour,' said Dogger, wiping his eyes with the back of his sleeve. 'Look at the poor bastard. He looks as if he's seen a devil-devil.'

Only Joolonga remained unsmiling. Eyre had taken on the challenge of Parilla against his advice, and won it; without bloodshed, and without any loss of dignity on either side. Joolonga stood to one side, his hands crossed behind his back so that they lifted up his coat-tails, and flapped them up and down like a cockerel's tail, intermittently baring his stringy brown buttocks.

The shot attracted more Aborigines, painted and feathered just as Parilla and his companions were. Parilla spoke to them in a harsh, imperative voice, and they stayed back in a respectful circle, waiting to see what would happen next. The chanting from the encampment continued, however, deep and melodious; so deep sometimes that it seemed below the range of human hearing. Two or three of the tribesmen who had come to join them on the ridge shouted back their responses towards the camp-fires, and there was whooping and rapping of sticks and boomerangs, until the night echoed and clattered and screeched.

'What are we supposed to do now?' asked Christopher, apprehensively.

'Now we do what they asked us,' said Eyre. 'We take off our clothes, and we follow them down to the encampment. But we don't let go of our rifles; and Midgegooroo can still bring his satchel of ammunition. Here, Midgegooroo, you might as well reload this one while we're undressing.'

'I'm damned purple if I'm going to undress,' said Dogger, ferociously.

'In that case, you can go back to the horses and wait with Weeip.'

'What, and miss the fan-dancing?'

Joolonga came over and said, 'You were lucky with this one man, Mr Walker-sir. He can laugh at himself. But there are many others who do not have the same facility.'

'Like you, for instance, my dear Joolonga,' said Eyre, unbuttoning his cuffs.

Joolonga gave a bitter little smile, and shook his head. 'I can laugh when the occasion warrants it, Mr Walker-sir. But tonight we must go warily, and treat our new acquaintances with respectfulness.'

Eyre stepped out of his britches, and unfastened his long cotton underwear, already stained and marked from days of sweaty riding, and from being washed out in nothing but muddy pools of stagnant water. He shook his shirt over his head, and then he was naked, very thin now, with protuberant ribs and a slightly curving stomach, and reddened thighs from the constant chafing of the saddle. Dogger, once he had struggled out of his combination underwear (A.L. Elder's finest), looked like a displeased Mr Punch. Christopher slowly took off his britches; but kept his shirt on. Parilla said something angrily to Joolonga, pointing and waving at Christopher, but Christopher said: 'Tell him I'm sick. Tell him I've got a rash. If I get the sun on my back, it'll kill me.'

'Come,' said Joolonga; and they followed Parilla and the other tribesmen down the sloping side of the limestone ridge, towards a second, less prominent outcropping.

Eyre felt curiously light-headed, walking through the night stark naked with these fierce and primitive-looking tribesmen escorting him on either side. But on the other hand he felt there was a naturalness to being naked in these surroundings; a oneness with the warm air and the raw rocks and the spiny grasses that stung his bare ankles. There was an ancient eroticism to it; the same blatant and unashamed sexuality that had first struck him when he landed in Adelaide last year. His penis half-stiffened as he walked, but it neither upset him nor embarrassed him.

During his days of isolation from Christopher and Dogger as they had crossed the salt lake, he had come to the understanding not so much that he should be more mistrustful of others, but that he should invest more trust in himself. That was why he had been able to turn to his companions at last and embrace them. That was why he

314

had been able to face up to Parilla so confidently. And that was why he could walk naked through the mountainous night with all the confidence of a warrior. Christopher had sensed the change in him, without even realising that it was his own betrayal of Eyre that had brought it about.

They reached the brink of the second outcropping; and Parilla said, in Wirangu, 'Behold.' And what they saw beneath them was so breathtaking and so moving that Eyre could only turn to Christopher and shake his head in astonishment.

The ground dropped steeply away below their feet into a deep layered gorge, scoured out of the limestone over thousands and thousands of years by a rushing array of waterfalls. The reddish crags on either side were in darkness now that night had fallen; but their terraces and balconies and water-hewn pulpits were sparkling with hundreds of cooking-fires and torches, so that the gorge had taken on the appearance of the grandest of civilised theatres, La Scala in the middle of the Australian outback, with chandeliers and footlights and carriage-lamps. Among these lights, shadowy primitive figures came and went, scores of them, and it was these figures who sang so resonantly as they roasted their meats or fed their dingo-pups or prepared their children for the night's sleep. It was the greatest gathering of Aboriginal tribes that any of them had ever seen; or even heard about. And the warmth of these people's humanity, the power of their family closeness, were overwhelming, rising from the glittering depths of the gorge as distinctly and as strongly as the smoke from the cooking-fires, or the vibrant harmony of the ancient songs. They were innocent feelings, yet proud; and under these skies on this most timeless of nights, they brought Eyre for the first time to an emotional rather than an intellectual understanding of the people who had lived in Australia for three million years.

'If all the centuries during which Australia has been inhabited were condensed to a single hour,' Captain Sturt had told Eyre, the night before they had set out, 'then the Aborigines would have lived here alone for fifty-nine

315

minutes and twenty seconds; and the remainder of the time would represent the white occupation.'

There had been Aborigines here in the Pleistocene age. There had been Aborigines here when the deserts were thick with trees, and giant kangaroo roamed the grasslands. There had been Aborigines here when the lakes of South Australia were vast sheets of water, teeming with fish, instead of crusted salt flats. And there were still Aborigines here, gathered together on this warm spring night to celebrate the coming-alive of one of their oldest legends.

Eyre found that there were tears in his eyes. 'Smoke,' he told Dogger, but Dogger understood, too, in his rough-and-ready way.

Parilla called to Joolonga; and Joolonga said, 'This way. There is a path down the side of the hill.' As the chanting swelled from the gorge below them, they climbed their way down through the rocks; at one point crossing a narrow waterfall, their fingers slipping on the lichen-covered rocks, the cold water splattering their naked bodies.

'I could murder a beer,' said Dogger, longingly. His belly was raw and scratched from scraping against the rocks as he shuffled from ledge to ledge. Eyre couldn't help glancing at his genitals: they looked like a mallee fowl sitting on her nest of gingery-brown vegetation, waiting for her eggs to hatch.

When they reached the floor of the gorge, they were immediately surrounded by a crowd of curious Aborigine men and women and children. The fires flickered and smoked, the chanting and the boomerang-banging continued as loudly as before; and all around them was chattering and laughing and scuttling; and a constant carnival of white-painted faces, scarred and decorated shoulders and chests, beads and feathers and shining teeth, wide eyes and wildly decorated hair, bare breasts and dancing feet. Dazed and dazzled, they followed Parilla to the centre of the ravine, where the greatest fire of all was burning, a huge stack of dried gums and emu bushes, spitting and sparking and roaring, and there, tied with twenty or thirty wallaby skulls and stuck with hundreds of emu feathers, stood a large shelter, or *tantanoorla*, of branches and brushwood.

'Parilla says that this is the shelter of Yonguldye the medicine-man,' said Joolonga.

'Well, then,' replied Eyre, 'I think you can announce us, don't you?'

'There is one thing to remember, ' said Joolonga. 'When Yonguldye asks you where you have come from, you must answer "Goondooloo".'

'What does that mean?'

'It is a name in the legend, that is all. But he must believe that you have come from there; otherwise our lives may be in danger.'

Joolonga told Parilla to call Yonguldye. Parilla shook his head, and launched into another of his long clacking lectures; but then knocked the end of his spear two or three times on the rock, and nodded, and went inside the shelter.

'What did he say?' asked Eyre.

'He said that Yonguldye is the greatest of all medicine-men, and that he must be treated with great respect because his revenge is very terrible and we will all have our heads cut off and our bones broken and be fed to the dogs.'

'That's reassuring,' said Christopher. He glanced beside him at a particularly inquisitive black girl, who was staring unashamedly at his nakedness. He crossed his hands over his genitals and the girl giggled at him.

Yonguldye kept them waiting for almost five minutes. They scarcely spoke to each other at all as they stood there; their faces and chests scorched by the raging fire, their backs chilled by the cool night air which was now beginning to flow into the valley. Eyre glanced at Christopher, but Christopher had his head bowed as if he were thinking deeply, or praying.

At last, however, there was a sharp clamour of sticks and boomerangs, and Parilla reappeared from the *tantanoorla*, raising his spear high into the air. A shout rose up from all the blackfellows clustering around them, and a chant of 'Yonguldye! Yonguldye!'

Yonguldye appeared before them with massive ritual dignity. He was a very tall, old Aborigine with a gigantic head-dress of fur and feathers and wallaby teeth that looked like some monstrous mythical creature which had decided to perch on top of him, and remain there to keep watch on his enemies. His face was painted grey with pipe-clay, with a broad ochre band across his forehead, and his withered chest was covered in curving and twisting *ngora*, or decorative scars. His penis was contained in a rolled-up piece of ghost-gum bark, tied around his waist with twine, which gave his protuberant belly the appearance of a brandy-barrel, complete with spigot. He was almost completely toothless, except for the stumps of his two top canines, which gave his face an even more devilish appearance.

Joolonga raised his hand and greeted Yonguldye in sign-language. Then he spoke to the medicine-man in a tone which Eyre had never heard him use before, low and quick and muttering, with none of his usual posturing or arrogance. Now and then he wiped sweat away from his upper lip with his hand. Eyre caught the words *'djanga'* and *'tyinyeri'*, which meant child; and *'milang'*; but Joolonga was speaking so quietly and so rapidly that it was impossible for him to follow the meaning.

Eventually, Yonguldye stepped forward, and stood before Eyre with half-closed eyes, scrutinising him in the firelight. He had a strange smell about him, Yonguldye, like herbs and sweat and lemon-grass.

'So,' he said. 'You are the *djanga*.'

'Yes,' said Eyre, as firmly as he could.

Yonguldye raised his hand and touched Eyre's shoulder. 'You feel like man.'

'Nevertheless, I am the *djanga*. I come from Goon-

318

dooloo.' Eyre hoped that he had remembered the correct pronunciation.

Yonguldye lifted his head towards the sky, and peered up at the stars. 'You speak like man,' he said. 'You speak like white man.'

'All men speak like white men in Goondooloo,' Eyre smiled, with as much confidence as he could manage.

'Hm,' said Yonguldye. He lowered his head again, and stared at Eyre with renewed ferocity. 'Why does *djanga* carry—' he was lost for the right word for a moment, and then he said, '—*oodlawirra*?'

'Weapon,' whispered Joolonga.

Eyre lifted up the rifle. 'For hunting.'

'*Djanga* no eat.'

'Ah, but sometimes the *djanga* wants to shoot a wallaby or two just for the sport of it; and give it to his friends and relatives. A kind of a gift, if you understand me. The dead nourishing the living.'

Joolonga translated, and Yonguldye seemed to be satisfied with that answer, for he walked all the way around them, nodding and sucking noisily at his gums, and then with a hand like a galah's claw, he beckoned them to follow him into his shelter.

Dogger hesitated at first, but Eyre took his arm, and they bent their heads down and made their way under the clattering skulls around the entrance into the darkness of Yonguldye's lair.

The stench inside the shelter was overpowering. Grease, and sweat, and aromatic herbs, and a smell like decaying fish, which turned out to be an overripe sea-bird which Yonguldye must have been keeping for his breakfast. There were already five other tribespeople inside the shelter; a thin-ribbed boy whom Eyre guessed to be Yonguldye's assistant; and four women; one of them grey-haired and elderly, with a face which looked as if it had been squeezed in a wine-press; the other three far younger. The youngest of them all, who couldn't have been much older than fifteen, was unusually attractive,

319

with very long black curly hair tied with twine, and that rare glossy look about her skin which the effects of harsh sunlight and an irregular diet had not yet dried away. Her face was as Aboriginal as any of her tribe but it was unmarked and unpainted, except for two tiny scars on her cheek and the more he looked at her, the prettier Eyre thought that she was. Her breasts were very large for her age, high and brown-nippled; although there was only the lightest fan-like growth of dark hair between her thighs. Christopher noticed the way that Eyre looked at her, and made a point of crossing the shelter in front of him, to obstruct his view.

'Sit,' said Yonguldye, and they eased themselves awkwardly down on the heaps of greasy-smelling kangaroo hides with which the floor of his shelter was carpeted. 'Food, and water?' he asked, and Joolonga nodded in appreciation, although Eyre realised with chagrin that because he was supposed to be a *djanga*, returned from the dead, he would not be able to eat anything.

Yonguldye knew very little English. Most of it he had picked up during the bad dry of 1838, when he and his tribe had been forced to camp close to a mission at New Norcia in order to survive the summer. He quickly lapsed into Nyungar, and Eyre had to depend on Joolonga's translation to follow the conversation. He felt uneasy about that: Joolonga seemed to be in a peculiarly uneasy mood this evening, snappy with Eyre and exaggeratedly subservient towards Yonguldye.

'You have come to ask me to journey to Adelaide and bury the boy Yanluga according to proper ritual?' Yonguldye asked Eyre, through Joolonga.

'That's right,' Eyre told him. 'He was given a Christian burial; but his soul will never join his ancestors unless he is given the rites in which he believed.'

'You were responsible for his death. Why should you be so concerned about his burial?'

'Because it is my duty.'

'And not simply because you are frightened that his spirit will never give you rest?'

'I am already at rest.'

Yonguldye nodded in assent. This was obviously a good reply.

'Will I be rewarded for journeying to Adelaide?' he wanted to know.

'Whatever you want. Food, clothing, knives.'

'Who will give me these things?'

'Captain Sturt. In fact, Captain Sturt will give you many more things if you help him further.'

Yonguldye looked suspicious. 'What further help does he want? This is not part of the legend.'

Joolonga interrupted here, and raised a hand towards Eyre to warn him not say any more. Yonguldye listened carefully to what Joolonga was saying occasionally sucking back the saliva from his toothless gums, and grunting to indicate that he understood.

'What's going on?' asked Eyre.

Joolonga said, 'Yonguldye has agreed to travel to Adelaide to perform the proper burial rites over Yanluga's body. He thanks you for your concern for Yanluga's soul. He says that you are obviously a wise and compassionate *djanga*.'

'Anything else?'

'He has agreed that in return for your magical knowledge, he will help us to locate a place he knows where there are firestones to be found.'

'Firestones?'

'Opals, Mr Walker-sir. He says there is a place near Caddibarrawinnacarra where firestones can be found; but this is a difficult place to reach, and he will have to guide us there. He cannot describe it to us.'

'Where the hell's Caddibarrawinnacarra?' Dogger wanted to know. 'I've never heard of the place.'

'Beyond,' said Joolonga. 'Yonguldye says *kononda*, which means northwest'.

'There's nothing out there but fried *charra*,' growled

321

Dogger. For Yonguldye's benefit, he had deliberately used the Aboriginal word for 'emu shit'.

'Nonetheless, Yonguldye says the firestones are there; very many of them. Tomorrow he can show us some of the firestones that his own people have dug up.'

Eyre said, 'What about the route to the inland sea? Does he know anything about that?'

Joolonga spoke to Yonguldye for three or four minutes. There was more nodding between them, and then Joolonga said, 'He knows of a route northwards, and he says his ancestors came that way, but he has never been further north himself than the place where the magic kangaroo came to slake its thirst.'

'Where's that?' asked Dogger, with a sniff. 'The Queen's Head Tavern in Kermode Street?'

'No, a place called Callanna,' said Joolonga, humourlessly.

Eyre put in, 'If the magic kangaroo came there to drink, then surely there must be water there.'

'Probably just a waterhole,' said Christopher.

Joolonga spoke to Yonguldye further, and this time Yonguldye rose up on to his knees, his ghost-gum spigot sticking straight out from between his legs, and stretched his arm wildly towards the north, again and again, and talked in a furious babble.

Joolonga said, 'Yonguldye has seen the ocean himself from Callanna. He looked in the distance and it was there. The sea-birds were flying that way, and he is sure that the shoreline can be reached in less than a day's walking.'

Eyre looked around at Christopher and Dogger and his eyes were bright with pleasure. 'Well, my friends,' he said. 'It seems that we may be able to achieve everything we set out to achieve. Yanluga's burial, Captain Sturt's opal mine, and the discovery of the great inland sea. We're going to be rich and celebrated yet.'

'If only you could drink to that,' said Christopher.

'Yes,' agreed Eyre. 'If only I could.'

Twenty-Four

That evening, the gorge rang with the chanting and singing of the greatest corroboree that had been held in South Australia since the days before the white men came. That, at least, was the opinion of the old grey-haired woman who turned out to be Yonguldye's senior wife, and to whom he always referred as *unkeegeega*, which, whether he meant it ironically or not, meant 'young girl'.

Eyre saw nothing that evening of the pretty young girl who had been sitting at the back of Yonguldye's shelter, but that was hardly surprising. He was surrounded all evening by warriors from six or seven different tribes, all of whom seemed to feel that sitting close to the mythical white-skinned *djanga* was a matter of great prestige; and all of whom were very curious about his paleness, and his uncircumcised penis. None of them spoke any English whatsoever; and so Eyre was restricted to smiles and nods and indulgent shakes of his head.

The food came first. Roasted emu, bloody and scorched, but smelling delicious to men who hadn't eaten fresh meat for days. Mallee fowl, their eggs served raw. Skinks, stripped of their legs and peeled of their skins, and dangled over the fire on spits. And with all of this feast, plenty of cold fresh water and Bunya Bunya pine-nuts.

Only Eyre had to remain hungry and thirsty; sitting cross-legged in the centre of his circle of inquisitive protectors; while Christopher and Dogger and Midgegooroo sat around a fire not far away, laughing and talking with a small group of Aborigines who had travelled here from Streaky Bay, and devouring as they did so whole breasts of emu until their faces glistened and the fat ran in rivers down their stomachs and into their pubic hair.

Later, the women silently withdrew to their shelters and to their own cooking-fires; and the men performed a sacred dance. Joolonga told Eyre that this was the dance usually seen at funerals, when the body had been interred, and fires were burned for days on end, while the family looked around for magical signs explaining what had caused the death.

The men looked ferocious and other-worldly in the firelight. Most of them had circles of white painted around their eyes, and skeletal outlines painted on their bodies. They jumped and shuffled and spun around; shaking their spears and swinging their clubs; while scores of sticks were tapped and beaten, and boomerangs were clapped together, and hollow wooden flutes blew that deep, vibrant song that now and forever would make the hairs rise on the back of Eyre's neck.

Sparks flew from the cooking-fires into the darkness; dancers whirled and shouted; and from the entrance to his shelter, Yonguldye the Mabarn Man watched the corroboree with the air of an elderly hawk, watching his revelling young.

After the dancing was over, the tribesmen gathered around, and Yonguldye stepped forward and spoke to them. His speech was long, and involved, and sounded very discursive, because Eyre saw several of the tribesmen yawning and looking impatiently around. It amused him to think that even in a primitive society which had remained almost completely unchanged since the dawn of time, there were still men who gave tedious speeches, and still men who had to stand around and listen to them.

Over and over again, Yonguldye talked about the *djanga*, and shook his bony arm towards Eyre; and every time he did so, there would be a responsive murmur from the assembled tribesmen. It sounded like *'moomoomoomery'*, and incongruously it reminded Eyre of Mrs McMurtry, Lathrop Lindsay's cook on the day that he had gone around to Waikerie Lodge to take Charlotte for a romantic constitutional.

Eventually, Yonguldye untied from his belt a kind of rattle, made of the skull of a young rock-wallaby hafted with gum on to the leg-bone of a kangaroo. Inside the skull there must have been pebbles, or dried macrozamia nuts, because when Yonguldye shook it there was a hollow, echoing sound, like a man desperately trying not to die of cholera. As soon as he shook it, a short imperative burst of noise, all the tribesmen sank silently to their knees, two hundred bowed black heads against a background of twisting orange camp-fires, and Yonguldye hopped and rattled and danced, and uttered a long, sharp, dry-voiced incantation.

'He is calling on Baiame to bless this meeting,' said Joolonga. 'He is telling the people here that this night will be remembered for all time, just as the gods of the dreamtime are always remembered.'

Eyre said nothing, but watched as the tribesmen began to disperse, and return to their shelters and their fires, some of them high up in the rocks, others beside the creek which splashed through the centre of the gorge.

Yonguldye called to Joolonga, and Joolonga said, 'He wants to talk to you before you sleep.' Eyre thought: thank God he doesn't think that spirits stay awake all night. Together they crossed the rocky ground to the entrance of Yonguldye's shelter, and there Yonguldye stared at Eyre and said, in what sounded like formal and dignified language, 'The story is complete. You have returned from the sunset and now you are here. Tomorrow you will give me all the magical knowledge that you possess; and we will take back all the lands and the sacred places that we have lost.'

Yonguldye paused, and then he said, 'You have the stone?'

Eyre beckoned Midgegooroo, who came forward with his satchel. Eyre reached inside it, and produced the engraved tektite which had been given to him on Hindley Street.

'You are truly the *djanga*,' said Yonguldye. 'Look—there is a shelter for you where you can sleep tonight. Tomorrow we will talk more. Tomorrow we will celebrate your coming, and your departure.'

Christopher and Dogger had been taken to a humpy shelter on the far side of the gorge. If Eyre knew anything about Dogger, he had eaten and drunk far too much, and had already fallen asleep. Christopher he knew would be awake, and fretful. Christopher always was. But tomorrow they would be able to set out on their journey to find the opal mine; and beyond, to the great inland sea; and that was exciting enough to overwhelm any apprehension that Eyre felt about their safety among the Aborigines. Tomorrow, they would set out on the journey that would make them great men; the journey that would discharge his moral debt to Yanluga; and which would win him Charlotte back. They would be heroes: Walker, Willis, and McConnell. Names to be taught in schools for the rest of recorded time.

Eyre's shelter was constructed of gum branches and brush, woven together, Like Yonguldye's, it was filled with kangaroo skins, in which Eyre could wrap himself up and sleep. His rifle, which he had left in Yonguldye's shelter during the corroboree, had carefully been laid at the far end of the shelter, still loaded, and respectfully polished for him.

Exhausted by a day of travelling and an evening of Aborigine celebration, Eyre crawled naked into the shelter and lay down on the coarse-haired kangaroo skins. He thought of going to talk to Joolonga about what they would be doing in the morning; and whether Weeip was safe, all alone on the far side of the ridge. But even with his face pressed against stinking kangaroo leather, his eyes began to close, and within four or five minutes the tapping rhythm of the boomerangs which was still going on outside began to fade from real perception, and reappear in his dreams.

He dreamed of murmuring voices, and silhouettes of blackfellows, like the strange lithographs of W.H. Fernyhough; black profiles and stylised poses. He heard rattling and shaking, and the whistling they called *bimblegumbie*. And all the time there was the over-and-over motion of boomerangs, vertiginous and sickening, like riding on a swing-boat at a fair.

He awoke with a shock. Someone had touched his thigh. He twisted his head around so quickly that he tugged the muscle, and hurt himself.

Black against the midnight sky was the shape of a girl, on her hands and knees. She had crawled into the shelter and woken him; and now she was waiting anxiously to see what his reaction would be. He recognised the long soft curly hair. He recognised the sightly slanting eyes. He also recognised the faintly herbal smell of Yonguldye's shelter, which she carried on her skin mingled with the aroma of sour grease and young-womanly perspiration.

'What do you want?' he whispered. Then, when she didn't answer, '*Minago*?' which was the same question in dialect.

She covered her mouth with her hand, to tell him that he should be very quiet. Then she wriggled up close to him, and lay down beside him on the kangaroo skins, and whispered back, 'My name is Minil. I speak English-language. They taught me English-language at mission-school. I was the class top at English-language.'

'If you speak English, what are you doing here?' Eyre asked her.

'I was at the mission-school at New Norcia when Yonguldye and his people stayed there. When they left, I followed them. I wanted to find my own people. No longer cooking and washing and learning Holy Scriptures. I wanted to be free like Yonguldye and his people.'

'But?' asked Eyre.

'But?' Minil frowned. 'I didn't say but.'

'You *say* no but; but there is but in your voice.'

Minil was quiet for a moment; then she said, 'Yonguldye is a strange cruel man. Now I wish to leave him, go back to mission-school. Mrs Humphreys.'

'Are you married to Yonguldye? Are you one of his wives?'

She shook her head. 'He does not like me. He says I

327

have devils in me. But he makes me work hard, cooking for him, making magic powder. Cure powder, for sick. Sometimes insect drink.'

She hesitated, and then she said, 'Wait,' and wriggled her way back to the entrance of the shelter. She came back straight away, with a wooden bowl full of water and a large curved piece of flaking bark, in which she had wrapped four or five large chunks of cold roasted emu breast.

Eyre propped himself up on one elbow, until his head was almost touching the main supporting branch of his shelter. But he was too hungry to worry about whether or not he might destroy his temporary palace. He crammed the half-cooked meat into his mouth, chewing it as quickly as he could; and then washed it down with gulps of cold spring-water. He belched twice; but he couldn't have felt less ashamed. He had sat there all evening, stark naked, watching hundreds of other people eat. Now it was his turn.

Once his hunger had begun to abate, however, and his chewing had slowed down, he turned to look at Minil with suddenly awakening suspicion.

'I'm a *djanga*,' he said. 'You realise that I don't usually eat this stuff. I'm only doing it so that I won't hurt your feelings. You realise that, don't you? Normally, in the spirit world, we survive on . . . well, on clouds, air, things like that.'

'You are not a *djanga*,' said Minil. Her nipple was pressing against his right arm, and he was beginning to feel surges that had nothing at all to do with Yonguldye, or Captain Sturt's opals, or tonight's corroboree.

'Of course I'm a *djanga*,' he insisted. 'It's in the story. The *djanga* returns to earth from the land where the sun sets; accidentally causes the death of a young Aborigine boy; and goes to the clever-man to seek forgiveness. That's me; that's why I'm here. Seeking Yonguldye's forgiveness.'

'Yonguldye knows that you are not a *djanga*,' Minil told him.

'What?'

'Yonguldye knows that you are not a *djanga*. He knows that you are nothing but a white man. You cannot be a *djanga* because *djanga* never eat.'

Eyre chewed even more slowly. 'Sometimes we do,' he said, in a petulant voice. 'Just to keep in practice.'

'Perhaps,' said Minil. 'But you are not one of them. And anyway Yonguldye believes that the old story foretells the landing of the white men, not the coming of the dead. A white man will kill an Aborigine boy; perhaps by mistake, perhaps not. But he will travel through the desert seeking a medicine-man who will forgive him for what he did.'

'All right, it's the same story,' said Eyre. 'The only discrepancy is that I'm a white man; a white man who eats cold roasted emu; and not a ghost.'

'What happens in the end is the same.'

'I don't think I understand you.'

Minil reached down and touched Eyre's bare thighs. Then, quite matter-of-factly, she grasped his penis, which was already erect, and began with a gentle black hand to stroke it up and down. Eyre knew that he should have told her to stop; that he was a *djanga*, and that *djanga* had no sexual feelings. But he found himself powerless to say a word. The feeling was too compelling. Apart from which, he didn't want to upset her until she had told him why Yonguldye didn't believe that he was a real spirit, returned from the dead.

Minil said, 'Yonguldye talks tonight to your man Joolonga; and your man Joolonga talks to you. But what Joolonga says to you is not the same as Yonguldye says to him. Joolonga says, "This is the white man who killed the boy in Adelaide. He is come here just like the story. He seeks forgiveness just like the story. Everything he knows I will give to you, if you tell me where to find firestones, and if there is sea to the north where men can sail." '

Eyre looked down. In the shadows of the shelter, he could just make out the black outline of Minil's hand, massaging him, and the whiteness of his own skin.

'I don't—' he began, but then he collected himself, and said, 'I don't see that it makes very much difference—whether Yonguldye believes that I'm a spirit returned from the dead or not. He's agreed to give poor Yanluga all the proper Aboriginal burial rites. He's told us where to find the firestones; he's even directed us towards the inland sea. I mean, I can't tell him much in return. I don't have a lot in the way of magical knowledge. But he's fulfilled *his* part of the bargain, and so I'll certainly do my best.'

Minil suddenly took her hand away, leaving Eyre highly aroused and crucially frustrated. 'If you really were a *djanga*, Yonguldye would not even dare to ask you for magical knowledge. He would be too frightened that you would drag him away to the land beyond the sunset. But, you are a white man, and he wants the white man's knowledge, and he is not frightened to take if from you. It is the white man's knowledge that he thinks will make him strong; and the leader of all the medicine-men, of every tribe. As well as that, he wants to stop the white men from exploring his country; to keep them away from his sacred places. He wants to use the white man's knowledge against the white man himself.'

Eyre said, 'Really, Minil, no matter *what* I tell him, he's never going to be able to keep white settlers out of his territory. Not for very long.'

'He thinks that he will.'

'Well, let him think it. As long as Yanluga gets his burial, and Captain Sturt gets his opals.'

'But I am trying to say to you that he will kill you for your knowledge. Tomorrow, he will kill you.'

'*What*? What are you talking about?'

'Yonguldye believes that if he strikes you down, and breaks open your head, and eats your brains, that he will take all your knowledge, all of it, even those things that you would try to hide from him.'

Eyre's erection shrank away like a frightened skink retreating into the sand. 'I can't believe that,' he told Minil. 'Eat my *brains*? But Aborigines aren't cannibals.'

'It is the way that Yonguldye believes he will learn everything you know.'

Eyre slowly chewed the last stringy mouthful of emu meat; although now he didn't feel hungry at all. He began to see at last what game Joolonga had been up to, right from the very beginning of their expedition; and, even more alarmingly, what game Captain Charles Sturt had been playing. There *was* an ancient Aboriginal story about a *djanga* returning from the dead and killing a boy; and although what had happened to Eyre had differed from the legend in several material ways, it had been close enough for Joolonga to excite the blackfellows around Adelaide into believing that at last it was coming true. Aborigine messengers must have taken the news to Yonguldye days and days ago; and to the kings of other tribes as well; and so this corroboree at Yarrakinna had been swelled not only by the tribes who normally would have come here at this time of year, but by scores of curious Aborigines who wanted to witness the great coming-alive of a celebrated myth.

It was the way in which Captain Sturt had so inventively used the legend that disturbed Eyre the most, however. Impending bankruptcy had obviously made the good Captain unusually sharp-witted. Sharp-witted enough to instruct Joolonga that he should tell Eyre about the legend just before they caught up with Yonguldye; so that Eyre would be prepared for Yonguldye's worshipful welcome; but also sharp-witted enough to conceal from Eyre the frightening truth about the legend which Minil had now revealed to him. In the days before the arrival of the white man, the Aborigines had thought that the *djanga* would be a real ghost; but over the past fifty years they must have come to believe that he would be a white man, and that his

331

appearance would signify the moment when they would at last learn the secret of white supremacy.

All of the complicated conversations which had taken place between Eyre and Yonguldye throughout the evening had been a sham. Yonguldye had known very well that Eyre was no resurrected spirit, and that Joolonga was tricking him. Between the two of them, Yonguldye and Joolonga had been doing nothing less than preparing Eyre for the final ceremony which would take place when the sun arose tomorrow morning. His sacrifice to the cause of Aborigine resistance.

Presumably Dogger and Christopher would be murdered as well: and even poor Midgegooroo.

Sturt's cunning appalled Eyre. Sturt must have known from his earlier encounters with Aborigines that there were opals to be found somewhere in the southern plains; and that a route could one day be found to the great inland sea. There was probably silver and gold, too, although Yonguldye didn't know where it was, or was not prepared to disclose it. But now Sturt had discovered exactly where the opals lay, and how to reach the sea, by offering the Aborigines the life of a fellow white-man. Sturt would reap all the profits, and the glory. He would probably hold a memorial service for those brave adventurers who had lost their lives in order that South Australia and Captain Sturt, could become rich again. And he would have risked nothing, not even the possibility of real resistance from the Aborigines, because of course Yonguldye would learn nothing at all from beating Eyre's brains out.

Eyre said to Minil, 'I must leave here at once. Do you think we can escape without being noticed?'

'There are watchers.'

'Well, we'll just have to take our chances, then. Listen, go across to the other shelter and wake my companions. Tell them they are in terrible danger. Don't try to explain why. Just bring them back here, and then we will try to get away.'

'I must come with you.'

'It's too dangerous. They will probably try to kill us.'

'I do not care. I must come with you.'

Eyre laid a hand on her shoulder. 'Go and find my companions first. Please. It will be daylight very soon.'

Minil touched his cheek with her fingertips. Then she nodded, and wriggled silently out of the shelter, and off to wake Christopher and Dogger. Eyre meanwhile sat up in the shelter, and retrieved his rifle, and made sure that it was ready to fire if necessary. His mouth felt very dry, 'like a lizard's gizzard', as Dogger used to say; and his stomach kept grumbling because of the half-chewed emu meat he had swallowed.

It seemed to Eyre that almost half-an-hour passed before the crouching shapes of Dogger and Christopher came into sight through the encampment, closely followed by Minil and Midgegooroo. They huddled up close to the entrance of Eyre's shelter, shivering in the pre-dawn chill. Dogger had had the sense to make himself an improvised *buka* by tying a kangaroo-skin around his shoulders.

'What's up?' asked Christopher. 'One minute I was dreaming about horse-racing; the next thing I knew I was being prodded through the dark by your lady-friend here.'

Eyre said quickly, 'It's too difficult to explain in detail. But Captain Sturt and Joolonga have betrayed us; and Yonguldye intends to kill us tomorrow morning. We're going to have to try to get away from here right away.'

'But they'll see us. We're going to have to climb right up that ridge again, in plain view.'

'Then we'll have to take a hostage,' said Eyre.

'Who do you have in mind?'

'The most valuable man in the tribe, of course. Yonguldye himself.'

'Now I know you're funning,' said Dogger. 'Let's get back to bed.'

Eyre said, 'It won't be as difficult as you think. Yonguldye knows the power of a rifle. He also speaks enough English for us to be able to make it clear to him what will happen if he doesn't co-operate.'

333

'Well, I can think of more pleasant ways of going to the great green pasture beyond the mountains,' said Dogger.

Christopher shivered, and raised his head, and said, 'It's getting light. Whatever we're going to do, we'd better do it right away.'

Eyre eased himself out of his shelter, dragging his rifle after him, and then stood up. Only a few yards away, the great fire that had burned during the corroboree outside the entrance to Yonguldye's *tantanoorla* was nothing more now than a huge heap of hot blowing ashes. Eyre said, 'Wait here,' and made his way barefoot across the rocks to the skull-hung entrance to Yonguldye's den. He glanced back for a moment at his friends, squatting apprehensively on the shadowy ground, all watching him; and then he crouched down and managed to penetrate the darkness of the shelter without making any of the skulls rattle.

It was so black inside the *tantanoorla* that Eyre had to rely on feel, and on the sound of Yonguldye's snoring, in order to make his way to the far end, where most of the kangaroo hides were piled. He was fairly certain that the great Yonguldye would have reserved for himself the warmest and most comfortable place to sleep. He edged his way forwards on his elbows and knees, holding the rifle clear of the ground in his right hand, and groping around in front of him with his left.

The smell of sleeping bodies was so rancid that Eyre had to suppress an upsurge of bile. Added to the usual grease and sweat, there was a stench of meat, and farts, and foul breath. And all around him there was the thick breathing of Yonguldye's wives, a chorus of congested bellows.

He touched something in the blackness. It felt like a foot. He circled around it warily; but as he did so, he partly lost his balance, and had to jab out with his left hand to prevent himself from tumbling over. His hand went straight into soft flesh: a woman's stomach. There was a jerk, and a screech of surprise; and a sudden harsh cry that could only be Yonguldye's.

Eyre stumbled up on to his feet, knocking his head

sharply against the main branch which supported the shelter. But then he threw himself forward, his left hand flailing around to find Yonguldye, and after two or three wild lunges he caught hold of a bony shoulder; and then a greasy, wrinkled-skin chest. He rolled himself forwards and sideways over the kangaroo-skins so that he was clutching Yonguldye from behind; and he rammed the muzzle of his rifle right up into Yonguldye's skinny back.

The medicine-man screamed with fury and fright, but Eyre shouted at him even more loudly, *'Keep still! Keep quiet! This is a rifle! Keep quiet or else I'll kill you!'*

Yonguldye twisted and struggled, but Eyre held him tightly around the neck with his elbow; and then gave him a hard punch in the small of the back with his knee. 'You want to die, Yonguldye?' he yelled at him. 'You want to meet Ngurunderi?'

The name of the god beyond the skies silenced the medicine-man almost at once. He lay still, panting a little, and Eyre could feel his withered skin sliding up and down over his protuberant ribs as he breathed. Now that he was at the very end of the shelter, he could see the triangular light of the dawning day at the entrance, and the startled outlines of Yonguldye's wives, one of whom was whimpering, and twisting her hair in anxiety.

'Very well, now,' said Eyre. 'I want you to make your way outside. Outside, do you understand me? But don't try to run away, or call for anybody to help you, because I will shoot you dead. Is that clear?'

Yonguldye said, 'A curse on you.'

'Save your curses for when I've gone,' Eyre told him. 'Now, let's get going.'

Grumbling and coughing, Yonguldye crawled out of his *tantanoorla*, and stretched himself in the pale blue light of early morning. All around the gorge, last night's fires were smouldering, so that the mountains were hazy with fragrant smoke; and the gathered tribes of Wirangu and Nyungar lay scattered on the ground in their skins and their shelters like the casualties of a massacre. But the

335

massacre was only sleep, and soon the tribesmen would be rising again, and Eyre would have almost no chance of escaping from the gorge whatsoever.

'Hurry,' he told Yonguldye, and prodded him towards his own small shelter, where Dogger and Christopher were waiting with Minil and Midgegooroo. Behind them, Yonguldye's wives crowded fearfully at the entrance to his *tantanoorla*, watching as their husband and Mabarn Man was taken away from them. Yonguldye lost his footing on the rocks, and Eyre prodded him again. 'Quick, or I'll kill you here and now, and take my chances.'

Yonguldye hesitated and stiffened when he saw Minil crouching there with Eyre's companions; and said something blistering to her in Nyungar. Minil turned her face away from him, and refused to answer, and Eyre said, 'Come on, Yonguldye. We don't have any time for recriminations.'

'Funny-looking bugger, isn't he, without his hat?' Dogger remarked.

Yonguldye haughtily ignored this gibe. His sparse woolly hair was knotted all over with bows of possum-skin twine, giving his head the appearance of a black decorated pineapple. He looked fiercely from one of his captors to the other, and Eyre was quite sure that he was silently wishing sickness and death on them all. Personally, Eyre preferred to risk any kind of curse, rather than submit to having his brains beaten out.

'Come on,' he said. 'Dogger, you go first; then Minil; then Christopher and Midgegooroo. I'll keep our friend Yonguldye with me as a shield.'

Tribesmen were beginning to wake and rise as they made their way through the encampment. Some were blowing on fires to breathe them back into life; others were going down to the creek-bed with gourds and skin bags to fetch water. They passed one family who were all asleep except for one of the wives, who had been woken up by her hungry dingo pup. She was yawning as she suckled the brindled wild dog at her breast.

336

Somehow, they seemed to pass through the smoke almost unnoticed as if they were ghosts. Perhaps nobody recognised Yonguldye without his head-dress. Perhaps Eyre and Christopher and Dogger were so dirty now that on first inspection they passed as blackfellows. It was only when they began to climb the rock-face back up towards the ridge that they heard a cry of distress, probably from one of the medicine-man's wives; and then a general clamour of alarm.

Eyre looked back quickly. He could see Joolonga in his midshipman's hat, running towards Yonguldye's shelter. All over the floor of the gorge, and up on the balconies of rock above them, tribesmen were rising and calling and taking up their spears.

'Now you will die,' crowed Yonguldye, toothlessly.

'Now you keep quiet and climb as fast as your skinny legs will carry you,' Eyre retorted. He could see that Dogger had passed the waterfall now, holding his kangaroo-skin *buka* in front of his belly in a rather matronly way to protect it from the abrasive rocks, and that Minil was close behind him, climbing with all the agility of a young rock-wallaby.

Eyre was necessarily slower. Yonguldye was elderly, and climbed the slippery rocks with difficulty; and Eyre had to keep the rifle pointing at his back. By the time Eyre had crossed the waterfall, grunting with the effort of levering himself over the green and greasy rocks, Joolonga and a rush of tribesmen had arrived at the foot of the rock-face, brandishing spears and clubs and fighting boomerangs.

Eyre twisted himself around, and called out, 'Joolonga!'

'Where are you going, Mr Walker-sir?' Joolonga shouted back.

'For a long walk, Joolonga; and I'd prefer not to have your company.'

'You must come back down, Mr Walker-sir. There is no escape that way.'

'We'll see.'

'These people will kill you, Mr Walker-sir. Yonguldye is their clever-man. You cannot take him with you.'

'I have no intention of taking him with me. He is my hostage, that is all. As soon as I am clear of the mountains, I will let him go.'

'I am only thinking of your own well-being, Mr Walker-sir.'

'I am very touched,' Eyre shouted back. 'I suppose you were thinking of my well-being when you brought me here. I suppose you were thinking of how salutary it would be for me to have my brains knocked out, and eaten for breakfast by this aged buzzard in return for his opals, and his route to the inland sea.'

'Why do you make such accusations, Mr Walker-sir?' called Joolonga.

'Because I know now what you and Yonguldye were saying last night.'

'Who told you, sir? That girl? That girl knows nothing; she is mad from sickness.'

'She may be, Joolonga; but in my opinion she's a lot less dangerous than you are.'

Eyre began to climb further, pushing Yonguldye ahead of him. At last he reached the crest of the ridge. Christopher and Minil and Midgegooroo were already halfway across the grassy slope up to the next ridge, heading back towards the creek where they had left Weeip the night before. The morning was quite bright now, and the first stab of sunlight appeared between the broken stumps of the mountains. Yonguldye limped as he walked, and groaned as if his feet hurt, but Eyre kept pushing him on with the muzzle of his rifle, and saying, 'Faster, come on, you can walk faster than that!'

As they reached the top of the next ridge, four or five Aborigines appeared on the lower ridge behind them, rapidly followed by more. Eyre shouted to Dogger, 'It's all right. They won't try to attack us as long as we have Yonguldye!' But even before he had finished speaking, there was the whop-whop-whop sound of a boomerang, then another, and two of them flew overhead like giant sycamore seeds and landed close by, in the grass.

It was then that Yonguldye dropped flat on his face on to the ground. Eyre seized hold of his shoulder, and tried to pull him upright, but the medicine-man crouched down and refused to get up.

'Do you want me to kill you?' Eyre screamed at him. But then he realised what Yonguldye must already have realised: that he was almost certainly incapable of shooting him in cold blood.

'Get up!' Eyre hissed at him. 'Get up, or I'll blow your head off your shoulders!' But still Yonguldye huddled amidst the lemon-grass, all ribs and bony spine, like an elderly kangaroo. Another boomerang flapped over Eyre's head, and this time he heard a cry. He looked up and saw that the boomerang had struck Christopher on the back of the leg, and brought him down.

'For God's sake, get on to your feet!' he shouted at Yonguldye; but the medicine-man only covered his ears with his hands, to show his contempt for all of Eyre's desperate threats. Eyre was about to leave him, when there was a tremendous report, and his rifle went off in his hands, recoiling so violently that it jumped out of Eyre's grasp and tumbled into the grass. Yonguldye let out a high, effeminate shriek, and jerked and writhed on the ground in agony, and then lay still, shuddering a little, like a lizard which Eyre had once accidentally crushed beneath the wheels of his bicycle.

Eyre left him, and ran through the scrub towards Christopher, who was trying to stagger up on to his feet. Eyre weaved and dodged from side to side as he ran, in case any more boomerangs were being thrown after them. But long before he could reach the limestone outcropping where Christopher had fallen, he heard another sound, far more frightening than the flackering of boomerangs. It was the humming of spears, launched from woomeras; and the next thing he knew, the sky was dark with what the Aborigines called 'the long rain' a torrential shower of quartz-tipped death-spears.

Three spears clattered on to the rock beside Christopher, who had fallen back down again now, clutching his leg. Another sang past Eyre and stuck into the ground, quivering.

Eyre shouted, 'Christopher! Christopher, get up!' But it was plain that Christopher's leg had been too badly bruised by the boomerang for him to walk; it was even possible that the bone was broken.

It was then that Midgegooroo appeared over the brow of the ridge, running low and quickly. He looked like a dark scuttling crab against the pale pink limestone rock. Eyre watched in relief and gratitude as he picked Christopher up without any hesitation at all and lifted him bodily on to his broad black back. He heard Dogger whistle shrilly in encouragement as Midgegooroo reached the brow of the ridge again, and shouted out, 'Back to the horses! Dogger, I've lost Yonguldye! Cover me!'

But then a death-spear came flying through the air as accurately as if it were a black pencil-line being swiftly drawn against the pale blue of the sky with a ruler. It struck Midgegooroo right in the back, missing Christopher by inches, and Eyre, who was much closer now, heard the crunch of quartz-tipped spear-wood dig right into his flesh.

Midgegooroo staggered, and let out a hoarse, high cry; but somehow he kept on balancing his way across the bare limestone ridge, with Christopher still dangling over his shoulders, until he had reached the other side, where the rocks fell away, and he was out of spear-shot. Then with the death-spear trailing noisily against the ground behind him, he slowly sagged to the ground like an emptying sack, letting Christopher fall awkwardly against an outcropping of rocks and bushes.

Minil, who had been halfway down the creek-bed to the place where they had left Weeip, turned and climbed back up the hill, kneeling down beside Christopher and feeling his leg, to find out how bad his injury was. Eyre was surprised to see that she completely ignored Midgegooroo, as if he were dead already; but then Eyre supposed that with a death-spear lodged in his back, that was probably true. He said, 'Dogger! Open fire! Hold the bastards off!'

Dogger knelt down on the limestone, and took aim at the Aborigine warriors who were now running towards them across the grass. He was an experienced shot, even if he was rusty, and the leading warrior fell into the bushes without even a shout. Eyre clambered over towards Midgegooroo, and eased the satchel of ammunition from around his neck; trying not to look into Midgegooroo's grey and desperate face, or at the bloody froth which bubbled at the corners of his mouth. He slung the satchel over to Dogger, and called, 'See if you can get another one in!'

Dogger reloaded with relaxed skill; and when the Aborigines were less than fifty paces away, he fired again, hitting another one right between the eyes, so that the blood sprayed up from the top of his head like an ornamental fountain. The other warriors hesitated, and retreated a few steps, while Dogger loaded up for the third time.

Eyre, keeping his head low, knelt down beside Midgegooroo and said, 'You're going to be all right. Don't worry. Once we get the spear out of you, you'll soon recover.'

Midgegooroo's expression was sweaty and strained, an agonised gargoyle. He shook his head again and again, and said, 'No, sir. No, sir.'

Dogger fired one more shot, which went wide. Eyre heard the bullet singing off the distant rocks.

'We'd better make ourselves scarce,' said Eyre. 'Here—give me some help with Midgegooroo.'

Dogger came over at a low crouch. He turned Midgegooroo over a little way, and examined the spear. The entire head was buried in Midgegooroo's back, and sticky blood was coursing over his black muscles, and on to the grass. As gently as he could, Dogger tugged at the spear, but Midgegooroo whimpered with such pitiful agony that

341

he let it go. Dogger looked at Eyre, and said, 'Death-spear, no doubt about it.'

'What can we do?' Eyre asked him.

Dogger shook his head. 'Not much, except push the whole thing all the way through him. There are teeth on the end of this thing, flakes of sharpened quartz. You can't pull it out the way it went in, not without tearing half his back off. I've seen it before. An old chum called Keith Cragg, out at Broken Hill. We had to push the spear right through his lung to get it out; and he only lived for half-an-hour after that. Kept coughing up blood and singing about his wife. Couldn't stand the name Madge ever after.'

'What then?' said Eyre, urgently, lifting his head so that he could see how close the tribesmen were approaching. Then he turned back to see how Christopher was getting on. It looked as if Minil had managed to help him on to his feet, because now he was hopping down towards the creek-bed, with his arm around Minil's shoulders.

Dogger sniffed, and wiped sweat from his forehead with the back of his hand. 'Can't see much option,' he said.

'What do you mean?'

'Well, either we leave him here; or we put him out of his misery.'

'*What*? We can't kill him.'

'That lot will do worse. Especially since we seem to have done for their clever-man.'

'For God's sake, the gun went off by accident.'

Dogger shrugged. 'They don't know that.'

Eyre said, 'We have to try. We can't just leave him.'

Dogger peered with infuriating thoughtfulness in the direction in which Christopher and Minil had just disappeared. 'Listen, old mate,' he said to Eyre, 'why don't you go and make sure that your chum's all right. That boomerang gave him a fair knock. And then there's your girlfriend, too.'

'You'll shoot him, that's why.'

Dogger rubbed the back of his neck. 'Well, you're right

about that. I thought perhaps you wouldn't want to see it.'

Impatient, angry at Dogger's defeatism, Eyre worked his way around Midgegooroo's shivering body until he was right up behind him. He rested the shaft of the spear on one bare knee, and grasped it in both hands as if he were cracking firewood. 'We're not going to give in,' he told Dogger, fiercely. 'If this were *you* lying here, with a spear in your back, I believe you'd thank me for what I'm going to do now.'

'Not I, friend,' said Dogger. 'I'd curse you all the way to Purgatory and back.'

Eyre pressed down on the spear's shaft with all his weight, trying to break it across his knee. Immediately, Midgegooroo threw up his arm and screamed. Dogger said, 'For pity's sake, Eyre, leave the fellow be.' But Eyre was determined. He pressed down on the spear again and again, until he heard the wood cracking, and at last the shaft broke off, leaving only six or seven inches protruding bloodily from Midgegooroo's back.

'Now,' he said, 'up with him, and let's get him down to the horses.'

Midgegooroo was roaring with pain, his eyes bulging and his mouth stretched open like a frilled lizard. But Eyre seized the Aborigine's arm, and bent forward, and lifted him up on to his back; and Dogger, with a quick spit of disapproval, took hold of his other arm, and made sure that Eyre wouldn't drop him.

Hunched over like gnomes or goblins, they hurried down towards the creek-bed; while a fresh salvo of death-spears came whistling over the ridge and rattled against the rocks all around them. One came so close that it scratched Eyre's calf, and almost tripped him over. Dogger, glancing back, said, 'They'll catch us if we don't run faster. For God's sake, Eyre, lay this fellow down and let's get away while we can.'

Eyre, panting under the weight of Midgegooroo's cold and sweaty body, could do nothing more than shake his

343

head. Then he began to slither down the loose shale of the creek-bed; half-tumbling, half-staggering, with the acacia branches whipping at his bare arms, and the rocks tearing at his bare legs. He managed the last few yards at jarring over-and-over roll, bruising his back and his hip; and Midgegooroo fell off his back and tumbled even further, at last lying concussed against a purple-flowered emu bush, his face grey.

Eyre stood up, just as Dogger came slithering down behind him. Two or three stray spears hurtled over the brink of the creek, and fell noisily down between the over-hanging banks.

Weeip and Christopher were ready with the horses; Minil was already mounted up. Without a word, Dogger and Eyre dragged Midgegooroo over to the nearest horse, and while Christopher held the animal's reins, and shushed it, they hoisted him across the saddle, and quickly tied his wrists and ankles to prevent him from sliding off. The broken-off spear protruded bloodily from his back and gave him the appearance of having been nailed on to the horse. His muscles quivered, and he let out a deep bubbling groan, but then he lapsed into unconsciousness again.

'Come on, let's get away from here,' Eyre ordered, and they turned their horses and began to pick their way back down the narrow waterway, riding as quickly as they could, but all of them aware that until they reached the open plains, they were far slower on their horses than a running man; especially a running Aborigine.

Dogger tried several times to reload his rifle as he rode, but it was impossible, and he scattered half-a-dozen balls on to the ground, as well as losing most of his priming-powder to the early-morning wind. Eventually, he cursed, and gave up, and slung his rifle back over his shoulder, and concentrated on making his way down the mountain-side as fast as he could.

At the foot of the mountains, they had to cross a maze of wrinkled gullies, where the water that ran down from

344

the higher peaks had washed down with it thick clay sediments, and then eroded them into a complicated pattern of passageways and dead-ends. Their horses' hoofs slipped on the crumbly yellow earth; and for one moment Eyre thought that his horse was going to slide sideways down one of the gullies, taking him with it; but with a flurrying scrabble of hoofs, the horse managed to regain its ground.

Behind them, startling them, they heard a great warbling cry, and a rattling of spears and boomerangs. Eyre twisted around in his saddle, and saw at least twenty Aborigine warriors running across the clay towards them, jumping from ridge to ridge and runnel to runnel, shrieking and calling, and occasionally pausing to fit a spear into their woomeras and launch it off.

Eyre shouted, 'Dogger! Stop here, and reload! One more good shot should keep them back!'

Dogger circled his horse around, and then dropped down from the saddle. While Eyre and the rest of the party began to make their way out of the clay gullies, he calmly loaded and primed his rifle, sniffed, adjusted his hat, and knelt down beside his horse's right flank; taking aim not at the leading Aborigine but at another, much further back.

Two spears landed close by, but he ignored them. He waited for the moment when the Aborigine at whom he was aiming was right at the top of the last steep slope, and then he fired. There was a flat *crack*, and a cloud of blue smoke drifted unhurriedly away from Dogger's rifle. The tribesman staggered, slipped, and then fell spectacularly head-over-heels all the way down the zig-zag creek-bed, spraying blood over the rocks as he went. He landed disjointedly at the bottom of the slope like one of the dancing beeswax figures at Mushroom Rock.

Dogger remounted, and cantered after Eyre across the powdery clay, letting out a high, harsh whoop. Behind him, the Aborigines threw another heavy shower of spears, but most of them fell short; and the tribesmen had been too frightened by Dogger's marksmanship to risk running very much closer. Even when it was launched from a woomera, a spear could only travel a hundred and fifty paces with any accuracy and force, whereas even an out-of-date muzzle-loading rifle like the Baker could bring a man down from over twice that distance.

At the top of the creekbed, Eyre saw Joolonga, his distinctive midshipman's hat silhouetted against the brightening eastern sky. As Dogger drew level with him, Eyre said, 'Look!' and pointed Joolonga out; and Dogger reined back his horse and squinted back towards the mountains, his face as creased and wrinkled as the dry gullies they were riding over.

'I should have picked *him* off, too,' sniffed Dogger. 'He's a dangerous fellow, your Joolonga. Educated savages always are. They gain the knowhow, but they never lose the wildness. Can't trust them, not an Irishman's inch.'

'He's clever just the same,' Eyre replied.

'Well, that's all very well; but my mother always used to say that you ought to give men like that legroom in case they kicked at you; and throwing room in case they chucked a stone at you; and that you should never tell them how much money you were carrying or introduce them to your wife.'

'Wise lady, your mother, by the sound of it,' Eyre smiled. For the first time since they had undressed yesterday evening, he was conscious that they were naked. 'It's probably a good thing that she can't see you now.'

Dogger slapped his big round beer-belly. 'Let's put a mile or so between us and these savages; and then let's get some britches between ourselves and these saddles.'

Christopher was waiting for them a little way away; holding the reins of Midgegooroo's horse. It was impossible to tell whether Midgegooroo was alive or dead; he hung over the saddle with his arms and legs trailing, and his entire bloody back was smothered with flies. Minil was riding next to him, and Eyre could see by the expression on her face that she didn't expect him to survive. As Eyre came closer, she said, 'This man was very brave. He was like one of the saints they told me about at the mission. St Philip, or St Jude.'

'If we can dig that spear out of him, he may live,' said Eyre.

'No,' said Minil. 'He is dead already.'

Twenty-Five

They camped at noon in the hot purple shadow of a limestone outcropping ten miles west of Parachilna. The temperature was 113 degrees Fahrenheit, and all around them the flat salt lake appeared to move up and down in slowly-undulating curves, as waves of superheated air flowed over it. The rust-coloured peaks of the Flinders also rose and fell, as if they were observing them through water. Eyre had the extraordinary sensation of being on a ship again, although he knew it was only an optical illusion.

The dryness was stunning. Two of their seven horses sank to their knees when they set up camp: and one of them, a three-year-old chestnut which had carried their main bags of water all the way from Adelaide, lay on his side after a while and began to pant and tremble.

'What do you think?' Eyre asked Christopher.

Christopher shrugged. 'There isn't very much we can do, except put him out of his pain.'

They deliberately avoided talking about Midgegooroo. He was still alive, although he had lost so much blood that he was barely conscious. Dogger had speculated that some herb or other had been rubbed on the tip of the spear to prevent the blood from clotting; certainly it had run out of

Midgegooroo's back in a wide sticky river, and they didn't even have enough water to spare to be able to wash him clean. He lay on his stomach in a small crevice in the rock, his eyes wide, scarcely breathing, his back teeming with huge grey sand flies.

They had dressed now: Eyre in his wide kangaroo-skin hat and bush-jacket and wide cotton ducks; Christopher in his white shirt and riding-britches; Dogger in his familiar faded trousers and shiny-toed suede boots. Eyre had offered clothes to Minil, and she had happily accepted a blue shirt and a silk scarf; although she had tied the sleeves of the shirt around her waist, so that only her bottom was covered, and crossed the scarf between her breasts, so that it did nothing more than lift them up even more prominently. She had combed her hair back now and tied it with twine; and Eyre was struck by the gracious black profile which this revealed, and by the flared curve of her bare shoulders. It unsettled him slightly to watch the way in which she allowed flies to settle on her, to walk across her cheeks or cluster on her back, and make no attempt to flick them away, as Eyre always did; but she had a hypnotic naked beauty about her which appealed to him more every time he looked at her.

Whether she was aware of what he felt, or not, he found it impossible to tell. She made no obvious effort either to ignore him or encourage him. She was sitting now in the shadows, her eyes closed, her forehead sparkling with sweat, her thighs unselfconsciously parted so that he could see how the grains of salty sand clung to her vaginal lips. He found he had to look away; and think of anything else instead; of the expedition; of what Captain Sturt had done to him; and of Midgegooroo.

They were four hundred miles from civilisation on a roaringly hot salt lake, with one desperately wounded man and another who could only limp; and only two young Aborigines who were little more than children to guide them.

They drank hot water from their flasks, and ate two

grey-faced terns which Weeip had snared the previous evening and charred over his camp-fire. It was Eyre's instinct to eat only a little, and to save the rest for later, but Dogger reminded him that the meat wouldn't last the day, not in this heat.

'Eat like an Aborigine,' he told Eyre. 'Cram as much into your belly as you can, because whatever you save will be stinking by nightfall. You can't keep anything fresh, not in the outback. I think the only food that I've ever seen the blackfellows store is wild figs, which they roll up in balls of ochre, and hide in the trees. The rest of it, they keep in here,' he said, pointing to his stomach.

They talked about Joolonga and Captain Sturt. Minil told them exactly what Joolonga had been discussing with Yonguldye; how Yonguldye wanted to break open the white *djanga's* head at once and take all the magic that was stored there. Apparently Joolonga had been arguing that if he allowed Yonguldye to kill Eyre so soon, he would no longer have any guarantee that Yonguldye would direct him to the place where the firestones could be found; or north to the inland sea.

Surprisingly, Yonguldye had been determined to travel south to Adelaide to give Yanluga's body a traditional Aborigine burial, as he had agreed. It was a crucial part of the coming-alive of the legend that he should do so. Presumably he would have asked Joolonga to take him to Captain Sturt, and Captain Sturt would then have arranged the burial with Lathrop Lindsay.

Christopher said, 'I really find this all rather hard to swallow.'

Dogger sniffed, with a dry catarrhal thump. 'You're dealing with people who believe in magic here, matey. I've heard tell of that story of the white *djanga* myself, although the one I heard had a slightly different twist to it. I think the *djanga* ended up eating the clever-man, instead of the other way about. And there was something about a waratah tree in it.'

'But it's quite extraordinary that the news of it should

have spread so quickly . . . and that we should have travelled all the way out here and found Yonguldye ready for us.'

'Not at all,' said Dogger. 'Once old man Lindsay's blackfellow had decided that Eyre here was the one true *djanga*, and told his friends, that story would have spread like a bushfire. The trouble with you, Mr Willis, is that you think that all blackfellows are as good-for-nothing as those idle buggers you see hanging around Adelaide, getting drunk on twopenny rum and running odd-jobs. Well, you're wrong, sir; eighteen hundred percentile wrong, because the chaps you come across out here beyond the black stump, they're clever and they're bright and if they want to carry a piece of important news from one end of this desert to the other in three days flat, then they'll do it. Look at the way they've been following Eyre around, ever since they decided that he was their man, taking care of him, making sure that he got out here safe and sound. If those fellows Chatto and Rose had tried to take him back to Adelaide, I reckon they wouldn't have gone for more than a mile before the blackfellows used them for spear practice. Mind you, I think they could do with some, the way they've been flinging them at us.'

'But can you really believe that Captain Sturt arranged all this?' Christopher demanded. His cheeks were red and flushed from the heat, and his eyes were bloodshot. 'It all seems so, well, *underhand*. So ungentlemanly. For a man of his stature to send another chap out to be killed by savages . . .'

'Christopher,' said Eyre, quietly, 'I know about the money. Joolonga told me.'

Christopher opened his mouth, and then closed it again. He flushed.

Eyre said, 'I know you didn't realise what Captain Sturt really had in mind. Well, I assume you didn't. Perhaps he didn't have *anything* in mind. Perhaps he knew nothing about all this ritual brain-eating and whatever; and perhaps Joolonga's been lying to me. But, if Captain Sturt is capable

350

of paying one friend to betray another—well, I would say that he's capable of almost anything.'

Christopher said unevenly, 'It was five pounds. I don't even know why I took it. But Captain Sturt did solemnly promise me that he would try to persuade you not to go off looking for Yonguldye.'

'Although of course he did exactly the opposite.'

'I still couldn't tell you, though, could I? How could I protest that he hadn't kept his word to me, when I had taken his money? What would you have thought of me? My God, what do you think of me now?'

Eyre looked at Christopher; and then looked away. 'Not much,' he said.

'I suppose if I were to say that I had nothing but your best interests in mind . . . that I was thinking of nothing else but protecting you . . .'

'Oh, for God's sake, Christopher, protecting me from what? From myself? From the Aborigines? If you ask me, the only person I need protecting from is you.'

Christopher's reddened eyes brimmed with tears. But then he sniffed loudly, and took a deep breath, and brought himself under control.

'Well, well,' said Dogger philosophically, and then, for no reason that anybody could think of, 'Rats in the cupboard.'

Eyre could think of a dozen cutting and hurtful things to say to Christopher; but there was no point in adding to the humiliation which he already felt. Besides, Christopher's suffering seemed trivial beside that of Midgegooroo, who was groaning again now, and calling out.

Eyre glanced at Dogger with a questioning expression.

'You're in charge,' Dogger conceded. 'Whatever we do, it's all up to you.'

'But you've seen wounds like this before.'

'I've seen worse. I've seen chaps with spears through their faces; and no way of getting them out. You should have left him, you know. He would have been dead by now; but at least you would have spared him all of this.'

'He stayed loyal to us; we had to stay loyal to him,' Eyre argued.

'Making him suffer like a dying dog isn't a very noble piece of loyalty, I wouldn't have thought,' said Dogger.

'Well, what do you suggest we do? Shoot him?'

'No,' said Dogger. 'I suggest we face up to what we've started to do, which is to try to keep him alive; and the only way we're going to have any chance of succeeding in that particular mission is by taking that spearhead out of him.'

'You mean pushing it right through him,' said Eyre.

'I mean pushing it right through him,' nodded Dogger.

Eyre stood up, and went over to the shadow where Midgegooroo was lying and knelt down beside him. A shower of flies rose into the hot afternoon air, and Eyre had to keep brushing them away.

'Midgegooroo?' he said, gently.

Midgegooroo's eyes flickered, but he said nothing.

'Midgegooroo?' Eyre repeated.

Again, nothing but a flicker. A fly crawled into Midgegooroo's open mouth, and out again.

Eyre sat back. 'Well,' he said, swallowing dryly, 'I think you're right. We're just going to have to try it. Weeip, will you bring my medicine-box?'

Weeip ran over to the pack-horse which was lying on the ground and unbuckled its pannier. In a moment, he came back to the rock carrying the polished wooden case, and set it down beside Eyre, wide-eyed. 'You cure Midgegooroo?' he asked, impressed.

'I don't know,' said Eyre. 'I can only do my best. Would you like to untie a scarf from my saddle-pommel, and see what you can do to keep the flies off while we operate.'

'Operate?' said Dogger, wryly. 'That's a fancy word for pushing a spear through somebody.'

'Just give me a hand, will you?' asked Eyre testily. 'And Christopher, could you hold his ankles? I think he's probably going to kick quite a bit.'

Between them, they lifted Midgegooroo out of the shadow of his crevice and laid him on his side on a crumpled green horse-blanket. Midgegooroo's eyes were still open, but Eyre wasn't at all sure that he was actually conscious. He didn't appear to be focusing on anything or anyone; and his breathing was rough and shallow, as if he were asleep, but having nightmares. His face had always looked very primitive to Eyre; very pug-like and Aboriginal; but now it was so ashen and stretched with pain that it scarcely seemed human. It reminded Eyre, chillingly, of some of the gargoyles on Durham cathedral.

Dogger said, 'Are you quite sure you want to do this? It isn't going to be easy; not on us, and especially not on him. It would be twenty times kinder to do away with him quickly.'

'We can't kill him, for God's sake,' Eyre retorted.

Dogger shrugged. 'If you say not. You're the one who knows everything about immortal souls, and stuff like that.'

'He's a human being,' Eyre reminded him.

'Well, exactly,' said Dogger, equivocally.

Eyre hesitated, and looked around, They were all watching him—Christopher and Dogger and Weeip and Minil—and none of them was able or prepared to take the decision for him. He was the leader of the expedition. Midgegooroo's life was in his hands; and the hands of God.

The day felt so immensely hot that he couldn't think. The heat was almost audible, an endless terrible drumming on the back of his neck. He realised that the atmosphere was so dry that he wasn't even sweating any more. His tongue lay in his mouth like a lizard, and swallowing required a complicated contortion of his throat muscles, as well as an act of will.

'I think we'd better begin,' he said, and opened the hot brass catch on his medicine-box, and took out surgical spirits and soft linen cloth. Weeip flapped the clustering flies away while Eyre cleaned as best he could around the lips of the wound, which were already stiff with crusted blood, and bobbled with whitish flies' eggs. Midgegooroo

353

remained limp and silent as Eyre was doing this, except when Eyre cleaned very close to the broken-off shaft of the spear. Then, his hand flailed out, and he clasped Eyre's knee; and let out a faltering breath, and a single word that sounded like *'yungara . . .'*

'He's asking for his wife,' said Dogger.

Weeip piped up, 'Midgegooroo have wife Mary-mary. Mary-mary died last Christmas, very sick.'

Eyre finished cleaning the wound, and wiped his dry forehead with the back of his hand, abrading it with salt grit.

'Right, Mr McConnell,' he said. 'Do you have any idea how this kind of thing is done?'

Dogger cleared his throat. 'You grab hold of the spear, and you push. It's as simple as that.'

Eyre took a painful swallow of hot air, reached around Midgegooroo, and clasped the spear in his right hand. Instantly, Midgegooroo screamed like a slaughtered cat, and jerked upwards, and thrashed his legs, and Eyre whipped his hand away from the spear and knelt there, shaking. 'Jesus,' he prayed. 'If I ever needed help, I need it now. Please help me to save this man's life; and please guide me so that I don't hurt him so much.'

Christopher was white. 'Please, Eyre, if you're going to do it, then do it.'

Eyre nodded. He firmly grasped the spear again; and again Midgegooroo shrieked so harshly that Eyre could imagine the flesh being stripped away from his larynx. But this time, Eyre kept on: pushing and twisting the spear-head into Midgegooroo's back, cutting through muscle and membrane and liver. Midgegooroo writhed like a beetle on a hotplate; and his screaming became so intense that he ceased to scream at all, but uttered an endless soundless cry that was more terrifying than all the screams of hell.

The point of the spear burst bloodily through Midgegooroo's chest, with a sound like a dinner-fork piercing the taut skin of a turkey. By now, however, the broken-off shaft was so deeply buried in his body that Eyre no longer had any purchase on it; and he was unable to grip the sharpened head and drag it through the front. He said to Dogger in a mouthful of jumbled words, 'Pass me that ramrod, from your rifle. Yes, the ramrod. Quickly.'

Dogger grimly did as he was told; and then Eyre lodged the end of the ramrod against the end of the spear, and gave one fierce push. The spear head cut its way out from under Midgegooroo's ribs, dragging with each quartz barb a shred of bloody muscle or black liver; and then at last it was out. Midgegooroo shuddered once, and then lay still, with his face pressed against the ground.

Christopher gingerly released his ankles. 'Is he dead?' he asked.

Eyre felt his wrist. His pulse was uneven, almost undetectable, but he was still alive.

'He can't last,' said Dogger.

'Perhaps if we could get him back to Adelaide,' suggested Christopher.

'I doubt it he'd survive it,' said Dogger. 'Look at the poor bastard; he's almost dead now. And what are we talking about—eight days on horseback at least. More like nine.'

'In any case,' put in Eyre, 'I wasn't planning on going back to Adelaide.'

Christopher stared at him; and slowly took off his hat. 'What? But what are you going to do?'

'I'm going to go on.'

'What are you talking about, go on? Go on to where?'

'Go on to the inland sea, where do you think?'

'But we no longer have the guide, or the supplies. Look at us—one poor fellow nearly dead—two young children—and my leg's coming up like a balloon after that boomerang hit it. How can you possibly think of going on?'

Dogger thrust his hands into his britches pockets, and whistled a dry little tune. 'In for a penny, in for two or three hundred pounds,' he said, and then whistled some

355

more. The sky above their heads was utterly cloudless, and the thermometer was creeping up to 115 degrees.

Eyre cleaned Midgegooroo's wound again, making sure that he squeezed out as many of the flies' eggs as he could. Then he padded both the entry wound and the fresh exit wound with folded gauze; and with Christopher's stunned and resentful help, he tightly bandaged the Aborigine's chest.

Christopher said, 'It's madness. We'll die.'

Eyre began to pack away his medicine-chest. 'There's an inland sea there, Christopher. Once we reach the sea we'll be safe.'

'But we don't have anybody to guide us.'

'The sea lies to the north. Due north. You heard what Yonguldye said.'

'But why, for Heaven's sake? Don't you think we've all suffered enough? I just assumed that we'd be heading straight back to Adelaide. I ask you, my dear chap, why should we carry on? Our sponsors have betrayed us; our guide has nearly had us sacrificed; what earthly reason do we have for continuing?'

Eyre made sure that Midgegooroo was as comfortable as possible, and then he stood up. 'I want that inland sea to be called the Walker Sea, that's why. I want this salt-lake to be named Lake Eyre; and I want that mountain to be called Mount McConnell; and that outcrop to be called Willis Hill. I want this place to be known as Midgegooroo; and we'll find other places and call them Weeip and Minil. We've sweated and fought our way as far as here; let's go back with the fame and the glory. Let's make our mark on this continent. What do you think would happen if we crawled back with our tails between our legs; whining that Captain Sturt had tried to feed us to the Aborigines? We'd be laughed out of Adelaide. No, Christopher, we've got to go back and announce that we've discovered the inland sea and maybe the opal mine, too; and then we'll see what our fine Captain Sturt has to say for himself; yes, and Colonel Gawler, too.'

Christopher walked two limping paces away from Eyre; then he turned around and kicked Eyre's medicine-box all across the sand, scattering bottles and tweezers and tablets.

'Are you mad?' Eyre shouted at him.

'You're asking me if I'm mad?' Christopher shouted back. 'What's the use of keeping a medicine-chest if you've condemned us to death? What's the use of salt tablets for men without water? Or laxatives if we don't have any food? By God, Eyre, we're going to be the healthiest corpses in the desert! Skeletons with rosy cheeks! You and your vanity! You and your damned vanity! I always knew that it would be the end of me! I always knew!'

Eyre took a deep breath, and held it. Then, without another word, he knelt down and began to pick up his bottles. Laudanum, syrup of Toulu, acid of sugar. He had almost finished collecting up the liver-pills when he saw that the tiny amber-glass jar of corrosive sublimate appeared to be empty. He picked it up and held it against the light. Absolutely empty; even though he knew that there must have been two or three drachms in it when they started out on their expedition. Usually, he kept it right at the bottom of the chest, since it was so intensively poisonous, and scarcely ever useful; but Christopher's kick had sent it flying out.

He thought of Arthur; and the sudden way in which Arthur had started vomiting those long stringy white masses of bloody mucus. He had suspected Joolonga before of poisoning Arthur; but the events that had followed had put the matter out of his mind. This empty sublimate jar was proof; at least as far as Eyre was concerned. The pointing-bone may have held some strange and dangerous properties; but none of them could have been half so strong as two drachms of corrosive sublimate. The only question that really remained unanswered was why Joolonga had considered it necessary to put Arthur to death. He had said, of course, that it was to protect them all from the vengeance of Ngurunderi. But nothing that Joolonga had said or done had turned out to be what it appeared to be. Eyre decided to reserve judgement; but to remain suspicious.

He also decided to say nothing to Dogger and Christopher, not yet. He didn't want them thinking that he had turned completely mad.

'Listen,' he said, closing the medicine-chest, 'if the inland sea is as close as Yonguldye said that it is, we should reach it in two or three days. But, if we turn back, we'll have at least a week of hard travelling; and nothing to show for it. Besides, Joolonga will probably still be after us; and the first thing that he will expect us to do is turn south. We'll ride straight into him, more than likely; and then where will we be?'

'Pickled,' said Dogger. 'And that's a dead bird.'

'Nevertheless,' Christopher retorted, 'I still think that it's foolishness, to carry on. Pride, and foolishness. My vote is that we try to make our way back to Adelaide.'

Eyre handed his medicine-chest to Weeip, to pack away, and then stood and looked at Christopher for a very long time, his hands on his hips, trying to give Christopher the opportunity to change his mind. But Christopher did nothing more than wipe his face with his red-spotted belcher and stare defiantly back at him. Eyre knew that Christopher would have to go; and Christopher knew it, too.

'Very well,' said Eyre. 'You and Weeip can leave us here and head southwards. Take Midgegooroo with you. I'll give you fresh bandages and spirits to clean his wounds with. If you're careful with him, he may survive. Use your compass, that's all you have to do; and head directly south. When you reach the ocean, follow it south-east, along the coastline.'

Dogger said, 'You seem to be assuming that I'm going along with you, you and your donah.'

'I had hoped that you would,' said Eyre. 'You're the only experienced man we have left.'

'Nobody has any experience when it comes to the inland sea,' said Dogger.

'Of course not,' Eyre agreed. 'But at least you know how to survive.'

'If I knew how to survive, I wouldn't have come with you at all,' Dogger told him. 'I wouldn't have shot those two gents, just for the sake of a grumpy old yoxter like Arthur Mortlock; and nor would I have followed you out as far as this. If I knew how to survive, I'd be back with Constance, well-pissed on home-made beer and tickling her garden-grove.'

'Are you coming?' Eyre asked him.

Dogger took off his hat, mopped away the sweat, and then replaced it. 'You know damn-well that I'm coming. If there's an inland sea, I want to wash my feet in it.'

He hesitated, and sniffed, and then he said, 'God almighty, if I took my boots off now, I reckon every one of those flies would jump off poor old Midgegooroo there and cluster on to my feet like berries.'

So, as the sun tilted away from its glaring zenith, and the shadows around the outcropping began to give Midgegooroo a few inches more protection, it was decided. Christopher and Midgegooroo should ride south to Adelaide, with Weeip as their guide and interpreter. Once in Adelaide, they would go to Captain Sturt and raise fresh supplies, which they would arrange to be taken to a spot on the salt-lake sixteen miles due east of Woocalla, buried under a stone cairn. These supplies would enable Eyre and Dogger to survive on their return journey, when they would probably be desperately short of almost everything, especially water. That was, unless they found the inland sea, and the freshwater rivers which must be feeding it, and the naturally irrigated forests which probably lined its shores. In that case, they would be bringing their own water, and their own supplies, and news of the greatest graphical triumph since Australia had first been discovered.

Eyre and Dogger would take the lion's share of the

supplies, as well as most of the water; and with Minil to help them in any encounter with Aborigines, they would strike due north, until they reached the ocean; and then south-west, to see if they could locate the source of Yongul-dye's opal diggings at Caddibarrawinnacarra.

By mid-afternoon, when they had finished dividing most of their supplies, it was clear that the sickest of their horses was finished. Dogger loaded up his rifle and shot it. The animal quivered and then lay still in the sunlight. The sound of the shot echoed through the burning afternoon like the clap of a stage-manager's hands.

Dogger came back with the rifle over his arm. 'Weeip,' he said, 'cut that poor old chap up before you go; and we'll share as much of his meat as we can carry.'

But Weeip was frowning towards the eastern horizon. 'No time, Mr Dogasah.'

'What's the matter? What do you mean, no time?'

Weeip pointed. Far, far away, a row of tiny black shapes moved in the wavering afternoon heat; like ants in syrup. And off to their right, carried above the hot distorted layers of air by the north-westerly wind, there was an ochre-coloured cloud of dust.

'Blackfellow,' said Weeip. 'Very many, running to fight.'

Dogger walked over to his horse, and took a shiny brass telescope out of his saddle-pannier. He slid it open, and peered for a long time in the direction of the Flinders mountains.

'Well?' said Eyre.

'They're coming after us, all right,' said Dogger. 'We're going to have to leave here right away.'

'And the horse?'

'Sorry, matey, we'll just have to leave it. No choice. Pity, though, I'm quite partial to horse-meat and pickles.'

Eyre and Christopher self-consciously said goodbye to each other. Eyre shook Weeip's hand and promised him a medal if they ever discovered the inland sea. Only Minil stayed aloof from their fond farewells; squatting on top of the limestone rock watching the gradual approach of the tribesmen from Yarrakinna.

'Well,' said Dogger, raising his flask of home-distilled rum. 'God loves you. Inside and outside.'

Eyre stood by his horse watching Christopher and Weeip ride off towards the south. Behind them, slung over his saddle, lolled the body of Midgegooroo, probably more dead than alive; but now heavily dosed with laudanum to dull the pain of his wound. Eyre stayed where he was until Christopher's horse appeared through the heat-haze to be ankle-deep in water; then Weeip's; and he didn't turn away until all three of them had begun to run and flow like a rainy painting.

'I wonder if we'll ever see *them* again,' said Dogger, pragmatically.

'I don't know,' said Eyre. 'But did you notice something, he didn't even turn around to wave.'

'Waving,' said Dogger, 'is for regattas only, and ladies on quaysides or clerical gentlemen on the top of God-permits.' God-permits was what Dogger always called stage-coaches, because their timetables carried the qualification *'Deo volente'*.

Eyre realised with some surprise that he was hurt by Christopher's temperamental departure. But at last he beckoned Minil down from her perch, and mounted up on to his horse with a squeak of hot leather, and said, 'Come on; we have some history to make.'

'Vultures to feed, more like,' countered Dogger.

Twenty-Six

It was cold, that night, out on the salt-lake. Dogger decided it was a dog-and-a-half night, not quite a two-dog night; but Eyre found it impossible to keep warm, and huddled in his blankets sleeplessly watching the moon curve from one side of the horizon to the other. The Aborigines often used their tame dingoes as bed-covers, and considering how hot and furry the animals' bodies could be, a dog-and-a-half night meant that it was almost down to freezing.

The next morning, they breakfasted on sugary tea and semolina, and set off early. There was no sign of Joolonga behind them, but Eyre knew that their former guide could follow their tracks as easily as if they had strewn him a paperchase.

The lake was flat for as far as they could see in every direction; and it glittered like ground glass. Their horses' legs soon became encrusted in salt, and they left a powdery trail behind them that even Eyre could have followed.

From time to time, Dogger turned his horse, and took out his telescope, and peered behind them at the distant waves of heat. But it was only towards late afternoon that he beckoned to Eyre, and handed him over the telescope, and pointed south-south-east.

'See them?' he asked.

The eastern horizon was beginning to darken; and the dust and the heat gave it a grainy appearance in which it was hard to distinguish anything. Eyre saw several black shapes that could have been Aborigine tribesmen, following them; or then again they could have been vultures, circling over a dead kangaroo.

'I see *something*,' said Eyre, hesitantly.

'You see Joolonga and Company,' Dogger asserted.

'How do you know?'

Dogger tapped his head. 'Long experience, chum.'

Minil reined her horse around and stood beside them.

She still wore Eyre's shirt as an apron in reverse, but she had unwound the scarf from her chest and now wore it on her head, tied loose at the back to keep the sun off her neck.

'If they catch us, they will surely kill us,' she said.

'We'll just have to make sure that they don't, then, won't we?' said Dogger, and turned his horse to ride on.

Towards nightfall, however, Eyre's horse suddenly lurched, and almost threw him out of the saddle. Eyre clicked at it to rear itself up, but then it lurched again; and Eyre looked down and saw that its hoofs had penetrated the crust of the salt-lake, and that it was buried up to its cannon-bones in thick grey mud.

'Dogger!' he called, and immediately dismounted. His own feet crunching on the salt, and made impressions in its surfaces as if it were the frosting on a soft cake. Dogger swung out of the saddle and came cautiously across, leading his horse on a long rein. Eyre said to Minil, 'Stay where you are, Minil; don't come any nearer.'

'*Koolbung*,' Dogger explained to her. 'Salt swamp.'

Eyre soothed and rubbed his horse's nose, and managed gently to coax it to step backward out of the mud. It shook itself and snorted, but the experience had obviously made it nervous.

'How deep do you think this mud is?' asked Eyre.

Dogger shrugged. 'Can't tell. The only other salt swamp I've ever been through, it swallowed a horse and a hay-cart, right up to the driver's hat.'

'Don't tell lies,' Eyre retorted. 'That's the same story they tell about Hindley Street, during the wet.'

'All I'm saying is, we can't tell,' Dogger repeated.

'Maybe we can ride around it,' Eyre suggested. 'After all, if there's mud under the surface, that's probably because there's a deeply buried watercourse down below. Perhaps it comes from the inland sea.'

'Yes, and perhaps it doesn't,' said Dogger.

'Well, wherever it comes from, it can't be limitless. No

wider than a river. So let's try riding westwards a few miles, and then strike north further along.'

Dogger took a measured swallow from his water-bottle. 'All right, then. I suppose it's worth a try. But we're better off camping right here for the night, where we know we've got solid ground to sleep on. We've still got some of that dried suet left, haven't we; and some dried plums. Maybe I'll boil up a hooting pudding.'

'What is "hooting pudding"?' Minil asked, curiously.

'My old mother used to make it, in the days when we were stony,' said Dogger. 'There were so few plums in it, they used to hoot to each other to let each other know where they were.'

Eyre looked southwards. 'You don't think there's any danger that Joolonga might catch up with us?'

'There's always a danger that Joolonga might catch up with us; but we'll be in a worser fix if we try to ride through that *koolbung* in the dark.'

They tethered the pack-horses and set up their hump-backed canvas shelter. Eyre lit a fire out of gum branches which they had brought with them; and the broken pieces of the box in which they had been carrying their dried fruit. Dogger's pudding would use up the very last of the fruit, and other essential stores were running low. There were only ten pounds of flour left, now that they had divided it with Christopher and Weeip and Midgegooroo, and they were also short of sugar, tea, and dried fish. Almost the only food which they had in plentiful supply were hard navy biscuits; but without an equally plentiful supply of water to wash them down with, these were harshly dry, and painful to swallow.

'We still have the horses to eat,' said Eyre, as they sat around their small, windblown fire.

'That's if Joolonga gives us long enough to butcher them,' Dogger replied.

Minil, her eyes sparkling in the reflected light from the fire, said, 'The Nyungar believe that food will always be given to them when they need it. Drink, too. They say

364

when they leave each other "never-starve"; it is a kind of goodbye, like "God-be-with-you." '

'Or, the Lord is mice pepper, as Weeip used to say,' smiled Eyre.

Dogger's pudding was so stodgy that when Eyre had finished it, he felt as if his stomach had been stuffed with kapok. He lay back on his blankets and looked up at the wealth of stars which sparkled overhead, and thought of Charlotte. Somehow, her face seemed less defined now; and he couldn't imagine her voice any more. But he still missed her. He still missed her softness and her silly innocence; he still felt aroused by her slyness and her smiles.

And while he thought of her, the cold pale moon rose again over the salt-lake; transforming it into a landscape of white and silver, a place of death from which only the spirits of those who had crossed it would ever return. A land without flesh, the Wirangu called it; and now Eyre understood what they meant. The body could not survive here; only the *djanga*.

He felt a dull, uncomfortable pain in his stomach. Perhaps he ought to walk out across the lake a way and try to empty his bowels. On a flat and treeless salt-swamp like this, privacy was impossible; and the most they could ever do to maintain their modesty was to turn away. He grimaced, and broke a little wind. No wonder Dogger's mother had called it hooting pudding. In actual fact, it was more like trumpeting pudding. On the other side of the shelter, Dogger broke wind too, and Eyre thought here we go, a musical evening; just when I'm really exhausted. He giggled, and then wished he hadn't. It wasn't very leaderly.

He slept and dreamed of Adelaide. When he woke up, he thought he was back at Mrs McConnell's, and for a moment he couldn't understand where he was. Minil was lying next to him, and when he sat up with a startled jerk, she said, 'What is it?' in a hot whisper; and then, '*Naodaup*?'

'I'm all right,' Eyre whispered back. 'I had a dream, that's all. I had the idea that I was somewhere else.'

Minil touched his shoulder. 'You're cold, that's why you dream.'

He twisted himself around in his blankets. 'I'll be all right. It was probably that hooting pudding.' He picked up his watch and peered at it in the darkness. Three o'clock in the morning. Another hour or so before it would be light enough to travel on.

Minil said, 'The other man, Christopher. . .'

'What about him?'

'I don't know. He is very strange. He seems to like you and yet also to hate you.'

'Well, he has own his particular way of looking at things. I don't think he really hates me. It's just that he wants me to be somebody else; somebody different. And when I'm not . . . well, it makes him angry.'

'You do not make me angry.'

'Why should I?'

'Sometimes white men make me angry. They call me "black polish". Sometimes they touch me. Mr Harris at the New Norcia mission used to touch me. But you are not like Mr Harris. You are like Prince Rupert.'

'Prince Rupert?' Eyre asked her, amused.

Minil lifted the side of Eyre's blanket and snuggled in close to him. Her skin was very soft and warm; a little greasy, but no greasier than Eyre's, who had been washing in no more than a pint of water for the past two days. She smelled of fat and woodsmoke and some musty but quite appealing fragrance that reminded Eyre of rosemary. Her breasts squashed against his arm, and she happily and immodestly thrust one thigh between his legs.

'What made you say Prince Rupert?' he said, although he didn't much care what the answer was. His penis had risen almost immediately, and touched her curved belly with a blind kiss. In response, she reached down and cupped his testicles in her hand, and gently rolled them.

366

'The Black Prince,' she whispered, as if that settled everything.

He lay on his back on the rumpled, uncomfortable blanket; and she climbed on top of him, not kissing him, but biting his shoulders and his neck and even his cheeks with her sharp, filed teeth. Her breasts swung against his chest, and he held them in his upraised hands, so heavy and full that they bulged out from between his fingers. Her nipples knurled, and he twisted and caressed them, and then pinched them hard, so that she pressed her hips against him, and shuddered, and let out short high gasps of pain and excitement.

She was fierce: she bit and gnawed at his nipples until he cried out loud, and he was aware then by the restless snuffling from the other side of the shelter that they had woken Dogger. But somehow, knowing that Dogger was listening made their coupling even more exciting; and when at last she grasped his erection in both hands and pressed it up against her warm, swollen vulva, it was all he could do not to spurt out immediately, and anoint their stomachs with semen. But he made himself think of how low their stores were; and how long it was going to take them to find the inland sea; and so when he slid inside Minil's body, so deeply that she bent her head forward and quaked with the feeling of it, he was able to thrust into her again and again, lifting her up with his hips so that he penetrated her even more deeply, but still keep his climax at bay.

'*Kungkungundun* . . .' she whispered; and he knew from Yanluga that she was calling him 'loved one'.

He kissed her then; the bridge of her nose; her forehead; her lips; and she accepted his kisses with shy passion.

'Loved one,' he breathed back at her, in English.

There was a moment when their bodies juicily slapped together; when her vagina squeezed him, slippery and hot; and when his penis began to jolt out the first tremblings of sperm. That was the moment of ultimate selfishness; when the demands of pleasure contracted tight inside their

367

own minds, and they both sought that bright white concentrated spark that would release all their feelings.

But, unexpectedly, Minil began to cry out first; and shake and shake and claw at Eyre's shoulders with her long broken fingernails until he knew that he must be bleeding. He had never known a girl reach any kind of climax before; and for a moment it put him off his rhythm; and his own ejaculation began to slide away like the mercury down a thermometer.

But then Minil thrust her hips at him again, and roused him up, and the wetness that ran down his buttocks made him feel that he had excited and satisfied her fully; and that gave him a pride that fuelled up his passion again. He suddenly groaned, and ejaculated right up inside her, right up against the neck of her womb; and it was then that she fell forward on him, and hugged him, and wiggled and wriggled her hips against him, and kissed him, and rolled her face against his, so that he could feel the tears, and the decorative scars on her cheeks, and her sharp teeth biting at his lips.

It occurred to him as they lay together afterwards, and Minil slept, that he may already have made her pregnant. She looked disturbingly young lying there against his arm, her mouth slightly parted as she breathed. She also looked remarkably black. But he didn't mind her blackness at all. It was rather like an exotic varnish on a body that was already beautiful.

Dawn cleared the skies again, and for an hour the air was remarkably limpid, so that they could see for miles. Ahead of them, the salt-lake looked flat and firm; although they already knew how deceptive it was. Behind them, they could see for the first time the encampment of the Aborigines who were following them: a strung-out row of improvised shelters and smouldering fires. Dogger spent a long time scrutinising the Aborigine camp through his telescope while Eyre tried to shave with nothing but soap moistened with spit. It was a slow and painful process; but Eyre was determined to be civilised, and not to grow a beard. Every now and then Dogger said, 'Mmm,' and Eyre said, 'Ouch.'

After a while, Dogger said, 'Have a gander at this,' and passed the telescope to Eyre. 'Look to your left,' he said, 'the big umpee second from the end.'

Towelling himself with one hand and holding the telescope with the other, Eyre inspected the Aborigine encampment. There were more than a dozen shelters altogether, and another score of blackfellows had probably slept out in the open, wrapped in their *bukas*. When he swung the telescope towards the left-hand side of the encampment, however, Eyre saw a larger shelter, and this shelter was decorated with feathers and skulls.

'That looks like a medicine-man's hut,' Eyre remarked, He turned to Dogger, and said, 'Joolonga?'

Dogger shook his head. 'Wouldn't have thought so.'

'But I shot Yonguldye.'

'Perhaps you didn't. You know how the balls tend to drop out of these old Baker rifles, especially when you shake them around. More than likely you did nothing worse than burn his bum with a charge of powder.'

'Then they're really after us,' said Eyre. 'Yonguldye too.'

'I would have thought so, yes,' sniffed Dogger.

'And they'll still be determined to sacrifice us,' said Eyre.

'Well, they'll still be determined to sacrifice *you*,' agreed Dogger.

'Thanks very much,' Eyre snapped.

'Don't mention it,' said Dogger, cheerfully.

Eyre finished wiping his chin, and put on his hat. Dogger said, 'You've humiliated Yonguldye, that's the worst thing. Humiliation is worse than death; at least as far as a clever-man is concerned. You can bet your hat that he's wearing the *Kurdaitja* boots; and you can bet your hat that he'll follow you now to the ends of Australia, wherever they may be.'

Eyre returned the telescope. 'It's time we left then, before they break camp.'

Minil came up. This morning she was wearing Eyre's

shirt tied around her shoulders, and her scarf arranged in peaks, like the wimple of a Brigittine nun. She came close to Eyre, but didn't touch him; but all three of them knew now that the triangle between them had changed during the night; and that Dogger was now the outsider. She said, 'Will we have time for breakfast?' But Eyre shook his head. 'We'll eat a few biscuits while we ride. I want as much distance between us and those blackfellows as we can possibly manage.'

'I heard you say Yonguldye,' said Minil, simply.

'Dogger thinks he may still be alive,' Eyre explained. 'One of the shelters has skulls on it; or what look like skulls.'

'Yes,' said Minil.

'Yes, what?'

'Yes—I too think that Yonguldye is alive. I feel it. He has a very strong—' she waved her hand around her head to try to describe mental power. 'When he calls me, even when he is far away, I am sure that I can feel it.'

'You feel that now?' Eyre asked her.

She stared at him. Her eyes were reddish-hazel and very wide. 'Yes,' she whispered. 'Yonguldye is still alive.'

All that day they rode westwards, skirting the edge of the salt swamp. The sun rose hot and white over their heads, and their shadows shrank beneath their horses as the thermometer rose to 112 degrees. Eyre wore his smoked-glass spectacles; but during the fiercest hours, just after noon, he felt as if the world were nothing but glaring white; white on white; and when he turned around to make sure that Dogger and Minil were following him, he thought that they looked like ghosts, bleached-out apparitions on a bleached-out landscape.

He drank as little as he possibly could; for their flasks were low now and there was no sign of a water-hole. But three mouthfuls during the course of the day was far too little to prevent his mouth from drying up, and his skin from cracking. At times he felt so hot and exhausted that he could have dropped off his horse and laid down on the salt and let the sun slowly bake him into a gingerbread man, stiff and smiling. A happy, mindless end. And there were plenty of times when he felt like giving it all up, and turning south.

They ventured again and again into the salt swamp; at least once every two miles. But each time their horses broke the crust of the lake, and began to sink. Then they spent valuable time coaxing the horses out of the mud, and calming them down, before they set off westwards once more, searching with increasing desperation for a northern passage.

At three o' clock in the afternoon, Dogger passed the telescope to Eyre without comment. Eyre focused sharply, about a mile-and-a-half away; and there was Yonguldye, in his tall head-dress; and beside him was that familiar midshipman's bonnet that belonged to Joolonga.

'We may have to stop and fight,' said Dogger.

'They will kill us,' said Minil, with frightening certainty.

Eyre focused the telescope again. Behind Yonguldye there was a large band of Aborigine warriors; fifty or sixty, judging from the spear-points which rose from the dust.

'We don't have a chance,' he told Dogger. 'Not out here, in the open. We're going to have to think of a way to balance the odds.'

'We've got rifles,' said Dogger.

'Not enough,' Eyre asserted. 'All they have to do is run into spear-range while we're reloading, and that will be the finish of us.'

'Well, don't ask me,' said Dogger.

They rode westwards for three or four more miles, but now it was clear that the Aborigines were catching up with them. Eyre observed the Aborigines through Dogger's telescope every five minutes or so; and they were running at a steady, even, lope. They must have scented that Eyre and Dogger and Minil were very close now; some of their sharpest-eyed warriors may actually have seen them, even through the dust and the distorted waves of heat.

Eyre drew his rifle out of its saddle-holster and made

sure that it was loaded; this time checking that the ball was still in place. Dogger did the same; and also unsheathed a large cane-cutting knife with a curved blade, which he tucked into his belt.

'What's that for?' asked Eyre.

'Topping and tailing,' said Dogger, without smiling.

Eyre looked all around for any kind of cover; any slight hillock or outcropping of rock where they could dismount and make a stand against Yonguldye. But the salt-lake's surface remained relentlessly flat and featureless, swirled with pink and grey; and he began to realise that if they were going to fight, it would have to be man-to-man, and face-to-face, and that they would unquestionably die. He muttered a prayer under his breath, and then part of the 59th Psalm: 'Deliver me from my enemies, O my God; set me securely away from those who rise up against me. Deliver me from those who do iniquity; and save me from men of bloodshed.'

Yet still, throughout the grilling afternoon, through the whiteness and the heat and the saline dust, Yonguldye and Joolonga followed him, guided by their native instincts and by the bloody *Kurdaitja* shoes, emu feathers stuck together with human blood, perhaps Yonguldye's own blood, or the blood of a tribesman who had been especially slain for the purpose.

At last, as the sun began to glower down through the crimson dust of the day, Eyre and Dogger were able to see their pursuers without using their telescope; and the trail of dust that the Aborigines left hanging in the air behind them was like the red steer, which was what the bush settlers nicknamed a bush-fire.

'They're going to catch us,' Dogger said, philosophically.

Eyre pulled up his horse, and sat in the saddle for a long time, looking behind him. At last he said, 'Could a man walk across that swamp, without sinking?'

'I haven't a clue,' said Dogger. 'You want to try it?'

'Yes,' said Eyre, and dismounted. He sat down on the ground and tugged off his boots, and then he began to walk due north, feeling the crusted ground gradually giving beneath his feet. He was able to walk nearly a hundred paces before the crust broke, and thick grey mud began to squidge up between his bare toes.

He walked further; and the salt crust broke again and again, until he was up to his knees in mud. At last he was floundering, and unable to walk any further. He fought against the warm mud clinging to his legs, but the more he struggled, the more deeply embedded he became. At last, panting harshly, he managed to drag himself clear, and crawl on his hands and knees back to firmer ground.

'You are so dirty,' smiled Minil. 'You look like the Mud-Man.'

'You certainly do,' agreed Dogger. 'And what have you proved? Yonguldye's only about a mile away now; they'll be with us in ten minutes.'

Eyre said, 'Don't argue, just listen to me. We'll ride on a little further, until we reach a place where the ground's unbroken; then I'll tell you what to do.'

They rode on for another half-mile, even though their horses were exhausted and stumbling. Then Eyre told them to draw up, and dismount, and unbuckle their saddle-panniers. Dogger frowned, and shrugged, but did as he was told. Eyre took their rifles, and their ammunition, and as many water-bottles as he could carry, and shared them out between them. Then he said, 'We have to buckle the saddle-panniers on to our feet, like big flat shoes.'

Dogger stared at him. 'You haven't got sunstroke, have you, chum? You want us to buckle these things on to our *feet*?'

'That's right,' Eyre nodded. 'Look, just watch me,' and he sat down and strapped one of the wide leather panniers to his right foot, buckling it tightly.

Dogger rubbed the back of his neck. 'I've seen some lunatics in my time, but this just about takes the biscuit.'

'Don't be ridiculous,' said Eyre. 'I got this idea from one

of my father's parish magazines. We can walk across the salt swamp without falling through.'

'Like Christ walking on water?'

'No, of course not. Like Eskimos walking on snow-shoes. The Eskimos wear wide flat shoes to spread their weight, so that they don't sink down through the snow. We can do the same on top of the salt swamp.'

Hesitantly, still sniffing and grumbling, Dogger eased himself down on to the ground and strapped his panniers on to his feet. He stood up, and danced a little shuffling trot, and said with distaste, 'I feel like a duck. What are my mates going to say if I die with a couple of satchels on my feet?'

'They'll say "clever, but unlucky",' Eyre replied. 'Now, let's walk out as far as we can.' He took Minil's bare arm, and began to guide her out on to the crust of the salt swamp.

The sun had turned bloody now, and was almost gone. They walked clumsily across the salt swamp, tiny figures in a red-and-purple panorama that stretched as wide as any of them could see. Eyre felt the ground give beneath his feet as he dragged his panniers along; but it didn't break. Soon they were more than a half-mile out on to the crust, in an evening that had now turned to boiling plum.

The wind smelled of brine, and dry dust, and distant mountains. The last vultures of the day spun lazily over their heads, looking for any stray creatures that might have died on the salt-swamps just before nightfall.

Eyre slowed down at last, and stopped, and said, 'Here. This should do us.'

Dogger looked around. 'This place is as flat as any other place; and any other place is as flat as a churchwarden's pancake.'

'Didn't you feel those last few hundred yards?'

'What do you mean?'

'Didn't you feel how soft the ground was?'

Dogger peered back. 'Yes. I suppose it was. But what does that have to do with anything at all?'

'Watch,' said Eyre. 'They're coming.'

Already, Yonguldye and his warriors had reached the edge of the swamp, where Eyre and Dogger had tethered the horses. Now, with Yonguldye leading them, his huge head-dress bobbing and waving in the evening light, they were running due northwards, to catch up with their magical prey. They wanted the *djanga* for their sacrifice. They wanted Yonguldye to have Eyre's brains, and devour them, so that at last they could stand equal to the white man, and keep him away from their sacred *corroboree*-sites, and their *bora*-grounds.

Eyre and Dogger had four rifles between them, all loaded. Eyre said, 'I'll fire first; then, when I'm reloading, you fire. And so on. But we may not need to kill very many!'

'I'm glad you're so confident,' said Dogger.

The sight of the Aborigines running towards them in the twilight was mystical and frightening. The tribesmen's eyes were surrounded by huge circles of white pipe-clay, and their bodies were outlined like boogie-men. This evening, too, they were completely silent, except for the clattering of their spears and the slapping of their bare feet on the salt. No fighting cries; no anger; no chants. Just fifty of them, running nearer and nearer; a dark and complicated outline of spears and head-dresses and running legs.

Eyre touched his cracked lips with the tip of his dry tongue, and lifted his rifle to his shoulder. He took aim at Yonguldye's head, and held it as best he could. Yonguldye was taller than most of his tribesmen, and so he made an easier target; but all the same he was bobbing and weaving as he ran, and Eyre knew that he would be very difficult to hit. 'Save me from men of bloodshed,' he repeated to himself.

Dogger said, 'God almighty, Eyre, they're going to murder us.'

Eyre, at that moment, felt equally frightened. The back of his neck prickled coldly, and he found it almost impossible to maintain his aim on Yonguldye. Any second now, he thought numbly, it's going to be the death-spear through the ribs, or into the belly; and after having seen how poor Midgegooroo had suffered, he knew what he would do next. Thrust the muzzle of his rifle into his own mouth, and pull the trigger. At least it would all be over in one catastrophic blast.

A spear whirred overhead, then another, and a third landed crisply in the salt soil not five feet away. Eyre fired; and his gunpowder flashed brightly in the gathering darkness; and he saw Yonguldye's head-dress collapse out of sight. Then Dogger fired, so loudly that it made Eyre's head sing, and another Aborigine went down.

Eyre took another rifle, and lifted it up; but at that moment he heard a cry from two or three of the Aborigines; then more cries, and shouts of panic. Their running feet had broken through the crust of the salt-swamp, and they had staggered headlong into the mud. Eyre fired at a knot of them who were struggling to free themselves; hitting one of them in the shoulder, but causing shouts of terror that far outweighed the value of the shot. Four or five more spears whistled around him, but now Dogger fired again and Eyre began to reload; and the Aborigines began to turn back in confusion.

For a few minutes, it sounded like a major battle. Six or seven tribesmen were stuck waist-deep in the mud, while at least twenty others tried to drag them out. The rest were running away; while Dogger and Eyre fired their rifles into the air, and screamed and yelled and shouted. 'Bunyip! Bunyip! and 'God Save The Queen!' Even Minil joined in, dancing and shrieking and banging two ramrods together.

Quickly, fearfully, the last tribesmen slithered out of the salty mud and ran away; grey ghosts in a thickening night; until only three of them were left. Yonguldye, lying flat on his back, his mighty head-dress plastered with blood; a young warrior whose spears remained unlaunched; and Joolonga.

Eyre and Dogger and Minil shuffled back across the salt,

with their saddle-panniers on their feet. Joolonga stood by their horses and watched them with arms folded.

'Well, Joolonga?' said Eyre, unbuckling his panniers.

'Well, Mr Walker-sir. It seems you were wiser than I first imagined.'

Eyre nodded towards the last of the running tribesmen. 'Will they be back?'

'I don't believe so, Mr Walker-sir. Not without Yonguldye the great Darkness to guide them.'

Dogger kept his distance from Joolonga, his loaded rifle over his arm. Minil crouched down and began to scoop a pit in the sand where they could light a fire.

'You deceived me, didn't you?' Eyre asked Joolonga. 'You knew that Yonguldye wanted to put me to death.'

Joolonga said nothing, but took off his midshipman's hat, and nodded.

'Did Captain Sturt know about this?' asked Eyre.

Joolonga closed his eyes, and swayed a little. 'I am wounded, Mr Walker-sir.'

Eyre handed his rifle to Minil, walked up to Joolonga, and opened the Aborigine's decorated coat. There was blood all over his chest; like a waistcoat of scarlet silk, and with each beat of his heart, there was more. Eyre looked straight into Joolonga's eyes. 'You'd better lie down,' he said, quietly.

Joolonga half-smiled. 'No need, Mr Walker-sir. Quite soon, I shall fall down.'

Eyre was silent for almost a whole minute. He glanced towards Dogger but Dogger could only shrug. He turned back to Joolonga, and repeated, 'Did Captain Sturt know what would happen if we found Yonguldye?'

Joolonga closed his eyes. 'Nobody knew, Mr Walker-sir; not even I.'

'But Minil heard you talking to Yonguldye about sacrificing me, and eating my brains.'

'Minil?' frowned Joolonga. His voice slurred; and his lips were sticky with blood.

'This girl; Yonguldye's protégée.'

'I shall have to sit down,' said Joolonga. Eyre took his arm, and helped him into an awkard sitting position, one leg raised, his back propped against one of their saddle-bags. He lowered his head for a while, so that his chin was resting on his blood-soaked tunic; and he snored blood-clots through his nose. Then he raised his head again, and said, 'Yonguldye wanted only your knowledge.'

'By killing me? By eating my brains?'

Joolonga shook his head. 'This girl does not understand Wirangu well, Mr Walker-sir. There are words which sound like Nyungar words, but have different meanings. Yonguldye would not have killed you, Mr Walker-sir; he was going to initiate you into the brotherhood of his tribe, so that he could share your mind. He did not say "eat your brains". He said "devour everything you knew." '

Eyre said tauntly, 'Are you sure?'

Joolonga nodded.

'You're not lying to me? Because, by God, if you are—'

Joolonga lolled his head back and looked up at Eyre with glassy eyes. 'Why should I lie to you, Mr Walker-sir? I shall soon follow Ngurunderi to the place above Nar-oong-owie, the island of the dead.'

Eyre glanced over towards Minil, who was deftly rubbing a fire-stick in order to start up their evening cook-fire. He said to Dogger, 'Give her a chuckaway, would you?' Then, to Joolonga, 'You lied to me about Arthur Mortlock. Why should I believe you now?'

'Mr Mortlock, sir? I said before. It was necessary for him to die; otherwise we would have been cursed by Ngurunderi. It was my fault, for burying those two bounty-hunters according to Aborigine custom. I am to blame. As it was, I think I was too late to save us.'

'But you poisoned him.'

'No, Mr Walker-sir.'

'You must have done. He died because he was given corrosive sublimate.'

'No, Mr Walker-sir. All I did was to point the bone.'

'How can a man die, just because you pointed your bone at him? Come on Joolonga, you're far more civilised than that!'

Joolonga coughed, and a great black gout of blood splashed out on to his gold braiding.

'Am I, sir?' he asked, in a gluey voice. 'I pointed the bone at him, and he died. Is that not proof enough?'

A billow of aromatic smoke engulfed them for a second; and an ash blew into Eyre's eye. Rubbing it with his finger, he asked Joolonga, 'You're serious, aren't you? I mean, you believe it. And did you really believe that I was the *djanga*?'

Joolonga's head fell forward again. The blood was so thick in his lungs that it was almost impossible for him to breathe. But after a moment or two he raised his head once more, and said, 'Whether you believe you are the *djanga* or not, Mr Walker-sir; you are the white man who came looking for Yonguldye because you wanted to atone for killing Yanluga.'

He hesitated, and then he said, 'Whether you believe you are the *djanga* or not, Mr Walker-sir; you are the man in the story. Captain Henry believed it, and from the moment Captain Henry believed it, and passed it on, it became true.'

Eyre knelt close beside him; felt the warm wet stain of Joolonga's blood through the knee of his britches. 'Joolonga,' he said. 'For God's sake, explain it to me. I don't understand.'

Joolonga almost managed a smile. 'It is easy to understand, unless you are white, Mr Walker-sir. The truth is that you are the man in the story; you have become a part of the dreamtime; Australia has made you her own.'

He caught his breath; and caught it again. But there was too much blood in his lungs now; and all he could do was to give one last desperate choke, splattering blood all over Eyre's shirt and trousers; and roll sideways on to the ground, as if he were dodging away from a blow, and lie with his face against the salt.

Dogger came over and looked down at him.

'Well?' he wanted to know. 'Did you believe any of that?'

'I'm not sure,' said Eyre. Stiffly, he stood up; then looked down at his bloody hands, and wiped them on his shirt. 'I always thought that men made up stories; rather than the other way about.'

Dogger put down his rifle, and stretched, and scratched his belly, and yawned. 'I don't know. They're a rum lot, these blackfellows. Old George Hubbard used to say that they'd all be better off dead. Well, save them some suffering. And, besides, who wants to end up as the figment of some savage's imagination?'

Eyre felt a grey wind across the salt-lake. He looked around, and although the body of the young Aborigine warrior was still there, lying twisted just where Dogger had shot him, the body of Yonguldye was gone.

'Dogger,' said Eyre, and nodded towards the broken surface of the swamp.

Dogger stared for a moment, not sure what he was supposed to be looking at; but then he spat, and said, 'Hell! The wily old bugger's made off!'

They crouched down by the spot where Yonguldye had fallen. Some of his blood-crusted emu feathers were stuck to the salt. Dogger traced the marks in the ground with the tips of his fingers, and said, 'You hit him, all right, but not too badly by the looks of it. He must have made off while we were talking. They can walk silent, some of these blackfellows, and some of them say that they can make themselves invisible.'

Eyre took off his hat and wiped the grit away from the band. 'Well,' he said, 'that means that Yonguldye's still out there; either looking for us because he wants to make friends, and devour my knowledge; or else because he wants to sacrifice us to the great god Baiame, and eat my brains.'

Dogger jerked a thumb towards Minil, who had begun to boil up a thick barley soup. In the intermittent firelight,

380

her face was quite impassive, a mahogany mask. 'It all depends on your point of view, doesn't it, chum? I mean, I'm the last man around to be a spoil-your-sport; but it does strike me that you ought to be taking her carefully; with a pinch of salt, if you know what I mean. If old squash-face was right, and *she* was wrong, then the consequences could be rather uncertain, if you understand me.'

'I'm not sure that I do.'

'Well, I'm not either,' said Dogger. 'But what I'm saying is, take care, and keep your powder dry.'

But it wasn't only the question of Minil that was troubling Eyre that evening; it was the question of Arthur Mortlock. For if Joolonga hadn't poisoned him; who had?

Twenty-Seven

Again and again, for over a week, they tried to strike out northwards, towards the shores of the inland sea. One afternoon, they managed to ride almost six miles further northwards than they had before, and Eyre was convinced that at last they had found a way through the salt swamp. Dogger even began to whistle, and Minil called to Eyre that as soon as they reached the other side of the salt-lake she would cook them a special meal to celebrate.

But then their horses' hoofs began to break through the crumbly crust again, and within ten minutes they were plunged belly-deep into thick, oozing mud.

Eyre shouted, 'Let's try to ride on! Perhaps the horses can find a footing!' But after quarter-of-an-hour of thrashing and wallowing, they were forced to dismount, and drag their frightened, miserable mounts out of the mud again; and stand filthy and bedraggled by the edge of the swamp looking northwards through the trembling heat at the distant horizon that Australia seemed to be determined to deny them. The 100-degree heat dried the mud on their clothes and on their horses' flanks in a matter of minutes; and so they looked like powdery white effigies of themselves; a monument to forlorn hope.

Through Dogger's telescope, Eyre could make out the faintly purple peak of two distant mountains. He pointed them out to Dogger, who collapsed the telescope with a soft brassy whistle of air, and then shrugged. 'You saw them first, you can name them,' said Dogger. 'How about Mount Constance and Mount Charlotte?'

'What would you call them?' Eyre asked Minil, who was standing a little way away from him, shading her eyes.

'I would call them *manaro*,' said Minil. 'That is north-language for breasts.'

'And what about you?' Dogger asked Eyre.

For the first time in days, Eyre gave way to frustration and bitterness. 'Mount Deception; and Mount Hopeless,' he said, and turned away.

Dogger said, 'Eyre—' But Eyre snapped, 'Never mind. We'd better mount up and make our way back.'

The following morning they tried for the last time to make their way northwards. It was one of the hottest days they had yet experienced, and they were becoming dangerously short of water and food. Eyre rode ahead wearing his smoked glasses, straining his eyes for any glimpse of hills or trees or even a gradual rising of the ground—anything to indicate that they could find a way across the terrible glittering surface of the salt-lake.

All the time, discreetly, Dogger kept a watch behind. Dogger knew Aborigines of old, and he was convinced that Yonguldye would be following them. It was Dogger's opinion that even if Yonguldye hadn't wanted to kill them on their first night at the *corroboree*, he would most certainly want to kill them now. They had slaughtered his tribesmen and wounded him twice and more importantly they had humiliated him in front of his people.

They paused for half-an-hour just before noon, and Minil brewed up a pot of tea. Now that she and Eyre had become lovers, of a kind, Minil seemed to consider that it was her duty to serve Eyre like a wife; and she did whatever she could to clean his clothes and cook him food and make him comfortable. Dogger had been a little peeved by this arrangement at first; but he was humorous and adaptable, and he soon accepted it. Eyre was grateful to Dogger for not making his usual relentless fun out of it; although he was still given to grumbling out loud whenever Minil was riding Eyre with too many screams and cries. He would bark, 'Keep that damned galah quiet, will you?' from the other side of the camp-fire.

Eyre was unsure whether he believed Minil or not. But, for the time being, her believability was unimportant. As long as she could cook for them, and help them to feed and water the horses, and as long as Eyre had a warm companion for the night, nothing else mattered. He would sometimes watch her, though, through the long glaring hours of the afternoon, her bare black back shining in the sunlight, her buttocks spread wide across her saddle, and he would wonder what and who she was; and whether she had a part in the dreamtime story, too. Then from time to time she would suddenly turn and smile at him, calm and erotic, and that smile would do nothing at all to make the mystery any more explicable.

They rode north until three o' clock; and then again the salt-lake began to deteriorate under their horses' hoofs, and one of the pack-horses sank to its knees and knelt there sweating and trembling, unable or unwilling to move any further.

Eyre sat on his horse in his smoked-glass spectacles, caked in white salty mud, his head bare under the relentless sun. 'This is where we have to turn back,' he said, in a voice that was little more than a hoarse croak.

Dogger stared at him silently; and then dismounted. 'Minil,' he called. 'Give me a hand with this horse.'

Together, while Eyre watched them, Dogger and Minil cooed and coaxed the stricken horse back on to its feet again. It still seemed bewildered, because it walked around and around in circles, until Minil was able to seize its bridle, and even then it kept twisting its head around as if it were wildly disoriented.

'Brain's gone,' said Dogger, tugging his hat further down over his eye. 'Thinks he's back in some pasture somewhere. Seen it before. Horses trying to chew the ground because they imagined it was grass.'

'Still, we have to turn back,' Eyre repeated.

'Yes,' said Dogger.

They both looked for the last time towards the north. In the gruelling afternoon heat, they could see the tantalising ripples of a horseshoe-shaped lake, glassy and clear, reflecting the peaks of Mount Deception and Mount Hopeless with crystalline clarity.

'That's your inland sea,' said Eyre, with cracked lips. 'A mirage. A dream. And nothing else.'

'Well, it's probably there all right; two or three hundred miles further north,' said Dogger. 'But the question is: how does anybody get to it?'

'Come on,' Eyre told him, and the three of them gathered their reins and began their long retreat south.

After an hour or so, Dogger said, 'What about the opals? Are we going to go and look for the opals?'

Eyre said nothing, but continued riding southwards, with his back to the glory of which once he had felt so sure. But now there was to be no glory, no great discovery; not even a clever-man to bury Yanluga according to the rites of his religion. He closed his eyes as he rode and tried to think about anything and everything else, in order to suppress the sharpness of his defeat. He thought of Charlotte, and of Adelaide, and of riding his bicycle again, if the piccaninnies hadn't stolen it. But again and again the bitterness of having to turn back rose up in his gullet like a cat's-cradle of regurgitated brambles. He cursed Captain Sturt and he cursed Joolonga and he cursed himself for being taken for a fool. He couldn't bring himself to curse Minil, although he began to feel that he ought to.

Neither could he bring himself to curse God.

That night, as they sat around their campfire, Minil said, 'We have no flour left. Tomorrow we must find fresh meat. Kangaroo, maybe. Emu.'

Dogger finished his mouthful of pasty, half-burned bread, and swilled it down with warm water. 'Won't be too soon for me, my lady.'

'I don't think I've seen a single kangaroo since we left Parachilna,' Eyre remarked.

'Don't you worry,' Dogger reassured him. 'We'll soon be back in Kangaroo country; and even if we can't catch any for the first couple of days, we can always survive on lizards until we do. Nothing like a good grilled goanna; what do you say, my lady?'

Minil knew that he was teasing her; for she leaned forward and kissed him with surprising demureness on his grey bearded cheek.

'Well, now,' said Dogger, his eyes bright. 'You'd better watch yourself now, Eyre old chum. Don't want your lady straying to an old dinger-hunter like me.'

On the morning of the following day, their sick pack-horse suddenly staggered and collapsed. They drew up, and dismounted, and Dogger felt the pulse in its neck. 'He's almost gone,' he said; and then 'He's gone.' The horse lay on the sandy ground with its purple tongue protruding and its eyes staring at nothing at all. Eyre looked away, thinking: my God, what has my conceit and my vanity brought to all of these people and all of these animals? Nothing but suffering and death. He began to feel like a Jonah, a curse on everything and everybody who had anything to do with him. It probably wouldn't be long before Dogger and Minil would be struck down with heat-stroke, and exhaustion; and then his devastation of all those whom he had ever loved or liked would be complete. And there would be no chance of him ever returning to Charlotte.

Dogger said, 'We'd better make the best of this poor beast. Are you any good at butchering; Eyre?'

'For God's sake,' said Eyre. 'Haven't you had enough?'

Dogger stood up. 'Now, listen here,' he said, and his voice was a rasp. 'You just stop behaving like Hunt's dog; which would neither go to church nor stay at home; and we'll all get on much better. It wasn't your fault that there were more salt swamps out there than you could manage; and it isn't your fault that we're having to go home with our tails between our legs. So let's make the best of what we have; and the best of what we have today is fresh horse-meat.'

Throughout the stunningly hot afternoon, Eyre cut up the dead pack-horse with a sharp sailor's-knife, hanging out some of the dark-red strips on a length of twine in the hope that they would be dried by the sun; and dividing the rest into bloody steaks. By the time he had finished there must have been more than 100 pounds of meat stacked up on every available plate and cooking-pan they had, clustered with grey sand-flies, but ready for a massive feast.

Minil built a fire out of dried bushes and twigs, and during the whole long evening they sat with lumps of horse-meat speared through by twigs, and roasted them in front of the glowing ashes.

Dogger said, 'Remember what I told you about surviving in the outback, old chum; eat whatever you can, and as much as you can, whenever you can get it; because you never know when you're going to get it next.'

Eyre's chin was glistening with fat and blood, and he didn't know whether he wanted to vomit or die, but he managed to eat nearly five pounds of meat before he lay back, his hands clutching his distended stomach, and decided that even Purgatory would be better than another mouthful of horse-meat. Dogger and Minil continued wolfing for another half-hour or so; but eventually even

Dogger had to admit that he didn't care whether he saw another horse in his entire life or not, and lay back on his blankets with a curse on all four-legged animals, and a ripping belch, and in five minutes or so was fast asleep.

Eyre was exhausted, both by days of riding and by disappointment, and he found it increasingly hard to keep his eyes focused on Minil as she sat by the fire. He dozed, and dreamed, and woke up; and she was still sitting there, naked, tearing voraciously at handfuls of horse-flesh, her attention focused on feeding, and nothing else; the single-mindedness of a wild animal. When she had sex with him, she thought of nothing but sex. When she drank, she thought of nothing but drinking. Now she was presented with nearly seventy pounds of uneaten horse-flesh, she thought of nothing but feeding.

The grease ran down her chin and over her breasts. Her eyes were half-closed but totally concentrated on what she was doing. As he watched her, Eyre began to feel very lonely, because he knew that he could never get to know her, not closely, not a girl who saw daily life as a continuous struggle to ward off the dangers of tomorrow. Minil was probably right and he was probably wrong; particularly in the outback of Australia; but all the same he would rather invest his trust in God, and the fairness of destiny, than in nine pounds of half-raw horse-meat.

He slept, and dreamed of Mount Deception and Mount Hopeless; and that future citizens of Australia would damn him for giving them such defeatist names. But then he woke up and thought that nobody would ever find out what he had christened them, because he would never reach Adelaide alive, or, if he did, it would be in deep disgrace, a waster of money and a wanton killer of innocent Aborigines. And if Captain Sturt had to wear the green bonnet simply because Eyre had failed to penetrate northwards to the inland sea, or discover any opals or gold and silver; then he could imagine what an outcast he would become. 'Not-Fall-Over' indeed. How could anybody have called him that?

He slept again; and woke up again; and when he woke up Minil was still squatting by the fire, devouring raw crimson lumps of horse-meat. Eyre looked at the stacks of meat remaining on the plates, and saw that she must have consumed nearly twenty pounds. Her stomach was bulging out as if she were pregnant, and glossy with fat; but she continued to pull at the meat with her sharpened teeth as if she were ravenously hungry.

He propped himself up on his elbow, and watched her in silent fascination. She had given up bothering to cook the meat, and now she was cramming everything she could into her mouth: bloody lumps of raw horse-liver, stringy shreds of neck; even lungs, like pale gory balloons.

Towards dawn, he lay back and dreamed of Yonguldye, disfigured and wounded, and hunting him to the ends of the desert. He woke up again with a peculiar jolt, and Minil was lying by the ashes of the fire, asleep at last. He crawled over towards her, and covered her with a blanket. He didn't know whether to kiss her or not. She seemed like a girl from another age altogether; not repulsive; not frightening; but utterly different from anyone he had ever met before, even Yanluga.

For a moment, he lifted the blanket again and looked at her. Her face, pouting and black, with its decoratively scarred cheeks, one hand touching her lips the way children do. Her breasts, swollen and shiny with grease. Her hugely distended stomach; and her unconsciously parted thighs, revealing labia as pink as parakeelya petals. He covered her up, and went over to the fire to brew himself a small pot of tea. Perhaps she disturbed him because she was the personification of Australia, this continent that he had so badly wanted to conquer, and failed.

Perhaps, on the other hand, she disturbed him because in an extraordinary way he had fallen in love with her; or at the very least, felt deeply reluctant to be parted from her. Unlike Charlotte, she had seen him both at his very best and at his very worst; and had accepted him without question. Charlotte had always adored his fashionable clothes, his silk neckties and his fancy patterned waistcoats. Minil had first met him when he was naked.

Charlotte had been delighted by his cheek and by his confidence. Minil had seen him stare at the endless salt-lakes of the Southern Australian outback, and give in.

What love do I owe, he thought to himself; and to whom? Do I owe anything to anybody? And he tried to think of his father in Derbyshire, and what his father would have said; and it was peculiarly dizzying to think that his father was probably awake now, and going on his rounds, all those thousands of miles away, on a winter's afternoon; safe and slow through the rain-dewed Dales of England.

He was woken up by the sun, lancing under his eyelids. He blinked, and raised his head, and his neck was stiff as a board. Dogger was already awake, frying up some slices of horse-meat with pepper and salt. Minil was squatting not far away, her hand covering her face, which meant that what she was doing was private. Dogger called it 'picking daisies'. Eyre stood up, and limped towards Dogger on a leg that fizzed with pins-and-needles.

'Good morning, chum,' said Dogger. 'Fancy a slice of beast-of-burden?'

Eyre shook his head. 'I feel as if I've eaten the whole of that horse, tail-first.'

'I think Miss Minil beat you to it,' grinned Dogger. 'Have you seen the size of her belly this morning?'

'I watched her in the night.'

'Well, I don't know how they do it, these Day and Martin's.'

Eyre said, 'Don't call her that. Do you mind?' and there was enough sharpness in his voice to make Dogger look up. Day and Martin's was a popular brand of boot-polish, and a name commonly given to blacks. Dogger prodded his frying meat, and made a face; but he was too much of an old hand to argue. Arguments caused bitterness; and even the best-equipped and most well-fed of expeditions could be ruined by bitterness.

'When you've finished eating, we'll go on,' said Eyre. 'We should reach our cache of food by nightfall tomorrow, if we make good time.'

'Always supposing there *is* a cache of food there,' said Dogger.

'Of course there's a cache of food there. Christopher promised.'

'Well, Christopher is Christopher, my old chum,' said Dogger, 'but food is food.'

'It will be there,' Eyre asserted.

Dogger said, 'You're a greater morepork than I thought you were.'

'What does that mean?'

Dogger grinned. 'It simply means that you'll always believe the best of people who are out to do you down; and the worst of people who like you. It's a common-enough disease. Poor old Joolonga had quite a dose of it, as far as I could see.'

'And what have you ever done?' Eyre demanded. 'You came along on this expedition uninvited, and since then we've heard nothing from you but philosophic advice, and salty aphorisms, and twopenny-halfpenny mottoes.'

'Did I ever offer anything else?' asked Dogger.

Eyre stood in the morning sunlight looking at Dogger carefully. His shadow stretched thin across the salt-lake; his hair was ruffled by the wind. 'You're trying to tell me something,' he said, at last.

Dogger turned his meat over, and sniffed at it with exaggerated relish. 'Only a twopenny-halfpenny motto,' he said.

'Tell me,' Eyre insisted.

Dogger sniffed. 'What about a rhyme?' he suggested.

'A rhyme?'

'What about, "When you fear the pointing-bone, Fear much more the John-and-Joan." Now, that's good, don't you think. You never knew I was a poet, did you?'

Eyre tugged at his curls, and then propped his hands

on his hips, and then turned away. 'God in Heaven,' he said.

Dogger forked out some curled-up horse-meat, and began solemnly to chew.

'God in Heaven,' said Eyre again; and then, 'Do you really think that?'

'Well, I didn't do it,' said Dogger, 'and I know you didn't do it; and nor do I believe that Weeip or Midgegooroo had any hand in it. So who does that leave?'

Eyre walked a little way away and stared for a long time at the western horizon. He knew what Dogger was saying; he had thought the same thought himself. 'John-and-Joan' meant 'homosexual'; and there had only been one homosexual on this expedition; and that was Christopher. The man upon whom they were relying so heavily for their next cache of supplies. The man who, for whatever motive he may have done it, was circumstantially most likely to have poisoned Arthur Mortlock.

Twenty-Eight

The following day, another of their pack-horses collapsed, this time with a splintered fetlock joint; and Eyre shot it straight away. Everything that the horse was carrying they had to discard; all their tenting equipment, all their spare clothing, their pick and their shovel.

They left the horse's body lying where it was, and rode on; while up above them the vultures began to collect, like flies on a dirty window.

The weather was unexpectedly cool, and the skies were overcast with thin woolly clouds. They enjoyed the relief from the overpowering sun; but the coolness brought higher humidity, and when they made camp for the night it was clear that all the half-dried horse-meat they had brought with them was begining to spoil. Eyre ate as much of it as he could, but he gagged on the last gamey piece, and gave up. The day after was blazing again, up to 115 degrees. They threw all their remaining meat away, and decided to ride as long and as hard as they could, until they reached the cache of provisions which Christopher was supposed to have left for them. Eyre had calculated that even if Christopher had taken ten days to return to Adelaide from Parachilna, he should have taken no more than another five days to reach the agreed spot, sixteen miles west of Woocalla.

They reached the cache late in the evening, under a sunset of trumpeting crimson. Eyre had seen from some way away that something was wrong; and that the stores had been disturbed.

'Maybe it's only dingers,' Dogger had suggested; but when Eyre dismounted and walked across to it, there was no question at all who had been here. Barrels of flour had been dug up, and emptied all over the sand. Biscuits, tea, sugar, and salt were flung around everywhere; not stolen, but wantonly destroyed. Most serious of all, three large barrels of water had been deliberately split open, and left to drain into the dry soil. There was no message, no letter, not even a marker to show who had left the cache, and for whom.

'I suppose the nearest water-hole is Woocalla itself,' said Eyre.

Dogger nodded, and couldn't even spit. 'We could try heading due south, to see if we could make it to Adelaide without taking on any water at Woocalla, but in this heat I doubt if we'd get too far. It's not us I'm worried about so much, it's the horses. And the last thing I've got a fancy to do is to walk there.'

'We'll go to Woocalla,' said Eyre. 'If we ride for most of the night, we should be there by morning.'

Minil asked, 'No rest tonight?'

Eyre shook his head. 'Definitely, no rest.'

They turned westwards, and rode through the thickening sunset with the sun glaring right into their eyes like the open furnace of an iron-foundry. At last, however, it was dark; although still stifling; and they rode through scrub and spinifex grass, their horses stumbling with almost every step, and they felt as if they were going to have to ride like this forever.

Just before dawn, after the moon had gone, they rested. They lit a fire, and brewed a little scummy tea; and then, when it was light, they set off again, leaving their fire burning in the way that Aborigines always used to. Aborigines believed that fire cleansed and fertilised the land; and so they would often burn hundreds of acres at a time, a style of agricultural husbandry which enraged the white settlers, especially the sheep-farmers. Sheep were too stupid to run in front of a fire; they invariably stood still as the flames approached, and allowed themselves to be roasted alive. 'I've been through some red steers,' Dogger used to say, 'when there so many sheep being burned that you only had to sniff and you could imagine yourself at Charles's Chop House.'

They reached Woocalla a little after ten. But as they neared the water-hole, with its white gum trees and its mulga scrub, Eyre lifted himself up in his stirrups and peered carefully ahead.

'What's the matter?' asked Dogger.

'I'm not sure. Just a feeling.'

'Aha. You're beginning to grow into a bushman. What kind of a feeling?'

'Well, look, there are no birds around the water-hole, like there usually are; and no animals. Not even an emu. Now, what could be keeping them away?'

'The same buggers who broke into our provisions, I'd guess,'' said Dogger.

'That's what I'd guess, too,' agreed Eyre.

Minil said, 'You think they wait for us?'

'This is the nearest water-hole. They must have been fairly sure that we'd head straight here.'

Eyre said to Dogger, 'Give me your rifle. The big one.'

Dogger drew his long hunting-gun out of its canvas holster, and swung it over. 'It's all primed and loaded,' he said. He didn't say that this was the first time he had ever allowed anyone else to use it.

Eyre lifted the heavy gun and aimed low towards the mulga bushes around the water-hole. He fired, a great bellow of a shot that echoed for miles; and foliage burst in all directions.

Immediately—even before the echoes had died away—twenty or thirty black warriors rose from the rim of the water-hole, raising their spears and their war-clubs; and they screamed at Eyre with a high, unearthly ferocity.

'Aha,' sniffed Dogger. 'I do believe they're trying to tell us something.'

'Where's the next water-hole?' Eyre wanted to know.

'Due west is the only one I've heard of,' said Dogger. 'A place the Aborigine hunters call Mulka.'

'West? But we want to go east.'

'There's nothing that way; not east; not within living distance.'

'All right,' nodded Eyre. 'In that case, we'd better go west.'

'We've got to get past these blackfellows first.'

Four or five Aborigines were already running towards them, screeching and waving spears. Eyre nudged his horse to the right, and clicked at it, and gradually they began to circle away from the water-hole, hoping that the tribesmen would be satisfied by having chased them away. But the tribesmen suddenly realised what they were doing, and changed course so that they could cut them off.

'Guns,' said Eyre, and handed Dogger's rifle back to him. They drew up for a moment while they loaded with powder-and-ball; and then Dogger said, 'Ready, let's give them a go.'

They rode towards the running tribesmen at a fast walk;

Dogger and Eyre and Minil and their two remaining pack-horses. Two or three spears were flung up towards them, but they fell short. As his first target, Eyre picked a warrior right in the middle of the crowd of tribesmen, lifted his gun to his shoulder and fired at him. He missed the man he was aiming for; but another warrior off to his left fell flat on his back in an explosion of blood and lay on the ground spreadeagled.

Now Dogger fired, and another Aborigine cried out, and dropped to his knees. Then, before they knew it, they were riding through them, with spears clattering all around, and Eyre grasped the barrel of his rifle and swung the stock around him like a club. It connected twice: once with another club, jarring Eyre's shoulder; and once with a warrior's jaw, smashing out his teeth with a noise like a breaking plate.

Their second pack-horse was brought down by four spears thrown almost simultaneously; one clean through its neck and the others bristling into its flanks. Most of their ammunition was strapped to this horse, and Eyre turned and watched it collapse to the ground with a feeling of alarm and helplessness. But there was no possibility of riding back to salvage anything; as it was, they would be lucky to escape with their lives.

One spear struck a glancing blow against the croup of Eyre's horse, and slid underneath the back of his saddle, piercing the leather and grazing his thigh. A second missed his head by less than two inches, and fell noisily in front of him, almost tangling his horse's legs and tripping it up.

But then, 'We're clear!' cried Dogger, and whooped, and waved his hat.

Minil was already well away, fifty yards off to Eyre's right. She was far lighter than both of them, and her horse was fresher. But all of them had passed through the gauntlet of Aborigine warriors unscathed, and as they turned around, it seemed that the tribesmen were reluctant to run after them.

'I think they've had enough lamb-and-salad for one day,

don't you?' shouted Dogger. And he lifted his hat again, and crowed, 'Brayvo, Hicks!'

As he did so, a heavy death-spear arched high through the air, seeming to travel so slowly at its zenith that Eyre glimpsed up and saw it hanging suspended. But then it appeared to accelerate, and by the time it reached them it was travelling so fast that Eyre turned his head too quickly and lost sight of it. It was only when he looked back again, perplexed, that he saw that it had pierced Dogger between the eyes and impaled his head, and that Dogger was sitting upright in the saddle with both his arms raised in a kind of stunned supplication; like a martyred saint, or a strange variety of balancing-act at a circus.

Eyre couldn't even speak. His horse carried him on; but Dogger remained where he was, his arms still raised, the spear still growing out of his forehead. Eyre thought: *Constance, oh God. What am I going to say to Constance?* And then he saw Dogger topple and drop to the dust, and the Aborigines running towards him, waving their clubs and their boomerangs.

His first angry temptation was to ride back, and swing his way through the tribesmen with his rifle-stock and his knife. But that would mean certain death for him, too; and apart from the plain fact that he didn't want to die, who would be able to go to Constance and tell her how Dogger had fallen? And how courageous Dogger had been; and how consistently reassuring, and what a friend could really be, when you really needed one; a mate; out beyond the black stump.

They rode westwards now with their single pack-horse and the sun behind them. Minil said nothing to Eyre and Eyre remained silent with shock and grief. But Minil seemed to know roughly the direction in which the water-hole called Mulka lay, because she walked her horse ahead of him west-north-west, and she kept her eye on the sun as the day progressed.

By noon, they were far out over a dry lake, shadowless, under a crucifying sun. Minil stopped, and climbed down from her horse, and shared out between them a few dry biscuits and a half-mouthful of water, which was all they had left. The horses shivered and sweated, and flared their nostrils at the scent of moisture, but if Eyre and Minil were to survive, there was to be none for them.

Eyre stayed in the saddle, slowly and dryly chewing his biscuit. Minil stood beside him, in her scarf head-dress, with Eyre's shirt tied around her shoulders. She said, 'Will you say a prayer for your friend?'

'A prayer?'

'He always told me that you were a man of God.'

Eyre wiped the sweat away from his face. 'He told you that? When?'

'One evening, when you were sleeping; and we were awake.'

'Well, you could hardly call me a man of God. Especially not now.'

Minil traced a pattern in the fine white dust that clung to Eyre's riding-boot. 'He said that he envied you.'

'He didn't have any reason to do that.'

'Oh, but he did, He always envied you. He said that you were the kind of man who makes days begin and years go by; whether you want to or not.'

Eyre coughed, and almost choked on his biscuit. 'Well, I don't want to, as a matter of fact.'

'What are you going to do now?'

'Go on,' said Eyre. 'Go on until we reach the water-hole. Then, drink.'

Minil smiled. 'Dogger was right. You are becoming a bushman.'

They rode on, and gradually the sun descended in front of them to scorch their faces and blind their eyes. By five o' clock, however, they reached a series of deep water-holes in the bed of the dry lake; and there they tethered their horses, and let down their water-bottles and water-bags on lengths of bridle and twine, all knotted together, and brought up gallons of water that was fresher and cooler than any that Eyre had tasted in weeks. They drank until the water poured out of their noses, and they felt as if they would drown in the middle of the desert. Then they watered the horses, and splashed their coats with hatful after hatful of fresh water, and rubbed them, and patted them, until at last the horses shook themselves, and stood calm and refreshed. There was even a scattering of tussocky grass around the edges of the water-holes for them to eat; but Eyre made sure that they were well-tethered before he let them graze. The water-holes were sheer and very deep, and if a horse were to fall down one of them, they would never be able to get it out again, even if it survived.

His caution proved itself only a few minutes later; for an emu came to the water-holes to drink; and while Eyre and Minil were sitting watching it, it toppled with a feathery squawk of fear and annoyance into one of the narrowest of the holes. It thrashed and cried, but couldn't extricate itself. Eventually, when it sounded as if it had grown tired, Eyre went across to the hole with his rifle, and shot it. Smoke rose out of the limestone well like a magic trick; soon to be followed by a dead female emu, dangling from the end of an improvised lassoo.

They had a feast that night. Eyre said it was for Dogger; a last offering from the mortal world. Minil dug a deep pit in the hard ground with a stick; lined it with brush and twigs and burned the wood until it glowed. Then she dragged the emu into the hole and buried it, leaving only its neck and its head protruding. Two hours later, steam began to puff out of the emu's beak, and Minil pronounced the bird cooked. Actually, it was half-raw; but they were ravenous, and ate the whole breast between them.

They made love that night, too, out in the open, for they had lost their *umpee*. And it was love, rather than coupling; warmth and companionship, rather than erotic excitement. Both of them were naked in the warm night air; with nobody around them for miles amd miles; only the scratching of the night-creatures for company, the Kowaris and fat-tailed dunnarts, searching for insects and other small mammals; and the explosive constellations of southern stars over their heads.

Afterwards, as they lay cuddled together under their horse-blanket, Eyre said, 'Was it true, that Yonguldye was going to kill me?'

Minil stroked his face with her fingertips, tracing the outline of his lips, and his nose, and his bristly chin. 'Did Joolonga say that it wasn't?'

'He said they wanted only my knowledge. Only what was inside my brains not the brains themselves.'

'And what do you believe?'

'I don't know. There doesn't seem to be any way of telling, not for certain.'

Minil kissed him. 'You are in the desert,' she said, softly. 'There is nothing certain here; only thirst.'

'Who are you?' he asked her; not for the first time.

'I am someone looking for something that is probably lost for ever,' she said.

'Yes,' he answered her. Then, 'Yes', again; because at last he began to realise what she meant. There would be no peace for the Aboriginals now; their innocent centuries of living alone in Australia could never return. All that lay ahead for them now was retreat; retreat from their old fishing- and hunting-grounds, retreat from their sacred places, retreat from their magical and mysterious way of life, even a backing-away from their own souls. No wonder such an electrified ripple of excitement had run through the Aborigine community when Captain Henry had announced that the *djanga* had at last arrived. Eyre had been seen as their very last hope against a bewildering and increasingly destitute future.

Whether Yonguldye had really intended to eat his brains or not, Eyre very much doubted whether he would have escaped from Yarrakinna alive. For when he failed to give Yonguldye the great knowledge and power of the white invaders, as he inevitably would have done, the wrath and disappointment of the Aborigines would have been catastrophic, especially for him. In one way, perhaps it was better for the Aborigines themselves that he had escaped, because as long as he remained alive, their hope of standing up against the white man would remain alive with him.

Eyre slept. When he awoke, there were dingoes prowling around their camp attracted by the smell of the half-charred emu. He called, 'Dogger?' and almost at the same time remembered that Dogger was dead.

Still, he said it again, a whispered name in the vastness of the cold Australian night. 'Dogger? Can you hear me, Dogger?'

But of course there was no reply.

Twenty-Nine

They had no choice now but to strike out west. There was little doubt in Eyre's mind now that Yonguldye was following them; and that it had been Yonguldye and his tribesmen who had destroyed Christopher's provisions. So if they tried to return to the water-hole at Woocalla, and then make their way south to Adelaide from there, the risk of running straight into Yonguldye would be dangerously high.

They knew of no more water-holes beyond Mulka, but Eyre could see that the ground was rising ahead of them; and in all probability they would be able to find an *aroona*, or a water-pool.

They rode for hours in silence across miles and miles of dry mallee scrub; and as they rode they were smothered in grey sand-flies, in their hair, on their faces, crawling inside their clothes. Eyre tried at first to keep them out of his mouth by tying a handkerchief across the lower half of his face, but the flies always found a way of working their way underneath it, and time after time he would snap it away from his face in disgust.

When they stopped at a little after one o' clock to eat as much of the emu as they could manage, and swallow a mouthful of water, Eyre found that he was crunching mouthfuls of flies as well as meat, and spat his food out on to the ground. But Minil seemed to be quite unperturbed by the glistening, clustering insects that clung around her lips; and giggled at Eyre for being so sensitive.

They rode on and on; Eyre using his compass to tend slightly southwards in the hope that eventually they would reach the coast. He estimated that if they continued on this bearing, they would probably see the Indian Ocean within four or five days, at Fowler's Bay, or Cape Adieu, or fairly close by; and with any luck at all they would be able to camp there and wait for a whaler or a merchantman to pass, and pick them up.

Minil said, 'If we ride westwards, we will come to my home.'

Eyre wiped the sweat from his face. 'Home? You mean New Norcia? That must be a thousand miles. I don't have the slightest intention of riding for a thousand miles.'

'I walked a thousand miles, when I came to Yarrakinna with Yonguldye.'

'You walked all the way across this desert?'

Minil nodded. 'There are many places to find water, for those who know.'

'All I want to do is find a ship,' said Eyre.

'You really want to go back?'

'Is there anything wrong in that?'

'I don't know. It doesn't sound like you; to give in.'

Eyre slapped flies away from his mouth. 'What are you talking about? Give in? You saw for yourself that we couldn't ride any further northwards through those saltlakes. And if we couldn't ride through them, certainly

401

nobody could ever run a road through them, or a railway-line, or drive stock through them.'

'But what about *this* way?' asked Minil.

'What about this way?'

'You could drive stock this way perhaps. Or just a road.'

Eyre stared at her. Her bright eyes were giving nothing away; no clues about her seriousness, nor why she was provoking him into thinking about carrying on westwards. But perhaps she saw in him something that he couldn't see in himself; a stamina and a sense of persistence that only needed the right cause, and a great enough inspiration.

'You can go back to Adelaide with nothing,' she said. 'Or, you can go back with a new stock-route to the west. Isn't that what you told me? That the farmers of Adelaide need to send their sheep and cattle to other parts of Australia, so that they can survive?'

Eyre said, 'Who was your teacher, at New Norcia?'

'Mrs Humphreys. She was teaching me ever since I was a baby.'

'Well, she taught you remarkably well. But your intelligence is your own; and you've got plenty of that.'

She said, 'Do you love me yet?'

'Do I *love* you yet? What a peculiar question!'

'I will stay with you for ever,' she said. 'If you want me to.'

Eyre laid his hand on her shoulder, and then brushed away the flies and kissed her. While they kissed, the flies crawled all through their hair and over their faces, but they did not part their lips from each other until they had shared everything they had grown to feel for each other since they had first met, in Yonguldye's shelter.

'No matter what happens to us, I will always love you,' said Eyre.

'You don't have to make that promise. I don't expect it.'

'Nonetheless, you have it.'

They rode on through a long and hazy afternoon. Now and then Eyre looked behind them, to see if there was any sign of Yonguldye and his warriors; but there was none. He wished very much that he had Dogger's telescope with him, and Dogger's long gun; and he wished very much that he had Dogger, too. But their lives were now reduced to nothing more than riding westwards, and surviving. There was no time for sentiment, and very little time for mourning. They were a dark, emaciated white man and a naked Aborigine girl, riding through a world of scrub and dust and relentless beige, and that was the sum of their existence.

Days passed; more days of dust; and they found no more water-holes. Every morning the sky-spirits lit the sun-fire; and every afternoon the scrub wavered with heat so great that the goannas and the skinks remained motionless, as if stunned by the 120 degree temperature, and even the vultures looked as if they were flying through clear syrup.

Still there was no sign of anybody pursuing them, and they were now as far from Parachilna as Parachilna was from Adelaide, and Eyre was sure that they would soon reach the coast.

But every morning the sun came up behind them, and there were no more water-holes. Their bottles were almost empty, and they had no water for the horses. They threw away everything they could, to save weight. They left their saddles behind in the dust, like abandoned tree-stumps. They left the two extra rifles, and Eyre's spare boots and even, at last, Eyre's copy of Captain Sturt's *Expeditions*.

They lay at night under their blanket, shaking with cold, and scarcely speaking to each other.

'When we reach the coast,' Eyre told Minil one morning, 'if we don't see a ship straight away, we'll turn back eastwards towards Adelaide.'

Minil said nothing. But both of them had begun to accept that staying alive was their only priority, and that the route to Western Australia could wait for another explorer, at another time.

By noon that day, they had run out of water completely.

Eyre turned his water-bottle upside-down, and a drop fell on to the palm of his hand, as precious as a diamond, and gradually evaporated in the heat. Minil looked up towards the sun, her eyes squeezed almost shut, and said, 'We have to go on.' The shine which fresh meat and fresh water had given her skin had now faded to a dull cocoa-brown; and her ribs and pelvis were showing, as if death were making a premature announcement of his imminent appearance.

They went on. Their last pack-horse was close to collapse, but Eyre was reluctant to butcher it in case they needed it later. Fresh meat lasted only a day or two in this heat, with all these flies; and although blood might see them through one more waterless day, it quickly congealed and went bad.

The following day was Christmas Eve. Eyre sat silent on his horse, his eyes closed, feeling the sun drum and drum and drum against his skull. Even inside his eyelids, the day was vivid scarlet, and too bright to look at. He thought: I shall probably die on Christmas Day, and that will prove what an Anti-Messiah I turned out to be. Everybody expected so much of me: destiny, history, the opening-up of a continent; and here I am, stupid with sunstroke, lolloping through the scrub on a half-dead horse without a saddle. *Brayvo, Hicks!* Dogger had cried, as the death-spear slammed into his forehead and right through his brainful of memories and laughter and drunken nights. At least he had died quickly; at least he had gone without any chance to grumble or regret, a cantankerous invalid on Hindley Street, without beer or horses. But he never got to see Constance again, and when he had been sitting on his horse dying in those last few instants he must have realised that; and what a woman Constance was.

Eyre thought: Christmas Day, whoever would have believed it? All these years, all through childhood, all through catechism, all through college, I've been destined to die on Christmas Day. By God, if I had known, I would have dreaded each succeeding Christmas, instead of merry-making, and eating too much, and dancing like a damned doomed marionette.

He saw Minil pitch off her horse like a falling shadow out of the corner of his eye. She dropped face-down on to the scrubby ground, and lay there still, while her horse came to an exhausted and obedient stop.

Eyre slid down from his mount, and walked quickly across to her in sweat-filled boots. He knelt down beside her, and gently turned her over, and she looked up at him with flickering eyelids, muttering and chattering with blistered lips.

'Minil,' he croaked. 'Minil, what's the matter?'

She lapsed into unconsciousness again, twitching nervously now and then as if she were dreaming.

'That's it,' he said to himself, out loud. 'That's it, that's damn-well it. She's going to die.'

He stood up, and took off his hat, and he was so dehydrated that he couldn't even bring tears to his eyes. But then he knelt down again, and slapped her face, one way and then the other way, and shouted at her in a high, broken voice, 'Minil!'

She wasn't dead; but he knew that she must be close to it. Her breath fluttered as delicately as a zebra-finch caught in a thorn-bush. He rolled back her eyelid and her eyes were white. She muttered, and jerked, but she didn't wake up.

He bent over her for a long time, fatigued and trembling and stricken with the pain of losing her. But then he sat up straight, and thought: I must find water. Where am I going to find water? If I try to take her any further, she'll be dead by the time the sun goes down. She'll probably be dead within the hour, in this heat. But supposing I leave her here, and go looking for water on my own?

He knew how desperate a chance it was. His only experience of bush-craft was the experience he had acquired on this one expedition. There was a high risk that he would go looking for water and never be able to find her again. And there was also a risk that when he was away, Yonguldye and his warriors would catch up with them, and kill her. But all he could do was trust in God, and his own judgement, and try to survive.

Carefully, he rolled her over on to a spread-out blanket. Then he propped up their second blanket on a dry branch, so that it formed a canopy over her head. She lay still, her mouth open, breathing faintly and roughly. God, he thought, how can I leave her? This may be the very last time I see her alive. But I must.

He remounted his horse, and rode westwards again; turning around from time to time to fix his bearings on the improvised shelter he had made. But after an hour, it was out of sight; and there was nothing but the rippling heat and the mallee scrub and the sky like a punishment above his head.

He thought of nothing sensible: the heat was too powerful. He rode with his thighs chafing against his salt-caked britches, his hat pulled low over his eyes. He didn't even have the strength to curse any more. He was sure that the sun was actually driving him mad, and that if he survived this journey it would only be as a lunatic, kicking and gibbering and nagging forever about roasted emu and weeks without water.

In a wandering, discursive way, he began to wonder what he was actually doing, riding westwards under this pitiless sun looking for water. Surely the most sensible thing to do would be to keep on going. Even if he did manage to find a water-hole, it would take him at least another two hours to ride back, and by then Minil would be dead. She was probably dead already.

It disturbed him that he could think about Minil so callously. But then it occurred to him that he must be very close to death himself, to be thinking so selfishly about his own survival.

He peered ahead through the sloping, glistening heat. There were imaginary lakes all around, lakes which could never be reached. He began to think that even when he eventually reached the sea, he would find out that it was nothing but a mirage, and that he would still be riding across dry sand.

What he didn't yet know was that he was riding thirty miles too far north to reach the sea, and that he and Minil had entered the eastern extremities of the land which the Aborigines called Bunda Bunda, and which the Europeans would one day christen the Nullarbor Plain; Nullarbor being dog-Latin for 'no trees'. The plain stretched all the way from Southern Australia, eight hundred miles to Western Australia, treeless, relentlessly flat, and with no running water from one side to the other. In the heat of Christmas Eve, it was more than the human imagination could bear.

Eyre began to think of Minil. At this moment, if she were still alive, she was the closest companion he had; or had ever had. They had now shared all the physical intimacies which any man and woman could share. But Minil remained strangely aloof; rather in the same way that Joolonga had done; and he still found it hard to understand her or what she was expecting out of her life. She had evidently been very grammatically schooled at New Norcia, and she had told him that she had always worn European dresses there, bonnets and parons and petticoats. And yet, for all of her education, she had gone with Yonguldye into the outback, leaving her dresses and her Christian upbringing behind her.

It showed Eyre just how strong the mysterious magic of Australia must be, that when Aborigines were classroom educated and taught how to question the world around them, the first question which they seemed to be drawn to; magnetically and inevitably; was the question of their own origin, their own being, and the reality of the dreaming. Cynical and sarcastic as he often was, Joolonga had plainly come to consider that the myths of the dreamtime had a greater strength and relevance to life in Australia than any of the beliefs which the white settlers had brought with them from the old country. The myths of the dreamtime were everlasting and immutable; they could not be adapted to suit the greed or the convenience of the believer. Joolonga's only tragedy, like Minil's, was that in rediscovering his own religion through European education, he had lost his natural and intuitive link with native magic; his ability to commune with the spirits of the sky, and the spirits of the rocks, and most importantly of all, the spirits of his ancestors.

Perhaps this link was what Minil had been hoping to regain when she had followed Yonguldye; and perhaps she had come into Eyre's shelter that night because she had realised at last that she could never regain it. Take me back, she had asked him; back to the white man's mission. There could have been no greater pain than living in a world of strange and limitless magic, but never being able to share in it.

Eyre could see now why Yanluga had pleaded with him to be buried according to Aborigine custom. It had been a last attempt to join in his people's spiritual heritage; even if it was after death.

'What are we *doing* to these people?' Eyre said, and surprised himself by saying it out loud.

He opened his eyes, which had gradually been closing as he was riding. About seventy-five paces ahead of him was a low limestone outcropping, on which four or five princess parrots were perched, pink-throated and yellow-chested. There were thick tufts of grass around the rock, and even a stunted gum. My God, thought Eyre, a water-hole. I can't believe it. I've actually found a water-hole.

He climbed stiff and awkward down from his horse, and hobbled like a very old man through the grass and scrub, until he reached the edge of the hole. It was dried up now, filled with sand, but when he knelt down and pressed his hand against the ground, he could feel that it was still slightly damp. He went back to his horse and took out of his saddle-bag the only implement he had which would serve as a spade: his curved brandy-flask, long ago emptied of brandy, but which he had kept with him as a water-bottle.

Watched by the inquisitive parrots, he began to dig into the sand. He was weaker than he had realised and he had to pause every few minutes to rest. But gradually the sand he was digging grew cooler and damper, and after an hour the bottom of his narrow excavation began to fill with clouded water. He lay flat on his stomach with his head down the hole and drank the water mouthful by mouthful, even though it was gritty and salt-tasting and even though he had to wait for minutes on end after each mouthful while the hole slowly refilled itself.

After he had drunk as much as he could manage, he dug the hole wider and deeper, and led his horse to it. The horse lapped at it for almost half an hour, while Eyre managed to dig another hole a little further away, and slowly fill up his water-bottle. He glanced up at the sinking sun: he would just be able to get back to Minil before it grew dark, and the water in his bottle would be enough to last them until they could ride back here tomorrow morning. Then: well, they couldn't be too far from the sea now. Another day's riding, perhaps. And if they were able to hail a ship, or find themselves a few fish, or washed-up mutton-birds, or cockles perhaps they might even think of going on, of doing what Minil had suggested, and finding a stock-route to the west. Destiny had brought him this far. Who knew where it might take him now? And it was extraordinary how much more alluring and accessible fame and glory both seemed to be, now that he had quenched his thirst. Minil had been right: it wasn't in his nature to surrender, and discovering a stock-route to Western Australia would make his name for ever.

It would also, he sincerely hoped, bring him Charlotte.

He looked around for his brandy-flask, to fill that up as well; but he couldn't find it. His horse must have trampled down the sand when he was drinking, and buried it. He dug for a while with his hands, but it was growing much darker now, and it looked from the clouds that they were building up in the north-west as if it was going to be a cold and windy night.

He rode back through the gathering dusk, clutching his one full water-bottle close to his stomach. His exhaustion had begun to overwhelm him now, and he had to make a sharp effort to wake himself up every few minutes, and check his compass bearing. His long shadow rode in front of him, across the dark orange scrub; and in the distance, towards the south-east, he saw four or five kangaroos bounding like rocking-horses against the thunder-black eastern sky.

The sun sank at last and the wind began to get up. Eyre dozed as he rode; only managing to jerk himself awake when he was on the point of overbalancing and falling off his horse. As he dozed, he dreamed, and sometimes he found it impossible to distinguish between the dream and reality.

It was only his horse drawing up beside Minil's horse and nuzzling it that at last woke him up. The sky was lighter now, with the moon just about to rise, and he could make out the dark triangular shape of the blankets under which he had left Minil. He clicked encouragingly to Minil's horse, and then dismounted. It was then that he realised with a physical shudder of horror and distress that he was no longer carrying the water-bottle.

'Oh my God,' he said to himself. He looked desperately around, to see if he could see it anywhere close. But he had just crossed miles of scrub and rough grass in the dark, and he could have dropped it anywhere.

Shaking, he went across to the shelter and lifted back the blankets so that he could see Minil. He thought she was dead at first, but when he bent down and listened against her lips, he could hear her breathing in shallow and uneven gasps, interspersed with occasional reedy whines, as if her lungs were congested.

'Minil,' he called her, and rubbed her hand. 'Minil, it's Eyre. Minil for God's sake, wake up.'

There was no response; except for a thin, dry cough. Eyre tried opening her eyelids with his thumbs, but even when she stared at him, it was obvious that she was unconscious, and that she couldn't really see him. 'Minil,' he repeated. 'Minil, you must wake up.'

He knew that she was close to death. She was so cold that he could hardly bear to touch her. Her body seemed to have shrunk even in the few hours that he had been away looking for water. Her hips protruded bonily, and her breasts had shrunk, so that they were soft and flabby.

He dragged together as much brushwood as he could find, and lit a fire. It flared up quickly in the northwest wind, and he had to stack on more brush every few minutes to keep it going. Then he walked back the way he had come, back towards the water-hole, following his horse's hoof-marks in the dust, searching everywhere for his lost water-bottle. He would have cried if he hadn't already been so exhausted, and angry with himself.

At last he walked back to the fire. The warmth seemed to have roused Minil a little, because she opened her eyes and whispered his name. He crouched down beside her, and took her hand between his.

'*Koppi unga,*' she said, so quietly that he could scarcely hear her. He knew what the words meant. Yanluga had said the same thing to him when he was dying. 'Bring me water.'

He licked his lips. 'There is no water. Not unless you can ride.'

He tried to lift her up into a sitting position, but she fell back on the blanket, her arms tangled uselessly.

'Minil,' he insisted, 'there is no water. We're going to have to ride and find it.'

He thought: I can lift her up, and tie her on to her horse. But will she survive another two or three hours, jolting on the back of an animal that itself is already on the verge of collapse? And will I be able to find the water-hole again in the dark? He felt that he had as good as killed her already, with his carelessness.

'Water,' she begged him.

'Minil, there isn't any. I found some, I filled the bottle, but I dropped it, somewhere in the scrub.'

411

She stared at him. 'Where is the water?' she whispered. 'How far?'

'Two, three hours. A little more.'

She said nothing for a very long time. Eyre watched her, while the brushwood fire died down behind him.

'Take me there,' she said, at last.

Eyre lifted her up, and half-dragged, half-carried her over to her horse. On the third attempt, he managed to lift her up on to its back, and she leaned forward, clinging on to the horse's neck, while Eyre tied a blanket around her, in the style of a *buka*.

There was no question of letting her ride by herself; she was too weak, and a fall from the horse's back would probably kill her outright. So Eyre walked beside her, leading his own horse and their one spare pack-horse by the reins.

The wind was stronger now, and as they left their makeshift camp, the brushwood fire was blown away across the scrub in fiery tumbling circles. Eyre pulled his hat down further over his eyes, and leaned forward against the wind and the cold and the stinging dust.

They walked for nearly five hours. The wind was at gale-force now, and it shrieked and howled across the plain of Bunda Bunda like Koobooboodgery. One blessing, thought Eyre: the wind and the sand will cover our tracks, and make it more difficult for Yonguldye to find us. But what will there be for him to find? Bones, and dead horses; nothing worth plundering, nothing worth punishing.

By the time the next day dawned, he knew that he had missed the water-hole; possibly by yards, possibly by miles. He stood on that endless expanse of scrubby plain and looked around him in the light of the early-morning sun, and nothing seemed familiar. He didn't even know where to begin looking for it.

He gently lifted Minil down from her horse, and laid her on the ground on her blanket.

'Are we near the water?' she asked him, in a peculiarly clear voice. But she looked much worse than she had yesterday: her eyes were dull and her thin arms were drawn across her chest as if even the act of lying down were painful.

'Not far now,' Eyre lied.

'You said two hours. Surely we have gone further.'

'I've, er . . . I've, er, lost my way . . . just once or twice . . . that's why. But, it won't be long now.'

He looked towards the sun. It was blazing brightly now, rising over the plain with bare-faced ferocity; causing every living creature at which it stared to scuttle for shadow, and protection. Eyre remembered that it was Christmas Day; and he knew that he would never survive it. Neither would Minil. She was already half-delirious, and her eyes kept closing in pain and fatigue.

'We have to go on,' said Eyre.

Minil shook her head. 'No more strength, Mr Walker.' She could still tease him, even now.

'We must go on. We can't just lie down here and die.'

'You go on. Let me stay here.'

'Minil, I need you. You must try.' But his voice sounded broken and weak and unconvincing, like an old man trying to persuade his sick dog not to give in. Minil would die first, probably within a matter of hours, when the sun grew really hot, of dehydration and heat exhaustion; and then Eyre would die shortly after. This patch of mallee scrub would be his last resting-place; and he didn't even know where it was. He looked around but there were no vultures; not yet; although he thought he could see some wild dogs in the distance. He just prayed that they wouldn't start to tear him apart until he was really dead.

Minil opened her eyes again, and lifted one hand to touch her lips. 'Water,' she said. Eyre didn't know what to say to her. 'Water,' she repeated. 'Water.' A soft and plaintive chant to her own extinction. 'Water.'

He sat up straight. He had remembered something that Captain Sturt had told him, about the way in which men had survived when they were stranded without water in the deserts of Western Australia. He pressed his hand over

413

his dry lips for a while, thinking; but then he made up his mind. If it would keep Minil alive for long enough for them to find the next water-hole, then there could be no vulgarity about it, and no indignity.

He stood up, unbuttoned his shirt, and loosened his belt, stepping out of his britches. His body was bony and dry-skinned and still pale, although his hands were as brown as gloves. He dropped his clothes to one side; and then slowly and carefully sat himself astride Minil's face, taking care not to kneel on her.

She opened her eyes again and looked at him. '*Urrabirra*,' he said, throatily. It meant 'drink'.

She reached up weakly and touched his bare stomach. She understood. Then she took him in her hand, and guided him between her lips. She closed her eyes momentarily to show him that she was ready.

There was very little; a sudden gush; but then in spite of everything he had drunk yesterday he had been very dehydrated. She drank thirstily, however, and even when he had finished she held him in her mouth, sucking from him the last possible drop. He eased himself up at last; and left her to rest, covering her over with a blanket; but he felt that in an hour or two she might have sufficient strength to ride for just a few miles more.

Those few miles more might lead nowhere. They might lead to another place just like this. Heat, and scrub, and flies, and imaginary oases. But on the other hand they might take them to the next water-hole, and save their lives. There was always hope. After all, there was nothing else.

He waited for her under the sun. At last, after an hour, he woke her and lifted her back on to her horse. Then they went on, south-westwards, into the hottest Christmas Day that Eyre had ever experienced.

Thirty

They saw the Aborigines from well over two miles away; thin black figures standing ankle-deep in a reflecting lake. They could have turned due south, and tried to escape, but Eyre knew that it was no use. So he kept on walking, straight towards them, and the Aborigines stood and waited for him with their spears and their clubs, a black etched pattern of naked figures against the hot horizon, as if somebody had been shaking a nibful of India-ink on to a sheet of glass.

They reached the Aborigines, and Eyre drew the horses in close and stood with his head bowed, waiting for them to approach him. He had no idea how they had overtaken him. Perhaps they had been running through the night. But he had no more strength to elude them; no more will to fight them. He could scarcely stand, and his horse was trembling and foaming dry foam at the mouth, and almost ready to collapse.

One of the Aborigines came forward, a dignified old man with a big pot-belly and a grey curly beard. He laid his hand on Eyre's shoulder, and said something in a dialect which Eyre didn't understand at all.

Eyre said, 'Where is Yonguldye? Let me speak to Yonguldye.'

The old man frowned, and shook his head.

'You are not Yonguldye's people?' Eyre asked him.

Again, the old man shook his head. He turned back to the blackfellows standing behind him, and said something long and excitable and emphatic. One or two of them answered him, and one began to point towards the northeast, and say over and over again, 'Yarrakinna, Yarrakinna.'

Eyre tried to step back to tell Minil that they had met up with a tribe that seemed to know nothing of Yonguldye, or what had happened at the great corroboree; but as he turned he felt the ground rising beneath him like the rising crust of a loaf; and suddenly he was deaf and stunned and lying on his side in the dust, although he was not at all aware that he had fallen, and there was no pain, no bruising; only the strange hot silence and the bare feet of blackfellows all around him.

'We have been travelling for many days without water,' he thought he said, although he couldn't hear his own voice. Then there was nothing at all: no sound, no sight, no feeling. His world dwindled away to a single speck of light, and then was swallowed up.

He was woken by the sound of tapping; the rhythmic tapping of musical sticks. He opened his eyes and saw that it was sunset, and that the sky was streaked with dark curls of cirrus. He was lying on a kangaroo-skin blanket; and not far away a fire was burning.

Stiffly, he raised himself up on to one elbow, and looked around. He was lying in the middle of an encampment of about twenty or thirty Aborigine men and women and children. The men were sitting in a group, tapping with their sticks, and humming. The women and children were squatting around the fire cooking sand-lizards. Two kangaroos were being roasted in pits filled with hot ashes: Eyre could see their leg-bones sticking up out of the ground. An elderly man was obviously in charge of this part of the cooking, for he sat scowling between the two ash-pits, and every now and then he would shout at the children who came hungrily sniffing around, and flick at them with a long whippy stick.

After a while, one of the younger men noticed that Eyre was awake, and came over to kneel down beside him.

Eyre said, 'Minil, the girl. Is she all right?'

The young man grinned, revealing several missing teeth, and pointed towards the far side of the fire. There, covered up by blankets, Minil was sleeping; watched over by an old woman.

'Thank God,' said Eyre.

'Thank God,' the Aborigine repeated.

Eyre pointed to his lips. 'Do you have any water?'

The young man grinned again, and produced a shaped wooden bowl, filled with muddy-looking water. Eyre took it, and finished it in three large swallows. It wasn't enough to quench his thirst, but it seemed impolite to ask for any more, particularly since the families may not have had very much to last themselves the night. Muddy water meant there had been hours of painstaking digging at water-holes. That much he knew from experience.

Soon the elderly chief who had first greeted him came over, and shyly shook his hand. He gave a long speech, occasionally turning towards the fire, and pointing towards the roasting kangaroos, and Eyre understood that he was being invited to stay for a while, and share in the meal. 'You're very kind,' acknowledged Eyre, nodding and smiling. 'I have been trying to reach the sea. Fowler's Bay, perhaps. Yalata, isn't that what you call it?' He made his fingers walk across the kangaroo-hide blanket, and said, 'Yalata.'

'Ah, Yalata!' said the old man, beaming back at Eyre, and clapping his hands. Then he pointed towards the south-west; in a far more southerly direction than Eyre had imagined that Fowler's Bay would actually lie.

'Thank God,' the young man repeated.

The old man placed his hand over his bony chest, and said, 'Ngottha . . . Winja.' Then he said, 'Winja,' again, and beamed some more. Eyre took this to mean that his name was Winja; and in return laid his own hand over his chest, and said, 'Eyre.'

For some reason, this caused great hilarity, and the young man fell on to his back in laughter, and kicked his legs. Even old Winja cackled uncontrollably, and had to wipe his eyes. He called out to the rest of the Aborigines there, and tapped his finger on Eyre's shoulder, and said, 'Eyre.' And there was even more laughter, and tapping of sticks, as Eyre's name was repeated all the way around the encampment.

The younger man recovered his composure enough to point to his own chest, and announce himself as 'Ningina.'

Ningina brought Eyre another bowlful of water, and watched him carefully while he drank it. It was only then that he decided that Eyre was fit enough to come across the camp and see Minil. He held Eyre's elbow solicitously, and talked to him all the time, as if he were a child taking his very first steps. In fact Eyre's knees felt so watery that he was glad of the encouragement. He squatted down beside Minil, and reached out to touch her forehead.

Minil stirred, and opened her eyes. Eyre suddenly felt overwhelmed with affection for her, and gladness that she was alive; and by sheer relief that Winja and his people had saved them from the desert. His throat tightened, and the first tears that he had been able to cry since they had started out on their expedition burst into his eyes.

'We're safe,' he told her. 'These people have saved us.'

Minil closed her eyes again and slept. Eyre was led back to the fire, where a *buka* was draped around his shoulders, and he was given some of the first of the kangaroo meat. He ate it very slowly; watched all the time with unblinking intentness by tribespeople all around him, who appeared to regard every movement of his jaw as being of almost magical interest. The meat was fresh, and well-cooked; and although Eyre's stomach had shrunk during his days without food, he forced himself to eat as much of it as he was offered. He remembered what Dogger had told him about surviving in the outback; and he had been through too much hunger to want to suffer like that again. He even sucked the grease from his hands.

Later that evening, Minil woke again, and one of the women fed her with dried quandong fruit and kangaroo-fat mixed with ground grass-seed into little flat cakes, and gave her repeated drinks of water. She came and sat by the fire with Eyre, tightly wrapped in a blanket; and Winja and Ningina soon came to join them, noisly chewing *pitjuri* leaves blended with ashes. Minil was a Nyungar, and could not translate everything they were saying, but they

418

managed to communicate haltingly; and Winja's natural good humour filled most of the gaps in their conversation with nods and smiles and cackles of laughter.

As she spoke, Minil repeated everything she said to Eyre, so that he could pick up as many Aboriginal words as possible, and occasionally join in. Both Winja and Ningina seemed to think that Eyre was irresistibly comic, and whenever he spoke they would hiss with suppressed amusement, and clutch their hands over their mouths to stop themselves from laughing out loud. Winja explained to Minil that they were not being disrespectful, but there was a long-standing joke in their tribe that somehow involved *earea* bushes, although they couldn't make it comprehensible to a white man. Minil tried to explain the joke to Eyre by saying that his announcement when he had first spoken to Winja was roughly the equivalent of having said, 'You, Winja, chief of your people—me, small bush.'

The conversation grew more serious, however, when Minil told Winja about Yonguldye, and what had happened at the Yarrakinna corroboree. 'Yonguldye is not dead, not as far as we know, and he is still following us with the *kurdaitja* shoes . . . his people have already killed Mr Eyre's good friend, and one of his black trackers. This is why we are travelling westwards. Partly, to find a new road to the west. Partly, because we cannot go back.'

Winja said, 'There is no road to the west.'

'*You* are travelling west,' said Minil.

'We are following kangaroo.'

'Somewhere, there must be a road to the west.'

'We have never seen one. There is no water until you reach Gabakile.'

'How far is that?'

Winja spat *pitjuri* juice, 'A whole lifetime if you die on the way.'

They talked well into the night. Winja had heard the ancient story of the *djanga* who returns from the land beyond the sunset, although the version he knew was slightly different; in that the *djanga* assuaged his guilt by asking the medicine-man to bring the boy back to life, and whispering all the secrets of death in the boy's ear. He gave the story one more twist, however, which may have explained why Yonguldye had been so determined to track Eyre down. In Winja's version of the legend, the *djanga* had to be prevented from returning to the skies, because then he would have told all the other spirits that mortal men now knew the secrets of the dead, and the other spirits in jealousy and anger might well have hunted down as many men as they could find, and kill them, as a punishment. 'The spirits will say, "if these men know the secrets of the dead, then let them die also." '

Eyre said, 'Do you believe that I could be the *djanga*?'

There was more laughter, and thigh-slapping. 'You! You are a bush! How can you be a *djanga*!'

But then Winja said, more seriously, 'You are a white man; not a *djanga*. We live well with the white people. We travel from the Murray River to the Swan River, to meet our kinsmen and to trade skins and flour. We also trade with the white people. We do not want any difficulty with the white people. Last year, two of my people were wrongly accused of burning a house; one of them was hanged. I do not want this to happen again. From what this girl says, you are an important man in Adelaide; therefore, we will take care of you, and make sure that Yonguldye does not harm you. I understand about the legend of the *djanga*; but life is changing. I do not believe that the black people can ever stand up against the white people. That is a lost dream. The best we can hope for is that we can live together side-by-side and that the white people respect our hunting and fishing places, and our sacred grounds. Already they have destroyed many of my kinsmen's fish-traps. Already many of our sacred places have been occupied by farms and settlements. But, we wish only to live our lives in peace.'

That night, Eyre and Minil slept together under a hide blanket close to the fire. They did not make love; they were too ill and too exhausted; but they held each other close, and kept each other warm, and when dawn came they were both much calmer and more collected, and they greeted each other with a kiss.

'I am beginning to see who you are,' said Eyre.

'Yes,' said Minil.

'You and I are just the same. I didn't understand that at first. We both went out into the wilds to look for ourselves; for what we were. You went to look for your people and I went to look for glory.'

Minil kissed him again, his lips, his cheeks, his closed eyelids.

'What do you think we found?' she asked him.

Eyre stroked her bare shoulder. 'I think we found that there is more than one truth. The truth of the desert is quite different from the truth of the town. All of the myths and the legends are alive out here; they all have reality and meaning. But back in Adelaide they will be nothing but traveller's tales. When you return to New Norcia, and put on your pinafore again, will Mrs Humphreys believe that you lived with Yonguldye, the terrible Mabarn Man? Will she believe what happened here, in the desert? Magic can only exist where people believe in it.'

Minil smiled. 'I do not understand you when you talk like this.'

'No,' said Eyre. 'But it doesn't matter.'

Winja happily agreed that Eyre and Minil could travel with his people as far westwards as they wanted to go. He declared that he was not at all frightened of Yonguldye; and that if Yonguldye and his warriors caught up with them, there would be a great *pungonda*, and that Yonguldye would be sent back to wherever he had come from. Ningina in particular seemed to relish the idea of a *pungonda*, and showed Eyre his axe, which was made of hard stones stuck to a kangaroo-bone with gum, and hung ostentatiously around his waist in a belt of oppossum-fur.

'Bong,' he said, and demonstrated the axe's use with a mock-blow to Eyre's head.

After gorging themselves with cold kangaroo-meat, the small tribe set off towards the south-west. Winja and Ningina led the men out in front, with their spears and their clubs, looking out for game. The women followed behind, carrying on their heads and on their shoulders their dilly-bags and wooden bowls, and digging-sticks, and the children who were too young to walk.

They were a strange but beautiful group. As they crossed the scrubby plains, Eyre rode behind them and admired their unselfconscious elegance, the dark curves of their bodies, the easy movements of their buttocks and legs. And the women walked with impeccable balance, even though some of them had bags and bowls and children to carry; their bare breasts pendulous and their stomachs protruding, but graceful beyond anything he had seen at an Adelaide ladies' tea-party.

For Eyre's sake, and Minil's sake, Winja ordered his families to rest halfway through the day; and they drank a little water and ate lizards and a paste of green ants. Eyre was too hungry to be squeamish. Last night's heavy meal of kangaroo meat had begun to restore his stomach to working-order, and it was demanding more. The lizard-flesh, singed over a small fire, was quite tasty. Firm, and slightly nutty, like smoked chicken.

That night they reached a water-hole, and made camp. Ningina had been unlucky, and had caught only a stray joey; but the women had brought in a collection of hopping-mice and lizards and a mallee fowl with a broken wing.

And so for three days they travelled this way, slowly heading south-west; while Eyre and Minil became gradually more accepted into the family, and Eyre began to speak a hesitant version of Winja's language.

On the morning of the third day, however, Ningina crawled into their shelter and said, 'We have caught sight of the warriors who are following you. They are less than two hours away. Soon there will be a great *pungonda*.'

Thirty-One

It was well past eleven o'clock before Eyre caught sight of them clearly. There must have been fifteen or twenty of them, well strung out, walking swiftly and with great deliberation. Soon he could see their spears, balanced over their shoulders, their hardwood shafts catching the high sunlight. Then he saw the great head-dress that belonged to Yonguldye, the Darkness, and he knew that his nemesis was at last going to catch up with him. He might have cheated death on Christmas Day, but sooner or later he was going to have to face up to Yonguldye.

Minil, sitting on her horse in a kangaroo-hide *buka* decorated with ochre, said, 'What can we do? We can't let Winja and Ningina fight our battle for us.'

'They want to,' Eyre reminded her. 'It's a question of honour. Well, I'm not certain that honour's the right word; but it's certainly a question of pride.'

'It seems terrible, to risk their lives.'

'I can give myself up.'

Minil stared at him. 'No,' she said. 'They'll kill you. I couldn't bear it.'

'Then we have no choice but to protect ourselves as best we can. And when I say ourselves, that means Winja and Ningina and all of their people.'

Eyre rode forward, between the walking women, and caught up with Winja.

'I wish to ask you a question,' he said, in Aborigine.

'Ask it,' said Winja.

'Do you truthfully wish to fight against Yonguldye, just for me? There is no thought in my mind that you are a coward. I wish only to protect your women and your children.'

Winja looked up at Eyre narrowly. 'You still do not understand, do you?'

'I do not know what it is that I am supposed to understand.' He stumbled over this phrase, and had to say half of it in English.

But Winja said, 'We found you; and saved your life. Your life therefore belongs to us, and the choice of whether to protect it or not is ours alone. We have decided. We will protect you; and the girl Minil. Some time in your future life you will return the favour. But for now, be prepared only to fight alongside kinsmen.'

Eyre shaded his eyes against the sun. 'There's some cover up ahead; a few rocks. Not much, but enough to give us some advantage. He translated what he had said into Winja's language, as best he could, using the word *bojalup*, which meant 'place of rocks', and ducking his head to illustrate 'cover from spears'.

The rocks were very sparse; only a scattering of lime-stone spheres littered across the scrub. They looked as if some giant god from the dreaming had tired of playing marbles, and thrown his handful across the desert. In fact, they were the remains of a ridge that had been undermined by water and by gritty wind. Winja and Eyre gathered the women and children as far behind the rocks as they could, with Minil to supervise them; and then they went to the front of the outcropping to arrange the men, with their spears and clubs.

Eyre said, 'Look—we will stand here, right out in front of the rocks—then, when Yonguldye and his warriors begin to throw spears—we can run back.'

'Run back?' frowned Ningina.

'Not out of fear. Out of wisdom. They will run after us in among the rocks, and then we can trap them, and kill them.'

'I do not want to run back,' said Ningina, pouting. 'I have never run back from my enemy.'

Winja glared at him. 'You will run back when you are told to. Are you my *ngauwire*, my son?'

'Yes, *ngaiyeri*.'

'Then you will run back.'

Eyre loaded his rifle while they waited for Yonguldye to

catch up with them. He would probably only have time for one shot; but this time he hoped he would be able to hit Yonguldye somewhere fatal. It was a miracle that Yonguldye had already survived what must at the very least have been a severe powder-burn, and then a glancing rifle-ball to the side of the head. Perhaps there was something in his magic, after all. Perhaps, like the fabled Mabarn Men of the past, he was invincible, and possessed of eternal life.

The sun began to fall to the west; and this to Eyre was another advantage. Yonguldye and his warriors as they approached would have the glare of the early afternoon in their eyes, as well as a quarry that was going to behave completely uncharacteristically, and run away. Running-away was not a recognised tactic in Aborigine battles; the tradition was to stand firm with club in hand and fight blow-for-blow until you or your enemy dropped dead.

Yonguldye looked unnervingly threatening as he approached. His huge black emu-feather head-dress dipped and blew with every step he took; and he walked with a long, awkward limp that must have been caused either by the two shots that Eyre had fired at him or by the exhausting length of his pursuit. At first, because of the rippling heat, Eyre was unable to see his feet; but as he came nearer, only a hundred yards away, he could distinguish the dreaded *kurdaitja* shoes, of emu feathers and human blood, the shoes which unerringly guided a Mabarn Man towards his victim. Yonguldye had followed Eyre for hundreds of miles now, through the heat and dust of high summer; and he had found him.

Eyre stepped forward with his rifle raised. Winja caught his arm, but Eyre said, 'No. Let me speak to him.'

Yonguldye stopped, and raised one hand in the sign that meant greeting. He was wrapped in a kangaroo-skin *buka*, the fringes of which were tied with coloured threads and rows of tiny bandicoot skulls, which rattled as he walked. The rest of his skulls and magical apparatus were being carried by two young boys who stood at the back of the group.

Eyre could see now that Yonguldye's face was scarred on the left side; a half-healed bullet wound which had tattooed his skin with black powder. The powder burns which Eyre had inflicted on him at Yarrakinna were presumably concealed beneath his *buka*. Yonguldye's expression however was haughty and disdainful; the look of a man of power and influence. A man who had proved himself to be the greatest of all clever-men: unstoppable and impossible to kill.

Eyre called, 'What do you want, Yonguldye?'

Yonguldye kept his hand raised. Some of his warriors shifted uneasily around him, and one or two of them lodged their spears into their woomeras. Behind him, Eyre could hear Winja's men moving forward a few paces, to protect the white man whose life they now owned.

Yonguldye let out a great harsh crowing, which made Eyre's back tingle with alarm. Then he spread his arms wide, and came out with a long screeching chant, punctuated by raucous and repetitive cries, which sounded like an imitation of a red-tailed cockatoo.

Winja called back something in return which sounded to Eyre like mockery. He couldn't understand any of the words, but Winja's tone was 'Come on, then, puffed-up one, come and fight if that's what you've walked all this way for.'

Yonguldye stopped screeching and crossed his arms over his chest. Then he said in broken English—English which Minil must have taught him, 'You, *djanga*, have killed many. You too must die.'

'You would have killed me first, Yonguldye. You and Joolonga.'

'Joolonga led you to find me. But now you must die. The story must finish.'

'The story is only a story, Yonguldye. I am not the *djanga*.'

Yonguldye shook his head, and all his skulls and his

426

beads shivered as he did so. 'The message came. I was in Woocalla; two men came from Tandarnya and spoke.' For a moment he couldn't think of the words; but at last he said, 'The *djanga* has returned, they said. He is here and he will come to find you. The story has come to be.'

'Why do you want to kill me?' Eyre asked him.

'You must not go back to the land of *tinyinlara*.'

'But I have not yet told you what is in my head.'

'You kill too many,' said Yonguldye. 'In your head is death. I will learn what is in your head when you are killed.'

'So it's true; you want to eat my brains.'

'The story says that you will give your head. The story must come to be.'

Eyre lifted his rifle and pointed it straight at Yonguldye's chest. 'I am not the *djanga*. And I am telling you now, unless you go back to where you came from, you and all your warriors, I will shoot you, and kill you, right here, and right now.'

Yonguldye looked at Eyre with eyes as dull and primaeval as grey creek-washed pebbles. Then he lifted a single finger; and immediately, one of his warriors leaned back, his spear poised in his woomera, and launched it towards Eyre's head. Eyre caught sight of the flash of movement out of the corner of his eye, and heard the whistling called *bimblegumbie*, and dropped smartly to one knee, and fired his rifle towards the knot of warriors. The shot was overcharged, and deafeningly loud; and a cloud of blue smoke rolled through the Aborigines like a frightened ghost. One of them cried out, and spun to the dust; and then Eyre was running back towards Winja and Ningina, shouting, '*Back! Back!*' and waving his arm at them to retreat.

Winja ran back towards the rocks straight away; but Ningina hesitated. Two spears whistled dangerously close to him; but then Eyre seized his arm and pulled him along after him, into the ambush they had prepared. Winja had already scrambled up on to the rocks and was standing there with his spear drawn back to catch the first of Yong-

427

uldye's men as they came running and whooping after them.

Eyre leaped up on to the rocks beside him, and picked up the stone-headed club that Ningina had lent him. Yonguldye, startlingly, was right behind him, and swung at him with a kangaroo-bone axe, tearing the leg of his britches and grazing his left calf. Then the rocks were crowded with howling, keening warriors, and a sudden burst of spears clattered down all around them like a hailstorm, followed by racketing stones and tumbling axes.

Eyre leaped higher up on to the rocks, but Yonguldye climbed up after him, his sharp teeth bared, his face contorted with concentration and anger. His huge emu-feather head-dress fluttered and blew in the afternoon wind, and the skulls around his *buka* set up a shaking, shattering noise, like the death-rattle of a dying man. Carefully, feeling the rocks behind him, Eyre backed away until he was right up against a sheer wall of eroded limestone.

Yonguldye hit out at him again; once, twice, and the kangaroo-bone axe made a soft *whew* sound as it flew past Eyre's arms. Eyre swung back at him; and their weapons jarred and clashed together, and for one moment they gripped each other and wrestled hand-to-hand. Then Eyre let himself drop back against the rock, and as Yonguldye lunged towards him, his axe raised, Eyre pressed his back against the rock to support himself, and kicked out at Yonguldye with both legs. His boots hit the medicine-man hard in the pelvis; and with a desperate shout, Yonguldye fell backwards off the rocks, and tumbled like an overbalancing emu on to the dusty ground. Eyre jumped after him, and struggled astride him, pinning him down. Then he lifted his club threateningly over Yonguldye's head, and shouted at him, '*Yonguldye! Listen to me!*'

Yonguldye stared up at him, wild-eyed. Eyre's heart was galloping, and he felt that he could hardly breathe.

'*Call your people off!*' Eyre demanded. '*Call them off! Tell them to put down their weapons!*'

Yonguldye spat, and struggled, and cursed Eyre in a

hissing stream of Wirangu that Eyre began to think would never stop. All around them, Winja men battled with Yonguldye's warriors; and even as Eyre knelt in the dust, pinning Yonguldye down, a spray of warm blood spattered over them both, and a man shrieked with agony, and fell heavily to the ground close beside them, bleeding and jerking.

Without any further hesitation, Eyre knocked Yonguldye in the side of the face with his stone club as hard as he could. Yonguldye grunted with pain, and twisted his head away, in case Eyre hit him again.

'Tell your people to drop their weapons!' Eyre shouted at him. 'Tell them to stop fighting! Otherwise, damn it, I'll beat your brains out!'

Yonguldye hesitated for a moment, and then closed his eyes; and let out a hoarse, commanding roar. It was so harsh and so supernaturally loud that it made Eyre's head ring; but then he had heard about medicine-men who could simply shout their victims to death. He looked up, and the fighting had suddenly stopped. The Aborigines eyed each other cautiously; and then Yonguldye spoke his command again, more softly this time; and one by one, clubs and spears and fighting boomerangs dropped to the ground.

Eyre climbed up off Yonguldye's body, and brushed down his shirt. 'That's it.' he said. 'That's the finish of it. No more story. No more coming after me with those *kurdaitja* shoes. It's finished, do you understand?'

Yonguldye was helped to his feet by two of his warriors. He stood and faced Eyre with undisguised malevolence; scowling like Kinnie Gerthe cat-demon, whose single pleasure was to eat men alive. Winja came forward and stood next to Eyre, as protective as before, holding his bloody club raised as an obvious warning that the battle was over; and that Yonguldye's men should not make any attempt to renew it.

'Are any of your people hurt?' Eyre asked him.

429

Winja said, 'Ningina has been wounded in the leg, but that is all. We have killed two of theirs.'

Eyre said to Yonguldye, 'This is what happens when you try to make a story come true. Men die. This bloodshed is your responsibility.'

Yonguldye held his hand to his reddened cheek. 'Truly you are the *djanga*.'

No, Yonguldye, I am not the *djanga*.'

'It is spoken that the true *djanga* will always deny his real name,' said Yonguldye, in Wirangu this time. Winja translated as best he could, into his own language.

Eyre said to Winja, 'Tell this medicine-man that he must go now and never trouble me again. Tell him that I am not the *djanga*, but that I will kill anyone who suggests that I am; or comes anywhere near me. Tell him that if he continues to track me, he will meet an extremely sticky end.'

'Stick-ee end?' frowned Winja.

'Yes. Tell him I will turn him into a grub and eat him for breakfast.'

Winja explained all this to Yonguldye, shouting to make himself understood in the same way that an English traveller would have shouted at a French douanier. Yonguldye listened with rage and mystification, glaring at Eyre as if he wished that death-spears could fly from his eyes and strike Eyre dead where he stood. At last, with an irritable chop of his hand, he indicated to Winja that he had heard enough. Then he limped forward two or three paces, and inspected Eyre even more closely, his face smeared with sweat-runnelled *wilga*, his eyes bloodshot.

'You are the *djanga* of the story even if you will not say so. You are the dead one who has come to give us knowledge. But you will not. Why?'

'Yonguldye, I am not the *djanga*. I am a perfectly ordinary human being, not a ghastly white spirit from beyond the sunset.'

'You have betrayed us!' screeched Yonguldye, with

spittle flying from his lips. 'I curse you! I curse you! I curse you!'

Shaking with anger, he plucked a shell-bladed knife from out of his possum-fur belt, and brandished it under Eyre's nose. Winja immediately stepped closer, his spear raised towards Yonguldye's chest, but Yonguldye waved him away again with that same impatient chop. 'We have waited for your coming for countless years,' he said, half in English and half in Wirangu. 'Now you have betrayed us; and left us naked in the face of the white-faced people who would steal our lands and break our fishing-traps and take our women. You have the secret. Why will you not give it to us? Is this a punishment? What have we done?'

Winja translated as much of Yonguldye's fulminating speech as he could follow. Eyre listened with apprehension; and with some sadness. There was nothing he could do for Yonguldye. There was nothing he could do for any of the Aborigine people. He was barely surviving himself.

He said at last, 'Go, Yonguldye. I will take your message to the white people; and do whatever I can.'

Yonguldye roared at him in utter frustration and fury. Then, turning the shell-bladed knife towards his own body, he ripped a deep diagonal cut all the way from his left nipple to his right hip, almost cutting the nipple right off. Blood ran down his belly in a bright red curtain, and rivered down his thighs. But then he transferred the knife to the other hand, and cut himself again, slicing a cross from one side of his body to the other.

The pain of his cuts must have been mortifying; but he threw down his bloody knife and stood facing Eyre with raw defiance on his face and both fists clenched like a madman. The lower half of his body glistened with running blood, as if he had been wading in it.

'If this is the end of our people; if we are betrayed even by the spirits; then so be it. We will fight to the very end of our existence, and that is the word that you can carry back with you to Ngurunderi.'

Winja translated a little of this, but very perfunctorily.

Winja himself believed that the fight against the white man was already lost; and that Yonguldye was trying to live in a world which had long ago come to an end. He also respected Eyre, and was anxious not to upset him by saying anything slighting about white people, or (if he did happen to be a spirit) about spirits.

But Eyre approached Yonguldye, trying hard not to look down at his terrible self-inflicted wounds, close enough to shake hands with him, and said, 'You are a proud and terrible man. You are a great wizard and a great chief. The greatest of all Mabarn Men.'

Yonguldye stared at him with those dark, unreadable eyes, and said nothing. Out of his shirt pocket, Eyre produced the mana stone which had been given to him by the Aborigine warriors on Hindley Street. With considerable ceremony, he held it out on the open palm of his hand, and offered it to Yonguldye.

'Your people gave me this totem. Now it is imbued with my magic. Let it now be your totem, as a gift from me. I cannot give you any more.'

Yonguldye swayed. The blood on his body had now begun to congeal; and Eyre could see that the cuts, although gory, were not fatally deep. They had not been an attempt at suicide. Rather, they had been meant as a gesture that Yonguldye could inflict on himself greater pain than anything that Eyre could force him to suffer; that he was master of his own fate.

Eyre continued to hold out the mana stone, and said, 'Please.'

Yonguldye took the stone, and held it up between finger and thumb, turning it over, and examining it, although at the same time never letting his eyes stray very far away from Eyre. At last he slipped the stone into a small bag he was carrying around his waist, and bowed his head.

'The future has now been altered,' he said. Winja translated this as, 'from tomorrow, all the days will not be the shape they were expected to be.' Yonguldye went on, 'There will be storms. This has been foretold. There will

432

be rain in places where there has never been rain before. The moons which live beyond the horizon will appear whole; instead of being cut up into stars by the giant who watches over them; and they will circle the world. But what these days will hold for my people, that is uncertain. The story did not happen as it was meant to happen. Therefore, everything will be different.'

Eyre realised that in his anger and his humiliation, Yonguldye was trying to rationalise what had happened. He could not bring himself to believe that Eyre was not the expected *djanga* after all; because when would a white-faced man ever again cause the death of an Aborigine boy, and come journeying through the outback looking for absolution as Eyre had? Not for years, perhaps not ever, whereas Yonguldye badly needed to believe that his people would learn the magic knowledge of the white people now, and have the strength and the knowledge to stand up for what they believed to be rightfully theirs.

He was still furious at Eyre; still bitter and grieved about the men who had died; but in spite of his anger he had to accept his defeat at the hands of the *djanga*, or else he would be unable to believe in the *djanga* at all, and that would mean despair.

'I will go now,' he said to Eyre, with terrifying gravity; and still bleeding he turned and beckoned to his warriors. The sand beneath his feet was speckled dark with blood. But without any further ceremony, he limped away towards the east, under the hot mid-afternoon sun. Neither he nor his warriors looked back; and none of them made any attempt either to pick up their weapons or to bury their dead. Let the dead bury their dead. Let the *djanga* take the responsibility for the havoc he had wrought.

Ningina came hobbling up. The spear-wound in his thigh was now wound tightly with bloodstained hide. He shaded his eyes and watched the wobbling black figures of Yonguldye and his warriors grow steadily smaller.

'You should have killed that medicine-man,' he said. 'You would have been a great hero.'

'No,' said Eyre. 'This is not a time for heroes.'

'What do you mean?'

'Eyre took off his hat. Behind him, there was the *pick-pick-pick* of digging-sticks, as Winja's people dug graves for their dead enemies. It was 109 degrees, out here on the treeless plain called Bunda Bunda, and it looked as if the heat had liquefied the whole world. A molten blue sky, and a desert that rippled like the surface of a muddy lake. Through the liquidness, Yonguldye and his men walked and walked and walked, heading towards a new destiny; and leaving littered behind them the remains of their very last dream.

Thirty-Two

They journeyed west through the desert, following the kangaroo. Week after week, under skies that were devastatingly blue, living on charred meat and half-cooked lizards and whatever water they were able to suck out of the mud.

Eyre discarded his soiled and tattered shirt; and his back reddened and peeled and burned and then tanned as dark as wood. He was surprised to see, one morning, the birth of an Aborigine baby, slithering out of its mother's vulva as pale as a white baby; and he realised then how close to the European races the Aborigines were. Just because they had migrated to this strange desert continent, millions of years ago, and just because they had adapted to heat and drought, and a nomadic way of life, that had not denied them their ancestry, nor their intelligence, nor their racial heritage.

Eyre, as he rode along with them, thought of the words that Captain Cook had written, only seventy years ago, when he had tried to describe the natives of 'New-Holland' to his English readers:

> They may appear to some to be the most wretched people upon Earth, but in reality they are far happier than we Europeans. The Earth and the sea of their own accord furnishes them with all things necessary for life, they covet not Magnificent Houses, Household-stuff &c, they live in a warm and fine Climate and so they have very little need of Clothing, for many to whom we gave Cloth left it carelessly upon the Sea beach and in the woods as a thing they had no manner of use for. They think themselves provided with all the necessarys of Life and that they have no superfluities.

For Eyre, these weeks of journeying across the land of Bunda Bunda with Winja and his people was like an extraordinary but revelatory dream. He hardly ever thought about Captain Sturt, or Christopher, or even of Charlotte. He was completely preoccupied with hunting kangaroo, with helping to skin and roast whatever game they could find; with digging for water and building fires. After five weeks, he went naked, and tied his trousers around his neck to protect his shoulders from the sun. There seemed to be very little point in being the only dressed-up man in a friendly company of people without clothes. Winja's women laughed openly at his white bottom; until Winja shouted at them, and threatened to prod them with his spear. Winja still thought a great deal of Eyre; especially after the way he had defeated Yonguldye; and he would not have him insulted.

Eyre and Minil grew closer all the time; for both of them were discovering the simple truth of survival in the outback; and at the same time the complicated truth of

435

Aborigine beliefs. A love developed between them that no longer required explanations or understanding. It consisted of touches, and close embraces, and looks, and kisses, and of holding each other in the night, when the moon was high and the wind was freezing cold. Sometimes it expressed itself in affectionate silence, when they rode together during the day, with their last solitary pack-horse following obediently behind them. Two naked people, a man with a wide-brimmed hat and a girl with a tight kangaroo-skin headband and wild black hair, on horses, on the hottest of all imaginable days. At other times, it expressed itself in violent lovemaking; when Eyre would force Minil on to her back and raise her legs high in the air and lance her and lance her deep into her vagina until she tore at his hair and screamed out loud, regardless of who could hear or who could see.

It was a life of incendiary passion and unreal tranquillity; when the days and the weeks no longer mattered, and were no longer counted; when Eyre rediscovered his basic thirsts and his fundamental hungers, his throat and his stomach and his penis; but with a force and a dignity that gave new meaning to everything he felt. Nothing could be cruder than to have to squat in the sand, in front of the girl you loved and the people you knew, and excrete. But nothing could be more spiritual than to sit with them around their various wind-blown fires; just before the sun had set across the plain; and offer prayers to the greater Gods who had created the world, and all the abundance that it could offer.

They reached the coast one morning in March, on a cool and breezy day when Eyre had decided to put on his shirt; although he still wore his trousers tied around his waist. They came across it quite suddenly. One minute they were walking through thick mallee scrub; the next they were standing on the edge of a cliff overlooking the shore.

After so many months traversing the desert, Eyre was peculiarly moved by the sight of the sea. He climbed slowly down from his horse, and walked to the very edge of the cliff, and looked down at the tumbling, seething surf as if he had never seen anything like it before. Winja stood a little way off, watching him with quiet paternalism, as if he in his turn had been waiting for this moment, and expecting what Eyre's feelings would be. Minil came up, too, and stayed close to Eyre, holding his arm, and for a long time they watched the long curve of the ocean, from east to west, and the gulls which dived and screeched for Goolwa cockles.

Some of Winja's men clambered down to the shore, where they found a dead pelican lying among the rocks, its beak rising and falling in the tide. Whooping, they brought it up to the clifftop, and hacked it open, so that they could drag out its entrails. Tonight, the families would all share a treat: pelican's intestines filled with heated fat. Eyre watched them cutting open the bird, and the white feathers flying in the wind, and smiled.

'You have become one of us,' said Winja, quietly.

'No,' said Eyre. 'I can never become one of you. I only wish that I could. Even poor Joolonga could never become one of you; not again. I have to go on; to finish this journey. I have learned now that God wills it, whoever God may be.'

'God is in your heart,' said Winja.

Eyre took Winja's hand, and squeezed it hard. 'God is in you, Winja. God is in all of us. That's what my father used to say, and it's true.'

The sea surged and splashed below them. Far away, beyond the ocean, lay Antarctica. Behind them stretched the hot and desolate land called Bunda Bunda. Eyre felt as if he had arrived at last at the conjunction of the Lord's hugest and most impressive creations. This was not the place where He had run out of ideas. This was the place where He had foregone conventional beauty in search of truth, and found it. It was apposite that it had cost Eyre such suffering to reach this place; because no truth could be reached without suffering. Eyre got down on his knees, and closed his eyes, and while Minil laid her hand on his shoulder, he repeated the words of Psalm 86. 'Give ear, O Lord, to my prayer; and give heed to the voice of my supplications! Teach me Thy way, O Lord; I will walk in Thy truth. Arrogant men have risen up against me, and a band of violent men have sought my life. But Thou, O Lord, art a God merciful and gracious, slow to anger and abundant in loving kindness and truth.'

That afternoon, on the beach, while the women baked cockles in the sand, and the men fished, Eyre baptised Winja and Ningina in the foam; and there was singing and stick-clapping, and the fires were lit for a family corroboree.

Winja said, as they sat around the fire eating the cockles, 'Tonight we must begin your *engwura*, Eyre. You have become one of us; but you are still an *utyana*, an uninitiated youth. Your *engwura* is your initiation ceremony. You must be a man, not only among the white-faces, but among the black-faces.'

Eyre scooped another cockle out of its shell. 'Can't we leave it until tomorrow? It hurts, doesn't it?'

'What is pain?' asked Winja.

'Pain is when your body hurts,' Eyre answered him, tartly.

Winja pressed both hands against his head. 'Your body will hurt, but inside your head you will feel nothing but peace.'

Eyre frowned, and Ningina laughed. Eyre turned to him crossly, and said, 'I suppose *you* weren't nervous, when you were about to be initiated?'

'I was shaking!' laughed Ningina. Everyone around the fire joined in, and some of them threw pebbles at Eyre and cried, *'Utyana! Utyana!'*

Eyre said to Winja, 'Are you seriously inviting me to be initiated?'

Winja nodded. 'Seriously. You are one of us. It was Baiame's will that we met you in the desert.'

Eyre glanced at Minil. Minil looked remarkably pretty tonight, with her headband, and her patterned *buka* drawn

438

over her shoulders, and a string of red-painted beads decorating her plump bare breasts. He felt that she had found contentment now: with an Aborigine family to satisfy her need for freedom, and to get back among her own people; but with Eyre to love her and to give her the European sophistication which Winja's people lacked. He felt regretful in a way that she had found such contentment, because it could never last. Winja and his families would have to be on their way, and Eyre would have to return to Adelaide; and where would that leave Minil? Eyre could sense the pain that would inevitably end their relationship; he could sense it already, now that he was down by the sea, and closer to civilisation. He just hoped that it would not be so great that neither of them could bear it.

He looked at Minil laughing and clapping her hands by the fire. He smelled the brine from the ocean, and the sizzling aroma of charcoal-roasted cockles. He saw the clouds overhead, fine and golden-grey. And he wished then that this moment could last for ever; that it would never pass, and that he would always be here, on this evening, for the rest of his life.

But the night came; and passed; and in the morning the sun stretched itself across the ocean. Eyre noticed, however, that Winja's people were not making their usual preparations for travelling on. Instead, they were lighting fresh cooking-fires, and the women were preparing food, and the children were playing in the scrub. Winja came up to Eyre wearing a heavily decorated *buka*, and said, 'Today we have decided to rest and hunt. Perhaps you will take your gun and see if you can find kangaroo or *toora*.'

Eyre ate a sparse breakfast; and then took his rifle and the rest of his ammunition and set off alone towards the north-west to look for game. He was glad of the opportunity to think in silence. Usually, whenever they went hunting, Ningina came with him and chattered incessantly about the fights he had had with other tribes; and the time that he had outrun a big red, and jumped on to its back.

The morning was clear and sharp, and there was a fresh autumnal wind blowing inland from the sea; although once he was below the line of the cliffs, and walking through the scrub, the desert was more sheltered, and very much hotter.

He spent hours stalking a *toora*, a scrawny-looking mallee hen, and twice fired at it and missed. At last he caught it by throwing a stone at it, knocking it stunned and fluttering on to the ground, and then clubbed it with the stock of his rifle. It wasn't much to bring back to several families of hungry people, but it was better than nothing. There had been plenty of days when he and Ningina had gone out all day and come back empty-handed, except for a few lizards. The sun was beginning to go down, so he made his way back to the cliffs, following his own tracks in the dust.

Winja and Ningina and two other tribesmen were waiting for him a little way out of camp. As he came closer, Eyre was surprised to see that they were fully painted with pipe-clay and *wilga*. Winja called to him, 'How was your hunting?' and Eyre lifted up the *toora* to show what he had caught.

At that moment, all four of the Aborigines ran forward and seized him, snatching away his rifle and his game, and running with him as fast as they could back towards the camp. Eyre shouted, '*Winja! What the hell's going on! Ningina!*' but neither of them took any notice. He struggled and kicked and tried to leap away from them, but their grip on his arms was too firm, and they were obviously determined not to let him go.

As they ran through the camp, past the flickering fires and the brushwood shelters, the women and children came hurrying out, shrieking and ullulating, and calling out, '*Don't take him! Don't take him!*' in Wirangu. Some of the women tried wildly to snatch at his arms, but Ningina and his men pushed them away. Even Minil came struggling forwards, shrieking, '*Don't take him! Don't take him!*

Don't kill him!' but Winja pushed her out of the way with his spear-shaft.

The men hurried with him down the sloping pathway that led to the seashore, leaving the women behind. Eyre fought and twisted, but most of the time his feet weren't even touching the ground, and he was taken down to the beach with his legs kicking in the air, like the *toora* he had just managed to catch. He was badly frightened: it occurred to him that Winja and his people had been keeping him all this time as a living totem, as a human good-luck charm, and that now they were going to please Baiame by sacrificing him.

Perhaps they had come to believe what Yonguldye had said about him: that he was the true *djanga*, and that somehow he had betrayed the Aborigine people by not giving them the magic knowledge which had been promised by myth and by legend. Perhaps they believed that if they killed him, the true gods would look on them favourably, and protect them from white men and devil-devils. Yonguldye had wanted his brains; perhaps Winja had decided that he too had an appetite for the white man's magic.

Panting, terrified, coughing, he was dragged along the sand and around a rocky limestone headland, until he reached a cove that was out of sight of the main encampment. Here, there was a huge fire burning, its flames rolling and flaring in the dusk; and all the men of the tribe were gathered, their faces painted with circles and stripes; so that they looked like a rabble of horrifying demons, hot from hell. Eyre shouted, *'No!'* but the men forced him down on to the sand, first on to his knees, and then flat, face-down.

Winja came up and stood over him. 'Eyre-Walker, you are about to die. Everything you have been, up until now, has been a way of getting ready for this death. All of your life; all of your thinking; all of your friendships. All your prayers, too, have been directed to this one moment.'

Eyre was turned over on to his back. He looked up at

Winja; and to his surprise, the grey-bearded old man was smiling at him.

'This is your *engwura*, your initiation ceremony. Tonight, the Eyre-Walker you once used to be will die; and the new Eyre-Walker will be born. You will take a new life, and a new name.'

Eyre said, 'You scoundrel, Winja.' His relief was enormous.

Winja prodded him in the shoulder with the point of his spear. 'Tonight is not a night for you to be disrespectful. Tonight you are a boy. Only when you are initiated will you become a man. Now, you will lie there, and Galute will paint your body with the totem of our people.'

Eyre lay flat on his back on the sand while Galute and Ningina stripped him completely naked and rubbed his skin all over with pelican-fat. Then, with tongue-clenching care, Galute began to paint Eyre's skin with moistened pipe-clay and ochre, an inverted white crucifix pattern with red stripes and triangles on it. Galute painted his face, too, a mask of white with diagonal red arrows, which tightened as it dried and made Eyre feel that his whole face had turned into a clinging, rigid mask. Finally, Galute painted pipe-clay into his hair, so that it looked like a wild configuration of plumes. When Galute had finished, Eyre lay back with his arms raised, looking up at the stars and the sparks that blew from the fire, while Winja and Ningina led their people in a long song that told of the boys who came for their initiation, and discovered the secrets of the tribe.

Out of a kangaroo-skin package, they produced flat, boat-shaped wooden *churingas*, attached to long twists of twine, and as they sang they spun these around and around over their heads, producing an eerie droning noise. Winja said to Eyre, 'The women and children believe when they hear this noise that they are hearing the voices of the dead. Only initiated men know that it is the sound of the sacred *churingas*.'

The singing and the chanting continued for hours; until

442

at last Galute returned, this time with a knife and a wooden bowl of ashes from the fire.

'We will mark you now with the marks of a man,' he said. Eyre watched him with a tingling feeling of anticipated pain. He could have stood up now, and refused to take part in any of Winja's initiation ceremony; but he knew that it was going to be an important step forward in his life; and that it was probably going to be the ultimate expression of his radical belief that every race and every religion must be respected, no matter how bizarre it might seem to be to those brought up on the Prayer Book.

While another young man tightly held Eyre's wrists, Galute produced a sharp shell knife, and knelt down beside him. 'This is the mark of a great hunter,' he said, and before Eyre could wriggle, he sliced his shoulders, left and right, in two swift stinging strokes. Eyre bit his tongue to keep back his pain, and most of all to stop himself from crying out loud. But then Galute said, 'This is the mark of the warrior,' and cut his chest in a herringbone pattern, one deep incision after the other.

'Now the mark of Pund-jil, the great god, who caused men to wander throughout the world.' And Galute slashed his thighs.

The *churingas* whirled around and around, and the evening was overwhelmed with their endless humming, and with the sound of the surf breaking on the shore. Eyre lay mute and helpless while Galute rubbed ashes into his bloody wounds; although the stinging was almost more than he could bear; and the edges of the cuts flapped open in a way that made his nerves shrink like sea-anemones.

He closed his eyes and tried not to think of the pain. The pain seemed to wash in with the surf, in waves of scarlet. And all the time the *churingas* droned and droned, and the sticks tapped, and Winja sang his songs of Baiame and Yahloo the moon goddess, and the days in the dreamtime when men had walked the earth like gods.

Winja told him how their families had first been born. Eyre could understand very little of it: it was a lengthy

and complicated fable involving all the gods who had
helped and guided them. He told of the first *churingas*,
and how these thin pieces of wood, when they were
twirled around and around in the air, could bring back the
voices of spirits and demons. He told of suffering and
drought; of days when there were so many kangaroo that
the desert had rippled like the sea; of moons and lyrebirds
and Bunyips and wallabies. He told of pain and punishment; of joy and laughter; and above all of friendship and
love. It was desperately hard, surviving in the desert, and
the love that grew between both men and women was
defiant and beautiful.

Eyre saw pictures in his mind. Dark figures, dancing
through a dark night. He heard noises, too; hollow hums
and strange sibilant whirrings. And when they approached
him at last with the circumcision knife, he was prepared
for what they were going to do. He lay back on the sand,
watching as they lifted the blade, and as they blessed it;
and when they knelt down beside him, and took his soft
penis in their hands, he closed his eyes and offered no
prayers to the Lord, but only to those spirits who would
now accept him as a man and a warrior, to those ancient
gods whose land he had chosen as his home, and these
people he had chosen as his kinsmen.

Galute pinched his foreskin, and drew it out as far as
he could. Then he inserted two fingers inside it, stretching
it wide, and began to cut through it with his knife. Little
by little, the skin bloodily came free, until the purple glans
was naked. Eyre no longer thought of the pain. The pain
was too dull; too much; too insistent. He looked at Winja
and gave him a slow, bleary smile. Winja nodded, and
held up the little fold of skin which Galute had cut off.

'You must swallow this,' he said; and offered it to Eyre
on the ends of his fingers, with a wooden bowl of water.

Eyre raised his head, and opened his mouth, and
accepted on his tongue the soft salty-tasting envelope of
skin. He was beyond nausea now; beyond anything but
going through this initiation ceremony until the end; until

444

it was over. Winja pressed the water to his lips, and he drank, and swallowed.

But now came the greatest of all tests. Galute inserted the point of his shell-knife into the cleft of Eyre's already-blooded penis, and made the first cut downwards, to open out the urethra in the same way that Joolonga's urethra had been opened out; and Midgegooroo's, and Weeip's.

Agonising as it was, Eyre's penis rose into a stiff erection; and Galute held him tight in his fist like a spear-shaft. Then, without hesitation, Galute cut deep into the underside of his flesh, right down to his tightened scrotum. He splashed the incision from his bowlful of water to make sure that it was clean; and then stood up, and lifted both hands, and cried out loudly, 'This is a man now!'

Eyre felt hot, and then chillingly cold. He couldn't feel his genitals at all. The tapping of sticks faded; the surf sounded as if it were pouring all over him. And the drone of the *churingas* went on and on; until he couldn't decide if the droning was inside his mind or outside on the sea-shore. He shivered with a pain that he was too far gone to understand. All he wanted to do was to sleep, and to forget it forever.

Winja covered him gently with a *buka*. However harsh the initiation ritual might have been, Winja knew how to cope with the bodily shock that always followed. Keep the initiate warm and quiet for at least a day; and then gradually begin to tell him what had happened; and why; and all the stories and fables that were connected with his new totem. There were hours of stories to tell, and Winja knew them all, just as his grandfather had told them; and his grandfather's father; right back to the days of the giant kangaroo.

Eyre slept fitfully for a while; then woke in agonising pain that made him cry out. The night passed in torrents of suffering, and there was nothing he could do but lie crouched-up on the sand and endure it; while the chilly wind blew from the Indian Ocean, and the fire popped and crackled and died down, and the sun gradually rose again from the eastern horizon.

They kept him hidden away from the rest of the tribe for two weeks, while Winja told him all the stories of the dreamtime, and how their people had come to be. He was shown all the magical artefacts; all the *churingas*, all the totems, and the significance of each was explained to him in detail. He woke, slept, dreamed, and suffered. But gradually his wounds healed themselves, and he was able to walk again, sometimes down to the seashore to watch the surf deluge through the rocks; sometimes along the cliffs, with the gulls screaming over his head.

One morning he examined his penis and saw that it had stopped suppurating; and that the lips of his ceremonial incision had crusted with healthy scabs. The fountain of urine that sprayed out whenever he relieved himself was still a surprise; but at least it no longer stung him, and he was almost completely recovered. His mind was still detached, still swimming in a half-world of legend and pain, but gradually he found that he was able to focus more clearly on what had happened to him, and understand what it was that he had become, and also what it was that he could never become. He would never become a true Aborigine, he knew that. He had no desire to be. But he would always be one of their kinsmen; a *ngaitye* both physically and mentally, a friend, and no matter what happened to him during the rest of his life, nobody would be able to take that away from him. He had achieved at last what he had set out to achieve, when he had first left Adelaide on this long expedition. He had become a man, and he had discovered his soul, and what it meant to him.

Winja had said, 'Your body will hurt, but inside your head you will feel nothing but peace.' And that was true.

They brought him back to the encampment on the clifftop twenty days after he had left to look for the *toora*; and he was greeted by the women and children with shouting and clapping and singing. And there, at the far end of the camp, standing in front of her shelter naked, in

446

spite of the wind, was Minil, her hands raised, her face shining with welcome.

They roasted kangaroo that night, and mutton-birds, and cockles, and Government House for all its pomp could never have laid out such a feast; nor excited such happiness. And any whaler passing close to the shore would have seen six or seven fires on the clifftop, and heard tapping, and music, and the voices of those to whom Australia had always belonged, and always would.

Thirty-Three

In the morning, standing amidst the smoke of the burned-out fires, Winja said, 'This is where we have to part.'

Eyre said, 'You're not going west any further?'

Winja shook his head. 'The wet season is coming. We will go back towards Yalata.'

Eyre looked at Ningina. It was a grey, overcast morning. The sea shushed dolefully against the rocks. 'You understand that I have to go on?'

'Yes,' said Ningina. 'We always knew that. We always knew that we would have to say farewell to you, sooner or later. You were not born one of us. You have become our kinsman. But you have other duties, in another world.'

Eyre looked out over the ocean. Today, it was relentlessly dull. A few gulls circled and swooped, but they were silent. The wind nagged at the clifftops, and rustled through the scrub, like a cold hand rubbing up a dog's coat the wrong way.

'I shall miss you for ever,' he said.

'No,' said Winja, taking his hand. 'It is we who shall

miss you for ever. You came from the desert; you return to the desert. We knew always that you were not a spirit, but a man. You were also one of us, even before you met us. It was prophesied when you were born that you would become one of us, and you will stay in our minds for ever, as one of our stories. Our ancestors will speak of you long after all of us have joined Ngurunderi. Eyre-Walker, who came from the east, and vanished in the west; and who defeated with one blow the great Mabarn Man Yonguldye.'

He paused, and then he said, 'There is one thing more. You are one of my people now; and therefore your son is one of my people; and your son's son.'

'I have no son,' said Eyre.

'You will,' replied Winja, looking towards Minil, 'and when you do, your son must be ours. You must return him to the tribe so that he may grow up amongst his kinsmen, and learn our ways, and undergo his *engwura*.'

Eyre held Winja close. 'My son is yours,' he pledged him. 'You gave me my life, you looked after me and protected me, you accepted me as one of your people. The least I can do is observe your laws.'

'Do not forget, then,' nodded Winja. 'On the first hour of the first day of the boy's second year, we shall be waiting for him. Our arms will be open to welcome him, and make him ours.'

'I promise it,' said Eyre.

Less than an hour later, Winja and his people were ready to leave. They stood watching as Eyre and Minil mounted their horses, and turned westwards; but it was only when they were almost out of sight, a line of black silhouettes on the clifftops, that they set up a hair-raising ululation, a warbling primaeval cry that swelled and faded on the wind, and raised their spears in salute.

Minil said, 'I am sad to leave them.'

But Eyre could say nothing except, 'Let's go,' because his feelings of pain and separation were even sharper than Winja's initiation knife.

They rode west for week after week; and gradually the

weather began to break, and the winter rains came. For days they were riding through a bright yellow landscape of mud and puddles; and then there were torrential storms, with the rain hurtling out of the sky at them like watery spears, leaving them drenched and bedraggled and silent. There was almost a whole week of sunny humidity and steam; when it was hot, but impossible to see the horizon, but then the clouds rolled back again, and the rains cascaded down, cold and unforgiving, until their *bukas* were soaked all the way through, dark and heavy, and they felt as if they had never seen a desert in their lives.

Eyre lost count of how far they had travelled. Every evening, he went to catch game; and now that the wet season had arrived, he was usually lucky. They sat close to damp, smoky fires, trying to roast bandicoots and lizards; and then they huddled up close together under whatever shelter they could improvise, while the rain clattered down, and the clouds fled past, and the whole world seemed to be flooded. Minil prayed every night to Birra-Nulu, the flood-sender, the wife of Baiame, that they should not be overwhelmed and drowned, but Birra-Nulu seemed to take very little notice of Minil's prayers; because by the time June arrived, they were riding through gullies that were waist-deep in muddy water, under skies that were as black as blankets.

Eyre's initiation wounds healed, although they were still quite tender; and by the beginning of July they were able to make love again. Some intensity, however, had gone out of their coupling, some feeling of closeness. Perhaps it was the nearness of civilisation, the anticipation that within a few days now, their extraordinary journey would be over. After their third unsatisfying bout, Minil twisted herself up in her wet *buka* and tried to sleep, while Eyre sat by the fire and chewed *pitjuri*.

'What will happen when we reach Albany?' Minil asked.

'What do you mean, what will happen?' The rain dripped off the leaves of their makeshift shelter.

'Do you want me to stay with you?'

'I don't understand. Haven't I said so?'

'You said that you loved me.'

He looked at her; and then held out his hand to her. 'I do. You know I do. Nothing's changed.'

'Something has changed.'

Eyre took the wad of wet *pitjuri* out of his mouth, and threw it aside. He wiped his lips with the back of his hand. 'My feelings for you haven't changed, if that's what you're trying to suggest.'

'Still, something has changed. I feel it.'

'It's just the weather,' said Eyre, trying to sound light-hearted.

Minil sat up, and leaned close to him. For a long time she said nothing at all, but then she stroked his arm, and asked, 'Do you really want me to stay with you, once this journey is over?'

'I'll have quite a few things to do,' said Eyre. 'I'll have to look for a new job, to begin with; and perhaps a new place to live.'

'Will you let me live with you?'

'I can't. Not to begin with. I only have one room, at Mrs McConnell's. But I expect that I can arrange something for you.'

Minil said, 'You are trying to tell me that you do not want me any more.'

'Of course not. That's ridiculous.'

'No. You are trying to tell me that when you are back among white people, you cannot have an Aboriginal girl with you. It would not be right. Other white people would not like it.'

'Minil—' he said, but she quickly shook her head.

'I have felt your love drawing away from me, mile by mile. I have already started to accept it. When you did not think that you would ever see your Charlotte again, you loved me. I was glad of your love; and I still am. But now you are thinking of returning to your friends, to your own people, and I will have to let you go.'

Eyre said, softly, 'Nothing will ever change the fact that I love you.'

'I know,' she said. 'But many people who love each other cannot live with each other.'

After that, Eyre could think of nothing more to say to her. He was still trying to work out inside his own mind what he was going to do; and he knew that to make her any more promises now would be futile and hurtful.

He had not yet allowed himself fully to face up to the truth that even this long and torturous part of his expedition had degenerated into failure. He had been trying to discover a stock-route from Adelaide to Albany; and all he had found was a wild and inhospitable coastline and a desert without water or trees or grazing. He had dreamed as they journeyed through the land of Bunda Bunda that he would be welcomed as a hero when he returned, but the closer he came to Albany, the more threadbare the dream became. He had found only that it was impossible to reach the inland sea, if there really was one; and that the Western desert was impassable to cattle. He had found no opals, no silver, and no lakes that could be used for irrigation. He hadn't even discovered any new plants or insects.

In the process of failing so completely, he had lost the lives of two black trackers and one of his dearest friends, as well as a dozen Aborigine tribesmen. Worse than that, he had squandered all of Captain Sturt's finances, and thrown away all his valuable equipment: guns, books, compasses, tents, saddlebags, shovels and picks.

Up until recently, he had fondly pictured his return to Waikerie Lodge, to claim Charlotte; but on this chilly rain-soaked night on the coast of Western Australia, crouched under a shelter of sticks and leaves with an Aborigine girl, the prospect of that, when he thought about it seriously, was dismally remote.

He would be lucky to be noticed when he finally trudged back into the municipality of Adelaide. He would be even luckier to find any employment. And there was a consider-

451

able risk that Captain Sturt would have him locked up for fraud and incompetence and God knows what other charges he could devise. Then there was the matter of Arthur Mortlock to be considered, and the deaths of Messrs Chatto and Rose. He hadn't thought about that for weeks now; but it had returned to worry at him like a bad tooth.

There was a choice, he supposed. He could stay in Western Australia, or even take a ship back to England, if he could somehow raise the money. But he knew that he would have to return to Adelaide to settle matters; whatever the outcome might be. And he did want to see Charlotte again, if only through the palings around her house, from a distance, as an elegant young fantasy that might have been his.

He slept, and snored, and had nightmares. He saw a man with a beard, smiling, and a baby who cried. Towards morning, the rain began to trickle in underneath him. He opened his eyes and saw Minil looking down at him, her face concerned.

'What is it?' he asked her.

'You were shouting out in your sleep,' she told him. 'You kept calling for the man called Dogger.'

Eyre stiffly sat up. He rubbed his eyes. Outside their shelter, the rain was still falling in heavy, rustling veils.

'Dogger,' he said; and for some reason the name sounded curiously unfamiliar, like a name in another language, from another age.

Then he looked at Minil, and frowned, and said, 'Do you think you might be having a baby?'

'Why do you ask me that?'

'I don't know. Something I dreamed.'

'Minil said, 'Since we nearly died in the desert, I have had no bleeding. I do not think that I can have babies, not now. Perhaps when this journey is over my bleeding will start again.'

Eyre crawled out from under his *buka*, and began to scrape together a few twigs and branches so that they could start a fire. The rain fell on his bare back, and made him shiver. Minil watched him with infinite sadness and care, as if she were trying to remember every movement he made, so that they would be imprinted on her mind, for ever.

Thirty-Four

They reached the crest of a hill and there below them among the gums and blackboy trees was the township of Albany. It was the first white settlement that Eyre had seen since he had left Adelaide the previous year, and he stood and stared down at it with an indescribable feeling of relief and thankfulness; but also with a surge of something that could almost have been fear. For just a moment, he saw the white people as an Aborigine might have seen them; their neat houses with thatched roofs and white-painted walls; their fences and their streets; their gardens lined with flourishing vegetables. Everything so tidily arranged, and so constricted. He saw carriages and ox-carts moving to and fro through the rutted streets, and beyond, in the curve of water that the Aborigines called Monkbeeluen and which the English called King George's Sound, there were sailing-ships at anchor, and ware-houses, and smoke was rising from office chimneys.

'Minil,' said Eyre, and reached across and took her hand.

'Yes,' nodded Minil. 'I know what you are saying to me. You are saying goodbye.'

They began to ride slowly down the muddy track that took them towards the outskirts of town. They said nothing. Their pack-horse walked obediently behind them, as he had walked for nearly a thousand miles. It had stopped raining now, and a watery sun had emerged from the clouds, making the rooftops and puddles glitter brightly.

They passed a garden where a curly-headed Aborigine boy in a white shirt and britches was hoeing vegetables. He stared at them as they passed; and Eyre raised his shapeless kangaroo-skin hat, and said, 'Good morning.' He realised that he and Minil must look two dishevelled scarecrows; he with his bushy black beard and lumpy *buka*; Minil with her tattered scarf wound around her head. The boy dropped his hoe and came to the fence and watched them as they rode further down the street; and then suddenly shrieked out, '*Minil! Minil!*'

Minil reined back her horse. The boy came running after them, his bare feet splattering in the puddles. 'Minil!' he cried. His eyes were bright, and he jumped and danced all around her.

Minil said, 'It's Chucky! It's Chucky! I didn't recognise you! How you've grown up!'

'Minil!' sang Chucky. 'How everybody tells stories of where you went! They say you went with some Wirangu; and then the Wirangu told stories that you left them and went with Mr Walker, the great explorer-man!'

'What?' asked Eyre, in an unsteady voice. 'Who told these stories? How do you know about me? Who said these things?'

Chucky stopped skipping, and touched his curls respectfully. 'Are you Mr Walker, the great explorer-man?'

Minil smiled. 'This is Mr Walker.'

'Minil is my cousin, sir, from New Norcia mission. Many people here in Albany know her, sir. All of her family work at the Old Farm once, with Mrs Bird!'

'But how did you know that she was with me?' Eyre repeated.

'A ship, sir, from Adelaide. Everybody in Adelaide thought you were dead and gone, sir, dead and gone. You were all the talk! Then some Wirangu came to Adelaide, sir, and said that you had gone off to the west with Minil, and with Winja's people. Then there was great excitement! You have been in all the newspaper, sir, my missis told me.'

At that moment, an elderly white man came walking down the street from the house where Chucky had been hoeing. He called, 'Chucky! Chucky! What are you doing, talking to those people? Get back to your gardening at once!'

Chucky piped up, 'But this is my cousin Minil, Mr Pope; and this is Mr Walker, the great explorer-man!'

Mr Pope stepped gingerly across the puddles and up beside Eyre's horse. He frowned at him through his spectacles. 'You are Mr Eyre Walker?'

'Yes, sir,' said Eyre. He suddenly found that there was a sharp catch in his throat.

'But, you are dead, sir,' said Mr Pope rather bewildered. 'The news came by ship from Adelaide that you had been lost between Woocalla and Fowler's Bay.'

'I am not dead, sir,' said Eyre. 'I am only tired. This girl and I have ridden and walked all the way. I believe it is something over nine hundred miles. We have just arrived.'

He couldn't say any more. He burst into tears, and sat on his horse sobbing with exhaustion and emotion. Mr Pope looked up at him worriedly for a moment, and then took hold of his horse's bridle, and gave him his hand to help him dismount.

'Since you are not dead, Mr Walker, I suppose it is incumbent on me to welcome you to Western Australia,' said Mr Pope. 'Come along, let me help this young girl to dismount, and we will see what we can do for you. I believe Mrs Pope has some fresh mutton pies just out of the oven.'

Eyre was shaking; and so was Minil, as Chucky and Mr Pope helped her to slide off her horse. Eyre said, 'I believe I could do with a glass of beer, if you have any.'

'Beer? Yes. I think we can furnish a beer.'

'Thank God,' said Eyre. And then, to Mr Pope, 'And thank you, too, sir.'

They were taken back to Mrs Pope's kitchen; hot and whitewashed and snug; where Mrs Pope heated up large bucketfuls of water for them to bathe, and Chucky laid the kitchen-table for them and served them with pies and boiled potatoes and beer, although Minil drank milk. They were both too stunned to say very much, and they sat huddled together at the end of the table like refugees from some appalling disaster, and in return the Popes gave them a respectful amount of room, partly out of sympathy, partly because they were so impressed at what Eyre had done, and partly because both he and Minil stunk of rancid pelican grease, and filth, and sodden kangaroo-skin.

After they had eaten, Mrs Pope took Minil to bathe outside in the shed while Mr Pope poured out a basinful of hot water for Eyre on the kitchen flags. Mr Pope drew up a kitchen chair, and lit a pipe; and said, 'As soon as you feel refreshed enough, we ought to take you to see some of our local dignitaries. It would hardly do for me to keep you to myself.'

Eyre turned his back on Mr Pope as he washed. Mr Pope puffed away for a while, and then said, 'Some bad scars you have there, if I'm not being too personal, Mr Walker.'

Eyre looked down at his chest, patterned with the purplish welts of *ngora*, and at his circumcised and sub-incised penis. 'Yes,' he said. 'We had some difficult times in the desert.'

He finished soaping himself, uncomfortably aware that although he had been welcomed back into white society for less than an hour, he had already denied his Aboriginal kinship for the first time.

Later, when he was washed and shaved, and dressed in one of Mr Pope's Saturday suits, which felt impossibly huge and baggy, and which seemed to weigh on his body like a heap of woollen blankets, Eyre was taken to shake hands with the neighbours; and then Mr Pope suggested they visit Albany's town hall, and make themselves known to everybody there. Eyre was tired, but curiously elated, and he agreed.

'Minil should come with me,' he said.

'Well,' said Mrs Pope, fussily tying her bonnet, 'the poor lamb's fast asleep now; and I think it better not to wake her, don't you? And you *are* the explorer, aren't you? The achievement has been yours; and yours alone.'

'I couldn't have done it without Minil,' Eyre told her.

'In that case, she should be proud to have had such an appreciative employer,' smiled Mrs Pope. 'Where are my spectacles, Frederick? Have you seen my spectacles?'

'I wasn't her employer,' said Eyre, although Mrs Pope wasn't really listening to him. 'I was her—'

He looked away. Outside the front door of the house, some of the neighbours had already gathered, and he could hear them chattering loudly; and some of them were whistling and cheering. Mr Pope's neighbours must have spread the news to all the surrounding streets, because the excitement sounded considerable; and there was the sound of running feet on the puddly road, and the rattle and creak of carriages.

'You were her *what* Mr Walker?' Mrs Pope asked brightly, staring at him with her milky-blue eyes.

Eyre said, 'It doesn't matter. I suppose things are rather different in the outback.'

'I should say so,' put in Mr Pope. 'Now, listen to that hullaballoo outside!'

'Come on,' said Eyre. 'We mustn't disappoint them, must we?'

Mr Pope opened the front door, and there was a burst of cheering and clapping; and it looked as if the whole street was packed from end to end with people, tossing up their hats and singing and dancing, and waving Union Jacks. There was even a one-man band there, with accordion and knee-cymbals and a dancing monkey.

When Eyre stepped out into the Pope's front garden, there was a deafening roar of welcome and enthusiasm; and he stood bewildered for a while until Mr Pope raised one of his arms for him, as if he had just won a fisticuffs match; and then the crowd screamed and whistled and cheered again. Two young burly men came in through the white-painted gate, and grinned, 'Come on, Mr Walker, we'll chair you!' and between them they lifted Eyre up on to their shoulders, and carried him right into the middle of the throng, so that the men could grasp his hands and slap at his thighs and the ladies could blow him kisses.

Then, in spite of his shouts of protest, they bore him off down the street, and across the market-place, where more people came running out to see what all the cheering was about.

They took him down to the docks, where stevedores in their brown aprons and peaked caps put down their bales and their grappling-hooks and applauded him as if they were opera-goers at the finale of *Cosi Fan Tutte*. 'He's arrived! He's alive!' That was the cry everywhere. 'He's arrived! Eyre Walker's arrived!' And nobody seemed to care whether he had discovered the inland sea or not; or whether or not it was possible to drive cattle from Adelaide to Albany, or sheep from Albany to Adelaide. All they cared about was Eyre; and his extraordinary journey, and the fact that he had walked and ridden all the way across the treeless plains of Southern Australia to arrive here alive.

He was finally allowed down to the ground outside the steps of the civic hall, where he was greeted by one top-hatted official after another; shaking hundreds of hands; and where even the loudest of speechmakers was unable to make himself heard over the cheering and shouting. From out on King George's Sound there was a dull, pressurised booming; one boom after another; and that was Her Majesty's naval supply ship *Walrus Bay* according Eyre an eleven-gun salute, followed by four ruffles on the drums.

He was showered with flowers; and then taken inside the civic hall for champagne, and more hand-shaking, although the crowd outside refused to go away; and after

458

a while an impromptu silver-band struck up with 'My Lily and My Love' and 'Dragoons'.

The editor of the Albany newspaper came up at last, in a tight-fitting blue coat, and a yellow-checkered waistcoat, with chestnut moustaches perfectly waxed into points.

'Well, Mr Walker, my name's William Dundas, of the *Albany Mail*. What an achievement.'

Eyre felt battered and out of breath, and said, 'You'll excuse me if I sit down.'

'Of course,' said Dundas, and drew him out a chair. Eyre sat down, and a smiling man in a very high collar poured him some more champagne.

'I'm surprised that I seem to have excited so much interest,' said Eyre.

'Well,' said Dundas, taking out a small cigar, 'You're a hero now. A genuine hero, in a country that's rather short of heroes. You mustn't blame us all for making rather much of you.'

'There is no route from Adelaide to Albany suitable for stock,' said Eyre.

'Bad country, hm?'

'The worst. Desert, mallee scrub, mud. No running water for over eight hundred miles.'

'Then how on earth did you survive? What did you drink?'

'I'm beginning to wonder. But, there are springs if you know where to find them. Muddy pools of water that you have to dig for. In extremes, you can dig for frogs.'

'I beg your pardon?'

'I never had to do it; but I was told about it. There are certain frogs that retain water in their bodies. You can dig them up and squeeze them out, if you're really thirsty.'

Dundas reached into his pocket for notepaper, and a pencil. 'Did the Aborigines teach you how to do that?'

'They taught me many things,' said Eyre.

'And what would you say was the most important thing that they taught you?'

Eyre lowered his head. The champagne had already

begun to make him feel drunk; what with the noise and the jostling and the music, and the sudden sense of suffocation he felt, enclosed inside a room after months of living in the open air.

He said, haltingly, 'The most important thing that they taught me was that the white man's way of life is blind, greedy, and completely lacking in spiritual values. They taught me that there is magic in the world, and mystery; if only we can be humble enough to commune with our surroundings, and to respect what God has given us.'

Dundas tapped his pencil against his thumbnail. Then he glanced behind him to make sure that nobody was listening, and leaned forward, and said to Eyre in a cologne-smelling undertone, 'Listen, Mr Walker. You must be very tired after your journey. Perhaps a little lightheaded. I think it might be a good idea if I made sure that you got back to wherever it is that you're staying; and that you didn't say very much more about magic or mystery or spiritual values. You're a hero now. If I were you, I'd take full advantage of it; and play it for what it's worth. And if I were you, I'd think twice before I upset people. You won't change them, after all, no matter *what* you discovered in the outback. Tell them how you were taught to squeeze frogs. Tell them how you roasted emus, and how you ate lizards. That's all very fine. Guaranteed to make the gels shudder. Good dinner-party stuff. Fine newspaper copy. But don't try to convert them with all this talk about greed, and blindness, and whatnot. Doesn't go down well.'

Eyre was silent. A fat woman with a coarse English accent and a very purple dress came up and kissed him, without being asked, right on the nose. 'You're a *hero*! she squealed.

Eyre raised his eyes and looked at Dundas with tiredness and resignation. Dundas shrugged, and twiddled at his moustache.

'Yes,' said Eyre. 'I'm a hero.'

When a carriage returned him at last to the Pope's house,

Mrs Pope greeted him on the doorstep with the news that Minil had gone. There was no message; nothing. She had told Chucky that she had gone to see her relatives at Swan River.

Eyre opened the door of the bedroom where Minil had been sleeping that afternoon, and stepped inside. The bed was crumpled, the sheets twisted. He sat down on it, and traced with the palm of his hand the wrinkles that her sleeping had made.

'*Minil*,' he whispered to himself, in the dusk of that room. He looked towards the window; and outside, in the blueness of dusk, he saw a gum-tree dipping and waving in the north-westerly breeze. She had left nothing behind, only these twists and wrinkles on the bed. He sat there for a few minutes, trying to think of her; but somehow he couldn't quite remember what her face looked like, or how she felt, or even what she had said to him, the very last time they had spoken.

He got up at last, and went to the window, and looked out. Mr Pope came into the room, smelling of tobacco, and stood there for a while, and then said, 'Is everything all right? Mrs Pope tells me that the blacky girl's gone.'

'Yes,' said Eyre, without turning around. 'Everything's all right. And, yes,' he said, 'the blacky girl's gone.'

'You'll want some supper, then,' said Mr Pope. 'Chicken casserole do you, with dumplings? And how about a beer? I'm glad of the excuse, to tell you the truth. Mrs Pope doesn't usually allow me a beer, not until Saturday. But, you know, seeing as how it's a special occasion.'

'I suppose it is,' said Eyre. 'Yes, you're very kind. I'll have a beer.'

Thirty-Five

He arrived back in Adelaide three weeks later on the merchant-ship *Primrose*; which was laden with grain and ironware from England. The people of Albany had given him everything he might possibly have needed; from a constant supply of French champagne to shoes and shirts and tailor-made coats. When he had left King George's Sound, more than half the population had turned out to cheer him and wave him goodbye, and sparkling maroons had been fired into the grey July sky. Now he stood in the wind on the *Primrose*'s poop, dressed rather formally in a black tail-coat, with dark grey britches, and a two-inch collar, with a black tie, and a pearl stud which had been presented to him by the Albany Commerce Club.

The *Primrose* leaned against the stiff north-westerly, her timbers creaking like the stays of an elderly woman. Then, across the ruffled waters of the Gulf of St Vincent, he saw the foaming outline of Henley Beach, and the outer harbour; and the masts of all the vessels that were moored there.

As the *Primrose* slowly rounded the point, her sails flapping against the wind, a rocket was fired from the end of the new McLaren wharf; and as soon as she passed the harbour entrance, Eyre saw that the water was clustered with scores and scores of small boats, lighters and bumboats and skiffs, bobbing and dipping, all of them flying bunting and pennants, and crowded from stem to stern with waving and cheering people. There was a sharp crackling noise as Chinese fireworks were let off all along the quayside, and then there was a roar of welcome and approval from the wharf where the *Primrose* would tie up; as hundreds of excited people poured along it from the direction of the Port Road.

'Well, seems as if they're anticipatin' you,' remarked the *Primrose*'s mate, hawking loudly. He himself had never been further ashore anywhere in Australia than Kermode Street in Adelaide for the British Tavern, or the worst alleys off George Street, in Sydney, for the boozers and the cribs, and he understood nothing of what Eyre had achieved. 'They're on one button here,' Eyre had heard him say to his captain, two days out of Albany. 'A fellow like that takes a stroll in the countryside, and they treat him like he's God-Amighty.'

Eyre said, 'You should be proud of your seamanship, to have got us here on the due date. They sent the *Ellen* on ahead of us, to tell them that we were expected to arrive today, and so we have. So take some of these cheers for yourself, master-mate.'

'Oh, bung it,' said the master-mate, irritably; although Eyre could tell that he was quite pleased by the compliment.

The *Primrose* was towed in by rowing-boat, and tied up, and from his place up on the poop, Eyre waved his hat and acknowledged the cheers and shouts from the huge assembly below. He saw Captain Sturt standing at the front, looking severe; and next to him a tall man with silver hair and deep-set eyes who looked important, but whom Eyre was unable to recognise. There was no sign of Christopher, nor of Lathrop Lindsay.

As soon as the gangplank went down, Captain Sturt and the tall man with silver hair were escorted aboard by marines; and up to the deck where Eyre was still waving and smiling. Flowers flew through the air and littered the planks all around Eyre's feet.

'Well, sir,' said Captain Sturt pushing aside some of the blossoms with his shoe. He was wearing a black jacket and a crimson satin waistcoat that was far too tight for him, and although he was grinning he looked particularly displeased; as if he had bitten into an apple and found it unbearably sour.

Eyre carried on waving, and nodding, and smiling. 'Well, yourself, Captain,' he replied.

'It seems as if you have made something of a name for

yourself,' said Captain Sturt. 'Allow me to congratulate you.'

'I don't think I really deserve your congratulations, do you?' asked Eyre; and Captain Sturt did not fail to miss the sharp double meaning of what he was saying.

'You have undertaken and completed a great journey of discovery, Mr Walker,' put in the tall man with the silver hair. His voice was deep and rich as plum-pudding, and his chins bulged over his necktie. 'You have crossed a desert that no white explorer has crossed before. That in itself is worthy of praise.'

'I'm sorry,' said Eyre, indicating that he had no idea who this gentleman might be.

'This is Governor George Grey,' said Captain Sturt.

'Then Governor Gawler is no longer with us?'

'He returned to England in May,' explained Governor Grey. 'Let us say that it was simply a matter of having drawn a little too enthusiastically on the London Commissioners. Although, of course, one has to acknowledge that in his short time here he achieved great things.'

Eyre shook hands with Governor Grey; but somehow he and Captain Sturt contrived not to.

'You must be tired,' said Sturt. 'Perhaps you would like to come back to my house and take some luncheon.'

'Yes,' said Eyre, 'I think I'd like that, thank you. But not right away. First of all, I think a procession is called for. That is, if I have your permission, governor.'

'By all means,' nodded Governor Grey. 'It isn't every day that we have such cause for celebration. Today you are Adelaide's most celebrated son, Mr Walker. It is only befitting that we should fête you.'

Eyre went to shake hands with the *Primrose*'s captain, and to wave to the crew, and then he slowly descended the gangplank to the wharf, with both arms raised in acknowledgement of the crowd's tremendous applause.

As he had been in Albany, he was lifted off his feet by enthusiastic young swells, and carried shoulder-high along the wharf, while flowers flew all around him, and

464

fireworks popped off, and so many black top-hats were tossed into the air that the crowd looked for a while like a bubbling, spitting tar-pit.

A carriage was waiting for him outside the port, decked with shrubbery and flowers; and then with seven or eight young men clinging on to the sides, it was driven ceremoniously towards the town centre, followed on either flank by cheering riders and rattling gigs and running children. Eyre turned around and looked behind him, and saw to his amazement and delight that there must have been well over three thousand people following him, hurraying and laughing and waving flags.

At the western end of North Terrace, where the road from Port Adelaide ran at a sharp diagonal into the city, they were met with a fanfare by Captain Wintergreen and his musicians, who had formed themselves into a marching-band, twenty-five strong, especially to celebrate Eyre's arrival. The driver of Eyre's carriage had been told to proceed straight to Government House; and so had Captain Wintergreen; but Eyre shouted to the driver, 'Left, left, over the bridge!' The carriage turned left and rumbled over the bridge, and behind it came Captain Wintergreen and his band, drumming their drums and blowing their trumpets and clashing their cymbals. Behind them, still cheering, still waving their flags, came the first of the riders who had followed them from the wharf; marines and dragoons and cocky young gentlemen in plumed hats. Then the gigs and the broughams and the rest of the carriages, crowded with Adelaide's prettiest girls, in their yellows and pinks and bright blues, spinning their umbrellas and singing like birds. Then the great rush of people on foot: children and farmboys and clerks and shop-assistants and Aborigines, skipping and clapping and chanting.

'Now, make for Waikerie Lodge!' Eyre instructed his driver, and with a nod of his head the fellow turned the carriage along the street towards Lathrop Lindsay's house.

'Why, that's Mr Lindsay's place,' cried one young

Narangy, who was hanging on to Eyre's carriage by the folded-down hood. 'He's going to be as mad as a cut snake if you parade past him with this lot! He's your worstest enemy; allowing for what he's been saying about you, since you've been gone!'

'Well, we shall see about that,' Eyre declared. He leaned forward, tapped the coachman on the shoulder, and told him to draw over to the side of the road, and stop. The driver did as he was bid, and then Eyre stepped down from the carriage, and waited while Captain Wintergreen and his marching-band caught up with them. They were playing 'Sons of Caledonia', one of the most stirring marches they knew, with plenty of drumstick whirling and cymbal-clashing, and their trumpets and bugles were wildly off-key.

Eyre neatly stepped in, right in front of Captain Wintergreen, and led the parade alongside the white fencing which surrounded the lawns of Waikerie Lodge, until he reached the front gate. Then he cried, 'Right—turn!' and held out his right hand, and marched confidently up the path to Lathrop Lindsay's front door.

Every window of the house was flung open; and at every window an astonished face appeared. In the drawing-room window, Lathrop Lindsay himself, in his emerald-green smoking-jacket, his mouth wide open. In the day-room window, Mrs Lindsay, her hair awry, clutching her tatting. Upstairs, in her parlour window, Charlotte, in a sugar-pink afternoon gown.

'Around the house!' Eyre cried to Captain Wintergreen; and with a flourish of bugles the marching-band split right down the middle into two columns, one parading smartly around the left-hand side of the house, and the other parading around the right. Each of these columns was followed by a stream of cheering, dancing, applauding people, some on horseback, one or two on donkeys, but most of them on foot, swarming and swelling into the gardens of Waikerie Lodge, hundred upon hundred of them, until the house was completely besieged with

466

people, none of them knowing why they were there, but all of them festive and happy, and ready for a great celebration.

The marching-band appeared from around the back of the house, and formed up on the front steps, marching on the spot, and playing 'Scotland The Brave'; which in less apoplectic times was Lathrop Lindsay's favourite tune.

'*Mr Walker!*' screamed Lathrop.

Eyre raised his hand to Captain Wintergreen, and the band died away in a few raggedy hoots, toots, and jingles.

'*Mr Walker!*' screamed Lathrop, again. His face was plum-coloured with wrath.

Those nearest to the house heard him screaming, and cried 'Oooooh!' in response, like a music-hall audience.

'*Mr Walker!*' screamed Lathrop, for the third time.

'Mr Walker!' cried the crowd, in huge amusement. 'Mr Walker! Ooooh! Mr Walker!' And then they burst out cheering and clapping and laughing again, and shouted, 'Mr Walker! Speech from Mr Walker! Let's hear him! Come on now, Mr Walker!'

Eyre climbed up two or three steps, and raised both hands. There was more applause now, and somebody let off a tremendous chain of fire-crackers, that jumped and spat and frightened all the horses.

'Listen!' Eyre shouted. 'Listen!' And at last, still hooting and laughing occasionally, the crowd quietened down. Lathrop stood in his drawing-room window shaking with disbelief and rage, while Mrs Lindsay had clapped both hands over her mouth, as if she were suppressing a high shriek.

'I have travelled as far north to the interior of Australia as a man can go!' Eyre cried. More shouting, more clapping, and some cries of 'bravo! bravo, that man!'

Then Eyre said, 'I have travelled westwards, all the way from the spring called Woocalla to the town of Albany, through desert and scrub, over a thousand miles!'

Now the cheering was so loud that Eyre found it almost impossible to think. His blood was racing and his face was flushed; and even though he had been given nothing to drink, he felt as if he were intoxicated.

'I have travelled all that way,' he shouted, his voice becoming hoarse from the strain, 'I have travelled all that way . . . just to claim the hand of the most beautiful girl in Adelaide, Miss Charlotte Lindsay!'

The crowd screamed their delight and approval. Hats flew up into the air again, even umbrellas and bonnets, and the band rushed into one of those little pieces called a 'hurry', which were usually used to accompany a variety player on to the stage, or off again.

Eyre raised his hands for silence once again. Some of the women in the crowd were openly weeping, and two girls and an elderly grocer had fainted, and had to be laid under the wattle-bushes.

'There is one thing that I must do before I can claim Miss Lindsay's hand, however,' Eyre announced. 'And that is to ask the forgiveness of her father, Mr Lathrop Lindsay; whom I have caused embarrassment and pain, not just once, but several times; and each time worse than the last. I admit to him that there was a time when I was a brash, ill-mannered, and incontinent young man, and I can only ask that he can find it somewhere in that generous heart of his to forgive me.'

Eyre slowly turned towards Lathrop, and held out his hand, as dramatically as Adam holding out his hand towards God on the ceiling of the Sistine Chapel. Lathrop, framed in his window, stared at Eyre in complete horror.

'Forgive him!' cried a wag, in the front of the crowd. But then the cry was taken up again and again, more seriously, until nearly a thousand citizens of Adelaide were standing in Lathrop's garden, trampling his wattles and his orchids, crushing his carefully rolled lawns, roaring 'Forgive him! Forgive him! Forgive him!'

Lathrop disappeared from the window and eventually appeared at the front door. Behind him, halfway down the stairs, Eyre could see Charlotte although her face was hidden in shadow. Until he had conquered Lathrop, however, he didn't dare to look at her. She had meant so much to him for so long that if he were to lose her now, when she was almost within his grasp, he would rather not remember her too sharply.

'Mr Lindsay,' said Eyre, 'I come to you today not as an impertinent young clerk who was too ebullient to mind his manners. I come to you as a man who has crossed a whole continent; and who has been matured and humbled by his experiences. I come to you as a man who has nurtured his love for your daughter through indescribable exploits, through starvation and thirst and terrible loneliness. I come to you as a man who is ready to apologise to you; but also as a man who has gained strength, and courage, and also a lasting reputation.'

At that moment, Captain Sturt forced his way through to the front of the crowd. Lathrop was about to reply to Eyre, but whatever he was going to say, Sturt raised a cautionary and advisory finger to him, and he swallowed the words before he had spoken them, as if they were liver-pills. He stepped heavily forward, and stared at Eyre with the expression of a man who cannot believe the persistence of his personal ill-fortune. There was sweat on his forehead, and his lower lip juddered with all the emotion that Captain Sturt had forbidden him to express.

He knew that he was beaten. The crowd was so enthusiastic about Eyre; Eyre was Adelaide's darling of the day; and if he were to slam the door in Eyre's face and refuse to forgive him, the consequences for his business and social life would be disastrous, at least for the next few months, if not for very much longer. Adelaide took warmly to its heroes; but treated its villains with unrelenting disfavour and scorn.

Captain Sturt was not even a friend of Lathrop's. In fact, he despised him. But Sturt was anxious not to see an important municipal businessman sent to Coventry; and he was also anxious to seek Eyre's favour too. There was much unfinished business between them, Eyre and Captain Sturt; and Captain Sturt was not particularly relishing the idea of settling it especially if Eyre was in an uncompromising mood.

Eyre held out his hand, and Lathrop took it. His grip was like cold moulded suet. 'I accept your apologies,' he said loudly, looking around at the crowd, and attempting a smile. 'Though God alone knows why,' he muttered, under his breath.

And then, loudly again, 'I will also consider giving you permission to marry my daughter Charlotte, if she is so disposed. Obviously, we shall need a little time to consider the matter more seriously, away from this . . . circus.'

The roar that rose from the crowd made the sash-windows rattle in their casements; and two horses threw their riders, leaped over the picket-fence surrounding Lathrop's garden, and bolted down the road. The band played 'Here Comes the Bride' in double-time, and Charlotte ran down the last few steps of the staircase, and came running out on silk slippers with her arms wide, her blonde curls bouncing and be-ribboned, as deliciously pretty and as small and as soft as ever before, and threw herself with a squeal into Eyre's arms, and hugged him tight, and kissed him, and wept and wept.

'I thought you were dead!' she cried, 'Oh, Eyre! My darling! I thought all this time you were dead!'

He held her close to him, feeling her warmth, breathing in her perfume. Then, very slowly, very strongly, he kissed her; until her eyelids trembled and closed, and her little upraised hand started to clench itself involuntarily into a fist.

Behind her, Lathrop snorted in disgust, and loudly blew snuff and phlegm out of his nose with an extra-large hand-kerchief. Captain Sturt watched with his arms folded and his face quite flinty.

'Thirty-three cheers for Eyre Walker and for Charlotte Lindsay!' cried one of the narangies. 'And thirty-three cheers for Captain Sturt and Mr Lathrop Lindsay!'

The crowd cheered and cheered and cheered again; until, defeated and despondent, and very close to angry tears, Lathrop Lindsay had to turn away and go back inside his house. Eyre stood with Charlotte on the steps, raising his hands again and again, and kissing Charlotte to show the whole of Adelaide how much he loved her.

At last, as the crowd began to disperse, and make their way back towards the river, and to Government House, where George Grey had promised band music and free drinks for everybody, Eyre took Charlotte into the hallway, and held both of her hands.

'I've asked your father,' he said. 'Now I want to ask you.'

There were tears in her eyes, but he wouldn't release her hands so that she could wipe them away.

'Yes,' she whispered. 'I will.'

Thirty-Six

They lunched very late, and neither of them were particularly hungry. They ate a little cold mutton and beetroot salad; and shared a bottle of '37 claret, which had either travelled badly, or been bad to begin with. The afternoon light filtered through the lace curtains as weakly as the light from half-remembered days gone by; and somehow it made Captain Sturt look even older, and tireder.

'George said that he's planning a proper municipal reception for next Thursday,' said Captain Sturt. 'Dancing, tables out on the lawns, even races. I won a three-legged race you know once, when I was in France, with the Army of Occupation. They gave me a goose. Well, that was the prize.'

'You were telling me about Christopher Willis,' Eyre

reminded him. Captain Sturt seemed to be ready to discuss almost anything at all, except Eyre's expedition.

Sturt sniffed, and helped himself to more wine. 'Your friend Christopher Willis, yes. From what I gather he acted with considerable fortitude. That's the word. He arrived back here in Adelaide only six days after he had left you out on the salt lake; and he was in very good spirits, though anxious, of course, that you and Mr McConnell should not come to any harm. He set off the very next morning with the boy Weeip and five other blackfellows to leave you those provisions. I gather that he even waited out there for a day, to see if you would appear. But, well, you didn't, and so he came back.'

'Did he tell you anything about Arthur Mortlock?'

'Only that he had become grievously sick, and died.'

'What about Mr Chatto and Mr Rose?'

'Hm?'

'Those two bounty-hunters who came looking for Arthur the day we left.'

Captain Sturt shook his head. 'What about them? They left Adelaide, didn't they? That's the very last that I've heard.'

'Then nobody's been looking for them?' asked Eyre.

'Should they have been?'

'No. But I wondered, that's all. They seemed like very persistent fellows.'

'Persistence is not always a virtue,' said Captain Sturt.

Eyre looked at him over the rim of his wine-glass, and then said, 'I hope you're not trying to suggest that *I* have been unduly persistent.'

'You were persistent enough to travel all the way from the salt lakes to Albany.'

'Yes,' Eyre said, warily.

'An expedition of great heroism. A journey of remarkable courage. An achievement which will no doubt be recognised for generations yet to come.'

Eyre said nothing, but watched Captain Sturt get out of his chair, and walk across to the window with his hands

472

thrust into his trouser pockets, and the tails of his coat cocked back. Sturt frowned out through the curtains at the muddy prospect of North Terrace, and the gum trees which bordered the Torrens River.

'Unfortunately,' he said, 'nothing of what you did was of any practical or commercial use whatsoever. Of course, I dare not say so. Isn't that ironic? I financed an expedition, and sent it off to discover a way through the continent and whatever riches might be there for the taking; and when it failed, with considerable loss of life, and abandonment of irreplaceable equipment, I have to appear to be cheerful about it, and shout 'huzza' along with the rest of the *hoi polloi*.'

Eyre said, 'It was scarcely my fault that the terrain was impassable.'

'You *tell* us that it was impassable,' Captain Sturt retorted. 'That's what you *say*. But terrain that is impassable for one man may well be quite easily negotiable for another.'

'Are you trying to suggest that I didn't do my very utmost to find a way through to the inland sea?' Eyre asked him, sharply. Even as he spoke, he could picture in his mind the horses wallowing and struggling up to their chests in grey, glistening mud.

Sturt pouted, and rocked on his heels. 'I'm only suggesting that my expedition might have been better served by a leader who was less *dogged*, and more astute.'

Eyre leaned forward in his chair, his spine as tense as a whalebone. 'Captain Sturt, just because a discovery is not to your personal liking; just because it doesn't help to line your purse; that doesn't make it any less of a discovery. My companions and I found out that the land due north of here is nothing but miles and miles of treacherous salt lakes; and that the land to the west of here is treeless desert; both completely unsuitable for the driving of cattle. Now at least we know that there is nothing we can do but cling to the coast of this continent, and raise our livestock as best we can, and leave the interior to the lizards and the Aborigines.'

'You didn't even find opals.'

'We were given the name of a site where opals can be found.'

'You were given the name of a site where opals can be found!' parroted Captain Sturt. 'My dear chap, how naive you are! It's astonishing that you weren't killed on the spot, by the first Aborigine you met with a sense of fun. Of course you were given the name of a site where opals can be found! What was it? Bugga Mugga, or Mudgegeerabah? That's eastern Aboriginal for the place of lies.'

He leaned forward and stared right into Eyre's face, his eyes bulging and bloodshot. 'Could you ever *find* this place, if you were to set out to look for it; or if anyone were to be foolish enough to finance you? Of course not! It's a mirage. An illusion, partly caused by the desert heat; partly by exhaustion. But most of all, it is caused by vanity, irrationality, and an immature impulse to make a hero out of yourself and a fool out of me.'

Eyre stared back at Captain Sturt for a moment or two, and then leaned back in his chair again and folded his arms.

'You're being more than unjust, Captain Sturt,' he said, as quietly as he could, although his voice was on the very brink of trembling. 'I personally believe that the discoveries we made were quite considerable, when you think how small our party was, how inexperienced, and how hastily prepared; not to mention the fact that our sponsors sent us off in complete ignorance of the mortal dangers that we would eventually have to face; if and when we achieved our goal.'

Sturt frowned at him. 'Mortal dangers? *What* mortal dangers? What are you trying to imply?'

'You knew about the legend of the *djanga*, the spirit returned from the dead.'

'What?'

'You know what a *djanga* is, surely; you know enough about Aboriginal mythology by now.'

'Well, yes of course I do,' blustered Sturt, 'but—'

'Captain Henry told Joolonga that I was the *djanga*, and Joolonga told you.'

'My dear Eyre—'

'Is there any use in denying it?' Eyre snapped at him. 'Well, *is* there? I know everything about it; why and how. Joolonga told you how long the Aborigines have been looking forward to the appearance of the *djanga*, for more centuries than anyone can count. And he also told you how desperate their prayers have become ever since the white people began to trample over the sacred places, and how they have been hoping against hope that the legend should at last come true. A saviour will come, and give us the magical knowledge, and set us free from the white man! And how callously you traded on that belief, didn't you? and on my life; and the lives of all my companions. Not for glory, though, or patriotism. Not for any greater purpose than to balance the books of South Australia to the satisfaction of the London Commissioners, and to make sure that you yourself did not become a candidate for the green bonnet of bankruptcy.'

Captain Sturt stood with his mouth ajar. His face was the colour of fresh calves'-liver.

Eyre said, in a more controlled voice, 'I have not yet been able to discover whether you knew that Yonguldye would murder us all; or, to be fair, whether Yonguldye was really thinking of murdering us or not. There was a misunderstanding of language; whether to eat a man's brains means literally to eat his brains, or whether it simply means to acquire all the knowledge within him. But when I was out at Yarrakinna, surrounded by hundreds of Aborigine warriors with spears and knives and clubs, I didn't see much wisdom in waiting to find out. Nor did those poor souls who were with me.'

Captain Sturt was silent for a very long time, his hands resting on the cresting-rail of one of his dining-room chairs.

475

At last, gravely, he said, 'I consider your accusation to be completely fantastic, Eyre, and unreservedly malicious. Why you wish to believe such things of me, I cannot think. All I can tell you is that I know nothing whatsoever of the legends of which you speak; and that certainly I never would have been foolish or irrational enough to send you off on an expedition which I myself financed, knowing that its success depended on nothing more than Aborigine superstition.'

He stared at Eyre and his eyes were chilly and displeased.

'I knew that it was important to you to seek an Aborigine medicine-man in order that the remains of your young black friend should be properly interred. And, yes, I admit that to some extent I used you. But I sought only to harness your spiritual mission to assist my temporal explorations; so that both of us would profit in our different ways. What you have suggested now is that I deliberately offered your life to the Aborigines in return for profit. Well, the notion is beneath contempt. Contemptible! You have hurt me, Eyre, deeply.'

Eyre took a sip of wine and then set his glass back on the table. 'Well,' he said, 'I'm sorry you're hurt. But I have to say that Joolonga was quite specific.'

'Joolonga? You're prepared to take the word of that rogue against mine? Joolonga was irrational; his mind wandered. Drink, *pitjuri*, drugs. He was always trying to pretend that he had magical powers; always threatening to strike people dead and nonsense like that. I'll say that he was a marvellous tracker. One of the best in the whole of South Australia. But up here,' Captain Sturt tapped his forehead, 'Joolonga didn't know whether he was white or black, real or imaginary, coming or going.'

Eyre said, 'Of course he's conveniently dead now, and can't support me.'

'He wouldn't, even if he weren't. The man was a story-teller; a joker; he was probably trying to frighten you, that

476

was all, a novice out in the wilds. It was regrettable to say the least that you took him so seriously.'

'I'll tell you how seriously I took him, Captain Sturt. I killed him.'

Captain Sturt smiled, and slapped Eyre on the shoulder. 'Then serve him right, really, wouldn't you say? Poetic justice.'

'Captain Sturt, Joolonga was a very cultured and intelligent man.'

Captain Sturt blew out his cheeks, and quickly shook his head, 'Opinionated, yes, as most blackies are, but not cultured. They seem bright, you see, because you don't expect any kind of intelligible conversation at all out of a face as primitive and as ugly as that. An orang-utan would only have to say three words and we would say that it was cultured. The same with the blackfellow.'

He reached over and rang the bell on the table. He seemed to have settled down now, and to have forgotten his annoyance at Eyre's accusations. In fact, his little burst of temper seemed as far as he was concerned to have cleared the air altogether, and to have put him into a mood of rather sickly good temper.

His housemaid came in: a Kentish woman no more that five feet tall, with a hooked nose like Judy and a flouncy old-fashioned bonnet. One of her eyes looked towards the window and the other towards the portrait on the adjacent wall of Captain John Hindmarsh, the first governor of South Australia.

'We'll have the pie now, Mrs Billows,' said Captain Sturt. 'The pie, Eyre? It's apple and cinnamon, with cheese pastry. Quite capital.'

Eyre said, 'I don't think so, thank you. I'm rather tired.'

'Ah,' said Sturt. 'A man who is too tired to eat some of Mrs Billows' pie is tired of life itself.'

'To paraphrase Dr Johnson,' Eyre retorted.

'Well, yes,' said Sturt, uncomfortably. 'I, er—I think I'll have mine a little later, thank you, Mrs Billows. Perhaps with some of the cheese and pickles, for supper.'

Mrs Billows allowed her eyes to revolve independently over the entire compass of the room. 'I did 'eat it up, Captin, like as what you required; 'arf a nower in the huvven.'

'Yes, and I'm sure that's very dutiful of you,' said Captain Sturt. 'But I don't think either of us has an appetite just now. Why not ask Tildy to clear up now.'

'Tildy? Tildy 'asn't done a tap since brekfist; nor's likely too niver. Giv 'er the 'eave-'o, I would; 'septing it's not my plice.'

After Mrs Billows had cleared up, very noisily, with a tremendous jangling of cutlery and a clashing of plates, Captain Sturt directed Eyre through a gloomy glazed conservatory, and then out into the unkempt garden, where there was a wooden seat situated under the shade of a stringy-bark gum.

'I vow that you're a good fellow, Eyre,' he said, lighting a small cigar, and blowing smoke upwards into the wind. 'You have your hasty moments, but anyone of your age can be liable to that. Speed's Disease, my father used to call it. He'd catch me running down the corridor, and seize me by the ear, and cry, "What's ailing you, young Charlie? Speed's Disease?" A wonderful man, shed a few tears when he passed over.'

'This all seems so contrary,' said Eyre. 'You think the expedition was a disaster; mainly because of me; and yet here you are telling me how much of a great chap I am.'

'Ah, that's because I have an eye for opportunity. You have to, in business; and even more so in politics. We didn't find the inland sea; no. But you're a hero now, and we must make whatever use of you we can. George Grey suggested that we give you a rather special job.'

'Job?' asked Eyre. 'I was rather supposing that I would go back to the Southern Australian Company.'

'Pfff, a man of your stature, as a shipping clerk? Think of it, you're a hero now. A great gilded hero. And in any case, we don't want you to feel that all of those months of traipsing through the outback went to waste. A man achieves something, and no matter how disappointing it turns out to be in terms of pounds, shillings, and pence; well then, he must be rewarded.'

Eyre looked down at Captain Sturt, who was sitting with his legs crossed, confidently smoking his cigar as if he owned Australia.

'You're buying me off,' he said, in a voice as clear as the afternoon wind.

Captain Sturt licked a stray fragment of leaf back into position. Then he glanced up at Eyre, and gave him a small, confidential smile.

'You're going to be the Protector of Aborigines for the whole of the Murray River district,' he said. 'Important job; suit your new understanding of the blackies. Pay you well, too. Seven hundred pounds the annum, with house. Dignified job enough for you to marry Miss Lindsay in style.'

'You're buying me off,' Eyre repeated. 'You did know about the *djanga* legend, after all.'

'Well, my dear fellow, that's what *you* say. But then you've spent several arduous months with the sun baking your brains and the sand roasting your feet, in the company of savages and other assorted riff-raff. Who's going to take the word of a fellow like you, for all that they admire you?'

'You're buying me off,' Eyre repeated, with even greater sharpness.

Captain Sturt lounged back, and smoked, and smiled at him. 'Yes,' he said. 'But you will never force me to admit it in any court of law; or in front of any inquiry; or within earshot of anybody save yourself. If I were you, my dear fellow, I would enjoy what I had. The name of a hero, and a comfortable job for life. Oh yes, and a pretty wife, too; won at the expense of some considerable chagrin from poor old Lathrop Lindsay.'

Eyre covered his mouth with his hand. He didn't trust himself to answer; and besides, he needed to think. Somewhere along the terrace, in a neighbouring tree, a kookaburra began to laugh at him. The sun waned behind a cloud, and the garden looked for a moment like a daguerreotype of a day already gone by; colourless, cold, and half-forgotten.

'You say that Midgegooroo survived,' he said.

Captain Sturt nodded, without taking his cigar out of his mouth.

'But, crippled?'

'Won't walk again. But you can thank your friend Christopher Willis for saving his life.'

'Hm,' said Eyre. 'Not that it will be much of a life, will it? A blackfellow, unable to walk? What will a poor soul like that be able to do?'

'Beg,' smiled Captain Sturt. He paused, and knocked a little ash off his cigar. 'But then, you know, we all have to beg at times; in various ways. It's the way that life happens to be.'

Thirty-Seven

He stood outside the house on Hindley Street for almost ten minutes before he climbed the steps to the front verandah and knocked at the door. Below him, already rusted, its wheels entwined with weeds and creepers, his bicycle was propped against the wall. Dogger had promised to look after it for him, but of course Dogger was gone.

He could see her approaching the front door through the frosted glass panes; a dark shadow, with rustling skirts. She opened the door without asking who it was, and stood there, white-faced, black-bonneted, dressed in black satin, with a necklace of jet and ribbons of black velvet.

'Constance,' he said.

'I knew you'd come,' she said, stiffly. 'You'd better step inside.'

He followed her into the parlour. The curtains were half-drawn, and it was musty, and smelled of pot-pourri, and camphor.

'Sit down,' she said, and he did so, holding his hat on his lap. She sat down opposite him, arranging her skirts, and clasping her hands together in a gesture of piety and disapproval.

'When did you receive the news?' he asked her.

She lowered her eyelids. They looked like crescents of white peeled wax. 'A gentleman came from Albany. He said that he'd spoken to you; and that Mr McConnell had been murdered near Woocalla by savages.'

Eyre nodded. There was a very long silence. The clock on the mantelpiece whirred, and then chimed eight.

'You must be very tired,' said Mrs McConnell.

'Yes,' said Eyre. 'I think I am.'

'Then, you may stay here tonight. But tomorrow, I must ask you to go. I would also ask you to take all of your possessions; your pictures; your clothes. I want no trace of you here, nothing.'

'Constance—' he began.

She opened her eyes and stared at him sadly. 'He wasn't very much, Eyre. He was cantankerous and awkward and usually drunk. But he was Dogger, and he was all that I had.'

'I know,' said Eyre.

'He died—quickly?' asked Constance. 'There wasn't any pain?'

Eyre shook his head. 'It was all over in a flash. He only had time to shout one word. He sat in the saddle and lifted up his arms and shouted just one word.'

Constance was waiting. The clock had finished chiming now, and was ticking onwards towards nine o' clock, and the end of another day without Dogger. Eyre said, 'He shouted, Constance! And that was all.'

Constance clutched her arms around herself. In the gloom of the room, her eyes sparkled with tears.

'He called for me? His very last word?'

'Whatever his first word was, when he was born; your name was his last when he died.'

'Oh, God,' wept Constance. She covered her face with her hands. 'Oh, God, he called for me. He called for me, and I wasn't there. I'm his wife and I wasn't there. Oh God forgive me.'

Eyre knelt down on the carpet beside her and took her hand. She shook and shook, and her sobs were so deep that they sounded as if they were tearing her lungs. But at last she raised her head, and took out a black lace handkerchief, and wiped her eyes.

'I haven't cried much,' she said. 'I was dreading you coming back, because I knew then that I would. I knew then that I would have to admit that it's really true, and that he's gone.'

'Constance,' said Eyre. 'Let me fetch you a sherry. Or a brandy perhaps. Come on, something to calm you down.'

'Oh, I'm calm enough,' she sniffed. 'I'm calm, don't worry. Why shouldn't I be calm? There's nothing to get excited about any more, is there? Not even an old dingo-hunter who snores.'

Eyre spent the night in his old room but scarcely slept. He heard Constance walk down the creaky stairs in the small hours of the morning, presumably to make herself a cup of tea. But she didn't disturb him; and when he woke in the morning and went down to the kitchen, he found hot meat porridge waiting for him on the stove, and a note saying that she wouldn't be back until late in the afternoon, and could he please have left the house by then.

He packed the few things that were left in his wardrobe; his carriage clock and his pictures of his mother and father; and these he took across the road to the little notions store run by Mrs Crane and her sister, two ladies who had emigrated to Australia in search of husbands and ended up selling ribbons and needles instead. They agreed to keep his cases in their back room until the evening, and blushed when he kissed them both and promised to tell them about his adventures in the land of Bunda Bunda. Then he went back and retrieved his bicycle from underneath Mrs McConnell's verandah, tugging the weeds out of the wheels; and cycled slowly off towards the racecourse, and Christopher Willis' house.

It was a strange still day; not very hot but humid. As he pedalled out along the racecourse road, between the thick rainy-season bushes and the tall green grass, he heard no jacks nor finches, not even an insect chirruping. He felt as if he had cotton packed in his ears.

Only the monotonous squeak of his bicycle reminded him that he could still hear. That, and his panting. He had forgotten, after months on horseback, how strenuous it was to ride a bicycle.

Christopher was sitting on his verandah drinking tea and reading the Adelaide *Observer*. He was wearing a large floppy calico hat, and from a distance he looked very thin. Eyre dismounted from his bicycle when he was about twenty yards away from the house, and wheeled it the rest of the way over the damp earth.

'What ho, Christopher,' he said, propping the bicycle up against the steps.

'What ho, Eyre,' replied Christopher, without looking up.

Eyre climbed the steps and walked across the boarded verandah to stand right next to him.

'What do the newspapers have to say?' he asked.

Christopher shook the paper and peered towards the editorial column. 'They say that Adelaide is one of the filthiest cities on God's earth. Most people's basements are flooded with filthy water, and that there are open cesspools, dung heaps, and pig's offals lying everywhere.

The population are drinking unfiltered water and dying like flies.'

Eyre sat down on the verandah rail. 'Anything else?'

Christopher looked up. Eyre was startled to see how old he seemed to have become, how wrinkled his eyes were, and how washed-out.

'Yes,' said Christopher. 'They say that an erstwhile shipping-clerk of the South Australian Company has returned to the city in triumph. A great hero, after travelling all the way from South Australia to Western Australia, with only an Aborigine girl for company. They don't even mention the Aborigine girl's name.'

Eyre said, 'You didn't come to meet me at the dock.'

'Is there any reason why I should have done?'

'I thought we were friends.'

'Well,' said Christopher, 'we were.'

'Are you jealous?' asked Eyre. 'Are you jealous because I rode all the way to Albany and you didn't? Are you jealous of all this fame; all this public hoo-ha?'

'No,' said Christopher.

'What is it, then?' asked Eyre, softly but insistently.

Christopher said, 'I'm over you, that's all,' He looked up, with a challenging expression on his face.

'Is that a good thing or a bad thing?' Eyre asked him.

'I don't know,' said Christopher. He folded up the paper and laid it down on the table. 'It's just a fact.'

'Does that mean we're not pals any more? Not even pals?'

Christopher shrugged. 'I think I would really have preferred it if you hadn't come.'

'Don't you want to hear what happened?'

Christopher picked the paper up again, and dropped it. 'I can read it all in here, thank you. They say they're going to publish your entire account of the journey. "With Eyre Walker Through The Outback." '

'But I want to hear what happened to you.'

'Nothing happened to me,' said Christopher, off-hand-edly. 'Midgegooroo groaned and shrieked all the way to

Adelaide; but in the end we got here, God knows how, and took him to a doctor. The doctor said it was a miracle that he was still alive, although he would lose the use of both of his legs and one of his arms, and that the experience had probably damaged him mentally; you know, made him into something of an idiot. But otherwise, well, he was fine, and still is. Still breathing, still eating, still excreting.'

'It wasn't my fault, you know,' said Eyre.

'I didn't say that it was. You asked what happened, and I told you.'

'And you?'

'Me? I'm all right. Well, reasonably all right. Not *quite* the same person.'

Eyre walked down to the end of the verandah. Three or four racehorses were prancing across the course on a morning exercise. He heard a man shouting, '*Up, Kelly! Up, Tickera!*'

'You've just got over me, is that what you said?' Eyre asked Christopher.

'I suppose that's the decent way of putting it.'

'What's the indecent way of putting it?'

Christopher looked at Eyre cuttingly, and then looked away.

Eyre said, 'I was very hurt that you didn't come to see me. You know that, don't you?'

'Oh, I don't think you were,' Christopher replied. 'You see, the only person you really care about is you. I'm not blaming you; but it's in your nature. It's the way you are. That's why you're able to survive while everybody else around you dies or collapses or gives in. That's what made it possible for you to cross that desert. Unless you had cared about yourself with such intensity that nothing could possibly have stood in your way, you would still be there now, or at least your bones would be. You have all the makings of a hero, Eyre. I should have believed you when you said that destiny had marked you out for some

485

magnificent and honourable task. It takes perfect self-love. *Un amour-propre parfait*. And I congratulate you.'

Eyre stood where he was, saying nothing.

Christopher watched him, and at last said, 'Would you like some tea? I could get some fresh.'

'Yes,' said Eyre. 'I think I'd like that.'

Christopher clapped his hands smartly, and the door of the cottage opened and out came the boy Weeip. He wore a cream linen sailor-suit, although he still kept a woven headband around his hair for decoration. He looked at Eyre cautiously, and then bowed his head. 'Welcome, Mr Wakasah.'

'Well, well,' said Eyre, 'welcome yourself. I see you've found yourself a comfortable billet with Mr Willis. How are you?'

'You're very well, aren't you, Weeip?' Christopher interrupted.

'Yes, sah, very well. Prays beetroot God.'

'Bring us some fresh tea, would you, Weeip, there's a good chap?' said Christopher.

'And buns, sah?'

'Eyre?' asked Christopher.

'No thank you. No buns for me,' said Eyre. He watched Weeip go back into the house, and then raised an eyebrow at Christopher.

'It's everything you think it is,' said Christopher. 'An innocent young savage who asks no questions and will do anything I require of him.'

'Have you given up Daisy Frockford?'

'Of course not. One must still have lady companions to take to dinners; although I must say that I've been invited to precious few since I've been back. Being a hero may be one thing; all fine and good; but being a hero's helper is of no distinction whatever.'

'You *are* jealous,' Eyre chided him.

'No, I'm not. I've told you I'm not. I just wish that I'd never gone along at all. I wish I'd never set eyes on you; or that damned Joolonga; or Dogger; or Midgegooroo.'

'Or Arthur Mortlock?' asked Eyre. 'We mustn't forget about poor old Arthur.'

Christopher made a face to show that he didn't particularly care to talk about Arthur Mortlock. But Eyre said, 'It was an odd thing, you know, about Arthur.'

'What was odd?'

'Well, despite the fact that Joolonga claimed to have killed him with his pointing-bone, he suffered the symptoms of a man who had swallowed a quantity of corrosive sublimate. You know, the vomiting, the diarrhoea.'

'I don't really wish to be reminded,' said Christopher.

'Well, nor do I,' said Eyre. 'But, it was still odd. And the oddest thing was that when I went through my medicine-chest, I discovered that my bottle of corrosive sublimate was empty; although I had used none of it during the journey.'

'In that case,' Christopher retorted, 'it seems to me that the likeliest explanation is that he inadvertently poisoned himself. He would have drunk anything, that man. Methylated spirits, horse liniments. A yoxter like him wouldn't have cared.'

'I can't see anyone drinking corrosive sublimate on purpose,' said Eyre. 'My God, the smell of it alone would have put him off. Apart from the bottle, which was ridged, and clearly marked corrosive poison.'

Christopher drummed his fingers sharply on the table. 'I'm afraid the mentality of people like Arthur Mortlock is a closed book, as far as I'm concerned. And even if you were to open it, you would probably find that it contained nothing but blank pages.'

'You're being very unkind to him,' said Eyre.

'The man was a scoundrel; a ticket-of-leave man, on the run. He could have had all of us arrested and hung.'

'Christopher, why on earth are you so nervous?'

'Nervous?' Christopher demanded. His face was grey and glistening, like an oyster. 'Of course I'm not nervous. Why in the world should I be nervous? I haven't been very well, that's all, since coming back from that expedition. I was down with influenza for two weeks, and the doctor said that I was quite fortunate not to go down with pneumonia.'

'Luckier than Arthur, then,' said Eyre.

Christopher said, 'I have no desire to talk about Arthur. He was a low scoundrel, that's all; and whatever happened to him, and however it happened, he got only what he deserved.'

Eyre considered asking Christopher straight out whether he had poisoned Arthur; but then he thought better of it. After all, back here in Adelaide, it did seem rather improbable that Christopher should have murdered him. What possible motive could he have had? Perhaps Arthur had made homosexual advances to him, and Christopher had poisoned him as a punishment; but Christopher was not ashamed of his inclinations, and had made no secret of them, even to Eyre. Therefore, the motive could not have been blackmail either: a threat by Arthur to reveal that he was a catamite.

Eyre decided to hold his peace; and so when Weeip brought the tea, and poured it out for them, they discussed nothing more than Eyre's journey across the desert, and even this was done awkwardly and with an exaggerated lack of interest on Christopher's part. At last, after half an hour, Eyre stood up and held out his hand.

'I have to get back. The artist from the *Illustrated Post* wants to make a drawing of me.'

Christopher shook his hand, and nodded. 'Being a hero has its chores, no doubt.'

'You won't lose touch altogether, will you?' Eyre asked him.

Christopher said, 'Of course not. But you'll be very busy, won't you?'

'Never too busy to talk to a friend.'

'An erstwhile friend,' Christopher corrected him.

'Well, whatever you like,' said Eyre.

Eyre retrieved his bicycle and began to wheel it away. He

turned once, but Christopher had picked up his newspaper again, and was making a big show of ignoring him. All right, he thought; if that's the way you feel; and he mounted up and prepared to ride off.

At that moment, however, Weeip came running up to him.

'You drop your kerchy, Mr Wakasah.'

'That's not mine,' said Eyre, peering at the crumpled handkerchief.

'No, sah, I know sah. But I have to bring it to speak to you, sah.'

'You want to speak to me?'

Weeip glanced anxiously back towards the verandah, but Christopher was still ostentatiously absorbed in his newspaper.

'Can you come tonight, sah; at seven? Then look in the second window at the back.'

'What? What for?'

Weeip said anxiously, 'You will know then, all about Mr Mortlock, sah. Bless his hole. Please come. Then you see. Mr Willis is good to me, sah; take care of me. Please come. Don't blame him, sah.'

Just then, Christopher looked around to see why Eyre hadn't yet bicycled away; and Weeip crammed the dirty handkerchief into Eyre's hand, and ran back towards the house. Eyre, baffled, waved the handkerchief at Christopher to show why he had been delayed. Christopher gave him a half-hearted wave in return.

Eyre made his way back into Adelaide quite slowly. He was puzzled by Christopher's prickly behaviour, and yet not completely surprised. Upsetting Christopher was not like upsetting a man-friend. It was like distressing a lover. But what could he possibly see through the second window at the back at seven o' clock in the evening, which would explain everything about Arthur Mortlock? Had Christopher really had anything to do with Arthur's death, or not? And even if he had, what could be discovered by

489

creeping back in the evening, and looking through his window?

He was so preoccupied that he allowed the front wheel of his bicycle to get caught in a rut in the road, and he staggered and hopped on one leg and nearly fell off.

Thirty-Eight

There was one more visit to be made; and this visit more than any other made Eyre understand that the purpose of his journey across Australia had been accomplished. For while he had failed to discover the inland sea; and while he had failed to bring back a medicine-man to bury Yanluga; he had been initiated into an Aborigine tribe, and could therefore bury Yanluga himself, according to the proper rituals. And as for the inland sea; well, Captain Sturt himself could go and look for that, if it really existed. The seagulls had been flying north, but then they could have been seeking nothing more than moth larvae, or a swampy patch on the salt-lake where worms could be pecked; and perhaps that was all that Captain Sturt would find.

Eyre talked to Lathrop Lindsay's secretary, at his offices on Morphett Street; and Lathrop Lindsay's secretary talked to Lathrop Lindsay; and Lathrop Lindsay sent back a message saying that there would be no objections of a material nature if Yanluga's body were to be exhumed from its resting-place next to Lathrop Lindsay's favourite horse, and re-buried according to tribal rituals. In fact, a complimentary article would appear in the following day's

Observer, praising Mr Lindsay for his 'humanitarianism and religious liberality'.

Eyre went along that afternoon with four hired Aborigines and several shovels, and in an unexpected drizzle, they dug up Yanluga's coffin from beneath the gum-trees, and laid it on the wet grass, and opened it with a pick. Yanluga lay inside, crouched like a huge spider, half-skeletal, his eyeless face grinning at the Bible which had been interred beside him.

'The Bible,' said Eyre, picking it up. 'And yet àll of this poor boy's religion was told by word of mouth, and painted on rocks.'

The hired labourers stood around in their soaking-wet shirts and stared at him uncomprehendingly. They were city Aborigines; black boys who had learned to make a living by scrounging from white people; selling rubbish and clearing out stables. They knew very little about tribal myths, or what had happened during the dreaming. They had already become what Yonguldye had feared all Aborigines would one day become; inferior white men lacking in tribal knowledge, or any of the skills of survival. With them, all the ancient crafts would die away in two or three generations. Some of the languages and myths had already been forgotten, or erased by epidemics of tuberculosis brought ashore by white settlers. A whole way of life was dying, and Eyre knew that the funeral he was giving Yanluga was only a personal gesture that would have no effect on the greater course of history.

The coffin was carried to a sacred place close to the reed beds on the River Torrens, where black-and-white cows grazed, and the gums twisted into the water. The rain had cleared but the soil was still heavy and aromatic and damp as the Aborigines dug Yanluga a grave. After an hour of excavation, Eyre and one of the boys lifted the corpse out of the coffin, and then set it down on a bed of branches at the bottom of the hole, its knees drawn up in a sitting position. The body was so light and brittle, Eyre could hardly believe it had once been human. One of the hands broke off as Eyre was bending it into the ritual position, and the finger bones burst out from the tightened skin like seeds from a pod.

Eyre cried out over the grave, loudly and unembarrassed, the lamentations that were due to a dead warrior. One of the labourers joined in; and for almost twenty minutes they cried and keened together over the corpse that had once been Yanluga. Then they covered the crouched-up body with earth, and brushed his grave with twigs and branches, and lit a fire beside it. The labourers had been paid to keep the fire burning for a week; and Eyre would revisit it from time to time; and say the prayers that would ensure Yanluga's eventual arrival in the land beyond Karta, the isle of the dead, to join Ngurunderi.

'Yanluga,' said Eyre, quietly. Across the river, the cows moved slowly through the long grass. 'Yanluga, you have led me to discover things that I never believed were possible. You have shown me a world that I can still scarcely comprehend. But I promise you that I will always keep faith with you; that my brotherhood with the Aborigine people will never be broken, not until the day I die; and join you beyond the sunset.'

He stood there for over an hour, while the fire smoked and twisted in the early-afternoon wind. This, more than anything else, seemed like the end of the journey. He took off his hat, and closed his eyes, and said the words of the funeral prayer which Winja had taught him, during the days of his *engwura*.

'You will live beyond the stars,
You will live in the land of the moons.
Happiness and friendship will always be yours.
And the laughter of those you left behind will always
    rise to you.'

At last, he left the graveside, and walked back along the path which would lead him to Adelaide. The rain began again, suddenly: a scattering of silver droplets on the dark earth track. The coinage of sadness, the currency of repentance, and the specie of tears.

He had booked a room at Coppius' Hotel; and during the early evening he moved his belongings there from Mrs Crane's notions shop. By half-past-six he was both tired and hungry, and thinking of dinner at the Rundle Street Restaurant. But, as he undressed to take a bath, he remembered what Weeip had said, about going out to Christopher's house at seven o' clock.

He was undecided. If he were to dress again, and risk missing his dinner, he could probably get out to the racecourse and back. But the Rundle Street Restaurant closed early; as most restaurants did; and if he came back very late, he would be lucky to get even a bowlful of warmed-up broth.

He looked at himself in the cheval-glass in the corner of his hotel-room. Well, he thought, there's no point in beating about the bushes; do you want dinner or do you want to know who murdered Arthur Mortlock? The thin figure in the long white combination underwear stared back at him seriously. It looked like a figure that could do with dinner. But then he had never taken very much notice of what images in mirrors had to say for themselves.

A chilly wind had got up as he bicycled out towards the racetrack again. It was prematurely dark now; and there were random spots of rain flying in the air. He hoped very much that he wouldn't meet up with a drunken Aborigine, or one of the cosh boys who occasionally attacked evening travellers. His journey had left him nearly two stones lighter than when he had set out, and he was still decidedly weak. Captain Sturt had called him 'all horns and hide', which was how local farmers described a starved yearling.

At last he reached the racecourse, and left his bicycle on the ground, its front wheel still spinning. He could see the lamplight shining through the orange calico blinds of Christopher's house from quite a long way away, silhouetting the branches of the grove of gums in which it was set. The rain clattered harder against the bushes, and something rustled and jumped; a bird or a joey or a dingo pup. Behind the mountains, the sky was oddly light, where the rainclouds had begun to clear, but here it was still dark and still furious, and the rain was sweeping down even more noisily. Wet and hungry, his collar turned up, Eyre made his way around to the back of Christopher's cottage, and trod as stealthily as he could through the unkempt garden, lifting his feet up like a performing pony so that he wouldn't trip up in the weeds.

He reached the side of the house, and leaned against it, breathing hard. More rain poured down, and the guttering at the back began to splatter into the rain-barrel. Eyre took out his watch and peered at it by a thin crack of light which penetrated the cottage's blinds. Two minutes to seven o' clock. He had only just got here in time; although so far he was at a loss to see how he was going to be able to look inside the house, with every single blind drawn. His stomach gurgled, and he was beginning dearly to wish that he had never come. Let Arthur's death remain a mystery, he thought. So much of what had happened in the outback had been without reason or explanation; as if it were a mysterious land with physical laws of its own. How many times had explorers returned baffled from Australia's interior? It was a continent which defied normal interpretation, a land of superstition and inverted logic. Perhaps Arthur had done no more than fall victim to that logic, and a destiny which this upside-down country had been keeping in store for him ever since he was born.

It was seven o' clock. Eyre could hear talking inside the house, and the shuffling of feet on the boarded floors. But another five minutes passed, and still the blinds remained tightly closed. He decided to give Weeip only two or three minutes more, and then leave. The rain had become steady now, steady and cold, and he was shivering.

He was just about to move, however, when the blind closest to him was lifted by an inch, and a pair of dark eyes peeped out into the night. It was Weeip. Eyre waved his hand quickly, and Weeip blinked to show that he had seen him. Then he disappeared from the window and went back into the middle of the room; but left the blind slightly raised.

Eyre was tall, but not quite tall enough to reach the window. He felt around in the long wet grass, and at last found a wooden fruit-crate which had been left beside the rain-barrel. He upended it, and cautiously stepped up, gripping the window-sill so that he didn't overbalance backwards.

The window was partly steamed up, but Eyre could still see clearly into the room. It was a bathroom, very spartan, with a bare floor and a rag rug, and an old-fashioned zinc tub, the kind of bath in which Marat had been assassinated. Beside the bath was a tall enamelled jug, full of freshly steaming water. On the far wall was a crucified Christ, in bronze.

Weeip was kneeling beside the bath, naked. His penis was erect. He had filled the bath with hot water and now he was arranging the soap and the towels. Almost immediately, as Eyre watched, Christopher walked in, wrapped in a striped Indian robe, maroon and green, the kind which travellers were offered for sale whenever their ships docked at Trivandrum or Colombo. He said something to Weeip, touching the boy's shoulder, and then walked across the room and back again. At length he leaned over, testing the water in the tub, and smiled. Weeip stood up, and Christopher reached down with his wet hand and clasped his erection, rubbing it up and down two or three times and then laughing when the boy shivered.

Now Christopher loosened the tie around his waist, still smiling. He was facing Eyre directly, and Eyre flinched, certain that Christopher would notice his eyes looking in at the bathroom window. But Christopher must have had his mind on his youthful lover alone; for he smiled, and then laughed, and moved away out of Eyre's line of sight. Weeip stood up, and followed him, and then reappeared again, tugging at Christopher's sleeve. It was obvious that he was trying to get his master to stand in front of the window.

495

But what am I supposed to see? Eyre asked himself. Two catamites bathing each other? Is that all? And what can this possibly have to do with Arthur Mortlock? But he could see Weeip glancing towards the window making sure that he was still there; and frowning; and so he decided to stay for just a minute or two longer.

Now Weeip suddenly started to dance around, and tease Christopher, dodging out of reach whenever Christopher put out a hand. Christopher at last held his wrist, and stepped back into sight. Weeip quietened down, and approached his master submissively, and put his arms around his waist. Christopher kissed the boy's curly head, and must have said something endearing, for Weeip nodded.

At last, Weeip managed to draw Christopher around so that his back was towards the window. Eyre saw Weeip's hands loosening Christopher's robe, and the tie fall to the floor. Then Weeip slowly tugged the robe away from Christopher's shoulders, and drew it down to his waist.

Eyre had been unsettled enough by the sight of Weeip and Christopher kissing and embracing; but what was now revealed was a hundred times more horrifying.

He stood in the rain on that lopsided fruit-box, his mouth open in shock. Then he stepped back, losing his footing for a moment in the overgrown garden; stumbling; but recovering himself enough to return the box to where he had found it; and to make off through the gum-grove in the same high-stepping way he had come.

He found his bicycle and awkwardly wiped the rain off the saddle, but he was too dumbfounded to ride it. Instead he wheeled it back towards Adelaide; as the evening lightness at last broke through, and the puddly ruts in the track turned to quicksilver.

Weeip must adore his master; both adore and respect him; and do anything to keep him safe. Otherwise he would never have arranged for Eyre to see what he had seen tonight. It had been an extraordinary act of loyalty on Weeip's part; and more than that, a supreme act of love; although Eyre found acts of love between men to be almost as mysterious as the inland sea. It had been an act of trust in Eyre, too, a trust that had first been forged out in the desert.

It was quite clear to Eyre now that it was Christopher who had killed Arthur Mortlock; and that poor Joolonga had been quite mistaken in thinking that he had done it with his pointing-bone. Joolonga had probably pointed his bone at every one of them, but had convinced himself when Arthur had begun to die that it was Arthur alone who was really guilty; and that it was Arthur alone who was being sacrificed to Ngurunderi.

Eyre also knew that he would do nothing further. He would forget Arthur and as far as possible he would forget Christopher. Christopher had already been punished enough for one lifetime; and it could only have been desperation that had made him take such a risk.

Eyre cursed himself for not having noticed what was going on during the course of the expedition. He had realised that Arthur and Christopher had never got on particularly well; but if only he had begun to understand why.

For when he had looked in at the bathroom window, Eyre had seen that Christopher's bare back was scarred with the criss-cross weals and twisted tissues that identified an ex-convict. Christopher must have been a ticket-of-leave man, like Arthur; perhaps they had even been imprisoned together at Macquarie Harbour, and Arthur, after a while, had recognised him. Perhaps Arthur had simply guessed from one or two words in Christopher's vocabulary. In any case, it was likely that Arthur had marked him for a yoxter, like himself. And what had he threatened? Exposure, unless Christopher paid him? Or set him up with a job, perhaps, and a place to stay, and a never-ending supply of rum money? Whatever it had been, Christopher had decided to save himself from the sweated anxiety of interminable blackmail, and the terrifying threat of having to return to prison.

After a while, when the lights of the city came into view, Eyre mounted up on his bicycle and began to pedal. His tyres splashed through the puddles. Knowing for certain that Christopher had killed Arthur, and why, was a huge relief. He began to sing as he rode for the first time since he had got back.

'All round my hat, I will wear the green willow
All round my hat, for a twelvemonth and a day . . .'

He was back on Rundle Street in time for a bowl of green-pea soup and a large pork chop, topsidey as they used to say, with an egg on top. He drank a quart of stout, and then went back to Coppius' Hotel for a hot bath and a long sleep.

He was accosted on his way back by several prostitutes; some of them smartly bonneted and pretty. The girls of Hindley Street had become a public embarrassment in Adelaide lately; and several respectable citizens had written to Governor Grey and complained that there were more women of disrepute than the municipality's population could possibly warrant, especially if it had any pretensions to morality at all.

One dark-haired girl linked arms with Eyre and skipped along beside him, nudging him with her breast and smiling and winking most invitingly.

'Give you the best time you've ever had, darling,' she coaxed him.'Get your gooseberries in such a lather you won't know whether you're here or Sunday.'

On the steps of Coppius' Hotel, Eyre at last managed to disengage himself, and shake his head. 'Not tonight,' he told her, and kissed her on the forehead.

'Give us a deaner, then, for tea,' asked the girl.

Eyre gave her a shilling, and she cocked her bonnet at him and twirled off. He watched her go, and then climbed the steps to the hotel foyer with a smile of memory, rather than amusement.

Thirty-Nine

It was to be the wedding of the year; the most spectacular social event in Adelaide's calendar for 1842. Even Lathrop, who could still be tetchy with Eyre whenever his heart was playing him up, and who had been known to refer to his future son-in-law after two or three brandies at the Commerce Club as a 'penny gentleman', insisted on marquees, and orchestras, and a special white carriage shipped from Van Diemen's Land, where it had once been the property of Lady Jane Franklin.

Eyre had spent most of the six or seven months after his return from Western Australia writing up his memoirs for the *Observer*, who paid him £350 in regular instalments for the privilege. He said nothing of Arthur Mortlock in his story; save that he was 'a trusted family friend from London'; and that he had died 'of a stomach-complaint, brought about by eating bad shellfish'. He did however dramatise their escape from the great corroboree at Yarrakinna, adding a few more skirmishes with the Aborigines for good measure, and including a long and genuinely heartfelt obituary for Dogger McConnell.

'Was there a man more natural and brave, a man whose loyalty to his friends and associates was of such a degree that he saw in danger only delight, that he might serve them more truly, and in death only accomplishment, that he had demonstrated the great nobility of his spirit? The last name upon his lips was that of his beloved wife; and though he has no memorial in the desert, that name will be forever engraved upon the air, even as he spoke it, just as the legends and myths of the first Australians are still spoken by the winds, and by the dust-storms, and by the creatures of the wild.'

When he had written those words, and sat back to sprinkle sand across his manuscript, he thought of Dogger sitting upright in his saddle, transfixed by that terrible death-spear, even as his last words echoed across the plain. *'Brayvo, Hicks!'*

Eyre was given a house on Grenfell Street, overlooking Hindmarsh Square. It was a smart, flat-fronted house of native bluestone, with white-painted shutters, and a small enclosed front garden. His office to begin with was a stuffy little room in the old part of Government House, so positioned that whenever Governor Grey's luncheon was being cooked, most of the smells wafted in through the window, but stubbornly refused to waft out again. There was also a cockatoo which habitually perched on the top of the open sash, and chattered to him irritatingly when he was working, and occasionally flew into the room to speckle his papers with guano.

Eventually, however, Eyre was promised a new house out at Moorundie, near Blanchetown, on the River Murray, where Governor Grey believed he could do the most useful work in helping the Aborigines to cope with the white invasion of their territory.

'We cannot hold back the eventual settlement of all of South Australia,' Grey would say to Eyre, at least once a week, whenever they met for sherry. 'So, rather than preside over the indiscriminate destruction of the Aborigines, we must arrange for their survival—which, in line with the policy of the Colonial Office, means that we must assimilate the blackfellows hook, line, and sinker into the British community. They already have rights as British citizens, rights granted to them generously and without stint. In their turn, they must behave like British citizens.'

Eyre thought to himself: Yonguldye had been right. The magical age of the Aborigines, which had lasted for thousands and thousands of years, was finally over. The great ark of Australia had been boarded, and captured, and towed into the harbour of European commerce.

Almost every weekend, and two or three evenings a week, he would make a call at Waikerie Lodge to pay court to Charlotte. They would have supper; some of Mrs McMurty's leek-and-potato soup; and perhaps mutton cutlets, with carrots and turnips; or sheep's trotters; or mutton collops with cabbage; or boiled sheep's cheek; and everybody knew very well that if they complained about the persistence of lamb on the menu that they would be immediately chastened by Lathrop Lindsay's famous recitation of Thomson's poem about 'the harmless race' whose 'incessant bleatings run around the hills'.

Afterwards, in the parlour, there might be singing; or Lathrop would read from the newspapers any selected titbits which he thought might be amusing and instructive to his wife and family; always concluding with the market prices for sheep. Then Eyre and Charlotte would be allowed a half-an-hour by themselves, although the doorway to the hall would always be left wide open; and quite often Mrs Lindsay would sit sewing in the living-room opposite and smile at them indulgently from time to time.

Charlotte had matured in a year; she was not only prettier but wiser, too, and more independent. She had grown her hair longer, so that it curled into masses and masses of shiny blonde ringlets, which she tied with velvet ribbons. And there was a slight hint of voluptuousness about her which Eyre found pleasantly disturbing, although he did occasionally wonder whether it had anything to do with any experiences she might have had while he was away on his heroic journey.

They went to church together regularly at the Trinity Church at the western end of North Terrace; Eyre in the fashionably tight black morning-suit he had bought with his first payment from the *Observer*; Charlotte in grey watered silk. They were always applauded as they emerged, Eyre for his newly won fame, and Charlotte for her beauty, and both of them for giving Adelaide the gleeful anticipation of the most lavish wedding that the colony had ever seen. It was generally rumoured that Lathrop was spending more than £2,500 on the catering, and that a special order of French champagne was already on its way from Epernay, in France.

Eyre and Charlotte were sitting out on the verandah of Waikerie Lodge in early March, drinking lemon tea and eating Maids of Honour, when the subject of children came up. It was only eleven days now to the wedding, and two men in faded blue overalls were pacing the lawns with one of Lathrop's gardeners to determine where they were going to pitch the largest of the three marquees. The Lindsay's pet kangaroos hopped along beside the wattles; and there was an aromatic smell of eucalyptus in the afternoon air.

Charlotte was dressed prettily in cream lace, with yellow ribbons. The sun shone through the brim of her straw bonnet and illuminated it like a halo. The angel of Adelaide, thought Eyre, and felt most content. He had been putting on weight since his return last year, and he decided that his white waistcoat must have shrunk a little.

'I think five is a good number,' said Charlotte, sipping tea.

'Five what, my darling?' asked Eyre. Then he said, 'That marquee is going to be absolutely enormous; look how far away they've placed that marker.'

'Children, of course,' Charlotte replied.

'Children?' blinked Eyre.

'Yes, five children. Three boys, and two girls. A family of seven.'

'Well,' said Eyre. Then, 'Well, I must say I hadn't really thought about it.'

'But we must. And we *can*, now that you're so successful; and such a hero. And when we're out at Moorundie, or wherever else you're posted, we're going to be glad of the company. Oh Eyre, I can almost see them now! Five, happy shining faces!'

Eyre was silent for a very long time. The day was still bright; the birds still chittered and cackled in the stringybark gums around the house; Charlotte still talked about how she would teach the children to ride, and to play the piano, and what fun it was going to be at Christmas. But a sudden dark feeling had risen up inside him, like a strong cold undercurrent, lifting him up and then dragging him back to the past.

'*You are one of my people now,*' Winja had said, on that grey windy day when they had parted. '*Therefore your son is one of my people; and your son's son.*'

And Eyre had held Winja close to him, and said, '*My son is yours.*'

A pledge, a holy and magical pledge. A promise that could never be broken. *My son is yours.*

He was quiet and withdrawn for the rest of the day. At last, after supper, when Mrs Lindsay was snoozing in her chair in the living-room and the servants were clearing up the dishes, Charlotte asked him what was wrong.

'You're not sickening, are you?'

Eyre shook his head.

'But you're so pale; and you haven't said a word all evening. It wasn't my talk of children, was it? That hasn't put you off? Oh, Eyre, if there's anything worrying you my darling, you must tell me! We must never keep secrets from each other.'

Eyre hesitated for a moment. Then he stood up, and went over to the parlour door, and gently closed it. Charlotte looked at him anxiously in the light from the engraved-glass lamp. A diamond pendant sparkled on the soft curve of her cleavage, and he thought that he had never seen her look so enticing.

'Listen, Charlotte,' he said. He could hear his own voice in his ear, flat and expressionless, as if he were standing on the opposite side of the room. 'When I was travelling across the desert . . . well, certain things happened to me. I haven't written about them in the newspaper, because I wanted to keep them to myself.'

'What things, my darling? What do you mean? Was it something terrible?'

He lowered his eyes. 'Not by the standards by which I was living at the time. In fact, what happened was quite uplifting. Quite spiritual. It gave me the hope and the faith to be able to finish my journey, and to survive. But . . .

503

well, how can I explain it? Now that I'm back here in white society, certain commitments I made might seem rather surprising. Rather difficult for other people to understand.'

Charlotte said, in a barely audible voice, 'Tell me. Eyre, you must tell me.'

He hesitated, and then he said, 'Well, you remember I told you that I was initiated into an Aboriginal tribe.'

'Yes.'

'It was quite a painful initiation. I mean physically painful. They—scarred me. Scarred my body. It's all part of the ceremony. All part of showing that you're a man, and that you're able to stand suffering without crying out. Also—well, they consider the scars decorative, and beautiful.

Charlotte whispered, 'You have scars?'

'Yes.'

'Why didn't you tell me? Why didn't you tell me before? I would have understood.'

Eyre turned away. 'I was going to tell you. In fact, I was going to *show* you. But somehow I could always think of some excuse why I should wait until later. I thought you wouldn't exactly take to them. I don't know. I just felt that they were something secret, something which I didn't truly understand myself.'

This time, the silence between them was even longer. The ormolu clock on the mantelpiece ticked tiredly, and outside they could hear the clopping of horses as the groom returned them to their stable. Somewhere in the servants' quarters, an Aborigine woman was singing some sweet, monotonous song. At last, though, Charlotte stood up, with a rustle of petticoats, and went to the parlour door, and opened it, and looked out. Then she came back and took Eyre's hand.

'Show me,' she said. 'Mother's still asleep. Show me now. I want to see.'

'Charlotte—' Eyre began, but she pressed the fingers of her right hand against his lips, to silence him.

'Show me,' she insisted.

Quickly, with several sharp tugs, Eyre loosened his collar, stripped off his necktie, and unbuttoned his shirt. Then he opened his underwear, and bared to Charlotte his chest, with its whorls and lines and zigzags of bumpy purplish scars; each one of which had been drawn by his Aborigine kinsmen, and rubbed with ash.

Charlotte stared at them, and then gradually traced them, every one of them, with her fingers. She looked up at Eyre, and her eyes were glistening with tears.

'They're beautiful,' she said. 'They're simply beautiful.'

'You don't *mind* them?' he asked.

'Why should I mind them? They show that the Aborigines think you're a hero; as well as the British. What other man in Adelaide has scars like these, to prove what he's done? I'm proud of them, Eyre; I shall cherish them. And I shall cherish you.'

She kissed his chest four or five times, and then stood up on tiptoe and kissed his lips. 'You should have shown me before, my darling,' she murmured.

Eyre said, 'There's something else.'

'Tell me. Come on, Eyre, you promised to tell me, and so you must.'

'My—' he started. Then he closed his eyes, and blurted out quickly, 'They also circumcised me.'

'Yes?' asked Charlotte, although she blushed a little. 'And is that enough to stop me from loving you? Eyre, don't you understand, I love you; dearly, and passionately; whether you are scarred or whole. I always have done, and I think I always will.'

He took a breath, and said mechanically, 'They circumcised me with a sharp knife made out of a cockle-shell. They also . . . well, I believe the correct term is sub-incision.'

'What does that mean? Eyre, please.'

Eyre knew now that there was nothing for it but to show her. They had attempted to make love before, on that hideous night when Yanluga had died; and there was no question that Charlotte was a full-blooded young woman

505

who expected sex as a vigorous part of her coming marriage. It would also be impossibly unfair of him to expect her to go to the altar without knowing what Winja and Ningina had done to him.

Pray God that her mother doesn't wake up, he thought, and opened his trousers.

Charlotte slowly sat down on the brocade-covered sofa. She stared at his penis so intently that he went red, and began to perspire. I'm embarrassed, he thought; me, who rode naked for hundreds of miles across the plain of Bunda Bunda. Embarrassed, and for some extraordinary reason, humiliated.

But Charlotte reached out with a gentle hand and grasped him, lifting him up so that she could see how deeply the Aborigines had cut into him. The urethra was open all the way from the glans to the testicles; open, and glistening with the lubrication of nervousness and passion.

'Will this . . . does this make it impossible for us to have children?' asked Charlotte, in a trembling voice.

Eyre shook his head. 'No. All the Aborigines have it done; at least, all the Aborigines that I met. It makes no difference, physically; and none of them seem to be lacking in offspring.'

Charlotte stroked him, with exquisite slowness, and he rose in her hand. 'If it makes no difference,' she said, 'then I shall accept it proudly.' She kept on stroking him, still slowly, until his penis reared up like a red sceptre, with a deeply cleft shaft.

'No,' he said, unsteadily. 'No more. We only have eleven more days to wait.' And with extreme difficulty he pushed himself back into his tight evening trousers, and buttoned himself up again. Charlotte touched the thick protrusion on his trouser-leg, and unexpectedly giggled.

'I think it's marvellous,' she said. 'Eyre, it's *marvellous!* I shall be the only lady in the whole of Adelaide to have a baby the Aborigine way! Isn't it exciting! Oh, it excites me! Oh, Eyre! I can't wait eleven days!'

He kissed her on the forehead. She tasted of perfume.

'I'm afraid that we shall have to,' he said. Then he kissed her again, and she lifted her mouth to him, and kissed him in return, her hard white teeth pressing against his lips.

'Now,' he said, 'we come to the most difficult part of all.'

'What?' she asked, her eyes bright, 'Eyre, if it's only as difficult as scars, or a circumcision . . .'

He sat down. He looked at her, and tried to smile. She was so expectant, so alive, so gleeful. How was he going to tell her that he had solemnly promised to give his first-born son away to Winja and Ningina, to be raised as a member of their tribe for ever more?

'It concerns the baby,' he said, his mouth dry.

'But we're going to have *five* babies!'

'Yes,' he agreed. 'Five. But it concerns the first. Well, the first son, at least.'

Why did he have to tell her? Why did he have to give the baby away at all? Who was going to force Eyre Walker, the Protector of Murray River Aborigines, a great white celebrity and a man of influence and income, to give away his first boy-child to a pack of blacks?

Only Eyre knew why; only Winja knew why. The answer lay in the desert, and the scrub and the dry limestone mountains. The answer lay in the integrity of people who have to depend on whatever they can find, and whatever help they can offer each other. Eyre's destiny had become mysteriously interlinked with that of the Aborigines from the first moment he had spoken to Yanluga as a human being deserving of equal respect; instead of thinking of him as an animal or a savage. He realised that there was a terrible primitive justice to what he was going to have to do. He had taken one boy away; and now he would have to give them a boy in return. There was no escaping it. Not if he was going to be able to think of himself as a man of honour; as he had always hoped he would be.

But he looked at Charlotte, sitting next to him; and she

507

was so excited and aroused and pretty, thrilled with the erotic naughtiness of having touched Eyre's exposed body, and intoxicated by the thought of marrying him in just eleven days' time; and he couldn't say it. How could he explain to her what had happened out there in the desert? How close he had been to death, and despair? How could he tell her about the magnificence of the dreaming; the majesty of Baiame; the thirsty enormity of a land which shimmered with mirages and throbbed with magic?

It was inexplicable; and his duty to Winja and his people was inexplicable. And so he said, hoarsely, 'Our first son, I'd—well, I'd like his second name to be Lathrop.'

And after Charlotte had kissed him in delight, and run across the hall way to tell her mother how marvellous he was, he stood up, and thrust his hands into his pockets, and stared up at the portrait of Lathrop's grandfather Duncan over the fireplace. There was laughter in the house, and the clattering of feet up and down the stairs. But all Eyre could think of was his son, not yet conceived, not yet born, but whose destiny was already entwined with this strange continent as surely and as inextricably as his own had always been.

The parlour door opened wide, and Mrs Lindsay came in, followed by Charlotte, and Lathrop Lindsay himself, and Mrs Lindsay held open her arms for Eyre and said, 'My darling Eyre. What a fine boy you are. You can't possibly imagine how happy you've made us. *Lathrop!* How marvellous! And how generous, too!'

Eyre held her in his arms, and smiled over her shoulder at Charlotte, but it took all of his strength not to cry.

Epilogue

On August 15, 1844, Captain Charles Sturt left Adelaide with an expedition of his own in an attempt to find the inland sea. He was so confident of his success that he carried with him a boat with which he hoped he and his companions would eventually sail from one side of the sea to the other.

Heading eastwards at first to avoid the salt-lakes which had bogged down Eyre, he made camp at Broken Hill, and then headed north. As each day dawned, however, all he could see in front of him was a country of 'salty spinifex and sand ridges, driving for hundreds of miles into the very heart of the interior as if they would never end.'

The daily temperature was higher than 130 degrees in the shade, and nearly 160 degrees in the sun.

At last, 400 miles north of Broken Hill, after crossing a desert of crippling stones, and miles of matted spinifex, Sturt was confronted with what would later be called the Simpson Desert. Ridges of deep-red sand succeeded each other 'like the waves of the sea'. Sturt realised that he could go no further with the resources he had brought with him, and was forced to turn back.

The expedition broke his health and his pride. In 1853, he returned to England, where his journals about his explorations had made him a celebrity, and it was in England that he died, in 1869.

He left many letters before his death. One, which was opened by his executors, was addressed to Mr Eyre Walker. When they read its contents, Captain Sturt's executors decided that it would probably be prudent to destroy it, since its contents, although rather mysterious, might constitute an admission of liability which could cause complications with the distribution of the Sturt estate.

So it was that on a foggy January afternoon in Chancery

Lane, London, twenty-nine years after Eyre had set out from Government House in Adelaide, the last words about the great corroboree at Yarrakinna were burned in an office fireplace; Captain Sturt's firm sloping script gradually being licked and scorched and charred into ashes; the simple words 'Forgive me.'

Empress

For Wiescka

When Henry came home that thundery afternoon and stood in the hallway shaking his umbrella and called out, 'India, my darling! They've given me India!' her immediate thought was not of palaces or elephants or princes with diamonds in their foreheads. As if they had flown open in her mind with a sudden and general clatter, she thought of those black tinplate boxes on the back shelves of the Darling general store; and how she had breathed in their mysterious dust-dry pungencies; and wondered what kind of extraordinary country it could be where people ate foods that tasted of shoe-leather and gunpowder and dried flowers and fire.

She had seen real live elephants, of course, whenever the circus had come to town, and she had seen pictures in magazines of snake-charmers and bazaars and the Taj Mahal. But prising open those lids and smelling those spices had given her the immediate understanding that for all of its farness, and for all of its strangeness, India was not a story but *real*.

And now Henry had returned home with rain spots on his shoulders and cheerfully announced that to all intents and purposes this far, strange country was actually *his*, and consequently *hers*, too.

'Fenugreek and cumin,' she recited, holding out her arms for him. 'Chili and turmeric and garam masala.'

'What?' he laughed.

She kissed him. His sidewhiskers were wet. 'India!' she told him. 'India!'

Yet – when she lay in their brass-pillared bed that night and Henry slept – she realized that Fate had brought her India

I

much earlier in her life. Fate had brought her India almost five years before and four thousand miles away, in Kansas, in early June; that day her Uncle Casper had reappeared.

She hardly ever allowed herself to think of what had happened that summer. It still made her feel dry-mouthed and upset. She stared up at the ceiling in the overwhelming darkness and wondered if God had given her India in belated consolation for what had happened; or if what had happened had been the price that she had been obliged to pay for a dream that she had never really asked for.

I

She was balancing like a tightrope-walker on Mrs Sweeney's back fence when she heard the train whistle; but of course she didn't know that Uncle Casper was aboard it, and so she paid it no attention.

Quite apart from which, it required all of her concentration to balance on top of the fence, arms held wide, parasol held high, one foot in front of the other, swaying a little, hesitating, and then high-stepping forwards. She looked as if she couldn't be real, a pretty mechanical marionette. The sunlight shone through her long blue-and-white striped skirt, and her white cotton bonnet.

'Steady, now! Back straight!' called Mrs Sweeney. She was watching Lucy intently; as if she could will her to keep her balance. 'And whatever you do, don't look down at your feet!'

The train whistled again, high and doleful. Lucy took two more steps, paused, then another three, paused, and then teetered quickly to the guttering, and held on.

'Well, that wasn't too bad,' said Mrs Sweeney. 'Not sure what Forepaugh and Sells would've thought about it; but it'll do for me.'

She helped Lucy to jump down. Lucy tugged her skirts out of her bloomers, brushed them down, and then perched herself on a backless kitchen chair to put on her button-up boots.

'Do you think we could dance some more?' she asked Mrs Sweeney, one eye squinched up against the sun.

'Oh, no, no, I'm all danced out, thank you very much,' Mrs Sweeney told her. ''Sides, I have to go along to Leonard Judd's in just a while, and deal with his correspondence.'

Mrs Sweeney always finished up Lucy's dancing-lessons by making her balance along the fence. 'It makes your feet strong; it gives you balance.' Before she married, she had walked the slack-wire for Forepaugh and Sells, travelling all over the country. The stories she could tell, the hearts she had broken.

'Just one more waltz?' Lucy begged her. 'You know me, I could dance all day!'

Mrs Sweeney took her to the gate, and opened it. 'You're just like my Samuel. I could die dancing, he used to say! And bless him, he did! The Lord called him at the Stockbreeders' Ball, right in the middle of a polka.'

Lucy tightened the ribbons of her bonnet. 'He's still dancing, I'll bet you, somewhere in Heaven.'

'Well, that's as may be,' sniffed Mrs Sweeney. 'But not the polka. I can't see the Lord God and his Heavenly Throng dancing the polka. Not with him, anyhow.'

Lucy was never quite sure if Mrs Sweeney was serious. Her pinched, triangular face appeared to be permanently vexed, and she always wore mourning-black. But she had an irreverent Irish wit; and because of that, and because of the dancing-lessons she gave, most folk in Oak City called her the Skipping Widder. She probably wasn't much more than forty-two years old; she could have passed for sixty.

But Lucy adored Mrs Sweeney because she chattered endlessly while they danced together round and round her creaky upstairs room, one-two-three, one-two-three. Like

3

two little people on the top of a musical-box. Mrs Sweeney told her all about the dances she had been to in New York, when she was a young girl, before she had fallen with a capital F and joined the circus. Oh, those dances, my dear! White gloves, ostrich feathers, gaseliers and sparkling jewellery! High-varnished carriages, and men with collars so tall they had to spend the entire evening staring at the ceiling!

By contrast, there was very little dancing in Oak City, Kansas; and not much reason to dance, either. Oak City wasn't much more than a wind-sucked collection of wooden buildings on the Kansas Pacific railroad track between Hays City and Fort Wallace. From time to time, some of the local sodbusters got up a barndance; and every year the Army arranged a Christmas ball at Fort Hays, where a local girl might have the chance of dancing with one of the officers (but what an ignorant, spotty, bay- rum-smelling collection of stumbling young giddy-goats *they* were!).

But apart from that, only the grass danced, only the dust danced; and the only music you could hear was the roller-organ in the corner saloon, or singing in the church on Sunday mornings. '*Rock of Ages, cleave to me . . .*' Oak City had more than its fair share of sky; and more than its fair share of wind; and when there wasn't any wind, like today, it had more than its fair share of silence.

'See you next Thursday, Mrs Sweeney!'

Lucy closed the yard gate behind her, and held up her skirts as she negotiated the alley that led to the main street. Today, the street was hot and silent; not even the rattling of a buckboard disturbed the quiet. That distinctive smell of prairie filled the air: hay, dust, and cattle, intermingled with a fragrance like dried spices.

She began to walk back towards her father's store. The heels of her button-up boots echoed on the plank sidewalk. She was seventeen years old, very small-breasted, very slim-hipped, and very tall; but then her mother had been tall, too. Her hair was so fair and fine that her mother used to

4

tease her that Rumpelstiltskin had spun it. Her nose was quite long but very straight, with just a sprinkling of freckles on the bridge, and her eyes were such an intense blue that people used to look twice, because they couldn't believe that anybody could have eyes as blue as that, as if she had tinted them with two meadowsful of squeezed-out cornflowers.

The only part of her face that Lucy didn't like was her mouth. It could look pouty and sulky, even when she wasn't feeling pouty and sulky in the least.

She hummed the *German Hearts* waltz, and skipped around in a circle. *One-two-three! One-two-three!* Over at the depot, she heard the deep-chested chuffing of the train, and blossoms of black smoke rose up into the sky.

Most of the doors of the stores along Main Street were open, because of the heat and the lack of wind. Inside, the shops and offices were shadowy, and each harboured its own particular smell. The musty ripeness of the Meat Market, where the butchers chopped up steer carcasses in their derby hats and their brown-bloodied aprons; L. Judd Real Estate & Loan Agent, where Mrs Sweeney worked in the afternoons, letter-writing, all lavender-water and papers; the Helmsley Drug Store, cough-candy and cloves; J. A. Overbay's Dry Goods & Clothing, sour new denim and boot-polish.

Two of the younger butchers were leaning outside the Meat Market with their arms folded, one high-coloured and the other white as milk. They were smoking cheroots and narrowing their eyes against the brightness of the morning. Lucy knew them both: Bob Wonderly and William Zang. They had attended the Oak City school together.

'Lucy! You been dancing, you pretty thing?' the ruddy one shouted out. 'How about a dance for your old pal Bob?'

Lucy smiled at him quickly under the shadow of her hat-brim, but shook her head.

'Hey, Lucy!' the butcher-boy persisted. 'Hey, come on over here! Don't you go acting all high'n'mighty-like! Listen here, how'd you care for some ox-liver?'

His colleague exploded with mirth. 'Smack me, Bob! Ox-liver! Romance aint dead yet! Hey, look! She's walking on! Maybe you'd better ask her if she'd fancy some washed tripes thrown in!'

'You can fun,' Bob Wonderly complained. 'I'm sure glad some folks can afford to turn up their nose at it. First-grade ox-liver, damn it. Don't grow on trees.'

Lucy crossed the street, and passed the wide dusty tract of land in front of the railroad depot. As she did so, a tall broad-shouldered young man appeared from the shadows of the entrance, his chestnut-coloured hair shining bright in the sun with brilliantine. In his right hand he was carrying a heavy brown-paper parcel tied with twine: his left arm was raised to balance the weight.

She stopped and waited for him and smiled, shading her eyes against the sun.

'Jamie!' she called.

He came up to her, and set the parcel down on the ground. He wiped his forehead on his shirtsleeve. 'Ned wouldn't wait for me,' he told her. 'Said his haircut was urgent, case he met Dorothy Oosterman.'

Lucy kissed the tip of her fingers and touched Jamie on the nose. 'Didn't expect to see you in town today.'

'Oh. Well, no. I wasn't coming till tomorrow. But since Ned was coming in anyway.'

He hefted up the parcel again, and together they began to walk slowly along Main Street. She and Jamie weren't exactly courting; not formally; but when the Cullens had settled close to Oak City just over two years ago, Lucy and Jamie had immediately made friends, and everybody naturally assumed that they would marry one day. People talked about them in the same breath, 'Jamie'n'Lucy.'

'What's that?' Lucy asked Jamie, nodding towards his package. 'Not more Bibles?'

'Bibles?' said Jamie. 'Not on your life. These are law-books.'

6

'That won't please your father,' Lucy told him.

'Don't care if it doesn't,' Jamie replied. 'Respecting your father is one thing. Pleasing him, well, that's another.' He paused, and then he added, 'Specially since he's so darned difficult to please.'

Jamie's father Jerrold Cullen was religious to the point of spontaneous incandescence, and had given a Bible to every man and woman who worked for him, and a few to people who didn't. He held every word in the Bible to be true indisputable fact, and you could guarantee that even if you started talking to him about cattle-diseases, or the price of feed, he would soon be lauding the suffering of Job, or discussing how Jonah got out of the whale, or considering the lilies as they grew.

Jerrold Cullen was sorely displeased by what he regarded as Jamie's unnatural determination to be a lawyer rather than a granger, and he frequently said so. To toil on the land was divine, as far as he was concerned. Jamie should be out in God's good air, ploughing and fence-mending and branding calves, not sitting in stuffy schoolrooms squinting at lawbooks. Book-learning in Jerrold Cullen's estimation came somewhere a little lower than taking the Lord's name in vain and only a little higher than coveting thy neighbour's maidservant.

To be truthful, Lucy didn't really understand Jamie's passion for the law, either. She had tried to read some of his books on Precedent, and they were boring beyond all human reason. But she liked Jamie. She liked him because of his slow, serious manner; and she liked him because he was so tall. She stood five-feet-seven in her stockings, overlooking most of the short squat Oak City boys by almost an inch. But Jamie was six feet two inches clear, and when he wore his riding-boots he stood out in a crowd like a man taking a leisurely swim in a lake of bobbing hats. He always made her feel small and delicate and feminine.

He was handsome, too; at least Lucy thought he was.

With age and experience his face was developing some edges. An angular chin, and a nose with the hint of a bump in it, and deep-set eyes which were grey like thunderstorms and very bright. He looked as if he couldn't make up his mind whether to hit you or laugh.

She liked him so much that she almost loved him; but she still had her secret dream of marrying a prince, or a lord, or a millionaire.

'Hudson's Law of Torts, in seven volumes,' Jamie explained. 'Had to order them special from Monkey Ward.' He used the derisive nickname for Montgomery Ward in deference to the bitterness that Lucy's father felt for the big Chicago mail-order houses. Montgomery Ward and Sears Roebuck had brought scores of small main street stores close to the brink of bankruptcy, Lucy's father included.

A farm wagon for $50, sent by railroad express? Seventy-two dozen shirt buttons for 35c? Which small-town store-keeper could compete with that? Especially when – once read, and re-read, and dreamed over, and ordered from – the mail-order catalogues supplied the entire Western frontier with an inexhaustible supply of free toilet-paper?

'Torts? What are torts?' Lucy asked him. 'They sound like some kind of cookie.'

Jamie said, 'Pfff!' in derision and shook his head. 'You must know less than just about any girl I ever met!'

'I'm going to be a socialite,' Lucy retorted, sticking her nose in the air. 'A socialite doesn't have to know what torts are. *Do* have another tort, Mrs Vanderbilt.'

'Are you trying to make a clown out of me?' Jamie demanded.

'I'm sorry! Oh, Jamie, I'm sorry! Don't sulk! Tell me what torts are! Do!'

Jamie could see that she was teasing him; but he cleared his throat and said gravely, 'A tort, see, is when you cause injury or damage, either by something you did, or by something you should've done and didn't.'

8

'Well that's as clear as mud,' said Lucy, skipping as she walked.

'Listen —' said Jamie. 'Suppose your father left the lid off the blasting-powder and then one of his Saturday boys went looking for a pound of nails with a lighted candle?'

'And then what?' asked Lucy.

'And then the boy got himself smithereened, of course, because your father should have put the lid back on the blasting powder!'

'And that's a tort? When a boy gets smithereened?'

Jamie gave her a serious nod. 'Well, yes. That kind of thing. Smithereened boys, trampled crops, ladders not fixed, you name it. Mr Collamer says there's a good steady future in torts.'

Lucy held on to his sleeve. 'It all sounds gigantically dull to me. I thought you were going to be a crime lawyer. You know, defending murderers and bank-robbers.'

'You know something about you?' Jamie asked her.

'No, what?'

'You'd tease the fleas off of a mule, you would. No mistake about it.'

They had almost reached Jack Darling's General Store. It was a two-storey frame building, painted stray-dog yellow; store below, living accommodation upstairs, the very last building in the street; where Oak City finished and the rest of Kansas began. To Lucy, the house where she lived had always marked the definitive end of the world. Street one side: High Plains the other. She sometimes felt that it was like living on the very edge of the Earth.

There are no mountains in Kansas. The plains-dwellers called it the land 'where you can look farther but see less'. But on days when the distant sky was gun-barrel black and the whitish-yellow prairie grass waved like a soft and silent sea, Lucy could still feel an alarming sense of vertigo.

In Kansas, it was easy to remember that you were glued on to the world only by the soles of your feet.

Jack Darling was waiting on the store verandah, a grey-haired man with a frame as bony as a bicycle, in a long shopkeeper's apron. Above his head, a weather-blistered sign announced that he was Jack Darling Leading Merchant of Western Kansas, and that he had a stock of Farm Supplies, Fine Groceries & Family Provisions; Clothing in Suits Nobby & Modest; and Stetson's Hats in all the Latest Styles.

The sign said nothing about him being a widower; and times being so hard.

'Poppa!' Lucy called out, and waved; and her father inclined his head to acknowledge that he had already seen her.

'Care for a sarsaparilla?' Lucy asked Jamie.

'Sure. But I can't stay too long. Ned said to meet him at twelve. I have to help out with the herd this afternoon. Dehorning, something real grisly like that.'

They climbed the steps on to the verandah, and Jamie set down his parcel and lifted his hat. Jack Darling smiled and said, 'How're you keeping, Jamie? Your pa working you hard?' And then, to Lucy, 'I've got a surprise for you, sweetheart, of sorts. Guess what just arrived on the eleven o'clock train?'

'Not those eyeglasses you sent away for?'

Jack Darling shook his head. 'It's not a what, it's a who.'

'Oh, pity. I'm dying to see you in eyeglasses.' She put her arm around him and kissed him. 'I expect you're dying to see me, too!'

Jack Darling gave his daughter a playful smack. 'You're going to be the death of me, one day, with all your teasing.'

'Takes after her mother,' he told Jamie, as they went inside. 'Never could be serious, not about nothing.'

'Yes, sir,' said Jamie, but that was all. Lucy had warned him that Jack Darling had almost died from grief when he lost his wife. Hadn't eaten, hadn't slept, and still groaned into his pillow at night.

Jack Darling was sallow-faced, with a drooping grey

moustache, and a slight stoop to his shoulders; but he was still good-looking. Most people reckoned that was where Lucy's eyes had come from; and that clear, determined profile of hers. It was her mouth that was different. You would have to look in the parlour, at a photograph of her mother, to find that alluring, pouting, wilful mouth.

'Sarsaparilla or lemonade?' asked Lucy.

'Either. Or a Prickly Ash tonic, if you have one.'

'Ugh! I don't know how you can drink that stuff!'

'Supposed to be good for the married side of life,' Jack Darling remarked. He was a moral man, a good churchgoer, but he wasn't prudish.

'Jamie's not married,' Lucy retorted.

'Not right now,' Jamie told her, defiantly. 'But when I get my law degree, and hang up my shingle – well, then, there's one or two girls in this town that better watch out.'

'There's one or two girls in this town that better watch out, already,' Lucy warned him, as her father topped up a glass of Prickly Ash bitters with soda-water.

'How about you, sweetheart?' her father asked her. 'Sarsaparilla?'

Lucy shook her head. 'Where's the surprise?' she wanted to know. The store didn't look any different from usual; shadowy and cool with the green blinds drawn down over the windows; its rafters hung with hams; its shelves crowded with everything from apple-butter to bushel-baskets to women's winter long-johns.

Around the stove (cold, of course, because it was summer, but still Oak City's social focus) the usual loungers were sitting, playing poker and sipping the whisky that Jack Darling provided for free. Henry McGuffey, a bearded old-timer who had somehow become beached on the High Plains on his way to the goldfields of California: 'run out of funds and enthusiasm'. Samuel Blankenship, former engineer for the Leavenworth, Lawrence and Galveston railroad (known in Kansas as the 'Lazy, Lousy and Greasy') who had

11

crushed his best friend while he was shunting and lost his nerve for driving locomotives. Osage Pete, half-Indian, half-Norwegian, able to speak five different languages and all of them badly.

Jack Darling smiled, and called out, 'Cass!'

There was a moment's pause, and then the stockroom door opened up and a stocky black-bearded man appeared, dressed in a tight tan-coloured suit. He had a large leonine head, a deep barrel of a chest, but disproportionately short legs. His face had been barbecued crimson by the sun, so that to begin with Lucy didn't recognize him. He came forward with a sly smile on his face; and then stopped and held out his arms.

'Uncle Casper?' breathed Lucy. She turned to her father. 'It's Uncle Casper!'

'It surely is!' her Uncle Casper told her; and then smacked his hands together, and picked her up in his arms and twirled her around. 'Heyyyy-hooooooo!!'

Lucy hugged him and kissed him. His hair was still wet from washing his face, and his hands smelled strongly of Peet's Almond Cream soap.

'Did you *know* Uncle Casper was coming?' Lucy asked her father, bright-eyed and excited, and when her father nodded, she said 'Why didn't you tell me?'

'Your daddy thinks I'm not to be relied on, that's why,' Uncle Casper told her. 'Thought I wouldn't show up, see, and didn't want you to get your hopes up unnecessary-like.'

'But you've never let us down before!' Lucy replied. 'You never forget my birthday, do you? And you never forget to send me the flower-money on momma's anniversary!'

'Couldn't forget my dear sister and my dear sister's little girl, now could I?' Uncle Casper asked her. 'What do you think of the beard?'

Jack Darling was smiling cautiously. They had seen Casper only twice in the last five years. The first time, on that stark February day when Lucy's mother had been buried in the snow. And the second time, two years gone, when he had arrived late one night to beg for money; and Jack Darling had given him a hundred dollars for the sake of his dear dead wife.

Casper had eventually paid most of the money back. All the same, Jack's expression showed that he was still wary and reserved about his brother-in-law. Jamie noticed it, even if Lucy didn't. Enough bad news had come through the door of the Jack Darling General Store in the past few years for Jack not to know its face when it put in yet another appearance.

'How long are you staying?' Lucy asked Uncle Casper. 'Oh, Jamie, meet my favourite uncle!'

'Fav'rite and only,' Uncle Casper remarked, laying his hand proprietorially around Lucy's shoulders. He ignored Jamie's outstretched hand, and said to Jack Darling, 'How about shot of that genr'l-store liquor, Jack, just to ease the old pie-eating equipment? And —' nodding to Jamie '— some for my friend here.'

Jamie said, 'Thanks, but I have to go. My father's expecting me back before lunch.'

'Come on, you've still got time for a shot,' grinned Uncle Casper, his eyes glittery and black. 'The first time I ever tasted whisky, my father was expecting me back before lunch, too. That was thirty-five years ago, and I haven't been back for lunch yet.'

Jamie shook his head. 'Thanks all the same. I have my law-studies, too.'

'Law-studies, huh?' asked Uncle Casper. 'Let me tell you something, young fellow — no man ever got rich by studying *nothing* — nothing except for life.' Jack Darling handed him a shot-glass of whisky, and he tossed it back as if he were throwing a bucketful of water on to a blazing barn. 'Women, and fighting, and how to make money, that's all you have to study.'

'And that's what you studied?' Jamie asked him. Lucy

didn't much care for Jamie's tone of voice. It was throaty and expressionless, the voice he put on when he was upset, or jealous, or angry.

Uncle Casper nodded and grinned. 'Women, and fighting, and how to make money.'

'And that's the way to get rich?'

Uncle Casper carried on nodding.

'By that token,' said Jamie, 'I guess you must be richer than most?'

Uncle Casper's eyes narrowed, and he sniffed in one nostril. 'No need to get smart, Sonny Jim.'

'Millionaire, are you?' asked Jamie. 'Multi-millionaire? Billionaire?'

There was a lengthy pause. Then Uncle Casper said, 'There's rich and there's rich. I may not be rich now. Not rich in the sense of having much money –'

'Is there another kind of rich?' asked Jamie, in exaggerated surprise. 'I always thought that rich, by definition, meant having a lot of money.'

'I'm right on the *edge* of being rich.' Uncle Casper snapped back at him. 'I'm rich in ideas, rich in plans, rich in assets. If'n my plans turn out the way they're s'poster, I'll be rich in money, too.'

He held out his empty glass without even looking at Jack Darling; but Jack Darling refilled it for him. He was a storekeeper after all; and it was a long-standing tradition that storekeepers kept one or two bottles for the sake of sociability.

'Oil,' said Uncle Casper. 'That's what I'm after. I'm taking the railroad clear to California, and I'm going to drill myself a fortune, right out of the ground.'

'Fixed your lease?' Jamie asked him. 'Sorted out your drilling rights?'

'Things are arranged,' Uncle Casper told him, offhandedly.

'Good,' said Jamie. 'In that case, all I can say is good luck,' and turned to go.

14

Uncle Casper snatched his hand out and caught hold of Jamie's sleeve. 'Don't you turn your back on me, Sonny Jim. When I come back here from California, you're going to be turning your back on a man of means.'

Jamie gently but firmly prised Casper's fingers away. 'I did wish you good luck, sir.'

Casper let out a loud, braying laugh, and tossed back his second shot of whisky. He said, 'Sure. Sure you did.' He was too much weakened by alcohol and poor eating habits to take on a burly young man like Jamie. He held out his glass with a noticeably trembling hand for another shot. Jack Darling hesitated, but then poured it out for him.

'Will you have a drink with me, then, to show that you mean what you say?' Uncle Casper challenged Jamie.

'Sir, I *always* mean what I say,' Jamie told him. 'I don't need to take a drink to prove it, to you or anybody else. Besides, I don't want to get home smelling of liquor. My father's a temperance man, can't tolerate the breath of Satan.'

Uncle Casper squeezed Lucy's shoulder and smiled. 'The breath of Satan, hey? Upright lad you've got here, young Lucy. Upright!'

Lucy didn't catch the sarcasm in Casper's voice, but Jamie did. Apart from that, Jamie didn't at all care for the way that Casper was hugging Lucy and kissing her hair, as if he owned her. Lucy didn't mind. Lucy didn't think anything of it. To her, Uncle Casper was Uncle Casper, and that was all.

Tightly, Jamie said, 'Believe me, sir, I can drink with the rest of them, when the time's right.' He hesitated, and then he added, 'Unlike some, I can hold my liquor.'

'How's that?' Uncle Casper demanded. 'You trying to tell me that I can't take my drink?'

Jamie stayed calm. 'No, sir. I'm not telling you anything at all. I'm just leaving. Goodbye, Lucy. Goodbye, Mr Darling.'

But Casper said, 'Ho no!' and reached across and tugged the bottle of whisky out of Jack Darling's grasp. He held it up high above his head, noisily sloshing its contents from side to side.

'Come on, now, you're a God-fearing young man, I'll bet you five dollars that you can't drink five shots of whisky without breathing in between; and then say the Lord's Prayer backwards.'

'Casper, that's foolishness,' said Jack Darling. 'Give me the bottle.'

Jamie looked away. 'I'm not taking any bets on anything, sir, least of all liquor, and certainly not prayer. My brother Ned's meeting me outside the barber-shop at twelve noon precisely, and he's going to be plenty sore if he has to wait.'

Casper glanced up at the clock. 'Come on, friend, plenty of time! No wonder you're studying law! You're just like a lawyer, you're all puff! Lucy – you should watch yourself with a fellow like this! All puff and no stuff!'

Jamie looked quickly at Lucy, then lowered his head.

'Puff! Puff! Puff!' mocked Uncle Casper, and sloshed the whisky with every word.

Jamie lifted his eyes. 'Mr Darling,' he said, in a quiet voice, 'would you give me a shot-glass?'

'Oh, *no*, Jamie,' Lucy begged him. 'Uncle Casper was only ribbing. Weren't you, Uncle?'

'Sure,' grinned Uncle Casper. 'I was ribbing, that's all. You High Plains folk don't know a leg-pull even when you trip right over it.'

But without a word, Jamie walked around the stove, and took down a glass from the shelf. He came back, twisted the whisky bottle out of Uncle Casper's hand and uncorked it.

'Jamie!' Lucy protested. 'If you drink so much as one drop of that whisky, I shall never speak to you again, ever!'

But Jamie stared at Uncle Casper and said, 'A bet's a bet. Do you think I'm going to walk out of here with your uncle or *anybody*'s uncle thinking I'm a coward?'

'Be serious, Jamie,' Jack Darling told him. 'Casper's a joker, that's all.'

But Jamie took a deep breath, then another, and filled up the shot-glass to the brim. He paused for a moment, and then knocked it back. Without hesitating, without breathing, he filled the glass again, and knocked that back, too.

'Jamie!' Lucy protested. 'Jamie – it was only a joke!'

Red in the face, Jamie filled his glass again, and swallowed it. Two more to go, and already tears were running down his cheeks. Uncle Casper put his arm around Lucy's shoulders and squeezed her tight and said, 'He's plucky! I'll give him that much! Most men would've breathed by now!'

Jamie splashed more whisky into the glass, and drank it with shaking hands. The liquor dribbled down his chin and trickled on to his shirt. One more to go. Jack Darling turned away, shaking his head. Old Henry McGuffey whooped hoarsely and called out, 'That's showin' 'em, son! That's showin' 'em!'

Almost purple, his forehead bursting with sweat, Jamie poured out a final shot. He hesitated for a moment, struggling not to breathe, struggling not to choke. Then he tilted his head back, and swallowed it.

He wiped his mouth with the back of his hand, set down the empty glass, and then breathed out.

'Don't nobody light no matches,' Samuel Blankenship cackled. 'That boy's going to have dangerously inflammable breath for just a while.'

Lucy clapped her hands. 'The Lord's Prayer backwards!' she laughed. 'Oh, come on, Jamie, you can do it!'

Jamie swallowed two or three times. Then he said, 'Amen, ever and ever for, glory the power the –' and recited the entire prayer from end to beginning with scarcely a single hesitation.

When he had finished, Lucy broke free from Uncle Casper and waltzed up and down the store with him. 'Whoopee! You did it. Jamie! You did it!' Uncle Casper watched them wryly, picking in between his front teeth with his thumbnail.

At last Jamie came up to Uncle Casper and held out his hand. 'That's five dollars you owe me.'

Casper gave him a sloping grin. 'I told you, didn't I? Didn't I make myself clear? That was a leg-pull, that's all. No bet. Just a leg-pull.'

Jamie took a deep, patient breath. 'Sir, that was no leg-pull, and you know it. That was a legal bet, square and legal; and what's more I won it square and legal.'

Casper looked around the store, smiling at everybody; Henry and Samuel and Osage Pete. 'What did I tell you? No sense of humour west of Leavenworth.'

Lucy said, '*Uncle* — you're cheating! Jamie drank the whisky and he said the prayer.'

Casper looked back at her, and shrugged. 'No concern of mine if the boy's too fond of the bottle, and an atheist to boot.' But when Lucy folded her arms and frowned at him crossly, he shrugged, and sniffed, and dug into the inside pocket of his suit, and one by one brought out a handful of crumpled-up bills. Painstakingly, he smoothed out a five-dollar bill, and held it out. 'Here — seeing that you won't take a joke for what it's worth; and seeing that it's Lucy here who's appealing on your behalf, here's your money. I wish you joy of it.'

Jamie let his hands drop to his sides. 'Forget it,' he said. 'I'm not a betting man, in any case.'

'Come on,' Uncle Casper encouraged him, flapping the money up and down. 'Take it, you've earned it.'

Jamie said, 'Forget it, do you mind?' and took hold of Lucy's arm. 'Will I see you Sunday?' he asked her. 'I thought we could go horseback-riding, down along the river. We could take those two new bays from the Williams place; they're really special.'

Lucy nodded. 'All right, then. Two o'clock. Three?'

'Two o'clock's fine by me.'

'Take the money,' Casper insisted. 'Come on, now. You've won it. Take the money.'

'Unh-unh,' Jamie told him, without taking his eyes away from Lucy. 'If it hurts you so much to give it away, then I'd rather you didn't. But you can pay Mr Darling for his whisky.' He swayed a little, and sidestepped. He was obviously beginning to feel drunk.

'Hmh. Suit yourself.' Uncle Casper folded up the five-dollar bill and tucked it back into his pocket. 'If that's the way you feel.'

Lucy took Jamie's arm and stepped out on to the verandah with him. 'I'm sorry,' she said. 'Uncle Casper can be kind of sharp sometimes. He doesn't mean any harm.'

'Sure he doesn't,' said Jamie. 'But, you know, be careful, all the same. A man who drinks that much.'

'Oh! You can talk! Five straight whiskies and no breathing!' Lucy stood on tiptoe and kissed his cheek. Jamie caught hold of her hand and pressed it tight between his.

'I think I like you, Mr Jamie Cullen,' Lucy told him.

'Well, yes, Miss Lucy Darling; and I think I like you, too.'

He picked up his parcel of books; and then lifted his hat to her, and began to make his way down the street towards the barber-shop. Lucy could see Jamie's brother Ned waiting in his buggy, dressed in black, his black hat lowered over his eyes, as motionless as a photograph. Jamie turned around to wave Lucy goodbye. As he did so, he lost his balance and fell flat on his back in the dust, with his legs in the air.

'Jamie!' screamed Lucy, and ran to help him up.

Jamie sat up with dusty-white shoulders and a glassy smile. 'It's those damned books!' he protested. 'Shifted my weight from left to right; and these damned books – swung around and tippled me over!'

Lucy was almost breathless with laughter. 'You're drunk! You're totally drunk! Ned's going to kill you! And what's your father going to say!'

'I'm all right, I'm all right,' Jamie told her, and started to laugh, too. 'But you tell that uncle of yours –'

He paused, and then he looked serious. 'You keep an eye 〒 that uncle of yours. I've seen men like that before.'

'Men like what?'

'Cardsharps, riff-raff. Devilish so-and-sos.'

'Jamie, he's not riff-raff. He's my *uncle*!'

Jamie climbed on to his feet, and collected his books. 'All the more reason.'

Lucy watched him teeter across the street towards his brother's buggy; and over the warm soft noises of the morning, she heard them arguing. *'Where the blue blazes have you been? Have you been drinking? Smell like a darned saloon!'*

At last, Ned whipped up the buggy, and it turned a circle in the street and headed back towards the Saline River. Lucy called, 'Jamie!' and waved, and Jamie waved wildly back. 'See you Sunday! Two o'clock! And you take care!'

Over a supper of pan-fried corned-beef hash, with a bottle of whisky on the table, Uncle Casper told them stories of what he had been doing since he had last visited. They sat in the cramped little dining room upstairs, with its greyish wooden furniture and its red chequered curtains. By contrast to the meanness of the room, the view out of the window was startling: an endless undulating ocean of grasses; an evening sky so clear and so wide that it could make your head spin.

Uncle Casper kept the whisky bottle beside his plate and drank almost three-quarters of it during the meal. Lucy loved him. The more he drank, the funnier he became; until the two of them were screaming with laughter. Lucy's father joined in, too; but less wholeheartedly, and sometimes Lucy caught him grimacing instead of laughing, or simply staring out of the window.

'I've made a fortune and I've lost a fortune,' Uncle Casper declared when they had finished eating, rolling a Durham cigarette one-handed. 'But this time, I'm out to make a fortune so big that it can't be lost. This time, I'm going to have silk shirts and velvet collars, and beautiful naked women to warm up my long-johns before I put 'em on.'

'Come on, Casper', said Lucy's father, with a smile. 'Let's keep the smoking talk till later.'

'Lucy doesn't mind, do you, Lucy?' grinned Uncle Casper, resting his hand heavily and affectionately on Lucy's arm, and breathing whisky fumes at her. 'Lucy and me, we're friends; and always will be; and always *have* to be. Because Anna was exactly like Lucy. My poor, poor Anna; rest in peace. But Lucy has the same looks, what do you think, Jack? And the same way about her. You can't deny it. Anna all over again.'

Lucy's father said nothing, but cleared away the plates, and went through to the kitchen to find them some plain cheese and an apple pie.

Uncle Casper leaned forward. 'Let me tell you something, darling. A schoolteacher told me this one, on the train from Leavenworth. He said the definition of good education is the ability to be able to describe a woman without using your hands.'

'Oh, Uncle,' Lucy protested, although she didn't understand the joke at all.

Uncle Casper laughed and tilted back in his chair and swallowed another mouthful of whisky. His eyes were pink around the edges and his words were beginning to sound blurry. 'You've grown up beautiful, do you know that? Beautiful! I can't even understand why you stay here, out in this –' he turned towards the window, where the grass waved for mile after mile. '– this isn't even a *place*.'

'It's home,' said Lucy, defensively.

'And you're going to stay here all your life?'

'Of course not. I'm going to be a socialite.'

Uncle Casper sucked at his cigarette, and blew smoke out of his nostrils. 'A socialite, hmh? All diamonds and pearls, I suppose, and ostrich plumes? I've seen women like that; in Washington, and Baltimore, and Charleston.'

21

Lucy lowered her eyes. She didn't mind being teased; but not about that one particular dream. That dream was precious. Without that dream, she didn't know how she could have tolerated the long glaring summers and the bitterly-cold winters and the weather-scraped faces of men and women who were trying to scratch a living out of nothing much.

'Need money, if'n you want to be a socialite,' Uncle Casper told her. 'Need money and plenty of it. And what have you got?'

Jack Darling came back into the room, carrying a plate of strong yellow cheese. Uncle Casper looked up and said, 'How's business, Jack? Thriving, is it? Can't hear yourself think for the register ringing?'

Jack sat down. He glanced at Lucy first, because she looked a little upset, but then he said, 'Look around you, you can see for yourself. Times have been nothing but thin since the cattle-drives finished. Everybody's living off credit, including me.'

Eleven years ago, when Jack Darling had first opened his general store, Oak City had still been a thriving railhead for Texas longhorns, and every cattle-drive between May and November had brought thirsty, hungry, and well-paid drovers – a seasonal trade for sure, but enough to keep Jack Darling's General Stores and most of the other Oak City businesses bustling.

But the prosperous days of the cattle-drives had been short-lived. Immigrant grangers like Jerrold Cullen had started to complain about the ticks which the Texas cattle brought with them – ticks to which the Texas cattle themselves were immune, but which had decimated the domestic herds with splenic fever.

In the end, the Kansas legislature had been forced by the grangers to declare a quarantine line, north to south, halfway down the territory. No Texas cattle were to be driven into Kansas anywhere to the east of that line; and as the grangers moved further westward, so the quarantine line had to be moved further westward, too.

One by one, the riotous railhead towns had lost their seasonal trade. 'The wild and reckless sons of the Plains' no longer congregated in towns like Abilene, Ellsworth, Wichita, and Ellis; and community after community dwindled and died. At the very last, even Dodge City, the wildest and wealthiest of all the railheads, had collapsed into poverty, too.

Lucy could remember the days when her father's store had been crammed with luxuries and fancy goods. Canned oysters, silks, perfumes from Paris, and nickel-plated .45s with carved ivory handles. At one time he had even sold diamond rings and stickpins. She could remember him giving her pretty new dresses almost every week; and soft kid boots, and ribbons, and bonnets. These days, he was hard put to keep them both in bacon and flour.

Uncle Casper nipped out his cigarette between finger and thumb and cut himself a stout chunk of cheese. 'Lucy wants to be a socialite,' he remarked. 'But that takes a whole consideration of money, being a socialite. How're you going to manage to dress her in furs, Jack? How're you going to decorate her with pearls, and such?'

Now Jack Darling understood why Lucy had been looking upset. He reached across the table and grasped her hand. 'Everybody has the right to have a dream, Cass. It's written in the Constitution. I have mine, you have yours.'

'Ah, yes!' Casper replied, with his mouth full. 'But the difference beween your dream and my dream is that my dream is going to come true! When I bring in that oil-well, I'm going to be rich, Jack, I'm going to shine with diamonds from top to toe. Lucy can dream about being a socialite, by all means; she can dream and dream. But only money can make a dream like that happen for real. Otherwise believe me it's Oak City, Kansas, for ever, and marriage to a hayseed lawyer with as much sense of humour as a half-a-pint of buggy paint, and five squalling babies, and lose your looks before you're turned thirty.'

Jack said, 'Cass, you listen to me, I'm a patient man, and you're Anna's brother, God rest her poor spirit, but don't try my goodwill.'

Casper leaned forward with an unabashed grin. 'Oh, you know me, Jack! I speak my mind, that's all; and sometimes it aint so difficult for people to take offence. But I don't mean nobody no harm, especially you, and especially young Lucy. If'n I've done you any discourtesy, well then, accept my apologies.'

He took hold of Lucy's hand again, and squeezed it tightly; and gave her an exaggerated wink. 'Trouble is, you know that I'm telling you the truth. It's money, or else it's Oak City. And Oak City's no place for a girl who looks the way you do.'

Casper smoked, and smiled, and poured himself another whisky. Lucy had never seen a man drink so much whisky and still remain coherent. At last Jack Darling looked up at the clock and said, 'I'd better get back downstairs. Sam's being taking care of the store. God knows, he's probably given everything away for free.'

'Good for him!' Casper remarked. 'I like a man with a generous heart.'

That evening, when the store was all closed up, Jack Darling and Uncle Casper sat in the parlour for a drink and a smoke. Lucy joined them for a while, sitting at the table with her crochet, but all Casper wanted to talk about was money and how to make it, and so at nine o'clock she made her excuses and left them to it.

She had just finished turning down the beds and lighting the lamps in the bedrooms; her father came out of the parlour and took hold of her arm. She was already in her nightdress; a plain cotton gown with a high-buttoned neck and a yellow-ribboned yoke.

'Goodnight, sweetheart,' he told her.

She kissed his prickly cheek. 'Goodnight, poppa.'

24

Jack Darling hesitated. He looked strangely old tonight; and tired. 'You know, sweetheart, if I *could* take you away from here. . .'

Lucy kissed him again. 'Was momma content, being here?'

Jack Darling pulled a face. 'Sure, in her way, she was content. But your momma, well – she was my wife, she had a duty to be content. She always stood by me, no matter what.'

'Then you don't have to worry. I'll stand by you, too, if you want me to.'

Jack Darling tried without much success to smile. 'I know that, sweetheart. But I've been thinking about what your Uncle Casper said at supper.'

'Poppa . . . if momma was content, then *I'm* content. You always do your best.'

'But you should have dresses, parties, dancing. That's what you really want.'

Lucy gave him another kiss. 'Everybody's entitled to have a dream. You said so yourself.'

'Even if it never comes true?'

She looked away. She didn't say anything. Her dream was too important for her to risk it by tempting fate. *You should have seen them*, Mrs Sweeney had told her. *The ladies in their white silk gowns, with all their ostrich feathers; and the men like gods.*

Jack Darling said, 'Lucy, what can I give you? Nothing but hard work, and more hard work, and when the good Lord calls me, what do you get? A patch of dry land, and a general store in a town where nobody can't scarcely afford to buy nothing.'

'Poppa, I'm content!'

Jack Darling looked away, disconsolate. 'The things I promised your mother! The jewellery, the high life! All that turned up was ruin and more ruin, and then the enteric fever.'

Lucy squeezed his hand. 'Poppa ... don't blame yourself for everything. It wasn't your fault that they stopped the cattle-drives. And momma getting sick, that wasn't your fault, either.'

Her father looked back at her, and his cheeks were glistening with tears. 'Just so long as you never curse me, Lucy, for all of my failures.'

'Poppa, you never failed me once. Not once.'

He held her tight. 'Goodnight, sweetheart. Sleep well. Me and Cass'll be turning in, too, in just a while.'

'Don't drink too much. And don't let Uncle Casper drink too much.'

Jack Darling wiped his eyes with his fingers, and grunted in amusement. 'That man must be hollow from the neck down.'

He went back to the parlour. As he closed the door, Lucy glimpsed Uncle Casper opening up another bottle of whisky. She stood where she was for a while, thinking. Then she went into her room.

Lucy had always felt secure in her room. It was small, wallpapered with roses, just big enough for her mahogany-veneer bed with its patchwork quilt, and a light-oak cupboard which a German family had brought all the way from Münster, in Westfalia. Jack Darling had accepted the cupboard in settlement of five months of unpaid credit. It wasn't worth anything, but it was handsomely carved, and to Lucy it represented the first time that she had been grown-up enough to understand an act of human charity.

She could remember the faces of the Hartmann family as they delivered the cupboard on their handcart. Grim, undernourished, with that defiance that characterizes people who face poverty and hardship without any foreseeable end to it, but who have come too far to go back.

When they had gone, Lucy had asked her father what the cupboard was worth.

He had walked around, slapped it, and shrugged, 'Four or five dollars, maybe nothing at all. Folks around here may be short of cash and food and shoe-leather, but they aren't exactly short of furniture.'

'But how much did the Hartmanns owe you?'

'One hundred and eight dollars and four cents.'

'But you told them that if they gave you this cupboard, that would leave them square!'

Her father had nodded, opening and closing the cupboard door. 'Well-made piece. We could put it in your room.'

'I don't understand,' Lucy had protested. 'If you didn't mind losing a hundred dollars, why did you take their cupboard at all? That was plain mean!'

Jack Darling had looked at his daughter for a while, and then he had said, 'If I hadn't taken their cupboard, Lucy, I would have taken their pride. They have to believe that they can pay their way, otherwise they don't have no reason for carrying on. In one moment of thoughtlessness, I would've done to them what five thousand miles of travelling and ten years of suffering couldn't do, and what ten more years of suffering won't do, either.'

He had laid his hand on Lucy's shoulder – and, tonight, all these years later, Lucy unconsciously laid her own hand on her shoulder in fond imitation.

'A man can live without a place to hang up his clothes, Lucy. But he can't live without hope.'

She sat on her bed brushing out her curls and thinking about what her father had said. Sunday-school talk, really; cracker-barrel kindness. But if a man showed genuine charity, it was always easy to accuse him of being sentimental and simple-minded.

Lying back on her pillow, she thought about Uncle Casper, too. Now that she was older, she felt that she could perceive in him some complications of character that she had never noticed before. It was not so much that he was a mischief-maker (although the more she thought about the

27

way in which he had taunted Jamie into drinking all that whisky, the more deliberate devilishness she saw in it). It was his self-destructiveness that unsettled her – the way he drank whisky as if he wanted to drown, and the relish with which he had told them about his catastophic schemes for making money, as if he revelled in ruination and disaster.

He had lost thousands of dollars of his own and other people's money trying to set up a steamboat service on the Platte River in Colorado (too shallow). He had fitted out an expedition to go to Peru, to dig for silver (it had never left Charleston harbour.) He had built the grand façade of a fifty-room hotel in Huron, South Dakota, believing (mistakenly, as it turned out) that Huron would be chosen as state capital.

Whether he was planning majestic follies on the Western plains, or keeping himself in whisky money by playing faro and find-the-lady in small-town saloons, it seemed to Lucy that her Uncle Casper was constitutionally incapable of doing anything successful – that he *needed* to lose; that he *needed* to be hurt.

But for all that, he had a louche magnetism that Lucy found hard to resist. He spoke his mind, even when it was impolite or offensive or even downright dangerous; and seemed from experience to know the price of everything, especially the price of dreams. This evening, he had disillusioned Lucy deeply, by telling her just how much her dream would cost. But by putting a price on it, he had somehow made it seem more possible. Yes, she would need a fortune to enter high society, but wasn't America a land in which there were still fortunes lying around to be made?

She opened the top drawer of her bedside table, and lifted out the inlaid jewellery-box which had once belonged to her mother. She unlocked it, and opened it up, and took out the pieces of jewellery one by one, and arranged them on the bed.

One cameo brooch; two necklaces, one pearl and one

sapphire; three pairs of earrings, one pearl, one jet, one silver; two rings.

In the prosperous days, her mother had owned much more; but by the time she died, this was all she had left. Lucy picked up the silver earrings and stood in front of her mirror, holding them up to her ears.

One day, she would dance, with these earrings on. One day she would have diamonds and rubies and emeralds.

She heard Uncle Casper laughing in the parlour; then her father's voice, lower and less distinct. Then Uncle Casper again. '– can't fail. They've already spudded three wells and every one of them's –' A long pause. The clinking of glasses. Then her father's voice. '– just don't have that kind of cash available – everything's tied up in stock – not to mention two-and-a-half thousand dollars' worth of credit – and who knows when that's going to be –'

Lucy put away the jewellery box; and then tiptoed across to her bedroom door, and opened it. She could just see a triangle of lamplight shining across the rumpled Indian blanket on the landing floor. However, she could now hear her father and Uncle Casper very much more distinctly.

Uncle Casper was saying, '– Jack, I can't deny that I've had my share of thin luck. Sure I've had some failures! The old Peruvian silver expedition didn't work out too good. Bold idea, bad organization. Probably just as well. Turned out the ship's captain thought Peru was someplace in Africa. But anybody can make mistakes, and I've sure learned by mine.'

Jack was silent for a while. Then he said, 'Cass, I simply don't *have* five hundred dollars; not to hand; and even if I did I'm not too sure that I'd give it to you.'

Casper coughed. 'Well . . . I guess I could scrape by with less. Say three hundred and fifty? Especially if I stay with acquaintances, and eat plain, and manage to pick up some second-hand drilling equipment. Come on, Jack, I'd cut you in for ten per cent.'

'I don't know,' said Jack. 'It took you two years to pay me back the last loan I gave you, and I was a whole lot flusher then.'

'I paid you back, though, didn't I? With interest, too!'

Jack said, 'Yes, you did. But this drilling for oil . . . you don't even know if there's anything down there!'

'My friend in California, John Ferris, he's sure of it. That's why he wrote me, asking me to come in with him. You might say they owe me a favour.'

'It still sounds like a long shot t'me,' Jack replied.

'Oh come on, Jack,' Casper urged him. 'Stop acting so damn glum! Just take a look at me! What do you see in my eyes? What's that brightness you see? Aint that the shine of good luck? Don't you see luck? Hey? Look in my eyes!'

There was another protracted pause. Then Jack said, 'Cass, when I look into your eyes, I'm not too sure *what* I see. I'm worried I might be seeing myself, reflected back.'

Casper laughed. 'You just won't trust me, will you, Jack? You plumb refuse to trust me!'

'The question of trust doesn't even arise,' Jack Darling told him, rather stiffly. 'I don't have the money, and that's all there is to it.'

'What about y'r property? Couldn't you raise five hundred with an extra mortgage?'

'Casper, it's taken me twenty years to build up this business. These days, I'm scarcely breaking even. If I went bankrupt now, I wouldn't have nothing. Not even the clothes I stand up in. And I have to think about Lucy, too.'

'Oh, well,' Casper sighed. 'Anna was always saying about you that you was the cautious sort.'

'The hell you say!' Jack barked at him. 'You leave Anna out of this!'

Casper sniffed. 'All right, all right! Don't get yourself aerated! Sometimes the liquor says somethin' what the heart don't mean. But think about it, Jack. Don't dismiss it out of hand.'

'Cass – let me put it to you this way,' Jack Darling told

him. 'I could raise the money, I guess, if I had the mind to. But I was never a man who believed in something for nothing. If you want that money bad enough, well, I'm not preaching at you, but I think you should earn it.'

Lucy heard the clinking of bottle against glass, and guessed that Casper was pouring himself another drink.

Then she heard him say, 'Every man has to take a chance, Jack, just once in his life. Otherwise – well – he might as well climb into his grave here and now, and whistle f'r his dog to fill it in for him.'

Later that night, after the moon had set, Lucy was woken up by Uncle Casper stumbling heavily against the corridor wall. There was a pause, and then her bedroom door swung open. She slitted her eyes open, and she could see him leaning against her closet, peering at her in the darkness. He was breathing harshly and heavily.

'Weave 'em up and weave 'em down,' he sang, under his breath. 'Weave 'em pretty girls round and round . . .'

He suppressed a cough. Then, 'Lucy?' he whispered, after a while.

She didn't answer.

'Lucy, you awake?'

Again she didn't answer.

Uncle Casper took three shuffling steps into the room. He hit his foot against the end of her bed, and almost fell over. 'Sssh!' he told himself, and giggled.

He came right up close, and knelt down beside her. She could smell the sourness of whisky on his breath, and the sweetness of Durham tobacco.

'Lucy? You sleeping? I just came to say goodnight. Goodnight kiss.'

She closed her eyes and kept them closed. *I'm asleep, can't you see that I'm asleep?* although her heart was beating in long slow bumps, and her fists were clenched so tightly that her fingernails dug into the palms of her hands.

31

'You've grown up a treat, Lucy, did you know that?' Uncle Casper slurred. 'You've grown up beautiful, Lucy like a – like a princess.'

He leaned right over her, and brushed his beard against her cheek. 'Just like a princess,' he repeated.

He waited for a long time, so near that she could feel his breath on her neck. Then he climbed back on to his feet again, staggered, and muttered to himself. 'Goddamn call o' nature.' He swayed back out of her room, colliding with the cupboard door as he did so. Lucy heard him wrestling open the kitchen door so that he could go down to the yard and use the privy.

Immediately, she jumped out of bed, hurried breathlessly across to her bedroom door, and turned the key.

She lay awake for almost an hour, waiting for Uncle Casper to return, but she heard nothing. At last she fell asleep, and dozed until sun-up, dreaming of frocks and silk stockings and people laughing. A little after five, the kitchen door slammed again, and Uncle Casper's footsteps came trudging through the parlour. She heard him cursing to himself as he passed her door. 'Goddamned stiff neck, stiff as a goddamned board.'

He must have fallen asleep in the privy and stayed there for most of the night. Lucy buried her face in her blanket to stop herself from laughing out loud. She heard him drag his way along to the spare room, and collapse on to his bed with a crunching of springs.

Sunday was windy and bright. Lucy and Jamie rode down to Overbay's Bend by the Saline River, and tied their horses to the scrubby bushes that grew right down to the water's edge. Overbay's Bend wasn't much more than a shallow oxbow, but the river had eroded the soil deeply enough to give some protection from the wind.

'So how long is this beloved uncle of yours going to be staying?' asked Jamie, shaking out a blanket and laying it on the grass.

32

Lucy shook her head. 'I don't know. Three months maybe. It depends how long it takes him to make enough money to go on to California. He's working in the store, and he's been doing some vet work, too. Poppa says that he's a wonder with animals.'

'He must have been pretty mad at your father for not grubstaking him.'

Lucy shrugged. 'If he was, he didn't show it. But it's hard to tell what he's thinking, most of the time. He talks a lot but he never really tells you anything about himself. And he has this peculiar smile, too, like something's funny, but he's not going to tell you what it is.'

'Here, sit down,' Jamie told her.

Lucy perched herself as elegantly as she could on the edge of the blanket. This afternoon she was wearing her maroon embroidered blouse and a long camel-hair riding-skirt. Her hair was brushed up under a plain-straw pillbox hat, which she had renovated by sewing a maroon velvet band around it. Primly, she covered her buttoned riding-boot with the hem of her skirt.

Jamie sat down beside her and scooped up a handful of pebbles. 'You should have seen me! I was drunk as a duck all afternoon, after drinking that whisky. At least Ned didn't snitch on me, that was one thing. But drunk! I nearly dehorned the dog, instead of the cow.'

'Well, serves you right. Uncle Casper was only ribbing.'

'Oh, no,' said Jamie, tossing pebbles across the wind-ruffled river. 'That man wasn't ribbing. Not one bit of it.'

'He'll be gone before too long, anyway,' Lucy replied.

Jamie glanced at her. 'What's wrong? He hasn't upset you or anything?'

'I don't know. I used to love him so much, when I was younger. But – I don't know – he seems different now. Kind of *mean*, in a way. Kind of strange. But definitely different.'

'Most likely it's *you* that's different,' Jamie suggested. One of his pebbles skipped and skated across the river, and then *plopped* out of sight. 'Maybe you've grown up, that's all, and now you can see him for what he is.'

Lucy took off her hat and lay back on the grass and watched the clouds sailing by. Huge cumulus clouds, dreamily floating fortresses, with battlements and towers and walkways and bridges. She could almost imagine people living in them, kings and queens and princes.

'I'm not sure what he is,' she replied. 'He talks real strange. He frightens me sometimes. But you can't stop yourself from listening. He can make you feel that you can do anything, anything at all – that anything you ever wanted can come true. Just so long as you're strong enough, and so long as you don't care what people think about you, and so long as you're ready to give up absolutely everything.'

Jamie frowned at her. 'Would you do that?'

'Would I do what?'

'Give up absolutely everything?'

Lucy looked at him. 'I don't know. I think I'd be scared to.'

'How about me?' Would you give me up?'

She didn't answer. Jamie rolled over and lay on his stomach and looked into her eyes, really close. He said, in a different kind of a voice, 'You know that I want to marry you, the day that I get my law degree.'

He hesitated for a second, and then he kissed her; a brush of a kiss at first, and then more deeply, his tongue-tip touching her teeth.

She closed her eyes and slowly wound her arms around him. They kissed again and again, and she could feel the wind blowing her hair across her forehead.

'Oh Jamie,' she whispered; but suddenly she had to open her eyes and stare at him, to make quite sure that he wasn't Uncle Casper.

★

On Monday morning, summoned by the president of the Kansas Farmers' & Stockbreeders' Bank, Lucy's father took the ten-oh-five train to Hays City. Lucy saw him off at the Oak City depot, which was little more than a lock-up warehouse and a gingerbread ticket-office that had once belonged to a now-defunct town called Willis. You could still see the name Willis in faded paint on the side.

It was a grey, overcast day, not too cold, but overnight the wind had grown friskier. Jack Darling leaned out of the passenger-car window and waved his hat as the train pulled away across the plains. Its smoke was visible for miles before it finally dwindled below the horizon. It was like watching a steamship sail off across a windy sea.

On her way back to the store, Lucy almost collided on the corner of Main Street with the Skipping Widder, who was hurrying to the depot to collect Mr Judd's mail. 'Been to the store,' Mrs Sweeney told her. She sounded very Irish. 'Who's the fellow serving today? Can't say that I've seen him before. Can't say that I'm sorry!'

'Oh, that's my Uncle Casper. My poor momma's brother.'

Mrs Sweeney narrowed her eyes and looked back towards the store. 'He staying permanent?'

Lucy shook her head. 'He's saving up enough money to go to California.'

'Hm! Best place for him, I'd say! Or China, maybe! That's further!'

Lucy was startled by Mrs Sweeney's vehemence. 'He wasn't rude to you, was he? He does have a way of speaking his mind, sometimes.'

'Rude? No. But I've met men like him, met 'em before. Not the kind of man you ought to dance with.'

Lucy couldn't think what to say. She smiled, and shrugged, and said, 'I must be getting back.'

Mrs Sweeney clasped her wrist. 'Well, you watch your step, young Lucy. That uncle of yours has got the devil perched on his shoulder, in my opinion. The very devil.'

35

Without saying anything else, she hurried off towards the depot, her black skirts billowing in the wind. Lucy shielded her eyes against the whirling dust, and watched her go. Then, puzzled, she headed back along Oak City's deserted main street, to the yellow-painted building where Oak City ended and the rest of Kansas began.

Uncle Casper was up on a stepladder at the back of the store, sorting out boxes of shoes. Samuel Blankenship was there, too, sitting by the cold stove with his sippin' whisky and a three-day-old copy of the Kansas City *Daily Journal*. Lucy closed the store door behind her to keep out the wind, and untied the ribbon of her bonnet.

'Your poppa make the train okay?' asked Uncle Casper. He wrote a large cardboard notice Shoes At Cost and propped it up on the shelf.

Although there were only two trains a day to Hays City, and you could see them coming for miles, Uncle Casper's question wasn't so strange. Western trains had a disconcerting habit of sliding out of stations and depots unannounced; with no whistle, no flag, and no cry of 'All aboard!' They arrived with a fanfare, left silent.

Uncle Casper said, 'You could sort them notions out, Lucy, if you've got a mind. They're all of a-tangle.'

'Oh, sure,' said Lucy, absent-mindedly.

Uncle Casper climbed down from the stepladder and came towards her, wiping his hands on his long white storekeeper's apron. 'Something wrong?' he asked her. 'You look kind of distracted.'

'I was just talking to Mrs Sweeney.'

'Oh, yes? You mean the little old Irishwoman? She wanted pickled fish and ground coffee. She wanted a bottle of Dr Kilmer's, too, but we're out.'

'Was she – was she *unhappy* about something?' Lucy asked him.

'Unhappy?' he sniffed.

36

Samuel Blankenship looked up from his newspaper. His expression was oddly expectant.

'I mean, was she upset about something?' Lucy asked.

Uncle Casper slowly shook his head. 'Not that I could see. Maybe dithering, you know, the way that old women do. But not upset. Why – what did she say to you?'

Lucy began to sort through a cardboard box full of tangled-up elastic. 'Nothing. It was just that –'

Uncle Casper was standing very close to her. He must have been drinking already that morning because she could smell the whisky, mixed with eau-de-cologne. An alarmingly masculine smell: the smell of vanity and self-destruction, mixed.

'Do you know something, Lucy,' he told her, and his voice was soft enough for Samuel Blankenship not to be able to make out what he was saying, 'you're going to waste here; here in this store; here in Oak City. Truly going to waste.'

Lucy blushed. She felt hot and cold at the same time. Uncle Casper smiled at her and she wanted desperately for him to go; but also for him to stay. She had never come across anybody who confused her so much. She glanced at him quickly and his eyes were dark and glittering like widow's beads, and he was still smiling.

Just then the store door gusted open and Mrs Barnaby came in, fussing and brushing the dust from her skirts. Uncle Casper gave Lucy a long slow wink, and then turned away. 'Good morning, ma'am; how are you today, ma'am? Mr Darling aint here today, but my name's Casper Conroy and I'm his brother-in-law, and whatever I can do to please you, I surely will.'

He dragged over a bentwood chair so that Mrs Barnaby could sit down, and fuss with her fraying ginger hair. 'Well, you wouldn't have three cans of wrinkled peas, would you, and a cake of that white floating soap?'

Lucy carried on tidying the drawers and boxes of notions;

37

but for the rest of the morning she was aware that Uncle Casper was staring at her.

He caught her in the stockroom during the lunch-hour, when Samuel Blankenship had at last eased himself out of his chair, and gone off to the Demorest Home Restaurant for pie and boiled potatoes. She was looking for more mother-of-pearl blouse buttons, right at the back of the stock-room, between the narrow rows of shelves, amongst the musty-sweet bolts of fresh fabric. She heard the door close but she didn't pay it any mind; the wind was up, and the draught was always banging doors around the house.

It was only when Uncle Casper appeared around the side of the shelving, smiling, and without his apron, that she began to realize that something was different; something was wrong.

He approached her, quite close, and watched her without saying anything as she sorted through cards of pearly buttons.

'You haven't left the store empty?' she asked him. 'The kids'll be coming back from school soon. They're always pilfering the cough-candy.'

'Store's locked,' said Uncle Casper, unblinking.

'Locked? Who locked it?'

Uncle Casper didn't answer, but looked around the stock-room as if he were trying to make up his mind about some-thing.

'We don't close for lunch,' Lucy told him, aware that she sounded faint.

'Oh, we do today,' Uncle Casper replied. 'Staff meeting.'

'Uncle Casper, if poppa finds out that you shut for lunch –'

'Oh, yes? And who's going to tell poppa that we shut for lunch?'

'Well, me, of course!'

Without warning, Uncle Casper snatched her left wrist,

38

and held it tight. He kept on staring at her, and smiling, although his smile was frighteningly tight-stretched. He was breathing deeply, whisky and tobacco, as if he had been running hard to catch up with her.

'Now, why would you choose to do a thing like that?' he asked her.

'Uncle, will you please let *go* of me,' Lucy asked him. She was beginning to feel the first quick surges of panic, but something inside of her warned her, *stay calm, don't over-excite him, don't make trouble*. She had the fearful idea that he might have gone mad, tipped over the edge of sanity by whisky and bankruptcy and her father's refusal to lend him any more money.

'Let you go?' he grinned at her. 'I aint likely to let *you* go! I aint *never* going to let you go! A prize like you! A prize like you, in Oak City, Kansas! Ha!'

He suddenly lunged forward and snatched at her other wrist. She dropped the cardboard box of buttons, and they sprayed over the floor. 'You're hurting!' she gasped at him, but he took no notice. He jerked her closer, so that they were almost face-to-face.

'What did I tell you?' he whispered. He was so near that she could see the open pores in his cheeks; the grey curly hairs in his black tangly beard. She could hardly breathe for the foulness of his breath. 'You grew up just beautiful. Better'n any man could've wished for.'

'Uncle Casper,' she pleaded, both wrists raised. 'Uncle Casper, please let me go. If you let me go now, I won't say a word to poppa. I won't tell anybody. I promise.'

Uncle Casper looked intently into her eyes. Then his gaze dropped to her white linen blouse, and the slight swell of her breasts. 'You grew up a looker, you know that? Even better'n Anna.' His breath went in and out, in and out.

Lucy swallowed. She was trying not to cry, but she could feel the tears springing into her eyes. 'Uncle Casper, please.'

For a moment, she really thought that he was going to let

her go. He lowered her wrists, although he didn't release them, and he dropped his head so that she could see the irregular parting in his scalp.

'Are you going to be accommodatin' to me?' he asked her, without looking up.

'Of course I am.'

He looked up. No smile now. 'I mean, are you going to be *real* accommodatin'?'

'Uncle, I —'

He lunged his head forward like an attacking rattlesnake, and tried to kiss her. She twisted away, yanked one wrist free, but he caught her round the waist and pulled her back towards him.

'I said are you going to be *accommodatin'*!' he shrieked.

She heard somebody screaming. She didn't realize at first that it was her. Uncle Casper gripped the hair at the back of her neck and clamped his mouth against hers, trying to force his rigid tongue in between her lips.

She pushed against him wildly, and staggered back, two steps, and then fell against the bolts of linen and percale that were stacked on the floor between the shelves. Uncle Casper scrabbled himself on top of her, forcing her down on to her back, grunting, grunting, and grabbing for her wrists.

She couldn't find the breath to scream again. She kicked and struggled, but Uncle Casper knelt astride her waist, gripping her tight between his thighs.

He looked down at her, panting. He sniffed, and twisted his head so that he could wipe his nose against the shoulder of his shirt. Then he said, 'What was all that for? Hunh? What was all that? What kind of a way was that for a niece to treat her uncle?'

Lucy was gasping and her eyes brimmed with tears. She shook her head. 'Uncle, let me go, please.'

'I told you, I wouldn't let you go. A princess like you? A man would have to be crazy in the head to let you go.'

Keeping her wrists held fast, Uncle Casper looked around

at the scattered boxes of notions. Buttons, reels of thread, crochet hooks. At last he saw what he wanted, a roll of red silk ribbon. He shifted his grip so that he was holding both of Lucy's wrists with one hand, and then he leaned over, grunting, and picked the ribbon up. He held the end of it between his teeth, and let it unroll from his mouth like a long lascivious tongue.

Dear Jesus, she thought, *he's going to strangle me!*

'Uncle, please!' she begged him. All she could manage was a throaty whisper. 'Uncle, please, don't strangle me. Please don't strangle me! Please!'

Uncle Casper let the ribbon drop out of his mouth. He stared at her in bewilderment. Then suddenly he realized what she meant, and picked up the ribbon, and brayed with laughter. 'You think I'd —? You must be crazy in the head! Strangle you? I aint going to strangle you! Have to be crazy in the head, to strangle you.'

Still laughing, still shaking his head, he wound the silk ribbon around Lucy's wrists and lashed them tightly together, two or three dallies and a half-hitch, above her head. He did it with all the deftness and expertise of a man who has tied up struggling heifers and panicking horses.

'Good strong stuff, silk, for something that comes out of a worm's rear end.'

He was calmer, now that he had tied her up; less jittery. He lifted himself off her — although when she tried to struggle herself up into a sitting position, he shoved her roughly back down. 'You just stay there, princess. Don't you move.'

'What are you going to do?' she whispered. Her lower lip was trembling uncontrollably. She felt as if she were just about to faint.

'Do? What am I going to *do*?' He heaved her further up on the stack of fabrics, so that she was lying flat on her back with her bound hands almost touching the wall. There were four or five iron hooks in the wall, and he unwound two

41

more feet of red ribbon and tied it around the largest hook, using the figure-eight knot that trailhands favoured when they had to lash down a really wild steer. He checked that the knots were tight by tugging at them, and sniffed.

'Uncle, it hurts! Please, it hurts! Please let me go! Please! Think of momma!'

Uncle Casper bent over her and kissed her directly on the lips. 'Well, I *am* thinking of momma,' he smiled. 'Believe me, I am.'

With that, he took out his clasp-knife, and opened it with a bitten thumbnail. Lucy thought for a moment that he was going to slit her throat, but he hardly looked at her. He cut the remaining ribbon free, and then he climbed down from the bolts of fabric, lifted Lucy's right ankle, and wound the ribbon around it, knotting it tight.

'Weave 'em up and weave 'em down,' he hummed to himself. 'Weave 'em pretty girls round and round.'

He bound the other end of the ribbon around one of the slatted shelves where the notions were stacked. Lucy screamed, '*Let me go! Let me go! Let me go!*' and kicked at him furiously with her free left leg. But Uncle Casper simply dodged, and said, 'Hey . . .' and batted her kicks away with his hand. Then he caught hold of her flailing ankle, and tied that, too, to the shelves on the opposite side.

The rows of shelves were nearly five feet away from each other, and so Lucy's legs were stretched painfully wide apart.

'There, tied up good and tight,' Uncle Casper told her. 'Chinese woman showed me how to do that. Chinese.'

Uncle Casper loosened his black spotted necktie. Lucy stared up at him wide-eyed, shivering. She knew there was no use in screaming, nobody could hear. She wrenched and twisted at the silk ribbons, but they were far too tight for her to break free. Uncle Casper said, 'You can struggle all you want, princess. You won't get away.'

'How can you call me a princess when you're doing *this*

to me!' Lucy screeched at him. 'Poppa's going to *kill* you! He'll *kill* you!'

Uncle Casper's eyes looked peculiarly distant, as if he were thinking about somewhere else, and somebody else. 'Well, princess, you know what they say. Love comes in all kinds of different disguises. Love wears all kinds of different masks. This just happens to be mine.'

Oh, Jesus save me, she thought. *He is mad! He's completely mad!*

He climbed back up on to the bolts of cloth next to her, and stroked her cheek. His fingers were gentle and surprisingly soft. She tried to turn her face away, but he wound his fingers into her hair, and breathed, 'Still! Keep still!'

He kissed her forehead, then her eyes, then her nose and her lips. His beard and his breath almost suffocated her, and she couldn't stop herself from retching.

But Uncle Casper didn't seem to be offended by her disgust. In fact, it seemed to arouse him all the more. He kissed her and kissed her, and stroked her face, and after a while his hand strayed down the side of her neck, until he was touching the cameo brooch that pinned together the collar of Lucy's blouse.

'Oh, don't break it,' she gasped, in desperation. 'Please, don't break it. It used to be momma's.'

Uncle Casper carefully unfastened it, and held it up for a moment, turning it this way and that. 'I wouldn't break it,' he told her. 'Where d'you think your momma got it from?'

He laid the brooch aside, and started to unbutton her blouse. She wanted to scream, she wanted to plead with him to stop, but somehow she couldn't make her jaws work. Perhaps it was fear that was keeping her silent. Perhaps it was pride. She knew that he wasn't going to let her go, no matter what; and that he would only relish it more if she begged.

Perhaps more than anything else she was silenced by shame. Nobody had seen her undressed before, not Jamie, not anybody. And worse than that, there was the shame of feeling excited. In spite of her helplessness, in spite of her panic, in spite of her revulsion, she felt a dark breathless anticipation, as if something inside her *wanted* it to happen.

'Oh please dear Jesus,' she murmured, and closed her eyes for a moment, and tried to picture Christ. 'Oh please forgive me.'

Almost matter-of-factly, Uncle Casper opened her blouse to the waist, and tugged it out of her skirt. She opened her eyes again, and stared at him. He stared back, and then smiled. 'You've grown up pretty, princess,' he told her. 'Pretty as a picture, that's what they say.' He reached out with both hands, hesitated for a moment, and then grasped her breasts through the thin muslin of her corset cover.

'Stop,' she mouthed, although she wasn't sure that she was speaking out loud. Could he hear her? Perhaps he couldn't even hear her.

'You know what my rule-o'-thumb is, for the perfect woman's breast?' he asked her. 'My rule-o'-thumb is that the perfect woman's breast should fill a man's hand, no bigger, no smaller. That's my rule-o'-thumb. The perfect woman, that's her proportion. Filling a man's hand.'

Between finger and thumb, he rolled her nipples through the muslin. She swallowed, she shivered; but at least he had stopped kissing her. Those foul kisses, bristly and suffocating and thick with sour-tasting saliva.

'I saw a girl once, in San Francisco,' Uncle Casper remarked. 'She danced naked, in a parlour-house on Commercial Street. And do you know something? Not a man in the place so much as took off his hat. Stark, stark naked, she was; and all those men there dressed to the nines. And do you know something, she was the most beautiful girl I ever saw, ever. After Anna, that is; and now you.'

Slowly, Uncle Casper lifted Lucy's corset cover. He smoothed the palm of his hand over her flat white stomach, around and around. 'Of course, she's probably dead now, poor creature,' he added. 'Once their looks go, those parlour-house girls ... well, they usually prefer the razor. Once across the throat! Then it's goodbye despair, hallo heaven!' He carried on smoothing for a while, thinking and smoothing. Then, with sudden impatience, he seized the muslin corset cover in both hands and tore it the rest of the way up. Lucy cried out, and thrashed from side to side, but Uncle Casper immediately leaned his weight on her and clamped his hand against her mouth and ordered, 'Sssh! Now, sssh, now!'

She said, '*Mmmf!*' and tried to bite his fingers, but he pressed his hand so tightly over her mouth that she could hardly breathe.

After a moment, he took it away.

'You goin' to be quiet?' he asked her.

'I hate you,' she raged at him. 'I *hate* you!'

'Good,' he smiled. 'But stay quiet.'

He lowered his head and kissed her lightly between her breasts. 'Beautiful,' he said, 'you smell of violets. What's that, violet soap you use, eau-de-violets, something like that?' He cupped her right breast in his hand, and closed his mouth around her nipple. She could feel his beard brushing her bare skin. She could feel his tongue-tip, drumming her nipple against the roof of his mouth.

'Please let me go,' she whispered. 'Please let me go.'

But she was sure now that Uncle Casper wasn't listening to her. It could be that he wasn't listening to anything at all, except some private carnival that was going on inside his head. Roll up, roll up, and see them dance. Roll up, and claim your prize. Prize princesses, yours for the taking! Lucy strained her head up a little to look at him. He was kissing and licking and squeezing her breasts, and occasionally murmuring, '*Perfect* ... perfect ... and tastes of violets, too.'

She watched his tongue-tip circle around her nipples until they tightened. Tight, and hard, and tiny, like unripe buds. For a split-second he gripped each nipple between his teeth,

45

nipped it, as if he were going to bite it off. Then he looked up and smiled at her, triumphant.

With two twists of his hand, he unfastened the waistband of her brown cotton skirt. It was impossible for him to pull her skirt right off, because her ankles were both tied. But he took out his knife and cut through the hem, so that he could rip it from top to bottom. It dropped on to the floor, leaving Lucy in nothing but her calf-length drawers and her white lisle stockings.

Uncle Casper stood watching her for a while, no longer smiling, distant, mad, and she wondered if he were going to go away now and leave her. Please, God, let him leave! But what would her father say, if he came home and found her like this! She was just about to ask Uncle Casper to untie her when he started to unbutton his shirt, and then to unbuckle his belt.

He undressed calmly, humming as he did so, although in time-honoured Western tradition he dropped all his clothes on the floor ('so's they don't fall off the hook and get lost'). He wore no underwear. He must have known since he woke up this morning what he was going to do to her. His chest was bosomy and suntanned and marked with a diamond of black hair, but he didn't look fit. His belly was slack from years of whisky, he wore a girdle of fat around his hips, and beneath their black shagginess, his short shapely legs were as white as Lucy's stockings. He must have caught the sun on his chest when he was labouring at some time with his shirt off, gardening or ploughing or laying railroad track.

'I was in Bodie once,' he said, as if he were continuing a conversation that had been briefly interrupted. 'I saw a girl dive off the roof of a hotel. Naked, she was, too. Death was what *she* wanted. What did she care about modesty? She was pretty. Redhead, I recall. But she lay in the street naked, with everybody looking at her, and of course she didn't care. Women take on a special kind of beauty, when they're dead.'

He approached Lucy slowly and stood next to her, naked. In his fist he held the totem of his perversity. He was gripping it so tight that its clefted head was almost maroon.

'You see this?' he asked her.

She turned her head away. Her heart was racing.

He grabbed her hair again, and forced her to face him. He held his swollen glans within an inch of her nose. 'You see this?' he repeated. His voice was beginning to crack.

She closed her eyes, nodded.

'Open your eyes,' he demanded.

She kept them shut.

'Open your eyes!' he shouted at her, and wrenched her hair until she felt her scalp crack.

She opened her eyes. They were sparkling with tears.

'This is yours now, princess,' Uncle Casper told her. 'This is your pleasure, morning, noon'n night.'

She stared at it. It looked more like a blind, angry creature than part of Uncle Casper. She didn't know what he wanted her to say. That she was so terrified that she was numb? That she was close to being sick? That she wished that God would strike him dead? In an unexpected release of fright, she wet herself; the way that a child does when there seems to be no escape, anywhere, in any direction. She sobbed with humiliation; but Uncle Casper hadn't appeared to have noticed, or if he had, to care.

Uncle Casper climbed up on to the fabric between her thighs, picked up his knife, and cut open her sopping muslin drawers. 'Beautiful . . .' he breathed. Then he looked at her, sharply. 'Have you been touched?' he snapped. 'Has any man touched you before? That hayseed lawyer? Any of them bug-ridden butcher boys?'

Lucy, trembling, shook her head. This response seemed to please Uncle Casper, because he smiled, and reached out, and stroked her gently with his hand.

The feeling of his fingers made Lucy shiver with cold. She

47

strained desperately at the ribbons that bound her hands until they cut into her flesh. She tried to heave her body from side to side, to break her ankles free. But she was tied up too securely, there was nothing she could do. The tears poured down the sides of her face, but she was too overwhelmed to sob; too frightened to cry out.

His fingers opened her and explored inside. She closed her eyes tight and bit her tongue and tried to believe that this wasn't happening, that she was back in bed, dreaming; and that she would soon wake up.

Her eyes were still closed when Uncle Casper shuffled himself forward, and began to press his glans against her.

'Defloration, that's the proper word for this,' he murmured. 'Dee-flaw-rayshun.'

He pushed, and he pushed again, and as he forced his way into her, Lucy screamed out loud. 'It's too big!' she screamed. 'It's too big! Take it out! It's too big!' But Uncle Casper forced himself all the way into her, and then crouched over her, panting with achievement.

'You know what you are now?' he breathed into her face. 'You're a woman. You've got yourself a man inside you. You should be proud of yourself. A woman.'

He drew himself out, and for a split-second Lucy thought that it was all over. But then he rammed himself back in again, harder this time; and then again; and then again. He went on and on, gasping and panting and spitting, until he roared out 'Aaaaahh!' and shuddered, and shuddered again, and then abruptly collapsed.

He sat on the bolts of fabric for a long time; still naked, smoking and drinking whisky out of the bottle. He didn't take his eyes away from her once.

At last, he said, 'Time to open up the store. People're goin' to start wonderin'.'

Lucy said nothing, but lay on her back staring at nothing, her eyelashes spiky with dried tears.

'Question is,' said Uncle Casper, 'what are you going to say to your poppa?'

Still Lucy said nothing. She could hear him talking but her mind was empty. All she could think of was the plains, the plains that stretched for ever and ever, and the silvery-grey grass that waved like the ocean in the wind.

Uncle Casper stood up, and found his pinstripe pants. He struggled his way into them, and buttoned them up. 'Tell you what you're going to say to your poppa. Nothing, that's what you're going to say. Nothing at all.'

He leaned over her, buttoning up his shirt. His eyes were crimson from drinking. 'You're not going to tell your poppa nothing.'

'Please untie me,' Lucy whispered.

Uncle Casper fastened his cuffs. 'You just listen to me first, princess. You're not going to tell your father nothing; and there's a very good reason why you're not going to tell him nothing.'

Lucy turned away. Her wrists hurt and her ankles hurt and her whole body felt swollen and bruised.

Uncle Casper said, 'You're not going to tell your father nothing because if you do, I'll have something to say to him, too, about your mother and me. Oh, yes. Don't you turn your face away from me. Your mother and me, we was only half-related, you know that, different mothers. And when we was young, your mother and me, we was close like two spring chickens in the same pot. We was lovers for a while, your mother and me. Might have been a sin in the eyes of God; but we was lonesome and friendless and each other was all we had.'

'You're lying,' whispered Lucy. 'I hate you.'

'Certainly you hate me, but I aint lying. It's the Bible truth, so help me.'

'My momma would never have done anything like that. Never.'

'Maybe she did and maybe she didn't,' said Uncle Casper. 'But you'll never know, will you? And if you want to keep your poppa sane and happy, you'd better make sure that *he* never knows, neither.'

Lucy couldn't think of anything to say in reply. She was beginning to tremble with shock; and with the dread that Uncle Casper would never let her go. She let her head fall back on the bolts of fabric, and the tears streamed out of her eyes and into her ears.

Uncle Casper leaned over her again. 'How about it, then?' he asked her. 'What you going to say to your poppa?'

Lucy shook her head. She was too distressed to be able to speak.

'You goin' to tell him what happened? You goin' to tell him what we did? That aint goin' to please him much, now is it? His own little girl, playin' parlour-house girls with his brother-in-law? Because then I'm goin' to have to tell him all about me and your momma; and then I'm goin' to have to tell them that you was leading me on, to show that you was just as good as your momma used to be.'

'No!' Lucy choked.

Uncle Casper seized hold of her hair. 'No, what? No, you're not goin' to tell him? Or what?'

'No,' whispered Lucy. 'I'm not going to tell him.'

Uncle Casper stared at her for a moment, and then slowly smiled and nodded his head. 'You're a good girl, Lucy. I could tell that, moment I saw you again. No witchery, no bitchery. Just the kind of girl I go for.'

He cut her ankles free, and then her wrists. He stood and watched her as she miserably buttoned up her blouse, and dragged her skirt up from the floor. 'There has to be a first time sooner or later,' he told her. 'No point in waiting till you're too darned old. I mean the best age is sixteen, for a girl. That's the best age. You've wasted a year already; don't want to waste no more.'

Lucy climbed off the stack of fabric, and stood up, holding her skirt around herself with her hand. She didn't look at Uncle Casper; couldn't; but he didn't take his eyes away

50

from her once, even when he lifted up his bottle of whisky to take another swig.

'You'd better open up the store,' she told him, so quietly that he could scarcely hear her.

Uncle Casper swallowed whisky, and wiped his mouth, and sniffed. 'Okay.' Then, 'Are you all right? Didn't hurt you or nothing?'

Lucy shuffled past him, opened the stockroom door, and went back into the store. Samuel Blankenship and Henry McGuffey were both outside, their faces pressed against the window. When they saw Lucy, Samuel Blankenship rattled the doorhandle, and waved.

'All right, you old coot, keep your goddamned wool on!' Uncle Casper shouted at him. He reached out and laid his hand on Lucy's shoulder.

'Listen . . . if I hurt you or anything –'

Lucy twisted herself away. 'Don't you dare to touch me,' she shivered. 'Don't you dare to touch me, ever again.'

Uncle Casper was about to say something, but decided against it. He blew out his cheeks in silent acceptance of what she had said, and picked up the keys from the counter. 'You'll want to change y'r clothes, right?' he suggested.

Without a word, Lucy unlocked the side door, and stepped out, and closed it behind her. The wind was gusting even more strongly now, and she had to keep her skirt together with both hands. Unsteadily, she climbed the stairs at the side of the store, and let herself in. She went straight to her bedroom, locked the door behind her, and sat on her bed.

Her face in the mirror looked like the face of another girl altogether; a girl she didn't know.

'Who are you?' she whispered. The girl didn't reply.

Jack Darling came back just after dark. Lucy had closed the store at six, and now she was serving out pork and beans in the kitchen. Uncle Casper was already eating, hunched over his plate, a half-empty bottle of whisky close to his elbow.

'Well,' said Jack Darling, briskly chafing his hands together, 'you'll be happy to know that the Farmers' & Stockbreeders' Bank is more than happy to extend my credit.'

'Is that good?' asked Casper, with his mouth full. 'Gettin' yourself even deeper in debt?'

'Oh, times'll turn,' said Jack, as he sat down at the table. 'I'll have some of that buttermilk, Lucy, if there's any left.'

'Interest you in a whisky?' Casper asked him.

Jack shook his head. 'One drunk a month is enough for me.'

He began hungrily to fork up beans. It was only after the third mouthful that he realized that nobody was talking. He looked from Lucy to Casper and back again.

'Something wrong?' he asked them.

'Not as far as I know,' Casper remarked. He had only eaten half his supper but now he pushed his plate away. 'Everything's fine, as far as I know.'

'How was the store today?' Jack inquired.

'Fine,' said Casper.

'What was the take?'

'Sixteen dollars and nine cents cash money; thirty-seven dollars and fourteen cents credit.'

Jack turned back to Lucy and said, 'Mrs Barnaby come in?'

'Sure,' Casper told him. 'Mrs Barnaby came in. Bought herself some peas, and some soap, and one of them self-righting cuspidors.'

'The twenty-cent or the forty-one cent?'

'The twenty.'

Jack put down his fork. 'You should've sold her the forty-one cent, the way John Barnaby spits.'

Lucy brought over a glass of buttermilk. She tried, but she couldn't bring herself to look her father in the eye. As she turned back towards the sink, her father said, 'Lucy? What's the matter, sweetheart?'

'Nothing,' she said, without turning round. *Oh God*, she thought. *If I try to talk to him, I'll burst into tears.*

'Come on,' Jack coaxed her. 'I know when there's something wrong.'

He looked at Casper but Casper simply shrugged, and swallowed more whisky.

'Lucy –' Jack began; but Lucy untied her apron and hung it up on the back of the door and covered her face with her hands. Jack got up from the table and stood beside her.

'Lucy, what the heck's wrong?'

She smeared tears away from her eyes. 'I've got a headache, that's all. It's the weather.'

'Hey, now! Did you take anything for it?'

She shook her head. Her throat was too tight for her to speak.

Jack put his arm around her. She stiffened, but she managed to tolerate it. Jack said, 'Listen, sweetheart, you're looking awful flushed. Take yourself off to bed. Cass'n'me, we'll do the cleaning-up. I'll bring you some hot milk and some Bromo Vichy later on. You've probably tired yourself out, that's all, what with two thoughtless men to take care of.' He winked at Uncle Casper.

Lucy nodded. She allowed her father to kiss her on the cheek; then she walked woodenly off to her room. She locked the door behind her and stood with her back to it, her eyes tightly shut, trying to make herself believe that today had never happened; that it had all been a nightmare.

But her face was flushed because she had been scrubbing around her mouth with a nailbrush and witch-hazel soap, to take away the taste and the memory of Uncle Casper's saliva. She had rubbed her breasts, too, with a rough flannel facecloth, and douched herself over and over with a Wearever syringe she had taken from the store. She had hidden it behind her closet, and prayed that her father wouldn't discover that it was missing.

'Oh, Lord Jesus, please forgive me my terrible sin,' she

prayed. Then she sat down on her bed, her hands in her lap, her eyes closed, too exhausted to cry any more.

After a while, however, she turned to look at her bedside table. She frowned at it for a moment, thoughtfully. Then she reached over and opened her bedside drawer, and took out her mother's jewellery box.

She was still sitting there half an hour later when her father knocked at the door.

The pawnbroker spread the jewellery out on top of the counter. He was a tiny man, with wild white hair and pince-nez eyeglasses. Lucy noticed that his shirt-cuffs were frayed, and from that she assumed that he was probably a widower. He took out a handerchief and blew his nose, and then he said, 'What did you think this was worth?'

Lucy looked down at it. The necklaces, the rings; everything except the cameo brooch, which she was wearing. 'I don't know. It used to belong to my mother.'

'It's good quality,' the pawnbroker told her. 'Modest, but good quality. The trouble is, I have to think about market values. Know what I mean by market values?'

'I think so. My father owns a general store.'

'Ah well, in that case. But take a look at my poor emporium! Most of this stuff I can't give away for nothing, and it's supposed to be security.'

The tragedy of what had happened to western Kansas since the quarantine laws was illustrated nowhere better than here, at Lilienthal's Pawnbroker, in Hays City. Scores of Sunday-best suits hung from the ceiling; as well as hats and umbrellas and walking-sticks and violins. The window was crammed with dusty silverware; one corner of the floor was crowded with shoes. The saddest cabinet was filled with wedding-bands, dozens of them, many of them inscribed. *For Ever and Ever, Your Joshua.* But nothing was forever when your children were hungry and the bank was threatening to foreclose.

'Folks around here can't afford to buy bread, let alone violins.'

Lucy waited while the pawnbroker inspected the necklaces through a magnifying-glass. He nodded a couple of times, and then he said, 'Two hundred eighty. That's the very best I can do. It's worth more. To be honest with you, it's worth four hundred, maybe five. But two hundred eighty is the very best I can do.'

'Can't you make it more?'

He picked up one of the earrings, and turned it over. 'Maybe three hundred, but that's stretching it.'

'But I need three hundred-fifty.'

The pawnbroker shook his head. 'I'm sorry. I'm truly sorry. It's just not possible.'

'Please,' Lucy begged him. 'It's real important. I just have to have three hundred-fifty dollars.'

'Miss – what can I do? Put yourself in my shoes. You want me to cut my own throat? You want me to open my veins in front of you, so that you can watch me bleed to death?'

Lucy said, 'I can pay you back the extra fifty in six weeks' time. Or maybe even a month.'

The pawnbroker took off his pince-nez. 'You *say* you can pay me back the extra fifty in six weeks' time. But what happens if you don't? I wouldn't have a leg to stand on.'

Lucy felt as if she were suffocating. She watched with rising panic as the pawnbroker began to wrap up the jewellery in the chamois-skin she had brought it in. If *he* didn't give her the money, she didn't have any place else to go. She couldn't take the train all the way east to Salina. It had been difficult enough persuading her father to let her come to Hays, on the pretext of seeing her childhood friend Marjorie Smith, whose parents used to run the Smith Hotel in Oak City (empty these days, and derelict). If she went on to Salina, she wouldn't have any hope of getting back home before tomorrow morning.

She placed her hand protectively over her cameo brooch. *Momma, I'm sorry, I know how much you loved this brooch.* Then – as the pawnbroker held out her chamois-skin – she unfastened it, and held it up.

'If I give you this, too?' she asked him. 'It's French, genuine French. From France.'

'French, from France? No kidding.' the pawnbroker took it and inspected it through his eyeglass. 'This your mother's too?'

Lucy nodded, and swallowed. 'It was her favourite.'

'Well, I'm not surprised. It's very fine. It's Dutch, as a matter of fact, not French.' He turned it over and scrutinized the back, and then he said, 'Sure.'

'Pardon?' asked Lucy.

'I said, sure, yes, I'll give you the money. Golden eagles suit you?'

Lucy was shivering as she watched the pawnbroker count out three hundred-fifty dollars in $10 gold coins, and shake them into a small canvas bag. He escorted her to the door, and then handed them to her. 'You take care, young lady. That's a whole lot of money you're carrying there. People have been killed for a whole lot less.'

'Thank you,' she whispered, and stepped out of the shop on to the wide windy sidewalks of Main Street, Hays. It was five after twelve. There was a train back to Oak City at twenty after, if she hurried.

It was only when she was back in her room that evening, and emptied the gold coins on to her quilt to count them, that she discovered at the bottom of the bag a small package wrapped in brown tissue paper. Puzzled, she unfolded it; and there was her mother's cameo.

She held the cameo tightly in her hand, and her eyes filled with tears. How could the same world contain people who were so generous, and people who were so irredeemably foul? She waited until well past eleven o'clock. Her father had gone to bed at nine-thirty after a hard day's stocktaking, and she could hear by his breathing that he was deeply asleep. When she heard the parlour clock chime a quarter after eleven, she quietly left her room, and crept along the corridor to the small spare room where Uncle Casper was staying. She hesitated for a moment, with her heart pounding, and then she knocked.

'Who is it?' Uncle Casper demanded, in a thick voice.

'It's me, Lucy.'

There was a pause, and then the bedsprings scrunched. Uncle Casper opened the door and stood there tousle-haired in his long-johns, a hand-rolled cigarette dangling out of one side of his mouth. His room was dense with tobacco-smoke and the stink of whisky.

'Well, well, well,' said Uncle Casper, his cigarette waggling. 'If it aint my fav'rite princess. Acquired the taste for it, have we? Come back for some more of your old Uncle Casper's special treatment?'

Her skin felt freezing-cold, and her mouth was dry. She was wearing her nightgown and a dressing-robe, both tightly fastened, and she had taken the precaution of wearing a pair of winter drawers as well. 'I want to talk,' she told him.

'Well, certainly!' slurred Uncle Casper, in a genial tone. 'Come on in. How about a drink? This is the last of the real good whisky.'

Hesitantly, Lucy entered the room. The smoke was so thick that she could hardly breathe. Uncle Casper sat on the iron-framed bed and patted the mattress beside him, to indicate that Lucy should sit down.

'I think I'll stand, if you don't mind,' said Lucy.

'Whatever position takes your fancy,' Uncle Casper grinned at her.

Lucy licked her lips. 'I want you to leave,' she said, her voice breaking with nervousness.

Uncle Casper looked her up and down, but said nothing.

57

'You came here to borrow money from my father, so that you could go to California and look for oil.'

Still Uncle Casper remained silent.

'Well, I have some money . . . enough for you to start drilling, anyway. You can have it, all of it, as long as you promise to go.'

'How much?' asked Uncle Casper.

'Three hundred–fifty dollars.'

Uncle Casper raised one eyebrow. 'Is that in gold, or paper?'

'It's in gold. You can see it if you don't believe me. But you have to promise to leave tomorrow. There's a train for Denver at ten after twelve.'

Uncle Casper swallowed whisky, and sniffed. 'You're in some kind of a rush to see the back of me, Lucy.'

'Yes,' she quivered, keeping her back pressed against the wall, and the doorhandle well within reach. She had never been so much afraid of anybody in her life: not even the Oak City schoolmistress, who used to scream at her, and thrash hysterically at her hands with a leather strap.

'Is that it?' asked Uncle Casper. 'You give me the money, and I go?'

'No,' she told him. 'It's my money. I pawned momma's jewellery to get it. Everything except the cameo.'

'Ah,' grinned Uncle Casper. 'So *that's* why you went rushing off to Hays this morning. Nothing to do with visiting no friends. You aint so apple–pie innocent as you look, are you, my lady? Still – glad you kept the cameo. That was always sentimental, that cameo. Worth something, too.'

Lucy said, 'You must promise to pay me back. You know – as soon as you've found your oil.'

'Well, princess. There's no cast-iron guarantee that we *will*, or even if we do, when. Could take years. You may lose your shirt along with the rest of us, if you'll excuse the expression.'

'I know that,' said Lucy. 'But poppa doesn't know what I've done. I must redeem momma's jewellery if I can. He'll be so angry.'

'Well, princess, sure. If God decides to smile on us and we *do* strike oil –'

'And a percentage,' said Lucy, swallowing hard.

Uncle Casper stared at her, one eye wide, one eye half-closed. He had been drinking so much that he found it difficult to keep her in focus.

'A *percentage*?'

'You offered poppa a percentage.' Her voice was shaking; and even though she tried to sound brave and confident, she didn't feel it.

'Well, now,' said Uncle Casper, 'what I said to your poppa, that was a different kettle of fish altogether. Your poppa wasn't trying to ride me out of town on a rail.'

'But you want to go anyway, don't you? And if I give you my three hundred and fifty dollars, that's an investment, isn't it? That's what you told poppa. Ten percent, that's what you said.'

Uncle Casper sniffed, and swallowed phlegm. 'You got yourself a cold ear, from listenin' at keyholes?' he asked her. ''Sides,' he added, 'now I'm here, and cosy, and now you and me are rubbin' along so well, there aint such a burnin' attraction for me to move on, is there?'

'I still think you ought to pay me a percentage.'

Uncle Casper laughed, a cracking, humourless laugh. 'You're a tough nut, and no mistake. All right. You can have a percentage. Say, two-and-a-half percent of whatever profits I make, net of expenses, and net of your original stake.'

Lucy didn't really understand what he meant, but she countered, 'Five percent. You offered poppa ten.'

'I keep telling you, princess, that was different. But, all right, for the sake of peace'n'tranquill-ity, let's say five.' He held out his hand. 'How about shaking on it?'

59

Lucy opened the bedroom door. 'I never want you to touch me again, ever, as long as you live.'

'Come on, princess,' Uncle Casper cajoled her. 'Don't take it so hard. I'm still your good old Uncle Casper. You'll look back on this, one day, and you'll think different about it.'

He stood up. 'Come on, let's shake on it. Make it legal.'

Lucy backed away. 'I'll get it all down in writing. Then you can sign it. I don't want you to touch me again, never.'

'You're a tough nut, Lucy, no mistake about that.'

'I loathe you and I despise you,' Lucy whispered at him. 'I'll see you in the morning with the money, and the paper to sign. Make sure you pack your bags. And if you say one single word to poppa about the jewellery, I'll kill you. I swear on the Holy Bible, one night when you're asleep, I'll kill you.'

Uncle Casper raised his whisky glass. 'Sleep tight, princess. Don't let the bugs bite. I always liked a girl with fire.'

Lucy closed the door, and stood in the darkened corridor with the blood rushing through her head with a sound like longhorns stampeding through dry prairie grass. She stayed where she was, taking one deep breath after another; but then she heard his bedsprings squeaking, and so she hurried back to her room, and locked the door behind her.

She heard Uncle Casper lurch his way noisily outside to the privy. She took off her dressing-robe and her winter drawers, and climbed into bed, and prayed; every prayer she could think of. The moon was setting, but her room was still burnished with silver light. '*In my trouble I cried to the Lord,*' she prayed. '*Deliver my soul, O Lord, from lying lips, from a deceitful tongue.*'

On his way back to bed, Uncle Casper rapped softly at her door.

'Lucy?' he called her. 'Lucy?'

She didn't reply. She lay rigid; willing him to go away.

'Lucy . . . I want to tell you this. I'm sincere now, Lucy,

so you listen. I love you, Lucy. I love you more than you can ever know.'

'But, Lucy, I can't, I'm not qualified,' Jamie insisted. 'Supposing I make some kind of terrible mistake. It could ruin my legal career for ever.'

'Jamie, I *can't* ask anybody else. Mr Judd would go directly to poppa, and tell him all about it.'

Jamie propped his rake against the side of the stall, and brushed down his shirt with his hands. He had been mucking out his father's horses when Lucy had arrived. His sleeves were rolled up tight and there was straw in his hair. Lucy thought he looked very scruffy and very handsome.

'All I need is a simple piece of paper,' she pleaded. 'And all it has to say is that I'm lending Uncle Casper three hundred and fifty dollars to help him drill for oil; and that if he actually makes any money, he has to pay my three hundred and fifty dollars back, as well as a five per cent royalty.'

'Well,' said Jamie, reluctantly, 'I guess it doesn't have to be all that complicated. A simple deed should be sufficient. Even exchanging letters would stand up in a court of law.'

'And it doesn't matter my being under age?'

Jamie shook his head. 'Not at all. Minors enter into legal contracts every day of the week. When a kid buys a poke of cough-candy, that's a legal contract. Actually, the advantage is yours, because if your Uncle Casper fails to pay your money back, you can sue him; but if *you* break your contract in any way, there's nothing much that he can do about it, because you're too young.'

He closed the stable door, and pinned it. 'Mind you, I still think you're wasting your time. A deed's only as good as the intentions of those that put their names to it; and I wouldn't trust your Uncle Casper's intentions further'n the next corner. But come on across to the house. I'll look up something in Sansom's Contract Law.'

Lucy followed him out of the stables and along the track that ran beside the corral. On the far side, shaded by three gigantic red oaks, stood the Cullen farmhouse, an L-shaped weatherboarded building with a split-shingle roof and vivid green shutters.

Jamie's brother Ned was in the corral, yanking at the reins of a wilful chestnut pony. As Jamie and Lucy walked past, he called out, 'Where you sloping off to this time, Jamie? Thought pa told you to muck out them stables!'

'Ladies first, muck later!' Jamie retaliated, and took hold of Lucy's arm.

They went into the house. Through the open door at the end of the hallway, they could see Jamie's blonde-haired mother busy in the kitchen. She was baking biscuits, and the whole house was tuneful with the aromatic music of pecans and syrup and gingersnaps. The house was decorated austerely, in a godfearing fashion, with whitewashed walls and simple furniture. The only decoration was provided by religious samplers, embroidered by Jamie's two sisters.

'Come on upstairs,' said Jamie; and led Lucy up to his room. It was a small room in the eaves, with a view to the north-east, toward the Saline River, and Oak City beyond. Down below, tethered to the fence, Lucy could see the grey pony she had borrowed from Mr Overbay to ride down here. Next to the window stood a home-made bookshelf crammed with leather-bound lawbooks. Jamie sat on the bed, and tugged out Contract Law.

'Hey, don't close the door,' he told Lucy. 'My father doesn't approve of unmarried people being in the same room together. Not with the door closed.'

Lucy said nothing. *If only you knew what had brought me here*, she thought to herself.

Jamie thumbed through the book for a while. Then he tore a sheet of paper out of his study-book, and began to draft an agreement. After a lot of scratchings-out, Jamie produced a deed between Casper Conroy, of Wappoo Creek,

Charleston, South Carolina, and Lucy Darling, of the Jack Darling General Store, Main Street, Oak City, Kansas.

'You're sure you want to do this?' Jamie frowned. 'I wouldn't trust your uncle with a bent nickel.'

Lucy stood with her arms folded. 'I'm sure.'

'Three hundred and fifty, that's a lot of money. Supposing he comes up with nothing but dust?'

'Then I'll have spent all my savings on nothing at all.'

Jamie waved the agreement dry. 'You don't seem unduly perturbed about it.'

'A person has to take risks, sometime,' said Lucy. 'Otherwise a person might just as well crawl into her grave and let her dog fill it in for her.'

'That sounds like your Uncle Casper talking.'

Lucy didn't answer. She read the deed quickly, and then handed it back.

'I suppose you want me to come into town with you, to sign it?' Jamie asked.

'Would you mind?' I'm sorry I'm such a nuisance.'

'No,' he told her, giving her a quick kiss on the cheek. 'You're a princess.'

She swallowed a dry swallow and stared at him. 'Please don't call me that,' she told him.

'What's wrong?' he asked her. 'Something's upset you, hasn't it?'

She tried to smile. 'It's nothing. It's just that I don't like deceiving poppa that's all. If I told him that I was giving Uncle Casper all of my savings — well, he'd go crazy. He thinks that Uncle Casper ought to work for his grubstake.'

'Well, personally, I agree.'

'Don't argue about it, Jamie, please. It's something I want to do, that's all.'

'I don't know,' said Jamie. 'It's pretty hard to believe that you're so darned fond of your dear old uncle that you're prepared to give him all of that money, no questions asked, regardless of what your father thinks about it. Holy smoke,

Lucy, you don't even know if he has the legal rights to drill anywhere!'

Lucy looked away. She made it plain that she wasn't going to discuss it.

Jamie watched her for a moment, and then said, 'All right, if that's what you want. But let me tell you this, Lucy, I don't approve of what you're doing, not for one second.'

'You don't have to,' she replied.

Uncle Casper was waiting with theatrical patience at the railroad depot, pacing this way and that, and fanning himself with his hat. His two carpetbags were packed, and he was wearing his tan suit and his best brown boots. There was no sign of the train yet; but at this time of the year it was very rarely late.

He greeted Jamie with a broad grin, and pumped his hand. 'Here's the fellow who can drink,' he said, loudly, turning around to smile at two elderly ladies who were also waiting for the train.

Lucy could hardly bear to look at him. 'We have an agreement,' she said, with her eyes lowered. 'Five per cent, that's what you said, wasn't it?'

'That's c'rect, five per cent. And darned generous, too, if you don't mind my saying so.' He snatched the agreement and scanned it quickly and sniffed. 'Looks all right t'me. Show me where it says five per cent.'

Jamie stood beside him and pointed to paragraph three. 'Ah, yes,' said Uncle Casper. 'That's good. That's fine, then.'

Jamie unscrewed his pen and offered Uncle Casper his back. Uncle Casper signed his name, and then Jamie signed his. They were just shaking hands when they heard the train whistling, piercing and mournful, as it approached Oak City across the prairie.

'Time for the money, then,' said Uncle Casper.

64

Lucy opened her leather squaw bag and took out the canvas sack.

'Do you think I should count it?' asked Uncle Casper, loosening the drawstring and peering inside.

'You can if you want to. It's all there,' Lucy told him.

'All right then, I'll trust you,' grinned Uncle Casper. 'If an uncle can't trust his niece.'

The train drew in to the depot with its bell clanging and its brakes squealing as if it were running over a litter of piglets. Uncle Casper climbed aboard, and then walked along the car so that he was right next to Lucy and Jamie. He slid open the window and stuck out his head.

'You wait,' he told Lucy. 'I'll be back here before you know it, richer'n My-das.'

The train waited at the depot for almost fifteen minutes, chuffing and clanking with monotonous regularity. Jamie wanted to get back home, but Lucy didn't want to leave the depot until she had seen Uncle Casper disappearing into the distance with her own eyes. Only then would she feel safe about leaving her bedroom door unlocked at night.

At last the conductor climbed up on to the step; and the locomotive blew out a deafening salvo of steam. Uncle Casper said. 'That's it, looks like we're off.'

Lucy stepped nearer. 'Uncle Casper!' she called him. Her voice was white.

He looked down at her. 'You wait,' he promised her. 'I'll be back.'

She was almost choking, having to talk to him. But she had to know. 'Uncle Casper—what you said about you and momma—'

'What about it?'

'You made it up, didn't you, just to keep me quiet?'

Uncle Casper grinned. 'What do *you* think, princess? What's your opinion?'

'I think you made it up.'

'If that's what you think, it's not my place to try to change your mind.'

'Uncle Casper! Tell me the truth!'

He shook his head. 'Bye-and-bye, princess – as you grow older – there's one thing you're goin' to find out for yourself. And that is – the only truth is, that there aint no truth.'

The train pulled away from the depot, and Jamie came up and took hold of Lucy's arm. She stood quite still until the train was out of sight.

'Do you want to tell me what that was all about?' asked Jamie, quietly.

Lucy whispered. 'No. Not yet, anyway.'

They left the depot building and walked across to Jamie's buggy. Jamie handed her the deed and said, 'You'd better keep this paper someplace safe. You never know.'

'Jamie,' said Lucy, 'thank you for everything. Thank you for not asking too many questions.'

Jamie climbed up on to the buggy and released the brake. 'I can wait. Will I see you on Thursday, when I come into town?'

She nodded and smiled.

Jamie cracked his buggy-whip and drove off back towards the Cullen Farm. Lucy watched him for a while, and waved, and then walked home, feeling empty and tired.

'Casper gone?' her father asked her, as she walked into the store.

'Yes,' said Lucy.

'Well, he's probably gone for good this time,' her father remarked. He was weighing out tea by the half-pound; and the brass scales made a clonking noise as he reached full measure.

'I hope so,' said Lucy.

'You didn't get on with him too good this time, did you?' her father asked her.

'No,' said Lucy. 'Not too good.'

'He drinks like a whale, I'll allow you that. Never seen a man drink like that before.'

66

Jack Darling wrapped up another packet of tea, and then he said, 'I'd love to know where he managed to get hold of three hundred and fifty dollars, though, just like that.'

'Didn't he tell you?' asked Lucy.

Jack Darling shook his head. 'He's a conundrum, that man. Never did understand him, nor trusted him much, neither. If he weren't your momma's brother –'

Lucy went upstairs to change into the plain blue cotton dress she usually wore in the store. She brushed up her hair, and then she opened her jewellery box to find her barrettes. When she looked inside, she went cold. She sat down on the bed with a feeling of grief deeper than anything she had felt since her mother died.

Apart from her tortoiseshell barrettes, the jewellery box was empty. The cameo had gone.

2

It was mid-January when Jamie rode up to the store in the middle of a snow-blizzard, and tied his blanketed horse to the hitching-rail outside. He came in through the door in a whirl of snowflakes and a high shriek of wind.

The stove was hot and all the usual loungers were sitting around it, drinking whisky and discussing President Cleveland's love life. The President was fat and ugly and nearly fifty. Was he truly going to marry twenty-two-year-old Frances Folsom, or was he more interested in her mother?

Henry McGuffey said it didn't matter how old a man was, he still enjoyed the company of pretty young women.

Lucy was serving Mrs Ottinger with Rubens shirts for her one-year-old son Thomas, who was sitting in the corner of the store solemnly sucking a stick of bright crimson candy. Jamie gave Lucy a smile and a wave, and waited by the stove until she had finished, warming his hands.

'How's Saint Jerrold today?' asked Samuel Blankenship, referring to Jamie's father. 'Saved any more sinners, has he?'

Jamie grinned. 'A little religion never did anyone any harm, Mr Blankenship.'

'Couldn't agree more,' said Samuel. He chewed off another cheekful of Union Leader Cut Plug. 'Trouble is, I never could understand having a taste for it, breakfast, lunch, and dinner.'

'You want nourishment, Mr Blankenship?' Jamie told him. 'My father says the scriptures are just as good for you as pork'n'beans.'

Samuel laughed, and spat tobacco-juice into the pan of ashes in front of the stove. 'Never argue with the son of a saint.'

At last Lucy was finished with Mrs Ottinger. She never hurried the farm women when they came into the store to browse and to buy, even when they asked to see muslins and calicoes and ready-to-wear dresses that they obviously couldn't afford. They would stand transfixed in front of the old cheval-glass in the corner, holding in front of their plain wool dresses some of the finest and prettiest fabrics, and for a moment their faces would light up, and their eyes would be far away. It didn't matter that the fashions were already a year behind the times in the East, and two years behind in Paris. They were new in Oak City, Kansas.

Jamie leaned across the counter and kissed Lucy on the cheek. She smiled, but these days it was always the same – she never let him kiss her on the lips. She never let him put his arm around her, either, and when he asked her why, all she ever said was, 'I'm sorry, but I think we ought to wait.'

He tugged a folded letter out of his glove. 'I just picked this up at the depot.'

'Did you see if there was anything for us?' Lucy asked him. Today's train had been the first in four days, because of the snow.

'Couple of cases of Heinz fruit,' Jamie told her. 'Didn't see anything else.'

He handed Lucy the letter and she read it slowly. It was headed Kansas State University, Manhattan, Kansas.

'You're going to study law at the State University?' she asked him, in surprise.

He nodded. 'That's right, the whole three-year course.'

'When do you start?'

'Next semester, isn't it great? Well, I have to ask father about it first. I mean he's going to have to pay for it. But he's been a little more easy-going about my law studies lately. You couldn't say enthusiastic, but more easy-going.'

'What about Mr Collamer?' asked Lucy. 'I thought Mr Collamer was teaching you just fine.'

Jamie shrugged. 'Well, sure, but Mr Collamer doesn't have anything else to teach me. He admits it himself. He hasn't practised for fifteen years, and what I need now is proper up-to-date lectures, you know, and real practical experience. There aren't even any proper law firms in Oak City, only Lloyd Judd's.'

'Does that mean you're going to be living in Manhattan?' Lucy felt breathless and upset, as if the world had suddenly come unstuck at the seams. She hadn't realized until now how much she had depended on Jamie since Uncle Casper had assaulted her. Not as a lover; she still couldn't help tightening up whenever he touched her; but as a constant friend. Somebody who protected her, and reassured her that some men could be gentle and protective.

'I'll *have* to live there,' said Jamie. 'But I'll be back for vacations, and maybe some weekends.'

Lucy hardly knew what to say. She folded up the letter and handed it back to him.

'You don't look too pleased,' Jamie told her.

'Of course I'm pleased. I'm really proud of you.'

'I'm pretty proud of myself, to tell you the truth.'

Lucy called to Henry McGuffey, 'Hear that, Mr McGuffey? Jamie's been accepted for the State University, to study law.'

69

Henry McGuffey raised his whisky-glass. 'Congratulations, young Cullen! How about a drink?'

'How about five drinks, without taking a breath, and the Lord's Prayer back'ards?' Samuel Blankenship suggested, and slapped his thigh in amusement. The social circle around the general store stove hadn't let Jamie forget last summer's wager. It had now become part of Oak City folklore.

Jamie shook his head. 'I have to get back. The cattle need feeding something desperate, with all this snow on the ground.'

Lucy walked to the door with him. She was looking white, and the reflected light from the snow outside made her appear whiter still. It was partly the winter, and the lack of sunshine. It was partly the memory of Uncle Casper, and what he had done to her. She had imagined that it would fade, and that one morning she would be able to wake up and go through the day without thinking about it once. But it remained raw and recent and startlingly vivid, as if it had happened only yesterday. Sometimes when she thought about it she found herself rubbing her wrists, as if Uncle Casper had only just cut her free.

Jamie touched her fine blonde hair. 'You look like you could use a tonic. Mother always swears by Dr Bradfield's.'

Lucy smiled faintly. 'I'm not surprised. It's two-fifths alcohol.'

'I'll call in to see you on Sunday, okay? If the snow's not too bad,' he told her.

'All right,' she said. Then, 'Do you really *have* to go to Manhattan?'

He looked at her questioningly. 'Of course, if I want to be a lawyer.'

'But what about us?'

Jamie took a deep breath. 'Us?'

'Well, if you're gone for three years –'

Jamie waited for her to finish, but she didn't. Instead, she reached out and touched the horn button of his coat, twisting it between her fingers.

'Lucy,' said Jamie, in a low, gentle voice, 'the way I see it, right now, there isn't any "us". Leastways, there hasn't been for six or seven months. You never kiss me, you never let me hold you, you never say you love me. You didn't want to come to the barndance; you didn't want to come to the carnival; you didn't want to come to Hays City, for the cavalry dance. Whenever we're together, you scarcely say two words to me. Now, let's be fair about it, we're still friends, but you can hardly call that "us".'

'Jamie –' she said, suddenly tugging at his button.

'I'm sorry, sweetheart,' he replied. 'There's so much I want to see; so much I want to do. The world is *huge*, Lucy, and I want to be part of it. I don't want to spend the rest of my days mucking out horses in Oak City, Kansas.'

Even more softly, he said, 'Remember, you used to have a dream too. All that stuff about being a socialite, going to dances. Rubbing shoulders with the rich. What happened to that?'

'Maybe I grew up,' said Lucy; although she didn't mean it. She didn't feel any more mature. She just felt dirty, and spoilt, like a brand-new doll that somebody stepped on, and then carelessly dropped into a muddy ditch.

Even now she couldn't convince herself that her lost purity didn't somehow show on her face.

Uncle Casper had robbed her of her dream that day in the stockroom. She didn't even bother to take dancing lessons any more. What was the use? She lived hour by hour, working in the store, cleaning the house, sweeping the floors and cooking the meals and ironing her father's worn-out shirts. Life at least seemed safe that way.

Jamie said, 'I promise I'll write.'

'I thought you wanted to marry me,' she persisted.

'Well . . .' he said, 'sure . . . but things can change.'

'Does that mean you don't love me any more?'

'Of course I love you. But, come on Lucy, it isn't easy to go on loving somebody who doesn't show any signs of loving you back.'

71

She lowered her head and looked down at the floor. Jamie stood watching her for a while, and then said, 'I have to go. I'm sorry.'

'You don't have anything to be sorry for,' she said.

'Well, maybe not. But I'm sorry things didn't turn out different.'

She looked up, and then she kissed him, on the lips. 'Me too,' she said, and turned away.

Jamie tugged on his gloves, and opened the door. Snow came tumbling into the warm interior of the store, and Samuel Blankenship looked up gravely.

'You inning, young fellow, or outing? Whichever it is, make up your mind before this stove freezes over.'

Lucy lay in bed that night and silently wept to herself. Then she stopped weeping and lay staring at the ceiling. The wind had died a little and the town lay eerily silent. She could hear icicles dripping along the eaves; and the roof cracking under the weight of the snow.

She thought of her dream. She thought of dancing, and laughter, and varnished carriages. She thought of silk ballgowns and rows of pearls.

Uncle Casper had been right. It had been one of those fantasies that would never come true. She didn't even have her mother's jewellery to wear to the Oak City barndance; let alone diamonds to wear to a New York ball.

Ever since she had been able to read the labels in her father's store, she had fancied that she would travel all over the world. Bourjois' Violette de Parme, from Paris, France. Myron Parker's Bay Rum, from Puerto Rico. Lea & Perrins' Worcestershire Sauce, from England. And all those extraordinary spices from the Bombay Trading Company, Bombay, India.

But now the names had shrunk back to being nothing more than names; far-sounding cities, in tiny print, on dull-coloured labels. Lucy felt as if the whole globe had dwindled

72

to the size of the Jack Darling General Store, and that she would never escape.

She was almost asleep when she heard a train-whistle blow. The blizzard must have died down for a train to be able to get through. She wondered which direction it had come from, east from Kansas City or west from Denver. Trains from the east usually brought them goods they had ordered, and they were running very low on sugar and washing-powders and navy beans. Well, she would find out in the morning, when she took the buckboard along to the depot.

Not a quarter of an hour had passed, however, before she heard footsteps on the wooden sidewalk below her window, and then somebody climbing slowly up the stairs at the side of the building. There was a knock at the kitchen door, then another, then another. The knocking went on and on, loud and insistent. Whoever it was, they weren't planning on going away.

Lucy sat up. She doubted if her father had heard it. His bedroom was at the back, overlooking the yard, and he was usually so tired by the time he got to bed that he slept like a dead man.

She climbed out of bed, took down her dressing-robe from the hook on the back of the door, and went through the parlour to the kitchen, tying up her robe as she went. A dark shape was visible through the spiderweb glass in the kitchen door, one arm lifted as it beat against the frame.

Lucy went up to the door and called, 'Who is it? What do you want?'

There was a long pause. She could hear the wind whining through the cracks around the sides of the door. Then a hoarse voice said, 'Lucy? That you?'

She felt as if she had been dropped into a tub of freezing-cold water. There was no mistaking that voice, however hoarse it was. Uncle Casper had returned.

'Uncle Casper?' she whispered.

73

'Open the door,' he demanded. 'I'm dyin' of frostbite out here.'

Lucy took hold of the door-key, but she found it impossible to turn it. Something inside her simply wouldn't let her do it. Her heart danced a slow waltz, *one-two-three, one-two-three.*

Uncle Casper drummed at the door yet again. 'Lucy, I'm dyin'! For Christ's sakes, let me in!'

But she couldn't turn the key. He rattled and banged and shouted out 'Lucy! Will you open the damned door!' but she couldn't turn the key.

At that moment, however, her father came into the kitchen. She couldn't see his face because it was so dark. But she could see the silhouette of his sleep-scruffed hair and his worn-out robe. 'Lucy?' he said. 'What in hell's going on? Who's making all that noise?'

'It's Uncle – Casper,' she told him, turning away from the door.

'Uncle Casper? Well, let him in, for pity's sake! You can't leave a man standing outside on a night like this!'

But Lucy stayed where she was, with her back to the door, unable to touch it. She was shaking with fear, as if she expected Uncle Casper to come roaring through the door like Satan himself, and to rape her where she stood.

Jack reached out and held her arm. 'You're cold, sweetheart,' he said. 'You're freezing.'

Lucy said, 'Poppa, I –' but then without hesitation, Jack turned the key in the lock and opened up the door. Uncle Casper came stamping in, whacking his gloves together, as big and as black and as shaggy as a bear.

'Jesus, Jack! A man could have perished!'

Jack shut the door and locked it again. Then he went over to the hutch and lit the lamp. Uncle Casper was wearing a huge fur coat and a huge fur hat, and black boots. He was carrying a large leather portmanteau. His beard and his eyebrows were encrusted with ice, and there were thick

74

icicles underneath his nostrils. When he saw Lucy standing with her back to him, he didn't say anything, not even 'hello', but he didn't take his eyes away from her as he eased himself out of his coat. Underneath he was wearing a well-tailored Norfolk jacket and knee breeches. He sat down on one of the kitchen chairs and Jack handed him the bootjack.

'Taken me over a week to make it here from California,' he remarked, easing off his boots. 'We were stuck solid for a day and a night in the High Sierras. It's taken me two clear days to get here from Denver.'

'How are things in California?' Jack asked him. He went across to the range and picked up the blue-enamel coffee-pot. 'What about some coffee? The hob's still hot.'

'Not for me,' said Uncle Casper. 'Keeps me from sleeping.' He reached into the inside pocket of his suit for a silver flask. He unscrewed it, lifted it up, and said, 'Good health. Here's to the dollar, and to whisky, and to immoral ladies wherever they may be!'

He took three long swallows of whisky; then burped into his fist. 'Don't know if I would've survived that journey, without this flask here. Jesus, it was cold in them railroad cars. Cold? We considered setting light to the seats, just to keep ourselves warm.'

'You're looking real good, if you don't mind my saying so,' Jack remarked. 'Did you find any oil?'

Uncle Casper was about to take another pull from his flask, but he lowered it and stared. 'Did I find any oil? Didn't you get my wire?'

Jack shook his head. 'Telegraph service is pretty irregular around here.'

Uncle Casper threw back his head and let out a great shout of laughter. 'Did I find any oil! Here –' he said, and opened his coat, and lifted his pocket-watch out of his vest pocket. 'Look at this, and then ask me if I found any oil!'

Jack took hold of the watch and held it in the palm of his hand. The watch was solid gold, its face engraved with scrolls.

'Turn it over,' said Uncle Casper; and when he did so, Jack saw a rose design, on a background of pavé-set diamonds, with petals of real rubies and leaves of real emeralds.

'Well, I'm damned,' he said. 'You actually struck oil.'

Uncle Casper nodded. 'Ferris and Conroy Oil Company, of Seal Beach, California.'

'Well, I'm damned, ' said Jack.

Uncle Casper took his watch back and grinned widely. 'Now, Jack! You regret you didn't back me now, don't you? Hunh? Just think about it! If you'd have been a little more foresighted – if you'd have been a little more trusting, a little more free-and-easy with your money . . . well, you could have been a wealthy man, as of today. They told us we was mad, me and Ferris, drilling where we did . . . but we kept on drilling and we kept on drilling, and November first we struck oil. And now I'm rich, Jack, and I'm making a thousand dollars a day without lifting a finger.'

Jack slowly rubbed his unshaven chin. 'A thousand dollars a day?'

'A thousand dollars a day. Maybe more, by now! Maybe fifteen hundred.'

'Fifteen hundred?' Lucy's father turned away with such a look of defeat and injustice on his face that Lucy could hardly bear it. He filled the coffee-pot with water and put it on the hob to boil.

'You're sure you don't want a whisky?' Uncle Casper asked him. 'You sure look like you could use it.'

Jack said, 'No thanks, Casper. I have to get up early tomorrow. I have a store to run.'

'Ha!' laughed Casper. 'Sure you do! Sure you do! Weighin' out butter, shovellin' out beans! It's a hard life, Jack! It's a real hard life!'

'You can use the spare room again, if you like,' Jack told him. 'Lucy – would you make sure that the bed's made up?'

Lucy nodded. She kissed her father, and then crossed the kitchen towards the door. As she did so, however, Uncle

76

Casper stuck his leg out in front of her to block her way, and gave her a wary, suggestive grin. 'Aint yo goin' to kiss your old Uncle Casper? He's a man o' means, now. Somebody to look up to. Why – you aint said one p'lite word to me since I walked through that door.'

Lucy stood stiffly with her hands by her sides. 'I have to make your bed,' she told him, in a cold voice.

'Not one little kiss?' Uncle Casper asked her, tapping his lips with his finger.

'I'm sorry,' said Lucy. 'I'm tired.'

Uncle Casper smiled at Jack and shifted his leg out of the way, but as Lucy tried to walk past him, his arm came out as quick as a bullwhip and snatched at her sleeve, pulling her on to his lap. Before she could struggle free, he kissed her, wetly and ferociously, right on the mouth.

Lucy wrenched herself away from him, and struck at him with both fists. As he tried to protect his face, he lost his balance and toppled sideways off his chair. He landed noisily on the floor, surprised and winded. Lucy wiped her mouth with her sleeve, almost hysterical, again and again, and spat out Uncle Casper's saliva. She felt as if he had infected her with every kind of foul disease there ever was.

'Lucy! What the heck!' Jack exclaimed, shocked. 'Casper, are you all right?'

Uncle Casper heaved himself up again, laughing. 'Bruised my butt, I think, Jack! But nothin' more serious than that! What a spitfire, hey? What a spitfire!'

Lucy stared at him wide-eyed; still shaking; still rubbing at her mouth with the sleeve of her robe.

'Come on, Lucy,' her father told her. 'I think you'd better say you're sorry to your Uncle Casper for that. He was only funning.'

'Funning?' said Lucy. 'Look at him, he's drunk! I can't stand to be kissed by drunks!'

Uncle Casper laughed, and sniffed, and took out his flask.

'How many drunks have you been kissed by, Lucy Darling my darling?'

'One too many,' Lucy retorted. She stared at her father to make it quite clear that she didn't have the slightest intention of apologizing, and then she stalked out of the room and slammed the door behind her.

She heard her father say, '... little upset ... her boyfriend's going off to law school ...'

'Oh, you mean the drinker,' Casper replied, and laughed some more. 'Five whiskies, without a breath; never saw anybody do that before. Never did it myself! Didn't even think it was possible!'

Lucy didn't make up Uncle Casper's bed. Goddamn him, he could sleep on the floor for all she cared. She hated him so much she could hardly breathe. She locked her bedroom door, then she filled her washbasin and scrubbed at her mouth with her facecloth.

She blew out her lamp and went to bed; but she couldn't sleep. She lay on her back listening to the murmuring of voices from the parlour. Then she heard the kitchen door open and close; and she could guess what was happening. Her father was going down to the store to fetch up another bottle of whisky. She could almost have hated her father for being so weak; but of course he didn't know what Uncle Casper had done to her, and she knew that he was entertaining him only because her mother would have wanted him to.

It was just after two o'clock in the morning when she heard her father retire to bed. She heard him tread carefully along the darkened corridor to the spare room; and then pause and murmur, 'Goddamn it,' when he discovered that she hadn't made up Uncle Casper's bed. She waited, holding her breath, expecting him to knock at her door, but he didn't. She heard him open the blanket chest, and make up the bed himself.

'Oh, poppa,' she whispered to herself. 'I'm sorry.' She

loved him so much for his patience and his kindness and his daily suffering. If only she could have told him what had happened.

She closed her eyes and tried to imagine her mother. She tried to remember her all dressed up in her blue silk dress, laughing. She tried to remember her at Christmas-time, singing carols and stirring the puddings. She tried to remember her dancing. But all she could picture was a hunted desperate face, white as ivory, and wrists as thin as wooden spoons, and eyes that were losing all of their life.

Her mother had died the week after her thirty-sixth birthday. Lucy wondered what it would be like when *she* was thirty-six – and when she was thirty-seven, and older than her own mother.

She was almost asleep when her doorhandle was clumsily turned around; and then there was a scratching at the door. She went cold. She lay with her eyes open, not moving, not even breathing.

'Lucy . . .' whispered Uncle Casper. 'Lucy, c'n you hear me?'

She didn't reply. She waited and waited, and for a moment she thought he might have given up and gone away, but then he scratched at the door a second time.

'Lucy . . . I came to give you y'r money back . . . y'r three hundred-fifty dollars. I've got it all here . . . golden eagles just the same like you gave me. C'n you hear me, Lucy? Are you awake? I've got your money. So's we're quits, you understan' . . . you can buy back y'r momma's jewellery.'

Still Lucy refused to reply. Uncle Casper sniffed and shuffled his feet, and then he said, 'I've come a long way, Lucy, just to square things up. All I want is for us to say that we're quits. I don't want nothing; nothing at all. C'n you hear me, princess? Just that bitty paper, that's all I want, so's we're quits.'

So that was why Uncle Casper had toiled all the way back to Kansas, in the middle of winter! He wanted to revoke their agreement, so that he wouldn't have to pay her five per cent of his oil profits.

No, she thought. *Five per cent is your punishment for what you did to me. I'm not letting you out of this one, uncle. I'm going to take my share and I'm going to go on taking my share until you die or your oil-well runs dry, and I know which of those two things I want to happen first.*

Uncle Casper scratched at the door-panel yet again. 'Lucy, are you hearin' me? I've got y'r money, Lucy, plus interest if you want it. Two per cent, now that's fair. You're lucky to get y'r stake back so quick, princess, plenty of people lose their money for good. And let me tell you this – I'm givin' you back this money before I've earned it. We aint broke even yet, me and Ferris, and I aint going to see any kind of profit out of that well for years and years. Maybe never will.'

My God, thought Lucy. *You're so grotesque!* She had seen the word 'grotesque' in a magazine, under a steel-engraving of gargoyles at Rouen Cathedral, in France. There had been something about the bulging eyes and stretched-open mouths of those gargoyles that had reminded her of Uncle Casper, that day that he had assaulted her.

'Lucy?' called Uncle Casper; but this was followed by an even longer silence.

Lucy strained her ears. Had he tiptoed off to his room? Had he fallen asleep in the corridor? She was just about to climb out of bed and go to look when he cleared his throat, and said, 'Lucy? If you're awake, you sweet thing, you listen to me. I'm tryin' to do right, you understand me? I'm tryin' to make up for treatin' you wrong. You can have y'r money, and another hundred besides. How's that? And, there's somethin' else, too. Your momma's cameo brooch? I guess you realized it was me that took it; but believe me, Lucy, I had to have all the money I could lay my hands on, and I pawned that brooch and got me thirty-nine dollars and that bought me all the drilling-bits I needed.

'But I redeemed it, when the well came in; and I've brought it with me. And if you give me that bitty paper, princess, you can have it back, and welcome, even though it's sentimental to me, too.'

Lucy sat up rigidly in bed. She was tempted for one moment to open the door and demand her mother's brooch back right away. But she took a deep breath and gripped the blankets and stayed silent. Uncle Casper was wily and violent, and there was no telling what he might do.

No, she thought. *He's going to bed now. He must be exhausted after travelling all the way from Denver in this weather; and apart from that he must have drunk the best part of a bottle-and-a-half of whisky. He'll sleep like a log.*

She felt a thrill of fear at what she was thinking. But she was determined that Uncle Casper had got the better of her for the very last time. She would have her five per cent; and her mother's cameo brooch; and Uncle Casper would never touch her or kiss her again.

I'll wait till he's asleep, and then I'll go through his pockets and steal the brooch back again.

There was a bumping noise. It sounded as if Uncle Casper was pressing his forehead against the door. 'Let me tell you somethin', Lucy . . . you may not think it, sometimes, but I'm real fond of you. When I was out in California, I used to think about you . . . you're a fine-lookin' girl, Lucy, I tell you that true. I used to think of you tied up in them ribbons . . . and I used to *shake*, Lucy, I used to *shake*! And it weren't them California earthquakes, neither.'

He paused, and sighed, his forehead still pressed against the door. 'Tied up in them ribbons, Lucy . . . you was a man's exotic-est dream come true.'

At last, after sniffing and coughing and shuffling a little longer, Uncle Casper dragged himself along the corridor to the spare room. Lucy heard the clunking of the whisky bottle that he was carrying against the door-jamb. Then the door shut, and she heard him collapsing into bed.

She was deeply tired, and it was hard for her to stay awake. She waited until three o'clock struck, then half-past three. At last, when she was sure that Uncle Casper must be sleeping, she climbed out of bed and wrapped herself in her robe.

Outside her bedroom window, Oak City lay white and silent under two feet of snow, a collection of wooden dollhouses out of a child's wintry dream. She unlocked her door and stood in the corridor for a long time, listening. All she could hear was her father's deep, regular breathing; and a crackling snoring from Uncle Casper's room.

She had never thought of herself as brave; and she had never imagined that she would ever feel vengeful. But she was so determined to punish Uncle Casper for what he had done – no, for even less than that – for being alive, for being what he was – that she made her way along the corridor with a set face and clenched fists and nothing but the abrupt appearance of the Devil himself could have persuaded her to go back.

She reached Uncle Casper's door. He had closed it; but his lamp was still lit, and she could smell tobacco-smoke. She waited for a moment, keeping her eyes on the dull little picture of Charlotte, North Carolina, which her mother had always kept in the corridor to remind her of home. A farmhouse, in Mecklenburg County, with ducks in the yard. Then she turned the doorhandle, and eased open the door.

Uncle Casper was lying on top of his quilt, still dressed, still wearing his boots. His eyes were closed and his mouth was open and if he hadn't been snoring Lucy would have taken him for dead. The smell of whisky and sweat was so overpowering that she had to clamp her hand over her mouth to prevent herself from gagging.

As Lucy crept around the foot of the bed, she saw that

Uncle Casper had taken a bottle of whisky to bed with him. He must have fallen asleep while he was drinking it, because the bottle had fallen over sideways and emptied all over his vest and his trousers. One hand curled lightly around the bottle, twitching every now and then as Uncle Casper dreamed.

Dear God, she thought, *what kind of dreams can a man like this be dreaming*.

She went to the bureau, where he had scattered his loose change and his tobacco-pouch and cigarette-papers. There was no sign of the cameo brooch there. She slid open the top two drawers, one after the other. One was empty; in the other lay a hammerless .32 pocket revolver, and some grey-looking handkerchiefs.

All the other drawers were empty. Uncle Casper hadn't bothered to unpack yet. He must have the cameo in his bag; or in one of his pockets.

Watching him carefully, Lucy knelt down beside the bed and unfastened the clasps of his bag. He snorted, and stirred, and said something that sounded like, 'Ferris, you sumbitch . . . no damn good at all.' Lucy froze, her knees trembling with the strain, her eyes wide; but Uncle Casper went on snoring.

It was difficult to see inside the case when it was opened. The lamp was on the opposite side of the bed, and so Lucy was crouching in shadow. She lifted out one or two silk shirts, and a handful of crumpled silk drawers, and a pair of corduroy trousers with some stiff yellowish stain on them. But she couldn't make out what was in the bottom of the case. She could feel some papers, and some pens, and some metal bits and pieces that must have been something to do with drilling for oil.

She stood up, and made her way around the bed, and cautiously picked up the oil-lamp. It was a heavy glass Bordeaux parlour-lamp, embossed with bunches of grapes coloured true-to-life. It had been a Christmas present from some friends of her mother's, and even though it must have cost more than three dollars, her mother had always hated it.

Lucy took the lamp around to the case, and held it up while she explored inside. The bottom of the case was awash with rubbish – railroad schedules, police suspenders, buttons, hairbrushes, Kissingen Salts (for obesity), Methylene Compound (for gonorrhea), valves, spring-loaded catches, a box of four barbers' razors, and a dog's-eared copy of *Illustrated Day's Doings and Sporting World* with a cover-line which promised pictures of 'frisky women' inside.

She didn't dare to tip up the entire contents of the case on to the carpet, but she was fairly sure that the cameo brooch wasn't there. She pushed back the shirts and the underwear, and stood up again, holding the oil-lamp like the Statue of Liberty. Uncle Casper must have the brooch in one of his pockets.

Biting her lip, she approached the bed. Uncle Casper had stopped snoring now, but his breathing was harsh and slow and regular. Carefully, Lucy tugged the purple silk handkerchief out of the breast pocket of his coat, and then slid two fingers inside, to see if the brooch were there.

Next, she lifted the other side of his coat, and explored his inside pockets. Nothing, except for a folded-over pamphlet.

She tried the ticket pockets at the front of his vest, then his side pockets. All of them were empty. She was shivering with cold and concentration, and with the effort of holding up the heavy lamp. She was just about to try his trouser pockets, however, when a strong hand closed around the wrist in which she was holding the lamp.

'*Ah!*' she cried, and looked up in fright. Uncle Casper, bleary-eyed, was smiling at her.

'Well, well . . .' he said, in a voice still clogged with sleep. 'I was right, then, was I? You want some more pleasurin'? You came back to your old Uncle Casper for more of them fun and games.'

'Let go of me!' Lucy hissed at him. 'Let go!'

Uncle Casper tightened his grip. 'What you whisperin' for? Frightened your poppa's goin' to find out? Well, we can keep quiet about this, if that's what you want . . . I don't mind. Romantic chatter aint totally necessary, in spite of what the women's papers say.'

'Let go of me! I want my mother's brooch!'

'Oh . . . so that's it? You didn't want no lovin' at all! You just came in here to steal my property! Well, let me tell you somethin', I don't take kindly to that. I don't take kindly to that at-all!'

He squeezed her wrist so tight that the lamp shuddered in her hand. 'I'll tell you what, though, princess, we can make a deal, you and me. An agreement, let's say! You can give me some of your lovin' now, and maybe I'll think about giving your momma's brooch back!'

Lucy thought of the revolver in the top bureau drawer, and wondered wildly if it were loaded. And, if it were – if she would have the courage to pick it up and use it.

But Uncle Casper was holding her in such a vicious grip that she couldn't get free. He was grinning at her, showing his teeth, as if he were quite prepared to bite a chunk out of her living flesh. *That uncle of yours has got the devil perched on his shoulder*, that's what Mrs Sweeney had told her, and Mrs Sweeney had known her men.

'Please, uncle,' she pleaded. 'I'm going to drop this lamp in a moment.'

Uncle Casper blew her a kiss, then smiled again, with strings of saliva stretching between his lips like spiderwebs. 'You and me, I do believe we was born for each other. Even if we wasn't, I must say that I've taken a fancy to you.'

He sniffed, and then he said, 'Seems to me like you've got yourself a choice, princess. Either you treat me nice; or else I shout out to your poppa that you came to my room, lookin' to misbehave yourself. And what's he goin' to say to that? Because the supportin' evidence is, that here you are.'

'Uncle Casper, I'm asking you, let go!' Lucy demanded;

and she knew that she wasn't going to ask him again. If he didn't release her, she would scratch his face.

Uncle Casper reached out with his free hand to take the lamp away from her. But as he did so, Lucy twisted her arm, and the lamp dropped on to his chest. The globe rolled off on to the floor, and the wicks flared up, and before Uncle Casper could say, 'Son-of-a-bitch!' his whisky-soaked clothes roared up into a sheet of flames.

Uncle Casper yelled. Lucy screamed, although it was more of a moan than a scream; and stumbled back, suddenly free of him.

'I'm on fire!' Uncle Casper raged at her. 'I'm on fire, Goddamn it!'

His coat and his vest were furiously ablaze. He tried to knock the lamp off his stomach, but the glass shattered, and he was suddenly awash with a lapful of fiery oil. He screeched a terrible high, harsh screech, and jumped off the blazing bed, enveloped in flames from the knees upward.

'God help me! I'm burning!'

He spun and danced and flapped his arms and screamed, trying to beat the flames out with hands that were themselves alight. His beard was alight, his hair was alight, fire rippled out of his cheeks. Backing away from him, horrified, Lucy could see his agonized face, eyes wide open, as it wrinkled and shrivelled and melted right in front of her.

'Poppa!' she shrieked 'Poppa!' She knew that you were supposed to roll people on the ground, if they were burning, or cover them up with a blanket. But the bed was burning, too, and the room was filled with whirling fragments of cotton quilt and smouldering hanks of horsehair; and through this maelstrom of fire, Uncle Casper was blazing like a tar-barrel, so hot that she couldn't get close.

The bedroom door hurtled open, and Jack Darling tumbled into the room, in his nightshirt. The draft of the door opening fed the flames with a huge rush of fresh oxygen, and Uncle Casper virtually exploded in front of them, in an incandescent pillar of human flesh. Lucy glimpsed his arms, held up in front of him in the stiff fetal posture that everybody adopts when they are burning to death; and his diminutive blackened head, like a lump of tarry coal.

Then her father snatched her out of the room, and pushed her whimpering and hysterical into the corridor. He slammed the bedroom door shut, and shouted at her, 'Fire-extinguishers! Go down to the store and bring me up as many as you can carry!'

Lucy hesitated, shaking. She felt as the night were closing in on her from all sides. But Jack Darling hustled her along the corridor and into the kitchen. He opened the kitchen door for her, and pressed the keys to the store into her hand. 'You understand me! Fire-extinguishers! I'm getting to work with the bucket!'

In bare feet, slipping and stumbling, her robe snapping in the penetrating wind, Lucy went down the icy steps to the back of the store. Behind her, she heard her father furiously trying to prime the kitchen pump. If it had frozen during the early hours of the morning, there would be no hope of putting out the flames, and the store could easily burn down to the ground.

Fumbling with cold and shock, Lucy opened up the stockroom and hurried to the far end, where they kept the blue glass hand-grenades for putting out fires. She cleared six or seven parasols off the top of the crate of hand-grenades with a sweep of her arm, and hefted it up. Panting, almost losing her balance, she climbed back up the stairs to the smoke-filled kitchen.

She needn't have hurried. When she reached Uncle Casper's room, coughing and gasping, the hand-grenades rattling in their crate, she found that the flames were already out. Her father had drenched the bed with two bucketfuls of water, and now it was simply smouldering. Behind the bed – although she hadn't wanted to look at it – she saw the twisted branch-like creature that had been her Uncle Casper lying face-down on the floor, its blackened teeth exposed.

Jack had opened the window, and already the smoke was shuddering off into the night. He took the crate of fire-extinguishers out of Lucy's hands, and said quietly, 'It's all right, sweetheart. It's over.'

Lucy covered her face with her hands. Her eyes were watering from the smoke, but she wasn't crying. She didn't feel anything at all. She felt completely detached from herself, as if she were somebody else altogether, the girl she had seen in the mirror after Uncle Casper had raped her.

Dearest Jesus, she had wanted revenge; but nothing like this.

As the night began to fade, and the sky lightened to the colour of ice-water, they sat in the parlour, wrapped up in their overcoats, and shared a potful of black coffee and brandy. The smell of smoke was piercing and sour.

'He must've reached out to turn off the lamp, and toppled it over,' said Jack, trying to be calm, trying to be logical about it, trying not to give way to shock, although he couldn't stop himself from flapping his hands as he spoke, like two snared doves. 'God above ... I told him that whisky was going to be the death of him ... but I didn't expect it to kill him *this* way.'

Lucy asked hoarsely, 'What are we going to do now?'

Jack said, 'I don't know. I guess we'll have to call Ernie Truelove, down at the funeral parlour. Then we'll have to get word to the county coroner, one way or another, to see if he feels like travelling two hundred miles in the snow to look at a man who was burned up to nothing but ashes. Don't suppose the sheriff'll want to know. Accidental death, after all.' He paused, and then he said, 'You heard him screaming, was that it, and you ran into his room and there he was, burning?'

Lucy nodded, tight-mouthed. She didn't want to think

about it. She knew already that she was going to have nightmares about it.

Jack was quiet for a while, blowing the steam from his cup of coffee. 'Natural justice, I guess. The hand of God. It was bound to catch up with him sooner or later. The drink, you know, or the drunkenness.'

Lucy said, 'Do we have to talk about him any more?'

Jack reached out and laid his hand on hers. 'No, of course not. I'm sorry. Why don't you ride out to Jamie's place, and spend the day there, while me and Ernie Truelove clear the place up?'

Lucy thought it about for a while, and then said, 'All right, poppa, that's a good idea. I don't think I can stand to – well, I think I will, that's all. Jamie's always been kind; even when I didn't deserve it.'

'Maybe you can persuade him to make an honest woman of you,' said Jack; in an off-key attempt to say something light-hearted.

Lucy stood up, and went across to her father's chair, and kissed him on the forehead. He took hold of her hand, and said, 'Whatever you do, you make sure you rest. You look tired out.'

'Yes, poppa. I love you, poppa.'

'I love you too, sweetheart.'

She filled up a kettle of water to heat on the kitchen stove. While Jack went down to see Ernie Truelove at the Truelove Funeral Parlour on Cross Street, she washed her hair in the basin in her bedroom, and combed it out. At least it didn't reek of smoke any more. While she was rouging her cheeks, so that she wouldn't look so tired and ghastly, she thought she heard a creaking noise from Uncle Casper's room, and the skin on her scalp crawled in instantaneous terror. She could imagine him lifting himself up off the floor, charred and black, and walking stiffly along the corridor to take his revenge.

She listened and listened, but then the creaking came

again, and she realized that it was only the bedroom door, creaking in the wind from the open window.

She dressed in her blue-velvet riding-habit. It was warm, even if Jamie had seen it dozens of times before. Then she put on her dark blue broadcloth overcoat, and her white-fox scarf, and her riding-boots. By the time her father came trudging back up the stairs, she was ready to leave for the Cullen farm.

'I'm off now, poppa,' she told him, as he coughed and sniffed and stamped the slush from his boots.

'Okay, sweetheart, you take care. It looks like more snow before lunchtime.'

'That's all right. If it snows too much, I'll just stay over.'

She kissed him, and squeezed his hand.

'You'll be all right, won't you?' she asked him, glancing back towards Uncle Casper's room.

'Sure. I'm afraid of one or two things in this life. I'm afraid of God, and being alone, and I'm afraid of the Devil. But I'm not afraid of the dead.'

Lucy left the store and made her way along the snowy street to Overbay's to borrow their grey pony. Although the drifts were so deep, a few people had stuggled in from outlying farms for provisions or medicines or human company, and their blanketed horses stood patiently tied to the hitching-rails.

Oak City was silent; a tiny silent town on a vast silent plain. But somehow Lucy felt *shut in*, as if she could hardly catch her breath – as if the world ended where the buildings ended, and the snowy landscape and the snowy sky were pressing in on all sides like fat suffocating pillows. She took two deep lungfuls of ice-cold air, and then she lifted her skirts and stepped over the snowdrifts to the Overbay's store.

She found Jamie up in the hayloft, bundled up in a sheepskin coat, his ears covered by the flaps of a havelock cap, forking bales of hay down to his younger brother Martin. It was gloomy and cold and aromatic in there, and Martin kept sneezing.

'Lucy!' called Jamie, brushing the hay from his overalls. 'What brings you down here?'

'Can we talk?' asked Lucy.

Jamie said, 'Sure,' and forked down one last bale. It thumped on to the floor of the barn only inches in front of Martin's feet.

'Hey, watch it!' Martin complained. 'You darn near beaned me with that one!'

Jamie climbed down the rickety loft-ladder, pulling off his gloves. 'Martin – how about loading up the wagon? I'll give you a hand in just a minute.'

Martin lifted up a bale in each hand, and sneezed yet again.

'Bless you,' said Lucy.

'Oh, don't fret yourself, it's always me that has to do the hard work,' Martin grumbled. 'Soon as anything that looks like effort rears its ugly head, Jamie finds a nickel-plated excuse for quitting.'

Lucy smiled. 'I'm glad to know that I'm nickel-plated, anyway.'

Jamie took hold of her arm. 'Surprised to see you down here,' he told her.

'Why are you surprised? We're still friends, aren't we?'

'Well, sure. But things haven't exactly been lovey-dovey between us, have they?' His eyes were bright: he was provoking her on purpose.

'Oh, Jamie,' she said. 'Have I really been that much of a shrew?'

Jamie pushed open the barn door. 'Come on over to the house,' he said. 'Mother's been baking hermits.'

'Can I talk to you alone?' Lucy asked him.

Jamie shrugged. 'Of course you can.'

'I mean now, out here.'

'Well, okay, sure. I don't mind the goddamned perishing cold if you don't.'

She covered her eyes with her hand. She hardly knew where to begin; or what to say. Out here in the snow, on the Cullen ranch, the events of last night seemed absurdly theatrical, like some kind of monstrous marionette-show, as if they hadn't happened at all. Lucy looked away, towards the empty corral, and the house, and the snow-burdened oaks. She wanted to cry but somehow she couldn't. She felt shocked; but she felt no grief for Uncle Casper. She hoped that he would continue to burn in hell, the same way that he had burned in front of her eyes.

'Something's happened,' said Jamie.

Lucy nodded. 'Last night . . . Uncle Casper came back from California.'

'Oh shoot, not that chiseller.'

'Jamie, please listen,' Lucy begged him. 'He came back because he struck oil.'

'He struck oil? You're kidding me! He actually struck oil?'

'Yes,' said Lucy. Her eyes were watering in the wind. 'I'm not exactly sure where, or how. Some place called Seal Beach, that's what he said.'

'Well,' Jamie replied, 'I guess that's good news. You get your five per cent. Congratulations, you're rich! Or you could be, anyway!'

'Jamie . . . he came back because he wanted to cancel our agreement.'

Jamie vigorously shook his head. 'Unh-hunh, that's not possible, he can't do that. That agreement is legal and binding. You're entitled to your five per cent no matter what.'

'I suppose I would have been,' said Lucy. 'But he's dead.'

Without warning, she found that she was crying. Not quietly weeping, but scrunching up her face like a small child, and sobbing in deep, frosty gulps. Jamie held her

tight, and patted her back, and said rather lamely, 'Hey now
. . . *Dead*? How come he's dead?'

'He – burned,' Lucy sobbed. 'He – stole my mother's –
brooch and I – was looking for it – when he was asleep.
And I was holding – the lamp and he – grabbed hold of my
arm – and he was all soaked in whisky and he –'

'Jesus,' Jamie exclaimed. 'You mean he really caught fire?'

'He was all burned up. I mean, like firewood. It was
awful.' She pushed herself away from Jamie, though gently,
and pulled her handkerchief out of her glove. The tears on
her eyelashes sparkled in the pearly, unfocused daylight.
'Poppa's called the funeral parlour . . . he told me to come
down here, to ask if I could spend the day.'

'My God, Lucy, of course you can spend the day! You
can stay here as long as you like! Look, come on in. It's cold
enough to freeze the cluck out of a chicken.'

They walked across the snowy yard. Jamie put his arm
around her, and squeezed her tight, and for the first time in
a long time she didn't find a way to duck him or dodge him
or twist herself free. Inside the house they hung up their
coats, and Jamie took Lucy through to the parlour.

Unlike most parlours in High Plains farmhouses, which
were ostentatiously stuffed with clocks and china and plants
and pictures, and thickly draped with lace and bobble-fringed
velvet, the Cullens' parlour was modest and severe. A large
leather chair stood by the fireplace (father's); and next to it,
slightly further away from the fire, a smaller sewing chair
(mother's) with an unfinished sampler resting on the seat.
Apart from two lamp-tables, the only other furniture was an
upright piano and a glass-fronted china cabinet, displaying
the plainest of German china; and the only decoration was a
framed Currier & Ives' lithograph showing a faintly-smiling
husband and an idealistically devoted wife reading the scriptures together.

The fire had burned low; and so Jamie stacked more logs
on to it. 'Here – come warm youself up. No, you can sit in

father's chair, he won't mind. He's a little short on temper, but not on Christian charity. You look just awful.'

Lucy took hold of his hand. 'Dear Jamie. You're the first person who's ever said that to me without my minding.'

'Mother'll bring you some hot milk and cinnamon.'

As the fire crackled up, Lucy began to feel better, although she still couldn't stop her hands from trembling.

'You should have seen Doctor Satchell,' Jamie told her. 'Shock can make you pretty ill. We had a cousin back east who saw his baby get caught in a feed-grinder. He couldn't speak for months. Just literally couldn't speak.'

'I'll be all right,' Lucy assured him. She gave him a rueful smile, and touched his hand. 'The worst of it is, I do believe I'm *glad* he's dead.'

Jamie said nothing. Asked no questions, expressed no surprise. Lucy glanced up at him with a quick, forced smile, and said, 'I suppose you think I'm dreadful, saying that.'

'I don't know,' said Jamie. 'What do you want me to think?'

'I'm not sure. I'm confused. It seems so much like justice, what happened to Uncle Casper, but it can't be right. It can't be right for *anyone* to die like that?'

Jamie shrugged. 'Father says that you shouldn't try to gainsay God.'

Just then, Jamie's mother came in with a blue china mug of hot milk on a tray. She was a handsome fair-haired woman, half Swedish; and Jamie and all his brothers looked strikingly like her. 'You'll stay for supper, yes?' she asked. 'We have fried salt pork and apple dumplings.'

'I'd love to,' said Lucy. The thought of sitting at a crowded supper table with a friendly and devoted family like the Cullens seemed very appealing. When she thought about home, all that she could picture was the burned-out bedroom where Uncle Casper had died, and that grinning stick-like body.

That body was going to haunt her. She knew that with

dreadful certainty. Still grinning, it would run after her in dreams.

When his mother had gone, Jamie drew up the sewing-chair and sat close to her. 'Listen, there's one thing that you *don't* have to worry about, and that's your share of your Uncle Casper's oil money.'

'I don't understand you. He's dead now, isn't 'he? How can I share his money when he's dead?'

'Lucy,' said Jamie, 'did you read that agreement?'

Lucy hesitated, shook her head. 'It just said five per cent, didn't it?'

'What kind of a lawyer do you think I am? That was a model partnership agreement copied out of Newman's *Contracts, Agreements, Deeds, Indentures & Bonds*. You could have smacked me with a bellyband when your uncle signed it without even reading it. Mind you, I got the distinct feeling that he couldn't read too good.'

'But what does it *say*?'

Jamie leaned forward and said. 'The agreement provided for you to receive five per cent of your uncle's oil profits when he was alive. Yes? But if he were to die – and the way I saw him drinking, that wasn't exactly a remote possibility – you inherit his entire interest.'

Lucy stared at him. She could scarcely understand what he was saying; but somehow she knew that it was moment-ous.

'Lucy,' Jamie repeated, 'now that your Uncle Casper is dead, you own not just five per cent of his oil, but all of it.'

'All of it? How can that be? He said he was making a thousand dollars a day. Maybe more. Maybe fifteen hundred.'

'Are you complaining? You're rich!'

Lucy didn't know whether to squeal out loud, or cry, or dance, or what to do. 'You're not fooling me? You wouldn't be mean enough to fool me? The agreement really said that?'

Jamie took hold of her hands between his, and held them tight. 'Lucy – I don't know what in the world possessed you to give your uncle all of your savings, and if you don't want to tell me, then I don't want to know. It's your business. But whatever the reason, Lucy, sweetheart, you surely did yourself a good turn.'

Lucy's eyes brimmed with tears. She had never felt so guilty or so wretched in her life; but at the same time she was ridiculously happy. How could you feel so bad and so good, both at the same time? She had treated Jamie so off-hand, all of these months; she had pushed him away and rejected him, and all the time he had already made sure that the dream for which she had been craving all her life had actually come true.

It was a fairytale; like looking under your bed and discovering a brimming chestful of gold and diamonds from a pirate story, or the Arabian Nights.

'There's one thing, Jamie . . .' she whispered. 'The money I gave to Uncle Casper. It wasn't my savings. I pledged my mother's jewellery.'

'You pledged it?' Jamie demanded. 'You took it to a pawnbroker? Shoot! What the heck did you do that for?' He sat back, angrily; and almost crushed his mother's embroidery. But then she could see the realization breaking in his mind that – the way things had turned out – it was just as well that she *had* pledged her mother's jewels. 'It was heck of a risk, wasn't it? A heck of a risk! And why?'

'I wanted – to be rid of him,' said Lucy. She didn't think that she could admit to any more; not yet, anyway. Jamie, of course, thought that she was still a virgin. She didn't know what he would say if she were to confess that she had already been taken by Uncle Casper. She knew that Jamie would be furiously jealous and deeply hurt; and all the more jealous and hurt because Uncle Casper was already dead, and there was nobody on whom Jamie could take his revenge. Nobody, that is, except Lucy herself.

She could still feel with unnerving clarity the bright red ribbons cutting into her wrists and ankles; and Uncle Casper grunting and spitting and bludgeoning himself into her. It made her feel as if the floor were tilting beneath her feet. She had tried desperately to drown the feeling in the bottom of her mind, but it proved as futile as trying to force a sodden mattress to stay under water. It surfaced, drearily, time and time again, as ugly and as unforgettable as ever.

Jamie said, 'Lucy – your uncle didn't ever upset you, did he?'

'What do you mean? Of course not.'

'It's just that I don't understand why it was so all-fired important for you to be rid of him. You told me you loved that jewellery; it was all you had to remember your momma by.'

Lucy picked up her milk, and stirred the cinnamon powder into it. 'I didn't like him, that's all. He drank too much. I don't know. He was crude. He cussed a lot. He upset poppa.'

'And that's all? He didn't try to get too friendly?'

Lucy blushed and lowered her eyes, but didn't answer.

'All right,' said Jamie. 'I'm sorry. I shouldn't have asked.'

They sat by the fire in silence while the flames took hold of the logs. After a few mintues, however, they heard the back door slam, and voices in the kitchen. Jamie's father appeared, brambly-bearded, meaty-shouldered, with piercingly clear green eyes and a big fleshy nose that had always reminded Lucy of some variety of ripe vegetable squash.

'Lucy!' he smiled, his voice thick with phlegm. He cleared it, and blew his nose, and said, 'I'm sorry. It's that cold wind. Makes your nose run faster than your feet.'

'Old joke, father,' Jamie complained. 'Listen – you don't mind if Lucy warms herself up a bit. She had a shock last night. Her uncle came back from California and ended up setting fire to himself in his bedroom.'

'Dear God!' said Jerrold Cullen, sitting down on the sofa. 'Was he badly hurt?'

'Dead, I'm afraid,' Lucy told him.

'Dead! That's terrible! Lucy, I'm so sorry!'

Lucy caught her breath. 'To tell you the honest truth, Mr Cullen, my uncle and I weren't exactly the best of friends.'

'I see,' said Jerrold, soberly. 'But all the same, he was a human soul; and his Maker has now drawn him back to the place from whence he came.'

'Amen,' said Jamie. His father turned and glared at him, not quite sure if he were serious or not. A pious man had a great deal to put up with in a household of irreverent sons.

'Can you tell me how it happened?' he asked Lucy.

But Jamie interrupted, '– Father, I don't think that Lucy really wants to talk about it.'

'Are you her advocate?' Jerrold inquired. 'Can't she speak for herself?'

He turned back to Lucy and said, 'This boy and his passion for the law, I never knew a boy so stubborn.'

'You must be proud of him, though, winning a place at the State University.'

Jerrold said, 'Hmph! The only place with which any man needs to concern himself is his place in the Kingdom of Heaven.'

'You're letting him go, though?'

'All the tribes of Israel couldn't have stood in his way,' Jerrold replied; and although he knit his eyebrows and tried to sound stern, Lucy had the feeling that he was secretly proud of Jamie's determination. Jerrold knew himself to be a formidable father, and if Jamie could stand up to *him*, Jerrold reckoned that he could stand up to anyone.

'Guess Jamie and me don't see eye to eye on what constitutes the law,' said Jerrold. 'As far as I'm concerned, the law was given by God, at Sinai. God is the moral governor of the world, and the redeemer of his people, and because of that, only God has the authority to legislate for the wellbeing of all of his creatures, and for righteousness on earth.'

'Amen,' said Jamie.

'Oh, you can mock me,' snapped Jerrold, turning around on the sofa. 'But you're breaking a fine family tradition, too. The Cullens have always been grangers, ever since they came here from Scotland, granger fathers and granger sons, and heartily proud of it, and the Lord be praised.'

He reached into his pocket for his pipe. 'But what can I do?' he asked. 'I can't do anything more than speak my mind; and then help him on his way. At the end of the day, that's all fathers are good for.'

Just then, Mrs Cullen called for Jamie to pump up some water for her. Jamie stood up, kissed Lucy on the forehead, and then went through to the kitchen.

Lucy said, 'You're going to miss him.'

'Hmph!' Jerrold replied. 'I'm going to miss his appetite, and I'm going to miss his argufying; but that's about the sum of it. He's the slowest stable-mucker I ever saw, and he rides about as elegant as a sack of beets. The law's welcome to him, that's my opinion. He sucks bullseyes in church and he never remembers the words of his hymns and he's always provoking his kith.'

'*I'm* going to miss him,' Lucy told Jerrold.

Jerrold looked at the fire, and tiny orange flames pirouetted in his eyes. 'Jamie's not the man for you, Lucy. You should be looking for somebody well-heeled, and reliable, a man of good stock.'

'I didn't say that I was going to *marry* him, Mr Cullen. I simply said that I was going to miss him.'

'Well, don't miss him too much. He's a wayward character, at best.'

Lucy was about to tell Jerrold that she had never met anyone more loyal and reliable than Jamie, but something in his expression cautioned her not to; and so she stayed silent, while the fire sizzled and crackled, and the minutes passed, and Jerrold Cullen stared unfocused into the flames as if he were remembering things that might have been, but which had never come to pass.

★

Jack Darling listened thoughtfully while Jamie explained about the deed; and to Lucy explaining that she had pawned her mother's jewellery; and then he untied his long brown apron.

'I never heard anything like it,' he said. He sounded angry, but controlled, and in some way, defensive. 'But – well – if you say that it's true, then I'll have to believe it, won't I?'

'I'm sure sorry about your brother-in-law, sir,' Jamie told him. 'My father sends his condolences, too. But it's an ill wind that blows nobody some good fortune.'

'What do we have to do now?' Jack asked him. 'Do we have to register our interest, something like that?'

Jamie said, 'I was going to suggest that you went to California, or sent somebody on your behalf, to look into things. After all, we don't even know the well's exact location, do we? Neither do we know whose land it's on, or who granted the lease, or who was supposed to be taking care of it while your brother-in-law came back here to Kansas, and if *they* have an interest in it, too.'

Jack sat down. It was still early morning, the thin sunlight was arranged across the floor like cut-up pieces of dress-pattern. The regular loungers hadn't shown up yet: in this weather, Henry McGuffey didn't usually ease himself out of the sack until he grew too hungry to stay there any longer.

'Who can I send?' asked Jack. 'I can't go myself. I can't leave the store.'

'Poppa, we're *rich*,' said Lucy. 'You can leave the store for ever if you want to. You can close up right this minute, and walk out of the door, and never come back.'

Jack looked at her with serious, unfocused eyes. 'Your mother and me built this store up together, Lucy. It's not just a store to me, it's part of my life. When I stand in here, and I'm alone, I can still hear your mother singing. I can still see her smiling at me, the way she used to, when she was weighing out the sugar for me.'

He lowered his head. 'Besides, this supposed oil-well may not turn out to be anything at all. Nothing else that Cass ever did was any darned good. I could close up the store and find myself bankrupt.'

Lucy suggested, '*I* could go, couldn't I?'

Jack looked up again. 'You? A seventeen-year-old girl all on your own? That's the dumbest thing I ever heard. 'Sides, it's more than likely a wild-goose chase.'

Jamie put his arm around Lucy's shoulders. 'Sir – I really believe it's worth going. And if you allowed Lucy to go, I could go along, too, sir. I've always had a strong yen to see California; and I have two clear months before I have to start college. That's if you'd trust me.'

'Trust you?' Jack seemed distracted, gruff. 'Any reason why I shouldn't?'

Jamie grinned. 'Then you wouldn't mind?'

'Well . . . I don't know. Let me think on it. I guess it would make some kind of sense for you to go, seeing that you're a lawyer. Or nearly a lawyer, anyhow.'

He tilted back his chair and reached for the bottle of sipping whisky. 'I'd better open up,' he said. 'You want a warmer before you go? That's a long cold ride back to your place.'

'No, thank you, sir,' said Jamie. 'I shouldn't be here at all. I just thought I'd better come along with Lucy to explain the way things stood.'

'You realize you're turning your back on a man of means?' teased Lucy.

Jamie smiled broadly. 'Yes, I do. And congratulations.'

Jack poured himself a drink. 'Thanks, Jamie. 'Preciate what you've done.'

When Jamie had left, however, Jack put down his drink untasted and turned to Lucy with a serious face.

'I think you owe me some kind of an explanation,' he said, clearing his throat.

Lucy was spooning coffee into the chipped red enamel pot. 'What do you mean?' she asked him. 'I've told you everything.'

'You and your Uncle Casper, that's what I mean, and you know it. There's more to this business than meets the eye.'

'I told you. Uncle Casper said that he needed the money really quickly, otherwise he might have lost his chance of drilling the oil-well altogether. I guess I felt sorry for him, that's all.'

'Don't lie to me, Lucy,' her father told her. He reached into his shirt pocket and took out her mother's cameo brooch and held it up in front of her. 'I found this in your Uncle Casper's valise. I thought it was dear to your heart. And all the rest of your mother's jewellery. I thought it meant something to you. Something precious.'

'It does,' whispered Lucy. 'It did.'

'Then how could you think of pawning it? Was your Uncle Casper more precious to you than your mother's memory? You've hurt me, Lucy, you've hurt me bad! Just – just giving away those things that meant so much! And then flying straight in the face of what I told you was right! You knew darned well that I wanted Cass to work for his grubstake! Even if I'd had the money, cash in hand. I *still* would've made him work for it! But what did you do? You not only gave him the money for nothing, you pawned your dead mother's jewellery to raise it! And by cracky I believe I'm entitled to know why!'

Lucy was shaking. 'Poppa –' she said. But her father was too angry to let her speak.

'Don't you 'poppa' me! I wasn't going to shout at you in front of your Jamie. He did his best, and he just about saved your skin, with that agreement of his. But I'm going to shout at you now! What you did was wrong, Lucy. It was disrespectful, it was disobedient, and it flew straight in the face of what was right!'

Lucy felt the tears coursing down her cheeks. She opened

her mouth but the words refused to come out. All she could do was shake her head, and then cover her face with her hands.

Jack stood up and watched her for a while, fidgety and uncomfortable.

'Do you want a drink or something?' he asked her.

Lucy whispered, 'No. No, thank you.'

'Well . . . I guess I'm sorry I yelled,' Jack told her. 'But the trouble is, Lucy, we only have you and we only have me. We don't have anybody else. If we can't trust each other, then who the heck can we trust?'

Lucy wiped her eyes. 'I'm sorry, too,' she told him.

'Do you want to try and tell me what was going on?' he asked her.

She was silent for a very long time, like a woman who has suddenly forgotten who she is. She and her father became a tableau, two figures standing motionless in a store filled with shadows, their faces pale as lamp-globes in the snowy light from the street outside.

After a while, however, Lucy sat down, her grey skirts arranged around her, and told her father what her Uncle Casper had done to her.

The weather eased a little the following week, although it was still far too early for a thaw. The skies were brilliantly clear and the snow was dazzling and the north-west wind was as hard as a hammer.

Lucy and Jamie took the Kansas Pacific Railroad west to Denver, where they spent two nights at a cheap but well-scrubbed boarding-house on 16th Street, waiting for a delayed connection to Cheyenne.

Lucy was delighted by Denver. She had visited Kansas City, on a hot summer weekend two years ago, but Denver by comparison was glorious: proud and high and rich with silver. Almost all of the buildings, by city ordinance, were built of brick; and some of them were astonishingly grandiose, like the Windsor Hotel, which boasted 176 rooms, and flags snapping on its Gothic rooftops, and a taproom (which Lucy peeked into) with three thousand real silver dollars embedded in the floor.

They went to Riverfront Park and listened to band music in the snow. They visited Elitch's Zoological Gardens, and saw a tiger and a lion and a camel, morose and sleepy in the mile-high winter, but fascinating all the same.

Horse-drawn streetcars rolled along the wide city thoroughfares. Lucy was particularly taken by the streetcars which travelled up neighbouring hills, and then rolled back down again, with their horses riding on the rear platform as passengers. And the stores! You could buy absolutely everything, from a solid gold watch-fob to a silk Paris gown to a 'festive Bowie knife'.

And everybody strolled the well-swept sidewalks looking so fashionable and wealthy and nonchalant.

But, more than anything else, Lucy was enchanted by the mountains. If she stood on her chair in the Miller Boarding-house and leaned out of the back window, with the brisk sub-zero wind blowing directly into her face, she could see the high clear summits of the Rockies, and the distant crest of Pike's Peak. She could scarcely believe what she was seeing. The mountains seemed completely unreal; as if they had been cut out of cardboard. After a lifetime spent on the Kansas plains, she couldn't believe that the people of Denver could walk the streets and not even give the mountains a second glance.

On their second night in Denver, as Lucy was brushing out her hair in readiness for bed, Jamie knocked at her door, and called, 'Lucy? Lucy, it's me. Can I talk to you?'

Lucy fastened the ribbon of her robe, and opened the door for him. He was dressed in shirtsleeves, with fancy embroidered suspenders. Lucy thought that he looked tired, and a little flushed.

'All right if I come in ?' he asked her.

'I guess it is,' she smiled. 'Just so long as Mrs Miller doesn't see you.'

They sat on the iron-framed bed. The room was very small, but a hot fire fumed in the grate, and heavy brown drapes kept too much of the draught from blowing in from the window. On the yellow-papered walls hung uninspiring engravings cut from religious magazines, such as *The Faithful Seneschal* and *Titus and His Family*.

Jamie said, 'I didn't feel like sleeping. Too excited, I guess.'

'What time are we supposed to leave tomorrow?' asked Lucy.

'Six o'clock, if the train's running. We should reach Cheyenne by lunchtime; and then we join the Union Pacific at three-thirty. Again – that's always provided that it's running.'

Lucy gave her hair a last quick brush. 'I love it here. When we come back from California, I'm going to come here again. In fact, I might even live here. Can you imagine that?'

'You'll be rich by then,' Jamie reminded her. 'You'll be able to go anywhere you like. New York. Paris, even.'

'No,' said Lucy. 'I want to live somewhere with mountains.'

Jamie shrugged. 'Guess you can grow tired of mountains, same way that you can grow tired of anything else.'

Lucy laid down her hairbrush and stared at him. 'You don't think that I'm tired of you, do you, Jamie?'

'Heck, no, you're only seventeen. I don't have any right to think anything like that. Now you're rich, well, you can go out and find yourself anybody you care to. Maybe one of those princes you were always talking about.'

'Oh, Jamie . . . we'll probably get to California and find out that I'm not rich at all.'

Jamie smiled ruefully. 'Forget it, Lucy. You're rich right enough. I looked at your Uncle Casper's clothes. A family with ten children could live off his shoes for a month.'

'So you think that I'm going to go off and leave you behind, and never think about you again?' Her blue eyes were dark in the lamplight, dark as ink.

'There's no "think" about it. If you had seven thousand dollars a year, you wouldn't stay in Oak City for a minute. And if what your Uncle Casper said was correct, you're going to have seven thousand dollars a *week*.'

'Jamie –' Lucy began, but Jamie shook his head.

'You know it's true. You're going to go off and be a socialite; and I'm going to go off to learn to be a lawyer. It's our calling, that's all. You can't fool around with your calling.'

'But if I'm *very* rich, you wouldn't have to be a lawyer, would you? We could both live off Uncle Casper's oil! We could stay together all the time!'

Jamie said, 'Lucy, you don't understand. I *want* to be a lawyer. It's my vocation. I haven't been fighting my father all these years, just to sit around on my duff all day, eating Turkish delight.'

Lucy giggled. 'Is that what rich people do? Sit around on their duffs all day and eat Turkish delight?'

'You're impossible, you know that?' Jamie told her.

'But I want you with me! If you study law, I won't see you for three years! And, who knows, I might meet somebody else.'

Jamie looked at her gravely. 'That's a risk I'm going to have to take. I always knew that.'

'But what if I get married? And have children?'

'I don't know. I'll have to think about that when it happens. *If* it happens, which I hope it doesn't.'

Lucy held his hand between hers. 'Jamie – I know things have been difficult between us – but it wasn't your fault, it was mine. I'm still fond of you. I still love you.'

She believed at that moment that she was telling the truth, that she really did love him. Sitting next to her in this boarding-house bed on a freezing-cold night in Denver, he looked tonight like the man who had everything she wanted. Handsome and gentle, but strong, too; and unselfish.

At the same time, she was conscious that she might not love him forever: that if he didn't agree to stay with her now, she might not give him a second chance. Life was too exciting for second chances.

Jamie said, 'I can't give up the law, Lucy. It's something I have to do, whether I lose you or not.'

He gave her a quick, buttoned-up smile. 'I suppose you're angry with me.'

'Why should I be angry with you?'

'For loving the law more than I love you. Isn't that what you're thinking?'

She squeezed his hand tight. 'I'm not angry with you. I never could be. I love you. It's only me I feel angry with.'

'Oh, yes? And what do *you* have to be angry about? You're young, you're rich, and you're pretty. What more could a girl want?'

For one unbalanced second, Lucy was about to tell Jamie about Uncle Casper. But then something inside her warned her not to; that he would take it too hard. She turned her head away, and stared unfocused at the hot sparks rushing up the chimney, although she could still feel Jamie watching her profile.

'Can I ask you something?' said Jamie.

She nodded.

'Do you really want to stay with me for the rest of your life?'

She turned back to him. 'Right this minute, that's what I want, more than anything else in the world.'

'Why? Because I won't give in to you?'

'No,' said Lucy. 'Because I really need you.'

He kissed her, two pecks on the lips, and then another; and then he stopped and looked straight into her eyes. She could see the little green flecks in his irises; the fine blonde hairs on his cheekbones.

They kissed each other again, very slowly this time and Lucy thought it was just like the sun sinking below the prairie on a clear winter evening, when you look and it hasn't quite gone, and you look again and it still hasn't quite gone, and at the very end there's a glimmering molten bar along the western horizon, the day clinging to the edge of the world by its fiery fingernails. Lucy closed her eyes. She couldn't think that she was cold; that this was winter-time. All she could feel was the heat from the fire and the heat from her cheeks and the heat from her own blood.

'Lucy...' said Jamie, touching her hair, touching her cheek.

'I'm sorry, Jamie,' she whispered. 'I was so *stupid*, and so selfish; and everything went so wrong.'

Jamie kissed her again. 'It doesn't matter. Everybody's selfish sometimes. You and I were born for each other. You know that, as well as I do.'

'How can people be born for each other?'

'You'll see,' said Jamie. He tugged the plain silver ring off his little finger, and slipped it over Lucy's wedding-finger. 'What's mine is yours, no matter what happens. You'll see.'

They held each other tight. Jamie kissed her again and again; her lips, and then her neck. His shirt rustled; her robe rustled; his breath rustled in her ears. The bedsprings creaked, the fire popped, the mountain wind sang through the window-frame. She did love him! She *did* love him! Even when she became a socialite, and she was surrounded by admiring young men – men like gods, men wearing starched collars so high that they had to stare at the ceiling all evening, Jamie would always be there to take care of her, in a way that her father had never been able to take care of her. She loved him! She loved him more than life itself! She could feel an extraordinary sensation rising up inside her, as if her womb were being flooded with warm water. She murmured, '*Jamie, Jamie*...' and it sounded like somebody else altogether.

Jamie's hand traced the long curve of her back, and the flare of her hips. He was breathing hard, and his eyes were closed. He reached upward, and his hand brushed her breast through her robe. He took hold of the ribbon that fastened it, and pulled it.

It was then that Lucy opened her eyes and saw Uncle Casper staring at her, his face on fire. Flames poured out from between his teeth, and his eyes were wrinkling like frying eggs.

She didn't cry out. She couldn't. But she pushed Jamie hard in the breastbone with the heel of her hand, and snatched her robe tightly together, and sat panting and shivering and staring at him in horror.

'Lucy?' he frowned at her. 'Lucy, what the hell's the matter? Jesus Christ, Lucy! Are you all right?'

She opened her mouth and closed it again. 'Jamie, I –'

Jamie gently put his arms around her, and shushed her. 'Lucy ... we were always meant to be together, you and me. No two ways about it. Lucy, I *love* you!'

'I can't,' she whispered. 'Just – can't –'

He kissed her cheek. She could feel for herself how cold and sweaty her skin was. 'Lucy you darling bobbasheely,' he coaxed her, 'there's nothing for you to be afraid of. Nothing! It's the naturalest thing in the world. And I love you, there's no question about that. Hey!' he joked. 'Maybe we could get married in Cheyenne, make it legal!'

She swallowed tightly, and shook her head.

'Well, just a suggestion,' he told her. He took his arm away, and clasped his hands together, and looked at her warily.

'It's not me, is it? I don't smell or something? You know, cheesy feet, something like that?' He was trying to be funny but she could tell that he was badly upset.

She shook her head, and said, 'It's not you.'

'Well, I'm sorry,' he told her. He kissed her quickly on the forehead and stood up. 'I guess I'd better get some sleep. Don't know how easy it's going to be, but I'd better try.'

Lucy, with tears in her eyes, reached up and took hold of his hand. 'Jamie, it's not you. I promise.'

'It's all right,' he told her, with the petulance of chronic frustration. He tried a smile.

'You do understand, don't you?'

'Sure. Sure thing. I understand.'

He left her room and closed the door quietly behind him. Lucy stayed where she was, sitting on the bed, with her robe wrapped tightly around her. She had wanted Jamie so desperately that she was trembling, the way you tremble when you have to hold the same position for too long. But she was terrified that he would immediately discover that she was no longer a virgin, and refuse to have anything more to do with her. In spite of his defiance of his father over the matter of law studies, she knew how religious he was, and she knew what it said in the Bible about harlots.

She was even more terrified of those incendiary visions of Uncle Casper; and the way that he was still clinging on to her, even in death.

She could picture her father's face, when she had told him at last what Uncle Casper had done to her. He had sat like a man chiselled with infinite patience out of ironstone.

She had tried to tell her father everything. She had spoken quietly and slowly, her eyes brimming with tears, occasionally pausing to compose herself, so that she wouldn't distress him too much.

At the last moment, however, with the words already taking shape on her lips, she had choked on Uncle Casper's lascivious claim to have slept with her mother. She had wanted desperately to talk about it, to find out the truth. The poisonous doubt that Uncle Casper had planted in her mind troubled her just as sorely as the memory of his raping her. But she hadn't been able to bring herself to hurt her father as much as that; and now that Uncle Casper was dead, it no longer seemed to matter whether he knew or not.

To Lucy, however, it remained just as much of a nightmare as ever. *We was close, like two spring chickens in a pot.*

At last her father had laid his hand on her shoulder, the way he always did, and had said hoarsely, 'I don't understand why you didn't tell me at once. I would have killed him.'

'I was ashamed,' she had told him.

'Good grief, Lucy. I'm the one who ought to be ashamed, for doubting you,' her father had replied. He had hesitated for a moment, his mouth working with emotion, and then he had said, 'I'm the one who ought to be ashamed, because I never protected you; same way I never protected your mother, neither.'

With tears sliding down his face, he had smacked his fist into the palm of his hand, and said, 'I wish to God I had burned him myself! I wish to God I had burned with him!'

After that, they hadn't spoken about it any more. There was nothing more for them to say. But Lucy's father had remained edgy and withdrawn for the rest of the day; and even Henry McGuffey's hilarious reminiscences about his boyhood in Mobile, Alabama, had failed to tickle him. Twice during the afternoon, Lucy had found her father standing and frowning at nothing at all, his hands by his sides. And when they were sitting together in the parlour in the evening, she had caught him staring at her over his newspaper as if he couldn't think who she really was.

When the morning had arrived for her to leave with Jamie for California, their railroad fares paid for by selling Uncle Casper's jewel-studded pocket-watch, she and her father had kissed each other goodbye with a brief display of forced tenderness that had almost amounted to relief.

Hatred can cool; envy can be assuaged; but guilt never forgets, and guilt never forgives, and guilt eats the spirit like fire consumes flesh.

According to Jamie's guide-book, Cheyenne was the largest city on the Union Pacific railroad between Omaha and

Sacramento; and after the luxuries of Denver, Lucy could scarcely wait to see it. As the train came clanking in to the depot, however, she was disappointed to see that Cheyenne was nothing more than a ragamuffin assembly of wood and canvas buildings.

Gathered around the station was a solemn audience of stray dogs, Indians wrapped in filthy blankets, and dangerous-looking men with big boots, broad-brimmed hats, and revolvers. It was just beginning to snow.

The train slithered to a halt on the icy rails, and immediately the more experienced travellers jumped down from the steps and made a rush for the railroad dining room. This was a flat-fronted barn of a building beside the tracks, set out with rows of refectory tables and wheelback chairs, its walls hung with stuffed buffalo heads. By the time Lucy and Jamie managed to push their way in, the noise inside had grown tremendous: an ocean-like roar of shouting and laughing and clattering cutlery. They had to wait for over twenty minutes before they could catch the eye of the harassed Chinese waiter, and then they were served (without being consulted as to choice) with two large steaks, sizzled black on the outside and bleeding-raw on the inside, fried eggs, boiled Indiań corn, and a heap of hoe-cakes and syrup.

The price was one dollar – but only seventy-five cents if you paid in silver.

As she sawed at her meat with a knife as blunt as a bricklayer's trowel, Lucy shouted to Jamie, 'What kind of steak is this? It's like trying to eat a horse-blind!'

A red-bearded man sitting opposite shouted back, 'It's beef, miss, if you'll forgive me; but when it's tough they usually call it antelope. Kind of makes it sound more enticing; you know, for your tyro traveller.'

He sniffed, and swilled hot tea around his mouth, and then added, 'I don't know which way you're headed, but you should keep clear of the dining station at Sidney, Nebraska. They do you an excellent-tasting stew they call chicken-stew, but I know for a sure fact that it's made from prairie-dog.'

They crossed Wyoming in an endless blizzard, although the hot-air stove in their Pullman car kept them as warm and comfortable as if they had been sitting in their own parlours. The only excitement was that now and again the train had to be halted, and the passenger-cars had to be disconnected for half an hour, so that the locomotive could be run ahead of them at full speed into a snowbanked cut, to clear the track. This procedure, the conductor laconically informed them, was called 'bucking the snow.'

The snowstorms whirled themselves away when they entered Utah, and Lucy couldn't keep herself away from the window as the train ran through roaring tunnels into Echo and Weber Canyons, where rocks towered above them in fantastic and dreadful shapes. The landscape was so strange that nobody on board the train seemed to be able to agree if they were travelling through God's sublime wilderness or the playground of Satan.

She and Jamie remained courteous to each other, but much more guarded than before. Neither of them was in the mood for a serious conversation about Lucy's abrupt disinclination to carry on with their love-making, although Lucy couldn't help turning it over in her mind again and again. *I want him; I'm sure that I love him; and perhaps he can help me to forget about Uncle Casper. But what if I see that blazing face for ever and ever? What good would I be as a wife?*

She smiled at him from time to time, and he smiled back, but their smiles were both strained with uncertainty.

At the moment, however, they were both too tired to think of much more than reaching California. They were both much farther away from home than they had ever been before. They had passed the Thousand-Mile Tree, one thousand miles west of Omaha, and the journey was both awe-inspiring and exhausting. They ate, slept, talked to their fellow-passengers; read books and newspapers supplied by the train attendant; and stared sightlessly out the window.

At last, however, the train began to climb the Sierras, the last great natural barrier to California. For almost forty miles they toiled upwards through gloomy wooden snowsheds, which kept the track clear in mid-winter. The snowsheds covered not only the main tracks but also depots, turntables, switch tracks, and even houses where railroad workers lived in permanent eerie twilight with their wives and children.

Still inside a snowshed, the train reached Summit station, seven thousand feet above sea level, in time for breakfast. The passengers ate a huge meal of rainbow trout and fresh-baked bread and good hot coffee. Lucy wrapped herself in her coat and took a walk outside. The air sparkled. The Sierras rose all around her, snowy and shining and forested with pine. She felt that she was standing on the threshold of Heaven. 'Mother,' she whispered, as if her mother would be able to hear her more easily.

Jamie came to stand beside her. He pulled off his glove and took hold of her hand. For a long time he said nothing, but at last, with his breath smoking, he said quietly, 'There's no need for you and me to be so chilly.'

She turned to him. Her eyes were watering with the cold.

'It's my fault,' she said. 'If only I didn't feel so darned muddled.'

'You're muddled? Muddled about what? Muddled about us?'

'No,' she told him. 'Muddled about myself. And about being rich, and you going off to university. I thought it was all going to be wonderful, but I don't understand it. I feel like I'm being swept away.'

Jamie held her tight. The train whistled, to gather its passengers. 'You're growing up,' Jamie told her, his breath smoking against her fur collar. 'That's all that's happening.' He smiled. 'It happens to everybody, sooner or later.'

*

The western slopes of the Sierras drop from seven thousand feet to thirty feet in less than a hundred and fifty miles, and the train flew down without using steam – coasting so fast and so silently that Lucy felt as if she were dreaming.

The train rushed round curves with nothing but its brakes to hold it. The axle-boxes smoked with the friction, and the Pullman cars were acrid with the smell of burning wood. The wheels were red-hot, and when they ran through the darkened snowsheds, they glowed like discs of fire.

They sped round embankments with a harsh metallic whisper, they glided softly through cuts and snowsheds; and then suddenly burst out into the sunlight and swung around the stomach-turning curve of Cape Horn, at which point Jamie's guide-book advised nervous passengers not to look out of the windows.

There, two thousand feet below them, was the American River, a silvery artery in the morning sunlight.

Lucy stared in fascination as the train twisted and turned its way around the head of the canyon, sometimes doubling back on itself so tightly that she felt she could throw a breadroll from her table and hit the tracks on which they had just been travelling.

Throughout the morning, they descended into the Sacramento Valley; and Lucy nodded in her seat and slept. She dreamed about her father, sitting mortified and silent in the parlour ('*Why didn't you tell me sooner? I would have killed him.*') and for some reason he was counting dry beans from hand to hand. She dreamed about her mother's picture on the shelf. Her mother spoke to her, in a tiny voice, almost inaudible. *Lucy! Lucy!*

When she opened her eyes again, the train was running swiftly through orchards and fields of flowers. The sky was clear blue and the air was so warm that the passenger-car windows had been opened. She sat up, and rubbed her eyes.

Jamie appeared, freshly-shaved, wiping his towel around

his neck. He smiled at her, and leaned forward and kissed her. 'Welcome to California,' he told her.

Lucy had conjured up in her mind all kinds of wonderful visions of the Puebla de Los Angeles, the town of the angels. But when they arrived on the steamer from San Francisco, she discovered that it was far from being the city in the clouds which she had imagined. Although some of the stores looked prosperous and well-stocked, and there were one or two impressive business buildings and a scattering of elegant private dwellings, the rest of the town was a higgledy-piggledy collection of adobes, saloons, warehouses, and flaking hotels.

The weather, however, was hazy and warm; and there was no real need for grandiose architecture to keep out the weather. Orange groves and vineyards clustered around the town on all sides. When Lucy unpacked her trunk at the Pico House and leaned on her elbows on the clay-tiled windowsill, she could look directly out over a small dark-green orange grove, while the mission-church bells clanged dolorously over Sonora, the Spanish quarter.

And there were flowers everywhere, on the last day of January! Tuberose and jasmine and fragant stock in the hotel garden; and heliotrope trained up the side of the open brick-paved court which you had to cross to reach the dining rooms.

They spent their first morning in Los Angeles resting. Lucy slept, fully-dressed, stretched on her bed. When she woke up, the sun was shining brightly, and she lay still for a while, thinking about her father, in snowbound Kansas; and about Jamie, in the next room.

For the first time, she allowed herself the heretical thought that she might not need either of them, now that she was rich. Perhaps she had been feeling muddled because she didn't love them as much as she felt she ought to.

But she still couldn't manage completely on her own. She

admitted that much. The thought of striking out completely alone, without anybody to take care of her – well, she wouldn't know where to start. Even if you were rich, how did you go about finding someplace to stay? How did you buy a house? How did you get yourself introduced into society?

She felt, however, that she was at a momentous turning-point in her life. She felt as if every step she had ever taken, every word she had ever spoken, had brought her at last to this: to an unexpected paradise where oranges ripened in mid-winter, and farmers went by with carts heaped with pumpkins, and strawberries, and green pod-peas, and lemons, and even lambs!

And what would be next? Society, fortune, and a thousand dollars a day!

She reached out to the table beside her bed and took down the photograph of her mother. Anna Darling, soft of eye, in a sepia picture that was already fading away. She kissed it; and she felt closer to her mother than ever; as if she hadn't died at all, but was always there, watching, waiting, and protecting her.

'He's dead, you tell me?' asked the russet-whiskered attorney, sucking at his empty pipe, his brown boots perched up on his desk like two glossy red squirrels.

'Yes, sir, dead,' said Jamie. He reached into his coat pocket, and produced Doctor Satchell's death certificate. The two squirrels jumped off the desk as the attorney swung himself around to read it.

'Burned dead, it says here,' he remarked. '"Cause of death, burned".'

Lucy was about to interrupt, but Jamie lifted his hand to hush her. 'That's correct,' he said. 'Burned dead. Accidental house-fire.'

The attorney cracked his knuckles, one by one. The plaque on his desk said that his name was Thurloe Daby, and Lucy had thought that if anybody in the world could have fitted such a peculiar name, it was him. He looked very Thurloe; and very Daby, too.

'What happens now?' Thurloe Daby asked handing the death certificate back.

Jamie unfolded a copy of the deed which Uncle Casper had signed at Oak City depot. 'This deed provides that, in the event of his death, all of Mr Casper Conroy's oil-leases and the proceeds thereof should pass to Miss Lucy Darling.'

Thurloe Daby grimaced at Jamie's tiny handwriting. He found his eyeglasses, and wound them around his whiskery ears, and scrutinized the agreement narrowly.

'Looks reasonable to me,' he drawled. He was a very slow speaker. 'I'll have to authenticate the signature, of course. But otherwise . . . well, it's all written in plain English, aint it? And I can't see any court in the Union denying the rights of a young lady so charming as this.'

The squirrel-shoes obediently bounded back up on to his desk, and Thurloe Daby settled himself back in his chair. 'You can't say that it hasn't been a story of dire tragedy, Ferris and Conroy Oil Company, now can you? One tragedy after another. But I guess that all's well that ends well.'

'I'm sorry?' said Lucy.

'Well, my dear, the whole shooting-match is yours now, the whole kit and caboodle.'

'What about Mr Ferris?' asked Jamie.

Thurloe Daby pulled a face. 'What you mean is, what about the *late* Mr Ferris.'

'You mean he's dead, too?'

'That's right. Last Thursday before Christmas. Shot dead. Clean as a whistle.'

'Well, I'll be darned,' said Jamie. 'How did that happen?'

Thurloe Daby shrugged. 'Nobody correctly knows. But the circumstantial evidence points to Mexicans, trying to rob his house. Surprised them, you see; and they were too fly with a forty-five. No head left, excusing your sensitivities.'

Jamie was obviously finding it difficult to suppress his excitement. 'So what you're trying to tell us is that the whole oil-well now belongs to Miss Darling?'

Thurloe Daby nodded. 'That's what I said. The whole shooting-match. The whole kit and caboodle. I'll have my clerk rustle up the lease for you. It's Congress land, which is one blessing, rather than railroad land. Less in the way of paperwork; and a whole 'ot less interference. Encouragement rather than avarice, if you know what I mean.'

He leaned over his desk and lifted the lid from a pottery cookie-jar in the shape of Charles Frémont's head. Lucy had already recognized Frémont's sad, worried eyes, and his neatly-trimmed beard.

'Cookie?' Thurloe Daby asked, taking out a handful. 'They're good. My maid bakes them for me. Never got married, don't know why. A radiant face and a well-shaped ankle – well, I always had an eye for a radiant face and a well-shaped ankle. But marriage? I don't know. Maybe I care too much for my peace and privacy.'

He walked around his desk, snapping cookies in half as he did so. He went to the open window of his ochre-washed office, and sprinkled cookie-crumbs on to the sill. Outside, the winter sunshine to which Lucy still hadn't become accustomed sparkled and danced on the leaves of palo verde and fan palm.

'Leave these out for the quail,' Thurloe Daby explained.

Jamie said, 'What's happening about the well now? Who's in charge?'

'Oh, it's pumping; and it's pumping good. No need to worry yourself about that. Mr Ferris was a stickler for organization. There's a foreman out there; fellow called Griswold; and sixteen or seventeen men; all properly pay-rolled. No need to worry yourself about that. The Ferris and Conroy Oil Company just about runs itself. With a little assistance from yours truly, of course.'

'Do you want to quote me some output figures?' asked

Jamie, taking out his pen and his notebook. 'How many barrels a day, and what price they're fetching?'

'Offhand, no,' said Thurloe Daby. 'But there won't be much risk of Miss Darling here having her bank account swelled by less than twenty-five thousand dollars a week.' He sniffed, and brushed cookie-crumbs off his button-strained vest. 'John Ferris hit the spot first time; pay-dirt; and after that he never looked back.'

'But surely they did it together,' Lucy put in. 'Uncle Casper told me they were partners; and that they drilled and drilled all over the place before they first struck oil.'

Thurloe Daby shook his head, his jowls wobbling. 'John Ferris had this oil-well spudded some time in May.'

'Then why did my uncle need money to buy drilling equipment? He even pawned my mother's cameo brooch to buy drill-bits!'

'Well, he may have *told* you that,' said Thurloe Daby, returning to his desk. 'But the truth was that John Ferris bought that lease, all on his own; and John Ferris drilled that well, all on his own; and your Uncle Casper didn't appear in the picture for quite some pretty time. Then, when he did, he and John Ferris were always shouting and arguing. They weren't friends. I saw them fight two or three times. I witnessed them fight in this very office. Throwing punches, tossing paper all around. You see that canary?'

They all turned to inspect a small yellow-and-white bird perched in a cage in the corner of the office. 'They threw that canary across the office, cage and all. Poor darned creature hasn't uttered a cheep since. His name's Chorus, on account of the way he used to sing. Now he's so silent I'm thinking of changing his name to Grave.'

'What percentage of the well did Mr Ferris give to Mr Conroy?' asked Jamie.

Thurloe Daby sat down again. 'Near on half. Forty-nine per cent or therebouts. They signed a paper about it.'

'Mr Ferris gave Mr Conroy forty-nine per cent of an oil-well that was already producing oil?'

'That's correct.'

'But *why*?' asked Jamie. 'Did he ever tell you why? People don't usually go around giving other people any per cent of a fortune, let alone forty-nine per cent, and for no reason whatsoever.'

'Do you want to know the truth?' asked Thurloe Daby. 'The truth is, I don't know, but I have my suspicions. You don't like to speak ill of the dead, do you? They're dead, they can't answer back. But on the other hand, if they can't answer back, what does it matter *what* they think?'

'What are your suspicions, Mr Daby?' asked Lucy, loudly; although she found him quite intimidating.

'You want to know what my suspicions are? Well, I'll tell you. My suspicions are that Mr Ferris and Mr Conroy knew each other from way back. They always talked as though they did; although they never fessed up to it in so many words. My guess was that they'd probably been involved in some kind of business arrangement together, back east. Who knows? The one thing I *do* know for sure is that Mr Ferris wasn't Mr Ferris's real name. And my suspicions are that Mr Conroy had been looking for him for quite a time; and that when he got wind of the fact that Mr Ferris was out here in California, pumping up the old black gold, he came hotfooting it out here to claim his share of the proceeds.'

Lucy turned to Jamie, and frowned. 'I still don't understand why Uncle Casper needed three hundred and fifty dollars so badly?'

Thurloe Daby opened one desk drawer after the other, searching for his tobacco-pouch. 'Who knows? Probably we'll never know. My suspicions may be completely groundless. But let me put it this way: I've been working out here in California ever since the war, and I know two fallen-out thieves when I come across them; and Mr Ferris and Mr Conroy were two fallen-out thieves.'

He licked his finger and made the sign of the cross in the air. 'May they enjoy eternal tranquillity, of course.'

He leaned forward, and told them in a harsh whisper, 'My suspicions are that Mr Conroy had a little bit of business on Mr Ferris; a little bit of business that Mr Ferris was reluctantly willing to give him forty-nine per cent of his oilwell for, just to keep it under his hat.'

'Oh, yes?' said Jamie.

'Oh, yes, Mr Cullen; because the commonest cause of a changed name is a shady past.'

'That still doesn't explain why he wanted three hundred and fifty dollars from Miss Darling here.'

Thurloe Daby found his tobacco-pouch, and flapped it open, and stared at the contents in disappointment. 'You're right,' he said, as if he were speaking to the tobacco-pouch. 'It doesn't explain it. Not unequivocally. But my suspicion would be that Mr Conroy wanted three hundred and fifty dollars to buy the testimony of Certain Parties who might have been willing to establish that Mr Ferris wasn't Mr Ferris at all; but that Mr Ferris was in actuality Somebody Else – a Somebody Else who was wanted by Certain Other Parties for – what? Who knows? Enbezzlement, cheating, making off with funds that weren't quite his? I mean, let's consider for one sober moment where Mr Ferris might have found the money to purchase his oil-lease and start drilling operations. There's a thought, yes?'

'But the oil-well still belongs to Miss Darling?' asked Jamie.

'Oh, yes. Legal and watertight. Mr Ferris and Mr Conroy signed a partnership agreement; and since Mr Ferris had no wife and no issue; and nobody else laid a claim to it; his share passed to Mr Conroy when he died.'

He held up Lucy's deed, and waved it from side to side. 'And here it is – provided the old John Hancock pans out. Mr Conroy's share and Mr Ferris's share; both. Congratulations, Miss Starling, you're an exceedingly wealthy woman!'

'Darling,' Jamie corrected him.

Thurloe Daby stared at him; and then fidgeted in his seat, and said 'Aha!' and adjusted his polka-dot necktie.

That afternoon, they walked on the beach; watching the grey-gold Pacific foaming and thundering on the sand. Lucy took off her shoes, so that her small bare feet made waif-like tracks. The breeze ruffled and flapped at her primrose-yellow dress, and made her ribbons fly.

'So that's it, you're really rich,' said Jamie, his eyes squinched up against the wind.

'I still can't believe it,' Lucy told him.

'You saw the oil-pump. You saw the oil!'

'I don't know, it all looked so scruffy. All those men in red-flannel shirts, and all those filthy black barrels.'

'You're rich, Lucy,' Jamie insisted.

She took hold of his hand, and together they walked barefoot into the foam. Although the weather was so warm, the water was bone-cold, and Lucy was soon shivering.

'I won't believe that I'm rich until I go out and buy my first diamond necklace.'

'Is that the first thing you're going to do?'

'No. The first thing I'm going to do is redeem all of my mother's jewellery; and then I'm going to buy my father a new Sunday-best suit; and then I'm going to buy myself one of those three-dollar walrus handbags I saw in the Sears catalogue. *Then* I'm going to buy myself a diamond necklace.'

'You'll be able to buy yourself a hundred diamond necklaces,' Jamie grinned. Then – watching her narrowly out of the corner of his eye – he asked, 'You think you'll leave Kansas?'

She stopped, and looked around her; at the sand-dunes; and the sunshine; and the gulls turning in the wind.

'Oh yes,' she said. 'I think I'll leave Kansas.'

They walked up the dunes towards the dilapidated surrey

that they had rented. Their old grey horse was tearing at the salty beach-grass with its teeth.

As she climbed up into her seat, Lucy turned to Jamie and said, 'I wish you'd come with me.'

Jamie shook his head. 'Sorry, sweetheart, it just isn't possible.'

'No duff, no Turkish delight?'

'Hit it in one,' he told her.

He climbed up beside her and took hold of the reins. Then, before he geed up the horse, he leaned across and kissed her, a long lingering kiss.

'Don't forget me,' he told her. 'I won't forget you.'

3

It was his voice that first attracted her attention: high, clear, and crisp as an English apple. She could hear him all the way from the tennis-court, in spite of the string quintet, and the children chasing the peacocks across the lawn, and the laughter of four hundred fashionable guests.

She turned, frowned, and said to Evelyn Scott, 'Who *is* that man? He sounds very pleased with himself, whoever he is.'

'Oh, you mean *him*!' said Evelyn, lifting her lorgnettes and peering at him across the garden. 'I should think that he has every right to be pleased with himself. That my dearest dearest, is Henry Carson.'

'Should I know him? I don't think I've heard of him.'

'My dearest dearest!' hissed Evelyn, between clenched teeth. 'He's just about the best-connected Englishman ever! He's a Member of Parliament, very well thought of! The Coming Man! You really must make more effort to become *oh coorong*. Especially when it comes to men.'

Lucy gave her a rueful pout. 'There seem to be *so* many

people one has to know. And I can never work out if I'm allowed to like them or not.'

'For goodness' sake don't say that you "like" people,' Evelyn chided her. 'You may as well eat mashed-potatoes with your knife.'

'I don't *like* mashed-potatoes, so I don't eat them with anything.'

'Oh, Lucy! Heavens! You'll be the death of me!'

Lucy twirled her parasol and gave a little skip and laughed. She knew just how much she irritated Evelyn when she 'behaved Kansas'. Evelyn was so shiveringly sensitive to etiquette that if a man took his gloves off when he was visiting for only ten minutes she positively *shrank*; and the sight of finger-bowls on a breakfast-table could make her quite nauseous.

Of course Lucy used to tease Evelyn on purpose – calling to see her well before two o'clock, and leaving well after five – asking the servants how they cared for the weather – or picking up her skirts and kicking off her shoes so that she could run in her silk-stockinged feet along the corridors of the Scotts' enormous cottage. Being rich was still too much fun for her to fret about etiquette.

But Evelyn was very dear to her. The whole Scott family was very dear to her. They had advised and protected her ever since she had arrived in the East, and Evelyn had been the sweetest of all.

Evelyn's father was Dawson Scott the Pennsylvania coal baron (walrus moustache, hair parted dead-centre, eye for the ladies, current market value $32 million.) When Lucy and her father had left Oak City in a fanfare of local publicity, they had been commended into Dawson Scott's care by Colonel George McNamara, the owner of the *Kansas Daily Journal*, who had grown up with Dawson Scott on a slummy street in North Side, Pittsburgh. Both George McNamara and Dawson Scott remembered whey-faced fathers with flour-sack pants and mothers with two dresses to last the year; and how frightening it could be to find that you were suddenly wealthy.

Evelyn was the Scott's middle daughter. All three Scott daughters were tiny and 'well-covered'; but Evelyn was particularly diminutive and plump-breasted and sweet-faced, with bushy coppery hair. She spoke in a high educated chirrup, like a caged canary; and had a special fondness for yellow. Yellow dresses, yellow gloves, and yellow hats.

She and Lucy went almost everywhere together, and Mrs Cornelius Vanderbilt (with unaccustomed wit) had christened them Primrose and West, after the famous burnt-cork theatrical entertainers. Primrose, of course, being Evelyn; and West, of course, being Lucy.

Lucy's Kansas accent had been described by Mrs Stuyvesant Fish as 'rather like a Jew's-harp, continually twanging, entertaining, not unpleasant in any way that one could name, but altogether *strange*.' The Fishes were old money but not too much of it, and so they couldn't afford to be rude to the Johnny-come-latelys like the Lehrs or the Darlings. There was a point at which wealth became so prodigious that it overwhelmed class.

Of course Lucy and her father were parvenus; but they had been accepted by the leading ladies of established society with far more gentleness than most of the newly-rich. For one thing, Lucy was very pretty to look at, and always laughing; while Jack Darling remained bemused and melancholy and gentle. He might not yet have learned that one raised one's hat only on the *first* occasion that one happened to pass an acquaintance on an afternoon drive; and that one certainly didn't wink and wave and shout out, 'How's tricks?' even to the Belmonts or the Goulds.

But he rarely offended anybody, and the husbands liked him because he wasn't boastful, and he could tell one or two robust stories after dinner, especially the one about the woman who could smoke three cigars at once. He turned out to be useful on a yacht, too, because he could tie knots, and sing songs, and even rustle up steak-and-eggs. Yachts were important to the monarchs of America's burgeoning wealth. They were an ideal way of showing off one's money in the guise of being 'sporty' and 'athletic'.

Lucy occasionally caught her father looking sad and a little lost; as if he were daydreaming about being back in Oak City, shooting the breeze with Henry McGuffey and Samuel Blankenship round the old general-store stove; but he never complained that he was homesick, and most of the time he seemed to enjoy their wealth as much as she did.

At the moment, he was sitting on the stone balustrade at the far side of the house, eating strawberry sorbet with a little spoon and telling an entranced audience of large-hatted ladies about the hard life that was daily endured by women living on the High Plains of Kansas. They listened with gasps of delicious dismay, as if he were describing the life of a primitive African tribe.

'And then of course it's time for them to leave, and they have to make their choice between the rustling Lucinta petticoat and two weeks' worth of kitchen-soap. But who's going to hear that petticoat, out on the farm, except their husband, and he's too tired to see, let alone hear.'

Lucy heard Henry Carson let out a sharp, brisk laugh. It sounded like the echo of somebody chopping down a tree.

'Oh, do introduce me,' Lucy begged Evelyn. 'He sounds such fun.'

'My dearest, I'd be amazed if Mrs Harris lets you approach within fifty feet of him,' said Evelyn. 'She's absolutely *frothing* to pair him off with Henrietta. He's thirty-one, he's one of Lord Salisbury's favourites, he's so intelligent he makes me feel ill, and his family own a house in Derbyshire, England, that makes The Breakers look like a toolshed.'

Lucy stared across at Henry Carson, one hand prettily raised to her cheek, as if she were posing for a Valentine fan. After studying him for a very long while, she said, 'Well, y'know, he must be a *lunatic* if he's thinking of marrying

Henrietta. She's so darned *plain*! And I don't think she can even read. There you are! Listen! He sure *laughs* like a lunatic.'

'You're incorrigible,' said Evelyn. 'All Englishmen laugh like that. Well, all rich ones, anyway. It's something to do with the schools they go to. Or inbreeding, or something.'

She hesitated, and then she sniffed, 'Papa says the only sure way you can tell if an Englishman is sane is to ask him what he thinks about the Irish. If he says that he finds them quite decent, on the whole, then that's it.'

'What's what?'

'He's mad. One hundred per cent guaranteed.'

Lucy was silent for a while, watching Henry Carson with unselfconscious absorption, occasionally moving her head from side to side when passing picnickers obstructed her view.

'Don't *stare* so,' whispered Evelyn, uncomfortably. 'He'll think you're interested in him.'

'I *am* interested in him.'

'Well, I know you are, but it's not done to show it,' said Evelyn. As far as Evelyn was concerned, almost nothing was 'done' when it came to men. It even offended Evelyn's sense of propriety if her boyfriends tried to pay for her theatre tickets, in case she was morally compromised.

'He's short, too, isn't he?' Lucy observed, after a while.

'Well, most Englishmen are,' Evelyn told her. 'It's the diet. They eat too much variety meat, that's what mamma told me. Liver and brains and things.'

'Short and mad,' said Lucy, opening her parasol and thoughtfully spinning it around on her shoulder. 'He's handsome, though, isn't he? And he must have the highest collar I ever clapped eyes on.'

'*Saw*,' Evelyn corrected her.

'Beg pardon?' asked Lucy.

'The highest collar I ever saw. Apart from the fact that it's coarse to make remarks about gentlemen's collars.'

The string quintet played a lilting polonaise. Some of the children danced on the verandah, the little girls garlanded in flowers. Behind them, the house that the Harrises called their summer cottage rose grandiose and marble-flanked amongst mature elms; a forty-room mansion in the style of a German *Schloss*, with towers and spires and a hundred-foot ballroom, and stabling for eight carriages.

The Harrises' summer cottage was just like one of the cloud-castles that had sailed over Lucy's head as she lay by the Saline River in Kansas, a cloud-castle translated by sheer wealth into stone and stained-glass and imported marble.

Mrs Harris adored picnics and today was perfect for a picnic. A warm south-westerly breeze blew across the gardens, and the peacocks wailed like lonely children, and rich and stunningly beautiful women strolled the greensward in linen and lace and hats that burst from their heads like flowering gardens in their own right. Occasionally the music and the laughter were punctuated by the civilized knock of a croquet mallet. A man passing close by said to his lady companion, '– but then again, it takes a high level of surrounding culture for – say – the invention of bicycles.'

Lucy said, 'I think I'll go say hello.'

But Evelyn snatched at once at her sleeve. 'Lucy, you can't do that!'

'Why ever not? He's only a man!'

'Exactly! He's a man! And you haven't been introduced!'

'I know, Evelyn. That's why I'm going to go introduce myself!'

Still Evelyn clung on to her. 'You can't introduce yourself until somebody else has introduced you first!'

'Well, *you* introduce me, then.'

'I don't know him! Besides, it's just not done. Mrs Harris will explode.'

'Oh, good! I love explosions! Do you know, in Kansas once the Army fired cannons into the clouds, to see if they could make it rain. It made such a noise! It was wonderful!'

'And did it?' asked Evelyn, almost hysterical with apprehension at what Lucy might do.

'Did it what?' said Lucy, and began to walk across the lawn towards Henry Carson and his companions. Evelyn hurried in pursuit.

'Did it rain?' Evelyn panted.

Lucy frowned at her. 'When?' she wanted to know.

Henry Carson had already glanced at her once or twice. No man really could have resisted glancing once or twice at a tall blonde girl in a silk day-dress the colour of poured cream, with a wide cream hat heaped with yellow silk roses, and a four-strand pearl choker that must have cost the better part of thirty thousand dollars.

He had smiled, too. Or half-smiled. Or looked amused, anyway. Lucy was in no doubt that she would like him the moment she spoke to him; and that he would immediately warm to her.

But (after the famous Mrs Pembroke Jones) Mrs Harris was the most experienced society hostess in Newport, and she was sensitive to the slightest tremor in the social fabric. Before Lucy could approach within thirty feet of Henry Carson, Mrs Harris fluidly excused herself from the conversation in which she was engaged and sped across the lawn at a sharp diagonal, intercepting Lucy beside the steps.

'Miss Darling!' she exclaimed, in a purposeful coo. 'I've been meaning to tell you all morning how *interesting* you look!'

'Well, thank you,' Lucy replied; not realizing that *interesting* was a small but calculated insult. 'I'm enjoying myself.'

Mrs Harris took hold of Lucy's elbow, and piloted her away from the steps and back across the lawn. Mrs Harris' complexion was uncannily flawless for a woman of sixty, as if she were wearing a pale mask of porcelain bisque, and she always dressed herself in the frilliest and fussiest of frocks. This morning's frock was white, with burgundy ribbons.

'You must meet young Charlton Bright,' she said. 'He

comes from Omaha, so you and he must have been neighbours, almost!'

'I was sort of hoping you might introduce me to Mr
Carson,' said Lucy.

Mrs Harris tightened her mouth, as if she had just dis-
covered an ulcer on the end of her tongue. 'Well, my dear!
Mr Carson is far too busy for girlish chit-chat, I'm afraid!
He's here on official business, for the British government.'

'He's *laughing*,' Lucy observed, turning her head.

'My dear girl, even politicians are allowed to laugh. And
he is so fond of Henrietta! Look! Here's Charlton!'

'Mrs Harris —'

'Charlton! You dear boy! Come and meet Lucy Darling!
Isn't she just a picture!'

Charlton Bright turned out to be as tedious as he was tall.
He was beakynosed, with a straggly brown moustache, and
a concave chest. He stood six inches away from Lucy and
addressed three one-minute sentences about horsebreeding to
somebody who (judging by where he fixed his eyes) must
have been sitting on Lucy's hat. Three sentences was all that
Lucy could endure. She excused herself when he made it
clear that he was going to attempt a fourth sentence, and
made her way back to Evelyn.

'Told you so!' said Evelyn, triumphantly.

'If I hear one more word about the private life of horses,
ever, in the whole of my life, I shall *drown* myself!' Lucy
told her.   'Charlton's *sweet*, once you get to know him,'
said Evelyn. 'He'll do anything, if you ask him! Anything at
all!'

'I don't care for men who do anything at all,' Lucy
replied; trying to sound airy. 'I only care for men who say
no; or that they *might* if you say pretty-please.'

Evelyn gave her an odd look that was partly regret and
partly envy. 'I knew another girl like you, once.'

'Oh, yes?'

'Well, she married an actor, and she was famous for a

while. But he beat her; and in the end he beat her so hard that she died. Or else she went mad, nobody quite knew.'

'That's not going to happen to me,' Lucy protested. 'I think you've got yourself an all-fired cheek to say that it might!'

'Lucy, it isn't *done* to say "all-fired".'

Luncheon was served at long tables under the trees; on starched white tablecloths and flower-decorated Limoges porcelain. Lucy ate a little cold lobster salad and a small slice of game pie; and drank only one glass of champagne. She was too interested in keeping her eye on Henry Carson to concentrate on eating.

She was fascinated by his obvious authority; and by the way in which everybody around him nodded and laughed at what he said. And now that she was closer, she could see that he was very handsome indeed. He had a high forehead, and a short nose with a slight bump on the bridge, and a firm cleft jaw. If she hadn't known him to be a politician, she would have taken him for a sportsman.

Lucy's father had been talking to Mrs Curwen Phelps, a fussy woman with huge white ostrich plumes on her hat; but now he turned to Lucy and smiled at her. 'I forgot to tell you. I heard from Mr Hardenbergh this morning. The house should be ready in about six weeks.'

'As soon as that?' said Lucy. 'That's marvellous!'

'I offered them a bonus if they finished quick. Well, I guess you'd call it a bribe.'

Since they had arrived in the East, Lucy and her father had been staying in a suite of rooms at the Holland House, on Fifth Avenue at Thirtieth Street, while a house was being built for them in the up-and-coming neighbourhood of Central Park West. Their bankers had advised them that they would soon be able to afford to build a cottage at Newport, too; although not on the scale of the Harris mansion.

The oil kept on pumping, and they had become what Evelyn liked to call 'medium-rich'.

Jack Darling sipped his champagne, and then turned around in his chair to see what Lucy was staring at so intently.

'Got your eye on some feller?' he asked.

Lucy smiled. 'Henry Carson. I wanted Mrs Harris to introduce me, but she wouldn't. And Evelyn said it wasn't "done" for me to introduce myself.'

Jack laughed. 'All this etiquette. Must say it gets good and tedious at times. I'd give fifty bucks to pick my teeth.'

'I'm going to meet him, though,' said Lucy.

'Oh, yes? And how're you going to manage that?'

'I'll manage.'

Jack looked down at his champagne glass. A curved reflection quivered on the tablecloth. 'Sometimes I wonder if you and me was meant for this kind of life.'

She took her eyes away from Henry Carson. 'Aren't you happy?' she asked her father.

'Oh, I guess so, sweetheart. Mustn't complain. I've got everything a man could wish for. But sometimes I feel like loosening my collar and putting my feet up and pouring myself a glass of sipping-whisky and just being myself.'

He paused, and then he said, 'I wish your mother was here, too. All those years of hard work, and she never lived to see the reward. I miss her real bad, Lucy, to tell you the truth. I miss her badder now than I ever did before. I don't even have her ghost to look at.'

Lucy held his hand. 'Oh, poppa, you'll get over it.'

But Jack shook his head. 'I don't want to get over it, Lucy. I want to mourn that mother of yours till the day I go to join her.'

The luncheon continued. The cloud-shadows sailed silently across the lawns. When the meal was finished, the forty-strong chorus from the New York musical *Father's Day* sang a selection of light operatic songs, and were rewarded with garlands of flowers and glasses of champagne.

After the entertainments, the women went to play croquet, while the men changed to swim in the indoor swimming-pool, or to play tennis. Lucy and Evelyn sat under an elm by the tennis-court, sipping champagne.

'You're quiet,' Evelyn remarked.

'Am I?' said Lucy.

'Yes,' Evelyn replied. 'I do declare that you're almost behaving yourself.'

At that moment, however, Lucy sat up stiffly, because Henry Carson and his friends had appeared from the direction of the house, dressed in tennis whites. They were laughing loudly, and Henry Carson was swishing his racket from side to side, as if he were clearing his way through some invisible underbrush.

'– you simply won't get the Bengalis to lift a single finger if you talk to them like that,' he was saying, as he passed Lucy by. 'You have to make the beggars feel that it was *their* idea, and that they're doing you some kind of tremendous favour.'

Lucy stared at him as he walked past; and for a split-second he looked over his companion's shoulder and stared back at her. He didn't smile. He didn't even blink. But there was something in his eyes that told her that he was interested in her. And what eyes! Dark brown and disturbing; the sort of eyes that could melt chocolate.

'Criminies, he's handsome,' she said breathlessly.

'I'd loosen my corsets if I were you,' Evelyn told her, tartly.

'And that *accent*! Snip-snip-snip! Doesn't it just make you quiver all over!'

'Lucy, for goodness' sake, I thought you were going to behave.'

The men began to play doubles; not particularly energetically, although Henry Carson hit two or three hard and accurate backhand shots. There were polite smatters of applause whenever anybody scored, and occasional cries of

134

'bravo!' All the time, Mrs Harris' footmen weaved their way discreetly through the guests, refreshing their glasses with champagne.

Henry Carson and his friend won the first game. While they were changing sides, and chatting to each other, and patting their faces with towels, Lucy abruptly stood up. She was still breathless, not because of her corsets, which were tight enough; but because she had made up her mind what she was going to do to attract Henry Carson's attention, and she knew that Mrs Harris wasn't going to approve one bit, let alone Evelyn, and she didn't suppose that her father would be particularly pleased, either.

'Where are you going?' Evelyn demanded.

'For a walk, that's all,' Lucy told her, and began to make her way towards the tennis court, dragging her chair behind her.

'Lucy!' Evelyn called her. But Lucy was determined to be deaf. She walked right up to the tennis-net post, and set her chair down beside it. Then she took hold of the net, to test how tight it was; and turned the crank-handle three times more, so that it was stretched to the maximum.

'Now, then, what are you up to, Miss Darling?' called Barry Wentworth in a jocular voice, walking towards her. 'We leave that kind of thing to the ground staff.'

Lucy said nothing; didn't even turn to look at him. Instead, she climbed up on her chair, and then placed one foot on top of the net post.

'Hey now, you better come down!' said Barry Wentworth.

But Lucy took a quick breath, and balanced herself on one foot; then carefully put out the other foot, and placed it on the net itself.

There was a sudden hush around the tennis-court as people turned to look. Lucy swayed a little from side to side. *Concentrate*, she told herself. *And remember what Mrs Sweeney told you. Don't look down at your feet. Back straight, eyes front. And be utterly, utterly confident.*

She stepped out on to the net. She kept her arms out-stretched, judging the way the net was swaying, feeling for that perfect centre of gravity. Unlike Mrs Sweeney's fence, the tennis-net had a disconcerting way of double-wobbling beneath her feet, and as she took a second step, and then a third, she began to fear that she wouldn't be able to do it, that she would have to jump down, even though everything depended on her crossing from one net post to the other, without a slip.

To tightrope-walk across Mrs Harris' tennis-court would be dramatic. To try to tightrope-walk across Mrs Harris' tennis-court and to fall off halfway through would be ridiculous.

There was a hush on all sides as she reached the centre of the net. Even the quintet stopped playing. She hesitated for a moment as the net gave a sudden sharp swing to the right; and for one moment she was sure that she was going to lose her balance. She put another foot forward, then another. She heard somebody gasp; and somebody else say, 'No! No! She's doing it! She's doing it!'

Now she was making her way 'uphill', towards the post on the other side of the court. There were only six or seven more steps to go; and the garden-party guests began to gather around her in fascination and amusement.

The soles of her feet felt as if they had been cut in half; and her calves were trembling uncontrollably. She closed her eyes for a second, admonishing herself, *confidence! back straight! you can do it!* and when she opened them again she saw that her exhibition had already brought her what she wanted. Henry Carson had elbowed his way discreetly forward through the crowd of guests, and was standing by the net post, his hands on his hips, smiling, and waiting for her.

Three more steps; two; she couldn't even smile back at him, she was concentrating so hard. But then he held up his arms for her; and she swayed once; and wobbled; and jumped lightly down on to the grass.

Henry Carson held up her hand, and called out, 'Three cheers!'

There were whistles and applause and laughter, and somebody shouted out, 'We ought to start a circus! Barry, old man! You can ride a bicycle, can't you?'

Lucy, flushed with effort and embarrassment, turned around and curtseyed, and there was more applause; although she glimpsed Mrs Harris at the back of the crowd with a face like a prairie cyclone. She couldn't see Evelyn anywhere.

Henry Carson was taller than he had appeared from the other side of the lawn. He smiled at her and said, 'Well! That was jolly impressive, I must say! Did you have to train for it?'

'My dancing-teacher showed me. She used to walk the slack-wire for Forepaugh and Sells.'

Henry Carson laughed that sharp woodcutting laugh. 'Forepaugh and Sells! There's a name for you! Nothing to do with dogs and prisons, I shouldn't suppose?'

'No, Mr Carson. Travelling showmen. They used to be famous, in the West.'

'Now, look here,' said Henry Carson, 'you really mustn't call me "mister". Plain Henry will do. George, would you bring us two glasses of champagne? You do care for champagne, I suppose, Miss Ah –?'

Mrs Harris had now managed to bustle her way across the tennis-court.

'Mrs Harris, you've been very remiss,' Henry Carson complained, before she could open her mouth. 'You haven't yet introduced me to this delightful tightrope-walking protégée of yours.'

Despite the porcelain smoothness of her face, Mrs Harris' eyes were pink with annoyance. 'Well, Mr Carson,' she said, between tight-stretched lips, 'the fact of the matter is that we didn't know that she could perform in public. She's been hiding her light under a bushel as it were.'

'Is that true?' Henry asked Lucy. 'I wish you'd show me how you do it. The Prime Minister keeps telling me that I ought to keep my lights hidden under bushels. Ha! Ha! Can't manage it!'

'Mr Carson, allow me to present Miss Lucy Darling,' said Mrs Harris. The words stuck to her tongue like fine-grained sand. 'Miss Darling, I have the honour of introducing the Honourable Henry Carson, member of Parliament for Southport.'

Henry Carson took Lucy's hand and kissed it, and Lucy bobbed a little curtsey.

'I'm charmed,' he told her.

'Well, I guess I am, too,' Lucy replied.

Mrs Harris raised her eyes to heaven.

They strolled across the lawns together, and down to the artificial lake which the Harrises had created by damming a tributary of the Wansicut River. A flotilla of bafflehead ducks came swimming up to them, hoping for bread-crumbs.

'You know, this reminds me awfully of home,' said Henry Carson, standing with his hand in his pocket, sipping champagne. 'Well, the family park, actually, at Brackenbridge. Not so Capability Brown, of course. But, still, awfully similar. I've been trying to build a cascade – you know, a kind of staircase of water.'

Lucy watched him for a while without saying anything.

'You come from Kansas, they tell me,' he remarked. 'I can't say that I've ever had the pleasure of visiting Kansas.'

'It's not much of a pleasure. Most of it's flat.'

'You're not sorry you left it, then?'

Lucy looked away. 'I don't know. I miss it sometimes. I miss the people more than anything. In Oak City, there was no pretending you liked folk if you didn't; and you never had to worry which fork you picked up.'

Henry Carson laughed. 'I never pretend that I like people

if I don't! And I certainly don't worry which fork I pick up! In fact I eat with my fingers whenever I can. It's only these dratted society matrons who worry about etiquette. They're so terrified that they're going to betray their' – and here he whispered confidentially, – '*lack of breeding.*'

'Well, I don't *have* any breeding to speak of,' said Lucy, quite defiantly. She didn't like to think that all of those lessons that Evelyn had given her in which fish-server to use for buttered haddock and what to do with your napkin after you had finished eating (*never* refold it!) were all in vain.

Henry Carson looked at her closely but she couldn't read the expression on his face. It was too complicated, too masked. She had never spoken to a man with this much poise, this much maturity. She suddenly felt as if she were very seriously out of her depth.

'You shouldn't worry yourself about it,' Henry Carson told her. 'Some people work all their lives at acquiring breeding, and never do; while some are simply born with it. I know at least three peers who are absolute pigs. Besides, why give a fig about breeding, when you have so much oil?'

Lucy turned to him suspiciously. 'You seem to know a whole lot about me.'

'Of course I do. I asked.'

'When?' she retorted.

'The moment I first saw you. I said to George, who's that entrancing creature? And George said, Lucy Darling, daughter of Jack Darling the oil millionaire. Jack Darling inherited his oil from his late brother-in-law; and now he's well on the way to being a very wealthy chap indeed. And everybody thinks that Lucy is the prettiest debutante of the season.'

Lucy blushed. She wished she had brought some cake to throw to the ducks. Anything to divert Henry Carson's attention. He wouldn't take his eyes off her, and it was so *embarrassing*!

Henry Carson said, 'I couldn't possibly have left Newport

without meeting the prettiest debutante of the season, could I? Blanche would never have forgiven me.'

'Blanche?'

'My sister. She's dying to see me married. She says it'll be good for me. Well, a great many people want to see me married. Especially Mrs Harris.'

'Mrs Harris tells everybody that you and Henrietta are practically engaged.'

Henry Carson nodded. 'I know. Frightful, isn't it? How can you tell a doting American mother that her beloved daughter is tiresome and fussy and plain as a pikestaff?'

He paused, and then he said, 'I shouldn't have said that. She's quite a sweet girl really. But the ladies of Brackenbridge have always been rather special. And when I get married, I want my wife to be the most special lady of all.'

Lucy didn't know quite what it was, but there was an inflection in Henry Carson's voice that seemed to suggest that he was talking about *her,* as if he had already made up his mind that it was *she* that he wanted.

They walked a little farther around the lake. They reached some low stone steps where a rowing-boat was moored, and where the whole Harris house was reflected in the water.

'The drowned palace,' said Lucy.

Henry Carson glanced at her. 'You should see the Taj Mahal.'

'In India? I'd love to go to India.'

'You'd adore it,' he told her. 'India is — well, India is beyond words.'

'You've really been there?'

Henry Carson nodded. 'Twice now. And each time I loved her more. Sometimes I feel that my whole destiny lies in India.' He smiled. 'That's if the Prime Minister allows it, of course. I may end up in Ireland, God forbid.'

'Don't you care for the Irish?'

'Of course not. They're beyond all comprehension, and they smoke their pipes upside-down.'

'You're sane, then,' said Lucy.

'*What?*' Henry Carson laughed.

He took hold of her elbow and escorted her slowly back up the hill. The grass was poisonously green and shiny, as if it couldn't be real. Lucy would have loved to have lain on her back on it, and watched the clouds go sailing past. It was one of those afternoons when she felt that everything was changing, that the world was pivoting beneath her feet, and carrying her away with it.

'I think I've monopolized you too long,' said Henry Carson, as they reached the parapet around the back of the house. The orchestra was playing a minuet; sprightly, prissy, and light. 'I really must go and talk about trade tariffs.'

Lucy said, 'I hope you don't think it was too forward of me. The tightrope-walking.'

Henry Carson laughed, and kissed her hand. 'I thought it was magical. I'm not sure that Mrs Harris approved, but don't worry about that. If we let ourselves worry about the Mrs Harrises of this world, nobody would ever walk on tennis-nets, would they? or swallow swords, or misbehave themselves, or fall in love at first sight.'

He grasped her hand. 'I would like very much to see you again, Lucy, before I return to England. May I call on you?'

Lucy suddenly felt hot and confused. She knew from Evelyn that the etiquette of accepting gentlemen callers was extraordinarily sensitive; and that she must avoid compromising herself at all costs. She opened her mouth and then she closed it again. The simple truth was that she didn't know whether it was proper to say yes; or if no would really be understood to be no; or whether there was something else she could say that would make it clear to Henry Carson that she would adore him to call, but that she couldn't say so in so many words.

'You're staying in Newport all summer?' Henry Carson asked her.

Lucy nodded, still flushed with confusion. 'Until the second week in August.'

'Well, I have ten more days here. Then I have to take the train to Boston, and the ship back home.'

'I – I'm not used to callers,' Lucy managed to choke out. 'In Kansas, when a gentleman called –'

'Yes?' Henry Carson encouraged her.

'Well, he just came up, and said, "how about a soda?"'

Henry Carson laughed out loud, and smacked his thigh in amusement. His eyes were bright, and Lucy thought that she had never seen a man so handsome and so darned debonair in all of her life.

'You really shouldn't worry,' he told her. 'I shall call on you with the greatest of propriety. You are a very rare specimen indeed, and I shall treat you with all the respect to which any rare specimen is entitled.'

Mrs Harris reappeared, off-balance and flustered. 'You *will* dance with Henrietta, Mr Carson?'

'If you insist, Mrs Harris, just a quick scurry.'

Mrs Harris linked arms with Henry Carson, and tugged him away; but not before she had swivelled her head around and glared at Lucy with an expression that could have crushed glass. Lucy airily looked away. After all, what had Henry Carson said to her? If we all took notice of the Mrs Harrises of this world, nobody would tightrope-walk on tennis-nets, or swallow swords, and nobody would fall in love at first sight.

She was about to walk back across the lawn to rejoin Evelyn when she hesitated; and turned; and frowned intently at Henry Carson as he accompanied Mrs Harris to the garden steps. Love at first sight? Had he really meant it? Love at first sight with *her*?

She returned to Evelyn looking preoccupied.

'Lucy! you look as if you've seen a ghost, my dearest dearest!' Evelyn exclaimed. 'You'd better have some more champagne.'

'No, no thank you,' said Lucy. 'I think I'd just like to sit down, as a matter of fact.'

'You never told me you could walk on a *tightrope!*' gushed Evelyn. 'You ought to hear what people are saying! They can't make up their minds if you're the debutante of the year, or a circus-performer! It's such fun! And, of course, when Henry Carson was there to help you down! What did he *say?* He's so dazzling! And Henrietta went absolutely *green!*'

'Yes,' said Lucy. 'I expect she did.'

She sat down under one of the elms. She felt giddy and strange, as if she had drunk too much. She was still sitting there when Mrs Stuyvesant Fish came past. Mrs Stuyvesant Fish hesitated, almost passed her by; but then stopped, and came back, and laid her hand on Lucy's arm. She was veiled and perfumed; her diamond rings flashed in the afternoon sunlight.

'My dear Lucy,' she whispered, 'I thought you were *encroy-able!* I haven't seen Wilhemina Harris so cross in *years!*'

'Thank you,' said Lucy; and it was then that she saw her father walking towards her, his white yachting pants flapping in the breeze. To think of Jack Darling wearing yachting pants! He took off his hat and she could see that he was smiling; and it was then that she knew everything was going to be dandy.

She dreamed about Henry Carson every night for the next three nights. The dreams were magnetic and dark and exciting, but also peculiarly frustrating. In each one she heard that clipped English voice calling, 'Lucy! Lucy!' But when she approached him, he immediately turned away from her, so that she couldn't catch sight of his face.

In one dream he was on the lawn at Mrs Harris' house; in both of the others he was in Oak City, just outside her father's general store. In the last dream she almost managed to reach him, but at the last moment he turned away again, so that all she could see was the dark straight hair on the back of his collar.

There was music in the dreams, too, but she didn't know what kind of music it was. It was thin, sad, pipe-like music, carried on the wind.

On the third morning the dream woke her just after seven o'clock. She lay with her eyes open looking up at the buttermilk-coloured curtains that hung over her bed. She had the prettiest of bedrooms; with tiny scarlet flowers on the wallpaper, and gilded walnut furniture that had been imported from France.

They had rented the house from the McPhersons, who had made their money in real estate. It was bijou by Harris or Vanderbilt standards; only eight bedrooms, and seven reception rooms, and stabling for two broughams and a tea-cart; but it was idyllically located on a small wooded hill overlooking the sea, and on a bright day you could see as far as Sakonnet.

She turned to look at the little enamelled clock on her bedside table. Then she drew back the quilt, and climbed out of bed. She was wearing her hair tied up in pale blue ribbons, and a pink French nightdress with a lacy bodice. She crossed to the window and looked out at the gardens. The waters of Rhode Island Sound glittered through the cedar trees, and gulls were sloping in the morning wind.

She slipped her feet into her white silk mules, and picked up her dressing-gown. Then she opened her bedroom door, and stepped out on to the galleried landing. In the hallway below her, illuminated by the muted amber sunshine that fell from the skylight, one of the maids was mopping the marbled-tiled floor, while another was polishing the doorhandle. From the direction of the breakfast room Lucy could hear the cutlery being set out for breakfast. She padded downstairs to the hall, and said, 'Good morning, Jane! Good morning, Dorothy!'

'You're powerful early, Miss Lucy,' smiled the maid with the mop. She was plump and white-faced and Irish, and had once thought of taking holy orders. 'First time I seen you up and about before nine o'clock.'

'Couldn't sleep any longer,' Lucy told her. 'It's such a beautiful day!'

'That's one thing that comes free,' the maid replied. 'God's good sunshine.'

Lucy tiptoed over the wet marble tiles, and Dorothy stepped back and opened up the front door for her. Dorothy was mulatto, graceful and calm, almost beautiful except for one wandering eye.

'You going *out*?' Jane asked her, in disbelief.

'Of course I'm going out,' Lucy replied.

'Well, then, you take good care of yourself,' the maid told her, as she skipped down the steps. 'If your poppa finds out that I let you go dancing around the garden in your nightclothes, why, he's going to skin me like a squirrel.'

Lucy turned around and waved at her, and called back, 'Tell him I was sleepwalking, and you didn't dare to wake me!'

She crossed the formal gardens in front of the house, past semi-circular rosebeds and stone statues of lions and gryphons, until she reached the woods.

She passed through the fragrant shadows beneath the trees; and at last emerged on the hillside overlooking the sea. The waves were as bright as smashed-up sugar; and already the first yachts of the day were leaning into the wind.

She stood with her arms stretched wide, so that the wind caught her dressing-gown, too, and made it ripple and flap. She closed her eyes, and thought to herself, this is what it's like to be a bird; this is what it's like to be a yacht.

This is what it's like to be in love.

'How happy I am!' she sang. 'How happy I am! How happy! how happy! how happy!' She opened her mouth, so that the wind made a hollow blowing sound across her lips. She felt that she could almost eat the wind, like bread, it blew so strongly, and it tasted of salt and freshness and sunshine.

Her eyes were still closed and her mouth was still open

when she heard somebody cough. A polite, formal cough, obviously intended to warn her that she wasn't alone. Immediately, she opened her eyes and crossed her hands over her breasts.

Half-concealed in the shadow by the edge of the woods, smiling at her mischievously, his hat and his riding-crop held in his hand, stood Henry Carson. On the far side of the woods she could see his Arab horse silhouetted amongst the trunks of the cedar trees.

'Good morning, Miss Darling!' he called out. 'You'll have to forgive my fearful lack of manners; but when I saw you there I simply couldn't resist coming to investigate!'

Lucy swallowed, and blushed, and all she could do was to chirp at him 'Oh! It's you!'

She was thrilled to see him. At least she would have been, if she hadn't been standing on this windy hill in her dressing-gown, with no powder or rouge or jewellery, and her hair all tied up in ribbons. She didn't know whether to run off down the hill, or hide behind a tree; or pretend that she wasn't there at all.

'Please, Miss Darling, don't be distressed,' Henry told her, moving out into the sunlight. 'You make a perfect picture. Perfect! But I'll go away if you want me to.'

'No, well, you don't have to go,' Lucy flustered. Her cheeks felt as if they were shining like plums. 'I was only – looking at the sea.'

Henry lifted his head up and sniffed the morning breeze, and nodded. 'It's a very fine day. Reminds me of the Isle of Wight, rather.'

'It was such a beautiful day I came out early,' said Lucy. 'I don't usually get out of bed until it's almost lunchtime.' She bit her lip. She wasn't sure if it was 'done' for a young lady to mention 'bed' to a man she scarcely knew.

However, Henry didn't seem to be at all scandalized. 'I wish to goodness that *I* could lie in bed all morning!' he replied. 'Got out of the habit, though; and once you're out of the habit, you can't go back to it. Myself, I always go for an early ride. Tones up the brain for the day's business. Sharpens the wits. This morning I thought I'd kill two birds with one stone; and leave you my calling-card while I was out.'

'You don't have to leave a card now,' said Lucy.

'Oh, Miss Darling, I must! Otherwise it wouldn't be proper. Besides, I was going to ask you and your father whether you would care to come to dinner with me tomorrow evening. Rather sadly, I have to leave on Friday; it's going to be my last opportunity to entertain you.'

'You're leaving so soon?'

'Affairs of state have to take priority over affairs of the heart, I'm sorry to say.'

Lucy looked up at him, with an unspoken question on her face.

In return, Henry lowered his eyes and tapped at his hat with his riding-crop, as if he expected to be able to conjure a rabbit out of it.

'I know I'm laying waste to all of the usual social conventions; especially here in Newport where they count for so much. I shouldn't be talking to you at all, let alone talking to you alone, in your night-attire, unchaperoned, in a field. But the plain fact of the matter is, Miss Darling, that when I saw you at Mrs Harris' the other day, you did something that no woman has ever done to me before.'

Lucy had already anticipated what he was going to say; and her heart began to rise inside her ribcage like a hot-air balloon.

Henry looked up. 'The plain fact of the matter, Miss Darling, is that you have quite captivated me. Ever since the day of that picnic, I have thought about nothing else but you; and seeing you again.'

'Well,' said Lucy.

Henry's expression was oddly little-boyish, almost plaintive.

147

'Well,' Lucy repeated; and then laughed. 'Here I am! You're seeing me!'

Henry nodded, and smiled. 'I am, yes; as clear as day; and it is the greatest imaginable pleasure.' He held out his arm to her, and said, 'If it isn't too bold a favour to ask, Miss Darling, perhaps you would allow me to escort you back to the house, so that I can leave you my invitation in the conventional manner.'

Lucy dipped him a mocking little curtsey. 'Am I still allowed to call you plain Henry?'

'But of course! You must!'

'In that case, hadn't you better call me plain Lucy; instead of "Miss Darling"?'

'Lucy isn't plain at all! But very well, Lucy it shall be! If I may offer you my arm?'

'Delighted,' smiled Lucy; and together they walked arm-in-arm through the woods. A squirrel scampered up a tree right beside them, and Lucy said, '*Psshh!*' and laughed to scare it even more.

'I sense a teaser in you,' said Henry.

'Isn't it done, in England, to tease an Honorable?'

'You mustn't call me that,' said Henry. 'I'm only a man, after all. No better and no worse than any other.'

'I haven't met any man better,' Lucy replied. 'But I've sure come across worse.' She thought this was quite a witty retort.

Henry looked at her narrowly. 'I can't believe that you know any men at all.'

Lucy turned away; suddenly alarmed that her lack of purity might somehow show in her eyes. 'Well, no, of course not,' she said.

'You're not – walking out with anybody?' Henry asked her. 'You're not engaged, perhaps, or spoken for?'

Lucy shook her head. 'I did know a boy in Kansas. His name was Jamie. Everybody thought that we were going to be married one day; but of course that was before we had

148

any money. He went off to study the law in Manhattan, Kansas, and I came here.'

Henry said, 'Did you love him?'

Lucy couldn't think what to say to that, but he added quickly, 'Please – forgive me if I'm being too inquisitive. It really is none of my affair.'

'Oh, I don't mind,' said Lucy. 'I suppose I did love him, in a way. I surely depended on him. But depending on somebody, that's not the same as being in love with them, is it?'

'It can certainly be *part* of loving them,' Henry observed. 'But, no, it's not really the same thing at all. When you're in love, well –' he looked down at her, and his eyes were dark-brown, and alive with amusement. 'When you're in love, you're on fire.'

For one horrific and unexpected instant, Lucy had a furious vision of Uncle Casper, with his face blazing. Then she found that she was standing in her slippers on the sunlit lawn, staring at Henry instead.

'Lucy?' he asked her. 'Lucy, is something the matter?'

Lucy shook her head. 'I'm all right. I felt a little queer, that's all.'

'Let me take you inside. It's not terribly warm, is it? Perhaps you got up too early!'

'Yes,' she said. Her mouth felt dry. 'Perhaps I did.'

He helped her up the wide stone steps into the hallway. Jane and Dorothy stopped their floor-washing and their polishing and curtseyed.

'Jane, would you go tell Herrick to come to the door?' Lucy told her. 'Mr Carson wishes to leave his card.'

'Whatever you say, Miss Darling,' Jane replied, disapprovingly, and bustled off to find the butler.

Henry grasped Lucy's hands between his. 'I'm sorry. It seems that I've upset you somehow.'

'No,' said Lucy. 'It wasn't you. I guess I need my breakfast, that's all. Too many late evenings, too much backgammon, too much champagne.'

'A young lady should take care of herself,' Henry told her, and pressed her hands warmly and strongly, as if they were two flowers he wanted to preserve. In that particular downward-straining light in the hallway, she noticed for the first time the curving scar over his right eye. It gave him a quizzical expression, like a man surprised at his own good fortune. She didn't dare to remark on it, or to ask him how he had come by it.

Henry was staying in Newport as the guest of the Widgerys; who were friends of the President; and rich as all hell; but comparatively cultured. That is to say, they were cultured enough to have heard of Mozart, and not to think that the plays of Shakespeare were what he had done at weekends, when he had finished his works.

The Widgerys were dining that evening with the Pembroke Joneses, a big Yacht Club do; but they had made a point of waiting for Lucy and her father to arrive at The Seasons, so that they could welcome them. The Seasons was a titanic Second-Empire mansion set in a seventy-acre park. It had cost Milford Widgery more than four million dollars to build, an exact reproduction of the Château de Larroque, in Gascony, France, except that the quality of the stonework was very much finer.

As they jostled and squeaked in their brougham up the two-mile drive, Lucy saw The Seasons appear in the summer twilight huge and dark, with rows of lighted windows; more like a cliff than a house; a cliff in which scores of cave-dwellers lived, and kept their fires.

Jack Darling coughed, and said, 'I heard that Milford Widgery didn't exactly live in no outhouse. And, by Jiminy, look at this bulger.'

'Poppa,' Lucy admonished him, squeezing his hand. 'Stop talking so *Kansas*.'

Jack Darling grunted. 'Don't give me that society nonsense. You should hear some of the conversations that go on over the port'n'cigars. If you ask me, the richer the fellow, the fouler his mouth.'

They arrived at the door. One green-liveried footman opened their carriage-door, and put down the steps, while another was on hand to help them out. Henry was waiting for them at the top of the steps, immaculately dressed in tie and tails, with a high white collar.

'Mr Darling, Miss Darling. I'm delighted to see you! Come inside and meet Mr and Mrs Widgery. They're off in a moment; but they wanted to say hello.'

They entered a hallway as vast and echoing as a cathedral. Sparkling chandeliers hung high above their heads, and a curving marble staircase swept down from the landing to the highly-polished floor. Milford Widgery obviously had a taste for the acceptably erotic, since every niche around the hallway was occupied by a hefty mock-classical Venus, and the staircase was hung with oil-paintings of romping pink nudes and grinning satyrs.

Mr and Mrs Widgery were ready to leave; but they were still talking to each other with fierce animation in one corner of the hallway.

'Henry!' called Milford. 'Come right on over, let's see if your friends can settle an argument for us.'

Milford was small and neat and smooth, like a seal that had just emerged from the water; while Ethel his wife was large and blurry, as if she hadn't had the patience to keep still while she was posing for a daguerrotype. She had frayed silk fringes and fraying white hair and a disconcerting habit of suddenly swinging her arms to emphasize what she was saying, so that her circle of listeners were constantly ducking and diving and stepping back out of range. She welcomed Lucy with an exclamation of delight, drawing her towards her bejewelled bosom as irresistibly as a flood tide drawing a dinghy on to the rocks.

For one awkward moment, their brooches became entangled.

'My dear,' cried Mrs Widgery. 'I heard *all* about your exploits at Mrs Harris'! What a marvel! I would have given the Perry Diamond to have seen it! You know that Milly gave me the Perry Diamond, don't you? I always said that the Harris' picnics needed pepping up, didn't I, Milly? And to walk the tightrope on her tennis-net! Henry was quite breathless about it!'

'I was admiring, certainly,' smiled Henry.

Milford said, 'She's a charming young lady, Henry. No mistake about that.'

'You said you wanted us to settle something,' put in Lucy. She loved compliments, but she still wasn't sure how she should deal with them. Saying 'thank you' seemed so vain, as if you knew darned well how charming you were; so she had taken to smiling and blushing instead.

Mrs Widgery replied, 'It's our daughter's fifteenth wedding anniversary next month. Milford says it's her ivory wedding but I say it's crystal.'

Henry shook his head. 'Not my line of country, I'm afraid. Haven't the foggiest.'

But Jack Darling said, 'That's an easy one. Crystal.'

'Well, that's jolly knowledgeable of you, Mr Darling,' Henry remarked. 'How did you happen to know that?'

Jack said, 'Lucy's mother died the day before *our* crystal wedding.'

'Oh, I'm fearfully sorry,' said Henry. 'I didn't mean to upset you.'

'Pay it no mind,' Jack told him. 'She was sick for quite a while. I bought her a chandelier, though. Real crystal. She always hankered after a chandelier. She'd have loved this'un. She never saw the one I bought her. Died without opening her eyes.'

'Well!' Milford exclaimed, in an attempt to break the moment of morbidness. 'We really must be going! Mrs Pembroke Jones is a stickler for punctuality. The sport of princes!'

'The *courtesy* of princes, you mean,' Mrs Widgery corrected him.

'The politeness of kings, actually,' said Henry. 'Attributed to Louis the Eighteenth.'

'I didn't even know there *was* a Louis the Eighteenth,' Milford replied, in surprise. 'He sounds like a golf-caddy.'

'Oh, you don't know *anything*,' Mrs Widgery chided him.

'I was joking, for God's sake,' Milford protested.

The Widgerys' butler brought them their coats, and they left for their dinner, Mrs Widgery waving as if she were going on a day-trip by train to the seaside. They were still arguing – whether it was 'cabbages and kings' or 'cauliflowers and kings.' Henry said to Lucy and her father, 'Please, come on through to the drawing room, I'm sure you'd like some champagne.'

He took Lucy's arm, and together they walked through to the principal drawing room. Lucy's sky-blue silk dress whispered on the Persian rugs. The drawing room was the size of the main concourse of a railroad terminus; with chandeliers and a painted ceiling and vast gilt-framed mirrors. An entire family of Kansas sodbusters would have been quite content to set up house inside the fireplace alone.

'Always bickering, the Widgerys,' said Henry, as he led Lucy to one of the eight velvet-cushioned ottomans. 'They're delightful people, though. Rich enough to make one's eyes water, but completely unaffected by it. And every year they personally give more money to charity than the entire state budget of Delaware. They never stop telling me; but then it's something worth telling, don't you think?'

Lucy saw herself in one of the mirrors. She had curled up her hair, and pinned it with diamond-and-sapphire combs, which flashed as she turned her head. Her gown was watered silk, very low-cut, and on her bosom wore a diamond-and-sapphire necklace.

'You look marvellous,' Henry complimented her. 'Mr Darling, you have a captivating daughter.'

'Well, takes after her mother,' said Jack, sitting himself

down and tugging at the knees of his pants to make himself comfortable.

The butler came into the room on soft kid-soled shoes, carrying a silver tray of champagne glasses. After he had taken his, Jack glanced at Lucy, and sniffed, and cleared his throat, and then said, 'Mr Carson, would you be offended if I asked for a shot of sipping-whisky?'

'Not at all,' said Henry. 'Leonard, would you mind?'

The butler brought back a glass of whisky. Jack accepted it, and winked; and then promptly tipped it into his champagne.

'Well, that's fairly novel,' Henry remarked. 'That's an eight-year-old Prieur-Pageot.'

'Too weak, that's the trouble,' Jack replied, taking a large mouthful and swilling it noisily between his teeth. 'Measure of whisky gives it a decent kick.'

Lucy blushed at her father's Kansas manners; but Henry said, 'That sounds like a capital idea to me. Leonard – bring us some more whisky.'

The butler brought the bottle, and Henry tipped a measure into his own glass of champagne.

'A toast!' he proclaimed, rising to his feet. 'To Lucy, who is easily the most alluring girl that I have ever met in the whole of America, if not the world; and to you, Mr Darling, for giving us not only Lucy, but the most practical cocktail that I have ever encountered!'

They drank. Henry coughed, and his eyes widened. 'That's wonderful!' he gasped, pummelling his chest with his fist to get his breath back. 'Absolutely magnificent! My friends in London will adore it!'

'Well, it's better than a poke in the eye with a bradawl,' said Jack, although he was obviously pleased.

'It has to have a name!' Henry exclaimed.

'What about the Oak City Special?' suggested Jack.

'No, no! Let's call it the Tightrope!' Henry told him. 'Then I shall always remember how I first made its acquaintance.'

'Sounds all right t'me,' Jack replied, pouring a little more whisky into his glass before the butler could hurry round to do it for him, and topping it up with champagne.

Dinner went on for four enchanted hours. The three of them sat together at one end of the Widgerys' hundred-foot mahogany dining-table, their eyes sparkling in the light from a twenty-branch candelabrum, eating and laughing and drinking Tightropes.

The Widgerys' servants discreetly came and went with asparagus soup, lobster timbales, broiled wild duck, and fruit. Milford Widgery was almost as serious about food as he was about money, and he had bribed one of the best chefs at Delmonico's to take over his kitchens.

Henry talked ceaselessly and enthusiastically throughout the meal. As Lucy's father said afterwards, 'He sure wasn't short of chin music.' He told Lucy and her father all about Brackenbridge, his family home, and how much he revered and adored it. 'In January, in Derbyshire, it can of course turn fearfully cold and depressing. But to approach Brackenbridge from the north, and to see the winter sun shining on the statues over the portico; to walk through the park and see the geese flying through the mist; there is no enchantment like it.'

He told them about his schooldays at Eton, and how he had confounded his tutors by pretending to be lackadaisical and ill-disciplined. 'I used to sneak up to Ascot races; not because I cared for racing particularly, but because it was forbidden.' In the First Hundred Examination, however, he had come well ahead of absolutely everybody. 'First of the whole school! My tutors were furious! But of course they hadn't understood that I will *always* be first, in whatever I undertake.'

After his fifth Tightrope, Jack began to ramble about Lucy's mother again, his voice squashy with drink. But with considerable care, Henry steered him off the subject, and consoled him in a strange way, too, by describing the death of his own mother. A corroded pipe had exuded sewer gas into her bedroom, and eventually she had caught a fever. (It was nothing unsual, he remarked. The sewers at No 10 Downing Street were so foul that the Prime Minister himself was frequently feverish, and one of his private secretaries, a good friend of Henry's, had almost died.)

'Once her spirit had left her, you know, my mother lay in bed smiling, the way I always remembered her; although her face was grey, like marble. My Aunt Elisabeth had strewn the entire bed with white camellias. I still have one of them, pressed in the first copy of my first book.'

'You've written a book?' asked Lucy, deeply impressed.

'It didn't sell very well, I'm afraid,' said Henry. 'It's rather portly, and it costs two guineas.'

'But all the same! Is it an adventure?'

Henry laughed. 'I'm afraid not! But it was certainly an adventure to write it. It's called *Persia and the Persians*. It covers absolutely everything that you would wish to know about Persia, and quite a few things that you *wouldn't* wish to know, too.'

'Persia! It sound so romantic!' said Lucy.

'Don't you believe it! They're elegant, the Persians. More scrupulous than any Parisian. But they're filthy beyond any description, and corrupt, and they make a science of lying, and they have an indifference to suffering which I can only describe as bestial.'

He forked up a slice of duck, and then he added, 'Do you know, the last time the Shah of Persia visited London, he had sheep killed in sight of his suite every morning, blew his nose on the curtains, and offered to buy Lady Margaret Beaumont for his harem for half-a-million pounds.

'I have travelled through Persia more than any other European observer, and if there is any romance anywhere, I have yet to come across it.'

'In that case, I guess I'll stay right here in Newport,' Jack remarked, peering into his drink.

'I can't say that I blame you,' smiled Henry. 'But some of us have a duty to save the Oriental races from their own ignorance and cruelty. Quite apart from protecting our Indian Empire from the ambitions of the Russians.'

'You're an educated man, Henry,' Jack told him. 'You've got yourself a destiny, too. You're way above *my* head, I'm sorry to say.'

'Yes,' said Henry, without even a hint of false modesty. 'But all of us have our part to play, Mr Darling; and no man who can bring a daughter such as Lucy into the world can be thought of as anything but blessèd.'

He paused for a moment, and then he said, 'I have a proposition to put to you, to both of you. I have to return to England next week as you know; and after that I have to spend some considerable time on Parliamentary business. In the autumn, however, I should like you both to visit England as my guests. I can make all the arrangements from London, and write to you.'

'Oh, Henry! England? Truly?' Lucy cried out.

'England, how about that!' said her father, trying to focus his eyes. 'I never thought for one solitary moment that I'd ever see England!'

The only sign of agitation that Henry betrayed was his re-arrangement of his knives and forks. 'The truth of the matter is, Mr Darling, that I cannot bear to think that it might be months or even years before I see Lucy again.'

Jack raised his eyes, and looked at Henry carefully. He knew what Henry was saying: that his feelings for Lucy were serious. 'What do you say to that, sweetheart? It's your decision.'

Lucy gave Henry a coy little smile. She didn't mean to be coy. She didn't *feel* coy. But Henry was so direct about his interest in her, and she had never come across such candour before, especially when it came to courting. Bob Wonderly had at least tried to offer her a pound of liver, by way of foreplay.

'I'd like to come, very much,' she said, trying to sound demure.

Henry's face broke into a broad, satisfied smile. 'I knew you would! Thank you! We shall have such a splendid time! I can show you London, and Brackenbridge, and introduce you to all of my friends! And I know that my father will adore you as much as I do!'

'Henry —' said Lucy, cautiously. He seemed almost to have taken her acceptance of a trip to England as an acknowledgement that she would marry him.

'No ifs and buts!' said Henry. 'Let's have another Tightrope, to celebrate! To England! And to happy chances! And to you, Lucy, for lightening up my life!'

It was past midnight before they left. The footmen were yawning behind their white gloves. Jack Darling weaved his way off to the lavatory, because his back teeth were afloat, while Henry and Lucy waited for him in the hallway.

Henry gently took hold of Lucy's hand. 'I hope you don't feel that I've been too obvious,' he told her. 'There's been so little time; and you struck me so devastatingly. I really had no choice at all.'

'I'm flattered,' said Lucy. 'And at least you've been truthful.'

'Well, I told you before, didn't I? I'm no good at all at keeping my feelings to myself. Not very English, I suppose, but there's so little time. I want so much out of life; and I'm not particularly rich. I have to write, and work, and there's never much time for being social. I don't want to end up like Robert Browning, who dinnered himself away.'

He hesitated for a moment, still holding Lucy's hand, and then he said, 'You must forgive me for being so immediate, Lucy. The very last thing I want to do is to frighten you off.'

'I don't think you've managed to do that,' Lucy replied; conscious of her long-drawn-out drawl. 'But everything's still so new to me. New York, Newport, picnics, yachts. I'm trying to take it calm and easy; but sometimes I can't believe it's me.'

She squeezed his hand quickly; then released it. 'Just be understanding, Henry, that's all I ask. Up until· last spring, I'd never seen a house, ever, that didn't have its privy standing out back.'

Henry laughed out loud. 'I love you! You're perfect! You'll scandalize everybody; and rightly so! I can't wait to take you to London!'

'Henry,' said Lucy, 'I don't want you to make any kind of show of me.'

'My dearest Lucy,' Henry told her, and reached into his coat pocket to produce a neatly-folded sheet of paper. 'I wrote you a poem last night. Take it home and read it; and when you read it, please understand that I mean it with all my heart.'

Lucy accepted the sheet of paper with bewilderment. 'A poem?' she asked him. 'You've written a poem?'

'Of course! It's for you!'

'You've written a book, and you've written a poem?'

'My dearest girl, I've written thousands of poems, and I shall write more books! At Oxford, we wrote a poem about almost everything! Our tutors, our chums, the government, anybody we didn't care for, and anybody we *did*.'

At that moment, Lucy's father reappeared, smiling and blinking. Lucy quickly tucked the poem into her reticule.

'Goodnight,' said Henry. 'I shall never forget this evening as long as I live.'

Jack slapped him on the back. 'You're lucky, my friend! I haven't just forgotten this evening, I've forgotten who I am!'

Lucy deliberately tantalized herself by waiting until she had washed and changed into her nightgown before opening Henry's poem.

She drew the bedside lamp closer, and unfolded it. It was written in dark blue ink, in a firm, sloping hand. It read:

159

Yes, though I saw the rising day,
In Hindostan and far Cathay,
I never saw it shine so fair,
As on Miss Darling's golden hair.

I never saw in any time
A beauty that was so sublime.
I never saw in any place
A vision that could match her face.

Now, though I toil to Samarkand,
Through rain and snow and stinging sand
I'll see Miss Darling's darling smile
Which shrinks by half each weary mile.

She read the poem again and again, her eyes dewy. She had read poetry at school, of course. She remembered *The Ancient Mariner*, and the wedding-guest beating his breast. But somehow it had never occurred to her that somebody had actually sat down and written those poems; that they had been invented out of somebody's head. And she had never realized that real people could be included in poems; not just kings and princes and heroes; but real ordinary people like her.

She felt light-headed; almost uplifted; as if by becoming a character in a poem she had somehow become more beautiful, more radiant, more famous.

I am so happy! I am so ha-a-ppy! I am so happy I could die!

There was a soft knock at her door. It was her father, in his quilted smoking robe, pink-eyed from too many Tight-ropes. 'Can I come in?' he asked her.

'Of course you can,' said Lucy. 'I thought you'd have dropped straight off to sleep.'

He sat down on the bed beside her and gave her a kiss. 'I don't know; my head's whirling tonight.'

'I'm not surprised, with all that whisky-and-champagne.'

He nodded at the poem which still lay on the embroidered pillow. 'What's that you're reading? Billay-doo?'

'Henry wrote me a poem.'

Jack Darling picked up the piece of paper and read the poem, softly moving his lips as he did so.

'That's pretty,' he nodded. 'That's a real pretty sentiment.'

Lucy said, 'You do *like* him, poppa?'

'Sure. Sure I like him. I thought he was kind of a blow the first time I met him, but he grows on you, don't he? I mean you'd think he'd stand on ceremony being English and a member of Parliament and all, but he's straight and fair, even if he does talk the leg off the table.'

Lucy watched her father for a while and she could tell that something was troubling him. She held his hand, and gently squeezed it, and said, 'You're worried.'

'Well, I don't know,' he replied. 'Maybe I'm fearful for no good reason at all. But you were always so happy, back in Oak City.'

'I'm happy now.'

'Sure you are. But you understand that if you take up with this Henry, you'll be starting a whole new 'nother kind of life. Dukes and duchesses, that kind of company. I mean you've got to decide if that's what you truly want.'

Lucy smiled, and kissed him. He smelled of Hilbert's Wood Violet Toilet Water. She had tried to wean him on to French colognes, but Hilbert's had always been his favourite, because it was made in Milwaukee and it was good and strong.

'Poppa, you mustn't worry. I can hold my own, even with dukes and duchesses.'

'There's something you should know,' he told her. His voice was low and hoarse. 'I never told you before, because it didn't matter, and it was best all round that we just let sleeping ducks lie. But now you're growed, pretty well, and you've started courtin', and it looks like sooner or later some fellow is going to want to marry you – well, I guess it had better come out.'

'Poppa, tell me,' Lucy insisted.

Jack gave her a wry smile. 'The truth is, Lucy, that – damn it, I don't even know how to begin to say this.'

'Poppa, you can tell me anything, you know that. Since when did you and me ever have any secrets?'

'Sweetheart, I've kept a secret from you all your life.'

She reached out and touched his cheek, he was so obviously distressed.

'Poppa – what secret?'

'That's it,' he said miserably. 'That's the secret. I'm not your poppa. Not *truly* your poppa.'

'What?' she asked him, in astonishment. 'What do you mean?'

'I raised you,' he explained. 'I always took you for my own. But the fact of the matter is that it says on your birthing papers that your true poppa wasn't known.'

'I can't believe it,' whispered Lucy. She couldn't stop herself trembling. 'Why didn't you tell me before?'

'Your momma didn't want you to know. She was ashamed of it, I guess. And besides, what good would it have done you, even if you *had* known? You loved your momma and you loved me, and that was all that was important.'

'But why does it say that my true poppa wasn't known?' Lucy asked him. 'Momma must have known who he was.'

Jack nodded sadly. 'Yes, she knew. But she never told me. She wouldn't. I asked her once, that was all. Just once, one Sunday morning. She said that if I asked her again, she'd pack her bag and she'd leave me for ever, and I knew that she meant it.'

Lucy suddenly realized that she was holding hands with a man who wasn't even her father. She couldn't believe that her mother could have deceived her all those years. Even when she was dying, she hadn't told Lucy the truth. Lucy felt her throat tightening and tears prickling in her eyes, and she didn't know which of them she felt sorrier for — her poppa or herself.

Jack Darling said, 'It was soon after we moved out to Kansas. We had a bad winter and everything seemed to go wrong. I started drinking because I was so worried; and when I drank I used to hit her. She said she couldn't take it any more; and rightly so; and so she went back to Charlotte where she was raised.'

He sniffed, and wiped his nose on the back of his hand. 'She stayed away till spring. By that time, I was beginning to get things straight, and make some money. It isn't too difficult to work your butt off when you're all on your own, without nothing to distract you but your own unhappiness.

'One day in early May she just appeared in the doorway, with her bag, and said she loved me, and would I take her back, I said yes, of course. But before she would take even one step inside, she told me that she was pregnant, and that she wanted to keep the child; and that she expected me to raise it like my own, no matter what.'

'And you said yes to that, too?'

'Sweetheart, I loved your momma with every single bone in my body. She could've told me she was expecting sextuplets, I still would have said yes.'

Lucy took out her handkerchief and dabbed at her eyes. 'And she never gave you any idea who my father might have been?'

Jack looked at her, his face disassembled by tiredness and drinking and grief. 'It could have been some beau she'd known from childhood. That's what I like to think. Some fellow she loved from way back before I met her. I sure don't like to think that it was anybody casual, a man on a train, or a hotel porter, or whatever.'

He cleared his throat, and then he added, 'I'm sorry I had

to tell you. But it's time you knew. I didn't want it coming out on your wedding-day, and ruining everything.'

'Poppa . . .' she said.

He leaned over and held her tight. 'Sweetheart, I'm still your poppa, and I always will be. I'll love you just the same as always.'

'Do you know something?' said Lucy touching his dear face. 'I always thought that we looked so much alike, you and me.'

Jack kissed her. 'Guess that was God, being kind to us.'

They sat together for a while, and then Jack eased himself up off the bed. 'It's time I hit the hay.'

When he reached the door, Lucy said, 'Poppa!' and he turned and looked back at her, although he wasn't smiling.

'Poppa,' she repeated. 'I love you, poppa.'

'I love you too, sweetheart,' he replied, and quietly closed the door.

She lay for a long time in the darkness after everybody else had gone to bed, listening to the house creaking. The night was still and humid, with only the slightest wind stirring the curtains. It was what the Eastern farmers called 'corn wea-ther,' ideal for ripening the corn crops, and the darkness was intermittently illuminated with distant flashes of 'corn light-ning'.

When Lucy heard the clocks chiming two, she climbed out of bed and went to the window, and opened it wider. The lightning was close now; and she could hear the banging of thunder, over to the south-west. A heavy rainstorm was making its way up the coast from Westerly, and it wouldn't be long before it was overhead. The trees began to rustle and whisper among themselves, and a wave of wind ran across the lawns.

Lucy brought over her dressing-table stool, and positioned it under the open window. She stepped up on it, and carefully climbed out of the window on to the parapet outside.

She peered down to the garden. The gravel path was forty feet below her, but she wasn't afraid of heights. She balanced her way along the guttering until she reached the corner of the roof, where she could see Rhode Island Sound, beyond the trees, and the white foam breaking over the shoreline. She sat down cross-legged, in her white nightdress, and felt the warm breeze blowing against her face.

I wonder who I am, she thought to herself. *I wonder where I came from. Lucy Darling, whose little girl are you?*

She raised both hands in front of her face and turned them this way and that. Whose fingers had she inherited? Whose talents? She had always believed that her personality was an equal mixture of her mother's vivacity and her father's gentle reserve. Now she felt completely fragmented, like a broken jug that wouldn't fit back together again. How could she begin to understand the world around her if she couldn't even understand herself?

She watched the lightning flicker on the ocean; catching the waves in an instant photographic flash, so that they looked as hard as hammered glass. She said, 'One grasshopper, two grasshopper –' but the thunder rumbled almost immediately. The first few drops of rain pattered on the roof, and on to her shoulders.

Whose little girl are you, Lucy Darling? You're not even a Darling at all.

Her mother had gone back to Charlotte. But who had she met there? Some childhood beau, as her poppa liked to believe? Or some stranger? Some carpetbagger with an eye for a pretty young wife?

The trouble was, there was one thought that wouldn't stop repeating itself, over and over, in the darkest part of her mind.

'We was lovers for a while, your mother and me,' that's what Uncle Casper had said, with that sly mischievous grin on his face. 'Might have been a sin in the eyes of God; but we was lonesome and friendless and each other was all we had.'

The lightning crackled so close now that Lucy could smell the air scorching. The thunder collapsed right over her head. The rain started abruptly, trailing in fuming sheets across the lawns and pattering on the slates.

At once, Lucy was soaked. The rain dribbled from her nose and her chin, and her hair was stuck darkly on to her scalp. Her nightgown hung heavily and chilled, like the shroud of a girl found drowned.

'We was lovers for a while, your mother and me.' My God, supposing her mother had gone back to Uncle Casper. Supposing he had told her the truth. Supposing Uncle Casper had been her real father?

The rain clung to her eyelashes like tears, and turned the whole world to blurry stars. Gasping with effort, Lucy pulled herself up into a kneeling position, and began to tug off her wet nightgown. It stuck to her body and her face like cold slime, but at last she managed to drag it over her head, and unbutton the wet lace cuffs, and pull it right off.

Now she knelt naked in the guttering, her face lifted to the rain. The lightning flickered again, so that her skin gleamed blueish-white. Then the sky split open, and the whole house shook, and the rain pelted down even harder than before.

Still gasping, still trembling, Lucy washed her face with her hands; then her shoulders and her breasts. She gripped her breasts tight, twisting her nipples until they hurt. She had to be clean. She had to be utterly pure. She had to wash off every single trace of Uncle Casper, and what he had done to her.

Her discarded nightgown had blocked the drain outlet behind the parapet, and so the guttering gradually filled with two or three inches of water. She knelt forward and frantically washed her hair, rubbing and massaging her scalp until it was sore. Then she lay back in the water, and parted her legs wide. She splashed herself again and again with scooped-up handfuls of chilly rainwater, her eyes squeezed tightly shut, her teeth clenched, praying that this would purify her.

Dear God, I want to be clean again. Dear God, I want to be clean!

After a few minutes, she turned over and lay on her stomach in the gutter, panting and shuddering with cold. The worst of the storm was already passing; like a circus striking its tents and moving to another town; and the grumbling of thunder was muffled behind the ridge of the roof. The gutters gurgled; the chimneys dripped. The lightning lit up the gardens again, but fitfully.

Lucy closed her eyes, but she wasn't crying any longer. She was too cold to cry. The rain fell steadily on to her naked back, her hair trailed in the gutter like weed.

At last, however, she climbed to her feet, and wiped the rain away from her face, and sniffed. She felt calmer now, after her moment of hysteria. She felt at least as if she had purged her own sins; if not her mother's, or Uncle Casper's. Dragging her sodden nightgown after her, she climbed back in through her bedroom window, and tiptoed across to her bathroom.

She wrapped herself up in a deep white Turkish towel, and sat for a moment on the edge of the bath, shivering, trying to quieten herself, and to get her breath back.

At last she stopped shaking, and her skin began to tingle with warmth. She stood up, and slowly combed her hair in the bathroom looking-glass, pausing between every stroke.

Facing her, expressionless, was a pale-faced girl with unnaturally blue eyes and a faint sprinkling of freckles on her nose. She snarled at herself. Then she stared at herself with her eyes popping. Do you *look* like Uncle Casper? she asked herself. Do you have Uncle Casper's eyes; or Uncle Casper's nose? When you smile, do your lips curl up like Uncle Casper's?

She couldn't tell. She would never be able to find out. Her mother had left her with nothing but a legacy of doubt and bewilderment. She went back to her bedroom, and sat down, still combing her hair, over and over.

When she had left the window open, the rain had spattered in, and blotched the poem that Henry had written for her. It looked as if the poem were stained with tears. Lucy picked it up, and read again,

I never saw in any time
A beauty that was so sublime.

But the line which she liked the most, the line which made her smile again, and the one which she repeated over and over, was *'I'll see Miss Darling's darling smile.'* When she whispered that line, she knew that Henry was telling the truth, and that he had really fallen for her.

Her bedside lamp was still burning when she fell asleep. By dawn it had flickered out. But Lucy slept and slept, undisturbed, while the sun came up, and dried away the puddles from the night's rainstorm; while yachts angled their way across Rhode Island Sound; while gardeners trimmed the roses and clipped the lawns; a girl in a dream.

It was early September before they could move into their house on Central Park West. It stood two blocks north of the Dakota building; between 74th and 75th Streets; and directly fronted the park.

The whole district was in riotous turmoil. Only a few years ago, it had been nothing but rocky fields and shanties and market-gardens. The Dakota building had been given its name because it had been so far away from the genteel homes of Fifth Avenue that it might as well have been built in the Dakotas. But all around it, streets were being graded and buildings were being thrown up, and the Darlings' accountants reckoned that building a house on Central Park West was the best investment they could have made.

Lucy wasn't at all sure that she liked the house when it

was finished. It was a four-storey limestone building in the style of a Loire château, with a circular turret at each corner. Sixteen bedrooms, five bathrooms, a huge mirrored drawing-room, and a mosaic-floored hall with *two* staircases, one undulating down on either side like twin waterfalls.

She was pleased with the view from her turreted bedroom: an uninterrupted vista of Central Park, which had recently been cleared of most of its garbage dumps and pigsties, and was now one of the handsomest city parks in the world. She felt like a princess up here, aloof from everything: the noise of traffic and the hammering of construction, and the metallic clashing of the Ninth Avenue elevated.

She felt, however, that there was something about the house which was rather cold. Everything was just a little too elegant, and a little too stylish. Marble-clad walls, perfectly-proportioned pillars, banister rails that were heavily silver-plated. Perhaps it was her fault, too. Perhaps she wasn't yet ready to lend it her own enthusiasm, and her own radiance.

Jack's delight in his new home, however, was huge – at least to begin with. For the first week after they moved in, he kept stepping out on to the front porch, and standing with his thumbs in his waistcoat, so that passers-by would realize that the house was his. Occasionally, if one of them lifted his hat, or nodded in his direction, he would take his cigar out of his mouth and announce, 'Lit by electric light! Whole place, totally lit by electric light! And an elevator, too!'

He sent wires to Samuel Blankenship and Henry McGuffey and several more Oak City cronies, inviting them to visit New York at his expense (although Lucy drew the line at Osage Pete.) None of them answered, but Jack told Lucy that they were probably daunted by the length of the journey, and by the prospect of having to put on 'fancy manners'.

But one rainy morning in the middle of September she found him in the morning-room, standing by the window, watching the raindrops dribbling down the glass; and when she came up to him, and touched his arm, she saw that his eyes were filled with tears.

'Poppa?' she said, gently. 'What's wrong?'

He sniffed, and wiped his eyes with the heel of his hand. 'Oh, nothing. Just regrets, I guess. And why should you call me poppa, when I ain't?'

'I'll always call you poppa. You're not crying for that, are you?'

'I don't know. Maybe I'm feeling lonesome, that's all. Maybe I'm feeling out of my depth. Maybe it's raining and I just feel low.'

Lucy tiptoed up and kissed his cheek. Her affection for her father had not been diminished by his revelation that he wasn't her real father. She still loved him as much as ever; and she still trusted him to take care of her. But a distinct note of reserve now strained their relationship, mostly on Lucy's part and mostly unconsciously. She no longer sat on his lap in the evenings, when they were talking beside the fire. She no longer kissed his lips. She no longer talked about her boyfriends, and the way she felt about them, not in the same way. The unavoidable truth was that in spite of their closeness, in spite of the fact that he had brought her up, she could no longer treat him as if he were flesh of her flesh.

'Why don't you go out, try to make some new friends?' Lucy suggested. 'Harold Stuyvesant had you elected to the Sportsman's Club, didn't he? You could always go down there.'

'What, and listen to a whole lot of stiffnecks talking about stocks and futures and who's married into whose fortune; and why the price of copper keeps falling? Some sport! I spent two hours at the Sportsman's Club last Thursday afternoon, and nobody so much as said "how d'ye do", or knew the latest baseball score, and none of them would have known a joke if it had stood up on its hinder legs and bitten them in the backside.'

'But poppa, we're in society now! You can't expect men to spit and chew tobacco and tell bawdy stories around the stove.'

Jack loudly blew his nose. 'Maybe they ought to try. Maybe it would do them some good.'

'Poppa – maybe you ought to give it another go.'

Jack looked at her. The sun suddenly came out, and reflected dazzling gold light from the stable rooftop outside, and for a moment Jack appeared quite different. All the colour was bleached out of his hair and his eyes and he could have been a hundred years old.

'All right, maybe you're right. Maybe I'll give it another go.'

Jack went upstairs to dress; and not long afterwards Evelyn called to take Lucy out shopping, and then for lunch. Lucy was measured at Francine's for four new gowns; one of them sewn all over with patterns of tiny seed-pearls, one black taffeta, one scarlet silk, and one in sumptuous pale-velvet, with a wide collar made of Brussels lace. They lunched at the New Netherland hotel, lobster mousse and rocket salad, and then they shopped for evening purses and shoes.

Lucy stayed at the Scotts' house until well after five o'clock, and by the time the Scott four-wheeler had taken her home, it was nearly six.

'Is my father back?' she asked Amy the housemaid, who let her in.

'Yes, miss,' Amy replied, and then pressed her lips tightly together.

'Just here will do, thank you,' she said to the Scotts' footman, who was carrying in her shopping. But as he carefully set down her parcels on the marble bench beside her, she heard bellowing laughter from the drawing room. It wasn't Jack's laughter, either; and it was followed almost immediately by the high-pitched screaming of a strange woman.

'Amy?' she frowned.

'Friends of Mr Darling, miss,' said Amy, and bobbed her a hurried curtsey.

Lucy took off her gloves and her osprey-plumed hat, and Amy helped her out of her coat. Then she walked with a brisk step to the drawing-room doors, and opened them wide.

At first she could scarcely believe what she was seeing. Jack was sitting crosslegged on the floor, with a bottle of champagne beside him, smoking and dealing out playing-cards on to the polished parquet. Beside him, laughing, knelt a blowzy-looking girl with raven black hair and huge white bosoms that were almost spilling out of her gown. Opposite him, lying back luxuriously on a heap of cushions, reposed a plump young man with black pomaded hair and one of those shiny emerald-green satin vests that Jack's store card would once have described as 'nobby'. He was alternately puffing at a large green cigar and swigging champagne out of the neck of a bottle, and busting himself with laughter in between.

It wasn't the blowzy black-haired woman or the plump young man in the vest who startled Lucy so much, however. At the end of the room, half-silhouetted against the window, a very slender young girl was dancing, although there was no music for her to dance to. She was naked except for an embroidered silk bustier and rolled-down silk stockings. Her scraggly fair curls had been heaped up on top of her head and pinned with tortoiseshell combs. Her eyes were closed, and she was singing to herself. Although her bottom was bare, she sported a huge and luxuriant blue tail of ostrich plumes, which bobbed and dipped as she danced; and it was only as she raised one leg in a mock-balletic step that Lucy realized where the plumes had been inserted.

Lucy turned to Jack in shock. The drawing room was dense with cigar-smoke, and the smell of strong perfume. Jack was laughing so much that at first he didn't notice her.

The plump young man on the cushions had seen her at once, however, although he didn't seem unduly concerned. He set down his bottle of champagne and lay back comfortably admiring her through slitted eyes, his podgy fingers laced over the front of his vest, his green cigar tilted between his teeth.

'Now that,' he declared, 'is class with a capital K.'

Jack stopped laughing and looked up. When he saw Lucy, he stiffened, and nervously wiped at his nose, and stopped dealing, and sat watching her, wary as a hunted stag. The girl by the window opened her eyes, and stopped dancing, and tippytoed quickly to the piano, where she had left her petticoats. Her ostrich-plume tail bounced behind her. Both girls made a great bustling fuss of covering themselves up.

'Poppa,' said Lucy, walking around the back of the sofa.

Jack nodded towards the plump young man. 'Lucy, want you to meet Tom Brach.'

The plump young man made no attempt to rise from his heap of cushions. 'How dedo,' he grinned, saluting Lucy with his cigar.

Lucy said coldly, 'Don't get up.'

Jack cleared his throat. 'This is ... Alice,' indicating the girl with the basque and the raven-black hair. 'This here is ... what's your name, honey?'

'Mavis,' lisped the young dancer. She couldn't have been older than thirteen or fourteen.

'That's it, Mavis, my little songbird,' said Jack, and blew her a kiss. The girl smiled uneasily at Lucy.

Lucy said, 'They can leave now.'

Jack stared at her, then shook his head emphatically. 'Ho, no. You said find yourself some friends, I found myself some friends.'

'Not at the Sportsman's Club,' Lucy retorted. She felt so furious at Jack that she could hardly speak. It was everything she could do to stop herself from bursting into tears.

'Well, yes, as a matter of fact, at the Sportsman's Club. I

173

sat in the lounge of the Sportsman's Club for twenty minutes, and believe me those twenty minutes were the most tedious twenty minutes of my whole life, bar none. I've had more fun watching paint dry. So I asked Cyril the doorman if he knew where there was anything lively going on, and I tipped him twenty bucks, and lo and behold he directed me to Miss Collings' on West 25th Street, and there I met Tom here, and Alice and Mavis, and we've had nothing but fun all day.'

'Poppa,' Lucy declared, 'I want these people out of my house.'

'Well, that ain't at all what I call sociable,' Tom Brach remarked.

'Uppity, I call it, 'specially when we've been invited,' added Alice.

But Lucy held her ground, staring at her father with such fury that after a moment or two he flung down his cards, and climbed up on to his feet, hobbling for the first two or three steps with pins-and-needles, and said to his friends, 'Come on, now, ladies and gentlemen, time to call it a day.'

'You don't mind if we dress,' said Alice, pointedly.

'Poppa, you and Mr Brach can wait outside,' said Lucy.

She stayed with Alice and Mavis while Mavis removed her tail and they helped each other into their clothes. Even when they were fully dressed they were a pretty bedraggled pair. Half of the plumage was trailing off the side of Alice's hat, and Mavis in her tight green velour bodice and her frayed straw skimmer looked like nothing much more than a scruffy schoolchild.

They shuffled out of the front door on worn-down shoes, watched by Amy with a mixture of awe and disgust.

When the door had closed behind them, Lucy went to find Jack. He was sprawling with feigned disinterest in the library, with a huge glass of whisky balanced on his knee. The tail of his shirt was hanging down in front. He took a large defiant swallow, and then he stared at Lucy with reddened, resentful eyes.

'When I'm lonesome I get on your nerves. When I find myself some friends you get angry. What the hell else am I supposed to do?'

'Your friend gone?' asked Lucy.

'You bet. Said he had all the frosty women he needed at home.'

'Poppa, I'm not being frosty. But this is our home. You can't bring gamblers and women back to our home. What would momma have thought?'

Jack banged his glass down on the wine-table beside him. 'Do you think what your momma did was any more moral than me bringing a couple of women back home?'

'I don't know what my momma did, except look for love, and raise me the best she could, and die.'

'Your momma was my wife. But you aint my daughter. God only knows whose daughter you are, your momma never said. That's what she did to me. That's what your momma did. And you have the sheer barefaced gall to say that I can't bring a couple of women back home, just for the fun of it?'

Lucy stepped forward, and swung her arm to slap Jack's face, but Jack snatched her wrist and stopped her. She twisted her hand away, and glared at him in white-hot temper. 'You call those women? One was not much more than a child! And that drunk of a cardsharp! What kind of friends are those?'

'Friends who ain't sour or snobby, that's what kind of friends they are. Friends I can laugh with.'

Lucy said, 'You didn't . . .? Not with those girls?'

Jack blew out his cheeks dismissively, and shook his head. 'They danced for us, that's all. Dance of the seven veils.' He waved his arms from side to side in a cursory imitation of an Egyptian houri. 'Christ, Lucy, I aint had so much fun since we left Oak City.'

Lucy was tempted to snap back at him, but she stopped herself. She walked across to the window and stood looking out at the street. She heard Jack swallow more whisky, cough.

After a moment or two, she said carefully, 'I think it's about time you remembered whose money this is; whose house this is.'

'I haven't forgotten. But no matter whose house this is; no matter whose money this is; that doesn't mean that I have to live like St Jack the Pure. None of those other rich guys live like that. You should of seen some of things they got up to on those yachts, back at Newport. That was an education and no mistake.'

Lucy turned around, her silk dress swishing on the rug. 'Poppa, you brought me up. What's mine is yours. But believe you me, this money cost me more than you could ever understand, and you're not bringing home gamblers or whores and that's final. If you want that kind of fun, go find it someplace else. I don't want to see even a whiff of it. Because if you ever bring people like that home again, you and me are finished for good and all.'

Jack considered this with sudden sobriety. He sniffed, and said, 'You know that I love you, don't you, Lucy?'

'Yes,' said Lucy, 'I believe that you do.'

'Well, then, for the sake of that, I'll keep my fun to myself. But don't think I'm going to live like St Jack the Pure, because I won't.'

That day changed everything between them; not just for a week or two, but for ever. Jack seemed increasingly to regard their wealth as an enraging kind of fairytale curse; money which had to be spent and enjoyed at an ever more furious pace. The simple shopkeeperly morals by which he had lived his life up until now collapsed under the sheer weight of wealth, like the rotten floorboards of a robber-baron's counting-house. Lucy, finding him drunk or depressed or boastful or over-elated, began to take pains to avoid him, and to lead a life that was more and more fanciful.

She stayed in bed longer in the mornings, daydreaming about being married, and having a husband of her own. By the time she came down to breakfast, Jack had usually left the house, either to gamble or to go drinking, or to go to the new Polo Grounds to watch the Giants. In common with thousands of others all over America, he had developed a passion for baseball.

During the last two weeks of September, they hardly saw each other at all. Every morning she lay in her French four-poster bed, in her grey-and-gold bedroom, with her Burmese cat Rangoon sitting on her feet, doodling Henry all over her writing-paper. Henry, Henry, Henry, with curling 'ys' and 'Hs' as elaborate as the Brooklyn Bridge.

After straightening her pillows for her, her red-headed maid Nora picked up one of the sheets of doodles, and remarked, 'Sure, you're fond of this Henry! Which one is he? It wouldn't be Henry Massenheim would it? He doesn't look like the type to interest you! Well, what with his nose!'

'Henry Carson, MP,' Lucy replied. She was growing her hair, and every night she curled it in ribbons. 'An English gentleman of the first water.' She had learned that phrase from Evelyn.

'Do I know him?' asked Nora. She was green-eyed, direct, with a sharpish tongue and a very busy way about her, but Lucy had preferred her to the prim and prissy 'yes-miss-no-miss' maids that she had interviewed first of all.

'No, you don't know him,' Lucy sighed. 'He's in England and I'm supposed to be going to England to visit him. But I haven't heard yet. So I'm moping, you see, and writing Henry all over everything, and dreaming.'

'But a prosperous young lady like yourself shouldn't be moping. You could have any man you want. Just a snap of the fingers. Any man in New York.'

'My dear Nora, Henry is the man I want.'

With an oil fortune worth close to $11 million, there was no question that Lucy was highly eligible, and there was no shortage of wealthy young bachelors who wanted to make her acquaintance. The tightrope story had spread like wildfire, and so wherever Lucy went heads would turn and fans would be spread so that women could whisper, '*That's the girl who –*'

Evelyn introduced her to scores of amusing boys, and steered her expertly away from adventurers and dandies, and those with a vaguely unsavoury reputation. The two of them were escorted almost every day to the theatre, or to supper-parties, or out dancing. Life became one glittering carousel of shining carriages and chandeliers, and men whose collars were so high they had to stare at the ceiling all evening.

They went to see William Gillette's *Too Much Johnson* and *The Prisoner of Zenda,* which Lucy found thrilling. They went to supper with the Jeromes and the Stewarts and the W. K. Vanderbilts. Lucy ate truffles for the first time, and decided she was going to live off nothing else. Truffles and champagne! They went to Mrs Douglas' September Charity Ball on the third floor of Delmonico's, overlooking the brightly-lit greenery of Madison Square, and Lucy danced and danced under the sparkling lights, exhilarated and laughing and prettier than ever.

With Evelyn guiding her, Lucy charmed New York society, and was named by the *New York Post* as 'Miss Lightbulb', because the men clustered around her like moths at every social function.

But although she met five or six boys whom she really liked – especially John B. Harriot IV, whose father owned most of Nevada – she was still waiting for her invitation from England. Her daydreams of being married were daydreams of him; and of that smile of his; and Derbyshire in winter. She could close her eyes and see the sunlight on the statues of Brackenbridge House, and the geese flying through the silver mist.

Henry's poem lay pressed in the front of her Bible,

together with a pink rose from the dinner-table at the Widgery's house. She read the poem every day. She watched herself in the mirror. She began to wonder if he had been deceiving her; if he were ever going to write.

On the first day of October, their newly-appointed butler came in to the drawing room while Jack was warming his back by the fire and Lucy was embroidering a handkerchief. With a great deal of ceremony, he handed Lucy a card on a silver tray. Jeremy had once buttled for Mrs James P. Kernochan, and he was the acme of haughty discretion. Jack had wanted to hire him for his imposing profile – 'like a bald-headed eagle wondering whether to lay an egg or not' – but Lucy had been entranced by his English accent. He came, in fact, from Massachusetts, but he had worked hard to develop an impressively butlerish voice.

'There is a gentleman without,' he remarked, inclining his head.

'Without what?' Jack cracked, although he cracked the same joke every time anybody came to visit.

Lucy read the card. 'It's Jamie! Poppa, it's Jamie! Oh, Jeremy, do show him in!'

Jeremy said, 'Certainly, Miss Darling,' and turned around on a rubber heel; but Jamie had already entered the open doors, and was standing with his hat on his hand, staring around the drawing room in open-mouthed admiration.

'Your hat, sir?' asked Jeremy, icily, quite unused to people who thought they were welcome to wander around his employer's house without being invited.

'Oh, sure, thanks,' said Jamie, quite oblivious, and handed it over. Jeremy flicked from it the tiniest speck of invisible dust, and carried it away.

Lucy stood up, and rushed towards him. Her hair was curled; she was wearing an exquisite dress of rust-coloured velvet, sewn with pearls. She took hold of his hands and said, breathlessly, 'Why didn't you wire? You could have wired! This is such a surprise!'

Jamie kissed her, and grinned. 'I didn't know I was coming till just about an hour before the train was due.'

'How're you doing, Jamie!' called Jack, from over by the massive marble fireplace. 'Good to see you, glad you could come! You're our first guest from Kansas, very first one!'

Jamie went over and shook his hand. He still couldn't stop himself from gazing around the room; at the arched and gilded ceiling, at the long drapes of pale-yellow velvet, at the three gilded chandeliers, at the mirrors and paintings and curvaceous French furniture.

'Some house,' he breathed. 'Never saw anything like it.'

'Electric light all through,' Jack told him. 'Got our own elevator, too.'

'How long are you here for?' Lucy asked. 'You are going to stay with us, aren't you?'

'I can only stay for a week,' said Jamie. 'I'm on my way to Washington. I'm attached to a law firm in Manhattan, Van Cortland & Paley – you know, doing some practical training. We're handling a land claim case against the Indians, and I have to check up on a whole lot of stuff at the Office of Indian Affairs. You know, land treaties and all that kind of thing.'

'So, they've finally got you doing some real work,' Jack remarked.

'Well, not really, sir,' said Jamie. 'I'm running errands, that's all.'

Jack nodded. 'You like the house? It's what they call a shat-oh. A Loo-wah shat-oh. Cost more'n three million dollars, and that's *ex*cluding the gold dinner-service. You ever eat with gold knives and forks? I mean, real gold knives and forks? You stay for supper tonight!'

Lucy said, 'I'm so pleased to see you. You look so well! And is that a moustache?'

Jamie sheepishly rubbed his upper lip. 'It could be. I guess it's still trying to make up its mind.'

Lucy hugged him and kissed him. 'You didn't *write*!' she protested.

'Write?' laughed Jamie. 'I haven't had time to eat, let alone write. But then neither did you write. Well – not that it mattered. I've been reading all about you in the newspapers. The *Kansas City Journal* always keeps us up to date on the doings on the Sunflower State's favourite daughter.'

'The banister-rails are plated in real silver,' Jack put in. 'Made in France, hand-made. Fifty-two thousand dollars, banister-rails alone.'

'I read about you tightrope-walking on somebody's tennis-net,' said Jamie. 'Was that really true?'

Lucy nodded, and smiled. 'It caused a terrible commotion! But I think they got over it. I was only showing-off.'

Jack said, 'How about some champagne? Jamie?'

'Well, sure, that'd be swell,' Jamie replied. 'But I don't want to make any kind of nuisance of myself.'

'You could never be a nuisance,' said Lucy. She couldn't believe how pleased she was to see him. 'Come and sit down. Where are your bags? You must come and stay here! We've got plenty of company rooms!'

'I'm booked in at the Metropolitan,' Jamie told her. 'Mr Van Cortland recommended it.'

Lucy wrinkled up her nose. 'When was the last time *he* stayed in New York? You can't stay at the Metropolitan! It's so – *urrgghh!* It's so down-at-heel!'

'It looked all right to me,' Jamie replied, a little defensively. 'Mind you – when you're used to a place like this –'

'Oh, I'm sorry,' said Lucy, reaching out and holding his hand. 'I didn't mean to be cruel. It's just that everybody in New York society is so worried about which places are fashionable and which places aren't! It's all they talk about! Things change so fast here! I mean that's why we've built our house way up here on the upper west side! People have built six-million dollar mansions on Fifth Avenue, and by the time they're finished the neighbourhood's gone to the dogs!'

'Kind of different from Oak City, then,' Jamie remarked.

Lucy looked at him closely and warmly. He was older, maybe a little tireder, but still very handsome – although handsome in a way that now seemed very Western and countrified. His suit was too tight across the shoulders and he wore boots instead of pumps and how *anybody* could walk around with a stringy necktie like that! She couldn't help noticing, too, how drawling his accent was. Every word seemed to drag on for ever. And Evelyn accused *her* of talking like Calamity Jane! Evelyn hadn't been having much luck in trying to train her to say 'fine' instead of 'faahn' and 'particular' instead of 'puhtickulluh', but Lucy had already managed to clip most of her vowels and sharpen most of her consonants, so that at least the Mrs Vanderbilts of this world didn't keep frowning at their friends and saying, 'Is that girl speaking Chinese?'

'You will stay, won't you?' asked Lucy. 'I'm dying to hear all of your news.'

'You're sure it's no trouble?' asked Jamie.

'Fourteen bedrooms, all going begging. Take your pick. I'll send a boy down to the Metropolitan to collect your bags.'

Jamie paused, and lowered his head; and then glanced across at Jack. But Jack was busy relighting himself a cigar now, and was out of earshot.

'I guess I should tell you that I purposely didn't write to you,' said Jamie.

Lucy hesitated, and then she said. 'You *purposely* didn't write? Why?'

'Well . . . look at us, Lucy. We could never be any kind of match for each other, now could we? The society princess and the hayseed lawyer? What could I ever hope to give to you now? A frame house in Manhattan, Kansas? A law business turning over three thousand dollars a year? You and I said goodbye to each other that day on the beach, in Los Angeles. You know that.'

He paused, and then smiled. 'I loved you once, Miss Darling, and I still love you just as much now. I've been thinking about you day and night, day and night, ever since you went away. I don't want you to feel obliged to have me stay here if you really don't want me to. But I don't want to have to sit this close to you and kiss you and hold your hand and pretend that it doesn't make my heart go bump and my stomach turn over, because it does; and I guess it always will, for ever and ever.'

'Oh, Jamie,' said Lucy. 'I love you, too. You know that.'

'Well,' he replied, 'there's love and there's love. I guess that you and I might have been married, if your Uncle Casper hadn't showed up. Everybody expected us to. But he did show up, didn't he, and maybe he saved the both of us from making a fool mistake.'

Lucy said, 'Oh, Jamie, it wouldn't have been a mistake. How can you say that?'

Jamie looked around the drawing room. 'It may not have been a mistake then, but *now* – well, just look at this place! I thought it was going to be grand, but I didn't have any idea. You've got to marry into society now, Lucy. You've got to marry into wealth. Some man who can walk into a place like this and not stand around like a Rocky Mountain trout with his mouth wide open.'

'Jamie –'

'Ssh,' he said, and raised his finger to his lips. 'I just wanted to be honest with you, that's all. I just wanted you to know where you stood.'

'I want you to stay,' she whispered.

'You can say it louder if you like.'

She grinned broadly, and threw her arms around his shoulders, and kissed him on the nose. 'I want you to stay! So there!'

Jack, puffing cigar-smoke, turned and grunted in amusement.

'There's something else,' said Jamie. 'I brought somebody with me.'

'Somebody from home? Who?'

Jack nodded. 'She's waiting outside. She wouldn't come in, not straight away. Not till I'd talked to you first.'

He gestured towards the doors. 'May I?'

Lucy watched him in pleased bewilderment as he crossed the drawing room, opened the doors, and disappeared out into the hallway. She heard him open the front doors; then heard him talking, although she couldn't make out who he was talking to. Then he returned; caught for a moment in the pearly October daylight; and he was ushering ahead of him the diminutive figure of Mrs Sweeney, the Skipping Widder, in a store-bought hat heaped up with artificial roses and swooping thrushes, and a worn but well-brushed fur-coat, and a duck's-head umbrella.

'Oh, Mrs Sweeney, you darling!' said Lucy, and hurried across the room to greet her. 'I can't believe that you're here!'

Beneath her fur-coat, Mrs Sweeney's ribs felt as fragile as a cat's; but she smiled so broadly that her eyes filled up with tears, and she held Lucy tight. 'I read all about you in the papers! How you walked along the tennis-net! And I said to myself, Molly you taught that girl to do that, and wasn't I proud! And when I heard that you were Belle of New York; well, I just had to come to see it for myself; I had to see you dance; and I had to see New York again, too, just once before I died. The varnish, the gaseliers, the young men like gods!'

'How did you get here?' asked Lucy. 'Poppa – look, it's Mrs Sweeney!'

Jack Darling had never liked Mrs Sweeney overmuch. Too fussy a customer, always complaining that he diluted his boot-polish with white spirits, and that he short-weighed his sugar. But she was Irish; and he had always had a soft spot for the Irish; and he knew how much she had delighted Lucy with her dancing-lessons.

'Well, well, Mrs Sweeney,' he said, waving his cigar at her. 'Fancy seeing you here.'

'Fancy seeing *you* here,' retorted Mrs Sweeney, looking querulously about her at the opulent drawing room. 'Jack Darling, the storekeeper. In a house like this! In New York!'

Jack clenched his cigar between his teeth and thrust his hands into his trouser pockets, and rocked back on his heels like a man with plenty to say if he had a mind to be sharp; but who had decided that there are times when it is better to say nothing, and this was one of them.

'Mind you,' said Mrs Sweeney, 'I wouldn't have known New York, the way it is now! All the railroads, and the cable-cars, and those buildings – you have to stand back and stretch your neck and you still can't see the top of them! And all those telephone wires, what a cat's cradle!'

'How long're you planning on staying, Mrs Sweeney?' asked Jack.

'Oh, not too long, don't you worry. Just long enough to look up some old acquaintances, and to dance, just once, if all my old dancing haunts haven't been torn down.'

Lucy said, 'There's a charity ball at the Waldorf tomorrow night, to raise money for the Henry Street Settlement. You can come along to that, if you'd care to. And you too, Jamie, I'd love it if you could come.'

'Don't you have an escort already?' asked Jamie. 'I've seen the society columns – "Miss Lightbulb," isn't it?'

'Oh, well, John was supposed to be taking me . . . John B. Harriot IV. But he won't mind if I tell him that you're escorting me instead. He's been dying to escort my friend Sylvia Park . . . not that he'll like her, once he gets to know her. She's so bossy with men, and John just hates to be bossed!'

Jamie smiled at her. 'You haven't changed, have you?' he told her.

She lowered her eyes. Her blue, blue eyes. 'I wish I could say that was true.'

That evening, Jamie and Mrs Sweeney were moved into the

Darling mansion; and they dined that evening on scrod and spit-roasted quail, sitting yards away from each other around a huge circular cherrywood table that they had imported from England, in what Jack loved to call 'the *cosy* dining room', as opposed to the 'grand dining room'.

The table was polished like a black pool. It reflected the electric chandelier and the whiteness of Lucy's face. She wore an off-the-shoulder evening gown of ice-pink silk, and a necklace of white diamonds, with diamond earrings to match. Jamie couldn't take his eyes off her.

'How are things in Oak City?' asked Jack, as Jeremy poured him another glass of champagne, the Dry Royal de Saint Marceaux, very popular in New York just then. 'I still miss it sometimes, you know; the old days around the stove.'

'Money always buys a man rose-tinted eyeglasses,' retorted Mrs Sweeney. She was dressed in black, as usual, with her hair scraped back and fastened with combs. 'Life's harder than ever. Samuel Blankenship died this summer; and Osage Pete's so blind now that he can scarcely find his way around.'

'Old Samuel Blankenship gone?' asked Jack, with distress. 'How come nobody wrote me?'

'What's the passing of some no-account railroad engineer, way out in the back-end of Kansas, to the sixteenth richest man in New York?' Mrs Sweeney taunted him. Lucy couldn't think why she was being so cutting.

'Samuel Blankenship wasn't no-account,' said Jack. 'He was my friend.'

'Oh, yes? How much of a friend? Soon as you got your claws on your money, you absconded, didn't you, Jack Darling, and never came back to visit him? And not a penny of all of your riches ever did anything for Oak City.'

'You listen here, I wrote off all my credit,' Jack retorted. 'There were folks in Oak City owed me hundreds. I wrote off fifteen hundred bucks' worth of clackers alone.'

'How much did you say them silver-plated banisters cost you?' said Mrs Sweeney. She lifted her solid gold fish-fork. 'And look at this here utensil. This here utensil would keep an Oak City family in pork and navy beans for an age of years.'

Lucy could see that her father was badly stung by Mrs Sweeney's gibes. She said, 'Poppa ... you did what you could. You can't support the whole world.'

But Jack asked Mrs Sweeney, 'Is that all folks've got for me now, back in Oak City? The black word? Do you say that I was tight? Do you think that I could have done anything at all to ease your burden? You listen to me, Mrs Sweeney, the only thing that could ever ease their burden is to bring back the cattle-drives, and you and me know that the cattle-drives are history, and never coming back.'

'They call you tight, yes,' said Mrs Sweeney. 'They say that you've forgotten them, and turned your back. Things are pretty bad these days, they've had the choleric fever, too.'

Jamie said, 'Mrs Sweeney ... let's change the subject, shall we? We're guests here, at Mr Darling's house, and we owe him our courtesy, at the very least.'

But Jack jabbed his finger at Mrs Sweeney and snapped, 'We'll see who's tight. You just wait, Molly Sweeney. We'll see who's tight.'

With that, he thrust back his chair, stood up, tugged the napkin out of his collar, and stalked out of the dining room.

There was a long, awkward silence. Then Mrs Sweeney turned sheepishly to Lucy and said, 'I'm sorry, Lucy. I guess I made a bad bust, talking like that to your pa. It's just that sitting here, eating with golden forks and drinking out of crystal glasses ... well, I can't help thinking of all the downright poorness back in Kansas – all the children dressed in flour-sacks, and the workworn wives, and your poppa thinking he's so all-fired much.'

Lucy said, softly, 'Poppa gave everything to Oak City,

Mrs Sweeney. His whole life; and my momma, too. Don't be too hard on him now. The money came by chance. He didn't ask for it, and to begin with, he didn't even want it. It may not last for ever, either. The oil-wells could run dry one day. So don't begrudge him this.'

'I'm sorry,' Mrs Sweeney repeated. 'But it's such a hard world; and here's the rich living like there's no poor folks at-all, like it's sunshine and money for everybody. And some of them rich folks not such good folks, neither.'

Lucy said, 'It's not all sunshine, Mrs Sweeney; even for the rich. Money never eased anybody's heartache.'

She glanced at Jamie. He didn't smile at her, but he continued to watch her with the wary intentness of a man who doesn't dare to think that he might be loved in return.

4

When Jamie saw Lucy rustling down the stairs in her dark crimson taffeta ballgown, he didn't say anything, but took one or two steps back, plainly impressed, and glanced at Mrs Sweeney, his eyes alive. Lucy's gown was deeply décolleté, in the latest fashion, and her white skin was decorated with a blood-black necklace of Czechoslovakian garnets.

'Well, there's the magical picture, isn't she?' said Mrs Sweeney, and she was crackling with pride, almost as if Lucy were her own daughter. 'And just to think that it was me what taught her to cut the pigeon wing.' – by which she meant elegant dancing. 'I looked just like that myself, once upon a time. Just like that! Thinner, maybe.'

Jamie held out his hand as Lucy crossed the hallway. 'You look simply fine,' he told her.

She curtseyed. 'You look very fine yourself, sir,' she replied. Jamie was wearing a high starched collar, and a new black tailcoat which Lucy had ordered for him from Woodbury's and which had arrived that morning accompanied by two tailors in case it required alteration.

Lucy thought Jamie looked distinctly dashing. In fact, now that he was dressed formally, the way that Henry Carson had always been dressed, she began to realize what a strong, attractive young man he really was. His tailcoat had given him unexpected style, and a look of masculine authority, in spite of his youthfulness, and his slow country drawl.

'We'd better be going,' said Lucy. 'Jeremy! Is the brougham ready? And where's poppa?'

'The brougham is waiting without, Miss Lucy,' Jeremy replied, from his position by the door. 'Your father will be down directly.'

'I hope he's still not sulking over what I said to him yesterday,' said Mrs Sweeney. 'I think a man should take his criticism, don't you think so? square on the chin. He needs a dance or two, that's what he needs. He needs some fun!'

But Jack — with the ludicrous promptness of a minor actor who has been waiting for his cue — appeared at that very instant at the top of the staircase. He took two or three steps, and then stopped. His face was as pink as anchovy sauce, and he was swaying very slightly from side to side, as if he were trying to keep his balance in a streetcar.

'I suppose you're waiting for me,' he announced. 'I suppose you're waiting for the tightwad of Oak City, Kansas, the man who turned his back on his needy friends.'

Lucy took two or three steps back up the staircase. 'Poppa, you've been drinking,' she said, resentfully.

Jack stared at her. 'Well?' he demanded. 'I'm in the best of spirits, the very best! Nothing like a few glasses of agurforty to make a man feel on top of the world! There you are, Molly Sweeney! Are you going to dance for me tonight? Are you going to show me what you're made of?'

'If he isn't fighting drunk!' whispered Mrs Sweeney; half in disgust and half in awe.

'Poppa,' said Lucy, gathering up her skirts and hurrying up the stairs to meet him halfway. 'Poppa, you can't go the ball like this. Everybody's going to be there! Mrs Vanderbilt! Even Mrs Astor. And Mr McKinley; and Mr Hanna, too. Poppa, *please!*'

Jack stopped and stared at her as if he didn't recognize her. 'I'm feeling *wonderful*,' he told her, confidentially, leaning forward so that she could smell the whisky on his breath. He'd been drinking Tightropes; but his own particular mix, which was more than half whisky and less than half champagne. 'Besides,' he whispered, 'Who are you to tell me where I should go, and when? Hm? You're not even my –'

Before he could say any more, Lucy snatched his sleeve, and braved the whisky fumes to whisper closely and directly into his face. 'Poppa, we're in society now! We've spent months and months, haven't we, making new friends, trying to learn how to do things properly, trying to give ourselves some standing. This is New York, poppa, not Kansas! If you go out drunk tonight, what will everybody *say?* We'll be cut by everybody, we'll never live it down!'

Jack wrinkled his mouth in disdain. 'Are these society folks such simlin-heads they never saw a fellow cheerful before?'

'Of course not, poppa, but this is a charity ball. And you're not cheerful, you're falling-down drunk. You don't go falling-down drunk to a charity ball!'

Jack stood up straight and stiff. He looked down at the hallway below, and pointed a finger at Mrs Sweeney. 'That woman accuses me of downright meanness. That woman accuses me of showing my back to my friends. Samuel Blankenship died because of me, that's what she said, and Oak City was ravaged by poorness, and what she said was, I never even cared.'

'Holy Godfrey's tonic, Jack Darling! I never said nothing of the sort!' Mrs Sweeney protested.

But Jack turned back to Lucy and now there were tears in his eyes. 'What have I done?' he sniffled. 'Look at this house! Look at me! Look at you! Your poor mother! What have I done?'

'Poppa, you'd better off in bed,' Lucy told him. 'Please – don't try to come tonight, you're far too upset. I'll find some dancing-partners for Mrs Sweeney.'

Jack stared at her. 'Mean, that's what she said! Mean, and didn't care!'

'Poppa –' said Lucy, reaching out for him.

He twisted himself away from her. 'Not you! Not you, too! I've had all the goddamned sympathy that any one man can stand! Even Casper felt sorry for me, and who can blame him? A faithless wife, no child of my own, a store that was nothing but grind and punishment! And now this! A fortune that I never deserved, heaped on top of me like – like saddlebags full o' rocks, heaped on top of a mule. It weighs me down, Lucy, it weighs me down! and I don't have the strength to get up again.'

Lucy made one more effort to take hold of his arm, but he wrenched it away, breaking one of her fingernails. 'Now don't you touch me,' he warned her, 'because you're no blood-relative of mine. You're anybody's child.'

Lucy felt stingingly hurt, as if she had smashed through a silverbacked mirror, and been sliced clean through to the bone. She turned to Jamie in distress. But Jamie clearly didn't understand what Jack was raving about, because he frowned, and mouthed, '*what*??' and shook his head.

It was Mrs Sweeney, mysteriously, who calmed Jack down. She came up the stairs neat-footed in her mourning-gown of stiffened black silk, and stood just two steps below him, composed, a little irritated, but contrite, too. 'Jack Darling,' she said, all Kansas-genteel. 'I spoke out of place. I'm sorry, that's what I've got to tell you, an awfully lot.'

'I never forgot them, none of them,' Jack insisted. He didn't even appear to have heard what Mrs Sweeney had said. 'Not Samuel, not Henry, not Osage Pete. I never forget the Lapps or the Foresters, nor yet the van Houtens.' He slowly tapped his right temple with his finger again and again, like a blind man determined to find a bellpush.

'They're all in here, all pictured in my mind's eye, every single one of them, forever and ever.'

Mrs Sweeney crooked her elbow as an invitation for him to link his arm through hers. 'Come on, Jack Darling,' she coaxed him. 'Some of that cold night air will fresh you up; that and some dancing. Look at me now, all dyked up in my brand-fired new dress! You can't let me step out without squiring me.'

'I never forgot none of them,' Jack repeated. 'Do you hear me? Do you hear what I say? And I was never untrue to Lucy's mother, not once, not ever.'

'Well, we hear what you say,' cooed Mrs Sweeney, 'but you just listen to this.' She beckoned him closer, and caught hold of his head, and lowered his ear close up to her mouth. She hesitated for a moment, but then she whispered something that only he could hear.

Whatever she said, the effect on Jack was instantaneous and extraordinary. He stood up straight, and stared first at Lucy, and then at Jamie, and all the alcoholic flush drained from his face.

'Poppa?' asked Lucy.

But Mrs Sweeney beckoned him yet again, and whispered something else; and Jack nodded.

'Poppa?' Lucy repeated.

'All in good time,' said Mrs Sweeney. 'Your poppa's just fine, now, aren't you, Jack? Ready for skipping?'

Mrs Sweeney guided Jack down to the hallway, where Jeremy was waiting to drape his evening-cloak around his shoulder. Jamie held out his hand for Lucy, and she could see that his face was congested with questions. *Anybody's child? What did that mean?* But Lucy was just as perplexed by what had happened as he was.

★

They drove to the Waldorf in the Darlings' high-varnished maroon brougham. The interior smelled suffocatingly of leather and perfume. As they passed one streetlamp after another, and the brougham's interior was intermittently lit by geometric patterns of gaslight, Lucy's face appeared and disappeared under the brim of her grey-beribboned evening hat. All the same Jamie kept staring at her from the opposite seat, his opera-hat perched in his lap.

Mrs Sweeney kept up a tireless excited commentary on everything she saw.

'Look at this, will you!' she exclaimed, as they turned south by the Grand Army Plaza. 'You should have seen it when I was here, when I was a girl! This was all garbage dumps, and quarries, and stockyards, with scarcely a house in sight, and it wasn't paved at all. Now look at all these buildings! It's a miracle!'

'All hotels here,' Jack told her, leaning so close to the brougham's window that his breath fogged the glass. 'The Savoy, the New Netherland, the Plaza. All hotels.'

But soon they were passing the huge mansions of the Vanderbilts; the house built by Cornelius Vanderbilt II on the entire blockfront between 58th and 57th Streets; the ravishing Gothic Revival house built by his brother William Kissam Vanderbilt on 52nd Street; and the two Renaissance-style houses built by their father William Henry Vanderbilt on 52nd and 51st Streets, one for himself and one for his daughters.

'The cost!' Mrs Sweeney exclaimed. 'What must these houses cost?'

In a glum voice, Jack told her, 'A. T. Stewart spent four million, so the yellow papers say; and the Vanderbilts spent fifteen million between them. The Vanderbilts could buy me and sell me twenty times in one day. And so could most of them, Astor and Gould and Carnegie. I'm small fry. You should tell them that, back in Oak City, those that give me the black word.'

Mrs Sweeney leaned across and touched Jack's hand. 'I've said I'm sorry, Jack Darling; and I've told you what you ought to know; so come along now. There's no call for making too much of it.'

Lucy said boldly to Jamie, 'You're staring.'

As they passed the next streetlamp, she could see that her challenge had made him blush. 'I'm sorry,' he said. 'I didn't mean to. But under that hat, I can scarcely see you.'

Lucy smiled. 'What were you thinking about?'

'I was thinking about you.'

'Oh, go on, tell the truth, you were thinking about business. You were thinking about how to run the Indians off the prairies, and tarts.'

'Torts,' he corrected her, laughing. 'But, no, I wasn't thinking about business. I was really truly thinking about you. You haven't changed, you know. Well, you *have*, your manners have changed, you're the blue hen's chicken these days. But you're still Lucy Darling, aren't you? Still the dreamer. I was thinking to myself, can you still see the clouds, for all of these tall buildings? Do they look like ships, and castles, and islands?'

'You're embarrassing me,' she told him; and he was, especially when Mrs Sweeney glanced across at her.

Jack coughed thickly, and said, 'There's rich, you see, and there's rich. There's some so rich they can't even count it, and they're the tightest, but who ever hears the black word about them?'

He paused, and then added, 'I can see it, you know. Still see it. The store, and the stove, and my Anna reaching up for the candy-jars.'

He frowned at Mrs Sweeney and asked her fiercely, 'Where did it *go*? Where did all of it *go*?'

Mrs Sweeney pursed her lips. 'Back in time, Jack Darling, where Sean lives now; and Samuel Blankenship, too; and all of those who went before.'

Without warning, Jack began to sob. He beat his fists on

his knees, and the tears coursed freely down his cheeks. Mrs Sweeney tried to shush him, but he wouldn't be shushed. Jamie watched him helplessly. What can you do for a man whose whole life has turned out to be nothing but bitterness and lost opportunities?

But Lucy put her arm around him and held him close. 'Poppa, they're jealous, that's all. Folks are always jealous when you have good luck. They don't mean you any harm, not really. If you went back to Oak City tomorrow, they'd welcome you just like always. Forgive them, poppa. That's all you have to do.'

'Wise words for such a young head,' said Mrs Sweeney. 'Forgive them, that's right; and forgive me, too, Jack Darling. And most of all, forgive yourself. Come along, tonight's for dancing!'

Jack wiped his eyes with his handkerchief, and blew his nose.

'Smile,' Lucy ordered him.

Jack gave her a grin as tight as a tourniquet.

'That'll do for now,' said Lucy, although when he stopped grinning, his eyes still flew from side to side, and his fingers pattered impatiently on the brim of his hat.

They pattered like hail on the roof of the store painted stray-dog yellow, on the very brink of the world.

Uneasily, Jamie said, 'Well, you know what it says in the Bible. Matthew, chapter nineteen. "It is easier for a camel to go through the eye of a needle, than for a rich man to enter the kingdom of God."'

They were waltzing in the Waldorf ballroom, under sparkling electric chandeliers; with more than three hundred other waltzers. The music and the laughter and the roar of chopped-up conversation made it almost impossible for Lucy to hear what Jamie was saying. The orchestra played *Love's Dreamland* and *Spring And Love*.

Lucy had already met Evelyn Scott and several of her friends; and been introduced to Mrs Astor and the John

Pierpont Morgans (she had met Jane before, and adored her). She had danced a polka with James Gore King, who had tramped blithely on her maroon velvet slippers. She felt aerated tonight, as if she *ought* to be enjoying herself, but Jack's drunkenness had unsettled her, and made her unpleasantly panicky. Much to Jamie's irritation, she kept twisting her head around to look for him. She hadn't seen him so drunk since her mother had died; nor behaving so oddly. What on earth had Mrs Sweeney whispered to him? She was terrified that he was going to do something stupid. He had always been a man of charity and deep humility, but lately Lucy had been able to see that he was charitable and humble only because he seemed to believe (quite falsely) that he had committed the most unforgivable wrongs, and deserved God's punishment. Lucy's greatest fear was that tonight he might feel that he deserved even greater punishment than ever, and humiliate himself beyond redemption.

If he humiliated himself, he would humiliate her, too; and that would jeopardize her tenuous new-found place in New York society. 'Sweet girl,' Mrs Astor had called her. But sweetness would not be enough to save her from the social consequences of having a drunk and publicly-embarrassing father.

'Can you see poppa anyplace?' she asked Jamie, worriedly.

Jamie looked over the heads of the waltzers. After all, he was six-foot-two 'above snakes', as Mrs Sweeney would have put it. 'Can't see him,' he said, after a lengthy inspection. 'Maybe he's gone for something to eat. Or something to drink, more like.'

Lucy said, 'I'd better look for him. He shouldn't have come tonight. I wish Mrs Sweeney hadn't persuaded him.'

'I can see Mrs Sweeney,' said Jamie. 'Just take a look at her! Talk about the Skipping Widder! Reckon she thinks she's still no more'n seventeen years old!'

Sure enough, Mrs Sweeney twinkled past them in the arms of Henry Sturgis Grew, the Boston millionaire, her eyes ecstatically closed, humming as she danced.

'Mrs Sweeney!' Lucy called her, but Mrs Sweeney was obviously dreaming of another time, and didn't hear her.

'Don't you go waking her up, now!' Mr Grew admonished Lucy, with a smile. 'I've never danced this good before! She tells me she walks the high-wire, too!'

'Once upon a time,' said Lucy, just as Mrs Sweeney mischievously opened her eyes.

Jamie and Lucy danced close to a prickly-moustached young man with spectacles, and a plainish girl with blonde ringlets and a big nose. The prickly-moustached young man called out, 'G'd evening, Miss Darling!' and out of courtesy, Jamie asked him, 'How're things?'

'That was Teddy Roosevelt, with Hester French,' Lucy explained, as they danced away. 'Teddy's something to do with the Navy. Very up-and-coming, although some people call him Moses, because he's always so righteous. Hester's one of those silly girls who dances with every young man who's up-and-coming, and then whines about them behind their backs, because none of them ever asks her to marry them.'

Jamie said, 'Not too much different from any society anywhere. What about you?'

'What about me?'

'Do you think you'll ever be married?'

'Nobody's asked me yet. Nobody that I *want* to marry, anyway.'

'What about your famous Englishman? Your Member of Parliament?'

Lucy gave him a scarcely imperceptible shrug of her bare white shoulders and looked away. She didn't know when she had stopped believing that Henry would ever write to her; but she had. All the same, she found it difficult to let his memory go. It was a little like taking a photograph out of

197

her purse again and again, with the intention of throwing it away; but always hesitating, and putting it back.

'I'm still young,' she replied.

The orchestra finished the waltz; and everybody clapped and cried, 'Bravo!' so that whatever Jamie said next was swallowed by the noise.

'I'd love a glass of punch!' said Lucy, and Jamie steered her by the elbow to the side of the ballroom floor. Evelyn was there, in a pretty green gown tied with bows, in the company of a rigid young man who looked as if he didn't dare smile in case it compromised his perfect Grecian profile.

'Wait here, and I'll fetch us some punch,' said Jamie.

'What an *adorable* boy!' Evelyn exclaimed, after Jamie had shouldered his way through the crowd. 'But did I detect just a *soupçon de* Kansas accent?'

'He's just a friend from back home,' said Lucy.

'Well, they certainly grow them a generous size, "back home",' Evelyn observed, with an exaggerated relish that was obviously calculated to irritate her escort. Her escort, however, continued to stare into the middle-distance as if he were thinking about himself and his profile and nothing else.

'This is Ronald Prout,' Evelyn explained, raising her eyebrows to imply that Ronald wasn't up to much. 'Just another Gas House boy.' The Gas House was the most socially notable of all the Harvard 'final clubs' – even more prestigious than the Porcellian or the AD.

Ronald focused his bright grey eyes for a moment, and remarked drily, 'Kansas? Isn't that someplace out past 59th Street?'

Lucy was just about to ask Evelyn about next week's ball at the Holland House, when a strange commotion rippled through the crowd, the way that storms used to ripple through the Kansas grass. Heads began to turn towards the archway which led to the hotel lobby. A man's voice shouted, 'Don't touch her! Don't touch her!' and then another man's voice called, 'Stand away! Don't stand underneath!'

A young man with brilliantined hair came pushing his way across the ballroom. 'What's happening?' Lucy asked him.

'Great fun and games!' the young man replied. 'An old lady's balancing on the balustrade! Old enough to be my grandmama!'

Lucy clasped her hand over her mouth. *Oh God, Mrs Sweeney! It had to be!*

Evelyn frowned, 'Lucy? What's going on? Lucy!'

But without a word, Lucy elbowed her way through the excited throng of dancers, through the archway, and into the Waldorf's grandiose marbled lobby. As she did so, several of the women screamed, and the men let out a great low cry of alarm, like a mighty herd of beef on the hoof.

'Come down!' one of the men cried out. 'For the love of God, madam, come down!'

Henry Sturgis Grew was standing in front of the crowd, his arms outspread in perplexity. 'She said, "I'll show you!" That's what she said! "I'll show you!" And the next thing I knew, she was calling, and there she was, up on the rail!'

Lucy looked up, and felt a chilly prickling of fear all the way down her back. Mrs Sweeney was up on the marble balustrade of the hotel's mezzanine floor, her black widow's skirts raised up in one hand, balancing one black evening-slipper in front of the other. She was calmly smiling; but the look in her eyes was very far away. It was the look of a woman who has forgotten where she is, and whom the passing years have already robbed of almost everything.

There were crowds beneath her, in the lobby, and crowds all the way up the curving stairs, but those on the mezzanine kept well back, for fear of putting her off her balance. The lobby was thick with fear and cigar-smoke and expensive French perfume, and diamonds flashed everywhere, like fireflies.

'Has somebody sent for the engine company?' bellowed the Waldorf's portly manager. 'Ned! Bring blankets! If she falls, we might be able to catch her!'

Above the moans and the screams, Lucy could hear that Mrs Sweeney was singing to herself, high-pitched, off-key, a tremulous little song that must have dated back to her years with Forepaugh and Sells.

> *'Though in this sil-ly farce of love,*
> *You've often tried to play . . .'*

Lucy, tight-lipped, her heart pounding, pushed her way through to the foot of the stairs. When a large woman in a blue velvet gown turned to protest, her white breasts shivering like blancmanges, Lucy said, 'She's a friend, please, I know her. Please let me through!'

Halfway up the stairs, she called out, 'Mrs Sweeney! Mrs Sweeney!' but the crowd was too clamorous for Mrs Sweeney to hear; and even if she had, she probably wouldn't have taken any notice. She kept on balancing along the banister, thirty feet above the marble floor, one foot hesitantly in front of the other, and she was somewhere else altogether, in another time, walking the slack-wire in Omaha, perhaps, or Valley Falls, or Sutro, while upturned faces watched her in awe.

> *'Just rest assured that you'll not live . . .*
> *To see your wed-ding day!'*

She reached the end of the banister, hesitated, and swayed. The women screamed again, and the screaming at last seemed to penetrate Mrs Sweeney's fantasy, because she frowned down at the crowd below her through her glinting spectacles, and then she vaguely smiled.

'Mrs Sweeney!' called Lucy, thrusting her way up the stairs. 'Mrs Sweeney!'

It was then, right behind her, that she heard Jack bellowing, 'Molly! Molly Sweeney! You come down from there, you damp raddled old calico! What in hell do you think you're doing?'

Jack came plunging through the crowd, red-faced, bung-eyed, with the thrashing arm-movements of a man swimming to shore. 'Who are you shoving, sir?' one elderly man protested; but Jack lurched and staggered and stared at him so madly that the elderly man briskly turned away, pretending that he hadn't said anything at all.

'Molly Sweeney, you Goddamned biscuit-eater!' he raged. 'You come down from there right now!'

Although he had managed to remember the polite euphemism for 'bitch,' he was even drunker than before. He must have spent most of the evening in the bar, downing Tightropes. As he pushed Lucy, he glared at her, too, and snorted, and sniffed, and fumed, 'Your mother, by God,' whatever that meant. His face was smothered with sweat, and his pomaded hair was sticking up on end. Whisky fumes flowed after him like an invisible evening-cloak.

'Poppa, don't!' Lucy begged him. 'Poppa, if you distract her – if you surprise her – she'll fall!'

As it was, Mrs Sweeney was already standing sideways on the balustrade, her arms wide, right on the very brink of losing her balance. But she was still singing, in breathless little gasps, and still smiling.

'Just rest assured –'

'Molly Sweeney!' screamed Jack, as he reached the top of the stairs. Everybody around him stepped back.

'Is he a lunatic?' a plump elderly woman asked, inspecting Jack through lorgnettes.

'Drunk, more like,' her companion remarked.

'More like both, drunk, and a lunatic,' a tall ginger-haired girl put in.

Lucy turned around. 'He's my father,' she declared, bravely.

'Oh *dear*,' said the plump woman, and nudged her companion with her elbow. Mrs Sweeney swayed from side to side, and at last managed to turn right around, so that she could balance her way back along the balustrade towards the stairs. She looked white-faced now, white as linen, and she was biting her lower lip in intense concentration.

'That you'll not live –'

Jack shuffled towards her. His shirt-tail was hanging out, and he had lost one of his collar studs.

'Molly, Molly, Molly,' he said, much more quietly now. 'If this is a punishment, Molly, I'm not going to take it. Is this the way you get your own back on me? Is this it?'

Mrs Sweeney didn't even glance at him, but came teetering towards him step by anxiously-adjusted step, her back straight, her arms outstretched, with a terrible elegance that somehow made her performance all the more frightening.

Right foot forward, poise on the toes, carefully place the weight on the arch. Pause, balance; then left foot forward, poise on the toes.

She wasn't doing it to punish Jack, Lucy knew that. She had heard Mrs Sweeney talk too often about 'my sparkling days, when everybody flocked to see me'. She was thinking of herself and nobody else. 'See Nile demencher,' that's what Doctor Cooper would have called it; the same way he called cholera morbus, the 'coloured marbles'. An old woman's sparkling days revived, as if all those years had never passed.

Mrs Sweeney stopped, and then hop-staggered one more step.

'To see –' she gasped, breathlessly. The crowd below her shrank farther back. Over by the elevators, on the opposite side of the lobby, two bellmen were struggling to drag blankets and pillows out of one of the elevator cars, anything to break Mrs Sweeney's fall, if she should fall.

'Molly,' said Jack, shuffling nearer and nearer, both hands outstretched, quivering. 'I was never such a bad man, Molly, you know that. I've been wrong, Molly, I admit it. I had my difficult times, that was for sure. And you're right to punish me for it. But not this way, Molly. Come down, Molly, I'll dance with you now.'

'— *your* —'

Mrs Sweeney smiled. She lowered her arms stiffly by her sides. She looked at Jack for the first time, really *looked* at him, really saw him, and the expression on her face was exalted, like no human expression that Lucy had ever seen before, only in paintings of saints and Jesus, with eyes that followed you with pious regret wherever you went.

'— *wedding* —'

She toppled sideways. The crowd screamed; then instantly stopped screaming. My God, she was still smiling as she fell! Farewell, Forepaugh! Farewell, Sells! What a time to plummet, at the crescendo of her girlish dream. Farewell, all you uplifted faces, all you laughing, glowing admirers!

But Jack covered the ten feet between them with two extraordinary lopes, and lunged out across the balustrade, and caught her around the waist, far too late, and the two of them fell together, clinging tight. The crowd remained silent: so that when they dropped into the outstretched blanket and then hit the marble floor beneath, everybody heard the crack of Mrs Sweeney's back as clear as a snapped-in-half walking-stick.

Now there were shrieks, now there was chaos. Arms flung up. Women fainted on all sides, dropped like shot cattle, and the crowd on the stairs swayed dangerously. Lucy, dumb with panic, pushed her way back down to the lobby, and in between the ramparts of heaving shoulders.

She found her way blocked by the broad unyielding back of the Waldorf's manager. 'Get back!' he was bellowing. 'Give them air, will you, give them air!'

Lucy tried to wriggle her way past him, but he reached around behind his back and shoved her away.

'He's my father!' she screamed, pummelling his tight-shouldered frock-coat with her fists. 'He's my father!'

The manager stepped back, crushing the toes of a young girl in orange velvet, who was whimpering, 'Let me see! Let me see! I never saw anybody dead before!' He laid his arm around Lucy's shoulders, and said, 'I'm sorry, ma'am. You'd best think of saying goodbyes. It looks like he's broken his neck.'

Jack and Mrs Sweeney were lying side by side, Mrs Sweeney on her back, Jack face down. The fawn blanket had become tangled around them so that they looked as if they had restlessly slept together on the lobby floor. Mrs Sweeney's bleached green eyes were wide open, her spectacles lay broken on the floor beside her. She was staring sideways at Lucy with a quizzical smile on her face, as if she were asking, *What am I doing here, Lucy? I should be dancing.* There was no blood; no sign that she was dead except that she didn't blink, not once, and her black widow's dress had collapsed around her like a smashed umbrella.

Jack was quivering violently. His face was pressed against the floor, so that only his right eye was visible. The pupil darted desperately from side to side.

Lucy knelt beside him, and gently touched his hair. 'Poppa . . . oh, poppa, it's Lucy.' Tears poured down her cheeks, and sparkled as brightly as any diamond necklace. The women in their silk and velvet ballgowns stood around her and watched her in horrified fascination. 'Poppa, please speak to me. Please say something.'

He tried to look at her, but he couldn't seem to focus. 'Lucy . . .' he slurred, his eye wandering. 'What's happened to me, my darling? Am I dying, or am I dead?'

'No, poppa,' she told him. 'Everything's going to be fine. You've hurt your neck, that's all. They've sent for a doctor.'

'What about Molly?' he asked her. 'Is Molly hurt, too?'

Lucy glanced quickly at Mrs Sweeney's collapsed and angular body; at her fixed green eyes. A moment ago, Mrs Sweeney had looked as if she were sleeping, but still alive. Now death had claimed her completely, and she had stiffened like a waxwork.

Lucy wondered for a moment if she ought to tell Jack that Mrs Sweeney was still alive; that he hadn't broken his neck for nothing. But she couldn't lie to him, not now. She stroked his cold sweaty forehead two or three times, and then she shook her head.

'She's dead, poppa.'

His single eye stared without compassion at the floor. 'Dead? Well, she probably deserved it. You can't say that I didn't do my very best to save her, now can you?'

'She never blamed you, poppa.'

Jack said nothing for a very long time. Only his quivering reassured Lucy that he wasn't dead. At last, he hacked up a little mucus, marbled with blood; and then he said, 'I never knew she still felt so bad about me. I never knew.'

It was then, kneeling beside the man who had raised her, but who had never been her father, that Lucy understood for the first time that men and women know nothing of each other's ambitions, and nothing of each other's fears.

She looked up, and Jamie was standing close beside her. 'Lucy?' She lifted her hand, and he took it. 'The doctor's here,' he told her. He sounded as if he were speaking inside a belljar.

'Is he going to die?' asked Lucy.

The doctor sported white muttonchop whiskers and a gravy-stained cherry-red vest, and a slack brown bag, which he dragged behind him like a somnolent spaniel.

He cleared his throat, and looked around, as if he couldn't decide where Lucy's voice had come from.

'Die? Die? Good God, no. None of my patients ever die.'

He knelt beside Jack, and asked loudly, 'How're you feeling, old man?'

'Are you a doctor?' Jack retorted.

'Sure I'm a doctor.'

Jack coughed up more phlegm. 'I feel like I'm going, doctor.'

'Poppa!' Lucy pleaded.

'Can't help it,' Jack told her. 'It's dark and I'm cold and your momma's calling.'

The doctor opened up his bag and rummaged around. 'You die on me, friend, in front of all of these people, I'm going to kick your back end from here to eternity.'

'Can't help it,' Jack whispered. His quivering became more convulsive.

'He's not going to die,' the doctor said, confidently, gently squeezing Jack's neck. 'Can you feel that, friend? How does that feel?'

'Hurts,' Jack told him.

The doctor lifted Jack's tailcoat, tore open the peach silk backing of his fancy vest, and then tugged his shirt out of his pants, to expose his bare back. He looked around at the silent assembly of richly-dressed onlookers. 'Anybody lend me a brooch, or a hatpin?'

Without hesitation, Mrs Grew unfastened a diamond and emerald star that must have cost more than two hundred thousand dollars, and handed it over. The doctor opened it up and pricked Jack's shoulders with its pin, deeply enough to draw blood.

'How about that? You feel that?' the doctor demanded.

Jack said, 'What? Feel what?'

The doctor prodded the back of Jack's hands. 'How about that? You feel that?'

'I don't know what you're talking about. I don't feel nothing.'

The doctor stood up, sniffed, and handed Mrs Grew's brooch back. 'Obliged, ma'am,' he said, taking out a large soiled handkerchief and noisily blowing his nose.

'Well?' asked Lucy. 'Is he going to live?'

'Depends what you mean by "live", my dear. He aint a-going to die, if that's what you mean. God don't want him yet. But he aint never a-going to walk no more, nor move a solitary muscle below his chin.'

'You mean he's paralysed?' asked Lucy. Her head felt empty and echoing, as if she were going to faint.

'Is he rich?' the doctor replied. 'I suppose he must be, if he's here.'

Jamie had pushed his way forward, and now he took hold of Lucy's arm. 'He's rich all right,' Jamie told him. 'Jack Darling, the oil millionaire.'

'Well, that's going to help,' said the doctor, closing his bag.

Lucy said, with a surge of hope, 'Is there somebody you know who could give him his feeling back?'

'Oh, no, no, no!' the doctor told her. 'Nothing like that. Once your neck's broke, your neck's broke. Can't be undone. Just like bashing your brains out, can't scoop them back in again. But least, you see, he can pay for nursemaids, to feed him and wash him and generally take care of him. He's going to be just like a baby, for the rest of his natural life, but there's a bright side to it, seeing he's rich. Least he's going to be a *pampered* baby.'

Outside, a thin glittering drizzle had started to sift through the gaslit night. Crowds had gathered on the sidewalk outside the hotel, and Fifth Avenue was clogged with carriages as the guests called for their coachmen and went home early. Whistles blew, policemen shouted, people jostled and collided. Inside the hotel, on the floor, Jack's head was lifted a little by two bellmen, so that he could take a sip of brandy, as if he wasn't drunk enough already, and then lifted on to a stretcher, still face downward, and taken by ambulance to Bellevue Hospital. Mrs Sweeney was covered by a blanket and left on a table at the side of the lobby, her black dancing-slippers at ten to two. Eventually two painfully thin young policemen arrived, to carry her off to the morgue.

Lucy sat on a gilded bentwood chair, her face as transparently pale as a fairy queen, her shoulders draped in a borrowed ermine wrap. She had insisted on staying at the Waldorf until she had seen Jack carried away; but a little after ten o'clock she allowed Jamie and Evelyn to take her home.

On the way back towards Central Park, she sat in the most shadowy corner of the brougham, saying nothing. She felt exhausted, as if she scarcely had the strength left to walk up the steps to the house, and she felt guilty, too – guiltier than anybody would ever be able to understand. She felt as if every single event that had led to Mrs Sweeney's death and to Jack Darling's injury had been her doing – that it had been her vanity and her wilfulness and her immorality that had caused them both, at last, to topple from that balustrade.

If she hadn't bargained her lost virginity with Uncle Casper, she would never have become so rich. Jack would still be poor, and hard-worked, but at least he would be whole. Mrs Sweeney would never have relived her long-lost dreams of dancing in New York, but at least she would be still alive.

Lucy felt as if the glutinous stain of what had happened in the storeroom with Uncle Casper had crept wider and wider across her life like black oil spilled across unbleached linen.

Washing hadn't been enough to cleanse her. Nor had prayer. When she washed, when she prayed, there was always the unspoken question, *perhaps you enjoyed it, princess; perhaps you still think about it, what it was like, and wish you could have some more.* And then she would picture that grinning fiery face, with flames gushing out of its cheeks, and it would leave her trembling, and dry-mouthed, and disoriented.

Evelyn stayed with Lucy while Nora, flustered with shock and sympathy, undressed her and drew her a hot bath. Jamie stayed in the drawing room downstairs, drinking whisky, and pacing up and down in front of the reeking coal fire.

'Did they say how long your poppa might have to stay in the hospital?' Evelyn asked Lucy, through the partially-open bathroom door.

'A month at least, they weren't sure,' Lucy told her. 'The doctor said they have to find out which of his neck-bones are broken, and make quite certain that they heal properly. Otherwise he could catch the infectious fever.'

Frances the little cherry-cheeked kitchen-maid tiptoed in with a blue-and-white cup of hot chocolate, which she left on the table in the turret.

Eventually Lucy came out of the bathroom in a long nightdress of fine embroidered cambric, with Nora following her, trying to rub her hair dry as she walked.

'It's all right, Nora,' said Lucy. 'I'll wrap it in a towel, and sit by the fire.'

'You're sure, miss? I don't want to be the one responsible for you catching the grippe.'

Lucy held her close, and hugged her. 'You've been so kind to me, Nora.'

Nora blinked tears from her eyes. 'Such a poor man, your poppa. Always so confused. Do you know what he used to do, he used to call me to the morning room, and say, "Nora, you're wise, what should you do when you don't understand where your life has taken you to?"'

Evelyn looked up. 'What did you say to him, Nora?'

'What could I say? It was such a question! But I used to tell him what my grandfather always told me. "Today and tomorrow are just like gold and silver, one today is worth sixteen tomorrows; and don't forget that tomorrow is the day after you're dead."'

'Well, I'm sure *that* cheered him up no end' Evelyn replied.

Nora wound Lucy's straggly dark-blonde hair into a towel-turban. 'I'll come up by-and-by to brush it out for you, miss. And, miss – I'm so sorry, miss. Your poor dear poppa.'

She left the room, and Lucy sat in her plaited French basketwork chair by the hearth, and watched the flames licking and dancing for a while.

'How do you feel?' Evelyn asked her.

'I don't know quite. Numb.'

'You should have taken those powders the doctor offered you.'

Lucy shook her head. 'I don't want to sleep. Not yet.'

'Why do you think he did it?' Evelyn asked.

Lucy looked up. The fire sparkled in her eyes. 'You mean, did he do it on purpose?'

Evelyn hesitated, but then she said, 'I heard one of the policemen suggesting it. "Here's a classical suicide," that's what he said. And I saw your poppa for myself. He jumped right out, he couldn't have saved her, he couldn't have saved himself.'

Lucy was silent for a long time. A pretty little silver clock ticked above the hearth. She felt as if she ought to cry; and she knew that she would, but not just yet. At last, looking towards the fire, she said, 'He always thought that whatever went wrong, it was always his fault. My momma left him once, and he always blamed himself for that. She came back, but then she died, and he always blamed himself for that, too. He could never believe that he was any good.'

He blamed himself for Uncle Casper raping me, too, she thought, but she didn't tell Evelyn. If she told Evelyn, the whole of New York society would know it by dinner-time tomorrow; and they'd be talking about it in San Francisco by the week's end.

True or false, stove-talk or not, Mrs Sweeney's news that nobody thought well of him in Oak City had somehow been the last straw that had broken Jack's spirit completely. What more she had whispered to him on the stairs, Lucy couldn't guess. He hadn't achieved much in Oak City: a store, and just enough to live on, and a small circle of friends, but at least he had achieved it himself. At least it was something he could be proud of. When that last reassuring memory had turned into ashes, Jack Darling, for all of their money, had been left with nothing.

He had been a High Plains storekeeper. He knew all too well what happened to people who were left with nothing.

Lucy sipped her chocolate. It was rich and bitter and scalding hot. Evelyn said, 'I'd better go soon. Daddy and mommy always retire at ten. Daddy says it's the secret of a long life, retiring early. And about a million Mellons are coming for luncheon tomorrow. I think it's so impolite to have such hordes of people in your family, don't you?'

'I don't have anyone at all, except for poppa,' said Lucy.

'Well, it's high time you married,' Evelyn told her. 'You could start your own family then. But for goodness' sake don't propagate like the Mellons. I know they come from Pittsburgh, and that must excuse them some lapse in manners, but really! You should be nicer to John. You could do worse, and he's almost unbearably rich.'

Evelyn stood up, and came over to Lucy, and embraced her. 'I'll call by tomorrow, my dear, to see how you are. Don't despair, will you? There are simply dozens of people who love you dearly.'

Evelyn left. Lucy stood in her turret and watched the brougham turning around on Tenth Avenue to take her home. Nora knocked gently at the door, and said, 'Shall I brush your hair now, Miss Lucy? I should brush it out before it dries.'

Lucy nodded, and went through to her dressing room, and sat down in front of the mirror. She hadn't realized how anaemic she looked. The ghost of Lucy Darling.

Nora started to brush, counting under her breath.

'What's Jamie doing?' Lucy asked her.

'He'll be retiring now, Miss Lucy. Jeremy drew him a bath.'

'Would you tell him that I'd like to see him, before he retires?'

Lucy could see Nora's eyes flicker with uncertainty. 'Where, Miss Lucy?'

'Here, in my sitting room, of course. We'll be quite *safe*, for goodness' sake! I've known Jamie since I was a little girl!'

'You're not a little girl now, begging your pardon, Miss Lucy. And your poppa's not here.'

'Nora, please just tell him to come up and say goodnight.'

'Very good, then.'

'And ask cook for two more cups of chocolate.'

'Yes, Miss Lucy.'

Jamie knocked at the door, and Lucy answered it herself. Jamie had bathed, his hair was smartly combed back, and he smelled of eau-de-cologne. His long maroon dressing-robe was tightly tied, and underneath he wore a popular pattern of Sears Roebuck pyjamas, green-and-blue stripes.

'Hallo, Jamie,' she said, and immediately hugged him close.

He glanced around her rooms. 'I don't think your maid approved of my coming up here,' he told her.

'Oh, Nora! She's just being a fussbudget. Come on in, cook's sending up chocolate.'

They sat together by the hearth. The fire had died down now, almost to the bars, and Lucy reached for the bell for the scullery-maid. But Jamie said, 'You don't have to trouble about that. I don't think I've been living with you rich folks so long that I can't remember how to tip coal on to a hearth.'

He raked over the fire, and then shovelled on more coal. He hunkered in front of it, watching the thin flame-tongues licking, and then he said, 'I can't tell you how sorry I am. You know, about everything. Your father, Mrs Sweeney. It was just too bad.'

Lucy looked tired but unusually pretty in the firelight. Nora had brushed out her hair until it gleamed, and tied it with pale blue ribbons for the night.

'Jamie, can I ask you a question?' she said.

He frowned at her. 'Sure, whatever you like.'

'Well,' she hesitated. 'Do you think I'm at all – *evil*?'

'Evil? What makes you say that? Of course you're not evil.'

She wiped tears from her eyes with her fingers. 'I can't help feeling – well, I almost wish that poppa dies. Does that sound terrible to you? I don't know how he's going to stand it, being paralysed. Being spoon-fed, just like a child. I don't even know how I'm going to take care of him.'

'You can have nurses living-in, I guess. You can afford it, can't you?'

'Oh, I don't know. It's not just the nursing. It's living with him, when he's a cripple. How can I leave him? How can I think of getting married? I feel desperately sorry for him, but I feel so angry with him, too. He's spoiled everything.'

Frances tapped cautiously at the door, and then came in with two more steaming cups of chocolate, and a plate of wasps' nests and kisses. She curtseyed goodnight, and then hurried away, leaving the door slightly ajar. Lucy touched Jamie's hand, and said, 'You wouldn't close it, would you? I don't want Nora listening.'

Jamie got up from the hearth, crossed the room, and closed the door firmly. 'I don't think I could ever get used to servants. I'd miss my privacy too much.'

Lucy said nothing, but turned back to the fire. Jamie stood watching her for a while, the slender back of her neck, where fine blonde hairs gleamed.

'I guess you have a right to feel angry,' he said. 'You're still young. You have everything that any young girl could possibly want. And now this, poppa hurt so bad, and for no real reason at all.'

Lucy lowered her head. 'There was a real reason,' she said, softly.

'Anything you want to tell me about?'

'Come and sit down,' she asked him, and turned, and held out her hand. Jamie approached her slowly, trying to anticipate what she was going to say by the look in her eyes.

'He didn't have anything left,' said Lucy. 'When Mrs Sweeney told him that none of his friends in Oak City thought well of him any more . . .'

'He has *you*, doesn't he?' said Jamie. 'Why should he worry what his old cronies back in Oak City thought about him?'

Lucy whispered, 'No. He didn't have me. He didn't have anything.'

'He said something,' Jamie remarked. He was being careful now. 'Early this evening, on the stairs, before we left for the ball. He said something about your not really being his kin.'

Lucy nodded. Her blue eyes were blurred with tears, and now she couldn't stop them. 'The truth is, I'm not even his real daughter. My momma was my real momma – but –' she was so choked up with tiredness and shock that she could scarcely continue. Jamie knelt close to her, and held her close, and shushed her.

'You don't have to tell me any of this, not tonight,' he told her. 'The best thing for you to do is to finish your chocolate and get yourself some sleep.'

'Jamie – she died – and I never even *knew* – and she never told poppa who my father really was –'

'Come on, shush, he was always good to you, wasn't he?'

Lucy smeared her eyes against the sleeve of her robe. 'Oh God, Jamie, I feel so darned miserable.'

He held her and rocked her for nearly ten minutes, until the little pretty clock on the hearth chimed eleven o'clock. Then he passed over her cup of chocolate, and wiped her eyes for her, and kissed her forehead, and said, 'Come on, wash your teeth and then get yourself to bed.'

She turned to him, and nestled her face into his shoulder. She felt so sorely distressed; her throat and her chest hurt her from crying. But Jamie was so comforting. She gripped his arm through the sleeve of his robe, and his arm-muscle was broad and strong. She felt as if she wanted him to hold her like this, not just for tonight, but for day after day, and night after night, until the seasons flew flickering past her turreted sitting-room windows like dancing pictures in a nursery picture-show, and the fire flared and died, flared and died, year after year, until her grip failed at last, and she fell suddenly back to the carpet with silver hair and desiccated skin. If he held her like this for ever, she would never have to dress, never have to cry, never have to fall in love, never have to face the world of pain and surprises and irrational guilt.

Without raising her face, she said, 'Will you stay with me, at least till I fall asleep?'

Jamie kept on holding her tight, but she could feel the tension in him. 'You recall what happened in Denver,' he told her, and his voice sounded thick and vibrant beside her ear.

'I mean just holding me,' she said. 'I feel so all-alone.'

'Just holding you?' Cautious, but perhaps a little hopeful, too.

'Like now, till I can fall asleep.'

Jamie was silent for almost a whole minute. Then he said, 'Here? By the fire? Just until you fall asleep?'

'Umh-humh.' She was almost asleep already. Tiredness had risen up inside her like a moonless tide, and she found it almost impossible to keep her eyes open.

'Well . . .' said Jamie. 'I guess there's no harm.'

Lucy snuggled closer to him. 'I like you when you're all proud, and principled, and angry. You forgave me for Denver, didn't you?'

He stroked her hair. 'I'm not so sure that I ever did.'

'It wasn't *time*,' she murmured.

He kept on stroking her hair, over and over. 'Do you think that it could ever be time?'

She smiled. Even though her face was pressed close to his

robe, and he couldn't see her, he guessed that she was smiling, and he smiled too.

'You must keep on trying,' she said. 'You must keep on asking.'

'What happens if I don't?'

'You know what they say. He who doesn't ask, doesn't get.'

'What happens if I find somebody else? Somebody else who says yes, instead of no?'

She looked up at him. 'If you find somebody else, Jamie; then I shall cry. But I shall try not to be selfish. I shall try to be glad for you.'

She lowered her head again, and squeezed him tight. 'Anyway, I don't want to talk about it.'

A long silence passed between them. The clock chattered, the coals in the fire began to dislodge themselves. Somewhere far away, they heard the night-flattened clanging of a fire-bell.

Jamie said, 'Do you really not know who your father is?'

'Momma always refused to say,' Lucy told him. 'When she died, well, the secret died too; that's what Jack said; so nobody will ever know.'

'Does it bother you, not knowing?'

'I don't know. Sometimes it does and sometimes it doesn't. When I feel angry, or depressed, I think to myself, maybe that's my father's evil temper coming out in me. My momma always seemed to be so sweet. But sometimes I feel good and brave; like I think I'm beginning to feel good and brave right now; and then I think, maybe *that's* what my father was like, because I can't imagine my momma with any man who wasn't worthy of her.'

She paused, and she was about to say something else, but she stopped herself. She didn't want to tell Jamie about Uncle Casper. Only Jack knew about Uncle Casper, and what he had done to her; and even if Jack had ever suspected that Uncle Casper was her real father, then he certainly hadn't gone so far as to voice his suspicion out loud. It was more than Lucy could bear to think about.

Gradually, she fell asleep. She was conscious of Jamie embracing her, and of the fire fuming and crackling in the hearth, but she couldn't think about Jack any longer, her mind wouldn't let her. Jack and Mrs Sweeney remained frozen in her mind, tangled together as they toppled from the balustrade; but they fell no further. Perhaps, in her dreams, they would never hit the floor.

She didn't know how many minutes passed; but after a short while she felt Jamie easing himself away from her. He laid her gently on the rug. She felt the prickle of close-cropped wool against her cheek. Then Jamie stood up, hopping slightly, as if one of his ankles had gone dead.

'Don't go,' she heard herself whispering.

'Ssh, it's all right, I'm not going,' he reassured her. She heard him sitting with a complicated creak on the basketwork chair, and she opened her eyes for a quivering fraction and saw his faded green-and-blue pyjamas, and his slipper; and closed her eyes again, convinced.

She heard him yawn, and sigh; and the sound of his hands rubbing his chin. He must be exhausted, she thought to herself, and then she slept.

She didn't dream; but she thought she heard voices. Her mother was sitting in the next room, talking about ribbons. 'They haven't sent us ribbons, Jack.' She felt like calling out, but she knew that her mother was dead. If she called out, she might wake herself up, and then her mother would vanish. 'Momma?' she mouthed. 'Please don't go.'

The next thing she knew, Jamie was kneeling beside her, and carefully picking her up. She murmured something like, '*Don't . . . evening . . .*' but he lifted her right off the floor, holding her close against his chest. She kept her eyes shut, and she allowed her arm to swing limply, and she continued to breathe with the harsh and regular breathing of somebody who has fallen deeply and abruptly asleep.

But she was quite conscious as Jamie carried her through to the bedroom, and laid her on the bed, where the sheets had already been neatly folded back ready for her. When he laid her on the bed, and covered her up, and leaned over to kiss her goodnight, she half-opened her eyes, and reached out, and clung on to the lapel of his robe.

'Jamie?' she whispered.

'Goodnight, Lucy,' he breathed.

'You're not going?' she said, sleepily.

'I have to. I can't stay here.'

'I'm not asleep yet.'

He squeezed her hand. 'Lucy ... it isn't right. I have to go.'

But through her treacly feeling of drowsiness, Lucy knew that she wanted him to stay with her. She clung tighter to his robe and refused to let go; and when he gently prised her fingers loose, she clung to his cuff with her other hand.

'Stay,' she demanded. She felt quite petulant about it now. He had to stay, he had to hold her, otherwise she would never be able to sleep. There would be two dreadful apparitions trailing their way through her dreams from now on: Uncle Casper, blazing like forty squibs; and her poppa, choke-throated, and stiff with paralysis.

She closed her eyes again, and dozed, but she didn't really sleep. She could feel Jamie sitting beside her on the bed, and staying there, even when she was too tired to keep her grip on his cuff. He waited beside her for what seemed like hours. But when he shifted, even a little, she took hold of his hand, with an even more possessive grip, and mumbled, 'Stay.'

He wasn't to go, she needed him there. Jack was waiting for her, somewhere down in her dreams; Jack and her Uncle Casper. She couldn't face them alone.

Jamie was still sitting beside her when the clock chimed a quarter after one. Then, gradually, she felt him fall sideways, until his head was resting on her hip. She closed her eyes, and the next thing she knew, the clock was striking two, and Jamie was still leaning on her, lightly snoring.

She shook him. 'Jamie? Jamie?'

'*Mmerrh*?' he replied.

'Jamie, get into bed. You're so tired.'

'*Mmhh.*'

The next time she opened her eyes, her bedroom was gradually filling with grainy grey light. She lay back on her pillow, staring at the ceiling. Then she turned her head, so that she could see the carriage-clock beside her bed. Five after seven. She lifted her head from the pillow, and there was Jamie, sprawled all over the other side of the bed, fast asleep, in his green-and-blue Sears Roebuck pyjamas.

She ruffled his hair. Then she kissed his ear. 'Jamie?'

It took him a long time to stir.

'Jamie?' she repeated. 'Jamie?'

He lifted his head and peered at her frowzily. 'Oh crims,' he told her. 'I must have fallen asleep.'

'It doesn't matter. Stop, don't go. It doesn't matter.'

He stared at her for a very long time. 'You're sure?'

She nodded, and smiled. 'Of course I'm sure. It's too late now, anyway. It's gone seven o'clock.'

Jamie sat up, and dry-washed his face with his hands. Neither of them said anything. But then Jamie turned and looked down at her, and said, 'I'm sorry.'

'What for?' she smiled.

'I fell asleep. Now what's your Nora going to think?'

'I don't know. I don't care. She's only my maid. I can dismiss her, you know, if I don't like her.'

'Guess I'm not so used to servants,' Jamie admitted. 'That Nora of yours, she can be pretty intimidating when she wants to be.'

Lucy reached up, and unfastened the top button of Jamie's pyjamas. 'I can sack her, whenever I feel like it.'

Jamie bent over and kissed her forehead. 'I guess you can.'

She ran her fingers into his hair, and she wouldn't let him go. 'I can do anything I like,' she told him. 'I can hire and fire, and who's to say different?'

'Jack?' Jamie suggested.

'Jack? It's not even Jack's money! It's mine! And Jack's not even my father!'

She hesitated, and then she added, 'Even if he was, he still couldn't tell me what to do; nor what not to do.'

She kissed him, forcefully, straight on the lips, but Jamie didn't close his eyes. She kissed him again.

'I love you,' she told him.

'No, you don't. I wish that you did.'

'I love you, simlin-head!'

She crossed her arms, and seized hold of her cambric nightdress, and wrestled it upwards, right over her hips and her breasts and her head, and then tugged it off, and threw it away. Then – naked – she clung close to Jamie, and kissed him, and kissed him again, while he tried to push her away, and to twist his mouth to one side.

At last, lifting himself up, panting, half-laughing, he had to look at her. Her tangled blonde hair, and her tiny pink-nippled breasts. Her narrow hips, and her long, slender legs.

She stared at him. She opened her thighs, on purpose. His eyes glanced sideways, he couldn't help it, then glanced again. She kept on staring at him, wanting him to want her, opening herself up, but irrationally fearful that just one look would reveal to him what Uncle Casper had done to her.

It was a test, a challenge, both dangerous and frightening. Her heart lolloped like a jackrabbit.

With a strangely grave face, Jamie unbuttoned the rest of his pyjama jacket. His chest was deep-tanned and ridged with muscles, from all those growing-up years of farmwork, with just the faintest whorl of dark chest-hair. He was breathing hard. He tugged loose the cord of his pyjama pants, and pulled them down; and up bobbed his penis, rearing out of its nest of hair, thick and knotted and sculptural and already glistening for her.

Lucy swallowed. Her cheeks felt hot, as if she were standing too close to a bonfire. She was so frightened by what she was doing that she closed her eyes. But then she felt Jamie's fingers stroking her cheek, and Jamie's lips kissing her face.

'I dreamed of this,' he murmured. 'You know that? I dreamed of this for years and years.'

She said nothing but, 'Sshhh, don't speak, . . .' and arched her head back on her pillow.

His hands cupped her breasts. They were small enough to fit perfectly into his palms; as if they had grown to just that size especially for him. Her tightened nipple brushed his lifeline. His lips brushed roughly against hers, and then brushed again.

'Jamie,' she said, although she wasn't sure that she had said it aloud.

He knelt between her parted thighs. He still looked so serious; almost reverential. Of course his father had brought him up to respect women and to fear God, and not to sin. With his paired thumbs, he parted the pale pink lips of her vagina, and stared in fascination as a single crystal drop of liquid ran slowly downwards, and disappeared like a lost diamond into the dark cleft of her bottom.

She felt the droplet slide. She looked into his eyes; and saw him smile; but failed to understand that, given the cause, he would have killed for her.

Lucy watched him, hypnotized by the expression on his face, as he raised himself up and pressed the swollen head of his penis between her lips; and then allowed the irresistible forces of gravity and desire to plunge him slowly inwards, until his dark curly hair tangled with her blonde silky hair.

His love-making was quite different from Uncle Casper's frantic coupling. Slow, rhythmic, with kisses and whispers of love. At first Lucy didn't think that it would excite her nearly as much. Perhaps she was a harlot after all, who could only enjoy love if she were forced into it, and degraded. But then the feeling of Jamie's penis pushing in and out of her began to give her a warming, vertiginous sensation that she had never experienced before. She clutched Jamie tight, and kissed and bit his muscular shoulders. And still his penis pushed, and pushed, and seemed to swell larger and larger inside her with every push.

She looked down, and as he half-withdrew, she clearly saw the thick reddened shaft of his penis, with her own petal-like lips moistly clinging to it as if they couldn't bear to let it go. She thought that she had never seen anything so strange or so beautiful. Two people, a man and a woman, actually joined together, one inside the other.

Jamie pushed harder and quicker, and he began to pant. His chest gleamed with sweat, and Lucy could feel the backs of his thighs tensing into knots of muscle. She gripped his buttocks and tugged him into her, deeper and deeper; and still his penis seemed to grow, until she couldn't imagine the size it must be. How could she possibly have room for it? It felt as if it were stretching her wide apart, filling up her whole body.

She felt as if she couldn't breathe. She couldn't even think where she was. She wanted to scream. She wanted to shudder. She wanted to bite him hard. He pushed and he pushed, and then suddenly he said 'Jesus God,' and pulled himself abruptly out of her, and she felt something warm and wet splatter across her stomach and her breasts, and touch her cheek.

Suddenly, everything seemed to have finished. She opened her eyes, and Jamie was kneeling between her thighs, gasping for breath. His penis was already sinking. She touched her cheek with her fingertips, and found that her face had been anointed with something like glutinous milk. There were more drops of it shivering on her stomach, and a drop sliding from her nipple.

Jamie was plainly embarrassed. He picked up one of Lucy's lacy handkerchiefs from beside the bed, and wiped her face, quickly, but with tenderness.

'I'm sorry,' he told her, hoarsely. 'I'm really sorry. I shouldn't have done that.'

She reached up and stroked his cheek. 'I loved it,' she whispered. 'I could do it again and again, for ever, as long as I did it with you.'

He tried to wipe her breast. 'I didn't want to risk you having a baby. That was why I –'

She looked down at herself, and curiously touched the droplets on her stomach. 'Is this what gives you babies? Truly? I somehow imagined you might be able to see them, swimming around. Very tiny, of course. I didn't expect them to be big.'

She frowned at the fluid, and sniffed it. 'What a strange smell it has. Does it really have babies in it? They can't feel anything, can they? It doesn't hurt them?'

Jamie began, 'Didn't your mother –' but then he realized what he was saying, and said, 'It has seeds in it, that's all. Human seeds. They have to be planted before they grow.'

Lucy reached for her nightgown. 'Was it so wrong of us, do you think?' she asked Jamie. 'It *was* wrong, wasn't it?' For some unaccountable reason, she suddenly felt as if she had sinned far more devastatingly than she had with Uncle Casper. She had seen Jamie naked; she had allowed him into her body; she had seen the seeds from which babies are made, and actually touched them. She felt as sinful as Mary Magdalene; but it had felt wonderful, too; and *important*; as important as living, as important as dying. How could anything so wonderful and so important be so sinful?

Jamie buttoned his pyjamas. Then he reached across the silk quilted bedcover and touched her hand. 'It wasn't wrong. God can always forgive human passion, that's what my father always said. Especially since we're going to be married.'

Lucy stared at him. 'Married?'

'We'll have to wait until your father's well enough, of course. We can't become engaged with his permission. I mean, he may not be your real father, but he's your legal guardian, isn't he, and you'll want him to give you away.'

'Jamie –' Lucy began. She loved him; she had adored making love to him; but she couldn't understand how one act of love had already become, in his eyes, a full and formal betrothal.

'We can wait, anyway, can't we, until I've finished my legal business with the Indians?' Jamie told her. 'Besides, we shouldn't make any announcement until Mrs Sweeney has been decently buried and decently mourned. Christmas would probably be the most appropriate time, what do you think?'

Lucy was trying to find the words to tell Jamie that she couldn't possibly think about marrying him; not yet, if ever; when Nora knocked at the sitting-room door.

'Miss Lucy? I've brought your tea.'

Jamie frantically tugged on his pyjama trousers, rolled off the bed, and looked around for somewhere to hide.

'Behind the drapes!' Lucy hissed at him, flapping her hand; and he stepped quickly into the window and wound himself into the heavy yellow velour curtains.

Nora came in directly, carrying a breakfast tray with tea and muffins, and the morning newspapers.

'Good morning, Miss Lucy,' she said, crisply. It was plain by the tight look on her face that she knew very well that Jamie was there. She never usually knocked before she came in; and she usually put down the breakfast-tray and chattered and fussed around opening the drapes and plumping up Lucy's pillows. This morning she set the tray down, arranged the newspapers beside it, and turned immediately to leave.

'There's no word from the hospital yet,' she said. 'But Doctor Crossley will be calling at twelve o'clock, to give us the latest intelligence.'

She hesitated. She was a chapel-goer, she disapproved of shenanigans with men, in fact she disapproved of men altogether, but she was too fond of Lucy to be difficult for very long. 'Perhaps you should look at the newspapers, Miss Lucy,' she said. 'I regret that they're rather on the excitable side.'

'Thank you, Nora,' said Lucy. 'I'll call you when I need you again.'

When Nora had closed the door behind her, Lucy, with shaking hands, picked up *The New York World*. The front-page headline read SOCIETY TRAGEDY AT THE WALDORF! Woman Killed – Oil Parvenu Critically Injured! They Plunge Thirty-Three Feet!

Trembling, she picked up *The Sun*. The headlines were even bolder. THE FATAL FALL! Oil Baron Paralysed, Woman Dies!

Both newspapers recounted every detail of the accident with breathless salacity. 'As they plummeted from the mezzanine, a dread hush fell across the assembled socialites. "Oh God, can no miracle save them!" a bejewelled woman was heard to scream.'

Worse than the sensational way in which the accident was described, however, was the bald statement at the end of the *World*'s article, which said, 'Coroner's Physician Donlin reported that Mr Jack Darling was in a state of acute intoxication, almost to the degree of alcoholic poisoning. In Dr Donlin's expert view, he would have been in no condition to effect a rescue of the late Mrs Sweeney, and his precipitate lunge towards her may even have contributed to her fatal fall.'

Jamie came out from behind the drapes. 'You haven't forgotten me?' he asked her.

She handed him the newspaper, and her eyes were filled with tears. 'They say that it was poppa's fault.'

Jamie studied the article for a moment, and then said, 'That's not true. We know that's not true. She was already falling when he jumped after her.'

225

'But he was drunk, wasn't he? Completely drunk. You can't deny that. And even if we say that it wasn't his fault, who's going to believe it?'

Jamie picked up his robe, and put it on. 'I'll write to the papers myself, and tell them what really happened.'

'Oh, Jamie,' said Lucy, miserably. She felt as if she would never be happy again.

Doctor Crossley arrived at the house just before lunch. He was very clean and dapper, and smelled of peppermints. He sat in the morning room with his case beside him, his hands clasped together just below his breast bone. Lucy sat opposite him, dressed in sober grey silk. Nora had braided her hair for her, and she wore a small black lace cap, fringed with dangling jet beads. In the foggy golden light that penetrated the room she looked far older than her eighteen years, but very collected.

Jamie stood behind her, in a tight off-the-peg suit from Hunt & Maxwell's in Manhattan, Kansas, nervously clearing his throat.

'I saw your father just an hour since,' said Doctor Crossley. 'His condition has not worsened, I am pleased to tell you; although it has not improved. His neck is broken, but this injury is not the direct cause of his paralysis. His tenth and eleventh vertebrae were displaced in the fall, resulting in irrevocable damage to his spinal column.'

'What does that mean?' asked Lucy.

'I am dreadfully sorry, my dear. It means that in common with the consultant surgeon at Bellevue, I have to conclude that your father will never regain any sensation below his chest. In time he will have limited use of his arms, and he will be able to breathe, to eat, and to digest without serious difficulty. However, all remaining bodily needs will have to be catered for by nurses; and he will never again be able to walk.'

Lucy clasped Jamie's hand. 'Oh God,' she said. 'He may as well be dead.'

226

Doctor Crossley shook his head. 'Not at all, my dear; although I quite understand your feeling. Many of the seriously handicapped lead comfortable, pleasant, and even useful existences. At least he will have the use of his hands. He will be able to get about quite nimbly in a wheeled chair.'

Lucy couldn't stop the tears from trickling down her cheeks. 'He's had such a terrible life, he's lost everything he ever wanted; and now this.'

'I will leave you a list of nursing agencies,' said Doctor Crossley. He paused, and then he said, very carefully, 'If I may, I will also recommend another physician.'

'Another physician?' asked Lucy. 'What for?'

Doctor Crossley tried to smile, but couldn't manage it. 'I regret that it will be difficult for me to continue as your doctor.'

'I don't understand.'

'When I took you and your father on to my list this summer . . . well, I may not have explained it very *clearly* at the time, but it could only be on what you might call a stop-gap basis. Now, I regret that the pressures of caring for so many patients has obliged me, well, to *prune* my list somewhat. I'm sure you can understand how sorry I am . . . but, truly, I have no choice.'

He took out a visiting-card, unscrewed his pen, and scribbled a name on to the back of it. 'Here – I'm quite sure that Dr Schumann will give you the greatest satisfaction.'

'But you were recommended by the Scotts,' Lucy protested. 'You were recommended most specifically.' In fact, what Evelyn had said was that 'Doctor Crossley is the *only* doctor in New York. Mrs Astor wouldn't be seen dead with anybody else. How many doctors do you know who spend the summer on E. C. Benedict's yacht?'

Doctor Crossley stood up. 'Of course, Miss Darling, and may I say that I have been honoured to make your acquaintance, and to be of service in some small way to you and your unfortunate father. But it is simply a question of practicality. I cannot effectively see to the needs of more than a hundred patients, especially when all of those patients demand the most personal and considerate attention.

'One of those patients is expecting me even now. My apologies, I really have to hurry.'

He handed Lucy the card with Doctor Schumann's name and address, and bowed his head. Lucy could see that he clipped the hairs in his nose. 'My heartfelt condolences on your tragic loss; my deepest regrets for your unfortunate father. My respects to yourself.'

Lucy tinkled the small silver bell on the table beside her, and Jeremy appeared to see Doctor Crossley to the door.

'May I visit my father?' Lucy asked him, as he sidestepped away.

'Oh – of course,' said Doctor Crossley. 'Any time you wish. At the moment, however, I must warn you – well, he is suffering considerable pain, and may not be in the most amenable of humours.'

'Thank you, doctor,' said Lucy.

'Thank *you*, Miss Darling,' Doctor Crossley grimaced, and left.

Jamie thrust his hands into his pockets. 'Didn't think much of him,' he remarked. 'Seemed to me like he couldn't get out of here quick enough.'

Lucy looked down at the card that Doctor Crossley had given here. Doctor Eli Schumann, 210 West 23rd Street. Not exactly a fashionable address. 'He said he was in a hurry,' she replied.

'There's being in a hurry and there's scurrying off like your tail's on fire,' Jamie replied, with a sniff.

'Oh, you're not familiar with *society*, that's all,' Lucy told him. 'Sometimes people seem like they're being brusque, but that's just etiquette. Evelyn's always telling me that it's ill-mannered to stay too long when you visit; or to behave too familiar. Why, a gentleman shouldn't even take his gloves off unless he's asked. A certain detachment, that's what Evelyn calls it.'

'Well, I don't think much to that, and I still didn't think much to *him*,' Jamie persisted. 'Leaving your gloves on, for pete's sake. Supposing there's a fire in the grate and you're sweating bullets?'

'Jamie,' smiled Lucy. Ever since last night, a new conspiratorial affection had grown up between them. But Lucy still wouldn't talk about betrothal, and whenever Jamie tried, she changed the subject, or thought of something she had to tell Nora, or called for the scullery-maid to bring more coals for the fire.

'You planning on visiting your poppa now?' asked Jamie.

Lucy nodded. 'He's suffered so much. Are you coming with me? We can take him some candy. He has such a sweet tooth for pecan penuche.'

She called for Jeremy to have the brougham brought around; and for Nora to bring her coat. Although Jack had contributed very little to the running of the household, apart from drinking whisky and dropping cigar-ash on the rugs and suggesting now and then that the cook should rustle him up some lamb shanks or pressed veal and horseradish, she felt very much this morning as if she were the mistress of the house. She would have revelled in it, if she hadn't felt so much unhappiness for Mrs Sweeney, and for Jack's accident. But as she waited in the hallway now, with Jamie standing silently beside her, she wondered whether she ought to have felt even more grief than she actually had; because she certainly didn't feel like crying. Perhaps she was shallow and wicked for having taken Jamie as her lover on the very night that Mrs Sweeney had died and Jack had been hopelessly crippled.

But this morning it was difficult for her to feel that Mrs Sweeney had died in any other way except the way that she had always wanted to die, spectacularly, and surrounded by gasping crowds. At least she hadn't died alone and sick, in

Kansas, and in a strange way Lucy could almost feel happy for her. As for Jack – Jack had been blaming himself and punishing himself for so long now that his paralysis seemed like a self-inflicted purgatory which he had deliberately – even hungrily – sought out.

She wondered how her mother would have felt today. Her mother had turned her back on Jack. Had that been easy for her? How much had her mother loved the man who had made her pregnant? Had it been easy to leave him behind?

That morning, as she waited for her carriage in one of the most opulent houses in New York, Lucy began to understand that she had no idea of the nature and measure of human love.

Quite simply, she had never had anybody to show her.

Being rich, Jack was lying in a room of his own at Bellevue, with a view of the East River. The room was whitewashed, and filled with blinding white October sunshine, so that it looked to Lucy as if Jack were already lying in an ante-room to Heaven. There was an overpowering smell of pine tar soap.

Jack's face was drawn tightly over his cheekbones. If she had passed him in the street, Lucy would have found it hard to recognize him. His eyes kept up that constant roaming from side to side that she had first seen when he was lying on the floor of the Waldorf lobby. His neck was supported by a high white celluloid collar, and his skull was wrapped in white bandages.

'Poppa,' she said softly. 'Poppa, it's Lucy.'

He pulled a taut, painful smile, but his eyes kept up their restless wandering.

'How are you feeling, poppa? Doctor Crossley said you were hurting.'

Jamie brought across a bentwood chair, and Lucy sat down beside Jack's bed. She lifted his hand from the knitted cotton bedcover, but it was limp and cold, like a piece of dead pork, and so she lowered it again. 'Poppa? I brought you some candies, some of the pecan penuche.'

Jack nodded. 'They say I can't feel nothing, that's what they say. Broke my back, broke my neck. What *I* said was, if I can't feel nothing, why in hell does it hurt so bad?'

Lucy said, 'Shush now, poppa. Doctor Crossley said you'll soon be better.'

Jack tried to cough, but he couldn't draw enough air into his lungs to clear out his throat. 'Feel like I'm choking, half of the time. I haven't eaten nothing yet, but it's going to be broth for the next few weeks, that's what they told me.'

He glanced at Jamie, and said, 'Is that you, Jamie?'

'Yes, sir,' Jamie told him, his hat in his hands.

'When're you leaving, Jamie?'

'I have to be in Washington by Monday, sir.'

'And then what?'

'Then it's back to Manhattan, Kansas, sir.'

Jack said nothing for a while, breathing harshly. Lucy said, 'We're going to find you a nurse, poppa. Somebody to take care of you every minute of the day.'

'They say I won't walk. Did Doctor Crossley tell you that? Not with my back broke. You don't remember old Dan Leuchars, do you? He was rolled on by a steer, had his back broke, saddest damned man I ever met.'

'Poppa, we're rich; you can have everything you need. Just because you can't walk, that won't mean you have to be unhappy. We can still go out; we can still go to the play; you can still go sailing with all of your friends.'

'Oh, sure enough,' said Jack bitterly. 'Jack the cripple, happy as a sandboy. Do you know what they used to call me at school? Jack-be-nimble, because I could run and jump so good. Now look at me. I should of died.'

His roaming eyes were blotted with bright tears. 'Guess you blame me for Molly Sweeney dying, too. Guess you think that's my fault. But I did what I could to save her. She was falling anyway, I didn't push her or nothing like that. I thought for that moment, I had to fly. *Had* to. Dear God, let me fly!'

Lucy took out her handkerchief and dabbed his eyes. He sniffled, and choked, and then he said, 'God thought different, I guess. "You're not going to fly, Jack Darling, no sir!" God decided in His infinite kindness that He wasn't going to grant me a miracle, not just then. But God alone knows that I did what I could to save her. And I just hope someday before I die that God has the heart to show me why He wasn't going to let me.'

'Poppa, why was it so terribly important?' Lucy begged him. 'I loved her, you know that. But she was old, and she didn't know what she was doing. I guess she thought she was back at the circus. Still young, you know? She was doing what she wanted.'

Jack pulled a face. 'Twinge,' he explained, trying to shift himself in his bed.

'Poppa, *why* did you jump?' asked Lucy.

But Jack began to cough; and wheeze painfully for breath; and to shake his head to show her that he couldn't answer; couldn't even find the air to answer.

'I'd better call the doctor,' said Jamie, and hurried from the room.

Lucy sat beside the bed, clutching Jack's hand, feeling not only powerless to help him, but powerless to understand him. Of all the people in the world she would have expected him to risk his life for, the Skipping Widder was the very last of them. There had never been love lost between them. Lucy remembered Jack calling her 'that boss-eyed old busy-body', and being so rude to her once in the store that her mother had spoken to him sharply about it, and they had argued in front of everybody.

The doctor bustled in, hog-moustached, with a yellow chequered vest, the kind that men wore to go to the track. He was closely followed by a big-faced frizzy-haired nursing sister in a floor-length apron.

'Now then, Mr Darling!' the doctor proclaimed, chafing his hands. 'You've been breathing again! What did I say about breathing?'

'Breathing!' the nurse admonished him.

Even though Lucy insisted that she wasn't hungry, Jamie took her for lunch at Delmonico's; firstly because he had always wanted to lunch at Delmonico's, and secondly because he thought that Lucy was looking pale and faint.

Delmonico's was comparatively quiet today. Outside the window of the main dining room, the trees of Madison Square were rusting sadly with approaching winter. She ate a few spoonfuls of asparagus soup and a small chicken salad, with a glass of sweet white wine. Jamie tried his best to restrain his appetite, but he made short work of the roast ribs of beef, although he wasn't sure if it was manners to pick them up in his fingers.

Jamie talked about going back to Kansas, and how he was planning to take on more work, and make a whole lot more money; and maybe think about politics, too, the state legislature had room for enthusiastic young lawyers. But even though he was talking about himself, it was plain that he was assuming that, by Christmas, he and Lucy would be betrothed, and that, by spring next year at the latest, they would be man and wife.

After all, wasn't it rare enough for a girl to allow a fellow to hold her hand, or to kiss her cheek, let alone encourage him to come into her bed?

In his euphoria, Jamie appeared to have forgotten the manifest difference in their destinies; that she was wealthy now beyond his imagination; that he could never hope to be the master in her house, in the way in which his own father had been master in his. He had forgotten what he had said to her on the beach in Los Angeles, that he could never follow her to New York. No duff, no Turkish delight.

But if Lucy had learned anything at all, it was that

manifest destinies are not to be tampered with; that the gods are not to be challenged. Jamie's cheerful assumption that they would soon be married filled her with a terrifying uncertainty, as if even to mention it would open a trapdoor beneath her feet, and set off another tragedy. She had never felt such panic in her life.

Jamie said, 'Are you all right, sweetheart? You still look pale.'

The restaurant seemed echoing and hot; and there was something about the chinking of forks on plates that Lucy found especially upsetting.

'I don't know,' she said. 'I think I'd like to leave in just a minute.'

Jamie wiped his mouth with his napkin, and smiled at her. 'You're tired, that's all. Yesterday was pretty much of a shock. I could use an early night myself.'

'Jamie —' said Lucy. First pale, she now began to blush. 'What occurred last night . . . between us. I'm sorry, Jamie, I truly am. But it cannot occur again.'

Jamie looked serious. 'Good Lord, Lucy, of course not!' He laid his hand across the table, but she made no move to take it. 'I never expected it to. It was a . . . what could you call it? A gesture. A statement, if you like, of something that we couldn't say in words. A statement of mutual affection. Gee, I wouldn't *expect* it to happen again. Not until we're — well, you know. Not until we're properly together, in the eyes of God, and of the law.'

Lucy didn't know what she could say to him; especially here, in a public restaurant. She toyed with the tiny spoon they had given her to eat her apricot sorbet, and said, 'It's so very soon, that's the trouble.'

She was about to say more; to explain that she hadn't yet seriously considered marriage to anyone at all, not even John T. Hollis who was embarrassingly handsome and scandalously witty and fifty times richer than she could ever be.

But Jamie said, 'I understand, Lucy. I understand!' even

though he couldn't have understood, couldn't *possibly* have understood, because Lucy couldn't even understand it herself. And just at that very moment, she caught sight of Evelyn Scott approaching them across the restaurant, in the company of her mother, and of two elderly but obviously very wealthy ladies, all of them plumed and feathered and with every square inch of sail on; the maitre d' ducking and dipping in front of them like a bow-wave.

'There's Evelyn,' said Lucy, and smiled at the ladies as they came nearer.

To her complete bewilderment, however, the entire party angled their noses very slightly upward and away from her, Evelyn included, and swept past her table, less than three inches away, with a contemptuous whisper of broadcloth and velvet and faille.

Lucy turned around in her chair. '*Evelyn!*' she called, but Evelyn didn't even flinch. The whole party were seen to a table at the back of the restaurant, and surrounded by waiters. They didn't even glance across at her. She might just as well have been invisible and inaudible.

'What's going on?' Jamie wanted to know. 'Isn't she speaking to you, or what?'

'She's my best friend!' Lucy declared. This was nightmarish.

'She's your best friend and she isn't speaking to you? Hasn't she told you why?'

'She hasn't said a word!'

Jamie made a face. 'Whyn't you go across and ask her?'

'I can't!'

'Why not?'

'I can't! It isn't *done!*'

Jamie was unimpressed. 'I don't think it's "done" to go marching past your best friend without so much as a "how-you-keeping?"'

Lucy pressed her hand across her mouth. 'Oh God, what if it's because of last night?'

'I don't get it.'

'What if they're cutting me because of last night?'

Jamie shook his head. 'I can't see how they can blame you for that. It wasn't you that fell off of the mezzanine. And *you* sure weren't drunk.'

Lucy hesitated, her heart beating furiously. 'Go on,' Jamie coaxed her. 'Go on over and ask her. If she was ever a friend worth having, she'll tell you what's what. If she won't, then she's not worth knowing in any case. My father always taught me to face what I feared.'

Lucy lowered her head for a moment. Then she said, 'All right. I'll go.' She placed her napkin on the table, and immediately one of the waiters came across to pull back her chair for her. She stood up; and for the first time she was aware that several of the lunchers gave her a quick, shifty look out of the corners of their eyes, before concentrating too much attention on their plates.

They know, thought Lucy. *They all know. I've been cut, and not even my so-called best friend has had the decency to stand by me.*

She approached the corner table where Evelyn and Mrs Scott and their friends had just been handed their menus. Mrs Scott flickered a quick look at Evelyn, but none of them raised their heads.

'You'll excuse me,' said Lucy, her voice thinner than she wanted it to be. 'But you may be pleased to know that my poppa is recovering tolerably well today, although he is still in great pain, and although he has certainly lost the use of his legs.'

Mrs Scott sighed the sigh of the martyred, and at last looked up. Two stuffed swallows, transfixed in mid-dive by milliner's wire, quivered on the brim of her hat.

'Anyone who wishes to follow your father's misfortunes, Miss Darling, has only to read the yellow press.'

'And that's why none of you will speak to me?' asked Lucy.

'My dear Miss Darling, *all* societies, no matter how primitive, have certain standards of etiquette. It is for their own preservation; and the preservation of those values that are important to them.'

'You mean you're stuck-up,' Lucy retaliated.

Mrs Scott pinched her lips together. 'Our society, no matter what you may think of it, is unusually generous to those whom it welcomes into its embrace. We care not for background, Miss Darling, in this new nation of ours we cannot. But we do care for form; and for decent behaviour. Your father and his elderly lady friend showed neither last evening, and while the consequences of their lapse were tragic, they were also a scandal of the first degree.

'The charity ball was ruined; the charity committee was all but accused by the common newspapers of being a hotbed of drunks and circus-performers; and I can only quote Mrs Astor to you, who said that you may take the people out of the country, but you can't take the country out of the people.'

'Mrs Scott –' Lucy began; but Mrs Scott ostentatiously turned her head away, and presented Lucy with a conclusive view of the back of her hat. Two encircling wings, and a spray of dried flowers.

Lucy was right on the edge of tears. There was plenty that she wanted to say to Mrs Scott about form and decent behaviour, and about country people, too, but she couldn't trust herself not to cry. She looked quickly and hotly at Evelyn, and then went back to Jamie, who was standing waiting for her.

'I want to go now,' she said.

'You're not going to let those biggity old bitches drive you out?'

'I'm going to cry, Jamie, if I stay; and I don't want them to think that they can make me cry.'

'What in heck did they say to you? Are they really going to cut you? Can't you cut them back?'

237

Their waiter came up and asked if anything was wrong. 'Just bring me the check,' Jamie told him; and then to Lucy, 'I could go over there and give them an earful, if that'd do any good.'

'No,' she said. 'It would just make everything ten times worse.'

Jamie escorted her to the cloakroom. 'Well, who needs them, anyhow? If they think they're such big doings, just because they wear all that silk and satin, and they've built themselves an inside biffy.' He deliberately exaggerated his Kansas drawl.

He obviously thought it would make Lucy laugh. But she turned on him with all the fury she could muster up. '*I* need them!' she hissed at him. '*I* need them! They're the only friends I've got!'

Their white-stockinged footman Harry had already unfolded the carriage steps, and Lucy was about to climb aboard when Evelyn came rushing out of the restaurant, holding up her crimson skirts.

'Lucy! Lucy! Please, Lucy, wait!'

Lucy hastily wiped her eyes with her glove, but didn't turn around.

'Lucy,' Evelyn breathed, 'I'm so sorry! I'm really so desperately sorry!'

'And that's the way you show it, by sticking your nose up?' Jamie interrupted.

'Jamie, ssh,' said Lucy.

Evelyn said, 'It's all been so terrible! People have been calling all morning, poor mamma's beside herself! What on earth possessed your poppa to get himself so drunk? And that woman, that poor woman, balancing on the balcony-rail!'

'Just good old everyday country behaviour,' Lucy replied. 'Tell your poor mamma.'

'Oh, Lucy . . . please don't be angry with me. Everybody will forget about it by Christmas. But they must blame somebody.'

'And what am I supposed to do between now and Christmas?' asked Lucy, turning to face Evelyn at last. 'Am I expected to sit alone in my mansion, talking to nobody, going nowhere? Am I still welcome at Mrs Vanderbilt's next week, or would everybody breathe a sigh of relief if I made my excuses?'

Evelyn reddened. 'Well, it really would be better all round if you –'

'Made my excuses,' Lucy finished for her. 'Thank you. I suppose, at least, that you're candid about it.'

'Lucy, mamma's right. There must be rules.'

'Oh, rules,' put in Jamie. 'Rules that ease your conscience when you turn your back on your best friend.'

'Please, Jamie,' said Lucy, touching his arm. 'Evelyn at least has said that she's sorry. Haven't you, Evelyn? Do you remember when Mrs Vanderbilt used to call us Primrose and West?'

Evelyn – who had been Primrose – was watery-eyed. 'I can't help it, Lucy. Mamma's quite furious that I'm talking to you now. And there are so many people who thought suspiciously of you and your poor poppa, right from the very beginning. Mrs Harris, of course. She's never forgiven you for the tennis-net.'

Evelyn paused, trembling, and then she said, 'They were quite prepared to accept you when you could give them harmless amusement. But now they feel that you're threatening them. Now they think that you're going to bring death and drunkenness and tightrope-walking to every party you attend. Lucy, forgive them – they're frightened of you.'

'And you, Evelyn?' asked Lucy. Her face suddenly looked very pretty in the opalescent October light. 'Are you frightened of me, too?'

Evelyn clasped her yellow-gloved hands together, and swallowed. 'Yes,' she whispered. 'I'm frightened of you, too.'

★

On Monday morning, Lucy came down to breakfast to find that only one place was set. 'Is Mr Cullen not having breakfast?' she asked Jeremy.

'Mr Cullen has taken his breakfast already, Miss Lucy,' Jeremy told her. 'He's packed now, and ready to leave.'

Lucy, in a soft billowing dress of blue-and-white striped silk, with a large bow at the back, crossed the polished hallway floor, and her reflection billowed beneath her. She opened the double doors to the morning room, and there was Jamie, sitting at the small French writing-desk, writing a letter.

'You weren't going to leave without saying goodbye?' she asked him.

He looked up, smiled, and shook his head. 'I was just writing down a few sentiments I want you to read once I'm gone. A few thoughts, that's all.'

She approached the desk and stood behind him, holding on to the back of the chair. He seemed to feel uneasy, sitting where he couldn't see her.

'Will you come back here, after you've finished in Washington?'

'I'll try, but I don't think it's likely. Once I get approval to clear those Indians off of that land . . . well, then, the sooner they're off of it, the better the Kansas legislature is going to like it.'

He eased himself around in his chair. 'As soon as all *that's* cleared up, though, I can come back to visit. Just so long as all the restaurant checks don't mount up as high as Delmonico's.'

Lucy stood poised, not knowing what to say; not having the nerve for it; not having the experience for it. Her tongue touched her front teeth, and stayed there, as if she were trying to pronounce the one syllable which would begin her explanation that she loved him, she *loved* him, she knew that she loved him, but that they couldn't marry, couldn't even think of marriage. He would ruin her and worst of all she would ruin him. She was making forty thousand dollars a week; he was making six thousand dollars a year. He couldn't even buy her three spoonfuls of soup and half a chicken salad without repeatedly expressing his disbelief at the size of the check. Seven dollars and fifty-eight cents! Plus tip!

But her tongue-tip remained where it was, pressed against her teeth; and although she knew that it was wrong of her not to speak; although she knew that it was actually *sinful* of her not to speak; she could not speak.

He loved her, and she had nobody else who loved her. She could tell him the truth, the flat truth, flat as a hoecake, that she had made love to him because she had been shocked and lonely and vulnerable, and because she had wanted to expunge the memory of her Uncle Casper. But she knew Jamie too well. If she told him that, he would walk out of here this morning and she would never see him again, never. And her whole world would shrink to just herself; a rich and lonely girl with no family and no friends, in a city that was frightened of her.

Jamie left just after eleven o'clock. The morning was sharp and metallic as a butcher's knife, and her breath smoked as she waved him goodbye from the doorway. The carriage circled around and rattled off on its way to Pennsylvania Station, and she stood for a long time watching it go, rubbing her arms through her thin silk sleeves to keep herself warm.

Eventually, Nora came up behind her, and said, 'The fire in the morning room's burning bright, Miss Lucy. Come along inside.'

Lucy nodded, and came in, and Nora closed the huge door behind her, blotting out the street. They walked together across the hallway.

'He's a fine boy,' Nora remarked; although it was scarcely a maid's place to make remarks of that kind. It was a mark of Lucy's isolation from New York society (which, of course, all of her servants knew about) that she could make it.

241

Lucy said, evenly, 'Yes, he is.'

'He told me –' Nora hesitated, and then she said, 'He told me you were going to be married. You and he. When he's back from the West, that is; and when Mrs Sweeney's been put to her rest; and when all this terrible Waldorf business is forgotten about.'

Lucy stared at her. 'Is that what he told you?'

'Yes, Miss Lucy, that's what he told me.'

'Well,' said Lucy. 'That's as may be.'

'It's not that I meant to be intrusive, Miss Lucy. He volunteered it, as it were.'

'Thank you, Nora, that's all.'

Nora put her head to one side and beamed at her. 'I have to say that I suspected his honour at first, Miss Lucy. But he's a fine boy. Any girl could do worse than him. And so pleasing to look at, too! My mother used to say that husbands should be like views from the kitchen window, always pleasing to the eye.'

'Nora,' said Lucy, and her words came out like chips of ice. 'That will be enough.'

Nora was undeterred. 'It's just advice, Miss Lucy. Sometimes the wisest of heads can do with advice.'

Lucy said nothing, although she was tempted. She and Jamie had spent the quietest and most reserved of weekends together. On Saturday they had taken the carriage over the Brooklyn Bridge, and ended up eventually on the cold beach at Coney Island, where they had walked along the shoreline with the sand whipping their ankles, saying nothing of love or promises, and not even talking of duffs or Turkish delight.

On Sunday they had not gone to church; but prayed at home with the servants, in the living-room, and sung *Rock of Ages*.

Late on Sunday afternoon, as it was growing dark, Jamie had knocked on the door of Lucy's turreted room and found her standing by the window, looking out over the lamplit carriages, and the shadowy trees of Central Park. He had stood a little way away from her, not speaking, and of course there had been no need. They had said everything they needed to say to keep their friendship intact. Anything more would have been dangerous for both of them.

Jamie had asked just one question: 'What will you do when I'm gone?'

Lucy had turned to him with eyes that were almost mauve. 'Wait. Think. Bide my time. What else can I do?'

'You could leave New York. There's always Washington. There's power in Washington, as well as society. There's Denver, too; or San Francisco; or Los Angeles. There's even Chicago.'

'Yes,' Lucy had replied, but her reply had meant nothing at all. She had turned back to watch the firefly lamps of the passing carriages. She had been sad, without tears. She had felt that her present existence was quite empty; as empty as a room. But she had also felt with extraordinary certainty that something new was waiting for her; and she was just as certain now, as she closed the morning-room door.

God may not have granted Jack the miraculous power of flight, as he hurled himself into off the Waldorf balustrade; but He still granted favours to the young, and the innocent, and the very beautiful.

Three weeks passed. October died; and November blew away its ashes. Mrs Sweeney was buried on a sharp sunny day with the soil so hard that the gravediggers had to be tipped extra. The priest said that she had danced, and because she had danced, she was blessed. Only Lucy and Nora and the rest of the servants attended the funeral. They wore black coats and black plumes, and carried black prayerbooks. The hearse stood in the background with its nodding, patient horses like a pen-and-ink drawing. Mrs Sweeney had no surviving relatives that anybody knew of. A bearded artist from the *New York World* sketched Lucy as she dropped a

243

rose on Mrs Sweeney's casket, and the subsequent engraving appeared on the front page of the following day's paper, with the caption Shunned Millionairess Pays Last Respects To Tragic Childhood Dance Teacher.

After the funeral, Lucy visited Jack at Bellevue. His face had the look of sodden newspaper, grey, semi-transparent, slimily breakable. He was sleeping, mumbling, and occasionally weeping. The doctor with the hog-moustache and the racetrack vest was loath to make book on his chances. The nurse with the big face kept pushing gruel into his mouth, but all of it slid unswallowed on to his pillow.

'Jack?' Lucy whispered, but hopelessly; because his eyes kept roaming and he wasn't speaking any kind of sense any more. 'Jack, it's Lucy.'

That was all she said until it was time to leave. Then she clutched his dead-meat fingers and softly raged at him, 'Why did you do it? Why did you do it? Why? Why did you have to fly?'

The big-faced nurse was standing by the door watching her. Lucy pressed Jack's hand carefully back on to the bedcover, as if she had been caught trying to steal it. She stood up and tried to smile but discovered that she couldn't. The big-faced nurse remained in the doorway, and wouldn't stand aside as Lucy squeezed her way past. Lucy wondered what Jack might have been telling her.

'Goodbye,' she said, with a break in her voice.

The big-faced nurse watched her walk along the corridor, and was still staring at her as she reached the stairs.

When she came home from the funeral the young man was still waiting for her in the hall. He was rather wan, with a snubbish nose and polished brown hair thick with dandruff, and a lumpy frock-coat that seemed to be two-and-a-half sizes too large for him. He stood up as Lucy came in, and said, in a very swallowed English accent, 'Miss Darling?'

'Yes?' said Lucy.

'He's brought you a letter,' said Jeremy, as a grumbled aside.

'Miss Darling, I'm very gratified to make your acquaintance. My name's Clive Mallow, from the India Office.'

'The India Office?' asked Lucy.

'In London, Miss Darling. I'm a civil servant. I have a letter for you. I was charged to deliver it personally, by hand.'

He closed his mouth tightly, and stuck out his hand, and offered Lucy a large white letter. Lucy glanced at Jeremy, and then accepted it, and read the envelope. It was addressed in the firmest, most elegant handwriting, in purplish ink, to her; *Miss Lucy Darling, New York.*

She knew who had sent it at once. But she walked across the hallway, into the morning room, and opened it there, with the gold letter-opener that Jack had bought from Tiffany.

St Ermin's Mansions, SW,
October 1, 1894.

My own dear Lucy,

I apologize profusely for not having written to you sooner, but I have been travelling widely on affairs of study and affairs of Parliament, and this is the first opportunity that I have had to invite you and your father to visit me in England.

Of course I have no idea whatever if you have already made arrangements for the Festive Season, but if you would care to come over for Christmas and the New Year, I would be delighted to entertain you both at Brackenbridge, where we always have the most wonderful celebrations. We invariably eat until we explode, and spoil our guests with far too many presents.

My dear, while this letter may sound jovial, I have missed you with all my heart since I left, and have sat down several times to write to you, telling you of my travels, and of my feelings. But each time I have destroyed what I have written, because it has sounded far too maudlin.

Please write back just as quickly as may be, and tell me that you will be able to gladden my Christmas with your presence. I dispatch this letter with a kiss. No, not a singular kiss, a crowd of kisses, a bewildering sequence, an ardent succession, an ecstatic pell-mell!

Your
Henry

Lucy turned back towards Clive Mallow and her eyes were shining.

'Good news, I trust?' he asked her, although he must already have known what Henry's letter said.

'Yes,' she replied. 'Good news.'

5

Alfred George, 4th Baron Felldale, Henry's father, marched ahead of them through the fog, thrashing his knobby walking-stick, and shouting obscenities at his Dalmatians, a crowd of obscenities, a bewildering sequence. He was sixty-six, and the father not only of Henry, but of eleven other children besides, four boys and seven girls, and he daily took brandy and eggs for breakfast, but he kept up a cracking pace through the desiccated bracken, and was obliged several times to stop and wait for them, sniffing and saying, 'Come along, now, come along, now, plenty more to see.'

The 4th Baron wore a billycock hat, and a huge chequered cape. His eyes were bulbous, a little like Henry's, and his muttonchop whiskers were brambly and vividly white. His boots were wet and very muddy. Unlike Henry and Lucy, he didn't care a damn where he walked.

'You get a fine view of the lake from here,' he told Lucy,

loudly. 'At least you do when it's not quite so foggy. Here, Willy, you disobedient bugger!'

Henry walked close beside Lucy, his hands clasped behind his back. He wore a plain grey coat and a grey gamekeeper's cap. His cheeks were pale and his nose was pink from the cold; but he was still just as handsome as Lucy remembered him. She was wearing a beautifully-cut overcoat of raspberry-coloured tweeds, and a velvet bonnet with a silver brooch and pheasants' feathers.

'My father loves Brackenbridge,' Henry remarked, his breath fuming in the fog. 'He feels the very fibre of it with every step! Do you know that Dr Johnson came here once, with Boswell, in the time of the 1st Baron Felldale. Johnson didn't care for it much, or he claimed that he didn't. He said that it would have made a handsomish town hall, but not much else. I don't think my ancestor ever forgave him.'

They passed through a row of massive and ancient oaks, and now, through the sun-gilded fog, Lucy could dimly see the classical outlines of Brackenbridge itself. It was a huge, pale, Palladian house, with hundreds of faintly-glittering windows, and two curving staircases that swept down in front of it with all the grace of a ballet-dancer's arms.

In the chill of late November, the surface of the artificial lake in front of the house looked like a breathed-over mirror; but ducks still swam across it, leaving ripples behind them that caught the sun, and sparkled.

Leading down to the lake was a series of white marble steps: a classical cascade which Henry had been working on.

'This house means everything to me,' said Henry. 'It is romantic, historic, and noble. It runs through my life like a shining thread. Do you know something, when I was only eight, I was furious with my sisters for cluttering up the Adam fireplaces with their little ornaments, because it spoiled their classic lines.'

'I don't suppose your sisters cared much for that,' smiled Lucy.

Henry obviously didn't understand that she was joking. 'Those who strive to uphold the finer things in life are never popular.'

Lord Felldale had made his way down the hillside towards the house, and had almost reached the lake. His Dalmatians went bounding after him, like nursery rocking-horses. 'Come along, Jumper, you stupid sod! Billy! If you chase those ducks again, I'll damnwell gut you!'

'Your father's a hot potato,' Lucy remarked.

'The Carsons always have been,' Henry told her. 'It runs in the blood. Can't stand to be idle, that's the thing.'

Lucy lifted the hem of her coat to keep it clear of the long wet grass. As she started to walk down the hill, Henry said, 'I haven't had an awful lot of experience with women.'

Lucy stopped, and turned. He had remained for a moment in the foggy green shadow under the oaks, but then he emerged into the pearly-grey brightness and stood very close to her. 'I've travelled, yes; twice around the whole world; and I've made my name in politics; and when we see an end to this miserable Liberal government, which we most assuredly will, I know that I will be called upon to do great things. At least my friends expect me to, and so does the Press. But in front of you, I find myself tongue-tied. What can I say to you, except that you quite captivated me, right from the second I first saw you, and that nobody fairer of face or brighter of heart has ever walked the grounds of Brackenbridge, nor ever will?'

Far from being tongue-tied with her, Henry appeared to Lucy to be immensely talkative. He talked incessantly – about British policy in India, about the restoration work at Brackenbridge, about writers that he knew, about art, about the Persians, about Lord Rosebery and the Liberals, about food, about money, about servants, about living in London. He told her jokes and anecdotes; he described his arduous travels in Persia, and how (sick from exhaustion and self-neglect) he had subsequently gone to convalesce in Athos and Meteroa. 'I was hauled up hundreds of feet of rock face, like a trussed quail in a net, to look at the vinegar and sponge that were offered Christ upon the Cross.'

It was possible, however, that he found it difficult to talk to Lucy about matters of the heart. He had asked his father to take them out on this walk on purpose, so that he could speak to her privately, with all of the glories of Brackenbridge held up grandly and temptingly in front of her; for all that Brackenbridge was not yet his.

But now he had to talk about his feelings; about his real emotions; and there was no sharp anecdote to fit.

There was a very long pause. Lord Felldale, who was now skirting the lake, suddenly stopped, and shielded his eyes with his hand against the foggy glare, and stood watching them for two or three minutes before he shouted at his dogs, 'bastards! buggers!' and continued his walk back to the house.

'Do you love me?' asked Lucy.

Henry took off his cap. 'My dearest Lucy, I feel like such an amateur. I want you to be my wife.'

Lucy smiled, and said, *hmh!* just to tease him. Without even waiting for an answer, Henry looked away, and slapped his cap against his coat, and protested, 'It's no use at all. I simply can't find the right words. It was love at very first sight, Lucy! The instant I saw you walking across that tennis-net, you snatched my heart and you squeezed it in that little fist of yours, and you have never once let it loose. I want you to marry me. In May, my dearest, when the buds are out. Here – at Brackenbridge, in the family chapel.'

He unbuttoned his brown leather glove, and tugged it off, and offered Lucy his bare right hand. She lowered her eyes for a moment. He had amused and embarrassed her; but at the same time she felt extraordinarily meek and feminine. She had always been wilful. She had always teased the boys that she had known; especially the shy and the lovestruck boys; and even Jamie. But somehow she realized that Henry was not to be teased. For all of his apparent shyness with her, Henry was iron-willed and determined that he should have her.

'Of course,' Henry added, 'you don't have to decide anything directly. You can think about it for as long as you wish, although the sooner you make up your mind, the happier you will make me.' He didn't seem to have considered the possibility that she might refuse him.

He turned around and stared for a while at the ghostly views of Brackenbridge, and its woods, and its spectral lake. 'I can't offer you very much, my dearest. None of *this*, at the moment; although we can come here as often as you wish, and one day, God preserve my dear father, it all shall be mine. All I can lay at your feet at this particular moment is my Parliamentary stipend, which will hardly keep you in emeralds, and my book royalties, which were not much more than £34 last year. But – ' and here he lifted a single finger, and smiled at her triumphantly, ' – I can certainly offer you glory.'

Lucy had never been offered glory before. She wasn't even sure what it was. She had been offered money, and fun, and a great deal of undying passion, of one kind or another, but never glory.

She said, uncertainly, 'You'll have to give me time to think about it.'

Henry grasped her hand. 'You're cold! We'd better get back. But you won't keep me waiting, will you? As soon as I saw you disembark from the ship, I knew that I hadn't made a mistake. You're quite perfect, my dearest; in looks and in temperament. To have you as my wife would be the crowning achievement of my life.'

They walked down the hill together towards the lake – close, but not holding hands. Lord Felldale had already packed off his Dalmatians to the kitchens for a meaty bone, and he would be going upstairs to change now, and take his bath, before coming downstairs to the drawing room, for tea and scones, and a noisy half-hour snore in front of the fire.

'When do you have to go to London?' Lucy asked Henry.

'Tomorrow morning, I regret. It won't be for long. Two days at the very most. Next Saturday I wish to take you to see the dearest friend of mine, Margie Asquith. You and she will make such friends!'

They had crossed the wide shingled driveway, and reached the foot of the curving stone steps, when Lucy stopped, and said, 'Henry – I'm none too sure about this.'

'But my dearest Lucy, what is there not to be sure about? My God, look at this! This driveway hasn't been weeded in a month of Sundays.' He bent over and plucked up two or three tiny clumps of grass, and a straggling dandelion.

'Henry, all of my money came by chance. I wasn't highly born, I didn't work for whatever I got. I was rich by accident, and nothing else.'

'I know that,' said Henry, levelly, watching her, still holding the weeds in his hand. 'I know that, and it really doesn't matter two hoots.'

Lucy covered her eyes with her raspberry-gloved hand. 'I'm not too sure what I'm trying to say to you, Henry. I think I'm trying to tell you that I'm not very well learned, and so you soon might find me very uninteresting to talk to. I think I'm trying to tell you, too, that I wasn't naturally bred to manners, so no matter how much I learn, not to mix the fish-knives with the cake-forks, there could always come times when I let you down. I guess I'm trying to tell you that I'm frightened.'

'Lucy –' said Henry, warmly, and reached out to hold her hand.

'It's true!' she protested. 'You meet the Queen, and lords, and all kinds of aristocracy. You're going to be a lord yourself one day. You said yourself, you talked to the what's-his-name of Afghanistan, just like you'd played cricket together. I was born and raised a storekeeper's daughter in

No-Place-At-All, Kansas, and educated with chalk and black-board, and you and me just aint suited.'

Henry stared at her, stiff and expressionless. Then his face gradually cracked into a smile. 'Say that again,' he coaxed her.

She didn't understand. 'All of it?'

'No, no, just the last bit, *please*, when you said that you and me just aint suited.' His accent was so clipped that, to Lucy's ears, he sounded hilarious, like a gobbling turkey.

'You and me just aint suited,' she repeated, in fullblown High Plains whirligig Kansas.

'Again!' Henry begged her, with glee.

'Yewnme jessayn sootud.'

Very slowly, very precisely, Henry tried to imitate her accent. 'You-en-me, jist, aint, sewted. Ha! ha! Is that it!? You-en-me jist ent-sewted.'

'No!' Lucy giggled. 'Not sewted! *Sootud*! Yewnme jessayn sootud.'

Henry, without warning, took her into his arms, and held her much closer and tighter than was usually respectable. He stared at her very steadily, and said, 'You're wrong, Lucy Darling. Yewnme, we're sootud excellently!'

'An awfully lot, that's what we say in Kansas, when we're trying to be posh.'

'All right, then. We're sootud an awfully lot.'

Lucy looked into his eyes for a moment, and then gently pushed him away.

'There's nobody else?' he asked her.

She shook her head. 'There's nobody else.'

'Then please consider marrying me, Lucy; and please don't keep me waiting for too long. We've both been waiting far too long for each other already. Yes, my dearest, I know! It's been my fault, not yours! But I've written you so many poems, although I haven't dared to send them to you, and I thought about you every day, and everywhere I went, even in the castle of Baltit, when I was guest of the

Thum of Hunza, on my way to the high Pamirs, I thought of you, and spoke your name; and when I became the first known traveller to climb behind the glaciers of the Pamirs, and see the head waters of the Oxus, I whispered your name to the wind there, too.'

Self-satisfied, almost smug, he turned around, smiling, and clapped his hands together. ·

'Don't you *understand?*' he asked her. 'The name of Lucy Darling has been spoken in places where no man had ever been before, nor may ever go again; and if that isn't proof of the intensity of my affections for you, my dearest, then I cannot think what may be.'

Lucy stared back at him wide-eyed, and couldn't think what to say. Her feelings wobbled like a spinning-top. She was flattered – yes; exhilarated – yes; and she thought that Henry was everything that she could possibly want. Ever since she had received his invitation to come to England, she had known that she was going to say yes to him. But now she was terrified that he was far too much for her; that she would never be able to please him. Lucy had seen her own small share of the world. She had clung tight to fenceposts, deafened, while cyclones bath-watered their way across black Kansas skies. She had yachted with millionaires and lunched with visiting princes. She had danced along Fifth Avenue in the middle of the night, in a white silk ballgown. She had crossed the Atlantic on a German steamer (vomiting, most of the time, most dreadfully sick). But what was any of that, compared with what Henry had done?

Henry had been to Persia and China and India and places that most people had never heard of, like Chitral and Mastuj and Bozai Gumbaz.

Henry had hobnobbed with potentates. Henry had taken tea with Queen Victoria, and advised Her Majesty on the manners of the Persians. ('No manners, ma'am.')

Although Lucy had arrived at Brackenbridge only yesterday afternoon, Henry's abrasive energy and unstoppable outpourings of knowledge and wit had already made her feel that it might have been better for both of them if she hadn't come at all.

A summer flirtation on Rhode Island was one thing. But a serious proposal of marriage in the Derbyshire countryside, in winter, was quite another.

For goshsake, Henry knew French and Italian and classical Greek; he could quote foreign sonnets by the tailor's yard; he wrote articles and poems and worked furiously at his desk from first light until lunchtime; and his lamp was always burning until well after midnight, every night. As far as Lucy could make out he was expert at absolutely *everything*, from the plastering restoration in Brackenbridge's great gallery, to the political future of India, to what the cook was preparing for lunch.

This morning, Henry had been outraged when the kitchen-maid had come up with a suggested luncheon menu of lobster mayonnaise and cold rabbit pie. 'On a raw, chill day like this? You must be losing your senses!'

Lucy was excited and desperately flattered that he should have asked her to marry him. He was handsome, he was strong, he had offered her glory. Not only that, if she were to marry Henry Carson, the shameful shenanigans at the Waldorf would be expunged for ever. She would be able to step back into society; she would shine with even more social incandescence than before. Her only reservation was whether she could manage the task of being his wife. A girl who knew nothing about politics of any kind; a girl whose knowledge of society was limited to one summer season on Rhode Island, and a few months of dancing and theatre-going in New York?

What was more, she would have to live in England; and England seemed like such a damp and suffocating place, with stunningly offensive drains and air like a cold wet quilt. Nobody was welcoming or pleasant. The customs officers at Liverpool had rummaged through her trunks for hours, and reduced Nora's immaculate packing to a blizzard of tissue paper and crumpled dresses. The fat-legged maid who had taken Lucy up to her room at Brackenbridge had said, accusingly, 'Tha'll be axing for hot water, I don't suppose?' – an unmistakable warning that hot water was a nuisance, because hot water had to be fetched.

'Lucy – you will try to be quick, coming to your decision?' Henry insisted, with impatience.

'Have you asked poppa?'

'Indeed I've *tried*.'

'What did he say?'

Henry made a face. 'To be truthful, my sweet, I'm not altogether sure. He sang me a sort of song.'

Lucy tried to smile, but she found it difficult. Henry was not at all abashed by Jack – Jack with his fits and his roaming eyes, all bundled up in his invalid–chair like a huge and helpless infant. Henry was used to madness and senility. But Lucy found Jack an embarrassment, and a terrible burden, too – and in some ways worse than a burden, because he reminded her every time she looked at him of Uncle Casper's viciousness and her mother's unfaithfulness, and the enigma of her own birth. *Whose little girl are you, Lucy Darling?* Jack's eyes always asked her, helplessly; and how she hated those eyes.

Lucy said, 'Poppa's been worse, these past two days. He's probably tired.'

'Perhaps I ought to let Dr Roberts take a look at him,' Henry suggested. 'He's very modern, Dr Roberts, trained in Vienna. He did wonders for father's liverishness. Gave him Kissingen salts, and some kind of electrical treatment on his skin.'

Lucy asked, 'Is that all that poppa did? Sing for you?'

Henry nodded, obviously amused. 'It was something about dancing. "Swing them up, swing them down."'

'Swing them pretty girls round and round,' Lucy finished.

'You know it,' said Henry.

255

'Yes.'

Henry hesitated for a moment, and then cleared his throat. 'I love you, my darling; you have quite changed the way that I think. I used to believe that celibacy was the only sensible way of life; and that marriage was a puzzle. Now it seems as if it is celibacy that is a puzzle, and that marriage will provide me with the answer to everything.'

'Just give me a little time, Henry,' Lucy begged him.

'Thank you, my dearest, I will,' Henry replied; although he was plainly disappointed. 'But you won't keep me waiting for too long, will you?'

It was raining hard the next morning when the station fly was brought around to take Henry to Derby. Lucy stood in the high-pillared portico in her high-necked plum-coloured dress, and waved to him with her handkerchief. She felt like a character out of Jane Austen (she had found the author's early work, *Love and Friendship* in her bedroom). Henry lifted his hat to her and called, 'You will think very hard, won't you, my darling child? And you will try to say yes?'

The fly scrunched off across the wet shingle. Brackenbridge had taken on an exceptionally dismal cast today, with the rain driving through the oak trees and lashing at the laurel bushes around the house, and cascading noisily from the gutters. A stablehand walked across the driveway with a sodden coat over his head, leading behind him a large bay mare, her blanket black with rain.

Tessie, the disagreeable fat-legged maid, was waiting for Lucy when she came back into the hallway. 'Dr Roberts will be calling to see your father this morning, miss,' she said. 'Will you see him in the morning room, or in the library?'

Lucy was surprised. 'I don't know,' she said. 'Mr Carson didn't even mention to me that he was coming.'

Tessie sniffed. 'Well, *that* don't surprise me one bit. That's Mr Carson all over, that is. Arranges owt, but never tells nobody nowt.'

'Well, if he's arranged it – I guess, yes. We'll see the doctor in the morning room.'

'The morning room, miss. Very well, miss.'

Lucy would have done anything to have Nora with her now – even fussy, inquisitive Nora. But on their way from New York she had allowed Nora to disembark at Dun Laoghaire, in Ireland, so that she could visit her family in County Carlow. Nora hadn't seen her grandmother since she was three years old, when her father and mother had taken their nine children across to America. She would be coming to Brackenbridge to join Lucy just after Christmas, but at the moment Lucy felt as if she had no friends at all, nobody with whom she could talk about her feelings for Henry, no matter how obliquely. Jack had grown more and more morose and uncommunicative with every passing day, and Mary – the nurse whom Lucy had employed in New York to take care of him during their journey to Europe – had turned out to be so long-suffering and martyred that Lucy scarcely dared to speak to her.

If Lucy had asked Mary whether she should marry Henry or not, Mary would most likely have said, 'Don't ask *me* such a question. I was never asked to marry by anyone.'

Lucy went through to the morning room, where Mary was reading Jack a tract about the evils of travelling on a Sunday. Jack was lying back in his invalid-chair at an odd angle, his head half-propped on a stained needlepoint cushion, his eyes furiously roaming from side to side. Although he was sitting close to the fire, he was wrapped up head to toe in a large green blanket, and this blanket had been strapped around his waist with a leather belt. He was startlingly white, and he smelled of vinegar and urine, and something else, like cabbage that isn't quite fresh.

Mary looked up. She was Lithuanian by birth, gargoyle-like to look at and professionally despairing. She wore a nurse's cap of her own devising, which looked rather like a deep-sea fisherman's hat, in thick brown felt; and a coarse beige linen apron. Her eyebrows met thickly in the middle, and one of her cheeks was semi-circled with a bright crimson scar, where, during her public nursing days, a patient at Bellevue had attempted to kill her with a broken iodine bottle.

'Mary, did you know that Mr Carson had arranged for a doctor to visit Mr Darling?' asked Lucy.

Mary said, 'He did mention it, Miss Darling.' She had an odd, reflexive accent, that always sounded to Lucy like somebody talking backwards. 'Darling Miss, it mention did he.' There was an expression on her face that showed she was well-prepared to be sullen.

'I mean, you don't *mind* if a doctor comes to take a look at him?' asked Lucy.

'Not my position to mind, Miss Darling. This is Mr Carson's house, if Mr Carson wishes to send for the doctor, then who am I to say no?'

'He's supposed to be very up-to-date, this doctor.'

'I'm sure that he is, Miss Darling. But that won't make my duties any less burdensome, will it? And if I know doctors, and I *do* know doctors, he'll give me more to do than ever. "Now, then, nurse, make sure you cup the patient four times the day, and dose him up with Vichy salts eight times the day." It's always the nurse that suffers the extra work.'

Lucy sat down on the opposite side of the fireplace. 'I'm sure there won't be any extra work, Mary. If this doctor can make poppa just a little better, you might even have *less* to do.'

'Well that's the unlikeliest story I ever heard,' said Mary, gloomily.

'I'm just surprised that Mr Carson forgot to tell me he was coming, that's all,' Lucy replied.

'Has Mr Carson gone for long?' Mary wanted to know.

'No, no. Two days, that's what he told me. He had some important business, he couldn't get out of it. Something to do with Parliament.'

'I suppose he will travel back on Sunday,' Mary remarked. She shook her head and her huge brown hat flopped from side to side. 'What godlessness.'

Lucy looked across at Jack, but made no effort to speak to him, or to catch his attention. He lay tilted in his invalid-chair with his eyes darting around in his face like flies around a milk-pudding, and nobody could guess what he was thinking, if he was thinking anything at all.

Mary took out her noisy pocket-watch, ignoring the gilded clock above the fireplace. 'I will bathe him after the doctor has gone; and he can wait for his syrup of poppies, too.'

Without saying anything else, she lifted the pamphlet in her lap, and continued to read, 'Sunday travelling, encouraged by specially low prices, is a great evil. It encourages idleness, and the use of bad tobacco, bad drink, bad language, and bad company, while the profits go to the railway company.'

It was impossible to tell if Jack was listening or not. He appeared to Lucy to have hidden himself somewhere inside his own head – to have shut himself tightly in some dark cupboard without pain or memories or hopelessness.

'We'll be visiting London ourselves next week,' said Lucy, interrupting Mary's reading. 'Mr Carson has promised to take me to see the sights.'

'I hope that your father will be well enough to travel,' Mary replied, threateningly. 'In my opinion, it was ill-advised to bring him all the way to England; and in such rough weather.'

Lucy didn't answer. They had argued about this before. Lucy wouldn't have brought Jack to England at all, but propriety had demanded it and Henry had insisted. He didn't want to compromise Lucy's reputation or his own Parliamentary career by entertaining her at Brackenbridge for the whole of the Christmas season, unchaperoned, particularly since he intended to announce at the end of her stay that they would be married in the spring.

The London newspapers were far more discreet than Hearst's and Pulitzer's rags in New York, but there would have been smiles and raised eyebrows and a few 'aye-ayes' among Henry's Oxford set, and at the India Office, and even at Marlborough House, and Henry could not bear to be thought of as anything but spotlessly honourable, in particular when it came to women.

Besides, Henry believed that a change of scenery would do Jack some good; lift his morale; show him that life could still be interesting and profitable; and quicken his convalescence. With any luck, he could be out of plaster by Christmas.

For Lucy, the journey to England would have been heaps more fun if she could have brought Evelyn instead; or any of her erstwhile New York friends. But the six or seven telephone calls that she had made to the Scott mansion the week before she left New York had been stuffily rebuffed by the butler's 'not at home, Miss Darling, I regret,' and it had been the same story at the McPhersons and the Vanderbilts and the Frosts. None of her friends had come to wave her goodbye, even though her departure for England on the *Fürst Bismarck* had been announced in the social columns.

Mary closed her pamphlet. 'He is worse every day, your father. He used to speak just a little. Now he does not speak to me at all. I never know what he requires. I never know when he feels hungry; or when he feels thirsty; or when he wishes me to read; or when he wishes me to stop reading. I never know when he wishes to sleep. I never know when he wishes to wake up. It really is intolerable. I have always thought that patients have an obligation to their nurses to show a little consideration.'

She was still complaining when Tessie came into the morning room to say that Dr Roberts had arrived. Lucy asked her to show him in and Mary turned her head away.

Lucy didn't know what she had been expecting from Henry's 'up-to-date' doctor. An excitable young man with spectacles and wild hair, she supposed. But when Dr Roberts appeared in the doorway – extremely tall, extremely handsome in rather a satanic way, with black hair combed back from his forehead and slightly greying sidewhiskers, and lips that seemed to be curled up at the thought of all the mischief that doctors could get up to, if they chose, Lucy stood up quickly and said, 'Oh!' as if she had been caught in the act of doing something she shouldn't.

'My apologies,' said Dr Roberts, in one of the deepest voices that Lucy had ever heard. 'I had no intention of startling you. You must be Miss Darling. Dr William Roberts, at your service.'

He took Lucy's hand. There were dark circles under his eyes, as if he rarely slept. 'Mr Carson explained that your father had accidentally fallen, and broken his spine.'

'It happened in New York, two months ago now. He's still in plaster; but his doctors said it wouldn't hurt him to travel. They said it might cheer him up.'

'Which, quite manifestly, it has not,' remarked Dr Roberts, turning towards Jack and removing his gloves.

'He is worse than ever,' Mary volunteered. 'He never speaks, he never tries to feed himself. These days I am not very much better than his slave.'

'Who is this person?' asked Dr Roberts.

'My father's nurse Mary,' Lucy explained.

Dr Roberts approached Jack; leaned forward, and stared him closely in the face. 'Well, Mary,' he said, without looking at her, 'a nurse in a sense is always a patient's slave. She must give of herself without asking what is the cost. She must be gentle and attentive at all times, and think of nothing but her charge's welfare.'

Mary glanced indignantly at Lucy, her eyebrows dense, her mouth puckered.

'What is your father's name?' asked Dr Roberts.

Lucy came forward and stood beside him. 'It's Jack,' she said, quietly. 'He's not dying, is he?'

Dr Roberts ignored that question. Instead, he lifted Jack's eyelid with his thumb and watched his eyeball coursing from one side to the other. 'Jack?' he called him. 'Jack, can you hear me? I'm a doctor.' He asked Lucy, 'Can he normally speak? I mean, he's spoken since his accident?'

'He is play-acting, if you ask me,' Mary put in. 'Trying to win himself some sympathy.'

'I did not ask you,' Dr Roberts squashed her. He stood up straight again, frowning. 'What medication do you give him?'

'Something for the pain, that's all,' said Lucy.

'Laudanum,' Mary explained.

'How much laudanum, and how often?'

'As much and as often as he needs.'

'What is that unpleasant smell?' asked Dr Roberts.

'I was waiting until you saw him before I gave him his bath,' Mary explained.

'When was his last bath?' Dr Roberts wanted to know.

Mary was silent.

'When did you last bathe him?' Dr Roberts demanded.

'I could not say for sure. Not too many days ago. He complained the last time that it hurt him, so I left it for a while. It was his own wish.'

'I presume that he isn't continent?'

Mary shook her head.

'What does he eat? What does he drink?'

'Well,' said Mary, 'porridge mostly, and water. He cannot trouble himself to chew anything solid. He asks for a whisky now and again, but I do not like to give it to him, not while he's so sick.'

Dr Roberts unbuckled the belt that held Jack's blanket in place. He lifted one corner of the blanket a little, peered inside, sniffed, then dropped it again.

'Miss Darling?' he said, turning towards her.

Lucy had just lifted her hands to rearrange the dried flowers on the mantelshelf. She could see by Dr Roberts' face that something was badly amiss.

'I'm afraid it looks to me as if your father is in a very grave condition,' he said. 'You ought to leave the room. Perhaps you would be good enough to arrange for a carriage, so that your father can be taken to the hospital.'

'What's wrong with him?' asked Lucy. She felt a sudden cold sensation of panic. Ever since his accident, she had secretly prayed that Jack would die; she had believed with all of her heart that he would be better off dead. But now that Dr Roberts was looking at her with such dreadful gravity, she couldn't bear to hear what he was going to say. Jack might be better off dead, but if he were dead, then Lucy would have nobody.

Dr Roberts said, 'I have to examine your father thoroughly. You ought to leave the room. Please. This, er – this *nurse* can stay and help me.'

Lucy swallowed. Then she nodded. 'Very well. I'll ask for a carriage. Is the hospital very far?'

'Not quite twenty miles. But he has to go. He may very well need surgery.'

Lucy left the room without another word and closed the doors behind her. Tessie was crossing the hallway, and she stopped. 'Miss Darling? Are you all right?'

'Yes,' Lucy whispered. 'Could you ask the coachman to bring a carriage around?'

She took three steps forward across the hallway and her eyes switched off and her knees buckled underneath her. She heard Tessie crying out; she heard her own dress whooshing as she fell. She knew that she had cracked her head on the marble as she collapsed, but she was surprised to discover that it didn't hurt at all.

She opened her eyes and a dark man with glittering black eyes and a cleft chin was looming over her. She didn't feel afraid of him, but she was curious to know why he was here, in her bedroom. And why was he staring at her so intently? His chin was very dark, as if it had been rubbed with lampblack. She couldn't think why any man should want to rub his chin with lampblack.

She said, 'Lampblack. Why?'

The man abruptly turned away from her. A woman with a dying bird on her head was standing by the door. The room was so gloomy that Lucy could barely see. She heard a noise like somebody tossing gravel against the window, and then a roll of drums.

The dark man turned back to her. 'Miss Darling?'

She was recovering consciousness very quickly. She began to understand that the gravel against the window was rain; heavy rain; and that the drums were thunder. She recognized the woman with the dying bird on her head as Mary, Jack's nurse, and she recognized the dying bird as her nurse's hat, not a dying bird at all. But she still didn't understand who the man was, or what he was doing here.

'You swooned, Miss Darling,' the man told her. 'Just rest for a while. You'll be quite all right.'

Lucy looked around her. She realized now that she was lying in her bed in the yellow company suite at Brackenbridge. She reached up with one hand, and felt the embroidered initial F on the linen pillow-slip. F for Felldale. On the opposite side of the room stood a large mahogany bureau, and beside it hung a painting of Agnes, 2nd Baroness Felldale, who had died in childbirth the very same year that she had married. The baroness's face was pale, bulbous-eyed, and infinitely regretful.

'I swooned?' asked Lucy. 'I don't remember. My head hurts, though. My head hurts something awful. Did I hit my head?'

Mary stepped forward and the dark man stepped away. Mary looked even more displeased with life than ever. 'Are you recovered, Miss Darling?'

Lucy was exploring her forehead with her fingertips, and suddenly found a large and painful bump. 'Ow! There it is! It's enormous! How in the heck did I manage to do that?'

The dark man reappeared on the other side of the bed. 'You were lucky it wasn't any worse, Miss Darling. I'm afraid you'll have a magnificent black eye, though, for a week or two. You should eat more regularly. Eating doesn't have to be fattening. Small regular meals are quite sufficient; and they are an excellent insurance against such swoons.'

'You're Dr . . . Roberts,' said Lucy.

'Yes, my dear,' he smiled at her. 'That's right.'

'How's poppa? Have you had time to look at him yet?'

Dr Roberts nodded. 'You've been unconscious for almost an hour. I've examined your father as well as circumstances would allow. I wanted to talk to you, however, before dispatching him to the hospital.'

Lucy tried to focus on him. Her vision was still blurry, and she couldn't quite manage to make out if he were smiling or not.

Dr Roberts sat on the bed beside her, and took her hand. Now that he was closer, she could see that his expression was very serious indeed. It was so serious that she had an almost irrepressible urge to laugh; especially since he was so good-looking (in his satanic fashion) and he was holding her hand with such uninvited familiarity.

'I must be truthful with you,' he said. 'Your father has very little time left to live. Amputation may stave off his demise; possibly for several weeks. He may even last until Christmas, but not longer. You will at least be glad to know that his pain will not be great, and he will be given sufficient opiates to render his last hours bearable.'

'Tell me,' Lucy whispered.

Dr Roberts lowered his eyes. Like many dark men, he had very luxuriant eyelashes. Lucy stared at them in fascination.

'It would probably be better for all concerned if your father were removed to the hospital; and that you said your goodbyes to him quite soon.'

'What's wrong with him? The doctors in New York said that he would live.'

Dr Roberts said, 'There is no point in trying to spare your feelings, Miss Darling. He is suffering from what we call necrosis. In other words, his nerves and his blood-vessels were subjected to such injury that his legs below the knee are already dead. The rest of him is speedily following.'

He paused and licked his lips, and then he said, 'It may be some consolation to you that nothing could have been done for him, not by the doctors in New York; nor by anybody here; and that while his nursing was sometimes lax, it was not the direct cause of his condition. He was beyond hope, Miss Darling, the very moment he fell and broke his back.'

In spite of herself, in spite of everything, Lucy's eyes filled up with blistering-hot tears. She felt so wretched, as if she were to blame for what had happened, as if she had been Jack's cross, from the moment she was born. She bent her head forward on the quilt and sobbed until it hurt; while Mary stood by the door in her fisherman's hat looking as if she were about to go to sea and Dr Roberts uncomfortably patted her back and told her to *sshh, ssshh,* everything was going to turn out all right, Jack would scarcely suffer, he would die by quiet degrees, as he was dying already, and that the Lord would welcome him quietly home.

She entered Jack's bedroom silently, and stood for a long time watching him. It was a sombre room, with dark blue walls and carved oak panelling. Through the window she could make out the greenish-grey outlines of the oaks, bowing and dancing in the rain. Jack was lying back on his pillow, awake, his eyes still flickering, but somehow less fretfully than usual. Lucy approached his bed and smiled at him with the smile of the truly sad.

'Jack?' she called him.

'Hello, sweetheart,' he croaked at her. He hadn't spoken a word to her for over a week, but now he seemed quite rational.

'Jack, they're going to take you to the hospital.'

'They could save themselves some time, and take me straight to the cemetery.'

'Jack, you're not dying.'

'I'm dying, sweetheart. Dying, it's just like being in love. It's one of those things you know for sure. Nobody can fool you otherwise.'

He coughed, and then he said, 'That Dr Roberts told me, in any case. I asked him straight and he told me straight. Dry gangrene, that's what he said. Instead of dying all at once, I'm dying piece by piece. Let's just hope my head is the last to go. I'd hate my hands to be still alive when my head wasn't there to know it.'

Lucy drew up a small ribbon-backed bedroom chair and sat close to the bed. She didn't take his hand, she couldn't. His hands felt as if they had been dead and buried for weeks.

'I loved your momma, you know that,' Jack said, in a clogged-up voice. 'I loved her so much, if I just hadn't of hit her. This is my punishment, lying here today, half dead already.'

'Jack . . . she must have loved you too.'

Tears slid out of his eyes, and on to his pillow. 'If she ever did, I killed it, didn't I, then her, now me.'

They sat in silence for a very long time. The light died outside the window, but the rain continued to clatter, and the guttering chuckled at Jack's self-inflicted plight, and draughts blew soft mockery under the doors.

'Jack . . .' said Lucy, at last. 'Jack, why did you do it?'

Another long pause. Then, 'Why did I do what?'

'Why did you jump? Why did you try to save Mrs Sweeney?'

'Oh . . . that. Didn't I tell you? Well, maybe I didn't, at that. I had to jump. I had to save her. She was the only person who knew.'

'What do you mean? The only person who knew what?'

Jack coughed, and coughed, and then awkwardly wiped his mouth. 'She told me on the stairs . . . just before we went out. She said, you behave yourself, Jack Darling . . . and you dance with me tonight . . . and maybe, just maybe, I'll tell you something you'd truly like to know.'

He said nothing more for almost a minute, but lay back on his pillow wheezing. High-pitched, tubercular wheezes. Then he coughed again, and caught his breath, and coughed some more.

Lucy asked, in a voice as transparent as water, 'What was it you truly wanted to know? Nothing worth *dying* for, surely?'

Jack turned his face towards her, and for the first time since she had left Oak City railroad depot with Jamie, to go to California in search of her fortune, Lucy saw the Jack who had brought her up, lean and sad and kind, the Jack she had always believed was her father.

'Oh yes, it was worth dying for. More than worth dying for. Molly Sweeney told me she knew who your poppa was. Your true poppa. She knew for sure.'

'But how? How did she know?'

'She birthed you, that's how; she was the Oak City midwife; and your momma must've told her then. She and your momma were always close friends. She treated your momma like her own daughter; and your momma returned the compliment, and that's why she gave you all of those dancing-lessons for no charge at all.'

Lucy felt unreal, as if she were still half-concussed. 'Mrs Sweeney *knew*?'

Jack nodded, and coughed. 'She knew all right. Only person who did. Then and there, right on the stairs, that's what she told me. You behave yourself tonight, Jack Darling, you dance with me, and I'll tell you something you'd truly like to know.'

'But she didn't tell you?' asked Lucy. 'She didn't give you any idea?'

Jack was still fighting to catch his breath. 'She was — teasing me. Know what I mean? She was torturing me.

Paying me back. She never liked me . . . never liked me one bit. What she was doing was paying me back. Far as Molly Sweeney was concerned, your momma was just like a daughter . . . that's what she used to say. And when she died . . . when your momma died . . . Molly Sweeney laid the blame on me.'

He gasped, and coughed, and coughed again. 'That's what she came for . . . that's why she came to New York. She came to dance, and she came to settle that score. Well, she sure settled it. She sure settled it good. She told me she knew and then she died without telling me . . . and that's something I'm going to have carry with me on a handcart to Hell.'

'Jack,' said Lucy, her cheeks shining with tears. 'Jack, you're not going to Hell. Momma's waiting for you. You'll see, Jack, and all those people you took care of.'

Jack closed his eyes, anything to blot out his dancing vision.

'I wish,' he said. 'I only wish. At least, if Molly'd told me, you could have gone to your wedding-day knowing who your real poppa was.'

Lucy sat in silence beside the bed. The room was so dark now that she could hardly see. The tears dried on her face.

'Jack?' she said, after a long time.

'What is it, sweetheart?'

'Jack, do you want to go to hospital?'

Jack didn't answer.

Lucy said, 'If you don't want to go, we'll take care of you here. I can ask Henry to find us another nurse.'

Jack coughed. 'I'll go, sweetheart. I'd rather go. I don't want you to watch me dying. I know what it's like, watching somebody die – whether you love 'em or not.'

His breathing grew thicker. He shifted his hand on the quilt and Lucy thought for a moment that he was reaching out for her, but he wasn't. He was almost asleep.

'Jack?' Lucy whispered.

'The brooch, that's what she said,' Jack murmured, then coughed explosively.

Lucy felt the back of her neck prickle. 'The *brooch*? What brooch?'

But Jack had already fallen asleep, and his mumbling had degenerated into a thick, crackling snore.

Lucy sat in the darkness listening to him struggle for breath. *The brooch*, that's what Mrs Sweeney had told him. It must have been a clue; a teasing clue. Jack hadn't understood it. But Lucy did. It confirmed the dread that she had kept to herself, ever since Uncle Casper had taunted her about her mother. If the brooch were the clue to the identity of Lucy's father, then without a doubt it had been Uncle Casper. She was the daughter of a brother and a sister; the child of unholy intercourse.

She didn't shed any more tears. She had shed enough. But as she sat next to this dying man, with the rain rattling against the windows like the skeletal fingertips of death, softly seeking admission, she made up her mind that everything that had happened in Kansas would be forgotten now; that she would marry Henry, and become Mrs Lucy Carson.

Lucy Darling, whoever Lucy Darling had ever been, would die when Jack Darling died.

She was still sitting with her head bowed when the door creaked open slightly. She didn't turn around; the house was alive with creaks and groans and abrupt cracking noises. But after a very long pause she heard an incredulous voice say, 'Vanessa?'

She lifted her head. Silhouetted in the open doorway stood Lord Felldale, in a bulky woollen dressing-gown, perched heavily on his cane.

'Vanessa?' he repeated.

Lucy drew back her chair and stood up. She approached the doorway, so that the lamplight from the landing fell in a triangle across her face.

'It's Lucy, Lord Felldale.'

The old baron stepped back, and focused his clouded eyes. 'Lucy? Lucy? Well, I'll be buggered! I could have sworn for one moment that you were Vanessa. Back of your neck, identical! Good Lord! Gave me quite a shiver, I can tell you!'

Lucy glanced back into the room, listened for a moment, then closed the door. 'Poppa's sleeping,' she said.

Lord Felldale nodded towards the door. 'Is he poorly? Dr Roberts said he may not last the week.'

'He's very ill, yes, sir.'

'He can stay here, don't you know, if that's what you'd prefer. Don't mind visitors dying here, plenty have before.'

'He says he'd rather go to the hospital.'

Lord Felldale offered Lucy his arm, and together they walked around the galleried landing until they reached the wide white marble stairs. On all sides hung immense oil paintings of classical scenes, shipwrecks and thunderstorms and torrents of hugely-upholstered nudes. Lord Felldale remarked, 'A man, ideally, should die at home; his own home; with a small orchestra to play him out with his favourite airs; and perhaps a choir. I myself wish to close my eyes for the last time to the strains of the *Eton Boating Song*.'

They went slowly downstairs together. They had almost reached the hallway when Lucy said, 'Who's Vanessa?'

'Ah,' Lord Felldale smiled. 'Vanessa is my fifth daughter, a year younger than Henry. She's married now, married some banker bugger. What's his name, Y-Stancombe, some bally ridiculous name like that. Wealthy, but you should hear him laugh! Won't let him go near the horses, in case he laughs. But handsome enough. And wealthy, as I say. Very pretty girl, Vanessa, very pretty. Fair hair, like yours; could have sworn you were her, for just a moment.'

'I'm flattered,' said Lucy.

'Well, my dear, you deserve flattery,' Lord Felldale told her, as a footman opened the doors of the drawing room for them. 'You're quite pretty enough in your own right. No wonder Henry fell for you so hard. When he came back from America, he could talk of nothing else. And never seen him scribble so hard! Always scribbles when he's in love! Desperate drivel, of course, quite desperate; but the girls like it.'

From the way in which Henry had spoken to her, Lucy had supposed that he had known very few girls, and that his overwhelming interests in life had been politics, and exploration, and dinners with his friends from All Souls.

'Is he *often* in love?' she asked Lord Felldale. She couldn't help herself.

'Not often, always,' Lord Felldale replied. 'But I've never seen him so much taken as he is by you. Never. He talks too much, that's Henry's trouble; and he's what we call a Clever-Dick. But you shouldn't take too much notice of that. He's very sentimental, underneath. It's a Carson trait. Weakness, if you like; along with a certain amount of godlessness; and a belief in doing everything correctly; and a liking for the pork they serve on Sundays at the Bell Inn, in Derby.'

Lucy wasn't certain what she should make of this; but before she could reply, Lord Felldale inclined his head close to her ear, and said, 'I know that Henry has asked you to tie the knot, my dear girl; and if you find it in your heart to say yes to him, then all I can say is, I'd be very content.'

Lucy, unexpectedly, found herself blushing.

Dr Roberts was waiting for her in the drawing room, with a half-finished glass of tawny port on the mantelshelf beside him. He looked tired and serious. The drawing room was decorated in Adam green and gold, with green silk curtains, and figured green upholstery. In the summer it must have been exceptionally fresh and bright. On a wet November night with the curtains drawn tight and the log-fire sullenly filling the air with acrid oak-smoke, it felt damp and unwelcoming and claustrophobically enclosed, almost submarine.

'Another port, Roberts?' Lord Felldale asked him.

Dr Roberts shook his head. 'I have to be going. Do you wish me to take Mr Darling into hospital tonight?'

Lucy said, 'He'll go, Dr Roberts. He thinks it would be better if he did. But he'd prefer to go tomorrow, if that's all right. He's asleep now, anyway.'

'Very well,' Dr Roberts told her. 'Sleep is probably the best condition for him, the way things are. I'll call again tomorrow morning, if you could have a carriage ready for him, and blankets to wrap him in.'

He finished his port, then came up to Lucy and said, 'As for yourself, Miss Darling, how does your head feel?'

'Sore,' she declared.

'Remember what I told you about eating regularly,' he admonished her.

He collected his hat and his coat and his gloves, and went to the door. 'I gather you're still keeping well, Lord Felldale,' he added. 'You haven't complained of any twinges.'

'I wouldn't either, if it meant taking any more of your repulsive salts,' Lord Felldale retorted.

One of the footmen had been sent out in the rain with a message to be telegraphed to London, to summon Henry back to Brackenbridge.

Meanwhile, there was nothing that Lucy could do but take a bath, which Tessie filled for her without complaining, and prepare herself for bed.

In spite of what Dr Roberts had told her, she couldn't bring herself to eat more than a few mouthfuls of supper. It was cold spiced mutton and lentil soup, and she didn't fancy either. Henry was right to complain about the kitchens at Brackenbridge. She could have cooked better herself.

The kitchen-maid plainly didn't mind that Lucy had eaten so little. Any leftovers from the upstairs tables were immediately devoured downstairs. Henry had told her that he had once changed his mind about a chop which he had left on the side of his plate, and had called the footman (who had only just reached the dining-room door) to bring it back. The footman had about-faced, with the chop already gripped between his teeth.

Shortly after eleven o'clock, the great house began to close down. Fires were guarded or damped, dogs were kenneled, shutters were closed. Lucy went to Jack's room to see if he needed anything, but he was still asleep. She didn't go too close. He smelled sour. He smelled like a man dying. She stood beside his bed watching him, and thinking of Kansas, dust and sky, and thin-faced men and women with eyes like funeral beads, scratching a living out of nothing.

The windows rattled in the wind. Lucy said, quite loudly, 'Goodnight, Jack,' and went back to her bedroom.

In the middle of the night, the rain died away, but the gale blew even more fiercely. It screamed between the chimneys, and shook in frustrated fury at the shutters, and sent leaves and branches tumbling and galloping across the parklands, skeleton riders on skeleton horses.

Lucy heard the great Tompion clock at the end of the corridor chiming three. She lay in bed with her eyes open for a while; then she pushed back the covers and got up. The room was draughty, but now the rain had passed, and the south-west wind had risen, it was noticeably warmer. She stood by the window in her long white cambric night-gown, watching the clouds shrivel away to the east, and the trees toss themselves wildly from side to side.

It was then that she heard a creak; the same creak that Jack's door had made when Lord Felldale had opened it that afternoon. She listened; and then four or five minutes later she heard it again. She tiptoed to her bedroom door, quickly and quietly opened it, and looked out along the corridor.

She thought she saw a shadow, flickering for a second on the oak-panelled walls. A shadow that could have been a monk, or a fisherman. But there was nothing else; nothing but the wind and the rattling windows; and the stuttering bang of a kitchen-yard gate with a broken latch.

She drank a tepid glass of water, and went back to bed. She wondered if she ought to pray; but she didn't know what to pray for. She hoped she wasn't godless, like the Carsons. She needed God now; she needed Jesus; and the bland kind face of the Virgin. She hoped they were watching over her, even if she wasn't praying.

She hoped more than anything that they would save Jack from suffering; and give her strength; and help her to discover who she was.

Tessie woke her up shortly before seven o'clock, shaking her shoulder. She said, 'What? What is it?' then pushed Tessie away, and covered her shoulder with her hand as if Tessie had hurt her or dirtied her nightgown. It was unthinkable for a servant to touch her like that.

'Sorry, Miss Darling, but you'd best come.'

She sat up. Tessie was already crossing the bedroom with Lucy's robe billowing around her like wings. 'What's happened?' Lucy asked; although even as she asked it, she knew.

'Dr Roberts has been sent for,' Tessie told her.

Quickly (why was she hurrying?) Lucy walked along the corridor to Jack's room. The door was wide open, as if it were a prison cell from which a convict had escaped during the night (and, in a way, it was). Lord Felldale was standing just outside the door, looking weary and desiccated. His valet Michael was hovering at his elbow with a steaming glass of brandy and hot water, with an egg floating in it.

Lord Felldale opened his arms for Lucy and hugged her. He felt bony, and smelled of tobacco. 'I'm so sorry, my dear child,' he told her; and she couldn't reply, because her throat was tightly choked, but she managed not to cry. She didn't want to cry. She refused to cry for anything, ever again.

'When Dr Roberts said he might last until Christmas . . .' Lord Felldale began. 'Well, I didn't imagine for a moment that it would be so damn quick. Diagnosed and dead, all on the same damn day.'

Lucy looked into the room. Mary was standing by the

275

window, against the watered-milk light of morning, her face hidden in crumbly shadow under her nurse's hat. Lucy couldn't tell if she were sad or relieved or just indifferent. On the bed, Jack lay still, his head slightly tilted to one side, the pupils of his eyes still for the first time since he had fallen from the Waldorf's balcony. He seemed to be staring at a point somewhere on the left side of Lucy's robe, and Lucy instinctively looked down at her robe to see what he was staring at. He didn't look dead; but then he didn't look alive, either. His right hand lay open on the quilt; his left hand lay closed.

Mary said something that sounded like, 'Darling Miss, sorry am I.'

'Yes,' said Lucy. Then, 'Thank you.'

Her mouth was filling with saliva, and she felt suddenly flushed and hot.

'I'm sure that he didn't suffer at all,' Mary intoned.

Lucy glanced at Jack as if she were annoyed at him. But now she kept having to swallow more and more saliva, and she felt almost as if she were drowning. She took one last look at Jack, pushed quite abruptly past Lord Felldale, who was drinking his brandy-and-egg, and walked stiff-legged back to her room. She walked slowly at first, then quicker and quicker. She could feel her stomach tightening as she reached her door. Tessie had been hurrying along behind her, trying to keep up with her.

'Is there owt you'd care for, Miss Darling? Cup o' tea, mebbe?'

Lucy's mouth flooded with bile. Keeping her lips tightly pressed together, she shook her head.

'Mebbe some nice warm milk? The cows'll be milked by now.'

She couldn't answer, couldn't speak at all. She slammed her bedroom door behind her, crossed over to the washstand in three urgent strides, and vomited into the water-jug.

After a few moments, she lifted her head, her eyes

crowded with tears. Then her stomach curdled and groaned and she vomited again.

Tessie rapped anxiously at the door. 'Miss Darling? Miss Darling?'

Lucy didn't reply. She walked in unsteady criss-cross steps back to her bed, and sat down on it. She was shivering all over, and her nose was filled with sick. Tessie knocked again, and this time she opened the door. 'I don't want to intrude, Miss Darling, but are you feeling under t'weather?'

Without a word, Lucy rolled over on the bed, and entwined herself tightly in her sheets. How could she feel so hot and so cold, both at the same time? She couldn't stop shaking. She felt deaf and blind and suffocated, and her throat burned with stomach acids.

Tessie said, 'Dr Roberts is here. Best that I fetch him in, aye?'

Lucy was shivering too much to speak. She was conscious of Tessie waiting by the bed, then leaving the bedroom and closing the door behind her. She could see her own hand lying on the pillow in front of her, so close that she could hardly focus on it. She could see the pale green veins in her wrist. Jack's hand had looked like that. Not dead, but not alive. Perhaps she was dead, too.

After a long time, the bedroom door opened again and she heard voices outside, including the deep reverberating voice of Dr Roberts. He came around the bed, and drew up a chair. Lucy heard Tessie say, 'Shall I bring you your tea now, doctor?' but Dr Roberts saying, 'Not just yet, Tessie. You wait here. We have to think of proper appearances.'

'Yes, doctor.'

Dr Roberts reached across and held the palm of his hand very light and dry on Lucy's forehead. He left it there for a while, so low down over Lucy's eyes that she found it difficult to blink. Then he sat back, and waited for her to open her eyes naturally.

'How are you feeling?' he asked her. He was wearing a

tweed coat and a yellow silk cravat, as if he had dressed in a hurry.

'I don't know, just awful. Boiling hot and then freezing cold.'

Dr Roberts drew up the sheet over her shoulder. 'You've had a serious shock. I want you to stay in bed for the rest of the day; perhaps tomorrow, too, if you're still feeling upset.'

He waited for a moment, and then he said, 'There's nothing wrong with you, Miss Darling, don't worry. The death of someone close to them . . . well, it affects different people in very different ways.'

'I saw my uncle die. He was burned to death, right in front of me. That upset me something awful but it didn't make me sick. Not like this.'

'Ah – but the deceased you saw this morning was your own father. That's quite a different kettle of fish. His very blood flows in your veins. You were related by destiny and by genetics; body and soul.'

Lucy almost felt like telling Dr Roberts that she was no more related to Jack Darling than she was to him; but somehow the protest seemed too futile to be worth finding the words for it. Dr Roberts stroked her hair, and her forehead, and said, 'Plenty of rest, plenty of fresh air. Keep the room well-ventilated, Tessie. Then some beef tea for luncheon, and something light for supper. Once the shock has diminished, you'll feel right as rain again. I promise.'

He was about to leave, when Lucy grasped his hand. 'He's dead, isn't he?' she asked. She did want to make absolutely sure. She didn't really believe in ghosts, or corpses that walked in the night, but she did want to make absolutely sure.

'Yes, Miss Darling, he's with God now.'

'He said he was going to go to Hell.'

Dr Roberts gave her a strained smile. 'I really don't think so. You've prayed for him, haven't you?'

'Yes,' agreed Lucy. 'I've prayed for him.'

Dr Roberts hesitated for a while, as if he were trying to make up his mind whether he should say any more to her or not. But then Lord Felldale's valet appeared in the doorway, and stage-whispered, 'Begging tha pardon, doctor. Lord Felldale's axing if tha wants t'send for t'pleece.'

'Please,' said Dr Roberts, irritably, waving him away.

'Sorry, doctor.'

Lucy lifted her head from the pillow. 'Did he say police?'

'It's nothing for you to concern yourself with, Miss Darling.'

'But why the police?'

Dr Roberts sleeked back his hair with the palm of his hand. 'I regret to say that your father did not pass away under entirely natural circumstances.'

'What do you mean?'

'As far as I can ascertain without a post mortem examination, your father died from a massive over-adminstration of some narcotic – most likely laudanum.'

'He was killed? Somebody *murdered* him?' Lucy tried to prop herself up on her elbow, but Dr Roberts immediately took hold of her arms and pressed her firmly back down on to the bed.

'Please, Miss Darling, we mustn't talk about murder! It's too early for me to say for certain. But I have my suspicions that Mr Darling's nurse Mary may have been – shall we say, less than attentive in her measurement of his nightly medication. That is all. I cannot say murder, nor must I. And nor must you.'

Lucy lay back on her bed with her hand across her forehead, watching Dr Roberts intently. Dr Roberts sat down at the small French bureau on the other side of the room, then reached inside his pocket for a pen. 'I'm going to prescribe something for you. Something to settle you, keep you calm. Laxative lithia ... not a strong preparation. It should set your system to working again ... improve your appetite.'

'I wish to see Mary,' said Lucy.

'I beg your pardon?' asked Dr Roberts.

'Mary, I wish to see Mary, my father's nurse.'

'Well, I'm not at all sure –'

She suddenly became irritated by his Englishness. 'I employ her, Dr Roberts, I pay her. She works for me. I wish to see her.'

Dr Roberts finished writing his prescription. He looked vexed, rather than grim. 'Very well, Miss Darling. If that is your wish. But I would like you to know that if you insist on doing anything but resting, and taking this medication, Lord Felldale cannot hold me responsible for your further wellbeing.'

He left the room with uptilted chin to call for Mary. If he had really been as satanic as he looked, he would have left behind him a sharp reek of sulphur smoke. Lucy lay back on her pillow. She still felt wretchedly nauseous: she wasn't sure if she was going to vomit yet again. But she managed to hold it back while she waited for Mary to appear.

When she came, Mary came so silently that Lucy didn't hear her. She opened her eyes and Mary was there, only inches away, white-faced, so grotesque in her appearance that she scarcely looked real. She could have been a changeling, or a troll. She had taken off her nurse's hat, and stood beside Lucy's bed with a shock of grey hair like a burst-apart telephone cable.

Lucy slowly inspected her, up and down. Her shapeless brown dress; her beige apron. Mary announced, 'The doctor said that you wanted to see me.'

'Yes, Mary.'

'If it concerns Jack, if it concerns the laudanum, then the answer is yes.'

Lucy said nothing, but waited, her hand on the pillow.

Mary said, 'He asked me.' It sounded to Lucy like 'Me asked he.'

'He asked you?'

'The doctor said that I was lax with Jack; but I cared for him, and both of us hated what happened to him. He was a burden and I made no pretence. He knew he was a burden. Why say otherwise?'

'He *asked* you?' Lucy repeated.

'Of course he did,' said Mary. Her tone was quite flat and repetitive, like somebody wiping a window with a leather cloth. 'He told me many times that he would be better off dead, and I agreed. He was dead already, I knew that and he knew that. His thighbones were dead, sequestrum they call it.'

'But he was alive,' Lucy protested. 'He was *alive*.'

'Oh yes.' Mary sounded unconcerned. 'But why was he alive? Jack himself, he would much rather have been dead. It was only you that wanted him alive because you have no family, and nobody in New York to speak to you now. And of course there was Mr Carson, who wanted him alive for the sake of appearances.'

'What are you saying to me?' Lucy whispered. 'What are you saying?'

Mary rocked up and down on her rubber-soled nursing shoes. 'Miss Darling, he was so fond of you. But I am saying that nobody wanted Jack alive for himself; not you; not anyone he knew; not even me; and that was why he was better off dead. Nobody had ever wanted him alive for his own self, that was what he told me. Nobody loves a storekeeper, that was what he said. The more you gave, the more they hated you, because they had to pay you back, and at the end you accepted their hatred because you deserved it, you should never have given them anything. A storekeeper with human sympathy is a fool, that is what he said; because who can reasonably ask a man to settle his credit for last week's beans. They have been eaten and become excrement. Cash for beans, yes. Cash for excrement, never.'

Lucy said blurrily, 'I don't understand any of this. You killed him! You gave him too much medicine!'

'Yes, I gave him too much laudanum. He asked me to. He begged me to. I am not ashamed of it. He was a miserable burden to me and I was a miserable burden to him. It was the very best way. That doctor, and all his talk of being a slave! If you are a slave to a patient, you take away his human dignity, in the same way that any slave strips his owner of his human dignity. You take away his reason for staying alive.'

Lucy couldn't follow what Mary was saying. It seemed like another language altogether. But she sounded so sure and so reasonable that Lucy found it impossible to be angry with her; or even to disagree with her. What was more, she could hear Jack speaking through Mary's mouth. A different accent, a different intonation. But it was Jack all right. By the time Mary had finished, and stood silent, Lucy could think only that she had done them all a service, and given Jack welcome relief from a life which had always been close to unbearable.

Dr Roberts reappeared. He stood darkly in the doorway, tugging at his fingers one by one.

'Miss Darling?' he inquired.

Lucy turned around. In a clear voice, she said, 'Doctor Roberts, I think we should wait for Mr Carson to return from London. It seems that my father took too much of his medicine on purpose; and that Mary tried to save him, but couldn't.'

'If this be true, how, pray, did he *reach* his medicine?' asked Dr Roberts. 'It was on the chest-of-drawers, on the opposite side of the room.'

'Dr Roberts,' said Lucy. She was aware that her accent sounded very American, in this temple of Englishness. 'We don't want to make too much of a damn fuss, do we?'

Dr Roberts looked at her with black glittering eyes. Then he smiled faintly, and nodded. Very well, *nolo contendere*. So long as everybody was content that Jack's passing had been all for the best; then he would be content, too. The very last thing that any of them wanted at Brackenbridge was an accusation against Mary of unlawful killing, with an inquest, and a court hearing, and newspaper reporters. Especially since the Liberal government was looking shakier every week, and it was accepted without question (in the better Press, anyway; and amongst his friends) that Henry would soon be called to some distinguished political office.

Boats were better not rocked.

Lord Felldale appeared. 'Lucy, m'dear!' he called her. 'Is everything all right? Roberts told me you'd been feeling queasy!'

'Everything's very well, thank you,' Lucy replied.

'Damned sorry about y'r pater,' Lord Felldale told her. 'Comes to us all, though, doesn't it? What?'

'Yes,' said Lucy. 'I guess that it does.'

Only a dozen weeks ago, nobody could have persuaded Jack Darling to believe that he would be buried in England, under a thunderous English sky, in the small medieval churchyard at Brackenbridge.

Rooks shrieked like fishwives from the nearby elms; and the church bell clanked; and the Rector of All Souls crisply declaimed, 'As he entered the world, unencumbered, so shall John Darling leave it; and face his Maker.'

There could have been no burial-place less like Kansas. The rector was unhealthily florid, everybody else's faces were as deathly-white as mushrooms. The cypress-trees rustled stiffly and proprietorially beside the grave. The tree of mourning, with somebody unfamiliar to mourn. But Lucy felt that Jack would be peaceful here; it was all God's earth; and when she turned away from the grave, to return to Henry, who was standing by the churchyard wall with his hat in his hand, she felt relieved, rather than sad.

Thunder rumbled in the distance; but for now, the church-yard was still radiant with coagulated orange light, and the cypresses were lit like flames. Henry asked, 'Are you well, my darling child? Do you want to go home directly?'

Lucy said, 'Yes, I think so.'

Henry offered his elbow. 'We're having drinks in the morning room, then luncheon afterwards. It's a pity there's so few.'

They had assembled only the smallest of funeral-parties: butlers and footmen and kitchen-maids, dressed in their Sunday-black; Dr Roberts; and Mary; but that was all. Lord Felldale had suffered an attack of gout in the early hours of the morning, and none of Henry's brothers and sisters had been able to come.

'Henry, you've been so kind,' Lucy told him.

Henry patted her hand. 'You're family now, Lucy, whatever you decide. Carsons always take care of Carsons. Look what it says on this gravestone *Let Courson Holde What Courson Helde.* My family have been here in Derbyshire for eight hundred years, since William the Conqueror.'

Lucy had never heard of William the Conqueror; but eight hundred years seemed like more than a coon's age, and she could understand that. Dressed in a black velvet hat, with a black silk veil; a black velvet dress and a black velvet coat; her breast patterned with glittering black beads, she walked beside Henry to the family clarence, be-ribboned with black.

They sat in silence as the clarence rattled and swayed up the hill towards Brackenbridge. The servants were taking the shorter path across the park. Raindrops sprinkled the carriage windows, and clung to the glass like tears, and Lucy could see the servants begin to hurry. A rainbow appeared behind the oaks, then faded.

'Ah, Blanche has arrived,' said Henry, as they reached the house. A small green victoria was standing by the steps, and a footman was carrying baggage into the shelter of the portico. Henry helped Lucy down, and gave her his arm as they walked into the house. Blanche was taking off her bonnet and cape, and giving them to Tessie, along with a teeming list of instructions about how to hang up her gowns, how to perk up the flowers on her hats, how to mix her hair-wash, how to clean her black boots. 'Treacle, sweet-oil, and an ounce of lampblack, and do it tonight, so that they have dried quite hard by the morning.'

'Blanche!' called Henry, taking off his hat. 'My dear Blanche, how perfect to see you!'

Blanche was also dressed in black; in respect for Jack. She was tall and fair and willowy and surprisingly unlike Henry, except that she shared that slight bump on the bridge of her nose.

'Blanche, I'd like you to meet Lucy Darling. Lucy – this is my beloved older sister, Blanche.'

'My poor girl!' Blanche declared. 'You must accept my heartfelt condolences!' She kissed the air on either side of Lucy's veiled face. 'Henry has never stopped talking about you!'

'I'm flattered, Miss Carson,' Lucy told her. She wondered if she ought to curtsey.

'You must call me Blanche, or Sha-sha, if you like. That's what Henry always called me when he was little. Tessie! Be careful with that hatbox!'

'It was very good of you to come,' said Lucy.

'My dear one, I was coming anyway, next week, to start the preparations for Christmas. One week early was no hardship. Besides, father could do with some looking-after. Less port, less snuff, and less rotten pheasant; more fresh vegetables and lentil soup. And less pretending to be twenty! Tessie! Tell the kitchen-maid to send for some ginger and Columba-root, as soon as she's back. Has Dr Roberts been?'

'He came this morning, before the funeral,' said Henry. 'He gave father a dose of Kissingen salts, and a telling-off.'

'Kissingen salts!' said Blanche, dismissively.

Outside, the rain began to lash hard across the park, and Lucy glimpsed the servants hurrying the last few yards to the back of the house, skirts lifted, hats held tightly on to their heads. Another carriage arrived: it was the Rector, Dr Williams, and Mrs Williams.

Henry said, 'When you're quite ready, Blanche, join us in the morning room.'

He caught Lucy's eye. Lucy looked back at him steadily but didn't smile. She felt too sad today to smile. But she knew that she had made up her mind. Or rather, fate had made up her mind for her.

'My dear Henry!' called Dr Williams, shaking out his frock-coat as if he expected rabbits to fall out of it. 'And my dear Miss Darling!'

She sat with Blanche in her sitting room overlooking the lake. The morning was dull and misty and silent, very late Novemberish. In two days it would be December. Blanche was busily embroidering a handkerchief. She had shown Lucy how to do French knots, but Lucy had given up after half an hour, and was sitting with her feet tucked up in the window-seat, watching the ducks make patterns on the water. It was the first Tuesday after the funeral. Henry was working in the library downstairs, but he had promised to take her into Derby that afternoon, for tea and a little shopping. Because of Jack's death, they had postponed their trip to London until the New Year.

Blanche kept glancing up at her. 'You ought to keep yourself occupied, you know. God gave us time in order that we might use it profitably.'

Lucy didn't know what was profitable about embroidering a handkerchief, especially since embroidered handkerchiefs could so easily be bought. But she was growing used to the Carson family's inexhaustible appetite for work; and especially their obsession with detail. Henry had been dissatisfied with the way in which one of the groundsmen had restacked a dry stone wall; and had spent two-and-a-half days dismantling it and rebuilding it himself.

From the minute that Blanche had appeared, the household had started running at double-quick time, everything polished, everything dusted, everything organized down to the last possible second. '*When* do we dust our hats?' she had demanded of Tessie. And to Lawrence, the coachman, she had given her own recipe for oil and Tripoli powder and instructed him to remove every last stain from the clarence's upholstery by four o'clock that day.

Blanche said, 'Henry is waiting on you, you know.'

Lucy leaned her head back against the shutter, but didn't say anything.

'He is absolutely captivated by you,' Blanche went on, satin-stitching as she spoke. 'He can scarcely sleep, waiting for your answer.'

Lucy said, 'I don't mean to upset him.'

'Will you marry him?' asked Blanche.

Lucy gave the slightest of shrugs.

'Do you care for him?' Blanche wanted to know.

'Yes,' said Lucy. 'I care for him very much.'

'Do you *love* him?'

'Yes,' said Lucy. 'I believe I do.'

'Then why not say yes to him? You would make him so happy!'

'I don't know,' Lucy frowned. 'I'm worried I won't be good enough for him. I mean *interesting* enough. I try to follow everything he's saying, and I try to take an interest in everything he does. But I wasn't schooled well, Sha-sha. What happens if I let him down, in front of Lord Salisbury, or even in front of the queen? What happens if he tires of my looks, and realizes that he's married a woman with no breeding and no education; nothing but money, and business-money at that?'

Blanche laid her embroidery in her lap. 'You have no idea, have you, how much Henry adores you? He wouldn't care if you were deaf-and-dumb, and knew nothing whatever. He is simply in love with you; and Henry has very seldom been in love. It is quite real, you know, quite genuine. He wouldn't have asked you to marry him if he wasn't completely sure.'

Lucy said, 'I want to say yes. I want to say yes with all my heart.'

'Then I'll tell you what,' Blanche enthused, 'I shall give you lessons in all of those subjects in which Henry has an abiding interest. I shall teach you history, and geography, and art. I shall acquaint you with politics, and protocol, and how to manage an English household. I shall give you some Horace, and some Ovid, and some Plato; but not Virgil, too liberal, *deus nobis haec otia fecit*, indeed! Moreover, I shall instruct you in French. I adore your American accent, you would sound wonderful speaking French!'

Lucy swung her legs down from the window-seat. 'Would you do that?'

Blanche set aside her embroidery and stood up and opened her arms. 'My dear Lucy, I have known you only a few days, but I feel already that I have known you since childhood! You have that sweet doubting nature that is a natural gift, and that is what Henry has fallen in love with! He adores your innocence, he is intoxicated with your uncertainty! But do not be uncertain about him. You will be the mistress of his heart for ever!'

Lucy hugged her. 'You'll really teach me to speak French?'

Blanche laughed. 'Of course I will! It's not at all difficult! Well – not as difficult as it might sound! Come here to the mirror . . . that's right, stand beside me. We can start straight away!'

They stood side by side in front of the large oval cheval-glass. Two slim, tall young ladies, dressed in black mourning silk, arm-in-arm.

'You must watch my lips as I speak, then imitate the same movements with your own lips,' Blanche told Lucy.

'Okay,' Lucy agreed.

'And you must *not* say "okay",' Blanche admonished her.

'Okay, then, I won't.'

'Very well,' Blanche began, 'say after me *faites énergique-*

ment votre tâche longue et lourde. Perform your long and
onerous task energetically.'

Lucy hesitated, then stuttered, 'Fate zenner . . . fate zenner
. . . *jeeka mon –*'

'Bravo!' Blanche applauded her. 'Now let's try it again!
Faites énergiquement votre tâche longue et lourde.'

Slowly and hesitantly, Lucy copied Blanche's precise
French pronunciation.

'There!' said Blanche. 'You have the accent! All we have
to do now is to learn the grammar!'

Lucy laughed, and Blanche laughed, too, and they hugged
each other. Seeing herself in the mirror, hugging Blanche so
closely, Lucy was surprised how much they looked alike.
They could have been sisters.

Henry was out in the garden that afternoon, supervising the
finishing-off of his cascade. It would carry water three hundred
and fifty feet down in descending steps all the way from the
Brackenbridge brook to the lake beside the house. The cascade
had been envisaged by Robert Adam when he was working on
Brackenbridge, but the 2nd baron had run embarrassingly short
of money (gambling, and a fertile and demanding mistress), and
so the cascade had remained as nothing more than a sketch. That
is, until Henry had written a short history of Brackenbridge,
and discovered Adam's original drawings in the library.

Henry had determined to build the cascade, exactly to
Adam's specifications, including the carrara marble steps,
and the Venetian-style bridge across the top of it; and he had
met almost the entire cost out of his own money.

Lucy walked diagonally up the hill on the south-west side
of the house, her long black velvet coat sweeping the grass,
her face veiled. She found Henry standing right at the top of
the cascade, while three workmen struggled with the sluice
mechanism. Henry was wearing a shapeless old shooting-cap
and a huge muddy coat and mittens, and he was barking at
the workmen relentlessly.

'Unjam it, you fool, if it's jammed! What's it jammed with? Twigs? What? Twigs?'

Lucy came up and stood a little way distant, watching him. He stretched out his arms like a penguin, and shook them. 'For goodness' sake, you blasted hammerheads! Easy with it, easy! This is machinery, not a mule!'

He wiped his mouth with the back of his hand, and stepped back, and almost stepped on Lucy's foot.

'Lucy!' His cheeks and his nose were bright red, like robins' breasts. 'I didn't realize you were here! My darling child! You must forgive my language!'

Lucy smiled and shook her head, but kept her lips pursed, as if she had a mouthful of water. She was desperately trying to remember the words that Blanche had taught her, as she left the house.

Henry took hold of her elbow, and led her towards the brink of the cascade's sluice. 'Here, look at this! You're just in time! As soon as these idiots open up the sluice-gate, the waters from the brook will be channelled all the way down these steps, and will pour straight into the lake.'

He lifted his fist triumphantly. 'Three-and-half years, it's taken, for me to finish this! But isn't it magnificent! Exactly as Adam first imagined it!'

One of the workmen lifted his head and said, 'Think we've cleared it now, Mr Henry sir! Twigs, sir, blown by that gale I shouldn't wonder.'

'Very well, then, open her up as soon as I give the word.'

Henry gleefully thrust his hands into the pockets of his coat. 'This will be quite magnificent! I did want father to be here, but he's suffering too much this afternoon, and I wasn't going to hold this up for *him!*'

Lucy touched his arm. He turned quickly and grinned at her, his breath smoking in the late-November sunlight.

'*Je . . . t'aime,*' she said, infinitely slowly.

Henry's grin gradually died away. 'What did you say?'

She could feel the tears prickling her eyes; but she had promised herself that she would never cry.

'*Je . . . t'aime,*' she repeated, trying to remember exactly how Blanche had pronounced it. '*Ma reponse . . . c'est oui.*'

Henry stared at her for a very long time without saying anything. Untidy as he was, in his oversized coat, he looked even more handsome than ever – well-built, broad-faced, with that deep cleft in his chin, and those eyes that were sparkling with gusto and determination and irrepressible self-confidence. Looking at him then, Lucy thought how silly she had been to doubt that she could make him happy. He had known from the very beginning just how innocent she was; how little she understood of politics or classical literature or art. It was her apparent innocence that had attracted him so much – that, and the prospect of teaching her everything he knew – the priceless anticipation of instructing a beautiful and ingenuous young girl in the ways of the world, not to mention the ways of the Carsons, and the ways of Henry Carson in particular.

'You do, then, wish to marry me?' he asked her. Down below, in the stone-lined sluice, the workmen were patiently waiting for him; with the authentic patience of men who have been trained since birth to do their master's bidding. Lucy nodded, and whispered, 'Yes,' behind her veil, like a ghost whispering 'yes' behind a curtain of smoke.

Henry took hold of her black-gloved hands, and squeezed them with pleasure.

'Lucy,' he said. 'Lucy! You don't know what you have done to my life already! You have brought me light, and joy, and meaning. And, as my wife –'

He paused. Then, gently and cautiously, he raised her veil. He looked into her eyes as if he found it impossible to believe that she was true, and that she was going to be his. There was nothing sentimental in the way he looked at her. There was nothing romantic about it, either. It was a look of pleasure, of possession – and also, quite unexpectedly, of something that resembled alarm. Not fear, but the jangle of nerves.

Did she *frighten* him? she wondered.

'I always believed that you would say yes,' Henry told her. He sniffed from the cold. 'I always believed that you would. But until you did – well, I haven't been sleeping very well.'

'Sha-sha told me.'

'And that was why you decided to say yes?'

Lucy shook her head. 'No. I decided to say yes because I decided to marry you.' *And besides*, she thought, with Jack gone, I have no other family left. Just you, and Sha-sha, and your father.

'I am delighted beyond all telling,' Henry grinned. He turned to the workmen down in the sluice, and shouted out, 'Now! Open it up! The very moment!'

'Good enough, sir,' the workmen said, and turned the wheel. The wooden sluice-gate was gradually raised, and muddy water began to surge out across the white marble steps. It foamed over the first step, and then the next, and then the next, until it was rushing all the way down to the lake, a sparkling stairway of water.

Henry took in a huge triumphant breath. 'I shall remember this day for the rest of my life!' he declared. 'My dear God, Lucy, you have made me so happy!'

Far down below them, Blanche and several of the servants had come out of the house to see the cascade. After a few minutes, Lord Felldale appeared too, in an invalid-chair, pushed by their coachman, Lawrence. Blanche waved and Lucy waved back, and Lord Felldale raised his stick.

Then Henry cupped his hands around his mouth and bellowed out, 'She said yes, papa! She said yes!'

Early on Christmas morning, before it was light, snow fell across the Derbyshire dales as soft and as thick as if the angels had been plucking geese. Lucy woke up on Christmas morning and knew that something was different. Her room was filled with a strange blue fluorescence, and when she climbed out of bed and drew back the heavy velvet curtains, she gasped at what she saw.

The whole of Brackenbridge, white with whirling snow. Even the lake had vanished. She stood enchanted, with the palms of her hands pressed against the cold window-glass, and felt as if they had been transported while they slept into another world. A world of silence. A world of softness. A world of white.

She was still standing there when Tessie knocked, and came in with her tray of morning tea.

'Happy Christmas, Miss Darling!' said Tessie.

Lucy turned away from the window. 'And happy Christmas to you, too, Tessie!'

'Church at eight o'clock, Miss Darling,' Tessie told her, setting down the tray beside the bed. 'I'll be in to dress you directly.'

'Thank you, Tessie.'

'Oh, and Miss Darling –' said Tessie, almost coyly, as she turned to leave. 'Mr Carson axed me to point out his gift to you . . . there, on t' tray.'

Lucy glanced towards the tray and saw a small rectangular box, wrapped in red tissue, with a white silk ribbon around it. She turned back to Tessie and smiled, and Tessie giggled and rushed out, closing the door behind her.

'*Henry*,' Lucy said to herself, as she walked across to the tea-tray in her long white embroidered nightgown. She picked up the box, and turned it this way and that; and shook it. It seemed quite heavy, for its size, but it didn't rattle. '*Oh, Henry,*' she repeated.

She sat on the bed, untied the ribbon, and tore open the tissue paper with her thumb. Inside she found a cardboard box, decorated with patterned paper. Carefully, she lifted the lid, and inside the lid was more tissue paper, perfectly folded. Only Henry could have folded tissue paper like that.

When she spread open the tissue paper she found a necklace. It was an evening necklace, designed to decorate a deep *décolletage*. It was arranged as three sunbursts of gold, two lesser sunbursts, and one large central sunburst, each set with diamonds. The central diamond was enormous, nearly as large as Mrs Widgery's, one of those flawless but tea-coloured diamonds which some collectors spurn but others would kill for. Nine carats, nearer ten.

Her hands trembling, Lucy lifted up the necklace and carried it in front of her to the mirror in her dressing room.

'*Henry, what have you done?*' she whispered. She held the necklace up to her nightgown, but it didn't look right; so she unbuttoned her nightgown and slipped her shoulders out of it, so that she was sitting in front of the mirror bare-breasted. She fastened the necklace and arranged it over her bare skin and the effect was startling. She looked so classically beautiful. She lifted her hair at the back, and turned her face sideways. She could have been Cleopatra, or Helen of Troy. She could have been Marie Antoinette. Sha-sha had told her about Marie Antoinette.

She was still sitting in front of the mirror when she heard the door of her sitting room open. Immediately she tugged up her nightgown, and called, 'Tessie?'

There was a long silence. She hoped it wasn't that awful foot-dragging Matthew, who cleaned out the grates. She had caught him several times trying to spy through the keyhole into her bedroom, and Sha-sha said he was epileptic, and ought to be locked up somewhere safe.

'Tessie?' she called again. 'Is that you?'

'Actually, it isn't,' said Henry's voice.

'Henry?'

'I'm sorry, Lucy; I apologize. This is really not proper. But I wanted so much to wish you a happy Christmas; and to find out whether you cared for the necklace or not. I'm afraid my usual enthusiasm got the better of me.'

'Henry, I haven't dressed yet.'

'Well, yes, of course. I shall retreat. Have you tried on the necklace? Does it look well on you? The diamond was given to me as a parting gift by the Amir of Afghanistan, Abdur Rahman Khan, probably the cruellest man I shall ever meet. I never knew what I should do with it, until I met you.'

'You had this necklace specially made for me?'

'By Asprey's, yes. It arrived by special messenger two days ago. I was terrified that they wouldn't be able to finish it by Christmas.'

'But, Henry, it must be worth a fortune!'

'My dearest dear, compared to you, it is worth nothing at all.'

Lucy took a deep breath, watching herself in the mirror as she did so. She and Henry would be married in May: Lord Felldale was going to announce it today, after their Christmas dinner. They would be man and wife, sharing everything. And what could she not willingly show to Henry that she had not already been forced to show to Uncle Casper, her own father?

'Come in, Henry,' she said. 'Come and see your necklace, how well it looks.'

She turned on her seat; and as Henry came into the dressing-room, in his blue Chinese dressing-gown, she let her nightgown slip down.

Henry stood staring at her. She stared at him, challengingly, back.

'It's beautiful,' he said at last.

Lucy stood up, holding her nightgown around her waist,

so that it would slip down no further. She approached Henry and stood in front of him, quite close.

'Thank you,' she said, her voice catching. 'It's wonderful. I've never seen anything so wonderful.'

His eyes were searching her eyes. What was he looking for? What did he expect to find? Some kind of clue that Lucy wasn't everything he thought she was? She tilted her chin up just a little, and half-closed her eyes, and Henry kissed her. Not a long kiss, but a searching kiss, the kind of kiss that asked a question.

He lifted his left hand, hesitated for a moment, and then touched her bare breast. Her small pink nipple immediately crinkled. Lucy looked at him, looked at his eyes, but they were closed now, and he was breathing like a man asleep.

'Henry?' she said.

'*Couvrez ce sein que je ne saurais voir,*' he murmured. He was quoting, she didn't know what he was quoting, but she had learned enough French from Sha-sha to be able to understand it. '*Par de pareils objets les âmes sont blessées, et cela fait venir de coupables pensées.*'

His fingers encircled her nipple. She would have done anything then, if he had only touched it. *Touch it, kiss it.* But he wouldn't. He took one step away from her, and opened up his eyes.

'Molière,' he told her. "Cover those breasts, I must not see them. Souls are wounded by such sights, and they arouse wicked thoughts.'"

'Is it wicked to look at your wife?' Lucy asked him.

Henry gave her the smallest shake of his head.

'But I'm not yet your wife,' Lucy suggested.

'No,' he told her. 'You're not yet my wife.'

'You're so proper, Henry.'

'And you're so innocent. What do you know of properness; or of improperness? And it's Christmas Day! And I shouldn't be here!'

'Henry –' she said. She didn't know what she was going to tell him. There was nothing to tell him. Her innocence had not been given freely, not with Uncle Casper, anyway. *Fumes! Fire! Laughter!* She was not to blame. Unlike Jack, she *knew* she was not to blame. So there was nothing to be gained from telling Henry what had happened. No forgiveness, no absolution. But, like all victims, she still felt guilty for what had happened. She still refused to believe that anything so drastic could have happened to her without her having been responsible for it.

She still dreamed of those ribbons cutting into her wrists. She still woke up, smelling the heated sourness of Uncle Casper's breath.

Henry said, 'I love you, Lucy. If you can be ready by ten minutes to eight . . . the carriages will be waiting outside to take us to church.'

Lucy came forward and kissed his cheek. She looked so young and slender and pretty in the strange reflected light from the snow; her blonde hair fastened in curl-papers, her nightgown around her waist, wearing the viciously-glittering diamond necklace of the cruellest of Amirs, her breasts tiny and upcurved and white, Arabian moons.

'You destroy me,' said Henry. 'You lay waste to me. But a happy Christmas, nevertheless.'

Brackenbridge became a noisy carnival on Christmas Day. A dozen of the Carsons' friends had arrived the previous day, as well as most of Henry's brothers and sisters, with all of their children. The corridors echoed with screaming and laughter and the scampering of little shoes. Henry was a genial uncle, but he was acutely conscious that, despite the fact that he was the eldest son, he had not yet married and produced any grandchildren of his own.

As they chattered in the carriage on the way back from church, his brother Charles recalled that Li Hung Chang, the Chinese diplomat, had expressed extraordinary surprise that a man of thirty-four should have no sons. The Emperor of Germany had six!

'Henry said, *very* stuffily, "I am not yet married, I regret." But Li Hung Chang had said, "So? What have you been doing all this time?"'

Charles shouted with laughter. 'You should have seen Henry's face! He couldn't answer him then; and if Li Hung Chang asked him the same question today, he *still* couldn't answer it!'

Henry did his best not to look annoyed. Lucy smiled behind her glove. She liked Charles. He was very robust, a much broader and more robust version of Henry, and he didn't seem to think very much of propriety or manners. He was astonished that Henry had summoned Blanche so promptly to act as Lucy's chaperone. 'But there we are, that's Henry for you, always watching his back! He wants to be Viceroy of India, when Elgin goes, and he daren't have anybody whispering about him. Everything proper, everything correct, and there had better *not* be any children to bob up and call him papa!'

'Charles, dear boy,' Henry scolded him. 'This is neither the day, nor the place.'

'Aha!' Charles retaliated. 'But haven't you chosen this day to tell us something special?'

'What do you mean?' retorted Henry.

'Oh, come along, Henry! Father can hardly contain himself! You know what father's like about lineage! "Let Carson Holde What Carson Helde." For ever, and ever, and you can't hold anything for ever, not without sons!'

'I don't know what you're trying to suggest,' Henry retaliated.

'Well, if you don't,' said Charles, clapping him on the back and winking at Lucy, 'you've been leading some young lady well up the garden path!'

Back at the house, they were greeted in the principal drawing room with hot punch and little mince pies, dredged in sugar. A tall aromatic pine stood in the window-bay, twinkling with dozens of tapers, and decorated with ribbons. The foot of the tree was heaped with gift-boxes, wrapped up in green and silver and gold, and an avalanche of nuts and sweets and gingerbread men had been spilled pell-mell across the floor, to give the impression that this profusion of presents had simply fallen from the sky.

Lord Felldale excitedly propelled his invalid-chair this way and that, toasting his guests and his family. 'Roberts says I shouldn't get myself aerated! Well, damn Roberts, that's what I say! This is Christmas! And this will be the very best Christmas ever!'

He rapped his cane against the side of his chair, and called to Blanche, 'Can't you let the children in yet, Sha-sha? I'm just bursting to see the little buggers' faces!'

Blanche waved and smiled, and said, 'Very well!'

She signalled the footmen to open the drawing-room doors; and all the children, fifteen or sixteen of them, came squealing and giggling into the room. They began to gather up the nuts and the sweets, the girls in their uplifted skirts, the boys in their knickerbockers, while their parents laughed and applauded and egged them on.

Then it was time for the gifts to be handed out; and Lucy had never seen so many clockwork monkeys and Dresden dolls and varnished toy yachts. One of Charles' boys, Edgar, came up to Henry with his face glowing, holding a cardboard box of painted lead soldiers, the 15th Bengal Cavalry.

'Uncle Henry, thank you!'

Henry scruffed Edgar's hair. 'Now you can play at putting down the sepoys,' he smiled. 'But if you play at the Mutiny, you must remember that in those days this regiment was known as Cureton's Multanis.'

'Yes, Uncle Henry.'

When he had gone, Lucy said, 'I would just adore to visit India. Poppa used to keep Indian spices in the back of the store. I used to take off the lids and smell them, when I was small, and imagine what India was like. Elephants, princesses, palaces! Poppa used to be cross with me, he said the spices would lose their smell if I kept on opening them.'

'You shall certainly see India,' Henry assured her. 'You shall see India and very much more. India is what I want out of life. I have never thought of myself as doing anything else, ultimately, than governing India. And if I govern India, then you'll be there beside me.'

'Just listen to him!' taunted William, Henry's youngest brother. 'The Viceroy of Pipe-dream!'

'You should do something about that moustache,' Henry replied. 'Shave it off, and put it out of its misery.'

'Have I met all of your family now?' Lucy asked.

'All save Vanessa,' said Henry.

'Will Vanessa not be here?'

'Vanessa . . . well, Vanessa doesn't come to family gatherings. She sees father two or three times a year, but usually when the rest of us are not here.'

'Have you quarrelled?'

Henry looked away. 'All families have their little differences, don't they? Would you like some more punch? We'll be opening the grown-ups' presents now.'

'That night that poppa died, your father actually mistook me for Vanessa.'

'Oh, yes? Well, he's growing a little old, you know. His sentiment waxes while his eyesight wanes. Look, here you are! This is the first of your gifts!'

'But I've already had this beautiful necklace!'

Henry took hold of her hand, and pressed it between both of his hands. 'I told you that we always over-indulge ourselves at Christmas; and you shall be the most over-indulged of all!'

Lucy was used to what wealth could buy. In New York, she had all the gowns and all the jewellery and all the ostentatious knick-knacks that eleven thousand dollars a day could stretch to. But she was not used to taste. When she opened her gift-boxes and discovered the most exquisite

300

solid-silver dressing-table set, enamelled in France in rusts and golds; when she lifted out a Blue John vase; and a pair of perfect eighteenth-century miniatures; and a travelling-set of perfume bottles in crystal, fused with a tracery of gold; and French pearl earrings; she felt that she had graduated into a world in which wealth was regarded as something much more than champagne and carriages and dinners at Delmonico's. Wealth in this household had meaning and substance. It sustained tradition, it sustained artistic sensibilities. In a hundred years, her silk gowns would all be rags, but some unthought-of grand-daughter of hers would be wearing these earrings, and brushing her hair with this dressing-table set.

There were many more gifts. Brooches, rings, bracelets, a porcelain loving-cup, from the Derbyshire potteries. And Lucy had gifts of her own to give – a diary with a solid-silver binding, for Blanche; a silver monogrammed flask for Lord Felldale, both bought in Derby.

For Henry, however, she had a very special gift. It was wrapped in a large flat package, decorated with white paper flowers and green silk ribbons. He opened it up carefully, with a small reflective smile on his face which she would later recognize as a tell-tale sign of anxiety.

'I expected nothing,' he said, looking up at her; conscious that the rest of the family had now drawn around him to see what it was.

At last, he took off the paper, and held it up. An oleograph, in a gilded frame, of Lucy standing by Henry's beloved cascade, in her black velvet dress and her black velvet bonnet.

'I'm sorry,' Lucy told him. 'I didn't have the time to have my portrait painted. I asked in Derby; and Sha-sha offered to paint me in watercolour. But you don't mind an oleograph, do you?'

Henry shook his head without saying anything. By giving him this portrait, she had of course completely confirmed what everybody in the Carson family gleefully expected: that before Christmas Day was over, he would announce their forthcoming marriage.

At that moment, however, Lord Felldale wheeled himself over, demanding, 'What have you got there, Henry? Let me take a look at that!'

Henry tilted it around so that his father could see it. Lord Felldale frowned at it, and grunted.

'Do you like it, father?' Henry asked him.

'Like it, yes. It's pretty enough.'

'Father?' Henry queried, sensing the reservation in Lord Felldale's voice.

'It's pretty enough, that's all I said. But what do you want with a portrait of Vanessa?'

There was an embarrassed silence among the grown-ups. Only the unselfconscious laughter of the children kept the spirit of the room alive. Blanche knelt down beside her father, and stroked the back of his thick-veined hand, and said, 'Papa . . . it's Lucy, not Vanessa. Mr Entwistle came from Matlock to take her picture just two weeks ago, by the cascade. You remember.'

Lord Felldale realized that he had said something out of place, but he still didn't understand what. He turned to Blanche in perplexity. 'Not sure that I –' he began. Then, 'Not sure that I –' He leaned forward in his invalid-chair and whispered hoarsely in Blanche's ear, 'Aint that Vanessa?'

'No papa, you're muddled-up. It's Lucy.'

'Ah, Lucy!' Lord Felldale declared. 'Lucy! Of course, Lucy! yes, yes, yes! *Lucy*!'

Henry stepped forward, and raised his hand. 'I had intended to save this announcement for later, when we were all well-filled with roasted goose and good red wine. But strong feelings are very difficult to conceal, especially amongst family and friends, and everybody here is more than aware of the affection I have for our American guest, Miss Lucy Darling.'

302

There was applause now, and a burst of relief, and Charles shouted out, 'Bravo!' The children cheered too; although not for Henry's sake. A division of dolls and Noah's-Ark animals had just broken through the ranks of Cureton's Multanis, and reversed the course of Indian history.

Henry said, 'I first came across Miss Lucy Darling in circumstances that, in American society, have now become legendary. She was slack-wire walking across the tennis-net, at the home of Mrs Gregory Harris, in Newport, Rhode Island. She impressed me so much with her beauty and grace that I decided, then and there, even before I had spoken one word to her, that I was in love with her, and that I would not be content until she consented to become my wife.'

Henry paused, and then he said, 'You all know me well. You know that I have always been one of the most determined bachelors of my age. But the minute I saw Miss Lucy Darling, the notion of bachelorhood suddenly appeared absurd. I could no longer think of a single reason why I should live without her.'

'Hear, hear,' William interrupted, but Blanche immediately shushed him.

'I have asked Lucy if she will be my bride,' Henry continued. 'To my unmitigated joy, she has said yes. Accordingly, we will be married in May, here at Brackenbridge, and the member for Southport will be wed not just to his country, not just to his party, but to the most beautiful lady in the western hemisphere.'

Charles cried out, 'Three cheers for Henry and Lucy! Hip-hip-hurra!' and William shouted, 'A toast! We must have a toast!' and Lord Felldale rapped his stick against the side of his invalid-chair and bellowed, 'Give the children some punch, poor buggers!'

At last, they drank to each other, Henry and Lucy, out of the loving-cup which Henry's sister Maude had given them. Everybody clapped and cheered, and the little girls skipped around them as if it were already May.

Henry took hold of Lucy's hand, and said, 'I love you, my darling, with my whole heart; and always will.'

'Henry,' she said, 'I love you too.' And she looked all around her at her new-found family. Charles and William and Blanche and Maude; even Lord Felldale, who had returned to his games with the children; and she felt secure again, and happy, and safe, and no longer alone in the world.

She began to feel sick about three o'clock, shortly after the family had finished their Christmas luncheon. The men had decided on a bracing walk through the snow, and a snowball fight, too, before it grew too dark, while the women retreated to the small drawing room to gossip. After only five or ten minutes, however, Lucy began to feel the lumps of roasted goose she had eaten sliding around in her stomach in their own grease, as if she hadn't even chewed them. She pressed the back of her hand to her forehead and it was chilled and perspiring, and she began to shiver.

'You must tell us what wedding-presents you want,' said Sha-Sha. 'You'll never guess what Arthur Balfour gave to Charles and Elisabeth: a silver-gilt tureen, in the shape of the galley of Sebastiano Venier at the Battle of Lepanto. Magnificent, but not at all suitable for leek-and-potato soup.'

Lucy tried to smile but found that she couldn't. 'You'll have to excuse me,' she said. 'I'm not feeling very well.'

'Too much excitement, for a Christmas Day,' Charles' wife Elisabeth suggested.

'You should lie down,' said Sha-sha.

She rang for Tessie and Tessie helped her upstairs to her bedroom.

'Stays too tight,' said Tessie, unbuttoning Lucy's dark red velvet dress, and then helping her out of her corset cover. 'You should do what Lady Brett always does, leaves off her stays at Christmas, and breathes in whenever a gentleman's looking.'

At that moment, Lucy felt herself turning shudderingly cold. She grasped Tessie's sleeve, and tried to say, *Help me*, but immediately she gagged and choked and splashed her lap with vomit. Goose, pease pudding, fricasséed kidneys, crimped cod, meringues; the very finest Christmas luncheon that Henry had been able to bully the kitchen into serving up.

There was nothing that Tessie could do, except to hold Lucy until she was finished; and then to help her weeping out of her dress, and bring hot wet towels to help her clean herself. Lucy felt as weak and as shaky as if she were dying, and her teeth were chattering so wildly that she was unable to speak.

'There,' Tessie soothed her. 'There, now. Let's sponge you, and put on your nightgown, and you can get into bed. Then I'll have young Kevin run for Dr Roberts.'

'What's wrong with me, Tessie?' Lucy shuddered. 'It isn't the typhoid, is it?' Henry had told her such grim stories about the bad drains that had killed his mother and several of his friends that she was always frightened to use the water-closets at Brackenbridge, and avoided every open drain-cover as if it were a trapdoor to Hell itself.

Tessie said soothingly, 'You're tired, that's all, Miss Darling. Over-excited. Dr Roberts'll doubtless give you something to calm you down. My goodness! Think of what happened today! No wonder you're feeling the way you do!'

Lucy managed to sip a little water. Then she lay back on her bed and tried to sleep, but sleep refused to come. Tessie sat in the chair beside her, saying nothing, waiting for Dr Roberts. The fire played criss-cross patterns on the ceiling.

It was almost dark outside. The windows were black. She heard laughter as the men returned from their walk. She touched Tessie's hand, and said, 'You'll tell Mr Henry, won't you? But don't alarm him, will you? Tell him I'm tired, that's all. Tell him I was over-excited.'

'All right, Miss Darling,' Tessie told her. 'Whatever tha likes.'

But it wasn't two minutes before Henry knocked at the door, and called, 'Lucy! Lucy! It's Henry! Sha-sha's just told me that you were sick!'

Tessie went to the door, and Lucy could hear their low, quick conversation. '– *over-excited, that's all – nothing to worry about – but called the doctor, anyway – well, you know, just in case –*'

Eventually, Henry said, 'All right, then, very well. She's your responsibility. But keep me informed.'

Tessie came back into the bedroom. 'Mr Henry's very upset, Miss Darling. But I told him it were nothing terrible. Just the collywobbles.'

'Thank you, Tessie.'

Tessie smiled in the firelight. 'Oh, miss, tha'll make a grand bride. I can't wait till May.'

'I hope I feel better than I do now.'

She didn't have long to wait, however. Dr Roberts appeared, chafing his hands, his face grey with cold.

'I'm sorry I brought you all the way out here on Christmas Day,' Lucy told him.

'No, no! Not at all! If we can't perform philanthropic works on Christmas Day, when can we do them? How are you feeling? Not too well, by the look of you. You look pale!'

Dr Roberts felt her pulse and checked her temperature. Then he asked, 'You haven't been lacing your stays too tightly?'

Lucy shook her head. 'I don't care for them too tight.'

'Have you noticed any swelling, however, of your bosom or your abdomen?'

Lucy was embarrassed; but Dr Roberts said gently, 'I'm sorry to be personal, Miss Darling; but I have to know.'

'Well – I'm putting on a little weight,' Lucy admitted. 'But Mr Carson is very insistent that I take my meals three times a day, even when I perhaps don't feel like it.'

306

'Have you seen anything this month?'

'Seen anything? Like what?' asked Lucy.

'Your period. Have you experienced any difficulties with that?'

Lucy swallowed. 'As a matter of fact, since coming to England . . .' she looked towards Tessie for support.

'Yes, Miss Darling?' asked Dr Roberts.

'Since coming to England, I haven't had a period at all.'

'Ah,' said Dr Roberts and rubbed his nose with the crook of his finger. 'No period at all? Not even a trace?'

Lucy shook her head.

'Ah,' Dr Roberts repeated.

'Do you have any idea what's wrong with me?' Lucy asked him. 'It isn't typhoid, is it? Henry and I are supposed to be marrying in May.'

'Yes, I heard about that, congratulations – and no, it's not typhoid. Would you mind if I were to feel your abdomen?'

Lucy stared at him blankly. 'All right. Go right ahead.'

Dr Roberts briskly rubbed his hands together. 'My fingers might feel rather cold . . . it's quite a journey from Matlock, on a night like this.'

He adjusted his expression to one of complete professional detachment, staring unfocused over Lucy's right shoulder while he carefully palpated her stomach. He took his time doing it, but he finished quite abruptly, and said, 'Thank you. You may cover yourself now.'

Lucy's stomach felt quite sore from all his prodding. 'Do you know what's wrong?' she asked him.

He nodded. 'I believe so. Would it be possible for your maid to step outside for just a moment, so that I can have a word with you alone? She may leave the door ajar, of course.'

'Tessie?' asked Lucy.

'Whatever you say, Miss Darling,' and went outside, into the corridor; where she stood sentry-duty over Lucy's honour.

Dr Roberts leaned forward, and in a peculiar throaty murmur said, 'You're pregnant. Do you understand? You're going to have a baby.'

Lucy stared at him. 'What?' she demanded. *Pregnant?* He must be making it up, like a character in a play. She couldn't possibly be pregnant. She had only made love once, with Jamie, and Jamie had made absolutely sure that his seed hadn't gone up inside her. She had read enough in *What A Young Woman Ought to Know* to understand that a woman couldn't become pregnant unless his seed 'entered the temple of her body'.

'I can't be pregnant,' she whispered.

'I will have to make some confirmatory tests,' Dr Roberts whispered back at her. 'But your symptoms are extremely unequivocal. You are pregnant, as much as two-and-a-half to three months. You can expect to have your baby sometime in mid-July.'

'I can't!' Lucy hissed back. 'I'm supposed to be marrying Henry in May!'

'Miss Darling,' Dr Roberts replied, 'it isn't a question of can't. "Can't" doesn't enter into it. You *are.*'

Lucy lay back on her pillow. Dr Roberts watched her with his dark-ringed eyes, not censorious, but not sympathetic, either. There was a shuffling noise outside the bedroom door, Tessie tying to position herself so that she could hear more clearly.

'Do you know who the father might be?' asked Dr Roberts.

Lucy glanced up at him. 'Yes,' she nodded, her mouth dry.

'It isn't –?' he asked, nodding towards the door, meaning Henry downstairs.

'No,' mouthed Lucy. 'It isn't Mr Carson.'

'Well,' said Dr Roberts after a while, 'you must consider what you are going to do. As you are probably aware, there are ways in which pregnancies may be terminated. But I should warn you that I will not personally be able to assist you in such a matter: it is something to which I am ethically opposed. Besides, there is danger enough in natural child-bearing, without tampering with God's intended procedure.'

He smiled at her. 'To die in the course of giving new life is a divine reward. To die while attempting to destroy new life is a divine retribution.'

Lucy whispered, 'When will it begin to show? I mean, really show?'

Dr Roberts shrugged. 'You have already noticed yourself your increase in weight, the swelling of your bosom and abdomen. Of course you may be able to conceal your condition for some time, with the aid of looser clothing. But it will be extremely difficult for you to keep it a secret until May; and impossible, of course, for you to keep it a secret on your wedding-night.'

Lucy lay back on her pillow. 'He won't marry me now, will he?' she said; more to herself than to Dr Roberts.

'That's impossible for me to say,' Dr Roberts replied. 'I *have* known men who have married women who are great with the child of another. There is a certain type of man who does; usually a man who is shy with women in his own right; but who is ready to take advantage of their special weakness at a time like this.'

'Henry's not that type of man,' said Lucy, emphatically. 'I'm glad he's not. I couldn't tolerate it if a man were to marry me out of pity.'

Dr Roberts reached down, picked up his bag, and snapped it shut. He stood up; and he looked peculiarly mournful, as if perhaps *he* were that certain type of man who would have married her. Sha-sha had already told her that he was single, and that he lived alone in a large grey-and-yellow stone house in Matlock, and that it was rumoured that he smoked opium, grieving for a long-lost love.

'Miss Darling . . . I can only say this . . . that if you have need of me, you have only to send for me. I will give you all the attention that you deserve and require. Meanwhile I can recommend only that you exercise frequently, perhaps by walking; that you eat healthy foods; that you leave off your stays; and that you try to remain of carefree mind.'

'But I *must* have the baby?' Lucy asked him.

Dr Roberts nodded. 'Would you count it an honour to have a murderer for a friend? It's horrible to think about, isn't it? So how could you talk to yourself, if you yourself were the destroyer of a human life?'

Lucy said nothing. She didn't know what to say or what to think. Dr Roberts waited for a moment, and then called, 'Tessie! I think your mistress could be given some tea!'

Tessie reappeared, and looked from Lucy to Dr Roberts and back again for some clue to what they had been talking about. She had obviously heard whispers, and murmurs of distress, but very little else.

'Tea,' Dr Roberts repeated; and then 'I shall call again tomorrow, Miss Darling, if you should wish me to. Just to ensure that your fever has died down; and that you are feeling better.'

He left, saying nothing more. Tessie reached over and plumped up Lucy's pillows. 'Would you care for some tea, Miss Darling? And some Christmas cake, mebbe?'

Lucy tugged at her tangled hair. 'No, thank you, Tessie, nothing. I still feel sick.'

'Did Dr Roberts tell you what were wrong?'

'It's nothing,' Lucy told her. 'Woman's sickness, that's all.'

'It's t'change in climate, I reckon,' said Tessie. 'I spent a fortnight in Whitby once, and I didn't see anything for months afterwards.'

Lucy tried to smile.

'Then there's your da passing over'n'all,' Tessie added. 'Bound t'upset your workings, one way or t'other. I took glyc'rine suppotteries for it, got me going a treat.'

'I think I need to sleep for a little while,' said Lucy.

310

Tessie finished straightening out the bed. 'Whatever you like, miss. I'll tell Mr Henry not to disturb you.'

Tessie crept out of the room on tiptoe, and closed the door behind her as carefully as if Lucy were already asleep. But Lucy lay on the pillow with her eyes open, wide awake; and she would remain wide awake until morning.

Henry exlaimed, 'You look wonderful! Do you think you'll be well enough to come down to London tomorrow?'

Lucy had appeared for family breakfast the day after Boxing Day, looking pale but otherwise healthy. She was wearing a chequered wool walking dress which she had always disliked because of the way its pleated front concealed her waist, which she was proud of. But now she was grateful that she had brought it with her, because whatever she looked like in it, she didn't look pregnant, and that was all she cared about.

Blanche was being fussy with a pair of hairy-boned kippers. She glanced up at Lucy, and remarked, 'You look ready to storm up East Moor Peak.'

'I've reserved us a compartment on the ten-past-nine from Derby,' said Henry. 'We'll easily reach London in time for luncheon. Wilfred Blunt's meeting us at King's Cross. We've been invited to dinner with Lord Salisbury the following evening; and we'll be spending Saturday and Sunday with the Hawthornes. On Monday we'll go to Reigate. My friend Billiam's found us a house there, which we might rent. You'll have a marvellous time, my dearest child, I swear it!'

Lucy was trying to do her best with two triangles of toast and a little soft-scrambled egg. 'I'm sorry, Henry,' she said. 'I'm not sure that I'm well enough.'

Henry was crestfallen. 'But, darling . . . it's all arranged. I'm sure you won't find it strenuous. It will mean so much to me, to be able to show you off! Especially to Lord Salisbury! When it comes to preferment, it is a great advantage to be well married.'

Lucy signalled with the faintest lift of her fingers for the footman to take her plate away. She had forked her eggs over two or three times, but left them untouched. 'I'm sorry, Henry. I would love to go with you. You don't have any idea how much I'm longing to see London! But I still feel so weak. I would be a liability to you. You don't want Lord Salisbury to think that your wife is sickly. Surely, in politics, a sickly wife is worse than no wife at all.'

Henry finished his tea and set down his cup. 'I don't know what to say. I really don't. I care for you, Lucy, more than life itself. But it would be impossible for me to pretend not to be bitterly disappointed. First we had to postpone your coming to London because of your father's death; and now you're unwell. And I am simply exploding to introduce you to everybody I know!'

'Perhaps you are being saved from making a mistake,' said Lucy.

Blanche had been fighting with her kippers and keeping well out of this particular conversation; but now she looked up sharply. 'Mistake? What mistake?'

'I'm sorry,' said Lucy. 'I haven't been myself. I've been trying so hard not to let Henry down ... but I feel so unwell.'

Henry pushed back his chair and came to kneel down beside her. 'Lucy, my sweetest girl. I'm sorry! I'm allowing my own ambition and my own feelings to overtake me completely! You mustn't worry! I don't expect you to come to London if you don't feel strong enough! We can go in March, when the snows are all gone. Lord Salisbury won't have to see you in person to know how happy I am!'

Lucy laid her hand on his shoulder, then leaned forward in her chair and pressed her cheek against his. 'Oh, Henry. Sometimes I wish that you weren't so understanding.'

Blanche stared at Henry for a long, noticeable moment, and then returned to her kippers. Henry had seen her, and he said, with a false lightness in his voice, 'I'm not always known for being understanding. It's not a vice of mine, if that's what you mean.'

Lucy was aware that some kind of hostile communication had passed between Henry and Blanche, but she didn't have any idea what it was. But as an intensive, Henry snapped, in a surprisingly Northern accent, 'You're making a mess of that fish, Sha-sha. What did it do to deserve that?'

'If a kipper could but talk,' Blanche retorted.

Later that evening, after Lord Felldale had retired to bed, and Lucy was sitting in the green drawing room with Blanche, embroidering, Henry came in and drummed his fingers on the back of the sofa, and cleared his throat, as if he had something to say. Blanche had been brought up in a family of men, and knew what was required of her. She finished her knotting, and then put down her silks and her needles.

'Did you wish to speak to Lucy alone?' she asked him.

Henry was standing with his hands held tightly behind his back. 'General idea,' he told her.

'Very well,' said Blanche, rising from her chair. 'I shall see to tomorrow's luncheon. That is, unless *you* have already done so, Henry. I was thinking of pea-soup, made from the boiled-pork liquor; then boiled chicken perhaps, with celery sauce; and baked-apple dumplings for pudding.'

'Whatever you like,' said Henry, uninterested. 'I won't be here, whatever it is.'

He waited until Blanche had closed the door behind her. Then he approached the fire, where Lucy was sitting, and said, 'Well.'

Lucy didn't look up from her satin-stitch. 'You're angry with me,' she said.

Henry sat down in the chair beside her. He lifted his hand as if to touch her; then withdrew it, as if to touch her would be an act of commitment which he was not yet prepared to make. Not until he was sure that she loved him, anyway.

313

'I, er, I just wanted to ask you one question,' he said.

She paused in her stitching. Her needle gleamed orange in the firelight. 'I just wanted to ask you if your sickness was quite as serious as you purport; or whether it is a diplomatic sickness; so that you don't have to travel down to London with me.'

Lucy looked at him with more sadness than he could have understood.

He flapped one hand in frustration. He was very rarely lost for words. '*I ask* – well, I hope you see why I feel I have to ask. Perhaps I'm making a fool of myself. But you seemed quite well before Christmas, before our betrothal was announced. Now you say hardly a single word to me, and spend all your time with Sha-sha, sewing. You said you despised sewing; but look. Needles and threads, cottons and silks.'

Lucy touched the flower-pattern that she had been embroidering. She had been thinking to herelf, while she stitched it, imagine all the baby-clothes that I can embroider, all the little day slips and coats and nightgowns, all the bibs and bonnets. She had decided almost as soon as Dr Roberts had told her that she was expecting a baby that she would keep it. It wasn't that prenatal murder was a crime, and that she couldn't face the idea of killing her own baby. It wasn't that Jack had just died, and that one life seemed mysteriously to have replaced another.

It was partly the fact that the baby was Jamie's; and that Jamie represented another world for which she was still desperately homesick; and that Jamie was friendly and comforting and loved her dearly.

It was partly the fact that Henry loved her so intensely; and expected so much of her, *now*, at her very weakest, so far away from home, with Jack recently buried, and the Derbyshire countryside bleak and hilly and cold as a stone-bladed knife.

It was partly the fact that she was terrified of being

Henry's wife. And, most of all, it was the fact that she was terrified of *not* being his wife.

An extraordinary thought passed through her mind, as she looked at Henry in front of the fire. *You want to be my husband, yet I'm expecting another man's baby. You want to be my husband, and yet I've never even seen you naked. Another man's penis has been inside me, and made me pregnant, and yet I've never even seen your penis, let alone touched it.*

She flushed at what she was thinking. It aroused her, in a strange way, but it didn't embarrass her. If anything, it gave her a little strength, a little superiority.

Henry said, 'You agreed to marry me. You haven't changed your mind?'

'No, Henry.'

'Lucy – I need you, and I love you beyond all reason. You do know that, don't you?'

'Yes, Henry.'

Henry took a deep breath. 'Can you say that you love me, in return?'

Lucy stared at him boldly. 'Yes, I can say that I love you, in return.'

'And this sickness –'

'This sickness is a sickness. Maybe it's tiredness. Maybe it's the weather. Dr Roberts seems pretty sure that I'm going to survive.'

'You don't think that yewnme jessayn sootud?'

The fire hissed. Lucy's embroidery lay unfinished. It was almost nine o'clock, and 1895 lay not far away. Lucy felt that sense of fate that always characterizes the turn of the year, in that hushed week between Christmas and New Year. All you can hear is the billowing of dustcovers, shrouding old memories for ever; and new covers sliding silkily off. All you can hear are whispers and frustrated prayers and hollow regrets. How small things are, in the tiny hours of that week! Hopes for the future are as small and as bitter as caraway seeds, being thumb-pressed into infertile clay.

315

And still the clocks will strike to chime the New Year in; and still the bells will ring out across the dales, even when there is nobody to hear them.

There were days of terrible indecision. Sha-sha knew that something was crucially wrong but Sha-sha wouldn't say.

Sha-sha would turn her face away; but never speak an unkind word. Lord Felldale would come up to her (he was walking again now) and lay his hand on her shoulder, absent-mindedly and paternally. Sometimes he would stand like that for five or ten minutes at a time. 'Good girl,' he might say at last. 'Good girl.'

She had accompanied Henry to Derby station, and waved him off on the train. His disappointment and unhappiness had been so obvious that she could have cried. But how could she tell him what was wrong? She had stood on the platform in her black henrietta coat, amidst the noise and the steam and the piercing cold, and he had leaned from his compartment window and cupped his hands around his mouth and shouted, 'I love you! Never forget! I love you!'

And what could she say in return, except that she loved him too; but that another life had intervened which already she cherished much more? Not because it was Jamie's, but because it was hers, it belonged to her, and she knew who it was. Even if she never married, she could say to this dearest of babies, 'Your father is Jamie Cullen, of Oak City, Kansas; that is his name; and he is a lawyer; and you know who your mother is, because your mother is me.'

On the very last morning of the year, when she was doing a jigsaw on the sewing-table in front of her sitting-room window, Sha-sha came into the room and said, 'We've had a telegram from Henry.'

Lucy was trying to fit a brown piece into *Stanley in Africa*. She hesitated with the piece on her hand and said, 'What does he say?'

'He says he has to stay a few days more. He's going down

to Reigate on Thursday morning. He says he misses you very much.'

'I see,' said Lucy. She tried not to sound cold. She didn't mean to sound cold.

Sha-sha came up to Lucy and stood close beside her. 'Lucy, my dear . . . none of us wishes to see Henry hurt. If you feel no love for him . . . well, you really should say so. It is better that he knows the truth now, and suffers the pain of it, than suffers a loveless marriage.'

Lucy replaced the brown piece of *Stanley* into its box. She would never be able to find where it went, not now.

'The truth is, Sha-sha, that I do love him.'

'Sufficiently to be his bride?'

'Sha-sha, I love him.'

'Are you aware how much Henry fears that you don't? That you feel *obliged*, rather than impassioned?'

Lucy didn't know how to answer that question. She did know that Henry was unsure of her affections, yes. But she didn't know how far she herself was responsible for his uncertainty. She was beginning to learn that real love is a dangerous business, every man for himself, no prisoners. She had learned even more from her pregnancy. She had learned that love comes in many different and baffling guises. Love comes open-faced, love comes masked. But – just as Jack had said, '*It's one of those things you know for sure. Nobody can fool you otherwise.*'

She loved her baby. She loved Henry. She loved Jamie, after a fashion. But most of all she loved her baby.

This dark little mystery that was curled up inside of her!

Sha-sha said, 'What is it, Lucy?'

Lucy looked up at Sha-sha and couldn't stop herself from smiling. 'I can't tell you. But everything will work out fine, believe me.'

'You're crying,' said Sha-sha.

'No, I'm not. When poppa died, I made myself a promise, that I would never cry again; not once.'

'You're crying,' Sha-sha repeated, much more softly than before, and laid her hands on Lucy's shoulders.

But her mind was made up that first Monday morning of the New Year, which was blindingly bright. The sun shone brilliantly on the Derbyshire dales, and by eleven o'clock the frozen icicles along the guttering began to drip, and cook reported a flood in the scullery. Lord Felldale had taken his bloody buggers for a walk, whooping and whistling. Blanche was packing her trunks in preparation for leaving at the end of the week. There was a feeling of excitement in the air, although most of January was still to come, and February, too; and people died in those months in Derbyshire, just as they did in Kansas.

Lucy was standing by the window with her hands unconsciously clasped across her stomach. She was thinking of what she might say to Henry when he came back from London tomorrow. She had almost decided that – no matter how much it would hurt him – she ought really to tell him the truth. At least he would know that she really did love him, and that her sickness was genuine. The trouble was, he was so concerned about his honour and his reputation. He wanted so much to be Viceroy of India. A viceroy was stand-in for the queen herself. A viceroy was royalty, practically. How could a man who aspired to royalty marry a girl of no family, who was already pregnant by a two-bit Kansas lawyer?

How could a girl of no family expect him to give up everything for which he had been born and educated, just for her?

She was just about to turn away from the window when she saw a fly come struggling up the driveway through the snow. She paused, and raised the curtain a little, so that she could see better. The fly stopped a few yards away from the portico, because of the snow, and so Lucy was able to see who was stepping out. A long green coat, a snow-white face, a tilted black hat. It was Nora!

Lucy picked up her skirts and hurried along the landing. When she reached the head of the stairs, however, she stopped and allowed herself a very deep breath. The stairs were slippery, and she didn't want to fall. Not with Master Darling inside her. Or Miss Darling, whichever it was. She descended the staircase very sedately, holding on to the banister-rail; so that by the time she reached the hallway, Nora was already inside, kicking the snow from her shoes, and brushing herself down, and looking as vexed as always.

'Nora!' Lucy's voice echoed around the hallway.

Nora looked up, and then smacked her gloved hands together with delight. 'Why, Miss Darling, you've blossomed! I wouldn't have known you! And look at me, what a B-flat polony I am, after all those weeks of potatoes!'

They hugged tightly. Nora said, 'The driver told me your poppa was gone. Well, bless his soul to heaven, poor man. I shall miss him, him and his mournful ways. But is your Henry here? The driver told me all about that, too, how he proposed to you on Christmas Day! He said they was ringing the bells in the village, that's how pleased they were; and Lord Felldale sending around free wine for everyone.'

Lucy beckoned to one of the footmen. 'Could you leave those bags in the hallway, just for now?'

Nora frowned at her. 'What's the matter? Is my room not yet prepared?'

'It's not that,' said Lucy. 'It's just that we have to leave, as soon as we can. This morning, now, if I can arrange it.'

'This morning, Miss Lucy? But where are we going? I'm only this minute arrived!'

At that moment, Blanche appeared at the head of the stairs. 'Lucy?' she called. 'Is this your lady's-maid?'

Lucy turned around. 'Yes, Sha-sha. This is Nora, just arrived from Ireland.'

Blanche came halfway down the stairs. 'She can have the room next to Tessie's. It's most agreeable. It has a view of the lake.'

'Actually, Sha-sha –' said Lucy.

'Yes?'

'Actually, now that Nora's here, I've decided to go to London, to see Henry.'

'Well,' said Blanche, with a bowtie smile, 'that's what I've been hoping to hear. Nora – Matthew will take your bags upstairs for you. The downstairs-maid will fetch hot water, if you require it.'

'Actually,' said Lucy, 'we're going now.'

Blanche stared at her with eyes that couldn't quite seem to focus.

'Now? What do you mean? *Now?* You won't get to London until six or seven o'clock, even if you hurry! You have so much to pack!'

Lucy seized Nora's arm. 'Nora will help me, won't you, Nora? We'll pack together! We need only two trunks, at the very most!'

'Lucy,' said Sha-sha, with a little patronizing whinny through her nostrils, and a rustling downstairs of her skirts, 'this will never do! You cannot leave *now*. Not now-this-very-minute. I've arranged the menu for luncheon, everything; and the Pearsons will be here for tea. Diana Pearson is simply dying to tell you about her travels to Turkey.'

Lucy said, 'I'm sorry. I'm sorry, Sha-sha, I really am. But now that Nora's arrived ... well, she's made me feel so much stronger. And she can act as my chaperone, of course. And I do miss Henry so dreadfully much.'

'Sure and you're talking like an Englishwoman,' Nora complained.

'Well, Englishwoman or not, I'm still going.' Lucy declared.

There was a moment's awkward silence between the three of them. Then Sha-sha clapped her hands and cried out, 'Why not? What a surprise Henry will have! He won't believe it, when you turn up on his doorstep! I'll help you to pack myself! Matthew, call for Lawrence! Tell him to bring

320

the clarence around to the front, as soon as he can! And when I ring, bring him up for Miss Darling's trunks!'

Nora unbuttoned her brown broadcloth coat. 'If you please, Miss Lucy; if I mightn't have the smallest cup of tea before we start to pack?'

They folded and packed away Lucy's clothes as fast as they could; giggling and chattering as they did so. Tissue flew through the bedroom like soft and spectral seagulls. The sun shone; Nora's hands smoothed out silk. Dear fussy Nora! She had seen her uncles and her aunts and all of her cousins; and every one of them had treated her like royalty, and fed her on the best they could; the best fowls, and waxy potatoes, and the very best beer. And the general opinion in County Carlow was that she was beautiful, and fit for the Queen of America, and rich as Crazes.

They were ready by lunchtime. Blanche absolutely insisted that they stay for lunch. It was roasted hare with redcurrant jelly. Lucy could eat very little. She was far too tense and excited. But Blanche was thrilled by the idea of Lucy surprising Henry in London, and did enough talking and eating for the two of them.

'He'll be so serious! You know what moods he gets into! I really wish that I were invisible, and could be standing right beside you when he opens the door! You must telegraph, when you have the time, to tell me what happened!'

Blanche smiled at Lucy lovingly. 'At least I shall leave here knowing that Henry is happy at last.'

At half-past one, the clarence was loaded and they were ready to make their farewells. Lucy and Blanche embraced each other tightly, and Blanche's eyes were filled with tears.

'*Au revoir*, Sha-sha,' Lucy told her. 'Thank you for everything. You've taught me so much.'

'Goodbye, my dear,' said Blanche, kissing Lucy's cheek. 'I hope with all of my heart that you will be happy and contented.'

Lord Felldale was waiting by the clarence, with his dogs. He kissed Lucy, and patted her shoulder appreciatively, as if she were a glossy young mare. 'Good girl, good girl. Look after yourself. And look after that son of mine. Don't let him get above himself. Less of the Clever-Dickery, got it?'

Lawrence the coachman climbed up to his seat and took the ribbons, and Gerry, one of their more reliable footmen, climbed up beside him. Blanche and Lord Felldale waved to them as they drove away from Brackenbridge. A little way behind them, Tessie waved too, flapping her handkerchief frantically from side to side as if she were signalling to an express train that the bridge was washed away.

They circled around the lake, and through the trees, and at last the house disappeared behind a hawthorn hedge and a dry stone wall.

'Well, well, and that was hello-and-goodbye and no mistake,' Nora exclaimed.

'You're not too tired?' asked Lucy.

'Not at all. It was a wonderful rest, seeing all the relations. I've got plenty of stamina. And it'll do me good, to work off some of those potatoes.'

She opened up her purse, and took out a small packet of violet cachous, and offered one to Lucy. Lucy declined it, with a shake of her hand.

'They're marvellous for the breath, if you have to talk to somebody holy after you've been eating onions.'

She sucked for a while, and then she said, 'I'm looking forward to seeing London, that's one thing. I've always wanted to see London.'

Lucy continued to stare out of the window at the bleak Derbyshire skyline. 'We're not going to London,' she said, in a matter-of-fact tone.

'We're not? But you told Miss Shoo-shoo or whatever her name is —'

'It doesn't matter what I told Sha-sha. We're not going to London. We're going to Liverpool.'

'But didn't I just this very morning come off the boat from Liverpool?'

'Yes, you did, and now you're going back; and you and I are going to book ourselves a passage on the very first ship to New York.'

Nora was aghast. 'But what about your beloved? What about Mr Carson? You're not running out on him are you? You're still going to be married?'

'I can't marry him.' Lucy's throat felt tight with misery.

'What do you mean, can't? Don't you love him? You said that you loved him!'

'I do love him, very much. But I can't marry him. And the worst of it is, I can't even tell him why.'

Nora was silent for a very long time, as the clarence jiggled and jolted through the snowy landscape on its way towards Derby. 'Can you tell *me*?' she asked at last.

Lucy said, 'Give me a little time, Nora, and I will. At the moment, all I want to do is to escape.'

They reached Derby station. Lawrence and Gerry climbed down from their seats, banging their mittened hands together to warm them up. Their woollen scarves were thick with frozen breath.

'I'll take you to the London train, Miss Darling,' Lawrence told her. 'Gerry will find himself a porter, and buy your tickets for you.'

Nora frowned at Lucy, but Lucy pressed her fingertip to her lips. She didn't want anybody to know where she had gone; not until she could write to Henry herself. Besides, there might not be any sailings from Liverpool for two or three days, and the last thing she wanted was for Henry to come after her, and try to persuade her to come back. She would have time to send him a letter from Liverpool, before she sailed. She wouldn't vanish out of his life without an explanation. But she wasn't brave enough to tell him to his face.

Derby station was swept with gusts of wind as cold as

iron plates. Lawrence led them on to the London-bound platform, where the train was just about to arrive, and called for the porter to help them with their baggage. Gerry came hurrying up with the tickets just as the train came scraping and squealing and chuffing into the station; followed closely by three more porters, wheeling their trunks on barrows, brisk and professionally panicky, especially for a sixpenny tip. The slamming of doors and the echoing of whistles and the roar of steam was hellish; but dangerously exciting, too. Their trunks were loaded into the guard's-van; Lawrence saw them to their first-class seats. There were six seats in each compartment, Gerry had bought them all.

'Please, you don't have to wait until the train leaves,' Lucy told Lawrence. She pressed two half-crowns into his hand, and said, 'Thank you so much for taking care of us. You've been marvellous.'

'Any time, Miss Darling; any time at all. We're all looking forward to seeing you back at Brackenbridge.'

The instant that Lawrence had left the train, however, Lucy pushed down the window. She could see Lawrence walking through the barrier, sharing out his tip with Gerry. She waited until they had disappeared behind one of the iron pillars, and then she frantically beckoned to the short Kitchener-moustachioed guard, who had taken out his pocket-watch and his furled-up green flag, and was now waiting for the very second to be off.

'Conductor!' she called him. 'Conductor!'

The guard looked around, then caught sight of her. 'Talking to me, madam? I'm sorry, I'm the guard.'

'Well, guard, conductor, whatever you are! There's been a terrible mistake! I'm supposed to be going to Liverpool. My servants have put me on the wrong train!'

The guard stared at Lucy with a slight cast in his eyes. The 2:32 London express was due to leave Derby in fifty-five seconds; the platform barriers were closed; all the doors were closed; the engine-driver was leaning out of his cab waiting for the green flag; and a pale-faced young girl in a black-plumed hat was leaning out of a first-class compartment and telling him that she was on the wrong train.

At the same time, the Liverpool train was just arriving on the opposite platform, in an ill-orchestrated clamour of steam and protesting brakes.

The guard half-raised his whistle to his lips, watching Lucy all the time. Lucy immediately opened her purse, took out a sovereign, and held it up between finger and thumb. She turned it this way and that, so that it would catch the wintry sunlight.

'Guard, conductor – please! It's absolutely desperate!'

The bright whistle stayed where it was. 'Port-aaah!' screamed the guard. 'Porter! Quick as you like!'

Nora, being Irish, loved the hysteria of it all. The guard's-van was flung open, all of their trunks were found and unloaded, and madly carried over the footbridge; while passengers curious and irritable opened their windows and stuck out their heads to find out what was happening; and the Liverpool train was firmly held in its place like an impatient dog, *stay, sir!* by the stationmaster himself, with a stern expression and a red flag.

All of their baggage was re-loaded, the London express was whistled off; and Lucy and Nora were found a first-class compartment close to the front of the train. Another whistle, and they were off, too, with a jolt and a jerk, and a frenzied barking of steam.

They were gradually pulling out of the station, still going very slowly, when Lucy glimpsed a familiar figure on the platform, queueing just like all the other passengers to show his ticket. Immediately, she sat back in her seat, and pressed her hands over her face.

'Miss Lucy?' asked Nora, still panting from their frantic rush across the footbridge. 'What's the matter, Miss Lucy?'

'It's Henry!' Lucy exclaimed, quite aghast. 'He must have come home early! He must have come back from London on this very train!'

They were pulling clear of Derby now. Outside the window were rows of huddled houses, cluttered back yards, freezing washing-lines, and patches of snow. Smoke from the locomotive's chimney went rolling across the countryside like grubby cauliflowers. Lucy sat back in her seat feeling suddenly emptied of all of her energy, and tired, and despondent. Oh crims, poor Henry! She could picture so clearly his return to Brackenbridge, only to discover that she had just left for London. She could picture him telegraphing London; or hurrying back by this evening's train; and finding her gone.

She had saved her own feelings by running away; but what had she done to Henry's?

The train was late; and it rattled and rocked through Belper and Clay Cross and Chesterfield, shouting its way through tunnels and cuttings, blurting over bridges. Lucy watched the dales and the villages unravelling past the windows, grey and luminous. Nora kept an eye on her for as long as she could; then folded her arms and rested her chin on her collar and began to nod off.

Lucy stayed awake; grittily exhausted but unable to think of sleep; frightened by her own fear; frightened of what the future might bring; but determined to keep her baby safe, no matter what happened.

Liverpool, January 9, 1895
  'On Board The American Line "St Louis".'

My dearest Henry,
  I pray that I have not caused you too much suffering. I am leaving in an hour on the liner St Louis, bound for New York. I shall not return to England, nor trouble you ever again, as if I hadn't caused you sufficient trouble for one lifetime.
  The truth is Henry that I feel I would disappoint you in so many ways. In disappointing you, I would disappoint

*myself. You deserve a wife who was born and bred to be the
consort of an English nobleman. Whereas I am nothing of the
kind. All the French I know was taught to me by Blanche, and I
can still speak only a few words.*

*You will probably not be able to forgive me, after all your
kindness and consideration too. However there are times when
we must be honest with ourselves, and this is such a
time.*

*You will never know how deep my affection was for you, nor
how much I wanted to be your bride. I will dream of it for many
years to come. Please do not think of me badly, or punish me by
being unhappy.*

With all my love,
Lucy.

It was the worst time of the year to cross the North
Atlantic; for all that the *St Louis* had been launched less than
a year ago, and that she had been blessed by President
Grover Cleveland with American champagne. A savage
January storm struck her shortly after she had left the shelter
of the Irish coast, and she spent two days wallowing and
lurching in thunderous troughs.

Lucy was chronically, painfully, seasick. She spent most of
her time lying in her stateroom, praying that God should
not punish her any more. The ship creaked all around her,
and she was sure that it was going to burst, and let in the
sea. Nora, on the other hand, seemed to thrive on the ship's
friskiness, and ate more than ever – not only her own food,
but the split-pea soup and milk-boiled haddock which the
stewards brought for Lucy on a tray, and which Lucy
couldn't touch.

After the third morning, however, the wind suddenly
dropped, and the sea became surrealistically calm. The *St
Louis* made speedy headway across an ocean as black and as
glossy as India ink. The air was still bitingly cold; and even
the bravest passenger could only remain on the promenade

deck for five or ten minutes at a time. Ice floes spun past them, white on black, like frightened memories, and Lucy looked out for penguins, or stranded polar bears, but the floes were empty, as if the polar bears and penguins had deliberately hidden.

Several of the men passengers attempted to flirt with her. A bridge-building tycoon from St Louis, very handsome, like a lion, but far too old, with deeply lined cheeks and fetid breath. A German with Junkers ancestry, fresh breath, no lines, but very prickly-headed, with a broken nose. A Frenchman who pretended to be sad, an actor and an adventurer, who drank too much brandy and couldn't remember why he had decided to visit America at all, or so he said. Lucy tried to speak French to him, but he refused to understand, and kept bending his head forward and kissing her hand, as if he were a customs official, rubber-stamping a passport. '*Mam'selle, ce n'est pas le temps d'être prude à dix-huit ans.*'

But for most of the voyage, Lucy kept herself to herself, and spoke only to Nora; and not often to her. She had thought that she would confess to Nora that she was pregnant as soon as they set sail from Liverpool; but now that she had left Henry behind, she no longer felt such a pressing need for confession. As her pregnancy progressed, she lost interest in Henry. She lost interest in Nora. She lost interest in the whole wide world. All she cared about was what was growing inside her; stronger and more assertive every day. She wasn't ashamed. She thought sometimes that she ought to be. But she felt so happy and so much at peace with herself that she couldn't believe that it was wrong for her to bear this child.

The *St Louis* was delayed for another day because New York harbour was icebound. Lucy stayed in her stateroom most of the time, playing cards with Nora. They could see New York from the promenade deck, across the cracked white ice. The tall spires of the business district, the skyscraping palaces of Mammon. The Washington Building, the Produce Exchange, the Manhattan Life Building, the New York *Times*.

They were sun-gilded and self-enclosed, like the castles of haughty princes.

Nora tried her very best not to be inquisitive; but as evening fell, and the lights of Manhattan began to twinkle, she asked Lucy, 'Will you tell me what it was that made you run out on Mr Carson with such a rush?'

Lucy stared at her cards. 'I didn't really love him enough to marry him, I suppose.'

'But surely you could have told him that to his face, instead of rushing off? He didn't look like the kind of fellow who would have taken it so terribly badly, so long as you told him the truth.'

'Nora ... I couldn't marry him. There wasn't anything more to it than that.'

Nora dealt her cards. 'I'm sorry that you can't confide in me, Miss Lucy. What else can I say?'

'Nora, I *will* confide in you. But give me time.'

'You're pregnant,' said Nora, boldly.

Lucy looked up, wide-eyed, white as the ice, startled by Nora's acumen; offended that her lady's-maid should have said such a thing; but relieved, too, because Nora had guessed it before she had found it necessary to confess.

'How did you know?' she demanded.

'Oh, come along now, Miss Lucy, I've guessed it for days. I'm a family girl. Isn't my own cousin Kathleen pregnant again, three months' gone, and isn't she behaving the same as you, sweet one minute, fickle the next? And all you can think about is baba, isn't that true?'

Lucy said nothing, but lowered her hand of cards with all the grace of a fan-dancer.

'I'm pregnant, yes.'

'But not with Mr Carson's child?'

'Mr Carson and I –'

Nora lifted both hands. 'Please, Miss Darling. You don't have to act like an Englishwoman when you're with me. You may sack me if you wish, for my impertinence. But it seems to me now that you have no family; and very few friends; and for all of your money you're just eighteen years old. It's a poor kind of human being that would let you fend for yourself just now, pregnant and confused.'

'Nora –' Lucy began, but didn't know what else to say.

'Have you told Mr Cullen yet?' Nora asked her.

Lucy shook her head.

'I'm suspecting that it's Mr Cullen's child? Him who hid behind the curtains, and all?'

'Yes,' said Lucy. She almost smiled. 'Him who hid behind the curtains.'

'Are you thinking of telling him?'

'I don't know,' Lucy admitted. 'I'm afraid.'

'Afraid?' What are you afraid of?'

'What do you think? I'm afraid that he'll want to marry me.'

Nora fanned out her cards. The king of clubs, the queen of hearts. 'You could do very much worse,' she said, with a moral neatness that would have finished a game of patience.

'I want to be married for love,' said Lucy.

Nora made a face. 'Hmph! There's many an old maid's said that, and no mistake.'

'Nora, I can't marry Jamie just because I'm having his baby. It's not the right reason! It wouldn't be fair! We'd end up like Jack and my mother; and the baby would end up like me!'

She paused, flustered, and then she said, 'I don't want any other child to end up like me; not ever.'

Nora stirred the cards around with her fingertip, without raising her eyes. She said nothing more; there was nothing more to say. Nobody could persuade a spoiled and hugely wealthy girl of eighteen years old to marry a man she didn't want to marry, could they? Especially when she wouldn't marry the man that she *did* want to marry.

Holy Mother, thought Nora; and they blame the Irish for being contrary.

It seemed colder in New York than Derbyshire. That hard New York cold; like somebody hitting you straight in the face with a roughcast brick, the second you step out into the street. New York seemed unfamiliar, too, not unfriendly but entirely self-interested, a city that had been carrying on with its business while she was away; a city that didn't care about her any more.

Lucy and Nora left their baggage at the American Lines office, and took a cab back home to Central Park West. It was a slow, traffic-jammed journey. The gutters were heaped with mountain-ranges of filthy cleared-away snow, and so at most places the streets would admit the passage of no more than a single line of carriages on each side. Lucy sat silently and shivered.

At last they reached Central Park West. Lucy had been so impressed with Brackenbridge that she had forgotten how titanic her own mansion was. It looked especially dark and bulky in the slate-grey light of a January afternoon. As Nora paid the cab-driver, Lucy stood on the icy sidewalk with the wind ruffling her furs, staring up at the turreted window of her bedroom.

They climbed the steps and Nora rang the bell. It took a long time for Jeremy to answer. When he did, he appeared diffident and strangely unsurprised. 'Miss Darling . . . come in.'

He took her fur coat. The house was echoing and dark and very cold.

'I received your wire concerning your father,' Jeremy told her. 'I was very sorry to hear of his death. Perhaps, under the circumstances, it was a blessing.'

'It's so *cold* here,' Lucy complained. 'In fact, it's *freezing*! Jeremy – haven't you been lighting the boilers?'

'We've been out of coke for a week now, Miss Darling.'

'Out of coke? Why didn't you order some more?'

Jeremy's hooded eyes slipped sideways. 'Obviously you haven't received my letter.'

'Letter? What letter?'

'Miss Darling . . . there is a fire in the morning room. Come warm yourself, and allow me to explain.'

Lucy followed Jeremy to the morning room. His shoes squeaked plaintively on the marble floor. She had a feeling that something terrible had happened. The house seemed so dead and dusty. And where were all the other servants? Nobody else had come to welcome her back.

A small fire of heaped-up slack was pouring out dense yellow smoke up the morning-room chimney. Outside the window, the stable roofs were thick with snow; which was odd, because the heat of the horses should have melted it by now.

Lucy sat down beside the fire. She kept her gloves on, because the room was so chilly. 'What's happened?' she demanded. Nora waited, standing, in the doorway.

Jeremy said to her, 'Nora, this is no concern of yours. You would be better occupied lighting a fire in your mistress's room, and unpacking her clothes.'

'Sure and why should *I* be lighting fires?' Nora wanted to know.

Jeremy turned back to her, his face a mask of well-trained superciliousness. 'Because there is nobody else to do it, my dear; that is why.'

Nora was about to protest further, but Lucy raised her hand and said, 'Nora, if you would. I must talk to Jeremy in private.'

'Very good, miss,' Nora told her, and gave her a formal curtsey; as if to indicate that the intimacy they had shared during their journey from England had now been summarily brought to an end.

Nora closed the door behind her. Jeremy waited until he

was sure that she was gone, and then he said, 'On the second of January, Miss Darling, your attorneys paid me a visit. Mr Greenbaum came in person. He said that he would be sending you a wire, and writing to you personally, but it seems as if the wire failed to reach you, and as if you and the letter crossed in mid–Atlantic.'

'What did he say?' Lucy asked. 'What on earth's the matter?'

'Mr Greenbaum could tell me very little, Miss Darling, since I am only your *major domo*. But was necessary for him to inform me that there had been legal action taken in California, and that the oil-wells which you believed to be yours had been successfully established in the California courts to belong to somebody else.'

'*What?*' said Lucy, shocked. 'What do you mean, they belong to somebody else?'

'Please, Miss Lucy . . . I was told only what it was necessary for me to know. Mr Greenbaum said that all your bank accounts have been frozen, and that I should immediately cut down the household budget to the absolute minimum. I had to sell the horses and the brougham just to pay the rest of the staff their severance wages, Miss Darling; and I myself have not drawn wages for two weeks.'

'I don't understand,' said Lucy. She felt faint and shivery, as if she weren't here at all. This was a practical joke, surely? Any minute now, the boilers would fire up, and the coal would start to crackle brightly in the hearth. Any minute now, the electric lights would sparkle, and all her staff would appear to welcome her home.

But Jeremy continued to look at her through the strained winter light, the skin of his cheeks as criss-crossed with crumples as a handkerchief, and she knew with a terrible empty dread that he was telling her the truth.

'What am I going to do?' she whispered. (Who said that? Did I say that?) She really had no idea. In a few short weeks, she had fallen from being the incandescent darling of New

York high society, the Lightbulb Girl, pampered and flattered and followed by the gossip-reporters from ball to ball, asked to marry by English aristocracy, to nothing whatsoever, not worth a mention, a penniless parentless girl from Oak City, Kansas. All she had to show for her briefly-sparkling career was an illegitimate baby and a few steamer-trunks packed with silken gowns.

Jeremy intoned, 'I have sought other employment, Miss Darling. I hope you will forgive me. But I will remain here until you have sorted matters out with your attorneys.'

Lucy swallowed, and nodded, and said, 'Thank you,' although she didn't feel like thanking him. He should be taking care of her, especially now that she was pregnant; just like Mr Greenbaum should be taking care of her, and all of her servants, and Jamie, and Henry. Why had Henry been so full of himself? If Henry had been more sympathetic, she would have been able to tell him about the baby, and he wouldn't have minded, and then she wouldn't have had to run away.

And as for Jamie, it was *his* child; but what concern had *he* shown for her? He hadn't even written, when she was in England.

And as for Nora, all she could do was to sulk, because she hadn't been asked into the morning room; and because Lucy had treated her like a servant, which she was.

Jeremy said, 'Mr Greenbaum left me some money for you, Miss Darling, two hundred dollars; for incidental expenses such as food and carfare.'

'Thank you,' Lucy repeated, very quietly. She had a strange feeling that she had once said 'Thank you' in just that way before. Outside the window, it looked as if it were snowing again, but it was only a gust of chilly wind blowing around the corner of the house, and whirling flakes of snow from the stable roof.

Ira Greenbaum, she supposed, was as considerate as anybody

could have expected, for an attorney whose fees could probably not be met. He had a squat, compressed body, and his head rolled around in his collar like a large plum-pudding about to roll off a plate. His office was intensely dark and smelled of sour paper and sausage and damp flannel trousers.

As he spoke, he restlessly winnowed through sheets of paper and folded letters as if he were searching for something crucial which he never really expected to find.

'Shortly after you and the late Mr Darling had left for Europe, Miss Darling, we had a communication from Mr – what-was-his-name – your company attorney in Los Angeles –'

'Mr Thurloe Daby,' said Lucy. She was dressed in chocolate-brown velvet this morning, with darker brown piping, and a pheasant-feather hat. She felt tired. She knew she had mauvish circles under her eyes. But she felt much more composed than she had yesterday.

'*Daby*, that was his name ... *Daby*. Odd name that, Daby. Sounds like Baby. But, anyhow, Mr *Daby* told us that a fellow called Beaumont had been arrested in mid-December by police in Charleston, South Carolina, after a fatal stabbing of a sea-captain on the dockfront. They charged him with murder in the first degree. Seems like Beaumont had been out to get his revenge on this sea-captain on account of some contraband deal between them that had turned sour.

'Anyhow, that isn't here and that isn't there. The point was that when the police searched Beaumont's house, looking for contraband as evidence, they found amongst plenty of other fascinating goods a gold ring and a boxful of papers belonging to a man called Nathaniel Touchstone, of Los Angeles, California.'

'What does that have to do with me?' asked Lucy. 'I don't know anybody called Touchstone. I *never* knew anybody called Touchstone.'

'Please, bear with me,' said Ira Greenbaum, still winnowing, still searching. 'It really isn't that complicated. When the South Carolina police wrote to the Los Angeles police, asking for information about Nathaniel Touchstone – asking for his whereabouts, you see, so that he could claim back his jewellery and his papers, they were told that Touchstone had once lived in Charleston, years ago, but that he had gone west to California to prospect for oil.

'He'd been pretty successful, too. Had a splendid house, plenty of land, owned an orange-grove, too. But, you know – in spite of all this – house, money – about three years ago, he committed suicide. Took poison.'

Ira Greenbaum's head wobbled from side to side, as if he were addressing a jury. '*Why* had he committed suicide? Well, because of remorse, apparently. He left a letter saying that about a year previous he had gotten very drunk one night with some old friends from South Carolina, and finished up the evening's entertainment by visiting a house of ill-repute in the Mexican district. He had woken up in the morning to find himself in bed with a young Mexican whore of not much more than ten years old, dead she was, stabbed to death, and himself covered in blood, and his own claspknife between the sheets.

'*God forgive me for what I did to that girl*, that's what he said in his letter, and he went to his grave convinced that he had murdered her. At the time, of course, what with the suicide letter, that looked to the Los Angeles police like the close of the matter. Great many people commit suicide in California, that's what they said, disappointment, broken dreams, whisky and suchlike. But now Nathaniel Touchstone's ring and papers had turned up mysteriously in Charleston, at the home of this fellow Beaumont.

'Well, the Charleston police talked to Beaumont; and in exchange for some leniency in the matter of the stabbed sea-captain, Beaumont told them what he knew about Nathaniel Touchstone.

'Years ago, Beaumont had been partners in the contraband

business with Touchstone, as well as a man called Weale and a man called Conroy.'

'Conroy?' asked Lucy. 'You mean *Casper* Conroy, my uncle?'

Ira Greenbaum nodded, and sharply sniffed. 'The same man, your uncle. Those three had made their living by smuggling everything and anything, apparently – guns, liquor, children. You name it. But after some kind of a disagreement, all three of them had broken up and gone their separate ways. Weale tended bar in Charleston for a while, your Uncle Casper went to Denver. At first, Touchstone seemed to have disappeared without trace. But it wasn't too long before Weale accidentally discovered from a California sea-captain that Touchstone had gone to Los Angeles and made himself a tidy profit in oil, legitimately, too . . . and that was when the mischief began.

'Weale rounded up Beaumont; and the two of them travelled by railroad to Los Angeles and re-acquainted themselves with Touchstone. Touchstone wasn't at all pleased to see Weale again, that's what Beaumont said. They had never been the best of friends, but Weale persuaded Touchstone to go out drinking. He knew from experience that Touchstone couldn't hold his liquor particularly well. By the time they took Touchstone to a house of ill-repute in the Mexican district, Touchstone was well-nigh unconscious.'

Ira Greenbaum paused, and looked sharply at Lucy, and asked, 'You're not feeling unwell, Miss Darling? You're looking a little pale.'

'I'm . . . fine,' Lucy told him. In actual fact, she felt as if the book-crowded office walls were shuffling closer and closer; and that she would soon be pressed to death between stacks of legal encyclopedias and choked on sheaves of musty paper.

'I could have my secretary bring you a glass of water? Or maybe some tea? She makes terrible tea, enough to revive anybody.'

337

Lucy shook her head. 'I haven't been quite myself, that's all.'

Ira Greenbaum rocked his head from side to side. 'It's this winter weather. *Paskudnak*, disgusting. I feel just the same.'

'You were telling me what happened to the man called Touchstone,' Lucy reminded him.

'Sure I was! And it was terrible, too. Weale and Beaumont found and killed a young Mexican girl. Killed her, just like that! Then they rolled her up in a blanket, and took her to the room where Touchstone was sleeping. According to Beaumont, Weale did the murdering . . . although of course there's nobody left alive to say that it wasn't Beaumont who did the dirty work himself. Then they left, so that Touchstone would wake up next to the dead girl, and think that *he* had committed the murder himself, when he was drunk.

'Which of course is what he *did* think, and went into a blind panic.

'He showed Weale the girl's body, and begged for help. He was a respectable oil magnate by now; the last thing he could afford was a scandal like this. Weale made a great pretence of shock and horror, but helped him to dispose of the girl's remains; and agreed to cover up the evidence. But in return, as insurance, Touchstone would have to make over to Weale a percentage of his Seal Beach oil holdings. Touchstone had two other equally profitable oil holdings further down the coast. What Weale was asking apparently didn't seem too much. Not to keep him from hanging, anyway.

'So that's how Weale got his hands on the title to the oil holding. By murder, you see; by blackmail. He even formed a company in the name of Ferris. Kind of a joke, you understand, Ferris Weale.

'But it wasn't long before Weale began to be discontented with his share of the oil, and he threatened Touchstone yet again, unless Touchstone gave him more. They had a terrific argument, apparently, but we don't know what the outcome of it was because Beaumont wasn't with them at the time. But the very next day Touchstone was found dead by arsenic poisoning. He had written a long suicide letter about "remorse" for murdering the Mexican girl, and another letter making over all of his oil to Weale.

'If Weale killed Touchstone, which he undoubtedly did, it was a pretty clever thing to do ... the police were relieved that they had managed to solve two deaths at once. Two birds with one stone. They didn't take the trouble to look any further for murderers.

'The story doesn't end there, though. Weale told Beaumont that the oil-well wasn't producing more than a few barrels of poor-quality crude every day; and paid Beaumont off. Pretty well, fifty or sixty thousand dollars. Beaumont went back to Charleston and bought himself a grand house, and a carriage, and a wine-cellar, and a different lady every night. But it wasn't more than a year before he'd spent everything that Weale had given him. He returned to California and quickly discovered that Weale had been lying and that the oil-well was prospering, and had made Weale astronomically rich.

'Beaumont didn't have the wit to tackle Weale on his own. So he wrote to your Uncle Casper Conroy and asked him to come to California to help him. He had found a druggist who was prepared to swear that he had supplied Weale with arsenic, and that Weale had told him it was "for settling a score with Mr Touchstone". Beaumont intended to blackmail Weale, in just the same way that Weale had blackmailed Touchstone. But he needed money, to pay off the druggist; and a maid who would say that she had seen Weale writing Touchstone's so-called suicide letter, and was prepared to *say* that she had, in court, but only for a price.'

'How much?' asked Lucy, faintly.

'I'm sorry?'

'How much money did he need, to pay these people off, the druggist and the maid?'

339

'I'm not sure exactly. The figure of three hundred dollars was mentioned.'

Lucy thought of her mother's jewellery; of Uncle Casper's eyes, watching her.

Ira Greenbaum said, 'Your uncle went to California. He met up with Weale; and presumably threatened to tell the police about Touchstone, if Weale didn't give him a share in Ferris Oil. Your man *Daby* said there were furious arguments, but that Weale agreed, in the end, and signed over forty-nine per cent. Hm! Your uncle was a real forty-niner, and no mistake!

'But then there was a strange shooting incident, and Weale was killed, supposedly by Mexicans, but nobody knows why. Certainly not Beaumont; or if he does, he's not telling. The oil-field passed in its entirety to your uncle, and thus, when your uncle died, to you.'

'But my deeds are legal,' Lucy protested. 'They were legally drawn up. My friend Jamie Cullen did it for me. And nobody ever proved that my uncle killed Mr Ferris, or Mr Weale, or whatever his name was, did they?'

Ira Greenbaum shrugged. 'Your deeds are legal in the sense that *you* did nothing illegal. But Weale obtained his holdings in Touchstone's oil by fraud and murder and forgery; and so whether your uncle was implicated in the death of Mr Weale or not, the oil-holdings should rightfully have passed to Touchstone's closest next-of-kin, or failing that, back to the railroad company. Whoever those holdings belong to, Miss Darling, they surely don't belong to you.'

Lucy sat in silence for a very long time. Then she stood up. She didn't know what else to do.

'You mean that I have nothing at all?'

'I'm afraid that's the way of it. Strictly speaking, you may owe the legitimate leaseholders a great deal of money – everything you've spent. But I expect that I can negotiate you out of that one.'

'I can't even pay *you*.'

Ira Greenbaum's head tilted to the left; he smiled, a little archly. 'Let's just say that I prefer to tie up loose ends. What are you going to be doing for your dinner tonight?'

'I don't know. I hadn't thought.'

Ira Greenbaum lifted up papers, let them fall. 'Maybe I could take you to a restaurant I know. It's not exactly Delmonico's, but then it's not exactly Bode's, either.'

'Thank you, Mr Greenbaum, I'd rather not.'

'You have to eat, Miss Darling.'

'I can find ways to feed myself, thank you.'

Ira Greenbaum stopped shuffling his papers for a moment and watched her with passive regret. 'You have to vacate the house by the end of the month.'

Lucy swallowed, and nodded, but didn't say anything.

'I'm sorry things had to happen this way. My father always used to say that it's no disgrace to be poor, but it's no honour, either.'

'Your father sounds as if he was a wise man.'

'My father ... I don't know. My father knew nothing about anything. And he was never rich, either. The *goldeneh medina*, that's what he used to call America, the Golden Land, but I could never tell if he was being serious or sarcastic.'

'Good day, Mr Greenbaum.'

'Good day, Miss Darling.'

In one of the fiercest February blizzards that the Middle West had ever seen, Lucy and Nora travelled westward through Indiana and Missouri to Kansas City, where they boarded the Kansas Pacific for the last leg of their journey through Topeka and Fort Riley and Salina, the snow blinding out the names of the towns at every stop, the snow turning the whole journey into a whirling, freezing dream.

The only warmth in the whole world seemed to be inside her, inside her own womb, where her baby nestled. As the train slowly clanked through the snow, she held her hands clasped over her stomach and closed her eyes and tried to feel what it was feeling; think what it was thinking. A tiny life, depending entirely on her.

Nora watched her with steady devotion. She had never been farther west than Elizabeth, New Jersey; but she and Lucy had developed a curious bond between them which seemed to have grown stronger and more intricate since Lucy had lost all of her wealth, and neither of them had questioned for a moment that Nora should accompany Lucy back home.

The blizzard was still screeching when they reached Oak City. They climbed down the ice-slippery steps to the ground. There was nobody to meet them: nobody knew they were coming. They carried their own bags across to the depot building. The snow was blown into snakes around their boots; their scarves whipped and curled and lashed their cheeks.

'Sure it's powerful chilly here!' Nora shouted over the blasting of steam from the locomotive. 'If this isn't the chilliest place on God's good earth!'

'It gets colder!' Lucy shouted back at her.

'That's a lie! It couldn't! I think that the tip of my nose just snapped off!'

They were lucky. They found old man Maeterlinck waiting outside the depot with his enclosed business-wagon, waiting for anyone who wanted a ride through the snow. He looked more like Santa Claus than ever, white-bearded, cherry-nosed, wrapped up in a thick green coat. He was too old for joinery these days, so he picked up pennies by giving rides, and doing oddjobs. He helped them with their bags, and then they climbed into the wagon, and brushed the snow from their coats, and unwound their scarves. Inside the business-wagon it smelled of pipe-tobacco and old man Maeterlinck's lunch, and it wasn't much warmer than it was outside, but at least they were protected from the wind.

'How's things?' old man Maeterlinck asked Lucy.

'Thought you would've had your own train by now, and twenty blackies to carry your bags.'

'I didn't want to appear too high'n'mighty,' lied Lucy.

'Well, something to be said for that,' old man Maeterlinck sniffed. 'Always said that poor folks never have no real enemies, but rich folks never have no real friends.'

He sniffed noisily, and then he said, 'Too bad about your pa, wodden it? And the Skipping Widder?'

'You heard about it?'

'It was all in the papers. How they fell off of that balcony and all. Don't know what the hell Molly Sweeney thought she was doing; but then she always was that way, wodden she? Always dancing and dreaming, dreaming and dancing.'

'There are worse things,' Nora retorted.

'Oh, sure, there are worse things,' old man Maeterlinck agreed. 'Like getting your great toe stuck fast in the faucet. Or biting into a cracky-wheat loaf and finding your wife's front tooth.'

Lucy didn't tell him that Jack was dead. She simply didn't want to.

They descended the gradient towards the Saline River. The snow was still flying, but not so fiercely now, and the wind appeared to have dropped. There wasn't much else for them to talk about, so they sat in silence. The wagon's springs creaked; old man Maeterlinck sniffed and cleared his throat; snowflakes pattered against the windows, soft as the finger-touches of forgotten women. Lucy could almost believe that they were the wind-blown spirits of all those wives who had died on the High Plains of Kansas, work-worn, bearing children, diseased, or just broken-hearted.

At last they reached the Cullen farm. Old man Maeterlinck whoaed his horses just outside the front door; and helped them down; and just as he did so, Jerrold Cullen appeared, in a thick sheepskin coat with the collar turned up, and the flaps of his muskrat hat pulled down over his ears.

'Lucy Darling!' he called out, in surprise. 'This is an honour!'

Lucy lifted her skirts as she stepped through the snow. She took hold of Jerrold Cullen's hand and squeezed it tight. 'Mr Cullen; it's so good to see you. This is Nora ... she's my – well, she's my companion. And my friend, too.'

Old man Maeterlinck heaved down their bags and dropped them in the snow. 'You want to drag 'em into the house, m'friend?' Jerrold asked him.

'Not me,' coughed old man Maeterlinck. 'Getting a sight too old for lugging ladies' portmantooties.'

Jerrold shrugged. 'Don't worry about it. I'll have Martin carry them in.'

Old man Maeterlinck came shuffling up to them and took off his hat.

'How much do I owe you?' Lucy asked him.

'Three dollars even.'

Lucy lifted her purse and unfastened it, but made no attempt to open it. She knew that after their railroad fares and their meals she had only $1.78 left. She had been hoping to raise a little more money in Hays City tomorrow by pawning the remainder of her mother's jewellery; but right now she was almost flat-busted.

Her eyes caught Jerrold's eyes. At first he wasn't quite sure what she was silently asking him. But then she looked meaningfully sideways at old man Maeterlinck, and appealingly back to Jerrold, and Jerrold understood.

'Oh, sure, I'm sorry,' he said, and dug into the pocket of his sheepskin coat, and brought out two silver dollars, and handed them over. Old Man Maeterlinck bit them, sniffed, pushed them into his glove, and then shuffled away. Meanwhile Martin had appeared at the door.

'Dad?'

'Yes, Martin. How about carrying these bags inside for Lucy? Looks like she's staying for a little while. And this is Nora, Lucy's friend. Looks like Nora's staying for a little while, too.'

'Hi, Lucy,' grinned Martin. 'Thought you millionairesses had electro-plated carriages, and hundreds of servants.'

'Not me,' Lucy smiled.

'It's great to see you. Does Jamie know you're here? He's coming back from Manhattan Friday or Saturday. He'll go crazy to see you.'

'Well, I'm looking forward to seeing him, too.'

They went into the house. It was just as puritanical in its decor as ever, but all the fires were well stacked up, and it was wonderfully warm. Mrs Cullen came out of the kitchen with floury hands to kiss Lucy welcome. 'They tell us all about you, at the store. The new owner's a really good man. Nothing like your poor pappa, but a real good straight-forward man.'

Lucy was given a plain blue-decorated room overlooking the river valley; Nora was found a smaller room over the kitchen. Lucy's room was sparse. A single mahogany bed with a blue throwover; a blue rag rug; an oval cheval mirror, and a washstand. She unbuttoned her boots and then collapsed back exhausted on the bed. She couldn't believe that she was really back in Oak City, as poor as ever. But then she couldn't believe that she had really been away, either. The past months of silk dresses and champagne and handsome young men seemed no more substantial than something she might have read in a book. And she had been to England, too!

She had owned gold knives and forks, real gold. Now everything she owned was locked up in two large port-manteaux; and in her mind; and in her womb. But, strangely, it seemed like quite enough.

On the wall of her room hung an embroidered sampler. Its simple message read, *Naked came I out of my mother's womb, and naked shall I return thither: the Lord gave, and the Lord hath taken away; blessed be the name of the Lord.*

She closed her eyes. She slept for a while, and dreamed of trains, and flying snow, and half-remembered faces in a blur of winter whiteness, as if somebody had been trying to obscure them with fence-paint.

Jerrold said, with his fingers steepled, 'Lucy, you'd better tell me what's wrong.'

Lucy's eyes glistened in the firelight. It was after supper now. Nora was helping Mrs Cullen in the kitchen with the pots and pans. The boys had gone out to lock up the cattle and the horses. The house was still fragrant with the aroma of chicken pot-pie and freshly-baked bread. The clock ticked, the fire spat. The cat sat in front of the hearth with its paws tucked in, its eyes slitted, dreaming of Egypt.

Lucy's hands lay white on her dark maroon dress. The only jewellery she wore was her mother's cameo brooch.

'There's nothing wrong,' she replied. 'Really, there's nothing.'

'What made you come back here to Oak City? Don't tell me you're just visiting. If visiting was all you had in mind, you would've come in the summer.'

Lucy remained silent, staring at the fire.

'You know what it says in the Bible,' said Jerrold. '"The truth shall make you free."'

Lucy smiled, without looking at him.

'You've lost your money, haven't you?' Jerrold asked her, very gently.

'Yes,' whispered Lucy.

'Everything? You've really lost everything?'

'Everything. The oil-well wasn't even mine to begin with; never was; we had no right. A man was killed for it; and then the man who killed him was killed for it; and then the man who killed *him* was killed for it.'

She looked up; and her face was so sad that Jerrold could have taken her into his arms and comforted her like one of his own daughters.

'It was never mine. Not for one minute. I was lucky they didn't make me pay everything back. I was never the Lightbulb Girl, not truly: I was never anything at all.'

'How's Jack taking it?' asked Jerrold. 'Is he coming out to join you?'

'Jack's dead,' Lucy told him. 'He died in England. We buried him there.'

'I'm sorry,' said Jerrold. 'I really am truly sorry.'

'Spilled milk,' Lucy replied. 'Nothing but spilled milk, that's all.'

'He wasn't in pain?'

'No,' Lucy whispered. 'He wasn't in pain. Not in his body, anyway.'

'He was a tortured man, your father, if you'll forgive me.'

'Yes,' said Lucy; and in spite of the fact that she didn't want them to, her eyes filled up with tears. 'Yes, he was a tortured man.'

Jerrold reached across and laid his hand on top of hers. 'What are you going to do now? You're going to stay with us here for a while, I hope?'

'For a few days, if you'll let me. I have to go to Hays City to get some money. Then I'm going to start looking for some work. Maybe the new man at the store might have me.'

'Lucy, you can stay here, long as you like. There's plenty of work on a farm this size, and never enough people to take care of it. And your Nora seems a real friendly willing woman. You can both stay, however long you like.'

Lucy knelt down on the rug beside Jerrold, and took hold of his hands and pressed them between hers. 'Forgive me for coming here,' she pleaded. 'After they told me that everything was gone, I was stranded in New York with no money, no carriage, no servants, nothing – nothing except my railroad fare west, and Nora, and a memory of just what a loving family home this is. You can throw me out whenever you wish; and as soon as you wish. I know that. I don't want charity. But this house is home to me, Mr Cullen; the only home I have.'

Jerrold stroked her shining blonde hair. 'You can stay for ever if you want to. And you're certainly not leaving before Jamie gets home.' She could feel his voice rumbling like

347

distant thunder. But it was reassuring thunder. The kind of thunder that makes you feel glad that you're at home.

Nora came in, and stood by the door, smiling; and it was then that Lucy knew that everything was going to turn out all right.

Jamie arrived home on Saturday afternoon, off the three o'clock train from Manhattan. Lucy hid behind the front door as soon as she saw the wagon arrive from the depot, and when Jamie came bursting in, stamping his snowy boots on the mat, she sprang out at him, and cried, 'Surprise!'

Jamie whooped like a cowhand, and lifted her up, and whirled her around.

'Careful!' she said. 'Careful!'

'Oh, I wouldn't drop you,' he grinned. 'You're precious to me like china.'

'When you were a kid, you broke half of momma's Carlsbad dinner service,' Martin reminded him.

'Hey now, you helped me,' Jamie retorted. 'I did the cups, but you did the saucers.'

He took off his cap and hung up his coat. 'What brings you all the way back to Oak City?' he asked Lucy. 'Thought you would have taken the grand tour of Europe, while you were there. Paris, Rome, Madrid.'

Mrs Cullen came up and kissed Jamie, and then put her arms around Lucy's shoulders. 'She's had some bad fortune, Jamie. You just be kind to her.'

They went through to the living room, where Nora brought them coffee (with just a nip of whisky for Jamie, to warm him up after his train-ride). Lucy told Jamie what had happened, and Jamie listened without saying a single word. It was only when she had quite finished that he knocked back his whisky, and wiped his mouth, and asked her, 'You're not going to marry Henry, then?'

'Of course not, I can't.'

Jamie rubbed the back of his neck. 'You can't? Just

because you lost your money? What difference should that make, if Henry really loves you? Rich or poor, shouldn't make no difference at all.'

'Oh Jamie, of *course* it makes a difference. Henry fell in love with an oil millionairess. He would never have fallen in love with a shopgirl.'

'Well, more fool him,' shrugged Jamie. 'Rich or poor, that doesn't make any difference to me. The only riches that are worth bothering about, as far as I'm concerned, are the riches of happiness.

'Amen,' said Jerrold, from the far corner of the room. 'The unsearchable riches of Christ.'

Lucy sat quiet for a moment, with her hands clasped in her lap. Then she said, 'There was another reason why I couldn't marry him.'

Jamie waited for her to tell him what it was, but she didn't.

'What other reason?' he asked, at last.

'Could I talk to you privately?'

'I don't think father's going to snitch on any of your secrets, are you, father?'

Jerrold grunted in amusement. He was reading *The True Measure of Christian Forbearance* – 'Wherefore, if meat make my brother to offend, I will eat no flesh while the world standeth, lest I make my brother to offend.'

'All the same,' said Lucy. 'I'd like you to be the first to hear it.'

Jerrold closed his book and tugged down his vest. 'Don't worry, I have work to do. I'll leave you two alone.'

When he had left the room, Jamie sat back in his chair with his cup of coffee, and Lucy thought that he was not only beginning to talk like a lawyer, he was beginning to *look* like one, too. He was just as handsome as ever, but he was too pale from sitting in offices and courtrooms; and paleness didn't suit him. 'What's this fearful secret, then?' he asked her, sucking his coffee-spoon. He would never have done that two years ago: that was an office habit.

349

'It wasn't the money,' said Lucy. 'It wasn't the money at all. I didn't find out about the money until I got back to New York.'

'Well, if it wasn't the money, what was it?' Still playing the lawyer.

'You don't have to *badger* me, Jamie. I'm not a witness in court.'

'I'm sorry. But you *can* tell me. Listen, I promise you! I won't snitch and I won't bite.'

'Maybe you won't. But you may get angry.'

Jamie laughed. 'Why should I get angry? I resigned myself a long time ago to the fact that you don't actually love me. You wrote and *told* me that you didn't love me.'

'Jamie, I do love you. You know I love you. I was confused.'

'*You* were confused? How do you think *I* felt?'

'I'm sorry, Jamie. I'm truly sorry. Henry was so —' Thinking of Henry, she couldn't stop the tears. Damn them! Tears, just when she didn't want them!

Jamie put down his cup of coffee and tugged a clean handkerchief out of his vest pocket. 'Henry was so *what?*' he asked her, quietly and kindly.

She wiped her eyes. 'I didn't mean to cry. I promised myself when Jack died — I promised myself that I never would.'

'That was a pretty stupid promise. How could you keep a promise like that?'

'I thought I'd try.'

She waited for a moment or two, and then she said, 'Henry was everything that I'd ever dreamed about. That was all. Well, that was more than enough. He was aristocratic and wonderfully educated and full of life and he would never take no for an answer.'

Jamie didn't say anything, but waited for her to tell him what her secret was. The secret why she couldn't marry the man she had always dreamed about.

350

When she actually said it, however, the words sounded like Chinese. He heard her speak; he thought that he had understood what she said; but his mind obviously refused to interpret the sounds that she had made into intelligible English.

'You're what?' he asked her.

Then, 'You're *what*?'

He offered, of course, more than once. But her mind was made up. She didn't want to think of marriage until the baby was born. She was still unsure of how she felt; and the last thing she wanted to do was to marry Jamie and turn his life into a never-ending purgatory of unreturned love. She had seen what a marriage like that had done to Jack Darling. It had eaten him like acid, inch by inch; and in the end it had killed him before his time.

Jerrold, to Lucy's relief, was neither angry nor disapproving. It would have been understandable for a Christian zealot to send Lucy out into the snow; and Jamie along with her. But when Jamie broke the news to him, with Lucy watching from the hallway outside, Jerrold said nothing at all. He seemed bemused, more than anything else, as if Lucy's pregnancy had presented him with a moral problem which he was unable to understand. If Jesus had been born in Oak City, what would Jerrold have done then? She saw Jerrold nodding; saw him frown; his hair shining in the blue-white light from the snowfalls outside the window.

When Jamie left, he said nothing; but sat in his rocking-chair with his hands clasped in front of him, not rocking, slightly hunched.

Later that day, Jerrold came into the parlour where Lucy was embroidering, and stood by the door watching her. Lucy looked up at him, and smiled, and then laid her embroidery down in her lap.

'You're not angry with me, are you?' she asked him.

'Angry? Why should I be? You know what the Lord said. Judge not, that ye be not judged.'

'This is your grandson,' said Lucy, laying her hand on her stomach.

Jerrold came into the room, and sat down, and looked at Lucy for a long time, his head couched in his hand.

'Do you know something, Lucy?' he asked her. 'I knew your mother very well. She used to come here often; for flowers, for cheese; or just to talk to Mrs Cullen, whenever she felt lonely. Your mother was what you might call an independent spirit; not like your father at all. She took whatever the world had to offer.'

Lucy didn't interrupt him, but watched him carefully. She could sense strongly that he was trying to tell her something; trying to give her clues to what she should do.

'The thing is,' said Jerrold, looking down at his hand as it rested on his knee; 'the thing is that your mother followed her own sense of what was right and what was wrong. Sometimes she shocked me, you know, the things she said; because she was pious and churchgoing and believed in the Lord, but she believed in happiness, too, everybody seeking their own fulfilment; she believed that the Lord expected every one of us to be happy and fulfilled.'

There was a long pause, and then Jerrold said, 'You've heard me talking strict to Jamie, specially when it comes to his law studies. But Jamie doesn't take too much notice of that, and nor should he. Jamie's going to be happy no matter what I say, Jamie's going to be fulfilled, because he's following the course that his heart dictates. The Lord has given him a path to tread and he's treading it. My advice to you, Lucy, honey, is that you should do the same. You've seen the elephant now, haven't you? You've seen New York, and London, and the way that rich folk live. There isn't much in Kansas that can match up to that kind of living.'

In a lacy-soft voice, Lucy asked him, 'Are you trying to say that I should leave?'

'Oh, no, not at all, sweetheart! you can stay for ever, if that's what you want!'

'Then what? I don't understand.'

Jerrold took a deep breath. 'I love Jamie, you know that; and I love you, too. And by all the Christian principles that I hold dear, I know that you should marry him. He's the natural father of your baby, after all. But if I'm going to be truthful, I think that you've been right to say that you won't. If you two married, then believe me, there wouldn't be nothing in it for either of you but pain.'

Jerrold had obviously said his piece, and had nothing more to say, because he sat back now, and watched Lucy anxiously, to see how she had taken it.

Lucy reached over and touched his hand. 'Thank you, Mr Cullen,' she told him. 'I can guess how hard it was for you to say that.'

'Sure thing,' said Jerrold, and stood up, and kissed her forehead, and went to round up his dairy herd for their evening milking.

But Lucy sat for a very long time alone by the fire, thinking about Jerrold's words, and almost feeling the world turning around her.

Spring came to the High Plains of Kansas; and then summer; and the grasses waved and whispered like the driest of oceans. Lucy spent her time helping Mrs Cullen in the kitchen, paring vegetables; or sewing. Her stomach was big, and very low, although she hadn't put on very much weight; and Mrs Cullen was sure that it was going to be a boy.

'What are you going to call him?' she asked Lucy one brilliant morning, as they sat together in the kitchen, cleaning wild fiddleheads for lunch.

Lucy could feel the baby pushing and stretching at her stomach. It kicked like an excited pony in the evening, when she sat down after supper, but during the day it stretched itself luxuriously and slowly, as if it were waking up from a long and befuddling dream.

I dreamed that I never existed, but now I do . . . She wondered if babies ever had dreams like that; or if they had memories of Heaven.

'I thought of Thomas,' she told Mrs Cullen.

'Well, Thomas is a good given name,' Mrs Cullen nodded. 'But what of a family name?'

'I don't know,' said Lucy.

Mrs Cullen stopped scraping the fuzz from the fiddleheads for a moment, and looked at Lucy with her intent grey Scandinavian eyes.

'Jamie worships you, you know that, don't you?' she said.

Lucy lowered her eyes.

'Jamie would die for you, Lucy, if you asked him to.'

'I never would. I would never do anything to hurt him, ever.'

'You're hurting him now, by carrying his child and refusing to marry him.'

'But what if I marry him and I just don't love him enough? What if I end up by being cruel to him, and vexatious, and hating him?'

Mrs Cullen took a deep breath. 'I don't think you would. I don't think that you have such spitefulness in you.'

'My momma wasn't spiteful; but she ruined my poppa. She *destroyed* him! I don't want Jamie to end up like Jack.'

'Perhaps Jamie's stronger than Jack,' Mrs Cullen suggested.

Lucy stared directly back at her. 'How can anybody be strong when the person they love doesn't love them in return?'

Mrs Cullen reached across the scrubbed deal table, and held Lucy's hand. 'What do you know about love and marriage, at eighteen years old? Some people marry for love; some people marry for money; most people marry for companionship. When you meet a man who loves you the way that Jamie loves you, you should think real seriously about what he is offering. Care, and friendship, and physical devotion. You must have found him physically attractive, that night you became pregnant.'

'I did and I do,' Lucy answered, boldly.

'So will you think of marrying him? Will you think of giving young Thomas his family name?'

Lucy scraped back her chair, and stood up, and walked across to the open door. A warm May wind was blowing softly through the oaks. On the grassy horizon, six or seven horses were galloping, as if they were runaways from a fairground carousel. Just in front of her, beside the brick pathway that led to the kitchen door, a bed of yellow-and-orange nasturtium flowers trembled. She thought: Jamie's so dear to me. Jamie's so good-looking. But I never wanted to have the family name Cullen; and I never wanted my children to have the family name Cullen, either. I know there's more, I've seen it! There are jewels and dances and fabulous people!

Please dear God don't let me end up here, married to Jamie. Please dear God. Otherwise my face will fade just like the faces of all those Kansas women fade; and my soul will tire of trying; and my spirit will end up pattering as a snowflake on some other poor girl's window, trying to warn her, trying to warn her, but melting too quickly to be seen.

She had a nightmare that hot July night of a moon that filled up the whole sky; and dragged everybody off the ground and into the air. Trees were wrenched up by their roots; shingles came flying off houses. Women screamed, cattle bellowed. Then the fences were ripped up and the soil itself was dragged into the sky in a blinding blizzard.

'*No!*' she shrieked, and woke up. She found that she was sweating, her nightgown was soaked and clung to her skin. Her stomach was drum-hard, and her muscles were gripping her as fiercely as Uncle Casper had gripped her.

'No,' she repeated, in a whisper, conscious that her first shriek had been silent, the swallowed shriek of a dreamer.

It was only when Mrs Cullen lifted the baby out of her that Lucy actually believed it. It was alive, an actual living baby. It steamed and it smelled and it coughed, and it clenched its tiny fists. In the fraction of a second, she had seen that she couldn't call it Thomas, because it was a little girl, and had counted its fingers and toes.

'A girl, God bless her, the little angel!' cried Mrs Cullen.

Mrs Cullen's face was ivory-white with exhaustion and varnished with perspiration, but she couldn't stop herself from clapping her hands together with joy, and saying, 'Thank you, Lord!' and 'Ettie, go tell your father, he's a grandpa! And it's a girl!'

The lamps around the bed were still alight; even though it was well past seven o'clock, and the sun had already dimmed their flames into flickering transparency. Jamie's fifteen-year-old sister Sarah was so affected by the baby's sudden appearance that she was giggling and sobbing at the same time, which made her sound as if she had hiccups. With serene deftness, Mrs Cullen tied and cut the baby's rainbow-coloured cord (she had cut several of her own) and handed the baby to Nora with no more ceremony than if it were a fresh-baked loaf, just taken out of the oven.

'Wash her, please, Nora. There's a towel on the chair. Now then, Lucy, one more push to get out the after-birth.'

'Let me see her,' begged Lucy, in a croaky voice.

'Juh-juh-juh-juh! Just one minute. First of all, I want you to push.'

Mrs Cullen disposed of the afterbirth in a wrapped-up copy of the Kansas City newspaper. Then she sponged Lucy with cool water and her best lily-of-the-valley soap, and soothingly shushed her, and told her what a good girl she was, and helped her to change her nightgown. At last, Nora came forward holding her baby, washed and patted dry, and dressed in a daisy-cloth wrapper.

'She's not crying,' said Lucy. 'Isn't she supposed to cry?'

'Oh, she will, I promise you, she will,' said Mrs Cullen, 'Just as soon as she's hungry, or cold.'

Lucy held her daughter in her arms with caution and exhilaration and the feeling that her whole life had altered completely, that she wasn't even Lucy any more. Those tiny red crinkled hands, with miniature fingernails! That ugly crinkled red face, with plumlike eyes, and a mouth that pouted like a goldfish! and most of all that pungent and unforgettable aroma of somebody freshly-arrived from Heaven.

It was then that Jerrold came into the room, and stood in his shirtsleeves with his arms by his sides.

'My grand-daughter?' he asked Mrs Cullen; and Mrs Cullen nodded, with tears in her eyes.

Jerrold came forward and sat on the side of the bed. He delicately touched the baby's fingers, and brushed her cheek, and slowly shook his head.

'I'd forgotten,' he said, with a catch in his voice, 'I'd simply forgotten. You tiny one! Have you any idea what you're going to name her?'

'I'm going to call her Blanche,' Lucy told him. And then without warning she let out a sob as painful as a stab with a kitchen-knife; and clutched hold of Jerrold's shoulder; and cried so bitterly and uncontrollably that she started to gasp for breath, and Mrs Cullen had to lift the baby away from her.

'Oh God,' Lucy wept. 'Oh God, oh God, oh God.' But at last she managed to take in six or seven deep breaths, and steady herself, and wipe her eyes with the sleeve of her nightgown.

'There now, there now,' Mrs Cullen soothed her. 'It's just the birth. It's all the strength God gives you, letting itself out. Every woman cries, when she has her first baby.'

Lucy, with her lips clenched tight and her throat aching with emotion, looked across at tiny Blanche and nodded. 'Yes,' she tried to say, but she couldn't; because it wasn't true. She had wept when she had called her baby Blanche because it was the first time since she had left Brackenbridge that she had allowed herself to think about Henry, and how much she loved him; and how much Henry loved her.

Mrs Cullen said, 'Would you like her back now?' and Lucy nodded, and took her back.

'Sha-sha,' she whispered, in Blanche's petal-delicate ear.

Mrs Cullen smiled. 'We've sent Martin to the depot, to telegraph Jamie.'

Lucy said, 'Thank you,' without taking her eyes off Blanche.

Jerrold glanced at his wife, and twitched his head two or three times towards Lucy, to encourage her to speak. Mrs Cullen hesitated, and licked her lips, and then she said, 'You haven't yet thought any more about your baby having a father?'

'Sha-sha,' Lucy cooed at Blanche. 'You beautiful Sha-sha.'

'What I mean is,' said Mrs Cullen, 'you haven't thought any more about marrying Jamie?'

Lucy pretended not to hear, although she heard. She kissed Blanche's forehead, and hummed to her, and tried not to think about anything but babies and angels.

7

Old man Maeterlinck's business-wagon came rattling down the track between the oak trees a little after eleven o'clock on the ninth of August, a glaring Tuesday on the High Plains. Old man Maeterlinck came right up to the kitchen door and banged on the side of the hutch, and whistled between his teeth, and called out, 'Letter! Just arrived!'

Nora took the letter and tipped old man Maeterlinck two bits. 'It's for you, now, Lucy, from Washington.'

Lucy was sitting in the key-shaped arrangement of sunlight that fell through the kitchen door, stitching lace on to one of Blanche's bonnets, and at the same time easy-rocking Blanche's crib with her foot.

So far, Blanche had been the quietest of babies, except when she was bathed. Then she clenched herself up and screamed and shuddered without taking a breath until she was all wound up in her wrapper again, and rocked, and cooed to, and told what a darling little Darling she was.

It was obvious from the taut expression on Jamie's face that it hurt him to hear his daughter called 'Darling'. But Lucy still avoided talk about marriage. She was too happy as she was to talk about marriage. She loved Blanche, she loved the Cullen family; she loved Jamie, too. But she was terrified that if she married him that she would gradually tear him to pieces, and herself too.

And there was something else: if she married Jamie, she knew that she would be closing off forever any chance she might have of returning to that glamorous and privileged world of the wealthy.

She didn't allow herself to think about that very often. It seemed unbearably selfish. But when she was rocking Blanche's crib in the evening, after her feed, she would close her eyes and imagine herself sailing at Newport, or dancing at the Waldorf. It was bitterly hard to have been forced to give it all up.

After a week or two, Jamie no longer brought up the subject of getting wed. But he cuddled Blanche whenever he could, and played with her, and called her 'ma'am', or 'my little lady', and sang nursery-rhymes to her, and treated her just like his own daughter, which she was. Blanche, however, slept in Lucy's room at night; a room to which Jamie was not admitted; and when Blanche was breast-fed, she was breast-fed behind closed doors.

Lucy overheard Jerrold on several occasions trying to talk to Jamie about what he should do, but Jamie obstinately refused to discuss it. 'If she won't marry me, she won't marry me. There's nothing I can do about it.' Whenever he spent a few days at home, Jamie would go to his room early with a bottle of whisky and read law reports. Sometimes Lucy would hear him in the night, stumbling over his shoes or his bedside table, drunk with whisky and frustration.

Nora gave her the letter. She recognized the handwriting at once, and her heart tightened. *Now, though I toil to Samarkand, through rain and snow and stinging sand . . .*

'It's from Henry,' she said.

She opened it up carefully. Inside was a single sheet of paper embossed with the letter-heading of the British Embassy in Washington. Nora watched her while she read it, trying to discover what it said from her expression.

Washington, August 3, 1895

My dearest Lucy,

I have written you a score of letters, but posted none of them until now. I have to confess that your sudden departure from Brackenbridge filled me with the greatest grief, and in spite of your letter, I still find it inexplicable. I experienced a sense of loss unequalled in my life before, except when my dear mother died. This was superseded by a sharp resentment that you could not have confided in me.

Lucy, if you truly do not love me, then you have to do no more than tell me. I will accept whatever you say — not with joy, perhaps, but with good grace. Before I first saw you, I was a man for whom bachelorhood seemed to be the perfect state of affairs; after you left, I was a man for whom bachelorhood was the only future.

I was destined to have only one wife, or none at all; and that one wife is you.

If I am intruding on your new life, then please forgive me. I discovered your whereabouts from a colleague in the Embassy here in Washington, whom I had asked to monitor copies of the New York newspapers. Sure enough, he sent me two months ago the intelligence from the Wall Street Journal that your oil-holdings had been transferred to the Southern Pacific RR, and that you had returned to Oak City.

Lucy, if it was the loss of your wealth that caused you to run away from me, then have no fear whatsoever. I do not love you for your money; I love you for your darling self. You may not have heard in Kansas that Lord Rosebery's Liberal government was defeated in the House of Commons in June; and that there has since been a general election, which we have won triumphantly with a majority of 152.

Lord Salisbury has appointed me Under-Secretary of State at the Foreign Office, which was a slightly less exalted position than the Press and my friends had expected for me. But in order to assuage any possible embarrassment, he nominated me for membership of the Privy Council (a honour usually reserved for senior Ministers), and I have already been sworn in the presence of Her Majesty.

I am therefore financially capable of taking care of both of us; and I have rented excellent apartments at Carlton House Terrace.

My darling innocent Lucy, you broke my heart. If it is your decision that it must remain broken, then so be it. Only you have the wherewithal to repair it.

Give me at least the consideration of thinking carefully on this matter; and please reply, even if your answer is a final no. I am staying here in Washington until the last day of August, before returning to England. You may telegraph or write.

You are in my heart always,
Your loving, Henry.

Lucy re-read the letter, her eyes blurred and her hand trembling.

'What is it?' asked Nora, voraciously. 'What does he say?'

'He still wants me to marry him. He wants me to go back to England with him. He knows that I've lost all my money, but he says that it doesn't matter.'

'But what about Blanche? Does he know about Blanche?'

'I don't think so. All he knows is what appeared in the *Wall Street Journal*.'

'Do you still want to marry him?' asked Nora.

Lucy lowered the letter on to the table. 'I don't know. Yes, of course I do.'

'Would you take the baby with you?'

Lucy looked across at Blanche, sleeping in her crib, her eyes tightly closed, one little fist gradually uncurling.

'Henry thinks I'm innocent.'

'There's a difference between innocence and purity.'

'He thinks I'm pure, too.'

Nora laughed uncertainly, then stopped. 'You wouldn't leave Blanche, would you? You couldn't!'

'No,' said Lucy, 'I couldn't.'

She didn't sleep at all that night. She read Henry's letter again and again. Privy Councillor! Her Majesty the Queen! Carlton House Terrace! And more than anything else, those words of despairing endearment, '*I was destined to have only one wife, or none at all; and that one wife is you.*'

While she sat up in bed, reading the letter, she could hear Blanche's breathing from her crib. The harvest-dust had given her a little sniffle, so that each breath had a little catch in it. Lucy climbed out of bed and stood beside the crib, and thought that Blanche was the most perfect of all babies.

But then Lucy stood up, and saw her own face in the cheval mirror. A pretty young girl of eighteen years old, in a long cotton nightgown. A girl who had tasted wealth and society, and lost everything; but who had now been offered a second chance. Not just a second chance, either. A final chance. If she refused Henry now, then she might as well marry Jamie and stay in Kansas for the rest of her life, the wife of a country lawyer. Picnics in the garden, with blankets hung up on the clothesline to keep off the prairie wind; church socials and Kensingtons. Middle-age coming on before you know it. 'You want to trade that receipt for slipped custard pie?' She'd heard it.

'Sha-sha,' she sang to her baby. 'Oh, Sha-sha, my darling.'

Blanche stirred in her crib. Lucy picked her up, and held her close, breathing in her hot milkiness.

Take my heart sweet child of mine,
And promise to be true,
Then come what may I promise
I'll be overfond of you.

Blanche's head nestled against her neck, and her fingers clung tight to the ribbons of Lucy's nightgown. Even if she could have seen the tears that were streaming down Lucy's cheeks, she wouldn't have been able to understand them.

Mrs Cullen sat in the parlour window, with the sun shining through the bird-embroidered net curtains behind her, so that Lucy could hardly make out her face. However there was no mistaking the sadness in her voice.

'I don't know who you will be hurting the most,' she said. 'Your baby, or my son, or yourself.'

'I can't stay here in Kansas,' Lucy told her. 'Not when I have the chance to go. Mrs Cullen, I shall suffocate.'

Mrs Cullen turned her face in profile. Curved Swedish-looking forehead, tilted nose. 'Can you really leave Blanche?' she asked. 'Do you think you have the strength?'

'I can't take her, and I can't stay.'

'Does this man Henry mean so much to you? What can he give you that Jamie couldn't? If you were to stay here, and to marry Jamie, you would have a family, a complete family. You would always be cared for, you know that.'

'Yes,' said Lucy. 'I know that; and I'm grateful. I can never pay you back for what you've done for me.'

'You can pay me back by deciding not to go,' Mrs Cullen suggested.

Lucy bent her head forward and covered her eyes with her hand. Her mind refused to work any more. She had thought over Henry's letter again and again and again, until she was numb. But she had known from the moment she had opened it what she was going to do. No matter how agonizing it would be to leave Blanche behind. No matter how much she would be hurting Jamie and all the rest of the Cullen family; she had to go. She couldn't explain it in a way that Mrs Cullen could understand. Blanche was so desperately dear to her. Blanche was not only *hers*, Blanche was *her*.

But out beyond the embroidered net curtains, across the yard, far beyond the grassy horizons of the High Plains, the spires of New York rose like the castles of haughty princes, and beyond New York lay the whole Atlantic Ocean, and England, and Italy, and India. Cities teeming with thousands of people!

How could any of that be comprehensible to Mrs Cullen, who would probably meet no more than fifty more people in the whole of her life, and was apparently quite content?

Even if Lucy were to stay in Oak City, and bring up Blanche, what would she tell Blanche about the world beyond? And when Blanche was eighteen, and wanted to go off and live her own life, what would she say then? You can't go because I didn't?

Mrs Cullen said, very quietly, 'I'm more than happy to raise Blanche as my own daughter, you know that.'

Lucy nodded behind her hand. She wasn't crying. Just at the moment, she couldn't cry. But she didn't want to show her face, not yet. In the darkness behind her hand, no decisions had to be made, and the clock, for a few moments, stood still.

*

She wrote to Henry that same evening, and took the letter to the depot herself, on horseback. On her way back she reined in her horse at Overbay's Bend, where she and Jamie used to lie on their backs and watch the cloud-castles. The wind was warm; the sky was clear; the river was furrowed with ripples.

What a time in her life, she thought. Too old to dream; too young to bear any burdens.

When she arrived back at the Cullen farm, Mrs Cullen was already feeding Blanche in the kitchen. Lucy stood in the doorway watching her, and felt that she had already given her up. She could still change her mind, she knew that. She could leave and travel to Washington and *still* change her mind. But something was waiting for her, far away to the east; and whether it was love or destiny or something else altogether, she knew that she would have to go.

When Jamie arrived home the following Saturday, Lucy was sitting in the apple-orchard. Blanche was lying on a blanket in the long grass, looking up at the way the sunlight flickered through the leaves, and gurgling. Jamie walked through the lines of apple-trees and then rested his arm against one of the winesaps.

'Hallo, Lucy,' he said. His voice was expressionless and flat.

Lucy looked up from under her straw skimmer. She was wearing a green-and-white candy-striped blouse and a green skirt. The sunlight shone on her hair, and made it look to Jamie as if she had a golden halo.

'I brought you a telegram from the depot,' he told her, and held it up. 'Just arrived from Washington DC, that's what Mr Perkins told me.'

Lucy waited with her head held up and her back quite straight while Jamie walked across and gave her the wire. She didn't take her eyes away from his; not once.

Jamie watched her open it. 'Mother told me all about you and Henry,' he said.

The wire read, ECSTATIC STOP COME SOONEST STOP WIRE AHEAD STOP LOVE HENRY. Lucy folded it up, and tucked it back into its envelope. Then she took it out, unfolded it, and read it again.

Jamie said, 'I can't believe that you're going to leave Blanche. I just can't credit it.'

Lucy was silent for a little while, then she replied, 'I can't believe that I'm going to leave any of you.'

'Then why go?'

'Jamie, I have to.'

'I don't understand you at all.'

'Why? Because I'm acting on impulse? Haven't you ever done anything on impulse?'

'You're telling *me* about impulse?' Jamie demanded. 'Where do you think Blanche came from?'

Lucy smiled down at Blanche, who was kicking her legs in the air. 'She came from love, Jamie. And that's what she deserves. Nothing but love. Not arguing or bitterness or anybody feeling regretful because she was born.'

'Do you regret that she was born?'

Lucy shook her head. 'No. But I have my own life, too; and I haven't even started to live it yet.'

'I can give you a life. I love you, Lucy. I can give you everything that any wife could ever wish for.'

Lucy watched Blanche trying to snatch at the flickering patterns of sunlight. Maybe she was just the same, trying to grasp a bright illusion that wasn't really there. But she had to try.

Jamie said, 'I'll ask you just one more time, Lucy. Then I won't ask you ever again. Will you marry me, will you be my wife? Will you let me be Blanche's father?'

'You already are Blanche's father. Nobody will ever be able to take that away from you.'

But that was all she said. It was difficult enough to

explain to herself why she had to leave, without trying to explain it to Jamie. The apple branches nodded in the breeze, the grasses whispered, and bees hummed like snatches of half-remembered songs. Over to the west, thunder-bumpers began to rise, layer on layer, and by nightfall the sky would be crackling with electricity.

Jamie said, 'It's Blanche's feed-time. I'd better take her in.'

He picked Blanche up, and carried her away, and Lucy was left in the orchard by herself, among the Jonathans and the winesaps, with a crumpled blanket still warm from her baby daughter. Now she was innocent and pure and childless, but at a price which was impossible to guess.

She stepped down from the train that afternoon at the Baltimore & Potomac Railroad Depot; hesitantly, in her long coffee-coloured travelling-dress and her feathery hat, and Nora stepped down behind her.

Almost as soon as she did so, the steam vanished dram-atically, like a swirled-away curtain, and there stood Henry, bare-headed, in a grey frock-coat, carrying a stick.

They approached each other slowly, quite shyly, through the drifting fragments of steam. All around them, people hurried and shouted and called for porters, but Lucy scarcely noticed them. All she could see was Henry, not as tall as she had remembered, but very handsome, very relaxed-looking, smiling, with his hair swept back, and a beautifully-folded grey silk cravat, with a pearl pin.

They shook hands.

'Hallo, Lucy,' said Henry. 'I didn't truly believe until I saw you that you would come.'

Lucy was amazed how crisp and English his voice sounded, after only eight months in Kansas. 'I said I was coming,' she told him.

'I have a carriage outside the depot. There are rooms for you, at the Embassy. Lady Spiers will take care of you. She's absolutely charming. Is that your bag?'

They walked through the waiting-room, followed by Nora, and a porter carrying their two portmanteaux. 'Do you know something,' said Henry, 'President James Garfield was shot in this very waiting-room – July 2, 1881. And the interesting thing is that, while he lay in hospital, Alexander Graham Bell the inventor of the telephone hurriedly devised a metal-detector so that the doctors could locate the bullet in the president's body. Unfortunately, the metal-detector was confused by the steel springs in the hospital bed, and they couldn't find the bullet, and the president died.'

He suddenly stopped, and turned to Lucy, and grasped both of her arms. 'Why the devil am I rattling on about President Garfield, when I haven't kissed you since Christmas!'

He kissed her there and then, in the waiting-room where President Garfield had been shot, and he felt strong and urgent and passionate, like he always had before. There were whistles from waiting passengers, and laughter, and clapping; and Lucy blushed; but Henry stood and looked at her with his eyes steely-bright, and said, 'I love you more than life, Lucy. You are absolutely everything.'

He linked arms with her, tightly, and they left the depot. An Embassy barouche was waiting outside, with a spiffy top-hatted black man on the box.

'We're having a private supper tonight,' Henry told her, 'but tomorrow we're having a formal dinner with Mr McKinley and Mr Hanna, and we're going to talk about trade tariffs and protectionism; and then the following night we're going to the theatre to see *George and the Dragon*; and the night after that we're holding a party, with dancing, and service *à la Russe*.'

Lucy sat back in the deep-buttoned maroon leather seat and smiled at him, and then laughed. 'I'd forgotten how busy you always are!'

'Busy, nothing! Those are just the amusements! I have twenty-three meetings between now and next Thursday; as

368

well as three lunches, nine committees, and a formal visit to Gallaudet College.'

'And what am I supposed to be doing, while you do all that?' Lucy asked him.

'Shopping, I hope. One portmanteau can hardly be carrying all the gowns that you're going to need for half-a-dozen dinners, two operas, two visits to the theatre, and an Embassy party.'

'Henry –'

Henry raised his fingertip to his lips. 'Don't you dare speak to me about money. I know what ill-fortune befell you. I love you for what you are; and whatever I can give you, I shall.'

Nora obviously liked the sound of this, because she nodded her brown feathered hat enthusiastically.

They drove along Pennsylvania Avenue under a blotting-paper sky. Streetcars with tied-back curtains came clanging noisily alongside them; but the horses seemed not to mind. Lucy found Washington humid and suffocating after Kansas, where there was almost always a wind blowing. Washington was breathless and oppressive, and there was a smell of summer fever in the air.

'You're not alarmed by all these parties, I hope?' Henry asked her. He was referring to the letter she had written him, in reply to *his* first letter. She had explained her sudden flight from Brackenbridge by saying that she had felt 'terrified by all the responsibilities of being a politician's wife; and alarmed by your energy'.

'No,' said Lucy. 'I'm not alarmed.' She was quiet, though. She was thinking of Blanche; and the moment when old man Maeterlinck's business-wagon had rattled through the oak trees, and her view of Blanche had flickered, blurred, and at last been blotted out. Blanche, in Mrs Cullen's arms, waving at the sky, waving at the wind; but not realizing that she was waving goodbye to her own mother.

Lucy told herself strictly, almost petulantly, you've chosen this course. If it hurts you, you're going to have to endure it. But whenever she thought of Blanche, the pain was close to the brink of being unbearable, like a terrible scald.

'That's the White House,' Henry pointed out. 'That's where President Cleveland lives. He has the most memorable telephone number in Washington. It's 1.'

Lucy nodded, although she didn't look around. She didn't want either Henry or Nora to see that there were tears in her eyes.

It was peculiarly dark on the day they left Washington. Accompanied by Nora and by Henry's private secretary, Walter Pangborn, they travelled by rail to New York; where – on a far brighter morning – they boarded the Cunarder *Oregon* bound for Southampton. Lucy and Henry stood together by the rail of the first-class promenade deck as they sailed past the Statue of Liberty, and headed out for the open boats. A warm sea made Lucy's long white scarf wave like the wing of an albatross.

Lucy's single portmanteau had already been joined by three brass-studded steamer-trunks, carefully packed with new clothes. Most of her gowns had been bought ready-made, since there hadn't been enough time to have more than three evening-dresses fitted; but Henry promised her that when they arrived in London, she would be able to dress herself 'as befits the wife of a Privy Councillor'.

She had made such a determined effort to put Henry out of her mind that she had forgotten what amusing company he was; and how feminine and pretty he always made her feel. His energy could be tiring, and his insistence on supervising every little detail of daily life could be irritating. But he was always so boisterous, always so *interested,* and even when he was talking about foreign policy he never bored her.

He was particularly entertaining when he described the pomposity of Kaiser Wilhelm II, complete with an hilarious

German accent. Although the Kaiser was the nephew of the Prince of Wales, he insisted that his Uncle Bertie treat him like an emperor, not only in public but in private, and he had made that fact officially known through the German ambassador in London. The Queen had been outraged. Such *perfect madness*, she had complained to Lord Salisbury. It was really too *vulgar*. She added that '*if* he has such notions, he had better *never* come *here*'.

Lord Salisbury had bluntly told the Prince of Wales that he thought the Kaiser was 'not quite all there'.

'Shall I meet the Queen?' asked Lucy. 'And the Prince of Wales, too?'

Henry smiled widely, 'Of course you shall! I've already dined at Windsor twice this year; and there are always dozens of social occasions during the season when you can be presented. I'm sure Her Majesty will adore you. And His Royal Highness certainly will.'

The Atlantic crossing was so smooth that Lucy felt as if they were gliding across a dark blue ballroom floor. The journey seemed quite unreal. During the mornings they talked and played pontoon and made wedding-plans. Henry was drawing up a comprehensive list of guests and family, and arranging on a huge sheet of paper where they should sit in Brackenbridge's chapel, according to a seating-plan which he had drawn up entirely from memory. They had agreed that Lord Felldale should give Lucy away, in the absence of her own father, and that Blanche should be matron of honour. There were so many Carson grand-children that there would be no shortage of bridesmaids and pages.

During the afternoons, Henry retired to his cabin to work on Foreign Office papers, and to send scores of telegraphic messages to his parliamentary private secretary Ian Bruce and to other officials at the Foreign Office. Lucy was end-lessly amused by the way in which he addressed his colleagues as 'My Dear Beano' or 'My Dear Giglamps'. But most of

Henry's closest associates came from the same aristocratic class as himself, and all of them had been together at Eton and Oxford.

She noticed with an odd sense of unease that Henry gave Walter Pangborn very little to do. While Henry was still scribbling letters at eleven o'clock at night, Walter would be standing on deck smoking a small cigar and watching the stars.

'He always works so hard,' Lucy complained to Walter one evening, when Henry had left them in the *Oregon*'s lounge after dinner to finish off a long memorandum.

'Don't *trust* anybody, that's Henry's trouble,' Walter remarked, laconically. He was a slender, blasé young man with a hawklike nose and lidded eyes. 'Always says that by the time he's explained what he wants other people to do, he might just as easily have done it himself.'

He helped himself to a musty-looking chocolate. 'The Cussboss never keeps his valets for more than six weeks at a time. I think the valet who stayed the longest was a fellow called French, stayed for a year and a bit. When he gave his notice, Henry asked him to recommend a suitable replacement, and French said, "The only name that comes to mind, sir, is Jesus Christ." The Cussboss expects his servants to be perfect, you see, and they never are. He expects *himself* to be perfect.'

'You don't think that he'll always expect *me* to be perfect?'

Walter chewed and smiled. 'My dear Miss Darling, excuse my impertinence, but you *are* perfect. Henry's a fearfully lucky man.'

In her stateroom that night, when Nora undressed her, Lucy found that the front of her corset-cover was stained with milk. Nora said nothing, but Lucy looked at herself in the mirror and said, in a transparent voice, 'I shouldn't have left her, should I?'

Nora unfolded her nightgown for her. 'You did what you felt was right.'

'Right for me, yes,' said Lucy. 'But what about Blanche?'

Nora took hold of Lucy's hands. 'You must think no more about Blanche. Blanche is being well taken care of, and Blanche will flourish, just as you did, for all that you didn't know who your father was.'

'I miss her so much,' Lucy whispered.

Nora pretended not to hear. It was probably the best thing to do.

Lucy slept badly that night. It was almost dawn before the beating of the *Oregon*'s engines finally induced her to close her eyes. Even then she dreamed that she was walking down the slope beside the Saline River that led to the Cullen farm, and that Blanche was waiting for her in the orchard, under the dancing sunlight, under the winesap trees.

They were married in October, in the small York stone chapel at Brackenbridge, by the Rector of All Souls. The choir sang the *Salve regina* from the Eton choirbook; and then *Hail, Gladdening Light*.

Although it had been so chilly in the chapel that they could see their breath, it was unseasonably warm and sunny when they stepped outside, and on the bright green grass the leaves lay like huge curls of ship's rust. The bells echoed across the dales; and Lucy came down the chapel steps in a white silk dress, wearing a high crown of Belgian lace, and a three-layered lace-trimmed veil. Her fifteen-foot train was held up from the ground by a serious bevy of Carson grandchildren, pages and bridesmaids, the boys in blue velvet jackets and cream silk knickerbockers, the girls in cream silk gowns.

They posed for their wedding photographs on the steps outside the chapel; and in later years historians would trace their faces with their fingers, and say, here, this is Lord Salisbury, the Prime Minister, white-bearded and balding, his hat in his hand; and here is Lord Felldale, looking unnecessarily fierce; and here is Sir Thomas Sanderson,

Permanent Under-Secretary at the Foreign Office; and Francis Bertie, assistant Under-Secretary, son of the sixth Earl of Abingdon; and Eric Barrington, son of the sixth Viscount Barrington; and here are all the other Etonians, Ian Malcolm and Pom McDonnell and Eyre Crowe; as well as Henry Asquith (looking slightly detached) and Margot Asquith (looking secretly amused); Margot's sister Charty, now Lady Ribblesdale, with her husband Lord Ribblesdale; and Henry's chum George Wyndham, with his wife the Countess of Grosvenor, whom Henry had once 'fancied rotten', as his brother Charles put it.

As the photographer folded his tripods and packed away the last of his wet-plates, Henry took hold of Lucy's hand and said, 'Happy?'

Lucy nodded. 'If only my mother could have been here today.'

'I'm sure that she is, in spirit.'

Margot Asquith came up to them, in a coat of pale lavender trimmed with fur, and a hat crowded with pale lavender flowers. She kissed Lucy, and then she kissed Henry, and then she stood back a little way and smiled at them. 'You make such a picture, Lucy, there are many ladies here today who are quite *emerald* with envy.'

'I must thank you for that wonderful Dresden porcelain,' said Henry. 'We're going to take it down to Carlton House Terrace and use it right away.'

'Charty thought it too fanciful,' Margot told him.

'Margot,' said Henry, 'it's quite beautiful,' and there was a warmth in his voice which clearly suggested that, in his view, it was the giver of the gift which lent it most of its charm.

As Lucy met more of Henry's women friends, she began to notice a distinctive pattern in the way that he spoke to them. He always engaged them in a form of playful erotic teasing; the kind of teasing that takes place between adolescent boys and girls who are too shy to admit that they are attracted to one another. It was plain that Henry had never been short of admirers when he was younger, but Lucy was always left with the impression that none of his flirtations had developed into serious associations. They had been ballroom escapades; country house charades; winks and fumbles when nanny wasn't looking. He believed with an earnestness that Lucy found astonishing that only the comradely endearment of men for men could be truly noble. That was why he was fascinated by cricket, although he wasn't good at playing it.

There was no homosexuality in the love that Henry and his fellows felt for each other. In fact, it quickly became clear to Lucy that they were horrified by what Henry in his letters called 'b-gg-rs'. Until May of this year, one of Henry's closest and best-loved friends in the literary world had been Oscar Wilde; and in spite of Oscar's outrageous behaviour and his effusive notes of affection (he had once called Henry '*un jeune guerrier du drapeau romantique*') Henry had been thoroughly shocked and surprised when he had been tried and found guilty of the love that dare not speak its name.

Although Henry made a special effort to include Lucy in his conversations, she always felt like an outsider when he began talking to his women friends; or for that matter to *any* of his friends. Almost all of them came from that closely-intertwined circle of English and Irish aristocracy; almost all of them had been educated at Eton, or Haileybury at the very worst; almost all of them had been to the same dinners, played the same pranks, travelled on the same Grand Tour. They would roar with laughter when they talked of the time that Henry had hit all of George Leveson Gower's tennis-balls at a snappish dog, although Lucy could never understand why. Or when they remembered the time that Henry had sent a footman in search of Charles at a crowded country-house ball, with no more helpful description than 'he looks like me, d'you see, and he'll be very hot'

– only to be presented ten minutes later with a complete (and very irritable) stranger.

But Lucy supposed that – in time – she would learn what all of the private jokes and all of the facetious undergraduate vocabulary meant. For the moment, she preferred to listen, to act demurely, and to keep her peace. This morning she had innocently asked Henry if Mr Laxer had arrived in time for the wedding, only to be met with peals of laughter because 'The Laxer' was Leveson Gower's university nickname, and not a particularly polite one, at that.

Yet, as the wedding party crossed the bright well-raked shingle to the Great Hall, Lucy was bursting with pride and happiness that she had married Henry, because it was obvious how much he was admired among his friends and colleagues; and how much of a catch the women considered him to be; and that the Carson family was already dearly fond of her. Lord Felldale called her 'my dove', and Blanche called her 'sweetness'. It was a small sharp sadness to her that she was unable to tell Blanche about the tribute she had paid her, by naming her baby Blanche.

The Great Hall was filled with sunshine; so dazzling that Lucy had to shade her eyes when she first walked in. A string quintet had been brought up from Oxford, and as she and Henry walked between the two long tables on which the wedding breakfast was spread out, the lutist played *Fair Oriana, seeming to wink at folly.*

Henry took hold of Lucy's hand, and held it high, in the manner of a medieval king entering a court with his queen, and smiled, and bowed, and everybody laughed and applauded.

'Bravo, Henry! Bravo, Lucy!'

'My darling Lucy,' Henry told her, 'I feel like Alexander, after he captured Tyre. Or Cortes, when he entered Tenochtitlán.'

'Oh, yes?' asked Lucy. 'And how was that?'

'Triumphant, my dearest! Triumphant!'

Henry had arranged the wedding-breakfast down to the last possible detail. He had chosen the menu, selected the china, supervised the floral displays, arranged the seating, and written out three hundred place-cards in the italic handwriting that Queen Victoria herself had praised for its clarity and grace. 'The wedding will be perfect from beginning to end', he had promised her; and in a strange unbelievable way it was. Yet because it *was* so perfect, and because Henry had insisted on supervising absolutely everything, she felt almost as if she were just another guest; or even as if she had dreamed it.

Henry had demanded that each of the two long tables should be embellished by a boar's head, garnished with aspic jelly. Then there should be mayonnaise of fowl; boiled chickens in Béchamel sauce; hams and ornamented tongues; raised game pie and galantine of veal; roasted pheasants; larded capons; lobster salads; prawns; meringues; custards and fruited jellies.

Cautiously – concerned that Henry's menu might be attractive on the eye but rather bland on the palate – Lucy had suggested panned oysters and scalloped turkey and some of Delmonico's devilled chicken – a chicken split open and seasoned in paprika and coated in breadcrumbs. But Henry had shaken his head without even looking up from his papers, and said, 'You see, my dearest, the tastes and the textures are all perfectly balanced; we don't want to upset the balance now.'

'I *can* cook, Henry,' Lucy had insisted.

'We have cooks to do the cooking,' Henry had replied. 'You are going to be my queen; and queens don't cook.'

'But I *like* cooking.'

Henry had laughed. 'Let me tell you something, my darling. Government House in Calcutta, purely by chance, was built by Lord Wellesley as a replica of Brackenbridge. The thing was, the Court of Directors of the East India Company didn't care much for Asiatic pomp and display.

So when they came to build a viceregal residency, they chose to imitate Brackenbridge, because of its purity, d'you see, and its elegance. And the copy in Calcutta, well, it's almost perfect, except that they have used lath and plaster for their pillars, instead of alabaster.'

His accent was part Derbyshire, part eighteenth-century. He said 'lăth and plăster, instead of alabăster'. His London friends were forever teasing and imitating him.

But he added, 'One day soon, God willing, I shall be Viceroy of India, and take my seat in Brackenbridge in Calcutta; as well as my seat in Brackenbridge here in England. And you shall not set one foot in the kitchens there; not one step; any more than you shall set one foot in the kitchens here. You are my queen. You are my empress. You are above everything but praise and adoration.'

He must have been rather pleased with that little speech, because he actually made notes in the margin of his writing-paper. His nib scratched, the ink gradually dried. In the huge family-room at Brackenbridge, with its sun-faded velvet curtains and its sun-faded oak panelling, Lucy had looked back at Henry for a moment, with the sun shining on the brilliant-blue iris of her left eye, and she had wondered then if she had misunderstood him, if he were quite another man from the man she had imagined him to be.

But the wedding was wonderful; and the wedding-break-fast was boisterous and happy. Lucy was kissed by more personable young men and more giggling young women than she had ever met in her life. Lord Salisbury, bearded and soft-spoken and avuncular, to her at least, gave her his 'dearest blessing'. Lord Felldale treated her so proprietorially and so kindly that she felt as if she had found a new father, as well as a husband. As they stood in the portico, wrapped in furs, to wave goodbye to the last of the carriages, Lord Felldale took hold of Lucy's hand and gripped it tight, and said, 'This is a great day for Brackenbridge, my dove. This is the beginning of a great new age! Brackenbridge shall have a new mistress, in years to come; and Henry shall have heirs; and although I shall not be here to see it, my God, it makes my heart glad!'

'I'm glad that you're glad,' Lucy told him, and kissed his cheek. 'I know that Henry adores Brackenbridge, and so do I.'

Henry came out, smoking a cigar, his black astrakhan coat hung over his shoulders, looking as pleased as Punch and smelling of brandy. 'What a wedding-day!' he declared. 'We should be married every day, my darling! Then all of our friends can come around!'

'Once is enough,' said Lucy, linking arms.

Henry kissed her. 'For you, my dearest darling, nothing will ever be enough.'

Lucy said, 'Your sister Vanessa didn't come, did she? I did so want to see Vanessa.'

Lord Felldale descended two or three steps, and whistled to his dogs. Henry smiled tightly, with his hands clasped behind his back, and shrugged, and said, 'Well ... Vanessa has a mind of her own, you know. She always has. Do you want to come inside now? There are oysters for supper; oysters and champagne.'

'Just right for a wedding-night, eh?' Lord Felldale remarked.

'*Father,*' Henry admonished him, almost prissily.

Lucy turned to Henry with the luminous smile of a happy bride. Her blonde hair was brushed into curls, and pinned under her fur-trimmed hat. Her collar was raised up around her face, so that the fur sparkled in the lamplight like a dandelion-puff on the very brink of being blown. She looked like a winter-fairy; October's child. She felt transfigured; as if she had changed beyond any recognition; as if she had started life as somebody else. Lucy Carson. *Mrs* Lucy Carson. Elegant, well-connected, and envied. The correspondent from *The Times* had asked her a few respectful questions, and actually *bowed* to her when he was leaving. And even lords and ladies had stared at her, unabashed, as if she were an oleograph rather than a real person.

As she took Henry's arm, and walked back through crowds of applauding servants, butlers and valets and coachmen and kitchen-maids, she understood at last that she was home because she had been determined to make this her home; that her own beauty had created a heritage for her.

Henry said, '*Nunc scio quid sit amor.* Now I know what love is really like.'

But her wedding-night was frightening, like a night spent without friends in a fierce and foreign country, and by morning Lucy was left feeling perplexed and anxious. Henry loved her. There was no doubt about that. But it was *how* he loved her that confused her so much. Between Jamie's cautious tenderness and Uncle Casper's extreme violence, she had no experience of sex, so she was ready to accept that she was a victim of her own ignorance. Yet, in all the romances she had read, there had been nothing to prepare her for Henry's urgency, or for Henry's temperamental demands.

Lord Felldale had given them the Sun Room, so-called because it was painted in sunflower yellows, with curtains in saffron velvet. Originally, it had been decorated in cobalt blue, but because it faced north-eastwards, it had always felt cold and unwelcoming. Henry's mother had redesigned it in yellows to give it life and warmth; yet there was still something chill about it. Lucy had already sensed it when Nora came in to undress her, and prepare her for bed. A fire was crackling in the hearth, but the ceiling was so high that she could scarcely see it through the gloom; and a thin impertinent wind kept blowing under the door, *fyooooo, fyoooooooeeee, fyoooeeeeee!!*

Nora allowed the billowing silk nightgown to fall airily over Lucy's naked skin; a whisper, a promise. The hope of happiness.

'Well, you may not think too much of this,' said Nora, 'but my mother taught me how to sing it, years ago, and perhaps it might help. *"On the night of her wedding, a young maid will say, 'I have nothing, my Lord, but this tiny cup.' But give this same maiden a week and a day, and she will be begging, 'Please fill it right up!'"* '

Lucy said nothing but blushed; remembering Jamie's sperm scattered across her breasts. Pearls, seeds; and Blanche had already been conceived.

Nora brushed out her hair and at last she was ready for bed. Dry-mouthed, she looked at herself in the mirror. Nora smiled and kissed the top of her head.

'You love him, don't you?'

Lucy nodded.

'It's just nerves, then.'

Lucy said, 'He won't be able to tell, will he, that I've had a baby?'

'Is that what you're worried about?'

'He thinks I'm completely untouched. Perfect.'

'Then let him think it, if that's what he wants. He won't be able to tell. What most men know about the physical side of life wouldn't cover the back of a penny stamp, in big writing, too.'

Lucy swallowed. 'But when you're a virgin . . . isn't there supposed to be – well, *blood*? I read something about Italian women holding up the sheets, to prove that the bride was pure.'

Nora said, 'It isn't always so, believe me. A young girl can break her maidenhead just by horseriding or by carrying coals or scrubbing the kitchen step, and any man who looks to the linen for evidence is a fool. Besides, what does it matter, if you've given yourself to Mr Carson, in the eyes of God, that should be good enough for anybody, especially for him.'

She paused, however, and took a small glass-beaded hatpin out of the pin-cushion on the dressing-table. 'If you think it will make him feel better, you can prick your thumb with this, when he's sleeping, and mark the sheet. What you might call a little red lie.'

It was then that Henry knocked at the doors of the Sun Room, and immediately came in, smiling expectantly, and a little flushed. He was wearing a long woollen dressing-gown in bottle green. His hair was pomaded and combed sharply back from his forehead. Lucy caught the fresh floral smell of Floris toilet-water.

He looked at the huge curtained bed, with its ornate mahogany bedposts, its covers neatly triangulated on each side, ready for himself and his bride.

'Well, now,' he said, clearing his throat.

'Don't worry, sir, I'm all finished here,' Nora told him, rearranging the silver-backed brushes on the dressing-table, and quickly tidying up.

'You're a good woman, Nora,' Henry remarked, for no obvious reason. Perhaps he was trying to demonstrate to Lucy that he could handle servants appreciatively, after all.

'Thank you, sir. I wish the very best of happiness to you and Mrs Carson, in your married life.'

'Yes,' said Henry, without interest. Nora might just as well have wished that the weather would stay dry tomorrow. Without taking his eyes away from Lucy, he added, 'Would you cast a few more coals on the hearth, before you go?'

Nora briskly did as she was told, although Lucy could guess how she felt at being required to do the work of a housemaid.

'Goodnight, sir. Goodnight, madam,' she said at last, and closed the bedroom doors behind her.

Henry approached Lucy with an amused but cautious look on his face, as if he had just thought of a good joke, but didn't know whether he ought to share it or not.

'Well, my dearest; we are man and wife,' he announced. 'I could never have guessed that any woman could be so beautiful. I could never have believed that such happiness were possible.'

He took her in his arms, and he kissed her forehead, and her closed eyelids, and then her lips. 'I am not a man for praying, you know that. But every single night, I count it as a miracle that we should have met. If any of my friends had told me just eighteen months ago that I should marry a storekeeper's daughter from Kansas, I would have laughed in his face. And now look at me, with you in my arms!'

Lucy kept her eyes closed, enjoying the feeling of his arms around her, the warmth and the strength and the comfort of him. 'I always wanted to marry a prince,' she whispered, 'and look at me, I did. I wouldn't have laughed in anybody's face if they had told me that. I just plain wouldn't have believed them.'

'Think we're sootud?' he asked her, kissing her eyebrows, kissing her cheeks.

She nodded, and opened her eyes, and looked at him closely, every detail of his face, the mole on his cheek, the scar above his forehead.

'Let's lie down,' he suggested.

Henry helped Lucy out of her robe, and then untied his own dressing-gown, folding it over the arm of the chaise-longue. Lucy climbed into bed, and sat waiting for him. He went around in his ruffled nightshirt and his velvet slippers, turning down the lamps. 'I have always felt a special affection for this room,' he remarked, looking around. 'It reminds me so much of my dear mother. Always golden, always joyful.'

Lucy glanced at her bedside table. Underneath the lace cloth that covered it, her hatpin gleamed, ready to establish the loss of her virginity.

Henry climbed into the bed beside her, bouncing up and down as if he were testing the springs. 'Well, now,' he said. He leaned over and kissed her again, quite hard, so that she could feel his teeth pressing against her lips. Then he bounced up and down some more as he changed his position to make himself more comfortable – tugging his nightshirt where it had become entangled between his thighs. His forehead knocked against Lucy's forehead, and he said, 'Sorry! Sorry, my darling!' and promptly rested his elbow on her hair.

Lucy suddenly felt panicky. All through their wedding-day, surrounded by guests and friends and affectionate relations, she had been ecstatically happy. But now that she was alone with Henry, she began to feel that she had somehow trapped herself; that she had married him not for love, but for all the things that he could give her – the home, and the family, and the place in society. He kissed her again, and again, and her panic began to rise. She felt that he was smothering her, that he was a relentless conglomeration of elbows and teeth and knees and tightly-twisted sheets, and that he was going to bruise her and suffocate her and crush her to death.

He squeezed her breasts through her nightdress, pinching and pulling her nipples. She tried to twist herself away from him, but he was much too strong and heavy for her, and he was her husband, so what possible reason could he have for believing that she didn't want him to make love to her, on their wedding-night of all nights?

He was clumsy more than violent, but he interpreted her struggling as shyness rather than panic, and so instead of giving her the opportunity to calm herself, and to catch her breath, he persisted in his kissing and squeezing and pummelling.

'Henry, please – !' she gasped. She was drowning in tangled sheets. She grasped at her pillow, but she succeeded only in pulling it down over her face, smothering her even more. 'Henry, mmmmmfff! Henry, please!'

He dragged up her nightdress, exposing her up to her waist. She felt the chill of the Sun Room's draught on her bare thighs. Henry kept pushing his face into hers, and leaning on top of her.

His breath roared in her ear. 'Oh, my darling Lucy ... oh, my darling Lucy!'

His leg swung across hers. She felt the rubbery stiffness of his penis against her thigh. It was then that she managed to gasp out, 'No, Henry! Henry, please, no!'

He stopped thrashing. He lifted himself up on his elbow and stared down at her. His forehead was shining with perspiration, and he was panting.

'Henry,' she whispered, reaching up and touching his lips with her fingertips. 'Henry, you mustn't be so rough with me.'

She felt his penis curl. Very slowly, he lifted himself off her. All this time he didn't say a word, but continued to stare at her. He pulled down her nightgown, and straightened the sheets.

'I'm not –' he began, after a while.

'Henry, I'm your *wife*,' Lucy told him. She felt less frightened now, less panicky; but she still felt as if Henry were a stranger. As much of a stranger as Jack had turned out to be. As much of a stranger as Uncle Casper. She stroked his sidewhiskers. She wondered if she would ever be able to understand what went on inside men's minds. It seemed as if they were always in turmoil. An inexplicable churning of jokes, brutality, cleverness, violence, and sentimentality.

Henry lay on his stomach with his fists clenched above his head and buried his face in the pillow.

'Henry,' Lucy coaxed him. 'If you can just be *gentle*.'

'I haven't had many women,' he told her, in a muffled voice. 'I'm not experienced. Only whores, like everybody else at Oxford, and they didn't mind what you did. I've never made love to anybody I really loved. Only once, and that experience crucified me, too.'

'Henry, my darling, I don't want to crucify you.'

'Perhaps I deserve it.'

Lucy reached across and stroked the hair at the back of his neck, but he still wouldn't lift his face from the pillow. 'Henry, I love you. I'm your wife.'

'But you don't want me to make love to you.'

'Of course I want you to make love to me.' (Did she? She didn't know. But now Henry had placed her in the extraordinary position of having to prove that she did, whether she did or not). She lay next to him for a long time, staring at the back of his neck, wondering what she should do. She was married to Henry; yet until he turned over and claimed her she remained unmarried. She was more married to Jamie than she was to Henry, if consummation were the test of marriage. She was more married to Uncle Casper, her own father.

'Henry, I didn't mean to make you angry,' Lucy begged him. She could feel the tears prickling her eyes.

'It's all right,' Henry replied. 'Whatever you said, I deserved it.'

She put her arm around his shoulders and kissed his hair. 'Henry, please. This is our wedding-night.'

'I know. And I have been cruel and unthinking. You should punish me.'

'Punish you? Henry, what are you talking about? You haven't done anything that I should punish you for. I'm your wife!'

He turned over at last. There was an expression in his eyes which Lucy found difficult to comprehend. She wondered if he were drunk. He could be drunk. The men had been downing magnums of Jacquesson champagne all day, and for most of the evening. But somehow Henry didn't *look* drunk. Not aggressive drunk, anyway. He looked cowed, like a dog that expects to be whipped for misbehaving; and yet eager, too, almost as if he *wanted* her to hurt him.

In a man who had first attracted her with his sophistication and social bravado, Lucy found this sudden change of demeanour to be highly disturbing, even frightening.

'My darling . . . perhaps you'd better get some sleep,' she told him.

'Are you that cruel?' he asked her.

'Henry, I don't understand what you're asking me to do!'

Henry took two or three deep breaths. His eyes remained piggy and glazed. 'I'm simply asking what any man would ask . . . if he had treated his bride so badly.'

'Henry, it isn't my place to punish you!'

'It is you who has been wronged,' Henry insisted. 'The meting-out of justice is your privilege. Accept it! You must!'

Lucy sat up in bed, propped up on one arm. The veins showed blue in her thin bent-back wrist. 'What do you want me to do?' she asked him. There had to be some way out of this alarming impasse; but Henry alone could tell her what it was.

He didn't take his eyes away from hers, but he dragged aside the sheet, and then lifted his nightshirt. His penis was half-erect, its head nodding to the beat of his heart. 'This is the real offender,' said Henry, his voice throaty. 'This is the one you must punish. Too eager by half. Too rapacious.'

Lucy said nothing, but waited for Henry to explain to her what she must do.

He reached up and unlaced the thin pink-silk ribbons of her nightgown. He handed them to Lucy as if they were reins. But still his eyes remained fixed on hers, scarcely blinking.

'He needs strict discipline,' said Henry. 'He needs to be taught to behave himself.'

'Henry . . .'

'Here,' said Henry. 'Wind the ribbons around him. That's right. Wind the ribbons around him, once, there, and twice.'

With shaking hands, Lucy wound the pink ribbons around Henry's penis, in the groove just below the dark-crimson glans. His breathing as she did so was harsh and erratic. In a series of pulses, his penis began to stiffen and rise. Henry said, 'You must never – ever – allow him to get away with it scot-free . . . he will only become worse . . . ill-behaved, undisciplined. Come on, now, punish him! Pull the ribbons tight!'

At first, Lucy couldn't understand what Henry wanted her to do. But then he seized hold of the ribbon himself, and tugged them hard, so that his glans swelled darker, and the ribbons cut deeply into his flesh.

'Tighter!' he demanded. 'He deserves to be hurt! If you let him get away with it, he'll be worse next time! Tighter!'

Terrified that she would injure him, Lucy nevertheless wound the ribbons around her fingers, and pulled them tight.

'Tighter!' Henry winced. 'Oh God, tighter! Make him suffer!'

Shaking with alarm, Lucy pulled tighter still. Henry's penis reared up like a runaway horse; its glans glistening and purple, its shaft hugely swollen. The ribbons were so tight now that they had almost disappeared into his flesh.

'*Now*,' said Henry, his voice constricted. He sounded like somebody else altogether, not Henry at all. He rolled on to his back, and grasped Lucy by the hips, and helped her to climb on top of him. Then without a word, he pushed his massively-distended penis – still tied around with pink nightgown ribbons – deeply and forcefully inside her – so deeply that she shuddered.

It took no more than two or three strokes, and Henry cried out, 'God, my God, Lucy!' and discharged himself inside her, making a sharp sucking sound between his teeth as he did so.

Lucy crouched on top of him for almost five minutes, feeling the hair of his chest against her cheek, listening to his heart beating. The fire spat; but the Sun Room still felt cold. The coldness leaked glutinously out between her thighs. Henry sidled after it. Cold wet nightgown ribbons stuck to her skin. She couldn't understand what had happened at all. She supposed that she was now Henry's fully-consummated wife; but had that been holy consummation or unholy punishment? It must have been agony for him, having his penis garotted so tightly, yet it seemed to have excited him hugely. He seemed to have *needed* it.

She thought: men are such a mystery, their lusts are so frightening. What kind of love can this be, where your husband wanted you to hurt him? Uncle Casper on the other hand had wanted to hurt *her*. Was pain a necessary part of making love? Would she always have to punish Henry, before they had intercourse?

Henry put his arm around her, and said, 'You're cold. You're feeling cold. Come under the covers.'

He sounded like himself again: the Henry whose voice had carried apple-crisp across Mrs Harris' lawns.

She climbed off and lay next to him. He made no attempt to hold her. The shadows from the fire danced across the ceiling. One day she would see an Indonesian shadow-play, and she would be reminded of her wedding-night. The shadows had curved noses and pointed ears, and jiggling insect arms like praying-mantises.

Henry said, 'Dearly beloved Lucy,' as if he were beginning a letter.

Lucy turned to look at him. He was lying on his back staring directly at the ceiling. The firelight outlined his sharp, aristocratic profile, and sparkled like a stray cinder in his eye. There were so many questions she wanted to ask him, yet she didn't know how to begin. She was a young bride, not even twenty years old. As far as Henry had been aware, she had never made love to a man before tonight. Yet he had immediately involved her in some private ritual of pain and humiliation without even explaining why.

'Henry,' she said, quite distinctly.

He didn't answer, but lay perfectly still, with his eyes open.

'Henry?' she repeated.

'Oh, I'm sorry, my dearest,' he replied, turning to smile at her. 'I was thinking of India.'

However, he didn't think about India all night. Shortly after midnight, when the fire was beginning to burn hot and low, he turned over in bed and lifted up her nightgown again.

She had been sleeping. Too much excitement, too much champagne. But she was woken up by the feeling of his hands caressing the curves of her bare bottom, and sliding down her bare thighs. 'Lucy, my dearest darling, are you awake?'

'Yes,' she murmured.

'Lucy, you must forgive me.'

'Forgive you? What for?'

Henry hesitated, then he thrashed away from her, turning his back. 'I'm always so selfish, Lucy, so intolerant. What must you think of me? You're the tenderest of children, the sweetest of brides. And what have I done but treat you with a worse depravity than any Persian?'

He paused, and took a deep breath, and Lucy could hear the catch in his throat. She thought: *He's crying. He's actually crying.* She lay in the dying firelight, horrified.

'Lucy,' he breathed. 'Speak to me. Tell me please that you'll try to find it in your heart to forgive me.'

'Of course I'll forgive you,' Lucy heard herself saying. 'There's nothing for me to forgive.'

'I won't ask you to punish me again, I promise.'

'Henry, ssh, don't talk about it.'

'I promise, I absolutely promise, that it will never happen again. Categorically, never.'

'Sssh,' she soothed him, and tangled her fingers into his hair. Perhaps after all he had been drunk earlier this evening, drunk and mad like Uncle Casper. She had recognized the flames that surrounded him, recognized the terrible brutal urgency.

He kissed her, his face wet with tears. He kissed her again and again. Then he heaved himself over her, with a great dragging of nightshirt, and opened up her thighs. He seemed to blot out the entire world like a total eclipse of the soul. She felt his fingers unstick her lips, she felt the blunt fleshy chisel of his member, pushing into her body.

In spite of his weight, in spite of the great drowned

dragging of nightshirt and nightgown and sheets, Lucy clung to him, and pressed her face against his shoulder, which smelled of fresh linen and sweat and flowery toilet-water, and thought at last that *this is love, this is loving. It was nothing but the drink before, nothing but shyness and inexperience. He's only been with whores, after all.*

He thrust deeper and harder, and her vagina stickily and audibly kissed him with every thrust. She closed her eyes and let her head fall slowly back on to the pillow.

'Oh Henry, my darling,' she whispered. 'I love you so much.'

It was then, however, that he began to soften. He tried to thrust quicker, his muscles tensed, Lucy heard him swear to himself under his breath. The only result was that he grew softer and softer, until he slithered out of her altogether. He gave a strange muffled roar, and pounded his fist against the mattress, and then rolled off her in a catastrophe of twisted sheets, and lay with his back to her, quivering with fury.

Lucy lay in silence for a while. Then she raised herself up again, and touched Henry's shoulder.

'Henry, please. It's not your fault. It's only the drink. You must be tired, too.'

But Henry continued to shake with humiliation and anger, and there was nothing that Lucy could do to console him. The clock in the hallway outside struck one; the fire died and the Sun Room darkened. Lucy remained wakeful for over an hour, hearing the clock strike again and again, and at last hearing Henry sleep.

They were to take a month's holiday in southern France, in the Var, in the house owned by Alfred Dunning, the painter, who had made friends with Henry at Oscar Wilde's house in Tite Street, in Chelsea. Dunning and Wilde had fallen out the year before, over a very gentle remark that Wilde had made about his epic painting *The Triumph of Divine Providence*. Now Wilde was in Reading gaol, disgraced, and

Dunning was painting the largest *Rape of the Sabines* ever commissioned.

Lucy had quite expected Henry to be bitter and morose after their wedding-night; but he was smiling and cheerful when he awoke and he kissed her as sweetly as if their whole night had been filled with fresh and fulfilling love-making. He had risen to go to the bathroom, and Lucy, when she had risen, too, to draw back the curtains and look out over the frosty grass, had heard him singing *Love's Sweet Delight* while he washed his hands and brushed his hair.

He had marched back into the bedroom, chafing his hands together. 'Well! I shall have to ring for the fire to be lit! They're too shy to disturb us, that's the trouble! But I could do with some breakfast, couldn't you? Finnan haddock, and poached eggs, and back bacon, and a good strong cup of China tea.'

Lucy had glanced towards the rumpled bed. She had suddenly remembered that she had forgotten to prick her thumb, and to mark the sheet with blood. She had glanced uncertainly at Henry, wondering if he would notice, but he had bounded back into bed, straightened the sheet, laced his fingers together, and sat waiting for his breakfast as if it were any other day of his life.

'Henry,' she had begun, sitting on the edge of the bed.

Henry had smiled at her. He had still looked so handsome; and so debonair! She could have been desperately in love with him, if he hadn't been so relentlessly difficult. It was almost as if he *worked* at being difficult.

He had taken hold of her hand, and kissed it. 'My bride,' he had told her, with pride.

Now they were sitting on a shaded veranda in the South of France, underneath a rust-coloured awning, drinking chilled rosé wine and watching the heat shimmer over the valley below them. Henry was very nattily dressed in a white coat and white ducks and a Panama hat, a real Panama hat which could be pulled through a wedding-ring (he had demonstrated, partly to show off the hat and partly to show off the wedding-ring.) Lucy wore an exquisite white linen dress, with a wide lace collar, and a white straw hat that looked as if it were about to take flight.

Alfred Dunning was spending his last day there. He was about to go to Algiers to spend some time with another artist from the Tite Street days. He was unexpectedly large and coarse-featured for an artist. At a guess, most people would have taken him for a coal-heaver, or a drayman. He talked very loudly, and was funny, most of the time, and very well-informed, and even his coarseness had a certain appealing immediacy about it. It was known that Alfred Dunning was never short of female companionship, and that every one of the fifty-three models who had posed for *The Triumph of Divine Providence* had been given plenty of opportunity to stretch her legs in between posing sessions.

'I still can't envy you, Henry,' Alfred said, fanning himself with his stained white hat. 'London winters, London fog, crowds of clerks all smelling like wet trousers.'

'My dear Dunners, it's the centre of the known world,' Henry had retaliated. 'I can stand at Charing Cross, and turn about on my heel, and know that in every conceivable direction, the great British Empire stretches out before me like a glittering paradise. Civilizing, educating, converting, enlightening. Bringing law where there was no law; bringing peace where there was only strife.'

'I know. And squeezing as much profit out of the poor befuddled darkies as possible.'

'Even enlightenment has its price.'

Alfred swigged back wine and, with his cheeks still bulging, poured himself some more. 'It's the light here. Marvellous for painting. But then you don't need light to be a politician, do you, Henry? Keep 'em in the dark, that's your motto.'

'I hope not,' Henry replied, a little priggishly.

'Still keen on India?' Alfred asked him.

Henry nodded, and narrowed his eyes, and gazed out across the claytiled rooftops. The heat distorted the olive-trees, so that they looked as if they were greenish-grey ghosts, waving to him silently and desperately from the opposite slope. He always narrowed his eyes like that when he wasn't particularly keen on answering the question.

'Well, I don't envy you India, either,' sniffed Alfred. 'Algiers is about as barbarous as I can stand. They have some entrancing ladies there; absolutely entrancing. Bellies like underfilled velvet cushions. Mind you, *you* have an entrancing lady here, so why should you worry?'

'Dunners, watch your language, there's a good man,' Henry retorted.

'Oh, he's not upsetting me one bit,' Lucy smiled. 'I can stand a little flattery as much as anybody.'

'That Kansas accent!' cried Alfred, sprawling back in his cast-iron chair as if he had been felled by a blow with a knobkerry. 'That derrr-awwwll! It runs right up my spine and circles twice around my head and comes tingling out of my tympani!'

Lucy laughed. Henry tried to join in, but was plainly too irritated. Their love life was still awkward; and after ten days of marriage the strain was beginning to show. Henry managed to be equable most of the time, but occasionally he was inclined to snap, or to drum his pen on his desk, or to stop suddenly in the middle of what he was doing and fix his eyes on the near-distance and look as if he had forgotten who he was.

They had made love two or three times, but on each occasion it had seemed to Lucy to be hurried and peremptory, as if Henry felt that he had something better to do. She couldn't understand it at all. When he talked of politics, when he talked of the British Empire, he was more eloquent and more passionate than any man she had ever known. He still amused her, still entertained her; and quite obviously loved her just as much as ever. It seemed quite out of character that when he made love to her, he was like a man running for a hopelessly-missed train. For Lucy, the fear that she had felt on her wedding-night had changed first to anxiety and then to frustration. She felt so much for him. She wanted to make him the very best of wives. But Henry kept stimulating her without giving her any satisfaction. It was worse than being served with a delicious plate of food, only to have it whipped away before she had eaten more than two or three mouthfuls.

She found herself drinking too much rosé and flirting with Alfred during the afternoon while Henry worked on his papers. Alfred certainly didn't mind, although he was cautious enough not to return Lucy's teasing when Henry was about. That afternoon, however, after Henry had finished his wine and vacated his chair on the balcony, Alfred crossed his legs and looked at Lucy from under the brim of his disreputable white hat, and she could tell that he had something on his mind.

'The *truite bleue* was marvellous,' she remarked.

'Your French pronunciation is improving,' Alfred replied, 'and so is your taste in food.'

'I've always liked trout. Once I had trout in the High Sierras, when I was travelling to California.'

'Ah, California! I must confess I've never been.'

'It's beautiful.'

'So I understand. But there are no artists there, are there? Only growers of beans. A land can have beans planted on it from one horizon to the other, but it never truly exists until somebody paints it.'

Lucy smiled at him in the glass-bright sunshine. He wore no socks, and he swung his suntanned ankle from side to side. 'Are you happy here?' she asked him.

'After a fashion. I enjoy it when my friends are here. The natives are a trifle crude.'

She turned away but he was still watching her. 'What about you?' he wanted to know.

'I'm newly-wed,' said Lucy. 'I must be happy.'

'There's no compulsion, you know. I've known scores of newly-wed couples who were really quite miserable'.

'I'm happy. I really am.'

Alfred poured her a little more wine. 'They take time, you know, marriages. They're rather like jigsaw-puzzles. They come in a brightly coloured box, with a pretty picture on the front, but most people are extremely disappointed when they open up the box and find that they have been given nothing but heaps of disassembled pieces, and that they have to put them all together themselves.'

He sipped, his ankle still swinging. 'Sometimes, of course, there are pieces missing. But you can't tell that for certain until you have sifted through them, tried to make some order out of them.'

They sat on the balcony in silence for a time, then Alfred said, 'Why don't I show you how my latest masterpiece is coming along? Bring your wine.'

He took her down the steep stone steps and across the angled garden to his studio; a high-raftered barn overgrown with vines. He unlocked the cracked oak door. Inside, the studio had walls of limewashed brick and a huge grimy north-facing window with dozens of broken panes. It was stacked with canvases, mostly Italianate landscapes and classical scenes, and broken pieces of stone statuary, female torsos mainly, although there was a row of six or seven Greek male torsos, all with their penises broken off. A pale bright light illuminated the whole studio with pearly evenness, and vine leaves fluttered against the window outside.

In the centre of the room stood a massive canvas, almost twice as high as Alfred himself, draped with cheesecloth. Alfred dramatically tugged the cloth away, and revealed a half-finished torrent of luminous nudity, and muscled horses' buttocks.

'The Sabines,' he announced. 'My *chef d'oeuvre*.'

'It's very dramatic,' said Lucy. 'And there's an awful lot of women with no clothes on.'

Alfred shrugged. 'It's a question of economics, I'm afraid. Nobody will buy a painting larger than three feet by two, not unless it's positively swarming with nudes.'

'They didn't really walk around nude in those days, did they?'

'My goodness, don't ask me. If they did, I don't suppose this would have been the first time they had been raped.'

Lucy laughed. She walked around the studio, fascinated by the pungent and oily smells of it, by the wriggling silver worms of half-squeezed paint-tubes, by the brushes and the bottles of turpentine. Long sticks of charcoal stood in a white glass jar like an incinerated flower-arrangement. She came to the row of male torsos. She sipped her wine, and said, 'They're all broken.'

'Yes,' said Alfred, watching her. 'Everybody thinks that they were damaged by centuries of erosion, but in fact they were broken off by vandals almost as soon as they were erected.' He added, daringly, 'If "erected" is the right word.'

Lucy turned. She set down her glass. Alfred approached her, and took off his hat. He stared directly into her eyes for a moment or two, then he tossed his hat all the way across the studio.

'You have the most exceptional beauty,' he said. 'Quite original; ceaselessly startling. You're like the sun shining through sunflower petals. You're like molten gold.'

Lucy opened her mouth slightly, her teeth resting on her glistening lower lip in the faintest of overbites.

Alfred said, 'I should love to paint you, you know.'

'Not as a Sabine woman, I hope?'

He took hold of her hands, clasped them both. 'Simply as yourself.'

Lucy looked away. Alfred gave her feelings that she couldn't comprehend. He seemed to be able to see through her, as if she were quite transparent, like water. Perhaps it was just his painter's eye. Perhaps she was revealing more of herself than she realized.

397

'Would you think it impertinent of me to give you some advice?' he asked her. 'I haven't known Henry for awfully long, but I do know something of what he's like.'

'Do you think I *need* advice?' Lucy challenged him.

'Perhaps. Only you can be the judge of that.'

He kept hold of her hands. His thumbs circled around and around on her knuckles. The sensation was soothing but peculiarly arousing at the same time.

He said, in soft, thick tone. 'Henry is the kind of chap who feels personally responsible for everything and everyone. He lives for toil! He eats blame for breakfast and sprinkles his supper with fault! Why do you think he wants so desperately to govern India? Only India is chaotic enough for him! Only India will burden him with enough administrative difficulties, enough tangled bureaucracy, enough political upheaval, enough poverty, enough pomp, enough pettiness, enough fanaticism! To be responsible for governing India is a martyr's dream!'

Alfred hesitated, and then he added, 'Henry believes for some reason which I fail fully to understand that he has to suffer. It is partly to do with the sense of historic mission with which a man of his birth and upbringing will always be encumbered. There may be something else, some other obligation which he feels he has to fulfil; or some stain on his soul which he feels he has to purge. Whatever it is, I sense that you have already become conscious of it, and that it is unsettling you.'

Again, Alfred paused, but he must have known that he was right, because Lucy didn't answer, and made no attempt to take her hands away.

Alfred said, 'You are Henry's wife. You have agreed to share his life. But you are not necessarily obliged to share his agonies. His agonies belong to him. You should remember that you are a woman in your own right, with your own desires, and your own free spirit.'

He smiled. 'You are also very young and very beautiful. You have a *duty* to enjoy yourself.'

398

He leaned forward. Lucy looked up. She realized at once that he wanted to kiss her. Their faces approached each other, sun and moon, until Lucy could feel his breath on her cheek.

'You don't have to think of anything at all,' said Alfred; and kissed her. The tip of his tongue ran along her lips, then penetrated them, and touched her teeth. She opened her mouth wider, and let him in.

They stood for long timeless moments in the pearly studio light, closely embracing, while behind them the Sabine women tumbled pink and plump across the canvas, like a basket of peaches being emptied, and the vines whispered and scratched at the window.

Alfred's hand gently closed over Lucy's breast, over her white linen dress. But then he kissed her one more time, and stood away.

'You're more than Henry deserves,' he told her. 'Don't let him turn you into a task; or a memorandum; or a column of accounts.'

Lucy said, 'Why did you kiss me?'

'Do you think it was wrong?'

'I'm Henry's wife.'

'You're Lucy. You're Lucy first, and Henry's wife after. You shouldn't forget that. Henry's wife is *what* you are; but Lucy is *who* you are.'

'We'd better get back,' said Lucy.

Alfred shrugged. 'As you wish. But you don't think that Henry will suspect us of misconduct, do you, if we linger too long in the studio?'

'I don't think I understand men,' said Lucy, brushing her dress straight and feeling quite cross about it.

'Nobody understands anybody. If they did – my God, if there were to be an instantaneous lightning-bolt of world-wide understanding, fellow for fellow – then the globe would be immediately be plunged into the fiercest and most destructive war in its history. It is only our failure to understand each other which keeps us from tearing each other's throats out.'

They left the studio and climbed back up the steps through the garden. Yellow roses nodded on either side of the path, making the afternoon air smell musky, and dropping their petals like thick curds of clotted cream. At the top of the steps, Lucy turned to Alfred, holding her hat against the katabatic breeze. 'Why didn't you want to make love to me?' she asked him, testing her own boldness, and his.

Alfred, with his disreputable hat pulled sideways over his forehead, laughed out loud. 'But I did, dear Lucy! I did!'

At that moment, Henry appeared on the balcony, in his shirtsleeves, looking pale and hot. 'Lucy! How are you?'

Lucy took hold of Alfred's hand. 'I'm very well, thank you, my darling. Alfred's been showing me his paintings.'

'Good man, Dunners,' said Henry. 'Nothing too risqué, I hope?'

Alfred gave Lucy's fingers the tiniest of squeezes. 'You know me, Henry. You know me.'

It was late November when they returned to England, and to the house that Henry had rented at Carlton House Terrace. Lucy had seen scarcely anything of London when they had stopped off for two days *en route* for France; but now she could see even less of it. The capital was plunged into raw and impenetrable fog; and all she could distinguish from her dressing-room window were the ghostly shadows of horses and carts, and spidery leafless trees, and guardsmen marching along The Mall.

Now that he was back in London, and back at work, Henry returned to the Foreign Office with a dedicated fury that almost made Lucy despair. He would rise every morning at six o'clock, shave and dress, and work by lamplight until breakfast. At half-past seven he would leave the house for the Foreign Office, which was only a minute's walk away, down the steps, across The Mall, and past Horse Guards' Parade.

Before he went, he would tiptoe into the bedroom, kiss her lightly on each cheek, and then on her lips, and tell her, 'Good girl, see you tonight.' That would be the last she would see of him until nine or ten o'clock, or sometimes later, when he would return white and stunned and semi-articulate with exhaustion. There were days when she felt that she wasn't married at all. Henry was nothing more than a stranger who came and went.

The sexual difficulties that they had suffered during the early days of their marriage soon ceased to trouble them. Henry was usually so tired when he returned home from the Foreign Office that the question of love-making became academic. Lucy took to shopping to satisfy her frustrations, and she and Nora could be seen almost every afternoon, in and out of the fashionable shops along Regent Street.

Carlton House Terrace was so close that most of her shopping had already been delivered by the time she got home. Hats and jewellery, and evening-purses and gloves. Sometimes she bought gifts for Henry: brandy-flasks or shooting-sticks or country hats, all of which he already owned in abundance. Once, to surprise him, she spent £55 on a French painting at a Bond Street gallery, but Henry insisted that the gallery took it back, because its subject-matter was too intimate (in the domestic rather than the sexual sense: it showed a kitchen) and because (in his opinion) it was hopelessly badly painted. The gallery's managing director wrote Henry a personal apology: Mrs Carson would be shown no more Bonnards.

However, there were moments of glitter and glory, and great delight. They were invited in early December to stay at Sandringham with the Prince and Princess of Wales, along with Lord Rosebery, Arthur Balfour, and Mr and Mrs Joseph Chamberlain. A week before Christmas they dined with Lord Salisbury, when he entertained the Russian Ambassador, M. de Staal; and every 'week-end' (as Saturday and Sunday were now being called), Henry contrived to invite somebody of amusement and interest to Carlton House Terrace. Leafing through her guest book at the end of her first winter with Henry, Lucy read the signature of the Duke and Duchess of Rutland; Thomas Hardy, the novelist; Henry Adams, the American historian; Henry and Margot Asquith; Alfred and D. D. Lyttelton, Evan Charteris, and many more.

They went to the theatre twice a month, at least; they attended official banquets with a great many colourfully-garbed men with shining black faces and ostrich plumes in their hair. They began to be mentioned almost every week in the society columns, and the *Evening Standard* called Lucy 'golden and ladylike', as if it were quite a surprise that an American girl could behave like a lady but, by the criteria of a nation that owned most of the profitable world, it was quite a compliment.

Then spring came, and Lucy began to know London better. She made more and more friends, mostly the wives of other Tory members of Parliament, but particularly the one-time Tennant sisters, Margot Asquith and Charty Ribblesdale. The Kansas accent which Evelyn Scott had vainly tried to Easternize was never lost altogether, but anybody in Oak City who heard it would have considered it well-nigh incomprehensible, clipped as a cow's ear. As if she were an actress in a play which she was making up as she was going along, Lucy found herself in high-ceilinged room with watered-silk walls, taking tea with elegant English ladies; riding side-saddle in a high silk hat along Rotten Row, between the budding elms; and although there were unexpectedly hurtful times, when she would glimpse a baby in a carriage in Kensington Gardens, and think of Blanche, *oh God, my poor Blanche*, she knew that she was living the life that she had always dreamed of. She had survived without parents, and found what she had always wanted. Blanche would do the same.

In May, to Lucy's undiluted terror, Henry and she were

commanded to dine and to sleep at Windsor Castle. Lucy thought that she would probably run away when she met the Queen. She had heard so many fierce stories about her. But when she was presented, she found the Queen to be tiny and articulate; softly-spoken, pale, almost girlish, and given to occasional giggles, and to making pointed remarks of her own.

After breakfast, as they stood in the sunshine waiting for their carriage, Her Majesty came up to Lucy in her rustling black dress and addressed her quite solemnly. 'You have a very agreeable husband, Mrs Carson. He is clever and well-informed. In an Empire such as ours, he has the ability to advance very far.'

'Thank you, ma'am,' said Lucy. She was amazed how white the Queen's hair shone; how white her lips were. Even her eyes looked bleached.

'I must say, too, Mrs Carson, that you are very handsome. I trust that you were not quiet yesterday evening because you found the conversation tedious.'

'No, ma'am,' Lucy replied. 'I found it real interesting.'

'Oh . . . it is never *interesting*,' the Queen replied. 'Diverting, perhaps. But never *interesting*.'

During the late summer, Henry (without consulting her) took Inverlochy Castle in Scotland, for the grouse-shooting. Lucy argued at first. She didn't want to leave London. But when Henry assured her that *everybody* left London in the summer, she eventually agreed. (In spite of tantrums, doors slammed, arguments up and down the stairs so that the servants could hear.) And, as it turned out, she adored Scotland. It was wildly different from Kansas, but she adored its mountains and its mauvish melancholy. She could open her bedroom window and the heather smelled like honey and the air smelled like slate.

Perhaps the only irritation was that Henry continued to work, even when they were on holiday. He was up at six o'clock as usual, sorting through papers that had been sent up in endless dispatch boxes by the Foreign Office, and by the time he and his friends left for the butts, he had already finished what (for most of his colleagues) amounted to a full day's hard work. After dinner, he returned to his desk, and worked until well after midnight.

Lucy had worked hard at Jack's store, dawn till dusk, but it was difficult for her to understand the ocean of paperwork with which Henry had to cope. Henry had told her with some pride that nearly ninety-two thousand telegrams and dispatches engulfed the Foreign Office every year, and every night Henry had to read the better part of them, so that he would be able to speak confidently and aggressively in the House of Commons. Every government minister suffered under the same burden of toil, and many of them were very much older and sicker than Henry. All for £1,500 a year, and the greater glory of Her Majesty's Britannic Empire.

Lucy was lying awake in her wide oak bed at Inverlochy Castle when Henry appeared at last. The clocks had long struck two, and she was so tired that she kept dropping off, and dreaming that she was still awake. She had been walking in the hills with Loulou Harcourt all afternoon, exercising Loulou's assorted dogs, and she had eaten too much grouse at dinner. But she had kept the lamp alight; and when Henry appeared, she sat up in bed and smiled at him.

'Finished at last?' she asked him.

He nodded. His face looked like a plaster-cast of himself. 'If you only knew what questions I have to answer.'

'Tell me,' she coaxed him, patting the green plaid blanket that covered their bed.

He shook his head. 'It's quite bad enough that I should have to worry myself with such matters, without you having to worry yourself, too. Can the Mayor of Portsmouth accept a foreign decoration? Can the Colombian Chargé d'Affaires be given a ticket of admission to the House of Commons? Does the Regius Professor of Physics at Cambridge University require a letter from the Russian Embassy in London before visiting Moscow? Should the Court of St James go into mourning for the Empress Dowager of Japan?'

Lucy pretended to think of some sensible answers, while Henry sat beside her, knowing that she couldn't. At last she lifted her head, and smiled, and unexpectedly kissed him. 'I don't have the first idea,' she said. 'But I know that I love you, my dearest.'

He loosened his necktie and eased out his collar-studs. 'It's more than I deserve. Your understanding is quite enough.'

'Ah, but I don't understand you. Nobody understands anybody. You know what they say. It's only our failure to understand each other that prevents us from tearing each other's throats out.'

She was tired. She had eaten and drunk too much. Henry was tired too. But he stiffened, right in the middle of unfastening his cufflinks, and demanded, 'What does that mean? What exactly does that *mean*?'

Lucy hopelessly shook her head. 'Henry, I'm really not sure. I just said it.'

He stood up, his eyes bulging, his face furious. 'Do you really mean to tell me that you believe in such sentiments? That our inability to understand each other is all that prevents us from falling on each other, like wild animals?'

'Henry, somebody said it, that's all, and I repeated it. It was only a joke.'

Quivering, Henry snapped at her, 'Do you have any idea how hard I have to work to achieve the most rudimentary of understandings between one country and another? Even between Englishman and Englishman? We live in Babel! We agree to talk to the Russian Ambassador, but everything he says is like Virgil's mysterious verses: you can only understand the first four words of every sentence. We agree to talk to the Society of Friends about slavery, provided they bring a shorthand-writer, so that we can check what they give to the Press, and we end up opening a file on who shall pay this shorthand-writer her one-guinea fee – a file inches thicker than our file on slavery! Every day is a thicket of misunderstandings, both accidental and intentional, through which I have to hack my path! And you try to tell me that misunderstanding is – I don't know, whatever you said that misunderstanding was.'

Lucy lowered her eyes, twisted her diamond-and-sapphire engagement-ring. 'Henry, I'm sorry. But we *don't* understand each other, do we?'

'Don't we?' he barked.

'Perhaps it's just that I don't understand you. I don't know, perhaps it's better that I don't. You seem to prefer to lead your own life, in your own way, without me.'

'How can you – ' Henry began, but then he clamped his hand over his mouth, as if he were the ugly step-sister in the Grimm's fairytale who coughed up frogs; and stood silent, staring at his collar-studs on the top of the black Jacobean table.

Lucy said, 'There's something wrong, Henry, isn't there?'

'Wrong? Of course not.'

'I don't mean wrong. There's something – something you've done – something you have to make amends for.'

Henry said nothing for a moment, then he let out a half-humorous, half-dismissive, *'hah!'*

'Isn't that true?' Lucy asked him.

Henry looked at her. He appeared to be wondering what to say next.

'Henry,' said Lucy, 'if it isn't true, if you're punishing yourself for nothing at all, then I swear to God that I'm going to leave you.'

Henry, with strangely jerky motions, undressed. He stood in the lamplight naked, deep-chested, a little too heavy around the waist, but very strong and athletic; a true gymnast, an exerciser in the nude.

He lifted the sheet and climbed into bed beside her. She waited for him, hardly daring to breathe. He said, in a voice like rubbed charcoal, 'I've been bad to you, Lucy, haven't I?'

'You've given me everything I could have wished for.'

'But love? What about love? Sometimes I feel that I have no capability to love.'

She held his wrist, and kissed the heel of his hand, again and again. 'You're tired, that's all. You work too hard.'

'I have to. God knows, we have an empire to run.'

'You also have a wife who cares for you, Henry, and doesn't wish to see you collapse from overwork.'

Henry was silent for a time. She felt his steady breathing on her hand. Then he said, 'I've thought for some time that you need to get out more, especially in London. My work keeps me tied to my desk, but that is no reason why you shouldn't go to dances and parties and enjoy yourself.'

'Henry, I'm quite content.'

'How can you be? I'm always so busy. I'm scarcely ever at home. But it's my nature, I would become quite mad if I were obliged to spend all my time at ease. There is so much work to be done!'

'What do you suggest?' asked Lucy. She wasn't sure what he was talking about.

'Well,' he said, 'it's this. I have a dear chum, Bruno Maltravers, we were at Oxford together. Malty, we always called him. His uncle's the Duke of Nantwich.'

'Didn't we meet the Duke of Nantwich at that reception for President Faure?'

'That's right. Bald, bearded, can't stick the man. Personally, I can never think for the life of me how he manages to have so much influence with the P.M. Malty always calls him the Mighty Coconut'.

'So what about "Malty"?'

'It's just that Malty doesn't do much for living; he's quite well off and he doesn't really need to. But he's the perfect escort. He's charming, he's amusing. You'll love him. I was thinking of inviting him to dinner, as soon as we get back to Carlton House Terrace, and putting a proposition to him, that he should escort you to dances, and to dinner-parties, whenever Parliamentary business makes it impossible for me to do so myself.'

Lucy said, 'Are you *sure?* I don't think I ever heard of such a thing.'

'My darling Lucy, it's quite common practice, especially among politicians. The administration of a global empire is a hugely time-consuming business, for all that we have junior clerks playing cricket in the corridors all afternoon. If you yourself have no particular objections, you and Malty would be doing me the very best of services. I could carry on with my work each evening without worrying that you were bored or fretful, or that you were privately blaming me because your life had turned out to be so drab.'

He kissed her, twice, on the forehead, more like a blessing than a gesture of husbandly affection, and then he said, 'These are great days for me, Lucy. I am approaching the destiny for which I was born. Unless I throw myself into my Parliamentary work night and day, I may easily lose the opportunity to become Viceroy. I was born to rule India; and I was born to rule her young. It is too much of a coincidence of destiny that the viceregal residence in Calcutta was built in imitation of Brackenbridge. Lucy – you talked of the cloud-castles that you used to see in Kansas. Brackenbridge in Derbyshire and Brackenbridge in India – *they* are my cloud-castles, and I must have them – I *must* have them – as you had to have yours.'

Lucy, taken by surprise, said nothing. She knew how Henry burned for India. But she had never realized how much he was prepared to sacrifice in order to make sure that it was his. Lord Elgin, the present Viceroy, was close to the end of his term. Almost everybody assumed that Henry would be offered the viceroyalty as his successor. Everybody, that was, except those who considered him harsh and incautious, like Lord George Hamilton, the Secretary of State for India; and those who were competitively interested in the viceroyalty for themselves, such as the Marquess of Lorne, heir to the Duke of Argyll and husband of Queen Victoria's fourth daughter, Louise, who didn't care for Henry one bit, and showed it, and never hesitated to tell the Queen what an arrogant self-serving bounder Henry was.

But Henry wanted India. And tonight Lucy had abruptly been brought to the realization that if he had to give up her love in order to win the viceroyalty, then by God, without hesitation, he would give up her love. He needed a wife; he would never be given India without a vicereine. But India came first. *He won't let me go, even if I say that I hate him to hell. He will endure my hating him, if he can have India.*

Henry appeared to have perfect confidence in Bruno Maltravers. But it wasn't his confidence in Bruno that made Lucy feel so estranged. It was his hunger for preferment; his terrible hunger for power and responsibility. Tonight, he had made her feel like a wife who had caught her husband at two o'clock in the morning in the pantry, stuffing himself with cream cake. His sexual character had mystified and worried her. But his greed for public duty was beyond her understanding.

When he slept that night, murmuring in his sleep as he always did, she lay awake staring at the darkness, trying to divine in it some reassurance, some shape, some form, some reason why she might be here, in this bed in Scotland, with her baby daughter half a world away, committed body and soul to an ambition that wasn't even hers.

Bruno Maltravers arrived at Carlton House Terrace just after noon on the first Thursday in December, as arranged, and sat waiting for Lucy in the front parlour, his legs elegantly crossed, his silk hat perched on his lap. Outside, the day was unexpectedly bright, although St James's Park was still blurred with fog, and the clattering of horses and the grinding of carriage-wheels sounded unnaturally flat.

Henry had left early on Monday morning for Berlin, to talk to Baron Marschall von Bieberstein, the German Foreign

Minister, about provocative German troop-landings in Portuguese East Africa. Antagonism between the German and the British governments was growing increasingly bitter; although Kaiser Wilhelm still wrote affectionately to his grandmother, Queen Victoria, and their ministers and their ambassadors were always received with the greatest courtesy.

Henry was attempting to use his long-standing friendships with German aristocracy to talk them into behaving with less truculence. He would be gone for two weeks at least, and he had warned Lucy with great solemnity that he might not even be back for Christmas.

'I am going to try to talk to the Kaiser personally,' he had confided in her. 'If I can do that, and convince him that the British government is interested not in conflict but in co-operation, then my future at the Foreign Office will be assured. Salisbury considers me an amateur, when it comes to European affairs. If I can mollify the Kaiser, as an amateur, then perhaps Salisbury will understand at last what I can do in Asia, where I am an expert. Think of it, Lucy! I will have India practically in my pocket.'

'Bruno promised to take me to see *Trilby*,' Lucy had told him. She was conscious that she was trying to make him feel jealous.

'I hope you enjoy it,' Henry had replied. 'I hate Tree.'

'Sometimes I think you hate anything that makes people laugh.'

Henry had stared at her and his face had looked oddly like a hawk – beakish nose and intensely-focused eyes. 'Nobody has ever accused me of being lacking in humour before,' he had retaliated.

'Perhaps you have never been lacking in humour before.'

'And what is that supposed to mean?'

'That you don't care for anything, anything at all, except India.'

Henry hadn't blinked. 'India is my destiny. Is it wrong of me to care so much for my destiny?'

Lucy had stood up, and clenched her fists, and almost screamed at him, 'Don't keep talking to me about your stupid destiny! Nobody has a destiny! You get – swept along, that's all! Just swept along!'

When Henry had left Carlton House Terrace that Monday morning, Lucy had begun to suspect from his turned-away face and his abrasive demeanour that nobody had ever said anything so hurtful to him in the whole of his life. He was a Carson, after all; and what was a Carson, but destiny incarnate? He had kissed her with all the limp lack of surprise of a steamed-open love-letter. Then he had cantered down the steps, heels clicking, climbed into his carriage, and gone to Germany.

But now (thank God) it was Thursday; and time for luncheon; and Bruno was here, morning-suited, dapper and shiny. Whether Henry had known it or not, the choice of Bruno as an escort for Lucy while he was away had been inspired. Bruno was tall, taller than Henry; handsome in a bashed-up upper-class way; exactingly fashionable; sardonic; but capable of huge acts of affectionate mischief.

Henry was a practical joker, but Lucy found most of his practical jokes to be cold and occasionally cruel. He thought it was funny if his friends fell off chairs and jarred their backs, or caught their fingers in mouse-traps. Bruno on the other hand preferred jokes against himself. 'There is nothing quite so funny as oneself. Once you understand that, you understand everything. God, the Universe, one's fellow man, you name it. It's an insight.'

Bruno's hair was chestnut-brown and crinkled. He was always straining his eyes as if he needed spectacles, and his short-sightedness had given him a slight stoop. His nose was broken, and his teeth were crooked, but he had a marvellously engaging smile. He was also the most attentive of escorts that Lucy could ever remember. He never failed to open carriage doors, to walk on the outside of the pavement, to send her gifts, to leave his card whenever he called. But there was nothing effete or weak about him. He took care of her because Henry had asked him to; and because he was a gentleman.

Lucy came down to greet him that Thursday morning dressed in a skirt of cobalt-blue velvet, with a Brussels lace blouse and a small fur bolero. She wore the six-strand pearl choker that Henry had brought her back from Madrid. Bruno stood up, and gave her an exaggerated bow. 'My dear Lucy, you look exquisite. Now I shall have to go home and change, to match up to your exquisiteness. Can you give me – what, an hour, perhaps? I shall have to spend at least ten minutes choosing a new tie.'

Lucy kissed him. 'You're as silly as ever.'

'Oh, you slaughter me,' Bruno protested. 'Actually, we'd better be going. We don't want to arrive later than the Prince of Wales, now do we? People would frown.'

Lucy said, 'Very well,' and she rang for Warren, the butler, to bring their coats. They climbed into Bruno's smart bottle-green brougham, and started to rattle along The Mall towards Buckingham Palace.

Bruno took hold of Lucy's hand. 'So, my dear, how have you been amusing yourself since Henry departed for the land of the midnight sausage? You know what they say about Germany, don't you? "Demand the best, but expect the wurst!"'

Lucy pressed her fingers to her forehead. 'Bruno . . .' she said. 'Do you really want to go to this luncheon? I wonder if I might persuade you to do something else.'

Bruno sat back in his seat, and frowned. They had passed the Palace now, and were progressing up Constitution Hill. 'Not so sure what you're driving at,' he told her, warily.

'Well, Bruno, I know we're supposed to go to this luncheon, and that the Prince of Wales will be there, and all about that . . . but I think I'd rather go the country.'

'The country?'

'I don't know, somewhere different, where nobody knows us.'

Bruno thought about this for a while — then, when they reached Hyde Park Corner — he rapped his cane on the brougham's roof, and his coachman Romney opened the hatch in the roof. 'Sir?' he demanded, out of the corner of his mouth.

'Epsom,' Bruno told him.

'Epsom, sir?'

'The racecourse, that'll do us.'

'No races today, sir.'

'Romney,' Bruno told him, with undisguised irritation, 'take us to Epsom.'

'Yes, sir,' said Romney.

In less than two hours they were standing on what seemed to Lucy to be the roof of the world. To the south, she could see thick hazy woods, and the single triangular spire of a church. To the west, she could see for miles and miles, all over Surrey, and farther; a pale countryside from which the sun was reluctantly dragging its watery-gold light, hedge by hedge, tree by tree, as it settled towards the horizon. The air was so raw that she could scarcely breathe in: not brittle-cold, like Kansas, but damp and sore-throaty.

A few yards away, by the deserted grandstand, Romney fed and watered the horses. He was in better spirits now, since Bruno had allowed him to visit the Derby Arms for bread-and-cheese and a pint of bitter beer. Lucy could hear him clicking to his horses and cajoling them and telling them how fine they were.

Bruno stood with his hands by his sides, his breath smoking, saying nothing, but looking right and left.

'It's marvellous here,' said Lucy. 'I feel like God, looking out over His new creation.'

'Well,' said Bruno, wryly, 'you could feel worse.'

'*Bruno*,' Lucy protested.

'I'm sorry,' Bruno told her. 'It's just that I really have no idea what all of this is in aid of.'

Lucy said, quietly, 'You do like women, don't you, Bruno?'

He swung his stooping shoulders around. 'I beg your pardon?'

'You do like women? You're not a buh-guh-ruh?'

Bruno opened his mouth and then closed it again.

'I'm sorry,' said Lucy. 'I'm truly sorry. That was quite unfair. What could you answer, if you were?'

'What could I answer, if I *weren't*?' Bruno retaliated.

Lucy turned to him. Behind her, the sun had fallen over Hampshire. In an hour-and-a-half, it would be dark. 'Bruno, why did Henry ask you to escort me?' she asked.

'He said he was very busy at the Foreign Office. Early mornings, late nights. He was afraid you might be bored.'

'Was that all?'

Bruno wouldn't answer. He stood leaning on his stick, looking out over the misty and mysterious undulations of the Downs, the shepherd of his own secret.

'That wasn't all, was it?' Lucy challenged him.

Bruno said, 'Perhaps I made a mistake.'

'What mistake?'

'Lucy . . . Henry is a very special chap. Henry is one of these chaps who only appears once a century or so and *he's* aware of it and everybody else around him is aware of it. You know what they say about him in *The Times*, and in *Punch*.'

Lucy stood very close to Bruno, her hands enclosed in her fur muffler, her face pale in the winter sunlight. 'Bruno, you're trying to tell me something.'

'Well,' he shrugged. 'I am, and I'm not.'

'What is it?'

'Don't you see?' Bruno demanded. 'It's all to do with Henry's what-d'you-call-it. His calling. His birthright. God said to Henry, you're going to govern India, and ever since God said that, Henry hasn't taken any notice of anybody else.'

Bruno looked around, sniffed, as if he could smell wood-smoke in the air, or blood. Lucy felt peculiarly afraid; but brave, at the same time. She wanted to know the worst. It almost excited her, to know the worst.

Bruno said, 'Henry, well . . . he's unique. Just like the Duke of Wellington; or Disraeli. Ordinary people like you and me, we can love him or like him, we can give him all the semblance of friendship and family life . . . But he's not like us, you know, Lucy. You and I, we're simply mortal. Henry will be remembered long, long after there is nobody in the world who can remember that you and I even existed.'

Lucy persisted, 'Why did Henry ask you to escort me?'

Bruno breathed steam. The day was falling fast, and it was already bone-cold. He could have said so many things. One explanation is as good as another. Why say anything complicated, or hurtful? Why say anything true? But Bruno had already gone too far, by agreeing to bring Lucy out to the country, when they should have been lunching in Park Lane. The moment he had said, 'Epsom', he had committed himself.

'Henry said –' Bruno began.

'Bruno, Henry said *what*?'

'Henry said, "The devil you know is preferable to the devil you don't."'

Lucy clutched his sleeve. She felt almost as if she were drowning, as if she couldn't breathe. 'Well, what did he mean by that? What does that mean, "the devil you know"?'

Bruno tried not to look at her; then looked at her. 'I'm obliged to tell you, aren't I?'

'Yes, goddamn it, you are!'

'What he meant was, Lucy . . . what he obviously intended me to understand him as saying *was* – that he was too preoccupied with affairs of state at the Foreign Office – to give a young, vivacious wife everything that was required to make her happy.'

415

At that moment, Lucy grasped what Bruno was telling her; but the implications of it were so enormous that she remained silent, and waited for Bruno to say it out loud, word by word, as if it were a school recital.

Bruno said, 'You needed parties, that's what he said. Parties, and dances, and theatre, and entertainment.'

'That's what you've given me,' Lucy reassured him. 'That's exactly what you've given me!'

'I think he meant more,' Bruno told her, in a voice like wrung-out washing.

'More?'

Bruno was agonized. 'I have to tell you the truth, Lucy. I'm too fond of you now to lie to you. If you never want to see me again, then of course I'll understand.'

Lucy immediately tugged off her left-hand glove, and lifted her fingers to her eyes, to see if she was crying.

Bruno puckered his mouth, and said, 'I'm sorry. I'm sorry. Henry's my friend.'

They stood together on the Downs for almost ten minutes, in the biting wind. Romney came over, and took off his hat, and said, 'Horses gettin' cold, sir. Should we be gettin' back?'

Lucy looked at Bruno. She tried to keep her voice steady and level. 'There must be an inn, in Epsom.'

'Spread Eagle, sir,' Romney suggested. He didn't speak to Lucy, not even once. As far as he was concerned, Bruno might just as well have been standing on the Downs on his own. Romney was what most employers would have called 'the soul of discretion'.

'Spread Eagle?' asked Bruno. 'How far is that?'

In the darkest hours of the night, when the town of Epsom was completely silent, Lucy could hear the erratic thundering of Bruno's breath, and the sliding of the sheets. Then Bruno, naked, was on top of her, very lean, all bone and muscle. She reached down and clutched his stiffness; and almost at once guided it into herself.

He was very hard, like a long bone. He said nothing to her, while he pushed himself in and out; either because he had nothing to say, or because he was afraid to. She was conscious in a remarkable way that she was committing adultery, but she felt almost as if Henry had commissioned it, like a portrait, and whether he liked the portrait or not, he had to suffer the consequences.

Bruno shuddered. He was finished. He kissed her once, on the cheek; then he turned over on to his side and fell asleep. Almost an hour later, in the bathroom, Lucy stood in front of the mirror staring at her face. She didn't look like Lucy Carson at all. She was somebody else; although she didn't know who.

It was very cold, in the bathroom. The sun was very far away.

8

When Henry came home that thundery afternoon and stood in the hallway shaking his umbrella and called out, 'India, my darling! They've given me India!' her immediate thought was not of palaces or elephants or princes with diamonds in their foreheads.

As if they had flown open in her mind with a sudden and general clatter, she thought of those black tinplate boxes on the back shelves of the Darling General Store; and how she had breathed in their mysterious dust-dry pungencies; and wondered what kind of an extraordinary country it could be where people ate foods that tasted of shoe-leather and gun-powder and dried flowers and fire.

'The Queen has given her approval, and the P.M. will announce it next week,' said Henry, so excited that he couldn't stop stalking from one side of the parlour to the other, flapping his arms up and down.

'Fenugreek and cumin,' Lucy recited, holding out her arms for him. 'Chilli and turmeric and garam marsala.'

'What?' he laughed. 'Have you been learning Hindi already?'

She kissed him, and shook her head. His sidewhiskers were wet from summer rain. 'India!' she told him. 'I'm so proud of you, Henry! India!'

'Hamilton wasn't too pleased,' said Henry. 'He said I was too adventurous to be Viceroy. Too high-spirited! But there's nothing he can do about it now. He's written to Elgin already, giving him the news.'

'When do we leave?' asked Lucy.

'Well, not until December. We have so many domestic arrangements to make. I don't know whether Elgin will leave me an aide-de-camp; or a house steward. I don't even know if we're supposed to take our own carriages and plate and wine.'

Lucy said, 'You'll have to be a peer, won't you? Malty said you would, if they gave you the viceroyalty.'

'Ah, we've sorted that one out, too,' Henry told her, with a self-satisfied smile. 'They're going to make me an Irish peer, instead of an English peer, so that I can be free to seek re-election to the House of Commons when I get back. They haven't created an Irish peer for thirty years, and they may never create one again, but the Queen seems quite agreeable. I shall be Lord Carson of Brackenbridge.'

He gripped her arms tightly, and smiled at her wide-eyed with delight. 'And you shall be Lady Carson!'

Henry lunched at home, cold mutton and mustard pickles. Over the tapioca pudding, he asked Lucy, 'How *is* Malty these days? I swear that I haven't run into him for months!'

'Malty's well,' said Lucy, without looking up.

'Is he taking good care of you?'

'Excellent care, thank you. In fact we're going to Twickenham this afternoon, for a picnic tea on the river with Jeremy and Nellie Theobald.'

Henry nodded, meticulously spooning up the last of his pudding. 'I'm sorry you had to stay in Town so late. But as soon as they've announced my appointment, we can go up to Brackenbridge for a week or so. Shoot some grouse.'

'I really don't mind,' said Lucy, trying to sound offhand. 'I've enjoyed myself in Town. There's always something to do.'

'Would you like Malty to come up to Derbyshire with us?' asked Henry.

Lucy lifted her head and looked at him. The clouds must have been clearing outside, because a sudden gleam of watery sunshine illuminated the table, and sparkled on the glassware. Did he suspect that she and Malty had been going to bed together two or three times a week; in fact, almost every time they went out together? Lucy had taken every possible precaution not to be seen, unlike some other aristocratic ladies who flaunted their lovers as ostentatiously as they flaunted their new hats. Nora seemed to suspect her, but Nora had said nothing. Nora was concerned only that Lucy should be happy; and during this long busy summer of 1898, Lucy had been happier than Nora had ever remembered. She was twenty-one years old, the beautiful wife of a popular and successful politician. She was invited to all the balls and all the receptions and all the best banquets. The popular Press adored her, and had nicknamed her the Yankee Butterfly.

She and Henry were regularly invited to Windsor and to Buckingham Palace, and the Queen now called her by her first name.

She had all of that, and sufficient money to be able to dress herself in silks and velvets and furs. And even if it was a disappointment that Henry was so erratic and unsatisfying in bed, she had Malty. Equable, uncomplaining, ever-loyal Malty, who would take her wherever and whenever she wished, and make persistent love to her, on and on for as long as she could bear it.

He was always careful, however, and wore a French letter. The very last thing that she wanted was to be blessed with a wavy-haired baby with a slight stoop and a habit of humming *Another Little Patch of Red*.

She couldn't be sure that Henry didn't suspect her of adultery. Yet her love-making with Malty immeasurably improved their marriage. She became quieter, and more content, and because of her contentment, and the fact that she made no physical demands on him, Henry appeared to enjoy life much more, and to laugh more often.

The Carsons' obvious happiness was infectious, and they were popular hosts. They held scores of dinners and *soirées* at Carlton House Terrace; and early in 1897 Henry had taken a lease on a six-bedroomed Georgian house in Reigate, twenty miles to the south of London, called The Vines, where they held weekend parties, too.

The following week, when Henry's appointment as Viceroy was announced, there would be even more celebrations.

Henry wiped his mouth with his napkin, and then laid it on the table. 'I'll be back around eight o'clock this evening; no later. I have to write a letter to Elgin, and to my old Balliol chum, Walter Pinkerton. I'm going to need a first-class private secretary when I'm in Calcutta, and if anybody has any ideas who to go for, it'll be Pinks.'

He leaned over Lucy and kissed her.

'Henry, I'm very happy for you,' she told him, and kissed him back. Both were kisses of complete chastity, such as a brother might give to a sister, and *vice versa*.

There was a distant rumble outside, summer thunder. 'Better take your bumbersoll,' Lucy warned him.

But the same storm which came lashing down on Henry as he scurried across The Mall to the Foreign Office had already caused the abandonment of the Theobalds' picnic on the river at Twickenham. Lucy and Malty hadn't intended to go to the picnic at all. Malty had arranged to use the

Theobalds' house in Cheyne Walk while they were out, telling Jeremy and Nellie that he wanted to impress some friends on leave from India.

The Theobalds knew nothing of Malty's affair with Lucy. They were both good friends with Henry; and they certainly wouldn't have allowed their house to be used as a refuge for Lucy's adultery. Still, they were supposed to be picnicking in Twickenham until early evening, and what the Theobalds' eyes didn't see, Malty had declared, the Theobalds' hearts wouldn't grieve over.

It was a particularly convenient trysting-place because the Theobalds had taken all their servants, too, as a summer treat.

When Malty's brougham reached Cheyne Walk, however, the rain was clattering down furiously, drumming on the roof, and bouncing off the coachman's top-hat. Wiping the steam from the carriage window with his glove, Malty peered out and muttered, 'Oh, God!'

'What is it?' asked Lucy.

'Jeremy and Nellie. Look! They've been rained off.'

Sure enough, three coaches were drawn up outside the Theobalds' redbrick house, and servants were scurrying to and fro with umbrellas and hampers and folded tables.

'Well, that puts paid to that, I'm afraid,' said Malty. He rapped his stick on the roof of the brougham, and called out, 'Romney! Royal Academy! Let's go and look at some pictures!'

But Lucy snuggled up close to him and kissed his cheek, and said, 'Why do we have to go and look at pictures?'

'What else do you suggest? We have nowhere else. You're too well known for us to risk an hotel.'

'We could go home.'

'Home? You mean *your* home? Carlton House Terrace? You must be mad!'

'I'll give the servants the afternoon off.'

'And they won't suspect?'

'Not if you pretend to leave, and then come back later, through the kitchen.'

'Lucy, my darling, it's fearfully risky!'

She kissed him again, 'Perhaps it's about time we took some risks.'

An hour-and-a-half later, with the rain still pattering against the bedroom window, Lucy sat up completely naked in bed and wrote, *'My life in Kansas seems so far away that I find it difficult to remember it. Faces, names . . . they seem to have faded away, like a picture-book left on the windowsill. I remember the tornadoes, and I remember Uncle Casper, and Jack, and my mother. But they all seem like they never truly existed, something I read about, some story somebody told me . . . not real people at all.'*

She became conscious that the soft scratching of her pen had woken Malty up; and that he was watching her. The way the light shone faintly gold on the fine hairs of her forearms; the way her hair tangled across her cheek. He touched her shoulder, and then his fingers delicately circled her breasts, around and around and around.

'Do you know what I think?' Malty told her.

'No, what do you think?'

'I think that all men are monsters and all women are goddesses.'

'I'm not a goddess.'

'Yes, you are. Henry thinks you are. That's why Henry can never make love to you properly.'

'I don't want to talk about Henry.'

His fingers trailed down between her breasts, lingered around her navel. 'Do you think it's *de rigueur* for a vicereine of India to wear a ruby in her tummy-button?'

'I don't know. Do you think it would suit me? I don't think Lord Salisbury would approve. I'm surprised he gave Henry the viceroyalty in any case. He thinks he's too lively, too adventurous. He's quite sure that he's going to rock the boat.'

Malty said nothing for a while but ran his fingertips backwards and forwards in a light brushing motion on her bare thighs. She watched him. She wondered what he was going to say next. It looked as if he had something on his mind; something which he couldn't quite bring himself to express.

'Why didn't I meet you first?' she asked him.

'You mean, before Henry? With a view to what?'

'With a view to marriage, of course.'

'I wouldn't have married you. I'm not that kind of a fellow.'

'What do you mean?'

'Exactly that. I'm not that kind of a fellow. If we were married, well then, I'd have to work, wouldn't I, to keep you in dresses and hats and handmade shoes?'

'I thought you had a private fortune.'

Malty shook his head.

'You always gave me the *impression* you had a private fortune. You're always dressed so beautifully.'

'A man's clothes will never tell you anything.'

Lucy sat up. 'So, where *do* you get your income from?'

'From friends. From generous friends.'

'Not from Henry?'

'He gives me a little. He helps to defray the expense of taking you out.'

'But why should friends give you money, just like that, for nothing?'

'Because they're friends.'

Lucy supposed that she couldn't argue with the logic of that, but she lay back on her pillow feeling perplexed. She glanced at Malty, and he grinned at her, and touched the tip of her nose with his fingertip.

Lightning crackled, somewhere across the Thames. Then, almost at once, the house was shaken by a tremendous burst of thunder. It sounded as if it were directly overhead. The windows rattled in their sashes, and fine plaster sifted down from the ceiling. 'God's disapproval,' said Malty.

But Lucy clung to him tight and said, 'Please, make love to me. Please, while it's thundering!'

Malty kissed her, and then rolled over and busied himself with a French letter. Then he climbed on top of her, and made love to her with all of his usual slow and rhythmic grace. She closed her eyes. The lightning tore up the sky, like rotten linen; then the thunder collapsed. Malty pushed and pushed and pushed, murmuring sweet and filthy language to her while he did so.

She didn't know what it was that made her open her eyes. But as Malty's rhythm began to quicken, she turned her head on the pillow and glanced quickly towards the partly-open bedroom door. What she saw there made her go stiff with terror. She almost cried out, but all she could manage under Marty's ever-quickening onslaught was a high-pitched gasp. Malty thought nothing of it; she was always gasping when he made love to her.

It was Henry, standing tall and still and white-faced, in a light grey frock-coat with shoulders spotted darkly with rain. He was staring directly at her; unblinking. He had learned this morning that he was to be Viceroy of India, the glittering pinnacle of his career, the realization of his natural destiny. This afternoon, less than two hours later, he was witnessing his wife fornicating with another man. Worse than that, fornicating with one of his friends.

Malty shivered, and coughed, and then rolled off her, panting. Henry continued to stare at her through the half-open door, but Malty obviously hadn't seen him. Lightning sizzled over the Palace of Westminster; thunder bellowed. One second Henry was in darkness; the next he was bleached by dazzling blue-white light. Then he was plunged into darkness again, but the image of his face remained imprinted on Lucy's retina.

'What's the matter?' Malty asked her, as she reached for her robe.

She laid her hand on his shoulder. 'Ssh, nothing's wrong.'

424

However, she was quaking, and Malty detected the quivering in her voice, and lifted his head up. 'Where are you going? Lucy?'

'I'll be back in just a minute.'

She hurried out on to the landing. Henry had disappeared. She bit her lip anxiously, looking this way and that. She hurried along to his dressing room. It smelled strongly of leather brushes and Floris toilet-water, Henry's smell; but Henry wasn't there. She tried all the spare bedrooms. He wasn't in any of those, either.

'Lucy!' Malty called her. 'Lucy, what on earth are you doing?'

Lucy went back to the bedroom door and said, 'Shush, Malty, for goodness' sake!'

Malty said something in reply, but lightning filled the windows with unnatural brilliance, and his words were swallowed up by the subsequent thunder.

She ran barefoot downstairs. Henry wasn't in the parlour. Nor could she find him in the morning room. It was then that she heard a thrashing noise from the library. She crossed the hallway, and pressed her ear against the door. There it was again, *thrashh!* and then again, *thrashh!*

She laid her hand on the doorknob, but then she hesitated. Perhaps it would be wiser not to open it. Some things are better left unsaid, some things are better left unseen. Whatever Henry was doing, it sounded painful and it sounded dire. She allowed her hand to relinquish its grip on the doorknob, and slowly retreated.

Malty was waiting for her, dressed, at the top of the stairs. 'What the devil's wrong?' he wanted to know.

She mounted the stairs with the dislocated movements of a marionette. The thunder rumbled yet again, but distinctly further away, over towards St Paul's. Now it was raining, a gushing, bucketing summer storm. Gutters were flooded, omnibuses rolled through muddy lakes. Sightseers outside Buckingham Palace cowered doggedly under newspapers and stared at the grey-coated guardsmen as if they expected them to dissolve.

'Henry's here,' said Lucy. 'He saw us.'

'*What?*' asked Malty, wide-eyed.

'He saw us,' Lucy repeated, bleakly.

'God's witness!' said Malty. 'Where is he?'

'He's in the library. I'm not sure what he's doing.'

Malty took two or three steps downwards. 'I'd better –'

'No!' said Lucy, clutching at his sleeve. Then, much more softly, 'No. You'd better just leave.'

Malty slowly reached up and touched her cheek, letting his fingers slide into her tangly hair. 'Do you know something, Lucy,' he told her, 'I was more fond of you than any other girl I ever knew.'

'Aren't you fond of me any longer?'

He shook his head. 'I can't allow myself to be, can I? It's over, now that Henry's found out. I just hope that he doesn't punish you too severely; or himself, for that matter.'

Lucy stared at him and realized that this was probably the last time she would ever see him. Unless, of course, she was preparing to sacrifice Henry, and India, and everything for which she had abandoned Blanche. Malty had been escorting her for almost two years, and Lucy knew that it was his friendship she would miss, rather than his love-making. But he was right. It was over. She had too much to lose; and, in his way, so did he.

'I'll just get dressed,' he told her.

He put on his clothes as immaculately as usual, and tied his necktie perfectly. Then he leaned over and kissed Lucy's forehead. 'It was all wonderful fun,' he whispered. 'But listen, I can't find my *thing* . . . my *capote anglaise*.'

'Don't worry', said Lucy. 'I'll take care of it.'

Malty took one long look at her, and then he left. She heard him close the front door behind him. There were of course no servants to see him out.

She straightened the bed. She wasn't crying, but she

couldn't seem to make her arms do what they were told. She tugged the quilt, and as she did so, she saw Malty's French letter, which had dropped underneath the bed. She quickly picked it up, to dispose of it. She was on the point of flushing it down the water-closet, however, when she hesitated. Pearls, seeds, and a little baby like Blanche. Now that she was married, she could have a baby with no scandal at all. In fact, with nothing but joy.

She turned the slippery rubber inside out, and let its contents slide into her hand. 'Bruno Frederick James Mal- travers,' she recited, in a whisper, as she cupped her hand between her thighs.

'Please be born. Please be a boy.'

She stood in the bathroom for two or three minutes. Then she washed, and brushed her hair. In the looking-glass she looked perfectly normal. A little flushed, perhaps, but otherwise composed. She finished dressing, and then she went downstairs.

She didn't know how she had expected Henry to react. With rage, perhaps. With icy fury. With disgust. With contempt. With bitterness and sorrow. Whatever it was, she certainly hadn't expected him to behave with such grace and equanimity, almost as if he were *pleased*, in a way, that she had hurt him. He was sitting at his desk in the library when she came down, wearing the half-glasses which he used these days for writing. The thunderstorm had passed away com- pletely now, and although the library faced to the north, and was never sunny, it shimmered in reflected light from one of the windows opposite.

She remembered what Alfred Dunning had told her in the South of France: *'Henry believes for some reason which I fail to understand that he has to suffer.'*

In betraying him with Malty, perhaps she had somehow given him some perverse pleasure.

He looked up. His face had taken on the same swollen

appearance that she had seen on their wedding-night. Glazed, congested eyes; and piggy jowls.

'Has he gone?' Henry asked her.

Lucy nodded, still waiting for an outburst.

'Well . . .' said Henry, 'I suppose, when it comes down to it, I have only myself to blame.'

Lucy didn't say anything, but Henry smiled at her as if she had. 'Perhaps if I hadn't have been so preoccupied with work . . . perhaps if I'd paid you more attention.'

He kept opening and closing the lid of his brass inkpot. Open and shut, open and shut. 'Do you love him?' he asked.

Lucy shook her head. 'He doesn't love me, either.'

'So it's . . . carnal, that's all? Physical?'

'It's friendship.'

Henry's eyes wandered back to his desk. 'Friendship. Yes. I can understand that. I have been blessed throughout my life with true and loyal friends. I had hoped that, apart from being my wife, you were one of them.'

'Henry, I am. Or at least I would be, if you were to allow it.'

Henry thought about that, and then slowly nodded. 'I haven't given you much of a chance, have I? My poor Lucy.'

After a while, he got up from his desk and went to the window, and stood with his eyes slitted looking directly into the trembling reflected sunlight, as if he were daring it to blind him.

'How long?' he asked her, without turning around.

'Right from the very beginning, almost.'

'Was I really so careless?' He meant it in the sense that he hadn't cared for her.

'Henry – there's something inside of you I can't understand. I try to understand it but you always hide it. It's something to do with our marriage-bed; something to do with our love-making. But you will never explain it.'

Henry pinched his nose, and then wiped it.

'Henry,' Lucy continued, 'if you don't tell me what it is, then I can never help you.'

He looked around at last. His eyes were glistening, as if he were close to tears. 'Lucy,' he said. 'I ask only this. That you stay with me; that you be my Vicereine; and that all the matter of Malty be forgotten. I deserved it, and I was justly punished. Now perhaps we can forget recriminations and look forward. We have five years of greatness ahead of us! Let us open our hearts to it; and to our duty; and to each other.'

'Do you really mean that?' asked Lucy.

He gave a little wry grunt of amusement. 'My darling, I have very little choice. I have been chosen by fate; and so, in your way, have you. We *must* go to India. What else can we do? I could divorce you, I suppose, for adultery. But if all of those politicians whose wives had been adulterous were to be sued for divorce, the House of Commons would be a club for single men.'

He left the window and walked right up to her. 'As for what lies inside me . . . well, you're quite right. There *is* a feeling inside me to which I am not yet reconciled. A passion, as a matter of fact. But it is impossible for me to explain it to you. Not until I have conquered it myself.'

'Henry,' said Lucy, 'if you expect me to come to India with you, to be your Vicereine, then you must tell me what it is. Henry, you *owe* it to me. You're *obliged*.'

They heard the kitchen door slam. The servants were coming back. Henry said, 'If you imagine that you need forgiveness from me for what you did with Malty; then I forgive you. Nothing will ever shake my affection for you. We have a whole empire to administer, and that empire is far greater than either of our temperaments.'

Lucy said, 'Sha-sha taught me some French. *C'est une folie à nulle autre second, de vouloir se mêler à corriger le monde.* It is a stupidity second to none, to busy yourself with setting the world to rights.'

Henry smiled faintly. 'I remember the time that I first quoted you Molière. At Brackenbridge, when I gave you that necklace.'

'Yes,' said Lucy.

Henry approached her. He laid his hands gently on her shoulder. My God, he was handsome; and the fatigue that was marked on his face from all of those hours at the Foreign Office – somehow that fatigue made him look even more appealing. Tired, vulnerable, the kind of man who needed a woman's care.

But she looked beyond him, towards his desk, and on his desk lay a flat black leather strap.

'What's that?' she asked. He knew at once what she was referring to.

'It's called a tawse,' he told her. His eyes challenged her to ask him any more.

'Is it yours?'

'Yes.'

'What's it for?'

'It's for anything you like'.

'What was it made for?'

Now he turned around, and focused on it, as if he had never seen it before. 'It comes from Scotland. They use them in their schools there, to maintain discipline, instead of the cane.'

'But what do you use it for?'

Henry picked it up, and slapped it into the palm of his hand, quite hard. 'I use it to remind myself that we are different from the animals only in that we are capable of punishing ourselves. Animals avoid pain at all costs. Only the human intellect understands that pain has a purpose.'

Lucy knew what she wanted to ask him, but didn't know how to phrase it. *Why are you punishing yourself? What for? And why must you always punish me, too?*

When she lay in their brass-pillared bed that night and

Henry slept, she began to see that they *had* to go to India; that only in India could their lives be fulfilled, for better or for worse. She also began to see that Fate had brought her India right from the moment that Uncle Casper had reappeared.

These days, she tried not to think about Uncle Casper. She still dreamed about him, still woke up dry-mouthed and quivering and panicky. And she could never bring herself to think about his being her father. It made her feel as if there were a madness in her from which she would never be able to escape.

Henry stirred, whispered, '*We are different from the animals only in that we are capable of punishing ourselves.*'

But why does Henry punish himself? And more to the point, why did he forgive me so easily?

In early October they abandoned their packing for two weeks and visited Lord Felldale at Brackenbridge. It was a wet and dismal autumn, all overcast skies and mud and slippery leaves, but their friends and colleagues had given them one farewell feast after another – the Old Etonians, Henry's contemporaries from Oxford, and his fellow civil servants at the Foreign Office (even the dour and disapproving George Hamilton).

Lord Felldale was looking drawn and unwell and peculiarly *shrunken*, but he was bursting with pride for Henry's appointment. When the news had first been announced, he had written to Henry. 'I begin to realize what a splendid position you have deservedly won. Congrats pour in from every quarter and the country generally is as proud of you as I, your father, am, and more I cannot say.'

In the afternoons, when Henry was busy with papers from the India Office, and with his endless inventories, Lucy went for long walks on her own. She felt different, calmer, she didn't know why. Perhaps it was because she now had something exciting to look forward to: a voyage to India, an enticing new country, and the splendour of representing Her Majesty the Queen. She had been received with such affection by the Press and by Henry's friends, and even by those society ladies who might have been expected to wax exceedingly jealous that an American girl was soon to take up such an exalted position in the British Empire. She had received the kindest of letters from three other ladies of American birth who had established themselves in the English aristocracy, the Duchess of Marlborough, Lady Randolph Churchill, and Mrs Henry White.

On Sunday morning, at chapel, while the village choir sang a sweet and awkward hymn that had been specially written to speed them on their way to 'Eastern parts' (which of course rhymed with 'Loyal Hearts') Lucy felt so happy and so much at peace that she looked up to the foggy crimson light falling through the stained-glass window and wondered if God had seen fit to beatify her. On the way back to the house, she began to feel more and more light-headed. The darkness of the day grew darker, like an owl's eye closing. She collapsed on to the shingle and didn't even feel herself hitting the ground.

When she stirred, Dr Roberts was sitting beside her. The curtains were drawn, and the oil-lamp was lit. The bedroom door was open for decorum's sake, and Nora was standing outside in the hallway. Lucy wondered when Nora had started to look older. Perhaps she looked older, too. It was strange how the years passed, like walking through an empty house, room by room, and never being able to find your way back again.

Dr Roberts said, 'Hello, Mrs Carson.'

She smiled lazily. 'Am I ill?' she asked him.

'Do you *feel* ill?'

'I'm not sure. I ate some grouse yesterday. I knew that I shouldn't. Grouse never agrees with me, but I didn't want to hurt Lord Felldale's feelings.'

Dr Roberts took hold of her hand. 'I have good news for you, Mrs Carson. You're expecting your first child.'

Her smile faded, and she looked across at him with widened eyes. 'That's very diplomatic of you, Dr Roberts. But you and I both know that isn't true.'

'Nobody else has to know,' said Dr Roberts. 'By the way . . . purely out of medical interest, was the first child healthy?'

She nodded. 'A little girl. I named her Blanche.'

'You left her in America?'

'In Kansas, yes, with a family that I can trust.'

Dr Roberts could see that it hurt her to think about Blanche, and squeezed her hand. 'You mustn't blame yourself, you know, for leaving her. You're still young now. You were much younger then. At least you gave her the sacred opportunity of life.'

Lucy looked away, although she still held on to Dr Roberts' hand. 'Sometimes I wonder how sacred an opportunity that really is.'

Dr Roberts stood up. 'I think, in India, you will see that for yourself.'

On the first Saturday of December, on a morning stung with sudden snow-showers, Lucy invited a crowd down to The Vines, at Reigate, since Henry was packing the last of his library. Lord Elgin had warned him that 'in neither Calcutta nor in Simla is there a library worthy of the name.'

They had tried to underpack, but it had been difficult, since Elgin had advised them that the climate was not always warm, especially in the hills at Simla, at the beginning and the end of the season, where it could be 'bracing, if not actually cold'.

The hallway at The Vines was crowded with trunks and packing-cases, and the house itself was looking self-consciously half-dressed, like an old woman caught in the corset-cover. Still, it was a good time to have a weekend party, and Lucy had invited everybody for whom she genuinely cared, with the exception of Malty, who was spending the winter in Athens.

Margot Asquith and Charty Ribblesdale had come down; and so had the Brodricks, the Grenfells, Arthur Balfour, and (to Lucy's great delight) Charles, and William, and Blanche. She had invited Lord Felldale, but he was too ill to travel in the winter, and had sent instead a letter of farewell.

'My dears ... God speed, we know that the next five years will add lustre to a name that is already bright.'

The Vines was a plain but elegant Georgian house, white-painted, with green shutters, built in the lee of the chalky North Downs. It boasted only six bedrooms and two bathrooms, but both Lucy and Henry liked it because of its huge drawing room, where they could entertain twenty or thirty people at a time.

That morning, the drawing room was particularly noisy and crowded, and enough champagne had been passed around for the laughter to have reached a high pitch of hilarity. But Sha-sha drew Lucy aside, close to the windows that overlooked the garden, and said, 'You're looking pale, my sweet. This isn't too much for you? I know how Henry loves to pack. A place for everything, and an itemized list for every place. But it isn't really your *forté*, is it? Especially now that you're a mother-to-be'.

Lucy smiled. 'I'm just a little tired, that's all. I've only just gotten over my morning-sickness.'

'You have exacting days ahead of you, in India. You must take care of yourself, and your baby. And Henry will need all the support that you can give him. You must try to prevent him from overworking, you know. He has plenty of nervous energy but not much stamina.'

'I'll do my best,' said Lucy. 'It's not always easy.'

Sha-sha looked around the room at the Adam-green walls and the gold-framed paintings of horses and sheep. 'I've always adored this house, you know. If I had to choose a house to die in, this would be it.'

She was silent for a while, and then she said, 'Are things – all right – between you and Henry?'

'All right? I'm not sure what you mean. He's delighted about the baby. He's already decided to name him Horatio.'

'Horatio? *Horatio?* He must be losing his mind.'

'I thought of James, if it's a boy. Or maybe Jamie.'

'Too Scottish,' said Blanche. 'Still – at least you'll be giving him a child. We were all beginning to think that you never would. After all, my dear, you've been married for three years. Most healthy women would have had four children by now.'

'Perhaps I'm just the kind of woman who doesn't fall too easily,' Lucy suggested.

On the other side of the drawing room, Henry was laughing loudly and saying to Charlie, '. . . and there we were at this tiny country halt, Cole Green, in the middle of nowhere at all, and the local train had already left . . . so I gave a telegram to the stationmaster, demanding that they stop the express, and pick us up . . .'

At the same time, she caught a glimpse through the side window of a maroon carriage arriving outside the house. The maroon-uniformed coachman climbed down from the box, opened the carriage door, and lowered the steps so that a tall young lady in a moss-green coat and a green ostrich-feathered hat could climb down. She was accompanied by a slightly older woman in brown.

Blanche couldn't quite see who it was. 'More guests?' she asked, craning her neck sideways.

Lucy said, 'Excuse me, Sha-sha, for just a minute.'

She pushed her way through the crowded drawing room. Henry frowned and followed her progress across the room as he finished off his story. '. . . and the stationmaster read it out word for word . . . *Lord Carson of Brackenbridge, Viceroy Designate of India, hereby requires you* . . . and in the end he looked up and said, "Goodness me, sir, you'll get there yerself before this wire does."'

Lucy reached the hallway just as the butler opened the front door. Immediately she was brought face-to-face with the woman in green. They stared at each other, not speaking, each seeking the resemblance that had brought them together.

'Vanessa,' said Lucy.

'Hallo, Lucy. I might call you Lucy?' She was blonde, tall, slight, and very beautiful, almost Germanic, with eyes of watered green.

'I didn't believe you would come,' said Lucy.

Vanessa stepped confidently into the hallway. 'To be truthful with you, neither did I.'

She stood quite still for a moment, listening to the chopped-up babble of conversation from the drawing room, then she smiled at Lucy benignly. 'What a pretty house,' she declared. Behind her, the woman in brown said, 'This is a pretty house. Very pretty. Bumpy ride from the station, though. All those ruts and troughs.'

Vanessa said, 'Oh, forgive me. This is Miss Hope Petworth, my sister-in-law. You don't mind? But she's been staying for a while.'

'How do you do?' asked Lucy.

The butler took their hats and their coats and their gloves. Miss Petworth said, 'You *do* look alike, you two, no question about it. Peas in a pod.'

Vanessa scrutinized Lucy with embarrassing intensity. 'Lucy is expecting a baby,' she declared. 'There's *that* much difference, at least. I don't know, Lucy, what do you think? Do you think we look that much alike?'

She took hold of Lucy's arm and guided her over to the wide hall mirror. 'There!' she said. 'Utterly different, when you compare us side by side.'

In fact (and Vanessa must have seen this, too), the resemblance was uncanny; and all the more uncanny because, feature for feature, they were quite unlike. Their hair was a different shade of blonde; Vanessa's darker, verging on the coppery.

Vanessa's eyes were green; whereas Lucy's were positively blue. Lucy was slightly shorter than Vanessa, with smaller breasts and narrower hips. And Vanessa's nose was incontrovertibly longer. But they still looked like sisters; and there was more than a physical resemblance. There was something about the way in which they spoke, and carried themselves. They were so alike that both of them could see at once that they could never be friends.

'I didn't want to upset any applecarts,' said Lucy.

'Of course not,' Vanessa replied. She spoke with the same distinctive accent as Henry, part North of England, part eighteenth-century. Very few people except Northern aristocrats spoke like that any more. 'Anyway, applecarts are specifically made for upsetting. Henry's still my brother, after all, and I have to feel proud of him, whether I like it or not'.

Lucy had written to Vanessa at her Lancashire address, although Sha-sha had told her that she would be visiting London. *My dear Vanessa . . . you are the only one of Henry's brothers and sisters I have not yet met . . . I understand that you and Henry have fallen out, although nobody has told me why. But may I appeal to you to come to Reigate for our farewell weekend party . . . because whatever has happened to divide you, we must all be proud of Henry's great achievement, in being appointed to India. He wishes to reconcile the differences of an entire people . . . surely, before he goes, his own family can reconcile their differences . . .'*

'Let's go in now,' said Lucy.

Vanessa primped her hair. 'I'm nervous,' she admitted.

'He's still your brother,' Lucy reminded her.

'Yes,' said Vanessa. 'Precisely.'

'I think I'd like to powder my nose,' Hope Petworth announced.

'The lavatory is on the left,' Lucy told her; and Hope Petworth disappeared.

Lucy said to Vanessa, 'You're not cross that I invited you?'

'I wouldn't have come, my dear, had I been truly cross,' Vanessa smiled at her. 'But, yes, I will admit to butterflies.'

'We'd better go in.'

Inviting Vanessa may have been reckless. Lucy couldn't tell. But nobody in the Carson family seemed to have been prepared to tell her just how reckless it was. The only way to find out for sure had been to invite her, and to worry about the consequences if and when they came. In any case, Lucy was much less vulnerable these days to the Carson family's displeasure. She was to be Vicereine, whatever they said; and Henry was to be Viceroy. Even Henry had to mind his Ps and Qs. He didn't dare to argue outspokenly with Lucy in front of their friends; and he certainly wouldn't risk a major scene. He and Lucy were always seen smiling, arm-in-arm; and he called her 'sweetheart' these days, as a matter of course.

They opened the drawing-room doors and joined the throng. As they did so, however, the group nearest to them abruptly fell silent; then the next group; then the next. In a matter of moments, the whole drawing room was deathly quiet; and all eyes were focused on Vanessa, standing in the doorway, and Henry, leaning against the fireplace, where he had been arrested right in the middle of the joke about the horse with two masters.

Henry slowly straightened himself. His eyes shone black and protuberant, lobster's eyes, and his cheeks were flushed. He tugged at his waistcoat, and adjusted his necktie. Then he stepped forward and said, slightly too loudly, 'Vanessa! What a surprise!'

Vanessa came forward in her rustling green dress and took hold of Henry's outstretched hand. 'Lucy invited me. She thought that you and I ought to make up, before you left to take up your illustrious post in India. After all, you're not simply my brother any more, are you? You're a national institution. You can't bear ill-will against a national institution. It would be just as absurd as hating the House of Lords.'

438

Henry couldn't stop staring at her. 'You've changed, Vanessa,' he told her, so quietly that most people in the drawing room were unable to hear. 'You've changed very much'.

'Have I?' said Vanessa. 'Marriage, Henry, that's what does it. Marriage, and time. Perhaps time more than marriage. Or perhaps you've grown so used to Lucy that you've forgotten what I look like.'

'You're still very –' Henry began. Lucy guessed that he was trying to say 'beautiful', or perhaps 'outspoken', but his mouth opened and closed and no words came out.

He stepped forward, two difficult steps as if he were trying to catch the timing of a waltz, and embraced her. She made no attempt to embrace him in return; but stood quite tall and still, smiling at everybody else over his shoulder.

'You must have a glass of champagne,' Henry insisted. 'Lucy . . . where's the champagne?'

Gradually, the conversation in the drawing room began to pick up again. Arthur Balfour told a story about Indian servants; and how they could only be persuaded to do what you wanted by suggestion, rather than direct demand. If your wife had left her hat in the carriage, for instance, it was more effective to instigate a roundabout conversation about how hats might suffer in the enclosed heat of a carriage, rather than give your servant a direct command to go and fetch the bloody thing.

Lucy stayed close to Henry, guarding him, almost, from Vanessa's obvious hostility. They talked about packing; about parties; about Afghanistan. A long, stilted and ultimately meaningless conversation which even somebody who didn't know either of them could have identified as the wariest of fencing-matches. Parry, riposte, parry.

After twenty minutes, Vanessa left Henry's circle in midconversation and started talking to Charty. Lucy noticed, however, that Henry didn't take his eyes off her, wherever she went; and that when she laughed – a high, trilling laugh that everybody could hear – he actually winced, as if he had caught his finger in the door.

A little after two o'clock, when they had eaten *à la Russe*, pheasant hash and devilled whitebait and fruit-flavoured creams, Vanessa suddenly said, 'I should leave now, Lucy my dear. Henry! We have to go, I'm afraid. I want to get back to London in time to dress for the theatre.'

'Well, then, yes. It is a long trip back to Town.' Henry lifted his arms, and then let them fall. He looked terribly bowed and defeated, almost hunchbacked, and Lucy couldn't think why. 'I'm very gratified that you could come,' Henry told Vanessa. 'If you can possibly get out to Calcutta; or to Simla . . .'

Gratified? thought Lucy. Vanessa has treated him worse than a tramp who hasn't even asked her for sixpence. How can he be gratified?

She saw Vanessa and Hope Petworth to the door. Henry made a point of staying behind in the drawing room, laughing with unnatural loudness.

'Perhaps I made a mistake,' said Lucy, worriedly.

Vanessa smiled, and then kissed her, once on each cheek. 'Good luck,' she whispered.

'Good luck,' said Hope Petworth, and suddenly hugged her tight, as if they were cousins.

'Did I make a dreadful mistake?' Lucy repeated. She had invited Vanessa to The Vines in the hope that she might understand Henry more clearly; but now she was even more confused than ever. Why were Henry and Vanessa so antagonistic to each other? From the moment that Vanessa had walked into the drawing room, the air had been rattling with aggression.

Vanessa's carriage rolled away, leaving water-filled ruts in the mud. As she watched them disappear between the laurels, Lucy was conscious of Blanche standing close behind her. She turned, and climbed the steps, and then linked arms.

'Do you think I was wrong to invite her?'

'Adventurous, perhaps.'

'I don't see why.'

Sha-sha said, 'Henry is still our brother, you know, whatever happens. And Vanessa is still my sister.'

Lucy grasped Sha-sha's fingers. They were very cold. 'I know that,' she said. 'But I'm his wife.' She looked around. A thin wet snow was falling, but surprisingly it wasn't particularly cold. 'Can we talk in the garden?' she asked Sha-sha.

'All right. Let me get my coat. I could do with some good cold country air, to sober me up.'

They walked between the damp black rose arches, and the snow prickled on their furs. Somehow, in this silent bitterness, Lucy found it easier to talk.

She said, as bravely as she could manage, 'The truth is, our intimate life hasn't always been very easy. Henry is always working so late. Usually he doesn't come to bed until two or three o'clock in the morning, and then he's up again at half-past six.'

'So it's overwork, and nothing more?' asked Sha-sha.

Lucy shook her head. 'I think I could tolerate, if it were. But he seems to want to punish himself all the time. He doesn't seem to be able to make love to me unless he feels humiliated, or actually hurt.'

She hesitated. 'You don't mind my telling you this?'

'Of course not,' said Sha-sha. She thought for a moment, and then she stopped, keeping her huge fur coat wrapped tightly around her. 'Let me say something to you in utmost confidence. You are Henry's wife; you have a right to know. But nobody else must ever so much as *suspect* it.'

They carried on walking. It took Sha-sha a long time to find the right words to begin her story. Crows cawed harshly in the surrounding trees. The soles of their boots crunched on the gritty York stone pathway.

At last, Sha-sha said, 'One of the reasons that Henry fell for you so quickly and so absolutely was because of Vanessa.

You look very alike. Well, you must have noticed. But it's not just your looks. You have the same kind of personality as Vanessa, too. Sharp, amusing, independent. You could be Vanessa reborn.'

They reached the very end of the path, then stopped, and looked along the grey-green backs of the Downs, towards Box Hill.

Sha-sha said, 'You must have noticed by now that Vanessa never appears at family gatherings when there is the slightest possibility of Henry being there. I was quite amazed that she came today'.

'Sha-sha, he's the Viceroy Designate. It's almost like being the heir to the throne. I had to ask her. I had to give her the chance, if nothing else'.

'I know, Lucy. I know. But what happened between Henry and Vanessa . . .'

Lucy turned and faced Sha-sha, and clutched at her sleeve. 'Sha-sha, listen to me. I'm almost five months' pregnant, with Henry's baby. I'm going to India with him. I'm supposed to act as his Queen. If there's *anything* I ought to know . . .'

Blanche lifted her face; and in that wintry gum-coloured light she looked startlingly old, and tired, and the wrinkles under her eyes looked like badly-pressed silk.

She said, with self-protective weariness, as if she had become bored with telling it, 'They fell in love.'

'They did what?'

'They fell in love. Well, he more than her; but there was a time when she found him entrancing, and of course bad led to worse.'

'Tell me,' Lucy insisted.

'There's nothing to tell,' shrugged Sha-sha.

'I'm carrying his baby!' Lucy shouted at her. 'Who has more right to know than I?'

Sha-sha said nothing for a while, but tugged down her gloves and looked at Lucy pointedly.

'They fell in love,' Sha-sha said stiffly. 'Henry was just sixteen years old, and Vanessa was thirteen-and-a-half.'

'And they were in love?'

'How do you define love, my dear? Vanessa was infatuated, but Henry was obsessed. You can see how pretty she is, even today. When she was fourteen, she was magical. Henry was absolutely captivated. I know how hard he fought himself *not* to be in love with her. But there was nothing he could do. If you're obsessed, you're obsessed. He never left her alone. He was always writing her poems and drawing her pictures and buying her trinkets. He lived for every school holiday when he would see her again.'

Sha-sha's nostrils widened as she took a deep, steadying breath. 'You must remember that this is in the strictest of confidences, between you and me and nobody else. But you are going to a strange and difficult country, where every one of your personal resources will be tested to the utmost; and I believe that it will help you to improve your marriage and to understand your husband more sympathetically if you know the truth.'

'And what is the truth?'

Sha-sha took out her tiny lace handkerchief, and dabbed at her eyes, although she wasn't crying. 'Henry went into Vanessa's bed one night, and attempted to dishonour her.'

'You mean he –?'

'Forcibly, yes. And her screaming woke the entire household'.

'Oh, my God.' said Lucy. Her stomach tightened, and she held her hands across it. 'Oh, my God. What happened?'

'What do you think?' Sha-sha shrugged. 'The whole household came running. Henry was caught, Vanessa was hysterical. It was Bedlam. Henry – well, Henry was awash with shame and mortification. They would have sent him away, but he kept threatening to kill himself, and Vanessa pleaded that nobody should know that anything was wrong. In the end, the whole family decided that they would simply

443

forget it – pretend that it had never happened. Far worse disasters had struck the Carson family since they came over to England with William the Conqueror. Poisonings, rapes, and incestuous acts. They decided, I think, that it was simply a part of English history'.

'But is that why Henry keeps punishing himself?' asked Lucy.

Sha-sha nodded. 'Mm!' she concurred. 'That's right! And poor Henry has never stopped punishing himself since. That was why we were all so pleased when he brought *you* home to Brackenbridge. We all believed that you would be the miraculous solution to all of his difficulties. After all, you look so much like Vanessa – we felt that at last he might be able to stop castigating himself.'

Lucy stood in the foggy garden feeling quite unreal. So that was Henry's terrible burden; that was why he demanded that she hurt him, and that she punish him. That was why he had forgiven her so easily for sleeping with Malty. In his eyes, that had been nothing, compared with the sin that *he* had committed.

'Well?' asked Sha-sha, after a while.

Lucy gave her a small smile. 'I'm pleased you told me. It explains a whole lot'.

'You won't tell him I told you? You won't even hint that you know? You would almost certainly destroy him, if you told him that you knew'.

'He needs to feel forgiven, that's all,' said Lucy.

'Well, yes, I suppose you're right. But Vanessa obviously hasn't forgiven him, and of course he doesn't care much for God. If only he were a Catholic, he might have got over it all years ago! Two dozen Hail Marys and twenty pounds in the poor-box, and his guilt would have been lifted for ever.'

Later, when the winter darkness had clamped itself over the Downs, Henry came into the bedroom where Lucy was brushing out her hair. He stood by the dressing-table for a while, twiddling his silver pen between his fingers, watching the way the lamplight gleamed on her curls. Her hair had all the glossiness of healthy pregnancy; her breasts beneath her nightgown were noticeably fuller.

'Why did you do that?' he asked her, his voice parched.

'You mean, why did I invite Vanessa?'

He was plainly trying to control his temper. 'I've told you countless times that Vanessa and I don't get on'.

She kept on brushing. 'I thought perhaps it was time that you did.'

'Lucy ... certain events have taken place in this family about which you know nothing. I'd prefer it if they stayed that way. I can't stand your – meddling in affairs which don't concern you.'

Lucy was tempted to say that Sha-sha had told her everything about Vanessa; but she remembered her promise, and kept her peace. It was a pity, in a way, that she couldn't discuss it with him. She found his love for Vanessa quite understandable, especially in the light of the passion that Uncle Casper had exhibited for her; and for his own sister, her mother. Just because people were related, that didn't mean they couldn't find each other attractive. That didn't mean they were immune from falling in love.

Henry turned away, still fiddling with his pen. After a while he said, 'Well ... I suppose no real harm has been done.'

Lucy laid down her hairbrush. 'Couldn't you find a way of making up with her? It seems such a pity that you can't be friends.'

Henry shook his head. 'No, she won't have it. You saw how damned frosty she was. I don't know why she came. Just to brag that she's seen me, I suppose, when she goes back to Lancashire.'

'Are you coming to bed?' Lucy asked him.

'Not yet. I still have to finish listing my reference books. I shan't be longer than two or three hours.'

'Henry –' Lucy began. He paused with his hand on the open door. 'Henry, don't you want to talk about Vanessa at all? Maybe I could help.'

Henry thought about that for a moment, and then replied, 'As far as Vanessa is concerned, my dearest, I believe I am probably beyond help.'

They sailed for Calcutta two weeks before Christmas on the British India Line's *Star of Bengal*. Henry went up on deck to watch England melt into the pewter-coloured afternoon light, but Lucy stayed in her stateroom, flipping through magazines and eating crystallized violets.

Out past the Isle of Wight, the steamer began that steady tilting and rolling that she knew would make her feel sick until she got to Calcutta. She closed the lid of the crystallized violets box, and wished she hadn't eaten quite so many.

Henry had instructed her to read up all she could about life and protocol in India – especially the guide to the daily round at Government House that had been painstakingly written for her in mauve ink by Lady Elgin. But she hadn't even opened the books that he had acquired for her, and Lady Elgin's close-written notes remained unread in their envelope. There would be plenty of time for that; and besides, she didn't yet want to think about India. At first she had been overjoyed at the prospect of visiting the continent that had been ground up like magic powder and shut up in Jack Darling's spice boxes. But Henry had been working so hard lately that they scarcely spoke; and it was like setting out for a strange land with a man she scarcely knew.

What was more, she felt as if Henry were taking her even farther away from baby Blanche, to a world so remote that she might never come back; and that upset her far more than she had imagined it would.

She had been appointed a travelling-companion, Mrs Nancy Bull, the wife of the Collector of Benares, who was returning to rejoin her husband after a Christmas at Home.

446

After fourteen years of living in India, Mrs Bull was bustling and bossy, a wide-hipped woman with a waddling gait and a face that was an explosion of peppery freckles. She knew everything and everybody, and brooked absolutely no impertinence or inefficiency from anybody, especially Indians.

'They will do as little as possible,' she warned Lucy, about Indian servants. 'And they will expect as much as possible in return. They are all scallywags.'

But she possessed an understanding of what it meant to leave one's home behind that was almost lyrical. 'The first time I came out, nobody had told me about the cord that is paid out behind one as the boat moves on, seeming to link one with the country and the life that one has left. As one travels farther, you know, it stretches; but it is always tugging at one's heart as if to prevent one from turning one's face forward, to go on, as a free person, to the East.'

Apart from Mrs Bull, and Nora, Lucy had also been appointed a lady's maid, Etta Brightwater, a brisk young widow from Sussex who had previously been employed by the Norfolks. Etta had worked as a maid in Lady Elgin's household when she first arrived in Calcutta, but she had returned home after only a year, widowed. Her husband had drunk unboiled water at an Indian feast, and died within two days of cholera. Etta was small and quick, sharp like a little mouse, and remarkably pretty in a countrified way. She had told Lucy that she couldn't wait to get back to India.

'I thought as how I missed Home so badly. But when I got back, there it was, same as usual, green and grey, same old faces, same old England. And no colour to it, just like it had been washed, and all the dyes had faded.'

Nora was suspicious of Etta at first. 'Even the Vicereine of Injure doesn't have the need for *two* lady's maids.' But when she began to understand how much work there was for them to do, constantly packing and unpacking clothes, cleaning gloves and mending stockings, she began to appreciate

447

the wisdom of Etta's appointment, and to rub along well with her. It helped that Nora was marginally higher in the order of precedence, and could tell Etta which clothes to fetch from the 'Present Use' baggage, and which of Lady Carson's gowns to lay out, and which shoes to clean. Occasionally Lucy thought that Nora was far too demanding, all the sewing and sponging that she told Etta to do, but Etta didn't seem to mind, and Lucy guessed that once the novelty of exercising her bright new ha'porth of power had worn off, Nora would probably stop her ordering-about, and return to her usual tolerant and light-hearted Irishness.

Henry's moods changed wildly, almost by the half-hour. One minute he would be laughing and playing practical jokes – 'fizzy as champagne', as his valet described it. The next, he would be deeply morose, scarcely speaking to anybody. Then he would become furiously over-active, issuing dozens of instructions to his overworked staff, asking for letters, information, statistics, and estimates. Next he would become withdrawn and solemn and pompous. In those moments, Lucy knew that he was thinking about his glorious new position in the British Empire; not just as governor and superintendent of the greatest jewel in Victoria's crown, but as her embodiment.

He would speak almost mystically during moments like those; of noble duty; of dominions on which the sun never set; of the paramount power with which he would soon be invested.

But in those moments he would sound painfully lonely, too.

It wasn't just that, as Viceroy Designate, it was impossible for him to join in too boisterously with the social life of the ship. His private secretary Walter Pangborn was travelling with them, as smooth and as lazy as ever, as well as a relentlessly brisk wax-moustachioed ADC, Colonel Timothy Miller, eleven of his new staff, six officers of the Viceregal Bodyguard, and Sir Evan Maconochie of the

Indian Civil Service. But the remaining passengers were mainly Indian Army officers, engineers, civil servants, planters, and the wives and children of district officers and estate-managers.

The root of his loneliness was that, although Calcutta still lay thousands of miles distant, Henry was already becoming obsessed with the difficulties of governing a continent so vast and so tumultuous. In particular, it irked him that his mandate over India would not be complete. Historically, the Punjab government under its own British Lieutenant-Governor conducted its affairs more or less independently; and the British governors of Madras and Bombay – both important provincial presidencies – rarely felt it necessary to tell the Viceroy what they were up to.

They were talking about this difficulty as they sat at dinner in their stateroom, the night they passed through the Straits of Gibraltar. Henry suddenly raged, 'It's wrong! I can't understand how Elgin tolerated it! The Viceroy should govern India without any circumscription whatsoever!'

His loneliness was reflected in his day-to-day habits. He became obsessive about procedure and ceremony and correctness. He had always been an exact dresser, but these days he spent twice as long with his new valet, making sure that he always appeared immaculate. His valet was a Cockney called Vernon, a tall brown-eyed man with the looks of a handsome boxer, 'a little uncertain about his aspirates', as Henry liked to put it (he dropped his aitches), but always attentive and discreet. He was the first body-servant with whom Henry had been at all impressed. He was also the first body-servant who – within limits – could answer Henry back.

Lucy wasn't sure that she liked or trusted Vernon. She didn't like the deadness in his eyes. She always felt that he could see through her; that he could tell she hadn't been highly born. *Takes one to know one*, he was always saying, for no apparent reason whatsoever.

449

She talked to Henry about Vernon, in a roundabout way, but Henry ignored her. Henry thought of nothing but India, India, India. He could smell his power and his position, like the alluring smell of spices on the wind. He was so hungry for it that on his infrequent strolls on deck he would stand facing the East, cracking his knuckles.

He began speaking to everybody, even Lucy, with stilted formality. He would pay her compliments as if he were addressing an Indian maharanee. 'You have an exceptionally graceful air about you this evening,' or, 'your hair is combed in a very captivating manner.' At the same time, anybody who talked to her with what Henry considered to be a lack of deference to the Vicereine-to-be would be harshly and quickly brought to heel.

One critical reason for his stiffness towards her, Lucy guessed, was that he was tightly suppressing his sexual desires. He refused to risk making love to her, no matter how he might have wanted to. He wanted an heir, Horatio Henry Carson, and he would rather remain celibate for six months than risk provoking a miscarriage.

A few hours before the *Star of Bengal* was due to dock at Valletta for coaling, Sir Evan Maconochie took Lucy for a promenade on the deck. She wore a light French-grey coat and a plain hat tied with a scarf. Sir Evan wore a grey frock-coat.

'Lord Carson seems somewhat distracted,' Sir Evan remarked. 'I trust that everything is well?'

'I think he's preparing himself for India, that's all,' Lucy replied.

'Well, agreed, it won't be easy,' nodded Sir Evan. 'He knows India extremely well, of course. Better than some district officers. More *comprehensively*, anyway. But all the same, it is one thing to come to India as a district officer, and quite another to come to India as Viceroy.'

'It's difficult to understand what he's feeling,' said Lucy. 'He seems to be cutting himself off . . . shutting himself away from everybody.'

Sir Evan stood by the rail with his hands clasped behind his back and took a noisy breath of fresh air. 'He needs to *distance* himself, certainly. And so will you. To all intents and purposes, he will be king and you will be queen.'

'I thought kings and queens could do what they wanted.'

Sir Evan grunted with amusement. 'In fairy stories, perhaps. But not in India. In India, both British and natives will expect you to conduct yourselves as divine beings. Don't you understand? Both British and natives measure their standing by where *you* stand. The viceroyalty is the pinnacle of the entire society.'

Lucy leaned against the rail and let the cool Mediterranean breeze blow into her face. 'Mrs Bull was making a whole lot of fuss about – what did she call it? – the pecking-order.'

'Oh, yes,' said Sir Evan. 'I prefer to call it the order of precedence.'

'She said there was even a printed book about it, who's more important than whom.'

'Indeed, the Warrant of Precedence. The *burra memsahib's* Bible! No society hostess would ever dare to seat her guests without it. It's mostly a middle-class society, you see, a salaried society, in which the only way in which your social supremacy can be measured is by what you do, or by what your husband does.

'The élite are the members of the Indian Civil Service – governors, judges, district officers, members of the Viceroy's Council. Slightly below them are the members of the Indian Political Service, who take care of the Indian princes and the frontier people. Then comes the Indian Medical Service and the upper echelons of the Public Works Department. Then, Indian Army officers – depending on their regiment, of course – cavalry almost always preferred to infantry, although the Gurkhas are generally smiled upon. Members of the Education Department, however, tend to be sniffed at; and subordinate civil servants are right on the very frontiers of respectable society. Clergyman are practically pariahs;

and retail merchants are *never* invited anywhere, no matter how wealthy they may be.'

He paused, and took a small silver snuffbox out of his vest pocket, and helped himself to two sharp pinches of Rappee snuff.

'At the very base of the social ladder in British India are the Domiciled Europeans and those of mixed blood, the Eurasians, the *chee-chees*, so-called because of their sing-song accents. They are never invited to the best parties; or to join any of the clubs. Personally I think they are the saddest lot of all. They are always trying to ape their betters; and they are always talking with such nostalgia of a Home they have never seen, and never will.'

Lucy said, 'Do you know something, Sir Evan, I'm not at all sure I care for the sound of so much precedence. I mean, if there aren't any lords and there aren't any ladies, it just sounds like snobbery to me. Even in New York – '

Sir Evan gave her a tight smile, suppressing a sneeze. 'Calcutta is not New York, my dear Lady Carson. Precedence is the Indian way. The Indians themselves observe strict orders of caste. Amongst the Hindu, there are the pukka Brahmins, the heaven-born; the Kshatrias, the warrior-class; then the Vaisyas, the merchant and moneylending class, and so forth, down to the very lowest, the Untouchables. Lord Carson and your good self will be leading a very hectic life, socially. You will regularly be fêted with a lavishness which Her Majesty the Queen-Empress herself might envy. You will be regarded almost as demi-gods. But, after a fashion, yes, you will always be alone.'

Lucy slowly shook her head. 'I've never been alone in my life, Sir Evan. Believe me, I don't intend to be alone now.'

Sir Evan hesitated for just a moment, and then he cleared his throat, and sniffed, and added, 'This may sound impertinent, Lady Carson, but do believe me when I tell you that I intend it in the best possible of spirits. They say that it doesn't go down too well for women in India to be too –

well, this isn't meant to be denigrating – but women should make something of an effort not to appear too *clever*. There are some clever ladies, but generally they take considerable pains to keep it quiet.'

He paused, sniffed again, and looked at her warily. 'You do see what I'm driving at?'

The *Star of Bengal* stopped for twenty-four hours at Malta to take on coal. That evening, Henry and Lucy were given a dull dinner at Government House, under chandeliers so dim that they could scarcely see what they were eating (grilled sardines; followed by fatty leg of lamb, with carrots; and trifle for dessert). The dinner went on far longer than Henry had hoped, and he began to fret, especially when the Governor launched into an interminable story about a catastrophically incompetent butler who had once worked for him. 'Lifted the meat-cover, didn't he, with such a flourish, and there were my missing trousers, for all to see!'

That night, back in his stateroom, Henry stood quivering and speechless with tension for almost a minute. Then he clenched his fist and smashed it against his desk, so hard that he split the skin across his knuckles.

'Henry!' Lucy exclaimed.

'It's nothing,' Henry told her, winding a handkerchief around his hand. Then, much more quietly, 'It's nothing. I can't stand to waste time, that's all. Doesn't anybody realize how much I have to do?'

'Henry, you have to rest sometime.'

'When do you suggest?'

'Well, I suggest now. You're not going back to work tonight, are you?'

'Lucy, I have to. I have no choice.'

He turned to her. His face was grey with exhaustion. 'There's so much to do. So many dispatches to answer. An entire report on Kowait. Besides, I have to finish writing up our personal accounts. We have a salary of sixteen thousand

453

pounds per annum. How we're going to be able to afford to entertain all those nizams and maharajahs and rajas, I have no idea.'

'Henry, for goodness' sake, Walter is supposed to do your accounts.'

'It will take him twice as long, Lucy; and I will still have to satisfy myself that they're correct.'

'Henry, you're Viceroy now! You have a whole staff and hundreds of servants! When are you going to stop being your own servant?'

Henry tugged tightly at his necktie. 'Lucy, I'm a servant by destiny. Not only my own servant, but *your* servant, and my country's servant, and the servant of everybody in India, no matter what their colour, no matter what gods they worship.'

'Henry, your health is more important than India. Your health is more important than anything. Henry, I'm carrying your baby.'

She watched Henry's highly-polished shoes pacing from one side of the scarlet stateroom carpet to the other.

Then he stopped pacing, and walked across to his desk, and made a considerable performance of unrolling his large-scale map of India, all billowing paper and crackling folds, and weighing it down with a book and an inkwell.

'Come here,' he beckoned her. Then, 'Come here, Lucy, look.'

She came and she looked. 'Well?' she asked. 'It's pink and it's yellow.'

'That's right. It's pink and it's yellow. British pink, native yellow. In the west here, look – Baluchistan and Sind – separated from the rest of British India by a string of native states, running all the way from the Eastern Ghats to the mountains of Rajputana. In the south, we have the Central Provinces, and the two Presidencies of Bombay and Madras, divided from each other by the native states of Mysore and Hyderabad. In the east, we have the Bengal Presidency, and the province of Assam. And here, north-westward from Bengal, run the solid line of British provinces that make up the spine of British India: Bihar, the United Provinces, and the Punjab, all the way up to the North-West Frontier.

'There are ten British provinces, and five hundred and sixty-two native states. To all intents and purposes, they go their separate ways. We let the natives run their own affairs. Some of them are civilized; some of them are quite barbaric. There are two thousand three hundred recognized castes, sects, and creeds in India. We could not hope to administer them all closely, nor would we wish to. But they all have one thing in common: one thing! They all share a common allegiance to Her Majesty the Queen-Empress, in my person, the Viceroy.

'That is my responsibility. That is why I have to go on working, no matter how much of a burden it sometimes becomes. And that is why I am asking for your tolerance, and your strength, rather than your censure.'

He looked down at the map a moment longer; then lifted off the inkwell and rolled it up.

Lucy said softly, 'I'm sorry. I don't think I really understood just how hard it was going to be for you. I thought, well — I don't know. I thought you were going to be a figurehead, and that was all.'

'Well, you would, you're an American,' said Henry. 'But I am many other things besides. A king, an administrator, a judge, a general, a guiding light.'

'Thank goodness India has quite enough gods,' Lucy replied.

'You're not to mock,' Henry reprimanded her; although he knew that there was very little he could do to stop her.

'You'd better get to work,' Lucy suggested. 'I think I'll go to bed and read Lady Elgin's instructions. "At 9.35 pm their Excellencies will attend an out-of-door performance of *Merrie England* in aid of the Diocesan Women's Hostel."'

'You're going to be a queen, Lucy. You're not to mock.'

'Henry, I'm not mocking. I just don't want to be the queen in the nursery-rhyme, that's all, sitting in the parlour, eating bread and honey, while her king spends all his time in his counting-house, counting out his money.'

Henry walked back across the stateroom and took Lucy in his arms. Her stomach was protuberant enough now for him to have to stand a little way back.

'I will be your king, I promise you.'

She didn't hear Henry come to bed that night; and when she woke in the morning he was already gone. The sunlight was reflected from Valletta harbour, and played criss-cross patterns on the stateroom ceiling. She lay on her back for almost ten minutes, slowly waking herself up and thinking of India. When Henry had first told her that he had been appointed Viceroy, she had imagined a land of spices. But after what Henry and Sir Evan had told her, all she could imagine was a land as dark and stifling as a cupboard, a labyrinth of precedence and prejudice and never-ending toil.

A little after eight, she rang for Nora and Etta to dress her. She wore a skirt and jacket of maroon velvet, and a blouse of creamy-coloured lace, with lacy cuffs. She joined Mrs Bull for breakfast in the first-class dining room, with its parlour palms and its oil-painted landscapes of famous Indian landmarks, the Taj Mahal at Agra, the Palace of Winds at Jaipur, the Tower of Victory at Chitorgarh. She had lightly scrambled eggs. It was too windy and cool to eat out on deck; but it was just the weather for sightseeing.

'Do you think you could persuade that young officer with the Scottish accent and the black hair to take us on a tour?' she asked Mrs Bull.

Mrs Bull was mortified. 'Persuade him, Lady Carson? I'll *order* him!'

So by ten o'clock, they had made up a shore party with Mrs Bull and Nora and John McCrae, the *Star of Bengal*'s handsome young Aberdonian first officer, to act as guide, and two officers from the Viceroy's Bodyguard, Captain Roger Philips and Lieutenant Ashley Burnes-Waterton, in scarlet uniforms that were more gorgeous than anything worn by the Brigade of Guards. They took two victorias to the Strada Reale to shop for coral and silver and lace. Lucy managed to buy Henry a pair of coral cufflinks, and a silver hip-flask engraved with the cross of the Knights of St John, but it was only a few minutes before she was surrounded by noisy crowds of onlookers, some of whom guessed who she was, and cheered, 'Hooray for Lady Carson!' Captain Philips was looking strained and crimson in the face from all the jostling, so Lucy agreed to leave the Strada Reale and tour the rest of the town. Young Mr McRae reluctantly agreed to take them to see the embalmed bodies of members of the Carmelite Order, the famous 'pickled monks', but afterwards, in the brightness of the streets, Nora complained of feeling dizzy, and Lucy could feel her baby and her breakfast swimming together in one congealing emulsion, yellow and pink, like the Viceroy's map of India.

'You'll see worse than that in India, ma'am,' Mrs Bull promised her, waddling along beside her as they returned to their carriage, one hand keeping her wide-brimmed hat firmly clamped on top of her head. 'I hope we don't have that awful Solferino soup for lunch again.'

'Or pickled monk, what?' suggested John McCrae, grinning.

'That'll be quite enough of that,' Mrs Bull snapped back at him.

Slowly the *Star of Bengal* sailed the length of the Mediterranean, a blurred white ship on a misty blue sea. The weather was similar to an English September: sunny but cool. It was difficult to remember that they had left Southampton only a few days before on a scrapingly raw day, with threatened snow.

Port Said was the first truly oriental stop on the journey.

On a warm windy afternoon they were greeted at the dock by Sir Evelyn Bentley, the Consul-General, and Lady Bentley, and by the Khedive, Abbas Halmi, and by scores of ministers and officials and ADCs, and a fleet of black landaus that had been polished as bright as Army boots. For no comprehensible reason, a brilliantly-uniformed band played *Scotland the Brave* and then *It Came Upon A Midnight Clear*.

They were invited to a formal lunch at the Bur Said Hotel, in a huge cool dining room overlooking a blue-tiled courtyard, where a fountain splashed. Tall black-faced men in fezzes brought them *molokheya* soup, charcoal-grilled mutton, and *ful medames*, with marzipan *bakwala*. It was Lucy's first taste of Eastern food; but the white-haired Lady Bentley sat opposite her and gave her motherly guidance on what to eat, and how. 'The left hand, you see! Splendid!' and, 'for goodness' sake, don't try to eat that!'

The Khedive told a story about his father, Tewfit, and how he had won a wager when he was young by running all the way around the Pyramid of Cheops with an orange between his knees. Nobody knew whether to laugh or applaud or to receive the story in respectful silence, but the Khedive himself obviously thought it was hilarious, because he laughed so much that his servants had to bring him a glass of water.

Afterwards, the Khedive returned to Cairo and Henry withdrew to a private suite to talk to Sir Evelyn about Russian encroachment on the eastern Mediterranean and the Persian Gulf. Lady Bentley and an enthusiastic young ADC called Minchin took them on a sightseeing tour of Port Said, accompanied by Captain Philips and Lieutenant Burnes-Waterton, and two tall black officers of the Khedive's official bodyguard, who wore red fezzes and white uniforms with red epaulets, and carried ceremonial swords. Mrs Bull, of course, came too; and so did the bothersome lady wife of the Superintendent of Police at Coimbatore, in Madras, who was almost hysterically excited at being invited anywhere with the new Vicereine (whom she had been inspecting on deck from a distance, through opera-glasses).

'Duncan simply won't believe me!' she fussed. 'I'll be the talk of the *moorghi khana*.'

'What's a *moorghi khana*?' Lucy wanted to know.

'Strictly translated, a henhouse,' said Mrs Bull, grasping the handles of Lady Bentley's carriage as if she were preparing to wrestle it like an ox, and overturn it. 'A room for the ladies; most clubs have them these days.'

Port Said was noisy and chaotic and smelled like nothing that Lucy had ever smelled before: of dust, and charcoal-smoke, and heavy perfume, and sweet-potatoes, which were sold in the winter months like chestnuts and bagels in New York. As they left the Bur Said Hotel, their landau was surrounded by crowds of ragged boys, beggars, fortune-tellers, and men juggling with eggs and day-old chicks. They were pursued down the street as they were driven off, passing through light and shadow, past fruit-stalls and awnings and shops advertising Copperware and Best Quality Solar Topis.

'Just for fun, I'll take you to Simon Artz,' said Lady Bentley, fanning herself as they rattled through the streets. 'Everybody who comes out East has to go there at least once. They sell everything from topis to Turkish delight. And you'll see their striped shawls on the shoulders of practically every *memsahib* in India. But don't buy anything; especially their ghastly topis. I have a double terai for you, for the Cold Weather, and a Cawnpore Tent Club topi for the Hot. Much more practical. And some beautiful shawls I found in Cairo.'

They reached the marble-pillared entrance to Simon Artz's emporium, and young Minchin assisted Lucy and Lady Bentley down from the carriage. A party of Europeans were just leaving the store, fresh out from England on their first trip to India, all of them kitted out in huge and conspicuously brand-new topis. They were cleared aside by the Khedive's bodyguards, just like everybody else. One of the men declared, 'Here – I say!' and was about to remind the Khedive's bodyguard that white was white and black was black, but his girl companion caught his sleeve and pointed out that they were being pushed aside not just for anybody but for the new Vicereine of India.

'Sometimes I wonder how I bear it, you know,' Lady Bentley remarked, as they crossed the pavement. 'The heat, you know; and the general *hugger-mugger*. And I can't *tell* you how much I miss Eaton Square. But Evelyn adores it. He's in his element, all these *fellaheen* to bellow at.'

They had almost reached Simon Artz's doors when there was shouting and scrambling and shrieking from the English girls, and 'I say! Here! I say!' all over again from the English chaps. The crowds parted like the side of a water-filled *wadi* suddenly breaking down, and a staring-eyed long-haired beggar in a fluttering red cloak scrambled his way wildly through the crowds on the pavement and flung himself down at Lucy's feet, pressing his lips to her shoe.

He cried out, barely intelligibly, 'Oh queen, have mercy on me, for the love of Allah! Oh queen, have mercy on me!'

'Oh my God!' Lady Bentley declared. 'Oh my God, get him off!'

One of the Khedive's bodyguard stepped forward, and Lucy heard a sound which she had never heard before, but which she would never forget. Sharp steel, scraping against a scabbard. The bodyguard's sword flicked up, shining. Lucy glanced in horror at the bodyguard's face, and it was smooth and black and completely impassive, with tiny expressionless eyes. He looked as if he were doing nothing more interesting than cutting an offending bramble in the Khedive's garden. But his sword hacked into the beggar's face, right across the bridge of his nose; and like a conjuring trick the beggar's right eye fell out, and rolled across the pavement. Blood sprayed finely on to the bodyguard's leggings; and on to Lucy's shoes.

Lucy squeezed her eyes tight shut, praying that it hadn't happened, that she hadn't seen anything. 'Oh my God,' said Lady Bentley, in a voice like a French horn. 'Lady Carson, quick – back into the carriage! Mr Minchin, what on earth are you doing?'

Mr Minchin was windmilling his arms and staggering in bent-kneed indecision from one side of the pavement to the other. Captain Philips and Lieutenant Burnes–Waterton had run forward – Lieutenant Burnes–Waterton to stand in front of Lucy, brandishing his Webley revolver, although he hadn't cocked it – Captain Philips to guide her back to the landau. He seized her elbow and helped her up. 'Steady now, ma'am. All's well.'

On their way back to the docks, Lucy sat in the carriage trembling and cold. Lady Bentley gave her a shawl to cover her shoulders.

'What a shock, my dear. What a terrible thing to happen! But in the East, you know . . .'

'In the East, *what*?' Lucy demanded. 'That poor man wasn't doing anything at all!'

'My dear, he was touching you.'

'So? So what? He was touching me, so what? He was kissing my shoe, that's all. There's nothing threatening in kissing a person's shoe.' Lucy's Kansas accent came out serrated and twangy as a sawblade.

Lady Bentley patted her arm. 'My dear, he was a *lazar*, and you –'

'What am I?' Lucy wanted to know, her eyes wide, her face white in the Port Said sunshine.

'You are an empress. An *empress*, my dear. Haven't you understood that yet?'

At Port Said, cold weather wear was exchanged for tropical wear, which meant that Nora and Etta were furiously busy packing away all the dresses and skirts which had been marked as Lucy's cabin baggage, and unpacking all the clothes which had been marked Wanted On Voyage – embroidered linen blouses, white skirts, white cambric dresses, white shoes. Double awnings were erected over the decks, and Mrs Bull gave Lucy a stern warning to 'beware the sun'.

'The sun is your enemy, Lady Carson, make no mistake about that. You will never get used to it. Every time you come out into the open in India, it will hit you like a hammer. You should never venture anywhere between sunrise and sunset without your topi.'

Like a ship in a torpid dream, the *Star of Bengal* drifted its way down the Suez Canal. The heat grew more intense every day, and Lucy spent most of the time in her stateroom, lying on her bed, fanning herself with a giant ostrich-plume fan that Lady Bentley had given her, trying to read Jane Austen but thinking of Blanche. *'I am the happiest creature in the world, for I have received an offer of marriage from Mr Watts.'* But where was Blanche now? Tucked up in her bed in her upstairs room in the Cullen farmhouse, with the snow all around, and the fires crackling? She could hardly believe that Kansas in winter had ever existed. Perhaps it had all been a dream. Every time she went out on to the promenade deck to watch the dun-coloured desert gliding hypnotically past her, she felt that Kansas had shrunk smaller and smaller, like a toy snowstorm in a glass bottle, and that soon it would dwindle away to nothing at all.

She wrote a letter to Blanche, and picked open the stitches in the lining of her purse, and concealed it inside. Just in case the ship sank; or she died of cholera, or circumstances made it impossible for her to go back to Kansas, ever again. No letter from a mother to a daughter was ever written with such grief and pain, in spite of the fact that Lucy found it difficult to express herself on paper.

'My dearest darling Own One ...' the letter began. *'You will never understand how hard it was to leave you. One day, if we ever meet again, please don't turn your back to me, please*

don't blame me. I was young. I had my own life to lead. I gave birth to you, I gave you everything I possibly could. You always have a little crib-space in my heart, just like the crib that Mrs Cullen laid you in, when you were first born.'

Henry came into the stateroom, just as she was finishing her letter. He was dressed in immaculate white ducks, and a topi, and he was carrying a sheaf of papers which he had been working on. 'Writing?' he asked, in that same crisp carrying voice that she had heard on Mrs Harris' lawn.

She quickly picked up the letter so that he couldn't see it. He chuckled, and walked across to his desk, and filed his papers away. 'A *billet-doux* to your secret lover, perhaps? Who is it? Captain Philips? Or First Officer McRae?'

'I was trying to write a poem, as a matter of fact.'

'Aha!' He came across to her, rubbing his hands with his handkerchief. 'A love poem? For me? May I see it?'

She crumpled the letter up in her hand. 'It's not very good. Please. I'd rather you didn't.'

He tilted himself forward and kissed her forehead. 'Not to worry. Try and try again, that's my motto. *Fortuna transmutat incertos honores, nunc mihi, nunc alii benigna.'*

He kept on smiling at her. 'How's the child?' he asked her, at last.

For a hairsplit second, Lucy thought that he meant Blanche, that he had discovered everything. But then she realized that he was talking about the baby that was growing in her womb.

'Oh!' she smiled. 'Oh, the child is very well. I'm quite sure already that he's a he. And I'm already quite sure that he looks just like you.'

'You're not too bothered by the heat? It's going to get hotter, once we're past Aden.'

'Henry . . . whatever you can tolerate, I can tolerate too.'

He kissed her again. 'Do you know something, my darling? That first day I saw you, that very first instant, I knew that you'd make me a wonderful wife.'

Henry's ADC appeared, and asked him if he could spare some time to discuss the arrangements for their arrival in Bombay. Henry blew Lucy one more kiss, and then left. She waited for a minute or two, then she slowly uncrumpled her letter.

'*My Own One . . .*' she whispered.

They slid slowly through Ismailia, where bumboats came out to sell them an eclectic cargo of monkeys, onions, shoes and black bread. Some of the passengers amused themselves by throwing pennies at the small boys who ran alongside the ship, whooping and shrieking for money. Lucy had never seen monkeys before and was enchanted with them. One monkey in particular caught her eye: it was gingery and beady-eyed and mischievous, and reminded her of Malty. She would have bought it if Henry hadn't heard her calling out to the merchant, 'You! Hey, you! Let me see that monkey!' and stalked out on to the promenade deck.

'You're Vicereine-to-be, for God's sake! You don't buy flea-ridden monkeys from flea-ridden Arabs! You don't even *talk* to flea-ridden Arabs! As far as you're concerned, they don't exist!'

Lucy had felt hurt, and childish, and embarrassed. So embarrassed, in fact, that she didn't know how to say sorry; or even if she *should* say sorry. She rushed past him; and in through the doors that led to their stateroom, and threw herself on to her bed. *Jamie would have let me have it. Anybody would have let me have it. Anybody, except Henry.*

At last they reached Suez, a scruffy and bleached-out collection of rundown buildings, under a sky the colour of writing-ink. A few of the soldiers went ashore for donkey-rides and beer; the rest of the passengers stayed under the ship's awnings and began to realize what heat really meant.

The next day the *Star of Bengal* passed starkly through the Red Sea, dazzling white on intense blue. Already, Lucy had begun to notice signs that the passengers were arranging themselves into a strict social hierarchy. She and Henry, of course, were always treated with excruciating deference. But Lucy could see that, among the first-class passengers, certain little groups had begun to conglomerate. One group was made up of Henry's staff, and the officers of his Bodyguard, and the upper-crust members of the Indian Civil Service. Another group was made up of planters, who played cards as if their lives depended on it, and drank immense pink gins bobbing with pearl onions, and laughed much louder and much more desperately than the civil servants.

Among the women, it was glaringly obvious who were the *burra memsahibs*, the senior ladies. They sat at all the best tables; occupied all the best chairs; and were followed everywhere by shoals of lesser ladies. Lucy found herself looking eye-to-eye with *burra-mems* like Mrs William Smith-Carter, the wife of a cavalry colonel stationed at Meerut, and thought to herself: you ought to try living in Kansas. You ought to try eking out a living from the High Plains, those long dry summers when the wind blows everything away, those stone-hard winters when your cattle freeze solid. Then we'd see about you and your precedence.

Lucy had not yet encountered India.

Their last coaling station before they set sail across the Indian Ocean was Aden, which to Lucy looked like a dry and uncompromising collection of rocks with scarcely any vegetation to soften their the sun-blinded harshness. From Aden, they headed for the southern tip of India, and Ceylon, and every day the temperature increased. One morning, Lucy looked at the thermometer by the stateroom doors, and it was reading 115 degrees. She turned around to tell Henry, but he didn't even look up from his paperwork. 'That's nothing at all, sweetheart. In the plains, it goes up to one hundred and sixty, when it's really hot.'

But Henry didn't ignore Lucy completely. He remained formal, although he could occasionally act with surprising tenderness. One rare evening, he abandoned his letter-writing, and took her out on to the deck, to show her the Southern Cross glimmering in the night sky. Behind them, the ship's wake shone with silvery-greenish phosphorescence.

'It's all so strange,' said Lucy. 'I can hardly believe that I'm here at all.'

'That's the point,' Henry told her, obscurely.

They slept at night with all the stateroom portholes open, but the heat was still unbearable. Lucy envied all the passengers who had their bedding brought up on deck, the ladies on one side of the ship and the men on the other. In her own bedroom, she slept naked, the way she used to sleep on hot Kansas nights, her body shining with perspiration. Nora made some prudish noises about 'keeping the baby warm'. A pregnant woman with nothing on at all, holy St Anthony. But Lucy ignored her. Light as they were, her silk and cambric nightgowns all made her feel so sweaty and tangled-up.

During the day, whales and porpoises plunged alongside; and flying-fish sparkled in the water like showers of silvery needles. The women languished in the heat; the men competed (rather erratically) at clay-pigeon shooting. Lucy sat in a deckchair, with a tall glass of Rawlings' ginger-ale and ice, listening to the intermittent banging of shotguns, and thought, and dreamed. Inside, Henry sat at his desk in his shirtsleeves, writing and writing, and cursing quietly when his perspiring hand dimpled his paper, and caused it to repel his ink.

Scarcely anybody slept. The nights were too hot and starry; the excitement of India was in the air. Every morning the decks were hosed down with powerful jets of water. Every morning brought Lucy's empire closer.

They had sailed slowly all through the early-morning hours through the bright green Bengal countryside, manoeuvring their way between the treacherous sandbanks of the Hooghly River, towards Calcutta. The sky was now the colour of beaten brass. The heat was overwhelming. On either side of the ship, Lucy saw date palms and coconut-groves and banana plantations; and, in the distance, rice growing as emerald-green as corn.

Lucy caught sight of three or four pariah dogs, tearing at something on the silty riverbank, something that was intermingled crimson and brown. It was only when the ship drifted nearer that she realized it was the dead body of an Indian.

'Oh, my God,' she exclaimed to Mrs Bull. 'That's a man, that's a dead man they're eating!'

But Mrs Bull didn't take her eyes away from a group of laughing passengers on the deck below, whom she considered had already drunk too much. Live and misbehaving Europeans were much more interesting than dead and half-devoured Indians. 'What did I tell you, your ladyship?' she said. 'That's India. In the midst of life, etcetera, etcetera. I went to a dinner party once, during the monsoon, and I smelled this most awful smell. I was sitting next to a colonel of the IMS, and he said, "For God's sake, don't touch the fish, it's stinking." Well, of course I was terribly embarrassed, and I asked him what should I do? He said, "You can't possibly touch it, it's death." And, do you know, he meant it.'

After breakfast, exhausted by the humidity and the anticipation of arriving, Lucy went to bed, and lay draped under mosquito nets listening to the low, steady thrumming of the ship's engines.

She slept uneasily, and as she slept she said the name, 'Jamie.'

Henry heard her murmuring; put down his pen and came into the bedroom.

'Jamie,' she repeated.

Henry leaned over her and watched her for a while. Then he asked, 'Who's Jamie? Lucy, who's Jamie?'

'Jamie,' she repeated. Then, 'Blanche. Poor Blanche.'

'Ah, a friend of Blanche, is that it?' Henry asked her.

He waited for an answer, but it was obvious that she was still asleep. He kissed her perspiring forehead, and then he left the bedroom and walked through to the parlour to pour himself a hugely-diluted whisky-and-soda.

His body-servant Vernon knocked at the door. 'Lord Carson? Half an hour, sir, thereabouts, so Colonel Miller says. I expect you'd care for your bath, yes, before you puts on your uniform?'

'Very good,' said Henry. 'And send Colonel Miller up to see me.'

'Hat the double,' Vernon responded.

Henry glanced towards Lucy's bedroom; then he turned away again, his forehead furrowed in thought. He could still picture Lucy slackwire-walking across Mrs Harris' tennis-net, that shining golden day in Newport. My God, how beautiful she had looked that day! How beautiful she still looked today! Vanessa reincarnate, only prettier, and younger, and shining even brighter, and carrying his child!

Perhaps it would have been better for both of them if he hadn't asked Lucy to marry him. The way things were, he had a dread that he might disfigure the very beauty that he cherished so much; because of his ambition; because of his guilt about Vanessa; because he burned for India so badly.

In his prouder moments, he saw his viceroyalty crackling up into the Indian sky like rockets and Bengal lights. He saw himself brightly illuminate the whole of India, its buildings and its people, its cultures and its castes; he saw them all lift their faces to his dazzling brilliance, all across the sub-continent, from the Rann of Kutch to the Bay of Bengal, from Cape Cormorin to the Himalayas.

Lord Carson of Brackenbridge, Viceroy and Governor-General, and God!

But there were times when he saw the rockets tumble, when their fire was spent; and he saw the Bengal lights winking out, and smoking to the ground. Perhaps he had married Lucy as a constant reminder that he was only mortal, and that there was darkness inside his ambition, as well as light.

He laid his left hand flat on his blotter, wrinkling the blotting-paper with his perspiration. Then he picked up his pen in the other hand, stiffly lifted it up, and stabbed himself between the knuckles of his third and fourth fingers. He clenched his teeth, and hissed with pain, but he didn't cry out. Pain was not enough. Pain was never enough. He would have to make far greater atonement than this.

Lucy, dozing in her bed, could smell Calcutta even before she was properly awake. A smell that was unique; a fragrance of tropical flowers and trees; a smell of garlic and spices and burning cow-dung; a smell of heat and jasmine and sandalwood and dust. And she could hear a band playing, too, a distant band.

She dreamed that she was sailing up the Hooghly River, but all the time she knew that she was dreaming, because the river was more like a lily-pond, and as warm as a bath, and Blanche, her baby Blanche, was calling her name. She slept more deeply for that single hour than she had slept since the *Star of Bengal* had left Port Said. When she awoke, the ship's engines had slowed almost to a standstill, and there was a peculiar quietness on board, a feeling of expectation and excitement; but a tingle of fear, too. For those who were returning, their Home Leave was irrevocably over. For those who were coming out for the first time, there were hundreds of anxieties. How would they cope with such a strange country? How would they fit into the social hierarchy? What would they do if they found themselves face-to-face with all those dangers they had been warned about — scorpions, and cobras, and rabid dogs, and beggars? What if they contracted cholera, or dysentery, or malaria, or plague?

Not the least anxious were the girls who had come out to

find themselves a husband, the so-called 'Fishing Fleet'. What they dreaded was that when the hot weather started, they would be 'Returned Empty'.

But for most of the newcomers, the worst nightmare was simply that they might make fools of themselves. Perhaps Henry's relentless letter-writing and scrupulous research had been a way of ensuring that he was never laughed at. Perhaps he was more concerned about making a fool of himself than Lucy had ever realized.

She reached across to the bedside table and rang for Etta to bring her robe and her mules. Etta seemed quite radiant as she helped Lucy to dress. As soon as she had tied Lucy's sash, she flung open the doors to the promenade deck, and declared, 'There you are, m'lady; Calcutta!' with as much pride as if she had constructed it herself, during the morning.

Lucy crossed the stateroom to the open doors, and looked out at the capital of British India. Under a flawless blue sky, she saw a white and colour-washed city of unbelievable grandeur, of magnificent pillars and domes and gateways, of classical mansions and palatial public buildings and hotels, of church spires and monuments and parks.

All of this imperial magnificence, sprawled around the hot, torpid bend of an alluvial river, thousands and thousands of miles away from Oak City, Kansas.

'It's wonderful!' she told Etta, and there were tears in her eyes. 'I had no idea!' But her tears were not shed out of awe, or romance, or even out of joy. They were shed for everything that she had left behind; and everything that she had decided to become. Now that she had arrived in Calcutta, those decisions were irreversible.

At that moment, a military band struck up with *Lillibullero*, and she heard cheering from the waterfront.

Like a tired but well-dressed old lady, the *Star of Bengal* was gradually manoeuvred into the Prinsep Ghat, the dock just south of Fort William. The fort itself was a remarkable star-shaped construction, based on a seventeenth-century principle of fortification. Behind it lay a vast area of dusty open ground, the *maidan*, created originally to give the fort an unrestricted field of fire, but now the most elegant part of Calcutta, with magnificent shining public buildings all around it – including, to the north, the house which Henry had been born to occupy, Government House, Brackenbridge in India.

The river was crowded with ill-assorted tugs and barges and punts, most of them decorated with flags and flowers. The cheering was deafening, and baskets of flowers were emptied into the river in thick blossomy cascades, until it looked as if the *Star of Bengal* were sailing not on water, but through somebody's ornamental garden.

The warehouses lining both sides of the Hooghly were all decorated with bunting, and every available inch of riverside space was crowded with thousands of dark-faced people in brightly-coloured Indian fabrics, violent yellows and fiery scarlets and livid greens. Lucy looked up, and saw that the *Star of Bengal* herself was fully dressed with flags, and that she was flying the Viceroy's standard.

Fireworks popped, whistles whistled, and the military band played *Hearts of Oak*.

'There you are, m'lady, that's all for you!' Etta told her. 'You and his lordship, of course!'

Nora came in and clapped her hands. 'Now then, Etta, her ladyship has to be dressed quick. Disembarkation in twenty minutes. I've already drawn your bath, ma'am. It's the white lace dress with the seed-pearls, your ladyship?'

'Yes, Nora.'

'And the tararah?'

'Yes, Nora.'

Lucy went through to the bathroom and Nora undressed her. If anything, Nora was more excited than she was. 'I never saw such a crowd. And all blackies! I never saw so many blackies! I went to the rail and they was whistling and shouting and calling me *memsahib*, and I'm sure I blushed to my roots and couldn't think *what* to do!'

'Do we have any Pears' soap left?' asked Lucy, as she turned to step into the tub. But just then, as she stood naked at the side of the bath, there was a cautious knock at the door. Lucy frowned at Nora. 'Who can it be?' she mouthed. The knock was repeated, louder this time.

'Lucy, it's Henry. May I see you?'

Nora clucked like a chicken in disapproval, but Lucy smiled, 'It's quite all right, Nora. We *are* married, after all.' Nora passed Lucy her white silk robe, and then reluctantly opened the door. Henry stepped in; and he was already dressed in his full formal uniform: gilt-embroidered jacket, white silk breeches, and buckled shoes. Around his shoulders was draped a full-length cloak in a sumptuous blue, with white be-ribboned epaulets, and tied with gold tasselled cords.

'Henry!' said Lucy. 'You look wonderful! Aren't you hot?'

'Nora, would you excuse us?' Henry asked her.

'Well, your lordship, it'll have to be just for a minute,' Nora protested. 'Her ladyship's supposed to be dressed by now!'

Henry came up to Lucy and clasped her shoulders. His eyes were bright with excitement.

'Have you seen it!' he exclaimed. 'Calcutta!'

Lucy smiled, and nodded. 'I've seen it. It looks – well, it's beautiful.'

'Oh, my dear, it's not just beautiful! It's the heart of all India! The heart, the brains! It's the centre of the world! Lucy, my darling, this is the moment! This is the moment when you and I step into the pages of British history!'

He kissed her forehead, then he kissed her lips. She clung to him tightly, and he enveloped her in his cloak. It was heavy, but it was silk-lined, and the silk felt cool. He kissed her again, his tongue trying to probe in between her lips, but she kept her mouth closed and resisted him.

472

Concealed within his cloak, she felt his hand loosening her waistband, and gently parting her robe. He caressed her neck and her shoulders, and then held her close, so that her bare breasts were pressed against the gilt embroidery of his jacket.

Nobody who saw them could have guessed that beneath his cloak, she was almost completely naked.

'You want me,' he whispered.

She said nothing, but pecked his cheek. 'Henry, I have to get dressed.'

He held her for a moment, trapped inside his cloak, then he let it fall away from her, and let her go. She fastened her bathrobe, not looking at him.

'There's something I want you to remember,' he told her, softly, so that Nora couldn't hear; but not so softly that Lucy couldn't detect the serious tone in his voice. 'India is very strange, and India is very hot, and we shall both be kept very busy here. But no matter what happens – no matter what arguments we have or what difficulties we get into, remember that I love you, now and for ever.'

She said nothing at first, but turned away, so that all he could see was her tangled hair and her quarter-profile. 'Love has to be proved, doesn't it?' she said at last.

She let the robe slip with a whisper to the floor. Then she stepped into the bath, and slowly sat down. All this time he watched her; her distended stomach, her swollen breasts; and didn't say a word.

'You do still love me, don't you?' Henry asked her.

She looked up, her eyes slightly hooded. 'What makes you ask that?'

He shrugged. 'Ha! It's damned silly, isn't it? I don't know. I suppose every expectant father asks the same question. Jealousy, I suppose. It sounds ridiculous; but you always seem to be paying more attention to the baby than you do to me.'

'But, Henry, *you* pay neither of us any attention at all,'

Lucy replied, although not bitterly. 'That's what I meant when I said that love has to be proved.'

He opened and closed his mouth in melodramatic astonishment. 'Do I have to prove to you that I love my own child?'

'Perhaps,' Lucy challenged him. She was speaking as a mother who had abandoned her own dearly-beloved baby. 'You have a child already, don't you? You have a son, called Ambition. It must be hard for you to find quite enough space in your heart for all of us. Me, and baby, and Ambition.'

'Lucy – ' Henry protested; but Lucy didn't even want to hear.

'Please, Henry, go. I have to get dressed.'

'Lucy – ' Henry repeated, but then he stopped himself, and shook his head.

'Lucy,' he said again, much more softly, but much more emphatically, as if he had just discovered her name.

He waited, but she wouldn't answer. 'All right,' he said, and wrapped himself up in his cloak, and swirled out of the bathroom without a word. Seconds later, she heard the double doors clashing.

'Now, what was *that* all about?' asked Nora, coming back in again.

Lucy shook her head. 'Oh, I don't know. Nothing. I always argue with him, even when I don't want to. I can't help it. He doesn't seem to be able to talk to me at all, unless we're arguing.'

'He'll do well here in India,' Etta remarked, from the bedroom, as she buttoned up one of Lucy's blouses, and carefully folded it. 'There's nothing your Bengali likes better than an argument. And he always thinks he's right, too!'

It was late afternoon on January 3, 1899, in the warm amber light of a sinking sun, that the state carriage carrying the incoming Viceroy and Vicereine of India rattled through the monumental lion-topped gates of Government House, Calcutta, and into the wide tree-planted compound that surrounded it. Their carriage was escorted by the Viceregal Bodyguard, almost ridiculously resplendent in scarlet tunics and gilded epaulets, their horses gleaming in the sunshine as if they were oiled. As the state carriage reached the foot of the ceremonial steps, a hoarse-voiced gunnery sergeant screamed *'Fire!'* and they were treated to a thirty-one gun salute, a deafening salvo that echoed and re-echoed all over the *maidan* and across the river to the crowded Indian district of Howrah.

Their arrival in Calcutta had been triumphant. Their progress through the streets had been greeted by a wall of noise, and they had been thronged by tens of thousands of cheering Indians, and blizzarded with flowers. Every building had been decorated with flags and banners and signs saying WELCUM LORD AND LADY CARSONS; or HELLO Y.E.s! and one – where the two halves hadn't quite managed to join up – had read A GAL A DAY.

'I think they flatter me,' Henry had said, squeezing Lucy's hand.

Lucy stepped down from the state carriage in her white lace gown, and her gold-and-pearl tiara. She looked tall, and pale, and very calm, and a murmur of curious approval rippled through the assembled company. Henry took her arm with obvious pride; and the two of them walked up the wide stone staircase towards the portico. Arrayed on the steps on either side of them was a rigid guard of honour, with sabres drawn. At the top, waiting for them with smiles of welcome, stood the outgoing Viceroy, Lord Elgin, in full uniform, and Lady Elgin, in yellow silk; as well as the governors of all the British presidencies; and the residents of some of the larger native states; and the political agents of some of the smaller native states; and more than fifty bejewelled and turbaned princes, including the Nizam of Hyderabad, the Maharajah of Benares, the Maharajah of Jodhpur; and the Maharajah of Mysore.

In that golden January sunshine, Lucy ascended the steps of Government House as if she were dreaming. Lord Elgin took her hand, and bowed his head, and said, 'Welcome to Calcutta, Lady Carson. I hope the guns didn't frighten you. The Viceroy gets more than anybody else. Practically deafened me, over the years. Even our pal the Maharajah of Gwalior only gets nineteen.'

Lady Elgin was dark-haired, grey-eyed, and very older-sisterly. She took Lucy's hand and said, 'No curtsey, please! I've been told of your condition. Congratulations! A new country, and a new baby!'

It took them nearly twenty minutes to be introduced to all of the residents and political agents and princes and deputy commissioners and members of the Viceroy's Council. Lucy was fascinated by the princes. The most plainly-dressed was the Nizam of Hyderabad, who wore a grey frock-coat and a fez-like hat with a feather in it, but Lady Elgin murmured to Lucy that he was by far the wealthiest of all of them, and that he used one of his two 180-carat diamonds as a paperweight. Some of the maharajahs were dressed spectacularly. The white-moustached Maharajah of Benares wore robes of Paisley-patterned silk, and a white silk turban decorated with green silk tassels and incredible emeralds, as green as glass and as big as birds' eggs, at least thirty of them. The Maharajah of the Punjab was dark and black-bramble-bearded, and wore a towering silk turban draped around with strings of pearls.

'I hail your Excellencies' advent,' he said, bowing low. 'Let us thank our Heavenly Father, whose grace has today enabled us to see your sublime Ladyship in all her great glory.'

'Well, thank you,' said Lucy. 'Thank you very much.'

As he conducted Henry and Lucy into the vast high-ceilinged Marble Hall, Lord Elgin noticed Lucy's amusement.

'Indians have a great love of florid language,' he remarked.

'You'll get used to it. Before you laugh at it, however, remember that comparatively few Europeans ever learn to speak Urdu or Marathi or Tamil or Telegu; and even those who do could never compose sentences as marvellous as that. Here! This is the Marble Hall! This is where we hold our state dinners.'

He let them admire the Marble Hall for a moment; then he ushered them through to the Council Chamber, where Henry's Warrant of Appointment was to be read. 'Just the other day, I was addressed by one petitioner as the father of all of his children. He had eleven. I'm just wondering when I ever had the time.'

Lucy looked around Government House with a mixed sense of familiarity and strangeness. This is my house now, this huge palace! Its similarity to Brackenbridge was striking. As Lucy walked along the corridors she felt almost as if she were home. But this house was very different in many ways; not the least of which was the fragrant Bengal breeze which blew softly through its pillared vistas. There was no central staircase: instead, there were four separate staircases to each of the four wings, and the walls were built not of softly-coloured Derbyshire stone, but of brick, rendered with Madras *chunam*, which had been polished and painted to resemble marble.

What had struck a keen note of sadness in Lucy's memory was that the outside walls of the entire residency had been washed in the same stray-dog yellow as Jack Darling's General Store.

'Don't worry,' said Henry, as if he had been reading her thoughts. 'We'll soon get rid of that yellow paint. There's only one colour for a viceregal palace, and that's white.'

They assembled solemnly in the Council Chamber. The falling sunlight glittered on jewels and silks and gold. Henry stood forward, and Lord Elgin unrolled his Warrant of Appointment, and cleared his throat. The chamber was noisy with coughing and shuffling.

'We do hereby give and grant unto you our Governor-General of India and to your Council as the Governor-General of India in Council, the superintendence, direction and control of the whole civil and military government with all our territories and revenues in India ... and we do hereby order and require all our servants, officers and soldiers in the East Indies ... to conform, submit and yield due obedience unto you and your Council.'

Lucy saw Henry gradually lift his head; and, as he did so, by divine stage-management, the sunlight pierced the chamber in a brilliant diagonal, and illuminated his face. His expression made Lucy tingle. It was stern, arrogant, triumphant. She had never seen a man to whom God had apparently given everything he could have wanted, and she felt charged with the most inexplicable emotions, excitement, fear – dread, almost – and an admiration for Henry which she would never be able to describe to him.

After the Warrant of Appointment had been read, the assembled officials and princes retired to the Tiffin Room for champagne and tea and a spectacular array of canapés and Indian snacks, from pheasant vol-au-vents to *karela masala*, fried bitter gourds, and bowls of lemon-flavoured rice.

Lucy noticed that all the Indians ate with their fingers, and most of them drank nothing but water. She tried eating a little rice with her fingers, until Lady Elgin shot her a friendly but cautionary look across the room which obviously meant 'not done, to imitate the natives'.

She was approached by the Maharajah of Baroda, Saraji Rao, a plump courteous man with an impeccable English lisp and a necklace of the largest natural pearls that Lucy had ever seen. 'I have seven children so far,' he told her. 'Have you and H.E. any comparable number of children so far?'

Lucy hesitated, and then shook her head. 'I'm afraid we have no children so far. Although we're expecting our first baby in June.'

'Well, please permit me to congratulate you in advancement,' the Maharajah told her. Then he said, 'You will find that a child brings H.E. and yourself great joy.'

'I hope so,' Lucy smiled.

'A man who has no children is like a house with no doors,' said the Maharajah.

'I'm sorry,' Lucy replied. 'I'm not too sure what you mean.'

'He is always *closed,* you understand. Thief-proof. He will never be opening himself up to anything novel. A man without children would be better taking himself to the cemetery and lying down in his mausoleum to wait for death.'

Lucy didn't know what to say to that; but she was rescued by Colonel Miller, who greeted the Maharajah effusively, and asked him if he would care for more *pethi halva.*

'You know my weakness!' laughed the Maharajah.

As darkness poured over the twenty-six acres of Government House as thickly as warmed-up treacle, Lady Elgin took Lucy on a tour of the southern wings of the house, to see the private apartments. The drawing rooms were cool and quiet, with pale walls and linen curtains across the windows to keep out mosquitoes. They were furnished in traditional English style, with comfortable shapeless sofas and huge armchairs, but most of the fabrics were Indian. Lady Elgin showed Lucy to her dressing room, where all her trunks had already been unpacked, and all her dresses and shoes and underwear exactingly folded and pressed and put away.

'You must be tired,' she said, at last. Outside the window it was almost completely black, except for a last smear of crimson on the western horizon. A distinctive and romantic fragrance filled the air, the distillation of tree-sap and flowers and spices in the rapidly-cooling air.

Lucy said, 'Yes, I'm a little tired. But what a day!'

'Dinner is at seven, for seven-thirty,' said Lady Elgin. 'You may of course retire early, once it's over, if you're feeling at all fatigued. You're the *burra-mem* now.'

'Are you sorry to be leaving?' Lucy asked her.

Lady Elgin looked around the dressing room. It was here that she must have dressed herself for countless dinners and receptions and balls and 'drawing rooms'.

'Yes, I'm sad,' she said. 'I'm looking forward to going Home, quite naturally. But once you've lived in India, you know, you can never forget it. It makes an indelible mark on you. You can meet people who haven't lived in India for twenty years, but you can always tell. They have a faraway look in their eyes. They may be sitting on a park-bench in Surrey, but some secret part of them is still stretched out on a long-sleever in Bengal.'

She ran her hand along the top of the bureau, and looked at her glove. Perhaps it was a habit that she had acquired over the years of her viceroyalty, checking for dust. 'I think perhaps my greatest regret is that I came to India as Vice-reine. I have been pampered, certainly, and entertained, and carried around like a queen. But there are so many aspects of a woman's life here in India that I have never experienced. Some nights, don't you know, I used to stand here by my window and think of all those women scattered across the length and breadth of the entire sub-continent. Lonely, frightened; struggling with Indian servants and snakes and dysentery and drunken husbands; trying to bring up children in remote stations in the *mofussil*. And I would think to myself . . . you never knew India at all.'

She turned, and touched Lucy's shoulder, as if she were conferring on her the isolation that she herself had been feeling for so long.

'I hope you leave India with fewer regrets than I. And do take care of your baby.'

Lucy woke up in the morning to find the sun shining bright through the gauze mosquito-nets, and the sheet wrinkled and deserted beside her. She rang for Nora.

'Nora, what's the time?'

'Ten before nine, your ladyship.'

'Where's Lord Carson?'

'He's taken his breakfast already, your ladyship. He's down in his office, with Lord Elgin, and Colonel Miller, and the rest of them.'

Lucy sat up. 'It's hot here, isn't it? Somehow I always imagined that Calcutta would be cool. It's the name, I suppose, "Calcutta". It just *sounds* cool. And this is the Cold Weather, isn't it?'

'I said the same thing to Etta, but Etta said this *is* cool. Compared with the Hot Weather, anyway. Would you care for a bit of breakfast, your ladyship?'

'No, just tea. And I'll dress first.'

'You should eat for two, your ladyship. Think of the babba. The babba needs to feed.'

'Nora, just tea!'

'Yes, your ladyship. Not even an egg?'

'Nora, please, I'm just not hungry!'

Nora drew back the mosquito-nets and Lucy climbed out of bed. She went across to the window and peered out over the compound of Government House. She could see the wide dusty-golden expanse of the *maidan*, and the zig-zag walls of Fort William, and across to the south, the Chowringhi Racecourse. A little farther to the east, the tall Doric spire of the Ochterlony memorial rose high into the morning sunshine, a hundred and fifty feet tall, with an odd Turkish cupola on top.

'I think I may like it here,' said Lucy.

'Well, it's all very peculiar, that's all I can say about it,' said Nora. 'If I want a cup of tea, I have to ask some fellow called the *khansamah,* and the *khansamah* tells the *khitmutgar,* and the *khitmutgar* tells the *biwarchi,* and the *biwarchi* makes the tea, and back it all comes, along the line, and if it isn't stone-cold by the time it gets to me. And there's about a hundred blackies milling around with nothing better to do than open doors and close them again. And not just that. Etta and me are nothing but what you might call supervisory, because there's four *ayahs* to care for your clothes and the Lord knows how many people to make the beds. It's an ant's-nest, so help me, not a servants'-hall. And I'm not at all sure about the smell. It's not corned-beef and potatoes for luncheon today, you can count on that. More like boiled-up mothballs.'

Nora went to ring for tea. 'They do a fair omelette, I'll admit that,' she coaxed Lucy. 'Will you not have an omelette?'

Lucy shook her head. She had eaten enough at yesterday's dinner: quail, and rice, and bright red chickens, and all kinds of fruits, and chopped almonds wrapped in gold and silver leaf. Mrs Bull had warned her against experimenting too enthusiastically with Indian foods. '*Calcutta tummy*', she had warned, pursing her lips in the knowing way that only a collector's wife could purse her lips.

Lucy might not have been hungry; but as she sat in her private breakfast-room sipping milkless Darjeeling tea and talking to Nora, Henry suddenly appeared with a sheet of notepaper in his hand, and announced, 'Dinners!'

'Dinners?' asked Lucy. 'What do you mean, "dinners"?'

'Dinners, of course! Dinners! A formal dinner, every night of the week! And after the Inaugural Ball, dances every Saturday, without fail!'

'Did Lord Elgin hold dinners every night, and dances every Saturday?'

'No, my dearest, he didn't. But you and I will. Government House will become the social whirlpool of India. Dinners, and dances, and levées, too. Colonel Miller is drawing up a list of two thousand men who might profitably be invited to a "levée", so that they can meet their new Viceroy first-hand.'

'Henry, we've only just arrived.'

'All the more reason! I want to shake them up, Lucy! The Indian Civil Service in particular! I want to meet them, and inspire them! I want them to share my vision!'

Lucy smiled at him, and then laughed. 'All right, then! Dinners it is! So long as I can get used to the food!'

On Monday morning, as she sat drinking tea and eating rumble-tumble in the sun-blinded glow of her private dining room, the head *khitmutgar* appeared, Abdul Aziz, as if on wheels; and bowed his head, and informed her that Memsahib Morris had arrived.

'Who?' she asked, putting down her fork.

In spite of Nora's suspicions, Lucy had grown to like the *khitmutgar*, who was extremely tall and wore gorgeous maroon livery, with gilded braids. She had already nicknamed him 'Buffalo Bill'.

'Memsahib Morris, Your Excellency. Your so-shall secretary. His Excellency was especially requesting that you should see her as soon as humanly possible.'

'My social secretary? I didn't know I *had* a social secretary!'

'Memsahib Morris is your so-shall secretary, Your Excellency, madam.'

Lucy wiped her mouth on her napkin. 'You'd better show her in.'

There was a long pause, and then a bespectacled spinsterish woman of about fifty stalked through the doorway like a *kulang*, a crane, carrying a brown leather satchel. She wore a *terai* hat and an ecru linen suit, with a frilled white blouse.

Twenty years ago, she had probably been handsome, in her way. Today she was ordinary and very thin, with the fleshlessness of long-term malaria. She stretched out her hand.

'Elizabeth Morris, Your Excellency! Welcome to Calcutta!'

'I'm sorry,' said Lucy. 'Do I know why you're here?'

'First day at work!' Elizabeth Morris said, brightly. 'Must say His Excellency gets cracking, doesn't he! Golly!'

Lucy said, 'I'm really sorry, I don't know why you're here.'

Elizabeth Morris blinked behind her spectacles. 'I'm your social secretary, Lady Carson. Elizabeth Morris. Surely your hu – surely His Excellency mentioned my name.'

Lucy shook her head.

Elizabeth Morris said, 'Ah!' and clasped her hands together as if she were praying. For a moment, neither she nor Lucy said anything. Then Elizabeth Morris dragged out a chair, and sat next to Lucy at the breakfast-table, and said, 'The thing is, His Excellency interviewed me on Saturday afternoon, at two o'clock in the afternoon, on Lady Elgin's recommendation, d'you see, and said I was appointed, two hundred and fifty pounds per annum.'

'His Excellency hasn't mentioned anything to me,' Lucy retorted, although she was suddenly conscious that she might be betraying his trust.

'Well, he's a fearfully busy man,' smiled Elizabeth Morris. 'Perhaps he forgot! In any case, he was *very* scrupulous, when it came to interviewing me; and he asked all sorts of questions! Did I have my own teeth! Goodness me! What a question! Well, I do, as a matter of fact, touch wood and whistle. But my qualifications were obviously right! I've lived here for years, you see. My late brother was Sir Gordon Morris, you *must* have heard of Gordon, he was Chief Justice of the Supreme Court; and anyway I live in his house on the Chowringhi Road, which you can see from here, which is most convenient for both of us. You and me, if you know what I mean. But anyway, I've lived in Bombay, I've lived in Madras, I've lived almost everywhere in India that you could mention, well not Goa, of course, I'm not completely reckless, and not Udaipur, they're *very* strange there. They have a ritual of mass suicide called *johur*, and the Maharana wears full uniform and bare feet and stares.'

Elizabeth Morris picked up a rattan bag, and waved it as if it were a salmon she had just caught. 'I've bought a new leather-bound diary from the Army & Navy; and new pens; and a bottle of Stephen's blue-black. So, whenever you're ready, Your Excellency!'

Lucy stood up. 'Excuse me for just a moment, Mrs Morris,' she asked.

'*Miss* Morris, actually. Was engaged, once! But he was killed pig-sticking. Well, many years ago, now. Before Gordon passed over.'

Lucy left her breakfast room and walked swiftly through the long vista of *chunam* pillars, across the Marble Hall, to the Tiffin Room. Henry was sitting in a large gilded arm-chair, next to Walter Pangborn, and two other members of the Viceroy's Court whom Lucy didn't yet recognize, and the Nizam of Hyderabad, sitting elegant and perfectly-dressed in a grey silk frock-coat.

'Lucy!' said Henry, standing up as abruptly as if a spring had broken through the seat of his chair.

The Nizam and Walter and the other two gentlemen rose to their feet, and bowed, regardless of the fact that Lucy was wearing her white silk *negligée* and slippers, and that her hair was wound up in a white silk turban.

'Who is that woman?' Lucy demanded.

Henry made quick conciliatory faces to the Nizam, and then stalked across to Lucy and took hold of her arm. 'Have you no idea what face I will lose if I look like a man who can't control his wife?' he whispered at her, ferociously.

'Who cares about your face? Who's that woman? Elizabeth Morris, whatever her name is!'

'Elizabeth Morris is your new social secretary! I appointed her on Saturday! She knows the Warrant of Precedence off by heart, she knows everybody who's worth knowing in the whole of British India, she has tact, influence, and the ability to run your social life so smoothly and efficiently that you'll be able to organize the very best dinner-parties and the very best drawing-rooms that Government House has ever known!'

Lucy thought about that, and then, in a raging whisper, retorted, 'Good! Why the hell didn't you tell me before?'

Lucy and Elizabeth Morris became the kind of friends that are found only once in a lifetime. Elizabeth had been brought up with the Raj. She had seen Calcutta grow; she had seen great buildings rise and fall. She had seen terrible tragedies; friends dying of cholera; friends dying of drink or despair. At the age of eleven she had been taken by Lady Charlotte Canning to see the menagerie at the Viceroy's summer residence upriver at Barrackpore, and taken a pair of lynxes for a walk through Lady Canning's Italian garden.

The next year, 1861, Lady Canning had contracted malaria while returning from Darjeeling across the fever-ridden Terai, and died, aged 44. Elizabeth Morris had laid flowers on her tomb.

Every morning, Elizabeth took Lucy out in her carriage, to look round Calcutta. While Henry argued with his Council and his civil servants, Lucy went to Chowringhi to see the European stores, the Army & Navy, Hall and Anderson's, and Newman's. She saw Warren Hastings' house at Alipur, and the Esplanade, and Writers Buildings. But the saddest time was when she visited the South Park Cemetery, in Chowringhi, crowded with so many columns, urns, pyramids and obelisks that it looked as if they had been stored here, or washed ashore from a sunken funeral ship. Elizabeth said nothing as Lucy walked between the neatly-tended monuments, but watched her sharply. This was a lesson in the misery of Imperial India, as well as its glory. There were so many graves of girls who had married at 15 or 16, only to die of disease or in childbirth before their seventeenth birthday; and there were so many children.

After a long while, Elizabeth said, 'Two monsoons, no longer. That's how long most of them lasted. As Sir William Hunter wrote, "The price of British rule in India has always been paid with the lives of little children."'

The most regretful monument of all was the spiral column decorated with stone roses, dedicated to Rose Aylmer, who had died of dysentery at the age of 20.

Lucy read the elegy. *'Rose Aylmer, whom these wakeful eyes/May weep, but never see./ A night of memories and sighs/ I consecrate to thee.'*

Elizabeth said, 'That was written by Walter Savage Landor. He loved her, you know, and he never forgot her. My brother knew him. Rose died in 1800, and Walter lived until 1864. Sixty-four years of grief! He missed her every single day of his life.'

During the first weeks of their viceroyalty, Elizabeth guided Lucy through the treacherous brambles of Calcutta society. Together with Colonel Miller, she drew up the guest list for the first ball, and planned all the seating arrangements. The *memsahib* of a political officer would certainly not care to find herself sitting next to an assistant inspector-general of forests; and the wife of a lieutenant-colonel in Skinner's Horse would be mortified to be placed next to an officer of the 39th Garhwalis, for all that they were Gurkhas.

Their first ball was enchanting. Lucy had brought out from England a low-cut gown of white silk, with an overlay of white lace which had been especially made for her in Nottingham. The lace had the appearance of thousands of peacock feathers, and each feather was sewn with pearls.

Nora curled her hair for her and fastened it with two twists of pearls; and to crown her *coiffure* she wore her diamond tiara. When Henry led her into the ballroom that Saturday evening, all three hundred assembled guests broke out into spontaneous applause; and Colonel Miller led a call for three cheers.

'She has the appearance of a graceful swan,' wrote the correspondent for the London *Times*. 'If there is a woman more beautiful in the whole of India, then I have never seen her or heard of her.'

The ballroom at Government House was spectacular. It was supported on each side with shining white *chunam* pillars; and from its coffered ceiling a glittering array of cut-glass chandeliers hung down. Between the pillars were ranged sofas of blue satin damask, and sparkling mirrors that reflected the light even more brightly.

At the upper end of the ballroom, framed in an archway, a very rich Persian carpet was spread; and in the centre of that, a *musnud* of crimson and gold, which had originally formed part of the throne of Tippoo Sultan. On top of this stood a decorated chair and stool of state, for the Viceroy.

Henry and Lucy arrived in the ballroom at about nine o'clock, and the orchestra struck up, and dancing began.

'May I ask for this dance?' said Henry.

Lucy gave him a little curtsey. She was conscious that every man and woman in the whole ballroom was staring at her, swivelling their heads around so much as they danced that there were several awkward collisions in the middle of the floor.

Henry waltzed her sedately around the pillars.

'I haven't yet told you that you look very beautiful,' he said.

'Well,' she said, a little off-handedly, 'thank you.'

'Do you think you're going to like it here?' he asked her. 'How are you getting along with Miss Morris? She always reminds me of one of those umbrellas with a duck's head for a handle.'

'I'm getting along with her very well, thank you, and she does not look like an umbrella with a duck's head for a handle. If anybody looks like a duck's head with a handle, it's you. In fact you look like a duck. You certainly dance like a duck.'

Henry quickly glanced around, to make sure that nobody could overhear them. 'What on earth has got into you?' he demanded. 'We're supposed to be celebrating tonight, not arguing!'

'Oh, yes, and what are we supposed to be celebrating? Our first conversation in ten days? Henry, I didn't marry you to spend my life on my own. I haven't even *seen* you since Thursday morning!'

Henry was silent as they pivoted their way past a nodding, smiling group of senior civil servants. Then he said, 'I made it quite clear that my first few weeks would be very, very busy. I'm not starting up a mutton club, for goodness' sake, I'm ruling a continent!'

'Walter says you're doing it again.'

'Walter says I'm doing what again?'

'Walter says you're doing everything yourself. He says you're answering every single letter personally; he says that you've arranged to see the head of every civil service department at least once a week; he says you've arranged to make three speeches already; and to entertain almost a thousand people. He says you've been writing letters at breakfast, correcting proofs at luncheon, and working on your accounts halfway through the night.'

Henry said tautly, 'Shall we discuss this later?'

'How can we? You'll be talking to your Council about irrigation or something.'

'Lucy, I know I work very hard, but it's my nature. I can no more accept blame or credit for it than I could for having a well-turned calf, or a handsome nose.'

'There's nothing wrong with your nose.'

'For goodness's sake! I wasn't suggesting there was! I was

simply saying that I am industrious by temperament, and that I have more than enough to keep me fully employed.'

Lucy said, 'Your health's suffering. Look at you! You haven't been here two weeks and your hair's thinning and you skin's waxy and you cough all the time. And your temper's no better. I heard you shouting at Abdul the other day. Henry, you should have been ashamed of yourself. You sounded like a roaring lion.'

Henry was about to snap back something sharp; but Lady Ampthill beamed at him from across the ballroom, and he was obliged to beam back. 'It's very irregular,' he said, 'but let's go outside, and finish this conversation alone.'

He guided Lucy away from the dance-floor, between the pillars, and out on to the balcony. The night was fragrant, and echoed with music and laughter. The compound had been illuminated with lamps suspended from bamboos; and the wall of Fort William which faced towards Government House had been illuminated with dramatic starkness.

'Lucy,' said Henry, his face hidden in shadow, 'I have to ask you to bear with me, to give me time. I came here bursting with all manner of far-reaching ideas. I want to reform the tax system, so that people don't have to pay so much in times of dearth. I want to change the rules of famine relief. I want five thousand miles' more railways. I want better schools, and more doctors, and better safeguards against epidemic diseases.'

He paused, and took out his handkerchief, and wiped the perspiration from his forehead. 'I want all of those reforms, and I want them carried out urgently. This sub-continent will collapse if they're not! But the great slow-grinding bureaucracy that I have inherited! You cannot imagine how it frustrates me! If I suggest to my staff that something is done within six weeks, the attitude is one of pained surprise. If I suggest six days, one of pathetic protest. If six hours, one of stupefied resignation.

'I have the greatest and clearest vision for the transformation of the Indian sub-continent that any man has ever had. I could give India efficiency, profit, learning, and health. But what help do I have with which to implement these visions? The largest collection of chronic snobs, nest-featherers, hair-splitters, nose-pickers, blackguards and cretins ever assembled in one building, and a slow-grinding bureaucracy that dwarfs the Ziggurat of Ur.'

Lucy slowly shook her head. 'Henry – that is still no reason to do everything yourself.'

'For God's sake, Lucy, if I don't do it, who will?'

'You must *teach* them to do it! You must *expect* them to do it! I mean, Henry, this business about the chickens!'

Henry reddened. 'Who told you about the chickens?'

'Walter of course. He said you spent hours trying to balance the household budget.'

'And why not?' Henry protested. 'The cook was charging for literally hundreds of chickens which he never even bought! He returned five hundred and ninety-six as having been bought last month; but when we went to the trades-man, he said that he had sold us only two hundred and ninety. That's a saving of three hundred and six chickens in one month, for goodness' sake!'

'Henry!' Lucy crackled at him. 'You're running India, Henry, not a grocery store! What does it matter, three hundred chickens here, three hundred chickens there? There are three hundred little children lying dead in South Park Cemetery! How about making sure that there are never any more?'

Henry tightened his lips, nervously jerked his head, paced, preened. Then, much more quietly, he said, 'We have to get back to the ball. I'm glad we talked. I'll make a particular effort to talk to you every day. Perhaps then you'll gradually grow to understand that a moral principle is a moral princi-ple, and that it must be scrupulously applied to the petty things as well as the great. If fifty pounds is saved on chickens; if a hundred pounds is saved on wine; if a thousand

491

pounds is saved on misappropriated stores; then every year we will have that much more money to spend on saving children.'

Lucy took hold of Henry's hand. 'Henry, I know. Henry, I *know*. But why do all those petty things have to be done by *you*?'

He tugged his gloves, sniffed, looked away. He probably didn't know the answer to that.

'Perhaps you'd be good enough to save me the last dance,' he said, and went back inside, leaving Lucy alone on the balcony, under the starry Calcutta night, with the insects singing and the bamboo lamps flickering and dipping, and a faint cooling breeze blowing across the *maidan* from the Hooghly River.

But Henry kept his promise to talk to her every day for only three days; and even then he spared her only five or ten minutes, and paced, as if he wanted to be back at his desk. All he could talk about was the commissariat, or dinner arrangements, or what he should wear at next week's dance, or how much he distrusted Colonel Miller.

'I don't like all this moustache-tugging. Have you seen it? Tug, tug, tug; as if it isn't really his. I'm beginning to wonder if it's an insult. That's what the Sikhs do, you know, to challenge each other. They twirl their moustaches, and say, "Hmmm, hmmmm". That's exactly what Timothy Miller does to me.'

On the fourth day he sent Lucy a note with Muhammad Isak his head bearer, begging her forgiveness. '*Please look on me with mercy and sympathy, my dearest sweetheart, and don't be angry.*' Isak watched her with sad dark eyes as she read Henry's complicated excuse. He couldn't see her today. He had a critical meeting with his military secretary. He had just received news that the Russian War Minister intended to strengthen his country's defences in Central Asia and, what was more, to improve the Russian army's capability to attack India. To that end, he had ordered Russia's strategic railways to be advanced southward, toward the very borders of India.

That was on the first day of February. For the next two weeks, Lucy scarcely ever saw him, except at dinner, or their weekly dances, or whenever they were receiving princes or visiting dignitaries. Before February was out, he had instructed Muhammad to set him up a bed next to his office, so that he could stay up working late without disturbing her.

She lay in bed every night, listening to the endless chorus of the insects, and she had never felt lonelier. Sometimes she closed her eyes and pressed her pillow up against her ears, and tried to hear the wind blowing across the High Plains of Kansas, but she never could.

In the last week of February, however, while Lucy was out in the grounds of Government House, supervising the planting of a row of new *peepul* trees along the northern boundary, Henry unexpectedly appeared on their private verandah, and came walking towards her with great purpose along the diagonal paths of faultlessly-weeded Bayswater gravel.

It was an afternoon of glaring sun and black shadows, and sky that was crushingly blue. Lucy was dressed in a fine linen frock of saffron yellow, embroidered with knots of tiny white flowers. A *chaprassi* stood patiently behind her, holding up a huge white fringed parasol, to protect the *burra memsahib* from the slightest hint of the sun. He kept clearing his throat as if he were about to make a speech. Nearly thirty coolies were digging holes for each of the eleven trees, and raising them into position with ropes, while the head *mali* and the under-*mali* and six other *malis* argued and fussed and contradicted each other.

As Henry approached, the arguing and the shouting and the furious rustling of glossy green fig-leaves subsided, until all that could be heard was the sawing of insects and the calling of *koels* and the crunching of Henry's shoes on the gravel.

'Henry!' called Lucy. Her voice sounded peculiarly stifled in the afternoon heat. 'This is a surprise!'

Henry gave her an irrepressible little smile of acknowledgement, and took off his wide-brimmed white hat and wiped around the headband with his handkerchief. 'I've just finished my meeting with Colonel Belloc,' he told her.

'Oh, you mean that architect fellow from the Royal Engineers?'

'That's right.' He replaced his hat and clasped his hands behind his back. He seemed to have made up his mind about something important. 'I must say that it was quite an experience. He's still here, as a matter of fact, I've asked him to stay for dinner. He's taking a bath at the moment.'

'You're smiling,' said Lucy.

'Yes, well, I suppose I am,' Henry admitted. 'Belloc's extremely *individual*. No doubt about it. Miller says that he and his brother once welcomed their Commander-in-Chief to their home in Simla by standing on their heads, on either side of the doorway, like matching pillars; and today, absolutely unabashed about it, he supped his tea out of his cakeplate.'

'But?' asked Lucy. She could sense an agitation in Henry's voice that she hadn't heard since they had left England. It excited her, too – and when the chief *mali* called out plaintively, 'Your Excellency, *ap mai ma-bap hai* (your are my mother and my father) but we are not being able to hold up this tree very much longer!' she scolded, '*Sssh!* Sukumar, do whatever you want!' and waved him away.

Henry said, 'Eccentric or not, Belloc has some remarkable ideas about the restoration of classical Indian buildings. Really – he's quite inspired me!'

'He must have done, to get you away from your desk,' said Lucy. She felt like adding, 'More than *I* can ever do,' but she held her tongue. Henry was in such an ebullient mood that she didn't want to spoil it. He took hold of her hand and swung it affectionately. Under her parasol, in her wide-brimmed primrose hat and her white chiffon veil, she looked delicately blonde and as pretty as a freshly-opened flower.

Henry said, 'I've given myself the afternoon off, as a matter of fact. Cancelled everything! I have some reports on the unadministered areas to look at later tonight, but they shouldn't take long.'

'I'm pleased.'

He looked around the grounds. 'So! These are the fig-trees you talked about!'

'They're beautiful, aren't they? They remind me of great green fans.'

'Make sure the gardeners water them properly. They should flood them twice a day, until they're well-established. They'll probably die, though. They don't like being disturbed.'

'Do you hear that, Sukumar?' said Lucy, defiantly. 'You must water these trees twice every day, plenty of *pani*! If they die, I will never forgive you!'

'Your Excellency *memsahib*, they will be attended as if they are my own children,' the head gardener promised her.

Henry led Lucy away from the fig-trees and across the gardens, with the *chaprassi* and his parasol shuffling after them. The heat made the gravel paths ripple as if Lucy were looking at them through a clear running stream. She almost expected to see trout flickering their way along them.

'You were right, you know,' Henry told her. 'I've been driving myself too hard. Not delegating; trying to be master and dog and tail, too.'

Lucy didn't know what to say. She had the strangest feeling that he was asking for her approval.

'It's Belloc, I suppose,' said Henry. 'He doesn't give tuppence for bureaucracy or protocol. But he cares just as passionately about India as I do, if not more. Since we rule

India, we have the obligation to protect its cultural heritage, that's what he says, even if the poor black heathens can't be bothered to do it themselves. Do you know that the British government spent less than seven thousand pounds last year, protecting India's historical buildings? Seven thousand pounds, for a whole sub-continent! That wouldn't buy a single plasterwork ceiling at Brackenbridge!'

'So what are you going to do about it?' asked Lucy. She couldn't pretend that she wasn't slightly put out that Henry's sudden new surge of ebullience had been inspired by an eccentric sapper – not by passion, nor by romance, nor even by guilt that he might be neglecting her.

Henry was looking tired, but he was no less charming and no less personable, and his appointment as Viceroy had invested him with an almost visible aura of political power which attracted men and women alike, and which attracted Lucy more than ever, even when she thought that she hated him. But her failure to reach to the very heart of him was making her feel a little less adequate and a little more defensive every day. Even when she saw him, she had stopped telling him how much she loved him, because it had begun to sound dangerously like pleading.

Sometimes his endless absences and his emotional stone-walling frustrated her so much that she felt like blurting out everything Sha-sha had told her about Vanessa, and to hell with the consequences. But if she did that, she was sure that he would shut her out completely; and then she wouldn't even have those few moments when he forgot his grinding official responsibilities and his haunting private guilt, and was amusing and gay and loving, as he was today.

She could have beaten her fists against the chest of this Viceroy, and demanded that he let the real Henry free. But how could one woman prevail against Eton and Oxford and Parliament, and eight hundred years of English family history – no matter how beautiful she was, no matter how furious she was, no matter what she was prepared to sacrifice?

Now that they were Viceroy and Vicereine, divorce or seperation were out of the question. Lucy had chosen glory, and so glory she would have to have. But she still loved him; she still needed him; and, more to the point, she still *wanted* him. She refused to believe, as Henry seemed to, that love and duty had to be mutually exclusive. Henry could love her back, if he allowed himself. What he needed was something to release his soul from its self-imposed captivity.

Perhaps, in the end, India would do it, by granting him the magnificent destiny that he had always craved. Perhaps their child would do it, when he was born, by granting him a heritage, and by presenting him with a responsibility that wasn't black, or bureaucratic, or a building.

Lucy knelt by her bed and prayed every night with her eyes tightly shut that Henry would be released; that he would suddenly blink and smile like a man shaken awake from a dream. But every night after she had whispered *amen* she would open her eyes and there in front of her would be her smoothly turned-down bedcover, and an empty marriage-bed, and nothing to look forward to but an hour's reading *Tess of the D'Urbervilles* under the thickly-draped mosquito-nets until she fell asleep, and Nora came slippered and curl-papered to turn out her lamp.

As they reached the house, Henry said, 'If nothing else, Colonel Belloc has at least encouraged me to get my hands dirty. Bricks and mortar, rather than paper! He's suggested that we make an excursion to see some of the buildings for ourselves, so that we can decide what needs to be done to preserve them, and how much we're going to have to spend. I used to do it at Brackenbridge, after all. And this is a far, far more momentous task than the preservation of one English country house.'

They climbed the steps at the back of the house and walked together along the arched verandah, their feet echoing on the marble-flagged floor. The fragrance of flowers and tropical vegetation had somehow become entrapped and distilled in the coolness of the arches, and was so strong that Lucy paused, and took a deep breath, and knew that she would never forget such a fragrance as long as she lived.

'I promised to show you the Taj Mahal,' said Henry, 'So we're going on a tour. We're travelling to Agra and to Delhi, setting off on Wednesday morning next week.'

'Well, that sounds wonderful,' said Lucy.

Henry heard the flatness in her voice. 'You don't seem to be exactly overjoyed.'

'I'm pleased, yes. But it sounds like more work to me. More responsibility.'

Henry grasped her hands and looked brightly into her eyes. 'Lucy, it's just what I need! Something to lure me away from all of my beastly paperwork! Something recreational!'

'Isn't your wife enough to lure you away from all of your beastly paperwork?'

'Of course, my darling. But I can't be selfish. You have your own life to lead, your own pursuits. Your drawing-rooms, your embroidery, your reading, your gardening. I can't expect you to give those up just to entertain me.'

'My God, Henry,' said Lucy.

Henry frowned. '"My God?" What's that supposed to mean?'

'It means, here we are, emperor and empress, but what's become of us?'

'Oh, Lucy,' Henry chided her. 'You're not going to start being temperamental again? Beloved, it's the heat, nothing more. It's your pregnancy, too. It's bound to make you feel disaffected at times. Major French did warn me about it, you know.'

'Oh, did he? Well, well, a medal for Major French! I don't suppose it occurred to Major French that I could be disaffected by trying to live with a husband who nevers stop playing Emperor of India, not even when it's time to go to bed?'

'Lucy, please, there are servants around.'

'There always are. Goddammit, Henry, a women can't even break wind in this house without a *punkah-wallah* rushing in to wave it away.'

Henry was tight-lipped, shocked. 'Lucy, for goodness' sake, you're forgetting yourself.'

'Oh really? Maybe I'm remembering myself. Maybe I'm remembering that I'm a storekeeper's daughter from Oak City, Kansas, who was wooed by a charming and considerate Englishman, and who was innocent enough to think that when she was married, she would be treated not just like a social asset but like a wife.'

'Actually, I think that's quite enough,' said Henry. He turned his back on her, and began to walk away.

'Henry!' Lucy called him, in tight-throated desperation.

Henry slowed, stopped, turned. He took off his hat. 'Lucy, it's no good railing against destiny.'

'I don't care a toot about destiny, Henry. I care about you and I care about me, and I care about my baby.'

Henry stiffly lifted his arm, still holding his hat, and gestured toward the heat-hammered grounds, and to the Palladian rooftops of Calcutta beyond, and to India. 'It's an empire, Lucy, and I'm responsible. I've been responsible for it from the very second I was born.'

'Henry, nobody is *born* responsible for anything. Do you think that I was born to be an empress? You could turn your back on India tomorrow, the same way you just turned your back on me. India wouldn't sink into the sea.'

'I'm not pretending that it would. But I have to do my duty.'

'Why is it so damned important that you do your duty to India and so damned unimportant that you do your duty to me?'

Henry lowered his arm. 'I will make every possible effort to forget that you said that.'

'I hope you don't, Your Excellency. I hope you *never* forget it.'

Henry hesitated, then came back along the verandah. Dark eyes were watching them from all around: eyes that glittered from the garden, from the open doors that led to their private drawing room, from behind the billowing net-curtains of their bedroom suites, from the steps where the Untouchables were sweeping, those whose wealth would be measured only in dogs and donkeys, and whose clothes were the garments of the dead.

'Lucy,' Henry coaxed her, 'the very last thing I wanted to do was to make you unhappy. If I have, then I beg your forgiveness with all my heart.'

Lucy looked away, and said nothing.

'This trip to Agra ... I dearly hope that it will be affectionate, as well as useful. Perhaps you can give me another opportunity to show you how deeply I care for you.'

Lucy swallowed, and nodded. 'I'm sorry,' she said, and she was; although not for what she had said. She was simply sorry that it had been necessary to say it.

'What, then, friends again?' asked Henry.

'I suppose.'

He kissed her cheek. 'Sometimes you sound just like a Kansas storekeeper's daughter.'

She gave him a small tart smile. 'Sometimes you sound just like an Honourable I once knew.'

At that moment, Walter Pangborn came battling his way through one of the breeze-blown curtains, in a cotton suit that looked like a slept-in bed. 'You've had a telegram from London, Lord Carson. It concerns that last dispatch you sent to the Russian War Minister. Yes, *that* dispatch. I think perhaps it would be wise if you could attend to it right away.'

'What? Very well,' Henry replied, without any hesitation whatsoever. 'My darling ... I'll be back as soon as I can. Timothy Miller is taking care of Colonel Belloc for the time being, but it would be nice if you could make yourself known to him before dinner.'

In obedience to their usual parting ritual, Lucy obediently lifted her cheek so that Henry could peck it, and she watched him without smiling as he strode away.

Sukamar the head-*mali* appeared below the verandah as promptly as if he had been hiding in the bushes. 'Your Excellency *memsahib*' — and to Walter, 'pardon me, *hazur*, — is Your Excellency *memsahib* wishing to inspect the tree-planting now? They are all prodigiously straight and up-right.'

'Thank you, Sukamar, but later,' Lucy told him. 'Don't forget to give them plenty of *peenika-pani*.'

'Of course, Your Excellency,' Sukamar told her. 'The inspection will be at your convenience.'

After Henry had walked off, Walter had remained behind, grasping the stone balustrade. He seemed uncomfortable, as if he wanted to tell her something.

'Fine trees,' he remarked.

'Well, I don't know,' Lucy told him. 'Henry's quite convinced they're going to die.'

'Henry's not very optimistic about anything much these days,' Walter replied. He took out a silver cigarette case and asked, 'D'you mind if I smoke?'

Lucy shook her head, and watched him light up. 'Why isn't Henry very optimistic?'

'I don't think I ought to gossip,' said Walter.

'Walter, I'm Henry's wife. I think I have a right to know, don't you?'

Walter winced, and blew out smoke. He hadn't taken very well to India. Since his arrival, he had suffered from constant diarrhoea and he was looking waxy and sweaty and noticeably gaunt, and twenty years older than thirty-one. He kept insisting that he was quite well, but when Elizabeth had first met him at one of their weekly dances, she had remarked to Lucy that he had the unmistakable appearance of a man who would be celebrating Christmas in South Park Cemetery.

'Everything's about a hundred times slower and a hundred times more difficult than Henry expected,' Walter explained. 'He likes action, don't y'know – immediate results! But the ICS wallahs are grumbling and procrastinating and causing all manner of complications because Henry is trying to cut down their paperwork and reorganize their offices. The governors are going their own sweet way as usual, regardless of what Henry tells them. The maharajahs and the swats and the walis are jolly polite, but utterly unhelpful. The residents are utterly unhelpful without even bothering to be polite. And the Foreign Office has been screaming at Henry to stand up to the Russians, and then giving him all kinds of stick when he does.'

Walter paused, and smoked, and then he added, 'Henry came here with such a vision of what he was going to do. India was going to be reformed overnight! But, d'you know, he's like a man in a swamp, the more he struggles, the more he protests, the deeper he sinks. He can manage an awful lot, you know. And he'll change India quite dramatically, I'm sure. But he won't be able to achieve what he came here believing that he could achieve, he'll end up desperately disappointed, and that's the tragedy of it.'

Lucy said nothing for quite a long time. Then she smiled quickly, and nodded her hat, and said, 'Thank you for telling me, Walter. I appreciate it.'

Walter said, 'I hope I haven't –'

'No, no. You were quite right to tell me. And I won't say a word to Henry.'

Walter coughed. 'The Cussboss finds it quite difficult – well, I've known him for years and years, and he finds it quite difficult to admit that he might have made a mistake. India is India, don't y'know, and it has enough graves of disappointed men to prove it.'

He winced again, and coughed.

'Are you all right?' Lucy asked him.

'Oh, it's nothing. Just another twinge.'

'You should take some leave,' Lucy suggested. 'Did Henry tell you that we'll be taking a trip to Agra next week?'

'Yes, he has.' Walter didn't sound very enthusiastic. 'An architectural excursion, no less.' He peered out at the garden, squinting his eyes to focus against the sunlight. His pomaded hair shone, his eyes looked unusually bulbous. 'I expect H.E. will want me to tag along.'

Lucy suddenly realized that Walter's shoulders were shaking. 'Walter, you're shivering! You're not feeling ill again, are you?'

'No, no. It's nothing. I'll survive. We Pangborns were always made of sterling stuff. Unsinkable, that's us!'

Lucy laid a hand on his shoulder. 'I don't know, Walter; maybe you should talk to Major French again. Miss Morris says that even a chill can be ten times more serious here than it would be in England.'

'England!' Walter declared, with cheerful bitterness. 'My God, what I wouldn't give to be sitting in the Marlborough Arms, in Oxfordshire!'

'Do you really want to go back?' Lucy asked him. She hesitated, and then she said, 'You could, you know. Henry would understand. What do they call it? Getting your Blighty-ticket?'

'No, no, of course not,' said Walter. 'We've scarcely arrived, and there's so much to do. Can't let a little tummy trouble get me down. Anyway, look at the time! I've got heaps of accounts to sort out.'

He briefly grasped Lucy's gloved hand, and gave her a flustered smile, and went back inside. Just then, the head *khit* came out and bowed his turbaned head. 'Her Excellency would be caring for some refreshment? *Meta-pani*, perhaps?'

Lucy wasn't particularly fond of the head *khitmutgar*, a portly pale-faced Hindu called Tir' Ram, who was endlessly obsequious, but who managed to convey with his measured squeaky-sandalled walk and his slow, immaculately-accented English that he considered himself somehow superior to everybody around him, European or Indian.

'Just bring me some *cha*,' snapped Lucy – cross with him for no particular reason, except that he was full of himself.

She passed through the floating curtains into the drawing room. Inside, it was shaded and cool and she took off her hat. She saw that the latest issue of *The Illustrated London News* had been laid on the brass-topped table, and she went across to pick it up. The previous issue had contained an article on New York society, complete with photographs, and she had read it again and again, carried back for almost half an hour to the city that Mrs Sweeney had dreamed about; and that had once been hers.

As she flicked through the first few pages, however, she heard a hissing sound like a snake, suh-suh-suh-suh! and she turned in alarm and caught sight of Walter at the end of the corridor that led from the private wing to the state reception rooms. He was crouched tensely against the wall, as if he were battling with a stomach cramp.

'Walter!' she called. Then, when he didn't answer, she hurried up to him, lifting her skirts as she ran, and called shrilly for the servants. '*Koi-hai! Jeldi! Jeldi!* and tell His Excellency!'

'Walter?'

Walter was rigid with agony. Lucy gently took hold of his elbow, and helped him to slide down the wall into a crouched sitting position on the floor. His face was shining with perspiration, his mouth drawn as thin and as tight as scrimshaw.

'Walter, what's wrong?'

'I'm all right, really, I promise you,' he gasped. 'Just the *khrab*, that's all. I'll get over it.'

'We'd better get you to bed,' said Lucy. 'I'll call for Major French, too.'

'I'm quite well, really,' Walter insisted. He relaxed gradually, and straightened out his legs, and took out his crumpled-up handkerchief to wipe his mouth. Muhammad Isak had arrived now, with two other bearers.

'His Excellency will be coming immediately straightway instanter,' Muhammad Isak announced.

'Can you help the *sahib* on to his feet?' Lucy asked him.

But Walter said, 'Wait, Lady Carson, please, just one moment.'

He tilted his head back against the wall, and closed his eyes, breathing evenly but very harshly, as if his lungs were clogged.

At length he opened his eyes, and said, 'There's something I have to ask you. One small favour you could do for me.'

'Of course,' said Lucy. 'Just tell me what it is.'

Walter leaned forward, and spoke to her in the hoarsest of whispers. 'If I do have to go back Home ... you know, because of my health – you will make sure, won't you, that Henry doesn't lose heart.'

'I can't imagine Henry losing heart.'

Walter shook his head. 'He doesn't want you to worry. The only person who knows how hard it is, is me. But if I have to go back Home ... well, then, he won't have anybody but you. Nobody else understands him. Nobody else wants to. And – what I said to you before –'

Lucy waited. 'What is it, Walter? What's wrong?'

'Well, it was something of an understatement. Henry's panicking, almost, if you want to know God's honest truth.'

'But what can I do?' asked Lucy.

Walter coughed, and winced. 'You can't do any more than I've been doing ever since we got here. Give him courage, keep his chin up.'

Lucy grasped Walter's hand. 'Walter, this isn't the time or the place. You're ill, and I want you in bed.'

'I'm all right. Just let me sit here for a moment.'

'Walter, you'll feel better for a rest and some stomach powders. And I'm sure they won't send you back Home. Not unless you really want to go.'

Lucy stood up. 'Muhammad, please help Mr Pangborn upstairs,' Lucy told him. 'And be particularly careful, he's precious to us.'

Muhammad Isak had a thin ascetic face of extraordinary calmness; and the thinnest of black moustaches. 'The *sahib* will be regarded as china,' he replied. 'We have sent a runner for the doctor-major, too, Your Excellency.'

'Good,' said Lucy.

Walter was assisted to his rooms by Muhammad Isak and three more over-solicitous bearers ('pleased to be putting your next foot on to the stair, heaven-born sir.') After he had gone, Lucy stood at the foot of the staircase for a short while, with her hand raised to her mouth, thinking.

Of course it was quite likely that Walter was slightly delirious. Fever came with terrible suddenness in Calcutta. Elizabeth had told her of women who had woken fresh and healthy in the morning, and yet by nightfall the same day had died raving and screaming that their husbands were murderers and that their servants had all turned into monkeys.

But Walter was certainly right about one thing. Since he had arrived in India, Henry had become increasingly diffident and difficult to please. Even if it hadn't yet affected his health, the Augean task of administering India had already begun to take its toll on his morale. It had brought to the surface all of his worst characteristics: his short temper, his chronic inability to delegate, and his fear of showing how much he loved anybody and anything, apart from himself and public duty.

Lucy could begin to see why he had embraced Colonel Belloc's ideas with such enthusiasm. To restore India's architectural heritage would present him with a task of monumental detail; something grand and historic and far beyond the ambitions of anyone who wasn't obsessively seeking ever greater burdens with which to punish himself.

But it was a task at which he could achieve some immediate and visible success.

She had just turned away from the staircase when Henry appeared, closely followed by Timothy Miller. '*Khit* told me that Walter had been taken ill.'

'Henry, he's in a dreadful state. They've taken him upstairs.'

Henry propped his hands on his hips. 'I really can't understand it. He told me this morning he was feeling so much better. He's even put his name down for the polo competition.'

'Henry, he said that to please you. He says everything to please you.'

'Lucy, for goodness' sake!'

'I'm sorry, Henry, but it's true. I'm surprised you didn't see it for yourself.'

Henry looked at Lucy for a long, difficult moment. Behind him, Timothy Miller cleared his throat and tugged at his moustache and tried to appear as if he wasn't there at all.

'You've called Major French?' asked Henry.

'Of course.'

'Then I'll see you at dinner.'

'I thought you said you were giving yourself the afternoon off.'

Henry didn't even look at her. 'I was. Unfortunately Her Majesty's Government had other ideas. Besides –' and here he waited until Colonel Miller had begun to walk back towards the state reception rooms '– there isn't very much joy to be had in giving yourself an afternoon off if there is nothing to do during this afternoon off but to listen to interminable criticisms about how insensitive one is, and what a boorish husband one is, and how one's destiny is not a desiny at all, but simply a job, like ragpicking, or delivering coal, or selling cat's-meat from a wheelbarrow.'

'Henry –' Lucy began; but she could see that he wasn't listening; and that he didn't intend to listen.

'I'll see you at dinner, then,' she agreed. But, before he could turn to go, she added softly, 'And in bed, afterwards, Your Excellency.'

Henry gave her a look which she couldn't interpret. Not

hostile, but very strange, like a man dreaming with his eyes open.

They crossed the arid plains of Bihar, running north-west-wards under a dark carmine sky. The viceregal train was decorated with flags and ribbons, and the lacquer of its carriages gleamed so brightly that it ran along the horizon like the dawn breaking. As the train passed, peasants rose from their dusty fields and watched it, not waving, not moving. Bihar was one of the poorest and most backward states in India, run by wealthy landowners as if it were a feudal country from the Middle Ages.

Lucy sat for hour after hour by the curtained window of their silk-upholstered railway carriage with her chin resting on his hand, staring at the thin figures standing in the grainy morning twilight, just as they stared back at her. Crystal table-lamps set up a soft persistent jingle, like a rich man jingling his money.

When the sun rose higher, she saw that the plains were almost colourless, dun and flat and stretching to eternity. Occasionally the landscape was lit by the scarlet flame of a *mohur* tree, and as evening settled she saw horizontal lines of smoke from village fires, and the last golden veils of dust stirred up by cows. The thick perfume of evening penetrated the carriage's ventilation; and she began to feel the strong romantic pull of the continent of which she could call herself empress.

The train was running on Working Time Bill No. 25, a gilt-edged requisition announcing in printed copperplate that Their Excellencies Lord & Lady Carson were travelling from Howrah Railway Station in Calcutta to Agra Canton-ment on February 23, 1899. It consisted of ten carriages, including a lounge car, a dining car, and a sleeping car, pulled by a locomotive called the *Empress of India*. More than ninety servants and bearers attended to the needs of the viceregal party, which included Colonel Belloc, Timothy

Miller, Walter Pangborn, two secretaries from Government House, two captains from the Royal Engineers, Nora, and eleven officers of the Viceregal Bodyguard, as well as horses, tents, and wardrobes.

Lucy was delighted by Colonel Belloc. He was a small, smart, tightly-corseted man of sixty-one with florid cheeks and huge white muttonchop sidewhiskers. He wore white and canary-coloured coats, and embroidered vests with innumerable pockets, in which he carried a variety of six or seven pairs of spectacles – 'for mighty vistas' – 'for reading railway timetables and the personal columns of *The Times*' – 'for sizing up handsome ladies' – 'for the front stalls of the theatre'.

The first night she had met Colonel Belloc at Government House, he had talked incessantly about the great palaces and temples of India, and how so many of them were collapsing from neglect. 'You should see the palace of Udaipur, at sunset, white marble rising from the middle of a lake. Or Shatrunjaya, which is a temple-city of eight hundred shrines, in the mountains of Gujarat. Golden, with a thousand spires! Or the Temple of Konarak, south of Calcutta, which positively writhes, positively wriggles, with thousands of stone carvings of human carnality. Made me tremble, the first time I set eyes on it! Made my teeth shake! And all I had with me were my hymnbook-reading spectacles!'

On the long train-journey to Agra, Colonel Belloc divided his time between reading the works of the Bengali poet Chandidas, writing minuscule and copious notes in his black-covered notebook, and drinking *burra-pegs* of brandy. In the evening, however, when Henry had retired to his study at the further end of the lounge car to work on his papers, he relaxed in his armchair and talked to Lucy about Tantric Yoga and the Hindu view of life and love.

'Hindus believe, you see, that there is no such problematic thing as "life", with "you" confronting it. The problems of "life" are simply ridiculous games which you yourself have set in your own path. But the Hindus believe that "life" and "you" are one and the same thing – *Tat tvam asi,* "You are It".'

Lucy sat very upright, very correctly, dressed in a lace-trimmed evening gown of ice-blue silk, her shoulders bare, a pearl-and-diamond star shining on the white skin of her bosom. Her blonde hair gleamed in the lamplight. 'What of love, then?' she asked.

Colonel Belloc sniffed sharply and took off his half-glasses. 'Love?' he asked her. He glanced towards the other side of the lounge car, where Walter, pale-faced and gaunt, but reasonably animated, was reading *The Field*; and Timothy Miller was reclining in his chair with his eyes closed, humming Gilbert and Sullivan songs and waving his hand like an orchestra conductor.

Colonel Belloc had obviously sensed that she was doing more than making polite conversation. She was young, she was pregnant. She was married to one of the most powerful men in the British Empire.

'The *Brihadarankaya* says, "When a man is in the embrace of his beloved spouse, he knows nothing as within and nothing as without." In other words, my dear Lady Carson, real love – what the Buddhists call *vajra,* or diamond-like love – is achieved by concentration of both partners not on themselves but on their love.'

He could see that Lucy didn't quite understand him, but he leaned forward and continued gently, 'Lust comes in black and clerical habits, or bustles, crinolines, impenetrable corsets, black stockings and gloves, layers of lacy pettitcoats, leather riding-boots, derby hats and breeches and whips. But love in the Hindu world is nothing, or rather "no thing". When a couple come together they transcend their earthly personalities and become the primordial pair, Shiva and Parvati. He is *purusha,* the witnessing self; she is *prakriti,* the natural world. Each is both.'

Lucy said, 'I *think* I know what you're saying.'

Colonel Belloc leaned back again, and smiled at her

paternally. He wasn't in the least intimidated by her vice-regality. 'This evening, Lady Carson, you think that you know. One day, when you experience it for yourself, you will *know* that you know.'

Very softly, Lucy said, 'I hope you're not trying to suggest that I'm not really in love?'

'Should I answer such a question?'

Lucy hesitated, then nodded. 'Yes, you should.'

Tir' Ram was approaching with a decanter of brandy on a silver tray, balancing his pale bulk against the swaying of the train. She waited while he poured Colonel Belloc-*sahib* another *burra-peg*.

When he was gone, Colonel Belloc said, 'It's hardly my place to judge. But I know from experience that it is always difficult to give of oneself, when one is not at all sure that anything is being given in return.'

'You're very astute,' Lucy told him.

'My nanny always said that I was.'

The viceregal train crossed the border between Bihar and the United Provinces in the small hours of the morning, under a March sky bristling with stars. Lucy slept alone in her bed, on embroidered linen sheets, in the thinnest of linen night-gowns. Henry eased open the door of her sleeping-compartment to say goodnight to her before he turned in, but she was already asleep. He stood beside her bed, looking down at her with a sad and distant expression on his face. Her toes were slightly curled as she dreamed some dream, and he could have touched them and caressed them, but he didn't want to wake her up. Her skin glowed through the linen of her night-gown.

He kissed her curls. More gently, he kissed her cheek. Then he closed the compartment door behind him, and returned to his desk.

Although the United Provinces were watered by the holy river Ganges, they were almost as desolate as Bihar. The Hot

Weather was only two or three weeks away now, and the sun beat down on the plains with all the relentnessness of a brass gong. All that Lucy could see out of the window was beige dust and glaring sunlight.

She spent most of her afternoons lying on her bed, fanning herself and reading a book of Indian poetry that Colonel Belloc had lent her, while the viceregal train clattered and swayed, and the miles sped past beneath her. She was used to endless horizons and interminable train-journeys, but India seemed to unravel forever.

The poems of Chandidas brought her unexpected comfort, and she read them again and again.

> *I have taken refuge at your feet, my beloved.*
> *When I do not see you, my mind has no rest.*
> *You are to me as a parent to a helpless child.*
> *You are the goddess herself, the garland about my neck, my very universe.*
> *All is darkness without you; you are the meaning of my prayers.*
> *I cannot forget your grace and your charm, and yet there is no lust in my heart.*

Late the next evening she was reciting this poem to herself when Henry knocked on her door, and stepped into her compartment. He was wearing shirtsleeves and khaki shorts, and his armpits were dark with sweat. Lucy put down her book and looked up at him.

'You can come in, if you like,' she told him.

'Thank you.' He came into the compartment, and closed the door. Then he sat down on the end of her bed.

'There's something I seem to have forgotten to say,' he told her, with some awkwardness.

'Oh, yes?'

He gave her a boyish, evasive smile. 'Actually, I was talking to Belloc. About India, about buildings, all that kind of thing. And Belloc reminded me that Indian culture is inspired not just by aesthetics but by love. One human for another; and humans for their gods.'

Lucy smiled back at him. 'Belloc sets great store by love, doesn't he?'

Henry picked with his fingernails at the stitching of Lucy's bedspread. 'There was a time when *I* did, too. There was a time when I wrote you poems.'

'So what is it that you've forgotten to say?' Lucy asked him.

Henry's voice was unusually gentle. 'Hundreds of things; on hundreds of occasions. How pretty you looked, on the day we were married. How regretful I feel, for having hurt you so many times.'

He hesitated, and took hold of her hand, twisting her wedding-band around and around. 'Belloc reminded me that I should look on this tour as something of a romantic journey, not only for me, because I feel such an affinity with the classical buildings of India, but for both of us. This is the first time that you and I have travelled anywhere in India as husband and wife, not on official duty. On this journey, my darling, you are more than my Vicereine, you are my bride; and what I have forgotten to tell you is that in spite of all of the burdens I have to bear –'

He stopped, his eyes bright with tears, his mouth tightly-clenched, as if all the pain and the passions that he was unable to tell her about were bursting at last to be released. 'I do love you, Lucy, that's what I've forgotten to say. I worship you. I know that I can be difficult to love. I know that I can be irascible; inattentive; and selfish. I find it hard to express my adoration for you in words, and even harder to express it with my body. But never forget that I am yours, completely, and that I have entrusted you with my heart, for your safekeeping, for ever.'

With that, he leaned forward and kissed her lips, lightly at first, the faintest of brushes. Then he kissed her more urgently, again and again and again.

A surge of warmth and excitement rose up inside Lucy; a feeling that Henry hadn't aroused in her since they had first been married. She clung to him tightly and kissed him fiercely back, tangling her fingers into his hair, tugging up his shirt and his cotton undervest, and feeling the sweaty muscularity of his back.

'Oh, Henry, if you only knew . . .' she whispered, kissing his eyes, kissing his cheeks, kissing and biting at his lips.

'Lucy . . . my darling . . .'

He kissed her again, and then he sat up straight. He was searching for a way to explain something to her. 'Of course we cannot make love.'

Lucy swallowed, and nodded. Major French had warned her that 'husbandly penetration would pose an unacceptable risk to the foetal wellbeing.'

Henry took a deep breath, and allowed his words to stumble recklessly on, in case he lost his nerve and couldn't say anything at all. 'There are ways, however, you see, in which a man can worship a woman . . . Belloc was showing me drawings from the Temple of Konarak, well, not only drawings from the Temple of Konarak but other drawings as well, rooftops, spires, architectural plans – but at Konarak there literally hundreds of sculptures of every conceivable act of love. Erotic, but not lewd, if you understand what I'm saying. Lustful, but not corrupt. The pure enjoyment of the flesh – of a man for a woman, and a woman for a man.'

Lucy said nothing. It was plain that Henry had been highly stimulated by the pictures that Colonel Belloc had shown him; and perhaps that had been Colonel Belloc's deliberate and particular intention. Perhaps Colonel Belloc in his knowing old–India–hand way was encouraging Henry and Lucy to rekindle the natural urges which the pomp and formality of the viceregality had vitiated.

'I adore you, Lucy,' Henry repeated, and lifted the poetry book from the bedcover, and set it aside. He kissed her, and then he lifted aside the bedspread, too.

Lucy said nothing as Henry took hold of the hem of her thin linen nightgown, and drew it up over her knees. He kissed her bare thighs – then, serious-faced, he pulled away the pillow which she had propped behind her back while she was reading, and drew her gently down the bed, until she was lying almost flat.

She felt breathless, and she could feel her stomach tighten. But she allowed Henry to lift her nightgown right up to her breasts. He knelt on the bed, staring down at her naked body with an expression that she had never seen on his face before; reverent, but hungry, too.

He parted her thighs with his hands; and then with his fingers she felt him open the lips of her vulva. Their kissing had moistened her, and her lips parted with the tiniest of sticky sounds, as if they were the wings of a freshly-emerged butterfly. He lowered his head, and with a quake of shock and pleasure, she felt his tongue-tip sliding right down the cleft of her vulva and into her body.

'*Henry* –' she protested, grasping his hair.

But he refused to lift his head; and his tongue ran up and down, exploring every fold and niche. Then he began to lick her faster and faster, his tongue-tip flying across her clitoris in a dazzling *pizzicato*, scarcely touching it, but stirring up a feeling inside her that was deep and dark and tumultuous.

She lifted her head, panting. She watched in excited fascination as the dark red of his tongue flickered between the blonde curls of her pubic hair. His eyes were tight shut, his lips glistened. His face looked like a beautiful mask. Calm, intent, concentrated.

Beneath the bed, beneath the bedroom car, the train-wheels beat out a ceaseless clattering rhythm on the rails, and India flew by.

Lucy lay back, panting even more quickly. Something was happening to her, she hardly knew what. The beating of the wheels and the swaying of the carriage and the flickering between her legs seemed to compress themselves within her head; as if the whole sub-continent of India were being poured like black molasses into a single tin.

'Henry,' she said. Or perhaps she didn't. The train-wheels echoed; the carriage swayed. 'Henry, you mustn't.' But the flickering of his tongue-tip grew faster than ever, and every muscle in her body was locked tight, tighter and tighter, until she felt that she could never move again.

Without warning her body was seized by a spasm that was so violent that she cried out loud, and jerked wildly up and down on the bed, as if she were being furiously shaken by an invisible demon; the Pretas, the Hindu demon of unquenchable thirst and insatiable hunger.

She lay on her side, shivering, weeping; her stomach-muscles rigid, clutching the pillow. She didn't know if she had experienced ecstasy or not. The feeling was beyond description, beyond putting a name to. Perhaps it really had been *vajra,* the diamond-like love.

Slowly she turned her head, and saw Henry standing over her. He stroked her forehead, and then he said, 'Are you all right, my darling? I haven't hurt you?'

'No,' she whispered. 'You haven't hurt me.'

He carried on stroking her forehead. His eyes were gentle but distant.

'Isn't there anything I can do for you?' she asked him, her throat dry.

He smiled at her. 'Not now. It was long overdue – the time for me to do something for you, without asking for anything in return.'

'You're not leaving, though?'

'Not if you don't want me to.'

'Then stay, please,' Lucy begged him. 'Sleep with me tonight. Tell me all about these Indian buildings you want to restore.'

'For a while, then,' said Henry.

The train continued through the indigo-dyed curtains of

the night, across the plain, with the warm dust sizzling between its wheels. At ten o'clock, Nora came into Lucy's sleeping-compartment to ask her if she wanted anything. She found Lucy fast asleep, and Henry sitting beside her, gently stroking her hair with one crooked finger.

Henry said, 'Ssh,' and smiled. Nora hesitated for a moment, and then closed the door behind her, and made her way back to her own sleeping quarters. On the way she met Colonel Belloc, who was standing in the corridor smoking a cigar and watching the night pouring past the windows.

'Colonel,' she nodded.

'Good evening, madam. Have you said goodnight to Lady Carson?'

'Yes, sir, I have.'

'She was well, I trust?' asked Colonel Belloc, with the faintest touch of amusement in his voice.

'Yes, sir, very well. Was there any particular reason why you asked?'

Colonel Belloc blew out smoke, and then admired the glowing tip of his Havana. 'No particular reason. But we must always be concerned for the wellbeing of others, don't you think?'

They descended from their carriage under a flawless turquoise sky, and Henry turned to Walter Pangborn and said, 'Please keep everybody back for just a while. I want to show this to Lady Carson on my own.'

'Of course,' said Walter. He was wearing a small pair of green glass spectacles, and Lucy thought that he was looking distinctly unwell. Colonel Belloc, who had accompanied them in the same carriage, was standing up, his face shaded by his huge Cawnpore Tent Club topi, looking this way and that, and clucking to himself, which he always did when he was considering some architectural problem, or a crossword puzzle, or the price of zinc (his family fortune had been founded on zinc.)

Henry took Lucy's hand, and led her across a wide and dusty forecourt, between rows of unkempt cypress trees, past dried-up water channels and heaps of rubbish and stones and weedy pathways. In front of them was a scruffy bazaar, with sagging awnings and piled-up baskets, and smoky cooking-fires. There was a strong smell of burning lamb-fat and fenugreek. Pi-dogs snuffled around the bazaar, morbidly searching for bones and chicken guts.

Beyond the bazaar, however, something magical rose into the sky. A snow-white palace that lifted itself from the darkness of the cypresses and sparkled like a dream.

'It's utterly pure, utterly perfect,' said Henry. 'I had the same feeling when I first saw you. That mixture of loveliness and sadness which is essential to the highest form of beauty.'

'I can't believe it's real,' said Lucy.

They made their way through the bazaar until they were standing beneath the walls of the Taj Mahal itself. Two officers of the Viceregal Bodyguard followed discreetly behind them; but to the fruit-sellers and pot-menders and curry-cookers in the bazaar, they might just as well have been any other European tourists taking their almost-obligatory *dekho* at the Taj. Henry had insisted that this visit to the Agra presidency should be informal and unofficial, as far as any of their visits ever could be.

Off to their left, the River Yamuna slid calm and turquoise-blue, a mirror to the sky.

Henry took hold of Lucy's white-gloved hand. 'If I could have one wish, it would be that you and I could be entombed in a mausoleum even half as exquisite as this.'

Colonel Belloc approached, in his huge mushroom topi, swishing a fly-whisk against the back of his breeches. 'Well, Lady Carson, what do you think? True love, as expressed in marble and semi-precious stones. Not that many of the stones have been left intact. The sad passion of Shah Jihan for his beautiful Mumtaz Mahal, and Moghul architecture at its very peak. What a combination!'

Henry said, 'The very first thing we're going to do is clear away this bazaar. Then we're going to tidy up the gardens and the forecourts, and dig out the water-channels. The Taj should be reflected not only in the river but in the gardens around it, so that it appears to float suspended in the air.'

'Excellent,' said Colonel Belloc. He turned to Lucy and gave her a curious look, half amused, half knowing. 'Great beauty should always be well attended-to. Those who are careless about great beauty should not be surprised if it falls forfeit.'

'Who said that?' Henry asked him.

'I did,' Colonel Belloc replied.

They returned to Calcutta on the second Friday in March. For Lucy, their journey had been dreamlike and magical; not only because of the strangeness and beauty of the Indian countryside and its palaces and forts and extraordinary temples, but because of Henry's affection and attentiveness. He had stayed almost over-attentively close to her side, and for the first time since they had been married, he had treated her like a virgin bride.

She would never forget the two days they had been taken on a steamboat-trip down the Ganges; past the crocodiles grilling their spines in the sun, and the Indian women gracefully balancing pots of water on their heads. They had floated silently between high wooded cliffs which rose sheer from the water, past ruined Hindu temples, clusters of huts, and beautiful stone *ghats*.

Under the stars that night, sitting on a sofa outside their heavily-furnished tent, Henry had told her, 'Lucy, I shall return to Government House not just refreshed, but inspired. Shah Jihan was inspired by his love for Mumtaz to build the Taj Mahal. I shall be inspired by my love for you to work the greatest changes in India that history has ever seen.'

His words had sounded as grand and glittering as a palace.

But only two days after their return to Government House, Henry began to show signs of the same irritability and the same obsessive working habits that he had travelled to Agra to forget. In the two weeks that they had been away, his paperwork had piled up, and there were countless telegraph messages from the Foreign Office to deal with, as well as urgent memoranda from Kuwait (for which Henry was also responsible) and the North-West Frontier.

He appeared at their weekly ball on Saturday evening, but only for half an hour. He danced with her only once, and said scarcely more than twenty words. There were dark smudged circles under his eyes. On Sunday evening he failed to come down for dinner altogether. He was still at his desk as dawn broke on Monday morning.

Lucy found him at ten o'clock, sitting at his desk with papers spread out in front of him, writing with his right hand and forking up a breakfast of kedgeree with his left.

'Henry?'

He glanced up, finished his sentence, then wiped his mouth with his napkin, 'Lucy? Is anything wrong?'

'Henry, you look dreadful. Have you had any sleep at all?'

'I snatched an hour on the cot. Please don't worry, I'm quite all right. It's just that we've had a few local difficulties up at Landi Kotal. Tribal stuff, nothing to worry about.'

Lucy came and stood beside his desk in her long white dress. He sat tensely, his pen poised, waiting to continue his work.

'Henry, I don't want us to forget everything that happened when we went to Agra.'

He put down his pen as if it were actually painful for him to do so, a sort of rheumatism of the soul. He took hold of her hand, and kissed it. 'We won't forget, I promise you.'

'Then please come to dinner this evening. And please don't stay up all night.'

'I promise.'

At that moment, Henry's valet Vernon appeared, looking as smooth and as insolent as ever. 'Your bath's drawn, Your Excellency.'

'Thank you,' said Henry. He kissed Lucy's hand a second time, although there was no more emotion in it than a post-office clerk franking a letter. 'And don't worry, my darling, I'll be there for dinner, no matter what.'

Lucy left the library, her gown whispering softly on the polished floor. Vernon watched her go, with eyes as bright as a monkey's.

Later that afternoon, while Lucy was resting on a long-sleever on the verandah, and Nora sat beside her embroidering a pillow-slip, Timothy Miller appeared.

'Colonel Miller!' said Lucy. 'What do you think of my *peepul* trees now?'

'Very fine indeed,' Timothy Miller agreed. 'In fact, it's beginning to look like a *pukkah* garden, since you've been here. Lady Elgin didn't get on tremendously well with the head *mali,* that was the trouble.'

'He has to be nagged,' Lucy smiled. 'I'm very good at nagging.'

'Actually, Lady Carson, I have a message for you,' said Timothy Miller. 'I lunched at Peliti's today with the commanding officer of my old regiment. Leonard Ryce-Bennett – you met him about a month ago, splendid chap. But anyway an American chap came up to me and said that he knew you very well from Kansas, and presented his compliments, and asked to be remembered.'

Lucy was astonished. She laid down her fan and said, 'You met somebody from Kansas in Peliti's?'

Timothy Miller opened his wallet and produced a calling-card. 'He said he was sorry for not leaving his card earlier; but he'd been travelling all around India; and he'd only just arrived in Calcutta.'

Lucy took the card with trembling fingers and read the

name on it. *James T. Cullen, Attorney-at-Law*. She looked up at Timothy Miller and she was unable to conceal the astonishment in her voice.

'He's here? He's really here?'

Timothy Miller nodded. 'Talked to him myself, Lady Carson. Bearded chap, tall, well-built. Strapping, you might call him.'

'That's him,' breathed Lucy. 'Did he tell you what he was doing here?'

'Something to do with the United States Diplomatic Service, so I believe. He's staying at Spence's.'

'Then you must send Muhammad Isak to go bring him here!' said Lucy, excitedly. 'Listen, I'll write a note, and you must send two bearers and a half-a-dozen coolies, so that they can carry his bags! He has to stay here at Government House, he must!'

Timothy Miller rang for one of the liveried bearers, who brought Lucy her portable writing-desk. She propped it on her knees, dipped her pen in the crystal inkwell, and wrote,

> '*My dearest Jamie,*
> *While you are here in Calcutta it is positively unforgivable of you to stay in an hotel! You must come to Govt House at once, so that Henry and I can look after you! If you are not here within 1 hr I will come and get you myself!!*
> *Love, Lucy.*'

She flapped the letter in the heat to dry it; then she sealed it and gave it to Timothy Miller. The aide-de-camp took it and bowed his head. But as he did so, he caught the concentrated look of misgiving on Nora's face. Behind Lucy's back, as she shut up her writing-desk, his lips formed the silent question, '*What . . .?*' but before Nora could give him any silent clues, Lucy said, 'Haven't you gone yet, Colonel Miller?'

'*Ekdum*, Your Excellency,' replied Timothy Miller; using

the Urdu word for 'immediately' to hint that she was treating him like a native servant.

When he had gone, Nora continued to frown at Lucy, with her embroidery in her lap. Lucy glanced at her, then turned away – then, when she realized that Nora wasn't sewing any longer, she looked back again.

'Well – what's wrong?' she wanted to know.

'You know what's wrong, your ladyship. You shouldn't have asked Jamie to come here.'

'Why on earth not?'

'You know why not. The Vicereine must always conduct herself in a manner becoming to Her Majesty herself.'

'But I've known Jamie all my life! I'm not going to ignore him, just because I'm the Vicereine. In fact – *because* I'm the Vicereine – I'm going to welcome him all the more warmly, so there!'

Nora shook her head. 'I just hope His Excellency will understand.'

'His damned Excellency is too busy working on his damned papers to worry about anything.'

'Didn't you say that you and his lordship had fallen in love with each other, all over again?'

'We did! In Agra, and in Oudh, and on the Ganges. But where is he now? Back at his desk, back with his papers and his worries and his government reports. Back with his residents and his commissioners and his deputy commissioners and his collectors and his clerks.'

'Lady Carson, it's his life's calling, you know that; and a wonderful calling it is, too.'

'Oh, yes!' said Lucy, bitterly. 'It's wonderful! Pomp and power, parties and balls! But men are all the same, Nora! They tie you up with silk ribbons, and they take your honour, and then they leave you to fend for yourself.'

Nora said nothing for a very long time. Outside in the gardens, it was baking hot, and the gardeners moved along the row of fig-trees, flooding the roots of each of them in turn.

'Well, I suppose it's not my place to criticize,' Nora decided. 'All I can say is that you should have a care. You may not think that Lord Carson is possessive about you; or that he loves you as dear as you believe he should. But I know a man who won't trust women when I see one; and I know a man who's jealous. I also know a man who's been badly hurt by a woman, once in his life, and won't let it happen again.'

'Nora, you're always looking on the black side,' Lucy chided her.

'Yes, your ladyship, perhaps I am. But at least that way I never get disappointed.'

The maroon-varnished carriage which Timothy Miller had sent to Spence's Hotel came rattling briskly through the gates of Government House less than fifty minutes later; and drew up beside the steps. The afternoon rippled with heat. The carriage door was opened by a liveried Indian servant, and the steps put down, and Jamie alighted, removing his double *terai* hat as he did so.

Lucy had asked Muhammad Isak to tell her immediately the carriage entered the grounds; and as Jamie took his first steps up towards the pillared portico, she came sweeping out in her long lawn dress and her wide white hat, and stood at the top of the staircase to greet him.

He came up slowly, his shadow zig-zagging behind him down the steps. He looked as if he had lost weight; but he was as tall and broad-shouldered as she always pictured him, and he was smiling in the same wry way.

'Your Excellency,' he said, bowing his head. His face was deeply suntanned, in contrast to most of the European men whom Lucy knew; who didn't want to look like *chi-chis*. He wore a plain grey suit and a soft-collared shirt, with a bolo necktie. His beard was streaked with fair hair, and made him look much older.

'Jamie! Of all the people I never expected to see in India!' shone Lucy.

'Well, then,' said Jamie, looking around at Government House. Scaffolding had been erected on the north-eastern side already, and the painters were busy with their white-wash. The lazy slap of their brushes punctuated the afternoon heat. 'So you found your cloud-castle at last?'

Lucy looked him up and down. She felt brimful with pleasure. 'You haven't changed! Well, you have, just a little! You're thinner!'

'I've been travelling, that's all,' Jamie told her. 'Hotel food, can't be helped.' He accepted her arm, and she led him into the house; through the cool echoing corridors. He nodded, and said, 'This is quite some place you've got here, isn't it? Befitting, I'd say.'

'You're teasing me,' Lucy protested.

'When did I ever tease you? It's befitting. You always dreamed of living someplace like this.'

His hat was taken, his cane disappeared. Abdul Aziz appeared, on silent slippers, and asked if he would care for tea. They were directed into the small white drawing room next to the main private lounge, where the curtains rose and sighed and fell back again; and a decorated brass dish stood on the low Benares table, heaped with *shakar parre* sugar puffs and the sesame-seed meringues called *tiltandula* and Darjeeling tea for two, in thin palmyra-decorated china that had been specially designed for Government House by Minton. Four servants stood attentively behind their chairs to pass their cups, and to help them to sweetmeats with silver tongs.

'So you're expecting another baby?' said Jamie. 'I didn't know.'

Lucy nodded; and couldn't think why she felt so shy about it. 'Henry's hoping for an heir to all the Carson estates. But how's Sha-sha? She must be so grown up by now.'

Jamie shrugged. 'She's fine. She's very pretty. She has blonde curls and ribbons, just like you. She can sing, she can dance. The last time I saw her was late last fall, just before they sent me out to Manila.'

'I miss her, you know,' said Lucy.

'Well, me too,' Jamie told her. 'But that was the way it had to happen, wasn't it? There's no sense in crying over spilled milk.'

'I wish I could see her, just once.'

Jamie picked up his tea, and sipped it. 'That wouldn't do anybody any good. She thinks that my father and mother are her real parents. It's real strange to see her sitting on my father's knee, and calling him papa, when all the time *I'm* the one she should be calling papa, not him.'

'Did the porters bring your bags?' asked Lucy. 'You can have the Aurangzeb bedroom, it's marvellous, it's all decorated in the Moghul style of the eighteenth century. You have a wonderful view of the garden I've been planting.'

'I'm sorry, I can't stay,' Jamie told her. 'I'm expected in Delhi by the end of the week. Then I have to travel north, to Kashmir.'

Lucy felt sharply disappointed; almost insulted. Since she had become Vicereine, she had been used to having her own way. For Jamie to decline her invitation was almost as unthinkable as turning down the Queen.

'You can stay for just two days, surely? I can have a special train requisitioned to take you to Delhi.'

Jamie shook his head. 'I'm sorry. I have to leave tomorrow. And the people I'm seeing wouldn't appreciate my arriving by specially-requisitioned train.'

'You can stay for tonight, can't you? Come for dinner!'

'Lucy, I'd love to, but no.'

'But why on earth not?'

'It just wouldn't be much of an idea, that's all. There are

times when what's past is best forgotten. Besides which, I don't want to be seen as too much of a pal of the Viceroy.'

'Who on earth's going to think that? And what does it matter, anyway?'

Jamie bit into one of the meringues. 'These are good,' he told her.

'My cook makes them specially for me. He calls them Lady Carson's Wishes. The recipe comes from a Hindu play that was written about two thousand years ago. Eggs, butter, brown sugar, limes, and a grain of sandalwood. But you're changing the subject.'

'I know,' Jamie agreed. He kept his eyes averted. 'But, you know – it's probably best for both of us if we don't discuss the reasons for my being here.'

Lucy widened her eyes in mock-disapproval. 'Can it be that terrible? You haven't taken up with pirates, have you, or opium-smugglers?'

'Lucy –'

But Lucy was irritated now. 'You used to tell me everything down at Overbay's Bend! All of your dreams, everything! So why can't you talk to me now?'

Jamie lowered his head for a while; then looked up at her and said, gently, 'Times have changed, Lucy; and so have we. You're not Lucy Darling any more. You're Her Excellency Lady Carson of Brackenbridge, the Vicereine of India.'

'I know that,' Lucy retorted. 'But what are you?'

Jamie pulled a wry face. 'Me? I'm not a lord or a viceroy or anything. I'm just a man who suddenly woke up.'

'What am I supposed to understand by that?'

Jamie sat back in his chintz-covered armchair. 'You remember all that legal work I was doing, on Red Indian affairs? I made quite a reputation for myself in Washington. My crowning achievement was when I dispossessed the Comanche around Spanish Peaks. No trouble, no fighting, they just folded their tepees and off they went. The government liked the way I could soft-talk the Indians into giving up their territories without provoking Little Big Horn the Second! "Can-Do Cullen", that's what they called me. It became my speciality, I guess: the legal rights of indigenous populations. In other words, how to gyp natives out of everything they've ever been entitled to. I was offered a job by Hector McAllen, doing legal work for the US Diplomatic Service. Good job, too, travelling the world, plenty of expenses. All I had to do was dispossess unsuspecting heathens wherever I found them, without breaking the letter of the law, or the solemn promises of Uncle Sam.'

A *khit* came forward, as silent as a shadow, to pour Lucy a second cup of tea. Lucy said, cautiously, 'Jamie, you sound so bitter.'

'No, I'm not bitter,' Jamie assured her. 'I've woken up, that's all. While I was working in an office, I didn't realize that the law had any particular connection with justice. But last year I went out to the reservations and saw some of those Comanche and Sioux families being moved off their homelands, in the middle of one of the coldest winters in living memory – old people, women, little children – and all because of legal work for which *I* had been personally responsible. Back at my office, in Manhattan, my boss had clapped me on the back, and given me a big cigar, "Have a cigar, Jamie, by thunderation you've earned it!" and a pay hike, too. He never saw those tiny babies in the snow. I thought of Sha-sha, then, and I thought of you; and I thought of me. We suffered, yes, when times were thin. But we never suffered like those Red Indians suffered. You wouldn't even know the meaning of the word suffering unless you saw what they had to endure. And we never suffered because of God-fearing human rapacity, and God-fearing human greed; and laws that twisted this way and that like the Saline River.'

'So what are you doing here in India?' asked Lucy.

'You could say that the wind just blew me this way. I was in Manila just a couple of months ago.'

'Manila, that's in the Philippines. You're fighting a war in the Philippines. Well, the United States is.'

'That's right,' said Jamie, 'and I was part of it. It was my duty to draw up papers that proved beyond a shadow of a legal doubt that the new Aguinaldo government was unconstitutional, and that the Spanish were still the legal administrators of the Philippines.'

Lucy was perplexed. 'But why would you do that? Surely the United States is at war with Spain.'

Jamie gave her a ground-glass smile. 'That's the whole point. The United States is at war with Spain, so if the Philippines still legally belong to Spain, we have the legal right to invade the Philippines and to shoot anything that moves. It's the old story, Lucy. I was supposed to be preparing legal pontifications in support of justice and human rights, but all I was doing was protecting the United States and its sugar industry.'

Lucy sat back in her chair. She had spent enough time with Henry and his political colleagues to understand that this was dangerous talk. It had been the golden conviction of every imperial administrator from Clive in India to Andrew Jackson in America that the inferior races 'have neither the intelligence, the industry, the moral habits, nor the desire of improvement which are essential to any favourable change in their condition' and that 'they must necessarily yield to the force of circumstances.'

To suggest that natives had rights of their own was close to blasphemy.

Jamie brushed meringue-crumbs from his lap, and then he said, 'One morning in Manila I was walking to the office and I came across a *negrito* woman lying in the gutter. Very black, very ugly, her dress pulled right up to her waist. She had a bullet-hole in her forehead and flies were crawling in and out of the bullet-hole like clerks crawling in and out of a law office.'

He didn't even look to see how Lucy was reacting to what he was saying. It was all too sharp in his mind; he had walked past this woman and she had actually been lying there, dead.

'What did you do?' whispered Lucy.

'What would you have done, if you had seen for yourself the effects on one poor woman of high-minded colonial rule? A bullet in the head, is that what it all amounts to? A gutter, and nobody even to pull your dress down and give you that last token of human respect? I'll tell you what I did: I kept on walking, right past the office door, and down to the docks. I caught the next steamer that was going, and I spent Christmas alone at the Gia-Long Hotel in Saigon, with *thit bhot to* for lunch, and nobody to sing carols with.'

He stood up; and walked across the drawing room to the beige-shaded window. Lucy was conscious that there was something in his posture which had changed. Maybe it was experience. Maybe it was age. Maybe it was harsh reality; and the burdens of fatherhood. Not just to a child; but to his own ideas. Men with no guilt never stoop their shoulders, not the way that Jamie was stooping.

'I travelled to Bangkok; and then to Rangoon, and up-country to Pyinmana and Mandalay; and then I read that Sir Humphrey Birdwood was giving a series of lectures on colonial law, here in Calcutta. It wasn't much of an excuse to come here; but it was good enough. And so I came.'

'You knew that I was here,' said Lucy, quiet as milk.

Jamie said nothing; but she could tell by the way he held his head that he had thought of her; and that he had been drawn to India as much by wanting to see her as he had by his conscience.

'Are you sure that I can't persuade you to stay?' she asked him, in an accent so English that she noticed it herself.

'No,' he replied, 'I don't know why it is, but life always seems to conspire to put us on different sides. You have your destiny; I have my conscience. Oil and water, I'm afraid, immiscible.'

Lucy said, 'Do you feel the same way about me now as you always did?' She hoped that the smooth-faced servants standing attentively behind their chairs wouldn't be able to follow what she meant.

Jamie tightened his mouth, didn't speak, but nodded.

'I feel the same way, too,' Lucy told him, trying not to sound breathless.

Jamie turned quite suddenly and stared at her. His expression was dark and hard: the expression of somebody who doesn't want to be played with. 'Are you serious?' he demanded. 'You're Empress of India, in everything but name. You have three hundred millions of people bowing down in front of you. You're pregnant with Henry's first child.'

Lucy took a deep breath. She felt giddy, and too hot; and even the ceaseless stirring of the gathered-muslin *punkahs* did nothing to make her feel any cooler. 'You and I grew up together. Nothing can change that. You and I know how Sha-sha came to be born, and nothing can change that, either.'

Jamie came over and held out his hand and smiled. 'Just like I said. No use crying over things that can't be helped.'

Lucy pressed her napkin against her mouth, and told herself strictly that she wasn't going to cry, no matter what.

Jamie watched her for a few moments, and then said, 'I think I'd best be going now. Is there someplace private, where we can say goodbye? Someplace – well, you have a whole herd of servants, don't you? It's kind of difficult to be yourself, with half of Bengal looking on.'

Lucy took Jamie's hand and climbed to her feet. 'Come to my sewing room.'

Immediately, the servants drew back Lucy's chair, and prepared to accompany her wherever she wanted to go, in case she should need something to sit on, or drop her handkerchief, or decide she was too cold, or too hot, or felt like a stroll in the garden. But Lucy raised her hand, and said, 'That will be everything,' and they bowed their turbaned heads, and said, 'Thank you, Your Excellency *memsahib*,' and let her leave the room, although their proprietorial anxiety was as thick and as cloying as vanilla *halva*. They didn't take their eyes away from Jamie until Lucy had swung the sewing-room door closed behind them.

In the buttermilk sunlight of a Calcutta afternoon, Lucy grasped Jamie's hands, and looked up into his face, and saw the whole of their childhood there, as country-simple as a book, but all of his years of work besides. She saw the hours of ambitious lawyering that Jamie had undertaken, to get himself to Washington. She saw the pain, and the disillusionment, and the care.

She loved him, she knew she did. She always had. But he wondered how much of her love was memories, and nostalgia; and whether it was easy to love him now because she wanted for nothing, and because no matter how preoccupied Henry might be, she was always well-cared-for.

Nora had once remarked, 'It's always the well-cared-for women who stray.'

Jamie held her in his arms, and she felt his unaccustomed beard against her cheek. But there was nothing unfamiliar about the way he embraced her, and when she kissed him, they kissed as deeply and as caringly as two people who had always been lovers; sharing their hearts, even if they had rarely shared their beds.

They kissed again. They didn't need to speak. If they had spoken, it could only have been to say goodbye, or to regret the circumstances that had kept them apart, and always would. Lucy closed her eyes. The hardness of her pregnant stomach pressed through her dress against the hardness of Jamie's penis. Their kissing had immediately aroused him; so that his grey trousers strained stiff. But their affection for each other was so strong that neither of them drew away. His excitement was a fact, just as Lucy's new baby was a fact, and they accepted both with silent – even mischievous – delight.

When their kisses had lingered; and died; and lingered again, they stood in the centre of the room still holding each other tightly.

'You'll be careful, won't you?' Lucy whispered, in a throaty voice.

'I'll be careful.'

'You won't die for any lost causes?'

Jamie squeezed her even more closely. 'Justice for people who have never been given justice before is never a lost cause.'

Lucy lifted her head. It was then that she saw in the mirror on the opposite side of the sewing room that the door behind her was slightly ajar, and that a pale-faced figure in a dark suit had been watching them steadily from the corridor outside. She turned, and gasped, and instantly the figure vanished, but she was quite sure that it had been Vernon, Henry's valet.

'What's wrong?' Jamie asked her. 'Lucy – what's wrong?'

She pushed his arms away. 'You'll have to go! Please, Jamie, you'll have to go!'

'I don't understand, what's wrong?'

'Somebody was watching us. One of the servants.'

'So what if they did? They wouldn't dare to say anything, surely?'

'It was a European.'

'All the same.'

'Jamie,' Lucy flustered, 'I'm Vicereine! And if you *knew* what Calcutta is for scandal!'

Jamie was about to protest, but when he saw the anxiety in her eyes he lifted both of his hands in resignation, and said, 'Very well. I have to go anyway.'

Lucy opened the sewing-room door wide and called for the servants.

'I'm sorry,' said Jamie. 'I just hope you don't have any trouble.'

'Will you write?' she asked him. 'At least let me know where you are.'

'I'll try,' he told her. 'I'm not sure that my friends are always going to be too happy about it.'

'You and I weren't put on this world to make our friends happy,' smiled Lucy, with tears in her eyes.

'Trouble is,' Jamie replied, 'we weren't even put on this world to make each other happy.'

Vernon's approach came much sooner than Lucy had expected. Jamie had been gone for only a half-hour, and she was sitting on the verandah with a glass of tonic water and fresh lime juice, when he passed through the floating gauze curtains like a shadow, and was suddenly there.

'Lady Carson?' he asked her, his hands clasped behind his back. 'I was wondering if I might have a word.'

Lucy had always considered Vernon to be coarse. His East End accent, she supposed. But when he approached her this afternoon she realized that she had quite dramatically misjudged him. His grey suit was perfectly tailored. His hair was cut with the precision that only a straight-razor and an utterly steady hand could achieve. Only his eyes reinforced the threat implicit in his voice. They were like the eyes of an intelligent but soulless primate; the eyes of a man who hit women. He moved with suppressed athleticism, which made him appear even more threatening. You knew that if he hit you, he would hurt you.

'How can I help you?' Lucy asked him; in a tone that tried to suggest that she wouldn't lift a finger to help him, even if she could.

Vernon pulled a face. 'I don't know, your ladyship. I think it's more like a case of *me* helping *you*.'

Lucy raised her eyes. 'And how exactly do you propose to do that?'

'Born and bred to be useful, your ladyship, that's me. Keep me mincers peeled, keep me lugs open. Knowing what's what, and who's doing what, and who wiv; that's John Vernon's particular stock-in-trade.'

'I thought you were a gentleman's gentleman, not a one-man newspaper.'

'Same thing, your ladyship. Part of the job. I mean, what use is a gentleman's gentleman if he can't serve his gentleman in every way there is; from polishing his toecaps to brushing his hats; and letting him know what's what, from time to time. I've always made it my business to tell my gentlemen everything what passes my way; from the favourite runners at the races to the latest intelligence about who was going bankrupt and who was misbehaving themselves wiv whom.'

Lucy said, with as much calmness as she could manage, 'What do you want?'

Vernon feigned surprise. 'What do I want? My dear Lady Carson, I never wanted nothing. Only to serve Lord Carson to the best of my ability and to find favour, if at all possible, wiv yourself.'

Lucy swung her legs off her long-sleever. 'Oh, come on, Vernon, what do you want? Five pounds? Ten pounds? A bottle of brandy?'

Vernon looked at her with those black soulless eyes; and then he slowly cracked an apeish smile. 'Fair dos, if you're going to play it so straight. Two hundred rupees a month, that would do it.'

'And how on earth do you think I can pay you two hundred rupees a month? I don't even know what a rupee looks like, if you want to know the honest truth.'

'It's quite all right, your ladyship. All you have to do is sign a chit. A little scrap of paper, promising to pay the bearer two hundred rupees. That'll be just as good as money.'

Lucy stared back at him and hated him so intensely that she could have stood up and slapped him and spat in his face. Perhaps if she hadn't have been pregnant she would have argued with Vernon, fought him. Perhaps if Henry hadn't been so unpredictable, she could have told him to do his worst. But she felt physically unbalanced and emotionally defensive. She wasn't at all confident that Henry would believe that whatever she felt for Jamie was nothing compared to her need to be wealthy, her need to be great, her need to hold the balance over other people's lives. She wasn't at all confident that she believed it herself.

It was the most tormenting of paradoxes. She had achieved greatness; she had achieved all the social influence that any woman could dream of. Yet here in front of her was another smiling man, nothing but a servant, making a victim of her.

She looked at Vernon and knew where she had seen such eyes before. They were the eyes of Uncle Casper; and of all the other Uncle Caspers; men who ran through the understructure of civilized society like rats through a derelict building.

She walked through to her drawing room, sat at her desk, took out a sheet of notepaper and unscrewed the cap of her Chinese-enamel pen. *Please pay bearer on receipt of this two hundred rupees,* and signed it.

Vernon accepted it with a nod, and blew on it steadily to dry the ink. 'I overheard Colonel Miller saying that your ladyship was a most extraordinary Vicereine. Must say that I have to concur wiv him, wholehearted-like.'

That night, however, she dreamed that she was back in Port Said; being jostled by crowds, under a thunderous sky. She was pushing her way through hundreds of hunched-up women, their faces completely covered with black veils. They knocked her with their shoulders and nudged their heads against her, quite violently, like undisciplined puppies. She was crossing the pavement towards Simon Artz's emporium when a dark figure flung himself at her. She tried to shout out, but her voice sounded strangled. A sword flashed, and the figure's face was cut completely in half.

There was no blood, only two halves of a head lying on the pavement like a sliced-open watermelon. Both halves were smiling at her. One half was Uncle Casper; the other was Vernon.

She sat up in a sweat, her sheets knotted, screaming for Nora.

The following morning, Henry came into the drawing room just before luncheon and stood fanning himself with a copy of *Punch*.

'Anything wrong?' Lucy asked him.

'Yes, as a matter of fact. *Punch* says that I believe myself to be divine, which is probably true; and we're losing Walter. He was very sick again last night, and Major French says he ought to be sent back Home.'

'Poor Walter!'

'Yes, and poor me, too. I shall miss him very sorely.'

Lucy said, 'You shall have to depend on me a little more.'

'You're expecting our baby. I can't make any more demands on you than I do already.'

'You can't make any fewer.'

Henry frowned. 'What do you mean by that?'

'I'm not quite sure. I think I'm beginning to understand something about men, that's all.'

'Oh, yes!' Henry laughed. 'And what great insight have you come up with that will dazzle the world and impress us all?'

'I'm not sure how to put it. But it's all to do with love and hatred.'

Henry sat down on the arm of Lucy's chintz sofa, took hold of her hand, and kissed it. 'Surely you haven't come to believe that I hate you?'

'No, I don't. But you hate the fact that you love me. It makes you feel weak. It makes you feel obliged. You always seem to think that you have to be punished for loving me. You keep trying my patience, and trying my love – as if you're deliberately provoking me into lashing back and saying something cruel to you, something unloving. Then you'll be able to forgive me, and feel like the great benevo-

537

lent Sahib; and in secret you'll feel guilty because you made me beg your forgiveness, and you'll wallow in your guilt like you always do.'

Henry slowly lowered his head. A muscle worked in his cheek. Stiffly, he released Lucy's hand. 'You know, Lucy – I'm beginning to question whether you and I are suited.'

'There you are,' she challenged him. 'Doing it again!'

'Doing what again?' Henry demanded.

'Trying to make me feel guilty! Well, I won't!'

Henry tossed the copy of *Punch* across the room, so that its pages fluttered and burst out of its spine. 'Sometimes, my dearest, you're quite impossible. Will you dress for luncheon, please? We're entertaining the railway people today, as you probably know.'

'Henry!' Lucy called, as he marched off towards the door.

Then, 'Henry!' she repeated, her voice a little higher-pitched.

He turned, cross. She smiled at him with bright eyes. 'I love you, Henry, in spite of all.'

Walter came in to say goodbye. He was very thin; his face as yellow as the old newspapers you discover under twenty-year-old linoleum. He insisted, however, on walking unaided by his bearers, and in bowing to Lucy as a formal farewell.

'Goodbye, Walter,' she told him, taking his hand.

'You won't forget what I said? Won't let him lose heart?'

'No,' she whispered.

He nodded. 'Jolly good, then. I'd better be off. Nothing else I can do, is there?'

'Perhaps one thing,' said Lucy.

Walter raised an eyebrow.

'It's just that I was talking to a young ICS wife the other day . . . and it seems that she was seen by one of her servants doing something indiscreet.'

Walter leaned his hand against the table to support himself. 'Oh, yes? May I ask *how* indiscreet? It does happen, you

538

know, especially in hills, before the men go up; and in the Hot Weather.'

Lucy tried to smile. 'Not *very* indiscreet . . . a mistake, more than an indiscretion.'

'I see. So what are you asking?'

'Well, the fact of the matter is that her servant is demanding money not to tell her husband. Blackmail, I guess you'd call it, so that that *sahib* won't find out.'

Walter coughed, and narrowed his eyes. 'Is this an *Indian* servant?'

'I'm really not sure.'

'It doesn't sound like the kind of thing that an Indian servant would do. Not demand money from a European woman. They're too proud of their jobs; even the lower-caste servants. And they'd be too damned scared of the consequences if they were caught.'

Lucy said, 'I really have no idea. This young woman – she was, well – she was quite upset.'

Walter took out his handkerchief, and dabbed thoughtfully at his turkey-shrivelled neck. 'I don't know. The proper thing to do is to inform the police. But I suppose this young lady isn't keen.'

'She'd rather not.'

'I can't help you, then,' said Walter. 'I know what *I'd* do, if I were the young lady involved. But it's not a course of action I could cheerfully recommend, not to anybody.'

'What would you do?'

Walter gave a feeble grin, and cut his throat with his finger. 'There are plenty of obliging fellows in India, who would silence a chap like that for ever; and probably charge half what he's asking to keep silent now. That's India for you. Information is expensive, but life is extremely cheap.'

He hesitated, swayed on his feet, still grinning. 'But whatever you do, don't tell her I told you. Can't have young ladies assassinating their servants – now can we?'

★

On the last day of March, Lucy held a 'drawing room' for the wives of junior ICS officials. She always enjoyed the company of the younger women, even when they were stiff and shy (which they usually were). She could sympathize with their uncertainty: not only about the strangeness of India, but about the men who had brought them out here.

Most of them were fiercely snobbish, and all of them considered Indians to be racially and culturally inferior. But Lucy knew from her own experience how much of their prejudice was rooted in fear and ignorance. She also knew from meeting some of Elizabeth's friends that while the new arrivals seemed arrogant and reserved, they would eventually give almost everything to India. Their love, their loyalty; quite often their happiness, too; and their children's lives; and their own lives, too.

It wasn't easy for a young middle-class English girl to come out to India and run a household of six or seven servants, especially when she couldn't speak Urdu, and it had been firmly impressed on her that it 'wasn't done' for her to try.

It was an exceptionally hot day, even for the end of March, over ninety-five degrees, and all the shades were drawn, so that the Tiffin Room was bathed in a gloomy subaqueous light. The English ladies always shut out India, protecting themselves from its heat and its language and its customs. One of the young women was telling Lucy that she was worried about her garden. She always planted nasturtiums and phlox and chrysanthemums in the Cold Weather, and they grew wonderfully, but as soon as the Hot Weather started, they shrivelled to nothing. 'Every year, you see, you have to start all over again.'

Another young woman with a complexion like fresh milk sprinkled with cinnamon said that she found it difficult to get used to the idea of so many servants. If she dropped a spoon on the floor, she was not allowed by her servants to pick it up. If she went out in the garden, simply for a stroll, a *chaprassi* would patiently follow her around with a deck-chair, in case she should take it into her head to sit down. And when she had tried to plant some calendula seeds with a tiny little fork and trowel, an entire deputation of *chaprassis* and *babus* had called on her husband that evening and said that digging by the *memsahib* was not allowed. A dozen coolies would be summoned in the morning to do the digging.

Lucy had grown used to Nora and Etta's attentions for a long time now, but she still found it difficult to accept the constant and detailed care which she was given by their Indian servants. She was expected to do nothing for herself whatsoever. Not to wash herself, nor dress herself, nor brush her hair, nor lace up her shoes. Whenever she left Government House, even for a shopping trip to Chowringhi with Elizabeth, it was always in the company of twenty or thirty people, including four officers of the Viceroy's Bodyguard.

She discovered, too, that the Indian caste system was even more rigorous than the European order of precedence. Only yesterday morning, she had gone out to find a dead bird lying on the ceremonial steps. She had asked a *mali* to remove it, but the *mali* refused, because it was forbidden for him to touch dead birds. She had asked the *mali* to call for the *masalchee*, but he also refused to touch it. Then she had called for a sweeper, who usually cleaned out the lavatories, but he had refused, too. In the end, they had been obliged to send for a low-caste *dome* boy from the bazaar, and he had removed it.

Lucy found it frustrating and unreal; as if she were being deliberately prevented by some elaborate conspiracy from making any contact with India herself. You may rule, *memsahib*, but you may not touch.

She was listening politely to a young wife telling her that she was trying to learn Urdu, because she had nobody to talk to during the day, except for her servants.

'I said to the cook, *kab* the sahib *yeh chiz dekhenge,* he will go *gonga.*'

As Lucy nodded and smiled, she saw Etta hurrying across the Tiffin Room, followed by Muhammad Isak and two other bearers. 'Excuse me,' she said to the young wife. She could tell at once that something was wrong. Etta was white and perspiring.

'Lady Carson, it's Nora.'

'What's wrong?'

'I'd rather not say within earshot, ma'am.'

'What's happened to her?' Lucy demanded.

'She's ill, ma'am.'

'Ill? She was all right this morning.'

Etta nodded and grimaced at the young wife who was trying to learn Urdu. 'It'd be better if I told you outside, ma'am; if you can spare just a minute.'

'Well, all right then,' said Lucy, a little irritably, and followed her into the Marble Hall.

As soon as they had passed the screens that separated the Tiffin Room from the Marble Hall, Etta flustered, 'She's terribly sick, your ladyship. They've called for the priest.'

'The priest? What for?'

'The last rites, your ladyship.'

'You mean she's going to *die?* How can she die? She dressed me this morning. She was perfectly well. She said she wanted to do some shopping.'

Tears began to stream down Etta's face. 'We went to the bazaar. We bought some silk and some beads and some musk. Then I met an old friend of mine from when I was here before, Katherine Anderson, who works for the Army & Navy, and all I wanted to do was to find out the latest *khubber.* And Nora wandered off on her own.'

'Yes?' Lucy demanded. 'Then what?'

'When I found her again – when I found her – she'd only bought herself some some *mottongost* from one of the stalls.'

'Some *what?*'

'Some *mottongost*, mutton on a stick; and she'd eaten it. I told her not to eat anything in the bazaar, but she said it smelled so good.'

Lucy didn't want to hear any more. She told Etta to take her straight to Nora's bedside.

'I'm sorry, your ladyship. Major French says no.'

'Then I want to see Major French.'

'Yes, your ladyship.'

Major French was already waiting for her in her private drawing room. He was grey-haired, very refined-looking, with long white hair that was combed back from his temples, and a large nose that was patterned with broken veins. For a man concerned with keeping people alive, his eyes were chilly grey and extraordinarily dead.

'Good afternoon, Your Excellency', he said, rising to his feet.

Lucy said, in a voice as empty as an embroidery frame, 'I'm told that my maid is going to die.'

Major French displayed a variety of shrugs.

'What's wrong with her?' Lucy insisted. 'She was perfectly well this morning, before she went shopping. Etta said that she'd eaten some meat or something.'

'I regret that she fell into a trap so often waiting in this country for the unsuspecting novice,' said Major French. 'You are obviously aware that we have been suffering something of a small epidemic in Calcutta recently, and it appears that your maid has become its latest victim.'

'Can I see her?' asked Lucy, swallowing back tears.

Major French shook his head. 'Not recommended, I regret, especially for the Vicereine.'

'She's my friend,' Lucy told him. 'Not just my maid, *my friend*.'

'You wouldn't count her as friend if she passed on *cholera morbus*,' said Major French.

'She has cholera?'

Major French nodded. 'The classic symptoms, I regret.

Painless but copious diarrhoea, with simultaneous vomiting. Blueish skin, hoarse voice – the notorious *vox cholerica* – terrible feelings of thirst. To be absolutely blunt, Lady Carson, I doubt if she will last the afternoon.'

Lucy found that she was shaking. 'I want to see her,' she said.

'I really can't sanction it,' said Major French, trying to smile. 'The *burra sahib* would have my guts.'

'I want to see her,' Lucy repeated.

'Lady Carson, I really must insist that you don't'

Lucy turned to him, full-face, and blazed, 'How would you like to posted back out to the *mofussil*, major? Somewhere really, really remote?'

Major French shrugged and nodded some more. 'Of course, if Your Excellency puts it that way . . .'

He led her upstairs, to the third floor where Lucy had never ventured before, to Nora's bedroom. Their footsteps echoed on the bare oak boards. Nora's room was whitewashed plain, with a simple iron bed and a plywood locker. On top of the locker was a framed photograph of Nora's mother and father, hardbitten folk with wrinkled faces, frowning at the camera with deep distrust. On the wall above her bed hung a crucifix. The blinds were drawn, the room was stiflingly hot. Nora lay on her back, hollow-eyed, purple-skinned, and startlingly wrinkled, an indication of how much her body fluids had already drained away.

She was being attended by one of the *ayahs,* and a *punkah-wallah* was fanning her with a wide hand-held fan to keep her cool.

'You see she's very seriously ill,' said Major French. 'I must advise you not to approach too closely. You are wearing a cholera belt, I presume?'

Lucy whispered, 'Yes.' On Etta's advice, she always wore the white flannel belt that was supposed to give her protection against cholera; though nobody had yet been able to explain how it prevented one from catching a disease that was transmitted through the air like an invisible poison.

'All the same,' warned Major French. 'Not too near, please, for your own sake.'

Lucy rapped lightly at the door. 'Nora?' she called. 'Nora, it's Lucy! Can you hear me?'

Nora licked her lips with a tongue as dry as a lizard's, and coughed. 'Is the priest here yet?' she whispered. 'Is that the priest?'

'It's Lucy.'

'Who is it? Lucy? I've know so many Lucies. You're not Mrs O'Halloran's Lucy, by any chance? Or Lucy from the post office?'

'Nora, it's Lucy Carson.'

Nora was silent for a long time, still trying vainly to moisturize her lips, still trying to think. 'I known so many Lucies,' she repeated.

At that moment, there was a bustling sound along the corridor, the quick rip-rapping of men's shoes, and the jingling of medals and uniform. Lucy stepped closer to Nora's bed, and stood right at the very end of it, so that Nora could see her more distinctly. Nora frowned at her, and tried to focus, but she was very close to death now. Major French had given her tincture of Kino, and plenty of boiled water; but the cholera had taken hold of her so rapidly that there was very little else he could do.

'Nora,' Lucy called her. 'Nora, it's Lucy.'

'I knew a Lucy Darling once,' whispered Nora. 'She was such a pretty girl . . . whatever happened to Lucy Darling?'

'That's me,' said Lucy. 'I'm Lucy Darling!'

'*You're* Lucy Darling? You can't be Lucy Darling! Lucy Darling is dead!'

Lucy approached Nora and took hold of her hands. 'Oh, Nora. You're so cold!'

'No, no,' Nora contradicted her. 'I'm sleeping, that's all. I'm dreaming.' Then she looked up at her and smiled faintly, and said, 'You *are* Lucy Darling, aren't you? You really are!'

Lucy leaned forward and kissed her forehead. 'Yes, my dearest Nora. I really am.'

It was then that Major French grasped Lucy's arm, and respectfully but firmly pulled her away. She turned to protest, but then she saw Henry standing in the doorway, his face stony. Behind him stood Colonel Miller and two junior ADCs.

'I think you'd better return to your drawing room,' Henry told her, coldly. 'You have more than a hundred ladies in the Tiffin Room, all milling around with not the slightest idea whether they should stay or go.'

'Damned *moorghi-khana* down there,' added Colonel Miller, sarcastically.

With simplicity, Lucy said, 'Nora is dying.'

Henry glanced towards the bed. 'Don't you think I can see that for myself? *Cholera morbus.* And that is an even more convincing reason why you shouldn't be here.'

'Henry, Nora was more than a maid.'

'In two hours, my darling, or even less, she will be nothing at all but human clay.'

'Henry, she was my *friend!*'

Henry stepped into the bedroom himself, and took hold of Lucy's arm. She tried to struggle but he gripped her too tightly. She was watched with embarrassment by Colonel Miller and the junior officers as Henry pushed her past them, and out into the corridor. Once she was outside, however, she was able to wrench herself free.

'Who the hell do you think you are?' she snapped at him.

'Your husband, and the Governor-General of India,' Henry retorted.

'In which order?'

'For God's sake, Lucy, you're Vicereine!'

'Exactly,' Lucy told him. 'I'm Vicereine and my friend is dying in that room and I want to see her to say goodbye.'

'Do you have any idea how infectious she is? You've

546

kissed her! For God's sake, Lucy, you might have contracted it already!'

Lucy shook her head. 'Nora wouldn't do me any harm. Nora would never do me any harm!'

'That's absolute nonsense!' Henry bellowed at her. 'That's absolute bloody nonsense! That woman –' and here he jabbed his finger at Nora – 'that woman through her own stupidity has contracted one of the most fearful diseases known to mankind – and she has brought it back to our house – and *you* blithely tell me that she wouldn't do you any harm! That woman is as dangerous as a poisonous snake!'

There was a moment's pause; and right at that moment they all heard a whispering voice, calling to them from the bedroom. 'Do you remember now, the old songs we used to sing? Do you remember them at all?'

Lucy returned to the doorway; although Major French barred her access to the room with his arm. 'Which songs, Nora?' she asked.

'Oh, all of them ones. All of them ones we used to sing, walking to the horse-fair and all.'

'She's dying,' said Major French, emphatically.

'Which songs, Nora?' Lucy repeated.

'Well . . . you remember this one . . . *Tip, tip, my little horse?*'

Lucy's throat felt tangled up with grief. 'I remember it,' she said. Nora used to sing it when they were riding in their carriage down Fifth Avenue, on bright chilly days in New York.

'Will you sing it with me?' asked Nora.

Lucy wiped her eyes. 'Yes, I'll sing it with you.'

She stood in the doorway, allowed no nearer, while Nora's choleric whisper scratched out the words of her nursery-rhyme. Lucy sang high and pretty, although she was so sad for Nora that she could hardly manage to keep herself from crying.

> *'Tip, tip, my little horse;*
> *Tip, tip, again, sir!*
> *How many miles to Dublin town?*
> *Fourscore and ten, sir!*
> *Will I get there by candlelight?*
> *Yes, and back again, sir!'*

Nora's voice faltered, then failed. Slowly, Major French moved around the bed, and lifted up Nora's wrist. This time Lucy made no attempt to go any closer.

Major French raised his eyes. 'She's gone, I'm afraid.'

There was a difficult silence. Henry managed to say, 'Amen,' and Colonel Miller cleared his throat like a burst of rapid machine-gun fire.

But Lucy stood in the doorway with streaming eyes, and sang to Henry, as clear and high as she had before,

> *Tip, tip, my little horse*
> *Tip, tip, again, sir!*
> *How many miles to Dublin town?*
> *Fourscore and ten, sir!*
> *Will I get there by candlelight?*

'Yes –' she began, but she was too miserable to finish. She turned her back on Henry and stormed off along the corridor, her primrose skirt flouncing as she walked.

Major French looked at Henry in embarrassment. 'I'm sorry I brought Lady Carson up here, Your Excellency. But she was so insistent.'

'Is there any danger that she may have caught the cholera?' Henry asked him.

Major French slowly shook his head. 'I doubt it. It usually seems to require very prolonged contact for the poisons to be passed through the air.'

'What about the kiss?' Henry demanded.

'I really couldn't say.'

Henry thought about that for a moment, tapping his order-papers against the palm of his hand. 'I suppose you can make funeral arrangements directly?'

'Yes, Your Excellency. A quick funeral would be my own recommendation, in view of the weather.'

'All right, then, do it. And you can tell that *punkah-wallah* that he can stop fanning her now. And – Major French?'

'Yes, Your Excellency?'

'I shall be talking to your commanding officer about a new posting for you. You are attached to Government House in order to protect lives; not to place them wantonly at risk.'

'If I might say so, Your Excellency –'

Henry walked right up to him and grasped the collar of his jacket and twisted it ferociously. His face was distorted like one of the caricatures of him that had appeared in *Punch*. 'If Her Excellency catches even so much as a cold, Major French, I will have you prosecuted to the fullest extent of the law. If she dies, then God help me I will kill you myself.'

The abruptness of Nora's death left Lucy utterly stunned. She returned to her drawing room white-faced, and told her bewildered guests that they would have to forgive her. Then she retreated immediately to her bedroom and lay face-down on her green silk quilt, staring at nothing, too distressed even to weep.

At six o'clock, Etta came in to ask whether she wanted tea; but she couldn't even answer. At a little after seven, Henry looked in on her, and sat on the bed beside her, and felt her forehead with his hand, but said nothing. At eight, when it was dark, Elizabeth Morris appeared, wearing a long grey dress, and a black tasselled shawl over her shoulders. She sat in the armchair close to Lucy's bed and watched her for quite a long time, with a saddened look on her face.

'Did Henry ask you to come?' said Lucy, at length.

Elizabeth said, 'Do you mind if I smoke?'

Lucy looked up at her. 'I didn't know you smoked.'

'Only in private,' she said, opening her large alligator handbag and taking out a tin of cigarettes. 'I'm afraid Gordon got me on to it. We used to play backgammon after dinner, almost every night. Backgammon and a cigarette; then a cup of cocoa and lights out.'

Lucy said, 'Did Henry tell you about Nora?'

'It wasn't Lord Carson, actually. It was Major French. He called in to see me, and suggested I might pay you a visit. Give you some sympathy, don't you know.'

Lucy sat up. She watched Elizabeth light her cigarette and blow out twin funnels of smoke from her nostrils. 'I never knew that anybody could die so quickly.'

'That's Corporal Forbes for you,' said Elizabeth. 'I beg your pardon, that's slang for *cholera morbus*. Some of my friends have taken days to die of it, but most go very speedily.'

'I think I could do with a lemonade,' said Lucy. 'I feel terribly thirsty of all a sudden.'

Elizabeth stood up and, still smoking, went across to the room to ring the bell for the servants. 'You should rest,' she told Lucy. 'I'll ask your lady's-maid to draw you a bath.'

Tir' Ram appeared, large and pale and supercilious, and asked what was wanted.

'*Meta-pani* for Her Excellency the Memsahib,' said Elizabeth. 'And *juldi!*'

While Lucy was waiting for her bath, Elizabeth told her about some of the friends she had lost from cholera and typhoid and dysentery. 'I think about them sometimes. I imagine their faces, almost like faces in a photograph album.'

Lucy thought about Blanche. She wished desperately that she had a photograph of her, just to know what she looked like now. She would be four this year. Lucy wondered if she looked anything at all like her.

Elizabeth said, 'I'm afraid that death is very close to us, in India. If you've lived here for a long time, like I have, you get quite philosophical about it. But it still hurts, of course; and all one can do is think that it's probably worth it, when you see what we've managed to do for the place. We've given them peace, and a common language, and a legal system that's second to none. We've built roads and railways and irrigated vast tracts of land.

'Even if the Indians hate us, there's something to be said for that, too. At least it will bind them together in a common cause, as one nation; and nobody could ever say that about India before.'

'I don't know where Nora fits into that,' said Lucy.

Elizabeth crushed out her cigarette. 'Everybody fits in somewhere. Even me.'

At two o'clock in the morning, Lucy awoke to find that she was sweating and shivering, and that her throat was raw. She reached out of her mosquito-nets for a glass of water, but she was shivering so much that she dropped the carafe on to the floor, and smashed it. Almost at once, Etta came in, with her hair in papers, in a huge balloon of a cotton nightgown.

'Lady Carson? Are you all right?'

'I d-dr-dropped my w-water j-ju –,' Lucy juddered. She could barely swallow, and she couldn't stop her teeth from chattering. Her stomach felt as hard as a drum.

Etta felt her forehead. 'You're burning hot!' she declared. 'Listen, cover yourself up, and I'll send for the doctor at once!'

Lucy said, 'It's not C-corporal F-forbes, is it?'

Etta didn't answer that. 'Let me send for the doctor,' she repeated. 'And I'll tell His Excellency, too.'

Lucy lay back on her sweat-wrinkled pillow, and clasped her hands over her stomach. *My baby. My poor baby. Please let me live, if only for my baby's sake.*

She had never really thought about dying before; although she had seen Uncle Casper die, and Mrs Sweeney die, and

Jack, too. Somehow their deaths had seemed like part of a play; part of a carefully worked-out drama. She could almost believe that they were still alive somewhere, like party guests hiding in another room to surprise their host.

It was only a few moments before Henry appeared, his hair ruffled, tying up the cord of his green silk robe.

'Lucy, my dearest, how are you?'

'Mind out, Your Excellency,' Etta warned him. 'There's glass on the floor.'

'Is Major French on his way?'

'I sent Muhammad Isak with a carriage.'

'Good girl,' said Henry. 'Could you bring us some water?'

Etta called for *pani*, and also for ice and a flannel cloth, so that she could bathe Lucy's forehead.

Lucy opened her eyes. Everything appeared to be warm and distorted and swimming. Henry's face was stretched out sideways as if it were made out of indiarubber, and Etta's voice was so low and blurred that Lucy couldn't distinguish what she was saying. Lucy tried to turn her head so that she could tell Etta to speak more clearly, but the bed seemed to pour away from under her, like a silent white waterfall, and she found herself floating in crimson darkness.

Someone was breathing harshly in her ear. She wasn't sure if it was herself, or Henry, or Vanessa. It could have been Vanessa. After all, they were practically twins. Perhaps the secret was that they were Siamese twins, joined by their destinies.

Henry had loved Vanessa. Perhaps he still did. Perhaps Lucy was nothing more than a substitute, someone to remind him of the woman he truly loved, until she forgave him, and came back to him.

Someone lifted her head and gave her a little cold water. She felt it dribble on to her nightgown. Her mouth wouldn't work properly, it wasn't her fault. Her throat was sore, too, so sore that she could hardly swallow. And even though her eyes were wide open, everything was dark.

She heard a deep voice saying, 'She's running a high fever. Let me look at her tongue.'

Then she heard Henry coaxing her. 'Lucy . . . Lucy, my darling. Can you put out your tongue?'

She couldn't think what that *meant* – to 'put out your tongue'. Was it the same as putting out the cat? But in any case she felt a firm hand grasping her chin, and another hand grasping her upper jaw, and then the dry woody flatness of a tongue depressor.

'Is it cholera?' asked Henry, after a moment or two.

Lucy couldn't hear Major French's reply; but she did hear him say, 'She should be bathed in cool water and vinegar, then put to bed and kept warm. I'll make up a powder of scammony and jalap, grey powder and antimony, and this should be administered every four hours. I'll also give you a tonic of rose leaves and quinine and a little sulphuric acid. Give her ladyship one dessertspoonful before she sleeps, and then again in the morning.

'If her throat becomes intolerably sore, have a hot bran poultice made up, and apply it to her neck.'

There was a great deal of shuffling of feet in the room, and then Lucy was conscious of somebody leaning over to kiss her. It smelled like Henry. It must have been Henry. 'It's all right, sweetheart,' he told her. 'It isn't the cholera. You remember the children's hospital you visited last week in Ballyganj? You've caught the scarlatina. Can you hear me? You have the scarlatina. Major French says it isn't too serious.'

'What about the baby?' whispered Lucy. 'It won't hurt the baby, will it?'

'He doesn't think so. But just to make sure, we're going to send you up to Simla, in the hills. It's much cooler there, and you'll be able to rest.'

'I don't want to leave you, Henry,' she told him. She tried to cling on to him but she couldn't seem to find him.

'Sssh, my dearest. The best thing that you can do now is

to stay quiet. Then, when you're feeling better, I'll arrange transport to take you up to the hills.'

'As long as the baby's all right,' said Lucy.

There was a pause, and Lucy heard Major French murmuring something to Henry. Then Henry came back, and said, 'Don't worry, my dearest, really. You'll soon be as fit as a fiddle. And you'll adore Simla. It's almost like England.'

'Can Elizabeth come?' asked Lucy. 'I do want Elizabeth to come.'

'Of course Elizabeth can come. You'll have a wonderful time. I can finish off my work; and when the Hot Weather starts I can come up and join you.'

'Well, well,' said Elizabeth, somewhere in the background. 'It looks like early furlough this year.'

Lucy's scarlatina was more serious than Major French had first thought, and she was feverish almost all week, her skin reddened and prickly like a lobster's shell. By the following Tuesday, he had deemed her well enough to make the journey to Simla, although he warned her that if her condition began to worsen on the way, she should make a stop at Delhi. In any event, he would be sending a nurse along with her, Mrs Smallwood, whom he was privately glad to be rid of. Women were distinctly unwelcome in the Indian medical establishment, and Mrs Smallwood had only managed to make her way in Calcutta's hospitals by an attitude which the Civil Surgeon had described as 'untypical of her sex to the point of being terrifying'.

Messages were sent on ahead to Simla that the Viceregal Lodge should be made ready for the early arrival of the Vicereine. As usual, a tremendous entourage had to be assembled: not just Lucy herself and Etta and Elizabeth Morris and Mrs Smallwood and four *ayahs,* but a twelve-strong contingent of the Viceregal Bodyguard, and scores of bearers and *syces* to look after the horses, and more than seventy coolies, and Lucy's favourite cook, with all his scullions, and six large trunks containing Lucy's clothes, including all the new dresses which had just arrived from London and Paris, four chests to carry the clothes of the other European women, six casks of formal porcelain and ornaments, thirty cases of stores and provisions, two cases of books, two boxes of drawing-room sundries and coats for the servants, who were unused to the coldness of the hills, and four more boxes for saddlery, tennis poles, pardah bamboos, linen, and cheval-glasses. Last but most imposing was a German grand piano which would be carried up to Simla on a piano-cart.

There was no railway up to Simla yet, although a remark-able looping track was under construction in the lower reaches of the Hills, and was expected to be finished in four or five years' time. All of the Vicereine's baggage would have to be carried up to the hills by coolies and by camels, forty-one camels in all.

Lucy herself would be carried up the precipitous hill paths in a palanquin, an ornate ceremonial litter like a gilded sledge, with a folding tasselled hood which resembled the hood of a baby-carriage. Her four liveried porters had been given mercilessly strict instructions not to tilt her too much, or to carry her too close to the brink of the roads, or to drop her whenever they saw a poisonous snake, or to fall over any precipices.

By the time her party was ready to leave Calcutta late the following week, Lucy was still weak and shaky, but almost completely recovered, and on the whole she would have preferred to stay on the plains, at least until the Hot Weather started. But although she could have changed her mind about going to Simla if she had really wanted to, she felt that it would be wasteful and absurd to disassemble a company of over two hundred people who had worked so hard to pack so many things. Besides, she sensed that Henry wanted her to go, so that he could finish off his Cold Weather work uninterrupted, untroubled by any anxiety that he might be neglecting her.

He had still not quite forgiven her, either, for the way in which she had argued with him outside Nora's room, on the day that Nora had died; and once or twice, with ponderous sarcasm, he had called her 'Miss Darling' – presumably referring to the way in which she had spoken to Nora on her deathbed.

The morning she was due to leave, she walked with Elizabeth Morris through South Park Cemetery, to the Plot where Nora was buried. At the moment there was only a plain wooden marker. Lucy had asked Colonel Miller to commission a marble statue of an angel, her head bowed, her hands covering her face. She had seen a similar statue in a catalogue of monuments in Kansas, when she was a child, and it had always fascinated and saddened her.

'She's in brave company,' Elizabeth remarked.

Lucy looked around at the pyramids and pillars and domed mausoleums. It was another hot, humid day, with not a breath of wind. A bird chattered self-indulgently to itself in a nearby tree. Lucy said, 'I feel as if I've buried a part of myself here, too.'

'You have,' replied Elizabeth. 'So many of us have. Friends, little children. If you have sacrificed those for the sake of living in India, then nobody can ever say that you don't have the right to call it your own country, too.'

Lucy looked down at the marker on Nora's grave. 'I'll be seeing you,' she whispered, and then she turned and walked away, with Elizabeth following close behind.

Simla was both romantic and extraordinary, and Lucy fell in love with it as soon as they arrived. It was the most glamorous of all the hill stations, perched eight thousand feet on a series of ledges on one of the lower slopes of the Himalayas, a collection of English-style houses and boarding-houses and country retreats, all clustered around a main thoroughfare called The Mall.

It was like a dream about England, rather than England

itself; some said a nightmare. The Mall was lined with a remarkable collection of buildings that could only be described as Indo-Tyrolean; and these buildings housed cafés, shops that sold European goods, a theatre and a library. From The Mall, roads meandered off through stands of pine trees to English suburban houses, properly-constructed houses made of brick, with real glass in the windows, and fireplaces, and cosy names from Home like The Cedars, Ivy Glen, and Sunny Bank.

But it was all an illusion. Beyond Sunny Bank rose the pine-forested ramparts of the surrounding hills, and then the distant peaks of the snowcapped Himalayas; and monkeys clambered noisily on Sunny Bank's corrugated-iron roof.

Elizabeth Morris was personally sceptical of Simla. 'If I were told that the monkeys had built it all, I would say, "what wonderful monkeys, they must be shot in case they do it again."'

Lucy, however, was captivated by Simla's peace and its charm and its unselfconscious eccentricity. At the far end of The Mall stood a little Gothic church, just like a church in an English country village; but The Mall itself was busy with Indians pulling rickshaws and coolies carrying luggage. It was still early in the year, too early for the Hot Weather season to have started, and so the streets were comparatively quiet. The air was fragrant and cool, almost sharp, and as Lucy was carried towards Viceregal Lodge she closed her eyes and breathed in deeply. It was marvellous. She felt recovered already; and for the first time she was grateful to Henry for having sent her away.

The Viceregal Lodge was set on one of the most commanding sites in Simla; and, symbolically, one of the most commanding sites in all India. From one side of it, water ran westwards down to the Sutlej and on to the Arabian Sea. From the other side, the drainage flowed eastwards to Jumna, and into the Bay of Bengal. Beyond the trees of its silent and elegant gardens, the hills and the mountains were hazed in a silken blue that would have looked far too strange and silvery in any other country but India. The Lodge itself was approached by a winding sandy driveway, between a profusion of Alpine flowers and mature cypresses. Like every other building in Simla, it was highly idiosyncratic. It had all the appearance of an Elizabethan mansion, with a castle-like tower, and forbidding facings in blue and grey sandstone and limestone.

Elizabeth had complained to Lucy that she always found the Viceregal Lodge unbearably oppressive. 'It always reminds me of a Scottish hydro.'

They were carried to the *porte cochère*, and their palanquins set down. They were greeted by stiffly-saluting officers of the Viceregal Bodyguard, by an assembly of liveried servants, both European and Indian, and by Henry's assistant private secretary, John Frognal, who had set off on the seven-hundred mile journey to Simla as soon as he knew that Lucy would be convalescing in the Hills. Lucy liked him. He was young and amusing, with brushed-down hair and an unsuccessful foray at a walrus moustache, and although he was wonderfully diplomatic with all of the rajahs and maharajahs that Henry had to meet, he always found it difficult to take Government House protocol very seriously. When the ladies rose from Henry's formal dinners, and curtseyed to the Viceroy at the door, John Frognal would take bets on how many knees they would hear clicking.

'Your Excellency, you are heartily welcomed to Simla,' he told her, bowing. 'We all trust that you're feeling much recovered.'

'I think I'm better already, thank you,' smiled Lucy.

John Frognal helped her out of the palanquin and then introduced her to the Lodge's senior staff. They eyed her warily. Dressed as she was in mourning black, she looked very young and shy after Lady Elgin, and very pale too. The butler, Corcoran, a tall white-haired man with gelatinous eyes and caved-in cheeks, gave her a low bow, and said,

'Whatever Your Excellency requires can be provided, please be assured.'

'I presume that Your Excellency would prefer to rest for a few days before considering any social functions,' said John Frognal.

'Is there anybody here that I should meet?' asked Lucy. They had now walked into the Lodge's great galleried entrance hall. Although the hall boasted a huge teak staircase, which gave it enormous grandeur, it was teak-panelled right up to the ceiling, which made it feel dark and heavy and depressing. Large brass pots glowered in the corners.

'There are one or two interesting people around,' John Frognal told her. 'Not many, of course, yourself excluded. But I was thinking that you might care to hold a small drawing room, perhaps; or even a dinner-party, if you felt strong enough.'

'If I can endure being shaken up all the way up into these hills,' Lucy retorted, 'I truly think that I'm strong enough for anything. Half the time I thought they were going to drop me over the edge.'

'Well, it has happened,' John Frognal admitted. 'Lost a French ambassador once. But, look here, if Your Excellency is quite well enough to give a small function or two, I'll liaise with Mrs Morris,' he told her. 'There are two senior ladies from the Punjab secretariat; and Lady Leamington-Pryce from Delhi; and Mrs Talbot – Colonel Talbot's wife, Fane's Horse.'

'Aren't there any men?' asked Lucy. 'We're going to need some men to make up a dinner-party.'

'I'm expecting Sir Malcolm McInnes at the weekend; and Lord Pethick sometime next week, but I'm afraid that Lord Pethick is a little . . . well –'

'*Gonga*?' asked Lucy, irreverently; using the British Indian slang for batty.

John Frognal smirked in amusement. 'Yes, Your Excellency, *gonga* is just the word I was looking for.'

'Anybody else?'

'An American gentleman, Your Excellency. A special envoy from Washington, so I believe. I'm not quite sure of his rank, but he's visiting India on behalf of the United States Diplomatic Service.'

'Well, it would be pleasant to talk to an American.'

Accompanied by Corcoran, the butler, who walked ahead of them with creaking shoes and his hairy-nostrilled nose in the air, Lucy and her entourage were taken up to her suite of rooms. Corcoran flung open the double doors with a flourish, and revealed an enormous bedroom, with windows on two sides, and a view of the Sutlej valley, with the Suwalik range in the middle distance, and the ghostly outline of the Himalayas beyond.

Corcoran said, 'The Hindus believe, your ladyship, that the gods live in the hills; and who is to say that they don't?'

He walked around the massive Elizabethan-style four-poster bed, and opened the leaded casements. From down in the river valley came the sweet wooden notes of a cuckoo. 'First one this year,' smiled Etta, setting down her bag.

Corcoran added, 'All your trunks and boxes will be unpacked, Your Excellency, and your clothing made ready. Would you care to dine in your rooms this evening, after your long journey?'

'Yes, I think I would,' said Lucy. 'A very light supper; perhaps about seven o'clock. Do you have any quail?'

'Quail in abundance, Your Excellency.'

Corcoran left on his creaking shoes, and Etta took off Lucy's hat and coat and unlaced her shoes. 'Perhaps you'd like a bath, Lady Carson?' she suggested.

'In a while,' said Lucy. 'I think I'd like a rest first; just to take the place in. Look, there's the full moon up there, isn't it huge! Just over the mountains. I don't think I've ever seen anything so beautiful.'

'Oh, but ghostly, too, up here in the hills,' said Etta.

Lucy went out on to the balcony, and breathed in some

more of that crisp glorious air. The light in the garden was pale but very intense, like no light that she had ever seen before; and apart from the sound of the cuckoo she could hear another sound, much quieter, the sound of streams rushing deep in the valleys far beneath her.

Etta came and stood behind her. 'The Hindus are always superstitious about the hills.'

'I don't know why.'

'Oh, it's not just the Hindus, either. Everybody says there are ghosts in Simla. Some of the houses are haunted. People have seen women in white dresses walking around their verandahs, and it's turned out that a young *memsahib* died there, while she was waiting for her husband to come up from the plains. Always pacing the verandah, don't you see, waiting for him, and he never came. Or at least he came too late.'

Lucy shivered. 'I don't want to talk about death.'

'India *is* death, that's what I think, sometimes.'

'You told me you missed it.'

'Oh, I did. I wouldn't go back Home for all the tea in Darjeeling.'

'Are you really happy? It must be hard, not having a husband.'

Etta unfolded a white silk blouse, and shook the creases out of it. 'I miss the comfort of it. But I don't miss having a man around the place, especially in India. Men can get to grips with the country, can't they? See things, and meet people, and really get to live here. But how many Indians have *you* been introduced to, apart from rajahs? You might just as well be sitting in a bread-oven in England as coming out here. Just as hot, and you see just as much. And the same goes for most of the wives.'

Lucy said quietly, 'I wish Nora could have seen this place. She would have loved it.'

Etta nodded. 'I told her not to eat anything, you know.'

'Etta, I know. Nobody blames you.'

'I told her not to eat anything, nor to drink anything, neither. But she came up and said, "They smelled so delicious, I just had to have one." And do you know something, the fellow that was cooking them looked as if he had black shiny hair, but when he turned round suddenly you could see that his scalp was completely raw, and what he had on his head wasn't hair, but flies.'

Lucy swallowed. 'Etta – I really don't want to talk about it any more.'

'Sorry, your ladyship.'

'Can you find my blue silk robe for me? I want to undress, and have a rest. And get me some tea, would you? And find those powders that Major French gave me.'

'Yes, your ladyship.'

'And Etta?'

'Yes, your ladyship?'

'Nora's dead now, and buried, and she's at peace. Nothing we can say will bring her back.'

At that moment, from the far side of the pine-forested valley, they heard the highest of cries, almost like a woman calling out in grief. It echoed and re-echoed from one hill to another.

'Monkeys,' said Etta, and went to chivvy the *ayahs*.

Lucy ate a quiet dinner in her private dining room, waited on by Corcoran the butler and three maroon-liveried Indians, who stood to attention behind her chair and refilled her glass whenever it look as if the level of her wine had dropped a sixteenth of an inch, and whipped service plates away like conjuring tricks, and expertly removed the slightest crumb she might have dropped on the tablecloth with a complicated folding and unfolding of crisp primrose-coloured napkins.

She was served with *Potage St Germain,* followed by two perfectly-roasted quail, their skin crisp and seasoned with garam masala; and then a small portion of *gateau mille-feuille,* which was so light and creamy that it might have been brought direct from a *patisserie* in Paris.

Afterwards, she was joined in her drawing room by Elizabeth. They sat in large chintz-covered armchairs in front of a briskly-crackling fire, and Elizabeth told her stories about Simla in the old days, before it was decided to make it the viceregal seat of government during the Hot Weather. 'It was eccentric, even then, although it didn't matter so much in those days, because it was only a resort. We had marvellous gymkhanas at Annandale, which is a clearing in the forest among the hills. Not a meeting went past without some rider disappearing over the side of the precipice; sometimes horse and rider together. But there were some startlingly pretty girls here. I often wonder what became of them all. Married, I expect, or dead.'

Shortly after nine o'clock, with the moon shining across the hills, Lucy said, 'I think I'll go for a walk.'

Elizabeth frowned at her. 'A walk? On your own? You can't!'

'There's no danger, is there? You've said that plenty of young girls used to go around on their own.'

'But for goodness' sake, my dear. You're the Vicereine of India, you're seven months' pregnant, and you've only just recovered from scarlatina. What on earth would happen if you were taken ill? Or if some *dacoit* decided to kidnap you?'

'You could come with me.'

'And what use would *I* be? An old lady like me!'

'Oh, Elizabeth, I'm longing to go out without taking two hundred people with me. And it's such a beautiful evening!'

Elizabeth stood up and brushed down her dress. 'All right, then. But let's take our coats. And if we fall down a *khud* don't tell me that I didn't warn you.'

It wasn't as easy for Lucy to leave the Lodge as she had expected. She and Elizabeth took their shawls, and left her suite of rooms as quietly as they could. But in the corridor they were immediately confronted by one of the house-servants, in his green-and-gold livery, who bowed to them and asked their majesties what they required.

'Just going for a *howa-khana,*' said Elizabeth, imperiously.

'Then I am fetching you bodyguards and porters and torchbearers, your majesty.'

'Be off with you!' Elizabeth told him. *'Jow! Ekdum!'*

The boy couldn't understand why she was cross with him. With hurt eyes, he retreated along the corridor, and then disappeared around the corner.

'We'd better hurry,' said Elizabeth. 'He's probably gone straight to the *khansamah* and the *khansamah* will go straight to Corcoran, and then all merry hell will break loose.'

They crept together around the galleried landing, the teak flooring creaking with every step. Lucy began to get the giggles, and her stomach contracted so tightly that she had to stop and lean against one of the newel-posts and get her breath back.

'All right, my dear?' Elizabeth asked her, her eyes glistening with suppressed merriment.

'Lead on, Macduff!' Lucy told her.

They tiptoed down the grand staircase, across the entrance hall, and out by one of the side doors. Lucy had the presence of mind to take out the key and lock it after her, so that whatever happened they would be able to get back in.

Wrapping their shawls around their shoulders, they hurried as rapidly as they could through the gardens, keeping away from the winding path. There were two sentries at the front gates, but Elizabeth beckoned to Lucy, and led her through some dense rhododendrons and across the grass to a small side gate. 'I noticed this gate when we were being carried up here. The gardeners were using it, and if I know anything about *malis,* they never bother to lock up after them. Here, look, I was quite right, it's open!'

So it was that Lucy and Elizabeth found themselves strolling through Simla late on a moonlit evening, without bodyguards or ADCs or Indian servants.

Lucy said, 'I'd almost forgotten what it was like, to be alone.'

'You must have forgotten what it's like to dress yourself too,' Elizabeth remarked.

'No . . . I can still button up a button, if I have to. I still find it hard to remember just to stand there, and let my *ayahs* do it all for me. Sometimes I feel like I'm not a real person at all, just some large doll they're dressing.'

They had reached the junction of The Ridge and The Mall, where the Swiss-styled Post Office buildings stood. The streets were silent, only a few lights twinkled here and there. Somebody was playing a gramophone, some crackly tenor song that could only be English. The moonlight cast a pallid light on the Post Office buildings, so that they looked as if they had been fashioned out of cake.

Below The Ridge and The Mall, the hill tumbled steeply downwards in a labyrinth of bazaars and alleyways and shacks. It looked like a village that was forever frozen in a tumultuous landslide. From here came the strong smell of frying onions and cumin and *mehti,* and the sounds of arguing and plangent music.

'The native quarters,' said Elizabeth. 'We shouldn't really go farther. They're supposed to be a hotbed of spies and thieves. And they're quite a maze, too. Kipling said that if you knew your way around, from one verandah to another, the police could never find you in a thousand years.'

They stopped for a while, looking out over the hill, smelling the distinctive and unforgettable aromas of the Indian high country. But the moon was beginning to fall behind the mountains, and it would soon be dark. Elizabeth said, 'We'd better be getting back. They've probably sent half a regiment to look for us already.'

They turned to walk back toward the Viceregal Lodge. As they did so, however, a tall hatless man in a light grey suit appeared as if from nowhere, bare-headed, his hat in his hand, from the general direction of the native quarters, and began walking with apparent purpose straight towards them.

'European, thank God,' muttered Elizabeth. 'Probably just a poodle-faker, making his disreputable way home.' Poodle-fakers were men who took advantage of lonely married women while their husbands were still working down on the plains.

The man began to catch up with them, but neither of them could walk any faster. As they plodded up the hill towards Christ Church, he overtook them. He turned his head and glanced at them, unsmiling, and as he did so Lucy felt a thrill of terror so great that she gasped out loud, and flailed her hand out to catch Elizabeth's arm.

In the moonlight, the man's face was floury-white, and his eyes glinted like the eyes of the dead. Everything that Etta had told her about the ghosts of Simla rushed into her mind, and she felt the blood emptying out of her brain.

For a single occluded second — although she didn't fall — she fainted.

10

When she opened her eyes again, he was still there. Elizabeth was holding her steady and he was standing quite still, looking at her in pleasure and disbelief.

'Lucy,' he said, 'Lucy? Are you all right? I didn't mean to scare you.'

It was Jamie, although she could scarcely believe it. But he was quite real; and absolutely solid. The moonlight didn't shine through him; and he didn't float an inch above the ground.

'Jamie . . . what in the world are you doing here?'

'I guess I should be asking you the same question.'

Lucy let out two or three little coughs of surprise. 'I'm taking a *walk*, what does it look like! You gave me the shock of my life!'

'Well, ditto. But I did tell you that I was heading up to the hills.'

'Elizabeth Morris,' interjected Elizabeth, with ill-concealed impatience. Elizabeth wasn't fond of being ignored.

'I'm sorry; forgive me,' said Jamie, and shook Elizabeth's hand. 'James Cullen, I'm a friend of Lucy's from Kansas. That is, we kind of grew up together.'

'What a remarkable coincidence your being here,' said Elizabeth.

'Well, not exactly,' Jamie explained. 'I was in Delhi last week; and I read in the paper that the Vicereine was going up to Simla. I was on my way to Amritsar as a matter of fact; but I had some people to see hereabouts, so I made a particular point of being here. But I sure didn't expect to find the Vicereine taking walks. I mean – not like this – walks in the moonlight, without any kind of bodyguard.'

Elizabeth lifted her tightly-folded parasol. 'I can assure you, Mr Cullen, that I am bodyguard enough. Any *dacoit* who values his eyesight had better watch out.'

Jamie gave her an amused-alarmed grin, and fended off the aggressively-pointed ferrule. 'I can believe it, Mrs Morris.'

'*Miss* Morris,' Elizabeth corrected him. Then, to Lucy, 'Is he all right, my dear? What I mean to say is, is he *pukkah*?'

Lucy smiled, and nodded. 'He's perfectly *pukkah*. We used to go riding together, didn't we, Jamie, when we were children? We used to lie on our backs by the river, and tell each other what our dreams were.'

'Well, I *suppose* that makes him *pukkah*,' said Elizabeth.

Lucy suddenly and irrationally thought of Samuel Blankenship. She knew what *he* would have said. *You bet your rear-end that makes him pukkah!* Not that poor old Samuel would have known what *pukkah* meant.

Elizabeth took Lucy's arm. 'We'd better be getting back. They'll be kicking up all kinds of a fuss once they've found that we've gone.'

'Please . . . can I escort you?' asked Jamie. 'I thought that whenever the Vicereine went for a stroll, she took elephants, and bearers, and eight million coolies, and shot ibex and tigers.'

'Well, I do that, too,' said Lucy, a little haughtily. 'I haven't actually shot anything yet, but Colonel Miller's been giving me lessons with a gun. This is my first evening in Simla, that's all, and I wanted to see it on my own.'

Jamie looked up the empty street; and then back down again. 'It's real strange here, isn't it? It's not like India at all.'

'There are supposed to be ghosts,' said Elizabeth.

'Indian ghosts or British ghosts?' Jamie asked her.

'Both,' said Elizabeth.

'And which of those ghosts are in charge?'

Elizabeth gave him a quick, prickly glance. 'We British have given an awful lot to India, you know, including the lives of some of our bravest young men and women.'

'I'm sorry,' Jamie told her. 'I didn't mean to suggest that –'

'Quite all right,' said Elizabeth, briskly. 'I don't as a rule expect foreigners to understand what we've managed to achieve.'

Jamie shrugged, and said, 'Well . . .' but he didn't know what else to say to her, so he turned his attention to Lucy, 'You know something, your vicereineship, it's so good to see you. You're blossoming!'

'She isn't a bush,' Elizabeth complained.

'Listen,' said Jamie, 'I said I was sorry.'

Lucy laughed. 'Don't take any notice of Elizabeth; she's frightfully mother-hennish.'

'When is Henry coming up to the Hills?' asked Jamie, off-handedly.

'I'm not sure,' Lucy replied. 'He said he would come just as soon as he could, but he's terribly busy. Are you here for long? You haven't even told me what you're *doing*, not properly.'

Jamie shrugged. 'This and that, talking to people, not much.'

'Are you touring, Mr Cullen?' asked Elizabeth. 'Or are you on business of some kind?'

'Oh, touring, really. Looking around; meeting people.'

'You ought to go to Kashmir, if you get the opportunity,' suggested Elizabeth, in a tone which seemed to recommend that if he left this very minute it wouldn't be too soon. 'Kashmir is exceptionally pleasant during the Hot Weather. I remember punting across Dal Lake one August afternoon. It was quite wonderful . . . the white peaks of the Himalayas reflected in the water. And so utterly quiet, as if my boatman and I were the only people left alive in the whole world.'

'I don't think I'll have much time for boating,' said Jamie.

'Jamie's a lawyer,' Lucy explained.

'I see,' said Elizabeth. 'Is there anything in India which could possibly interest an American lawyer? India is run by British law.'

'I look around me, I see a whole lot that's relevant to American law,' Jamie replied.

Elizabeth seemed unimpressed. 'I was always led to understand that American law is very different from our own. My late brother was Sir Gordon Morris; perhaps you've heard of him. He used to say that American law was the law of vested interests. In trusts we trust.'

'Sounds like your brother was a cynic,' said Jamie.

'Perhaps. But he was a very gifted cynic.'

Jamie was silent for a while, as they slowly climbed the hill together; an incongruous party of three underneath a moon like a lamp. But then he said, 'The relevance of what's happening here in India today, compared with my recent experience in American diplomacy, is that in both cases, an indigenous population is being tricked, robbed, and buggered blind, and all in the name of the law.'

'Sir!' Elizabeth protested.

'Oh, you can "sir!" me all you like,' Jamie told her. 'But

ever since I arrived here in India, I've learned a whole lot. I've learned about oppression, I've learned about exploitation, I've learned about wholesale butchery in the name of some Queen who sits in a palace five thousand miles away and doesn't even think of her three hundred million native subjects from one weekend to the next.'

Elizabeth stiffened at this rabid affront to the British throne, and released Lucy's arm. 'Sir! You are not only foul-mouthed but unpatriotic. Our countries are bonded by a common language, a common ideal, and a common desire to do the right thing. The Raj is the jewel in the British crown. Long may it beam and glisten!'

'Well, hear, hear!' clapped Lucy.

But Jamie turned away and shook his head. 'You won't understand, will you? It's been staring you right in the face, Mrs Morris, from the moment you first arrived in India! The reason why India is the jewel in the crown is because the people here work for practically nothing. Without slave-labour – or the next thing to it – British India would collapse overnight.

He paused, and ran his hand through his hair. 'Let me tell you something, Lucy, I've been lucky, tonight, to meet you alone. Think how many people you normally take with you, wherever you go! What a magnificent spectacle it must be, when you and Lord Carson set out on your tours! Special train, two hundred servants! Who cares what it costs? But – well, as far as I can figure it out, one rupee spent on a specially-woven ceremonial carpet is one rupee taken out of the mouth of a starving child.'

'Oh, for God's sake, Jamie, stop it!' Lucy protested. 'I came out here to look at the moon, and the mountains, and to think what I might be wearing for Saturday's ball. I can't stand pomp, and I can't stand ceremony, and I don't want to talk about justice any more, either!'

Jamie gave her a look which she wasn't at all sure that she liked. 'Saturday's ball! Is that all you can think about?

Worrying your curls out of their curl-papers, stepping into your fine silk slippers. You're pretty beyond price; you're expecting a baby; and you're married to one of the most influential men who ever lived. Oh, yes – whatever you think about Henry, my darling, no matter how much you think you love him, no matter how much you think you hate him, he's clever and tenacious and he'll never give in to anybody. He represents the British Crown in India . . . he *is* the British Crown in India, and if there's one thing I know about him, he's totally dedicated to maintaining British rule, no matter what.'

'And what, may I ask, is so terrible about that?' Elizabeth demanded, quite white with indignation.

Jamie smiled. 'You don't see it, do you? You don't see what you've done, you British!'

'How dare you! I've seen exactly what we've done! We've taken a divided and primitive society – and we've pacified it, and educated it, and we've – we've bonded it together! We've given them law, and banks, and commerce, and a postal service second to none – and, and Scottish dancing – and goodness only knows what else!'

'Well, you're right, of course,' Jamie admitted. 'India these days – well, it's a spectacle. Buildings, railways, tea-plantations, docks, forts, cantonments. What a spectacle! But the spectacle can't exist without hunger, and filth, and disease, and beggary. It's a fact of history. The brighter the rooftops on the Golden City shine, the dirtier the sewers that run beneath.'

'You can talk!' Lucy protested.' 'What did you do to the Comanche? What did you do to the Sioux? Surely that was worse?'

'Yes, it was, in a way,' Jamie admitted. 'In Kansas and Colorado I took away their ancestral lands for ever. I desecrated their sacred burial-places. I robbed them of their self-sufficiency and I robbed them of their pride. In the end, to add injury to insult, I killed them, too. The American Raj is just as bad as the British Raj, and worse in some ways, because the sole aim of the American Raj was not to rule, not to administer, not even to exploit – but to destroy one people for the benefit and profit of another, under a banner called manifest destiny.'

'I'm glad to hear that you have *some* sense of shame,' put in Elizabeth, tartly.

'You're right,' said Jamie, 'I do. My father brought me up to believe in absolute fairness; and the sanctity of human life; and I betrayed both of those principles because I was flattered and because I was paid a lot of money to betray them.'

'In that case,' said Elizabeth, 'I really fail to see how *you* can be remotely qualified to criticize *us*.'

Jamie stopped. They had almost reached the crest of the hill, beside the dark Gothic silhouette of Christ Church. The trees whispered like conspirators.

'What I did in Kansas doesn't excuse what the British are doing here in India, what Lord Henry Carson is doing here.'

Lucy held her hand out. 'Jamie . . . let's forget about it for tonight. You sound as if you're all burning up!'

'And you don't know why?'

'Jamie, I don't even want to think about it, I'm too tired.'

'Yes,' he said; and suddenly he dropped his arms down to his sides, and looked away for a moment. 'Yes,' he acknowledged. 'I'm sorry. I've been tub-thumping and all you did to deserve it was to take a walk.'

'Perhaps we shall see you again, Mr Cullen,' said Elizabeth.

Jamie took her hand. 'Perhaps you shall.'

'At least you have manners,' Elizabeth smiled at him. In spite of herself, she had obviously begun to warm to him. 'It isn't often that one comes across a radical with manners.'

'Oh, I wouldn't call myself a radical,' said Jamie. 'Just because I don't believe in empires; and emperors.'

'And empresses?' asked Lucy. She was feeling very weary now, from talking and excitement and too much walking;

and she felt like provoking Jamie not so much because he irked her, but because she wanted him to go away; so that she could think about him when he was gone.

She thought to herself: Sometimes you can be so fond of somebody that you don't want them there. You want to relish them in memory and in anticipation and in dreams. Sometimes their actual presence is almost too much.

'Let me tell you something,' said Jamie. 'The British almost take it for granted, what they've achieved here in India. But they shouldn't. I mean what kind of a national character did it take to turn more than a thousand different ancient and holy civilizations into a single continent of obedient children – and then to swindle those children out of everything they have, year in, year out, for hundreds of years? You don't even have to invent some grand-sounding historical excuse, like manifest destiny! You just say, we know better, you ignorant little sooties, so behave yourselves! And the tragedy is that they do!'

Elizabeth asked, not altogether unkindly, 'Have you been drinking, Mr Cullen?'

'No,' said Jamie. 'I haven't been drinking; although I do. I've been visiting Indians, that's all. Indian villages, Indian towns, Indian families. Muslims and Hindus, makes no difference.'

He paused, and then he said, in a soft and almost regretful voice, 'I've been trying to understand what the people in this country have been suffering. That probably sounds ridiculous to you. Maybe it *is* ridiculous. Some of the people I've met, no education, no food, no sewage, no clean water – they don't even understand that they *are* suffering. They think that life is always like this – never known any different.'

He paused again. Lucy was very tired, but she was still listening.

Jamie said, 'You probably don't feel it, up there in Vice-regal House. But the ground is starting to shake. It's like an earthquake coming, you'll never be able to stop it, no matter what you do.'

Just then, they heard the clattering of horses from the direction of Viceregal Lodge. Down the hill, riding smartly and expertly and at very great speed, came Lieutenant Ashley Burnes-Waterton, followed by three more officers of the Viceroy's Bodyguard.

'Lady Carson!' called Lieutenant Burnes-Waterton, reining his horse to a spectacular sliding halt, its shoes striking bright orange sparks off the roadway.

'I'm quite well, thank you,' said Lucy, as clearly and as calmly as she could. 'I'm sorry that we alarmed you. I needed to walk by myself for a while. This gentleman was kindly offering his assistance.'

Lieutenant Burnes-Waterton nodded and saluted, and said, 'As you wish, ma'am. May we send for a rickshaw to take you back?'

'No, thank you,' said Lucy. She sounded like the young empress again. 'I walked here, and I shall walk back. Mr Cullen will escort me. You may follow at a distance if you care to.'

Lieutenant Burnes-Waterton dismounted, and led his horse along behind them, fully understanding that 'at a distance' meant out of earshot. The remaining officers walked their horses even farther behind, looking rigid and cross.

Lucy took Jamie's arm and the two of them walked up the hill very close together.

'When do you expect your baby?' asked Jamie.

'The middle of June, midsummer's day,' Lucy told him.

'What do you want? A girl or a boy?'

'Henry wants a boy. He's going to call him Horatio.'

'Jesus,' said Jamie; the old Jamie, from Oak City, Kansas, who once drank five shots of whisky in five minutes without taking a breath.

'How long are you going to stay here in India?' she asked him.

He made a face. 'I don't know. Until I've talked to everyone I feel I need to talk to, I guess.'

'You're not going to cause any trouble?'

'Trouble? What do you mean by trouble? Of course not. I'm just travelling around, asking awkward questions, and coming up with awkward answers. You know me.'

Lucy looked at him narrowly. 'I'm not so sure that I do.'

'I'm okay,' he reassured her.

'Are you happy?' she asked him.

'I'm still not married,' he told her.

'Courting?' she inquired.

'Unh-hunh.'

'You're not still pining for me? Now, that would be plain foolishness.'

He stopped, and Lucy stopped, and Elizabeth stopped, and Lieutenant Burnes-Waterton stopped, and all the other officers stopped. Jamie looked around him. 'By God,' he said, 'I sure know why you wanted to take a hike on your own.'

They carried on walking. They had almost reached the fence around the Viceregal Lodge. Lucy was beginning to feel chilly now, and tired.

'I don't know what it is,' said Jamie. 'I'm not ashamed to admit it, not now. The years have gone by and I've travelled all the way around the world and met dozens of women and lots of them were pretty. But I always felt that you and I were meant for each other, born for each other. I don't know why. It doesn't even trouble me any more. I just kind of take it as true. You know, like the world's round, and you and I were meant for each other.'

Lucy intertwined her fingers between his, and they were just as strong and reassuring as ever.

'I never took it for granted that the world was round,' she told him, in a voice too soft for Elizabeth to hear her.

'Maybe that's your trouble,' grinned Jamie. 'You're a dyed-in-the-wool flat-earther.'

She gave him a long, slow smile. 'You must come to dinner at the Lodge,' she said. 'I'll have Mr Frognal send you an invitation.'

'I'm staying at the Hotel Cecil,' he told her.

'That's pronounced Sessul; not Sea-sill,' she admonished him. 'And don't try to kiss me goodbye. Everybody in the viceregal court suffers from the same incurable disease, *gossipus rampantus*. We can't have the Viceroy thinking that his Vicereine is being pursued by a poodle-faker.'

Jamie slowly shook his head. 'Do you know how English you sound?'

'I love you,' mouthed Lucy, as he put on his hat and walked away.

She arranged a dinner for that very weekend, for the sole purpose of inviting Jamie; even though to balance her guest-list she had to invite the Reverend Hugo Watkins who was alleged by John Frognal to be a notorious bore on the subject of slavery, particularly about naked black women chained to trees, and particularly with his mouth full, so that he emphasized his evangelical fantasies by spraying out showers of crumbs all over the tablecloth. It had also been necessary to invite Doctor Kingston Lear, who lived in a huge rambling chalet on the brink of a hair-raising precipice on the south-eastern side of Simla. Doctor Lear had perversely called his chalet *Chota Bungla* – 'little bungalow' – because it was neither a bungalow nor little. It was rumoured among the service wives that if you were ever accidentally put up the spout while your hubby was still in Calcutta, Dr Lear was the man to go to. Fortunately the wives' behaviour (though flirtatious) was almost always so desperately honourable that even if Dr Lear had done that kind of work, he would have made very little profit out of it. Simla was not known for being a poodle-faking station.

It was a dull dinner party. Lucy hadn't realized how talented Henry was at talking, even with the silliest or most retiring of guests. Jamie said very little because he didn't want to appear too intimate with Her Excellency. The Reverend Watkins had plainly been warned by his wife not to talk about naked black women chained to trees, and so he spoke instead about trying to persuade the Simla Amateur Dramatic Society to put on *The Humility of Bishop Stewart on his Sickbed* at the Gaiety Theatre this season, instead of *The Geisha*.

Doctor Lear was yellow-skinned and hairy-wristed and almost equally morbid. He told two jokes as if they were physically painful to impart; one old chestnut about the brigadier who had dined a little too well at the Viceregal Lodge, and had tried to light his cigar with a geranium; the other a riddle asking, 'In which month do Indian civil servants drink the least?' The rest of the company had long turned to another topic of conversation before he perplexed them all by suddenly coming out with, 'February.'

After dinner, however, they retired to the panelled drawing room, where a large fire was roaring and *burra pegs* were poured, and everybody relaxed a little more. Lucy at last found herself able to talk to Jamie for a few minutes.

'I want to see you in private,' he said. 'I must talk to you.'

'Jamie, I can't.'

'Please. I can't stay in Simla too much longer.'

'Well, what do you suggest?'

'Come out to Mashobra. It's only six miles away. I don't know whether your ADC's told you, but there's a viceregal chalet there. It's real quiet and informal, not like this place. You won't have to take many servants. Maybe you could bring a picnic, something like that. I could meet you there about noon Monday.'

'I'm really not sure.'

'Lucy . . . I want to talk to you about Blanche.'

'Can't we do that here?'

Jamie looked around the gloomy drawing room at the chattering and laughing dinner-guests. The fire danced

577

wildly in the hearth, and everybody's shadows swivelled around the carved-oak ceiling. There was a feeling of madness in the air; of a century that was coming to a close.

Lucy said, 'I mustn't come, Jamie. What if Henry found out? He's finding things difficult enough already, without thinking that –'

'Without thinking what?' Jamie demanded.

'Well – without thinking that I might be interested in another man.'

Jamie's eyes were very dark and steady. 'But you're not interested in another man.' Long pause. 'Are you?'

'Jamie, I'm married. And being Henry's wife – being Vicereine – that's more than just being married.'

'You mean your commitment to Henry is public as well as private?'

'I suppose so.'

'Even if you don't particularly love him?'

There was a very long-drawn-out silence between them, as slow and as viscose and as transparent as melted sugar.

Jamie said, softly and wildly, 'Lucy, I made a terrible mistake, letting you go. My God, I should have locked you in the root cellar and never let you out. I should have made you stay, at least until you understood how much I cared for you, and how much you cared for me, too.'

'Jamie,' Lucy warned him, 'this isn't the place.'

'Well, I'm not too sure that I care about that any more. I thought that I could forget about you, forget what you looked like, forget what you felt like. But I couldn't, and I can't, and I don't want to.'

'Oh, Jamie,' whispered Lucy, and touched his hand. It was the greatest intimacy that she could allow herself, here in the drawing room of Viceregal Lodge.

Jamie laid his hand on top of hers. He couldn't have failed to notice her diamond and sapphire and ruby rings; heirlooms from Brackenbridge and gifts from Henry's wealthier friends.

'Blanche is growing up to look just like you,' he told her. 'Same eyes, same curls, same skinny legs.'

Lucy swallowed with emotion. It was still painful to think about Blanche.

'Lucy . . . I want to be Blanche's father, bring her up to know who her real parents are. But I can't do that less'n she has her mother, too. I can't take all of that responsibility on my own. Wouldn't want to, wouldn't be fair on Blanche.'

'What are you asking of me?' Lucy demanded, in a soft, intense voice.

'Maybe it's impossible,' said Jamie.

'Yes,' Lucy told him. 'It's impossible.'

'Couldn't we talk some more?' Jamie asked her. 'Some-place private; someplace alone?'

'The last time we did that, we —' Lucy began, then thought better of it. She didn't want Jamie to know that she had been forced to pay Vernon to keep their last meeting a secret. She regretted now that she had given in to Vernon so easily. In fact she had regretted it the very next day. But how could she possibly stop paying him now? She didn't doubt for a moment that Vernon had the brass East End neck to tell Henry what had happened; and no matter how innocent the kisses that she had given Jamie might have been, Henry would assume that she *must* feel desperately guilty, or else she wouldn't have paid up.

Jamie said, 'I don't want to upset you, Lucy; I promise. But I do want to talk. You know, just the way we used to. Otherwise — I don't know — it all seems so goddamned *unfinished*. You left me with your child, Lucy, and you left me with a broken heart, too. At least give me the chance to understand why.'

Lucy said nothing. She knew why. But how could she really explain it to Jamie without breaking his heart even more; and her own heart, too?

And she was frightened of much more than that. She was frightened that if she came to know Jamie better — this new, bearded Jamie, with his strong political conscience and his worldlywise ways she might have to admit to herself that she loved him more than she could ever love Henry. She might have to face what she already knew to be true – that Jamie would love her just as demonstratively in return, which Henry never would.

'Come to Mashobra, please,' Jamie begged her. 'Just for an hour. Just to say goodbye.'

Lucy lowered her eyes and looked down at the silk embroidery on her evening gown.

Jamie said, 'I have a photograph of Blanche, back at the hotel. It's the only one I've got; but if you come to Mashobra, I'll give it to you.'

Lucy lifted her head. 'You have a *photograph*?'

'My father took it. He bought himself one of those folding cameras from Sears. He took some views, too. The house, the river. And a whole lot of mother.'

Lucy hesitated for a moment, but the thought of having a photograph of Blanche was too much of a temptation to resist. 'All right, then,' she said. 'I'll fix up a picnic. But I won't be able to stay for long.'

She was conscious that Elizabeth was observing her intently from the other side of the drawing room, and she smiled and nodded as if Jamie were telling her something tedious.

The *khit* came around with more cognac, but Jamie covered his glass with his hand. 'I have work to do, people to meet; thanks all the same.'

He started to tell Lucy about his work in the Phillippines, and Lucy watched him as he talked with the softly-focused look of deep affection. I could have married this man; we could have lived together in Kansas for the rest of our lives, where the sunflowers grow, and the wind blows fresh.

'You'll marry someday,' she said, interrupting him in the middle of a sentence.

'What?' he asked her, baffled.

'You'll find somebody some day. I'm sure of it.'

'Well . . .' he said, glancing around the room. 'Maybe I will.'

'Jamie, you mustn't love me for ever.'

He looked back at her. 'That's not one of those things you can decide for yourself. You can decide to change the way you are, like I can try to make up for what I did to the Cheyenne and the Arapaho by doing some good here in India. But you can't decide who you're going to be in love with.'

'Oh, you'll meet somebody, when you're least expecting it.'

'That happened to me a long time ago.'

'Jamie . . .' she cautioned him. You never knew who might be listening.

But he wasn't to be cautioned. He sat forward on the sofa and took hold of her hand. Under his breath, he said, 'Tell me.'

'Jamie, let go of my hand. Somebody will see.'

'Not before you tell me that you love me.'

Her eyes were bright and very blue. 'Of course I love you.'

'You mean it?'

She nodded. She said it to calm him; she said it so that he wouldn't feel too hurt.

'You mean it,' he repeated, releasing her hand and sitting back.

'Jamie,' she said, 'I loved you when we were young and I love you now and I will never stop loving you for the whole of my life. But I made my choice. I made it of my own free will. And my choice was to marry Henry.'

A picnic at Mashobra was surprisingly easy to arrange. All she had to say was, 'I want to have a picnic at Mashobra on Monday,' and at eleven o'clock on Monday morning Corcoran knocked politely at her door to assure her that her entourage was ready to depart. It was a soft, bright day, with the sun sparkling through the pines, and a light breeze stirring the Union Jack above the Lodge's crenellated tower.

As she and Elizabeth stepped out of the main door, she saw that Jamie had been right: she hadn't required more than a *khansamah*, two *khitmutgars*, three *musolchis*, Etta, with *two ayahs*, two *syces* to take care of the horses, four officers of the Viceroy's Bodyguard, eighteen coolies for pulling the rickshaws and carrying the charcoal stoves and the ice-pails and the tables and the linen-boxes and the supplies, and six or seven assorted boys who seemed to be coming along for the fun of it.

'I do so love a quiet outing in the countryside, don't you?' Elizabeth remarked.

'It would probably be more peaceful if we took a travelling circus with us, don't you think?'

Mashobra was one of the few retreats where the Viceroy and Vicereine could behave with genuine informality. Lucy and her party reached it by travelling through a long dark tunnel through the hills, and then along a narrow road which clung to the side of a sheer steamy precipice thousands of feet deep. Although it was only six miles away, it was a small haven of primitive peace among the trees, and even the viceregal chalet, for all the grandeur of its fretwork balcony, had no hot water, and only iron tubs to wash in.

Sunlight played shadow-theatre patterns on the road as they ascended; and monkeys laughed in the trees; and the rickshaw coolies puffed and groaned as they pulled Lucy and Elizabeth and Etta up steadily-steepening gradients.

'Don't worry,' said Elizabeth, dismissively. 'They only groan as a matter of habit, so that people will pay them more.'

At lunchtime, they reached Mashobra, and the entire noisy jingling entourage dismounted. The chalet had been opened already. Carpets had been rolled out, curtains had been hung, dust-covers had been dragged off chairs. Pots of geraniums had been brought up from the Lodge and arranged along the verandah, as if they had always been there. With all these scurrying scene-changers accompanying her wherever she went, Lucy wondered if it would ever be possible for her to see India as she really was. She was escorted up to the verandah by Lieutenant Venables, who saluted with quivering exactitude, and ask for permission to fall out.

Lucy and Elizabeth drank a glass of champagne on the balcony, while the *khansamah* got to work with his charcoal stove, and the rest of the servants busied themselves with setting up tables and arranging napkins and plates and silverware. In the middle of the forest, in a chalet with no hot water and a corrugated-iron roof, surrounded by the jabbering of monkeys and the calling of cuckoos, on a warm misty April day, they would be eating from Minton porcelain and patting their lips with Irish-linen napkins, as if they were lunching at an English country house.

The head *khitmutgar* came out from the kitchen and bowed. He presented both Lucy and Elizabeth with a typewritten menu for their picnic. *Green Bean Toran, Biter Gourd with Union Stuffing, Hole Rose Chicken Vicereine, Stuff Okra, Black Lentle Chutni, Plantin Jaggery.*

'With your special allowance, Your Excellency, the *khansamah* has dedicated to you this special new menu for the whole roast chicken, especially and deliberately devised on purpose for Your Excellency as an initial well come to Simla for the first time.'

'How is it prepared?' asked Elizabeth, quite sharply. Even as Vicereine, Lucy still couldn't quite get used to the demanding way in which Europeans spoke to their Indian servants; although Henry had told her time and time again that they would take advantage, otherwise, and run you ragged.

'*They're just like children,*' John Frognal had explained; and she had remembered then what Jamie had said, under the fast-disappearing moon.

The *khit* said, 'The chicken is taken leave of its skin, Your Excellency, and then it is suffocated for six hours long in onions and paprika and chilli and saffron and cumin and garam masala and coriander, but it is the great secret of this whole roast chicken that it is choked in its interior with the chest part of six quails tied together and covered with coriander leaves.'

'It sounds marvellous,' said Lucy, ignoring Elizabeth's wrinkled-up nose. 'Tell the *khansamah* that I am pleased by his compliment.'

'Very honoured, Your Excellency,' the *khit* acknowledged, and bowed again.

The picnic turned out to be wonderful; one of the most ravishing meals that Lucy had eaten since she had arrived in India. The 'Hole Rose Chicken Vicereine', was one of those truly great dishes that can only be created when the stars are in the right conjunction – when inspiration and traditional skill address themselves to a mixture of limited, odd, but superb ingredients, and come up shining in glory. Even Elizabeth had to admit that it was exceptional; and ate almost half of it.

Plantain jaggery turned out to be peeled plantains, boiled in raw sugar and chilled. Lucy adored it, but was too full to do very much more than taste it.

After luncheon, they were served coffee on the verandah, and Elizabeth began to doze on her long-sleever, her *terai* hat nodding lower with every deep breath. But Lucy was beginning to grow anxious. There was no sign of Jamie anywhere. Although she had enjoyed herself, and her servants had treated her like the empress she represented, it looked as if Jamie might have been prevented from getting here; in which case she would simply have to tell the servants to pack everything up and return to Simla.

The *khit* had just come out on to the verandah to ask them if they wanted more coffee when she saw a light flashing in the nearby trees; a mirror, catching the sun. It flashed three times, and then it stopped.

She waved the *khit* away, and said to Elizabeth, 'I'm just taking a walk around the bungalow. You don't mind, do you?'

Elizabeth was asleep, under the brim of her hat. She was snoring with the noise that her servants usually called 'memsahib singing hymns'. The coolies were eating their midday meal, leaning their backs against the gardening-shed. The officers of the Viceroy's bodyguard were stretched out on camp-chairs, eating *moorghi masala* and laughing. Lucy was able to rise from her long-sleever and leave the verandah without anybody seeing, and cross the chalet garden to the trees, where the mirror had been flashing.

She crossed the pathway like a ghost, or a memory.

Jamie was waiting for her in a small rocky hollow, almost completely overshadowed by ferns. Not far away, a small stream gargled over the rocks; and barbets twittered; and there was a pungent smell of woods and mountains.

This time she opened her arms to him and kissed him without hesitation. He held her as closely as he could, pressing her tautly pregnant stomach up against him, and kissed her hair, and her face, and her eyelids, and her cheeks, and her lips.

'You don't know how much I've missed you, Lucy. It's been worse than a pain that just wouldn't go away.'

She stepped back a little way and looked at him. He was dressed in a canary-yellow suit with patch pockets, and an open-necked shirt.

'Where *did* you get that suit?' she asked him.

He tightened his lips, and then laughed. 'Everybody asks me that. Goddamit. Abercrombie & Fitch, no less. They told me that this was what the experienced traveller always wore to tropical climes. I've never been laughed at so much in my life. My topi was so ridiculous that I threw it away. If I could afford the time, I'd have a *derzi* copy this suit in white, and then throw this away, too.'

'Oh, Jamie,' Lucy laughed.

Jamie said, 'There's a blanket here . . . why don't you sit down?'

Lucy perched herself on the double-folded *durry* that Jamie had arranged for her on a rock. 'Goddamit, you look pretty,' he told her.

'You didn't forget the photograph of Blanche?' Lucy asked him.

'No, no.' He reached into his jacket pocket, and took out an envelope. When he handed it to her, Lucy noticed that his hands were trembling.

'I wrote the date on the back,' he told her.

Lucy opened the envelope and took out the small sepia picture. It showed a small girl in a sunbonnet and an apron, frowning at the camera. Her arms were chubby; and around her left wrist was woven a chain of ox-eye daisies. Lucy recognized the background at once: it was the yard out at the back of Mrs Cullen's kitchen.

Lucy sat on the folded *durry* under the breeze-flickered leaves and her eyes blurred with tears.

'She's pretty, isn't she?' said Jamie. 'Every bit as pretty as you.'

'You're quite certain I can keep this?'

'Sure. See what I've said on the back.'

Lucy turned the picture over, and across the back was written *Blanche Cullen, Saline River, 1898. From her father Jamie to her mother Lucy, with love.*

Nothing could stop the tears that ran down Lucy's cheeks. Jamie offered her his handkerchief, but she shook her head and said miserably, 'No.'

'It was your choice,' said Jamie. 'You made it of your own free will.'

'I know,' Lucy replied, smearing the tears with her fingers. 'That doesn't make it any easier.'

Jamie stood still, watching her. Then he said, 'You're sure you won't come back to me?'

'Oh, Jamie, it's far too late for that.'

'You said that you loved me. You said that you always will.'

'I know. And it's true. But when you make a choice for yourself you have to stick to it, don't you? You have a duty to stick to it.'

'Is that one of Henry's platitudes?'

Lucy took another sad look at the photograph of Blanche, then tucked it back into its envelope. She stood up, and brushed the creases from her dress. 'I think I ought to go now, Jamie. I don't want to hurt you any more.'

'I shouldn't worry about hurting me, Lucy. You've already hurt me just about as much as one man can stand. Besides, there's somebody I want you to meet.'

Lucy quickly turned her head. 'Here? There's somebody else here?'

'It's somebody I trust, believe me.'

Lucy felt alarmed, and stepped back two or three paces. 'I though it was going to be you and me, alone.'

Jamie spread his arms wide. 'I'm sorry. It is. I mean, he hasn't been listening.'

'Well, that's very nice to know,' Lucy retaliated.

'Lucy, I'm sorry. Believe me, I asked you to meet me here today because I wanted to talk to you. I mean just about Blanche, and us. I thought by some ridiculous chance you might have changed your mind. I don't know, I guess I thought that you might have decided that Blanche needed both of us – that maybe you and Henry – I don't know. I guess I was grasping at straws.'

'Jamie, who's here?' She looked around the hollow, this way and that. 'And where is he? Or she?'

Jamie said, 'Please don't be angry, okay? It was after I left your dinner party the other night. I was talking to some of the people I met here in Simla, and I told them where I'd spent the evening. And they couldn't believe that I was actually friends with the Vicereine. They said it was such a great opportunity, and they were right.'

'*What's* a great opportunity?' Lucy wanted to know. 'Come on, Jamie, tell me!'

'These people – these friends of mine – they're trying to change things. Trying to persuade the people of India to help themselves – you know, rather than depending on the British for everything.'

'I don't understand,' Lucy replied. 'I'm not even sure that I want to. Listen, Jamie, I'll have to be getting back.'

'Lucy,' Jamie pleaded with her, taking hold of both of her hands. 'I wouldn't have asked you to come here if I didn't think you were sensitive enough at least to listen. All right, you've listened to me, and thank you for listening, but you've told me no. Now at least listen to Tilak. You can always say no to him, too.'

'Tilak, is that his name?'

Jamie said gently, 'You rule this country, Lucy. Don't you realize that? How can you rule a country without knowing how its people feel? What their needs are, what their hopes are? Every day millions of Indians say prayers that their gods will keep you and protect you and guide your hand. And yet you don't even know how much they're suffering; or what they want. You don't even know who they are.'

Lucy said, with deliberate sarcasm, 'You should have been a lawyer.'

'You'll listen?' asked Jamie. 'That's all I ask.'

Lucy nodded; and waited tall and still in the intricate light of the hollow while Jamie cupped his hands around his mouth and shouted, 'Tilak! It's all right! Tilak! Come here!'

Birds screeched and whooped in alarm, and startled monkeys crashed furiously through the trees. Jamie watched Lucy very closely as the clamour died down. The undergrowth rustled, twigs broke, and a short middle-aged Indian appeared, dressed in a rumpled buff-coloured business suit, and a dark red turban. He was plump and anxious-eyed and perspiring, with a small hooked nose and skin the colour of cold tea; more like a Bombay shipping agent than anything else. He bowed his head to Lucy; but the look on his face told her that he had very little respect for her, or at least for the viceroyalty.

'This is Bal Gangadhar Tilak,' said Jamie. 'Tilak, this is Her Excellency the Vicereine, Lady Carson of Brackenbridge.'

'*Salaam*, Your Excellency,' Tilak told her. 'Mr Cullen has spoken to me much about you, extolling your virtues, praising your beauty. I confess that he spoke no lies; and that you are more beautiful than any European woman I have ever been honoured to meet.'

'Why are you here?' asked Lucy, aware that she was using the same sharp tones that Elizabeth had used when she was asking about the Hole Rose Chicken. 'What do you want?'

Bal Gangadhar Tilak gave Lucy the tiniest of smiles, like a heart-shaped hole in a pierced Indian screen. 'This is indeed an unusual opportunity for me, to meet one of those who call me a petty volcano. But Mr Cullen said that you would listen with sympathy, and consider what I say, and if possible pass on my message for the ears of His Excellency, so that he would consider our feelings with greater care.'

Lucy was immediately aware that this was wrong; that Jamie had coaxed her here not as Lucy, not as a lover, not even as a friend, but as Vicereine of India. She said, 'Jamie – I think I have to go. You shouldn't have asked me here, really. Whatever I feel about you, whatever I feel about Henry – Jamie, this isn't right.'

Jamie took hold of her hand, and gripped it tightly. 'Come on, Lucy, for once I want *you* to listen to *me*.'

'It isn't right,' Lucy reiterated.

Jamie ducked his head as if she had tried to slap him.

'Right?' he asked her. 'You tell me what's right! Is it right that a whole civilization should be dominated by a handful of people, your husband worst of all. Is it right that babies should be starving before they're even born? Is it right that five-year-old children should die of typhoid and cholera and dysentery? Let me ask you this – is it right that millions and millions of people should live their lives from birth to death without being given one single anna of the riches that their country has to offer them?'

'Jamie,' said Lucy, turning away, 'I can't do anything to help your guilt about the Cheyenne; and I'm not going to help you; and I'm not going to listen. Good day. And good day to *you*, Mr Gunga Din.'

She began to climb up the steep slippery sides of the hollow, holding her skirts up to help herself up, when Bal Gangadhar Tilak called, 'Mrs Viceroy! Wait!'

Lucy hesitated, and turned around. From out of the bushes, Tilak had beckoned a young girl, no more than four or five, only a little older than Blanche. She wore a blanket to cover her, but nothing else. Her hair was sticky with dirt and thick with nits, and her lips were crusted with yellow sores. All the same, her eyes were wide and dark and intelligent; and if she had been washed and dressed and treated by a doctor, she would have been captivatingly pretty.

'Your Excellency,' said Bal Gangadhar Tilak, 'this is the daughter of my cousin who lives close to Delhi. I visited him on my way to meet with Mr Cullen, and to talk to my people in Simla. I brought her with me because she is very sick, and will certainly die if she is left in the plains during the Hot Weather. Her name is Pratima, which means golden temple idol. She is almost starving; she has rickets and worms and many different diseases from which starving people suffer. Look at her, she is very dirty and sad.'

Bal Gangadhar Tilak laid his hand with great gentleness on Pratima's head. 'She is given to us from the gods, and if necessary the gods will take her back. But there is a way in which her suffering can be used to prevent the suffering of many other children, in many generations to come. Your friend Mr Cullen risked very much to bring me here to talk

590

to you. I risked much; and so did you. I am a wanted brigand with a price on my head. I am supposed to be a dangerous man, a murderer! But – look at this little girl; and ask yourself what has she done to deserve such suffering. Ask yourself that. And then say to me that you cannot at least speak to His Excellency for just a few minutes about helping the plight of such innocents.'

Blanche, thought Lucy. She climbed slowly back down the hollow, and Jamie lifted his hand to help her. She leaned over Pratima and touched her cheek with her fingers, and Pratima shivered.

Bal Ganghadar Tilak made a resigned-looking face. 'She may survive, she may not. She has more chance than most, because I have brought her here. But if she has persuaded you to talk to the Viceroy about her plight; and about the plight of so many millions of our people . . . well, she will have achieved something with her short life, won't she?'

'Pratima?' Lucy cajoled the little girl. 'Pratima?'

Then, softly, she sang to her:

> '*Tip, tip, my little horse,*
> *Tip, tip, again sir!*
> *How many miles to Dublin town?*
> *Fourscore and ten, sir!*
> *Will I get back by candlelight?*
> *Yes, and back again, sir!*'

Pratima smiled faintly, and then covered her eyes with her hand. Bal Gangadhar Tilak laughed. 'She is shy, you see! Even when you are starving, even when you are dying, you can be shy!'

Lucy thought of her picnic, of her Hole Rose Chicken, and her pain and her shame were almost too much for her to bear. She stood up straight, her lower lip trembling with grief and emotion, and said to Jamie, 'I'm sorry. I'm sorry I misjudged you.'

Jamie held her tightly in his arms. 'Sssh, hey. You don't have to be sorry. You haven't done anything at all.'

'But I love you!'

'I know. And I love you, too.'

She tugged a handkerchief out of her pocket and dabbed at her eyes. 'I'll do – I'll do what I can. I'll talk to Henry, in any case. How long are you going to be here?'

'Not more than two more days,' said Bal Gangadhar Tilak. 'We have very many people to see, up and down the whole country.'

'Oh, Jamie,' said Lucy, and hugged him close. 'What happened to those cloud-castles?'

'They're still there,' said Jamie. 'But, you know – I don't know. Maybe they were always just clouds, and nothing else.'

That night, in her study, by electric light, she sat at her small Regency desk and wrote Jamie a letter. Mauve ink, the same mauve that Lady Elgin had favoured, on vellum paper. On the wall beside her, engravings of Victoria and Albert regarded her with imperial seriousness. Outside, the monkeys still screamed.

'Viceregal Lodge, Simla
April 10 1899

'My darling Jamie,
There will be no opportunity for us to meet again before you leave. But never forget that I love you. Carry that thought with you wherever you go.
As for Bal Gangadhar Tilak, tell him that I will talk to Henry; and that I will try to persuade him that Tilak is a man of honour who cares only for the welfare of the young and the old and the starving.
Meanwhile, I love you, my darling Jamie. I love you, I love you. And in all the years to come.
Your Cloud-Castle, Lucy.'

When she had blotted the letter, and dropped scarlet wax on to it, and impressed the wax with the viceregal seal, she called for a messenger to take it to the Hotel Cecil. 'And guard it with your life,' she told the small barefooted boy.

'Yes, *memsahib*,' the boy had assured her, and scampered off.

Elizabeth had walked into the room just as the boy was running away, and seen Lucy putting away her pen and her blotter, and frowned.

She heard no word from Jamie the following morning; nor the morning after that. She sent a bearer to the Hotel Cecil, inquiring about Mr Cullen; but the bearer came back with a three-toothed grin to say that Mr Cullen had left Simla at eleven o'clock, with two servants and four coolies. He had left no message; he had left no forwarding address. He had vanished, without a word, without a goodbye.

Lucy spent the rest of the afternoon in her drawing room, staring out over the mountains; but as night had fallen the mist had closed in; and the mountains had looked eerier and stranger than ever before. She heard a cry that wasn't monkeys and wasn't men; but something else altogether.

After Jamie's unaccountable disappearance, Lucy slept badly. She lay in bed night after night, thinking about him; hearing his voice. *I wanted Blanche to have a mother and a father*. And all the time the spring winds whispered and rustled through the Lodge, lifting curtains, turning over pages of magazines, stirring the dreams of the sleeping *ayahs*.

There was nothing that she could do. She couldn't send anybody to look for Jamie, or to find out where he might have gone. He had told her that his next stop was Amritsar, and then Kashmir, and she was tempted to send a telegraph to the resident at Amritsar, asking him to look out for Jamie on the pretext that he had left a valuable cigarette case behind, when he had visited Viceregal Lodge for dinner. But in the end she decided against it. She had already tied herself up into enough of a tangle over Jamie.

On Wednesday night she sat up reading until well after one o'clock in the morning. Etta had come in to see her just after eleven, to ask her if she wanted some warm milk or a powder to help her sleep. But Lucy had shaken her head. She was tired; but she wanted to think about Jamie. She needed to churn her feelings about him around and around in her head, like shirts in a washing-machine, until she was certain that she didn't love him more than she loved Henry. Or until she was certain that she did.

At one o'clock, she slipped out of her mosquito-nets, wrapped herself in her long white cambric robe, and stepped out on to the balcony. The night was the palest lilac; chilly but fragrant; and the sound of streams rushing down the dark and precipitous valleys was like the sound of blood rushing through her veins.

She felt as if she had been thinking for so long that her mind hurt. If only she could forget Sha-sha; if only Jamie hadn't kissed her in just that particular way. If only she hadn't slept with Malty. If only she hadn't ever set eyes on Henry.

She took the photograph of Blanche out of her pocket and angled it towards the moonlight so that she could see that serious little face, those chubby little arms. Jamie had said that she had skinny legs now; so she must have grown since this picture had been taken. If only I hadn't left you behind, my darling daughter.

She was still peering at the picture when she heard a soft knocking at the door of her bedroom. Quickly, guiltily, she turned around, trying to push the photograph back into the pocket of her robe. She missed her pocket, and dropped the photograph on to the tiled floor of the balcony; and just as she reached down to pick it up, the wind caught it, and tumbled it through the railings, and out into the night.

She was still anxiously trying to see where the photograph had fallen when Elizabeth appeared, in her nightcap, and the most severe and modest of missionary nightgowns.

'Why, Lucy! What on earth are you doing? You'll catch your death! That's if you don't tipple off the balcony!'

Lucy turned around, tearful. 'I dropped my – hairslide.'

'Your *hairslide*?' Elizabeth went to the edge of the balcony and looked over, into the shadows. 'Do you want me to send a *chokra* to go and look for it.'

'No, no, I don't want to wake anybody up.'

'Was it valuable?' asked Elizabeth.

'No, really, it was sentimental, more than anything else. Henry gave it to me.' She wiped her eyes. 'I'm too sensitive, right now. Anything makes me cry.'

Elizabeth put her arm around her, and guided her back into the bedroom. 'Well, we'll find it in the morning, when it's light. And I've just heard wonderful news from Mr Frognal. Henry's coming up to Simla tomorrow. He should be here by teatime.'

'Henry? That's marvellous.'

'Well, you may not think it, my dear, but it is. Once the Viceroy's arrived, the social whirl will *really* start! Which is not to say that you haven't started it already, my dear. But in your condition, of course, it has been rather difficult for you.'

Lucy sat down on her bed and looked towards the open balcony windows, as if she half-expected Sha-sha's photograph to come tumbling mysteriously back in again. But it was gone for good, she knew it was gone for good, and so was Jamie. Perhaps the wind and the night were trying to show her the right thing to do.

'Elizabeth,' she said, still staring at the balcony, 'have you ever been in love?'

Elizabeth had been tightening the ribbons around her wrists. She paused; uncertain at the tone in Lucy's voice.

'Yes,' she said, 'I've been in love.'

'What was his name?'

Elizabeth finished tightening her ribbon. 'Richard, that was his name. Captain Richard Watson, 13th Bengal Cavalry. He married a girl named Minnie Forrester, in the end. She had a thick black moustache, almost as magnificent as his. I heard later that he died in Egypt. Not heroically, either. Food poisoning.'

'I'm sorry.'

'Don't be. He was a beast, really.'

Elizabeth waited for a moment or two, and then she said, 'Why do you ask?'

'I'm not really sure,' Lucy admitted. 'I just wondered if you knew what it was like.'

Elizabeth let out a little laugh. 'You're the expert, surely! Married to the most dashing man in the British Empire!'

'I just wondered how you could ever be *sure*.'

Elizabeth came over to the bed and sat beside her. She smelled of lavender-water, and some kind of clove-scented rub. 'You're having a baby, you know. Your affections go quite topsy-turvy when you're having a baby.'

'I suppose so.'

'Are you worried about what you feel for Henry?'

Lucy said, 'I'm more worried about what I *don't* feel for Henry.'

'Well, don't think any more about it. These days, your brain is concentrating on loving your baby. It doesn't have much time for Henry; but it will.'

'Did your Richard make you shiver?' asked Lucy.

Elizabeth stared at her. She had begun to realize that perhaps Lucy wasn't talking about Henry at all; but about somebody else.

'At first,' she said. 'But when I saw him years and years later, with Minnie and four diminutive Minnie-ettes, I shivered! Not from excitement, my dear — but from profound relief.'

*

Lucy called Etta to dress her especially early that morning.

'Miss Morris told me that Lord Carson's coming this afternoon,' Etta smiled, as she brushed out Lucy's curls in front of the gilded dressing-room mirrors.

'Yes,' said Lucy. 'Now the fun's supposed to start.'

Etta obviously noticed the flatness in her voice, because she caught Lucy's eyes in the mirror; and paused in her hair-brushing. A small hand on a heavy silver-backed brush, a wedding gift from Lord Salisbury.

'You're looking a little tired, your ladyship, if you'll forgive me,' said Etta.

'Oh, it's nothing. Sleeping in a strange bed, that's all. And you know what they say about Simla. One of those unquiet places, crowded with ghosts.'

'I can't truthfully say that I've ever seen a ghost myself,' said Etta, carrying on brushing. 'Not sure that I want to, either.'

She brushed out the back of Lucy's hair, and caught a tangle.

'Oh, for goodness' sake!' Lucy snapped. 'Nora never –!'

She stopped herself, 'I'm sorry, Etta. That was wrong of me.'

'I miss Nora, too, you know, Lady Carson,' said Etta.

'Well, I suppose we all do. It's just that Nora worked for me when I was living in America. She was more of a friend that a lady's maid.' Lucy didn't add, of course, that only Nora had known about Blanche. If Nora had still been alive, she would at least have had somebody to talk to; somebody to tell how upset she was that she had lost Blanche's photograph.

Etta pinned up Lucy's hair. 'I hope that I can be your friend, too, Lady Carson; given time.'

Lucy turned, and took hold of Etta's hand. 'Of course you can. You are already.'

Somebody knocked at the door. Etta went to answer it, and it turned out to be Mrs Smallwood, Lucy's nurse. She was a neat, busy-mannered woman with black scraped-back hair and a white cotton apron and the efficient thinness of a truly dedicated nurse. It was said that she had lectured the Senior Surgeon at Madras so ferociously about the admission of women to the medical profession that he had broken down and wept (albeit after a half-bottle of Spencer & Co.'s cognac). She reminded Lucy of Mrs Noah in a children's Noah's Ark – hard, varnished, and bossy.

'You won't mind if I take your temperature, will you?' she insisted, setting her brown leather satchel on the nearest table and taking out her thermometer. She always spoke in the form of challenging questions, like a nanny. It must have been that maternal hectoring which had finally reduced the Senior Surgeon to tears.

'But I was going out for a walk,' Lucy protested.

'A walk? At this time of the morning? In your condition? After scarlatina? With all that dew on the ground? I'm sure you aren't serious, are you?'

'I feel like some exercise,' said Lucy. 'I feel so cooped up.'

'There is sensible exercise and there is silly exercise,' Mrs Smallwood replied, popping the thermometer into Lucy's mouth. 'I'm sure you know that, don't you?'

'Mmff,' Lucy replied.

'When the dew has evaporated, and the air is clear, you may take a short walk, if that's what you wish. But you do understand that His Excellency is coming this afternoon, and His Excellency wouldn't care to find you tired and out-of-sorts – now, would he?'

'Muffuff,' said Lucy.

Lucy breakfasted with Elizabeth Morris in the Plassey Room; a small quiet parlour with arches of saffron-coloured tiles, and long linen curtains which blew in the morning wind like the flags of some ancient order of Buddhist monks.

Elizabeth like *khagina* for breakfast, an Indian spiced omelette mixed with bessan, coriander, cardamoms and onions, and cut into thick diagonal slices. Lucy had her usual porridge, with a little cream. Mrs Smallwood had told her that any Indian spices would affect her unborn baby's digestion.

Elizabeth wore a rather arty dress of crimson-and-indigo printed muslin; and pearls. As she helped herself to the rolled-rice pancakes called *dosha*, she said, as if it had only just occurred to her, 'You meant, of course, have I ever loved more than one man at a time?'

'What?' asked Lucy, startled.

Elizabeth smiled, with her mouth full. 'When we were talking last night. You meant had I ever loved more than one man at a time. At least – forgive me – that's what I *thought* you meant.'

Lucy said nothing, but sipped her tea and waited to hear what Elizabeth was going to say next.

Elizabeth swallowed the last of her *khagina*, and fastidiously wiped her mouth. 'There's a famous Indian story, about a millionaire who was looking for a wife. He went to rich households and he went to poor households. He talked to girls who were beautiful and to girls who were plain. He asked them all the same question: *can you make a good meal out of two pounds of rice?*

'Of course they all laughed at him. That is – until he found a dazzlingly pretty girl who said, yes, she could. She took the rice, and carefully threshed it, keeping the grains and setting aside the husks. She sold the husks to jewellers, who use them to polish silver; and with the money she bought firewood and two pans.

'She lit the wood, and steamed the rice grains; and when the wood was all burned she sold the charcoal; and with the money she made from the charcoal she bought ghee and curds and oil and myrobalan and tamarind.

'She was able to serve the millionaire with rice broth, and kedgeree, and buttermilk, and soup. She served everything beautifully, with water scented with aloe wood; and of course he fell in love with her and married her.'

Lucy finished her tea. 'I'm not sure what you're trying to tell me.'

Elizabeth gave a little dismissive shrug. 'I think I'm trying to tell you to make the best of what you have. Your marriage to Henry may sometimes seem as unexciting as two pounds of rice. But if you work hard, and attend to what you have, it will one day bring you joy and happiness and great satisfaction.'

She paused for a while, and then she said, 'You were born in modest circumstances, my dear, in a place very far from here; and what happened to you happened by extraordinary chance and by dramatic good fortune. But now the responsibility for your future happiness is yours. You have more than most women ever dream of. I know that you feel uncertain. I know that you are sometimes simply bored. You doubt Henry's love. You doubt your own love for Henry.

'But like those two pounds of rice, a marriage needs care and work and constant attention; exchanging each reward for another reward; until you have not just two pounds of rice, but a banquet.'

Lucy looked back at Elizabeth for such a long time without speaking that Elizabeth eventually said, 'Lucy? You're feeling quite well?'

'Yes,' said Lucy. 'I'm fine.'

But then she said, 'What if I'd done that, a long time ago, with somebody else? I mean, what if I'd worked just as hard at loving *him*?'

Elizabeth smiled. 'What if I'd married Richard Watson? What if the world ended tomorrow?'

She reached out and touched the knuckles of Lucy's hand. 'In India, questions like that are called "flowers that grow in the sky". They have no point, Lucy. They are idle thoughts that will make you sad, and lead you nowhere at all.'

The two of them remained at the table while the servants cleared away the dishes, and the curtains rose and fell; and outside they heard shouting and laughter and the clattering of feet, as the Lodge was made ready for the arrival of His Excellency Lord Carson, Lucy's husband.

She managed to slip out into the gardens shortly after eleven o'clock, with a light shawl around her shoulders. She skirted around the Lodge until she was standing below her balcony window; and then she carefully searched through the flower-beds and the bushes, trying to work out where Blanche's photograph might have fallen.

She was picking through the Apline rockery when a *mali* appeared, wheeling a wheelbarrow.

'Hey, you!' called Lucy, as he made his way down the sloping lawns. '*Koi-hai!*'

The *mali* stopped, and set down his wheelbarrow. He was very young; and his face was pockmarked and pale. '*Mem-sahib?*'

'Have you been working here all morning?'

The *mali* clearly didn't understand. For the first time, Lucy felt infuriated that she hadn't learned any Urdu.

'Have – you – been – working – here –' she began, much louder, but then she realized that shouting made no difference: all she was doing was frightening him.

'Have you seen a picture?' she asked him. 'A picture, of a little girl?'

He stared at her, nervous, desperate to oblige, but completely uncomprehending.

'A picture,' she repeated, drawing tiny invisible squares in the air. 'A *photograph*. Picture of missy *baba*.'

'Missy *baba*?' frowned the *mali*, completely perplexed. He hadn't seen any little girls around Viceregal Lodge. There were no European children here at all; no *chota* sahibs or missy *babas*.

Lucy took a deep breath, and then she said, 'If – you – see – a – picture – of – a – missy – baba –' But it was hopeless. He didn't know what she meant.

She turned, and walked back across the shiny overwatered grass. Tin-pot birds called from the trees around her, alarmed by the comings and goings of the servants and the officers of the Viceroy's Bodyguard. Elizabeth was waiting by the stone steps that led up to the conservatory.

'Did you find it?' she called.

For a moment, Lucy was perplexed.

'Your hairslide,' Elizabeth reminded her.

'Oh,' said Lucy. 'No. It must have bounced, or gotten buried in the bushes.'

Elizabeth took hold of her arm. 'It'll turn up. You mark my words. I've sent boxes and parcels from one end of India to the other. Once I even sent some children, some young cousins of ours, with nothing but a picnic box, and a cardboard label saying *Bombay*. I've never lost anything yet.'

Together, they went back into the Lodge. Already the servants were sweeping and polishing and hurrying from one room to another with huge bowls of sweetpeas and daisies. Corcoran the butler creaked into view like a pirate ship under full sail, and asked, 'You *did* say the summer pudding, your ladyship?' Then John Frognal came jingling past, in full uniform, and saluted, and said, 'His Excellency should arrive at three o'clock, Lady Carson. I've just had the word.'

'Well, my dear,' said Elizabeth, talking hold of Lucy's hand, 'it seems as if your two pounds of rice are being delivered.'

Lucy couldn't help laughing. 'Henry would be *furious* if he heard you call him that!'

Henry strode into the gloomy panelled hallway of Viceregal Lodge with his hat in his hand, looking hot. Lucy was waiting for him inside, in one of the huge brocade armchairs by the foot of the staircase, fanning herself. She had chosen her blue linen tea-gown; the blue made her eyes look even more blue; and Etta had pinned up her hair for her in the soft, loose curls that she knew Henry adored.

Long pearl earrings swung from her ears.

Henry stopped quite still, and looked at her. 'Lucy,' he said; as soft and sharp as a nutmeg chipped against a metal grater.

Lucy stood up and faced him. He was dressed quite informally, in a linen suit and breeches, and a black silk necktie. He looked exhausted; as if his skin had collapsed around his face. But she detected a certain burned-down pleasure in the way he had walked in; as if he had completed his work in Calcutta to his immediate satisfaction, and was now quite prepared for some recreation and entertainment in the Hills.

He came forward and carefully kissed her. 'I've missed you,' he said; and he couldn't have said anything that pleased her more.

'I've missed you too. Things have been pretty dull up here.'

'You're well, though? You're feeling quite fit? Mrs Smallwood has been sending me daily reports.'

'Well done Mrs Smallwood! Yes, I'm feeling wonderful.'

Lucy took hold of Henry's sleeve. 'Master Carson's been kicking. Especially at night.'

Henry's eyes creased with pleasure. 'Has he now? The little blighter! And is everything well?'

'Everything's fine, Henry. Everything's wonderful.'

'Horatio Carson,' Henry enthused. 'And what a mark he shall make!'

'Henry,' said Lucy. She could see that his sense of his position was taking over; his sense of history and grandeur. Carson upon Carson, down the centuries! Let them hold what they held! She could scarcely speak to him when he behaved like that. It might be hours before he talked like a husband again; or like a lover.

He blinked at her.

'Henry,' she repeated. 'I'm feeling so good because I've been resting. I feel like myself again. I want you to do the same. Rest, and spend some time with me.'

Henry nodded, and smiled, and kissed her forehead. As he

did so, Lucy glanced towards the door. Caught in the afternoon sunlight stood Colonel Belloc, in a perfectly-pressed white suit; and behind him, dark and humourless and attentive, stood Vernon. Their eyes met, Lucy's and Vernon's; and although Lucy immediately looked away, she felt herself flush with guilt and embarrassment; and with the sheer hatefulness of what she had done.

Colonel Belloc came forward and took hold of her hand, and kissed her glove. 'Lady Carson, what a delight! I was planning on a visit back Home, as a matter of fact; but H.E. wanted to spend the Hot Weather talking about buildings, so here I am! Probably just as well. Time I opened up the old house and gave it an airing, don't you think? You and H.E. must come to dinner! It's just along the Ridge – Bellocgunge. Named after me and my brother, don't you see?'

Henry was already climbing the stairs, followed by Corcoran and Vernon and Muhammad Isak and twenty or thirty bearers and coolies carrying Henry's trunks.

Colonel Belloc waited until Henry had reached the half-landing, and then he murmured, 'As a matter of fact, I was much more interested in seeing you, than in talking about buildings. Please don't misinterpret my intentions, Lady Carson. I'm an honourable man. But I'm also a great believer in offering my services to all who seem to require them. Spiritual, political, artistic, sexual. I'm like a bazaar, don't you see, with insights for sale, instead of sweetmeats and incense.'

Lucy wasn't offended; but she wasn't sure that she was pleased, either. She gave Colonel Belloc a fleeting smile, and said, 'I'll see you at dinner, Colonel. And tomorrow we're going for a picnic. Perhaps we can talk then.'

'Be delighted to, your ladyship,' Colonel Belloc replied, and bowed, so that she could hear the laces of his corset creak.

That night, Henry and Lucy slept together; although Henry did no more than kiss her and hold her in his arms.

When Horatio started to kick, Lucy took hold of Henry's hand and pressed it against her stomach, so that he could feel it. He said nothing at first, but looked at her in wonder and amazement.

'Horatio,' he whispered.

'Perhaps,' she replied.

He slept very deeply for most of the night, with his back turned towards her. Towards dawn, however, he began to whisper and tremble, and say 'No, father,' over and over again.

She shushed him, and stroked his shoulder. Somehow, in Simla, away from his desk at Government House, he seemed very much more vulnerable, very much more human – very much more like the man who had once said to her, '*when you're in love, you're on fire*.'

Dawn began to lighten the sky beyond the balcony. Henry opened his eyes and stared at Lucy for a long time, as if he didn't know who she was.

She kissed him. He tasted like Henry. Cedarwood, salt, some particular masculine flavour.

'You're in Simla,' she told him, when he still failed to show any signs of recognition.

'My father's not here?' he asked her.

'No,' she mouthed. 'Your father's not here.'

He sat up. 'That's strange, you know. I dreamed that he was. I wanted to ask him about plaster of Paris.'

'Plaster of Paris?'

'Yes, to –'

But then Henry stopped. He had suddenly realized that he was talking dream-talk; and that in fact he was here, in bed with Lucy, in Simla.

'Do you know something?' he said, frowning around the bedroom. 'I could have *sworn* that –'

Lucy kissed him again. 'Simla is known for its ghosts. Perhaps you just met one.'

She went back into the gardens the following afternoon,

after she and Henry had given a 'delighted-to-meet-you' lunch to most of the members of the Simla Amateur Dramatic Company, all of whom were excessively noisy and pleased with themselves, and half of whom had drunk too much hock.

But now the rickshaws had all rolled away; carrying officers and wives and paramours, shouting out Shakespeare as they went, 'What's gone and what's past help!'; and Viceregal Lodge seemed extraordinarily quiet. Even the birds seemed disinclined to sing. All that Lucy could hear was the indolent flapping of the huge Union Jack on top of the crenellated turret, and the faint clamour of washing-up from the direction of the kitchens.

She found herself a stick, and began to probe through the bushes directly beneath her bedroom window. She found a small square of pasteboard, and her heart jumped; but it was only a visiting-card from somebody illegible. She picked up her skirts a little, and carried on jabbing and poking in the thickest places.

She was still searching when she heard a slight noise behind her. She lifted her head, and looked around, one hand on her large straw hat to prevent the breeze from lifting it off her head. Not far away stood Vernon, with his hands held so tightly behind his back that he looked as if he had no arms; as if his body were a black limbless sausage.

'Vernon!' said Lucy. 'You startled me!'

'Sorry about that, your ladyship,' Vernon replied. 'I'm not a startler by nature.'

'I suppose you want another chit,' said Lucy, stepping out of the shrubbery.

'Oh! Well – that, yes. All in good time.'

'I should never have agreed to it. It was quite absurd. Mr Cullen and I – well, Mr Cullen and I were childhood friends, that's all.'

Vernon nodded: 'Quite sure of it, your ladyship. Quite sure of it.'

Lucy looked at him keenly. 'Then you'll stop asking me for all this money?'

Vernon contorted his face in a complicated squinting grimace, giving Lucy what Cockneys called 'the north eye'. 'Can't say that,' he told her.

'Then what can you say? I used to work once, the same way you work. You're not Jack-out-of-doors and you're not the gentleman, either; so we can understand each other.'

Vernon sniffed, and stood uprighter. 'I like you, your ladyship. You're straight.'

Lucy waited, and Vernon remained upright. In the distance, they could hear hounds yapping, and the sound of somebody shouting, 'Heel! Heel, sir! Heel.'

'I wonder if you've been looking for something,' Vernon remarked.

'Looking for something? What do you mean?'

'Well, the way you was jumbling that bush with that stick of yours, I thought you might of lost something valuable.'

'My hairslide as a matter of fact,' Lucy replied, primly.

'Your *hairslide*?' grinned Vernon; as triumphant as a parent who knows all the time what his erring child has done wrong. He gave Lucy the same terrible feeling that Jack had given her when she was six years old, and had stolen three twists of cough-candy.

'Do you want your chit or don't you?' Lucy demanded. 'I could arrange for cash, two hundred rupees.'

'Well, now,' said Vernon, 'a kiss and a cuddle in the sewing room, that isn't worth more than two hundred rupees, that's agreed. But what about this? What do you think *this* is worth?'

He produced one arm from behind his back, and held in front of her nose the sepia photograph of Blanche. Dangled it, danced it, flicked it.

'*Where did you get that?*' Lucy snapped at him, snatching at it.

607

Vernon whipped it out of her reach. 'Lovely little girl, aint she? Pretty little thing. And such a sentimental message on the back.'

Lucy was shaking, and her eyes were filling with tears. 'You bastard,' she hissed. 'Where did you get that?'

'Easy,' Vernon told her. 'One of the *syces* found it on the path, and the *syce* gave it to the *dewan* and when we came in through the gates the *dewan* showed it to me, and asked me if I knew who it belonged to, and I took a look at the back and said serpently, course I did.'

He grinned even more widely. 'Providence, I'd call it. God's provision. Manna from heaven.'

'Give it to me,' Lucy insisted, her heart beating painfully against her ribcage.

'Give up the goose what lays the golden eggs? *Juwaub* to you, your ladyship.'

'Give it to me,' Lucy repeated. 'It's mine, and I want it.'

'I'm sure of it,' Vernon taunted her. 'But the question is, how bad do you want it? I mean to say, what would His Excellency say if he clapped his mincers on young Fanny Adams here? What would His Excellency think, if His Excellency found out that Her Excellency had been playing mummies and daddies with some Yankee nosper?'

'Give it to me,' Lucy begged him; and her voice was quite naked. 'It's all I have of her, that photograph.'

Vernon held it between two fingers, turning it this way and that.

'Thousand a month,' he told her.

'A thousand rupees? That's more than fifty pounds!'

'Seventy-five, to be precise.'

'I can't give you seventy-five pounds a month. I just can't!'

'Course you can. You're the Vicereine, you'll find a way. Colonel Miller spends twice that much on sherry. And bloody awful sherry it is, too.'

'I want my photograph.'

'Course you do. And I'll give it you back, if you're obliging. But I'll make myself a copy first, just to make sure. This is my jury, chummage and couter, this photograph is – knife, fork and spoon. I couldn't let you have it without making myself a copy, now could I?'

Lucy felt her stomach tightening in a contraction. 'I'm expecting a baby,' she whispered. 'How could you do such a thing?'

Vernon shrugged. 'It's the weak and the strong, aint it, your ladyship? Some live by noble birth, but most of us live on our wits.'

'I wasn't nobly born, you know that.'

'Ah,' Vernon smiled. 'But you're wealthy now; and you're weak. And if the Lord God don't find you out, then His Excellency will; and which is worster? Tell me that?'

'Give me my photograph.'

'Yes, your ladyship,' said Vernon. The sun shone on his brilliantined hair. 'Just as soon as I have your chit for a thousand rupees. Fair dos for all, that's what I say.'

The next evening, after dinner, Henry went to the library to work on his diaries; and Lucy was left by the fire with Colonel Belloc.

'You seem sad,' said Colonel Belloc, spinning his cognac around in his glass.

'Sad? Do I?' asked Lucy. Her hair shone in silk-fine strands in the firelight. She was wearing a green velvet evening gown, quite low-cut, that showed off the deep cleavage of her swollen breasts. She looked beautiful; she felt beautiful; with all the glow of pregnancy. But Colonel Belloc was right. She felt sad, too. Sad that she had abandoned Blanche; sad that she had lost her photograph. Sad that she was unable to seek the advice and comfort of her own husband.

For reasons she couldn't fully understand, she was beginning to feel closer to Henry than she had before. Perhaps she was simply growing more used to her life in India. Perhaps, by meeting and talking to Jamie, and seeing how much Blanche had grown up, she had accepted the reality that there could be no turning back.

There was something else, too. When she had watched Henry at work today – surrounded by governors and residents and maharajahs – constantly busy, constantly talking, constantly writing – she had felt proud of him, proud of what he was doing, and proud that she was a part of it.

Somehow that made her sadness all the more acute, because she had betrayed him, if only for a few moments – and if only in her heart.

Colonel Belloc said, 'You shouldn't be sad, you know. You'd be quite amazed how devoted Henry is to you. While we were travelling up here, you know, we had quite a talk. He's very concerned that he doesn't show you often enough how much he loves you.'

Lucy raised her eyes. 'He's very busy.'

'Of course. He has India to govern; and his own enthusiasms to pursue. But he thinks of you constantly, you know, and how to make you happy.'

'Henry hasn't made me feel sad,' Lucy replied. 'I just feel sad.'

Colonel Belloc swallowed more cognac. 'You're allowed to feel sad on occasions, my dear. Why not? Sadness is one of the nine moods of dramatic art. Whenever I see a woman looking pensive, I always remember the *ragini* of the rainy season.'

'The what?'

'Oh, I'm sorry, I'm being obscure as usual. During the medieval centuries, some Indian poets composed series of exquisite poems which they called Ragamalas, which means garlands of *ragas* - that's the male form - or *raginis* - that's the female form. Little mood pieces, as it were. And the *ragini* about the rainy season says that she is "pale and weak, her voice like the Kokil singing; some cadence of the song reminds her of her lord".'

610

Lucy started to smile.

'Mind you, it's spring, and the *ragini* for spring says, "My heart dreams of the firm-breasted Hindola with broad hips, who wears bright-coloured clothes; with the flower of the lotus she worships Lord Krishna who sits on a swing hung among the twisted roots of the banyan tree. She hears the notes of his flute, her heart full of love, her beautiful limbs adorned with jewels."'

Colonel Belloc's eyes were bright as he looked at her. 'That, my dear – that reminds me of you.' He coughed into his fist. 'Well, all except the broad hips, perhaps.'

They talked together until well after half past ten. After spending three or four weeks in Simla, Colonel Belloc was planning on a visit to Mount Abu in Rajputana, to examine the lavishly-carved Dilwara temple. He showed Lucy pages of drawings that he had made on his first visit there; sinuous stone figures intertwined with demons and gods and snakes and horses.

He told her about the God Vishnu. He recounted the adventures of Krishna, and how he had copulated so deliciously with the village women of Brindaban that they had pursued him through thorn-thickets, tearing off their clothes as they ran. He told her about the male followers of Chaitanya, who perceived the universe as feminine, and dressed up as giggling, flighty girls.

He was like a talking library on Indian art and music and religion; and through his eyes she began to see that she could reach Henry after all; that she had been immature and selfish and stubborn, and that the barriers between them would cease to exist the moment she said, 'they cease to exist'.

When at last Lucy excused herself to retire to bed, Colonel Belloc stood up and gave her the courtly bow, back straight, head bent. 'I hope I haven't bored you,' he said, taking her hand.

'Quite the contrary, Colonel. You've taught me more in one evening than my schoolteachers taught me in seven years.'

'Just remember,' said Colonel Belloc. 'There are no problems, only solutions. If something is standing in your way, all you have to say is, "*there is nothing standing in my way*."'

While Etta waited for her in the hallway, Lucy went to the library to say goodnight to Henry. She found him furiously writing, his head in his hand, with books and reports lying open all around him, as if a flock of dead albatrosses had landed on his desk. He put down his pen, and raised his head, his expression cautious, as if he expected her to be irritated that he was still working so late.

She stood behind him and laid her hands on his shoulders and kissed his hair. 'I'm going to bed now. Don't get too tired.'

He turned in his chair and looked at her carefully. 'How was your evening?' he asked her.

She kissed him again. 'I enjoyed it. Your friend Gordon Belloc is absolutely fascinating. Maybe a little too fond of talking about the things that men and women get up to; but fascinating.'

'He's the real stuff of the Raj,' said Henry. 'You know, half of these Indians you hear jabbering about *Swaraj* don't even know half as much about their own culture as Gordon does. Gordon's devoted his whole life to it – the buildings, the paintings, the literature. Do you know that he can even play a *sitar*? I'll get him to demonstrate it for you.'

'What's *Swaraj*?' asked Lucy. 'I head Colonel Miller talking about it at lunch yesterday, to Saraji Rao.'

'*Swaraj*, my darling, is a rude word in this house. It means independence, self-rule for Indians, by Indians.'

'You mean, without us? Completely on their own?'

Henry nodded.

'But they couldn't manage to rule themselves, could they?'

'Of course not. But a few fanatics seem to have got it into their heads that they could.'

'But how could they run the railroads, and the post; and plant tea; and everything like that?'

Henry picked up his pen, and twisted the nib. 'They may be capable of it one day, in a hundred years' time, when all the work that we're doing here today bears fruit. All of the education, and the restructuring of government, and the engineering, and the agricultural development. But they're certainly not ready for it yet. The trouble is, most Indians are so gullible that it takes only a few agitators to stir up trouble amongst thousands of them, millions of them; and then the innocent suffer as well as the guilty.

'In fact,' he said, leafing through the papers on his desk, 'we've been having unconfirmed reports from Army intelligence that one or two of the most notorious agitators have been seen around Chandigar and Simla; so it's probably best if you don't repeat your little expedition of the other night.'

'Oh,' said Lucy. 'Lieutenant Burnes-Waterton told you about that.'

Henry grasped her hand, and smiled, and then kissed her fingertips. 'It was his duty to report it. After all, your safety that night was his personal responsibility. Don't worry, no harm was done. But I had to give him and John Frognal quite a severe dressing-down.'

Lucy said, 'Oh, I hope not too severe. It was all my fault.'

'No, my darling, not too severe.'

She left the library and closed the door behind her. As she did so, however, a black-suited figure appeared out of the shadows. It was Vernon, with his hands clasped behind his back.

'Good evening, your ladyship. A word with you, before you go.'

Lucy opened her pocket, and took out a thousand rupees, in new folded notes. She had told John Frognal that she needed the money for new dresses and hats. How she was going to explain it to Henry, when he came to audit the accounts, she had yet to devise.

'Here, this is what you asked for,' she told Vernon.

He took the money, licked his thumb, and quickly counted it.

'Well, most grateful,' he said.

'What about my photograph?'

'Ah,' said Vernon. 'I've got a little problem with the photograph.'

'What do you mean? You said a thousand rupees and I've given you a thousand rupees.'

'Yes, I did, and you have. But what I was thinking was, am I selling myself short? I mean, if the photograph is worth a thousand rupees, as ready as that; then maybe it's worth two thousand.'

'I can't give you any more!' Lucy protested. 'I just can't!'

'In that case, p'raps I'd better let his lordship have a *dekho* at it.'

'Vernon, I beg you! Give me back my photograph!'

'One thousand more,' Vernon insisted. 'Then, on my life, you can have it.'

'Vernon, I can't!'

'In that case, Lady Carson, suit yourself, that's all I can say. Those are the terms. One thousand more, or else that photograph lands itself on Lord Carson's desk, no messing.'

Lucy was shaking with frustration and anger. 'I can't possibly get hold of one thousand more. Perhaps – I don't know, perhaps five hundred.'

'One thousand or nothing, your ladyship. Those are the terms, and terms is terms.'

'How long will you give me?'

Vernon sniffed. 'Ooh . . . I don't know. Forty-eight hours, how's that? Sooner if you get it sooner.'

At that moment, Etta appeared at the end of the corridor. 'Are you ready to retire now, Lady Carson?'

'Yes, Etta!' Lucy called back. Then, to Vernon, in a soft poisonous hiss. 'All right, then. But this had better be your last demand; because if it isn't I'm going to tell the Viceroy what you've been doing myself, and damn the consequences!'

'Sleep well, your ladyship,' Vernon grinned, and disappeared back into the shadows.

*

That night, she lay awake for hour after hour. All she could think of was Sha-sha's face, in that tiny photograph; and Vernon; and what Walter had said to her, before he went back Home.

'*There are plenty of obliging fellows in India, who would silence a fellow like that for ever.*'

And then she thought of what Colonel Belloc had said, that very evening. '*If something is standing in your way, all you have to say is,* "There is nothing in my way."'

Very quietly, she whispered, 'There is nothing in my way. *There is nothing in my way.*'

She was out in the grounds of Viceregal Lodge the following afternoon, taking the air, her *chaprassi* shuffling behind her with her parasol, when a very tall Indian bearer came walking across the sloping lawn towards her, unusually quickly, and with an unusual sense of purpose.

She glanced around her, a little worried. Elizabeth wasn't far away, sitting placidly in her garden-chair embroidering a tray-cover. Two of Lieutenant Burnes-Waterton's men were standing at the corner of the house, by the verandah steps. But all the same, Henry had impressed on her twice more this morning that nationalist extremists had been reported in the district, and that she should take particular care.

Elizabeth had told her some terrible stories of attacks by Indian servants on British officers and women on the North West Frontier. Garottings, stabbings, and axes between the shoulder-blades — even in the street. For a week or two afterwards, she had watched her servants' movements with deep suspicion, particularly Tir' Ram, who was a Pathan, but even her *ayahs*, too. 'You see,' said Elizabeth, 'the Indian mind works entirely differently from ours. They're like Alsatians. They can give you love and affection and devoted service for twenty years. Then they can suddenly turn and bite your leg off.'

'The Alsatians or the servants?' Lucy had asked her.

'The Alsatians, of course. Most of the servants are vegetarians.'

But now the tall Indian was only a few feet away. He came right up to her, and bowed, and said, 'Salaam, Your Excellency.'

'What is it?' Lucy demanded. 'What do you want?'

Without lifting his turbaned head, the bearer said, 'Just a few words, if you can spare the time.'

Lucy stared at him. 'Jamie?'

He lifted his head and gave her a tight-lipped smile. He had shaved off his beard, and rubbed dark make-up into his skin, but now that she looked at him closely, she wondered why she hadn't recognized him at once. Maybe she never really looked at her servants; not as people; not as anyone she might be interested to talk to.

Jamie said, 'Tell your servant to give me the parasol. Then send him away.'

Lucy instructed the *chaprassi* to hand over the parasol; and then she and Jamie started to walk slowly down the gardens, beside the flowering shrubs. Elizabeth looked up once from her embroidery, but obviously saw nothing unusual in the tall liveried bearer who was following Lucy with a measured pace.

'I got your letter, thank you,' said Jamie. 'I'm sorry I couldn't answer. I had to leave in a hurry.'

'Why are you wearing this ridiculous disguise?' Lucy asked him. 'You could have come for tea, if you'd wanted to talk to me.'

'Well, I'm afraid not. And that's all part of the reason I had to leave Simla so quick.'

'I don't understand.'

'I've got British agents looking for me. They think I'm some kind of subversive. You know, whipping up unrest and dissension, that kind of thing.'

'But that's ridiculous! I could tell Henry that you're not! Then you could take all that stuff off your face. You look so silly in a turban.'

'I'm afraid it's not quite as easy as that,' said Jamie, as they made their way along the lower part of the lawn. 'Because I've been meeting people like Bal Gangadhar Tilak . . . well, it's going to be difficult for me to prove that I haven't been involved in stirring up trouble.'

'I haven't had the chance to talk to him about Bal Gangadhar Tilak yet.'

'Well . . . it's probably better that you don't, not now. I thought maybe that the British were becoming a little more receptive to the idea of Indian independence. Prepared to listen to some new ideas, at the very least. But they've had people looking for me ever since I left Calcutta.'

'Jamie, let me talk to Henry. Let me explain!'

'You could tell him how you feel about Indian self-rule. You could tell him that maybe it's time for the British to start listening to the people they govern, instead of ordering them around like three hundred million dumb animals.'

'But you can't go around with a blacked-up face all the time! Let me tell him you're here. I'm sure he'll understand!'

'Lucy,' said Jamie, 'there's a particular reason why you mustn't tell him that I'm here, not yet. It's too dangerous. Will you please just trust me?'

'But –'

'Trust me, Lucy, please.'

'All right, then,' Lucy agreed. Did she trust him, though? Could she? 'But if it's so dangerous, why did you come?'

'Just to see you. Just to make sure you're all right.'

'I'm fine, I'm really well.'

'You look tired.'

'Well . . . even empresses have their problems.'

They stood by the flight of stone steps at the bottom of the lawn, and looked out over the distant peaks of the Himalayas. The day was so warm and hazy that, beyond the deodar trees, the snow caps appeared to be hanging in mid-air, like starched and crumpled white flags.

'I heard that the Viceroy had arrived,' Jamie coaxed her. '*He's* not the problem, is he?'

'No,' Lucy replied, so softly that it was more like a breath than a word.

Jamie turned to her, frowning.

'What's wrong?' he asked her. 'You really do have a problem, don't you.'

'It's nothing I can't sort out for myself.'

Jamie said, 'It's nothing to do with me, is it?'

Lucy shrugged. For some reason, she found she had a lump in her throat. Being pregnant had made her so emotional, made her so quick to cry, and she hated it.

'Lucy, tell me, is it something to do with me?' Jamie insisted.

'Well, in a way, yes.'

'Then tell me. Come on, tell me. How can I help you if I don't know what's wrong?'

Lucy took out her handkerchief and wiped her eyes. 'That day in Calcutta . . . when you came to visit.'

'What about it?'

'We went into my sewing room, remember? We kissed?'

'What of it?' Jamie wanted to know.

'Nothing. I mean it wasn't wrong or bad or anything. But somebody was watching. Vernon, Henry's body-servant. It wouldn't have mattered so much if it hadn't been him. The trouble is, he's white, he's British, and Henry trusts him, thinks he's the salt of the earth.'

'Did he tell Henry?' asked Jamie.

Lucy shook her head.

'Then what do you have to worry about?' said Jamie. 'Surely Henry isn't going to take a servant's word against yours . . . even if the servant *is* white. Even if he *is* the salt of the earth. He wouldn't be much of a husband if he did.'

Tears started to cluster in Lucy's eyes again. 'It's not just that. I paid Vernon some money. I gave him a chit in my own handwriting, two hundred rupees. I know it was stupid, but it's too late now. And what's Henry going to think if he finds out that I've been paying Vernon to keep quiet? He's going to think that something terrible's been going on.'

Jamie half-lifted his hand, as if he were tempted to put his arm around her. But he had to remember that he was supposed to be an Indian servant, and he couldn't even touch her sleeve. He watched and waited, serious-faced, while she recovered herself.

'Don't you think it would be better to tell Henry the truth?' he asked her, at length.

'I wish I had. But something else happened. Something worse. I lost Blanche's photograph, it fell in the garden. One of the servants gave it to Vernon, and he made me give him a thousand rupees. Now he wants another thousand, by tomorrow, or he's going to show it to Henry.'

'Let him show it to Henry, for God's sake! What does it matter? You're not ashamed of Blanche, are you?'

'Jamie, don't you understand? If Henry found out about Blanche, our marriage would be finished, absolutely torn to pieces. It hasn't been especially happy, these past two years, it's just beginning to get better. I'm just beginning to understand how to be the kind of wife that Henry needs. It's been hard, Jamie. You have no idea how hard. I couldn't bear it if it all came apart.'

'So, what are you going to do?' said Jamie. 'Are you going to go on paying this leech? You'll have to, if you don't want Henry to know about us.'

'Jamie, there isn't any "us".'

'Not at all?'

'There can't be.'

'Well, whatever, you're still going to have to go on paying the money, now you've started.'

Lucy was silent for a long and difficult moment. She had thought about this, ever since she had talked to Walter in Calcutta, but up until now it had only been play-acting in her head, a ridiculous fantasy that could never come true. *There are plenty of obliging fellows in India, who would silence a chap like that for ever.*

'I suppose this sounds really evil, and absurd,' she heard herself saying. 'But that man I met, Tilak . . . I mean, was he joking when he said he was a murderer?'

Jamie wiped the sweat from his forehead with the back of his hand, leaving a smear of berry-dye. 'What are you suggesting?'

'I don't know. I'm desperate. I can't think what else I can do.'

'You want to have Vernon *killed*?'

'I don't know. No, of course not.'

Jamie was very thoughtful. The day was growing hazier still, all around them, until they appeared to be standing in a fog of evaporated gold. Lucy could hear the barbets singing, the tin-pot birds, down in the valley; and behind her the persistent and nearly-irritating tinkling of ice against glass, as Elizabeth swirled her glass of Rawlings ginger ale around and around and around.

'I'll think of something,' Lucy told Jamie. 'I didn't really mean –'

'No, no, listen,' said Jamie. 'I'm sure we can help you. Supposing we don't actually *kill* this Vernon fellow; but supposing instead we frighten him; warn him off. Tell him to give you back your photograph, and to stop blackmailing you, otherwise something very unpleasant is going to happen to him.'

'Could you really do that?' Lucy asked him. It seemed perfect. She had thought of killing Vernon over and over again; but the idea of frightening him half to death was so much better. So much more possible; so much more *exciting*.

Jamie said, 'All we'd have to do is smuggle one of Tilak's people into the Lodge . . . maybe dressed like a servant, like me. He could hide in Vernon's room; and when Vernon goes to bed, he could come out and hold a knife to Vernon's throat and tell him to behave himself.'

'Do you think it would work?'

Jamie grinned. 'What would *you* say, if somebody was holding a knife against your neck?'

Lucy laughed, a little hysterically. 'I think I'd say honest Injun!'

Jamie looked around. 'I doubt if I can find anybody to do it tonight. Let's say tomorrow.'

'There's a small side door by the verandah steps,' said Lucy. 'Tell the man to wait there about eight o'clock. I'll let him in, and show him the way to Vernon's room.'

'What about a password?' Jamie suggested.

'Kipling,' said Lucy.

'Kipling? For God's sake!'

'All right, then, *Swaraj*.'

'Very apt,' Jamie nodded. '*Swaraj* it is, eight o'clock tomorrow.'

'And your man won't do anything more than give Vernon a scare?'

Jamie said, 'Promise. He won't even be touched.'

Lucy tried to smile at him, but found that she couldn't. For the first time in all of the years that she had known him, she couldn't read in his eyes what he was thinking, what he was feeling. She had the disconcerting impression that she was looking into the eyes of a complete stranger; and it wasn't just the brown dye and the turban that made him seem so unfamiliar. She felt as if something had broken, somewhere inside of him. Hope, or ambition, or faith; or whatever it was that had made Jamie the boy she used to know.

Although she couldn't yet understand it, she felt intuitively that she was looking at a man who had loved and lost his only love; and in place of his love, embraced an ideal. An ideal that came knocking at poor men's doors.

'I'd better leave,' Jamie told her. 'I wish I could kiss you, but it wouldn't be very wise, would it? Especially if this Vernon fellow happened to see us. The Vicereine kissing the black help.'

'You'll tell your man, won't you, not to hurt him?'

'Not a whisker.'

Together, they walked back towards the Lodge. As soon as they reached the verandah, Jamie folded the parasol, propped it against the wall, and quickly made his way around to the side of the building, without turning back once. Lucy watched him go for a moment or two, then realized that it wasn't quite the thing for the mistress of the house to stare after one of the lowliest of her servants. She called for a *chaprassi*.

The next day was taken up with bitty little social events. In the morning, Lucy hosted a small bazaar in the conservatory in aid of Christian missionaries in Pondicherry. Very large women in very large hats stood behind rickety little card-tables draped with Union Jacks, stentoriously selling macramé plant-holders and hand-painted fans and tins of Huntley & Palmers Empire Assorted Biscuits.

Later, when the very large ladies had been bustled away in a procession of rickshaws, the Viceroy and Vicereine entertained to luncheon some of the more junior officers of the secretariat and their wives. The junior officers of the secretariat and their wives flushed a particular shade of boiled-ham-pink whenever they spoke or were spoken to, and afterwards Lucy remarked that for all their youthfulness she had seen more verve in a billiard-room full of stuffed bison.

'Thank you so much for your hospitality, Lady Carson,' one of the wives whispered. 'It was all so fearfully glamorous.'

Lucy smiled, and looked around her; at the baronial chairs and the massive mohogany dining-table and the mahogany-panelled walls; and she suddenly realized that, yes, to a young middle-class girl freshly out from England, this must seem almost impossibly glamorous. She remembered the first gowns she had bought for herself, from Uncle Casper's oil money – expensive and dowdy and years out of fashion – and she flushed a little pink herself.

She rested all afternoon, or tried to. But she kept thinking about what she would have to do during dinner this evening – go to the side door and whisper the·password *Swaraj*. That one word which was darkest tabu in Viceregal Lodge; and anywhere in India that Englishmen gathered.

Dinner at Viceregal Lodge when the Viceroy was staying there was always formal; although tonight's dinner was a little more jolly than most. Among others, they were entertaining the Blackguards Club, which was an association of Simla's wealthiest bachelors, and Lady Fitzsimmons, the wife of the Governor of Bombay, who was florid and excitable and possessed a notorious and distinctive shrieking laugh.

Lucy had taken a long time dressing, and felt more nervous than she could have imagined. She wore a simple grey silk evening gown, with a lace overdress to conceal her pregnant stomach, and a small pearl tiara, with matching pearl earrings. As she put the finishing touches to her hair, Etta remarked, 'You're looking a little pale, Lady Carson, if you don't mind my saying so.'

'Oh, tiredness, I suppose,' Lucy replied. 'I feel quite all right.'

As she went downstairs, she came across Vernon, on the first-floor landing. He paused, and bowed his head to her in the courtly bow, but said nothing. They both knew that Lucy's payment was supposed to be made tonight, or else Henry would be shown the photograph of Blanche. What only Lucy knew was that Vernon had another rendezvous arranged; a rendezvous with what she hoped would be fearsome retribution.

She was calmed a little by seeing him. He deserved it, after all; and Jamie had promised that he wouldn't be hurt. She couldn't wait to see his face tomorrow morning.

Henry approached her as she came downstairs, and offered his hand. 'You're looking very beautiful this evening, my dearest,' he told her. 'It looks as if Simla agrees with you. Come and meet Lady Fitzsimmons, but for goodness' sake don't say anything amusing. She might laugh.'

'Henry – ' Lucy began. She wanted to tell him that she was trying very hard to love him, that she was doing everything she could to come to terms with being his wife. But she couldn't find the words for it. When he said, 'Yes?' she simply shook her head, and said, 'Nothing. I'll tell you later,' and accompanied him into the huge panelled reception room, under the sparkling chandelier.

They sat down to eat at half-past seven, all forty of them, while the Viceroy's orchestra sat in their boiled shirts at the far end of the dining room and played light selections from the latest musicals. *We Shall Waltz Again In Springtime* and *Why Does Your Heart Tell Such Lies?*

Lucy scarcely touched her julienne soup; and ate only a tiny portion of her fillet of duck and peas. One of the Blackguards, a very handsome young cavalry officer called St John Teacher, asked her solicitously if she wasn't feeling well. It was almost ten to eight. It would take her only a minute to reach the side door, and open it, but Lucy was so tense that she took the opportunity to turn to Henry and say, 'You will excuse me, won't you, for just a moment? I need a little air.'

Henry rose, and immediately every man at the table rose with him. They stood silently to attention while Lucy was escorted to the door by two of the servants. Behind her, she heard them all sit down again, and resume their dinner.

'You wish to return to your room, Your Excellency *memsahib*?' asked Muhammad Aziz.

'No, please. I need a little fresh air, that's all.'

'I can escort you to the verandah, Your Excellency *memsahib*?'

'No, no. Please. I want to be alone, for just a few minutes.'

'Your Excellency *memsahib* is sure?'

'My Excellency *memsahib* is absolutely certain, thank you. Now, please, you have plenty of other duties to attend to.'

'Of course, Your Excellency *memsahib*.'

At last she was left alone in the hallway; apart from the two doorkeepers who stood waiting beside the entrance. She made her way quickly along the panelled corridor to the side of the house, holding up her grey silk gown so that it didn't rustle too noisily on the floor. The long-case clock in the hallway struck eight o'clock as she hurried down the short flight of stairs that led to the side door. She hesitated for a moment, took a deep breath, and then pulled back the brass bolts, using both hands, and turned the key.

She opened the door, and the cool night air flowed in. At first, she saw nothing, but she didn't dare to call out. She waited, feeling faint, her heart pounding against her ribs. Supposing he didn't come? Supposing the sentries had caught him? But then she heard quick, soft footsteps, and a small turbaned Indian appeared, dressed in the loose shirt and tight trousers of a rickshaw-coolie. He carried a wrapped-up bundle of cloth, which must have concealed his knife.

'*Swaraj*,' he whispered, in such a muffled voice that she didn't hear him at first.

'Oh, yes,' she said. 'Come in. Quick, I'll show you the way.'

She closed and locked the door while the Indian waited for her. She could smell garlic and onions and asafoetida on his breath, and his clothes were sour with sweat. He said nothing, but he had obviously understood what she said.

He followed close behind her as she led him to the servants' staircase. She was short of breath as she climbed, and she prayed over and over again with every step that none of the servants would appear, but they reached the second floor without being seen. Lucy led him along to the door of Vernon's room, and opened it for him.

'You know what to do?' she asked him.

His eyes glittered in the darkness. 'Yes, *memsahib*. I have been told what to do.'

'And you won't hurt him?'

'That is a promise, *memsahib*.'

Lucy waited for a moment, then closed the door behind him, and walked back along the corridor to the main staircase. As she slowly descended the stairs, her hands were trembling, and she was very close to fainting. On the first-floor landing, she stopped, and rested, listening to the sounds of laughter and conversation, and the orchestra playing *When We Meet Again, My Love*.

Then she went down to rejoin the dinner-party.

On her way up to bed that night, accompanied by Etta and two of her *ayahs*, Lucy paused on the first-floor landing outside Vernon's door. She was tempted for a moment to pretend that she had heard a noise, and to call for Lieutenant Burnes-Waterton, so that the rickshaw-coolie would be discovered and arrested.

On reflection, the idea of frightening Vernon into returning her photograph seemed much less appealing, even downright dangerous. Supposing the rickshaw-coolie were discovered, and caught? Supposing he admitted that the Vicereine herself had let him into the house?

Etta asked, 'Anything amiss, your ladyship?' but Lucy shook her head and said, 'No, nothing, thank you, Etta. I thought for a moment I might have forgotten something, that's all.'

She watched herself in the looking-glass as Etta prepared her hair for bed. She looked pale and preoccupied, an angel painted in thinly-diluted watercolours. Etta didn't seem to notice how pensive she was. She kept chattering on about a frilly blouse she had seen in Pearson's Modes, down by Scandal Point; and how pretty it would look with her new linen skirt. 'My very first mistress said to me, a lady's maid should always look smart, otherwise it reflects so poorly on her mistress.'

Etta brought Lucy a glass of hot milk to help her sleep, and 'to nourish young Horatio', but Lucy couldn't stomach it, and sat up in bed trying to read Jane Austen while the top of the milk crinkled, untouched, and formed a skin.

Shortly after eleven o'clock, Henry came in to bid her goodnight. 'Everybody's gone now, my darling. I'm spending a little time with Gordon Belloc; then I'm retiring to bed.'

She held his hand tightly. 'You won't be too late?'

'I promise,' he told her, and kissed his fingertip, and pressed it against her lips.

Lucy lay sleepless for another hour, listening to the servants preparing the Lodge for the night, closing doors and windows, extinguishing lights, carrying away empty glasses and dishes. Outside her open window the night sang with the steady chanting of insects; and the occasional whoop of a night-bird.

She wondered what Vernon would say to her, in the morning. Would he be angry? Would he be cowed? Would he give her photograph straight back? What if the rickshaw-coolie didn't frighten him at all? What if he called the guard?

She lay in bed listening and listening, until the clock in the hallway sonorously struck half-past midnight. She hadn't heard Henry come up; although she usually did, if she was awake. All those footsteps, and doors closing, and stage-whispered 'goodnights'. But Vernon would have returned to his room by now, to prepare Henry's clothes for the morning.

When the clock struck a quarter-to, Lucy couldn't stand the suspense any longer. She climbed out of bed, and went to the wardrobe and took out one of her dressing-gowns. Then she eased open her bedroom door, and looked out. The only illumination came from downstairs; otherwise the first-floor landing was in shadow.

She waited for almost a minute, listening. She could hear

servants talking quickly and softly downstairs, and the persistent *shushing* of a floorbrush. Then there was a long period of alarming silence.

It was high folly to think of going to Vernon's room. But she knew that she wouldn't be able to sleep until she had discovered what had happened, and she had a long and difficult day tomorrow, culminating in a visit to the Gaiety Theatre. Feeling more like an Oak City tomboy than an Indian empress, she gathered up her dressing-gown and tiptoed as quietly as she could across the galleried landing until she reached the mahogany-panelled door of Vernon's quarters; where she paused, and waited.

There was nobody around. No bearers, no cleaners. The lights were shining brightly downstairs, and so she assumed that Henry and Colonel Belloc were still talking in the library. Their plans for cleaning and restoring the Taj Mahal were already far advanced; and now they were working on the possibility of cleaning and repairing the Temple of Konarak.

Lucy knocked softly at Vernon's door. She waited, but there was no reply. She knocked again, and called, 'Vernon? This is Lady Carson.'

She waited almost a minute, but still Vernon didn't respond. Perhaps he was downstairs, attending to Henry. Perhaps he had fallen asleep. But if he had already been threatened with a knife at his throat by Jamie's rickshaw-coolie, it was highly unlikely that he had simply dozed off.

She knocked once more, as loudly as she dared. As she did so, the door swung open, by itself. Vernon must have left it unlatched. Inside, she could see that a lamp was still burning, on Vernon's desk, although the door wasn't open wide enough for her to be able to see any more.

'Vernon?' she whispered, Then, 'Vernon?'

Very cautiously, she eased back the door. Little by little, the room came into view. A smallish room, with slatted blinds, and a varnished desk, and a chintz easy-chair, and a single bed. On the wall, a frame photograph of an unprepossessing girl with a large nose, holding a bouquet of lilies – his mother or his wife.

Lucy took only one step forward; but one step was all that was needed for Vernon to come into view. He was lying back on his bed, fully dressed, and he was staring at her. She thought at first that he was wearing a maroon scarf, and she couldn't think why. But then she realized with a frizzling chill that he was dead, and that his head had been almost completely severed from his body. The maroon scarf was congealing blood.

'Oh God,' she swallowed. 'Oh God.' Her stomach muscles tightened, and she had to hold on to the edge of the desk to keep her balance. Shocked as she was, however, she found it impossible to take her eyes away from Vernon's grotesque body. The rickshaw-coolie must have panicked, and cut his throat. Perhaps he had intended to cut his throat, right from the very outset. Perhaps he intended to cut *all* of their throats.

Because what had Jamie really been doing, wandering around the gardens of Viceregal Lodge, disguised as a bearer? Now she came to think about it again, Lucy found it difficult to believe that he had gone to all of that trouble just to find out how she was. He must have been reconnoitring; seeing how easy it was for an Indian assassin to slip into the house. Perhaps he had even been carrying a weapon himself.

Lucy took one step nearer the bed. She would have to call Henry now. If the rickshaw-coolie hadn't escaped already, he would have to be flushed out of hiding, and arrested. If he happened to reveal to Henry that his wife and Vicereine had allowed him into the Lodge, then Lucy would have to accept the consequences. Perhaps she could think of some explanation that wouldn't involve telling Henry that Vernon had been blackmailing her.

She was about to leave Vernon's room when she caught sight of a crumpled manila envelope on the bloodstained *durry* next to his hand. Swallowing back a throatful of vinegary-tasting bile, she reached over and picked it up. One corner of it was soaked dark red. On the front, in Vernon's particularly nasty backhand, was the name *His Excellency Lord Carson.*

Her hands shaking wildly, Lucy tore the envelope open. Inside was a note which said '*May it please Y.E., the inclosure speaks for itself.*' Pinned to the note was Lucy's photograph of Blanche.

She tucked the photograph into the pocket of her dressing-gown, and then she took three deep breaths, holding her stomach in an effort to relax her muscles. Thank God she had the photograph back. Now Henry would never have to find out about Blanche. All the same – no matter how vicious and unprincipled Vernon had been, no matter how relieved she was to recover the picture from him, Lucy couldn't bring herself to think that he had deserved to die for what he had done.

She turned to leave the room, and to call for Henry and Lieutenant Burnes-Waterton. As she did so, however, the door of Vernon's closet swung open just behind her, she glimpsed its dark diagonal movement out of the corner of her eye, and a muscular arm gripped her fiercely around the neck.

'Not to speak!' a voice hissed, close to her ear. She immediately recognized the strong smell of garlic and spices and sweat. Something hard and greasy was pressed against the side of her head, an inch behind her right ear. 'You are speaking only one word, unless I am speaking to you first, and I am shooting off your head!'

'Please,' Lucy begged him. 'Please, I'm pregnant.'

'I am telling you not to speak,' the rickshaw-coolie repeated. 'Where is the Viceroy?'

'I don't know. I really don't. I've been in bed.'

'This is not true! You know where he is!'

'How could I? I've been asleep!'

The rickshaw-coolie gripped her even tighter around the neck, half-choking her. 'I am waiting for him and he is not coming! Where is he?'

'Please - can't breathe - '

Now the rickshaw-coolie took the gun-muzzle away from her head, and dug it hard into her stomach.

'You are wishing that I kill your baby? Is that what you are wishing?' He dug at her stomach again and again.

Lucy coughed, her eyes filling with tears. 'Don't hurt my baby, please! He's probably - in the library - with - '

'Show me the way!' the rickshaw-coolie insisted. 'And no calling, no shouting!'

He pushed Lucy out of the door of Vernon's room on to the landing. Then he edged her towards the top of the stairs, prodding her stomach again and again.

'Please don't hurt my baby,' Lucy wept. She felt as if the whole world was collapsing on top of her. She could scarcely move one leg in front of the other. But the rickshaw-coolie kept on jabbing her, and breathing, 'You are not crying out! You are showing me where is the Viceroy!'

At the top of the stairs, Lucy begged, 'Wait, wait, be careful! I don't want to fall!'

The rickshaw-coolie hesitated. At that instant, one of the landing doors opened behind them. The rickshaw-coolie turned around; and Lucy turned, too; and there was Elizabeth, in her white broderie-anglaise robe, staring at them both in astonishment.

'Lucy?' she called. 'Lucy, what on earth – ?'

'Elizabeth, no!' Lucy screamed.

'Lucy, who is this man? What's going on?'

Elizabeth came towards them, around the corner of the galleried landing. Lucy tried to scream at her again, to warn her to keep away, but the coolie's arm pulled viciously tight at her throat, and all she could do was to let out a high choking noise.

She heard the rickshaw-coolie shout something in Urdu;

she didn't know what it was. Then a deep thunderous booming sound; and Elizabeth stopped in surprise. Another booming sound, and blood burst out of Elizabeth's iron-grey hair, and she threw up her arms like a puppet and fell backwards on to the carpet.

'*No!*' shrieked Lucy. She tried to struggle free, but the rickshaw-coolie snatched hold of her wrist, and twisted her arm behind her back. '*No!*'

Downstairs, doors were flung open, and the hallway was flooded with light. The rickshaw-coolie cursed, and tried to pull Lucy down the stairs with him. There were shouts and banging noises and the sound of running boots. Lieutenant Burnes-Waterton appeared, in his mess trousers and shirt-sleeves, tugging his Webley revolver out of its brown-leather holster. Just behind him, Henry and Gordon Belloc were framed in the open doors of the library.

Lucy heard Henry shout, 'Lieutenant! For God's sake be careful! That's my wife!'

As he did so, the rickshaw-coolie lifted his revolver and fired twice into the hallway. Lieutenant Burnes-Waterton, with his gun still half out of its holster, performed a stagger-ing little dance, like a drunkard attempting a waltz. He fell on his side on to the floor, and lay shuddering and twitching. His blood ran across the polished floor.

'Which is the Viceroy?' the rickshaw-coolie screamed at Lucy. 'Which one is the Viceroy?'

'Please, you're hurting me!' Lucy gasped.

But Henry stepped across the hallway, and stood alone at the foot of the stairs, and announced clearly, 'I am the Viceroy. Release my wife at once.'

The rickshaw-coolie thrust Lucy aside. She staggered, and almost lost her balance, but managed to grasp the banister-rail. One silk slipper tumbled down the stairs by itself. Lucy watched in wide-eyed horror as the rickshaw-coolie took three steps further down the staircase, and lifted his revolver so that it was pointing directly at Henry's heart.

'I am being told to say that you and all of your people are oppressors and tyrants,' the rickshaw-coolie called out, his voice breathy with fear. 'This must be said by the newspapers when they tell of your death.'

Lucy thought she was screaming but she couldn't be sure. The rickshaw-coolie pulled back the hammer of his revolver and took two more steps down the stairs. Henry's face was extraordinary: rigid and bloodless, more like the face of a marble statue than a man. This was the way that a hero of the British Empire should die, facing his enemy, protecting his loved ones, his patriotism and his loyalty to the Crown untarnished.

Just then, though, with supreme casualness, as if he were out for a day's rough shooting in the *mofussil*, Gordon Belloc reappeared at the library door, holding up an enormous Savage 99 elephant-rifle. Calmly, but without any hesitation, he aimed it at the rickshaw-coolie and fired it.

The noise was devastating. Even the chandelier jangled. The hallway was filled with smoke. Lucy clapped her hands over her eyes as the rickshaw-coolie's body stood on the stairs for a moment, headless, and then flopped to the bottom of the stairs, to Henry's feet.

'*Facilis descensus averni,*' Colonel Belloc remarked. 'The way down to hell is easy.'

Henry, stiffly, climbed the stairs. He knelt down beside Lucy and held her in his arms. She was too shocked to weep. She shivered and shook like a small child with a high fever.

'Everything is all right now,' Henry soothed her. 'Everything is quite all right.'

Shortly after breakfast the following day, Etta came into Lucy's room and stood a little way away, as if she were afraid to come too close. 'They've arrested somebody,' she said.

Lucy shielded her eyes against the sunlight with her hand. 'They've arrested somebody? Who?'

'It was almost by accident, that's what they said, down in the native quarter. They wanted to talk to one of the rickshaw-coolie's cousins. They found a man sleeping in his house, somebody they didn't know. But it turned out it was somebody called Tilak, he's a well-known troublemaker. He's been around here for weeks, that's what they said! One of the gardeners said that he'd been planning to murder the Viceroy for months. It makes you shudder, doesn't it, just to think about it!'

Lucy stared at her. 'Where's Tilak now?'

Etta narrowed her eyes. 'Down at the police station, under guard, I'd say.'

'Has he talked to anybody?'

'Nobody's told me nothing, your ladyship.' said Etta. Then, 'Something wrong, your ladyship?'

'No, nothing. But I want you to find out what Tilak's been saying.'

'I'm surprised you care, your ladyship.'

'Of course I care! He killed Miss Morris! He killed Lieutenant Burnes-Waterton!'

'All right then, I'll do my best,' said Etta. 'Don't get fretful.'

Lucy said, 'Where's my hand-mirror? Bring me a flannel for my face.'

She looked at herself in her mirror while Etta poured out the water and wrung out the flannel. Very pale. Dark grey smudges under her eyes. She hadn't slept all night; except for a half-hour's fretful doze towards dawn.

'What do you think they'll do to him?' she asked Etta.

'What do I think they'll do to who?'

'Tilak, of course.'

'Oh, well,' said Etta. 'They'll hang him, won't they? No doubt about it.'

Lucy began to have a cold, sinking feeling of terrible dread. Now that Bal Gangadhar Tilak had been arrested, it was highly likely that he would soon tell the Simla police that he had talked on Monday to the Vicereine; and that the Vicereine had appeared to be sympathetic to what he believed in. In fact, Lucy's skin shrank at the thought that her meeting with Bal Gangadhar Tilak might have led directly to what had happened last night. What better way to demonstrate his impunity than to murder the Viceroy aided and abetted by herself?

Bal Gangadhar Tilak had been right. He was no 'petty volcano'. Bal Gangadhar Tilak could set India on fire, from end to end.

The confrontation between Henry and Bal Gangadhar Tilak's lawyer was informal but sober. Henry sat on a sofa beside the empty fireplace, while Tilak's lawyer sat brown and bespectacled nearby, ceaselessly rubbing his long brown fingers together, but obviously not intimidated by Henry's presence. It was plain that Henry found his lack of subservience to be irritating in the extreme. The day was bright and sharp. The light fell into the room like golden razor-blades. Henry was baffled and infuriated by Tilak's terrorism, and by his lawyer's intransigence.

'An act of political expression can scarcely be described as terrorism,' Tilak's lawyer suggested.

'None the less, he shot and killed a serving officer of the Viceroy's Bodyguard; and an innocent British lady; and a British manservant.'

'This is not denied.'

'What do you mean, "this is not denied"?'

'Exactly that, Your Excellency. The facts are unavoidable, and speak for themselves. The man who carried out the attack on Viceregal Lodge last night was one of the political fellowship of Bal Gangadhar Tilak; and was acting with Bal Gangadhar Tilak's approval, if not his specific knowledge. But I have to say that he was under the strictest orders not to harm the Vicereine.'

Lucy looked out of the windows. The peaks of the

Himalayas had vanished altogether behind a pearlized mist, like old Indian women concealing themselves behind their veils.

Henry was watching Lucy all the time, but he spoke to Tilak's lawyer. 'You realize what you're saying?'

'Yes, Your Excellency.'

'You realize what the penalty will be, if Tilak enters a plea of guilty.'

'Yes, Your Excellency.'

Henry took a deep, testy breath. 'Does he wish to be a martyr? I can certainly oblige him, if he wishes to be a martyr.'

'No, sir. He does not wish to be a martyr. He will plead guilty, you see, but with mitigating circumstances.'

Henry slowly took his eyes away from Lucy and focused on the lawyer. 'What mitigating circumstances? He sent an assassin to break into Viceregal Lodge to kill as many of us as he could, myself included.'

'Ah, but we have a letter, Your Excellency.'

The fire had reddened one side of Henry's face. 'Letter, what letter?'

'Here, Your Excellency,' said Tilak's lawyer, and shuffled in his case, and produced at last two sheets of paper. At once, with a sickening sense of shock, Lucy recognized the letter she had sent to Jamie at the Hotel Cecil, and a fair copy of it, written in large, angular italics.

'Here in my left hand the original copy which I do not wish to give to you in its actual bodily form at this moment, Your Excellency, for reasons that you will plainly under- stand. But this is a perfect copy in every respect.'

Henry read the letter with his hand faintly trembling. Then he handed it back to Tilak's lawyer in silence.

'It's a forgery,' he said.

'Your Excellency insults my intelligence. I am defending a man for his life. If I had only a forgery at my disposal, what chance would I stand in a court of law?'

'If it isn't a forgery, it was stolen. Stolen evidence is inadmissible.'

'Not stolen, great sir.'

'It's addressed to Mr Jamie Cullen, not to Bal Gangadhar Tilak. How else could Bal Gangadhar Tilak have acquired it, except by stealing it?'

'It was given to him freely,' said the lawyer, seriously. 'Mr Jamie Cullen wished to show Bal Gangadhar Tilak that the Vicereine was sincere in her intentions to intercede with you on matters of Indian independence.'

Lucy was so frightened that she could hardly swallow. Henry seemed to crouch lower and lower in his chair and she thought that he might crouch himself so small that he would concentrate himself into some black explosive demon, and turn on her with claws and horns and raging eyes.

But Henry was Viceroy; and he controlled himself. He sat without saying a word for nearly four minutes, and nobody dared to interrupt his deliberations, although Colonel Miller kept coughing and sniffing and shuffling his feet.

'Very well,' Henry said at last to Tilak's lawyer. His face was quite expressionless. 'No charges will be brought; Tilak will be released. I can only warn you that if anything like this ever happens again, mitigating letters or not, I will send up the Bengal Cavalry and I will order them to cut off your collective heads.'

The lawyer stood up, and bowed, and as he bowed, the firelight glinted from his spectacles. 'Your Excellency is very comprehending.'

He left. Henry sat silently for three or four minutes longer; then said to his own solicitor, and to Colonel Miller, and to Timothy Frognal, and to the small council of Indians who had accompanied them, 'The Vicereine and I wish to be alone for a while, thank you.'

Everybody shuffled quickly out of the room, and closed the doors behind them. Now there was just the two of them, husband and wife. Henry in his armchair, staring at the fire; Lucy on the sofa, staring at Henry.

'Henry?' asked Lucy.

Henry said nothing, but drummed his fingers on the arm of his chair.

'Henry, I'm sorry. I don't know what to say.'

He shrugged. 'There's nothing you can say. For some inexplicable reason you felt constrained to write Mr Cullen extolling the personal virtues of one of India's most un-scrupulous nationalists. The letter is writ; the deed is done. All I can do is to make the best of it. That's part of a Viceroy's job, you know, making the best of things. Part of the burden.'

'But they killed Elizabeth, right in front of me! How could you let them go!'

Henry took a deep breath. 'I had to, Lucy. They knew from the very beginning that I would have to. I can't think why you wrote such a letter. I'm not even sure that I want to know. But if we were to try Tilak publicly, he would produce it in open court, and I would have no choice but to resign.'

'So for the sake of your job, you're letting that murderer go free?'

He turned to her and his eyes were chilling. 'Don't be so damned ridiculous. It's not for the sake of my job, it's for the sake of Her Majesty the Queen, and India, and the whole course of British history.'

'Henry, you're a man, not a god.'

He stood up, and walked stiffly across to the window. 'I have never once deluded myself that I am a god, Lucy. But when the Duke of Nantwich recommended my appointment to Lord Salisbury, he wrote, *"There are some men through whose spirits the magnetic forces of historical inevitability can be felt to flow, and Henry Carson is one of them."*'

Lucy sat watching him for a while. Something rang off-key. Something she couldn't quite understand. 'I didn't know the Duke of Nantwich had recommended you.'

Henry turned his head for a moment, and nodded. 'Yes, that's right. The Duke of Nantwich.'

'The Duke of Nantwich is Malty's uncle.'

'That's right, yes, so he is.'

Lucy frowned, 'Why did he recommend you? I thought he didn't like you. You didn't like him. You called him the Evil Coconut.'

'I really haven't the faintest idea why he recommended me,' said Henry. 'I'm glad he did, though. Salisbury's always taken his advice about India.'

Lucy stood up, her stomach very protuberant and low. 'Henry, you're lying to me.'

'Lying? I'm tired, that's all.'

'Henry, you're lying.'

He swivelled around. 'All right, lying about what? What reason could I possibly have to lie to you?'

'You're lying to me about Malty! You pushed us together on purpose!'

'You needed somebody to amuse you, that was all. I thought we'd forgotten all of this!'

'Amuse me!' Lucy protested. 'He was my lover! And you didn't care, did you? In fact, you *wanted* him to be my lover!'

'That's absurd!' Henry snapped.

'Is it? Is it really? Then why did the Duke of Nantwich the Evil Coconut who couldn't even stand to look at you – why did he recommend you to Lord Salisbury for Viceroy?'

Henry stood very still. He sniffed, and took out his handkerchief, and wiped his nose, and then patted the sweat from his forehead. 'You want the truth?' he told her.

'Yes, Henry, I want the truth.'

'Very well,' said Henry, 'since this seems to be the time when our mutual mistrust of each other has almost brought the British Empire down to her knees – the truth. And the truth is, yes, that I did encourage Malty to become friends with you. Not your lover, perhaps; but I suppose that had to

639

be the inevitable consequence, with a woman as – physically active as you. A woman as young as you. As beautiful as you.'

He hesitated, but both of them knew that he had to finish what he was saying. Lives had been lost, reputations had been broken. He couldn't go back now.

'The day after you and Malty – well, the day after I found you together – I called on the Duke of Nantwich and explained what was happening between you. I said that there were several courses of action open to me. I could sue for divorce, citing Malty as co-respondent; but the scandal of that would have ruined the Nantwiches in society for several seasons, and would probably have killed Malty's mother. Or else I could say nothing and arrange for Malty to be reasonably employed in the India Office somewhere, playing cricket in the corridors for two hundred and fifty pounds a year; in return for which I would expect the strongest possible recommendation for my appointment as Viceroy.'

Lucy felt her stomach tighten, and she had to sit down.

'That's the truth, isn't it?' she whispered.

Henry couldn't even say the word 'Yes.' He simply nodded.

Lucy took five or six deep breaths, and gradually her contraction subsided. 'You sold me ... you sold my body ... you prostituted your own wife ... so that you could be certain of becoming Viceroy?'

'That isn't the way that I would express it. You needed things that I just couldn't provide. You needed amusement, fun, parties. You needed somebody who could – well, you needed somebody who could give you comfort in bed. I confess that I haven't served you very well in that particular part of our married life.'

Lucy swallowed. Then she said, 'You should have told me about Vanessa right from the very beginning.'

'Vanessa?' Henry frowned.

'Henry, I know all about Vanessa. I could have helped you.'

Henry sat down. 'I'm sorry. I'm sorry you know. There's nothing that you could have done to help.'

'Perhaps if we start telling the truth to each other, that will help.'

'Lucy! You can't understand!'

'I can't understand that you're still in love with her? Of course I can!'

'And don't you think that being irredeemably in love with your own sister deserves punishment?'

Lucy thought for a while, and then she slowly nodded. 'Yes, Henry, perhaps it does. But I can give you both of those things now, truth *and* punishment, all in one.'

He lifted his head. He didn't understand her at all.

'You're going to tell me you love this Jamie Cullen. You're going to tell me that you've been having an affair with him, even though you're pregnant.'

'No,' said Lucy. 'I haven't seen Jamie Cullen for years and years. Well – not until he turned up in Calcutta last month.'

'You said in your letter that you loved him,' said Henry.

'I did. I do. I always will. I knew him in Kansas. I can't pretend that I didn't. But I could never love him the way I love you.'

Henry stood up. 'In that case, my dearest, how could you possibly have been persuaded to write what you did about Bal Gangadhar Tilak? You said in your letter that he is an honourable man, a great benefactor, and that you will try to persuade me what a saint he is.'

'I made a mistake,' said Lucy, sitting down.

Henry approached her, his face starkly shadowed by the electric light. 'Yes, my dearest, you made a mistake. You made an appalling mistake. You are Vicereine of India, the representative of the Queen-Empress, and yet you decided to meet in secret with the most vicious and squalid terrorist that India has ever known. And what did you do after that?

Did you repudiate him? Did you send troops to look for him? Oh, no! Nothing like that! You wrote a letter to your friend or your lover or whatever he is, and told him that you supported Bal Gangadhar Tilak, the terrorist, the nationalist, and that you would try to persuade me to treat him with respect!'

Lucy realized that Henry was in such an emotional rage that nothing could stop him. His fists were clenching and unclenching, spit flew from his lips, and the veins on his forehead bulged.

'With one letter,' he seethed, 'with one letter, you brought the viceroyalty to the brink of destruction; and gave me no option but to release one of the most determined of India's nationalists. The man who killed Elizabeth will never be punished. You saw to that.'

Lucy, without another word, rose from the sofa, and stood in front of him. Then she spread out her black mourning skirts, and knelt down on the floor. Then she lay spreadeagled in front of Henry, stretched out on the carpet and kissed and licked the toe of his black polished shoe.

'Lucy, get up! Lucy, you're expecting a baby, for God's sake!'

'Sahib,' she said. She was half-laughing, half-weeping. 'Oh mighty, mighty Sahib!'

'Lucy, get up!

'Not until I tell you the truth that will always be your punishment, oh mighty Sahib!'

Henry, fearful and enraged, seized Lucy's arms and lifted her bodily up off the floor. 'What in God's name is the matter with you? Are you demented! You're expecting a baby!'

She smiled at him, a saucy humorous anguished smile that she knew would provoke him beyond all measure. 'The truth and the punishment, Henry, is that this child that you're so concerned about may be yours; but on the other hand it may equally well be Malty's. In which case, you have paid the price for your precious viceroyalty in blood; and so have I.'

Then her shoulders began to shake, and she wept the bitterest tears that anybody could ever weep, for Elizabeth, and for Blanche, and for Henry, and for herself, too.

They caught Jamie as he was boarding the train at Delhi for Bombay. He was dressed like a clerk, in a grey suit and a *terai* hat, and he was carrying a briefcase. He was immediately escorted back to Simla. It had not been publicly announced, but it was generally known throughout the Indian Army and Police that the Viceroy was prepared to reward anybody who apprehended him; and generously.

Lucy saw him again from her bedroom balcony as he was brought under guard to the Viceregal Lodge, at six o'clock in the morning. The Sutlej valley was so misty that she couldn't even see the opposite hills. He was brought to the side entrance, with his head bowed. Lucy watched him, and prayed that he wouldn't raise his eyes.

Jamie was questioned for six hours by Henry and by various Indian Army officers. Lucy sat in her room, knowing that he was there, a pale pregnant widow wearing black. As it grew dark, Colonel Miller came up and knocked at her door and presented his compliments.

'Mr Cullen has asked to speak to you, Your Excellency, and His Excellency the Viceroy has assented.'

Lucy glanced at Etta, then gathered her skirts and stood up. 'Very well,' she said; and followed Colonel Miller along the corridor. His highly-polished shoes barked briskly on the teak flooring.

Jamie was waiting for her in a bare whitewashed room that had once been used for keeping guns. He looked tired and unwashed, but otherwise he seemed to be well.

'Well, well,' he said, as Lucy walked in. The sergeant standing behind him prodded him, sharply, to make him stand up.

'Hello, Jamie,' she said. She didn't sit down.

'Did His Excellency tell you what he was going to do to me?' asked Jamie.

Lucy shook her head.

'His Excellency is going to deport me; directly back to the United States of America, and His Excellency is going to lodge a formal complaint with the United States diplomatic service.'

Lucy said, very carefully, 'Don't you think you deserve it? You tricked me. You killed my best friend. You would have killed Henry, too.'

'Lucy,' said Jamie, 'that wasn't anything to do with me. That was just one of Tilak's hotheads.'

'You killed my best friend, Jamie.'

'I'm sorry about that. There isn't very much else I can say.'

'You're *sorry*?'

Jamie lowered his head, and said nothing.

Lucy watched him for a while, and then she whispered, 'I never knew that anybody could ever be so jealous. It's been burning inside of you, hasn't it, for years and years? It's burned you more thoroughly than Uncle Casper was ever burned. And you would have killed Henry, wouldn't you? You would have killed him. Nothing to do with *Swaraj*. Nothing to do with justice. It was jealousy, and nothing else.'

She paused, and then she took a small bloodstained photograph out of her pocket, and held it out to him. 'You'd better take this. You're responsible for both of them. The child, and the blood.'

Jamie swallowed, but still didn't speak.

Lucy looked away for a moment. Then she said, 'One thing more. That little girl. That little girl that Bal Gangadhar Tilak brought to see me. Was she really his cousin's child?'

'No,' Jamie whispered. 'I just thought – well, there wasn't

much hope of you changing your mind, was there? There wasn't much hope of you talking to Henry ... not unless you could see some suffering that you understood.'

'You pulled my heartstrings, is that it?' asked Lucy.

'Something like that,' Jamie agreed.

'Where is she now? Do you know?'

'I don't know, somewhere in the native quarter; back where we borrowed her from.'

Lucy said, 'There's only one thing that I'm going to say to Bal Gangadhar Tilak, and that's to take care of that little girl. And there's only one thing that I'm going to say to you.'

'Oh, yes?' smiled Jamie.

'Oh, yes,' said Lucy. 'I've learned it from you and I've learned it from Henry. And that is, that I'm an empress. Not an empress of India; not an empress of anything at all, except the man I love, and myself.'

Jamie tilted his chair back, and leaned his head against the whitewashed wall. 'Empress,' he repeated, as if he would have to be satisfied with that.

On Sunday morning, June 24, 1899, to the sound of bells pealing from the Gothic tower of Christ Church, Simla, 'Horatio' Carson was born and named Nancy Victoria.

Nancy was blonde and curly, like her mother, but she seemed to bear no likeness at all to her father. To Lucy's secret relief, she didn't look at all like Blanche. She wouldn't have been able to bear it if she had given birth to yet another daughter just the same. Sha-sha would always have a very private individual place in her heart.

Although she didn't look like him, Henry was dearly fond of Nancy, and was always finding excuses to leave his desk and come through to the nursery and watch her; even if she was asleep. It didn't seem to upset him at all that she could have been Malty's daughter, instead of his. Quite the opposite; it seemed to give him a new calmness and balance in his life, as if at last he had been punished justly and sufficiently.

He never asked Lucy any more about Jamie, or why she had allowed him to introduce her to Bal Gangadhar Tilak. She sometimes suspected that he might have found out why, from the Simla Police, or from one of the Army's intelligence officers. Immediately after Henry had been obliged to let Tilak go, he had been noticeably distant with her; even testy at times.

But when Nancy was born, he seemed to make up his mind that whatever the failings of their marriage, whatever the burdens of his viceroyalty, he and Lucy had chosen their lives and they must live them honorably and affectionately, and with pride.

On Christmas Day, he gave Lucy a diamond-and-emerald ring. Inside it, he had inscribed the words, *I Will Love You Eternally, H.*

Lucy occasionally felt that she had been left with one unanswered question: whether it had been right for her to turn her back on Blanche and Jamie and choose the life of an empress, rather than the life of an Oak City wife and mother.

Jamie had killed with his jealousy whatever love she had once felt for him but she still thought about him; and about her younger days in Kansas, with the stormy sky hurtling above their heads as if it had a train to catch.

That is, until New Year's Day, 1900, the very first day of the new century, as she was being dressed by Etta in her dressing room at Government House for the traditional Viceroy's New Year's Day Parade.

Outside, she could hear the racketing echo of military drums across the *maidan*; and the clear-throated sound of bugles; mingled with the jingling of harnesses and the braying of elephants.

'Very well, I'm ready,' she told Etta, rising from her dressing-chair. 'I just want to say goodbye to Nancy.'

In her pleated and ruffled white dress, she crossed to the nursery, where Nancy was lying in her curtained crib, playing with her feet.

'How's my darling?' she asked her, leaning over her crib. 'How's my beautiful girl?'

The *amah* smiled fondly at Nancy, and said, 'Very sweet child, *memsahib*. Never weeping.'

'Well, she has nothing to weep about,' said Lucy. She reached into the crib to pick Nancy up. 'My darling, beautiful girl.'

Nancy tugged at Lucy's curls, and then at her earrings. Lucy kissed her, and was about to lay her back in her crib when her little fingers caught hold of Lucy's cameo brooch; the same cameo brooch which she had been left by her mother.

'Now careful, my sweetness!' Lucy cautioned her; but the brooch suddenly came apart, and the cameo dropped out of the silver backing, on to the baby's sheet. After it, a tiny oval photograph came fluttering, and landed beside it.

Frowning, Lucy picked the photograph up. It showed a serious-faced young man, with rather old-fashioned sidewhiskers. She turned it over, and on the back was written, *To My Only Love, On The Birth Of Our Daughter*.

It was only when she had studied the photograph for two or three minutes that it gradually dawned on her that she was looking at a photograph of her real father, Jamie's father, Jerrold Cullen.

That night, when the great New Year's Day Parade was over, she sat and wrote a short letter to Jamie. A letter without bitterness or cruelty; but a letter which told him who she had discovered herself to be; and a letter which she prayed would ease at last the pain of all of his wasted years.

She sat at her desk alone while the sun settled over Calcutta, thickening the shadows, turning the lazy reflective curves of the Hooghly River into polished bronze, and

647

filling her room with a strange amber light, as if her dress were fading, as if her tiara were tarnishing, as if she were a photograph herself, a curio to be wondered about far in the future.

She turned, and saw Henry standing at the door.

'I have never seen you look so beautiful,' he said. Then he turned, and left the room, and closed the door very quietly behind him.